DATE DUE

FEB 11 1988			
MAR 1 0 1988			
APR 2 6 1988			
JUN 2 2 1988			
APR 4 1989			
FEB 4 1991			

BOOKS BY GARY JENNINGS

Spangle (1987)

The Journeyer (1984)

World of Words (1984)

Aztec (1980)

SPANGLE

SPANGLE

GARY JENNINGS

NEW YORK   Atheneum   1987

This is a work of historical fiction. Except for verifiably historical characters and institutions extant in the late 1800s, all names, characters, places, and incidents are either the product of the author's imagination or are used fictitiously. Any resemblance of such nonhistorical incidents or figures to actual events or persons, living or dead, is entirely coincidental.

Atheneum
Macmillan Publishing Company
866 Third Avenue, New York, N.Y. 10022
Collier Macmillan Canada, Inc.

Library of Congress Cataloging-in-Publication Data
Jennings, Gary.
Spangle.
I. Title
PS3560.E518S6   1987   813'.54   86-47687
ISBN 0-689-11723-X

10 9 8 7 6 5 4 3 2 1

Printed in the United States of America

for Jesse and Penny

SPANGLE

AMERICA

I

"I'D SAY we've seen the last of the elephant, eh, Johnny?" said one of the soldiers in blue.

"Reckon that's so, Billy," said one of the soldiers in gray. Then he looked mildly surprised. "Hey, you Yankee fellers say that, too? About the elephant?"

"All the time, or used to," said the Union soldier. "Feller said he was going to see the elephant, it meant his outfit was off to tangle with you Rebs."

"Sure enough, same with us Cornfeds. I'm sorry we lost this war, but I ain't sorry I won't see that particular elephant no more."

"Me neither. What say to a smoke, Johnny?"

"Lordamighty, Billy Yank! You got tobacco?"

"Some. You got a pipe?"

"About all I have got." The Confederate soldier shifted the several horses' reins he was holding, so he had a hand free to scrounge in his pocket. "We been smoking and chewing raspberry leaves. When we wasn't brewing 'em up for mock tea. Imagine that? And all this part of Virginia hereabouts used to be prime tobacco country."

"Here y' go. Connecticut shade-grown broadleaf. Stoke up."

Several others of the enlisted men now unbent from the stiff parade-ground "stand to horse" postures they had been maintaining. They mingled, blue and gray together, and handed back and forth the reins they variously held, so they could pack their pipes or cut quids. They were on a grassy knoll off to one side of a triangular acre of bare ground, just down the road from the village courthouse,

3

and they were tending the mounts of the numerous Union and Confederate officers overseeing the final stacking of arms.

Those officiating generals and colonels at the edge of the ceremonial ground did not yet relax, but stood as straight and somber as if they were attending a military funeral. Which, in a way, this was, even to the melancholy music the Union band was playing—the more doleful of the campfire songs favored by one army or the other—the Confederates' "Lorena," the Yankees' "Tenting Tonight on the Old Camp Ground." Out in the fields beyond the drab Yankee tent city that had sprouted beside the village, the remnants of the Confederate Army of Northern Virginia were gathered in formation. Now, on command, those men marched by companies to the verge of the triangular bare ground and, on command, by squads stepped forward into it. The movements were done solemnly, but grudgingly and therefore sloppily, with the men all out of step and their lines never dressed.

In the triangle, they did not stack any of their arms in approved tripod fashion, but merely dropped their rifles, muskets and carbines—and the pistols and sabres of the cavalrymen—in a heap for the waiting Union armorers to bundle away. When each squad had disarmed, it abandoned all semblance of order and, without waiting for any command of "Dis-missed!" the men ambled separately wherever they chose. Some stayed to watch for a while. Others went to gather up whatever belongings they still possessed, and then simply went away. Some departed with broad grins on their faces, some with tears. Off in the distance, on the other side of the Appomattox River, the Confederate artillery's heavier weapons were being trundled by horse teams into one collection area.

There were several civilian spectators also on the scene, most of them reporters from northern newspapers. But one was an old woman, a local resident. She stood, gumming an unlit corncob pipe, all that morning on the rickety porch of her clapboard cabin at one side of the acre of stacking ground. A small white cat, evidently hers, strolled here and there, sometimes rubbing and purring against the old woman's bare feet, sometimes against the scarred leather boots of the generals and colonels, sometimes against the fetlocks of the officers' waiting horses. Meanwhile, the orderlies of those officers had lit up and were puffing gratefully, or were chewing and spitting luxuriously, and now they amiably began chatting about the horses they were tending.

"This-here big black beauty," said a Union sergeant, "is General Sheridan's charger, Winchester. And that gelding, Johnny—that's General Lee's famous gray, ain't it? The one named Traveller?"

"That's him. Been called Traveller ever since Uncle Bobby has owned him. Named Jeff Davis afore that. And my own name ain't Johnny Reb—not after today it ain't. It's Obie Yount."

"And I won't be Billy Yank no more neither, Sergeant Yount. I'm Raymond Matchett."

"Pleased to make your acquaintance, Sergeant Matchett. And I thank you for the smoke. This does taste mighty fine."

Around those two men, other sociable conversations went on, overheard in snatches.

"... Yessir, used to be in the United States Army myself. And when I joined this-here Secesh Army, you know what happened? I went to visit some old U.S.

Army friends, and they very rudely *turned their backs on me*. At First Manassas, that was. Them friends turned all the way back to Washington, D.C."

"I believe it, Johnny, 'deed I do. All the time I been in this war, our officers been telling us, 'Men, them Rebs is *retreating!*' But every damn time it turned out that them Rebs was retreating *at us!*"

"... Hell, yes, Johnny, just like you, I'm craving to get home to my gal and, hell, yes, do that. But I never in my life heard it called *doodling* a woman."

"Ain't surprised, Billy. It's kind of a private word. My wife is a piano teacher, see, and we used to call that 'making music.' But after the war begun, her and me thought up a new name. Now we call it 'playing Doodle without the Yankee.' "

"... Just offhand, Sergeant Yount, I'd take you to be too big and ugly and ornery-looking to be doing wagon-dog duty as an orderly."

"You're right, Sergeant Matchett. I'm only here because my colonel is, and he ain't no pigeonhole officer either. Colonel Zack and me, we're cavalry. It's just that General Lee wanted our side to make a presentable showing here at the surrender, so the officers he brung are them few that owned uniforms which wasn't all in tatters. This claybank horse here is Colonel Zack's mount, Thunder. This one of mine here, I named him Lightning, so they'd go together proper. Thunder and Lightning."

"Lightning?" said a Union corporal standing nearby. "That's a Percheron brewery horse!" He laughed. "No offense, Sergeant, but oughtn't you to call him something more suitable? Like Leviathan?"

"Don't go throwing off on him, sonny," Yount said affably. "I got this brute from your side. From some Yankee farmer up towards Gettysburg, after my own got shot out from under me."

"Well, now that I've took a good look," said the corporal, "the horse ain't a *hell* of a lot heftier than you are. Big horse for a big man. So them's Thunder and Lightning, eh? I kind of admire that notion."

"This-here horse of Sheridan's used to have another name, too. Rienzi," said the Union sergeant. "Little Phil changed it to Winchester, because it was from the town of Winchester that the general started the last Valley campaign, and won it."

Yount growled, "Little Phil Sheridan calls it a campaign, huh? Everybody in the Shenandoah Valley called it the Burning."

"You was there?"

"Me and my colonel both. He was only a captain then, Captain Edge, and that was only—Christ, that was only last autumn. We was there with the Thirty-fifth Cav. That time, we saw the elephant at a place called Tom's Brook."

"Me, I wasn't ever in the Valley," said Sergeant Matchett. "But I recollect hearing something about the Thirty-fifth Virginia." He scratched meditatively in his beard. "Wasn't that the battalion nicknamed the Comanches? And wasn't it—?"

"Disbanded right after that engagement," Yount interrupted abruptly. Then, as if to smooth over his brusqueness, he grinned and drawled, "I've always wondered why we call it that."

"What? Comanches?"

"No. Seeing the elephant."

The Yankee corporal said, "Come to think on it, I don't rightly know, either. It used to be a city folks' saying—*I've* seen the elephant!—meaning you can't fool me; I've been around. Nowadays it means I've seen action; I'm no green recruit. But I don't know how it came to mean that."

"I never heard any soldier say it down in Mexico or out in the Territories," said Yount. "Never heard it used so until this war commenced."

Sergeant Matchett exclaimed, "You was in Mexico?"

"Me and Colonel Zack both. And back then, we was both just *troopers,* no rank at all. When we was still . . ." Yount coughed and looked down, past his bush of black beard, at his shabby garb of gray and butternut. "We was both wearing blue then. Well, hell, so was Jeff Davis and Robert E. Lee."

"Why, so was I! In Mexico, I mean. Went in with General Scott at Veracruz."

"We went in earlier, at Port Isabel, up north."

The corporal, who had known only this one war, looked from sergeant to sergeant, respectfully silent.

"If you was in the northern campaign, then you probably didn't get into the action at Cerro Gordo. Or Chapultepec?"

"No. We fought at the Resaca. Monterrey. Buena Vista . . ."

The two newly met, once-allied veterans were still swapping the names of battlefields far from Appomattox Court-house—far from Virginia, far from this war—when this war ended. Someone barked, "Atten-*hut!*" and every enlisted man, in blue or gray, snapped to statue stiffness. All the Confederate arms were stacked, the Confederate army surrendered, and now the generals and colonels in blue and gray came to collect their horses. Colonel Edge, not the youngest of the officers, but the only one not wearing a beard or mustache, came and took Thunder's reins from Sergeant Yount.

There was a considerable noise of jingling harness, creaking leather and shuffling hoofs, as the officers and men mounted. Yount leaned across from his great Percheron and asked confidentially, "You sure, Colonel Zack, you don't want to fight no more? I'm game if you are. There's other Cornfed armies south and west of here that ain't quit yet."

Edge said quietly, "I've given my parole not to fight any more."

"Well, I ain't gave no parole yet. A lot of the men ain't bothering, and the Yanks don't give a damn. They know as well as we do, them certificates is just so many ass wipers."

Edge took out and looked again at the flimsy slip of paper he had been accorded in exchange for his word of honor. In smudgy print and scrawled handwriting, it informed all whom it might concern that "The Bearer, *Lt. Col. Zachary Edge, CSA,* a paroled prisoner" now had the United States Army's "permission to go to his home, and there remain undisturbed."

Yount said, "You being an officer, you still got a carbine, a revolver and a sabre. They outweigh that piece of privy paper. And we both got horses—like Devil Grant said, to use for the spring planting. But a lot of these men you see leaving here ain't scooting for home to farm. They're heading south to see can't they meet up with General Johnston in North Carolina, and fight alongside him."

"They won't, though," Edge said dispiritedly. "The news that Lee has surrendered will get there before they do. Old Joe will quit, too. So will Taylor and Smith and the others. They've got no choice, with Lee out of the war. Obie, it's all over."

Yount raised his bulky shoulders high, then let them sag. "Where *are* you going, then? You don't aim to hitch Thunder to a plow and start spring planting here in Appomattox County?"

"No. I reckon, just as it says here, I'll go to my home and there remain undisturbed." Edge tucked the paper in a tunic pocket, turned in his saddle and checked the secureness of his bedroll and pack behind the cantle.

"Come on, Colonel Zack," Yount said plaintively. "You know damn well you ain't got no home, no more'n I do, outside a barracks or a cantonment or a bivouac. Long as we've knowed each other, you and me, we ain't done nothing but soldier. Near twenty years of soldiering."

"There won't be much call for our soldier services, Obie, not for a long while. We'd better learn new trades."

"What, then? Where?"

"I can't tell you what to do. I'm not your troop commander any more. As for me, I figure I might as well go on back where I came from, be it home or not."

"Back to the Blue Ridge?"

"Yes."

"You'll go and be a hillbilly again? And me back to a mill town in Tennessee? We split up, after all these years?"

"No need to split up right now, anyway. Both places are west of here." Edge kneed Thunder to a walk, turning in the direction of the courthouse, where now was flying the United States flag.

Yount hastily checked his own gear and spurred his big Lightning to a reluctant and ponderous trot. The horse had to shoulder its way through the crowds of other horses, soldiers and vehicles of all sorts, so Yount didn't catch up to Edge until they were both out the other side of the village and on the packed-earth Lynchburg Pike. As they rode side by side past falling-apart worm fences and falling-down tobacco barns, the commotion and music of Appomattox—where the Yankee band was now playing a funereal rendition of "The Bonnie Blue Flag"—faded behind them.

Only then did Yount speak again, and gloomily. "You know what we are now, Colonel Zack?"

"I know what I'm not, and that's a light colonel, CSA. And you're not my troop sergeant any more. So let's scrap the ranks and go back to the way we first knew each other. Zack and Obie."

"All right by me. You know what we are now, Zack? What we are *right this minute* is history."

"Maybe so. More likely our history is all behind us. I reckon we ought to be grateful that we lived through it."

"Trouble is, we got to go on living. How do you calculate to earn a living in the Blue Ridge Mountains?"

"Well, it's been nearly a year since Hunter and his vandals burned down VMI. By now, I'd hope somebody has started rebuilding it, and it's only right that I should lend a hand to my old school. They'll need all the hands they can get. Yours, too, if you don't favor going on to Tennessee. And once it's rebuilt, it'll need professors and instructors again. Maybe I'll qualify. If I do, maybe I could get you taken on as a drill sergeant."

"Me? Teaching cadets at the Virginia Military Institute?" Yount went from gloom to wonderment to radiant cheerfulness. "Say, now, that would be some pumpkins!"

"We can go and see."

After all the hubbub of the commingled armies was behind them, they rode through an eerie silence and emptiness. They came to no sizable communities west of Appomattox, and the few farmhouses they passed were shuttered and smokeless, and there was no one else on the road except an occasional other soldier in gray, like themselves, riding or trudging somewhere homeward. The word had gone abroad, less than a week ago—when Lee's army pulled out of its long besiegement at Petersburg, to make a desperate dash for a new stronghold at Danville or Lynchburg—that it would have to come this way, and that Grant's armies were sure to pursue. So every inhabitant of these parts had grabbed up everything he or she could lift and had got out of what was bound to be a battlefield. As things turned out, the battling had stopped short of here, but there was no one around to hear that news.

Edge and Yount had not taken to the road until well after noon, so the early April twilight was soon upon them. They took shelter for the night in a deserted hamlet, in a ruined and vacant but still partially roofed frame building that, according to the dim signboard still over the doorless doorway, had formerly been the Concord Township School House.

They awoke the next morning to a gray, chilly and drizzly day, the rain not enough to make them stay put, but enough that the red-dirt road soon became a sticky red clay. That slowed the horses, so they made no more progress in a whole day of riding than they had done on the previous afternoon. A while before dusk, they came upon another vacant roadside building, also with a sign: GILES'S STORE. It was empty not only of Gileses but also, as Yount made sure to ascertain, of any kind of stores. The discouragement was enough to disincline them to stop there for the night, and they pushed on. This proved to be a mistake because, after only three or four more miles, the rain began to come down harder, and at the same time Lightning began to limp.

"Cussed animal," Yount grumbled. "Out of all this muck, you manage to pick up a stone."

A little way ahead, there was a wooden bridge visible through the rain, so they kept going until they were on its boards and out of the red mud. Yount dismounted, knelt, took up the hairy barrel hoof on his barrel thigh and began prying at it with his belt knife, meanwhile continuing to grumble:

"Folks around here are great ones for putting up signboards." There was one attached to the bridge railing, identifying the stream underneath as Beaver Creek. "Got to keep reminding themselves who they are, and where."

"We should have stopped at that last sign," said Edge. "This rain won't let up for a while. I vote we get under the bridge and make camp. There ought still to be some dry wood down there."

So they did, and there was, and they soon had a small fire going. They sat on either side of it in the gathering twilight, Edge heating over the flames a pan of sagamite, the cavalryman's iron ration of mixed cornmeal and brown sugar.

"I remember another Beaver Creek on the map," said Yount. "We crossed it coming from Petersburg. No, I recollect now, that one was Beaver *Pond* Creek."

"Oh, hell, there must be more Beaver Creeks in Virginia than there are Baptists," Edge said idly. "I've never seen a real live beaver in the wild, though." He chuckled to himself. "But I've seen many a wild Baptist." When Yount made no comment, Edge glanced up at him. Yount's eyes were wide and his mouth hanging open, a gap in his black beard. Edge said, "Why in the world should that remark surprise you so?"

"Beavers and Baptists be damned," said Yount, in a hushed voice of reverent awe. He was still staring intently, but not at Edge—over his shoulder, past him, down the creek bank. "Just yesterday... me and some fellers was talking about seeing elephants. And now, all of a sudden—by Jesus, Zack—right yonder *is* one!"

2

"MASSA FLORIAN!" came a distant but distinctly agonized wail from somewhere beyond the curtain of rain. Then the wailer materialized out of the wet twilight, a short and scrawny brown-skinned man. He came running barefoot toward the wagon train, his big turban askew and his gaudy robes flapping. "Oh, Lawdy, Mas' Florian!"

"Confound it, Abdullah!" snapped the more plainly garbed driver of the leading vehicle, a rockaway carriage. "Every time you get flustered, you forget to address me as Sahib."

As he came up to the carriage, the brown man panted, "I ain't flustered, Mas' Sahib, I got skeered."

"Damn it all, not *Master* Sahib, just..." Florian stopped, heaved a gusty sigh and shook his head. He reined the carriage horse to a stop. The four wagons in line behind also stopped, and all began quietly but perceptibly settling into the red mud of the road. "Now tell me calmly, Abdullah. What frightened you? And where is Brutus?"

"She yonder." He pointed a wavering brown finger up the road toward the wooden bridge with the sign: BEAVER CREEK.

"Hannibal Tyree, you cowardly black good-for-nothing!" said a pretty blonde woman, who leaned suddenly out the side opening of the rockaway. "You ran off and left poor Peggy all by herself?"

"I *wish*," Florian said fervently, through gritted teeth, "now that we're on the road again, Madame Solitaire, I wish to God we could all get back in character, and remember what character we're each of us in."

"Oh, piss on that," said the pretty woman. "If Hannibal's lost that bull, we might as well get off the road again and back to oblivion."

"Peggy she all right, Miz Sarah," the Negro assured her. "She got all foah feet in de creek yonder. She spouting water wid her trunk, happy as kin be."

"Then what is the trouble, Abdullah?" asked Florian.

"Spied two men a-hiding unner dat bridge, Mas' Florian. Sojer men! Jist happened to look, seen 'em crouched and waiting. *Rebel* sojers. Now dat de waw is ovuh, dey prob'ly turned bummers. Y'all drive 'cross dat bridge, dey spring up and *whooey!*" He turned to say reproachfully to Madame Solitaire, "I ain't no cowardy nigger, Miz Sarah. I come running to warn y'all."

Another two men and a half, from the other wagons, had come up in time to
hear the warning. The half, a man about four feet high, said sourly, "The lint-
head showed some sense for once. It was only that rube on the road said the war
was finished. Maybe it ain't. I kept telling you, Florian, we'd be taking a Christly
risk, coming out this soon."

One of the two taller men—this one not really tall, but slim and lithe, and
elegant-appearing despite his wagon-driver attire—said more temperately, "Oh, I
don't know. In this dismal desolation, it may be better to get shot, une fois pour
toutes, than to perish of slow starvation."

The other, a beefy man whose head was totally hairless except for a fierce
walrus mustache, bluntly asked Florian, "Vas ve do, Baas? Ve go chump dem
first? Feed dem to de cat?"

Florian considered, then got down from the carriage seat and said, "Well, it
may be that they're laying for prey. But right now, I'll warrant, they're goggling
bug-eyed at that unexpected elephant, and making the teetotal pledge to God
and each other. We won't take chances, though. Abdullah, you said Brutus is in
the creek. Which way from the bridge?"

"Left side, Sahib Florian," said the Negro, quite collected now. "Upstream of
dem two bummers."

"All right." To the woman inside the rockaway, Florian said, "Dear lady, would
you hand me our firearm?" She gingerly poked out to him an old and antiquated
underhammer buggy rifle. "I'll go first, men, and down the left bank to where
Brutus is. So you, Captain Hotspur and Monsieur Roulette, sneak down on the
right side of the bridge. If those lurkers jump me, you dart under the bridge and
take them by surprise."

The bald man cracked his knuckles and said, "Ja, Baas." The slim man only
shrugged languidly. The near-midget protested, "Hey, Florian! I don't count for
shit, do I?"

"Tim, Tim," Florian said soothingly. "You'll be the most necessary of us all.
You can tread lightly, so you walk right onto the bridge itself, and they won't hear
you. And here, you take the firearm. If you see us all about to tangle, you can get
off the one shot. Please make it a good one."

The little man took the rifle, almost exactly as tall as he was, and wickedly
bared his little teeth.

"But don't jump them first," Florian said to everybody. "Give me the chance
to introduce myself. They may be harmless tramps and—who knows?— they
may even have some victuals to share."

However, as he made his way through the wet underbrush and sniffed the
caramel-smelling campfire smoke in the air, he muttered unhappily, "No, they
won't, damn it, not if they're reduced to eating sagamite."

He halted behind the last dripping screen of creekside foliage and, dripping
abundantly himself, peered through at the two gray-uniformed men, a few yards
away. They were standing in the shallows right beside the elephant, the water
near their boot tops. As they regarded the animal, one of them reached out to
stroke its trunk, at which Brutus, seeming pleased, voluptuously raised and
flexed and curled the trunk. Florian glanced downstream, saw the small campfire aglow beneath the bridge and, beyond that, two horses browsing on the
shrub they were tethered to. Florian's eyes lighted, and he said under his breath,
this time not at all unhappily, "Well, well, well..."

Then he stepped boldly out toward the men and the elephant, and with great joviality called, "Good evening, good sirs!"

They gave no start of guilt or alarm as they turned, but one of them casually laid a hand on the big black holster at his belt.

With a seigneurial gesture, Florian said, "Allow me to present to you, sirs, *Big Brutus, Biggest Brute That Breathes!*" The men nodded civilly enough, to him and then to the brute. Florian addressed the one with the holstered pistol and with the two stars embroidered on his tunic collar. "Do you know, Colonel, what it signifies when you stroke the trunk, as you just did, and the elephant curls it in respectful salute, as Brutus just did?"

Edge said soberly, "No, sir, I do not."

"It means—according to a venerable circus tradition—that you will someday succeed in owning a circus of your own."

That made Edge smile. And the smile made Florian regard him with some puzzlement. The colonel's face, in repose, was personable in a craggy kind of way, like a benign rock sculpture. But his smile was ineffably sad, and made his face almost ugly.

The two soldiers sloshed out of the water to join the man on the bank, and Yount said, "Circus, hey? That explains it. Mister, I thought I was going crazy. Maybe I still am. Of all the things I might expect to see coming along on the heels of a war, a circus sure ain't high on the list."

"*Florian's Flourishing Florilegium of Wonders*. I have the good fortune to be that very Florian, owner and director of the enterprise." He stuck out his hand.

Edge took it, and noticed that the circus owner had a peculiar grip: it included a sort of extra pressure with his forefinger and thumb against the recipient's palm and knuckles. Maybe, thought Edge, it meant something among circus people, or in whatever foreign country this Florian haled from; he spoke English with too nice a precision for it to be his native tongue.

"A pleasure, Mr. Florian." Edge's uglifying smile was gone, and he looked pleasant again—but he did not act so. While he held onto the circus owner's right hand, his own unencumbered left hand undid his holster flap, drew the long pistol and thumbed back its hammer with an ominous triple click of steel moving against steel. "Sir, you'll do me the favor of standing still, right where you are."

"Oh, misery," sighed Florian, as Edge let go his hand and moved one step back from him, still pointing the revolver at his vest buttons. "Of a Yankee, sir, such behavior would not much astonish me. But I did not know that Southern officers ever fell from gentility to rascality. I had hoped you'd prove friendly."

"So I will be, sir, as long as you don't move left or right. Where you're standing, you are the shield between me and some other friends of yours. There's one up on that bridge and two beyond it. In this bad light, I might not hit all of them, sir, but I promise I can't miss you. Obie, go get the carbine."

"Wait," said Florian. "My own fault, sir. We hoped you would be on the square, but we couldn't be sure you were not bummers lying in ambuscade. If I may raise my voice, I will call those men peaceably in to meet you."

"You may give a call, sir. I recommend that you be persuasive."

Florian turned his head ever so slightly, and shouted, "Friends it is, men! Tim, come down with the gun reversed. Best, kapitein, komt u en ons ontmoeten. Soyez tranquille, Roulette, et venez ici."

After a moment, they could hear the scrabbling noise of the others approaching through the underbrush. Edge nodded approvingly, and recited, "Jamais beau parler n'écorche la langue," but he did not yet lower his pistol. "What was the other language?"

"Dutch," said Florian. From one frayed sleeve of his coat he plucked a fine lawn handkerchief, to pat his brow. "Actually the captain speaks the very crude Cape Dutch, but he comprehends the real thing. More readily than English."

Yount said suspiciously, "Then you and your friends ain't Yanks nor Secesh neither one?"

"My dear Sergeant, any circus is a menagerie of nationalities. I myself am an Alsatian..."

"I meant your political sympathies, mister."

"And we try never to inquire into another man's politics or his religion or any of his other superstitions. Here come my colleagues. If I may introduce you, sirs?" He waited until Edge reholstered the revolver. "In order of arrival, if not of stature, this is Tiny Tim Trimm, our world-renowned midget and hilarity-provoking clown, who doubles in brass as our cornet player."

The little man came dragging the buggy rifle at trail, and nodded grumpily, as if he resented not having had excuse to use the weapon.

Yount remarked, "I've seen smaller midgets."

Tim Trimm glared at him with eyes like those of a fish, colorless, and with that same hard, scaly sort of surface glaze. He snarled, "You can kiss my midget pink ass!"

Florian hastily said, "And this is Monsieur Roulette, champion acrobat, tumbler and ventriloquist."

"Enchanté," said the slim man, unenchantedly.

"And this is Captain Hotspur, our nonpareil equestrian, fearless lion tamer, expert farrier, cartwright and trustworthy wagonmaster to our entire train."

"Goeie nag," said the bald man, then, in translation, "Gut evening, meneers."

"You will have perceived, sirs," said Florian, "that in our circus each man in his time plays many parts... as another great showman once observed."

"You-all sure do have fancy names," Yount said admiringly.

"Les noms de théâtre." Florian flipped a dismissive hand. "Most of us find our noms de baptême unsuited to what we are these many years later in life. For one instance, Jacob Brady Russum's baptismal name is longer than he is, so we redub him more aptly Tim Trimm."

"En nee gut for hotspur horse rider, my name," said the captain, humorously waggling his mustache. "Ignatz Roozeboom."

"Hélas," said Monsieur Roulette. "My name is regrettably an only slightly fancified version of my real one." He held out to Edge a manicured hand from his draggled cuff. "Jules Fontaine Rouleau, late of New Orleans, and a malheureusement far way downhill from there. No doubt my people back home devoutly wish I would take a permanent alias. Even one like Ignatz Roozeboom."

To the company at large, Edge said, "We're pleased to meet all of you. I am Zachary Edge and this is Obie Yount."

"Well," said Florian, "we wayfarers met suspicious of each other, and now that is over, thank goodness. Also the rain is tailing off. But we are all wringing wet and the night is upon us. Brutus seems happy enough here, but I suggest that the rest of us adjourn to shelter in the wagon train. And you, Colonel Edge,

Sergeant Yount, maybe you would like to sup on something better than saga-mite?"

Those two looked at him as they might have regarded a mirage. The circus men also looked at him, and even more incredulously.

"Thank you, but, to tell the truth," said Edge, unwilling to be taken for a cadger, "we had a pretty good meal night before last. Some Yankee boys shared some with us."

Likewise trying to appear self-sufficient, Yount added, "And we had an onion, for a while." Then he weakened. "But it's been damned short commons for a damned long time."

"Ja!" Roozeboom said feelingly, still staring at Florian.

"Yes, yes," said Florian. "With us, too, it's chicken one day, feathers the next. But you lads won't say no to a pork chop tonight?"

"Hell, no, we won't say no!" Yount blurted, to forestall any polite demur from Edge.

As those two went to fetch their horses and other belongings, Rouleau said, "Pork chops?" as lusciously as if he could taste them, and Roozeboom continued to glare—with the space above his eyes, where his brows should have been, contracted into a frown.

Florian ignored them and said to the small man, in an urgent undertone, "Run on ahead, Tim. Tell Madame Solitaire to prepare her wagon for company, and to start a fire under the chops. She'll know what you mean."

Trimm protested wrathfully, "The last time *we* had pork chops was the day we left Wilmington. Ever since, the rest of us have been living on mush and molasses. And damn you, Florian, you and that yeller-haired bitch have been having chops all along?"

"Shut up and scamper. That last time you gorged, Madame Solitaire and I put our two chops away, to save them in hopes of just such an opportunity as this. Don't you see what those soldiers have got? Two capital horses! Go on, you vile homunculus, and do as I say!"

Trimm went, but still fizzing mutinously. The others waited to accompany Edge and Yount from the creek up toward the road again. Roozeboom, walking beside Edge and his Thunder, observed, "Goeie pards, your two horses, meneer. Dey nee have fear of olifant?"

"The matter never came up before," said Edge, with good humor. "I reckon a war horse gets accustomed to surprises."

Florian apparently thought it best not to show too much interest in the horses. He changed the subject. "Aren't you a trifle young, Zachary, to be a lieutenant colonel?"

"No, sir. These last months, promotion kept pace with attrition. Johnny Pe-gram was a brigadier general at twenty-three and dead just two months ago. I'm thirty-six."

"And alive. Well, it did look to me as if you know how to handle your weapons."

Edge shrugged. "I'm alive."

"I was a little astonished to see that you shoot left-handed."

"Either hand. But I'm right-handed by nature, and I prefer to shoot that way."

"You drew your pistol with your left hand."

"Because the cavalry holster is made the way it is. See? Belted on the right hip, pistol butt sticking forward. That's because a cavalryman is expected to use his sabre most often. And you draw the sabre with your right hand from over here, on the left of the belt."

"Ah. The pistol is supposed to be only a second resort."

"Supposed to be. So you learn to draw it left-handed and shoot that way, if you have to. Or flip it to your right hand, if you've got time."

"And you, are you accurate with it either way?"

Edge drily repeated, "I'm alive."

"Allow me to introduce you, messieurs," said Florian, as they got to the top of the creek bank, "to another valued member of our troupe. This is Abdullah, our irreplaceable juggler, drummer and bull man."

"Bull man?" echoed Yount.

"Abdullah is in charge of Brutus, whom you met first of all."

"The elephant? A bull?" said Yount. "I ain't no expert on that breed, Mr. Florian, but I'd reckon even your midget has got more pecker than your Brutus does. Might you be mistaken in supposing it a male critter?"

Florian laughed. "Brutus is a cow, true. And the name she comes to when called is Peggy. Practically all circus elephants are females. Easier to handle. Nevertheless, all circus folk call all elephants bulls. Just another old tradition, like the extravagant names."

"Yessuh," said the Negro to the newcomers. "My real name be's Hannibal Tyree."

They said hello, and Edge remarked that the young man's real name seemed suitable enough for an elephant handler.

"Again, true," said Florian. "You clearly have studied history. But the lad is hardly the right color for a Hannibal. Even more unfortunate, we don't have any armor to dress him as a Carthaginian. But his color *can* pass for Hindu, and an Abdullah requires only some scraps of bright cloth for costume. You will learn, my friends, that a circus, like a woman, lives by artifice and contrivance. We work things out as we go along."

They had come by now to the wagons still standing disconsolately in the darkening night, and rather deeper in the mud. The remainder of the circus troupe had managed to find wood for a fire. They stood around it, bundled in shawls and horse blankets, their eyes yearningly fixed on the frying pan that the pretty woman was holding over the flames. The pork chops, just starting to sizzle in that pan, were also the first thing Edge and Yount looked at.

"Good for you, my dear!" Florian said heartily. "Some provender for our guests."

The woman gave him a good-humored look; the others of the troupe did not. Yount said indistinctly, because his mouth was watering, "Ain't y'all eating?"

"The rest of us," Florian said very distinctly, "have already dined." A subdued growl answered him, whether from someone's throat or belly was indeterminable. Over it, Florian went on, "Let me finish introducing you around. The charming lady doing the cooking is our Madame Solitaire, équestrienne extraordinaire."

She gave them a smile, and it wavered slightly when Edge smiled back. The woman had dark blue eyes and curly, short hair of an antique-gold color. Up close, her pretty face could be seen to have weathered somewhat, and Edge supposed her to be about his own age. She shifted the frying pan to her left hand to shake the strangers' hands with her right; it was as callused as theirs were.

"The bonny young wench is Madame Solitaire's daughter, Mademoiselle Clover Lee, who is learning her mother's art as an apprentice rider."

The girl was thirteen or fourteen years old. She had her mother's cobalt eyes, luminous young skin, and her long, wavy hair was a cascade of even brighter gold, the color and flowingness of a satin cavalry sash.

"The dowager lady," said Florian, "is our farseeing soothsayer and all-seeing wizardess. I am not quizzing you, gentlemen. Perhaps you have sneered at palm readers and other such humbugs on other shows, but I guarantee you this is the genuine article. Some of her prophecies have astounded even me, when they so accurately came to pass, and I am the consummate cynic. I might also mention that the lady's name is no circus coinage; it is what she calls herself. Gentlemen, I have the privilege of presenting Magpie Maggie Hag."

"Good evening—er—ma'am," said Edge.

The old woman's dark face was a tight-tied knot, all wrinkles and puckers and creases, deep within the hood of an ancient cloak. Edge expected her voice, if she had one, to come creaky and feeble from in there. He was surprised when it came, as deep and resonant as a big man's, saying, "Mucho gusto en conocerles."

Yount, not at all taken aback, replied politely in the same language, "Igualmente, señora."

"Why, Mag," said Florian. "It's been a long time since I've heard you speak in one of your old tongues. Why now?"

"Because they speak it," she rumbled.

"Ha! You see?" said Florian. "Knows all, tells all. Well, now you have made the acquaintance of our whole troupe. Oh, except for the Wild Man—back there in the shadows."

They leaned and peered. The lurking one appeared to be nothing but a loutish youth of uncommonly unappealing looks. He had a tangle of long but scanty and colorless hair, slanted eyes, vestigially tiny ears and a repellently protruding tongue too big for his mouth.

"Don't bother to say hello," Florian said carelessly. "He'll take no notice, and he can't reply. We dress him up as a savage and bill him as the Wild Man of the Woods, but he's only a run-of-the-mill idiot."

To the women, Edge said, "I'd like to beg your pardon, ladies, for our coming among you bearing arms." He indicated the pistol at his side, the holstered carbine and sabre on his saddle. "I know it's inexcusable manners. It's just that these weapons are about the only valuables we have left to our name."

The basso voice spoke again. "They soon serve you better, gazho, than ever before."

"Uh, well... thank you, missus... ma'am..."

"Magpie Maggie Hag I am, and so you may call me."

Edge was incapable of addressing any grown woman by a nickname, especially a beldame apparently two or three times his age. So he bowed and turned away, to look at what Florian had described as the "wagon train," and regarded it with wry amusement.

The train consisted of five vehicles. The cooking fire's light was sufficient to show that they had all seen better days, and a multitude of bad days since. Their onetime coats of blue paint and multicolored lettering were faded and peeling, disclosing sprung seams and gaping cracks stuffed with rags. No two wheels on any wagon were in true, and few even leaned in the same direction, and a number of their spokes wore splints tied on with rawhide thongs. At the head of the line was the dilapidated rockaway riding carriage. The next three were high, heavy, slab-sided closed vans. The last, hard to make out in the darkness, seemed to have barred sides, like a jail cell. There was a decent enough horse, a white one, between the shafts of the rockaway, and another, a light dapple gray, to draw the first wagon. The next wagon in line was attached to a drayhorse that had once been as massive as Yount's Lightning, but now was an immense rack of ribs and knobby joints. The next wagon had no shafts or tongue at all, but a complex cat's-cradle of leather traces, ropes and whippletrees, patched together to enable it to be drawn by two very small, shaggy and dejected-looking animals.

"*Jackasses?*" said Edge.

"Disdain them not," Florian said airily and without embarrassment. "The little beasts have served loyally, hauling that museum wagon. They also inspired me to make up one of the few poems I have composed in my life. I have been saying it over and over to myself, over the weary miles:

> Far have we traveled,
> And slowly time passes.
> Tired are our feet
> And tired are our asses."

"Florian's Flourishing Florilegium..." muttered Yount. He was puzzling out the ornate and once brilliant legend on the side of the nearest wagon. "Southern Men, Southern Horses, Southern Enterprise... A Southern Show for Southern People!"

"To be honest," said Florian, "I borrowed that line from Mighty Haag." Edge and Yount nodded, though uncomprehending. "It went over well in North Carolina, where we've just come from. However, in real Bible-thumping-bumpkin land, I generally make it 'A Clean Show for Moral Folk.' It is usually necessary to overcome the typical intolerance of the provincial intellect for anything new or foreign. But come, friends! Let Captain Hotspur take your horses. While your supper is cooking, let us go inside this wagon and"—he nudged Edge with an elbow—"take on some wood and water, eh?"

They got inside by climbing a little stile, hinged to let down from the wagon's sagging rear, and then opening a narrow door in the wagon's back wall. The interior had only a constricted open aisle down its middle, because on both sides were shelves and racks and uprights from floor to ceiling, provided with many hinges, hasps, hooks, sliding bolts—all sorts of hardware, all of it rather rusty— so the sections of apparatus could be variously let open or stowed tight or made to do double duty, and every opening in that woodwork bulged with rolls of canvas, painted poles, coils of heavy rope, unidentifiable other gear. A coal-oil lantern was already alight and dangling from a ceiling hook. The atmosphere inside the wagon was pungent but not offensive, compounded of several major smells: old smoke, warm hay, feminine perfumes and powders, animal odors— and several minor ones: greasepaint, mildew, dried sweat.

Florian said, as he went stooping and searching for something, "Pull down that section there, Obie. It's a bunk you two can sit on. This is normally the tent wagon and the women's quarters, but I told Madame Solitaire to prepare it for guests and—ah, yes, here we are."

He stood up, holding a half-full bottle and three tin cups. Edge unbuckled and laid aside his belt and holstered pistol. Yount fumbled with latches and cautiously eased down one blanketed bunk shelf for himself and Edge, while Florian deftly let down another for himself across the narrow aisle, deftly uncorked the bottle and deftly poured. The guests took the proffered cups, and Florian, with his, made a gesture of toasting.

"Well met, gentlemen. Here's to you."

The guests murmured replies, drank, flinched, shuddered and meditated. After a moment Edge inquired, "Ought we to be drinking up your horses' liniment?"

"I admit it's not Overholtz rye," said Florian, looking a little hurt. "Wilmington city was fairly well provided with the luxuries of life, but not many of them percolated down to us. Still, this is whiskey of a sort, and not everybody in Dixie is drinking whiskey of any sort tonight."

"Amen!" said Yount, holding out his cup for a refill.

Edge said, "Was Wilmington your last stopping place?"

Both Edge and Yount, though they had not exchanged a word about it, now strongly suspected the real reason for their being so cordially received: that he would try to talk them into parting with their horses. So they sat back and studied Florian as he talked. What they saw was a small, compact, slightly plump man in a maroon frock coat and gray shoe-loop trousers that once had been exceptionally natty and now were stained, patched and threadbare. The lapels and turnback cuffs of his coat still bore remnants of what had been an expensive job of gold-thread embroidery. Florian's brown eyes were bright and lively, and he didn't seem to be much over sixty, but his hair and his neatly vandyked little beard were silver-white, and his ruddy face had been deeply stamped and rutted by the tread of his years.

"Wilmington," he said, not fondly. "It looked like Wilmington would be our last stopping place forever." He sloshed more whiskey into their cups. "Five years ago, when it was clear that a war was going to break out any day, practically every circus in North America hurried to make one last tour before the roads were barred. We owners and directors all convened at the Atlantic House in Philadelphia, to agree on which of us would go north, west or wherever. For a particular reason, I chose south, and here I've been ever since. Even the shows that got back safe and sound to their northern grounds haven't had an easy time of it over these last years, so I've heard. Dan Rice put his show on a boat, and he's been not very profitably working up and down the Ohio River. Spalding and Rogers took ship to South America to wait out the war. Howes and Cushing to England. Maybe some others got stuck behind the lines, the way we did; I don't know."

He paused to sip at his whiskey. Yount asked, "Can we smoke in here?" Florian bobbed his head, so Yount got out the last of the tobacco he had scrounged from that Connecticut Yankee. He and Edge filled pipes and lit up, and asked what was the particular reason that had brought Florian south.

"I wanted to acquire some good freaks. In America, North Carolina is the best source for them."

"Is that a fact?" said Edge. "Why?"

"Hell, man, up there in the Great Smoky Mountains those Tarheels have been inbreeding for centuries. Why else do you think the North Carolinians are called Tarheels? Because they stick where they are. Those hillbillies never move five miles off their home mountains in their whole lives, so they've got nobody to marry but one another. When sisters and brothers and cousins have been inter-marrying for generations, all they generate is Wild Men, Pinheads, Three-Legged Wonders, Bearded Ladies, you name it. And they'll gleefully give them away free gratis."

"I just bet," said Yount.

"So that's why I decided to head south. And immediately half my show walked out on me. Ten or twelve artistes and numerous animals they owned. Those performers just would not venture southward under the prevailing uncer-tain circumstances. That didn't surprise me much. In fact, I was considerably surprised and pleased that Abdullah consented to come, since he'd been freed only a few years before, from a Delaware plantation. And I wasn't too much bothered by the defection of those others. A smaller troupe was easier to trans-port, and still it was a good enough show to draw the yokels."

"You came with just what circus you've got now?" Edge asked.

"Yes. Except that we had better road stock than jackasses, and the wagons and gear and costumes were all in good condition and sparkling trim back then. We made a sufficiently awesome impression on the Tarheels. Better than they made on us. Which is to say that they were, for once in history, dismally short on freaks. All we picked up was that mediocre idiot. So there we were, working our way through the Smokies, and as remote from civilization as those hillbillies. We didn't even hear that the war had started until it was well under way. When we did, we came hellity-split out of those mountains. Made a dash for the coast, hoping to get a ship. We made Wilmington all right, and that was the end of our luck."

"Ought to've been grateful you had that much," grunted Yount.

"Oh, we were, indeed. Wilmington was a Confederate seaport—but even so, all through the war, it was a sort of little Switzerland between the belligerents. Both sides seemed tacitly to have decided on that. The Union warships block-aded the port, but only in a halfhearted way, so there was constant traffic through it—to and from both sides. It was the Confederacy's best access to foreign trade. And it served the Union as a channel for slipping in spies and provocateurs, for arranging prisoner-exchange agreements, that kind of thing."

"If so many other things were going in and out," said Edge, "why couldn't you?"

"For one reason, blockade runners don't use craft big enough to ship an elephant. For another, they had their pick of far better-paying cargoes. Going out of Wilmington, the runners could take cotton, tobacco, hoarded gold and jewels, passengers eager to pay any price—foreigners who'd got caught over here, wealthy Southern planters and their families fleeing abroad, young Southern gentlemen not caring to put on a gray uniform..."

Yount snorted in disgust, then said, "But it couldn't of been the worst place in the world for you to be stuck."

"No, no, not at all. A lot of the goodies going in and out clung to Wilmington's fingers, so to speak. The city lived royally, compared to most of the South. Not that *we* could afford many of the good things. But the gougers had to spend their loot somewhere, so they spent it on entertainment. Throwing gala balls and dinners, going to the theater, to the racetrack—and to the circus, which was us."

The three men sat silent for a minute, listening to the circus outside making ready for the night. There were muted whinnies as the horses and asses were unhitched and let loose to graze. There were some louder moos that suggested cows, but were apparently the noises of the Wild Man. There was shuffling and clatters and a rumbling of the gypsy's voice that sounded like conjurings in some unintelligible tongue. And once there came the light, young laugh of a girl.

Florian resumed, "We couldn't add to the troupe or even keep up our equipment while we were in Wilmington; the blockade runners didn't import circus gear or performers. Cloth was too expensive for us ever to afford new costumes. But we kept our tickets cheap to keep folks coming time and again. And by changing our acts and our program at intervals, we managed to show the folks some diversity. Every one of our people changed names so many times—that's why I am being insistent now: that they resume and remember their original characters. Well, that's it. We didn't thrive, God knows, but we survived."

"And now?" said Edge.

"Now we damned well *want* to thrive. We've had enough of poverty and misery and making do. Making the horses and poor Brutus learn to live on corn shucks. Feeding poor Maximus any guts and tripes we could scavenge, and the feet of the chickens we stole for ourselves, and any stray pet dogs and cats we could catch in the alleys."

Yount asked, "What's Maximus?"

"Our circus cat."

"You fed a cat *cats*?"

"Cat is the circus word for any feline—lion, tiger, leopard, whatever. Maximus is a lion. That reminds me...if you'll excuse me a moment, Zachary and Obie?" He opened the door, stuck his head out and called loudly, "Captain Hotspur!"

When Roozeboom appeared at the foot of the little stair, Florian spoke at some length in Dutch, except that the name Maximus occurred a time or two. Roozeboom replied, "Ja, Baas," and went away again.

Florian shut the door and continued, "Let me give you an instance of the troubles we've seen. These last days, coming inland from Wilmington, we've put on a show in every crossroads community on the way. I mean, here we are, in Backwater Junction, North Carolina; we might as well set up and perform. And here are some Backwater people to watch, and maybe they've got a spare copper or a turnip to pay us with."

He paused and chuckled richly. "No, I'll be honest. Circus folk will put on a show wherever there are people to watch. Admiration is our sunshine. We are like birds—we would sing and preen and strut in any case, and so any paying audience just adds extra warmth to the sunshine." He chuckled again, then sobered. "Well, North Carolina is swarming with tramp darkies—freed or run away—so we would give them a meal of whatever we had, in exchange for their running on ahead to the next town, during the night, and posting our paper."

Edge and Yount looked blank.

"Putting up our circus posters on walls and trees—sticking them up with flour-and-water paste. We'd give them a little pail of it to carry along with the paper. Well, we kept coming to new towns and seeing no paper, and the people not aware we were coming. What it was, the darkies were throwing away the posters and *eating the paste!* That's how bad things have been."

"Do you think things are any better here?" Yount asked, with a harsh laugh. "Mr. Florian, for the past ninety miles or so, you've been inside the Commonwealth of Virginia. You talk about people and coppers and turnips—hell!—we ain't even seen a loose *darky* in the last two days."

Florian looked glum. "We had no choice; we had to get out of Wilmington. The Federals finally invaded and took over, five or six weeks back, and the good life, so-called, came to an end. It was clear that the whole war was fast coming to an end. We didn't want to risk being marooned in Dixie for however long the Union decides to keep the Confederacy under severe martial law. Right now, we're aiming for Lynchburg."

"Just a short day's ride from here," said Yount.

"And it's a sizable burg," said Florian. "Big enough that it might provide some badly needed sustenance for us. Then we'll keep on north. On the way, maybe recruit new acts, find new gear to replace our worn-out stuff. If we can only get across the Mason-Dixon line..."

"When you came out of Wilmington and headed this way," said Edge, eyeing Florian curiously, "you were aiming straight across General Lee's intended route of march. Right this minute you might have been in the very middle of a shooting war. What fool kind of thing was that to do?"

"A gamble, yes, but a shrewd one, I thought. And so it proved. You see, we got word in Wilmington as soon as your army pulled out of Petersburg, and the word was that your men were deserting by the thousands from that moment on. The end had to come soon. I figured Lee's march would stumble to a stop, well before we crossed its route."

"I see," Edge said somberly. "Well, we realized the end was imminent when General Lee didn't issue any order against straggling. It was the first time he ever neglected to do that, and we knew it was deliberate, and everybody knew what he meant by it. We left Petersburg with something like twenty-seven thousand men, and they just melted away. At Appomattox, as best I could count, we had about eight thousand left to surrender. Yes, you judged right, Mr. Florian. I hope you keep on being right."

"If I could boast a Latin family motto, Zachary, I daresay it would be... let's see... 'In mala cruce, dissimula!' Rough Latin, maybe, but it says it: 'When in a bad fix, bluff!'"

There was a kick at the wagon door, and a voice announced blithely, "Flag's up!"

Florian leaned to unlatch the door. Madame Solitaire stood smiling on the little stile, holding two steaming tin plates. Each bore a single, very small, fried pork chop, a dab of cornmeal mush and some anonymous greens. Edge and Yount thanked her effusively as she handed them the pathetic meals and a tin fork apiece. They sat looking at the plates and politely hesitating and audibly gulping.

"Well, go on, eat!" said the pretty woman. "Don't wait for me. I've already had mine. We all have. Florian said so, didn't he?" She threw him a mocking glance.

So the two men pulled out their belt knives and pitched in, trying not to look voracious about it. Edge cut for himself a tiny fragment of pork, forked it into his mouth, chewed it for a savoring long time, swallowed, paused in appreciative deliberation and said, "Mighty fine, Madame Solitaire, and mighty welcome, and mighty hospitable of you folks."

"If you're going to make speeches at me while you eat, call me Sarah—it's shorter, and you can eat a lot faster. My real name is Sarah Coverley."

"Please, Madame Solitaire," Florian objected mildly. "I am trying to teach them circus ways."

"Oh, balls," she said, and the two men's eyebrows went up. "*I'm* circus, but I can't remember all the names I've had for all the ways I've performed. Princess Shalimar in harem gauzes, Pierrette in a clown suit, Joan of Arc in pasteboard armor, Lady Godiva in nothing at all..." The two men's eyebrows practically merged into their hairlines. "Will you two stop stopping? Go on and eat while it's hot."

Florian commented, "They may be hesitating over the taste of it. I'm sorry, lads, but that's how Nassau pork is. Coming all that way from overseas, it does tend to get a little greenish."

"No, no, it's fine, perfectly fine!" Edge said, and cut another minuscule bite. He chewed as thoroughly as if it had been an entire ham, swallowed and spoke again. "If your name is Sarah, ma'am, I reckon your little girl is not Mam'selle Whatever-it-was."

"No, she's Edith Coverley, but *her* stage name came sort of naturally. See, when she was only a teensy squirt, first learning to talk, she couldn't pronounce that name Coverley. Best she could do was Clover Lee. So she just kept it as she grew up."

"It *is* a nice name," said Yount. "And Mr. Coverley, what's he called?"

"'The late,' I hope, if he's in hell where he belongs. I haven't laid eyes on the son of a bitch since I notified him that Clover Lee was on the way."

Yount's eyebrows did some more twitching, but Edge hastened to say, "From your name, I take it you're not a foreigner."

"To you I probably am, Reb," she said mischievously. "I'm from New Jersey. Now shut up and eat. I'll be back for the dishes when you're done. Florian, pour them some more of your snake piss, to cut the taste of that pork."

She went out, and Florian did as he was bidden. Edge drank from his freshened cup and said:

"I was just trying to sort out the menagerie of nationalities you spoke of. It seems to me that most are Americans. That lady and her daughter, the Louisiana gentleman, the Tarheel idiot. I reckon you could stretch a point and call the elephant darky an African. You said you're an Alsatian, and the lion tamer is Cape Dutch. But the midget—from his lovable disposition and his cultured speech, I'd guess Deep South poor-white trash."

"Yes, Tim's just a Mississippi mudcat. But most circus people talk rough— you heard Madame Solitaire. If Tim talks filthier and louder, it's because he thinks he's talking *taller*. Of course, that's about as hopeless as a cross-eyed man trying to look dignified."

"The old dowager lady ain't American, Zack," Yount pointed out. He said to Florian with some pride, "We picked up a good deal of Spanish down in Mexico."

"But the old lady is no Mexican," said Edge. "She speaks her 'c' with a lisp. That's European Spanish."

"Right," said Florian. "Maggie's a Spanish-born gypsy." He looked at Edge long and thoroughly. "So you know Spanish well enough to spot the real Castilian. And down there at the creek you spoke to me in French."

Edge said deprecatingly, "A textbook proverb. My French has gone rusty, I'm afraid. I tried to keep it up—spoke it sometimes with General Beauregard. He's from an old New Orleans Creole family, like your Rouleau gentleman."

"And you?"

"I'm not. Not a gentleman, not anything. No old family, no exotic birthplace. Never been abroad, except for Mexico and the Territories. I'm just a Virginia hillbilly."

"I meant where did you learn French?"

"At the 'I'—when I was a rat."

Florian blinked. "I beg your pardon?"

"Well, you've been flinging circus slang at us all evening. I thought I'd retaliate." He smiled, and Florian blinked again, at the change it made in Edge's face. "A rat is what a new cadet was called at the Virginia Military Institute—the 'I.' That's where I learned French. One of the first books we had to crack there was the *Vie de Washington.*"

Florian continued to look keenly at him. "So you have some French and some Spanish. Any other languages, Zachary?"

"Well, I read Latin, of course."

"Of course. I'd expect that of any Virginia hillbilly."

"You know what I mean. We had to study Latin at VMI. Major Preston taught it, and he was a good teacher. Hell, all our teachers were top-notch. One of them you've probably heard of—Stonewall Jackson. Not that he was called Stonewall then. We called him Professor, and we took care to say it respectfully. He was pure-poison pious and strict. Anyhow, I was well taught, and I've tried to hang onto what I got there. I don't mean I could sit here right this minute and construe a passage in Tacitus, but . . ."

"But you have some Latin, some French and some Spanish. Quite a cultivated man, you are. You could easily make your way all over Europe. Have you boys ever thought of going to see it?"

Edge stared, smiled his woebegone smile, shook his head and sighed. "Europe? Mr. Florian, there's about as much chance of us going to see Europe as there is of it coming to see us."

Florian laughed, but went on sincerely, "Again I say that I am not quizzing you, friends, I am dead serious. Europe is where I came from, where I got my early circus experience. That's where I intend to go back to, just as soon as I can, and take my circus there. The United and Confederate States are going to be suffering turmoil and deprivation for a long time yet. If I hope to recoup my fortunes, and increase them—and everybody else's on the show—Europe is the place to do it. We shall forge on through this impoverished southland until we get to some northern cities where there is more money to be made, and make enough of it to take ship for England or France. What do you lads say to coming along?"

Edge said, with sardonic amusement, "All this while, I've been expecting you to make us some kind of offer for our horses."

"Well, ahem, yes. I'd like to have them, indeed I would. And when we first met, they were all I had eyes for. But now I'd like to have you two along with them."

Yount said unbelievingly, "Ain't you already saddled with enough poor-whites—and other colors—counting on you for support? Why in blazes would you want two more that can't earn their keep?"

"Because I think you could, Obie. Earn your keep and more. I told you I hoped to be adding new acts as we go."

"Acts? Hell fire, mister, I ain't no actor! All I know is soldiering. Why, the notion is pure moonshine. Me, at my age in life, running off like a schoolboy truant to join a *circus?*"

"No actor was ever an actor until he started acting. And nobody ever knows what extraordinary things he may be capable of, until he tries something out of the ordinary. That's what the circus is, Obie—a stretching of the limits of the possible, a defiance of the strictures of the commonplace, a realization that the impossible *can* be possible."

"Well, mebbe so," Yount mumbled, overwhelmed by the rhetoric. "But it ain't for everybody."

"When I first met Hannibal Tyree, he was shining shoes on a Pittsburgh street corner, and he never figured to be anything but a Negro shine-boy for the rest of his life. I came along. I saw the way he flipped those shoe brushes and slapped that shine rag in cakewalk tempo. Result? Today he is an artiste, a competent juggler, and a bull man besides. As long as there exists a circus on this planet, Abdullah won't lack for gainful employment at a job he enjoys . . . and he'll have admiration . . . and a measure of celebrity. He may never be a star turn like Léotard or Blondin or the Siamese Twins, but he'll never be just a low-down nigger again. Sergeant, what's the heaviest thing you ever lifted?"

"Uh, what?" Yount started at the unexpected question, and stammered, "Why . . . heavy thing? Jesus, I don't know. Heaving an artillery caisson out of a mudhole, I reckon."

"All by yourself?"

"Uh huh. See, it was like this—"

"Never mind. I just wanted you to realize. That's something not everybody could do. Now, I doubt that you could lift Brutus off the ground, but I wouldn't give odds that you can't lift that Percheron of yours. You certainly *look* like a strongman, and that's how I'll bill you. How does *The Quakemaker, Strongest Man on Earth* sound to you?" Yount gawked at him, stupefied. "As for you, Zachary, I've been thinking: something dignified, along the lines of Colonel Deadeye or Colonel—"

"No," Edge said flatly. "Don't squander your powers of persuasion on me, Mr. Florian. Anyway, I'm not a Colonel Anything any more. As soon as I can lay me down to sleep someplace warm enough to take off this tunic, I'm going to pick the damned embroidery off the collar so nobody'll mistake me again for what I'm not."

"Don't be a simpleton," said Florian. "At least you came by those two stars honestly. Hell, after this war, every measly militia man who spent his whole military career in the Saltpeter Corps—if he got even a brevet rank for it—will insist on being addressed as Major or Colonel to the end of his days."

"Let him, I don't give a damn. He can't outrank me. There are no ranks in civilian life."

"Anyway, Zachary, I was talking of a stage name. In everyday civilian life, outside the pavilion, you can call yourself what you like."

"Everyday civilian life is exactly what I'm going back to, thank you. Not a circus life of doing tricks for anybody who's got the price of admission, and deluding myself that that's celebrity."

There was a thump at the door again, and this time Sarah Coverley let herself in without waiting. She said cheerily, "The troops all fed? And what's this—nobody drunk yet? What kind of Southern gentlemen—?" She stopped and gazed around at them: Edge looking adamant, Yount looking uncomfortable and Florian apparently pondering deeply. "Did I interrupt devotions, or what?"

Florian shook his head and said to nobody in particular, "I was trying to think of some civilian occupation that does *not* consist of doing tricks for whoever will pay for them. And a civilian occupation that is *not* arrayed according to rank."

"Ah, you gents are playing at conundrums," said Sarah. "Do I get a turn?"

"Be quiet," said Florian. "Tell me, Zachary, what occupation *are* you going back to?"

"I don't know. Maybe I'll have to turn bandido or filibustero, like the leftovers from most wars. But I'm hoping that maybe I can get on the faculty of VMI. Teach cavalry tactics or something. Hell, after nineteen years in one uniform or another, I ought to be able to give the rats something worth their while."

Florian jumped to his feet and said loudly, in disbelief, "A man in the absolute prime of life, a veteran of nineteen years of manly action in the wide-open outdoors, and you're going to dwindle into a *schoolmarm*? A dusty, desk-bound, time-serving, nose-wiping warder of green and pimpled recruits? For that, you'd forgo the opportunity I am offering you? To stay on horseback, to go on using your skills and your weapons and your experience. To enjoy all manner of excitement and adventure, to be a man among men—*and* among gorgeous women like Madame Solitaire here—*and* to see the world into the bargain. Solitaire, tell Zachary what a fool he is!"

"What a fool you are, Zachary," Sarah said, biting back a grin.

Florian said, "Gentlemen, I offer each of you thirty dollars a month. And peck, of course." He indicated the plates the two men had cleaned. "Obie, you to be the Circus Strongman. Zachary, you to be our Exhibition Shootist. You heard what Magpie Maggie Hag said—that your weapons will serve you better now than ever before. For each of you, thirty dollars and peck. And prospects, gentlemen, *and prospects*. The prospects of advancement to positions of responsibility and unimpeachable respectability. Prospects of—"

"Of performing before the crowned heads of every country on the globe!" Sarah took it up as if she was reciting a speech heard often before, and now she was not hiding her grin. "Prospects of meeting and dazzling the wealthiest and handsomest young counts and dukes and even princes. Why, you could marry some European nobleman so far above your station, so far beyond your wildest New Jersey dreams..."

She desisted, for they were all laughing.

Florian took advantage of the moment to bring forth his bottle again. "Here, lads, have another dram of this dyspepsia."

"Thank you," said Edge. "But I still have to decline your offer, sir. It would actually mean a considerable comedown for me. My present wage is ninety dollars a month, all found."

"And when did you last get paid?"

"Oh, well."

"If you had a thousand of those Confederate butt-wiper dollars right now, you'd be lucky to exchange them for one Federal ten-dollar gold piece."

Yount exclaimed, "You're offering thirty a month in gold?"

"Yes, by God, I am. Gold, sterling, whatever is the specie of whatever realm we're in. Of course, you understand that it must be promissory for the time being. I think I've made plain to you the current situation. We are all of us working on speculation, as it were. However, strict account will be kept, and all obligations honored in full." While he went on talking to Yount, Florian gave Sarah a look, and she nodded almost imperceptibly in reply. "So, Obie, let's you and me step outside and discuss this, and we'll also decide where you two might spread your bedrolls tonight. In the meantime, Zachary, would you kindly lend Madame Solitaire a hand with clearing away the supper utensils?"

He was gone, with Yount in tow, and the door closed behind them, before Edge could ask why the woman should need assistance in gathering up two small plates, two forks and three cups. She didn't even pick them up. She picked up the bottle instead, held it to the lantern, then divided its remaining inch or so of liquor into two of the cups and handed one to Edge.

"Let us drink," she said, "to you being such a fool that you don't want to bedazzle a duke."

"Is that what you want to do sometime?" he asked, as they clinked cups and drank.

"Sure, why not? I've bedazzled lesser notables, and not just in the circus ring. Aren't you dazzled, Zachary?"

"Is that what you want me to be?"

"Yes," she said, and seemed to wait. She added, "I am extremely susceptible to compliments." When Edge responded only with a boyish flush to his face, she added, "I am a widow—of sorts—and I frequently suffer from the widow's complaint."

Exposed to so much feminine frankness, unprecedented in his experience of women, Edge could only say, "What is that complaint, ma'am?"

"Suppressed flirtation. If it should break out in boils, I could not sit a horse. I've got to think of my art and my livelihood."

Edge recklessly suggested, "Better not suppress it, then."

"I try not to. And right now the other ladies are doing their best to help me not to. Old Maggie and my Clover Lee are bedding down tonight in the property wagon—the white men's quarters—and they've booted the men out to sleep on the ground with Hannibal and the Wild Man and your sergeant. So you and I can have this wagon to ourselves. These bunks are not exactly commodious, but we can pile the bedding on the floor."

Edge cleared his throat. "I'm not at all averse, Madame Soli—"

"That's big of you. You're supposed to be as dazzled as a duke. And do call me Sarah, or we'll never get past these damned kittenish preliminaries."

Edge said patiently, "Sarah, I was only trying to remark, with apologies, that I haven't had this uniform off in I can't remember how long."

She shrugged. "Leave it on, then. Do you only perform by the manual of drill?"

"I mean, goddamn it, woman, *I need a bath!* Can you let me borrow a piece of soap? I'll slip down to the creek."

"Oh. Well, if we're going to be duke-and-duchess fastidious about this, I ought to have one too. I'll come with you."

"That water'll be cold. You may be a horsewoman, but I doubt that you've got the hide of a cavalryman."

"You can feel it all over, and tell me." Still carrying her cup of whiskey, she reached for the door. "Come on. You can even satisfy your cavalryman's curiosity. About whether this filly's tail matches her mane."

"Wait a minute. I want to ask—are you Florian's woman?"

She tossed off the dregs in her cup. "When he needs one."

"And when he needs somebody persuaded of something, he uses you for that, too?"

"That's not very flattering, Zachary. To yourself or to me, either one."

"I just wouldn't want you to do something under duress, and find out afterward it went for naught."

"Oh, crap. Now you're being the gallant Southron. Maybe there was a time when I wanted to be wanted. Now I'm satisfied just to be needed."

"Damned if I'm acting gallant, when I'm saying straight out that I *don't* need you. I mean, I don't need a woman so bad that tomorrow I'll join this road show out of gratitude or guilty conscience."

"Why don't we both simply shut up and let nature take its course? You never know, you may be so smitten that you'll join out, just hoping for more of me."

"You really reckon that you'll bedazzle me, Sarah? That you're so irresistibly good-looking? Or so talented in that way?"

She shrugged again. "The looks may have gone downhill over the years, but the talent could only have increased, right? . . . Don't do that."

"Do what?"

"Smile. Don't. You're a much handsomer man when you don't smile."

"Well, I don't, often. I don't find many things nowadays to smile about. I thank you for giving me cause to smile, just then—but if you say so, I'll try not to."

"Good," she said, and sighed a little. "So will I."

But later, in the dark, she did smile, and so did he.

3

AT THE SOUND of a shot very close somewhere, Edge came instantly awake and flung off the blanket that covered him. He was not quite awake enough to be aware of where he was, but he had recognized that the sound was not of friendly fire. It had been a rifle shot, but of a lighter-calibre weapon than his own familiar carbine. In the dark, he grabbed for his revolver, left within easy reach whenever and wherever he went to sleep. Instinctively he made for the nearest light in the darkness, a rectangular bright sliver indicating a closed door. He burst through that door, pistol foremost, and was in the full sunlight of a mild April morning, where he was greeted by an uproar of shouts, laughter and at least one piercing feminine screech of outrage. Edge realized that he was standing at the top of the little stair leading from the circus wagon in which he had slept, and that he was standing there buck naked, unaccoutred except for the revolver in his hand.

"Colonel Zack!" cried Obie Yount, scandalized. "You're out of uniform!"

"Superb entrance, Zachary!" caroled Sarah Coverley, already dressed and outdoors.

Jules Rouleau began to sing, in a syrupy way, the refrain of "Oh, Wake and Call Me Early, Call Me Early, Mother Dear."

"Hey, Colonel!" yelled Tim Trimm. "At least stick on your stars and braid!"

Even the elephant let out a mocking trumpet blast. And the outraged screech sounded again, from a middle-aged woman upon a lattice-sided tobacco wagon that had not been there the night before. She would only have had to turn her head and the immense coal-scuttle bonnet she wore would have blocked out any unwelcome sight. Instead, she dramatically flung her apron up over her head.

At least assured that nobody was under armed attack—though that did not much palliate his hideous embarrassment—the red-faced Edge popped back through the door and slammed it shut.

"Well, I never!" wailed the woman, from under her apron. "And in front of a good Christian woman and her innocent chillun! Oh, I had heerd of sich goings-on amongst you traveling folk, but never did I think to see the day—"

"Pay it no mind, Mrs. Grover," said Florian.

"He's gone now, Maw," said the middle-aged man beside her on the wagon seat, and spat tobacco juice over the wheel. "You kin unkiver your head."

Florian solemnly explained, "A case of what the military surgeons call soldier's heart—a nervous disorder brought on when a man has endured long service under fire."

"Lots of our sojers suffer from it, I hear," Mr. Grover said sympathetically. "You hadn't ought to of let that gun be shot off, without warning the poor feller."

"Too true, sir. Now, as I was saying, you folks will be in Lynchburg this afternoon, before we can get there, so we'll gladly reward you for doing us a favor."

The tobacco wagon had come along the road from the east and was waiting for the circus to clear the way for it to pass. Florian had already ascertained that Mr. and Mrs. Grover and family were refugees who had fled Lynchburg in expectation of its soon being under siege. Now that the war was over, they were going home again. Their wagon carried no tobacco, but was heaped and hung with all their household belongings, including numerous children. While the Grovers' collective attention was on the elephant and the other exotica roundabout—and, briefly, Zachary Edge's contribution to the spectacle—Tiny Tim Trimm and Magpie Maggie Hag were unobtrusively but industriously filching from the wagon every small item within their reach that was concealable in the gypsy's many layers of voluminous skirts.

"Just take these posters and this paste along with you," said Florian, handing them up to the woman. "Stick them anywhere you can—walls, trees, shop windows."

"They ain't nasty things, are they?" Mrs. Grover asked, looking disapprovingly at the rolls of paper on her lap. "Like that-there sojer's hard we jist seen?"

Florian turned away to cough for a minute, then said, "Madame, read the poster for yourself."

She said primly, "I don't never read nothing 'cept the Good Book. Rev'rend

Jonas bids us avoid everything what's unnecessary or unwholesome."

"You would avoid laughter, madame? Pleasure?"

"Rev'rend Jonas says laughter is seldom necessary and pleasure is seldom wholesome. So I don't never read nothing 'cept—"

"This is a perfectly respectable advertisement of our show. Perhaps you'll allow me to read it *to* you..." Flapping open one of the rolled sheets he still held, Florian began to do so, with appropriate gestures, vocal modulations from piano to forte, occasional suspenseful pauses and distinctly audible capitals and italics.

"'FLORIAN'S FLOURISHING FLORILEGIUM! Combined Circus, Menagerie, Educational Exhibition and Congress of Trained Animals!... Recently acclaimed at Niblo's Garden in New York City!... Crowned with *New Laurels of Success* in the Capitals of Europe and South America!... To be *Presented Here in Pavilion*... TOMORROW!'"

"Hooray!" cried all the little Grovers.

"... 'Under the auspices of an enlightened management whose sole aim has been to form a COMPLETE MODERN COTERIE comprising the *Male and Female Elite* of the Equescurriculum... and the *Crème de la Crème* of Acrobatic and Gymnastic Artistes, Coryphées and Vaulters, who, in their Astonishing Feats of Agility, defy the Earth's Own Gravity!'..."

"My!" breathed Mrs. Grover.

"... 'Plus the most MAMMOTH MENAGERIE of the Treasures of Zoölogy ever presented to a Discerning Public, including the *Man-Eating African Lion*, MAXIMUS, King of Beasts, trained and commanded by the daring Captain Hotspur... and BRUTUS THE ELEPHANT, the veritable *Behemoth of Holy Writ*, captured by his present keeper, Abdullah the Hindu Hunter, in the jungles of far-off Asia!'..."

"Is that a fact?" said Mr. Grover, staring at the elephant even more admiringly than he had been doing.

"... 'And all the other *Unique Attractions* which make up this WORLD-FAMOUS CONVENTICLE OF WONDERS!!!'..."

Florian glanced up and saw Edge standing nearby, dressed now, regarding the scene from under a skeptically cocked eyebrow.

"Well, ahem, there's a good deal more of just plain description like that, so I won't read it all. But do listen to this part: 'It is *too true* that very few of today's traveling establishments are suitable for ladies and families to visit. A laudable exception is Florian's GREAT MORAL EXHIBITION, wholly free from indelicate sights, sounds or allusions, and dedicated to the upholding of *Virtue and Piety*.'"

"It all does sound right respectable," said Mrs. Grover.

"Beats me why world-famous folks like you-all would *want* to spread yourselves in poky old Lynchburg," said Mr. Grover, spitting juicily again. "What's it cost?"

Florian read again from the poster: "'Notwithstanding the enormous outlay attendant upon such a SHOW OF SPLENDORS, the admission price is fixed at the trifling figure of only twenty-five cents; children under twelve and servants only ten cents...'"

"Fergit it, mister," said Mr. Grover.

Florian hastily took out a thick mason's pencil, scribbled on the poster and read the emendation: "'*Or* twenty-five dollars and ten dollars in Confederate scrip. *Or* barter in kind acceptable.'"

"That mean groceries?"

"Any local produce or commodities."

"Ain't much *in* Lynchburg 'cept a little tobacco."

"Well—heh heh—believe it or not, yonder behemoth enjoys a plug when it's offered."

"What, the Beast of Holy Writ? *Chews tobacco?*"

"Learned it from an Old Testament prophet, yes. But it will cost you good Grovers nothing at all to see our extravaganza. Merely post those papers today and, when you present yourselves at the Big Top tomorrow, I will personally hand to you and every one of your fine children a free ticket. To the best seats in the house."

"Hooray!" all the little Grovers cried again.

"I don't know as the Rev'rend Jonas would approve of us having dealings with show folk," mumbled Mrs. Grover. "But I reckon we cain't disapp'int the chillun. We'll do it, mister."

Roozeboom and Yount had by now moved all the circus vehicles to one side of the road. Mr. Grover clucked to his horse and the tobacco wagon clattered across the bridge over Beaver Creek.

Edge said to Florian, "I never heard such a pack of lies as you dealt to those poor hicks."

"Lies? Nothing of the sort. Only a trivial adornment of the truth, here and there."

"You and your posters make this outfit sound like something the Caesars dreamed up to embellish Rome." Edge looked around, with amused contempt, at the derelict wagon train and its shabby crew. "Aren't you kind of raising people's expectations too high? When they see what little you've really got to show them, you might just get stoned out of town."

"Not so, my boy," Florian said kindly. "You will learn that most people see exactly what they expect to see. If that constitutes deception, it is no fault of mine. Blame the deficiencies of the average human mentality."

"Want some breakfast, Mr. Florian, Mr. Zachary?" The golden daughter of Sarah Coverley came up to them with two tin plates, each bearing a very narrow wedge of some brown substance.

"Why, thank you, Clover Lee," said Florian. "This is a delightful novelty—breakfast! What is it, anyway?"

She giggled. "I know it looks like a piece of a cow flop. But it's sweet-potato pie. Tiny Tim snuck it off those folks' wagon. Not much to go around, but it was the only eatable he could snatch. Anyhow, Tim mainly wanted the baking pan it was in. For his act."

"My compliments to the chef de filouterie." Florian turned to Edge, who was glowering at the plate he held. "Say thank you, Zachary. Or if it troubles your conscience to eat someone else's pie, we can give it to someone else."

"No, no," mumbled Edge. "Thank you, Clover Lee." With two fingers, he put the tiny moist brown fragment in his mouth.

"Enjoy it, Mr. Zachary," the girl said brightly, and then, just as brightly, "Did you enjoy my mother?"

Edge choked on his pie.

"Of course he did, my dear," said Florian. "Anyone would, don't you fret. But run along now. Never interrupt the grown-up talk of your elders with childish prattle."

She sauntered away, and Edge said, "I'd hate to hear that kid talk any *more* grown-up."

"Yes, well, a child raised in a circus does tend to be somewhat precocious. Monsieur Roulette, who tutors her in her lessons, tries mightily to instill some good manners at the same time. But I suppose even the best education doesn't discourage a young girl's natural curiosity about things like sex and—"

To steer the conversation away from that very thing, Edge interrupted, "I take it thievery is not discouraged, either. That pie was probably intended to be a homecoming feast for that Lynchburg family."

Florian said tsk-tsk. "Really, Zachary. We sometimes have to live by foraging, just like your cavalry. Are you pretending that your men never conveyanced anything from the civilians?"

"I don't recollect that we ever pilfered from somebody who was already doing us a favor at our request."

"You heard what Clover Lee said. Tim did not steal the pie. The pie just happened to come along in the pie tin he wanted for a prop in his act."

"He props himself on a pie tin?"

"Prop. A property. A gimmix. A tool. Something he employs to enhance his act."

"How the hell could a pie tin—?"

"I don't know and I won't ask. It is considered impolite to be too inquisitive in such cases. I'll just have to wait and see what Tim does with the baking pan in the show. You can too, if you like, since you and Obie are going our way. As a matter of fact, he has very kindly offered his Percheron as a draft horse for us, as far as Lynchburg. Perhaps you'd also volunteer yours, and ride along with us? Stay to see our performance? As our guests, of course. Will your charger work in harness?"

"He won't like it, but he'll do it. In his time, Thunder has pulled caissons, ambulances—even a cold-meat wagon, once. All right, yes, you can hitch him up. I reckon I owe you that."

"Me? Or Madame Solitaire?"

Edge gave him a very chilly look and said, "I owe you for drinks and food and general hospitality, Mr. Florian. You'd have to ask Sarah if she feels *she's* owed anything. Or let her daughter ask, since you and the brat both seem to share natural girlish curiosities about such things."

Florian stepped a pace back and raised his hands. "I stand deservedly admonished. Now come, you'll want to supervise Captain Hotspur's harnessing of your horse."

But Roozeboom was busy with something else: skinning and quartering a dead animal. Magpie Maggie Hag was assisting, to the extent of holding a mug to catch some of the spilled blood. Yount and Rouleau also stood by, Yount keeping hold of the Wild Man, who mooed and blubbered and laughed, seeming eager to lend a hand in the dressing-out.

Edge saw the old underhammer rifle lying to one side, and said, "So that's what woke me up. You shot one of the jackasses."

Florian said, "They aren't needed, now that we've got Obie's horse to haul the tent wagon. We'll lead the other ass. And if your Thunder will draw the cage wagon, Brutus can be excused from that task for a while. The elephant has work to do when we get to the pitch. We try not to make the bull labor on the road unless it's absolutely unavoidable. That's the most valuable animal in this whole train."

"That little jackass might not have been valuable, but he was still sound," Edge said. "Just last night, you told us how loyally those burros had worked for you. And this morning, by way of thanking them when their work is done, you shoot one of them."

Florian looked chastened, and for once he did not seem to be acting. In fact, he winced from Edge's angry scowl and dropped his own gaze to his scuffed shoes, saying nothing at all. So Jules Rouleau spoke:

"Zachary, ami, you might not know it to look at me now, but I too was once an advocate of chivalry, of noblesse oblige, the beau geste and all that. I have had to learn expediency and compromise since I joined out with the circus, especially in recent years. Step over here and let me show you something."

He led Edge to the wagon barred like a jail cell. It was simply a big cage on wheels, measuring about four feet by ten, composed of vertical iron bars along the sides and at the back, where there was a barred gate for access. Up front, there was solid wood between the driver's seat and the cage, and the whole top was wood with a bit of gingerbread overhang, for some slight protection against the weather. Edge looked in, at what might have been a large, tan, crumpled and rather moth-eaten fur rug.

"That is Maximus," said Rouleau. "King of the Great Cats, His Majesty Maximus."

"Is he sick?"

"He is old. And he is famished. Tell me, Zachary. That piece of pie you ate, did it fill you up? Or are you still hungry?"

"Hell, yes, I'm hungry. I've been hungry for most of the last four years."

"Aussi moi-même. Yet you and I are young, so it is a miserable condition, but it is not intolerable. We know we won't starve. If it gets bad enough, we will cadge or steal. But suppose you were extremely old and weak, and helplessly penned up, and dependent on others to feed you."

Edge said nothing.

"Maximus depends on us. And we depend on him, for he is worth any three or four of us as an attraction for the canaille. No ticket-buying Reuben will ever properly appreciate *anything* another human being may do in the ring, however spectacular, but he will gawk avidly at this poor, sad, aged African lion. So we depend on Maximus, and all the cat asks in return is that we feed him when we can."

"What would you have fed him if the jackass hadn't been expendable?"

"Je ne sais quoi. But I can assure you of one thing. If all the rest of us were prosperous and well fed, and it was only the little *ass* that was going hungry, Florian would cut off his own hair and beard for hay for it. As things stand, the lesser must be sacrificed for the greater good, and Maximus desperately needs meat. Your scolding of Florian was unnecessary. He already feels bad enough. He is a good circus man, and every good circus man is kind to his animals above all else. Same way a good carpenter takes good care of his tools. In this case, Florian was being kind in the only way possible."

"I didn't mean to sound like some meddling little old lady," said Edge. "God knows a cavalryman doesn't get sweet notions about animals, because God knows the horse is probably the stupidest animal there is. But a cavalryman does learn respect for sound horseflesh, and he won't mistreat it. That's not little-old-lady sentimentality, and I'm not sentimental about anything else in the world."

Rouleau gave him a sidelong look. "Oh, a cavalryman has to sound manly and gruff, of course. But you can't make Jules Fontaine Rouleau believe that Zachary Edge doesn't have a sentimental regard for some things."

"What, for instance?"

"That, if nothing else." He reached out and touched Edge's sleeve. "The gray uniform. The lost cause."

"Oh, hell," Edge muttered. "There was a time once when I believed babies were brought by the stork. Are you going to throw that up to me, too?"

"Florian said you had worn a uniform for nearly twenty years. The gray one has existed for only four years or so."

"But there was a Virginia a hundred and fifty-some years before there was a United States of America. So all right, I'm a Virginian, and yes, I turned my coat."

"And you don't call that sentimentality."

"Call it what you like. I don't have it any more. The cause is lost. As dead now as Sam Sweeney's banjo. I won't spend the rest of my life weeping over it."

"Do not sound so defensive. I was not accusing you of any unmanly weakness. As I said, I too was once a person of some sensitivity and much sentiment. The circus is not a cruel place, but it is a demanding one. It demands much of all of us. I would like to think that I still possess sensitivity. But, for the good of the troupe, I learned to subdue sentiment. Every kind of sentiment." He looked away. "Sweet notions. Lost causes."

"Maxi-*moose!*" bellowed Roozeboom, as he came with a reeking and dripping blue-red haunch of meat. The crumpled fur rug responded to its name, or to the smell of the raw meat, by raising one end of itself, revealing that to be an immense head with a matted mane and rheumy eyes. Roozeboom said tantalizingly, "Was gibt es zum Festessen? Ha *ha! Fest-Esel!*" and shoved the haunch between two of the iron bars.

"Captain Hotspur makes a play on words," said Florian, joining them at the cage. "'Festessen' means a feast of eating. 'Esel' means ass. You noticed that he spoke German to the cat, not Dutch?"

"I wouldn't know the difference," said Edge.

"An old European circus tradition. Whatever a cat trainer's nationality, he addresses and gives orders to his animals in German. Mainly, I suppose, because the German language seems to have been *made* for command. A Russian trainer once pointed out to me how it would take him at least two Russian words to give his tigers a command that could be given in German with one—and might have to be given in a hurry. A syllable's fraction of a second can mean life or death when you're working lions or tigers."

Maximus did not leap for the meat, or even stand up. As if unable to believe either his trainer or his own nose, he only slowly raised his front end on his forelegs, and wearily dragged himself to where he could lick the offering with his vast tongue, then wonderingly mumble it with his capacious lips. But that first taste seemed to revive and cheer him considerably. He curled back the lips, showing a mouthful of teeth that were yellowed and blunt, but still formidable in number. And, with a muted growl, he began to tear hungrily and gratefully at his meal.

Edge asked, "Why was the old gypsy collecting the blood? Does she do some kind of witchery with it?"

"No," said Florian. "She was doing that for Captain Hotspur. He uses it in his act."

"And I forgot—I shouldn't be the inquisitive Reuben," Edge said. "I apologize. And I'm sorry I sounded off at you back there, Mr. Florian. An outsider shouldn't meddle in things he can't possibly know from the inside."

"I was only worried that you might retract the offer of your horse. I promise we won't feed him to the menagerie."

"Let's go hitch him up, and the others, and ride on to Lynchburg. I want to see your show."

It was a pleasant road from Beaver Creek onward, and dry now. The area was one of the few in Virginia that had not been fought over during the war, so, except for many farm fields left fallow for lack of hands, there was no ruination to be seen. The road ran alongside the broad, brown, swift-flowing James River. It was bordered by early-blooming wild flowers and overhung by willows and sycamores just coming into bright spring green. As the road got within a few miles of Lynchburg, it changed from mere packed earth to a corduroy of well-laid transverse logs.

There were more people to be seen now. On the road, in the fields, on house porches, around roadside inns and stores, the people all paused in their occupations to stare, with more head-scratching bewilderment than they probably would have shown if the wagons had been bringing Devil Grant or Vandal Hunter or any other of the Yankee conquerors. Most of the folk must have seen circuses on the move before, but not in recent years. And, as Yount had remarked, a circus could hardly have been one of the first things they expected to see traveling from the direction in which there had lately been warfare, devastation and desperation. Indeed, the circus looked as if it had never heard of the war: the horses ambling, the wagons trundling slowly, the riders aboard looking lazy and carefree.

As usual, the rockaway led the train, drawn by the show's white ring horse. Florian was wearing a high silk hat, not much dented, and the rest of his spiffy attire did not show its decrepitude from a distance. Beside him sat a Confederate officer garbed in dress gray that likewise did not, to the spectators, proclaim its age or the fact that it was Edge's one and only uniform. The weather curtains of the carriage were rolled up, exposing its interior, and its two pretty female occupants frequently leaned out to wave at the oglers, and their yellow hair shone in the sunshine.

Ignatz Roozeboom's bald head gleamed almost as brightly. He was driving the next wagon, with the Wild Man beside him, bundled in shawls to hide his uniqueness from nonpaying spectators. They were on the cage wagon, pulled by Edge's handsome claybank Thunder, which kept snorting and sneezing at the ammoniac smell of Maximus so close behind. Inside the cage, the lion was in its favorite—or only—position, lying down.

The next three wagons were the closed vans, not revealing what marvels they might hold, but they were the painted ones. And the April sunlight picked out what colors they still flaunted, and made the colors bright, and sparkled the traces of gilt on the garish lettering that proclaimed the Florilegium's name and character. One was the property wagon, drawn by the gaunt and shambling cart horse and driven by Jules Rouleau, no distinctive sight, dressed as he was in common country overalls. Next came the tent wagon, driven by Yount because his own big Lightning was hauling it, and it was trailed by the remaining ass on a lead rein. Next came what Florian had called the museum wagon, drawn by the circus's other ring horse, the dapple gray, and driven by Tim Trimm. To onlookers, Trimm's littleness was not much apparent up there on the high seat, especially because of the even littler dark thing on the seat beside him: the hooded, draped, clenched and mysterious-looking Magpie Maggie Hag.

But if the wagon part of the train was not flagrantly spectacular, the last part made up for it, because the last was the majestically slow-striding elephant. Peggy was swathed in a great blanket of scarlet velvet which, glowing in the sun, did not show its naplessness. With the grand animal, sometimes stalking beside it, sometimes perched aloof on its lofty neck, came the exceedingly foreign-looking brown man in turban and robes. His face was set as stern and determined as if he were the real Hannibal, and as if this gently rolling Virginia piedmont were in fact a craggy pass between ponderous Alps, and his elephant only one of hundreds, and sleepy Lynchburg yonder really an apprehensive and cowering Capua.

Though Florian led the wagon train at a leisurely pace, it arrived in the outskirts of Lynchburg before dusk, and he decided against going very far into town. The dark-leaf tobacco growers who had built the city for their auction-market center had set it prettily on a cluster of small but steep hills. That made its cobbled streets not so pretty to the teamsters and draft animals of the tobacco wagons that had to go up and down them. But the city looked good to the circus people, as they came into it along Campbell Court House Road, because the Grover family who had preceded them had kept their promise: the Florilegium's black-printed buff posters were visible on posts, trees and building walls.

Edge asked, "Did you get all those papers printed down in Wilmington?"

"No," said Florian. "Had a good supply left from before we came south. That's why they describe a number of acts and attractions no longer with us. But so grandiloquently that I can't bring myself to cross them out."

The wagon train rounded Diamond Hill and kept to the outer reaches of the city until it came to a railroad and warehouse district near the river. When Florian saw a commodious empty lot off the street, he turned the carriage into it. The rest of the train followed, from the cobblestones into the weeds. Between the farther extent of the lot and the banks of the river stood some derelict railroad sheds, and among them wound rusty rails on which stood long-sidetracked boxcars and platform cars. During the past year or more, as the fortunes of war and the battle lines had shifted, the South Side Rail Road had had either no goods to carry or no hope of carrying them through the blockades to where they might have been of use and profit. Nevertheless, this neighborhood still smelled faintly but distinctly of old engine smoke and steam-heated iron boilers.

When Florian stopped the carriage, and the horse immediately began grazing among the weeds for something edible, Edge said, "You don't ask anybody's permission to set up here?"

"If this run-down acreage has an owner, he'll show up soon enough. Or the city fathers may send a policeman to demand a fee for the pitch. But usually, these days, a few free tickets will suffice." He handed Edge the rockaway's reins and said, "Keep the carriage here, out of our way."

He hopped nimbly from the seat, stowed his silk hat and frock coat under it and began to pace the length and depth of the lot, occasionally bending down and cocking his head to check for irregularities in the ground. Then he yanked a clump of weeds to leave a bare spot, and shouted, "Gumshoe here!" He walked a dozen or so long paces toward the rear of the lot and shouted, "Backyard!" Then he came toward the street side of the lot again, shouted, "Front door!" walked a few more paces and shouted, "Red wagon!"

Every other member of the company had gone into action at the same time Florian had, and just as purposefully. The scene became one of confusion, but organized confusion. Sarah and Clover Lee got out of the rockaway, carrying pots and pans. Roozeboom handed the reins of his cage wagon to the Wild Man and got down, carrying something bulky in his arms. So he was right there when Florian shouted "Gumshoe here!" and he dropped the thing on the ground at that spot. As well as Edge could see, it was no kind of shoe, but a large, thick round of log, with a heavy spike jutting up from it to near knee height. Roozeboom got onto the cage wagon again and drove it to the place where Florian had shouted "Front door!" Meanwhile, Jules Rouleau was driving the property wagon past the gumshoe thing, and stopped the wagon a good distance beyond that, where Florian had shouted "Backyard!" Hannibal Tyree had stripped the immense red cover off Peggy and was carefully folding it for stowage. By the time Florian shouted "Red wagon!" Tim Trimm had the museum wagon there to stop on the spot.

Now the Wild Man scrambled down from the cage wagon's seat, and under that wagon, and began letting down some canvas flaps there, to hang like curtains from the cage bottom to the ground all around. Hannibal had got a heavy leather strap from somewhere and was buckling it like a collar around Peggy's big neck. Magpie Maggie Hag got down from the museum wagon, which had its rear toward the street, whence presumably the circus's patrons would approach. She opened two doors there, throwing open the whole back to reveal a sort of shallow booth where a ticket seller could sit behind a high counter.

Hannibal, Trimm, Rouleau and Roozeboom converged on the tent wagon, which Yount had simply brought to a halt some way in from the street. They unlatched its door and began dragging out the gear compactly stored in there— rolls of canvas, various metal objects, a great deal of rope and numerous tackle blocks, and three long, thick, smooth-rounded poles. Each of those was painted red, except for a narrow blue band near its middle, marking the balance point, so a man could seize the heavy pole there and carry it most comfortably.

Edge was half inclined to join the workers and lend a hand. But he was an old campaigner, veteran of many a tenting ground and redoubt construction, and he had too often seen hard work made harder by the awkward efforts of a new recruit pitching in among practiced professionals. Also, when Roozeboom bellowed something like, "Off-loaden de staubs out of de vay!" or Hannibal called something like, "Hyar come de bail ring!" Edge had no idea whether it was some circus jargon he couldn't possibly know, or just their native accents which he couldn't decipher. So he sat where he was and watched.

Hannibal lugged a heavy hoop of iron, as big around as a wagon wheel, and laid it on the ground so it encircled the thing called the gumshoe. Trimm, Rouleau and Roozeboom each brought one of the three red-painted poles and laid them nearby, end to end, while Hannibal ran again to the tent wagon and fetched two metal cylinders, open at the ends. The men fitted them like sleeves onto the separate poles to join them into one continuous pole, or mast, some forty feet long, that tapered from waist-thickness at one end to thigh-thickness at the other. In the thick end a hole was visible, drilled straight up into the pole's interior. Hannibal now fetched the elephant, while the others secured pulleys to both ends of the long pole, and reeved ropes several times back and forth between them. Another rope they uncoiled to reveal that it ended in a large metal hook, and Hannibal slipped that into the elephant's collar.

He said loudly, "Peggy, mile up!" and the elephant began very slowly to walk away from the group of men, while they snubbed the thick end of the pole. As Peggy's tugging brought the thinner end up off the ground, the men hefted the thick end so the hole in it went up and onto the point of the gumshoe's heavy spike. The elephant continued to draw on the rope, and the pole rose, all its pulleys and ropes rattling, until it was at the vertical, when its butt end slid down firmly on the length of spike. Hannibal yelled, "Tut, Peggy!" and the elephant stopped, leaning to keep the rope taut and the mast held steady at vertical. Edge now could perceive the function of the gumshoe. That high pole could have been stood on the bare ground, but if the ground were soft—and a sudden rain might make it so at any time—the pole would sink, without the gumshoe to provide a wider base for it.

While the other men had been engaged with the pole, Florian was kicking open the bundles of canvas laid nearby, and they unrolled to become tremendous triangles. Elsewhere, Yount was helping Sarah kindle a campfire with some dead weed stalks, and Clover Lee and Magpie Maggie Hag were moving about the lot, bent over, apparently in search of more substantial burnables. Of the whole troupe, only the Wild Man was not in sight. The elephant stood staunch at her station, and in the cage wagon even the lion Maximus seemed to have revived somewhat from his customary comatose state. Edge could hear from there a hollow grumbling and low roaring, accompanied by clinking and clanking, as if the lion were struggling against iron fetters.

When the workers were satisfied that the tall pole was firm and that its hanging pulley ropes were all clear of tangles, they turned to the next job. Trimm and Hannibal joined Florian, and those three arranged the immense canvas triangles side by side on the weedy ground, so they surrounded the gumshoe like slices of a pie. Then the men produced lengths of light rope and, running them through brass grommets in the canvas edges, began to lace the slices one to the next, as if they were making an unbroken crust over the weed pie beneath. Meanwhile, Rouleau and Roozeboom were making repeated trips to the tent wagon, bringing smaller poles—these painted blue, only arm-thick, about twelve feet long, each with a short iron spike at one end—and laying them spoke-wise around the perimeter of the canvas on the ground.

When the canvas sections were all laced together in a circle, the piecrust had a hole in its center just the size of the iron hoop still lying at the base of the upright mast, encircling it. The canvas had more grommets around that hole, which the men employed to lace it securely to the iron, and then the ring was fixed to the pole's pulley ropes. The men came off the canvas, walking delicately so they stepped only on the laced portions of it. Hannibal brought with him the end of another rope, this one running under the canvas from the pulleys at the center pole's base, and he attached that line also to Peggy's leather collar.

Florian and Roozeboom lifted up the outer rim of the canvas piecrust, a bit at a time, so Rouleau and Trimm could take the blue poles, insert their spike ends into still more grommets at the canvas's edge, then wedge the poles upright between canvas and ground. When the men had done circling the canvas, it was no longer like a piecrust, but hung like a vast, limp, wrinkled saucer, its inside at the base of the center pole, its rim supported some twelve feet above the ground by the ring of outer poles.

While Florian gave the result a looking over, the others made several more trips to the tent wagon, bringing unpainted wooden stakes about four feet long, sharpened at one end, flat and splayed at the other. They also brought three heavy sledgehammers, and now they put on a virtuoso performance as pretty as any Edge expected ever to see inside the pavilion.

Trimm held erect one of the stakes, about eight feet outside the nearest blue pole, and Roozeboom tapped it with his sledge to start it into the ground. Then he, Rouleau and Hannibal swung their sledges all together and repeatedly, so rapidly that they were a flickering blur, all hammering the one stake, but with such perfect timing that the blows were like the staccato stutter of a Gatling gun, and the stake sank as if into butter, until only a foot of it remained above ground. The men went around the circle of the tent, pounding home one stake after another, one stake to each blue pole, and their rhythmic tempo never faltered, a swing never missed its mark or collided with another sledge. Florian came along after them, with more lengths of rope, these each with a loop spliced in one end. He tossed a loop up over a support pole's spike protruding above the canvas, guyed the rope down to the ground spike, secured it there with the simple but reliable round-turn-and-half-hitch, and went on to do the same at the next pole and stake.

When that phase of the work was finished, the result looked less like a saucer and more like a spider: its canvas body sprawled among uplifted leglike side poles, each with a strand of web running to the ground. Florian again gave everything a close appraisal, then he and the others congregated around the elephant. Hannibal untied from the leather collar the rope with which Peggy had raised the center pole, and the men took hold of it to keep that pole steady. Hannibal again called, "Mile up!" and the bull again began slowly to walk, drawing only the rope that ran from under the canvas. The pole's numerous pulleys creaked, and their ropes rattled and twanged, and the iron hoop slowly ascended into view above the upturned canvas rim, bearing with it the center and the whole weight of that canvas. When the hoop touched the pole's top pulley, Roozeboom called, "Ja, klonkie!" and Hannibal instantly commanded, "Peggy, tut!" to halt her.

And now the canvas had ceased to look like a spider or a saucer or a piecrust. It was a shapely, round, pointed, dun-colored tent roof, some seventy feet in diameter, its peak about thirty-five feet above the ground, its slopes gently billowing and rippling in the evening breeze.

"C'est bon," said Rouleau. "All right, tie off the bail ring."

It was Tim Trimm who complied, no doubt because he was the lightest in weight. He shinnied up one of the side poles onto the roof of canvas, then scurried up the slope along one of the laced seams. At the very peak, he did some strenuous lashing of ropes around the iron hoop—the "bail ring," Edge decided —and the pole tip and pulleys, to hold everything firm up there. Then he just let go and slid down the slope of the canvas, whooping excitedly, swooped off the edge and was neatly caught in the stout arms of Roozeboom.

The tent's blossoming into recognizable shape was greeted by a scattering of cheers and applause. Edge turned and saw that a score or so of Lynchburgers had gathered at the street side of the lot. Most of them were children and most of those were black, but there were some adult males, all elderly. Florian was quick to take advantage of having an audience, calling to them:

"Welcome to the Big Top! And thank you, gentlemen and young folk, for your kind reception!" He spoke aside to Rouleau, "Get on with the sidewalling. But it'll be dark soon, so we'll save the ring and seats until morning." He raised his voice again to the onlookers: "Performance tomorrow, good people!" and, as he spoke, he was hurrying to the rockaway. There he put on his frock coat and top hat and snatched up one of the rolled circus posters. "Yessirree! Come one, come all!" Now properly attired, he strode over to the little crowd, still speaking in a loud voice but conveying a confidential tone.

"Performance tomorrow at two o'clock! However, since you fine folks are clearly the most eager and appreciative circus lovers in this fair city, we shall repay your good will with some of our own." The children goggled; the men looked interested but wary. "Tomorrow at show time there is certain to be a crush of people elbowing for the best seats. But, since you folks were the first to welcome us, we shall not only permit you to reserve your seats right now, we will offer them to you *at half price!*"

The men and children looked glum and embarrassed, and shuffled a little away from him. Florian flapped the poster to unfurl it, got his mason's pencil from a pocket and, with a flourish, scrawled on the bottom of the paper.

"Regard that, friend!" he said, shoving the poster in the face of the nearest white man. "You see what the regular price is? See also how I have slashed it precisely *in half!*"

The man mumbled, "Cain't read, mister."

"Right! As you say, sir, an incredible offer! Instead of the usual price of just two bits for you gents and just one thin dime for you tads—*instead* of that, I have cut the prices to twelve and a half cents and five cents respectively. Merely step over to the ticket wagon yonder"—he waved toward the museum wagon, where Magpie Maggie Hag had magically appeared inside the booth—"and our Chief Cashier will gladly dispense tickets to you gentlemen for only *one bit,* tickets to you children and persons of color for only *five pennies!*"

There was some more glum and embarrassed shuffling. "*Or* the equivalent in Confederate paper dollars!" Shuffle, shuffle. "*Or* barter in kind acceptable!"

The men looked dolefully at each other; so did the children. Edge shook his own head sympathetically and turned back to where the tent was still being worked on. Hannibal was under it, at the center pole, warping onto cleats there the ends of the ropes that had done the raising of pole and roof. Roozeboom was going about the outside, checking the ropes from roof to stakes, here and there tightening one or easing another to get the tension equal all around, then giving every rope an extra half hitch and tidily belaying the loose end so it would not be tripped over. Trimm and Rouleau were unrolling yet more canvas, twelve-foot-wide lengths of it that they hung from under the roof eaves and pegged to the ground. Peggy the elephant, released from duty, was desultorily plucking up weeds with her trunk, putting them in her mouth, spitting out most of them, occasionally and not very zestfully eating one.

"You have seen the mighty pachyderm putting up the Big Top!" Florian continued to harangue the onlookers, now with rather a cajoling voice. "Tomorrow come and see him at play—*Brutus, Biggest Brute That Breathes*—doing impossible tricks and imposing feats of strength at the command of his genuine Hindu master!"

When the canvas lengths were hung and pegged, the tent was walled all around, except in two places. At the side farther from the street a gap was left—for the performers to go in and out by, Edge presumed—and beyond it in the "backyard" was parked the baggage wagon. Opposite that opening, in the nearer wall, was the "front door" through which the patrons would enter after they had first stopped to pay at the ticket booth and then, between it and the entrance, had stopped at the cage wagon to admire the lion.

"King of the Great Cats, *His Majesty Maximus!*" cried Florian. "You can hear him, folks, roaring for raw human flesh, which is the only meat Maximus will eat! Tomorrow come and see the daredevil Captain Hotspur actually climb inside the cage and try to subdue that bloodthirsty beast!"

Edge saw that Yount was unhitching his Lightning and the little jackass, and back behind the tent Hannibal was loosing the other dray horse. So Edge got down from the rockaway and went to unharness Thunder from the cage wagon. He paused to look back toward the street when he heard Florian cry encouragingly:

"That's right, sir. Step on over to the booth. You too, lad." He raised his voice to shout, "Madame Bookkeeper, be so kind as to issue tickets to our first two patrons! Best seats in the house, make sure of that!"

Edge grinned in some surprise. Indeed, a gray old man and a towheaded boy, both wearing faded overalls, both looking sheepish but radiant, were crossing the lot to the wagon. The other men and children were watching them wistfully, and a few more rummaging deep in their pockets. Edge went on to the cage wagon to attend to Thunder, and got another surprise.

His Majesty Maximus was evincing no more vivacity than Edge had previously seen in the animal. He was lying on his side, his eyes closed, only his barrel ribs moving as he softly snored. The jangles of iron fetters and the hollow roars of bloodthirst were coming from *under* the cage. Edge bent and lifted the canvas that had been let down for a curtain below the base of the wagon. In the space underneath squatted the Wild Man, diligently shaking a length of rusty chain, and making more or less his normal vocal noises, but with his head invisible inside a zinc bucket that amplified and made the sounds passably leonine and ferocious.

"It's his only real talent," said Florian, coming up just then. He was patting his moist forehead with his handkerchief, as if his exhortation to the onlookers had been the hardest work he had done all afternoon. "And the poor idiot loves to do it, so don't look so disapproving."

"I swear..." Edge said softly, and shook his head. He dropped the canvas and stood up. "I see you sold some tickets."

"Only two, alas. The other gawkers were just the usual lot lice."

"What did those two pay you with?" Edge started undoing Thunder's harness.

"The old gent was carrying quite a wad of Rebel dollars, and he handed over thirteen of them. Said he'd been saving up for his funeral, but he'd rather see a circus any day than get buried. The boy had just come from the river. He was taking this home, but decided to part with it." Florian held up a string on which hung a medium-size dead catfish. "The lad went back to the river to see if he could catch another for the home folks before suppertime."

"A fish? What are you going to do with a fish?"

"Eat it, man! Did you think I was going to have it perform?" Florian laughed. "I grant you, though, I did do that once—with dancing turkeys."

"Dancing *turkeys*," Edge repeated.

"We, ahem, acquired a small flock of them. Took them along as provisions on the hoof, you might say. So while they lasted, we presented them as dancing turkeys."

"*Dancing* turkeys."

"Stand any turkey on a sheet of hot iron, and watch."

Edge shook his head again, and went on with the unharnessing, and said, "So now, for some worthless Confederate paper and a catfish, you gave those folks the two best seats in the house?"

"Well, two seats. Come along now. The flag is up—or it would be if we had a cook tent to hoist it on. We'll toss this mudcat into the nettle soup and it ought to make a delectable—"

"Nettle soup?"

"Old Mag is adept at living off the land. She was collecting the ingredients while we put up the pavilion. Nettles and wild onions. Not bad soup at all, you'll see. But it will be better with a dash of fish meat."

Edge stared at him. "These people of yours haven't eaten a bite since that sweet-potato pie this morning. And that was *just* a bite. They've traveled the livelong day, and now they've been working like niggers. And you're going to feed them nettles and catfish juice?"

"We eat what we have," said Florian. "The ass meat has to be kept for the lion."

"I swear," Edge said again, "I don't think I've ever come across such a scruffy outfit in my entire life. I've seen the Mexican militia and the Texans of the Big Thicket and I've heard all the jokes about the Yankees' pitiful Oneida Cavalry. But for sheer hangdog miserableness, I'm damned if you people don't beat them all—come day, go day, God save Sunday!"

"You are overwrought," Florian said kindly. "From hunger, no doubt. Tether your horse over there with Snowball and Bubbles and come and dine."

When they joined the others around the fire, Florian went to the far side of it and gave the fish to Magpie Maggie Hag. Yount hailed Edge with enthusiasm. "You watch the putting up of that monster tent, Zack? Wasn't that a pretty piece of work?"

Edge snorted. "Many a time, Obie, you've watched the reserves do maneuvers in peacetime, just as pretty and busy and self-important. And what was all their fuss ever worth?"

"Zachary, you sound like you don't think much of us," said Sarah Coverley. She gave him a wicked grin. "And I tried so hard to make a good impression."

"Mother!" Clover Lee exclaimed, as if scandalized, but then she giggled.

Edge said he was only trying to maintain a trace of common sense, which commodity seemed in short supply hereabouts. "Yesterday, your Mr. Florian yonder described himself as the consummate cynic. Never have I heard a man more wildly misread his own character. I've been trying to decide whether he's the world's most hopeful optimist or its most blithering nincompoop."

Sarah said quite sharply, "Lots of know-it-alls have refused to believe that Florian would do what he set out to do, and he has confounded them time and again. It's true enough that we're supping on pucker-water soup tonight." She started angrily slinging tin bowls around to the company. "But if Florian says we'll someday be dining on caviar and champagne, we don't laugh or jeer. We get our faces *set* for caviar and champagne."

There were only enough of the tin bowls for the regular troupe; to Edge and Yount she gave bowls of cheap chinaware. At that, Tim Trimm scowled and said testily, "You horseshit-kickers be careful of them good dishes. They're props for my act. You break one, you better watch out!"

"Ja! Make Tim mad, he *sting* you," Roozeboom said with a rumbling laugh.

"Little man," said Yount, "you're as mean as snot."

Tim gave him an ugly look and stalked off to the fire, perhaps to provoke the pot to the boil. Rouleau said to Yount, "Don't be misled by the defects of his personality. In the ring, in front of an audience, Tim is a passable joey."

"He is, huh. What's a joey?"

"Circus word for a clown."

"Ah," said Yount, and pridefully displayed his erudition. "Named for Joe Miller's Joke Book, I reckon. Our chaplain had one of them books, to spark up his sermons with."

Rouleau laughed at that and said, "Good guess, ami, but no. Named for Joe Grimaldi, the first clown—or at least the first famous one—in England, maybe fifty years ago."

Magpie Maggie Hag was just now crumbling the skinned catfish into her iron kettle, so the deplorable meal was not quite ready, and—this being the first time Edge had been among all the circus folk in close company—he was suddenly aware of how unwashed and unclean they smelled, as bad as so many soldiers together. He himself had had at least a cold dip and a quick shave the night before, but his uniform and undergarments no doubt contributed to the general odor. Anyway, he carefully set down his bowl and ambled away to fresher air. He left the lot and crossed the cobbled street, to take a close look at one of the Florilegium's posters pasted on a telegraph-line pole over the way.

The paper was common buff-colored newsprint, densely covered with a hodge-podge of different sizes and styles of type, from swaggeringly big bold black to mincingly elegant scripts. Among the clutter of words were muddy woodcuts. Some showed ill-drawn apes and elephants, and improbable creatures like unicorns and mermaids. Others depicted improbable events: a gentleman in striped drawers wrestling barehanded with a writhing heap of lions and tigers, and a dainty lady balancing on one toe on the withers of a horse weirdly levitating entirely off the ground, its legs extended fore and aft. The printed matter was equally improbable, describing performers and performances that Florian had once had in his Florilegium, or maybe only had wished he had:

"MLLES PEPPER AND PAPRIKA, charming Volantes and Figurantes, doing breathtaking *Aeronantic Oscillation* on the Vertiginous High Pole, dizzying exploits to make strong men gasp!

"ZIP COON and JIM CROW, the two Comic Mules, never failing to convulse the Audience with their *Knockabout Humor!*

"ALLEGORICAL TABLEAUX of Living Pictures formed by *Beautiful Young Ladies,* personifying Liberty Triumphant over Tyranny...the Queen of Sheba at King Solomon's Court..."

"Or barter in kind acceptable," said a voice at Edge's elbow, and he turned. Another Lynchburger in overalls was peering at the poster in the deepening twilight. "Says so, there at the bottom. You reckon, Cunnel, they'd take a couple sacks of smokin' tobacco fer a couple of tickets?"

"I'll personally see to it that they do." Edge steered him across the street to the campfire, where Florian was more than happy to interrupt his slurping of nettle soup to effect the exchange.

. Edge let Magpie Maggie Hag ladle some of the soup into his bowl too—only a meager portion, not because it tasted awful, which it did, but because he felt he ought not to deprive the men who had worked so hard. After he had got the soup down, Edge took off his tunic and, with the point of his belt knife, began picking the curlicue braid off the cuffs and the embroidered stars off the collar. The gypsy's cooking kettle was soon scraped empty, though none of the partakers could have been anywhere near full. So Florian next produced a paper bag and handed it around.

"Dried apples for afters," he said. "Get some of these inside you and the soup will swell them up. You'll swear you've just had a nine-course meal."

Then he passed around the newly acquired tobacco, and he and most of the other men—and Magpie Maggie Hag—packed pipes and lit up. After the indolent smoking session, everybody began preparing for an early bedtime. The Negro Hannibal, who customarily slept under one of the wagons with the Wild Man, solicitously led the idiot inside the pavilion for this night, and carried in pallets and blankets for them both. Because the night promised to be a mild one, the white men also decided to sleep in there instead of in a wagon. So Edge and Yount, too, lugged their bedrolls inside the tent and spread them on the cushioning mat of weeds. Soon everybody was asleep, except Edge.

There was a moon, and the worn old canvas did not much impede the light of it. The whole tent interior glowed a sort of dreamy blue-white, with brighter patches here and there, where the canvas was particularly threadbare. No one else awoke to admire the effect, or to deplore it, but Edge lay wide-eyed. He had once, in Richmond, seen a military observation balloon inflated—growing from a flaccid pile of fabric to the immensity of a wineglass elm tree, the cloth rippling and dimpling and billowing as it grew. Now he could almost imagine himself *inside* such a thing, vast and empty, translucent to the moonlight, whispering and sighing and chuckling in the soft night breeze.

Though he was dressed only in his long underwear, Edge got up and went outdoors, for another look at the Big Top's outside. It now looked like a pavilion indeed, like a fairy-tale rotunda built of moonbeams and spindrift and held to the ground only by a web of gossamer threads. None of the tent's worn places or patches or seams showed in the bluish half-light, and even its ordinary peaked roundness seemed blurrily mysterious of outline as it gently quivered and swelled and ebbed. Edge heard some quiet noises from the far side of the big tent, and he went around it to where the baggage wagon was parked near the back-door gap in the tent wall, and he saw a prettier sight yet.

The elephant was back there, chained by a clamp around one hind foot to one of the tent pegs, but with a decent length of chain, so it did not hinder what the animal was doing. And the great beast, mumbling softly, talking to herself, was doing some peculiar things. As Edge watched, she lifted one front foot, placed it on the splayed top of a tent stake, took it down, put the other front foot atop a different stake, then put both front feet on both of the stakes so her upper body was raised. Then she lowered herself to ordinary standing position, and stood thus as if meditating. Then she knelt on both hind legs, keeping the front ones stiff, so her back was steeply inclined. Then she stood up and meditated some more.

Edge wondered if the animal had perhaps eaten some kind of locoweed during her browsing of the unfamiliar ground. There was some elephant dung about, but it gave off no offensive aroma; it smelled fresh and garden-y and not at all unpleasant.

Now, quite suddenly, the elephant let her hind legs slide forward under her, sat back on her tremendous rump and raised her front feet, sitting erect, so she towered as high as the tent eaves. She waggled those front legs, playfully pawing the night air, then raised her trunk and curled it and whuffled softly through it what would have been a trumpet blast if she had really blown. And Edge realized what the elephant was doing. All by herself, without goading or command, all alone in the moonlight, the bull Brutus, Biggest Brute That Breathes, was rehearsing her circus act for tomorrow.

4

BECAUSE Edge had been the last to get to sleep, he woke to find work going on all around him. Florian, Roozeboom and Rouleau were bringing into the tent armloads of planks and oddly shaped other pieces of wood, and piling them close around the curved canvas walls. Obie Yount and the Wild Man were on hands and knees on the ground, working under the officious direction of Tim Trimm, all three of them yanking up the weeds and other growth to provide a clear floor for the middle of the pavilion.

"Rise and shine, Zachary!" Florian called, when he saw Edge sit up. "The boys went down to the river at dawn, and they got some decent fish for breakfast. Maggie's keeping one warm for you."

Edge hurriedly got into his clothes, rolled up his bedding and took it outside, out of the way. At the lion's wagon, Hannibal was using a long-handled hook, which he ordinarily employed for guiding the elephant, to poke gingerly through the cage bars and scrape out the lion dung from the floor of the wagon. Maximus himself was awake for a change, pacing up and down the cage, stepping daintily over Hannibal's scraping hook.

Sure enough, Magpie Maggie Hag had a fish fried and waiting for Edge on a tin plate, while she worked at cleaning the others' used dishes with a handful of sand. Edge thanked her sincerely and ate his breakfast with wolfish appetite, though it was only a small carp and as tasteless and textureless as all river carp. He could tell, from the well-cleaned but identifiable bones on the used plates, that the earlier diners had eaten catfish and suckers, much tastier fish, but he could hardly complain because the last one awake got the leavings.

"Now, gazho," Magpie Maggie Hag said, in her deep voice, "you go help with the tabernacle."

Edge gave her a look askance. "Godamighty. Florian calls it a pavilion and a Big Top. You call it a tabernacle. All it is is a tent."

"Tatcho, gazho. You see the words 'holy tabernacle' these days, you think a big church, no? Or saint's tomb, no? But you see word 'tabernacle' in Bible, all it meant then was hut or tent, easy to move around. Me, I know. My people, the Romani Kalderash, they have lived always in tabernacles."

"If you say so, ma'am." Edge obediently went to the tabernacle and inside it.

There, Florian was directing Rouleau, Trimm and a volunteer, Obie Yount, in the putting up of the spectators' seats. Those consisted only of long planks laid across the stair-step notches of stringer boards that slanted from high on the tent walls down to the ground. Each of the stringers was supported at its high end by a fork in the end of an ordinary upright sapling, and a small toe peg was driven into the earth at the stringer's lower end to keep it from sliding. When the seat planks were laid, they made a semicircle of five tiers from the tent eaves to near the ground, around each curve of the pavilion from front door to back door. Edge calculated that, if people really crammed in and sat tightly together and let their feet dangle unsupported, the tent would seat a capacity crowd of about five hundred. But he remarked to Florian that the whole arrangement looked pretty precarious.

"We rely on the natural laws of physics," Florian said equably. "Right now, the laws of friction and inertia are holding everything together. When the people come and sit on the planks, the law of gravity will hold everything more securely. Of course, if any crowd gets really excited and starts to bounce around, the whole works *can* come clattering down."

"Must be a continual worry," said Edge.

"Worry?" Florian repeated, as if the concept had never occurred to him. "Why, my dear Zachary, that would mean we had put on a truly thrilling show!"

Toward the middle of the now bare ground inside the tent, Ignatz Roozeboom was working at something else and getting some help from the Wild Man. To the center pole Roozeboom had tied a long string with a spike on its far end, and he had walked on his knees around the pole at the extent of that string, scratching the spike on the earth, to inscribe a circle somewhat more than twenty feet in radius, centered on the center pole. Then, with a short spade, he had started digging up the earth in a narrow band around that mark—then had given the spade to the idiot, who was continuing to dig around the circle. Roozeboom now was firming that loose soil with his hands into a little parapet enclosing the ring, about a foot high and a foot thick.

"American-style ring," Florian said, with a disparaging sniff. "In Europe, every respectable traveling circus carries a nicely painted wooden ring curb in portable segments. We'll have one, too, by damn, whenever I can afford it."

Edge said, "Mr. Roozeboom—I mean Captain Hotspur—seems mighty fastidious about the dimensions of his work."

Florian looked at Edge in amazement. "Lord, I thought *that* was something even a rube would know about. Every circus ring everywhere in the world, Zachary, is precisely the same size. Forty-two feet across, ever since the Englishman Astley started the first modern circus, and decided on that diameter. It *has* to be standard everywhere, or how could the horses and other animals be trained? And then be traded about and perform in one circus after another? There'd be ungodly confusion if all rings weren't the same size."

"Oh," said Edge.

"Not just for the animals. For the performers, as well. A bareback rider's horse, at performing pace, takes exactly twenty-two steps to go once around the ring. The horse knows that, and so does the artiste, and so does the band of musicians, if there is a band. So the horse and the rider know just where each of them is during each trick—every step of the horse, every movement of the rider —and the band music can keep perfect tempo, too."

"I reckon I must be a real rube Reuben," said Edge. "Something like that, I should have figured out for myself. In the peacetime cavalry, we've done dressage and other sorts of fancy riding, where you have to keep close count and all that. Sometimes with a brass band playing."

"One of these days I'll have a band," said Florian, more to himself than to Edge. "Someday I'll have everything just right. Decent seats, and with real jacks instead of saplings to level the stringers." He looked about the tent and then looked up. "And a decent pavilion, too, by God. A really *big* Big Top. And it'll be called the Big Top because it's the biggest, not just the only one. There'll be another top for the menagerie, and one for a sideshow. And we'll have horses that are matched and gaited, and grained every day. Not just the ring horses, but the wagon stock too. And we'll have the fanciest of spangled dress, and nickel-plated rigging, and plenty of slum to peddle at intermission..."

Edge noticed that he had started that soliloquy saying "I," but soon was saying "we."

"...And we won't be playing high-grass stands like this poor burg. We'll have a sharp advance man out in front of us, and he'll head for the smokestacks—the big, prosperous cities—and he'll arrange for the stand and the animals' feed and our own provender and all kinds of first-class publicity. We'll be a real low-grass show—won't play any city that won't mow its courthouse lawn for our pitch. And we'll parade into every town in full dress, right down Main Street. Not just the band playing, but a steam cally-ope besides!"

"A cally-ope?" Edge echoed.

"Ah, I was forgetting. You had a classical education. Yes, the steam organ was named for the foremost of the nine Muses, and it should properly be pronounced calliope. But every American circus man pronounces it cally-ope. And it was invented by an American, so who am I to correct the name? Anyway, I intend to have one of the things, and play it full blast."

As if to mock him, a single, forlorn drum began boomp-boomping outside. Florian left the tent and Edge followed, to see Hannibal Tyree dressed in his Hindu turban and robes, seated on top of Peggy's neck, banging a big bass drum that rested on his thighs and was secured by a strap around his back. Peggy was again wearing the scarlet, once-velvet covering, but Hannibal had reversed it. This side of the big blanket bore, on either flank of the elephant, tarnished letters that had once been gilt, commanding COME TO THE CIRCUS!

The Negro paused in his thumping to shout cheerfully, "We's ready to go whenever you say, Mas' Florian!"

"*Sahib* Florian, damn it, Abdullah." From a vest pocket, Florian took out and consulted a battered tin watch. "Well, it's nearly noon and we're nearly ready, so you might as well start. Make as many streets as you can, but make sure you can find your way back here."

Hannibal nodded, called, "Shy, Peggy!" and the bull made a smart right turn, to shuffle briskly across the lot to the street. There Hannibal ordered, "Come in, Peggy!" and the elephant made a smart left turn, to go toward the center of town. Hannibal resumed his pounding of the drum to punctuate the words he began shouting. "Follow me to de circus! Down by de railroad yards! Follow me to de Big Top!"

"He'll do that up one street and down another," said Florian.

"Won't he stampede every horse in town?"

"The children will crowd around as soon as they spot him. And they'll be happy to run ahead and yell 'Hold your horses!' By the time Abdullah returns, he'll come like the Pied Piper, leading all the kids that exist here. I trust their older folks will follow after."

"They might not," Edge observed. "They *might* think he's recruiting for the Union Army." The drum was painted on both drumheads: U.S.A. IIIrd DIV. HQ. BAND. "It would be kind of ironic if your black man got lynched in Lynchburg."

"Um, yes," said Florian. "The Yankees, ahem, misplaced that drum and sticks down in Carolina. If ever I come across some paint, I'll put our name on it."

Edge, feeling guilty that he had done nothing at all to deserve his having been given breakfast, went back into the tent to help Roozeboom with the ring curbing. Yount, having earned his peck by helping to put up the seats, had thereby worked off the meal and was hungry again. He suspected that everybody else was, too. So he said to Sarah Coverley:

"If you'll lend me that hook and line again, I'll go back to the river and try to catch us something else to eat before it's time for the show."

"Don't trouble, Sergeant," she said kindly. "We can ignore our gut rumblings if you can. Florian has predicted that we'll have a real straw crowd, bringing bushels of good things for us to eat."

"A straw crowd?"

"Overflow attendance. Too many for the seats, even, so some have to sit on the straw. On the ground. Anyway, Obie, we've probably scared off every fish in the river. We've been going down there, by ones and twos, for a quick sponge bath before we dress. It's my turn at the sponge now, so excuse me."

Yount sat down on an upturned tub—the circus women's wooden washtub, half of what had once been a flour or whiskey barrel—and watched those troupers who were not off bathing. One who clearly bathed very seldom was the Tarheel idiot, whom Hannibal, before departing on the elephant, had dressed in his Wild Man outfit. That consisted of a few skimpy animal skins draped around him in only sufficiency enough to avert public complaint, plus some lengths of very stout chain hobbling his ankles and wrists, and some campfire char daubed here and there like war paint on top of his natural dirt. The Wild Man spent a little while leaping about and jangling and making faces, apparently getting into character, then crawled under the canvas below Maximus's wagon and began again to grunt and roar inside his bucket, supplying the bloodthirsty noises for the lion sedately pacing up and down the cage.

Closer to Yount, Florian was doing his dressing, which meant only brushing his black top hat and maroon frock coat, and scraping some traces of animal manure off his boots and the stirrup ends of his trousers. Magpie Maggie Hag also did not have to dress for her rôle, beyond the cowled cloak and layers of skirts she already and always wore. So Florian said to her:

"Mag, there are some more rubes stopping along the street to give us the eye. Just in case they're not all lot lice, why don't you take your place in the red wagon now?"

She went to do that, and Yount got up from his tub to inquire of Florian why he referred to a "red wagon" that was no redder than any other wagon on the lot.

"Another circus tradition, Obie. I assume some circus at some time first painted its ticket wagon red for the sake of visibility. Ever since, the office and cash-box wagon of every circus has been called the red one, whether it is or not."

"Oh. Well, another thing. Couldn't your red wagon have been built more convenient? Look yonder. You can barely see the old gypsy woman up behind that high counter. Anybody that wants a ticket from her really has to stretch. Don't that discourage business?"

"More tradition, Obie, and more than tradition. It is set high that way not to discourage the patrons, but to encourage the walks."

"The walks?"

"The walkaways. People who walk off without scooping up all the change they've got coming. There's always crowding around the ticket booth, and everybody wants to hurry along for a good seat. So they may fling up a bill and just make a snatch for their tickets and their change. With the counter above eye level like that, you'd be surprised how many walks leave a few coins behind."

Yount said he'd be damned, and went to sit on the tub some more. Florian strolled over to the wagon under discussion and unlatched and let down the side panels of it, forward of the ticket booth. That disclosed the body of the wagon to be another sort of cage, only with wire netting instead of bars enclosing it. Yount remembered that the "red wagon" had also been referred to as the "museum wagon," so he got up again and went to see what it contained.

Not much.

The cage had a dirt floor and a branched section of dead tree pretending to grow from the dirt up to the roof. There were several animals standing or lying about the floor of the cage, and a few—including a snake—climbing about on the tree, and a number of birds in the branches. But all of them were as dead as the tree, and they had been so inexpertly embalmed and stuffed, and so gnawed by moths and mange, that they looked deader yet. The largest creature was at least a minor curiosity: a calf with two muzzles growing from its head, so it had two mouths, four nostrils and three glass eyes. The other animals and birds had been normal enough when they were alive, and none of them uncommon in these parts: a woodchuck, an opossum, some chipmunks, one skunk, a mockingbird, some cardinals and hummingbirds. Even the snake was an ordinary gray and brown, yard-long North American milk snake.

Yount said, "Excuse me, Mr. Florian, but there's not much of anything here that every person in Virginia ain't seen running around alive—and prob'ly cussed it for a varmint. Even a calf like that ain't nothing too out of the ordinary to a dairy farmer. A dairyman also won't appreciate looking at a milk snake— and, by the way, milk snakes don't climb trees."

"Thank you, Obie," said Florian, sounding not at all downcast by the information. "True, these species may be undistinguished, but each of these *speci-*

mens has some unique story connected with it. And when I relate those edifying stories, the rustics see the creatures through new eyes. Also, I might as well confide, I collected these exhibits not so much to amaze American audiences as those in Europe, when we get there. The hummingbirds, for example."

"Mr. Florian, even foreigners won't be amazed by hummingbirds. I've seen more of them in Mexico than here."

"You'll never see one in Europe, unless in a museum. They simply do not exist over there. No European ever saw or heard of a hummingbird until sometime long after Columbus, when the naturalists began to bring over specimens. Same with the opossum, and several others of these items. So my little museum will interest our European audiences, you may depend on it."

Yount said again that he'd be damned, and returned to his tub to mull over the wide-ranging education he was acquiring here.

Inside the tabernacle, Edge and Roozeboom finished tamping the earthen ring curb, and Roozeboom hurried out through the backyard to take his turn at the river and then in the property-wagon changing room. Edge went also to wash and shave, and he got back to the lot just as Tim Trimm emerged from the prop wagon, wearing his performing garb. It would have been no extraordinary costume for any ordinary man: merely a farmer's frazzled straw hat, plaid shirt, well-worn bib overalls and old gum boots, but all of a size that might have fitted Obie Yount. On Trimm, they were so vastly much too big that they made him look considerably tinier than he was. He could easily have put both legs into just one of the boots, and the straw hat came down below his nose. What little of him was visible between hat brim and boot tops was engulfed in voluminous folds of shirt cloth and overall denim, and the shirt's cuffs hung nearly to the ground. It was a costume that Trimm had certainly assembled on the cheap—possibly free, from some cornfield scarecrow—but it was effective. Even though Edge detested the little wart, he couldn't help chuckling at the sight of him.

"You shouldn't laugh, Colonel Zachary," said Clover Lee, who was already dressed for the ring.

"Why not, mam'selle? He's a clown. Aren't people supposed to laugh at him?"

"I mean *you* shouldn't laugh. You look nicer when you don't."

Edge sighed. "So I was told by your mother, too. You are your mother's daughter, all right."

"Not altogether. Whatever she says to a man, she's flirting. When I say something, I mean it seriously."

Anyhow, in Edge's opinion, Clover Lee was her mother's daughter at least in the matter of good looks, and she bade fair to outdo her mother in that respect. Granted, right now—dressed in flesh-colored tights from neck to wrists to feet, with a faded crimson torso-garment over the tights, and a gauzy tarlatan frill sticking out like a shelf around her hips—Clover Lee looked like a young stepladder, all legs and angles. But if she ever got enough to eat, her body would blossom and, with her pretty face, the bright blue eyes and the waist-length hair of golden satin, she gave promise of being a stunning beauty.

A pity she couldn't be better dressed, thought Edge. The flesh-colored tights had permanent large knees and elbows pouched in them, and the cloth was much darned at those bulges. Elsewhere her costume sported patches—minutely and painstakingly applied, so they were visible only up close, but patches nevertheless. And in other places the costume showed snags and pulls and small rips that had not yet been patched. At this moment, for some reason, Clover Lee was patting herself all over with a wet sponge. Edge asked why.

"Oh, this is the first trick every artiste learns," she said. "Put on your fleshings"—she rubbed the sponge along one leg of her tights—"and your léotard"—she ran the sponge over the little bumps her breasts made in the body garment—"and then damp them all over. When they dry, they cling tighter to your body."

"And I reckon that helps your agility in the tricks."

She stared at him for a moment before smiling the smile of a woman of the world.

"My, but you are an innocent, aren't you, for a colonel? It makes the fleshings look more like real skin, *naked* skin. Do you suppose the yokels truly come to see circus women do tricks? They come to watch us shameless, scandalous circus women expose ourselves. The men eye us to see how much of us they can catch a glimpse of. And the women only watch to see how much we'll dare to show of ourselves, so they can disapprove. Hell, if I was as good a rider as my mother— or even the Great Zoyara—the rubes would never realize it. But if they think they've had just one peek up my bare legs, right to where my legs join, then the gawkers go home believing they've had their ticket money's worth. And I don't even have shapely woman's legs yet—let alone anything real interesting up where they—I told you, Colonel Zachary, you look nicer when you're not grinning."

"I'm sorry. I was just thinking again: you sure are your mother's daughter, no doubt about it."

Their colloquy was interrupted by a sudden blare of horn music, not very well played, but recognizable as the opening bars of "Dixie Land." Edge sought the source of the sound and found it inside the tent. Tim Trimm was playing a cornet, holding its bell out the front door of the pavilion while he kept his costumed self behind the canvas and invisible to passersby. The cornet was recognizable, by its carrying strap, as having once been the property of an army band.

Edge stood and listened until the cornet wailed away the last "Look awa-a-ay..." Then he winced as it launched into "Listen to the Mockingbird" with a tooth-jarring bad note that no mockingbird would have tried to mock, and he departed the tent again for the backyard. Roozeboom, Rouleau and Sarah Coverley were also dressed by now, and had become Captain Hotspur, Monsieur Roulette and Madame Solitaire.

The captain had donned a wide-awake hat, a tunic with vast epaulettes and roomy side-stripe trousers. Except that he wore soft shoes instead of boots, his costume was a quasi-military uniform that obviously had been accreted from castoffs of Yankee blue and Rebel gray, all dyed now to a uniform purple unlike the uniform of any army in the world. The monsieur and madame each wore the second-skin tights that Clover Lee had called fleshings. Over his, Roulette wore underwear—an ordinary "combination" suit of short-sleeved top and knee-length drawers—in wide stripes of yellow and green. Over her tights, Solitaire wore a vest spangled with some silvery things like fish scales, and about her waist a translucent skirt of stiff silvery tulle that reached to her knees. Edge thought the glittery top showed off her handsome bosom just fine, but the skirt might deprive the yokels of some of their Peeping Tom pleasure.

He did not approach her, because she and the two men were busy, bringing things out of the property wagon. Monsieur Roulette lugged into the Big Top a short ladder and something that looked like a small child's teeterboard. Captain Hotspur and Madame Solitaire carried in some lengths of thick pink rope and some things like children's rolling hoops, only frilled with all-around ruffs of pink crêpe paper. Edge got out of the way, ambling on around the outside of the canvas wall toward its front door. He passed the two tethered ring horses, the white and the dapple—bareback except for a single girth band—and saw that somebody had braided colored ribbons into their manes and tails, and dusted their backs with rosin powder, and put on them bridles with extra-long reins, check-straps from jaw to girth, and head plumes that waved above the horses' ears.

When Edge got around to the front of the lot, he saw quite a number of Lynchburgers, white and black, male and female, grown-ups and children, standing along the street, wide-eyed and open-mouthed as they listened to the invisible Trimm, who was now raucously playing "Goober Peas," and to the invisible idiot roaring and jangling his proxy lion noises from under the cage, and to the very visible Florian, who was alternately bowing and stretching a-tiptoe, and waving his hat, and all but prancing, and loudly exhorting:

"Come one, come all! Come to the circus, where everybody is a child again, just for a day! Ladies and gentlemen, young folk and colored folk, even before the performance begins, you will fix your admiring gaze on our zoölogical and ornithological museum of rare creatures captured in the wild. Then approach as near as you dare to the den of the man-eating African lion, king of the jungle. Inside the Big Top, you will first thrill to the music and spectacle of the Grand Entry and Promenade of the entire circus troupe. Then—"

He broke off as the first townies to shake loose of their timidity—an elderly and shabbily dressed man and woman—approached him offering something in outstretched hands. Whatever it was, it was not money. Florian examined it, turned and shouted to the red wagon, "Madame Treasurer, two full-price tickets for our first two discerning patrons of the day!" then turned back to continue haranguing the onlookers:

"Come one, come all! You will disbelieve your own ears when the renowned Monsieur Roulette, master of engastrimythism, projects his voice into remote parts of the arena and engastrimythizes even inanimate objects..."

Yount came up to Edge and said admiringly, "Man, he sure can wrap his tongue around some heavy-artillery words, can't he?"

The people were coming, some singly, but mostly by couples and families, from the street toward the red wagon, and some appeared to be paying at the booth with cash money. But the greater number of them had to pause on the way, to have their barter offerings appraised by Florian. As well as Edge and Yount could see, he did not spurn anything presented and did not turn anyone away, but waved them all on to the ticket counter. Only a number of ragged children, with nothing whatever to offer for admission, remained at a distance.

Maximus and the Wild Man clearly knew their circus-day procedure. As the first patrons received their tickets and made their first stop to peer into the museum part of the red wagon, the idiot scrambled out from under the cage wagon and disappeared toward the backyard, leaving the lion to do his own rather poorer vocal imitation of a bloodthirsty man-eater. Now, besides pacing, Maximus was occasionally baring his teeth and emitting a hoarse, coughing grunt. But that seemed enough to impress the visitors. When they came to his cage, they stood at a respectful distance from it and eyed him with awe, and pointed him out to each other, and in hushed voices discussed his various leonine characteristics.

At a moment when there was quite a cluster of people at the ticket booth and Florian could take a break from his orating, he trotted across the lot and said to Edge, panting slightly, "Would you do me a favor, Zachary? Your uniform looks enough like a doorkeeper's—"

"I thank you kindly. So does the Confederate States Army."

"Yes. I wonder if you would do me the kindness of taking tickets at the front door. Don't tear them, just collect them, so we can use them again. Direct the darkies to the upper boards on the left. The whites sit where they please." Not waiting for Edge to accede, he added, "Ah! I see you are wearing your gun belt."

"Sorry. I didn't know any safe place to leave it, so—"

But Florian only raised his voice to address the rubes at the cage wagon: "Be not afraid, ladies and gentlemen! Just in case that vicious lion *should* break out of the cage"—the rubes all took a step away from it—"we have always in alert and armed attendance the noted English explorer of Africa and hunter of big game, Colonel Zachary Plantagenet-Tudor here—"

"Jesus."

"—And at the first sign of any danger, you may depend upon the colonel and his trusty six-shooter to dispatch the beast before he can mangle and maim any significant number of bystanders. Thank you, ladies and gentlemen. Now enjoy the exhibits. The show will commence shortly." And he strode back to his post near the street, leaving the people looking with even more respect at old Maximus, and with almost as much at Edge.

"By damn," Yount said, still admiringly. "That man can manufacture some advantage out of anything that catches his eye."

Edge gave him a look and left him, to go and stand beside the front-door gap in the tent, and flinch at Trimm's tootling of "Get Along Home, Cindy." Yount went the other way, to help Florian handle the arrival of still more patrons bearing barter goods. The crowd increased when, in a little while, Hannibal returned aboard Peggy and leading, as predicted, a retinue of children, all of them cheering and whooping and trying to imitate the elephant's ponderous walk. Not far behind them came the first of a train of wagons, carts, buckboards and buggies bringing older folk and whole families. And after them came still more, afoot.

"Begod, it *will* be a straw day!" Florian exulted. "Do you know what, Obie? Besides the edibles and usables and shinplaster Secesh paper, I've actually taken in seventy-five cents in good, hard, sound Federal silver coinage!" He called to Hannibal, as the Negro swung down from the bull's neck to her flexed trunk to her upraised knee to the ground, "Abdullah, rejoice! One lady traded me six china soup plates for tickets. So you and Tim can afford to smash one or two, if you like, when you do the mimic-juggling turn."

Hannibal beamed happily and, well in character now, called back, "Amen to Allah, Sahib Florian!"

The bargaining and bartering and dispensing of tickets went on, Yount running the received goods to the tent wagon for storage, while Hannibal and his drum joined Trimm and his cornet to play inviting music like "Nobody Knows What Trouble I Seen," and Edge stoically accepted the grubby bits of pasteboard from the people entering. When one female patron remarked in passing, "Gotcher clothes on today, I see," Edge smiled sheepishly, recognizing Mrs. Grover.

Eventually, and just about at the promised two o'clock, the outside lot was empty—except for the many vehicles left by the railroad sheds, a good distance away, so their horses and mules would not be spooked by the smell of lion or elephant—and every board seat inside the Big Top was groaning under the weight of expectant spectators. With so many people inside it, the pavilion had become rather warm and humid. The sun, high now, sent bright yellow shafts poking down through the dusty twilight of the interior, a large beam like a spotlight from the bail-ring aperture in the canvas at the top of the center pole, and thinner rays by way of the dozen or so unintended holes elsewhere in the roof.

Down by the red wagon, Florian graciously dismissed Yount to go and find a place to watch the show—"So you'll see it all, right from the come-in spec"— then he looked around with great satisfaction. In all of what he could see of Lynchburg, there was not another prospective patron in sight, except the several scruffy children still standing empty-handed and wistful on the cobbled street yonder. He beckoned to them. They came warily, as if expecting to be scolded, and they were.

"You brats don't show much gumption!" Florian barked. "When I was your age and size, I'd have sneaked under the sidewall long before now. What's the matter with you?"

A girl with a dirty face mumbled, " 'Twouldn't be right, suh."

"Claptrap! Think you're buttering up your Sunday School teacher? Come on, sis. Which would you rather be? Righteous and melancholy or sinful and joyous?"

"Uh, well . . ."

"Don't tell me. Go now and be joyous. When you grow up, try to be sinful." As he started around to the backyard, he shouted to Edge, "No tickets, Colonel, guests of the management! Let them pass!"

The children filed through the front door at a funeral shuffle, still wary, looking wall-eyed at the big holster on the doorkeeper's belt and the big, bearded Yount beside him. But, once within the portals, they scattered and scampered, giggling delightedly, and scrunched room for themselves somewhere on the crowded tiers, and the show began.

5

THE GRAND ENTRY AND PROMENADE consisted of most of the troupe coming in through the back door and marching three or four times around the pavilion between the banked-earth ring and the spectators' seats. It was led by Florian, walking with a swagger and flourishing his top hat. Behind him came the white horse Snowball with the glittery Madame Solitaire riding sideways on its bare back, facing the crowd, then the dapple-gray Bubbles with Clover Lee doing the same, both the steeds stepping high and prettily and nodding their heads so their plumes danced. Behind them marched the purple-suited Captain Hotspur, his fringed epaulettes flopping at each step. Behind him came Mon-

sieur Roulette, sometimes lightly bounding along, sometimes throwing somersaults and cartwheels. Brutus brought up the rear of the procession, bearing
both Tim Trimm and Abdullah on her back, and walking with a sort of rocking-
horse gait so as not to overmarch the marchers in front of her. Tim was playing
on his cornet, and Abdullah drumming in time to it, a sprightly tune that was
recognizable as having originally been "God Rest You Merry, Gentlemen." Everybody in the parade except Tim and the animals—and Roulette when he was
head over heels—was singing new words to that old music, singing lustily but
sounding feeble in the cavernous space under the canvas:

> All hail, you ladies, gentlemen,
> Let nothing you dismay!
> We're here to cheer you in your seats
> On this fine circus day...

"You reckon Florian wrote them words?" Yount asked Edge.
"If he did, he ought to be ashamed. 'Cheer you in your seats,' good God."

> And bring to you some gorgeous sweets
> We hope will make you say...

The words and meter might have been atrocious, but the tune was familiar
enough to everybody in the stands, so that, before the troupers had completed
their second circuit of the arena, the entire audience was humming or whistling
and clapping hands along with the song. What had begun as a piping bleat-and-
thump of drum, horn and voices became a music as clamorous as if it were being
played by a full brass band:

> O-oh, grand it is, that ci-ircus joy
> For girl and boy!
> O-oh, gra-a-and is that ci-ir-cu-us joy!

The song evidently, mercifully, had no other verses; it got repeated several
times as the company circled the tent. Then, at the peak of the spectators' participation, while they were still enjoying being performers themselves, Florian led
the procession out through the back door. The last tailing off of the noise was
Captain Hotspur's "... Dot cir-coo-oose choy!"

And immediately Florian, alone, frisked back into the tent, shouting, "Welcome, ladies and gentlemen, boys and girls, to *Florian's Flourishing Florilegium
of Wonders!* To commence today's performance, allow me to introduce to you the
first of our Educational Marvels—a mite-y artiste. Not mighty like an elephant,
mind you... but mite-y like a *mite!*" Florian held up a thumb and forefinger to
his eye. There came a scattering of polite laughter, which caused Florian to put
on a look of exaggerated surprise.

"Please, good people! Small things are not always insignificant. Think of diamonds. And the gem I am about to produce for you is our world-famous midget,
Tiny Tim Trimm!" There was a start of applause, but it died when Florian said
loudly, "Eh?" and held up a hand to his ear. "Did I hear some Doubting Thomas
ask: how small *is* this midget of ours?" Everybody leaned and looked about for
the Doubting Thomas. "I'll *tell* you how small this midget is. This irreducible
fraction of a man, this lowest common denominator, this midget is so *very* short
that, even when he is standing fully erect... when he stands as tall and upright
as he possibly can... *his feet barely touch the ground!*" Several people in the

audience groaned, but the mass of them gave a burst of laughter, while Florian, with a sweeping gesture, bellowed, "We take pride in presenting...Tiny...Tim ...TRIMM!"

A cornet fanfare blared from beyond the back door, and the audience quieted in anticipation. Then nothing happened.

After a moment, Florian did an exaggerated business of craning and peering, and said, "Told you, folks. Little tiny legs that barely reach the ground. Takes him a while to get here." From the audience, more laughter, and it increased as Tim gradually came out into view from between the two banks of seats. He was walking frantically fast, but doing it *inside* his great boots and billows of clothes, scarcely making progress, and again blowing his own fanfare, with breathless sputters and gurgles. He seemed to consist only of a large straw hat atop a heaving pile of laundry, with the cornet bell sticking out from between. Aboard the elephant during the promenade, he had been unremarkable, and in any street crowd he would have been taken only for a runt, not a midget—but now he contrived to look like a bug struggling across a pan of molasses. By the time he had flailed and floundered over the intervening ground to the ringside, the audience was roaring loud enough to drown out his horn squawking.

"Ah, there, Tiny Tim!" Florian bawled, when the laughter began to diminish. "You are late, my lad. Explain yourself. What kept you? We won't stand for slack here, you know!"

"Maybe *you* won't stand for slack," piped Tim, in a squeak meant to be a typical midget's voice. "But that lady yonder does." He pointed to a woman on one of the front benches.

"That lady yonder stands for slack?" said Florian, astonished. The woman looked flustered, and everybody in the stands looked wide-eyed at her. "Whatever do you mean, Tim?"

"She was *standing* on the *slack* of my britches!" squawled Tim, holding out a yard or two of his overalls. "That's why I was late!" But his last words were lost in the gales of laughter, and even the guiltless woman rocked and pounded her fists on her lap.

"I didn't mean that kind of slack," Florian protested. "You don't understand."

"Oh, don't I? *Look* at me, man! I understand *everybody!*"

Laughter continued in gusts through the comic duologue, which played every possible variation on words like standing, upstanding, outstanding and misunderstanding—"Miss Understanding? Why, she's my little sweetheart!"— with Tim getting ever more smug and cocky in his retorts, and Florian getting increasingly exasperated at being the butt of them. When the audience seemed to tire of laughing at the wordplay, Florian began slapping the little man every time he made one of his smart-aleck remarks—"Smart? I'm smarter than liniment!"—and the laughter got properly loud again. The slaps looked gentle, but they resounded—*thwack!*—and every one made Tim reel and fall and lose his hat. The spectators would howl at that, and go on howling, because Tim, scurrying for his hat and impeded by his swaddle of clothes, every time would kick it farther from his reach. When finally he retrieved it and returned to Florian, he would deliver another drollery and receive another slap, and he would fall again and have to repeat the fumbling for his hat.

Even Edge, looking on from the sidelines, was grinning, but not at the hilarity of the performance. He had just perceived something that he never had before, when he'd watched other such knockabout acts. Florian was not hitting the little man at all; his slaps never touched Tim's face. The loud *thwack!* was made by Tim himself, at the precisely right instant, by clapping his own cupped hands together—and that small fakery went unnoticed by those who saw only his violent recoil from the apparent blow.

Florian seemed to have some kind of gauge inside his head that alerted him to the exact moment when even the funniest act began to pall. The next time Tim demolished him with a witticism—"You can't hurt me! I don't have far to fall!"—Florian did not slap him, but waved his arms in despair and cried, "Enough of this! Let's have somebody with some intelligence out here!"

"Right!" squeaked Tim. "Right as a fellow with his left arm off! You go away, you dummy, and send in an animal!"

"We'll do just that! Let's let the young folks say what it will be. Sing it out, kids! Which animal do you want to see?"

The resultant shout was commingled of "Lion! Elephant! Horses!" but Florian pretended to hear a consensus.

"The elephant it shall be! Give us a fanfare, Tiny Tim!" Over the cornet's brassy arpeggio, Florian went on, "Ladies and gentlemen, I invite you now to sit very still. Do not move. You will feel the seats beneath you—the very *earth* beneath you—tremble to the thunderous tread of that mighty pachyderm I now have the honor to present... *Big Brutus, Biggest Brute That Breathes!*"

"Mile up, Peggy," was audible from the back door. Then the bass drum was heard—loud *boomp!-boomp!* and ominous *rumble-rumble*—in time and countertime to the elephant's steps as she strode into the tent. It was a masterly conjuncture of the program. The elephant made Tim Trimm look even smaller than he had seemed until now, and Tim made the elephant look even bigger than she really was. The turbaned drummer seated on her said, "Peggy, tut," and she halted at ringside. She stood with patient dignity while Florian indulged in some more of his flapdoodle:

"You heard, ladies and gentlemen—*peggitut*—one of the mystic Hindu words with which only the great beast's master, Abdullah of Bengal, can control the bull elephant's unimaginable power and gigantic size. To get some idea of Brutus's immensity, ladies and gentlemen, try to conceive of this. All of you *together* do not weigh as much as this single titanic pachyderm! To subdue a behemoth of such size and strength is an art known only to the natives of the far-off land of Bengal. Not I, not any other white man, could tame such a monster as Big Brutus, and teach him the performing skills which you are about to witness. Only a genuine Hindu, like Abdullah here, has the knowledge of those secret words of command..."

He went on for some while in that strain, then finally relinquished the arena to the performers and came to stand with Edge and Yount near the tent's front door. Brutus stepped delicately over the curbing into the ring, raised her trunk and one knee, and Abdullah did his lithe descent of her, from neck to trunk to knee to ground, bringing the drum with him. From then on, he seemed to have no need of his mystic Hindu commands, but only tapped the drum now and again to cue the bull from one pose to the next. Edge knew that even that was unnecessary, since he had seen Brutus go through her repertoire entirely unprompted.

She did the same things now. Abdullah ran to bring, from under the stands, a piece of equipment that Yount recognized as the circus's washtub, and upended it in the ring. At the *thump* of the drum, Brutus slowly raised and placed one foot on it. Suspenseful pause, then *thump,* and she took that foot down and put up the other. *Thump,* and she gathered herself, gave an exaggeratedly mighty heave and got both front feet up on the tub, her body at a steep slant, and stuck her trunk out stiff and blared triumphantly. The Negro spun around to give the whole audience a grin, and raised his drumsticks in the high V sign that every- one recognized as the signal for applause, and they all clapped delightedly. Ab- dullah gave the same high sign every time Brutus did something else spectacular—sitting on her haunches like a dog, then sitting up like a dog beg- ging, front feet pawing the air—and every time the audience responded with vigorous applause. When the elephant hesitated, and she did that at intervals, cannily aware that it made each new pose look more difficult than the last, Florian would dash into the ring and give a brief, edifying lecture.

"There are many curious things about an elephant, ladies and gentlemen, which Abdullah would wish you to know, but he speaks only Hindu. So allow me to inform you, while Big Brutus ponders the difficulty of his next feat. Among the peculiarities of the elephant, it is the only creature on this planet that has a knee in every one of its four limbs. Observe and count them, ladies and gentle- men—*four knees!*"

When the time came for Brutus's crowning achievement, she stood for a minute or two and frowned at the washtub—in the manner of Ignatz Rooze- boom, frowning without any eyebrows—while the Negro gently thumped his drum again and again and made pleading, encouraging gestures. Again the ele- phant put both forefeet on the tub, then reluctantly, cautiously hunched her massive body to bring one of her rear feet stepping up there, too. The audience rustled and whispered anxiously and waited. Florian bounded forth.

"While Big Brutus gathers his every muscle for this most arduous attempt at balance and precision, allow me to point out another unique thing about the elephant. You have all known your horses to get mired in the mud, I am sure. An elephant, though twenty or thirty times heavier, never does. Its tremendous feet have spongy soles; when the behemoth puts his weight on a foot, it spreads like a supporting mat. When he takes the weight off, it contracts. And so—but *hark!*" Abdullah had given a ruffle of his drum. "Let me not distract you, ladies and gentlemen. You are about to witness a feat that it is not given to many to see and marvel at."

Brutus waited for him to shut up, then lifted her fourth foot, so all of her was standing atop the tub, feet bunched together like those of a cat on a newel post. She trumpeted gleefully, and Abdullah danced around, alternately pounding his drum and throwing up his arms in the V sign, as if he had at last accomplished his whole life's purpose, and the audience was lavish with applause and approv- ing shouts.

"And now," boomed Florian, as the elephant daintily got down again, one foot at a time, "you have seen the extraordinary agility and grace of this mammoth creature. I invite you now to see his strength—I challenge you now to *test* his strength for yourselves. I call the ten biggest and burliest men among you to come forth and pit your combined muscularity in a contest of tug-of-war against this single specimen of the grandest mammal in all God's Creation!"

There could not have been ten really ablebodied men in all of Lynchburg, unless they were deserters or early retirees from the war. But there were at least some fat men and some fairly fit old farmers. After they had ducked their heads and said aw-heck and been prodded by their neighbors on the benches, ten men clambered down and bunched bashfully in the ring. Abdullah meanwhile fixed Brutus's leather collar around her neck, and Monsieur Roulette ran in with a length of the heaviest tent rope. It was hooked to the collar and the men took overlapping hold of its other end.

Tim and Abdullah played ruffles and flourishes, and the men—at Florian's "Heave *ho!*"—leaned back and dug in their heels and tugged mightily and Brutus eyed them humorously and never budged. The ten men took fresh hold and this time leaned back almost horizontal, and Brutus eyed them humorously and never budged. Florian said, "Very well, you've had your try. Abdullah, give the secret Hindu command." The Negro called, "Peggy, taraf." She began walking slowly backward, drawing the men as easily as a tent peg. Tim swung into a waltz tune on his cornet and Brutus walked faster, almost dancing as she dragged the ten men around the ring, one after another of them falling down, while the crowd rocked in convulsions that threatened the seating.

Florian cried again, "Big Brutus, Biggest Brute That Breathes!" and the elephant and Abdullah, pounding the drumheads near to bursting, exited to the loudest applause yet. So Florian's next announcement was audible only in fragments: "Monsieur... engastrimyth and ventriloquist... amaze you... voice projection and insinuation..."

Rouleau came in leaping, bounding, turning cartwheels, bouncing end over end. He stopped in the ring, upright, and immediately, but without moving his mouth, began barking like a dog—a sort of muffled barking, like that of a dog with its head in a sack—meanwhile pointing meaningfully to the still upturned washtub on the other side of the ring. He stood there and barked for some time, not getting much attention, then went and, with much theatrical posturing, tipped over the washtub to show *there was no dog underneath.*

It was just as well that the audience wasn't very attentive, because Monsieur Roulette's voice throwing was something less than prodigious. At one point, he began wailing like a hungry infant, with his mouth still immobile, then moved it to shout in his own voice, "Feed your poor child, madame!" and jabbed an imperious finger at a woman in the crowd who held a blanketed baby in her arms. She shouted back, "I'm a Christian woman! I ain' go' give tittie in public!" The spectators went into convulsions again, and Roulette, no doubt realizing he could never top that for audience appreciation, bowed and went bounding end over end out of the tent.

Florian hurried to cover his retreat, though again the new act's introduction was only fragmentarily to be heard: "... Late of the Boer Irregulars... against the Zulus... *Hotspur!*" The crowd finally quieted enough for all to hear: "... To thrill you with his spectacular reenactment of the *Saint Petersburg Courier!*"

Instantly, from outside, there came the noise of pounding hooves, together with Tim's blowing of the cavalry "Charge!" and Abdullah's beating of his drum, and a sound like repeated gunshots. Captain Hotspur must have started his run from a good way up the backyard, because the horses were at full gallop when they erupted into the arena. The white and the dapple careered side by side around the space between the ring and the stands, the purple-uniformed man standing on them, one foot on each horse's back, their reins gathered in his left fist, his right cracking a viciously long sjambok whip. The audience cheered as the trio made several thunderous circuits of the tent, the horses authentically wild-eyed and foam-lipped, as if they really were bearing an urgent message across the Russian steppe.

"Actually, in the classic Saint Petersburg turn," Florian said to Edge and Yount, whom he had joined on the sidelines, "the rider next forces his two steeds apart, so other horses can pass one by one under his legs, and he snatches up their reins, until he is driving a whole herd. Unfortunately, we do not have a whole herd."

The captain brought his two horses skidding to a stop, and they reared handsomely, their necks arched by the check-straps. Hotspur nimbly dropped to a sitting position astride the white horse. Clover Lee was suddenly present, to take the dapple's reins and lead it aside, while Hotspur neatly jumped the white over the curbing and inside the ring. There he bawled, "Mak gauw!" kicked it to a canter, circling the ring, and, as it went, he began to leap off the horse's back and on again. His wide-awake hat flew off, and Clover Lee ran to snatch it out of harm's way. Next Hotspur hung head downward from the horse, supported by one foot inside the girth band. Then he sat up long enough to leap off again and run alongside, then vaulted astride again, to work his way completely around the horse's underside, by way of the girth, while it continued unconcernedly to canter. The spectators admiringly applauded each new feat. Almost every one of them had owned at least one horse, and knew horses better than any other mode of transport, and could descry good horsemanship better than, say, good Hindu elephantmanship. Their approval inspired Captain Hotspur to repeat every trick he had done, until the sweat flying off him sparkled visibly in the sunbeams.

"It's called the voltige, that violent sort of circus riding," said Florian.

"Called gander pulling in the cavalry," said Yount.

"It also put a word into the formal English language," said Florian. "The word 'desultory' comes from the Latin. And in the ancient Roman circus, a 'desultor' was a performer who leapt from horse to horse."

As Captain Hotspur brought the white horse again to a rearing halt, Florian said, "It's time now for the Pete Jenkins." He strode into the ring, where Hotspur was taking bows. Clover Lee brought the captain his hat, and he carefully mopped his sweat-beaded bald head with a rag before he put the hat back on.

Florian called to the audience, "While Captain Hotspur takes a well-deserved pause for breath, I have an announcement to make. One of our patrons just a minute ago informed me that we have a birthday lady in the house." The crowd made noises of interest, and began to lean and look about. Florian consulted a scrap of paper. "And a very *significant* birthday—her seventieth! The biblical three score and ten!" The crowd made noises of being impressed. "Because of the coincidence—her celebrating such a momentous birthday on this Circus Day—I should like the lady to stand up and let us all wish many happy returns ... to Mrs. Sophie *Pulsipher,* of Rivermont Avenue!" He began clapping and the crowd joined in.

"I thought he said Pete Jenkins," murmured Edge.

"Must of been a Pete Jenkins that told him about her," said Yount.

"Come on, Mrs. Pulsipher!" Florian urged. "Don't be shy. Come and take a bow!"

"Hyar she be! Hyar!" shouted several voices. Florian shaded his eyes with a hand to peer up into the seats. In one of the upper tiers, a woman awkwardly fumbled to find footing to stand. The men around her gently helped her down the boards to the tent floor.

"Here she comes!" cried Florian. "Let's hear congratulations, ladies and gentlemen, for Mrs. Sophie *Pulsipher!*"

All previous applauding was surpassed now, and the crowd sang as well, when Tim began tootling "For He's a Jolly Good Fellow," and the kerchiefed, shawled, gnarled little woman hobbled to the ringside. Edge and Yount would have suspected it was the old circus gypsy doing some kind of impersonation, except that Magpie Maggie Hag now came from the other side of the tent, carrying a tiny cupcake on which stood a single candle. At that, Mrs. Pulsipher turned to flee from the attention she was getting, but Florian had hold of her arm. Some of the spectators stopped singing to call, "Blow out the candle!" "Make a wish!"

Mrs. Pulsipher wavered, hesitated, leaned over and—after several weak attempts—blew out the candle flame. "Wish! Make a wish!" cried the people. Florian smiled encouragement at her and bent his ear to her lips. Whatever she said seemed to surprise him; he gave her a very odd look. Then he laughed and shook his head in a firm negative. The audience, intrigued, went quiet and waited. Still shaking his head, Florian quietly said, "No, no," but everybody could hear him. "Mrs. Pulsipher, I thank you for confiding your wish, but no—that could not be permitted."

Several of the spectators yelled, "Tell! Tell!"

Florian looked a little perplexed. "Well...heh heh...this dear little old lady..." He paused, then reluctantly let it out. "She says she never in all her long life rode on a bareback horse. Heh heh. Can you believe this, ladies and gentlemen? Mrs. Pulsipher would like to go once around the ring, riding pillion with Captain Hotspur." The captain, inside the ring, also looked astounded, wrinkling his eyebrowless brow.

The women in the stands crooned things like, "Aw-w-w, the precious ol' critter..." and some young rowdies yelled, "Hey, let her do it! Let's see her ride!" The rowdies swung the vote; others took up the call, "Let her! It's her birthday wish! Let her ride!"

Florian looked even more as if he wished he had never started this. Mrs. Pulsipher stood visibly quivering, while Florian went and conferred with Captain Hotspur, who looked annoyed and impatient to get on with his act. But the two of them came back to Mrs. Pulsipher, and the crowd began cheering and clapping happily.

Clover Lee led the white horse close to the ringside. Florian and the captain gingerly lifted the old lady over the curbing onto Snowball. There was a good deal of awkward scrabbling, and even the horse looked back in inquiry, as they got Mrs. Pulsipher up to a sidesaddle position. Florian held her securely there while Hotspur made sure her hands were clasped on the girth band in front of her. Then he effortlessly vaulted up behind her, wrapped his arms about her waist and nodded to Clover Lee. The girl led the horse by the bridle, walking it very, very slowly. Even so, the old lady teetered considerably, and let out a high giggle that had a tinge of hysteria. The audience laughed with her, and began applauding again, as if she were performing some trick that outdid Hotspur himself. Tim blew a bray of fanfare.

The tent suddenly rocked to a mixture of women's horrified screams and men's hoarse bellows. The audience leaped to its feet, and Florian and Magpie Maggie Hag—even Edge and Yount—lunged toward the ring. At the blare of the cornet, the horse had started violently. Captain Hotspur, caught unprepared, slid off its rump, which scared the horse even more. It bolted, and flung Clover Lee sprawling, and now the horse was galloping madly around and around the ring, with Mrs. Pulsipher clinging for her life to the girth band, but the rest of her fluttering like a sheaf of rags from one flank of the horse to the other. The horse was terrified further by being chased by Florian, Edge and Yount, so it went even faster, while the tent's seating boards clattered as the men in the crowd tried to get down to ground level and lend help.

But before the consternation and uproar could get any worse, the old lady somehow got her legs bent under her and onto the horse's back, and she was whizzing around the ring in a kneeling position. Everybody else in the tent stopped and froze in silent astonishment. Then Mrs. Pulsipher let go of the girth band entirely. In one limber bound she was on her feet atop the runaway horse and she was shedding into the air a litter of flying shawls, kerchiefs, skirts and other haberdashery—and stood revealed as a shapely and pretty woman, glittering and smiling and riding easily upright.

"*Ma*-DAME *Soli*-TAIRE!" boomed Florian at his very loudest.

The spectators let out another roar of pleasure at the metamorphosis of old lady into spirited woman, now striking one graceful pose after another, as serene and confident as if the galloping horse were a parlor carpet. She balanced on one leg, she swooped and pirouetted, she made figures like a swan flying, and every time the horse carried her through one of the shafts of sunlight, her sequined bodice and white tulle skirt lit up the tent's twilight like a flare of summer lightning. Edge had seen players in spangled outfits before, but he had never previously noticed how the spangles reflected upward. Solitaire's face was iridescently dappled by their light and made mysterious, as might be the face of a naiad under rippling water.

The crowd settled back to the seat boards, the extraneous circus people cleared out of the ring, Yount and Edge retired to where they had stood before, near the front door. Florian joined them there, beaming in vast satisfaction at how well the imposture had gone over. They watched as Madame Solitaire continued and elaborated her lissome dancing on her moving perch.

Yount muttered, almost grumpily, "You said that act was called Pete Jenkins. How come?"

"Damned if I know," Florian said cheerfully. "Somebody by that name must have been the first to do the turn."

The white horse slowed to an easy lope. Tim began to play a melodious tune—he had hung his straw hat over the cornet's bell to mute it—and Madame Solitaire threw flirtatious smiles to the men in the stands, while at ring center Monsieur Roulette sang, in quite a good tenor, a most moving song:

> As I sat in the circus and watched her go round,
> I thought that at me she was smiling,
> And smiling so sweetly, this fairy completely
> The heart from in me was beguiling.

The spectators tilted their heads from side to side, to the lilt of the anapests. In the ring, suiting their actions to the lyrics, Solitaire now waved to the men while Roulette wrung his hands together and thumped them at his bosom.

> She waved to the audience—I knew 'twas to me,
> And the heart in my bosom was gay.
> Solitaire is the Queen of all riders, I ween,
> But alas! she is far, far away!

When the song stopped, so did the horse. Madame Solitaire jumped down, as lightly as any fairy, and flung up her arms in the V appeal for applause—which came generously—while Monsieur Roulette and Tim slipped out of the tent. Florian came running to give the lady a paternal hug, and shouted facetiously, "Mrs. Sophie Pulsipher thanks you, ladies and gentlemen!" Laughter from the crowd, and from Solitaire, too, as she departed, leading her horse.

Florian asked for, and got, a round of applause for the ring horses, then said, "Now... to make the moments pass pleasantly while we prepare the ring for the next thrilling spectacle on our program... here again is our own Merry Andrew of Tom Foolery and Joe Millerisms... the ever popular *Tim Trimm!*"

Tim arrived quickly and bouncily this time, no longer encumbered by the oversized farm garb. What he had been wearing under it, and was wearing now, might have been snatched off some household clothesline. It had originally been a boy's flannel combination suit of underwear, but was disguised by having enormous polka dots of various colors daubed all over it. He was also carrying Abdullah's drum instead of the cornet. He came in pounding on it and skipped spastically around the ring, while he told—in his normal loud voice, not the midget squeak—some of the oldest jokes known to mankind.

"The boss of this-here circus didn't want us to get this-here drum, you know!" Boomp-boomp. "He said the noise would upset him." Boomp-boomp. "So we promised him we'd only play it when he was asleep!" Ba-*boom!* Maybe some of the children in the audience laughed. So Tim set down the drum and tried a different theme. "Our boss is a furriner, you know? You got to be careful how you say things. When I told him I was hungry as a hoss, you know what? He tossed me a pitchfork of *hay!*" Not even the children laughed.

Meanwhile, Captain Hotspur, Abdullah and Monsieur Roulette were man-handling the lion's cage wagon in through the front door of the pavilion, and maneuvering it through the gap in the ring curbing. More people were watching that procedure than were attending to Tim, as he doggedly kept on:

"So the boss said eat up that-there hay, Tim, it'll put color in your cheeks. And I said who wants to look like a *high-yaller?*" No laughter at all, so Florian trotted out to his rescue, saying jovially and without preamble, "I hear you're thinking of getting married, Tim, my lad!"

Tim looked grateful for the new subject. "Well, I don't know, boss. After all, what does ma-tri-mo-ny mean? *A matter o' money!*"

Evidently a few men in the audience caught it. Anyway, a few men laughed.

"Yes!" boomed Florian. "You must look for a good wife, and a good wife should have certain qualities. A good wife should be like the town clock. She should keep punctual time and regularity."

"No, sir, that would be a bad wife! She would speak so the whole town can hear!"

By now, the cage wagon was positioned at ring center, so Florian tossed out just one more line: "Furthermore, a good wife should be like an echo. Speak only when spoken to!"

"No, sir, boss. A bad wife, that! She'd always have the last word!"

"Argh, get along with you!" And Florian sent a kick to his backside. It did not connect, but it sounded so, because Tim hit the drum at the proper moment. He threw himself asprawl, got up and scuttled out of the tent.

"And now, ladies and gentlemen!" Florian shouted, waving toward the cage wagon. "You have all had an opportunity to look closely at that beast yonder. You have seen the size of him, the sharpness of his dread fangs. You have heard his heart-stopping roar." Captain Hotspur poked the end of his sjambok in through the cage bars. The cat batted at it with a paw, and obliged with a coughing grunt and growl. "Now you are about to see a brave man actually get into the cage with that vicious predator, to demonstrate man's mastery over the brute creation. I ask you all please not to applaud or make any other sudden sounds, for if the lion is at all startled, or the lion tamer's concentration even for an instant distracted— well, the result could be horrible beyond description. So I beg for silence and, without further ado . . . I give you the daredevil *Captain Hotspur* . . . and the King of the Great Cats, the lion MAXIMUS!"

The crowd obediently ceased every whispered conversation. The captain dramatically flung away his curly-brimmed hat, then flung off his epauletted purple jacket to reveal a brawny bare chest and arms. Coiled whip in one hand, he cautiously undid the latch of the cage door. Maximus growled in what could have been a tone of malice and menace. Slowly, Captain Hotspur put a foot up to the cage entrance and, still very slowly, levered himself into the doorway, stepped slowly inside and swung the door to latch behind him.

He and the big tawny cat stood facing each other inside a barred area only four feet by ten. The captain let his sjambok uncoil and flipped the tassel end of it close to Maximus, who again batted at it and curled his lips to display his formidable teeth. "Platz!" commanded Hotspur, in a voice as gruff as the lion's, and, after a surly hesitation, Maximus lowered his rear end and sat. Someone in the stands involuntarily clapped twice, but Hotspur threw a glare in that direction. Next, he twitched the tassel to flick Maximus under the chin, and commanded, "Schön'machen!" The cat again balked and grumbled and looked gloomily about, as if for escape, but then sat up on his haunches, forepaws lifted.

The captain put the lion through its repertoire of not very sensational tricks —after all, there was not room in the cage for him and it to do very much— making Maximus jump over his whip ("Hoch!") and then lie down, and then play dead ("Krank!") supine with all four paws in the air. Then he backed the lion to the far end of the cage, and himself backed against the other end, and held them apart with the extended whip, while Florian reappeared to announce:

"Now, ladies and gentlemen, Captain Hotspur will attempt the most daring and death-defying feat of all. He will demonstrate his total power over the lion by opening its jaws with his bare hands . . . and putting his unprotected head into the killer animal's *jaws of death!* Let us keep silence . . . and let us pray!"

"Platz!" barked the captain, and Maximus again grumblingly and reluctantly sat down like a house cat. The spectators made not a sound, but their very breathlessness was almost evident, as Hotspur stalked step by step toward the lion, then dropped to one knee before it. Actually, he did not have to pry the animal's jaws apart; Maximus opened them as boredly as if in a yawn. Captain Hotspur turned his head sideways—he did have an admirable head for the purpose: bald and smooth—and put it between the lion's gaping jaws, and from there grinned hideously out at the enthralled audience. After a moment, he extracted his head, stepped away from the lion and bounded upright. There was no room for him to raise his arms in the usual V. Instead, he theatrically threw out toward the lion the hand that held his coiled whip, and insouciantly stuck his other hand in his trouser pocket—and so stood beaming in the storm of applause and cheers and whistles.

Then, again, the applause suddenly became screams and yells of horror—as Captain Hotspur's grin turned to an agonized rictus and his body contorted. Maximus had abruptly reached out his still-open jaws and closed them around the captain's bare forearm. Grimacing and writhing, Hotspur managed to yank the arm loose from the enclosing teeth, yanked his free hand out of his pocket and clamped it around that arm, and blood spurted from between the fingers.

The spectators were vociferous in their commotion as a number of circus people ran to help. Roulette and Abdullah and Tim Trimm got into the ring first, but stopped in their tracks when Captain Hotspur yelled, through clenched teeth, "*Bock!* Stay *bock!* Not yourselfs in danger poot!" To the lion he said firmly, "Zurück! Stille!" and stuck out the whip to keep him at bay.

Maximus was not pursuing the attack; he stayed where he was and looked more bemused than maddened by the taste of blood. Hotspur, with his uninjured arm holding the sjambok steady and the lion in place, thrust through the bars the arm smeared and dripping with blood. Abdullah quickly stooped, tore a long strip from the hem of one of his several robes, stepped close to the cage and deftly bound the rag about the protruding arm. The spectators' cries diminished to sobs and gasps and noises of admiration, as the staunch Captain Hotspur eased himself backward, step by slow step, to the cage door. Monsieur Roulette leaped to unlatch it and, when the captain had jumped backward out of it—reeling giddily as he landed—Roulette emphatically slammed and fastened the door again.

Though clearly unsteady on his feet, the captain insisted on a proper close to his turn. He raised both the whip arm and the bloody-bandaged one in the V, and got the applause he deserved—from most of the audience, anyway. Numerous women had swooned and collapsed, and were being fanned with the hats of their male companions.

"Have you ever noticed," Florian said to Edge, as Roulette and Abdullah helped the captain totter out of the tent, "how a woman never faints until there is nothing more to see?"

"Well, *you* don't seem to mind the sight of blood."

Florian looked mildly surprised. "Not when it's the blood of a jackass. You saw it being collected and saved. The captain had a bit of it in a sausage skin in his trouser pocket."

And, waving his arms, Florian went into the ring again to quell the crowd's agitation.

"Ladies and gentlemen, we regret the terrible accident, but I am happy to report—our company physician assures us that the gallant captain was not badly injured by the man-eater's assault. The captain will be with us again, just as soon as the wound is properly dressed and he has taken a short rest. So we shall now declare an intermission. The program will resume after half an hour, during which interval our talented musicians will render various popular melodies for your delectation."

On cue, Abdullah and Tim struck up "What Is Home Without a Mother?"

"You are welcome, ladies and gentlemen, boys and girls, to leave the pavilion and stretch your limbs with a stroll along the circus midway. At our Mobile Museum of Zoölogical Curiosities, I shall personally deliver an educational lecture on some little-known facts about the rare specimens of fauna to be seen therein. Adjacent to that area, you will be able to observe the recently captured Wild Man of the Woods..."

Most of the people were already climbing stiffly down from the benches, talking among themselves and gesticulating excitedly.

"If some of you ladies would prefer to remain in your places upon the grandstand, you may there avail yourselves of the prognosticatory and divinatory arts of the all-seeing clairvoyante, Madame Magpie Maggie Hag, who will move among you during the interval. At your request, she will accurately foretell what lies in your future, give sage advice in matters of love, health, money and marriage..."

After all the people who were leaving the tent had gone, Edge and Yount helped Abdullah and Monsieur Roulette haul the lion's wagon outside, and a considerable crowd of rubes collected around the cage to watch Roulette throw to Maximus a meal of jackass meat as his reward for having performed so nobly. Yount loitered there on the lot—what he had regarded only as "outside the tent," but Florian had grandly called the "midway"—to listen as Florian expatiated on the "little-known" aspects of the extremely well-known creatures stuffed and mounted in the museum wagon.

"...May *look* to you like an ordinary woodchuck. But in truth this is the *very* woodchuck that inspired the poet who wrote that immortal lyric of rustic humor: 'How much wood would a woodchuck chuck, if a woodchuck could chuck wood?'..."

Inside the tent, where Magpie Maggie Hag was at the moment tête-à-tête with a plain-faced but shining-eyed young woman, Edge sidled close enough to overhear the gypsy saying, "You want your man fall in love with you, juvel? What you do, you take long piece of string. Wait until he stands in sunshine, but where he no see you. Take that string, measure his shadow, cut string that long exactly. Remember, he must not know. Put string under pillow while you sleep. Masher-ava! He fall in love with you. Five cents."

Outside, the Wild Man of the Woods capered about at the end of his chain, gibbering and scratching himself in intimate places under his covering of animal skins and dirt and campfire char, while Florian informed the watching crowd:

"Since nothing remotely like him has ever been discovered before, the savants are unable to accord the Wild Man a specific native country. However, by examination of his peculiar dentition—that is to say, by comparing his teeth to those of known mammals—the scientists *have* concluded that he is part-bear, part-human. The conjecture from that can only be that he was miscegenetically sired by some deranged mountain man upon a she-bear. Or, even more horrendous to contemplate, that the Wild Man is the offspring of a he-bear which somehow..." Florian left that one dangling, and the eyes of the women in the crowd got wide and speculative. "As you would expect of a bear, the half-ursine Wild Man likes his meat raw. So perhaps some of you ladies would prefer to avert your gaze, for it is now the creature's feeding time."

None of them looked away. Monsieur Roulette threw to the idiot a jackass thighbone, which Maximus had at some earlier time picked clean and almost polished. The Wild Man seized it avidly and, with a delighted mooing, began to rattle his dentition up and down it. The rubes muttered among themselves, and Yount muttered to Roulette, "I think that's purely awful. Using that poor idjit so."

"Pourquoi?" said Roulette. "He enjoys it. He is happier here, being admired, than he was at home with his family, being despised."

"Still, it don't seem right."

Roulette said, somewhat tartly, "You and your ami ought to restrain your habit of chiding people for doing what they can do best instead of what you think they ought to be doing."

Inside the tent, Edge listened as Magpie Maggie Hag told a middle-aged but still handsome woman, "You maybe want get rid of old, rich husband, be merry widow! What you do, take string, measure shadow of him standing in sunshine, but not let him know. Roll up string, sneak it under his pillow while he sleeps. Soon—mulengi!—he be dead. Ten cents."

"Shit!" said Madame Solitaire, outside the tent, where she was examining the gear of her white horse.

"Is something the matter, ma'am?" asked Yount. He thought she might be cussing her own gear, for she had changed clothes since she had left the ring, and this outfit was even more sadly shabby than what she had worn earlier. There were more bare patches among the sequins sewn on her bodice, the tulle skirt was more frayed at its fringe. But that wasn't what was bothering her.

"I just noticed. Snowball's check-strap is about worn in two. Right here, see? And he's a great one for throwing his head back. If he does it while I'm a-straddle and bent forward—which is when he'll do it—I get a busted nose. I've had enough busted noses for one lifetime."

"When do you go in the ring again, ma'am? Can't it be fixed afore then?"

"I'm a fair hand at sewing, Obie, but not through leather. I'll have to ask Ignatz, but he's going on any minute." The cornet was playing "Wait for the Wagon," which meant that Florian was herding the rubes back into the tent. "The first turn is Clover Lee doing the garters and garlands, and Ignatz works with her."

Yount scratched in his beard. "If there's time, and if you've got an awl and a piece of waxed twine, I can fix that strap for you, ma'am. Us cavalrymen get to be pretty good at harness work."

"Oh, that's gentlemanly of you, Obie. Come on." They took the strap and went to the prop wagon. "There's Ignatz's tool kit. While you're working, I'll go and see what kind of barter Florian took in—what kind of peck Maggie and I can make of it after the show." She went away, leaving the wagon door open to give him working light.

"...And now, ladies and gentlemen," Florian wound up his introduction to the second half of the program, "here she is—cousin to the brave General Fitz-hugh Lee, grandniece of our beloved General Robert E. Lee—riding her horse Bubbles, which you will easily recognize as a son of Traveller, General Lee's own famous gray—and herself renowned as the world's youngest, most talented équestrienne, Mademoiselle *Clover* LEE!"

Tim and Abdullah blared and boomed into "The Erie Canal" and Clover Lee rode in, smiling radiantly, seated sideways on the bare back of the dappled horse. Captain Hotspur and Monsieur Roulette trotted in on foot and went to the center pole. Florian departed to the sidelines, where Edge said:

"How can you spout such flummery? That child's no more kin to Uncle Bobby and Nephew Fitz than I am."

"You know that, and I know it, but do these yokels know it?"

"If they know that Traveller is a gelding and never sired any get, they might doubt the rest of your rigmarole."

"They're not here to seek Clover Lee's hand in marriage, only to see her ride. But if it's even barely possible that she comes from a family they know, they'll be more kindly disposed to cheer her on."

The horse loped around the inside of the ring and Clover Lee bounded to a stand on its back, but her movements were rather less graceful and fluid than her mother's had been. When Tim and Abdullah swung into the chorus of the tune ("Low bridge, everybody down...") Captain Hotspur ran to the outside with a garter, merely one of the fluffy pink ropes Edge had earlier seen. One end was attached to the center pole and Hotspur held the other above his head to make a barrier in Clover Lee's way. The horse went under it and the girl cleared it with a bound, to come down safe on the horse's back again. Then Roulette ran out with a second rope ("Low bridge, for we're goin' through a town...") so, next time around, Clover Lee had to make two quick bounces.

When she had repeated that trick several times, the men dropped the pink garters and Captain Hotspur stood on the ring curb holding a garland—one of the hoops fringed with pink paper ruffles—out in her path. Clover Lee jumped, somersaulted through it and landed standing on the still-loping horse beyond it. Again Roulette stepped forward, with a second hoop, and now the girl was no sooner landing from one somersault than she had to throw another. It was a pretty sight, and she got tumultuous applause when she finally hopped down from the running horse. Bubbles was also applauded when Florian reminded the crowd again of the animal's distinguished lineage.

"And now, direct from Paris... where his astonishing agility amazed the Emperor Louis Napoléon and the Empress Eugénie... that master of tumblers, foremost of gleemen, the most accomplished of parterre gymnasts... I give you *Monsieur* ROULETTE!"

The man's acrobatic turn was immeasurably better than his voice throwing had been. Indeed, Edge thought it stupendous, and he could honestly believe that even emperors and empresses might well find it amazing to watch him. As Tim Trimm variously tweedled softly and blasted rollickingly, Monsieur Roulette did leaps and twists and turnovers that seemed to gainsay his having any bones in his body or any obligation to the law of gravity. He Frenchified every trick by crying "Allez houp!" before he began it and "Houp là!" when he succeeded, and occasionally even explained in French what he was about to do: "Faire le saut périlleux au milieu de l'air! Voilà!"

After an unassisted display of several-in-a-row forward and backward somersaults and numerous midair cartwheels and flip-flops, he ran and got from ringside the short ladder Edge had seen him fetch to the tent. He stood it upright in mid-ring, not leaning against anything, merely balanced on its two legs—and climbed swiftly up one side and down the other, the ladder somehow just standing there. He did all kinds of posturings and balancings on it, himself sometimes standing up on the rungs and sometimes horizontal to the ladder, held only by one heel against and one toe under the rungs, while the ladder teetered and swayed, but miraculously always stayed erect.

Then he scurried to the top of that standing ladder, stood up on its two uppermost points and walked the thing, like a pair of hobbled stilts, around the ring. Next, without ever getting down, with the ladder still vertical, he stood on his hands on those two upper stubs and again walked the thing around the ring. During much of Roulette's performance, the audience had sat silent, as if afraid to make a noise that might topple him. But that latest feat brought a tremendous burst of clapping and cheers and whistles.

Out in the property wagon, Yount was busy with sail twine, leather palm and curved needle, when Clover Lee suddenly breezed in past him and, not even closing the wagon door, began to undress, right down to the buff. Yount was too confounded even to turn politely away, but frankly stared and finally stammered, "Girl, what are you doing?"

"Changing for the closing spec—the closing promenade. Sweat is worse than moths for eating holes in clothes. Got to rinse them out right away. What's the matter, Sergeant Obie? Surely you horse soldiers know what sweat is?"

"Well, uh... sure."

"Ah. Then maybe you never saw a female naked before."

"Well, uh... not free gratis, no, miss."

"Enjoy it, then. I don't give anything else away for free. *That* I'm saving for when I'm grown, when I meet a duke or a count to give it to, over in Europe." Yount stared even more unbelievingly. "Meanwhile, you go ahead and look all you want at what little I've got to show." Then she laughed, as she realized the object of his gaze. "Oh, you're looking at this thing." She held up the small pad she had just removed from inside her discarded tights. "Every circus artiste wears one. Men, too—only in their case it's to make the bulge at their crotch less noticeable. For us females it's to cover our little cleft, so it won't wink at the audience. It's called a cache-sexe. That's French."

"I might of knowed."

She tucked the cache-sexe between her legs, swiftly slipped into clean clothes from the skin out and flitted out of the wagon. Yount wonderingly shook his head, finished the strap mending and went to take it to Madame Solitaire.

Inside the tent, Monsieur Roulette brought to the ring the thing Edge had thought might be a child's teeterboard. It turned out to be simply a slant short ramp for Roulette to run up and jump from. He did that several times, the board giving him extra altitude and a longer parabola in which to do his fantastic capers and head-to-toe backbends and legs-apart splits in midair. Meanwhile, Abdullah led Brutus into the tent again, and the climax of Monsieur Roulette's act consisted of his taking a run at his board, giving a mighty bounce on it, sailing high and far into the air, turning a succession of tightly tucked somersaults over the top of the elephant and coming down lightly on his feet on the other side of Brutus—"Houp là!"—and the crowd nearly lifted the tent roof with its acclaim.

After Abdullah had taken the elephant outside again, he bounded into the ring anew and Florian introduced him this time as "The master of those *other* Hindu secrets known in the Hindu language as the Art of the Hannibal-tyree. That tongue-twister Hindu word, ladies and gentlemen, means a worker of wonders. And here to *show* you what it means... is *Abdullah* of BENGAL!"

The Negro at first seemed to be empty-handed, but when he began moving his hands up and down, an onion suddenly appeared in one of them. It was flipped to the other hand, but that first hand somehow still held an onion, and that one was flipped into the air, but each hand still held an onion... and so on. Faster than the eye could follow, Abdullah produced onions out of nowhere and sent them arching from hand to hand in patterns so fast and quick-changing that their blurred trajectories looked to be an insubstantial cat's-cradle being woven and remade and made ever more complex. Then the number of onions began mysteriously to lessen, until the individual onions could be seen flipping from hand to hand. Then there was only one of them, and Abdullah was tossing it idly up and down and grinning at the audience. He gave it one last toss, higher than before, got his head under it as it came down, caught it in his mouth and took a loud, juicy bite out of it.

Over the applause, Florian said to Edge—and to Yount, who had just joined them—"To think, friends, that boy used to shine shoes!"

Tim Trimm ran in and handed Abdullah three lighted torches—sticks with bundles of pitch-pine splinters burning at one end—and Abdullah juggled those for a while, making them spin end over end while they were flying high over his head, from hand to hand, and they made a fine spectacle in the tent's twilight. When he had finished with those, catching all three in one hand and blowing them out, Tim ran in again, with a stack of what Edge and Yount recognized as the sort of bowls they had supped from the night before.

Abdullah sent them flipping back and forth between his hands, almost negligently, and this time Tim stood close by. He was playing the clown again, watching the act with an expression of imbecile-Reuben vacuity. He began to make broad gestures of imploring, and Abdullah responded with an inviting nod. So Tim got alongside him, and Abdullah abstracted one dish out of the number in the air and handed it to him. When Tim only gaped at it, Abdullah had to snatch it back from him to keep up the continuity in the air. So Tim repeated the business of imploring, and Abdullah again slipped him one of the soup plates, and Tim flung it at once, and Abdullah had to scramble half across the ring, juggling all the while, to get it into his stream of plates again.

The audience giggled at that, and then they guffawed, and before long were laughing constantly, as Abdullah and Tim rushed hither and yon, colliding, falling down, though still somehow keeping the dishes aloft. Finally Abdullah made a broad gesture of disgust and quit the whole affair—while the soup plates were helter-skelter high in the air—folded his arms and stood aside. Tim managed to skitter about and catch and hold the things as they came down, but there were too many for him, and he could hold only so many in his clutching arms—and the last one fell on his head and shattered to pieces, and the spectators howled and pounded their knees.

Tim looked contrite, then vexed, then indignant. He suddenly gave a yowl of rage—and the audience stopped laughing to duck and dodge. Tim had flung one of the soup plates so it whirled upside down, straight at the bank of seats farthest from him. But oddly the dish slowed in its discus flight and then paused, spinning above the massed and ducking heads—then reversed its direction and sailed back into Tim's waiting hand. The people straightened up again, astounded.

"Now you know why Tim acquired that pie tin," Florian shouted to Edge, over the renewed laughter and applause. "To gaff the mimic-juggling turn."

Tim and Abdullah went off, bowing, and immediately grabbed up cornet and drum to provide a fanfare for the reentrance of Captain Hotspur and Madame Solitaire and the two ring horses. The captain again stood straddled between Snowball and Bubbles, but this time the pretty lady stood right behind him, one hand lightly on his shoulder, the other raised in greeting to the crowd. Hotspur wore his purple uniform jacket, so no one could see whether he was still bandaged, but clearly he had full use of both arms. The horses went side by side around the ring, while the man and woman assumed various artistic poses, sometimes both of them using both horses, sometimes one of them on each horse, sometimes both on one.

Mostly the tricks consisted of Madame Solitaire's being assisted by the captain to an otherwise impossible position—as when she stood on Snowball's withers and bent backward, Hotspur from his stand on Bubbles extending an arm to support her, and she continued arching backward until her hands rested on her horse's rump—both the horses galloping like fury the whole time. The most impossibly perilous pose was of course saved for last. Hotspur knelt atop his horse, and the woman climbed up his back to sit astride his shoulders. The captain slowly stood upright and shifted one foot so he again stood upon both horses. Then Solitaire carefully lifted one foot at a time to Hotspur's shoulders, and unfolded herself so she was *standing* up there, holding onto nothing, her arms outstretched like wings, she and the captain leaning inward as the horses pounded around the ring. When the horses were slowed and she and Hotspur dropped lightly to the ring in their arms-up V stances, the cornet and the drum were drowned by the applause.

"Madame Solitaire and Captain Hotspur thank you, ladies and gentlemen!" shouted Florian, when he could be heard. "And now, before the Parting Salute of the Grand Closing Promenade, we have a very special treat for you, an addition to our regular program. Because you have received us so warmly, our wagon-train escort—Colonel Zachary Plantagenet-Tudor of the British Grenadiers— has volunteered to entertain you with an impromptu exhibition of pistol sharpshooting!"

"Why, the son of a bitch!" Edge exclaimed.

Tim Trimm immediately began a spirited rendition of the "British Grenadiers" march. Florian beckoned to Edge while he continued his blatant falsehoods: "...A fact little known, but our stalwart British sympathizers seconded some of their most expert marksmen to our gallant Confederate Army during our recent struggle against the Yankee invaders..."

"Colonel Tooter," said Yount, highly amused, "you better get out yonder, afore he runs out of guff."

"Let him, the presumptuous windbag. I'm damned if I'll go out there and make a fool of myself."

"You'll look more of a fool if you cut and run."

"God *damn!*" Edge looked almost frantically about and saw that everybody in the seats nearby was eyeing him expectantly.

Florian was still beckoning and still spouting: "However, since our show has already run overtime, Colonel Zachary will make only a single demonstration of his marksmanship. Therefore, I shall ask him to shoot just once—to put out a flame while I personally hold it up. That is how much confidence I have in the colonel's keen eye and consummate skill."

He took from his vest a match, bent and plucked a splinter of pitch pine from one of Abdullah's discarded torches, lit that and held it at arm's length.

"Christ," muttered Edge. "He's not only crazy, he's suicidal. Obie, quick, you got a worm handy?"

"Uh huh." Yount took out a formidable folding knife and opened from it a small corkscrew.

Florian went on, "To overcome the colonel's very British reticence, let's give him a welcoming hand!" and the people obediently started clapping.

"Damn it to hell!" growled Edge. He handed Yount his pistol. "Quick, Obie, pull one of the balls." And he went out into the ring.

"Colonel Plantagenet-Tudor!" bawled Florian, waving his little flame. "Not in British red coat now, but wearing the good honest gray of our beloved Confederate Army!" The applause got even louder. "Take a bow, Colonel Zachary." Edge did so, stiffly, and gave Florian a baleful glare. Then he strode again to the sidelines where Yount, with a nod, handed him the big revolver.

Edge glanced at the front of the pistol's cylinder, and gave the cylinder a slight turn as he stepped again into the ring. The crowd quieted, and the oily triple click of the gun's hammer being cocked was clearly audible. Edge stood with the weapon down at his side until Florian raised and held steady the tiny flame, ten feet away. Edge moved sideways so he had Florian between him and the tent's back door, empty of people. Then he raised his arm, seeming not to take aim at all, and pulled the trigger. Even in the considerable expanse of the Big Top, the shot was a concussive *blam!,* and several people jumped. But Florian did not wince, and the flame at the end of the pine splinter puffed instantly out.

The people clapped heartily, but Edge did not do any V-posturing or even stand still to be admired. He simply turned and went back to his former place by the front door. As if the gunshot had been their signal, the circus troupe and animals came parading in again. Florian stayed at ring center, turning as the parade went around him, as if his extended hand, holding his top hat, were directing it.

Edge commented, "They've most of them changed clothes, just to do this walk around."

"Sweat ruins their costumes," Yount said authoritatively. But then he gave due credit. "That girl Clover Lee told me so. Hell, she changed clothes right in front of me. These circus females've got about as much modesty as so many Injun squaws. You know what else that kid told me? She's saving what she's got atween her legs, until she meets a count or a juke over in Europe."

"I hope there are enough of those to go around," said Edge. "Her mother's got somewhat the same idea. I wouldn't be surprised but the old gypsy woman does, too."

"I mean to say," said Yount, "when I was that kid's age, I didn't know I *had* anything atween my legs, except a spigot to pee from." He paused and reflected.

"Hey, maybe I ought to save my thing, too, for some countess or—Zack, is there such a thing as a jukess?"

"Duchess. And I believe countesses and duchesses only get that way by marrying counts and dukes. Sarah or Clover Lee might have a hope of snagging a title, but you wouldn't. Obie, are you seriously thinking of joining this bunch?"

"Well, I ain't saying I ain't. Hell, I'd never even get to *see* such a thing as a countess in Tennessee."

The troupe had completed two or three circuits of the pavilion. Now Tim muted his horn and swung into the most popular ballad of the day, and Madame Solitaire and Mademoiselle Clover Lee sweetly sang it as they rode:

> We loved each other then, Lorena,
> More than we ever dared to tell...

The lyrics of "Lorena" were woefully lugubrious, but the tune was as beautiful and bittersweet as that of "Auld Lang Syne," and the spectators hummed or sang along with it as they began to clamber down from their benches and make for the front door:

> It matters little now, Lorena,
> The past is in the eternal Past...

Since Edge and Yount were the only apparently circus people in their path, several folks stopped during the come-out to give them a word of thanks for the entertainment.

"I don't reckon," said an elderly gentleman, "we should exactly be celebrating the *way* this war ended. But it's a comfort to have it over with. And you folks, coming along just now, have made us feel a lot better about things in general."

"Yes," said an elderly lady. "Thar ain't nothin' like a circus or a good rousin' camp meetin' to lift the sperrits."

"And y'all's is the fust circus to come since the waw begun," said her elderly lady companion.

"Maw and me'd been keepin' our jar of canned peaches," said a middle-aged man with a middle-aged wife, "for a slap-up dinner whenever our boy come home. But last week we got word he ain't a-comin' home. So we're glad we swapped them peaches for y'all's show. Maw and me, we made out like Melvin was with us, and so we enjoyed it a whole lot. Bless you folks."

6

"OUR TAKINGS, our profit, our plunder!" exulted Florian, standing in the door of the tent wagon where it was piled. He began to tally the acquisitions out loud, for the benefit of his colleagues gathered about the cooking fire. At any other time or place, the takings would have been accounted a pathetically paltry treasure.

"Foodstuffs first. Well, there are the eggs and sausage and mushrooms, some of which Mesdames Maggie and Solitaire are cooking at this very moment. Homemade sausage, said the lady who brought that, and I gallantly refrained from inquiring what went into it. We also acquired the onions you saw Abdullah juggle, and quite a quantity of other root-cellar produce. Potatoes and carrots and turnips and parsnips and some black walnuts. Two good-sized sacks of corn meal and a can of lard. *Four* combs of honey. At least twenty jars of preserved goods—um, let's see—tomatoes, snap beans, peaches, squash, plums, pickled watermelon rind. A fair-sized sack apiece of dried pinto beans and black-eyed peas and goobers in the shell. From the kids, three hefty strings of suckers and catfish. Ladies, I don't think we ought to let those lie around too long uncooked."

"We had fish for breakfast," said Sarah. "Now we're going to have eggs and sausages, with mushrooms and corn cakes, and honey for the cakes. *And* coffee. Well, parched-peanut coffee, but it's the first of any kind we've had in ever so long."

"If some of you would prefer another beverage," said Florian, continuing the tally, "we have spruce beer, persimmon beer and scuppernong wine. None of them tainted with the demon alcohol. *However,* for those who are not teetotalers, we also have here two stoneware jugs of what I was told is Lynchburg's own best brand of white lightning."

All the males except the idiot immediately handed up their tin cups or china mugs to Florian. He poured liberal tots of whiskey all around, including one for himself, and went on:

"Of plunder not edible or potable, but still useful—let's see. We have about a lifetime's supply of Lynchburg's prime product, tobacco in shag, plug or even leaf, if anybody wants to roll cigars. Here, Abdullah, take a plug and give Brutus a treat right now. We also acquired a quantity of mixed tableware, including those dishes for juggling. Some nails and screws and clothespins. A small mirror and some candles and a can of coal oil and some lamp wicks. A couple of not too threadbare horse blankets, a box of horseshoes of mixed sizes, and three or four nose bags, in case we ever get some grain to feed the poor brutes. Various townswomen contributed lengths of ribbon and braid and some paper flowers. Madame Hag, I'll let you determine what decorative use may be made of them. We also have various odds and ends of military uniform that we can dye, and we even got some pots of copperas and sassafras and sumac dyes." He paused to refresh himself with a sip of the corn whiskey. "It's almost more fun to do business like this than the orthodox way of just taking in money. Never know what you'll come up with. For example, this."

He held up a six-string banjo, in good shape except that it had only the chantarelle and two of the long strings.

"If we can procure three more strings, one of us will have to learn to play it. But I also got a musical instrument for *me*." He stuck a tin whistle in his mouth and blew a shrill blast. "I've been without one too long, and an equestrian director without a whistle is like an orchestra conductor without a baton."

He tucked it carefully in his vest pocket, then went on with the catalogue.

"Here's a nice portable library for us. Six or seven copies of *The Camp Jester* magazine and three Beadle dime novels. Let's see—*Nick of the Woods, The Indian Wife of the White Hunter* and *The Forayers*—ha! that's *us!* From the youngsters I took in a whole heap of these little 'comfort bags' their Sunday Schools were supposed to have sent to the troops. I think we can discard the tracts against drinking and cussing and such. But the bags do contain useful items like pins and needles and thread." He sipped again at his whiskey. "And now, last but not least, the actual cash money we took in. I am happy to announce the grand total of four dollars, eighty-seven and a half cents in good Federal silver and copper, eight *hundred* dollars in Confederate paper. Now I call that a pretty good take!"

All the circus folk applauded as exuberantly as the paying audience had done, but Edge spoke up:

"I reckon I'm as Confederate as they come, Mr. Florian, but I frankly don't understand why you're continuing to accept those shinplasters."

"I may be wrong," said Florian, "but I strongly suspect that we'll meet diehard Rebels, somewhere along our way, who will actually refuse to accept Yankee money in exchange for whatever we might want to buy."

"If you say so," said Edge, and subsided.

"Maggie," Florian called down to her. "How did you make out with the rubes in the interval?"

She looked up from her cookery to say, "Seven dollars."

That rather dampened Florian's glee. "Why, Mag, you used to do better than ... why, I'd have expected ... Hell, Mag, that's only worth about seven *cents* in genuine—"

"Not paper." She gave him a gap-toothed but very satisfied grin. "Real money."

"What!" Now Florian was stunned. So was everyone else. "Why, that's almost as much as *all* we took in at the red wagon, Federal and Secesh together."

Magpie Maggie Hag set down her cooking implements to feel about among her layers of skirts and underthings. She extracted a cloth bag that jingled richly and handed it up to Florian.

Jules Rouleau asked, "How in the world did you come by it, Mag?"

"Women," she said, and spat contemptuously. "Come war, come misery, come Doomsday, *all* women magpies. Sneak away penny at a time, hide away little nest egg. Any woman can pilfer good as any gypsy. She maybe won't spend for food, shoes for family, even frippery for herself. But she give nest egg to have her dream or her palm dukkered, if she think it maybe dukker affair of love. A man if she got none, a new man if she already got one. *Women!* Now come, everybody. Supper ready. Good supper."

It *was* a good meal, and a welcome one, not to say a necessity and long overdue, and the fire made a bonny gathering place in what was now the no longer warm dusk of the day. Only the Wild Man unmannerly slobbered and gulped his share of the meal and then drifted away. The others enlivened their dining with amiable chatter in the various jargons of their several arts.

Hannibal Tyree said to Tim Trimm, "Would it be easier for you, when you horn in, if I was tossin' a shower 'stead of a cascade?"

"Don't matter. But next time, after I throw the tin and skeer the rubes, we ought to give 'em a laugh to relax. So you kick me into the tub and roll me around."

Clover Lee said to Ignatz Roozeboom, "I think, instead of just a hop-down at the close, I should do a back lay-out from my last somersault to the ground."

"Ja, gut. But if you stop den, you sway, look unsteady. From dot lay-out, go into a one-hand round-off."

Edge leaned over to say to her, "I remember, mam'selle, that you called your tights 'fleshings.' But you call the other garment some foreign name?"

"A léotard. I don't know why it's called that."

"Shame on you, Edith Coverley," said Florian. "The man who designed it and gave it his name is the greatest trapeze artiste alive, Jules Léotard."

Rouleau said, "I hear that all kinds of things in France have been named in his honor—rissole à la Léotard, pâté Léotard—just the way we have the Jenny Lind bonnet, the Jenny Lind polka and so on, over here."

"How lovely!" said Clover Lee. "Maybe, when I get famous in France, they'll name something after me."

Edge turned to Magpie Maggie Hag, who was frying another batch of sausages, and said, "Ma'am, I hope Lynchburg is well supplied with string. Do you tell every woman that's the way to get a man—or get rid of one?"

"Why not, gazho? *You* ever try measure man's shadow with string, and him not know it? That can take long time to do. In long time enough, man going to fall in love with *somebody*. Likewise, sometime man going to die. Give it time, string *always* works."

"Hey, horse sojer," said Tim Trimm. "You axin' us questions, I want to ax you one. How come you don't wear a beard? Your sergeant does, and so does prac-tic'ly every other sojer I've seen. You think your face is too pretty to cover up?"

Edge said equably, "Is that why you don't wear one?"

"Shit, no. Circus men don't grow beards 'cause they kin git caught in the riggin' or somethin'. Dangerous. One of these days, old Ignatz here is gonna git his walrus mustache snagged on that old lion's teeth. And you'll be in trouble, won't you, Dutchman?"

Roozeboom only shrugged his mustache. Edge said to him, "I hope, if you do get in trouble, the whole troupe doesn't just think you're play-acting, like that trick with the bogus blood."

"That's called gaffin' the act," Tim explained. "To give it a toot. A li'l extry flash and dash."

Roozeboom chuckled. "Ven I vas a jong, first learning, my old Baas he told me: de trick is not to piss, it is to make de foam."

Edge laughed, too, and turned again to Tim. "Me, I shave my face so the fleas and lice will have one less place to roost." He added reminiscently, "All through the war, we had those daguerrian artists following us around with their camera boxes and cabinet wagons. Every time I'd see one of their pictures—of a bunch of heavy-bearded generals in war council or whatever—I'd wonder how in hell the generals sat still long enough for the man to catch their picture. I knew damned well they had to be itching and frantic to scratch."

Tim said grudgingly, "There's one thing I gotta admit, sojer. You done some nice shootin' back yonder. Can you do that every time?"

"I don't know," Edge grunted. "I haven't had much experience shooting at toothpicks."

He and Yount, having finished eating, emulated the others in the matter of disposing of their used implements. The wooden washtub—which had, in this one day, variously served as a washtub for persons and for soiled costumes, as a thing to be sat upon and as a ring prop for the elephant to perform on—was again right side up and full of river water, and the troupers swashed their dishes and cups around in it before giving them to Magpie Maggie Hag for more thorough scouring with sand. Edge and Yount then packed pipes and strolled about, smoking with great gratification. Yount paused where Hannibal sat, still eating, and asked him in all seriousness:

"Boy, do you really talk Hindu to that elephant of yours?"

Hannibal giggled and said, "Lawd, nossuh. 'Mile up' and 'tut' and them words, they jist circus-elephant talk I talks at ol' Peggy. Mas' Florian, he *tells* the rubes it be's Hindu, and they don't know no different. They ignernt."

"Oh," said Yount. "Then I reckon I am, too."

"Then we all are," said Florian, overhearing. "Hell, I don't even know if there is such a thing as a Hindu lingo."

"I'm surprised," said Edge. "In the little time we've known you, I've heard you spout at least three other languages. How many *do* you speak?"

Florian reflected, then said, "Fluently: French, German and American colloquial English. Well enough to get by: Dutch, Danish, Italian, Hungarian and Russian. That's what? Eight. Nine if you count the Latin I acquired at the lycée. Ten if you count Circus."

"Godamighty!" Yount exclaimed. "Why don't you dump the rest of this outfit and just charge people admission to admire *you?*"

"How did you come by so many?" Edge asked.

"Partly by accident of birth. I am from the Alsace, in the middle of Europe. Do you know it?"

"I know more or less where it is."

"To the west of it is the French Lorraine. To the east, the Duchy of Baden, which is a German-speaking land. They continually compete for the possession of Alsace, so we Alsatians grow up speaking both French and German, just in case. Meanwhile, the rest of the world never knows to whom the Alsace belongs. Witness, you foreigners prefer to call our Alsatian sheep dog a German shepherd, and our Alsatian water dog a French poodle. Anyway, my knowing French enabled me fairly easily to pick up Italian. Knowing German made Dutch not difficult. As for the others, I was once married to a Danish woman, and another time to a Hungarian, and yet another time to a Russian. If there's any better way to learn a language than pillow talk, it's mutual vituperation."

Yount murmured, "Well, I'm damned."

"So was I, fluently and frequently. Speaking of Europe, how did you enjoy playing the British grenadier, Zachary?"

"Well, I had determined that I wouldn't even speak of it, for fear that I would get to cussing, but since you broach it... For one thing, grenadiers don't shoot pistols. They throw grenades."

"Is that a fact? Yes, of course. I was being 'ignernt.' Thinking the word signified a corps d'élite. Well, I was sincerely trying to do you proud."

"I'd be more gratified if you didn't do it again. This time, since you hadn't given me any advance notice—whether you truly wanted to commit suicide—I wasn't sure whether to oblige you or not."

"Come, come. I had every confidence in your marksmanship. Are you suggesting that I was in some peril?"

"Not just some. It's a good deal easier to shoot a man than deliberately *not* to shoot him. Even if I were the world's champion pistolero, my first round might be a badly cast or badly seated ball that could go slewing off sideways. Now, a miss wouldn't matter much if I was shooting to *hit* a man; I've still got five more rounds to plug at him. But if I'm deliberately aiming left, where you held the torch, and that bad ball chances to go right..."

"Good heavens," Florian said faintly, looking at Edge's holster with new respect and some misgiving. "But—heh heh—it did not, after all. And you did shoot straight. You hit the flame."

"I didn't have to. Any wind would blow it out, and that's all I shot—a puff of wind. Obie pulled the ball while you were introducing Colonel Fancy-Pants."

"But—but there *are* professional shootists. If a gun can't be trusted..."

"Oh, this one's trustworthy. Remington 1858, calibre forty-four, six-shot percussion. None better among handguns. I was talking about the loads. If I were a trick shooter, I'd make damn sure about the loads beforehand. That is, if I was notified beforehand that I'd be called on to do some trick shooting."

"Yes, yes. See your point. Foolish of me... impetuous..." To take Edge's sardonic eye off him, Florian pointed at the pistol again and asked, "Standard issue, that?"

"To the Yankees," said Yount, with a snort. "All *we* was issued was permission to go and snatch any that we could."

"And you did."

"More than once," Edge said drily. "The first pistol I took from a Yank was the Colt forty-four. But it doesn't have the top-brace across the cylinder, and it begins to feel loose and rickety after a while. So next I went for a Yankee that had one of these."

"I'd think any forty-four would do to stop a man in his tracks. But I couldn't help noticing: that carbine on your saddle is bored like a young cannon."

"Fifty-eight calibre. That's for stopping a charging *horse* in its tracks."

"Ah, of course. Another bequest from the Yankees?"

"No, that one's pure Confederate. Made by the Cook brothers down in New Orleans. Well made, too."

The talk of the tools of his trade appeared to have mellowed Edge's mood, so Florian dared to say, "I realize I pulled a low trick on you, Zachary, but the audience was clearly pleased with your impromptu performance. And you brought it off with admirable savoir-faire. Are you really going to carry a grudge about it?"

Edge made a sour face, looked over at the Big Top and finally said, "Oh, hell, I reckon it wasn't *too* mortifying."

"Well, then!" said Florian, with a gusty sigh of relief, but he did not pursue the matter. "Tell me, what is the next nearest town of any size?"

"There purely ain't any," Yount put in. "Not this size, not in this end of Virginia. Lynchburg's the third biggest in the state, and the other two are 'way over east in the Tuckyhoe country."

Edge said, "If you want to take the shortest way north, up this piedmont side of the mountains, Charlottesville is the next town big enough to fill a shirttail. Or you can go north up the valleys, and the nearest town will be Lexington, where Obie and I are headed. But that's fifty or so miles from here, and westward beyond the Blue Ridge."

"A two-day run, and over the mountains," mused Florian. "If we were to go where you're going, friends, could we still have the loan of your horses and your companionship on the way?"

Edge and Yount exchanged glances and said they wouldn't mind.

"Then that's preferable to the easier route without your animals to help," said Florian. "We'll go with you to Lexington."

"We'd figured on going tomorrow," said Edge.

"Yes. Tomorrow. We'll start the teardown right now."

"You don't give any night show?" Yount asked. "Seems to me that other circuses do that."

"In big cities, and when we have lights enough, Obie, we do, too. But never in farm country. Folks have to get up at cockcrow, so they go to bed early. And this may be a city of some size, but it's still a farm town full of farm folk. And I rather suspect that we already have milked the town for all it's worth."

"I ought to warn you," said Edge. "Lexington is only a little college town, and it got raked over by General Hunter's Yankees less than a year ago. Poor pickings for you, I'd estimate."

"A college town. I assume that's where you intend to settle down as a schoolmaster. Where your military academy is."

"Was. VMI and Washington College, too. David Hunter looted and burned them both. The rest of the town exists only to peddle goods to the professors and cadets and students, of which there likely are not any, so the whole place may be deserted. It could turn out that *I'm* foolish in heading there, but I'm not responsible for a herd of other people dependent on me. You are."

"Ah, well. One must have a destination, however illusory or—what's that?" They had been interrupted by a thrumming, strumming sound. It went on, at first just a disorganized jangling, but then resolving itself into an attempt at music.

"Look yonder," said Yount. "It's the idjit. He found that busted banjo you took in today."

"Not only found it," said Florian. "He's playing it. Like he knows how."

They walked over to where the Wild Man sat on the ground, his back against a wagon wheel. Without missing a stroke, he looked up and gave them a loose-lipped grin, his tongue protruding through it.

"Listen," said Florian. "You can make out what he's playing, by damn!"

"Uh-huh. 'Lorena,'" said Yount. "And not too bad, with only half the strings. Lucky one of 'em is the thumb string."

Florian knelt and stopped the Wild Man's hands momentarily, gave him an encouraging nod, then whistled to him the first few bars of "Dixie Land." The idiot listened, gave an even more sloppy grin and began to pluck and strum the identical notes.

"Oh, hell," said Yount. "Every least nigger knows 'Lorena' and 'Dixie.'"

Florian stopped the young man's hands again and whistled something that neither Edge nor Yount could name. The Wild Man again listened and immediately played the same melody.

Florian straightened up, with a look of mixed triumph and awe. "Not many Negroes know that one. 'Partant pour la Syrie.'"

"What?" said Yount.

"The French anthem. Well... I've heard of such things, gentlemen, but he's the first I ever encountered. An idiot savant."

"And what's that?"

"What you're looking at. And listening to." The Wild Man was playing that scrap of anthem over and over. "An idiot totally devoid of intellect and capability, except in one area where inexplicably he excels—without ever having been taught, and probably without having the least notion of what he's doing. Sometimes it's mathematics—an idiot savant can do sums and calculations that would confound a whole roomful of professional accountants. With this one, it's music." Florian lifted his hat to scratch his head. "By holy Hades, I thought I was humbugging, but I bet the scientists *would* like to get hold of him. We could ask a substantial price..."

"We-ell," Yount said thoughtfully, "I don't know about scientists. But if there's colleges and professors in Lexington..."

Florian bounded erect and snapped his fingers. "You've hit it, Obie! So! We have a destination *and* a reason for going there. Zachary, we'll give your VMI first bid on the creature."

"Jesus! I go back to my old alma mater bearing an idiot for sale. Mr. Florian, you *are* determined to mortify me, aren't you?"

But Florian didn't hear; he was striding off, alternately blowing ear-splitting blasts on his new whistle and shouting names: "Hotspur! Abdullah! Roulette! Hop to for teardown. We're blowing the stand early in the morning."

"Reckon I'll lend a hand," said Yount. "You, Zack?"

"Oh, hell. I reckon."

The teardown was pretty much the setting up done in reverse order, except that it went a good deal faster, even in the now near-totally dark night. Magpie Maggie Hag, Sarah and Clover Lee all got lanterns from the wagons, lit them and went inside the Big Top to hold and aim them while the men bent to their work. That commenced with the dismantling of seats. Gathering up the unfastened bench planks was a quicker job than laying them in place had been, and so was the knocking loose of the sapling jacks and the toe pegs and the notched stringers they supported.

Edge found this operation more interesting than the daytime work had been, simply because every person and every thing looked somehow larger and grander in the dim lamplight than in the radiance of forenoon. The lanterns held by the women threw the shadows of men and equipment up onto the sidewalls and the canvas ceiling high above, making them gigantic and black and almost mysterious in the swift, well-practiced movements they made.

When the last of that lumber had been hauled out and stacked in the property wagon, all the men and women vacated the tent to work outside. The moon had not yet risen, but the lamplight made things even more eerie than moonlight would have done. The night's slight chill was bringing up a ground mist, so the lanterns threw not beams but a diffused, foggy, dreamy sort of light—and it was given a fairy flutter by the hordes of moths that followed the lanterns around and flickered like sparks detached from them and added their twinkling little shadows to the greater ones the lanterns flung about. Every man cast a tremendously long and attenuated shadow, either high on the tent's roof or from his feet across the lot into the far distance where the shadow was absorbed into the night, and when he walked the long shadows of his legs scissored like an immense, black, insubstantial pair of shears trying to trim the lamplit weeds off the lot.

Tim again shinnied up one of the side poles, then clambered up the billowy slope of the Big Top, along one of its seams, to undo the lashings with which he had secured the bail ring at the top of the center pole. And he slid down again, and again into Roozeboom's waiting arms. Meanwhile, Hannibal had put the leather collar on the elephant and was leading her around the staked perimeter of the pavilion's side ropes, followed by Clover Lee carrying a lantern. They stopped at each stake, Hannibal whisked around it a loop of the rope attached to Peggy's collar, the elephant merely leaned back and the stake—which three strong men had sledgehammered three feet deep in the ground—came up and out as if it had merely bobbed up from underwater, and they moved on to the next one.

Florian picked up one of the removed stakes and judiciously examined its pointed end, its arm-thick length and its hammer-splayed top end. "I suppose they'll do for a while longer," he said, as if to himself. But Yount was working nearby and threw him a questioning look. Florian explained:

"We usually cut new staubs every year, while we're in winter quarters, and we cut them five feet long. By the end of a season of setups and teardowns, they'll have worn down to useless nubbins. In Wilmington there weren't any new ones to be had, but there it didn't matter, because we weren't moving. Now—you see—these staubs have already been beaten down to some four feet long. I must remember to keep a lookout for every good stand of saplings where we can cut new ones."

Yount nodded solemnly and went back to what he was doing, which was helping Roozeboom and Rouleau to unrope and unpeg the sidewall sections of canvas, and roll them up and lug them to the tent wagon. But suddenly all work stopped as Florian blew another commanding blast on his new whistle. All over the lot, the men and women paused in their several occupations and looked to him, puzzled.

"Lads and ladies," Florian called. "You're all toiling away as morosely as if this were season's end. But we've had a straw stand, and we're on the road again tomorrow for new horizons. Why aren't we hearing a good rousing heeby-weeby?"

He blew the whistle again and waved his arms like a choral director. The troupers all laughed and, as they went back to their chores, began chanting:

> Heeby, weeby!
> Shaggid, taggid, braggid,
> Maggie *moo*-long!

"If that's a work chantey," Edge said to Florian, "it's one I never heard before."

"You'll hear it from the canvasmen on the ropes, some version of it, every time a circus sets up or tears down. A prosperous circus, that is. These poor folk haven't had much esprit de corps for a long time. But maybe today marks the start of better times—and higher morale. Maybe from now on they'll sing without my prompting."

Right now, anyway, they were repeating the chantey, over and over, in unison, and seeming to do it cheerfully. Edge listened closely, but finally said, "I give up. What are the words?"

Florian sang along with them, but carefully articulating:

Heave it, weave it!
Shake it, take it, break it,
Make it *move* along!

Edge took it up himself and, chanting, went back to what he had been doing, which was helping Tim Trimm undo the guy ropes from the uprooted "staubs," then flicking the loop ends of the ropes off the top spikes of the side poles, then neatly coiling the ropes. As they progressed around the guys, Tim also gave the side poles a kick, so they fell outward from under the tent roof eaves, but he left every sixth pole unkicked and upright. So, by the time the workers and the elephant had gone once around the pavilion, there was nothing left of the Big Top except the center pole and the tent roof depending from that to the few remaining side poles—a roof no longer trimly conical but sagging in wrinkled scallops from its high peak. Hannibal ran into the darkness under it and emerged with a single rope end. He stood holding it and looking alertly at Florian.

"Everybody clear?" called Florian. Then he put his whistle to his mouth and blew once more. Hannibal yanked his rope end. It evidently loosed some crucial hitch or warp among the many ropes and pulleys of the center pole, because the bail ring came with a rasping rush down the length of that pole, and the whole vast extent of roof canvas came with it. Everybody standing around felt the swoosh of wind from under it, and was pelted with blown dust, grit, bits of weed, straw and paper and other trash left by the audience. The tremendous canvas continued to belly and billow as it settled, and its eave edges fluttered quietly against the ground as the trapped air sighed out.

Edge and Yount followed the other men as they ran onto the canvas—being careful to step only on the lapped-together edges of the several sections—tramping down the last pockets of air. Still chanting the heeby-weeby, they quickly undid the ropes at the bail ring where all the canvas pie-slice points converged, then undid the lengths of the seams down to the eave edges. They did not bother to unlace the ropes from the grommets one by one, as they had so painstakingly laced them together, but simply pulled a rope end so it whipped out of a series of grommets in one yank.

"But don't pull *too* fast," Rouleau cautioned Edge. "In dry weather the friction could set the rope afire. Or the whole canvas."

When the sections were all separated, the men rolled them into bundles and tied them with the ropes that had just been removed. There remained only the center pole, standing rather precariously now, supported only by the spike in the gumshoe base. Hannibal again brought Peggy, attached her collar to one rope, the men took hold of another and—at Florian's whistle and shout of "Lower away!"—they tugged (*"Heeby!"*) to bring the high pole tilting to one side. On its other side, Peggy took the weight as it leaned (*"Weeby!"*) and moved to let it gently down toward the ground, the gumshoe careening over with it. When it was down (*"Shaggid!"*), Roozeboom ran to tug the gumshoe spike out of the pole's interior. Rouleau quickly (*"Taggid!"*) took off all the pole's pulleys and ropes and coiled them. Then (*"Braggid!"*) all the men combined their strength to slide the separate sections of the pole out of the uniting metal sleeves. When all the bundles of canvas, pieces of pole, pulley blocks and coils of rope (*"Maggie*

MOO-long!") had been stowed in the tent wagon, nothing remained of the Big Top except the heaped-up circle of the earthen ring curbing.

The cooking fire was only embers now, but sufficient for Magpie Maggie Hag to warm up the pot of parched-peanut coffee and give everyone a restorative mug of it. She and some of the men lit up pipes and passed around one of the jugs of moonshine, and Peggy got a chew of tobacco. Then they all jumped as Florian blew yet another whistle blast.

"Damn it all!" said somebody. "Wish you'd never got that gimmix."

"I was sounding curfew," said Florian. "Early day tomorrow."

He, Trimm, Roozeboom and Rouleau went to climb into their bunks in the prop wagon. Edge was unrolling his thin old pallet and blankets under that wagon—so were Yount, the Negro and the Wild Man—when a lantern shone over his shoulder and a voice sang softly at his ear a revised version of the ring song he had heard earlier:

> As you sat in the circus and watched her go round,
> You knew that at you she was smiling...

He turned and looked up into Sarah's lamplit face. She grinned mischievously and whispered, "It's been *such* a good day, oughtn't we to celebrate?"

"Not much privacy here," Edge whispered back.

"We'll move 'way over by the railroad sheds. Combine our bedding."

So they went over there, made a bed, undressed and, after a while, Edge remarked, "Obie was right. He said you circus women are shameless."

"Oh? What have any of us done to shock Obie Yount? What in God's name *could* anybody do that would shock a sergeant of the horse cavalry?"

"He said something about Clover Lee undressing in front of him."

"For Christ's sake, this is the circus. We don't have any privacy, so we cultivate the good manners to ignore such things."

"What you call good manners, I suppose some people would call not very good morals."

"Let them, and be damned to them. Manners are a lot more important than morals."

"That's an interesting theory."

"It's not a theory, it's the plain truth. What you and I are doing right now, most people would consider immoral, but—"

"I wasn't *complaining.*"

"—But we're doing it in private, where it can't possibly bother anybody. We people with bad morals don't parade them. But bad manners, why, they're right out in the open, where they can offend and upset everybody."

Edge said, "Then I don't know whether you'd consider this bad morals or bad manners, but I'll tell you something. When you were doing your act, up on that rosinback horse, and you did that backbend—where you curved all the way over backwards—you know what I was thinking then?"

"Hell, yes. I know very well," she said, pretending exasperation. "You gawks are all alike. Never admire the skill and grace and perfection of the pose. You just think *hey,* I never tried it in *that* position."

"Well... I never did. Did you?"

"No. I doubt that anybody ever did. It's not exactly an easeful position for me alone. It ought to be damned uncomfortable for two."

He said playfully, "Let's find out."

She laughed again, but eased out from under the covers and cast a wary glance over toward the distant circus wagons. The moon was up now; she could see nobody stirring. So she stood erect, naked, glowing in the moonlight, and easily arched over backward into a bow, her hands and feet on the ground.

"Well?" she prompted, looking at him upside down.

"I'm admiring you," he said truthfully. "Your skill and grace and perfection." In her backward-arched position, the uppermost part of her was her blonde little pubic escutcheon, and it gleamed in the moonlight like a night-blooming pale flower.

After a wary look about, Edge also got out of the bedding. There ensued a period of awkward movements, trials and retrials, whispers of encouragement and mumbles of frustration, and finally he confessed defeat. "I reckon you're right. Nobody ever did."

"One of us would have to be built different, or both of us," she said. "Can we resume the old, tried-and-true ways?"

After another while, when they were resting, Sarah said, "Now let me ask you something. Did you ever watch a klischnigg?"

"Jesus. I don't know. What is it?"

"Just another name for a circus posture-master, a contortionist. It's the word Florian uses. I think Klischnigg was the name of some old-time artiste. There are other names—india-rubber woman, human serpent, boneless lady. Anyway, it's a woman who does impossible wriggles and contortions with her body."

"Then no, I never saw one. Why?"

"Well, now that I know your secret tastes"—she gave a mock-melancholy sigh—"when you meet a klischnigg, that's when I'll lose you."

He laughed at that, then said, "You'll still have Florian."

"I told you. If I'm nevermore to be wanted, I would like at least to be needed. He doesn't need me very often."

"Well, there'll be all those dukes and counts. They can probably buy everything they need. So, when you captivate one of them, you'll know he really wants you."

She sighed and said she would hope so. "But until then...as long as I'm needed..." and she burrowed close beside him, and after another while they went to sleep.

7

THOUGH it was still very early, next morning, when the rockaway carriage lumbered off the lot and the other wagons followed, some of the local children were already "playing circus" in the abandoned earthen ring and the flattened weeds of what had been the Florilegium's pitch. Hannibal and the elephant again trailed at the end of the train, and the Negro kept running back and forth across the street, to peel off as many as he could of the pasted-up circus posters to keep for future use.

Florian said to Edge, on the seat beside him, "You overslept again," delicately not alluding to the fact that Edge and Sarah had come from the far margins of the lot just in time to partake of Magpie Maggie Hag's breakfast of cornmeal mush, preserved peaches and counterfeit coffee. "So you probably don't know—and I'll tell you, before you throw another tantrum about our cruelty to dumb animals—that I had Captain Hotspur shoot the other jackass and skin it out for Maximus. It also prevents our having to drag the poor creature over the mountains to no purpose."

"It also means," said Edge, "when Obie and I part company with you folks, you'll have one heavy wagon with not even a single jackass to hitch to it."

"Oh, I wasn't angling for sympathy—or charity. We can employ Brutus if nothing else offers. As I've said, I don't like to put a valuable bull in road harness. But, as always, we'll have to work things out as we go along."

Florian was keeping to Lynchburg's less hilly riverside streets. The few adults abroad at that hour stared in surprise or waved familiarly as the train went past, and the many children abroad at that hour frisked and capered behind the elephant. They came to Seventh Street and the city's one rickety wooden bridge across the James. When they had crossed, and all the children turned back for home, Edge pointed for Florian to turn west along the River Road.

"If these were normal times," said Florian, as he turned the horse, "we'd be following a route sheet made up by our advance man, telling us two or three weeks ahead of time where to be on what date. He'd know the condition of the roads everywhere, and what kind of ground we'd find at every pitch—good, bad, tolerable. He'd know, in every factory town, exactly what day the workers get paid. In farm country, he'd know when the farmers are plowing or planting and couldn't take time off to see us. And he'd know when they get their harvest in, and how good a harvest, hence how much money the yokels would have in their pockets. He'd know any places ravaged by flood or drought, and he'd route us around them. He'd know every local law and license imposed, and he'd either comply with them or he'd do what we call patch. Useful word, patch. It covers every kind of means to cut red tape and dodge blue laws and save unnecessary expense or trouble. Our advance man would also know the route of every other circus and minstrel show and medicine show, so we wouldn't find ourselves going day-and-date against any rivalizing outfit." He sighed and repeated, "If these were normal times."

"Well, I'm sorry I can't do any of those things for you," said Edge. "I can only take you through the easiest pass in those Blue Ridge Mountains yonder. It's called Petit Gap, where the James flows through, and this road hugs the river level a good part of the way. It has to skirt aside and climb a little way up a mountainside here and there, but none of those places is a rugged haul. If we don't stop for any midday meal we ought to make the other side of the mountains, where the North River runs into the James, right about camping time."

The day was fair, with big whipped-cream clouds floating about in an azure sky, and the scenery was splendid. To the left of their way, the wide brown river slid majestically along, dividing now and again to accommodate a green island in midstream. All around were the mountains of the Blue Ridge, not craggy and forbidding peaks, but gentle wooded swells and hollows and soft rounded ridges, voluptuous as women's breasts and bellies and buttocks. Any mountain near the road was all vivid green spring foliage and colorful wild flowers. But when the vista opened out so a mountain was visible at any distance, it was an all-over soft, misty blue.

"It's not the distance that makes them look so," Edge explained. "Of their millions of trees, maybe a third are pines, all breathing out a mist of resin. It hangs in the air and gives that pale blue tinge to everything."

The circus train made the fine day's journey with no trouble—except once, briefly, when Tim Trimm, again driving the museum wagon, got careless and let a hind wheel drop into a narrow roadside ditch. For all Tim's strenuous sawing back and forth, inching and pinching, and turning the Blue Ridge bluer with his profanity, the horse Bubbles could not hump the wheel out again. So Hannibal brought Peggy up. She had only to lean her great forehead against the wagon's back panel and give the merest nudge to put the wagon back on the road.

When the mountain hollows began to fill with twilight and a chilly mist began to rise from the river, Florian suggested to Edge that they could stop anywhere along here, since there was ample camping space and wood and water. But Edge said to keep on, and before long his reason was clear. For they came out of the Blue Ridge into a verdant and hospitable valley, where the sun was just now setting beyond another mountain range far to the west, and the air was still warm and golden.

"The Valley of Virginia," said Edge, as the wagons wheeled into a riverside meadow. "To the south it's the valley of the Roanoke River, to the north the valley of the Shenandoah."

"It certainly is a pretty place," said Florian.

"Even the old-time Indians thought so. The Catawbas, the Onondegas, the Shawnees—they were all rival hunters, and usually at war with each other, but they made a treaty. They agreed that this valley was so almighty beautiful, so full of game and other good things, that they would all hunt here, but never fight here." He added somberly, "We white men didn't have such good sense."

"You have fought here?"

"Not on this precise spot. Down the valley, several times. All the way to Gettysburg in Pennsylvania, once. But long before that, I lived hereabout. This is Rockbridge County, and I was born just a few miles farther on from here."

"No, is that so? What's the name of your hometown?"

"It wasn't a town, just a place in the bottomlands, and it wasn't called anything but Hart's Bottom. The house is long gone, and my folks long dead. But I lived here in Rockbridge until I was seventeen or so. Worked in the Jordan iron furnaces and forges. You'll see them as we go along the North River yonder. That river used to have coal and ore bateaux forever going up and down it."

While the women gathered wood and lit a cooking fire, Roozeboom fed Maximus another chunk of jackass, then went about the wagons, examining all the horses' shoes, before the men unhitched them and turned them loose to graze and drink. Night had fallen by the time the troupers sat down to their own meal. But it was a balmy and starry night, and the meal was another good one: fried fish, corn cakes, turnips and beans, with pickled melon rind for the sweet. The imitation coffee was getting low, so Magpie Maggie Hag decided to save that for the next day's breakfast. She found in the meadow some of the minty plant that the local folk called Oswego tea, and brewed up a pot of that. After supper, the men all lit up pipes and passed around one of the jugs of corn whiskey. Florian came to where Edge and Yount were sitting, and said, with a sigh of well-being:

"Yes, sir, Zachary, you picked a fine valley to be born in."

Yount grunted. "You won't think it so fine when you get a ways north of here. The whole damn valley, from about Staunton clear to the state line, was a wasteland last time we seen it, and that was only last fall."

"Big battle up there?"

"Big and plenty of 'em. But worse—the Burning. When the Devil and his inspector-general decided to relocate Hell in the Shenandoah Valley."

Florian cocked his head and said, "Setting conundrums, are you? I know Ulysses Grant is called the Devil. But I didn't think he had ever set foot in western Virginia."

"He didn't," said Yount. "He sent Little Phil."

"Now, that's Sheridan, am I right?"

Edge said, "The Shenandoah Valley was our army's commissary, so to speak. Grain, timber, garden truck, herds of cattle and sheep and horses. Grant sent Phil Sheridan to wipe it all out. We've even seen a copy of his actual orders; it said something like, 'Leave that valley so bare that even crows flying over it will have to pack their own rations.' And Sheridan did. That's why he's not so fondly known around here as the Devil's inspector-general."

Yount added, "But he didn't just grab the herds and the eatables. He burned the pastures and the forests, farmhouses and barns and mills. Left the *civilians* without roof or food or a rag to wear—old folks, women and children—and with winter coming on. That wasn't a soldierly thing to do."

"So you lads were among those who went to stop Sheridan?"

"Went to try," said Edge. "Lee sent every man he could spare. But the Yanks outnumbered us two to one, and they came armed with the new Henry repeater rifles. Obie and I were with the Thirty-fifth Virginia Cavalry in those days."

"The Comanche Battalion, we called ourselves," said Yount. "Never been whipped, not in any engagement during the whole war. Until then."

"And how did that happen?" Florian asked.

Both men went stony-faced, and looked away into the night, and were silent for a while. But then Edge hoisted the jug, and apparently found in it some resolution or consolation or absolution or something. He said grimly:

"Sans peur et sans reproche, that was the Comanche Battalion. Until last October, at a little stream called Tom's Brook, down the valley, near Strasburg. We were riding as part of the Laurel Brigade, advancing in support of some infantry moving against Custer's division. Then we were caught by flanking fire. That was no novelty; it never stopped us before; so there's just no explanation for what happened. Our advance became a retreat—no, a rout—running for the rear. What's worse, the whole Laurel Brigade *kept on* running—three or four miles from the fight—*and there were no Yankees chasing.*"

"Hell," said Yount. "Velvet-Suit Custer and his Yanks were busy, grabbing onto all our artillery pieces and supply wagons and caissons that had been left unprotected."

"When the remnants of us finally got rounded up," said Edge, "our Colonel White called the roll. It didn't take him long. Company F had deserted entire, and the other five companies could muster, in total, about forty men and six officers. We'd started with a hundred and fifty men. In less than an hour, what had been one of the proudest cavalry outfits in the CSA had lost two-thirds of itself, and pissed all over its fine reputation, and demolished its morale beyond recovery. Those few Comanches who were left didn't want any more association with it. Colonel White did eventually put together a whole new Thirty-fifth out of replacements, but it was never again trusted to do anything worth mentioning. Meanwhile, we others got parceled out amongst other outfits. Obie and I were posted to Second Corps—over east, with the others of what were called Lee's Miserables, holding Petersburg against the siege."

"Ah, well. The fortunes of war," said Florian, to put a merciful end to their recollected misery. Then he said, "What goes on here?" and stood up, a little unsteadily, to ask, "Is something wrong with Maggie Hag?"

The gypsy had disappeared, and only Sarah and Clover Lee were cleaning up after the meal.

Sarah said, "Something's got her out of curl, yes. But I don't think she's taken ill. She all of a sudden mumbled that a bad thing was happening somewhere, and she would have to consult the spirits."

"Oh, Lord," said Florian. "Did she say *what* might be happening?"

"No, but I can vouch that she's consulting the spirits. You can almost smell them from here. She took one of your jugs into the wagon with her."

Florian flapped his hands helplessly. Since Edge and Yount still had possession of the other jug, he sat down with them again, and explained, "Mag has these spells every so often."

Yount asked, "She really got second sight? She ever see anything worth-while?"

"Hard to say. Sometimes she suggests that we take some different road than the one we're on. And we always humor her, so of course we never know what might have happened on the other road." Florian took a long swig of whiskey, and changed the subject. "Tell me, Zachary. How did a hillbilly—such as you claim to be—manage to get an education and learn languages and wind up a field-grade officer, instead of remaining just another hillbilly bump on a log?"

Edge thought about it for a while before saying, "Curiosity, mainly. I remember, when I was a boy, my papa used to sing me that song about 'The bear went over the mountain, to see what he could see...' It goes on for about twenty monotonous minutes, the bear climbing all the time, and finally it finishes, 'The bear got over the mountain, and all that he could see—'"

"'Was the other side of the mountain,'" said Florian. "Yes, I've heard it."

"Around here, folks take it for gospel. What's the point in going over the mountain, when there's nothing yonder but the other side of it? I didn't believe that. So it was mainly curiosity that took me away from here—and dissatisfaction, too. I wasn't eager to spend my whole life toiling in old John Jordan's ironworks. That's why, when the Mexican War came along, I went for a soldier. Cavalry, of course."

"That was when me and Zack met up," Yount said proudly. "On our way to Mexico."

"Well," Edge went on, "I didn't figure to toil my life away as a trooper, either. But I turned out to be good enough at it that our Colonel Chesnutt took notice of me. And, when that war ended, Jim Chesnutt very graciously drew up all the applications and recommendations to get me into VMI—as what they call a State cadet, meaning free tuition and board and uniforms and books and all."

"Me, I just plugged along as a trooper," said Yount.

"Being a State cadet puts you under an obligation," said Edge. "When you graduate, you have a choice: take a military commission as a second lieutenant or go off to some country school and teach for two years. So, when I got out in 'fifty-two, I put on the cavalry blue-and-yellow again and was sent out to the Kansas Territories."

"And there at Fort Leavenworth," said Obie, "me and him met up again."

"Peacetime garrison duty?" said Florian. "Now that I *would* call drudgery."

"Not in the Plains, not in the fifties, hell no!" said Yount. "That was when the Territories came to be called Bleeding Kansas. All the border wars, you know—Pro-Slavers ag'inst Free-Staters. And whenever the wars simmered down, we could count on some kind of Mormon outrage against decency or some Injuns raiding an emigrant train that we'd have to go and make 'em sorry for."

"One of my fellow lieutenants out there was a fellow named Elijah White," Edge went on. "After a time, he retired from the army and came to Virginia to be a gentleman farmer. But when the War for Southern Independence started, Lije began raising his own company of Rangers for the Confederacy. It was about that time that I resigned my USA commission, and Obie his enlistment, so we came and joined Lije White. When his horse company was formally mustered into the CSA as the Thirty-fifth Cavalry, I got the grade of captain, with Obie as my troop sergeant. You know the rest. That's my life story. All resulting from curiosity—and dissatisfaction. Oh, and a lot of luck, too."

Florian firmly shook his head. "Considering where you started from, you've come a good way, and I'd wager you'll keep on upward. But luck means the aces that life deals you. Everything that's come to you, Zachary, you went out and did it yourself, or earned it, or had the gumption to take it."

Edge said, with a straight face, "I wasn't being maidenly modest about the thundering success I've made of my life. Hell, anybody can step up and admire that for himself. How I've worked my way up from hillbilly obscurity to this pinnacle of being an unemployed soldier, on the brink of middle age, living on handouts along the road—and with all the rosy prospects of a Free Negro running for elective office in Mississippi." Then he dropped the sarcasm. "No, I was being honest about the luck. And grateful. One more war is over and done with, and I'm still alive. That's aces enough. Now, this jug is done, too, and I'm sleepy. Good night, gentlemen."

The next day's journey, alongside the North River, was an even easier one for the circus train, because the road rose and fell in only undemanding grades over the valley's undulations. Magpie Maggie Hag rode inside the tent wagon, in her bunk and still nursing her jug, evidently still unstrung by whatever had spooked her the night before. The idiot rode strumming his banjo, playing over and over the last two tunes he had heard, regaling the countryside alternately with the national anthems of Dixie and France. That was enough to give notice of the train's approach to the few riders and other wagons they met on the road, but Florian, up front as always, was careful to call out, "Hold your horses! Elephant coming!"

Once, when the road detoured a good distance from the river, as if deliberately to take every wayfarer through a glen floored with white and yellow crocuses and daffodils, walled and perfumed with lilacs, Edge idly mentioned to

Florian, "This is Hart's Bottom, and I was born over yonder." He indicated some crumbling stone foundations where once had been a house and maybe a barn or a stable. But he showed no inclination to stop and meditate on the scenes of his boyhood or commune with any lingering ghosts.

In midafternoon, the wagons crossed a log bridge over a smaller stream and then had to climb the one rather steep and very long hill on the day's route. From the top of it, they were looking out and down, across meadows and woods, at a tidy little town a couple of miles distant—neat brick business buildings, pillared or porticoed residences and some rectitudinously tall and sharp church steeples —all clustered rather close together, considering how much empty land lay about.

"We're on top of Water Trough Hill," said Edge. "It actually does have a spring and a trough down at the bottom, for the sake of the horses that make this pull. That's Lexington yonder, and those jagged black things you can see on the near edge of it used to be the walls and towers of the VMI buildings. Out the other side of town, past the cemetery, there's a fairground that's probably the best place to pitch the circus, if we're allowed."

They went on down the hill, let the horses and the elephant thankfully take on water at the trough, then continued along the road and came to a mill dam and a covered bridge of brand-new, yet-unpainted wood. It took them across the North River and past the ruins of the military academy. As if the circus had been expected, all the local children immediately congregated to troop and dance along with it, or to run ahead crying warning of the elephant to everybody with a horse. The adult residents also collected on both sides of Main Street to watch the train's entrance—and these people were not dressed in everyday overalls and calico. The men wore hats and suits and even cravats; the women were in hooped skirts and flowered scoop bonnets—mostly old-fashioned clothes, and showing their age, but clearly the townfolks' best dress. Florian reined Snowball to a halt and tipped his own hat to a gentleman so respectably stout and full-bearded—the beard even scented with bay rum—that he had to be one of the town fathers. Florian politely inquired about the availability of the fairground for a circus performance on the morrow.

"Tomorrow!?" exclaimed the respectable man, as scandalized as if Florian had asked permission to undress and expose himself. "No such thing would ever be allowed on any Sunday, sir!"

"Oh, I do beg your pardon," said Florian, flustered. "I had been keeping track of the date, but not the day. We would never dream of profaning the Sabbath."

"Not just the Sabbath, sir. Your calendar must be seriously out of kilter. To-morrow is Easter Sunday."

Edge said, "So it is. Palm Sunday was a week ago. Day of the surrender. We stacked arms on Monday. It seems longer ago than that."

The respectable man went on, "Truly there is ample reason for special jubila-tion and rejoicing tomorrow, as there has been today. But the celebration will be done devoutly and with dignity, not with theatrics. And in church, not in a circus tent."

"Er...special rejoicing?" Florian asked. "Has something occurred, sir, that outshines the Resurrection?"

"Where *have* you been, man? The joyful news must be resounding up and down every road throughout Virginia. The despot Abraham Lincoln is dead!"

"What!?" blurted Florian. "Why, he was younger than I am."

"He did not die, sir, of natural causes. The government at Washington tried to contain the news, but every telegraph wire has been humming the day long. The tyrant was shot last night and died this morning."

Florian rocked backward on the seat of the carriage. From inside it came the stunned gasp of the listening Coverley women. Edge breathed, appalled, "Good God."

"God *is* good, sir," said the respectable man. "He helpeth those who help themselves. And it was about time, too, if I may say so without seeming to criticize the Almighty. The dispatches report that the perfidious Secretary Seward also was attacked last night, but his wound has not yet proved fatal. Wherefore the churches have been full all day, of supplicants praying that Mr. Seward may speedily go to join his—"

Edge cut him short, demanding, "Do they know who did those outrages? Did they catch him?"

"Outrages, sir?" said the man, raising his bristly eyebrows. "If I mistake not, you wear Confederate gray."

"That's why I'm anxious to know, damn it! Was it a Southerner that shot Lincoln?"

The man said stiffly, "Profanity uttered in public is a breach of the peace. And on Easter Eve—"

"Was it a Southerner?"

"One sincerely hopes so!" the man barked back at him. "The reports have been only fragmentary, but that is the assumption, yes. It would be a sad reflection on Southern manhood, sir, should the champion prove to be only some disaffected Yankee blackguard."

"Why, you sanctimonious imbecile—!" Florian jabbed a sharp elbow into Edge's ribs, and in the same motion flicked his reins to start the horse moving again, saying over his shoulder to the affronted and angry gentleman:

"We thank you, sir, for imparting the news. I have no doubt that everyone in our train will be joining tomorrow's churchgoers in their thanksgivings." They had left the man behind by then, and Florian turned to Edge. "You said you wanted to settle here. That's a fine way to court a welcome. What's the matter with you?"

"Settle here? If that pietistic old vulture was telling the truth—if Lincoln really is dead—there won't be *any* Southern place worth settling in."

Florian said incredulously, "Surely you had no personal fondness for Father Abraham?"

"No. Are you as dense as that damned driveler we just talked to? If Lincoln is gone, there goes any hope of a soft peace. Especially if he was assassinated by a Southerner. That'll be the excuse for Stanton and Seward and all the other no-mercy men in Washington to trample and gouge the South, the way they've wanted to all along. And if that drunkard Johnson is President, he'll be just their pawn. Lincoln talked reconstruction. What we'll get now will be retaliation, revenge, reprisal."

"Well, don't despair until we have more news. Maybe *everybody* in the Washington government is dead."

"I'll ask around, see what I can get." Without waiting for Florian to pull up, Edge swung down from the rockaway seat. Inside the carriage, Sarah and Clover

Lee looked shocked and pale as they rode past him. He waited in the street until the tent wagon came along, Yount on its driver's seat. Edge walked briefly alongside to shout the news up to him, adding, "I'm going to look for any old acquaintances I might be able to find. Learn more, if I can. Join you later at the fairground."

That fairground and, next to it, the Presbyterian Cemetery, occupied most of the crown of a small hill. When the wagons turned onto it, everybody got down and looked back the way they had come, where most of Lexington lay spread out before them. On the town's farther side were the black and broken remains of the buildings, barracks, armory and magazine of the Virginia Military Institute. Closer in, some once-fine residences were also burned-out shells, and even some of the substantial brick business buildings had holes in their roofs or chunks torn from their walls.

"Done by General Hunter's cannonballs," said Yount. "He bombarded the town for a while before he marched in. Then he done the looting and burning— all of VMI, the homes of some prominent people, the science building and library of Washington College—which is what got him the name of Vandal."

"Still, with all the damage," said Sarah, "Lexington is a pretty place."

"Let us pray," said Jules Rouleau, with nonchalant irreverence, "that the handsome town treats us handsomely."

It was well after dark when Edge got back to the circus. He found the Big Top set up and faintly glowing with lantern light inside, where the men were putting up the seat stands. Florian emerged from there, saw Edge and hurried to meet him, jerking a thumb to indicate the pavilion.

"Partly just to give the boys something to do. Partly to advertise our presence in the town, since I don't want to plaster posters around at such a time as this. Come and eat, Zachary. Maggie is up and working again, and she's saved you some supper. Have you learned anything more?"

"Yes," Edge said glumly. They went to the fire, and all the rest of the troupe gathered to listen, solemn-faced. Magpie Maggie Hag gave Edge a plate of beans and corn bread, and he talked between forkfuls.

"I found a man I used to know: old Colonel Smith, who was superintendent of VMI. He still is—what there is of it to superintend. He's General Smith now, and I gather he gets to read all the telegraph reports of the scouts and spies that are still reporting. Lincoln is as dead as a wedge, that's certain, and it's a Maryland man to blame. But there seem to have been a number of others in it with him, all ex-Rebs or Rebel sympathizers."

"Just what you were afraid of," said Sarah.

"Yes. What it amounts to is that they've broken the word of honor of Robert E. Lee. A week ago, General Lee downed arms—no more killing. So did Grant —no more killing. And then, goddamn it, *one of us,* in the most cowardly way possible, shoots Abraham Lincoln in the back. I wish *I* could catch the son of a bitch. I guarantee you, he has made 'South' a dirty word—far dirtier than it ever was before. And I can also guarantee you, the whole South will suffer for that."

Florian said, "I take it your General Smith feels the same way you do. Not gleeful, like that lout we met on the street."

"Francis Smith has good sense. He even broke out a bottle of prime Monongahela rye—and he's no drinking man—so we could drink our condolences to the South. Thank God, not everybody in Virginia has the jackass mentality of a clodhopper or a counterjumper."

"Rooineks, ve call such asses back home," Roozeboom said helpfully.

Clover Lee said, "Will you still be settling here, then, Mr. Zachary?"

"No, miss," Edge said, with a sigh. "I kind of hinted to General Smith that I could be coaxed back to VMI, but he threw cold water on that." He looked around at the troupe. "You know what he told me? He said this state isn't even the Commonwealth of Virginia any more. From now on, officially, this is nothing but Federal Military District Number One, and it'll be under an appointed governor, and probably under martial law."

"Ça va chier dur!" exclaimed Rouleau. "We'd better get north in a hurry, then, before we're trapped. Be worse getting stuck here than in Wilmington."

Yount said, "But, Zack, none of that ought to interfere with schoolteaching— what you figgered on doing."

Edge gave a wry laugh. "The Institute may survive, but it'll be one hell of a long time before it can call itself a military school, or its students cadets—or teach them military subjects, or dress them in uniform again. No, General Smith and the other remnants of the faculty are going to have a hard enough time fending for themselves. They don't need any added handicaps, like me." He said sardonically to Florian, "And they won't be wanting your idiot savant, either."

"What *will* you do, Zachary?"

"Well, General Smith says a lot of ex-Rebel officers are going to Mexico, to fight for or against Maximilian, whichever side will hire them. But, hell, I've already served a hitch south of the border." He looked up from his plate of beans. "Europe sounds better all the time. If your offer still holds, Mr. Florian, you've got yourself a shootist."

"Well, now!" said Florian, with vast delight.

"And a strongman," said Yount. "And two good horses."

"Well, now!" Florian said again. "Welcome, gentlemen!"

"Welkom, meneers," said Roozeboom.

"Bienvenue, mes amis," said Rouleau.

"Bater, gazhe," said Magpie Maggie Hag. "You now first-of-May."

Yount said, "It's still just April, ma'am."

"First-of-May is circus language," Florian said jovially. "Meaning any new recruit or temporary performer. Because we can get plenty of would-be's in clement times, when the season is well along, but only real troupers hit the road while the weather is still chancy. You yourselves will soon be greeting other newcomers as 'first-of-Mayers.'"

"Well, you can consider me as green as any new recruit," said Edge. "I may be a veteran at shooting, but I've never done it theatrical style. You're going to have to show me what part you want me to play."

"Me, too," said Yount.

"Gladly, gladly," said Florian. "But start by getting the terminology correct. Only actors *play*. Circus artistes work. We'll commence lining out an act for each of you as soon as—"

But he was interrupted. Six or seven soberly dressed townsmen came onto the fairground just then, and expressed a desire to have a private conversation with the owner of the establishment. So Florian and they went off to one side of the Big Top and talked long and earnestly. Then there was a lot of handshaking all around, the gentlemen departed and Florian came back to the fire, looking pleased.

"Fortune continues to smile upon us. Or perhaps I should say Providence—even Heaven—since those gentlemen were all preachers. Inasmuch as our pavilion will not be in use tomorrow, they have requested the loan of it for an ecumenical tent meeting."

Most of the troupers made exclamations of surprise or inquiry, but Tim Trimm said sourly, "Something smells fishy. I bet I've been saved in every kind of church there is. And there ain't no such a church as Ecumenical."

"The word means all-embracing, Tim. Various different sects getting together for a special occasion. This occasion being, of course, the spectacular coincidence of Easter and the assassination. The pastors expect to have a big turnout tomorrow."

"There's churches all over this town," Trimm persisted. "Why do they need a circus top?"

Florian said patiently, "True, the established sects all have quite imposing edifices. But the men who came calling are the pastors of congregations not so well endowed. They meet in each other's front parlors or empty shops or whatever. Adventists, Dunkers, Evangelicals, Quimbyists, Premillenarians—I forget what all of them are. But they expect an attendance tomorrow that would strain any of their facilities. So they asked for our Big Top, to accommodate a day-long, maybe even night-long service, one congregation after another. Possibly overlapping, truly ecumenical."

"And you said *yes?*" Sarah asked incredulously. "A rock-ribbed unbeliever like you?"

"My rock ribs enclose a gut, Madame Solitaire, just like the gut of the most devout, which requires occasional nourishment. Those services will each conclude with an offertory. I asked a rental fee of half the take. They proposed one-quarter. We compromised on one-third."

"Don't count on a largesse that will bulge your rock ribs," said Rouleau. "Not if I know those fence-corner cults."

"They won't make us wealthy, no," said Florian. "But it beats having a Big Top full of nothing but air."

Yount said hopefully, "Well, whether it brings in much money or not, a nice religious service ought to lend the tent some holiness."

At that, all the troupers laughed, and Clover Lee said, "Mr. Obie, if that canvas gets any holier, it won't keep off the dew."

"No matter," said Magpie Maggie Hag, addressing Edge. "I told you already, gazho, la tienda es un tabernáculo. Soon you *abide* in tabernacle."

"Yes," said Florian. "Let us to bed now, and tomorrow—Zachary, Obie—we shall commence the making of you into artistes. *Artistes,* my lads!"

8

IN THE MORNING, the circus women made use of the pump and troughs provided by the fairground to wash every piece of costume and spare clothing the show owned, including a quantity that had been long laid away in the property wagon's trunks, so the new artistes Edge and Yount would have articles from which to assemble costumes of their own. Roozeboom strung a line, zig-zagged back and forth between the tent wagon and the prop wagon, where the wet clothes were hung to dry. They made a spectacle of variegated color and glitter in the April sunshine: spangled léotards, diaphanous skirts, flesh-tinted tights, garish tailcoats and frock coats, faded drawers and combinations and stockings and an assortment of underwear, including the little trusses called cache-sexe.

Then Sarah and Clover Lee dressed in what Sunday-best civilian clothes they owned—outdated bonnets and gowns so old they were stiffened with crinolines instead of hoops, but the Coverleys looked surpassingly pretty in them—and went off to Easter services at the massive stone Presbyterian church just across the cemetery beyond the fairground. Most of the men also donned clothes nattier than overalls and also went to church: Trimm to the Baptist, Roozeboom to the Methodist, Rouleau to the Episcopal—that being the closest thing to Roman Catholic in Lexington—and even Hannibal went seeking a black congregation of some denomination.

By that time, the first tent-meeting pastors had arrived at the fairground, bringing in a wagon a portable rostrum and lectern and even a small foot-bellows organ to place inside the Big Top. Shortly afterward, the worshippers began coming, on horseback, afoot, in a variety of vehicles. Long before the preachers had drawn straws to determine who would lead off, the Lexington fairground was much more crowded than the Lynchburg circus lot had been. Though the people were of various religious persuasions, they seemed to have come not only to hear their particular preachers, but to stay through the services of all the others.

Florian kept the museum wagon shuttered and the lion wagon and the ele-phant positioned out of sight on the far side of the pavilion, so they should not be savored by the nonpaying public, but he could not very well chain up the Wild Man all day. Anyway, the idiot wasn't wearing his smudges and tattered furs, so he was given his banjo and bidden only to stay out of people's way. That satisfied him just fine. He went and sat outside the tent on its far side. Every time the organ inside laid out a hymn, he had only to hear the first couple of bars and, about simultaneous with choir or congregation breaking into song, he would start to strum—in perfect tune and time—so he was an addition to the music, not a distraction.

While the townsfolk and folk from the countryside all around continued to come from Main Street across the fairground and into the tent, Florian, Edge, Yount and Magpie Maggie Hag sat together in the shade of the tent wagon.

"Maggie is our wardrobe mistress and chief seamstress," said Florian. "But before we talk about what dress we'll put you into, let's talk about what you're each going to do. You first, Zachary. Now, you have a sabre, a carbine and a pistol..."

"There's not a lot I can do with the sabre, all by myself."

"You can whip it out as you ride in during the opening spec, and wave and flash it about."

"All right. Then, the carbine, it's only single shot. So most of my act will have to rely on the pistol."

"I've never owned a six-shooter. I'd be obliged if you'd explain the workings of that thing."

Edge took it from his holster. "It loads just like that old buggy rifle of yours, except that you load these short chambers in the cylinder, so you don't have to shove powder and wad and shot down the whole length of a barrel. You start by pouring your powder charge into the opening of each chamber."

"Since I don't imagine you got instructions from its Yankee owner, how did you find out how much to pour?"

"When I first got the gun, I worked out the best load by firing over snow."

"Over snow?" Florian and Magpie Maggie Hag said together.

"Stood in a snowbank and kept firing, using a little more powder each time. When I saw unburned specks of black powder on the white snow, I knew I was overloading, so I cut back to the proper load."

"Ingenious," said Florian.

"But now, for performance shooting inside that tent, I figure to use only a light charge of powder. Just enough to give me reach and accuracy, but not enough that the ball will keep on going full range."

Yount said, "So as not to bring down somebody's cow off beyond the lot."

"Next," said Edge, "I put a lead ball here on the opening of the cylinder chamber. The ball is just a hair bigger than that hole, so now I unlatch this rod from under the barrel. It swings down and—you see?—it's a lever pushing this plunger set here in the frame. The plunger seats the ball well inside the chamber, just like a ramrod. When you've got charges and balls inside all six chambers, you pinch a percussion cap onto each of these six nipples around the back of the cylinder. Then cock the hammer and pull the trigger, and it shoots. Exactly like your rifle, only here each cocking of the hammer brings a new chamber around, and you've got six shots before you have to reload again. I always—after loading—I always let the hammer down easy, so it rests between two of the nipples. Prevents it going off until I want it to."

"A beautifully made piece of machinery," said Florian. "It's even an elegant thing to look at." He stood up. "Excuse me one moment. There really are so many people, and still coming, I'd better go and see how the seats are holding out."

Yount strolled with him, and they peered around the front door opening of the Big Top. The tiered planks were close to capacity, mainly occupied by old folks, hoopskirted women and girl children. Since there had been no ring built, the younger men and boys sat on the ground around the rostrum. The crowd had just finished singing, to organ and banjo accompaniment, "Shall We Gather at the River?" They were now settling back, spangled with roundels of sunlight from the holes in the canvas overhead, to hear the preacher say:

"Brothers and sisters, this has been a month of Sundays. Just two Sundays ago, we got the dreadful news that General Lee's lines in the east had broken, that our President and Cabinet and Congress were refugeeing from Richmond and abandoning our capital city to the enemy. A week later, only last Sunday, we got the even more terrible news that General Lee was surrendering his entire Army of Northern Virginia. The noble war against Northern tyranny was ending here in the Old Dominion, and our gallant Confederacy would soon be no more."

The people moaned and there were a few sobs. The preacher raised his voice, and his tone rose from somber to exultant.

"Those were the darkest Sundays in many a year, but today is a brighter one. For this day, this Easter Sunday, while we sing hosannah that the Christ Jesus has risen from the tomb, we can also praise the Lord because Satan's chief emissary on this earth—known while he was here as Ape Lincoln—has been gathered back to the brimstone pit he came from! Yea, brethren and sistern, the old Ape is in Hell now, pumping thunder at three cents a clap!"

The people chorused, "Amen!" with fervor.

Florian said, "Obie, do you really think that kind of blather is going to make our pavilion holier? I'll be satisfied if the deity doesn't send down a lightning bolt and tear it all to shreds."

They returned to the tent wagon, and Florian said, "Let us look over the garments the ladies washed and hung up. See if anything gives us any ideas on how you lads might best perform."

Magpie Maggie Hag pointed among the array of haberdashery and suggested, "Leather jerkin?"

"Hm, a leather jerkin," said Florian. "Zachary, how about you doing William Tell's Triumph Over Gessler the Tyrant?"

"And who's to be the boy with the apple on his head?" Edge asked. "Tiny Tim? The Wild Man? Which can you spare? Mr. Florian, even a crack shot is going to shoot a little low once in a while."

Magpie Maggie Hag pointed again and suggested, "Feathers?"

Florian said, "Yes, there's that feather cloak that Madame Solitaire hasn't used for a while. We could pluck some plumes, fashion a feather headdress. You wouldn't need anything else but a simple loincloth..."

"Jesus. If you're going to rig me out as a redskin, why don't I save on lead and powder? Throw some tomahawks."

"Ah! Splendid! Could you do that?"

"No."

Florian sighed. "Oh, well. I suppose it's best that we go back to my original conception. Colonel Deadeye? Colonel Ironsides? Colonel Ramrod? That's it! That's a good one. Will you settle for being Colonel Ramrod, Zachary?"

"In a uniform?"

"Well, not that one you're wearing. You'll need that for street clothes. But we acquired quite an assortment of uniform pieces in Lynchburg. Mag, you can put together something dashing, can't you, and dye it?"

Edge asked, "Purple, like Hotspur's? I'd almost rather wear Yankee blue."

"No, gazho," said Magpie Maggie Hag. "Indigo and berry all I had, then. Now I give what color you like. Yellow? Orange? Black?"

"Black and yellow," Florian answered for him. "That sounds dashing, indeed. And while you're at it, Mag, cut up one of those vest-and-drawers combinations for Obie here. Cut it like a caveman's fur piece—you know, one shoulder strap, rest of the chest bare—and use the same dyes. Color it yellow with black leopard spots."

"Hot damn!" said Yount, grinning and thumping his chest in what he supposed was a caveman manner. "Here comes the Quakemaker!"

"Now, about your props," Florian said. "Something hefty."

"I already got some," Yount said proudly. He reached inside the tent-wagon door and yanked. One after another, three immense iron cannonballs rolled out and thudded heavily on the ground.

"Bless my soul," said Florian.

"Shells for the Yankees' ten-inch Columbiad," said Yount. "The leavings of General Hunter, no doubt about it. They burned out without exploding, or maybe they was never charged. Forty-eight pounds apiece, which is hefty enough for even a strongman to play with. But if we plug up them loading-and-fuse holes, folks won't realize they're holler. They'll look like pure solid iron and a damn sight heavier than they really are."

"Where did you find them?"

"Right yonder in the graveyard. There was a heap of fourteen, piled up nice and neat. I figgered three would do me for—"

"Christ, Obie!" said Edge. "They were a monument over Stonewall Jackson's grave."

"Is that a fact?"

"He's buried right here. It's probably the most sanctified spot in Rockbridge County."

"Is that a fact? Well, if I was Stonewall, I'm damned if I'd want a pile of Vandal Hunter's cannonballs laying on my belly."

Florian said, "Just don't let any of the townfolk see them until performance time tomorrow. Then we'll be decamping before they can realize where the balls came from."

"How *do* I perform with them?" asked Yount. "Juggle 'em, like Hannibal? I'd fall down as dead as General Jackson."

"Captain Hotspur will have some ideas. He has doubled as a strongman in his time. And here he comes now."

Roozeboom, Rouleau and Trimm had returned together from their separate churches. Rouleau threw a disapproving look at the Big Top and said, "Merde alors, Florian. What are your pet preachers doing in there? You can damned near hear that one downtown."

They all listened. A minister of one of the less temperate sects was now bellowing, "The Beast of Revelation, that's what Abraham Lincoln was! It says rightchere in Revelation thirteen, '*And there was given unto him a mouth speaking great things and blasphemies.*' And didn't Lincoln blaspheme, brothers and sisters? Didn't he utter the abominable Emancipation Proclamation?"

Response: "Lay it out, brother!"

"Look again at chapter thirteen. '*And it was given unto him to make war with the saints.*' And didn't he make war against us? Against all our sainted beliefs and traditions and Southern virtues?"

Response: abysmal groans.

"'*And he had power to give life unto the image of the beast.*' What that refers to, brethren, was Lincoln lettin' loose the black savages from their rightful masters!"

"Kushto," murmured Magpie Maggie Hag.

"Rooineks," grunted Ignatz Roozeboom.

Edge asked, "Are the more orthodox churches ranting like these gospel-grinders?"

"They're not exactly grieving that Mr. Lincoln is dead," said Rouleau. "But the Episcopalians at least are lamenting the fact that he was *shot* dead."

"That reminds me," said Florian. "Zachary, I once saw a shootist who shot little glass globes all to splinters as his assistant threw them high in the air."

"He must have been a wizard marksman."

"Not really. The audience thought he was firing balls, but he had actually loaded his rifle with bird shot. If we can find something for an assistant to toss up, could you smash that with your carbine?"

"Using bird shot, even the Wild Man could do it. But I don't have any. Bird shot is not standard issue ammunition in the cavalry."

"No problem there. I've got some."

"But won't the audience wonder how it is that I'm not punching a new hole in the tent roof every time I fire the carbine?"

"Audiences don't cavil when they're overcome with admiration. Very well, that will be the carbine part of your act. Clover Lee can assist. Here are the Coverley ladies now. And I had another idea—remembering how you shot out that flame the other night. Clover Lee, my dear, would you stand still while Zachary shoots his pistol at you and you catch the ball in your teeth?"

"*What?*" Edge exclaimed.

"That old chestnut?" said the girl, without concern. "How about a variation? Let Ignatz catch it in his mustache."

"Captain Hotspur is not a pretty girl. No audience is going to tremble for fear he'll get a hole bored through his head."

"Now see here—" Edge protested.

"Calm down, Zachary," said Sarah. "We'll show you how it's gaffed. We won't let you kill anybody."

There came a sudden, loud and melodious singing of "Bringing in the Sheaves" from the Big Top. Florian motioned to Trimm and Rouleau. "You two get inside the pavilion where you can keep an estimating eye on the collection, every time they take one. In the meantime, Captain Hotspur, would you kindly give Obie the Quakemaker some pointers on the art of being a professional strongman?"

Roozeboom and Yount each picked up one of General Jackson's cannonballs. "Kerst Jesus, man," Roozeboom commented. "You nee start small, do you?" They took the iron balls off to the very farthest limit of the fairground, where they could practice unobserved by Stonewall's local votaries.

"Obie, you know vas is spier? How you say ... muss-kle?"

"Uh, sure. Muscles." Yount flexed his biceps.

"Ja. Now, de muss-kles of de body are of differences, and you must learn de different abilities, if you be strongman. Some are long muss-kles, some are short, some are broad. Long muss-kles, like in your arms, dey for t'row, for lift. Broad muss-kles, dey for heavy strain. You know vas is trapezius?"

"It's that swing, 'way up in the air, where the acrobats—"

"Nee, nee, nee! Trapezius is muss-kle—here." He slapped Yount's beefy back. "Broad muss-kle, trapezius, toughest in body. Under it is splenius muss-kle"—he slapped the back of Yount's neck—"also broad, tough. Now, to begin. You have pick up heavy t'ings before, ja?" Roozeboom bent at the knees and got his hands under one of the iron balls.

Yount nodded. "I know you got to get the power of your legs and back into it. You don't just lift it, or you rupture yourself."

"Ja, correct." Roozeboom straightened up, with the ball in his hands. "Now, ven you got it dis high, you can t'row it up." He did so, tossing the forty-eight-pound ball some distance in the air. Then he simply stood and let it thump to the ground again. "You don't catch in hands from so high, or you break somet'ing. You catch on neck."

"On the *neck*? Are you crazy?"

Roozeboom made no reply. He hefted the ball again, stood upright, threw it a yard or so into the air, bowed his shaven head and caught the thing with a meaty thud on the back of his neck. He jiggled his upper body just slightly to balance it there for a moment, then let it roll over his shoulder and caught it in his arms.

"Kee-rist," said Yount, in awe. "I druther bust a gut than break my neck."

"Takes practice. You build up pad of splenius muss-kle, it takes de blow, de trapezius muss-kle takes de weight. I show you. Bend head."

Yount did so. Roozeboom gently laid the cannonball in the declivity between Yount's occiput and nape. "Put hand, feel. Ball must land in curve between back of head en dis first knob of backbone. Never hit dat knob or you bad hurt."

"Jesus."

"Takes practice," said Roozeboom, lifting the ball off him.

"Just how do I do the practicing?"

"First time—many times—put ball on top of head, bend head, let ball roll, catch on neck. After while, toss ball little bit in air over head, bend and catch on neck. Toss little bit higher each time. Dat you can do by yourself, Meneer Kvakemaker. For now, show me how you begin. Pick up." He let the ball thud onto the ground again. Yount squatted properly, knees on either side of it, got his hands under it and stood up. "Nee, nee, nee. You do it too easy, Obie. Make believe it ten times heavier. Strain. Do some sweat."

"Damn it, Ignatz. I can't sweat on command."

"Sies, who knows dat? Carry rag. Wipe face, hands, shake head in doubt, despair. Looks real to rubes." Yount, feeling rather silly, pretended to be mopping away beads of desperation and determination. "Ja, gut. And you have big beard, looks gut on strongman. But I say also shave your head. De scalp sweats most of whole body. Shiny wet head makes look real strongman."

"There's more to this than I figgered on," said Yount.

"Anyt'ing gut, worth working for. Even look ugly for. Now—you put ball on back of neck, practice balance it dere. Klaar? Walk around like dat all time, make muss-kles strong. But not dis minute. I see rubes on lot. Never dey should see practice."

Over by the front door of the pavilion, some of the congregation had come trickling out, either for a respite from the humid heat in there or because the organ and banjo had swung into "Stand Up, Stand Up for Jesus," and the baskets were being sent around. The women, once outside, undid their bonnets and fanned themselves with them. Some of the men lit up pipes or cigars. The children began to scamper all over the fairground.

A woman called to two of them: "Vernon, Vernelle, y'all behave! Come away from them people's things. Come away from that-there clothesline." Then she gasped, "Oh, mercy me!" She scuttled about, collected a number of other women, and they huddled in converse together. Then they approached the group of circus folk, and the mother of Vernon and Vernelle said frostily to Florian, "Be you the proprietor of this establishment?"

"I have that honor, madame." He swept off his top hat and smiled. "The main guy, as we say in circus circles. May I do something for you, ladies?"

A very large woman said severely, "You may cease displaying your loose morals among respectable folks."

"Eh?" said Florian, bewildered.

"Look a-yonder, sir!" a sharp-nosed woman commanded. "That-there clothesline!"

"Ah, the laundry," said Florian, properly contrite. "I grant you, ladies, Sunday should be a day of rest. But I beg your tolerance of the exigencies of road travel. We must do the necessary when we can. Surely it is a small enough sacrilege that—"

"Bad enough to be hangin' out wash on the Lord's day," said the mother of Vernon and Vernelle. "But look what's hangin' right out in the open, where mixed comp'ny can see 'em. Inexpressibles!"

Florian looked even more bewildered, but Magpie Maggie Hag inquired, "You mean underwear?"

The women recoiled at the word, but the large one rallied to say, "Yes! It is scandalous and indecent!"

Florian said, without contrition this time, "Ladies, over the years I have managed to cure myself of most of the depressing virtues. Nevertheless, I do believe that morality should consist of more than mere pudicity."

The sharp-nosed woman said, "You won't cozen us by usin' bad language at us, mister. I bid you again, look at what is hangin' on that line. Men's and women's unmentionables *together!*"

Sarah said mischievously, "Oh, I doubt they'll mate, dearie. They're too wet and soggy. Would you, in that condition?"

All the women gasped, and the mother of Vernon and Vernelle said, "Advertisin' your loose morals is indecent enough in front of your own girl child there, but *my* children is pure and innocent. Ladies, let's go straight to the police!"

"Fiddle-dee-dee!" Clover Lee said suddenly. "What makes you old biddies think children are pure and innocent?"

And just as suddenly, though she was still garbed in a full-belled gown, Clover Lee tilted sideways and turned a slow cartwheel. It let her skirt upend over her torso and bare the length of her legs before she was upright again. The women reeled away, squawking "Lordamighty!" and "Disgraceful!" and "Worse than disgraceful! Didn't you *see?* She wasn't wearing *anything* underneath!" and they scurried back into the sanctuary of the tabernacle.

"Shame on you, Clover Lee," Sarah said, mock-sternly. "You offended the tender sensibilities of those good modest women."

"Mokedo," sneered Magpie Maggie Hag. "Good modest women built no different from any other kind. Except they more troublesome. And Clover Lee, you maybe agitate them make trouble for us."

"Let's hope not," said Florian. "Anyhow, go and take down that clothesline, Mag, or conceal its depravity some way." She went, as Tim Trimm and Jules Rouleau emerged from the Big Top. "Ah, here are the basket boys. Let's see how we're doing so far."

"It looks like a lot," said Rouleau, handing him a paper bag. "But it's all Confederate torche-cul."

Tim said, "You know nobody's goin' to toss anything worthwhile into a stump collection. The preachers didn't even bother to filch any before we got our share."

"Thousand dollars or so, it looks like," said Florian, rummaging through the limp and tattered bills. "Worth about ten. Not bad, with the day only half gone. And we'll make use of it somehow, lads." Then he looked up, past Rouleau and Trimm, and said with surprise, "Hello, what's this?"

Hannibal Tyree was just now coming back from whatever church he had found, and he was not returning alone. The elephant was supposed to be still tethered out behind the Big Top, but here came Peggy trailing the Negro across the fairground from Main Street. The bull's trunk was draped over Hannibal's shoulder, and he was holding tight to it with both hands. Another man, a white man, was holding one of Hannibal's arms just as tightly captive. The elephant managed to look perceptibly guilty, and both men looked angry. All three marched up to the group of circus folk and Hannibal said:

"Mas' Florian"—but he said it in no servile mumble—"hyar I goes off to services and trust y'all to keep watch on our most precious propitty, and what happens? Down de church, us has a happy shoutin' time, den de church empty out and I hears screechin' like de Debbil outside de door. I step out, see ev'ry brudder and sister scatterin' ev'ry whichaway, and dere stand ol' Peggy, waitin' for me. Now, I hopes to tell you, Mas' Florian, she could o' been shot on her way dere, or fell down a well, or—"

"Hush up, boy," said the white man. He was Sunday-dressed, but he wore a tin star on his suit lapel. To Florian he said, "That big critter frisked like a goat through half the backyards in Lexington, and plucked up every green sprout from the kitchen gardens, and turned over privies, and part of the monument to General Jackson has gone missing, and I'm here to inform you that you-all are responsible for the damages. I am a depitty sheriff of this county, and *my own privy* was one that got turned over!"

Florian apologized profusely, and Edge thought it remarkable that he commenced by apologizing to the black man.

"I am terribly sorry, Abdullah, and we all stand convicted as charged. It is no excuse that we had quite a lot of other matters to occupy our attention here. Please accept my apology on behalf of us all. Go and stake Brutus where she belongs, and give her a plug of tobacco to settle her nerves."

Until Hannibal led the elephant away, Florian let the white man stand fuming, then turned to him and said, "Shades of Mary and her little lamb, eh, Deputy? Well..." He squared his shoulders. "Can you tell me what the damages are likely to amount to?"

"No, sir, not yet I can't. Practically the whole town was in church during that animal's foray, and half the town is still inside that tent of your'n. I won't know the total extent until everybody gets home and starts raising the dickens."

"At least let us begin by paying for your own, er, outbuilding."

The officer dismissed that with a wave of his hand. "Never mind. No real damage to speak of. Except that Maw was inside it at the time. No, what I want to say is that the property damage is the least of your problems. I could swear out a criminal warrant for you-all letting a dangerous beast like that run loose."

Florian chuckled richly. "That mild-mannered old pachyderm? Why, a cow elephant is no more of a menace than a cow *cow*." The other troupers had been staying carefully impassive, but at that remark Florian got sharp sideways looks from Rouleau, Sarah and Clover Lee. "You observed yourself, Deputy, that the animal is a vegetarian. Clumsy and awkward, yes. But vicious? Tut tut."

"Well..." said the deputy. "Well, there's still the matter of its committing a public nuisance. After eating up them gardens, the critter—if you'll excuse the vulgarity, ladies—the critter emptied its bowels all over them gardens."

"What? Great Scott!" blurted Florian. He whirled to Edge and Rouleau and Trimm. "Get shovels, men!"

The deputy blinked. "Is *that* stuff dangerous?"

"Dangerous, sir? Elephant dung is the most potent fertilizer in all Creation. Lexington would be a jungle of vegetable produce. Cucumbers climbing in your windows, corn on cobs you'd need two hands to lift, watermelons blocking the road traffic. However, we will scoop it up, it being rightfully our property. Whatever we are fined for the damage done here, we can sell that rich manure to any plant nursery along our way, for forty or fifty times what we have to pay your citizenry."

"It's that valuable, eh? Well, then, wait a minute, sir. Consider. You'll have to send your men all over town to find the sh—the stuff, and shovel it up, and fetch it back. Then you'll be detained while all the folks' damages are assessed, and then you'll have to pay. How about we settle for an even swap? Leave the elephant droppings, and I'll explain to the people, and them that don't want to use it themselves can sell it to Gilliam's greenhouse, and we'll call everything square."

"We-ell..." said Florian. "It's noble of you to save us work and time and penalties. I think we'd do better by peddling the manure, but"—Florian took the man's hand and pumped it—"I'll accede to the agreement. And here, sir, tickets for tomorrow's performance. For you and Mrs. Deputy, if she has recovered from her, er, discomposure by then... for any little deputies..."

The man went away happy, and Florian took out his sleeve handkerchief to pat his brow. The other troupers were looking at him with mixed expressions.

"I've known you to tell some Christly lies before, Florian," said Trimm. "But making Peggy out to be a cuddlesome pet lamb would have strained Ananias."

"If some rube had poked her with a pitchfork," said Rouleau, "or some brat had thrown a stone—ça me donne la chiasse!—you know damned well she'd have done a headstand on him. We'd have needed a shovel for sure."

"Of course I know it!" snapped Florian. "And I am sincerely thankful that no such thing happened. But I refuse to fret over every *what if?* until I have to. Now, Monsieur Roulette, Tiny Tim, get back in the tent there on basket patrol. Colonel Ramrod, go get the Quakemaker, and you two report to Maggie for costume fitting. Madame, mam'selle, get out of those fancy clothes and start preparing some peck. I'll go and try to make peace with Abdullah. This may be the Sabbath day of rest and tranquillity—*hah!*—but tomorrow we have a show to put on!"

Either there were not too many rubes fearful of indecency, or else the deputy sheriff had spread the word that the circus was passably decent, because the people of Lexington and vicinity came again to the fairground next day to attend the performance. There was not the crowd that had flocked to the religious services, but at least enough to fill the seats.

"Most have paid in Secesh paper, of course," Florian said to Edge. "But some seem to realize that we fleshly mortals require more tangible remuneration than the spiritual clergy. So a fair number have paid in silver, and the rest brought good edible or usable barter. I even had one boy offer me a fistful of Brutus's droppings."

Edge laughed. "You turn him away?"

"Hell, no. I told him a mere pinch of the stuff was worth a ticket, and let him keep the rest. A good lie is always worth the effort of sustaining it."

Magpie Maggie Hag was still dealing out tickets from the red wagon, and today Monsieur Roulette was being the talker to the crowd at the museum wagon. Inside the pavilion, Tim's cornet and Abdullah's drum had been joined in their musical medley by the Wild Man's banjo.

"Among the goods we've taken in," said Florian, "are some more cheap dishes. So Clover Lee can toss one in the air for you, and you can use your carbine to shatter it. Have you worked out the rest of your turn yet?"

"I've got my pistol sighted. I spent the morning practicing with the lighter loads, shooting dead persimmons off a tree at the back of the lot yonder. I reckon you heard me."

"Yes. And I saw Obie going around hunched under a cannonball. I'm pleased that you two are taking your apprenticeship seriously."

"Well, I can't fetch a persimmon tree into the tent. So I just sketched out a target." Edge showed it: on the back of a circus poster, with a bit of bullet lead, he had traced concentric circles. "If you'll lend me that pencil you carry, I'll black in the rings and bull's eye."

"No, no," said Florian. "You are a straightforward sort of man, Zachary, but sincerity does not make for showmanship. No, no, a paper target won't do."

"I've got to shoot at something."

"For today, at least, we will sacrifice some more dishes. Tell you what you do. Load the carbine with bird shot for knocking one dish out of the air. Load your pistol with five balls, and only powder in the remaining chamber. Clover Lee will set five saucers on the edge of the ring curb. Shoot them to pieces, as dramatically as you can. That'll convince the audience that you're shooting genuine balls. Then I'll talk you up some more, then you'll fire the uncharged chamber at Clover Lee. She'll know what to do then."

"All right. You're the boss. Or no—the main guy, you said."

"You're learning. The name comes from those guy ropes that hold the Big Top together." He gestured to the ropes that ran from the ground stakes up to the tent roof eaves. "By analogy, every performer and crewman is also a supporting guy, and the director of the whole works is the main guy."

Roozeboom and Yount approached them, Roozeboom carrying a wooden fruit crate and Yount one of his cannonballs. Because Magpie Maggie Hag had only begun on the new costumes, Yount had contrived one of his own. He was barefooted, bareheaded and mainly clad in his own long underwear, but around the waist he had draped some of the Wild Man's spare skins. From a distance, he looked like a very pale and muscular giant, nude except for the dense hair of his kilted furs and his facial beard. As he came close, Edge realized how *very* nude he appeared, and exclaimed:

"Obie, what have you done? Just *look* how you look!"

"Shaved my head," Yount said airily, "so it'll sweat. Hey, Mr. Florian, Ignatz and me had this idea for what he calls the capper of the act. What do you think of it? He'll prop Jules's ladder against the center pole, climb up it and drop a cannonball on this-here crate. The crate'll go all to smash. Then I'll kneel down in its place, and Ignatz'll drop the ball on me. How's that sound?"

"Admirable, Obie!" Florian turned to Edge and said, "Now see? That's showmanship. All right, everybody, get ready. I'll soon be giving the musicians the signal to play 'Wait for the Wagon' and that will signal Monsieur Roulette to turn the tip."

"Turn the what?"

"He'll cease the free show. He'll stop bragging on the museum and the lion, and turn the gawkers—the crowd, the tip—into the tent. As soon as they're all seated, it'll be time for our come-in and spec. Zachary, hadn't you better be loading your weapons?"

"I will, as soon as Madame Hag has sold tickets to those last few comers yonder. I need to borrow a little cornmeal from her."

"Whatever for?"

"I told you, I'll be using only a light load of powder in my pistol, so I want to top up each chamber with a little cornmeal before I ram in the ball."

"But don't you spray a cloud of yellow powder when you shoot?"

"No. It burns as it goes out the barrel behind the ball. And it burns out the powder residue from previous shots, so it helps keep the barrel clean. Every pistol shooter knows that little trick."

"Well, well. Live and learn."

Some ten minutes later, a tremendous blaring and booming of cornet and bass drum silenced the expectant rustle and murmur of the crowd in the Big Top. Then Florian's whistle blew a shriek.

This time the come-in commenced with Colonel Ramrod in solitary splendor. He rode headlong into the tent on his claybank Thunder and galloped several times alone around the ring, his sabre high. He still wore his old army boots, gray trousers and tunic with CSA brass buttons, but Magpie Maggie Hag had found for him somewhere a cocked hat, and stuck in it a huge plume that made him look as dandified as the notorious fops Stuart and Custer. But the crowd evidently did not see him so; it burst into appreciative applause. That, to Edge's surprise and gratification, made him feel less like a ridiculous posturer, more like a genuine performer, so he tried genuinely to perform. As he careered around the ring, he wielded his sabre in the thrust, the downstroke, the flank and cuff cuts, the banderole, the disengage—at least as well as he could without an opponent to fight or skewer—making his blade flash and flicker, and making the audience applaud ever more heartily. Some of the men in the crowd even gave the shrill, hair-bristling "Rebel yell."

The cornet blared again outside, and Colonel Ramrod hauled Thunder to a skidding stop at the back door. Then he let the horse go on again at a sedate, high-stepping walk, and held his sabre at the "charge" to lead the Grand Promenade of artistes, horses and elephant. He even joined in the song: "All hail, you ladies, gentlemen! Let nothing you dismay...!"

In the opening act, Tim Trimm again came laggardly to the ring, swaddled in his joey clothes, and was reprimanded by Florian: "You should get out of bed earlier, young fellow. It's the early bird that gets the worm, you know."

"Hah! Then the worm got up even earlier. I should imitate *him*?"

That and Trimm's other smart-aleck sallies drew the expected laughter. But then Florian said, "You claim you work so hard every day. I daresay you really enjoy your bed at night."

And Trimm retorted, "No, sir. The instant I get into it, I fall asleep. And the instant I wake up, I must get out of it." He leered and concluded, "So I get no *enjoyment* of my bed at all."

The audience laughed again, or most of it did. There came also some high-pitched cries of "Shame!" and "Nasty!" and "Such language!"

"Christ, it's the bunch of harpies from yesterday," said Madame Solitaire, watching from the sidelines.

Florian swung a slap at Trimm for that riposte, but instead of faking the slap sound Tim ran away, forcing Florian to chase him. Tim ran clumsily in his voluminous boots and trousers, and so fell flat on his face. Then he was up again, running *out* of the boots and trousers entirely, his bare little legs twinkling under his shirttails. The audience roared with laughter again—except for the mother of Vernon and Vernelle, and her companion females. They hissed, hooted and called, "Shame! For shame!" until the other people ceased laughing and sat uneasily quiet. One of the females stood up, turned slowly to sweep the stands with a stare like a scythe, and loudly declared, "Neighbors, it appears to me like you-all are enjoyin' yourselfs too much to be good Christians!" The rest of the people looked meek, as if the female had spoken true.

For once, Tim Trimm's poisonous disposition came in useful. He stopped short in his toddling run and angrily pointed at the women, who were still crying "Shame!" through cupped hands. He jumped up and down and screeched loudly, "This show ain't goin' on until *them drunken men in women's clothes* are made to behave!"

The audience rocked again with laughter—so did all the troupers—and many another finger was derisively pointed at the women. The females turned white with indignation, then red with embarrassment. Then they tried to sidle crabwise off their plank without standing up. But that brought catcalls from the crowd—"Them drunks is sneakin' out for a snort!"—so the women literally jumped from the stands and fled out of the tent.

Tiny Tim resumed his clown act, to laughter and applause considerably in excess of what he was accustomed to hear. And when he finally came out of the ring, he got an equally unusual acclamation and backslapping from his fellow artistes.

The remainder of the program's first half was as well received here as it had been in Lynchburg. The good folk of Lexington were as naïvely taken in by the Pete Jenkins act of the aged "birthday lady," and were as delighted when she turned out to be Madame Solitaire, and were as thoroughly horrified by the "vicious" Maximus's biting of ass's blood out of Captain Hotspur's arm. The ensuing intermission was something of a torment for Edge and Yount, because Florian had scheduled them both for the second half of the program. They several times remarked to each other that they hoped to hell something would occur to prolong the intermission indefinitely, and then several times remarked that they wished to hell it would hurry up and end, so they could the sooner have their début performances, success or failure, over and done with.

As before, the second half commenced with Clover Lee's being introduced as a near relation of Generals Fitz and Robert E., and her horse Bubbles's being introduced as an equally near relative of Traveller. When the act had concluded, and Clover Lee was still taking bows to the applause for herself and Bubbles, Florian came to the back door of the tent, where Yount in his underwear and skins was fidgeting, and said, "It's show time, Quakemaker. Any questions before I introduce you?"

"Yes," said Yount and, as if he had been addled by stage fright, he asked a question totally malapropos. "How come you always tell the folks to clap for them horses? They don't do no more than run around in a circle, and I've seen corralled Injun cayuses do that."

"You're right, Obie," said Florian, answering as seriously as Yount had inquired. "Our mounts could hardly compete with real show stock. But regard Bubbles, as he exits now. That horse is strutting as proudly as if he'd done an aerial ballet. Should I deny the animal a share of that admiration all artistes yearn for and revel in?"

"I reckon not. I don't begrudge him. I just wondered."

Florian murmured a quotation:

> Hath wingèd Pegasus more nobly trod
> Than Rocinante, stumbling up to God?

Yount asked, "Is that another poem you made up on the road?"

"No. I wish it were. Are you ready, then, Quakemaker?"

"Ready as I'll ever be."

Whether he had been nervous or apprehensive or downright terrified, the Quakemaker and the others participating in his act put on a very commendable show of showmanship. To a fanfare of cornet, drum and banjo, Florian gave him a flavorsome introduction as "the tremendous human being discovered by a scientific expedition exploring Patagonia, which name means in the Argentinian language 'The Land of Giants'..." This went on for some time. "And now, clad like Hercules in the skins of savage lions he slew with his bare hands...the world's strongest man, the *Quakemaker!*"

And Yount strode in through the back door with a tread almost as majestic as that of Brutus, who came right behind him, Abdullah on top pounding the drum. The elephant was hauling a rope net in which the three cannon balls dragged along the ground, clanking heavily—and Brutus took care to walk slowly, leaning forward, as if the weight were a load even for a behemoth. Ex-Sergeant Obie Yount followed all the advice Captain Hotspur had given, beginning by heaving and puffing audibly as he rolled the iron balls from the net to the ring center. He even improved on the advice, when he realized that taking his position directly in a sun shaft from one of the roof punctures would accentuate his newly shaven head.

After much rag-wiping of his hands and repeated, fractional, finicking adjustments of the way the three cannonballs lay around his feet, he struggled mightily—and took several minutes—to lift just one ball in both hands. While the audience ooh-ed and aah-ed, he put down the ball and did some more wiping—hands, bald head, black beard, even armpits—slowly lifted the same ball again, tucked it under one arm, stooped and with even fiercer effort lifted a second with the other hand. Eruption of applause. He swiveled that hand around to tuck the ball under that arm, so he was holding the two balls between elbows and waist on either side. That left his hands empty and, when he stooped again, just barely able to grasp the third ball with his fingertips. By the time he had struggled erect, two balls under arms, the third precariously held by the extended fingers of both hands, the Quakemaker no longer had to pretend to be sweating.

The capper went well, too. Captain Hotspur trotted in and climbed the short ladder propped against the center pole. The Quakemaker, again with many trifling little adjustments, positioned the fruit crate, then gruntingly heaved a cannonball up to perch upon the two ladder ends protruding on either side of the pole. Then Hotspur and the Quakemaker engaged in a dialogue of grunts and gestures, which occasioned some more adjustments of the crate's placement. Finally, at a signal, Abdullah rumbled his drum, from soft up to loud, the Quakemaker made a chopping gesture and Hotspur pushed the ball off the ladder. The old crate crashed all to flinders at the impact. The Quakemaker again muscled the cannonball up to Hotspur at the ladder top, and then went down on hands and knees where the crate had been. He was sweating now so profusely that the beads were visible as they dropped from his face to the ring ground he was staring at, bulgy-eyed.

After some more dialogue in grunts, and Abdullah's even more prolonged rumble from pianissimo to fortissimo, the drum gave one thunderous *boom!* and in the sudden silence Hotspur let the ball fall, so that its hitting the Quakemaker's neck sounded like a sledgehammer whacking a side of beef. The Quakemaker gave a mighty grunt, perhaps not mere showmanship, but his head stayed on, his neck stayed intact and the cannonball stayed steady there. After a suspenseful moment, keeping his head bent, he erected himself onto his knees, then slowly onto his feet, the iron ball staying put. He waited for the applause, which came prodigiously, then let the ball roll over his shoulder and down his extended arm. At the last instant, he flipped his hand so it was palm up, and the ball came to rest on it. He twirled the thing as if it weighed nothing, then dropped it so the audience could hear its convincingly heavy thud on the ground. Louder and longer applause, while Hotspur and Trimm rolled the balls back to the net for Brutus to drag out.

"You did it like a seasoned trouper!" Florian cried, and clapped Yount heartily on the shoulder, then ran to the ring to introduce the next artiste, Colonel Ramrod.

"I hope I do as well," Edge muttered uncertainly.

The seasoned trouper, so recently his troop sergeant, told him, "Just act like a real colonel out there, Colonel."

"Mr. Obie, you sure did sweat toward the close," said Clover Lee, and laughed. "I bet you were wishing you had left some hair on to cushion that cannonball."

"It wasn't that, miss," the Quakemaker said sincerely. "I just then realized that I'd get my neck broke for damn sure if somebody all of a sudden stood up in the crowd and yelled, 'Them is Stonewall's balls!'"

That remark so amused and relaxed Edge that, when Florian wound up his long introduction, he pranced into the ring almost as carefree as Clover Lee did.

"... Scourge of the Red Indians, hero of the Border Wars, officer of our own indomitable Confederate Cavalry... the world's premier sharpshooter, Colonel *Ram*-ROD!"

When Clover Lee gracefully assumed the V-pose, Colonel Ramrod did too, holding his brassbound carbine high in one hand, his plumed hat in the other. The audience clapped more than merely politely or expectantly, for they were applauding the gray he wore.

"As his first display of shootistic virtuosity, ladies and gentlemen..." said Florian, and went into another spate of superlatives. Clover Lee danced to where Ramrod's few props were stacked by the center pole, and the colonel, emulating the Quakemaker's painstakingness, frowned studiously and pretended to check over his weapon, from muzzle to percussion cap.

"...Only one shot, only one ball," bawled Florian, "so only one chance to hit the moving target, ladies and gentlemen. I will allow you five seconds to place any wagers you may care to make among yourselves." While Florian slowly counted aloud, Colonel Ramrod felt the fixity of the crowd's gaze as if he himself were the focus of a battalion of gun barrels. "Mam'selle... *throw!*"

She scaled the saucer edgewise, straight up in the air toward the tent's peak. Ramrod had been holding his carbine at port arms. He almost leisurely brought its butt to his shoulder, cocked the big hammer, pretended to sight as if he were really drawing a bead on the little pale object, but merely fired in its general direction, confident that some of the charge of bird shot would hit it. So loud was the blast of the carbine that the saucer seemed to dissolve silently into atoms up there.

Clover Lee skipped about, as delightedly as if she had bet on the shot and won. Tim Trimm came running to take the empty carbine, while the big cloud of blue smoke wisped away and the crowd applauded the man in gray. The colonel next unholstered his pistol, scowled at it and examined it: twirled the cylinder, counted the caps and so on. Florian reeled off some more rigmarole, while Clover Lee took the remaining five saucers to that arc of the ring backed by only the empty back door of the tent, and stuck each saucer's rim into the ring's earthen curb so it stood upright.

"Notice, ladies and gentlemen!" commanded Florian. "Five targets, and Colonel Ramrod has only six rounds with which to hit and shatter them." Et cetera, et cetera. Ramrod settled the pistol back in its holster on his right hip, its walnut grip facing forward, the holster's stiff leather flap unbuttoned and raised. He walked to the edge of the ring farthest from the target, then held both hands a little way out from his sides, a little below waist level, until Florian barked, "*Fire!*"

What followed happened so quickly that the pistol's *blam!* seemed to put the exclamation point to Florian's command, and the first saucer in the line disintegrated. Colonel Ramrod had flicked his left hand across his body to the holster, whipped out the revolver and thumb-cocked it as it came up level in front of his face. Then the left hand had dropped away, leaving the pistol apparently levitating there just long enough for his right hand to flash up, seize it, aim it and pull the trigger—all of that done so fast as to appear simultaneous with Florian's barked order. As the blue smoke billowed about, and the crowd applauded, and Clover Lee cavorted with pleasure, Colonel Ramrod spun the gun around his finger in its trigger guard, so it did a graceful twirl, and he plunked it down into the holster.

He could have blown to pieces the remaining four saucers as fast as he could cock the pistol's hammer—but "make everything look real difficult," the Quakemaker had advised. So the next saucer he shot from a kneeling position, the next with his left hand holding the revolver, the next shooting from the hip without appearing to take aim at all. And in between, he wiped his palms on his trousers, swiped the back of a hand across his forehead, knuckled his eyes, as if the strain and deliberation were almost too much for mortal endurance. When he blew the last saucer to pieces, Clover Lee and the audience responded as joyfully as if he had just shot the last Yankee in Virginia.

"Now!" cried Florian, when he could be heard. "Now that Colonel Ramrod has succeeded in the next to impossible, he will attempt the *truly* impossible. Mam'selle Clover Lee, do you have faith enough in the expertness of this gentleman officer to trust your life to his skill?"

The girl looked nervous and hesitant, but for only a moment. Then she looked noble and courageous, and gave a resolute nod.

"Gallant lass," said Florian, and turned to Ramrod. "Do you, Colonel, feel that your hand and eye are still steady enough to essay this hazardous feat? Are you willing to accept the risk of being the murderer of this lovely child?"

Colonel Ramrod looked staunch and masterful, and gave a resolute nod.

"Very well," said Florian. "On your head be it. Ladies and gentlemen, I must beg you now for absolute silence and stillness. For what Colonel Ramrod will now attempt is to *shoot directly into the face* of this brave child in such a way that she can *catch the ball in her teeth!*" Several people gasped. "Please! Absolute silence. Those who cannot bear to watch are requested to leave the pavilion this moment. Also any who are liable to swoons or epileptic seizures. Colonel Ramrod must not be discomposed by any sound or movement."

Colonel Ramrod could not suppress a smile at all that taradiddle, and a smile was not his most appealing expression. The people stared at him, some perhaps taking his look for one of melancholy at the prospect of doing harm to the girl, others perhaps believing he was expressing the true maleficent nature that had led him to scourge Red Indians. Clover Lee stood with her hands on hips, her back to the tent's back opening, head erect, with a farewell-cruel-world expression on her face.

Florian asked, "Are you ready, mam'selle?" She did not budge or even nod, only slid her eyes sideways to him. "Then commend your soul to God, my dear. Are you ready, Colonel?" Ramrod licked his lips, rubbed his trousers, readjusted his hat and nodded. "Very well, I shall say no more, and give no command to fire. From this moment, sir, you are on your own." And he stepped entirely out of the ring.

Colonel Ramrod spread his feet apart and assumed a solid, tense, braced posture. He really did aim most carefully—low, so that any sprinkle of still-hot cornmeal particles would patter harmlessly onto Clover Lee's léotard. After the longest and most suspenseful pause in the whole day's performance, he fired. Clover Lee rocked backward the tiniest bit, and her hands left her hips in an uncertain, steadying gesture, as the blue smoke briefly blurred her outline. Then she was seen to be smiling, showing her bright white teeth, slightly parted. The crowd released its pent breath in a whoosh. Clover Lee raised a hand to her mouth, plucked the bit of lead from between her teeth, held it up and danced around the ring, displaying it to the crowd that thundered in ovation. After a full circuit of the stands, she espied a wide-eyed, beaming, hard-clapping old man, and tossed him the ball.

"Examine it, sir!" called Florian, and the crowd began to quieten. "Pass it around so all may see. The ball shows clear evidence of its terrific impact upon the fragile teeth of the winsome lass."

As Colonel Ramrod walked backward from the ring, sweeping his plumed hat repeatedly from head to ground, he realized that Clover Lee had not swiped a clean ball from his possibles-bag of ammunition and implements. She must have picked one up from the ground behind the saucer targets: a ball that was plausibly misshapen for handing around among the rubes. He might be working now with tricksters, but they were *professional* tricksters, and good at it.

"You show promise of becoming a real artiste, Zachary, ami," said Monsieur Roulette, at the back door awaiting his own cue to enter. "That ugly grimace you made, just before the capper, that was masterly. Ambiguous. Intriguing."

Edge thought back, and said, "All I did was grin."

"I asked myself—even I—does he dread the risk of killing the girl? Or does he relish the idea, peut-être? Ambiguity is true artistry."

"All I did was grin," Edge said again, but his colleague was gone, flip-flopping heels over head into the tent as Florian cried: "... That swift, slippery, slithering, brisk and nimble limberjim... Monsieur *Rou*-LETTE!"

Edge and Yount had nothing more to do until they mounted Thunder and Lightning to ride in the closing spec and sing "Lorena" with the others. It was some time later, after the crowd had gone, while the troupers were waiting to eat supper, that Florian came to congratulate Colonel Ramrod on his maiden performance. Edge was sitting apart from the others, apparently rapt in deep study, and he murmured only an offhand thank-you for the compliments.

"What's the matter?" Florian asked. "Are the nervous conniptions just now catching up to you?"

"No. No, I'm all right. It didn't bother me at all. That's what bothers me."

"Eh?"

Edge took a deep breath. "I was just wondering if I'm really cut out for this sort of career. Practically all my life, I've been a soldier, dealing with hard realities."

"So will you here. The circus life is not too different from the military. Like an army, we're frequently on the move, concerned with the logistics of living off the land. Like soldiers, we adhere to discipline on duty, but we have liberty—even license—when we're off duty. The main difference between circus and soldiering is one I should think would appeal to you. We don't operate by manuals and rigid regulations, so we have infinite scope for improvisation and ingenuity. There are no two days alike with a circus. We expect the unexpected: surprises, obstacles, setbacks, the occasional stroke of good fortune. Dealing with such things will make a man fit for any eventuality. If and when you *should* go back to soldiering, I'd wager you'd be the better officer for the experience."

"The logistical part of a circus is reality enough, I grant you. But... the *showmanship* part? Forgive me, Mr. Florian, I don't mean to make it sound trifling, but..."

"We like to think of circus as an art, and I would hardly rank art as a trifle," said Florian, but not testily. "Indeed, ours is the oldest art there is—performing. Also the most ephemeral of arts, I have to admit that. We strike light across the air, yes. But, like light on air, we leave no mark, no trace, no history. Poets leave thoughts, artists leave visions—even warriors leave deeds. We do nothing but entertain, and we don't pretend we're doing anything more significant. We come into humdrum communities where pinched little people lead commonplace lives, and we bring them a bit of novelty, a touch of the exotic. For the space of a day perhaps, we give those people a look at gloss and gossamer, danger and daring, a laugh and a thrill they may never have had before. And then, like a dream or a fairy tale—or what the Scots call glamour—we are gone and forgotten."

"Well, there you are. A soldier may be just a pawn in a game, but the game itself is not a fairy tale."

"Warriors leave deeds, eh? You want to be remembered. We only want to be enjoyed."

"I don't mean that either. Hell, I doubt that General Stonewall yonder under the sod knows now whether he's remembered or not. I just mean that an officer, even the lowliest enlisted man, while he's alive, deals with solid, enduring things."

"With the eternal verities?" Florian said sardonically. "With immutable truths? Let me remind you, Zachary. A few years ago, wearing the Union uniform, you were fighting against the Mexicans. If you were still in Union blue, now that this war is over, what do you suppose your army would likely be doing next? Fighting *alongside* the Mexicans to drive the French out of the Americas."

"All right, not eternal verities," Edge said, a little uncomfortably. "But, *at any given moment,* a soldier knows where he stands. Who is enemy, who is ally, what is black and what is white. I'm trying to say that here—in the circus—one minute you think you know and the next you don't. Sure, you have realities, like worrying about getting enough to eat, money to go on with. But all of a sudden everything shifts, and you're dealing with sheer unreality. Like...take Sarah, for example. I know you know about her and me."

"No explanations necessary, Zachary, and no apologies. Long before you came on the scene, Madame Solitaire and I had arrived at an understanding and comfortable arrangement. A man of my age seeks not sole possession of a love, only tranquil enjoyment of it at intervals. An autumnal love gives a man the sober splendor and gentle warmth of a September sunset, but it does not buffet him with the springtime storms of resentment or jealousy."

"I wasn't apologizing. And I wasn't resenting your sharing her, either. What I wanted to say was—well, when she and I are Sarah and Zack, it's something real. When she turns into Madame Solitaire, it's—I don't know—she's fairy-tale gloss and gossamer." Edge paused, pondered and went on, "Maybe this comes closer to what I mean. This afternoon, I heard you recite that pretty little couplet about Pegasus and Rocinante. It sounded like something you sincerely believed." He waved toward the Big Top. "Nothing you ever say in yonder ever sounds sincere."

"Ah, well...showmanship," said Florian, and shrugged.

"It's not just you. It's the difference between Sarah Coverley and Madame Solitaire, Hannibal and Abdullah, Peggy and Brutus. One minute they're one thing, the next they're another. And now it'll be me, too. Zachary Edge and Colonel Ramrod. Right after I finished my turn in the ring, Jules Rouleau said he admired me for being ambiguous, when all I had done was—"

"Ah, well...Monsieur Roulette," said Florian, and shrugged again.

"It's everybody and everything. One minute it's practical business, like finding food and fodder. And sincere feelings, like yours about that couplet. And the next minute we're dealing in pure fantasticality. From real to unreal. Oughtn't even a *circus* to be one thing or the other?"

Florian meditated for some time, and finally pointed and said, "Look there."

Clover Lee had washed out her latest-used costume and was pinning it up to dry. The sun was just going down, and its level amber beams struck multicolored sparks and splinters of light from the léotard the girl was hanging there.

Florian said, "That garment is decorated with sewn-on sequins, brilliants, spangles, whatever you prefer to call them. Each of those is a thing—an entity—it exists—it is a tiny, thin flake of bright-tinted metal. In the circus ring, under sunbeam or limelight, it reflects a sharp flicker of color. And a circus audience, not being very close to the performer wearing it, sees only those coruscations of red and gold and green and blue. Now tell me, Zachary, which is more real. The flake of inert metal or the vibrant glint of color? Decide that, and you'll have answered your own questions. Furthermore, you'll be well on the way to becoming a philosopher of some eminence." Florian stood up, dusted the seat of his trousers and, before he went away, said again, "Which is more real? The spangle or the sparkle?"

9

MAYBE if the next morning had been the sort to remind a man that the realistic world is a jagged and granular place of harsh weathers, dreary duties, wan hopes and inevitable disillusionments, Edge would have waked still in his mood of perplexity, and he might have abandoned the circus then and there. But the day dawned so unrealistically spangled with light and beauty that the world seemed a pleasant place and brimful of promise. The sunrise turned the sky a rosy pink, fluffed with little clouds as white as innocence, and their shadows put dapples of emerald on the ordinary green fields, dapples of sapphire on the ordinary blue mountains. The balmy air might have been borrowed from May, and the new-leaved trees everywhere twinkled like tinsel. Even the cemetery next to the fairground looked festive, what with the tulips, hyacinths and jonquils the people had piled on the graves two days before. And Edge felt on his face that old familiar breeze that blows always from the far places and beckons: "come see what I have seen."

They were hitting the road early this morning. The next sizable town to the north was Staunton, some thirty miles away, and Florian wanted to make it in one day's run. So the Big Top had been torn down the night before, and the wagons packed with the heavier goods. Now most of the men were stowing the last few items and harnessing the horses, occasionally pausing to grab one of the hotcakes and rashers of fried fatback the women cooked and handed out in relays.

"Would you mind driving Lightning on the tent wagon, Zachary?" asked Florian. "Our Quakemaker is quaking a bit."

"A bit, hell," groaned Yount. "I do believe I *did* break my neck yesterday.

Damn my showing off!" With winces and grimaces and slow movements, he peeled his shirt partway down to show them his bruises.

Edge whistled and said, "Obie, you remember the sunsets on the Mexican desert? You won't have to perform any more. We can call you a panorama and charge people just to come and look."

"Not to worry, Obie," Florian said airily. "Our company physician will fix you up. Docteur-Médecin Roulette."

"What's good for a busted neck, Doc?" Yount asked him.

"Regardez," said Rouleau. My entire medicine chest—lint, liniment and laudanum. I will use the lint to dab on the liniment while you swig some of the laudanum."

"You can ride with me on the rockaway, Obie," said Florian. "It will give you the least jolting." Then, half an hour later, he said, "I *thought* it would. Sorry, Obie." The rockaway was truly rocking, also pitching and lurching and bouncing, over a grievously rutted and blistered and scabbed and chuck-holed road on which even the four-footed Snowball was having to watch his step. "What do they call this terrible road? And why is it so terrible?"

"This is the Valley Pike, from Lexington on north," said Yount, between grunts of discomfort. "Macadamized. At least it used to be. One of the few such high-class roads in all Virginia. Reckon we ought to be glad it's ruined. If it was still in good condition, we'd be stopping to pay at a tollhouse every few miles."

"Did the tollkeepers take the money and abscond? I thought the tolls were for road upkeep."

"It wasn't neglect that ruined this turnpike, Mr. Florian. It was the war. There's been one after another Rebel and Yankee army charging or retreating up and down it on wheels and hoofs for four years." He grunted at a bump. "That's one reason I was glad to be cavalry. We didn't have to stick to roads. We could go overland. Ride free and wide."

"Ah, yes. I gather that the cavalrymen have always been the knights-errant of every army."

"Well, I sure preferred ranging service to any other soldier's kind of life. It beat digging rifle pits and ditches with the webfoots, or dodging them big iron pumpkins the cannoneers slung at each other. All we ever asked in the cavalry was a fair fight in a fair field. That's why the *best* time to be in the cavalry was during the Mexican War. Wide open spaces to fight in, no civilians or settlements to get in the way of a charge. Best of all, you was far away from all the headquarters brass, the wagon-dog officers, the spit and polish."

Farther back in the train, riding with Edge on the seat of the tent wagon, Sarah was saying, "You mustn't get puffed up now, Zachary, just because that one audience applauded your act. It still needs a lot of practice and thought. You see, anybody can work up an *audience* trick in a couple of days, like you did. To work up a *performer's* trick may take a couple of years. Inventing and rehearsing and perfecting it."

"I won't ask what's the difference," said Edge. "I imagine you're going to tell me."

"It's the difference between the showy and the artistic. An ordinary audience will go wild over something that *looks* difficult or dangerous. But only other performers and a very few discerning spectators will appreciate a trick that *is* difficult but looks easy, because it's done with skill and grace and Jesus!" The wagon had given an exceptionally lively lurch. "Right now, we're practically doing a swaypole act."

There came a thumping from inside the wagon. Edge stopped the horse, and the wagon's back door opened. Magpie Maggie Hag emerged, explaining that she had been trying to work on the new costumes, but she couldn't do it in conditions that would scramble an egg. So she climbed up on the seat beside them, and Edge clucked Lightning into motion again.

He said to Sarah, "I gather that a real artiste would rather perform for the knowing few than for a whole crowd's hurrahs."

"Wouldn't you?" she asked. "Didn't you? In the cavalry? Wasn't it a better feeling to have the esteem of your fellow troopers than a lot of rube civilians who would clap for a silly garrison parade?"

"I reckon. But don't forget, a cavalryman *has* to be good at his trade or he'll soon be dead."

Sarah gave a ladylike sniff and said, "Shit. You want me to start naming risky circus acts and the performers who have died doing them?"

"Well, put it another way. The cavalry's work is *necessary*."

Magpie Maggie Hag said, "Listen, gazho, people need circuses much as they need soldiers. We been around at least as long. Jugglers and joeys, no different from Abdullah and Tiny Tim, they went along on the Crusades. Temple priests in old Egypt, they only voice throwers like Jules Rouleau, made the god statues talk. And circus people not always looked down on. Lots got up high in the world. There was daughter of animal trainer in old Rome, born and raised circus dancer. And her? She in history books as Empress Theodora."

"And in Philadelphia right now," said Sarah, "there's a freak singer called the Two-Headed Nightingale. Just a mulatto girl, she is—or they are—but I hear she pulls in six hundred dollars a week. United States dollars. I bet no cavalry *general* was ever paid that much."

"No," Edge admitted. He made no comment on the incongruity of the women's double-harnessing to their argument a Roman empress and a two-headed mulatto.

Sarah went on, "Well, maybe I'll never get as famous as a necessary soldier like Jeb Stuart or a legitimate stage artiste like Jenny Lind. But circus is what I *do,* so I try to do it as well as I can."

Edge nodded approvingly. "For the esteem of your colleagues, not just the ignorant civilians."

"Yes. Here in America, anyway. Florian says it's different in Europe. He says over there the commonest audience can tell the difference between real artistry and sheer toot."

Magpie Maggie Hag concurred. "American, European circus, they different as nigger minstrel show and theater ballet. One time in Spain I see limberjim *weep* when he finished his act, he brought it off so beautiful."

Edge asked, "Do you ladies reckon Mr. Florian really will get us to Europe?"

Sarah said, "He'll do it or bust a gut trying. And he may have to bust a gut. Last night, when he counted up our total take so far—counting in Mag's earnings and our share of the tent-meeting collections—we've got forty-some Federal dollars and about five thousand Confederate. If he can find some way to convert that—to fifty, say, in real dollars—it's still only about a hundred all together."

"And we're not likely to run into any more stump preachers that want to hire a tabernacle," said Edge.

Sarah went on, "He got out a map and decided that Baltimore is our best hope for getting a ship. And he calculated that there are ten or a dozen towns worth our making a stand in, between here and there. If they all pay about as well as Lynchburg did, and *if* he can cash in the Secesh paper we take, and *if* we can live along the way without having to lay out cash, and *if* we don't run up against any disaster that costs us money, we ought to hit Baltimore with a total of four, maybe five hundred dollars."

"I don't know much about ocean voyaging," said Edge. "But I'd think any shipping company would ask a lot more than that to ship all of us clear across the Atlantic."

"Not all of us," said Magpie Maggie Hag, "but more than all of us." Before Edge or Sarah could ask what she meant by that, she said, "Madame Solitaire, you no tell me any dream for long time now. You no have any dream needs dukkering?"

"Only the same old dream I always have," Sarah said cheerfully. "I take a fall from a horse, and there's a net that catches me so I don't get hurt, but somehow I can't get loose of the meshes."

"And I have told what it means. But still long time off."

Edge asked politely, "Does everybody relate dreams to you, Madame Hag? I don't mean the female rubes. I mean the people in the show."

"Everybody, yes. And you better learn to talk circus. Always say *on* the show, not in it."

Sarah asked her, "Has anybody else been having any dreams of any consequence?"

"Yes."

After a moment, Sarah said, "Well?"

"I no tell who. Or what the dreams. But from one I dukker a wheel somewhere turning. From another a trouble with a black woman."

Edge said, "We don't have any black women. On the show."

"And nobody works with any kind of wheel," Sarah said, reflecting. "Maggie, do you mean some of us are going to blow the stand? And is Hannibal going to marry some black wench? What?"

"No matter," said Magpie Maggie Hag. "We go to Europe, yes, and more of us than we are now."

Sarah persisted, "Then you mean someone new will be joining out?"

Deep within her cowl, the old gypsy nodded, but said no more.

Late that night, Edge said to Sarah, "Before you fall asleep, tell me, that dream you mentioned, do you have it every night?"

"No. Only now and then. I haven't had it any of the nights we've slept together, so I don't expect I will tonight. But when I do—and that's what is curious—it's always the same. I fall from a rosinback, but safe into a net."

They were again bedded apart from the other troupers, this time in a field outside Staunton. The wagon train had arrived after dark, and so they had made camp without yet erecting the Big Top.

Edge asked, "And how did Maggie interpret that dream?"

"Oh, a lot of hocus-pocus and horsus-shittus. The meshes of the net, me getting tangled in them—I'm going to fall into evil ways and then be abandoned. Something like that."

"You don't believe in such things, I hope."

Sarah shrugged in his embrace. "If and when it happens, I'll believe it. She was right about Abe Lincoln being dead."

"She never mentioned any such thing. She just went early to bed—maybe with a stomachache—and everybody took it for a portent after the fact."

"Well, I hope she's right about us getting to Europe. And it shouldn't be long before we know whether she's right about us having new people on the show." Her voice began to trail away as she drifted into sleep. "I wonder who or what we'll get first . . ."

"Abner Mullenax is the name," said a man, seizing and wringing Florian's hand. "That show of yours, gents, was just downright dandy!" It was the next afternoon, the circus had just finished its performance, and this man had emerged from the Big Top with the rest of the crowd. He wore farmer's homespun garb, but Edge estimated him to be not over forty, young enough to be in uniform—and probably he had been; he wore a black patch over one eye. "That show was so dandy that I'd like to show my gratitude, gents. I'm going to make you-all an offer of something special."

Florian only murmured noncommittally. He had been grumbling to Edge and Rouleau, before the man approached, about the sparse attendance of the Stauntonians and the poor quality of goods they had bartered for tickets. He was in no mood for further disappointment. But he looked surprised and a trifle less gloomy when Abner Mullenax went on to say:

"I got a great big colored circus tent you-all can have. Big as this one here and a whole lot purtier. And no, don't ask how much I'm asking for it. Just come and look at it and if you want it, it's yours for the taking. My wagon's yonder and my place is only three mile from here. If we hustle, we can get on the way before all these other folks clog the road. You could be back here with your new tent by nightfall. What say?"

The three circus men looked at each other, more than somewhat bewildered, but their looks agreed: why not? They went with Abner Mullenax to his ramshackle wagon and climbed aboard, Florian on the seat beside him, Edge and Rouleau sitting sprawled in the bed of it, Rouleau still wearing his gaudy ring dress. Mullenax briskly slapped the reins to prompt the plow mule, and they did get away while the rest of the circus audience still milled about. They drove a short distance along the Pike, then turned off onto a minor dirt road and, except for one digression—"There's a jug under the straw back there, gents. Help yourselves and hand it up here"—Mullenax was talking up his tent the whole way.

". . . Splendiferous thing and looks brand-spanking new. Been hoarding it all through the war. My wife and daughters wanted to cut it up, make themselves dresses and what not. Wouldn't let 'em. A thing like that, you don't want to use it up piecemeal. It belongs all together and, by God, I've kept it that way."

Florian finally got a word in. "Excuse me, Mr. Mullenax, but—"

"Call me Abner. Here, have a snort."

Florian took a sip of the corn whiskey and tried again. "Er, Abner, what circus were you with?"

"Me?" He laughed. "None yet, unless you count the Battle of First Man-assas." He took a healthy pull at the jug. "You mean where'd I get the tent? I found it. After I was invalided out of the army. I was early in, lost the eye I aim with—to a minnie ball at Manassas—and early out again. Come back to my farm and there was the tent in my crick hollow."

"You *found* a circus tent?"

Mullenax gave him a bloodshot look with his one eye. "You don't reckon I could *steal* a thing that size?"

"No, no, of course not. But it's almost as hard to believe that some outfit would set up its pavilion on your land and then go off and leave it."

"Wasn't set up. Just was laying there on the ground. Couldn't hardly believe it myself. Like it might of blowed from somewhere."

"Well!" breathed Florian, still nonplussed. "Blowdowns do happen. I've never seen one blow *away*, but it's conceivable. I just can't imagine the circus people not chasing and catching it."

Abner Mullenax alternately sucked at the jug and discoursed on his brief war service during the rest of the hour or so it took to reach his farm, a place about as ramshackle as his wagon. Only a halfheartedly barking hound dog greeted them there—none of the women Mullenax had mentioned—and a penful of pigs oinked and squealed with hungry vigor. The men got down from the wagon, Mullenax a little unsteadily, and he led them around behind the barn to a hay-stack, which he began tearing apart.

"Took good care of it, see? Out of the weather and out of sight. Even the two times the Yanks stopped by, they was satisfied to grab a pig or three I left out for 'em to find. Didn't go poking in here."

When he had scooped away enough of the hay, they could see that it con-cealed another farm wagon, ordinary enough, except that its bed was full of folded fabric and tangled rope. Edge and Rouleau moved in to help Mullenax fling away the hay, until they could make out that the cloth was part vermilion, part white, and had tremendous black cloth letters sewn on it. Curiously, the ropes were more slender than the usual circus ropes, and of finer fiber, and seemed to be a net of some sort. When the wagon was all uncovered, three of the big black letters were uppermost in a row. They spelled RAT.

"Ma foi!" Rouleau exclaimed in awe. "No wonder your women wanted to cut it up. This cloth is *silk*."

Florian gave him a sharp nudge to shut him up, but Edge was on the other side of the wagon, and couldn't be stopped from commenting, "Yep, pongee silk. Double thickness, besides. And these cords are linen." Then he laughed.

Mistaking the expression on Edge's face, Mullenax asked worriedly, "A silk tent ain't no good?"

"Oh, I'm sure we can make *some* trifling use—" Florian began, but he was overridden by Edge:

"Mr. Mullenax, this is not a circus tent."

"*What?!*" said the farmer, and hiccuped. "Why, the son of a bitch is twice as big as my whole house yonder."

Edge asked, "Did you find a sort of basket with it? A big wicker basket?"

"Uh huh," said Mullenax, regarding Edge the way rube women regarded Magpie Maggie Hag when she spoke oracles. "It's in there under the cloth. Big enough for a couple-three men to take a bath in, if it was zinc. And there's some other things—wood, brass, india rubber. I figgered 'em to be circus trappings."

Edge turned to Florian, who was looking simultaneously puzzled and annoyed. "You want us to unfold some of it, Mr. Florian? Those letters will spell out *Saratoga.*"

"Never mind," Florian said, a little peevishly. "I gather you've seen it before. What is the thing?"

"I never saw this one, but I heard about it. It's a Yankee observation balloon."

"Well, I'll be switched!" blurted Mullenax.

"Four years ago," said Edge, "after First Manassas, when the Rebs damn near took Washington, the Yanks got real apprehensive about the safety of their city. They laid out elaborate defense works all around, including their Balloon Corps. All the balloons had names. They had this *Saratoga* at Centreville, and a man went up in it every day, to keep an eye out for any more Rebel buildups at Manassas Station. Then a November gale came along, and a balloon can't stay up in a wind. The Yanks cranked the *Saratoga* down far enough for the observer to jump out, but then the whole thing got away from them. The norther blew it away like an autumn leaf. Nobody ever knew what became of it."

"Well," said Mullenax, "I'm glad to know I got *something* out of Manassas. But here I've been tending it all this time like the goddam family jewels and *shit!* It ain't no use to you-all at all?"

"Mais oui!" cried Rouleau, his eyes sparkling. "A circus that can feature a balloon ascen—ouch!" He had got fiercely nudged again.

"It's not *worth* anything to us, Abner," Florian said quickly. "But I daresay we can find something to do with it. The main problem is transportation."

"Oh, hell," said Mullenax. "Leave it in the wagon where it is. I'll just go fetch the mule and hitch him to this one. Tote it right back to the circus grounds for you."

"That's very kind, but *we* don't have anything to put it in. Our other wagons are already jammed full to the doors."

"Goddam it, man, Abner Mullenax don't give a gift halfway. I'm giving you this-here wagon, too, and the mule to pull it. You only got to say you want 'em."

"All right, yes, we want them," said Florian, but with a bewilderment verging on suspicion. "We just don't want to take advantage. It is a handsome offer you make, sir, but I can't help wondering..." He refrained from suggesting the possible influence of the whiskey jug in this unprecedented transaction. "I mean— you're not asking *anything* in return? You're giving us a balloon, which is something you'll never likely have use for. But the mule and wagon? Surely they are necessities to a farmer."

"Only if I stay a farmer," said Mullenax, and now there was something sly in his bloodshot eye. "Can I show y'all something else?"

He led them to the ill-smelling pigsty, where a hog, a couple of sows and three piglets wallowed in the mud, making more noise than Maximus the lion ever had. "You-all ever seen a performing pig?"

"Well... yes."

"You're about to see some more." A short, crude, homemade ladder was leaning against the outside of the pen. Mullenax lifted it over the fence and leaned it against the inside. Instantly, one of the piglets slogged through the muck to the ladder, fastidiously shook its little trotters as clean as it could, scrambled up the rungs as nimbly as a cat, paused proudly, turned and twinkled down again.

Another piglet came and did the same, then the third. Mullenax removed the ladder before they could repeat the sequence.

"Why, that was pretty!" said Florian. "You trained them, Abner?"

"No. I won't lie and brag that I did. The thing is, you set a ladder in front of any pig—a pig that ain't got too heavy—and it'll climb the ladder, same as it'll climb a stile in any field. For some reason, they just *like* to."

"I never knew that."

"Not many people do. I never did, either, until I found it out by accident. I just happened to put the ladder in there one day, and saw what went on."

"Bless my soul," said Florian. There was a short silence, during which Mullenax's one eye regarded him imploringly. Florian said, "I take it, Abner, you want to sell us the performing pigs as a condition of giving us the—"

"No, sir! All I'm asking is that you take the pigs along with the balloon and the wagon and the mule. *And me.*"

The circus men all goggled at him. Finally Rouleau said, "You wish to run away with the circus, mon vieux?"

"That's right. I want you to hire me and these shoats as your—whatchama-callit—your pig act. You set the wages, or we'll work for just our keep."

"Hm-m-m..." Florian said. "Let's see. Pigs. Boars. Wild Tasmanian Boars. Eye patch—pirate—Captain Kidd. No, we've already got a captain..."

"Gents, I don't like to rush you," said Mullenax. "But I got reasons for hurrying."

"Done!" said Florian. "Barnacle Bill and His Wild Tasmanian Boars!"

"*Yee-ee-hoo-ee!*" Mullenax gave the piercing Rebel yell, startling everybody in the farmyard. Even the pigs went silent.

Florian said, "You mentioned a wife and daughters, Abner. Oughtn't you and we have a word with them? After all..."

"They ain't here. I took 'em to see your circus."

"You drove off and left them there?"

"They'll walk home when they get tired of looking for me. Or some neighbor'll give 'em a ride. That's why I'm in a hurry. There's another road we can take, going back, so we won't meet 'em."

Edge said, "You're simply going to disappear? No good-byes? Nothing?"

"You ain't met my wife and daughters, Cunnel. If you're lucky, you won't. If you're even luckier, you won't never have no such things of your own."

"But aren't they sure to chase after you?" Florian asked. "We're not leaving town straightaway. Today was such a poor stand, we're staying to give another performance tomorrow. We won't depart until the next day, and even then we won't exactly whiz off over the far horizon. A circus travels at a slow pace."

"This hive of females has been *wishing* me good-bye for as long as I can remember. If me and the animals stay out of sight tomorrow, and tag along when you pull out, the womenfolk ain't likely to follow. They'll figger it was worth the loss of a mule and some pork to be rid of me. Come on, you fellers, give me a hand."

With Mullenax at the reins and Florian, Rouleau and Edge each holding a trussed, squirming and squealing piglet, and all of them crowded together on the driver's seat, so as not to risk damaging the precious silk and linen cargo in the wagon's bed, they took a roundabout route back to the circus pitch, and they encountered no Mrs. Mullenax or Misses Mullenax on the way. During the ride,

Rouleau eagerly inquired of Edge what else he knew about balloons and the technicalities of ballooning.

"Not a hell of a lot," Edge confessed. "I've seen several of them hanging up in the air. The Yankee ones. The Confederates only tried balloons a few times, I think, and I only saw one of those being actually sent up. That was in Richmond. They squirted it full of gas at the Tredegar ironworks."

"Arrêtez. What kind of gas?"

"Damned if I know. But the Yankee Balloon Corps had horse-drawn machines to make it on the spot, wherever it was needed. I've seen them through a spyglass, but I couldn't tell you anything about them. Just a couple of big metal boxes painted light blue, mounted on ordinary escort wagons, and a lot of hoses running here and there."

"We must learn all these things," Rouleau said decisively. "We must become aéronautes. To own a balloon and not to send it aloft, that would be a shame. An atrocity. C'est tout dire. It must fly."

The next morning, Hannibal rode Peggy all over Staunton, pounding his drum and shouting invitingly, and Tim Trimm rode about town on Bubbles, pasting and tacking posters. Obie Yount spent the morning painfully but doggedly practicing with his cannonballs. He had persuaded himself that yesterday's poor crowd was his fault because he had been too sore to appear as the Quakemaker—and he was undissuaded when everybody in the company pointed out to him that Staunton could hardly have been expecting a Quakemaker. The rest of the troupe more enjoyably occupied the morning by unbundling the balloon from its long confinement and unfurling it across the field to admire it. Abner Mullenax stood to one side, looking proud, and breakfasting from a jug—he seemed to have an unlimited stock of them—while his new colleagues paced up and down beside the awesome length of limp fabric, ropes and wicker basket, making comments variously laudatory, calculating and yearning.

Sarah read the name lettered on it and said, "*Saratoga*. I did the nude 'Mazeppa' ride in the convention hall at Saratoga Springs one time. Blow this thing up and it would be twice as high as that hall."

Roozeboom said, "Ja, verdomde big bag."

Florian felt of the cloth and said, "It has some kind of an elastic varnish all over it. Makes it leakproof, I suppose."

Edge said, "My grasp of geometry has slipped some, but I figure we're looking at something like twelve hundred yards of doubleweight pongee silk."

"Mishto!" said Magpie Maggie Hag, licking her thin lips almost lustfully. "How *many* nevi dress I could make. Nevi for everybody on the show."

"Jamais de la vie!" Rouleau said severely. "This is not a linen closet, madame, this could be the making of our fortune."

"Not unless we can contrive some way to inflate it," said Edge.

The object of their regard was, even in its detumescent state, a formidable thing indeed. The cloth part, laid out flat, was fifty-five feet across at its widest—"Inflated, that will be a thirty-five-foot diameter," said Edge, working his geometry again—and it was more than twice that long, a pear-shaped affair of alternate vermilion and white gores, the seams between them meticulously lapped, gummed and reinforced. The narrow end of the pear tapered to a hollow tube that ended in a brass cock, with a bright blue cord and a bright red strap dangling beside it. The blue cord went clear up through the interior of the balloon, connecting to a large and elaborate valve contraption, made of mahogany, brass and india rubber, sewn into the very top of the balloon's bulbous upper body.

"The red strap seems to go all the way up inside, too," said Florian. "But I'm damned if I can tell what it does."

"I think I see," said Magpie Maggie Hag, to everyone's surprise. "One gore, at top, only lightly lapped and sewn."

"Ah, bien entendu!" said Rouleau. "When one has used the blue cord judiciously, to open the top valve to descend and land, one then pulls that red strap to rip that panel loose. It spills all the remaining gas to collapse the balloon, lest the basket be dragged around on the ground. Then it must be resewn before the next ascent."

The upper half of the *Saratoga*'s red-and-white body was enveloped by a lozenge-meshed net of linen cord, loose and lank now, but it would closely embrace the bag when that was inflated. The linen cords' lower ends were gathered beneath the balloon, where they were firmly affixed to a stout suspension hoop of wood about five feet in diameter. From that, on fewer but heavier ropes, depended the oblong wicker gondola, commodious enough for two persons but a snug fit for three. Edge drew the onlookers' attention to the fact that an iron sheet had been fitted in the bottom of the basket.

"Armor plating," he said. "So the observer wouldn't get shot in the—uh—between the legs—by riflemen on the ground. He wasn't in much danger, though, except when he was first going up or nearly down again. In the air, he was beyond rifle shot."

"The silk has survived its storage undamaged," Florian noted. "But I notice that some of the linen network has frayed and parted here and there. Since that is what holds up the aeronaut, it had damned well better be secure. Captain Hotspur, I'd be obliged if, in your spare time, you'd do what splicing is necessary. And Mag, stop looking so deprived. Somewhere we'll find you some other pretty cloth to work with. In the meantime, you've already got the dress to finish for Obie and Zachary. And we'll want a piratical outfit for our new artiste, Barnacle Bill."

So Magpie Maggie Hag, though grumpily, took Edge away from the balloon and Yount from his strongman practice, for a fitting of the costumes she had by now basted together, and also took Mullenax away from his liquid breakfast. Florian, Roozeboom and the Wild Man began refolding the *Saratoga* to bundle it back into its wagon. While Colonel Ramrod and the Quakemaker were trying on their new clothes, gingerly, so as not to burst the temporary seams, the old woman gave Barnacle Bill a close scrutiny and decreed that he already possessed the most necessary item of a pirate's equipment, the eye patch. She simply gave him a gaudy gypsy bandanna to tie around his head and a faded green-and-white striped jumper to replace his denim shirt, and declared him costumed. She also dismissed Edge and Yount, after she had done some tucking and pinning of their new garments, and Yount went grimly back to his cannonballs. Edge wandered idly into the Big Top, and saw in use a piece of circus apparatus he had not previously seen.

From halfway up the center pole stuck out, at an angle, a second and slimmer pole, like the boom arm from a derrick mast. It was fixed there by a loose iron circlet that enabled it to swing freely around the center pole. The boom reached about midway across the ring and had a hole in its outer end. From the top of the center pole, a rope angled down and through that hole; its far end was tied to a leather belt worn by Clover Lee, who was standing on Bubbles as the horse loped easily around the ring. Ignatz Roozeboom, standing in the ring, was guiding the horse and occasionally tapping it with the tassel of his long whip. With his other hand he clung tightly to the other end of the rope that came from the top of the center pole.

"Is called rope-fall, dis t'ing," he said, when Edge asked. "I hold dis rope, see, it goes over pulley up top de center pole, comes down to boom end, den to mam'selle's safety belt. If she fall off horse, I t'row my weight dis end, she no hit ground. Rope-fall is for practice new or hard trick."

"I'm trying to teach Bubbles to do a left and right hand," Clover Lee called to Edge. "You know, frisk a little to the left and right, while I'm jumping the garters and garlands. Add a touch of toot to the trick."

She demonstrated. Roozeboom, still holding tight to the rope-fall end, flicked his whip. The horse, not slowing his lope, did a cross-leg to the left while Clover Lee bounded into a somersault, landing lightly and safely on Bubble's .rump. Then Roozeboom flicked the whip again, the horse did a cross-leg to the right, but this time awkwardly balked while Clover Lee was in the air, so he was not in the right place when she came down. Her feet skidded off the horse's rump, Roozeboom leaned into the rope, and the girl dangled in the air, laughing, still going around and around the ring some six feet off the ground. Roozeboom eased off on the rope and lowered her gradually as she slowed, until her feet touched earth and she skipped gracefully to a halt.

"Damned old rosinback just doesn't like cherry pie," she said.

"I never knew a horse that did," said Edge. "But what's that got to do with anything?"

Clover Lee gave him a look of patient toleration. "In circus talk, cherry pie means extra work laid on. Because you're supposed to get *paid* extra, but you usually don't. Anyhow, you can't be truly circus if you're too lazy to work. You might as well blow the stand. That means pick up and leave."

Edge left the tent, cogitating. He was aware that Clover Lee had not been chiding *him* as a shirker, but he was also aware that the girl was going to great pains to perfect a nuance of her act that would not even be noticeable to most of the rubes who watched it, and that meanwhile the Quakemaker was in the circus's backyard getting in shape to return to work, while he himself, Colonel Ramrod, was loafing. So he began trying to think of ways to improve his own act. And just then a little black boy came along the road, carrying a basket of dried and colorful gourds.

"Buy a gourd, massa? Make y'self a dipper?"

Edge gave him two tickets to the afternoon show, probably an extravagant overpayment, and got the whole basketful. The gourds would shatter when shot, as impressively as did the saucers, but they were a lot showier and, being all of different sizes and shapes, they would look to the crowd as if they were harder to hit. Colonel Ramrod felt quite pleased with his notion.

He used the gourds in his act that afternoon. The crowd, though still no-where near the tent's capacity, was gratifyingly larger than that of the day before, and it was properly appreciative of Colonel Ramrod's shooting. Among the loud applauders, two small black boys clapped loudest, and one was heard to shout to the other, with profound pride and glee, "Them's *my gourds* he busted!" Flor_an of course did not put Barnacle Bill and his Tasmanian Wild Boars on the bill that day, lest they be recognized and reported to the abandoned Mullenax women. Abner watched the show from concealment under the stands and said it was all right with him, not performing on his first day in the company.

"I got plans for them pigs," he confided to Edge. "Now that I've got 'em away from the distractions of farm life, I'm gonna teach 'em a lot more tricks than just going up and down a ladder."

Edge was slightly amused that a neophyte, who had not even been in the ring yet, should already be eager to contrive an act new and astonishing to the world. But Edge was to discover that no circus performer, however old in years and experience, was ever satisfied that his act was beyond perfectibility—and also that a circus director was never satisfied that the sequence and variety of his program was beyond improvement.

Now that Florian had the Quakemaker and Colonel Ramrod on his bill—and Barnacle Bill waiting in the wings—he told Monsieur Roulette, that afternoon in Staunton, to omit his bit of wretched ventriloquy. The decision was greeted with no outcry. Everybody on the show, Roulette included, considered it a mercy to both him and the audiences. Not at all repining, Jules assiduously practiced, from then on, to embellish his acrobatic act with even more spectacular flights of contortion—what he called monkey jumps and lion's leaps and souplettes and "brandies." He also procured a small coal-oil lamp, and at ensuing performances made his entrance holding it alight in one hand while he turned flips and layouts and one-hand walkovers all around it.

"It impresses people," he told Yount, "to see the flame go on burning while I do that."

"Hell, it impresses me," said Yount.

"Pourquoi? If you think about it, ami, why should *not* the flame stay alight?"

"I reckon you're right. But it sure is showy." He added, "I'll have to think up some new tricks for myself, if the Quakemaker's not to be totally outshined."

North of Staunton, as Edge and Yount had said, the Shenandoah Valley was pitifully war-worn. What should have been farmhouses, barns, stables, silos, fences and even stands of timber were now only crumbled stone, charred wood and stumps. The sprinkling of livestock to be seen consisted mostly of old, crippled or windbroken horses left behind by one army or another. In many places where the Valley Pike was supposed to vault over a creek or river, the road simply stopped at its brink in midair, the bridge having been a victim of Sheridan's making the valley untravelable as well as untenable by other armies. Some of those gaps were easily forded, but at others enterprising country folk—usually Negroes—had rigged up block-and-tackle ferry rafts, and man-powered the circus across, one wagon at a time. The charges were modest, and the entrepreneurs accepted Confederate scrip, but they never had fixed a rate for ferrying an elephant. It didn't matter. Peggy preferred to swim at every opportunity, and did so with more aplomb than was shown by the gawking ferrymen.

The valley's towns and villages still stood, but not undamaged. Sheridan had made his march and his Burning in too much of a hurry to take time to destroy every community utterly. He had been content to demolish mainly mills, warehouses, armories, granaries and the like. So the larger towns had a gap-toothed look about them: streets missing a building here, a row of buildings there, or whole squares flattened into rubble-strewn empty lots. The buildings that were still erect were much pocked by rifle shot, many were holed by cannonballs and some had even been knocked askew on their foundations.

Where people had been burned out of their homes, they had made at least habitable domiciles from scavenged and mismatched planks or discarded army tents. Here and there in the distance, off Sheridan's route of march along the very middle of the valley—hence remote enough for the Yankees not to have bothered with them—could be seen the occasional sturdy homestead and even a few plantation houses of estimable grandeur that had escaped the Burning. Wherever there lived an ablebodied man, woman or child, the farm fields had been at least in part resown and were showing early green. Elsewhere the soft Virginia springtime was decently clothing the fallow fields, the pastures and meadows and mountain slopes, if only with wild grasses, shrubs and flowers. Throughout the valley, dogwood trees were in full blossom and they scattered their big white petals so prodigally that even the miserable road surface was carpeted like a triumphal parade route, and the wagon train's hoofs and wheels flung the petals fluttering in a continuous gentle, warm snowfall.

The valley was coming alive again, albeit slowly and painfully, and the valley's people could hope that it would revive more quickly as the younger men came trudging home from the war. So they seemed to take the arrival of Florian's Flourishing Florilegium as a welcome augury, but they had pathetically little with which to pay or barter for tickets. This led Florian to decree that, in each of these northerly-valley towns, the circus would stay for two days of performance, sometimes three, to enable all the country folk to make their way into town from the surrounding areas. Thus, although it meant two or three times as much work, the circus realized approximately as much from each town—some good silver, a lot of Confederate paper, some edibles, wearables and usables—as it had taken in with just one show in the comparatively unravaged Lynchburg.

By the time the circus showed in Harrisonburg, Magpie Maggie Hag had finished the new ring dress for Edge and Yount. The Quakemaker proudly put on and strutted around in his bogus leopard-skin caveman attire, even in his free time. Colonel Ramrod, however much he felt a dandy and a sham in his black-and-yellow uniform, at least no longer felt he was subjecting the Confederate gray to disgrace. The gypsy had even found enough woolen material to make a cape to go with the uniform. It was black outside, yellow inside, had a stiff collar that stood up around his head like a coal scuttle, and was of a length that reached the ground. The first time he wore it into the ring, he wore it only long enough to accept his entrance applause, then unhooked it and let Tiny Tim take it while he did his shooting.

"No, no, no!" Florian scolded him afterward.

"Hell, that thing's cumbersome," said Edge. "I can't have it hindering me."

"Take it off, yes," said Florian. "But don't just *take it off*. Do it with a grand flourish. Watch me."

He put on the cape and strode around the empty tent with a swagger that made the cape billow dramatically behind him, while he gave gracefully slow arm wavings and swooping bows and arms-up V-signs to an imaginary throng.

Then, still striding, he unhooked the cape at his neck and, with one hand, gave it a twirl that made the whole thing a fluttery, swirling, black-and-yellow wheel that he slowly and dramatically let subside to the ground.

"That's how," he said. "Do it when you put it on, too, to take your exit applause."

So Edge dutifully went off to practice swashing his cape. Nowadays, all the troupers were practicing *something*, either their established routines or new ones they were trying. The addition to the program of the three new men had put a fresh competitive spirit into the old troupers, and that made those three first-of-Mayers work even harder to become old troupers themselves. The fact that the circus stayed now at each pitch for two or three days, instead of tearing down every other night and hitting the road every other day, gave the company ample time in mornings and evenings to work on their acts and refurbish their costumes and props.

When Hannibal Tyree wasn't in the ring or on parade as Abdullah the Hindu, he was forever practicing his juggling and balancing tricks, and with ever more numerous, more various and more outlandish props. He could now do showers and cascades of such diverse shapes and weights as a horseshoe, a posy of flowers, an empty lard bucket, a hen's egg and—after a while of that—snatch off and add to the array one, then the other, of his own shabby shoes.

Hannibal and Tim Trimm together also spent time adding to the Wild Man's banjo repertoire. They sat him down and played through every tune they used in the program, from the "Dixie Land" overture to the closing walkaround's "Lorena." They also taught the Wild Man the piece they had chosen to accompany the Quakemaker's exhibition of brute strength, "If Your Foot Is Pretty, Show It"—and, of course, "Barnacle Bill the Sailor" to go with the newest act. Abner Mullenax had never heard the song and hadn't even known there was such a thing, but he was gravely shocked when he heard the musicians working on it, because Tiny Tim sang along with the music, and he sang the bawdy lyrics to the *original* song, "Bollocky Bill."

"Ain't them words awful dirty for a mixed audience?" Mullenax anxiously asked Florian. "Me and my pigs do a clean act."

"Only the music will be played while you perform, Abner. Nobody will sing the words."

"Well, if that's so... all right, then. I don't want my pigs pelted with no rotten eggs."

It was not likely. The audiences were charmed by his pigs, even when, during their early performances, they did nothing but scamper up and down the ladder. By the time the circus got to Woodstock, though, Mullenax had taught the smallest and cleverest of the pigs to do something that absolutely delighted the rubes. During just a couple of practice mornings, Mullenax borrowed Roozeboom's rope-fall, tied the piglet to the rope, set it outside the ring curb and, with Roozeboom's sjambok, prodded it to a trot. It could only run in a circle around the curb, and Mullenax could make it stop simply by dropping the whip tassel in front of it. However, at the same moment he did that, he clicked one thumbnail. After only a few circuits, the little pig had learned to stop at the sound of the click, with no need of the whip at all. By the second practice session, Mullenax was working the animal without even the rope-fall attached.

Beginning with the first show at Woodstock, the piglet—which Florian in-

sisted be named Hamlet, though Mullenax thought the name "undignified"—
was the star of the pig act and very nearly the prime attraction of the whole
show. Barnacle Bill would set the pig to trotting around the tent, then call out,
"Hamlet, pick the girl what likes to be kissed," and, in the resultant rush of
laughter, nobody would notice the faint thumbnail click that made the pig halt
before some pretty girl in the first row of benches and set her blushing and set
the whole crowd on a roar. Barnacle Bill would touch Hamlet with the whip to
start him trotting again, to "pick the girl what likes to be kissed *in the dark!*" and
so on. At many performances thereafter, it was hard for Florian to summon the
pirate and his piglet out of the ring, for the audiences seemed never to tire of
them.

After one show's extended series of encores and bows, when Mullenax finally
made his exit, he said to Florian, breathing whiskily, "Might be that I'm ready
now for bigger things. Do you reckon Captain Hotspur would give me lessons in
lion taming? Like he does Obie Yount in the strongman routine?"

"Presumptuous man," Florian said, but genially. "Learn lion taming? You
have intrinsic talent, I don't have to tell you that, but it takes a lot of other
qualities. What makes you think you could learn?"

"The fact that I think I could makes me think I could."

Florian gave him an approving look. "Good answer, that. I'll put in a word for
you, Abner, with Captain Hotspur."

But Roozeboom already had plenty of work to occupy him, now that the
competitive spirit had infused the whole troupe. When he was not practicing
with one or both of the Coverley women on new tricks to do in the various riding
acts, and when he was not trying mightily to invigorate Maximus out of his
customary torpor so *he* might learn a new trick or two, Roozeboom was still
generously helping the Quakemaker to achieve new feats of strength. On what
had been the extensive battlefields around New Market, Yount had found a Yankee "bull-pup" cannon—half submerged and caked into a now-dry mudhole, but
quite undamaged—and employed his Lightning to drag it free and haul it to the
circus lot. At first sight of it, Florian was disinclined to add such a ponderous
prop to the show's transportation problems, but Roozeboom joined Yount in regaling him with reasons why he should.

"Is nee so heavy as it looks, Baas," said Roozeboom.

"And it'll look *damn* heavy," said Yount, "when the rubes watch it roll right
over me. Ignatz says I can lay down in the ring with two planks across my chest
and legs, and—"

"Like I haff told Obie, in de chest en thighs are strongest bones. Also, Obie
have chest like verdomde oak barrel en thighs like oak stumps."

"I'll have Lightning pace up the planks and right across—"

"Good God, Obie," said Florian. "That Percheron must weigh three-quarters
of a ton."

"We already tried it. As long as Ignatz keeps him moving, I only feel the
whole weight for just a second, when the planks tilt for him to go down the other
side. But he'll be hauling this-here field piece, and it'll roll right over me, too.
Naturally, I'll groan and thrash a lot—make it look good. It'll even outdo the part
where the cannonball falls on my neck."

"Well..." said Florian, frowning. "But the damn gun is so big. We can't carry
it. We'll need another draft animal to haul it."

The iron cannon itself was only four and a half feet long, but it perched atop a formidable carriage of timbers and swivel screws and dangling chains, attached to the iron-bound beam that was its trail and recoil-spade—the whole flanked by two wheels that stood higher than the gun itself.

"Shucks, big Peggy kin drag it," Hannibal said confidently. "Lookahere, Mas' Florian. Lift de trail and de whole thing balance puffickly delicate on dem two wheels. Be no load a'tall for Peggy to pull. And jist think how fine it look on de road."

"Well, all right," said Florian, spreading his hands. "Brutus is your responsibility. As long as the bull can continue to do her crew work and ring work, I can't complain. We'll keep the cannon."

By now, so many other troupers were adding so many refinements to their acts that Edge was inspired to add another to his—a trick he had heard of other shootists doing. Among the barter handed in at the red wagon, he found a woman's small hand mirror, and he began to practice firing his revolver backward over his shoulder, aiming with the mirror. It would have been difficult if he hadn't gaffed the trick. He loaded four chambers of the Remington's cylinder with regular lead balls, the fifth with bird shot and the sixth, as before, only with powder tamped down with cornmeal.

In the ring, after he had used his carbine to shoot out of the air a gourd tossed up by Clover Lee, he used the revolver to shoot at the other five gourds perched on the ring curb, and disintegrated four of them with the regular balls, fired from different positions. Then, turning his back and using the looking glass to aim over his shoulder, he had only to aim approximately at the fifth gourd to demolish it with the spray of bird shot. Finally, as usual, he fired the sixth and uncharged chamber directly at Clover Lee so she could "catch the ball" in her teeth.

Florian was so taken with Edge's new flourish that he promoted Colonel Ramrod to the coveted "close" of the show—the last act on the program before the final walkaround spec. That demoted the former closing act, Captain Hotspur and Madame Solitaire, to next-to-close. But Sarah was proud of Edge, "her protégé," and Roozeboom was stolidly incapable of jealousy, so they accepted second-best stardom without protest.

"Tout éclatant!" Florian said delightedly to Rouleau, as they stood together watching the close of the final performance at Strasburg. "We've worked up a more than decent show. Now, if only we had more of a midway outside. Something to bring us extra money at intermission."

Rouleau laughed. "And if the yokels could *pay* the money. Merde alors, they're paying little enough for the main show."

"I'm thinking ahead, Jules. Up the road. Up north, where they *can* pay. In the cities where the people don't go to bed at sundown, and we can put on evening performances besides these matinées. And Europe, where we can really spread ourselves. Let the poor think us rich; let the rich think us risque-tout."

"Bien, a balloon ascension would be just the thing for the midway. If only I can find out how to do it. All along the road, I have been inquiring of everybody that looks like a soldier-come-home—asking if he ever served anywhere near the Balloon Corps. You can imagine the kind of looks I get. Mais, sous serment— somewhere, some way—I am going to learn how to get that aérostat into the high blue sky."

"Well, until you do, I think what we need at intermission is a proper side-show. The Wild Man and the museum aren't enough. We need the real freaks—a Human Skeleton, a Fat Lady, an Intersex, things like that. While you're asking around about balloons, ask if anybody knows of any creatures of that nature available."

However, shortly after teardown that night, the circus discovered that it no longer had *any* resident freak. Tim Trimm was the first to notice. They were all eating supper around the fire when Tim said, "Has the idjit finally got tired of his nigger-fiddle? He ain't serenading like usual."

They all looked at each other, then roundabout. Sarah said, "He was here just a few minutes ago. He got his supper, all right. Nobody could miss noticing when the Wild Man eats."

"Well, he sure ain't anywhere around now," said Yount, after the troupers had scattered through the darkness to the farthest reaches of the lot and then re-gathered at the fire.

Magpie Maggie Hag said darkly, "One gazha woman today, she ask me dukker her palm if she ever have baby. This woman got wild eyes, like loco, so I tell her yes for certain she have shavora. But I don't tell her I think she damned old for begin family."

Florian looked mildly astounded. "Mag, are you suggesting that some woman, desperate for a child, has abducted the Wild Man of the Woods?"

The gypsy only shrugged.

"Shit, she could of had me," said Tim, with a giggle. "Serve her right, when she finds out she's adopted a fizzlewit."

"Well, she must have got his banjo, too," said Clover Lee, coming into the firelight. "I've just looked in the prop wagon and everywhere else, and it's gone."

Hannibal said wonderingly, "You know what? I bet dat boy done run off fum de circus 'cause he thinks he *is* a circus. Me and Tim shouldn't of learned him all dat music."

"It could be true," said Florian. "Even those most defective in intellect can possess a deep and devious cunning. I had a wife like that once."

"No use searching for him in the dark," said Edge. "But Obie, we'll saddle up at first light and make a cast."

They did, and Roozeboom and Sarah came with them, riding Snowball and Bubbles, so they could quarter the compass. But none of them found the Wild Man. By noontime, they had all returned to the lot, and Florian said resignedly, "I hope that childless female did give him a home, and I hope she enjoys banjo music. Now we've got a twenty-mile run to Winchester, and a late start. If you fellows will get those horses into wagon harness, we'll roll. And Barnacle Bill, I'm afraid this makes you our Wild Man until we can get another."

"What?" said Mullenax.

"Old circus saying: the newest clown has to take the water. Be the butt of every jest, the target of everything thrown. In other words, the newest man gets the dirtiest jobs. Before each show, you'll do the roaring and chain-clanking for Maximus. Then, during intermissions...hm...I think we'll make you the Croc-odile Man."

"*What?*"

"Nothing intolerable about it. Abdullah used to double as a crocodile until we got the idiot. We have to work things out as we go along. You'll still do your

Barnacle Bill in the first half of the program. Then you strip down to a loincloth, we pour poster paste all over you, and you simply roll in the dust. As it dries, it crusts and cracks and scales most realistically."

"Judas Priest."

"Can't do it with your pirate eye patch on, of course," Florian briskly went on. "Lift that up for a moment, Abner, let me see the hole. Ah, ghastly, yes. Good. That will add to the frightfulness. Your Crocodile Man ought to make as favorable a hit as your pig act."

"Jesus Christ."

While most of the men were still occupied with hitching up the wagons, Sarah said to Magpie Maggie Hag, with some awe in her voice, "You did predict that not all of us would go to Europe. Now, sure enough, we've lost one."

"But got another," said the gypsy, indicating Mullenax, who was moodily kicking at the dust he would soon be wearing. "We still same number. More yet to lose, more yet to come."

I O

IT WAS a Friday night when they arrived in Winchester and found a place to set up, near the Negro Cemetery. So they showed on Saturday, to a fairly good crowd, then had a lazy layover day on Sunday before performing again on Monday. Most of the troupers had chores or practicing to occupy their off-time, but some of them ambled up Loudoun Street to have a look at Winchester.

A whole block of buildings near the courthouse had been razed, and the emptied square was now being used as an open-air market, full of farm wagons, barrows and makeshift stalls displaying handscrawled signs—Produce, Fish, Baked Goods, Notions and so on—but only the fish stalls had much to sell. Edge, Rouleau and Mullenax were strolling together and paid not much attention when they were passed by a small black girl in a slimsy calico frock, hurrying to the market with a basket nearly as big as she was. But they did notice when the same girl passed them again, coming away from the market with her basket heavier on her arm, because she was suddenly accosted by a sinister-looking white man. Or a man who was mostly white. The three circus troupers had stepped into the doorway of an empty shop, out of the breeze, to light up pipes, so it chanced that they witnessed the scene unobserved.

"Little girl, let me see," said the man, stopping her and peering into her basket. "Loaf of bread, two fish, some packets of miscellaneous. Right. Exactly what you were sent to fetch. Now, do you remember where you were to deliver these things?"

"Why, sho," said the child, puzzled and wary. "I'se to fetch 'em to my ol' Mistis Morgan. At our house, suh."

"Quite so." The man held up a finger and cocked his head. "Now let me be sure that you are the pickaninny I was sent to meet. That would be your Mistress Morgan of—what street?"

"Why, Weems Street, suh, right down yon—"

"Precisely so. However, Mrs. Morgan has decided she needs these things in a hurry, but she is going out—visiting Mrs. Swink—and will not be in Weems Street when you get there, so she sent me to fetch them to her at Mrs. Swink's house instead. Here is a penny. You go and buy yourself a sweet, and I will take the bask—"

He was abruptly surrounded by the three men. None of them was small and none looked pleased to meet him.

Rouleau said to the girl, "Keep your basket, petite négrillonne, and hurry on where you belong." She obediently ran off.

Edge disgustedly blew smoke in the man's face and said, "That was just about the most low-down trick I ever witnessed."

Mullenax said to him, "Mister, let's you and us step around in yonder alley, where we won't bloody up the street, and discuss your ornery behavior."

The man smiled bleakly, shrugged and said, "Yes, let us do that. As well die of a beating as of starvation. And I deserve it. That *was* the lowest-down trick Foursquare John Fitzfarris ever tried."

"Hungry ain't no excuse for stealing," growled Mullenax.

"Why, it's the very best I've ever had," said Fitzfarris. "You should have heard some of my other excuses."

Rouleau said, "If you had a penny to give the girl, péteur, you could have bought at least a bun to stave off starvation."

"Alas, any tradesman would have seen that the penny is as counterfeit as I am," said Fitzfarris. "It's a Mexican centavo bit that some crook once passed off on *me*. I should have known then that I was losing my touch. Let us adjourn to the alley and get this over with."

"Wait a minute," said Edge. "You were in Mexico?"

"Well, not exactly." He glanced at Edge's uniform. "I was at the border, at Fort Taylor, when you soldier boys came marching back from down there. To sell you some of Dr. Hallelujah Weatherby's Good Samaritan Tonic. So you could cure the gleets you'd picked up from the señoritas, before you went home to your sweethearts."

Rouleau couldn't help laughing, and Mullenax asked, without growling this time, "Did it? Cure the gleets?"

"I sincerely hope so. The stuff had failed me miserably as a hair restorer, pain killer, corn remover, alleviator of women's distresses—I forget what else." He turned again to Edge. "No, soldier, my striking appearance doesn't date from Mexico. I had the good sense to stay out of that war. I got involved in the more recent one, however, and it was a gun's misfire that made me as picturesque as you see me now."

Edge contemplated him for a moment, then said to the others, "Fellows, I reckon we can overlook an honorable veteran's brief slippage from grace, don't you? And maybe offer him a drink and a bite?" The other two nodded agreeably enough. "Yonder's a saloon, and I've got some of Florian's Secesh money, if the barkeep will accept it."

The taverner was willing, or afraid not to, when four such specimens bellied up to his bar. He didn't even try to foist on them scuppernong wine or pumpkin beer, the only beverages on view, but brought up from behind the bar a keg of genuine mountain mule. He also, when asked for food, went into a back room and returned with some boiled eggs and slices of gray bread spread with lard. While Fitzfarris wolfed the provender and sluiced it down with whiskey, he gave his new companions a quick sketch of his history.

"At various times, I've pushed stocks, bonds, gold shares, other sure-fire investments. I have solicited funds for nonexistent charities. I have dealt in an ointment warranted to turn black persons white. Or *some* new color, anyway. Failing all else, I have always been able to pour some fluid substance into empty bottles and paste on my Dr. Hallelujah labels. But I can't very well peddle a cure-all when I am displaying this too, too obvious affliction of my own. A confidence man, by definition, deals in *confidence,* and the surest way to arouse it in other people is to possess it yourself. But how the hell can I radiate confidence now?"

Rouleau murmured, "Hm-m," and thoughtfully sipped at his whiskey.

"Worse yet, a confidence man should have an anonymous, medium, bland physiognomy. I used to have. Ten minutes after I had sold some commodity to some client, he could not have picked me out of a crowd of his own relations. Now I'm as visible as a cannibal in a church choir. I couldn't even stoop to doing snatch-and-run. Horses would bolt at sight of me. Children would cry."

"Perhaps," Rouleau said tentatively, "you should consider some other line of endeavor."

"Well, there's always mail order," Fitzfarris said gloomily, "if the postal service ever gets dependable again. I could solicit custom with newspaper advertisements."

Edge asked, "How can you radiate confidence and all that in a newspaper advertisement?"

"Once," said Fitzfarris, "when I found myself at loose ends and low on capital, I came upon a street pitchman selling hair ribbons for two cents apiece. Nice ribbons they were, all colors, about an inch wide, couple feet long. I thought to myself: there ought to be a more profitable market for such things. So I approached him, did some haggling and bought out his entire stock at a cent and a half apiece." He paused for an egg and a gulp of whiskey.

Mullenax asked, "Then what? Sold 'em to young nigger wenches for some fancy price, I bet."

"No, sir. Sold them to young men—of what complexion I cannot say, since we dealt entirely through the mails—and sold them for a very fancy price."

"To *men?*"

"I ask you, friend Mullenax, what is the all-prevailing, all-pervading worry of all young men? It is the fear that they have made themselves unmanly, enfeebled, unfit for matrimony, through their childhood practice of—" He broke off to look about. There was no one in the saloon except themselves and the bartender, who was pretending uninterest. Nevertheless, Fitzfarris lowered his voice to a confidential whisper. "The vicious and abominable practice of self-pollution."

Mullenax hiccuped and said loudly, "What the hell is that?" Rouleau leaned over to murmur in his ear and Mullenax said, "Oh. That. Homemade sin."

"With my remaining cash," Fitzfarris resumed, "I had some printing done and also took out a couple of discreet newspaper advertisements. Invited all young men worried about the state of their virility to send in a sample of their urine, which Dr. Hallelujah Weatherby would analyze free of charge. Well, I was absolutely inundated with samples. Didn't make me very popular at the post office."

"Nor very wealthy, as far as I can see," said Edge. "What was the point?"

"To each respondent, Dr. Hal sent back a horrifying analysis—printed in advance, of course—saying, in effect, 'Yes, dear sir, your specimen shows un-

mistakably that you have indulged in the dread habit. You will shortly be suffering loss of hair, teeth, eyesight, fertility, potency and your mind.' Also included
was a certificate, which entitled the sufferer to send in seven dollars cash money,
bringing him by return post a guaranteed cure for his condition. Money back if
not satisfied."

"The ribbons?"

"One ribbon to a customer. Meanwhile, as fast as I was mailing them out, I
was investing some of the seven dollarses in still more advertisements. Had quite
a thriving trade going—made a satchelful of money—before I deemed it prudent to leave that dodge and that city."

"I do not understand," said Rouleau. "A potion maybe, like your Samaritan
Tonic, or a pill or something. But a *ribbon?*"

"Each customer got instructions with his ribbon. Every night, he was to cross
his hands at the wrist and tie them together with it. Clearly, it would be *impossible* for him to flog his—I mean abuse himself. Clearly, Dr. Weatherby's ingenious
invention would break him of the pernicious habit straightaway."

There was a long, waiting, anticipatory silence in the saloon. Finally it was
the bartender who could bear it no longer, and asked:

"Did it?"

"Cure anybody? I doubt it, landlord. Did *you* ever try to tie your own hands
together?"

"Well... but... then you must of got an awful lot of demands for the money
back."

"Oh, yes. Some of them in flavorful language. To every complainant I sent
another missive, directing him to read the fine print in the guarantee. His money
would be returned just as soon as he sent to Dr. Weatherby three signed affida-
vits—one from his minister, one from some member of his own family, one from
any principal businessman in his community—each affirming that the subject
in fact *was* a notorious self-abuser and that, despite the professional aid of Dr.
Weatherby, the wretch was *still* abusing himself. I never heard another word
from—"

He was drowned out by the noise of the bartender, going into strangling and
flailing convulsions of laughter. When the man had recovered, he sloshed whiskey liberally into all their glasses and into one of his own, and said:

"Here, boys, this round is on the house. I ain't had a laugh like that since
before the war, when a Tuckyhoe run off with the preacher's wife. Funny part
was, Preacher Dudley went chasing after 'em and *he* got struck by lightning.
Here's luck, Mr.—er—"

"Ex-corporal Foursquare John Fitzfarris."

"Tell me, Mister Foursquare, do you get anything else out of your occupation
besides fun and money and lifelong enemies? Is that how your face got half blue
and half normal? You look a lot like Preacher Dudley did when they fetched him
home."

"No, sir," Fitzfarris said sourly, but civilly enough. "A defective gun burst and
sprayed hot gunpowder over that whole half of my face. Black powder embedded
under the skin looks blue. Just as neat a job as if I'd had myself deliberately
tattooed, from nose to ear and hairline to collarbone."

"Heck," the barkeep said, "you can always go into circus work."

"As a matter of fact," said Rouleau, "we three *are* in circus work. I myself am a parterre acrobat. The colonel is a shootist. The pirate works wild boars."

"Well, I'll be damned," said both the bartender and Fitzfarris.

"Florian's Flourishing Florilegium, presently flourishing out near the Negro Cemetery. To you, Monsieur Fitzfarris, I am empowered to offer employment. Wait. Attendez." He held up a hand. "Before you strike me, hear me out. To be a Tattooed Man is at least preferable to a career of swindling small servant girls for your victuals."

"Christ Almighty," muttered Fitzfarris. "I am heartily glad that my old mother and all my mentors are dead. To think that I should come to this. Invited to be a freak in a sideshow."

"Disdain it not," said Rouleau. "A traveling circus offers a man ample opportunity—how shall I put it?—to exercise *all* his talents. And also, allow me to point out, it never stays in one place for very long."

"Well, now..." Fitzfarris said thoughtfully.

Florian, an hour later, contentedly smoothing his little beard, said to Fitzfarris, "If you dislike the appellation Tattooed Man, we can bill you as—um—the Bluejay Man?"

Fitzfarris said resignedly, "That's like debating whether to dignify your asshole as an anus or a rectum. Call me your Tattooed Man."

And so, between the halves of the Monday program, the Winchester folk on the midway outside the pavilion heard Florian announce "the most gallant explorer of our time! Ladies and gentlemen, meet Sir John Doe, the Tattooed Man. For reasons you will shortly appreciate, Sir John prefers not to reveal his true surname, for it would be recognizable as one of the noblest in the English peerage."

The people gaped at Fitzfarris, who stood blackly shrouded in Colonel Ramrod's ring cloak, both to conceal his shabby civilian clothes and to make his particolored countenance even more striking. He stood trying to look as Englishly noble as was possible with a face half face-colored and half blue.

"While daring to explore remotest Persia," Florian boomed, "Sir John also dared to fall in love with one of Shah Nasir's own court favorites, the beautiful Princess Shalimar, and actually insinuated himself into the innermost harem chambers of the Shah's palace to woo that princess. Unhappily, Sir John was surprised and captured by the harem eunuchs, and the tender affair ended tragically."

Florian dabbed his handkerchief at his eyes. Fitzfarris looked stoic.

"The irate Shah exiled the lovely princess to a distant mountaintop, where she languishes to this day. And Sir John was punished as you see. The cruel Shah Nasir had his powerful black eunuchs hold this brave man helpless, while they scorched one half of his face with the blue flames of the terrible Bengal Fire. Now Sir John wanders the world as the Tattooed Man, unwilling to return to his own people—unable ever to return to his adored princess—bearing the ineradicable mark of love turned to tragedy."

Florian dabbed at his eyes again, and several women in the crowd were sniffling.

"Sir John is the only Western man ever to get inside a Persian harem and come out alive. And he is prepared to tell about it. If any of you gentlemen care to spend a paltry ten cents—or ten dollars Confederate—Sir John will relate to you all the scandalous secrets of the harem, of the maidens taken by force, of the mutilated eunuchs, of the concupiscent concubines. Of course, you ladies and young folks will wish to hear no such things, so, if you will accompany me, we will move on to the Crocodile Man, a fearsome creature discovered on the banks of the Amazon..."

Evidently none of the male patrons had ten cents or dollars to spare, or had no curiosity about harem secrets. They went with Florian and the women, to look at Abner Mullenax groveling on the ground.

When the circus train left Winchester the next morning, Fitzfarris rode beside Rouleau on the seat of the property wagon. He said, "You know, I always thought, by God, I possessed a fine line of patter. But that Florian is a nonpareil of cast-iron nerve and ossified gall and petrified impropriety."

Rouleau laughed. "Eh, bien, I still remember, when *I* was a first-of-May, long ago, Florian told me that we must never let ourselves be bound by propriety, precedent, convention or morality; those things are recipes for banality. I think, Fitz, you and Florian are going to get along like brothers born."

Florian, on the rockaway at the head of the train, with Edge again riding beside him, said, "That fellow Fitzfarris. Which side was he soldiering on when he got that curious disfigurement?"

"Didn't think to inquire," said Edge. "I doubt I'd believe him if he told me. Anyway, I figure such trifles don't matter any more." He pointed. "Yonder's where we turn onto the Charles Town road, if you still want the shortest way to Baltimore."

Florian steered Snowball onto the road forking eastward off the Pike. It was a firm dirt road, a much better surface than the ruined macadam they had been traveling on. But just making the turn seemed to put a finally unendurable strain on one of the wagons, because there came a splintery crash and then a spate of cussing. Florian drew Snowball to a halt and looked back. On the balloon-carrying wagon, a rear wheel had collapsed. The wagon sat tilted, stern down, its upraised shafts almost lifting the draft mule off his feet, and Mullenax was sprawled on the road, shaking a fist.

"God damn it to hell, all I do these days is roll around in the dust!" The other men gathered to look at the damage.

Roozeboom said, "Too long das vagon vas drying out under your haycock, Abner. De spokes all loosed. I should haff giff dose vheels a good soak in some creek on de vay. My fault."

"Well, the wheel ain't broke," said Tim. "Just fell apart. You can fix it, Dutchman."

"Ag, ja. Efery vheel on dis train I haff fixed sometime. But it means first I fix, den find creek or pond, soak it all night."

"At least it's the one wagon we can get along without," said Florian. "The rest of the train can travel while you work on it."

A new voice suddenly spoke up. "Are any of you people Yankees?"

They turned to see a man regarding them from across a rail fence. The fence was all entwined with honeysuckle in flower, and smelled delicious. The man was gray-haired and gaunt, but well favored and even well dressed for the time and place. Behind him stretched a rising slope of ground that had once been an expanse of lawn, now gone to weed and seed and rank growth. At the distant top of the slope was visible a manorial house fronted by two-story columns and surrounded by ancient oaks.

"No, sir," Florian said. "Some of us are émigré Europeans, but the rest all staunch Southerners. Right here is Colonel Edge, late of the Confederate Cavalry. Sergeant Yount, likewise, and Corporal Fitzfarris..."

"I am Paxton Furfew, erstwhile adjutant of the Frederick County Home Guard, now living in retiracy," said the man, in the soft accents of the well-born Virginian. "Forgive me for having blurted a qualifier even before the invitation, but would you-all care to rest here at Oakhaven while your wagon is being repaired? Mrs. Furfew and I simply will not abide Yankees, but we're grateful for the company of more decent sorts. Perhaps the ladies in your party would like to spend a night in a real bedroom. And we set a fairly commendable table here, such as it can be in the circumstances."

"Why, that is surpassingly gracious of you, sir," said Florian. "I think, as director of this enterprise, I can say that all of us accept your invitation with alacrity and with heartfelt thanks."

"It is we who should thank you, sir. We have never entertained a circus or an elephant before. If you'll simply continue on, you will find the entry to the drive. Leave the broken wagon where it is. Some of our darkies can take down this section of fence and drag the wagon up to our outbuildings. Your cartwright will find there a smithy with a forge and all the tools he'll require."

In some wonderment and considerable admiration, the troupers went along the road bordering the property, turned in through a stone-pillared and wrought-iron arch, in which was worked the name "Oakhaven," and followed a gently winding drive between walls of untended and overgrown shrubbery that had once been banks of flowers. The house, when they finally got there, proved to be even bigger than it had looked from the road, but in sad disrepair: the paint all peeling, windows broken and patched with pasteboard, the stucco sheathing of the wooden columns so crumbled that they resembled Roman ruins. Mr. and Mrs. Furfew awaited them on the veranda, and she was as pudgy as he was lean. Though she was equally well turned out—clad in a voluminous hoop skirt and a profusion of furbelows—and though she had the same magnolia voice, her speech was as rustic slovenly as his was precise.

"Ain't none of y'all Yankees, you claim," was how she greeted the guests.

"And mighty glad not to be, madame," said Florian. "Those of us who were not actually fighting for Dixie Land at least endured with her throughout the entire war."

"It's like I allus say," she said. "The Yankees may hold the ground now, but that's all they got. They ain't defeated the sperrit of the South. Ain't that what I allus say, Mr. Furfew?"

"Always, my dear," he murmured. Then, to the troupe, "Won't you-all come in, refresh yourselves? The stable boys will see to your animals. They will show your own darky to the quarters, too."

A number of black men, mostly barefoot, all clad in much-worn homespun, all acting as subdued and obsequious as if they had never heard of Emancipation, came to take most of the reins. But, muttering and walling their eyes, they left the elephant and Thunder with the lion wagon for Hannibal and Roozeboom to lead around to the stable yard. As the other troupers got out of and down from the vehicles—the females trying to step as queenly and daintily as if they were descending from barouches at a court ball—Mrs. Furfew continued to fulminate.

"Us bein' right smack on the enemy border here, we done already seen more'n we'll ever want to see of Yankees ever again. Them scoun'erls just about ruint our Oakhaven. Tell 'em, Mr. Furfew."

"The Yankees just about ruined Oakhaven," he patiently repeated, as he led the way into an entry hall that was immense but unfurnished. "They looted and smashed and—"

"And what them scoun'erls couldn't pilfer, they ruint. Tell 'em about the chandelier and the pitchers, Mr. Furfew."

He waved vaguely toward the ceiling and walls. "Here in the hall, there used to be a pendant chandelier of crystal lusters and prisms, and a gallery of the Furfew family portraits. The Yankees—"

"They drug down the chandelier, and what dangles didn't break they hung on their horses' harness for pretties. Then they got a pot of tar and dobbed mustaches on Mr. Furfew's Grandmaw Sophronia and Aunt Verbena and all. Just ruint 'em. The men ancestors in the pitchers already had mustaches, so them Yankees took their bayonets and slashed 'em to ribbons. Tell about the clocks and the books, Mr. Furfew."

He sighed. "They carried off all the clocks except the tall case clock. It was too big to haul, so they toppled it down the stairway to destruction. They burned all our books, including a hundred-year-old Bible that chronicled all the Furfew births and deaths and weddings. They burned all the other family records, land deeds, slaves' titles, everything on paper. Now, my dear, perhaps you'd show these ladies upstairs and have the maids bring them wash water."

Mrs. Furfew looked as if she'd rather continue reciting grievances, but she shepherded Sarah, Clover Lee and Magpie Maggie Hag up the long and curving staircase. That would have been an elegant feature of the hall, except that it was missing many of its banister posts and even some treads and risers.

"You must forgive Leutitia's stridency, gentlemen," said Mr. Furfew in an undertone. He gestured toward his wife as she climbed the stairs behind the other women. "Look at her shoes. Satin, you think. Yes, but the satin is of pieces carefully peeled from old notions boxes. That black blouse she is wearing was originally an umbrella covering. Ah, the pitiful little pretenses and brave little graces of destitution. If she seems obsessed with Yankee-hating, she has had provocation, God knows."

"Well, I suppose you ought to congratulate yourselves that you still have a house," said Florian. "Not to mention servants. I am surprised they didn't run off with the Yankees."

"I think they are all too afraid of Leutitia," said Mr. Furfew, with a chuckle that was not entirely humorous.

Fitzfarris asked, "Which Yankees was it, sir, that you got overrun by?"

"Just about any of the regulars you can name. McClellan's, Banks's, Shields's, Milroy's. Banks quartered his officers here, which is doubtless why the house didn't get burned. And of course, we did get to see an occasional one of our own Confederate commanders—Jackson and Early have dined at our table. Most recently, since that damned Sheridan pulled out, we've had bunches of bummers come looking to sack anything that the regulars might have left. The last straggle of rogues, a week ago, not finding anything they could use, despoiled what they could not. Look at this."

He had led them into what must once have been the drawing room, though its only piece of furniture now was a massive imperial-size grand piano. "This is a Bösendorfer with Erard action," he said. "Or it was." He lifted the tremendous lid and they looked in. The latest bummers had used the remains of the tar that had earlier been daubed on the Furfew family portraits. They had poured it all over the piano's strings and hammers.

"Fils de putain," muttered Rouleau. "Totally ruined."

Edge said, "I believe you mentioned, sir, that you'd been with the local Home Guard."

"Yes, damn it. Too old and rickety to serve. Didn't even have a son to send. And about all I could do in the way of Home Guarding was to give our neighbors the benefit of our own sad experiences. Very early on, we tried to preserve Leutitia's jewels, the family silver, other such things, by burying them about the yard. But the Yankees already knew that trick. They didn't even bother digging up the whole yard. They just went about jabbing their rifle ramrods deep in the ground until they hit something. Then they made our own darkies do the digging up. So the next time Oakhaven had a surcease from occupation, and any things worth keeping, we put them under the privies—very deep under—and the stable-yard manure pile. We managed to save a fair quantity of canned goods, root vegetables, even grain, and I advised our neighbors to do likewise. Oh, by the way, I've told Cadmus to grain your animals. They look as if they could use it."

"Oh, my dear sir!" Florian exclaimed. "You'll spoil the creatures. But it is a kindness beyond hospitality. Do let me pay you for that."

Mr. Furfew looked uneasy, and threw a glance at the hallway. "In God's name, man, if you're carrying Federal specie, don't dare show it around her. I mean around here. We've sworn to spend and accept only Confederate money until there is absolutely no other recourse."

"As it happens, I can pay you with some of that."

Mr. Furfew waved dismissively. "One day, a crippled Yankee happened by and, when our little black boy gave him a dipper of water, the soldier gave him a penny. Leutitia snatched the coin and threw it at the man. Then she birched the boy nearly bloody for accepting it." He sighed. "But, as I say, she has had ample provocation."

"It is so provoking, the war and all," Mrs. Furfew confirmed, when they all sat down to a midday dinner around an uncovered and improvised trestle table, eating off an assortment of tin and wooden plates with an even sketchier assortment of utensils. "I feel like Oakhaven has been defiled. Do you know—when them filthy Yankee officers was quartered on us?—they had the gall to bring their wenches from Washington to stay with 'em! Them hard and coarse Yankee women! Naturally, what bedding and linen them officers didn't steal when they left, we took out and burned. So it's poor pallets we're giving you, ladies, but if they look a little gray, think of it as Confederate gray."

Edge sneaked a look at Sarah and Clover Lee, those hard and coarse Yankee women, but they were keeping their eyes demurely on their plates, and he suspected that neither of them had said so much as a "damn" since they had come into the house.

He also saw how grotesque the circus troupe looked, sitting around a table in at least passably civilized surroundings. There were two glossily bald-headed men, one with a fierce walrus mustache, the other with an even fiercer black beard; the trim and dapper, silver-bearded director; a slat-thin, high-shouldered yokel who would be a typically Virginian bumpkin except for his sinister black eye patch; two fairly good-looking younger men, but one with his face in permanent blue half-shadow; a runt whose head barely topped the table; a pretty blonde woman, a pretty blonde girl and a hag whose nose and chin, though barely visible inside the hood she wore even to meals, nearly scissored every time she chewed. And then there was himself, Zachary Edge, whatever he looked like. Small wonder, he thought, that the little mulatto girl waiting on the table was warily goggle-eyed as she served them from pots and platters.

Florian swallowed a mouthful of the succulent stew on his plate and said, "I sympathize with all your deprivations, madame. But I must say you have coped well with them, and made the most of what provender you've managed to hold onto. This meal is delicious."

"Thank you, monsewer. Yes, our Aunt Phoebe can do wonders with little provisions. I just wish she could learn her high-yaller brats some manners." She raised her voice to the girl who was at the moment spooning stewed tomatoes onto Yount's plate. "You, miss! You're serving that gentleman from his right side. That's the wrong side! Come here, hussy!"

The girl, no older than twelve or thirteen and no darker than fawn color, rolled her eyes and wailed, "Mistis, I ain' nebber knowed. How kin de right side be de wrong side?"

"Hush your mouth!" Mrs. Furfew's face turned the color of eggplant, which made her rather darker than the mulatto. "I said *come here*, you sassy critter!"

The girl sidled reluctantly around the table to where Mrs. Furfew could reach out and give her a hard slap across the face. The girl flinched and started away, but Mrs. Furfew snapped, "No, miss, that won't do. I want to *hear* it. You puff out your cheeks, like I've learnt you." The girl puffed out her cheeks, making them an even paler tan, and Mrs. Furfew slapped her again, this time producing a *whap!* as resounding as any Tim had ever achieved in the circus ring.

When everyone else sat silent in some embarrassment, Mr. Furfew relieved the strain. He turned to ask Florian what was the destination of the northward-bound circus train.

"Baltimore, sir, on this side of the water. We intend to take our Florilegium on to Europe—if we can convert our Secesh money to pay for passage." Florian saw Mr. Furfew wince, and quickly said placatively to Mrs. Furfew, "We have to recoup our fortunes, but we are determined *not* to do it by touring Yankee land."

She had not turned purple, and indeed nodded approvingly. "Them's my sentiments, too. My dear brother lost his life in Tennessee. But I've done stopped grieving for him. I envy Henry now, I really do. He fought for the cause, and that was more'n any of us women could. We could only try to manage, try to keep on."

"At Petersburg," said Yount, "the city ladies used to come out, during lulls in the fighting, and visit the lines to *inspire* us soldiers." He said it acidly, but Mrs. Furfew did not seem to notice. "They used to bring us tracts. Them was to persuade us not to gamble or cuss or do improper things. Only fight and kill, like we ought."

Mrs. Furfew again nodded approval. "Yes, our work was to inspire. There was little else we frail women could accomplish. That's why I envy Henry. He at least got to *die* for what he believed in."

Fitzfarris spoke up, lazily, "What was that, ma'am?"

"Why—why, the *South,* of course. For the Southern culture and principles and morality. Henry must feel proud and good about having died so. Don't you expect, Corporal?"

"I don't know, ma'am. I saw many a dead man, and none of them looked proud to be that way. I imagine Henry just feels glad to be lying down and resting. And not having to be shot more than the once."

"He was not shot, Corporal. His colonel sent a nice letter of condolence, and said Henry died of dysentery."

"Ah! Then I'll wager he feels even more glad to be at rest. I had the scours once myself, and—"

Mrs. Furfew suddenly flared up. "Listen at you! Oh, a live man can afford to run down a dead one—can't he?—and throw off on the glorious cause. *All* you men may forgive and forget the whole war, because it was you what *lost* it!" She had gone eggplant again. "But the cause will not *ever* be forgot by us Southron women. *We* never surrendered, we never quit, and we never will!"

"My, my," said Florian, again hastening to placate. "Fruitcake for dessert. Will wonders never cease? As toothsome as everything else of the meal. Your cook is a real treasure, madame."

Mrs. Furfew's color ebbed, and she grudgingly accepted the change of subject. "Yes, Phoebe makes a right tol'able fruitcake, considering that all she's got to put in it is persimmons and hickory nuts and peppercorns."

"I think I shall go in person and compliment the lady chef," said Florian. "If I may?" He waited for Mrs. Furfew's condescending nod, then fled from the table to the kitchen outbuilding.

But the hostess threw no more tantrums, and the dinner party disbanded without further unpleasantness. Mrs. Furfew insisted that "all us ladies" follow the inviolable Southern-belle custom of retiring to their rooms for an afternoon nap. Roozeboom went off to the smithy to work on the broken wagon wheel. The other men went out on the veranda for a smoke, there breaking up into groups of two and three.

Mr. Furfew was discoursing to Trimm and Edge, "... Yes, Jeff Davis was much criticized. But, gentlemen, President Davis knew the temper of the South. He knew that, if there was ever to be amicable accommodation between us and the North, the South must win the war. Or, if she could not win, she wanted to be whipped—well whipped—*thoroughly* whipped."

"Well, she was," grunted Tim.

"Yes, we lost. But *ah!* was it not a most magnificent fight?"

Fitzfarris said to Rouleau, "Our host is a cultivated gentleman and she's no better than a swineherd putting on hoity-toity airs. How do you suppose those two ever got together?"

"Tiens, I am inclined to suspect that they met in a forest," Rouleau drawled, "when he took a thorn out of her paw."

Mullenax said to Yount, "That woman is rattling the shingles on her garret. I hope every female in Dixie ain't gone as crazy."

Yount growled, "If such women want to carry on the war after it's over and done with, I say let 'em. Miz Furfew may be short on shoes, and holding a grudge about that. But I ain't seen any women lacking *legs,* not even in Petersburg."

"Nor eyes," said Mullenax. "No denying it was us men that lost the war—but we lost a lot else besides. I'm with you, Obie. The damned old biddies can *have* the goddamned war."

In the kitchen shanty, which was separated from the main house by a covered breezeway, Florian had fulsomely complimented the cook, Phoebe Simms —a large, plump, glossy-black woman—and had proffered some further pleasantries, and now, a gleam in his eye, was pursuing a line of seductive inquiry.

"Haven't you thought of traveling, Aunt Phoebe, now that you're free to travel?"

"Ain' no place special callin' me to come," she said good-humoredly, as she washed dishes. "An' I got obligations hyar."

"Surely you feel no overwhelming obligation to Madame Furfew. I've seen the way she treats her help."

"Least she feeds 'em."

"You feed *her,* Aunt Phoebe. There are folks who would better value your services, and treat you better, and give you the respect you deserve. *And* let you be something more high-toned than help."

"Whut dat?"

"You could be a circus artiste. A star attraction."

She giggled and jiggled all her adiposity. "Hee hee! Me wear tights, Mas' Florian, an' jump around? I seen a circus onct, an' I marbled at dem pooty ladies. But laws-a-mussy, I be's black an' I be's fat."

"Exactly why I want you. I offer you a position of dignity. No funny dress and no jumping around. You'd simply sit on a platform and be admired. The one and only Fat Lady in Florian's Florilegium. I will even ennoble you with a title— *Madame Alp!*"

"Ain' nobody go' call no nigguh Ma'am. Anyway, shoot! I ain' much fatter'n ol' Mistis."

"But far more impressive. Your being so magnificently black adds to the impressiveness. You'd be fairly paid and—"

"*Paid?!* You means cash money, Massa?"

"Why, assuredly. It might be scanty for a while, until we get up north where the real money is. But yes, you'd be paid, and you'd get to see new country almost every day, and you'd have all the rights and privileges of a Freedwoman."

"Lawsy, lawsy..."

"And we would not neglect your other talents, either. You can cook for us, just as you do here. I guarantee it will be better appreciated than it is here. For one thing, you'd eat *with us,* not off in a corner. Everybody in a circus is one of the family. You can ask our own respected black companion, Hannibal Tyree."

"Wull...him an' me did talk some," Phoebe admitted, "when I guv him a dab o' dinner. He do talk mighty happy an' high an' mighty fo' a nigguh."

"Well, there you are, then. What more need I say?"

"But...how 'bout my chirren, Mas' Florian?"

"Eh?"

"My pickaninnies. Sunday, Monday, Tuesday an' Quincy."

"Is that how she spells Wednesday?" asked Edge, when Florian excitedly broke the news to him.

"The boy's a different litter. He's only eight years old. But the girls—"

"Mr. Florian," Edge said tolerantly. "I've had a look at that Aunt Phoebe. You've already got the world's tallest circus midget. Now you want to have the world's puniest Fat Lady? Hell, down in Rockbridge County, every third woman bloats up bigger than Phoebe Simms, just as soon as she's hooked herself a husband."

Florian waved in the elegantly dismissive manner of Mr. Furfew. "Maggie Hag can pad her out to hippo dimensions. Europe has probably never seen a *black* Fat Lady. But listen to this, Zachary. The three girls are all thirteen years old—*identical triplets!* And handsome, too. You saw the one that waited on table. I really had no idea what a splendid coup I was in fact engineering. We not only get a Fat Lady, but also three good-looking mulatto wenches who are triplets. No other circus can claim such a showpiece! The boy Quincy is blacker than Abdullah, but we can always find use for another Hindu."

"Curious. How did the woman come to throw a whole litter of yellow roses and then a single blue-gum black?"

"I wasn't so rude as to inquire too closely. But she used to belong to a different master, and maybe she herself was smaller and prettier in those days. He must have been a handsome man, to judge from the result. It probably would have gone unremarked, even by the man's own wife, if Phoebe had dropped just one half-breed daughter. But *triplets*—the whole neighborhood would have been a-buzz. So he sold her and them in a hurry. Little black Quincy dates from since she's been here at Oakhaven. I'd guess that that stable man Cadmus is the father."

"Well," said Edge, "I can't accuse you of taking up slave stealing. They're all free darkies now. But don't you feel you're ill repaying these people's hospitality?"

"Oh, indeed I do feel bad, on Mr. Furfew's account. Phoebe's cooking must be the only delight he has in life. But to deprive the *mistress* I think justifies the crime."

"I can't gainsay that," said Edge. "Even a gypsy life will be better for those pickaninnies than growing up here. How do you intend to do this?"

"The Simmses don't own more than the clothes they're wearing, so they're not coming freighted with luggage. All they'll have to do—right after breakfast tomorrow—is slip away to the farthest roadside corner of the property and hop the fence. We'll pick them up there. And now that we've got the balloon wagon, we've got something for them to ride in and sleep in. We'll just throw a protective canvas over the balloon. I only hope we can make some distance before they're missed and we're pursued."

"No problem there," said Edge. "Make eight more miles or so and we cross the border into West Virginia. Even if the Furfews had any legitimate claim, no Virginia lawman can press it there."

"Ah, good, good!" Florian exulted, rubbing his hands together. "Seldom has Dame Fortune so concatenated her blessings on our behalf. Why, with all these Negroes, we can even have our own troupe of Ethiopian Minstrels—no, no,

no—every show calls them that." He pondered briefly. "Aha! The Happy Hottentots! How does that strike you, Zachary?"

Edge only sighed and said, "Nothing surprises me any more."

Nevertheless, something did, the next morning after breakfast. The troupers
were dispensing thanks all around and making ready to depart, when Mrs. Furfew drew Edge aside and said:

"Colonel, seeing as how you're the ranking Confederate officer amongst this
crew, I want to show you something. I'd like your Monsewer Florian to see it, too.
And you might want to fetch along a pry bar, and somebody strong to use it."

Wondering, Edge went and collected Florian and Yount. After Mrs. Furfew
had made sure nobody else was paying any attention, she led the three men
around behind the house, beyond the outbuildings, across a long-fallow field
where they stumbled over old corn stubble. They came finally to a copse of trees
that had been left growing to conceal what would otherwise have been an un-
sightly rubbish dump: all the boulders, stumps, deadfall branches and other
trash removed when the fields were cleared.

"Monsewer," said Mrs. Furfew, "you said you wanted to convert some Confederate money to Yankee dollars." She gestured to Edge and Yount. "Start shifting them stumps and things, and see what you find in yonder."

Still wondering, they obeyed, and after some labor they uncovered the rear
end of a blue-painted, metal-sheathed wagon of unusual configuration. Edge
stepped back in amazement and exclaimed:

"That's an Autenrieth wagon! All fitted out inside with compartments and
pigeonholes. The Yankees used them mostly for ambulance wagons. But look,
Obie—the initials on this one: P.D. Not Medical Department, by damn, but Pay
Department! Ma'am, I don't know how this got here, but this is the wagon of
some outfit's *paymaster*."

"That's right," she said. "Can y'all get it open?"

"You knew it was here? You knew what it was?" said Edge, as Yount pried at
its padlocked door with his iron bar.

"Course I did. I had Cadmus and some of the other boys hide it here. Please
don't let Mr. Furfew know about it. Now, Monsewer, about that money of
yours—"

"But where did you get it?" Edge persisted, in bewilderment.

"From Little Phil Sheridan. Anyhow, from whatever part of his army it was
that left here last, going eastwards, back in February. It sprung a wheel rim and
the rest of the column went on without it, until it could be fixed and catch up.
The Yankees ordered me to give 'em dinner while Cadmus worked on it. There
was a driver, a lieutenant and two clerks that wore spectacles. I reckon Sheridan's still looking for 'em, or got 'em listed as deserters, but they're there in the
trash pile, if you want to see 'em."

"What?!" exclaimed Edge and Florian together. Yount glanced around, wide-
eyed, but went on working at the door.

"Phoebe fixed 'em a meal and I brung it from the kitchen myself, but I come
by way of the potting shed and mixed Paris green in the food."

"Madame, that is arsenic!" said Florian, horrified.

"Well, it kills garden vermin, so I figgered it'd kill blue-belly Yanks, and it did.
After they ate, they was in the smithy watching Cadmus work, when they fell

over and started squirming. Mr. Furfew thinks they went on and caught up with the others. I'd sooner that he keeps thinking so."

"Ah...um...yes," said Florian, in a strangled sort of way. There was a loud twang, as the paywagon's hasp and staple yielded to Yount's levering, and then a rusty screech as he forced the metal door open. "But why, Madame Furfew, do you disclose the secret to us?"

"You got some Confederate money. I'll buy it from you."

"Christamighty, she can, too!" cried Yount. He was inside the wagon, in the narrow aisle between the banks of shelves and drawers. "There must be a whole division's whole month's pay here! All in U.S. greenbacks!"

"I congratulate you, madame," said Florian. "That should go a long way toward restoring Oakhaven from the damage—"

"May the Lord strike me dead if I spend a penny of it," she said firmly. "The storekeepers hereabouts know I won't pay in nothing but Confederate paper. That's why I want yours."

"I'll be happy to accommodate you, madame. Were you thinking of paying the official exchange rate or the prevailing one?"

"I'll give you dollar for dollar."

When Florian found his voice, he breathed a prayerful exclamation in one of his native languages, something Edge and Yount had never before heard him do:

"Ich mache mir Flecken ins Bettuch... Er, I mean to say, madame, our exchequer comprises quite a *lot* of Confederate dollars. Something in excess of nine thousand. Were I to exchange them for Federal dollars anywhere else, they would be worth only about ninety..." Mrs. Furfew had begun to turn eggplant color again, so Florian ceased his protesting and said, "Excuse me, madame. If you'll allow me a brief consultation with my colleagues..."

Florian, Edge and Yount moved a little way apart from her, and Florian confided in a mutter, "This creature belongs in a cage. I've done some underhanded things in my time, but I do hesitate to take advantage of a sanctified and certifiable lunatic."

Edge murmured, "Nine thousand real dollars would sure get us to Europe, and probably with some left over to pay wages."

"Yes, but... ill-gotten gains? And blood money, at that?"

"Listen here, Mr. Florian," Yount growled. "I ain't often insubordinate, but let me say this. *I* got no scruples about skinning this particular old sow. You run and fetch that worthless paper of ours while I help her start counting out the greenbacks from them drawers in yonder. And if it still bothers you, *I'll* do the handing back and forth when you get it here."

So that is what they did, and then, at Mrs. Furfew's command, the three men piled the rubbish over and around the wagon again. When they returned to the house, Florian's frock-coat pockets were visibly bulging—with nine thousand, two hundred and twenty-four dollars in genuine, spendable, United States cash money—and none of the three men was able to meet the honest eyes of Mr. Paxton Furfew when shaking his hand in farewell.

The circus train maintained a sedate pace going down the drive and along the road as far as it bordered the Oakhaven property. But where the fence left the roadside to turn at the Oakhaven boundary, Phoebe Simms and her four little Simmses were waiting, as scheduled. The train paused while Mullenax helped the Negroes scramble onto the canvas-covered bed of the balloon wagon, and then Florian called:

"Now let's make tracks!" He flapped his reins and put Snowball to a canter, and all the animals behind hustled to keep up. "Never," said Florian to Edge, beside him on the rockaway, "never have I done so many dirty dealings in just one morning. Ha-*ha!* And never have I felt so downright happy in my unregenerate sinfulness."

"I have to agree. The money's a fine thing and, now that I've seen the Simmses climb aboard, I think they were worth acquiring, too. The boy's only a little ink blot, and his mammy's no sensational freak, but the three yellow roses do look as much alike as peas in a pod."

"Wait until we get them in spangles, Zachary—and now we can afford to. They'll look as pretty as *real* yellow roses. If only we can get clean away."

"If the Furfew place was pestered by Yankee bummers just a week ago, it argues that there isn't much law around this border area."

"Hell, I'm not worried about lawmen now. I'm purely terrified that *that woman* might come after us."

"She'd starch and iron us, all right. But any place where you don't have to worry about law, you sometimes have to worry about outlaws. Maybe you've noticed that we haven't passed anybody else at all on this particular road. Looks like the common folk avoid it."

They rode a couple more miles at the canter. Then the road began to slope gently uphill, so they eased the pace to the usual walk, and Edge spoke again. "We're climbing up toward Limestone Ridge. It marks the state line and the international boundary. Once we cross it, we're in West Virginia."

"Newest of the United States," mused Florian.

"Yep, a whole new state," said Edge, and shook his head. "I've seen many a change made by this war."

"Nonsense," said Florian. "That piece of land ahead may have changed its name, but it's still the same piece of land. You've read history, Zachary. Name me one war that ever made any change on the face of the earth that stayed visible or significant for more than maybe a century or two."

"Put it that way and, just offhand, I can't."

"No, the things that *do* cause changes—and irreversible ones—are usually less dramatic and more insidious. I can show you two of them right here and now. Look at that railroad running parallel to us over there, and the telegraph wires strung above it. Swift locomotion and far communication, they're already changing the world. When people can get quickly and easily from one place to another, every damned place worth going to will be overrun and overflowing with people. When they can talk by telegraph to anybody anywhere in the world, you can damned well bet they *will* talk. And pester and peddle and harangue and preach. Within your lifetime, Zachary, there will hardly be a place on this planet where you can find privacy from people and the yammer of people."

Edge said he was probably right, and it was a sobering thing to think about. They rode in silence for a while, and then he said:

"Time was, I did my best to *stop* the spread and spraddle of railroads. Back when Obie and I were with the Comanches, the battalion used to tear up railroads to interrupt the Yankees' supply lines. We'd pry up the rails, make a big bonfire of the cross-ties, lay the rails across the fire until they got hot and soft, then wrap them around trees to cool solid. We blew up bridges, too, but that was more sport than practicality."

"Why so?"

"Well, it seems that every iron bridge in America is made in Cleveland, Ohio. And some engineer in Cleveland figured out how to build portable bridges—in small sections that the Yankees could carry and bolt together and make a bridge wherever it was needed. So they replaced the bridges about as fast as we knocked them down." He laughed and added, "One time, we blew up a railroad *tunnel*. Did a good job of it. Brought the whole hill thundering down into it. But when the dust cleared, one of our boys said, 'What the hell, them Yankees'll just fetch another tunnel down from Cleveland, Ohio.'"

Florian laughed too, but stopped laughing when he noticed what Edge was doing. He had unsnapped the flap of the holster on his right hip. Now, without taking out the revolver, he cocked its hammer with that familiarly ominous triple click. Then he let the pistol stay there, snug in the holster, its butt facing front-ward as usual in the cavalry-carry position, but with his right hand resting on that butt.

Florian said, "I thought you always carried that thing with the hammer down for safety."

"It's another kind of safety I'm concerned about now. I said this might be lawless territory here. I had Obie carry my carbine handy, too, just in case. And I might as well tell you: ever since we got a little way from the Furfews' place, there've been three riders keeping pace with us, over the fields yonder to the right of the road. They've stayed well off behind the trees, so I've only caught glimpses of them, but they're still with us."

"And you never said anything? You must not be very worried about their intentions."

"We'll likely get an idea of their intentions when we breast the top of Lime-stone Ridge—when we're going our slowest. I figure they'll be waiting on the other side of the crest."

They were. The men had dismounted and left their three horses to block the road, so the wagons could not have made a dash past them in any case, but one of the men raised his hand and called amiably, "Hold a minute, folks. Like to have a word with y'all."

Florian said bitterly, "I should have known we'd had too much good luck. Here's where we lose it all."

Edge quietly advised, "Just rein in slow, so the other wagons come to a stop close behind us."

The three men in the road looked sufficiently ugly to be bummers or bandits or any other kind of undesirables. They were dirty, their beards had been trimmed by the ax-and-stump method, and they were dressed in a motley of Yankee and Rebel jackets, boots and forage caps, plus derelict items of civilian attire, belts and bandoliers of modern cartridge ammunition. Only in two respects were they elegantly fitted out. Their horses were prime animals, though wearing battered, old-fashioned Grimsley saddles. And each of the men, in addition to a belt pistol, was carrying a new-blued Henry repeater carbine. Holding those weapons casually, but with their hands ready on the levers and triggers, the men fanned across the road. One stayed directly in front of Snowball, an-

other slowly approached on Florian's side of the rockaway, and the third came
toward Edge, saying:

"Stay sittin' just like you are, sojer. I don't want to see that left hand sneak
acrost towards your pistol holster."

"We don't mean to sound unfriendly," said the man on Florian's side, in a
wheedling way. "But these are hard times, and you meet some hard characters
on these roads."

"What can we do for you, gentlemen?" Florian asked levelly.

"We seen y'all leave that plantation a few miles back," said the man, moving
closer to him. "We been there ourselves, and we left as poor as we arrived. Folks
not hospitable a'tall. Tightfisted as homemade sin."

"Yeah, damn 'em," said the man on Edge's side of the carriage, moving closer
to him. "And the only female yonder was so ugly she'd skeer a dog out of a
butcher shop. Hyuck hyuck." He spat a stream of tobacco juice.

"But you-all," said the other to Florian, stepping still closer, as if preparing to
pounce. "Y'all come ridin' spry out of thar, like you'd just got drunk and got laid
and got prosperous, all at onct."

"Yeah," said the other to Edge, spitting amber again. "We kinda wondered if
we might of missed somethin', and mebbe y'all got it instead. Anyhow, you got a
couple mighty purty passengers in this-yer rockaway... Say! Don't I know you,
sojer?" He stood right before and below Edge now, and stared up at him. "I'll be a
son of a bitch. Hyuck hyuck. Ain't you Zachary Edge, what used to be a Comanche?"

Edge said, just as bogus-cheerfully, "Sure am. Hyuck hyuck. How've you
been, Luther?" and shot him in the belly.

Edge had not made any sudden or overt move, and actually had fired his
revolver upside down. With his right hand resting on the backward pistol butt,
and that hand's ring finger inside the holster, on the trigger, he had only to twist
the holster a trifle upward and fire through its open narrow end. Before Luther
finished sprawling backward in the road, there came the heavy *boom!* of the
Cook carbine from Yount's wagon farther back in the train, and the bummer on
Florian's side of the carriage did an abrupt pirouette and also fell down. Meanwhile, the recoil of Edge's own gun had squirted it backward, free of the holster.
It was in his hand, right side up, the hammer thumbed back again, before the
third of the men, farthest up the road, even grasped what was happening—and
Edge had time to aim and shoot him in the breast. The three rapid gunshots
were echoed by a few weak feminine shrieks, from Clover Lee and two or three
of the Simms females.

When Edge jumped down from the driving seat, through the hanging cloud
of blue smoke, Sarah Coverley was leaning out of the rockaway, her eyes wide.

"My God, Zachary," she said, half-awed, half-appalled. "They hadn't so much
as threatened us."

He gave her a look. "Sometimes it's advisable to soothe a man a little before
he gets to the threatening stage."

His Remington cocked again and at the ready, he went cautiously to stoop
over each of the men. The one he had shot in the breast and the one Yount had
shot side-to-side through the rib cage were already dead. But Luther, flat on his
back in the road, was still alive, opening and shutting his mouth like a fish.

When Edge bent over him, he said crossly: "I swallered my damn tobacco. Don't never swaller yer chaw, Cap'n Edge. It makes yer stummick hurt like hell."

"You deserve to hurt, Sergeant Steptoe. You never were worth a damn as a soldier, and you haven't improved any as a road agent. You'd have died a better death at Tom's Brook."

"Shit, I warn't the only one what turned tail at Tom's Brook, and you ought to know that better'n—*ow!*—Christamighty, but that tobacco's gripin' my poor stummick!"

"I'll ease it for you," said Edge, and shot him again.

The other men of the company had got down from the wagons and now came to gaze at the victims, occasionally casting sidewise glances of genuine respect at Edge and Yount.

"Well, I'll be double damned," said Yount. "Pittman and Steptoe and Stancill. I thought they was dead long ago. So this is what they come to."

"How do you happen to know them?" asked Florian, his voice somewhat unsteady.

Yount said, "We told you about that battle where us Comanches got scattered. These three was among the men that never regrouped. They must of been bumming around the vicinity ever since." He paused and considered, then said, "I'd almost like to ride back and tell Miz Furfew, so she could share out some of that blame she puts all on Yankees."

Rouleau said to Edge, indicating the late Sergeant Steptoe, "Did you have to shoot him twice, ami? Might not that one have lived?"

"No. In a minute he'd have been screaming and writhing. A man gut-shot can take hours to die. Would you want to sit and hold his hand that long?"

"Well, do we just let 'em all lay?" asked Mullenax. "For the buzzards to deal with?"

"Better not," said Edge. He scanned the horizon. "These could be just outriders of a bigger bunch somewhere. If so, and if these are found—well, we're the only other people who've passed this way, so their bummer chums might come looking for us."

"Anyway, Mr. Florian, you've got three good remounts," Fitzfarris said. "None of them is wearing any brand, army or otherwise. Throw away the saddles—they're worthless old things—and chances are nobody will ever recognize the horses as anything but circus stock. We probably can find employment for these weapons, too. Zack, you might want to use a repeater Henry in your act, instead of your single-shot. The revolvers are two Colts and a Joslyn."

"Fine," said Florian, taking command. "Sir John, you collect the arms and ammunition. Captain Hotspur, unsaddle the horses and tie them on lead, one to each of the first three vehicles. Monsieur Roulette, bring some of our old pieces of canvas. We'll wrap the cadavers and stow them in the tent wagon. Then let's roll."

When they were again under way, Florian said to Edge, "Well, it *has* been a lucky day, thanks mainly to you and Obie." When Edge said nothing, Florian gave him a look. "Are you feeling remorse, my boy? I gather that those men were never exactly your bosom comrades, but I realize they were at least old acquaintances."

Edge shook his head. "They'd have been shot by firing squad after Tom's Brook, if they had been caught. Shameful as a retreat is, it's no capital crime—

but those three kept on running. They were deserters, renegades, and it's obvious that they'd become even worse things since then."

"Um, yes," Florian said thoughtfully. "After seeing what they did to the Furfews' fine piano, I can guess what they'd have done to Sarah and Clover Lee."

"The bastards figured they had us cold, and I wasn't inclined to sit idle until they really did. I don't feel any remorse at all. How long do you intend to play pallbearer for them? In this warm weather, they won't keep very well."

"We'll bury them when we get to Charles Town."

"That could cause some questions."

"I didn't mean we'd do it ceremoniously. No, there's an old circus way of disposing of potential embarrassments. When we're preparing the ring, we'll plant the departed under it. After two or three shows, with the horses and elephant pounding over them, the rogues will be well tamped down. Unlikely they'll ever be resurrected, to cause any questions."

I I

AT CHARLES TOWN, they found the old racecourse ground available for a pitch, and Florian put the men to work right away, erecting the pavilion in the twilight and then, in the dark, preparing the ring. It had to be spaded and forked deep, to accommodate their detritus of dead bummers, and then firmed flat again before the curbing could be heaped up around it. When the troupe finally sat down around the campfire to eat, they ate well, for Phoebe Simms had already taken over the cooking job, and she did wonders with the circus's scant supply of provender, as she had done with the Furfews'. After the meal, the men and Magpie Maggie Hag lighted pipes, and Abner Mullenax passed around one of his ever-present jugs, and Florian said, "Gather close, everybody. I have an announcement. Today is salary day!" and a cheer went up from the whole company.

Florian found an old shingle on the ground and, with his mason's pencil, did elaborate calculations on it, then began peeling off greenbacks from the wad he'd got from Mrs. Furfew. The artistes who had more recently joined out were paid in full, and consequently were not paid very much. Edge and Yount, for example, were owed for only some three weeks' work, and so were handed just twenty-two dollars apiece. The original troupers, dating back to long before Wilmington, got paid considerably more in lump sum but considerably less than they were due. Florian acknowledged that, and apologized for it.

"However, if our luck holds—and the attendance—I ought to be able to whittle down the deficits bit by bit. In the meantime, old friends, you understand that the greater part of our treasury must be kept by, for passage money."

At any rate, everybody had been paid in unequivocally hard currency, so nobody complained. Indeed, Sarah Coverley declared her intention of strolling downtown to buy for herself and Clover Lee something in the line of sheer frippery, just by way of celebration.

"Restrain yourself, my dear Madame Solitaire," said Florian. "In case our luck should *not* hold, I would suggest to all of you that you tuck away at least part of your wages in the good old traditional grouch bag." Sarah shrugged and sat down again. Florian went on, "Now that our Florilegium is to some degree approaching solvency, and has burgeoned in numbers, we must give some thought to the best utilization of our company. If anyone has any suggestions, I shall be happy to hear them. Anyway, I have some of my own on which to solicit the company's opinions." He looked around. "Comments?"

"Well, first off, what's a grouch bag?" asked Mullenax.

Sarah said, with a grin, "It's what your wife would wear, Abner, if you still had a wife."

"Eh?"

"A grouch bag is all *I* had when the late Mr. Coverley ran out on me. When there's a woman in a team of performers—especially if her man drinks much—she'll put away what money she can. Some women buy a teensy little diamond now and then, to carry in a chamois bag on a neck chain. Diamonds are easy to carry and they're sellable anywhere. So a woman's always got grouch money when she needs it."

Mullenax mumbled something about "uppity females," then avowed that he didn't drink so doggoned much, then took a pull at his jug.

"All right. Now my suggestions," said Florian. "First for you, Madame Alp."

It was a moment before Phoebe Simms realized it was herself that was being addressed. She said, "Oh . . . yassuh," and laughed delightedly. "Take a while t' git used t' not bein' called Aunt or Mammy."

"Well, among ourselves, we'll call you whatever you prefer."

"Don' matter," she said, with another laugh, this one slightly rueful. "I bin called darlin' honey and I bin called nigguh hussy. But I be's always me, and I knows who I am."

"Would to God more folks did! Anyway, as of your first appearance on the show, in public you'll be Madame Alp. But, first thing in the morning, I want you to take this money and go to market. Stock our larder with all kinds of staples and groceries—get some fresh horsemeat for the cat, as well—and get every kind of cooking and serving utensil you think we need. Buy plenty of everything because, once you're Madame Alp and a celebrity, you can't run around and give every yokel a free look at you."

"Yassuh. I go to market."

Florian turned to Magpie Maggie Hag. "Madame Wardrobe Mistress, I'd like you to get started right away on padding a tremendous dress for Madame Alp. Have her rigged out for showing as soon as possible. Also, think about some kind of dress-up for the triplets. I know I'm putting a lot of work on you, Mag, but at least those three all have the same measurements. And here's shopping money for you, too. Go and buy every gaudy piece of cloth and trimming you can find in Charles Town. You've been making do with scraps for too long."

The old gypsy mumbled something that sounded grateful.

"Next—Colonel Ramrod. Will you look over those new horses we acquired? See if they'll work in harness."

"They ought to," said Edge. "Considering who's been using them, they've probably done every kind of work. But I'll make sure."

"Then we'll need extra harness to equip them, Captain Hotspur."

"Ja, Baas. I go buy vas ve need."

"I have another job for you to attend to at the same time, Captain. Since you are also our boss rigger, I want you to do some *rigging*. Here is ample money. While you are in town, buy us some lights."

"Kerst Jesus!" Roozeboom exclaimed. "You mean it, Baas? Ve make night show now? I can buy *everyt'ing*? Chandelier and all?"

"All. You decide what we need, and you get it. Tomorrow, ladies and gentlemen, for the first time in this touring season, there will be two shows—afternoon· and night. Mam'selle Clover Lee, here is my pencil and here is a stack of our posters. Start adding at the bottom of each one—'Evening performance, eight p.m.' And Tiny Tim, I want you out early tomorrow, posting that paper. Abdullah, you and Brutus do the usual rounds, as well, but yell to folks now that there will be both daytime and after-dark shows."

"Yassuh, Mas' Florian."

"Abdullah, Abdullah, I am still *Sahib* Florian to you. And to your apprentice Hindu, too. Impress that on little Quincy. No—Quincy doesn't sound very Hindu. Ali Baba, that's it. From now on, professionally he is Ali Baba."

Roozeboom said, "Baas, now ve got Mevrou Alp en dem klonkies, dey can't ride alvays in open ven it rains. Ve going need 'nother vagon."

"Hm. Yes, I daresay you're right. Very well, procure one. As sturdy but as cheap as you can find. Thank goodness we've at least got enough draft animals now for all our wagons. And one of the new horses can take over the job of dragging that cannon, so Brutus doesn't have to do it."

"Ja, Baas."

"Everybody else on this show doubles or triples, and so should those new horses. Colonel Ramrod, do you think you could train them in some ring tricks? Since we now have more horses than equestrians, could you possibly work up a liberty act?"

"Possibly, if you'll tell me what a liberty act is."

"Horses working by themselves, with no riders aboard, with no controlling harness, only decorative plumes and such. You make them do drill and parade maneuvers on command. Or better, with unobtrusive signals of hand and whip, so they look like they're really doing it ad libitum."

"I can give it a try."

"Good. Do so. Do it well enough, Colonel Ramrod, and you will be promoted to one of the posts I now hold—equestrian director—what the rubes call ringmaster."

"Whoa, now," said Edge. "I don't have your gift of blarney."

"Oh, I'll still be the talker. But you'll wield the whistle and a whip. Get the acts on and off in proper order—including your own—and in good order. Find a way to cover up when things go wrong. Decide when to pull an act off early or let it run long. Things like that. You'll learn. And, as soon as I can afford it, I will double the pittance I am paying you at present."

Rouleau asked, "Florian, mon vieux, are you preparing to abdicate? Going to grab your grouch bag and run?"

"Au contraire. We have come some way toward being a real circus, not any longer just a mud show, and now the main guy must delegate some responsibilities to others. Which brings me to you, Sir John."

There was a moment of general puzzlement, everybody looking at everybody else. Then Fitzfarris gave a start and said, "Oh, yes. That's me. Shucks, it's been so long since I was called anything but Aunt Mammy or honey darling..."

"Sir John, you *can* tip off the blarney, so I'd like you to take over complete supervision of our growing sideshow. Build it into a real annex to our main program. For now, I will still introduce *you,* and relate your tragic history, so you won't have to brag on yourself. But then I'll step aside and you'll be the talker. Explain the lion feeding, expatiate on the Museum of Zoölogical Wonders, tell how the Crocodile Man was captured, introduce Madame Alp and her—what? —the Three Graces?"

"No, no," said Fitzfarris. "If I'm to be responsible for the sideshow I want *curiosities.* How about the Three White African Pygmies? Would you object to that, Madame Alp?"

"Dey still be's Sunday, Monday and Tuesday to me, and I still be's Mammy to dem. But dey good gals, dey do whatever you want."

"All right," said Fitz. "And let me suggest one other thing, Florian. You talked about not letting the public get free looks at Madame Alp, but everywhere on the road people are looking at the lion for free."

Florian said, "Well, a lion says *circus.* It's an allurement."

"You've got the elephant for that. I say let's put sidewalls around the lion's cage while we're traveling."

"There's not much allurement to a blank-walled box, Sir John."

"There could be. That wagon's got just an ordinary brake lever now. Ignatz, couldn't you take that off and whittle a great *big* one, near as hefty as a tree trunk, to put in its place?"

"Ja. But for vhy?"

"People see this closed cage rolling along the road. They see this monster brake lever sticking up beside the driver. They wonder what in Christ's name could be so big or so strong or so dangerous inside that box that it needs such a safeguard. Now *that's* allurement!"

Everybody around the fire stared at him, and finally Rouleau said softly, "Par dieu, this man *has* got circus blood."

Florian said, with admiration, "I wish to hell, Sir John, I could send you out ahead of us as our advance man. By God, you could get us talked about and newspapered like P. T. Barnum. But there—I'd be giving folks free looks at our Tattooed Man." He turned to the others. "Well, the other main item that's concerning me right now is that I sure wish we had some more music to go with the show. Does anybody here have any talent on any instrument?"

Phoebe Simms said, "Sunday can pick some on a pianner. Ol' Mistis used to show her."

"No! Well, I'm damned," said Florian. "That old dragon actually once did a good deed?" He looked at the three ragamuffin Simms girls, who had sat all this time in a row, moving only their eyes to gaze in concert at whoever happened to be speaking. "Which of you is Sunday?"

"Me, suh," said one of them, otherwise indistinguishable. They all wore identical garments: shapeless, frazzle-hemmed frocks of colorless homespun, apparently with nothing underneath, and none of them had shoes.

"Sunday, my dear, do you remember what you used to play?"

"Yassuh. A pianner."

"I mean the names—the names of the pieces that woman taught you."

Sunday looked blank. "I played music, suh. Music ain't no *thing.* It cain't hab no *name.*"

"Could you perhaps *hum* to us something you remember playing?"

Sunday walled her big brown eyes like a frightened colt, but then began shyly to hum, and gradually hummed louder, until it was audible.

Florian said "'Ah, vous dirai-je, maman.' That's what it is."

Yount said, "Sounded to me like 'Twinkle Twinkle, Little Star.'"

"Same song," said Florian. "It may not be great music, but it's international. Monsieur Roulette, maybe you can work her up into something. Any person that can play a piano can play an accordion, n'est-ce pas?"

Rouleau scratched his head. "I would guess so. Just have to learn the squeezing. I'll see if I can find one cheap in a pawnshop. Sunday and I between us can have a go at it. I will at the same time work on her abysmal dialect and diction."

Florian said, "I also want the children to become something more than side-show curiosities. Madame Solitaire, you take first try at the girls. See if they have any gift for equitation. We'll all have a try at them and see where their talents lie. Monsieur Roulette, regard the little boy there—Ali Baba. Isn't eight years about the right age for starting klischnigg practice?"

"Contortions? Oui. Before that age, the bones are too easily broken. After that age, the ligaments soon get inelastic."

"Would you undertake to teach the posture-master's art to Ali Baba?"

"I can get him started. Crack the instep. Begin the side practices."

"Hoy!" little Quincy cried faintly, but he was ignored.

Roozeboom was the first back from town next day, driving the new wagon he had bought—another slab-sided, closed van, similar to the tent wagon, and about as dilapidated—and he commandeered Mullenax to help him unload from it his other purchases. There were torch poles wound with turpentine-dipped wicking at one end, and fully forty small coal-oil lanterns, each with a tin reflector attached.

"And what the Jesus is this thing?" Mullenax asked, grunting under the weight, as they manhandled the largest piece of new equipment out of the wagon.

"Is a chandelier," said Roozeboom.

"Hell, I was expecting something fancy, like what Mr. Furfew said he used to own. All glass and bangles."

"Dis I made myself at a carpenter shop. Made it in fast hurry."

"It looks it."

A lot of rough, unpainted two-by-twos were nailed together to make a pyramid of square frames of diminishing size, with an iron hanger ring attached at the pinnacle.

"Komt u, klonkie!" Roozeboom called to the nearest of the Simms triplets. "You fix candles on here, ve vork on odder t'ings." He produced a tremendous box full of cheap tallow candles, and showed her how. He lighted one candle and used it to soften the bottom end of another and another, sticking them upright around the perimeter of the top chandelier frame. "Stick dem close togedder, en as many as you can on dis sqvare. Den move down to next frame, do de same. It ought to hold maybe t'ree hundred candles."

The two men went to distribute the pole torches, and Mullenax discovered that the four upper corners of the lion wagon and the museum wagon were already equipped with sockets for them. Roozeboom stuck other torches in the ground in a line, as guide lights from the street to the front yard, and a couple on either side of the Big Top's front door.

Inside the pavilion, Roozeboom showed Mullenax how to affix the small coal-oil lamps at intervals all the way around the lowest tier of seat planks, their reflectors positioned to aim their light at the ring. While Mullenax was doing that, Roozeboom went to the center pole and undid various hitches from various cleats, to let the boom angle out just a bit from the center pole and dangle its pulley rope. When the Simms girl had finished studding the wooden chandelier with a thicket of candles, the two men carried the big thing into the tent and attached its ring to the rope-fall. Roozeboom struck up the "heeby-weeby" chant while they hauled it up to the boom end, some twenty-five feet above the floor and necessarily a little off-center of the ring.

"Tonight ve let it down, light it, send it up again," said Roozeboom. "Be pretty. You vill see. Now—I also bring from town vagon spokes, hubs, shims, strip iron, axle grease. I go fire some charcoal, get my hammer en anvil, you en me start repair en true all our vagon vheels."

They were sweating at that job when the other troupers returned from town, with a wail and squawl of music. Jules Rouleau was jauntily perched atop one of the wagons and working an accordion, wheezing out "Frère Jacques," not very well but very loudly.

"It's almost a pleasure to be here in Yankee land," Yount declared to one and all. "Charles Town ain't no hub of all Creation, but it's better stocked than the whole of Dixie."

"Yes, indeed," said Florian, who was wearing a new high hat. This was a beaver, much richer-looking than his old silk one. "I decided, by damn, Monsieur Directeur, you're owed a treat, too. Voilà, le chapeau!" He gave it a juggler's twirl along his arm, then flipped it back onto his head.

"Nice, Baas," Roozeboom said dutifully, then anxiously, "You got meat for Maximus?"

"Half a horse, damn near," said Edge. "And for us, some beef. Not dried, not salted, not smoked. Real beef!"

Yount said, "I'm just about herniated from carrying Aunt Phoebe's grocery purchases."

That lady announced, with vast self-satisfaction, "I 'spect I done cleaned out eb'ry market in dat town."

"And Maggie every drapier," said Rouleau. "There's no great tonnage of cloth goods to be found, but what there is, she got it."

"And I see you got your musical squeeze box," Mullenax said to Rouleau. Then he turned to Fitzfarris. "How about the squeezin's I asked for?"

"Yessir, yessir, three jugs full," Fitz sang cheerfully. "In that crate there with all *my* bottles."

Mullenax took out one of the jugs, uncorked it, took a drink, happily smacked his lips and handed the jug around the circle of men. "How come, Fitz, you bought me full jugs and yourself only empty bottles?"

"They won't be empty long. They're for my tonic. And I'd like to ask a favor, Abner. Can I pour just a dab of your whiskey into each bottle? It'll give some authority to the other contents."

"I reckon. Just a dab, mind. What else is going in?"

"Mag says she's got some tincture of ipecac I can have. That's pretty authoritative, too, in its way. And Clover Lee says she's just washed out some red tights, so the wash water is a nice shade of pink. I shouldn't need anything else."

"Jesus. Dirty water and upchuck root and a dash of chain lightning. Is this the gleet-cure tonic you talked about?"

"Oh, no. I've got a new and splendid crocus to peddle." He turned, as Magpie Maggie Hag plucked at his sleeve.

"You come, get ipecac. Get something else I got for you."

"And you girls come try on these shoes I bought for you," said Sarah to the triplets. "Then we'll introduce you to Snowball and Bubbles. See how you like them and they like you."

"And then, Sunday—" said Rouleau, "whichever one of you is Sunday, you and I will go off and learn the accordion together."

So, as everyone else drifted away, Mullenax retrieved his jug and took it to where Roozeboom, resting from his exertions, sat leaning against a wheel of the cage wagon. Mullenax plopped down beside him and proffered the jug.

"Dank u, nee," said Roozeboom. "Not so soon before show time."

"It ain't often I can catch you not workin', Ignatz, and I want to ask something. Everybody else around here is gettin' up new acts. I'd like to broaden my own edjication. Florian said you might be willin' to learn me lion taming."

Roozeboom jerked a thumb over his shoulder. "Dere is a lion. Go tame him. Geluk en gezondheid."

"Oh, crap, man. That old hearth rug is already tamer'n my gran'daddy."

"You t'ink so. Stand up dere close en say hello to hearth rug."

Mullenax got up and put his face close to the cage bars. Maximus immediately showed his yellow teeth and roared menacingly. Mullenax backed away abruptly, sat down again, took a restorative nip and said, "I reckon that signifies he's in a bad mood. How do I know when he's in a good one? Does he purr?"

"Nee. Lions cannot purr. Of all de big cats, only cheetahs en cougars can purr. En *dey* cannot roar. A tiger, now, a tiger makes a noise only tigers can make. A rough sort of chuff-chuff—means good humor, same as purr."

"That's right interestin', Ignatz, but it don't help me much. All we got is a lion, and all he's done is roar."

"To trainer, roar don't mean much. Lion could be cross, hungry, playful, anyt'ing. Some say ven cat lashes tail he is angry. I say vatch—ven cat goes stiff, rigid, *den* he is dangerous. I say also, ven you vorking cat, remember alvays you are looking at five mouths. Vun full of teeth, four full of talons. I tell you, Abner, vunce you get in dat sqvare cage, you don't never be bored."

"Tell me what I *do* do. Ain't there some rules, like ABC's?"

"Dere probably are ninety-nine rules for cat trainers. None of dem can be trusted. But I recite you some of dem, sure. Eerste, Abner, never approach or touch cat timidly, alvays firmly, en never unexpected, never from behind."

"Well, I learned that much on the farm. Touch even a hog unexpectedly, he'll near jump out of his skin."

"Touch so a cat en he peel you out of *your* skin. Remember also, if a cat bite you, he can let go. But if he claw you, he *nee* can let go. His paw is made so by God Himself. Ven cat reaches to grab somet'ing, de tendons extend de talons en *fix* dem in hooked position. So, even if cat grab you by accident, en he is sorry, ven he pulls paw away he vill rake hunks out of you."

"All right. That's rule one to remember. What's second?"

"Tweede, grow yourself another eye."

"Eh?"

"Only vun eye, Abner, means you nee can judge distance too good. You should know alvays exactly how far you are from cat. Also many cats—like people—be right-handed or left-handed. Got to learn each cat, so you know vhich paw to keep eye on. A man vit only vun eye...en so much to look out for..."

"I can't grow another one. I'll just have to take my chances."

"Derde rule: *never* take chances. Vierde rule: stay avay from dat stuff." He indicated Mullenax's jug. "A cat vatches for every veakness, takes qvick advantage."

"Aw, hell, I've always worked better with a little Dutch courage."

Roozeboom said drily, "In Dutch, ve call it drunk courage, meaning don't rely on it. But come, Abner. Stand here vit me." He got up and stood close to the cage bars. "Let Maximus see us togedder. Soon he accept you as friend. Ve go in cage togedder."

Mullenax set down the jug and the two men stood at the cage for a time, Roozeboom occasionally reaching in to scratch the lion's head. After a bit, Mullenax was encouraged to do likewise, and the lion permitted it. After another while, making no sudden moves, the men edged around to the barred door and opened it. Maximus roared, but only in an absentminded way. Roozeboom went inside, talking softly and persuasively, then went close and affectionately ruffled the lion's mane, while Mullenax also sidled inside and prudently stayed at the far end of the cage.

That whole procedure was observed with great interest by one of the Simms triplets, standing a little distance away. In her absurd garb of ragged homespun frock and bright yellow brand-new high-top spring-heel shoes, she looked rather like a pretty duckling. As she watched Roozeboom and Mullenax cautiously enter the cage wagon, she wore a dreamy half-smile, and every time the lion rumbled her whole body trembled.

She in turn was being watched by Sarah, Rouleau and Florian. The latter remarked, "The girl is frightened."

"No, she's enjoying it," said Sarah. "She's a peculiar child. When I plunked her up on Bubbles, bareback, nothing to hold onto but his mane, and let him walk with her around the ring, I'd have thought that would scare her at least a little. But she said, 'This feels good,' and got that same funny smile on her face and that same tremor all over."

Florian shrugged. "Maybe she is a born équestrienne. Which one is that, anyhow?"

"That one's Monday. You'll soon be able to tell them apart. Sunday is the quick and lively and intelligent one. Monday is this dreamy one, kind of strange and contained. And Tuesday, well, she's a plodder. She'll tackle anything, and probably do it dutifully, but without any spark or sparkle."

"That is approximately my summation, too," said Rouleau. "So we have pronounced our expertise upon them; now let us decide how to employ them."

Florian said, "Well, naturally we'll show them as a trio in the sideshow. But in the ring, I think we ought to scatter them somewhat. Make our troupe look more numerous and various."

"Bien," said Rouleau. "Sarah, you and Ignatz take Monday and Tuesday for riders, and I will keep Sunday and Quincy. The boy holds promise as a contortionist, and I can start the girl with the same basic instruction, then bring her along to parterre acrobatics, eventually even to aerial, if we ever get any such rigging."

"I'm agreeable to that," said Florian. "Meanwhile, is the girl's piano playing adaptable to the accordion?"

"We have not got beyond 'Vous dirai-je.' But I think that girl Sunday could learn anything. She told me that she hopes to *be* something in this world, something better than her mammy. I suggested she could start by referring to her 'mother,' and now she does."

"Aunt Phoebe will be flabbergasted," said Sarah.

"I further suggested that speaking good English is a good way to get ahead in the world. So she *axed* me if I would *learn* it to her. I began by drilling her in the pronunciation of 'ask' and the difference between learn and teach. And she grasped them, à l'instant."

"Bless my soul," murmured Florian.

"I will teach that child to read and write, too, while I am teaching Clover Lee. French as well as English. All three of those little mulattoes are handsome chabines, Florian, but in that Sunday girl, you have made a real find."

They were interrupted by the voice of Magpie Maggie Hag, calling, "Olá, Florian, look what I bring you!"

They turned and, when they saw the stranger approaching with her, they put on polite smiles of greeting. Then, as the man came closer, their smiles changed to looks of incredulity.

"Well, I'll be damned," murmured Florian.

"I do declare," breathed Sarah. "Sir John Doe."

"Maggie Magicienne, you've worked a miracle!" said Rouleau.

For the first time since they had known him, Fitzfarris's face was all the same color, and that color all human. Not until he was standing right before them could they discern the cosmetic appliqué.

"However did you do it, Mag?" asked Florian.

"Barossan, you remember that toby clown we had on the show, long time ago, back in Ohio? Billy Kinkade? He leave me some his face paints when he blow the stand. I keep ever since. This color here, Billy the Kink called 'complexion ointment.' Always he put it on first—not zinc-white muck like most joeys—before he start with bright colors. I decide I try, see how it work on Sir John."

"It works wonders!" said Sarah. "Fitz, you're a good-looking gentleman."

"And do you know what this means, Sir John?" Florian crowed. "You can be our patch!"

"Patched is what I am, all right."

"No, no. Our advance man, our advertising agent, our fixer, our patch applier."

"Ah," said Fitzfarris, comprehending. "In my former trade, it was called a soap specialist."

"You'll have to scrub off the good face to appear as our Tattooed Man this afternoon and evening. But our next pitch will be Harper's Ferry, only six miles along the road. Tomorrow morning, you can put on the good face again and ride over there to start the publicity mill to grinding."

From the direction of Charles Town now came the boompty-boom of Hannibal's drum, and Tim Trimm rode onto the lot on the smallest of the new horses, carrying only his paste pot and brush.

"Looks like Tim has got this town all papered," said Florian. "And yonder comes Brutus leading the first of today's crowd. So let us get ready for show time. Monsieur Roulette, would you help Maggie open the red wagon for business?" He turned and called to Mullenax, who was just then descending from the lion's cage, "Barnacle Bill, ahoy!" Mullenax shambled over, looking slightly sweaty but extremely proud of himself. "I'm afraid you'll have to go on doing the Crocodile Man until we've got all our other curiosities costumed for showing." Mullenax stopped looking proud.

"And hey, Abner," said Fitzfarris, "I'll make a celebrity of you and some publicity for us. When I ride over to Harper's Ferry tomorrow, I'll spread the word. The circus is coming, and it'll be grateful if everybody will keep a lookout, because its Crocodile Man has *got loose*. That'll raise some noise and interest, you can bet."

The others regarded Fitz with dazzled admiration, but Mullenax only muttered, "Jesus," and went off to get into his pirate dress for the first half of the program.

The crowd at the afternoon performance was of estimable size, and paid more in currency than in barter—good Yankee coin and paper—and was properly appreciative of the show. Phoebe Simms was not yet accoutred to appear as Madame Alp at intermission, but Florian and Fitzfarris decided that the triplets were worth displaying even in their duckling-looking garb of threadbare old homespun and big new shoes. After Florian introduced Sir John Doe and recounted the woeful tale of how he had come to be a Tattooed Man, Fitz took over:

"And now, ladies and gentlemen, allow me the honor of presenting to you my companion unfortunates in this Congress of Curiosities and Abnormalities. First, cast your wondering eyes upon these three identical White Pygmies, discovered by missionaries traveling through deepest, darkest Africa. No one knows how these white women chanced to be there, among the black and savage pygmies of the Congo. But these are adult and full-grown white women, only disastrously pygmified and negrified—stunted of growth and given a dusky tinge to their skins—by the terrible environment from which the mission fathers rescued them..."

He spouted fictitious facts about every dusty and dubious marvel in the museum wagon, and prattled lies all during the lion's feeding, and made the Crocodile Man sound even worse than he looked—"cast up on the banks of the Amazon, just as you see him now, scrabbling on all fours like any other saurian beast, crusted all over with reptilian scales, except for that hideous gap in his face, where he was struck by the dart from an aborigine's blowgun. And that concludes our display of Wonders and Phenomena. But, gentlemen, when the ladies and children have departed, perhaps you will linger to hear one last announcement *for your ears only*..."

The females obediently moved away, children in tow, and a few dragged their men along with them. But Fitzfarris was left with quite a surround of male adults, variously grinning and looking skeptical.

"Gentlemen," Fitz said, in a just-among-us voice. "When I escaped from Shah Nasir's harem, I brought out one other thing besides this blue disfigurement. I stole the secret formula of the potion which enables that monarch to satisfy the nightly lusts of his sixty-nine young wives and four hundred beautiful concubines. And, using those same rare herbs and spices and extracts, I have compounded a limited supply of that powerful invigorating fluid, to offer to a few of my fellow men the veritable stag and stud virility it can give them."

He reached behind him, under the museum wagon, and dragged forth a crate clinking with half-pint bottles of all shapes, containing a rather vividly pink liquid.

"It is called in Persia the Potentate's Resurrection Tonic, but as you see I take care to put no such label on the bottles, so the compound is not susceptible to pilferage by womanizing scoundrels or—heaven forbid—by small boys, who might be impelled to molest their little girl schoolmates, or even their very schoolmarms."

"Mister... I mean Sir Doe," said a voice, in a fair imitation of the local drawl. The man was slouch-hatted and dressed in overalls, so none of the rubes recognized Jules Rouleau. "A pow'ful pecker bracer like that-there must be almighty scarce and hellaciously expensive. Kin folks like us afford it?"

"Sir, you cannot afford *not* to possess it. True, in the Orient, this manhood-enhancing medicament is dispensed only in tiny phials, and exchanged only for its equal weight in twenty-four-karat gold. However, I will frankly confess that it is only for the motive of avenging myself upon the hated Shah Nasir that I offer you his long-guarded secret *not* for gold, not for ten dollars—nay, not even for five. Take the Potentate's Resurrection Tonic, gentlemen, for only *two* dollars the bot—"

He was almost swept off his feet by the surge of them.

The night show was the first in a long time for all of the Florilegium's veteran troupers, and a novelty for those lately joined out. Edge had been worried that the poor light might adversely affect his shooting, but he found that, though the little reflector lamps and the cheap candles were individually feeble, all together they were ample for everybody's work. Hanging high above the crowd, where the crude wood frame was unnoticeable, the chandelier's constellation of some three hundred candles looked really splendid. They did, however, create a minor nuisance: a steady drizzle of wax pellets, melted up there and congealing on the way down. A drawback to the candles and lamps alike was the horde of moths and other insects they attracted—flickering like bright confetti around the lights, and sizzling and popping and giving off wee puffs of smoke whenever they hit the flames.

"I am particularly pleased to have the footlights," Florian said to Edge. "See how even more beautiful they make Madame Solitaire and Mam'selle Clover Lee appear out there. Set low, shining upward, casting a warm and gentle light, the footlights soften the jawline, enhance the forehead, make mysterious the eyes and merry the mouth. They accentuate the cheekbones and almost vanish the nose. I have never known a woman, Zachary—even the most gorgeous woman—to be entirely satisfied with her nose. Yes, I firmly maintain that Mother Nature never provided any light so flattering to a woman as the man-invented footlights."

In an unbusy interval, Edge stepped outside the pavilion to admire the look of the circus lot by night. Across the darkness of the racecourse grounds, the double row of torches outlined an avenue leading to the cage wagon and the museum wagon—also ruddily illuminated by their corner torches—and to the front door of the Big Top. The peaked canvas that was drab by day, now lighted from within and glowing ivory-white against the night, was a thing so soft-bright and immense that now it might well be called a tabernacle without disappointing anybody who expected a tabernacle to be an imposing edifice. When the performance concluded, and the people dispersed from the light into the darkness, they discussed the show as appreciatively as any daylight audiences had done, but less raucously and more reverently, as if the entertainment had also constituted some sort of devotional service.

The next morning, Fitzfarris, with his cosmetic face applied and with a roll of circus posters tied behind his saddle, rode eastward to Harper's Ferry. Magpie Maggie Hag sat down, with Phoebe Simms helping, to work on the costumes for Madame Alp and the White African Pygmies. Tim and Hannibal got out some newly bought buckets of paint and began to turn the balloon wagon and the newly acquired one from their weathered gray to a cobalt blue. Sarah took Monday and Tuesday to the ring, to give them their first riding lessons, and Yount accompanied them to lend his weight on the rope-fall when it was needed. Rouleau took Quincy and Sunday to start their acrobatic training. Edge, assisted by Clover Lee, began breaking-in the three new horses for a liberty act. When Roozeboom and Mullenax had finished refurbishing all the wagon wheels that needed it, they went again into Maximus's cage to continue the lion-training lessons. Florian circulated among all those arenas of activity, contributing advice, criticism or encouragement as required. There was not an idle person on the lot.

"That's all it takes?" said Clover Lee, with admiration. "Just tap the horse like that, Mr. Zachary?"

"Well, you've got to do a lot of gentling first," said Edge. "Stroke and caress him, get him nicely soothed. Then you strap up his off foreleg, like I just did. Then take the whip and tap him gently just below the knee, on the leg he's standing on. After a little, to stop his being tapped, he goes down to both knees. It looks to the audience like he's taking a bow. Caress him some more, to show him he did the right thing. Then stand off to one side, pull the reins gently toward you, and he'll ease over sideways and lie down. Caress him some more. Pretty soon you've only got to touch him just barely, to make him do either move."

"I've never had to learn much about horses except my own work on top of them." She added, with unconcealed jealousy, "Now that we've got those buffalo gals studying riding, too, I'm going to have to add some more toots and flash to my own act."

"Let me show you another trick I'm teaching them," said Edge. "Look, I take this pin and just barely prick this fellow here at his withers." The horse whickered in surprise and reared up on his hind legs. "Now I prick him again, back here on his crupper." The horse made another surprised noise and kicked up his hoofs behind. "Pretty soon I throw away the pin, just touch him with the whip tassel to make him rear or kick, either one. Or I touch him back and forth, both places, and he imitates a rocking horse."

Clover Lee exclaimed, "That's as pretty as can be!"

"*Ow!*" cried Quincy Simms. Then quickly, penitently, "I'se sorry, Mas' Jules, but dat hurt."

"It's supposed to," said Rouleau. He held one of the boy's bare, black, mauve-bottomed feet in his hands, and was bending the toes under and backward, toward the heel. "You must keep doing this yourself, just as I am showing you, and do it every chance you get. Every time, do it until it hurts so you can hardly stand it. And each time, the instep will bend a little farther and more easily. It is the only way to perfect the pointed toe, and that is essential to any limberjim. Now let's have the other foot."

"Ow-oo!" howled Quincy. "Sorry, Massa."

"Crybaby," Sunday said loftily. "And de man don't be's Massa, he be's Monsieur Jules."

"He *is* Monsieur Jules," said Rouleau through gritted teeth. "I *am* Monsieur Jules. There is no such word as 'be's.'"

"Hoy," said Quincy, bewildered. "Dem ain't bees yonder?" He pointed to the ones buzzing about a nearby clump of clover.

"J'en ai plein le cul," Rouleau muttered to himself. "Why do I let myself get saddled with eight jobs at once?"

"He talkin' Eur'pean at you, Quince," Sunday said brightly. "J'en ai plein le cul. I say dat right, monsieur?"

"Exactly right, chérie. And I expect you will say it often in times to come. Now take off those foolish stiff shoes. We've got to start cracking your instep, too."

He manipulated her fawn-colored, pink-soled feet, and she bravely resisted crying out at the pain. Florian came ambling by, and asked avuncularly, "How go things here?" He started slightly, and Rouleau burst out laughing, when Sunday piped up joyfully:

"J'en ai plein le cul, Monsieur Florian!"

"Before anyt'ing else, Abner," said Roozeboom, "must know *care* of cats. Poor Maximus here, he has learned to eat anyt'ing nearly. But now ve can afford skoff, he vill eat ten or tventy pounds of meat each day. Feed alvays lean meat; fat giffs lion boils. Also, alvays feed meat vit bones in, so cat has to eat slow, not gulp it down en get indigestion. Vun day each veek, no feed at all, let belly empty out. En vun day each month, giff him *live* skoff—chicken, kid, vun of your piglets, maybe."

"Hey, them pigs is my livelihood, Ignatz. At least until I'm a genuine lion tamer. Tell me about the *taming* part."

"Vell..." Roozeboom tugged at his walrus mustache. "Dere is taming...en dere is training. Here in America, most cat men imitate Thomas Batty—show off de tamer's mastery of de animals. In Europe now, many imitate de Hagenbecks —show off de animals' beauty, grace, de routines dey haff learned."

"Well, Maximus ain't no beauty, but he's beautifuller than me. I'll let the folks admire him and his tricks."

"Nee, cat never learns a *trick*—cat don't know trick from man in moon—cat learns a *habit*. En only two t'ings make it possible a man can train a cat to a habit. Vun is dat a man has patience, a cat has greed. Oder is dat a cat nee realize he is stronger dan a man. So you use his greed, your patience, to make in him a habit. Say you lay broomstick across inside his cage. He valks, steps over it, you giff him bit of meat. You raise stick inch each day, he must step higher en higher, you feed his greed each time. Vun day he vill have choice: make little chump over or creep under. You say, 'Springe!'"

"Why not say jump over?"

"Alvays giff command in Cherman. Is tradition, is also good sense. Sometime you buy cat from oder show, you nee have to vunder: does dis vun speak French, Zulu, Chinese? All cats obey Cherman."

"All right. I say 'Springe!' Then what?"

"Ven he chump, you giff bit of meat. Raise broomstick higher each day, he chump higher. In time, he make big high chump every time you say 'Springe!'"

"Wait. Back up. That first time he has to choose—suppose he chooses to creep under the stick?"

"You scold, sound angry, crack whip, giff no meat. Hit him if necessary, not to hurt, only to show you angry. Never do cruelty. Cat is dangerous enough, you nee vant make him enemy besides. If you must, start over from beginning. From broomstick down on floor."

"Jesus, such a simple trick. Does it have to take so long?"

"You de superior human, nee? You have de patience, you must use it. Get cat in a habit, he vill repeat it over en over. Die gewente maak die gewoonte. But if ever *vunce* he refuse, you must insist. He must never get idea he can disobey en get avay vit dat. He must never suspect he stronger dan you, in villpower or in muss-kle. If ever a cat scratch you, don't flinch, don't get angry, don't let cat know it *can* hurt. Klaar?"

"That's kind of a tall order, asking a man not even to flinch."

"Chust get out of cage soon as you can. Voetsak! Is best idea, anyvay, go get carbolic en bandage. Cats are clean animals except in mouth en under claws. Alvays bits of old meat dere, rotting. Small bite or scratch giffs you mortal infection. Also remember, if cat attacks you, de most tender spot on him is his nose. You nee can beat off a cat by main strength, but hit him on nose, he maybe back off."

"Maybe."

"Vatever happens, Abner, try stay on your feet, even if whole cage of cats go crazy. On your feet you taller dan dey are, you still superior. But you fall down, you look to dem like fresh kill of gazelle, laid out to eat. Dey vill eat you."

Mullenax swallowed. "You mean...if a tamer falls down even once in his career, he's a goner?"

Roozeboom shrugged. "Try to fall face down. Ven a cat kills in de vild, first t'ing he eats is entrails. You lie on stomach, he vill paw at you, try roll you over, get at your belly. Maybe dat giffs time for somebody come running en help."

"Maybe," Mullenax said again, looking at old Maximus with a new respect and apprehension. "Well, we're talking about cats already sort of tamed—and me in the cage with 'em. But suppose I was to get a new one, or a whole herd of 'em. How does a man *begin*? What's the *very first* thing you do?"

"You sit for long time at a distance en you vatch."

"Watch what?"

"Vas dey do. Kerst, Abner, you already know dat. You vatched pigs on your farm, you saw dey like climb ladders. You made act of pigs climbing ladders."

"That's it? That's the secret? Find something the animal already knows how to do?"

"Or likes to do, en can do better. Cats all playful. Lions, tigers, same as kitty cats. You vatch dem play, maybe you see vun dat chumps backvard, or vun dat likes to roll. See vas de cat does naturally, encourage him to exaggerate dat, make habit of it. After vhile, you haff cat dat can make big backvard chumps, or roll like barrel. Rubes t'ink you vunderful, make cat do somet'ing *un*natural."

"Well, I'll be damned. Here I was, learning lion taming in my own barnyard, and never suspected it!"

"I cain't let folks see me lak dis!" wailed Monday Simms.

"Laigs all hangin' out!" wailed Tuesday Simms.

"Dey's right, Miz Maggie," grumbled Phoebe Simms. "Bad 'nuff I looks big as dat tent yonder. My gals looks *indecent*."

Magpie Maggie Hag had finished basting together the dresses for Madame Alp and the White Pygmies, and had commanded a try-on. Madame Alp's blouse and skirt, voluminous to begin with, were now so padded inside that they bulged at the buttons and seams, and the skirt needed no hoop or crinoline to make it stand out all around. For contrast, the wardrobe mistress had made the girls' garb slim and sylphlike, mere tights that fitted like paint on their narrow torsos and willowy limbs. She had chosen cloth of a tan color that matched their own —so on these girls they were "flesh-colored"—and decorated them only with bursts of glittery sequins around their chests and loins: red for Monday, yellow for Tuesday and a blue-spangled outfit set aside for Sunday.

"Cain't even bend to sit down!" wailed Tuesday Simms.

"An' *I* cain't hardly stand up," growled Phoebe Simms.

The old gypsy did not argue; she went to fetch Florian. At his approach, the two girls squealed and hid behind their mammoth mother.

"Forgive me for speaking bluntly, Madame Alp," he said. "But I fail to understand the complaints about the children's fleshings. Since I've known the girls, they've been running about in nothing but a shift. At least now their bottoms are—"

"Dem gals is jist 'bout old 'nuff to start havin' der flars. I keeps 'em unkivered on dat account."

"Der flars?" echoed Florian.

"Their flowers," Magpie Maggie Hag translated. "The curse of Eve."

"Oh," said Florian. "Ah. Um. Well, ladies, I'll leave it to Madame Hag to explain to you about—ahem, napkins and clouts. I will say only that circus tights are called tights because they are *deliberately* tight. Those fleshings are not made for sitting, they are made for freedom of movement in your work, and to show off your legs and rumps while you do it."

"Mas' Florian, dey looks *buck nekkid!*"

"Madame Alp, I have seen more countries than you have seen counties, and nowhere in the world have I ever seen anything more beautiful than a beautiful woman naked."

"Ain't *decent*. To show demselfs like dat afore white folks."

"You've seen both Madame Solitaire and Mademoiselle Clover Lee wearing tights. If white women can parade their bodies, your girls have every right to do the same. Anyway, at their age, they don't have enough curves to be ashamed of showing them. By the time they do, they'll show them proudly. Now, let me hear no more complaints. And by the way, allow me to compliment you, Madame Alp. You look alpine, indeed. Maggie, try to have these dresses finished in time for today's intermission."

She did, and made the Simms females wear them, and Fitzfarris was back from his advance run just in time to take his own place in the sideshow, and to do the talking:

"Next, ladies and gentlemen, observe this living mountain of flesh... The market scale registered seven hundred and fifty-five pounds before it went wild and broke... Requires the elephant Brutus to lift her from ground level into her specially stout-sprung traveling wagon... Any lady in the audience may assure herself of Madame Alp's genuine obesity by pinching one of her massive ankles. In the interest of good manners, gentlemen are kindly requested to refrain..."

And the Simms females were so gratified at being made to sound so special that they abandoned their prudish grousing and self-consciousness, and settled back to enjoy celebrity and the crowd's massed eyeballs.

"I was lucky," Fitzfarris told Florian, as the rubes headed back into the Big Top for the rest of the program. "I hit Harper's Ferry just as the newspaper man was preparing to run off this week's issue. Got him to tear the paper apart and put in the warning about the savage Abner Mullenax on the loose. It should be on the streets right about now. Here, I brought one."

The Harper's Ferry *Herald* was printed on the blank side of old and faded sheets of wallpaper. And this edition had elbowed into corners the news of the week to make room for the galvanizing headline CROCODILE CREATURE ESCAPES FROM LOCAL TENT SHOW! and a story obviously set in type directly from Fitz's dictation.

Florian read it, smiling, handed it around for the other gathered troupers to admire, and said, "Sir John, that's the first time we've been newspapered in I can't remember how long. Wilmington got tired of writing and reading about us long before we left there."

"I've also got darkies putting up our posters all over town. And I've engaged a decent lot between Bolivar and Camp Hill. Cost me only a handful of tickets, all told."

"Very good. Listen, everybody. This will be an overnight run. We'll tear down right after tonight's show and hit the road. Everybody who is not driving, try to get some sleep on the way. And Barnacle Bill, stay in your crocodile crust."

"Aa-argh!" cried the creature, despairingly.

"No—better yet—slather on another coating of it before we leave here. Then bunk down on your balloon wagon; Fitz will drive for you. We'll have to pretend you got recaptured somewhere along the way, so we may have to produce a Crocodile Man on demand."

12

THE CIRCUS TRAIN was still half a mile from the Harper's Ferry peninsula, climbing the road that led between Bolivar Heights and the Shenandoah River, when Florian, in the lead, saw what appeared to be the lights of town reflected in the sky, unaccountably bright for this hour just before dawn. He was puzzled. Then he was startled, as the light rushed upon him and became a mob of men carrying torches, lanterns, shotguns, pitchforks and clubs.

"Y'all the ones that lost that crocodile critter?" bellowed a bearded man at the front of the throng. Snowball, terrified, reared in the carriage shafts. "We aim to keep it out of our town, by God!"

The drivers of the vehicles behind all hauled on their reins to keep from colliding with the ones ahead of them, and from inside the wagons could be heard squeals and curses from the troupers rudely awakened by the pileup. The

mob poured down both flanks of the train, thrusting their torches and lanterns
into the drivers' faces, and the horses all shied, snorted and danced in consternation. Fitzfarris had been dozing on the balloon-wagon seat, so he failed to halt
his draft mule and it tried to dodge around the vehicle ahead. That dropped the
balloon wagon's offside wheels into a ditch beside the road, and the whole wagon
tilted. Fitz merely fell sidelong on the seat. But Mullenax, who had been sound
asleep on the canvas wagon cover, awoke to find his blanket unwinding, twirling
him into the road. He lit on all fours—among the legs of a crowd of men and full
in the light of their torches—blinking his one good eye, dazed, but snarling
bestially. Whatever the men had aimed to do, they did not do it. Instead, they
recoiled, milled and cried in a clamor of voices:

"Jesus God!" "*Look!*" "It's loose!" "*Run!*"

And all the men on that side of the road leaped the ditch, flung away most of
their lights and weapons, and took off through the cemetery that abutted the
road there. Having come suddenly awake among a gang of grown men looking
appalled and screaming and running, Mullenax gave a hoarse cry of his own,
scrambled to his feet and took off in the direction they had gone, vaulting the
ditch and doing a broken run among the graveyard stones and mounds. Although still half asleep and totally confused, although considerably impeded by
his Crocodile Man encrustation, he ran creditably. Among the men running in
front of him, a few faces turned back, turned ghastly-looking and bawled,
"Christ!" "It's after us!" "Git a move on!" The retreating mob retreated even
faster, and Mullenax, disinclined to turn to see *what* was after everybody, gave
another hoarse bellow and accelerated his own run. His pumping arms and legs
shed flakes of dried mud and poster paste that joined the other discards of guns,
forks, torches, hats and chews of tobacco.

Those Harper's Ferry men who had been on the other side of the train when
all this commenced, now simply stood there gaping into the darkness in which
half of their company had vanished. So did the circus people. They all stood and
listened to the scattered, distant shrieks and shouts getting ever more distant
down the hill.

"Son of a bitch..." murmured one of the townsmen, in awe. "When they all
hit the river at that speed, it's gonna part like the Red Sea."

"Lookahere!" growled the bearded man who had spoken first of all, again
addressing Florian. "We tried to corral that monster. Now, if'n it kills or eats any of
our fellas, somebody's gonna get strung up. And I don't mean just the monster."

"Not to worry," said Florian, thinking fast. "We thank you for flushing the
creature. We had been seeking it all along the road. We have the one and only
means to subdue it. Abdullah!"

The remaining townsmen gave a start as the elephant suddenly shouldered
into the torchlight.

"Take Brutus and give chase," Florian commanded, pointing riverward.
"Bring back the Crocodile Man. Er—dead or alive," he added, for the crowd's
benefit. As the bull loped off into the graveyard, merrily kicking aside tombstones, Florian pulled a sheaf of tickets from his pocket and began dealing them
like a round of cards. "Nothing to fear now, gentlemen. We'll catch the monster
for you. And if we capture him alive, you can come and see him this afternoon,
safely chained. And meanwhile, congratulate yourselves that you did *not* encounter that savage creature without an elephant to hold him down."

"Christamighty, I'm gettin' more like a crocodile all the time," Mullenax said sullenly, dripping wet mud, river weeds and slime, when Hannibal and the elephant brought him to the lot where the troupe was just starting to set up. "But at least I stopped when I fell off the riverbank. Them other fellers swum right on. They must be rampagin' through the Chesapeake Bay by now."

"Why in the world," said Sarah, giggling, "did you chase those poor men, Abner?"

"Chase em?! Lady, I woke up and seen the whole world runnin' like hell, everybody yellin' 'It's done got a-loose!' I thought they meant the *lion*."

Not surprisingly, with so many tickets given away, the Florilegium had a straw house at the afternoon performance. But so many people came back again and again—the men of the vigilance committee returning to gaze repeatedly at the Crocodile Man and his elephantine subduer, and bringing their families and friends and remotest relatives to show them the monster and recount the horror story of That Night—that the pavilion was filled during every one of the four shows it gave in Harper's Ferry.

After the first day's first performance, while all the other troupers tried to catch up on lost sleep, Florian drove his rockaway downtown. The circus awoke to find that he had brought back to the lot a well-dressed gentleman who was assembling an immense camera on a sturdy tripod, and a good deal of other paraphernalia.

"Mr. Vickery is a photographic artist," Florian introduced him. "He is going to prepare for us some slum to sell during the sideshow. Madame Alp, if you and the Pygmies would get into costume, please..."

So the Curiosities and Abnormalities sat to the artist: Sir John Doe in full-face closeup, then the White Pygmies in trio, then Madame Alp in solitary majesty—sitting for nearly a minute, trying not to move or to squint in the light of the setting sun—while Mr. Vickery twiddled knobs, racked his bellows back and forth, slid plates of glass in and out of the big black box, took the cap off the staring lens and put it on again.

"Whuffo' we do dis, anyhow?" Madame Alp asked Florian.

"To make yourself some extra money. You're not just a waxworks for people to ogle, like the objects in the museum wagon. Folks will appreciate having a memento of you. Mr. Vickery will go back to his studio and print not just one picture of you, but a hundred, on little cards. What are called in Europe cartes-de-visite."

"Cartes-de-visite," Sunday repeated to herself.

"You and the girls and Sir John will offer those cards for sale to the circus patrons at four bits apiece. After my, ahem, considerable investment is recovered, those four bitses will be yours to keep."

Mullenax said, "I'll be damned if I'll leave anybody a reminder of me in crocodile getup."

"No, Barnacle Bill," Florian said genially. "I think you have done your utmost on the Florilegium's behalf. This town will see your last appearance as the creature."

"Well, thank the little Lord Jesus."

The next night, as Captain Hotspur was defying death and tedium in the lion-taming act, Florian said to Fitzfarris:

"During intermission, you might want to speed up the sideshow presentation a little. Then put on your traveling face and ride out straightaway for our next stop. Frederick City is twenty-five miles away, and you'll want to snatch some sleep when you get there. That will leave you most of tomorrow to do your advance work before we pull in tomorrow night."

"All right. I still need Mag's help with the face. I hope she's up to it. Says she's not feeling well tonight."

"Oh, Lord. She must be having one of her oracular spells."

"Is that what it is? She mumbled about something bad coming on. Across the water, whatever that means. Anyhow, I'll ride out right after the intermission. Any special instructions?"

"Same as before: stir up as much anticipation as you can. But, please, nothing in the escaped-monster line this time."

The next day, the circus train crossed the pontoon bridge over the Potomac River into the state of Maryland. The arrangement was that the troupe would find Fitzfarris waiting, when they entered Frederick City that evening, to guide them to the lot in that town. So Florian was surprised when, six or seven miles before they got there, Fitz came cantering up to the rockaway.

"I rode out to meet you," said Fitz, breathing hard, "because maybe Maggie Hag's premonition is coming true. I had darkies pasting our paper all over town this morning. But when I went out walking to admire their work, I found that somebody had been pasting other posters *over* ours. Another circus."

"Well, I'm damned," said Florian. "And tearing paper, eh? It's an old trick. I suppose we ought to be flattered that somebody thinks we're competition. But I'm amazed there's any other show at all working this territory. Whose is it?"

"Some Yankee, I take him to be, from his name," said Fitz, fumbling inside his shirt. "Here's one of his posters."

"Treisman's Titanic," muttered Florian, when he had unfolded it. "He's a flimflammer I never heard of, and I've heard of all that matter. Some parvenu just trying to get a start, I'd guess. He probably heard of the straw crowds we've been pulling and decided he'd make a stab at pilfering a piece of our good fortune. Go up against us, day and date."

He handed the poster down to Sarah and Clover Lee, who, in curiosity, had got out of the carriage. Sarah scanned it and said, "It's all balls, Florian. Here I was hoping we'd meet some old kinker friends, but there are no names at all. Just the acts—Wondrous Wirewalkers, Antic Acrobats..."

"Shows that he hadn't even hired artistes when he printed them up," said Clover Lee scornfully. "A pure piss-ant amateur. A professional would have *invented* some names, at least."

She passed the poster up to Edge, sitting beside Florian, and he read aloud, "TREISMAN'S TITANIC TENT SHOW, *an Omnium Gatherum of Truly Asiatic Splendor...*" then skipped to the bottom of the sheet. "It says they're pitching on the Liberty Turnpike."

"I went to have a look," said Fitzfarris. "Nothing there yet. I've got us a much better situation—right in the middle of town, little park on a creek—but they've got a bigger lot, if that means anything."

"Probably sheer posturing," said Florian. "But you haven't encountered their advance man?"

"No. He must have dashed in just long enough to hire a gang of paperers, then out again."

"Good. Here's some extra cash, Sir John. You go back, take a plentiful batch of posters, hire his crew in addition to your own, tear all his paper and post ours."

When Fitzfarris had cantered off toward town again and the circus train was moving on in his wake, Edge said to Florian, "You don't seem unduly perturbed."

"Oh, this is old stuff to any veteran showman. Why, in my time, I've known two shows to get so stubbornly rivalizing that they'd play a whole *season* day and date, one town after another. Sometimes they'd cut their own prices, sometimes they'd cut each other's tent ropes. And sometimes, if neither show could trump the other, one owner would just buy out the other, entire. Maybe that's what will happen here."

"Come on!" Edge scoffed. "That's crazy. You'd never sell this show. I've seen you work too hard and lovingly—"

"Heavens, no! I meant I might snatch Treisman's away from him."

"That's even crazier. I've learned enough about circusing to know that what money we've got wouldn't buy one elephant."

"Remember," said Florian, smiling, "when in a fix... bluff."

They were pleased, on arrival at Frederick City, to find it posted all over with only Florilegium paper, and they found Fitzfarris waiting for them at the municipal park. They hurried to set up the Big Top, and then Florian carefully brushed the road dust from his new beaver hat and his old frock coat, and started to climb onto the rockaway again.

"Hold on," said Edge. "There's plenty of muscle and weaponry here that you can take with you. And me, I wouldn't miss this."

"I had intended only a scouting expedition first. But you're right. We might as well make it a show of solidarity. Who wants to come?"

"Me and Obie and every other man, right down to Tiny Tim. What else would you expect?"

"We cannot leave the lot and all the ladies unprotected. The hostiles may get the notion of making a similar foray."

"Ignatz and Hannibal are still working on the ring, and Ignatz wants to do some bareback practice with the new girls. He and Hannibal ought to be enough of a garrison. Abner, fetch your balloon wagon. We'll all pile into that, Florian, and follow your carriage."

Fitzfarris rode with Florian, to direct him to the other lot. Night had fallen by the time they got there, but the other circus's crew was still laboring, by torch and lantern light, to put up its tent. They also had only a single elephant to help with the heavy work, but their Big Top was half again as big as the Florilegium's, boasting two center poles. Edge also noted that the men raising it were shouting a variant version of the work chant:

> Heeby, hebby,
> hobby, holey,
> *go*-long!

In no respect except tent size was the Titanic show visibly superior to Florian's, or even much different. Here, as at the Florilegium's lot, a considerable crowd of Frederick City folk had gathered to watch the setting up, and those lot lice appeared to be pressing too close for the comfort of one of this troupe. A man who could have been a grocery-store clerk—bespectacled, harassed-looking—was fluttering his hands at the onlookers to shoo them farther away. Florian dismounted from his carriage, approached that nervous individual—who shooed ineffectually at him, too—and inquired in a voice that carried over the noise of the lot:

"Have I inadvertently arrived at the city dump, sir, or could this possibly be what is advertised as Trashman's Trivial Tent Show?"

The clerk said, in a thin, peevish way, "*Treisman's . . . Titanic!* Are you simply insensitive, sir, or are you deliberately defaming my worthy—?"

"*Yours,* sir?" boomed Florian, with contemptuous astonishment. "Are you the *proprietor* of this squalid establishment?"

The clerk opened and shut his mouth several times, unable to make words, but two other voices squealed girlishly:

"That talk! That style! It could only be Florian!"

"Florian, love! Macushla!"

And two strikingly pretty, orange-haired women burst out of the darkness of the lot to fling themselves upon Florian in affectionate embrace, complete with loud, smacking, wet kisses.

"Florian! It really is himself!"

"It has been so long, kedvesem!"

The clerk Treisman watched, with visible vexation.

Florian, laughing, disentangled himself long enough to say, "Pepper! Paprika! My hot-spice beauties! What a wonderful surprise!"

"But what are you doing here?" demanded the one he had called Paprika. "Ürülék! Surely you do not seek a job on this trash pile."

"No, no. I still have my own show. No trash pile, that."

"You are seeking artistes, then!" cried Paprika.

"Faith, you came looking for *us!*" exclaimed Pepper.

"Well . . ." said Florian.

The clerk's vexed look turned to one of alarm.

"We have so much lamented leaving you, Florian."

"But when you never came north again, we thought you must have perished in the war."

"No, we all survived. Come and meet some old friends—and some new ones." He led them to the balloon wagon, ignoring the clerk's grimaces and feeble protests. Tim Trimm and Jules Rouleau immediately bounded from the wagon, and they and the women rushed together.

"Paprika, you Viszla bitch hound!"

"Jules, you dear old auntie!"

"Brady Russum, ye evil little leprechaun! How awful—ye've not grown at all, at all."

"And Pepper, the Irish washerwoman! Still doing the pole? Which one of you is on top these days?"

"Arrah, how dirty ye make it sound."

Florian introduced the other men—Edge, Yount, Fitzfarris and Mullenax—all of them looking dazzled by the onslaught of beautiful women and the tumult of insults and endearments.

"These carrot-tops, gentlemen, are Pepper and Paprika. In civilian life, Rosalie Brigid Mayo, of the county of the same name, and Cécile Makkai. Or Makkai

Cécile, as she would properly be called in Budapest, where she was oftener called improper names. It was I, myself, gentlemen, who brought them to bless America with their beauty and naughtiness. Pepper and Paprika are the best perch-pole act in the business. I assume, my dears, you do still do the perch."

Paprika, the brown-eyed one, said, "I'm doing the trap, too, since this show has the rigging. And Pep does a hair-hang."

Pepper, the green-eyed one, said, "But sure and what *are* you doing here, Florian? Heading north again?"

"Heading east, mavourneen. From Baltimore, we sail for Europe."

"*Europe!*" they exclaimed together, brown eyes and green eyes shining. Pepper said, "Yez're really going beyant?" And Paprika said, "Európa, igazán?"

"Európa, idenis," said Florian. "I am sorry you are already engaged."

"Engaged here we may be," said Pepper excitedly. "But married here, sure we're not!"

"Make us an offer," said Paprika.

"*Any* offer," said Pepper. "This creature Treisman, he's as tight as a nun's nooky."

"Oh, the hell with haggling," said Paprika. "Come on, Pep. Let's get our gear."

The clerk let out a wail. "Now, wait a minute, you people!" He wrung his hands at Florian. "Mister, you can't do this. Pepper and Paprika are my star attractions."

Pepper gave him a look of disdain. "You said it. The rest of your show is bozzy-makoo. Let's go, Pap." They started off.

The clerk showed enough spirit to snarl spitefully, "You touch that trapeze rigging, I'll have the law on you."

"Izzy, you can take that bar and bugger yourself," said Paprika. "The perch-pole rig is ours. Jules, come and lend a hand."

The clerk turned back to Florian and spat again, "You can't do this, mister. I'll have *you* up in court. First defamation and now... and now... alienation of affections!"

"Sir," said Florian, aloofly examining his fingernails, "I made no slightest enticement."

"This is unethical! This is illegal! This is criminal!"

Rouleau and the girls returned, he and Paprika carrying between them a theatrical trunk and a long apparatus of metal and leather, Pepper carrying an armload of spangled clothing and various other feminine belongings. As they piled the goods into the balloon wagon, the clerk made one last tearful try:

"What's this crook going to pay you? I'll better his top offer!"

Pepper said, "He can pay us anything or nothing, if he's taking us back to Europe. Piss off, Izzy. Let's roll, boys!"

When the rockaway and wagon got back to their own lot, there was another joyous scene of old friends reuniting, for the orange-haired girls knew all the others of Florian's original troupe. "Clover Lee, is it? But you were just a *baby!*" They even stuck their hands fearlessly into the lion cage to fondle "Macska" (as Paprika called him), and embraced as much as they could reach of "big old Peig" (as Pepper called her), while the elephant trumpeted and waggled her trunk in happiness at seeing them again. Then the two girls were introduced to Phoebe Simms, to Quincy, to Sunday and Monday.

"A twin act it is yez are, then?" said Pepper.

"They're not even twins," Florian said smugly. "Wait until you see the rest of the set. Where is Tuesday?"

Hannibal pointed to the Big Top, dimly glowing in the night with only a single work light inside it. "She still wukkin' wid Ignatz in yonder."

"Come, my dears," said Florian. "You haven't greeted your old friend Captain Hotspur."

"Jaj, I knew someone was missing," said Paprika. "The Dutchman."

Almost the entire troupe accompanied them to the pavilion, all chatting and laughing companionably. As they got near, they could hear Snowball's hoofs thudding rhythmically and patiently around the ring. They crowded through the front door, and Pepper brightly gave the traditional call of the Irish come visiting, "God and Mary to all here!"

Then she and the others stopped abruptly where they were, uncertain of what they were seeing. In the flickery light of the one basket torch bracketed on the center pole, the trotting Snowball cast a giant shadow that swung around and around the empty benches and billowing canvas walls. It must have been heavy work for the horse, and it must have been quite a while since he had been given the command to trot. Tuesday was astride him, gripping with her legs as hard as she could, and lying forward on the horse as well, her hands twisted tightly in his mane, holding on with all her strength. Her face was wet with tears, contorted with fatigue and terror and the strain of long crying unheard for help. She still wore the leather belt of the rope-fall about her waist, and the rope still connected her to the boom above, which creaked as it swung around and around the center pole. But the rope was stretched taut by an additional weight upon it.

Midway between Tuesday and the center pole, the rope was kinked about Ignatz Roozeboom's neck. Its tension held him almost upright and dragged him backward around and around the ring, so that his boots flipped and kicked and flopped as if he were playfully running in reverse. The bootheels had worn a fairly deep circular groove in the earth. The torchlight made his bald head glow healthily pink, and his eyes were open and his eyebrowless eyebrows were raised in an expression of mild surprise, but he had been dead for some time. The ex-soldiers were the first to unfreeze. Fitzfarris ran to stop the horse, Edge to free Roozeboom from the rope, Yount to lift Tuesday down, Mullenax to unbuckle her rope-fall girdle. Then the women came running to coddle and mother the girl while she hoarsely sobbed and wept.

"Strangled, did he?" Florian said sadly, watching Edge gently lay the dead man on the ring ground.

"No, sir. He'd be bloated and discolored in the face if he had. And Ignatz could have got himself loose before he choked. His neck is broken. It must have happened damned suddenly."

Tuesday, though terrified and incoherent, her voice weak and croaking, was able to tell them enough to confirm that it had been sudden indeed. She had been standing on Snowball, Captain Hotspur behind her, kneeling on the horse's rump so he could adjust her hips to some particular angle of balance, when one of her feet slipped. She had recovered, but only to feel a violent yank as the rope caught Roozeboom and flicked him away. The abrupt pull had made her drop prone and hold on, and she had been riding that way ever since—for hours, she thought— with the broad leather belt so constricting her that she could only feebly croak and wheeze for help. And the horse, having once been instructed by Roozeboom to trot, would trot on until Doomsday, waiting for Roozeboom's permission to halt.

"Get the child down to the fire," Sarah said. "Give her a hot toddy of Abner's whiskey. She's had a bad time."

"Better make toddy for everybody," said Rouleau. "Her sister looks just as bad."

Clover Lee, Quincy, Sunday and Monday had stayed outside the ring. Three of the youngsters looked on with wide and wondering eyes, but they were standing still. Monday was trembling all over and perceptibly chafing her legs together, and the expression on her face was as fixed and distant as the one Roozeboom now wore.

"Run all the kids out of here," said Florian. "Pity they had to see this. Maggie, would you attend to the laying out?"

There was no answer. Magpie Maggie Hag had not accompanied them to the tent. "Remember?" Sarah whispered to Edge. "She predicted that somebody on the show would have trouble because of a black woman. Tuesday's not black or a woman, but she's Negro and female." They found the gypsy still by the cooking fire, industriously sewing away on some purple garments.

"Mag," said Tim Trimm. "We got some bad news to—"

"Yes," she said, and looked past him to call, "Barnacle Bill!"

"Ma'am?"

"I made smaller the waist, made longer the legs." She held Captain Hotspur's old ring uniform up against him. "I think it fit you now."

Then she went to a wagon, got out some old canvas, and slowly, by herself, a tiny figure darker than the darkness, went to the Big Top.

"She'll clean him and shroud him," said Florian. "We'll bury him as soon as it's light."

"Where?" somebody asked.

"In the ring, of course."

"What?" blurted Yount. "Plant a good man and a good friend the same shameful way we did them dirty bummers? And then we give a show on top of him? Dance on his grave?"

"It is the ring he shaped himself," said Florian. "The ring is where he lived, where he was most alive. Captain Hotspur would wish no different interment. And his soul, if there is such a thing, will enjoy being present at one last show."

Pepper said softly, "There's only now the tellin' of the bees."

"Yes," said Mullenax. "Can I do that, Mr. Florian?"

"You are the one who should."

So Mullenax went off to break the sad news to Maximus the lion, and to keep him company for a while in his bereavement. The others went to comfort the children, and to take a drink with which to toast their late friend, and then went to their beds.

The next morning, while Tim and Hannibal on cornet and drum quietly played and ruffled a dead march, the troupers took turns dropping light spadesful of earth into the hole that had been dug for Ignatz, right under the ring chandelier he had built himself. Then Yount and Rouleau began filling the grave. Phoebe Simms said plaintively, "Ain't y'all even go' say some wuds fum de Scriptures?"

Florian pondered, tugged his little beard and at last said, "Saltavit. Placuit. Mortuus est."

Pepper and Paprika, hearing Latin spoken, sketched the sign of the cross on their breasts. Rouleau, the other Catholic in the company, looked up from his spade work, looking slightly amused, and said, "I don't believe that is from the Scriptures."

Florian shrugged. "I read it somewhere. Epitaph on a Roman circus performer. It serves."

They all waited, and when Florian did not translate, Edge did: "He danced around. He gave pleasure. He is dead."

As show time approached, the park got crowded with carts and wagons and a few carriages, and a lot of people afoot. They were not just lot lice; most were buying or bartering for tickets. Seeing them, Fitzfarris was inspired to take a horse and ride across town. He returned to report with pleasure to Florian that, perhaps because Treisman had lost his two leading artistes—with three different acts among them—the Titanic had folded its tent. "Like the Arabs," Fitz quoted, "and as silently stolen away."

"Well, I'm glad he got to steal *something*," said Florian, laughing. "But a real professional, even after his bluff was called, would have played out the hand, even if he played to empty seats. Proof enough, this fellow is small potatoes. Doomed to failure and oblivion."

"He left heading westward," said Fitz. "I asked around. So we won't be finding him in Cooksville."

"And after Cooksville, Sir John, you'll have only one more advance run to do on this side of the Atlantic. Now, come inside for a treat. You're just in time to see our new artistes perform."

Pepper and Paprika were taking what had been Captain Hotspur's place as the closing act of the program's first half, for Mullenax declared that it would be some while before he would feel confident enough to perform in the lion cage in public. Since the Florilegium possessed no apparatus either for Paprika to do her trapeze swinging or for Pepper to do her hair-hanging, the two were doing only their perch-pole performance. That pole was a twenty-foot metal column, rather dented and discolored, which splayed at the bottom into a padded leather yoke, and at the top end bristled with vestigial metal spokes and leather loops. The two girls wore only fleshings splashed with sequins—Paprika's as orange as her hair, Pepper's as green as her eyes—and the sequins were distributed in patterns to emphasize the girls' curvaceous bodies, though those needed no enhancement.

When Edge had whistled the girls into the ring and Florian had grandiloquently introduced them, the two men helped Pepper hoist the yoke to her shoulders and balance the pole at the vertical. Then top-mounter Paprika climbed up her under-stander's body and on up the twenty feet of the pole. While Pepper kept her gaze aloft and her feet ever shifting, her body ever swaying, to maintain the balance, Paprika stood unsupported on the metal nubs at the pole's tip, then did handstands on them, then put one hand in a leather loop, one foot against the pole, and struck various graceful poses. Then she put a foot in the loop, let herself fall until one hand gripped the pole, and did the same poses upside down. Then she scurried to the top again, stood on her hands again and did a series of upside-down contortions, backbends, center splits, when she spread her legs horizontally from side to side, and stride splits, when she spread them fore and aft.

"Well, here's where I lose you to a klischnigg," said Sarah to Edge, as they watched together. "Not only can they both twist like reptiles, they're at least twelve or fifteen years younger than I am."

"I don't think you have to worry," said Edge, with good humor. "Pepper was giving little Sunday some acrobatic lessons at noontime, and I heard her warn her, 'Never fall in love. It ruins your sense of balance.' I have a suspicion those girls are not much interested in men."

"You suspicioned right. They're toms. Fricatrices. They've never fancied anybody but one another. Still, some men find a tom a challenge." Sarah sighed. "God, but men are lucky. Women have to get old, and men never even grow up at all."

"I'm not men, I'm me," said Edge. He took his eyes off the ring long enough to give her an affectionate glance. "And you sure are not any Maggie Hag yet, by a long shot." Then he had to run into the ring, for Paprika had slithered down the pole and Pepper had nonchalantly let it fall clattering to the ground. Edge and Florian took a hand of each girl and all four threw up their arms in the signal for applause.

When Florian began to talk the crowd out of the stands for the sideshow, Obie Yount found himself in close proximity to Clover Lee, and both of them being rudely jostled by two ladies from the audience. The women were portentously shaking their heads and saying in exceedingly refined voices:

"Shameful!"

"Yes, disgusting!"

Clover Lee threw a conspiratorial grin at Yount and stayed close to the women as they bustled out of the tent, so Yount did likewise. The ladies continued exchanging what were patently opinions of the act just concluded.

"Unfit for Christians to see!"

"So absolutely true!"

Yount whispered to Clover Lee, "What ails these old sows? That was a purely clean act, and them girls is purely beauti—"

"Ssh!" said Clover Lee, and kept close to the critics.

"Probably Eye-talian, those trollops."

"I wager you're right. No Christian lady would let herself be seen in that heathenish condition."

"Two grown women—*unshaved under the arms!*"

Clover Lee, grinning more gleefully than ever, lagged back now, and let the ladies go on unattended. Yount eyed them and her with puzzlement, scratched his cue-ball head and said:

"Well, I never. Nobody'd give a damn if *them* two females sprouted *quills,* but they have the gall to criticize girls as gingham-pretty as Pepper and Paprika. Still, you seemed mighty interested, mam'selle. You reckon you learned something?"

"I don't know," Clover Lee said, giggling. "But if good Christian women disapprove of something, it's got to be pleasurable in some way."

And she ran off to change for the second half of the program.

The loss of Ignatz Roozeboom had deprived the show not only of the lion act, for a while at least, but also of Captain Hotspur's participation in the riding acts. Edge volunteered to replace him at least to the extent of taking over the voltige turn.

Since he and Thunder had often, in garrison times past, engaged in the cavalry's sporting contests of gander pulling, he was even better at the voltige than Roozeboom had been. With Thunder going at full gallop, Edge would bound off and onto the horse, swing himself under its belly and up to the saddle again, lean down at full speed to snatch things from the ground, fall off the horse's rump, seize Thunder's flying tail, let himself be dragged bodily around the ring, scramble to his feet at a pell-mell run and vault onto the horse again. In taking on that act, he took on yet another new identity. Florian insisted on his doing that turn as "Buckskin Billy, Dauntless Reinsman of the Plains," and Magpie Maggie Hag hurriedly sewed together a new costume of shirt and trousers that consisted predominantly of fringe.

Meanwhile, Roozeboom was also much missed during the teardown and setup of the Big Top, and on the road as well. The Florilegium now had more rolling stock than it had adult males for drivers, because Fitzfarris was always out ahead of the show and Hannibal, at the rear of it, had to guide both Peggy and the horse drawing the bull-pup cannon. Pepper and Paprika and Madame Alp all disclaimed any ability or desire to handle horses' reins.

So, when the circus rolled into Baltimore, late on a gray and rainy afternoon, Florian was still up front on the rockaway, but inside it the two redheads rode in leisurely comfort. Sarah Coverley was farther back in the train—and out in the wet—driving the balloon wagon, with Clover Lee on the seat beside her. Rouleau drove the tent wagon, and Edge drove the new box van with the whole Simms family inside. Mullenax, with Magpie Maggie Hag sitting beside him, drove Maximus's cage wagon—now shuttered from the public gaze by wooden panels fitted around it, and fancied up with the eye-catchingly massive brake lever that Roozeboom had fashioned.

Baltimore was the biggest city some of the troupers had ever been in, and the only real city Mullenax and the Simmses had ever seen. So there was much rubbernecking and peering out through wagon doors, as those troupers gaped more avidly than did the few people on the wet streets watching them roll in. Not that Baltimore was much to look at, or to smell either. The circus train came into town along the Old Liberty Road and, as soon as that road became a paved street with brick houses and other edifices along both sides, it also became a running open sewer, and the reek of it became first offensive, then revolting and soon nauseating.

"Jesus, it's worse'n I ever smelled around pigs," Mullenax said, his voice thick, because he was holding his nose.

"Some must come from the steam mills," said Magpie Maggie Hag, drawing her cloak's hood close around her face.

"Uh huh," grunted Mullenax. He looked at the profusion of immense and ornate signs, and mused, "I wonder how you bottle steam. Or print on it."

They were passing huge brick buildings that proudly advertised themselves as Steam Bottling Houses, Steam Printers, Steam Laundries and Steam Boiler Works, not to mention the Sulphur Match Works, Tanneries, Lard Refineries and Guano & Bone Dust Works that did not claim to have anything to do with steam. But it was evident to any nose that much of the prevailing stench came from the residential houses' backyard "earth closets," leaking the essence of their contents into the drainless streets.

Only one person in the circus train found something immediately to admire about Baltimore. Jules Rouleau stood up on the tent wagon's driving seat to call it to everyone else's attention.

"Voilà! Look! There is a thing we never saw in Dixie. Not even New Orleans has it. Gaslight!" The other troupers looked, without great interest. "Gas! We can send up the balloon!"

It was true: the central portion of Baltimore sported on every corner a modern gas lamp standard, its glowing globe casting a lovely peach-tinted white radiance on the grimy factory walls, on the sickly streetside trees, on the slimed and scummy cobblestones—and on Florilegium posters put up by advance man Fitzfarris. Many of those were beginning to peel or melt in the rain, so Florian hurried the train along through the dusk, because the posters marked the route to the circus's allotted setting-up place. The gaslight, for all its pearly beauty, did nothing to mitigate the other gases in the local atmosphere. And the farther Florian followed the route into town, the less he was inclined to do so, because the stink got more and more noxious. Finally, at Pratt Street, where the train crossed a bridge over "Jones Falls"—in actuality, a putrescently burping and belching sump of black water—Florian decided that downtown Baltimore was simply intolerable. As soon as he could find an alley opening, he swung Snowball left into it, then left again, to lead the train back the way he had brought it, some two and a half miles, up Eutaw Street to the cleaner heights of Druid Hill Park. When he stopped his rockaway on a wet greensward there, he addressed the company.

"I don't know what place the city fathers in their wisdom picked for our pitch. But I'll be damned if I'll set up any closer to that terrible town than right here, even if I have to pay double fees. We've got breathing room here, and yonder's a pond for fresh water. Will you boss the setup, Colonel Ramrod, while I follow the posters again and see if I can find Sir John? If he's still downtown, he'll probably be in some saloon getting drunk to numb his olfactory sense. Anyway, he and I will see about getting a permit to pitch here."

"Suppose the city fathers *won't* permit it," said Edge.

"This is a right swanky park," said Yount. "Bandstands and all."

"Possession is nine points of the law," Florian said. "You get that pavilion up and it's pretty possessive-looking."

Setting up in the rain was no easy job, since the canvas got wet and ponder-ously heavy as soon as it was out of the tent wagon, and the wet ropes were limp and difficult to put through grommets, and the tent stakes were so easily ham-mered into the wet ground that their holding power was suspect. But the men made sure that the seam-binding ropes were reeved only loosely, and the guy ropes left slightly slack. So the tent, when it was finally up, looked despondently saggy and wrinkled. But, if and when the rain ceased, the canvas and ropes would dry and tighten and the pavilion would assume its proper perky shape all on its own. Edge gave Hannibal the responsibility of staying awake all night, in case the rain stopped before morning, to keep watch that the shrinking ropes did not yank the surround of stakes right out of the ground.

The work was done and Phoebe Simms was cooking supper when Florian got back. He did have Fitzfarris in tow, and Fitz *was* perceptibly drunk, in a mild state of maudlin euphoria.

"I got a lot t' learn 'bout bein' advance and patch," he declared, with hiccups. "Here I come t' town and argue and wheedle and spread palm oil around, and ever'body in City Hall just sits dead as flies on a sheet of tanglefoot. The best I c'n get 'em to give me is the back lot of Weaver's Coffin Manufactory. *Wouldn't* that be a dandy place to set a circus! But this fella Florian comes along an' hunts up the city clerk an' prattles at him in sauerkraut lingo, an' by God we get a permit for this fine park."

"No great art to it," Florian said modestly. "I merely happen to be aware that every Baltimorean of quality or position is of German descent. You talk to a man in his preferred language, and you have a better chance of talking him into or out of almost anything. I did, in fact, get us more than this pitch. Monsieur Roulette, écoutez. The city folk are all buzzing about the surrender of the very last Confederate Army, down in your Louisiana, a day or three ago. The word just came in. So I persuaded the authorities that the city ought to celebrate, and that a fitting celebrate might include—"

"Une ascension d'aérostat!" Rouleau cried.

"That very thing. There'll be some men from the city gas works up here tomorrow to see about inflating the thing. Now, you must give them the impression that *you* know what's to be done."

"Trust me, I shall act l'aéronaute comme il faut. In return, I give you a gift. My protégée Sunday has at last mastered the playing of 'Vous dirai-je, maman' on the accordion, and her sisters and brother have learned the English words to sing along."

"Splendid," said Florian. "The perfect accompaniment to the balloon ascension. The Happy Hottentots caroling 'Twinkle, Twinkle, Little Star' as you mount into the blue empyrean."

"Is this really a good idea?" asked Edge. "The *Saratoga* blew away from its keepers once before, and they *did* know what they were doing. Jules, wouldn't it be better if you sort of practiced the first time or two in secret, not in public?"

Rouleau wagged a finger at him. "Ah, you are being reasonable, ami, not circus. I quote at you Pascal. 'Le coeur a ses raisons que—"

"I know the line, and it's a winsome one. But damn it"—he appealed to Florian—"you made me the equestrian director, responsible for the troupe's safety. I say this is not safe."

"I'd be inclined to agree," said Florian, "except...tell me this. Just how *would* one practice in secret with an object nearly as big as Baltimore's landmark Shot Tower downtown?"

"Well..."

"And Monsieur Roulette cannot simply slip the balloon's snout over a street lamp and twiddle the gas cock. He'll need the assistance of the technicists."

"Well..."

"Zachary, if I am to be exploded," said Rouleau, "or whisked off the planet forevermore, do you suppose I wish to do that *in secret*? Mais non, I want a great crowd and loud cheers as I go."

"Well..." said Edge yet again, and shrugged in resignation. "Abner, fetch a jug. Let's get an early start on the cheers."

13

THE BIG TOP did not collapse during the night, and the morning brought sunshine that would soon put it in proper shape. Edge delegated Yount to keep an eye on it, and he climbed into the rockaway to go downtown with Florian and Fitzfarris. They found the smell of the city slightly less offensive by daylight—or maybe, they speculated, some of the stink had run off with the rainwater. Fitz got out at the offices of the Baltimore *Sun*, to promote the newspapering of the circus's presence and the imminent balloon ascension, and also to order the job printing of special posters to proclaim that event. Right around the next corner of the street, Florian espied the offices of the Baltimore & Bremen Shipping Line. He and Edge went in, but Edge merely stood about while Florian conversed in German with the agent. He came away from the man's desk looking rather cast down.

"Their ships do go to Bremen, and to Southampton on the way," he told Edge, as they left the office. "But there's none due in port here in the near future, and Herr Knebel did not thrill at the prospect of transporting a circus aboard a passenger liner. He recommended that we apply to a freighting company called Mayer, Carroll—'out on the Point,' wherever that might be."

They drove to the waterfront and made inquiries. Baltimore's inner harbor, they learned, was reserved to the shallow-draft bay and coastal packets. To find the docks of the larger, oceangoing vessels they had to drive an extremely long way around the basin and out to Locust Point on the other side of the harbor. The wharf area, in any other seaport, would have been the foulest-smelling part of it. But Baltimore's waterfront smelled sweeter than its toniest residential districts, because here were all the city's coffee-packing plants, exuding the rich aroma of Brazilian coffee beans being roasted. When Florian and Edge finally found a dingy dockside warehouse bearing the sign "Mayer, Carroll" over its office door, they were somewhat nonplussed to see that the company described itself on the same sign as "Shippers of Cumberland Coal to All Foreign and Domestic Ports."

"I think we've been misdirected," said Edge. "Or do the words circus and coal sound alike in German?"

"Zirkus und Kohle," muttered Florian. "Well, as long as we're here..." He got down from the carriage seat, and Edge followed.

Florian and the gentleman in charge of the office conversed in German while Edge stood about some more. But this time the colloquy went on for quite a while, and Florian looked pleased by what he had heard. He waited until he and Edge were outside again before exclaiming happily, "All'Italia!"

"To Italy?"

"Did you know that the United States' chief export to that new nation is coal? Neither did I. But Herr Mayer has a shipment of it leaving for Livorno in Tuscany three days from now. Perhaps you have heard of Livorno—called Leghorn in English. And what better place for us to go than Italy? It was the home of Saint Vitus, and he is the patron saint of traveling showmen. Also, it will be autumn by the time we get there. The climate will be much more clement on the Mediterranean than up around the North Sea. Furthermore, from Livorno we will have only to go straight inland to reach Firenze—Florence, the capital of that just recently united kingdom."

"But... Florian... we're going on a *coal barge?*"

"Good heavens, no. On a modern steam collier. So very modern that it is driven by a screw propeller, not paddlewheels. Let us stroll around the warehouse to the waterside and have a look at it. The merchant ship *Pflichttreu*, how does that sound?"

"If you can pronounce it, I can ride it."

"A very good name. It means loyalty, dutifulness. And I should think that a fully laden collier will give us a nice, stable ride."

They came around to the loading dock, and Edge said, "Is that it? I thought you said it was new."

"Well... modern, not necessarily new."

A ship that carried coal all the time was bound to get dirty and battered, Edge charitably supposed. But he was glad to see that it had masts and rigging for sail, in case its newfangled screw propeller was as beat up as the rest of it. And it had loading derricks fore and aft that Edge hoped would serve to lift Peggy the elephant and the heavy circus wagons aboard, because the only gangplank the ship had was an ordinary wooden ladder leaning from the dock to the deck. Edge asked wryly:

"Tell me, what is this elegant pleasure cruise going to cost?"

"Ahem. Herr Mayer and I have not yet fully discussed that aspect of the matter. It will first be necessary to present ourselves to the *Pflichttreu's* Kapitän Schilz, and persuade him to consent to take us along as deck cargo and passengers. After all, a circus is not his customary freight."

They went on board and Florian inquired. A uniformed personage appeared and, after some converse in German, Florian said in English, "Colonel Edge, recently of the military—Captain Schilz of the good ship *Pflichttreu.*"

"Nein. Master I am," the man said gruffly, as he and Edge shook hands. "Kapitän a courtesy title only is, except in navy." His breath smelled faintly of schnaps. "You gentlemen are pill-grumps?"

Florian said, "Er—pilgrims? Pilgerin? No, captain, I am the proprietor and Colonel Edge is the director of a traveling circus. Wir möchten einen Seereise nach—"

"Zirkus? Nein, nein!" Schilz interrupted, violently waving his arms. In deference to Edge, he explained in English, "Animals all over my deck they shit!"

Edge started to remark that, having seen the *Pflichttreu,* he doubted that its deck could be further defiled by mere shit. But Florian simply stuck out his hand to shake the captain's in apparent farewell, murmuring, "A pity. You leave a brother in the craft beached on the sea sands."

Captain Schilz seemed surprised by the handshake and the remark. His rejoinder was still mostly in English: "At low-water mark, Bruder?"

"Or a cable's length from the shore. Es ist jammerschade. And all our beautiful women stranded as well."

"Beautiful women?" the captain repeated, so loudly appreciative that every deckhand in earshot looked up alertly.

"As easy as that," said Florian with satisfaction, as he and Edge went again toward the company office.

"A good thing the captain is susceptible to beautiful women," Edge observed.

"Oh, there was a little more to it than that," said Florian. "Now I hope we can settle the price as felicitously. Here, Zachary, here is a thousand dollars in paper. Slip it down inside your boot. Grouch bag, so to speak. Then I can honestly turn out my pockets in front of Herr Mayer and tell him, 'This is all I have.'"

He almost had to do that, too. Herr Mayer first commanded him to write a list of every person, creature, vehicle and piece of equipment he intended to take on board. Then the agent took the manifest and began writing a price for the fare alongside each separate item—steep prices.

"Mein Herr!" Florian protested. "Six of the passengers are mere children. Surely they should go at half fare. And only fourteen of the animals are alive— the lion, the elephant, eight horses, three small pigs and one mule. All those others listed there are dead."

"You transport dead animals?" said Herr Mayer, with distaste. "The customs house will never allow them to pass."

Florian explained that they were stuffed museum pieces. While Herr Mayer recalculated, looking annoyed, Edge said, sotto voce, "Even if you count Clover Lee a child, I can only count five children."

"We'll put Tim in short pants. Hush."

The fare still added up to more than Florian could have paid without dipping into Edge's boot. But finally, after much agonizing, he decided not to take along Mullenax's mule and Yount's Yankee cannon, and got Herr Mayer's price down to where he *could* pay it by handing over practically every dollar in his pockets. He might have gone on haggling, or deciding to leave other items behind, but it was past noon now and coming up toward show time. They drove at a trot inland from the harbor, Florian grumbling all the way.

"Damn it, I should have *hired* that man instead of paying him. He's better at fortune-telling than Maggie Hag is. He certainly estimated my fortune almost to the pfennig. That thousand in your boot, Zachary, is going to be considerably diminished when we buy feed for the animals for the voyage. So, unless we turn a handsome profit here in Baltimore—"

"Great day in the morning!" Edge interrupted. "Look at that!"

Even though Edge had seen an inflated observation balloon before, the sight was still imposing. Indeed, he and Florian could see the *Saratoga*'s bright vermilion and white rounded top and the big black letters of its name, towering above the bulge of Druid Hill, even before they could see the treetops of the park it stood in. As they breasted the hill, they could see that the balloon was securely tethered by four ropes pegged about the ground where its basket rested. The whole circus company and a gathered crowd of Baltimoreans stood about, admiring it. The smooth, silken, pear-shaped object, clasped in its upper net of linen cord, straining against its web of cords that converged on the wooden hoop below the bag, stood almost exactly twice as tall as the Big Top's peak. The two immense cloth constructions, one bulking lengthwise on the park's green, the other upright against the sky's blue, made a fine sight.

"Une beauté accomplie. No problems at all," said Jules Rouleau, when Florian and Edge found him in the crowd. "These two gentlemen have had prior experience." He indicated the men, wearing prideful smiles and overalls stenciled BALTIMORE GAS & COKE. "They say our *Saratoga* is the most gorgeous aérostat ever seen here, but she is not the first. Anyway, that bandstand yonder is fitted with gas lights. So the messieurs had only to arrange a long gum hose from there to the appendix of the bag, as we aéronautes call it."

The younger of the gas-company men volunteered, "This-here coal gas ain't the best for ballooning with. Don't have the lift."

"Really?" said Florian. "I'd say the thing looks absolutely eager to leap up in the air."

"Aye, she'll go up," said the older of the two. "And she'll take one man, but no more. And even with no ballast she'll be sluggish. What ye really want is hydrogen gas. With that in the bag, she'll lift three men. But for hydrogen ye'll need a generator."

"Also, y'all ought to take care of that beauty," said the other. "The outside varnish is weathered considerable, and the inside needs a new coat of neat's-foot oil. We took it on ourselves to put a new seal around the clack valve."

"Ah," said Florian distantly.

Rouleau explained, "So the gas will not leak until I am ready to let it out. And the messieurs were also kind enough to give me a tin of the sealing cement, left here by a previous balloonist."

"Very kind, indeed," said Florian, but then his face fell as the older man handed him a piece of paper, and said:

"Twenty-five thousand cubic feet, in round figgers. Naturally ye get a bulk rate, so I've rounded off the bill to just seventy-five dollars and no cents."

Florian said, in a strangled voice, "I understood that we were doing this performance to benefit a citywide celebration."

"All I know is that ye've got a cubic footage of gas that would light all of Baltimore for two or three nights. If ye care to argue with City Hall for your money, go ahead. But they'd likely demand to see proof of ownership of yon balloon, and the balloonist's qualifications, and surety money against any damage ye might cause..."

Florian made a wry face, but gave the nod to Edge to dig down in his boot. Edge brought out the wad of bills and peeled off the demanded payment. When the men had departed, Florian said reprovingly to Rouleau, "This is an expensive indulgence. That money would have bought a lot of hay and oats and horsemeat."

"I had no idea, mon vieux..."

Another wagon came up the hill just then, attracted by the looming balloon, and among the family tumbling out of it came Fitzfarris, who had hitched a ride from downtown. He was carrying a large round wooden object under one arm. As he approached, Florian was saying, "...Just hope the ascension brings enough extra people and extra money to offset the expense..."

"It will, it will!" Fitzfarris cried gaily. To Rouleau he said, "Be sure to make all your preparations slow and careful and long drawn out, Jules, old boy. Give the rubes plenty of time to get fidgety, so they'll turn for diversion to my interim entertainment."

He displayed the thing he was carrying. It was like a broad, shallow drum made of plain pine, a couple of feet across but only a few inches deep. The under surface of it was solid, the upper was bored with a circle of twenty-one holes, an inch in diameter, near its perimeter. In the shallow sidewall of the thing was cut a single opening, big enough for Fitz to get his hand inside.

"I didn't have time to construct any proper wheel of chance, so I simply had a carpenter knock together this mouse game for me. No time either to get it painted nice and gaudy, but it'll serve."

The others asked what the hell was a mouse game, but Fitzfarris had raised his voice to the crowd: "I'll give two bits to the first kid that finds me a field mouse!" All the children, black and white, scattered and scampered throughout the park, bent over, looking for burrows or nests. To the bewildered Florian, Fitz said, "May I borrow that stump of pencil you always carry?"

Florian gave it to him and Fitzfarris numbered each of the holes in the drum's upper face: 0 to 20. A small Negro boy ran up, holding in his cupped hands a tiny brown and white mouse. Fitzfarris took it, thanked the boy, said briskly to Florian, "Company expense. Pay the lad, would you, boss?" and dashed away to the prop wagon, to wipe off his cosmetic face and be ready for his rôle of Tattooed Man.

Both the afternoon and evening shows that day were only sparsely attended, obviously because most of the prospective patrons were waiting for the next day's added free treat of the balloon ascension. But, during each program's intermission, after the rubes had gaped their fill of the Tattooed Man, the Three White African Pygmies, the Museum of Zoölogical Wonders and Madame Alp—and even purchased a few of the cartes-de-visite—Sir John introduced his mouse game.

"Bet a dime, folks, win *two dollars!* The most honest guessing game ever devised. Bet a dollar, win *twenty* of 'em! It's a game of human intuition versus animal instinct. Simply pick the hole that little Mortimer the Mouse will run to."

He had set his new wooden apparatus on the circus's ubiquitous washtub. The game consisted merely of his putting the wee mouse in the middle of the board, when it instantly scurried for one of the holes around it and ducked into the dark interior. There Fitz's hand was waiting to snatch it, bring it out and set it on the board again.

A cluster of rubes quickly gathered, most of them male, and, after they had amusedly watched the proceedings for a minute, they began to dig in their pockets and plunk down dimes—even a few larger coins and one or two dollar bills—alongside one or another of the numbered holes. The mouse dutifully ran for a hole every time it was exposed to public gaze, and Fitzfarris dutifully paid off every winner, with a bellowed felicitation: *"Two dollars* to this clever fellow! Good going, sir! A return of *two thousand* percent on your investment!"

The noise brought others crowding around, so they had to reach over and under the tangle of arms to place their bets. Eventually, every time the mouse ran, almost every hole on the board bore a stake, and there was a winner almost every time—adding his shout of *"whoopee!"* to Fitzfarris's own congratulatory clamor: "Mind over mammal! Absolutely the fairest game you'll ever play. And there's *another* winner! Don't crowd, gentlemen. Give the ladies a chance at instant fortune, too!" The mouse never seemed to tire, and the game went briskly, the only interruptions consisting of Fitz's occasionally wiping the whole board with a damp rag. Even with the day's scant attendance, Fitzfarris kept the intermission running overlong, until the gamblers were either satisfied with their winnings or unable to go on losing.

"Seventy-five dollars and forty cents clear for the day," Fitz said happily, at the close of the evening's intermission.

"I'll be damned," Edge said admiringly. "That pays for the balloon gas, right there."

"If we get a straw crowd for the balloon tomorrow," said Fitz, "the game ought to fetch eight or ten times that much, easy."

"A marvel," said Florian. "How do you gaff it, Sir John?"

"Gaff it, sir?" Fitzfarris looked inexpressibly wounded.

"Well, one simply assumes... a midway game of chance... like the venerable shell-and-pea game..."

Fitz firmly shook his head. "Anybody can spot a rigged game. It doesn't take detective ability. Watch any confidence man doing the shell-and-pea. He's always got one long fingernail to hide the pea under. But my mouse game doesn't have to be rigged. Twenty-one holes to bet on, and I *say* I pay odds of twenty to one. Suppose twenty-one rubes bet a dime apiece. I scoop in all the dimes and give the winner two dollar bills. He's actually getting only nineteen dimes profit and I'm richer by one. The balance can seesaw, of course, depending on who bets how much, and where, but that extra hole—number zero—always gives the edge to the house, as we say in the profession."

"Yes, of course, I see," said Florian. "I had thought . . . that business of wiping with the rag . . . perhaps some secret preparation . . ."

"Only ammonia water. If a mouse runs to the same hole a couple of times, he might afterwards follow his own scent and go there repeatedly. Some rubes can be sharp enough to notice that, and bet on it. So I wipe the board clean after every few plays. That's to keep *Mortimer* honest."

Next day, the first thing Rouleau did was to hurry to his beloved *Saratoga*. There he opened the brass fixture at the very end of what he called the balloon's appendix. A quite copious stream of water gurgled forth, and he carefully directed it outside the basket.

"Instructions from the technicists," he explained to those watching. "The coal gas has a content of moisture, and it condenses during the cool of the night. No sense taking up more weight than I have to."

"Maybe no sense in doing anything today, kedvesem," suggested Paprika. "Maggie is staying huddled in her blankets this morning."

"Oh, damnation," said Edge. "Has she foreseen some disaster in the ascension?"

Paprika gave an expressive Hungarian shrug. "Of the balloon she says nothing. Only something about a wheel."

"Aha!" said Rouleau, relieved. "Go frighten Foursquare Fitz, then. He is the only one working with a gimmix like a wheel." He patted his wicker gondola. "I, Jules Fontaine Rouleau, am henceforth liberated from anything as earthbound as a wheel."

Paprika shrugged again and went on talking as she walked with Obie Yount to the backyard, where Phoebe was cooking breakfast. "Jules mentions earthbound. Ó jaj, I have known artistes of the most hair-raising acts to survive all manner of risks, and then get crippled or killed in a trifling and earthbound sort of accident."

"Such as what?" asked Yount, as they sat down on the ground to wait to be served. He was seated between Paprika and Pepper, and was eminently pleased to be so.

"In Paris, there was a girl aerialist who made herself notorious and acclaimed. She strung a cable between the towers of Notre Dame and danced upon it. She was famous, but the devout were scandalized, and they said Our Lady would punish her for the sacrilege. A week later, she fell off a bateau-mouche and drowned in the Seine."

"And remember, macushla?" said Pepper. "That joey in Warsaw what did the humpsty-bumpsty?" She explained to Yount, "That's a clown what does knockabout falls and sprawls. He was forever stepping in a bucket of water and sloshing hither and yon. Never broke a bone, did he, but one day he scraped his shin on the bucket. The dye from his stocking infected the scratch and, bedad, his leg had to be sawed off." She crossed herself and murmured, "Safe be my sign."

"Say, ladies," said Yount. "Since we've got to leave my bull-pup behind, I've been trying to invent Quakemaker tricks that don't need a cannon. I wondered —how about me pyramiding you two on my shoulders?"

"Not much flair to that," said Paprika. "How about we stand on your shoulders and the Simms girls stand on ours? We can easily hold them if you can hold us all."

"Nothing to it," said Yount, expanding his barrel chest to hogshead dimensions.

"It's fine with me," said Edge, when Yount sought him out and proposed the new bit of ring business. Then he gave Yount one of his ugly smiles and said good-humoredly, "I've known you to get smitten by a female here and there in the past, Obie. But only one at a time. Have you got your eye now on *both* those firetops?"

Yount bashfully pawed the ground with one big foot. "Not really. I grant that both of 'em are galuptious. But that Paprika, she's the real knee-weakener. I'd gladly tie the hitch with her and, if the opportunity comes, I'm fixing to tell her so. What do you think about that, Zack?"

"I think you'd do better, Obie, to get yourself tied to a whipping post."

"Well!" Yount said huffily. "I sure do thank you for them friendly good wishes."

"Whoa, partner, whoa. I just meant... well... redheads have a reputation for being prickly. God knows what a *Hungarian* carrot-top might be like. Take care you don't get stung."

Yount grinned and flexed his biceps. "That'll be a frosty Friday, when the Quakemaker is afeared of a li'l bitty girl." He strode off manfully, and Edge looked after him with something like commiseration.

Though it was still quite early in the day, numbers of local folk had already climbed the hill to the park, mainly to admire the balloon, but also to peer inquisitively at what they could glimpse of the circus's living arrangements. So the women of the troupe made haste to tidy up after breakfast, to take down the clothes they had washed and hung up overnight, and generally to make the backyard neat. Then, one or a few at a time, they climbed into the property wagon to change from their robes and wrappers into ring dress. Phoebe Simms went first and took Sunday with her, because she needed help to put on her vast costume—or rather, to construct it around herself—and while that job was under way, there simply was not room in the wagon for anybody else.

She emerged as Madame Alp and, so as not to be ogled for free by the gathered gawks, went to wait in the tent wagon, where she could be company for Magpie Maggie Hag, still enfeebled by her premonitions or whatever was ailing her. Clover Lee climbed next into the prop wagon, and she and Sunday were getting into their tights when they were joined by Pepper and Paprika. The two white women and the white girl engaged in chatter and banter while they dressed, but Sunday stayed silent, struggling amateurishly to wriggle into her fleshings and trying to stay out of the others' way. That was no easy feat in the close-quarters mêlée of their handing bits of apparel back and forth, doing up each other's laces and buttons, borrowing and lending little pots of rouge, powders and puffs, creams and pomades, and helping each other apply them.

The camaraderie of all-girls-together emboldened Clover Lee to tell Pepper and Paprika what she had overheard back in Frederick City: the good Christian women waxing indignant at having seen two other women with hair under their arms. The two were not at all embarrassed or chastened by the report; they laughed hilariously, and all but fell about when Clover Lee concluded, "They said you must be Eye-talians." Pepper and Paprika hung onto one another for support while they shrieked and guffawed.

"If that don't bang Banagher!" gasped Pepper. "I've near pissed me britches."

"Eye-talians, indeed!" snorted Paprika. "Ignorant old bawds."

"Well, I know you're not Italians," said Clover Lee. "But is it something you learned from Italians? Not to shave there for some reason? I asked Florian, but he just coughed."

That sent them into new paroxysms. When they had recovered, Pepper said merrily, "Colleen dear, it's sheer showmanship. Show-woman, I should say. Whenever folks see a female with bright-colored hair—not humdrum brown or black or mouse pelt—they think: aye, but is it her natural growth? Women do the wondering catty-like, of course. But men do the wondering *lustful*-like, because they seldom see aught but black or brown belly fleece on their ordinary women."

"So we make it plain that we are genuine, natural-born of this flame color," said Paprika. "When the jossers glimpse the pink tufts in our armpits, they know damned well that our furbelows are pink, too. Here, see for yourself, child. It drives men wild, the imagining of that secret place. And drives their womenfolk wild with envy."

"Sure and that's why we laughed at being called Italians," said Pepper. "Faith, why would a dark dago female want to advertise that she's naught but nigger-haired all over? No offense to ye there in the corner, alannah."

"Cela ne fait rien," murmured Sunday.

"You hear her? 'Sally Fairy Ann'!" cried Paprika in surprise and delight. "By Saint Istvan, this child is no longer a néger! Sunday, angyal, you are becoming a real cosmopolite!"

Sunday looked unsure of what that was, or whether she wanted to be it, but said shyly, "Monsieur Roulette is teaching me to talk like a lady. In American and French, both."

"Well, angyal," said Paprika, "if you would care to further your education on the way to Europe, I will be happy to help. Magyar is hopelessly difficult, but German will serve you as well when you are in Hungary, and I can teach you that."

Talking like a textbook, Sunday said, "Thank you, Mademoiselle Makkai. I do desire to learn all that I can apprehend."

Pepper looked dubious of that proposition, or disapproving, and when they all left the wagon she was intensely whispering something to her partner. Clover Lee, ever eager to overhear any secret thing she could, caught only the last few words.

"... Baring your bird's-nest to the one and calling the other Angel. I ken that much of Magyar."

Edge and Mullenax were shining the hoofs of the horses with stove blacking when Florian bustled up to them and said, "Look at this mob already here, a whole hour before show time. We'll have all of Baltimore up here today. The local darkies are even setting up snack stands all over the park. Selling pork cracklings, terrapin soup, lemonade..."

"Well, that won't profit us any," said Edge, "but it keeps the crowd in a good mood. I've told the musicians to tune up to entertain them, too."

Mullenax added, "Every rube that's not eating or just gawking is playing Fitz's mouse game. He must be raking in the shekels for us."

"Oh, I'm not complaining about the attendance," said Florian. "It's just that there clearly will not be anybody left in town to come see us tomorrow. And I see no profit in our showing to another bloomer stand, the way we did yesterday. So what I suggest, Colonel Ramrod, is that we simply cancel tomorrow's performances. We'll use the free day for a leisurely teardown, get everything packed good and tight, buy provisions for the voyage. That way, we won't have to hustle and hurry on the day after, getting down to the wharf for embarkation."

Except for a few lot lice, too poor or stingy to pay for admission, the people in the park all bought tickets and took their preliminary looks at Maximus and the museum. Then, when Tim and Hannibal played "Wait for the Wagon"—with a slightly faltering accompaniment by Sunday Simms's accordion—the people all packed into the Big Top. A good many of them had to sit on the ringside ground or stand wherever they could find room. After the intermission and the sideshow— and more mouse game—while the afternoon audience was still enjoying the second half of the program, the park outside again filled up with people come early for the balloon ascension before the evening show. They bought tickets enough to fill the pavilion once more, so, when a considerable number of the first audience decided they'd like to stay for the second show and applied again for tickets, Florian finally had to declare a turnaway. He did it with no dismay; with pleasure, actually, at having a turnaway crowd for the first time on this whole tour.

Jules Rouleau, as instructed, made his preparation for the ballooning with slow deliberation, giving Fitzfarris ample time to do a booming business with his game. Since the ascension required little more than the casting off of the tiedown ropes, Rouleau's only real preparation consisted of his fetching from the tent wagon a length of rope ladder and tossing that into the basket, for some purpose he did not confide to anybody. Meanwhile, Florian curled a circus poster into a cone and through that makeshift megaphone bellowed to the surrounding masses:

"Monsieur Roulette must await the sundown fall of the breeze... Such a daring feat demands absolute stillness of the air... Extremely hazardous even then..."

Between those repeated announcements, Tim and Hannibal loudly played music appropriate to a balloon ascension—"Nearer My God to Thee" and other such things—and Sunday pitched in with her accordion on every piece familiar to her. At last, when the crowd's muttering indicated that suspense was giving way to impatience, and when Fitz's marks were running out of betting money, Rouleau wetted a finger and held it in the air, gave a solemn nod to Florian to signify that he could feel no wind, then vaulted jauntily into the basket. Tim's cornet bleated a flourish and Hannibal's drum boomed a wild African tattoo and Florian shouted, "Stand by your cables!"... pause... and "Cast off!"

Edge, Yount, Mullenax and Fitzfarris all at the same instant threw off the four stake ropes, and the *Saratoga* gave a blithe bound upward. But the four men kept hold of the anchor-and-hauldown rope that had come with the balloon, already attached, when they acquired it. They payed it out hand over hand, so the balloon went up only slowly, in small jerks, and not very dramatically. To the onlookers, the taut rope might have been a stick *pushing* the contraption up from the ground. Tim and Hannibal and Sunday played, and she and the other Happy Hottentots sang—at about the same spiccato tempo that the *Saratoga* was rising—"Twin-kle, twin-kle, lit-tle star..." The balloon could not go very dramatically high, either, for there were only some six hundred feet of the anchor rope to pay out before the men belayed it to the stakes.

Nevertheless, the *Saratoga* was a beautiful object, and its ascent, if not exuberant, had been at least majestic, and it now hung at an altitude more than twice the height of Baltimore's Shot Tower, which was the highest thing any of the local folk were accustomed to seeing, and up there the brilliant vermilion and white silk had gone from ground shadow to where the setting sun's rays still shone, and the bag shone like a small sun itself. The crowd of watchers, after a long, sighing "Ah-h-h!" during the ascent, suddenly gave another "Ah-h-h!"—this time on an indrawn, gasping breath—for away up there Monsieur Roulette had gone insane and vaulted *out* of the basket.

Even the troupers of the ground crew were taken by surprise, for they had been busy with the belaying and had not seen Rouleau drop the rope ladder from the gondola before he leaped. He had caught onto the ladder, of course, and its upper end was secured somewhere inside the wicker rim, and now he was doing the same acrobatic poses and contortions and convulsions that he did in the ring on his wooden ladder, and the crowd was laughing and sobbing with relief, and cheering and applauding with pleasure.

Most of it was, anyway. Somebody plucked at Florian's sleeve, saying in a frigid voice, "Sir, I am told that you are the proprietor of this enterprise."

Florian turned to face a gentleman with a doleful long jaw stiffly fringed with an Anglican-inch beard. "That I am, sir. I trust you are enjoying the entertainment."

"Enjoyment is not our object in life, sir," said the man, indicating the other people with him—two or three more men and several women, all wearing the same expression of pious woe. "We represent the Citizens' Crusade, and it has been brought to our notice that your so-called entertainment includes a certain wheel of chance."

"Oh, Lord," muttered Edge, at Florian's elbow. "Maggie Hag was right again."

Fitzfarris nobly spoke up. "The wheel, as you call it, is mine. And if you are here to complain, I can assure you the game is honest."

"Honesty or dishonesty is not our concern, either," said the man. "We are interested only in succoring the innocent victim of outrage and indignity."

Fitz looked bewildered. "Well, some have lost money, I confess that. But outrage? Indignity? I don't—"

"We wish you to show us this game," said a dish-faced woman.

"I don't mind," said Fitzfarris. "But right this minute we've got our colleague dangling way to hell and gone up yonder in—"

"This instant," the woman said. "Or we can summon a constable to command you."

Florian said to Fitz, "Monsieur Roulette is all right. And he'll be cavorting for a while yet. Go get the board, Sir John."

Fitzfarris went to bring the washtub and the pine apparatus. Then he reached into a pocket and brought out his mouse, which he had to disengage from a morsel of cheese it was busy with. "You interrupted Mortimer's meal-time," he said, as he set the mouse on the board. "Now, what happens—the players guess which hole he'll run to. And Mortimer picks his own. No forcing, no trickery. See? Number seventeen this time. No earthly way this game can be diddled, doctored or deaconed."

"As we suspected," said a woman with an iron coiffure. "Cruelty to animals."

Prepared as he was to defend himself against charges of swindling, fraud or flimflam, Fitzfarris was staggered by this unexpected accusation. He said with some heat, "Lady, it was you folks who disturbed Mortimer's mealtime repose. Do you see *me* being cruel to him?"

"If not overt cruelty," said one of the men, "certainly a perversion of the animal's natural behavior and violation of its dignity."

"Dignity?" said Fitzfarris, unbelieving. "Man, this is a common, ordinary field mouse. Not some noble horse being mistreated. Just a *mouse*—doing what mice *do*—running for a hole."

"But at your bidding," one of the women said flintily. "Not of its own accord. The creature is being callously degraded."

The half of Fitz's face that was not blue had now gone red, and he seemed apoplectically speechless, so Florian intervened.

"Madame, perhaps you accord this mouse an undue amount of concern, be-cause the mouse currently occupies, so to speak, the limelight of celebrity. But consider. If you were to find this rodent running about your kitchen, would you not regard it as unwelcome vermin? Would you not kill it, just as you would a cockroach?"

"Entirely different circumstances," said the woman, unswayed. "In that case, the animal would be pursuing its normal way of life, and taking its normal chances at survival. Here, it is being forced to unnatural acts."

Florian also looked stunned now, and could only sputter, "Unnatural acts? ...A field mouse?..."

Edge would have preferred to stay apart from this farcical imbroglio. But he realized that the zealots could easily widen their area of interest and demand the emancipation of the lion, the elephant, Barnacle Bill's pigs. Even if the meddling resulted in no worse than nuisance, it could also mean delay, and the *Pflichttreu* was sailing two days from now.

He said amiably, "Excuse me, folks. I take it you object to the use of a *mam-mal* in Sir John's little game. Someone just now mentioned a cockroach. Would your sensibilities be soothed if we substitute a cockroach for the mouse?"

Nobody laughed at this further descent into the ridiculous. The Citizens' Crusade exchanged inquiring glances. The man with the Anglican-inch beard scratched meditatively in it and murmured, "Hm...well....a cockroach *is* an invertebrate...certainly a being rather lower in the order of Creation..."

Edge quickly said, "Sir John, a sturdy bull cockroach would serve as well, wouldn't it?" Then, before Fitz could reply or shriek with laughter or tear his hair, Edge as quickly said to the citizens, "There we are, then. A cockroach it shall be. And we thank you folks for helping us mend our ways. Now, would you, ma'am, care to take possession of this Mortimer Mouse?" The woman he ad-dressed cringed away, aghast. "Then we set him free? Very well. Sir John, let Mortimer return to his, er, natural habitat."

Slowly shaking his head in incredulity, Fitz knelt and tenderly set the tiny creature on the ground. It scurried off in a hurry, as Florian, Edge and Fitzfarris turned away, returning to their posts at the balloon's hauldown rope. Florian was growling, "By Christ, I'll be glad to get out of this sanctimonious, sniveling country! We have been flayed for our language, for hanging out our laundry, for not shaving under the arms, and now for giving gainful employment to a—"

He was interrupted by another concerted gasp from the crowd, and then everybody dodged as the hauldown rope came tumbling in a loose coil down among them. They all looked up—to see that Rouleau had finished his acrobatics, climbed back inside the basket and cast loose his only tie to earth. The *Saratoga* immediately soared higher aloft and drifted sideways over the hilltop. But obviously Rouleau was not going to take *too* much of a chance at free flight. He had immediately afterward pulled the rope that communicated with the valve on top of the balloon's crown. The bag gradually elongated from pear shape to carrot shape, and descended as it did so. Getting ever thinner and longer—and wrinkling so that its broad red and white gores became only narrow stripes—it sank to the ground some distance away, but still in Druid Hill Park. The basket gently touched the grass, Rouleau pulled the ripcord, the bag lost the last of its gas, and came billowing and fluttering and flattening out on the ground.

With more cheers and hurrahs, the crowd surged to the descension spot. Edge, Fitz, Florian and Mullenax ran, too, to prevent the crowd's stepping on the precious silk. As Rouleau wriggled his way out of the gondola and out from under some folds of the fabric, the people mobbed him with handshakes and thumps on the back. When he got free of his congratulators, he came beaming and perspiring and all but glowing, to say, "Forgive me, Monsieur le Propriétaire —and Monsieur le Directeur—but I simply could not resist one brief moment of absolute freedom."

"That's all right, Jules," said Edge, "as long as you and it are all right. It made a grand finish to the act."

"And God knows when we can afford to give you the opportunity again," said Florian. "But let's bundle up this thing, lads, before the rubes get the notion of tearing off pieces for souvenirs."

Fitzfarris and Mullenax were already straightening out the fabric and lines, and Edge went to help. Rouleau ran to bring the balloon wagon. The three men were still lapping and folding the *Saratoga* when they heard a commotion back there at the lot—a number of confused shouts and the noise of feet running about, and then a clear cry, "Is there a doctor in the crowd?"

"Something has happened yonder," said Florian, but he hesitated to leave the balloon. "Why doesn't Monsieur Roulette come with the wagon for this thing?"

Little Quincy Simms came instead, running barefoot, saying breathlessly, "Hoy! Mas' Jules done hurt he se'f. Y'all come."

"What? How? What happened?"

"He jump fo' wagon, de hoss give a start. Mas' Jules, he leg in spokes when wheel turn. Ker-rack!"

"Oh, Jesus," said Florian. The other men were already running. "Ali Baba, you stay here and guard the *Saratoga*. Don't let anybody near it." And Florian went running, too.

Rouleau was laid out on the tarpaulin in the bed of the balloon wagon. His face was stark white and his teeth were gritted, and an elderly gentleman wearing pince-nez was gently palpating the length of his left leg. Some of the troupers were solicitously peering over the wagon sides at him, others were keeping the crowd away. When Florian leaned in, Rouleau unclenched his teeth enough to give him a tortured grin and say weakly:

"I risk my bones twice a day on the ground... and today in the sky... and now, regardez. Perhaps I brought it on myself. Péter plus haut que le cul..."

"Chut, ami. C'est drôlement con. How bad is it, Doctor?"

The physician shook his head, removed his pince-nez and pursed his lips. Then he climbed down from the wagon and drew Florian aside before he spoke. Edge stayed close to them.

"Broken in three places, and curiously so, for his age. The man must have the bones of an adolescent."

"Yes, he is exceptionally limber. That is good, right? They will knit and heal quickly?"

"That is bad, sir. Because the bones *are* so flexible, these are greenstick fractures, and compound. The splintered ends have pierced the flesh and skin. Even if the fractures could be properly reduced, it would mean a month or more of complete rigidity. And during that time of depleted blood circulation, the flesh wounds are bound to mortify."

"What are you saying?" Florian whispered.

"I am saying amputate."

Edge blurted, "Good God! The man's a professional acrobat!"

"You are of course at liberty to solicit a second opinion. I suggest you make haste."

Florian wrung his beard. Edge whirled and barked, "Abner!"

"I ain't no medic!" said Mullenax, recoiling.

"You can carpenter. Go and find some planks, at least five feet long. If you can't get them elsewhere, rip them off that bandstand. You there, Sunday! You and Tim and Hannibal strike up some music. Fitz, start talking up the lion. Florian, get the show ready to commence, and turn the tip as soon as it is. Doctor, will you stand by while I have a word with the patient?"

"Saint Joseph's is the nearest hospital. The quicker we can get him there—"

"Let's at least solicit *his* opinion. I'll be right with you."

Edge climbed carefully into the wagon, not to jounce it, knelt and said, "There's no time to sugarcoat this pill, Jules. You've got a choice—live with only one leg or maybe die with both of them." Already chalk white, Rouleau went slightly green. Edge continued, "The doctor can saw it off, and you'll be lopsided but alive. Or I can give it the treatment that once saved a good horse all intact. Say which."

Rouleau did not hesitate. He gave again the tortured grin and said, "If I am not as good as a good horse, ami, I deserve to die."

"Try to bear that in mind, so you'll whinny and not screech when it hurts." Rouleau laughed outright before he gritted his teeth again. "Doctor," Edge said, over the wagon side. "He's decided to take his chances. We thank you, anyhow."

"What *chances*?" the man protested, but Edge had turned away and was shouting for Sarah. The doctor shook his head and followed the rest of the crowd to see the lion Fitzfarris was loudly advertising.

Mullenax came with an armload of light planks, a hammer, saw, nails and one of his ever-ready jugs. Rouleau drank deep of the whiskey, while Edge instructed Mullenax in the hurried construction of a shallow, narrow wooden trough, rather like a window box for flowers. It was made with one end open, so Rouleau's leg could be laid in it and his foot pressed against the closed farther end. At the bottom and on the inner side, the box was just long enough to reach from Rouleau's crotch to the sole of his foot, but the outside plank was made long enough to extend all the way to his armpit.

Edge turned to Sarah. "You run and fetch a sack of that bran we got for the horses, and some carbolic acid, and some long, thin sticks from our stock of firewood, and some strips of cloth I can use for tying. Abner, you're going to hold Jules firm and steady while I pull on this leg and see if I can set the broken bone ends. And Jules, you're just going to have to whinny like a whole herd of mustangs, because this will hurt like hell."

Edge waited until the music and crowd noise from the Big Top was at its loudest, then started the pulling, just below the topmost break. Rouleau did more than whinny; he howled and screamed. Sarah grimaced and clapped her hands over her ears. But Edge felt one after another of the three bulges in the leg diminish, and watched the jagged ends of bone slip back under the bloodied flesh and—he hoped—fit back where they belonged. Before the job was done, Rouleau had ceased screaming and Mullenax did not have to lean on him to hold him motionless, for he had fainted dead away. Then Edge placed the sticks along the leg for splints, and with the cloth strips bound them tightly in place. He and Mullenax carefully laid the trussed leg in the new-built box, positioned the longer board up along Rouleau's left side, between his body and his arm, and bound that firmly with cloth strips running around his waist and chest.

"Sarah," said Edge, "before he wakes up, give those flesh wounds a good burning dose of carbolic."

While she did that, Edge ripped open the sack she had brought. He poured the bran into the box, packing it tightly under, around and over the leg.

"There," he said, wiping sweat from his forehead. "That'll hold it pretty near immobile, but let some air circulate around it. Sarah, you and Maggie can dig through the bran whenever you need to treat those wounds. I reckon Maggie will know how to sew them shut and what to put on them. Then pack the bran back tight again. Jules is going to have to lie still and stiff for maybe two months. But with luck he'll live, and come out of that box with a fairly usable leg. It worked with a horse, once, anyway. Come on, Abner. While he's still out, let's move him to the prop wagon where he's accustomed to sleeping."

When they had done that, Edge and Mullenax took the balloon wagon to collect the *Saratoga* and Quincy, then hastened to join the show in progress. It was the last time the Florilegium would perform in the United States of America, most likely, and also the troupe had to make up for the absent Monsieur Roulette, so the artistes exerted themselves to give their best performances. Barnacle Bill decided he had been reluctant long enough, and tonight brought the lion cage into the tent, got inside it himself and put Maximus through most of his repertoire—sit down, sit up, lie down, roll over, play dead—only stopping short of sticking his head in the lion's mouth or doing the bogus business of being "bitten."

The Quakemaker let the bull-pup cannon—because this was its last performance ever—roll back and forth over him so many times that he was almost too sore to do his new trick, but do it he did. He let Pepper, then Paprika, climb up him and stand erect, one on either shoulder. Then the Simms triplets, not quite so gracefully, climbed up him and up the women, to stand three abreast on the women's shoulders—all the females leaning sideways from their linked hands —making a three-high fan of six bodies. Florian and Tiny Tim threw local landmarks into their knockabout routine—"Ow! That kick caught me on Pratt Street!"—and when Sir John substituted for Monsieur Roulette in singing Madame Solitaire's anthem, he changed some words:

> ... And the heart in my bosom adores.
> Solitaire is the Queen of all riders, I ween,
> But alas, she is now Baltimore's!

Magpie Maggie Hag had recovered from her prostration, now that her premonition had come to pass—whichever of the "wheel" troubles was the one she had foreseen—and at intermission dukkered a whole forest of palms. Out on the midway, Sir John, deprived of his mouse game, made elaborate and florid presentations of every exhibit, concluding with Madame Alp: ". . . and the phenomenon will now hand out mementos of her monstrosity, classic photographic replicas of herself. Yours to keep, ladies and gentlemen, for the trifling sum of fifty cents. Biggest bargain in Baltimore. You can take Madame Alp home with you for only one-fifteenth of a cent per pound!"

"Did you notice, Fitz?" Pepper said to him afterward. "When the rubes had got done buying the Fat Lady's cartes-de-visite, there was one man—a darky— what bought every one of them she had left?"

"No, I didn't notice. But so what? Some men admire women who are beef to the heels."

"No matter. Except that it put me in mind of them maggot-brains in Europe that I've seen come slinking and asking to rent a freak for a night or two."

"I'll keep an eye peeled. But I doubt anybody'll *carry* her off."

No one did. At any rate, after the "Lorena" walkaround and the come-out and the crowd's dispersal, Phoebe Simms was still among the company, and already had a hearty hot meal waiting to resuscitate them after the long day's exertions. Sunday carried a plate to the property wagon, to feed Rouleau, but he had kept Mullenax's jug by him, and was feeling no hunger pangs nor any other kind. After the troupe had eaten, most of them simply lay about in the summer darkness, chatting and smoking. Edge took a final stroll about the lot, partly to see that the animals were all comfortable, partly just to look at the last setup he would see on American soil in the foretellable future. The Big Top looked metallic now, sheened with dew that reflected the moonlight, and only palely shining from within, where Hannibal and Quincy slept under a single watch lantern. The tent itself seemed sleepily to breathe, like a living creature, for the little random breezes that wafted through it made the canvas whisper, and the ropes and chandelier and bail ring rustled and creaked and clinked. When Edge went to spread his bedroll in the open, under the stars, only Phoebe and Magpie Maggie Hag were still awake, sitting together beside the embers of the fire, conversing in murmurs.

After Phoebe had waddled off to her wagon, Magpie Maggie Hag stayed awake most of the night, to look in on Rouleau at intervals. Most of those times she found him asleep, but feverish and restless. She was reluctant to pour laudanum into him, on top of his considerable whiskey content, unless he should go into such a thrashing delirium as to budge the heavy box he was tied to—and he did not. Indeed, in the morning, when Edge came in to take stock of him, Rouleau was hale enough and in good enough spirits to smile and say:

"Zut alors, those mice of Fitzfarris's have been getting their revenge. All night, they kept coming to nibble at the bran in my box. I can endure the pain and the boredom, ami, but am I to pass every night with vengeful vermin tickling up and down my leg?"

"Be glad of them," said Edge. "As long as you can feel the mice tickling, that leg is still alive, and so are you."

The teardown of the Big Top was not done "leisurely," as Florian had phrased it, but it was certainly done slowly, with now another man missing from the crew. The job took until noon, and by then the women had accomplished all the other complicated packing of the wagons, deciding what things could be kept stored away throughout the voyage, and what should be accessible for use. When everybody had had a bit of midday peck, Florian called the troupe together.

"Ladies and gentlemen, I am now going to pay out another round of salaries. Then all who wish to accompany me downtown may do so, and can pass the afternoon shopping for any items needed for the trip."

The women nodded to each other and began comparing notes on what they ought to be buying. Edge began ticking off, on his fingers, the amount of provender the animals would require. Mullenax muttered that he had better lay in a good supply of liquid refreshment and, while he was downtown, he could damn sure use some horizontal refreshment, too.

"One word of advice to you all," said Florian. "Buy no more than you really *need,* just to get you to Italy, for I can assure you that things will be cheaper over there than here."

"Mas' Florian," said Phoebe Simms. "Kin I go, too, dis time?"

"Most certainly, Madame Alp. It won't matter now if the public sees you en déshabillé."

"Well, I warn't goin' on dere. I'se goin' to Darktown."

"Mother!" Sunday murmured in embarrassed exasperation. "He meant being out of costume."

They all went except Maggie Magpie Hag, who stayed to look after Rouleau, and Hannibal, who stayed to guard everything else. And they all managed to pile into Florian's rockaway and the least loaded wagon, which was the one carrying only the balloon. They descended from the heights into the miasma of downtown and stopped at the base of the Merchants' Shot Tower.

"This edifice is visible from everywhere in the city," said Florian. "So this is where we will reconvene, at sundown."

Edge and Yount drove off in the balloon wagon, to find a feed store and a meat market. The other troupers scattered by ones and twos and groups in various directions, Phoebe Simms even going off separately from her children. And, some hours later, she and Florian were the first to reconvene. He was slouched on the rockaway seat, idly flicking his coach whip at flies on Snowball's rump, when Phoebe came plodding determinedly up to him.

"Ah, Madame Alp. Finished your business in Darktown? I see you bought a hat. That's, er, quite a hat."

"Thankee kindly. An' kin I ax you somep'n, Mas' Florian? Does de law say I be's bound out to y'all becuz I runned away wid you?"

"Why, no, of course not. There is no such thing as bound out any more. You're as free as any white woman walking this street. Good heavens, have we somehow made you feel that you're just a slave to us?"

"Nawsuh. Das why it mek me feel bad now to tell y'all good-bye."

"What?"

"I'se gettin' ma'd, y'see."

"You are getting *married*?"

"Yassuh. Dey's a fine cullud gemmun bin co'tin' me. Mebbe you seen him. Yaller shoes an' a high-dome hat? He come to all foah shows we done give here in Baltimo', jist to marble at *me*. Bought all my pitchers, jist so he could talk wid me. Now I done meet up wid him at he house, an' we decides we go' git ma'd."

"But . . . but . . . Madame Alp, you are our irreplaceable Fat Lady."

"Das whut Roscoe like. He a li'l disapp'inted t' see I ain' really as fat as in my pitchers, but he say he go' plump me up some. He kin affo'd to do it, too. He got a high fo'man position in de Ches'peake an' Maine Dry Dock. Das a *nigguh* comp'ny here. Begun by Free Nigguhs, and all cullud dat wuk dere, an' it thrivin' fine. Roscoe he a big man dere. Got him a nice house, a hoss an' buggy . . ."

"Well, I certainly congratulate him, and the company, and . . . and you, too. But this comes as a thunderbolt. On the very eve of departure, losing you and the triplets and—"

"Nawsuh. Roscoe he ain' too fond of udder men's get. He want us start all over, hab he own."

"Madame Alp! You would go off and abandon your children?"

"Dem gels ain' chil'rens no mo', Mas' Florian. Dey all done got der flars in de pas' couple weeks. Dey be's wimmens now, an' dey kin take keer of Quincy. You don' need worry none."

"Woman, I'm not thinking of myself! I'm thinking of them. How they will miss you."

"You want t' see how dey miss me, suh? You want t' see how much *anybody* evuh gets missed? Go to dat pond in dat park we at, stick yo' finger in de pond, den look at de hole it leave in de water. Mas' Florian, a mammy knows, once her chil'rens git 'shamed of her, a mammy's wuk is done."

"Oh, come, now. If that's some tidbit of folk wisdom—"

"Das mammy wisdom. Black mammy, white mammy, make no differments. Nawsuh. Me an' Miz Hag, we done talk dis out, an' she agree. Dem chil'rens soon be impawtint folk, wid rich prospecks out ahead of 'em. Sunday she awready talk fancier'n ol' Mistis Furfew. Dem chil'rens won' want no ol' fat, ignernt, black mammy draggin' after 'em."

Florian tried every argument and persuasion he could think of, including the dangling of rich prospects for Phoebe herself—"Why, Europe is just full of visiting African monarchs!"—but she was adamant in maintaining that an executive foreman of the Chesapeake & Maine Dry Dock Company was all the husband she required, and far better than she had ever expected to find.

"Well, we've lost you," Florian finally sighed. "And we regret it, but we wish you and Roscoe all the best. We'll even give you a wedding present. I know the Yankees promised every freed Southern darky 'forty acres and a mule.' I don't have forty acres to give you, but when we depart tomorrow I'll leave our mule tethered in the park. You and Roscoe can go up and collar it whenever you like."

"Mighty good o' you, Mas' Florian. We be much obliged."

"Meanwhile—much as I'd hate losing the triplets—I must ask you this again. Would you not wish to entrust them to some aunt, some uncle, some other of your family?"

"I *am* leavin' dem wid fambly, Mas' Florian. You-all is it."

"I daresay that was meant as a compliment to us," Florian told Edge and Yount when they drove up later, the balloon wagon heaped high with bales of hay, bags of grain and slabs of smoked meat. "But she is gone, and how I am to break the news to those pickaninnies, I do not know."

"Better worry about how you're going to tell Fitz," said Edge. "Here he comes now. He's just lost a hefty hunk of his sideshow."

Fitzfarris, Sarah and Clover Lee came up the street together, their arms laden with small parcels. Florian uncomfortably made the announcement that Madame Alp was off to get married.

"And from the seats," said Sarah. "To think that she'd be the first of us females to snare a beau out of the audience."

"Shit," was all that Fitzfarris said.

"Yes," said Florian. "I immediately thought of going to the local orphanage, Sir John, to see what it might have to offer as a replacement. A pinhead or whatever. But, without plausible credentials, I've always found it laborious work to convince a superintendent or a mother superior that I am a medical doctor engaged in scientism and seeking specimens for my studies. No, there wouldn't be time."

"Here come most of our others," said Yount. "I'll start perching 'em on top of that wagon load."

"Put the Simms children in my rockaway," said Florian. "And Madame Solitaire, you squeeze in there with them. On our way back up to the pitch, break the bad news to them as gently as you can. Try to convince them, as Phoebe said, that they've still got a family."

Evidently Sarah succeeded in that, or perhaps the children were by now accustomed to cataclysms occurring frequently in their lives. Anyway, they did not try to run away to find their mother, and did not weep or show any other overt signs of deprivation. Nevertheless, their elders—as soon as all had gone to look in on Rouleau and give the invalid a cheery greeting—exerted themselves to keep the little Simmses too busy to grieve. Edge and Sarah hoisted Monday and Tuesday onto horses and put them through their riding paces around the now open-air ring, and Pepper and Paprika drilled Sunday and Quincy in an exhausting routine of acrobatic exercises. The trouper most affected by Madame Alp's defection was Magpie Maggie Hag, since the cooking of supper devolved upon her, and she went about it grumblingly.

"Serves you right," snapped Florian. "You could have talked the woman out of it. You could have dukkered that her Roscoe is a notorious wife-beater or something."

"I dukkered honest—that he a good man. I flimflam rubes, yes, but never a sister on the show. Go away. Let me cook."

Florian went away, to the park pond, and squatted beside it in what appeared to be solemn meditation. Several passersby gave him looks askance, for he repeatedly stuck a finger into the water and then morosely contemplated the resultant ripples as they quickly subsided and vanished.

The steam collier *Pflichttreu* looked even uglier than when Florian and Edge had earlier seen it, for its main holds were now filled and it sat ungainly low in the water, so the grime-encrusted upper works and masts and yards were more easily visible. It also had steam up, so its tall, thin single stack exuded an ooze of dirty smoke and a steady drift of soot that did not go very high in the air before descending, on deck and dock impartially, like a sticky black snow. Though the chute loading was all done, the ship's derricks were still working, bringing sacked pea coal aboard. Their booms creaked and groaned as they swung the pallets of sacks from dockside to deck hatches, where the crewmen, as black begrimed as everything else in sight, wedged them down into the remaining hold space.

Florian brought the train to a halt at a distance from the activity and the clouds of dirt enveloping it. There were already plenty of supernumeraries and loafers crowding the wharf to see the ship off. They were presumably unemployed or off-duty seamen and stevedores, seated on rope coils or leaning on bollards all over the cobbled waterside area, all of them smoking stumpy pipes or chewing tobacco, all keeping up a running commentary—mostly derogatory— on the *Pflichttreu*'s loading procedures and its crew's competence at the work. But even from a distance Florian could notice that, notwithstanding the ship's generally repellent look, Captain Schilz had made at least one chivalrous provision for his oncoming female passengers. The only gangway from shore to ship was still the same ordinary open ladder, but it was now fitted with a "virginity screen," a strip of canvas slung below it from top to bottom, so the workers and loiterers on the dock could not peek up the ladies' dresses as they ascended.

Florian climbed down from the rockaway. "Take charge, Zachary. Make sure nobody else runs off as Madame Alp did. I'm going to the office to get a refund from Herr Mayer for her." He paused. "Now what the devil is this?"

He backed defensively against the carriage as three men sped across the cobbles toward him, gibbering in excited, high-pitched voices. They were not just running, they were gleefully leaping and bounding as they came, and pointing at the wagons and wigwagging at the elephant as though they were old acquaintances of hers. The language they gabbled was totally incomprehensible, but one locution—"kong-ma-jang!"—was recognizably repeated over and over. They were very small men, not much taller than Tim Trimm, and exceedingly skinny. They had simian faces, of yellowish-tan complexion, and were patently Orientals, but of indeterminable age; any of them could have been anything from thirty to sixty. They wore blousy tunics and trousers that had originally been of white cotton but were now mostly gray rags, and wore no shoes at all.

Arriving before the astonished Florian, they did an extravagant number of elaborate Oriental bows. Then two of them fell supine on the cobbles, in opposite directions, and stuck their legs in the air. The third man jumped straight up from the ground, curled himself into a ball in midair, and the other two began kicking him back and forth through the air between them, making him spin first one way, then the other.

"By damn!" Florian exclaimed. "Antipodists. A risley act."

"What?" said Edge, who had protectively joined him on the ground.

"Antipodists. Foot jugglers and upside-down acrobats. They're doing what's called a risley—after an old-time English performer, but it's really from the Orient."

"So are they," said Fitzfarris, also joining them. "Bunch of Chinamen, I'd guess."

"How in the world do they happen to be on a Baltimore dock?"

"The railroads out west use a lot of Chinks for coolie work," said Fitz. "I'd bet this trio booked steerage passage—or more likely stowed away—on a China-trade clipper they thought was bound for California. They probably don't know where the hell they are. They don't seem to know a word of English."

The Chinese, if that was what they were, had got to their feet and were again frantically jabbering and gesticulating. Whatever they were saying sounded urgent and importunate. When they pointed to themselves they said gloomily "Han-guk" and proudly "kwang-dae." When they pointed to the wagons they said imploringly, "Kong-ma-jang."

"I'd reckon that means circus," said Edge. "They can't read the words, but they recognize circus wagons when they see them."

"And I'd say they're asking to come along with us," said Fitz.

"Then so they shall," said Florian, with instant decision. "We have just lost a freak and our star acrobat is an invalid. We can use a new act. We'll take them."

Edge suggested gently, "Oughtn't we to try telling them where they're going? I mean, if they think they're in California right now, what will they think when they wind up in Italy?"

"It won't be any more alien to them than Baltimore. They are obviously stranded, lost, no doubt bewildered by the local customs, out of work and desperate. We will give them employment and sustenance."

"You were just about to demand money back from Mr. Mayer. Now you're going to shell out for two more fares."

"No, sir," said Florian, still being decisive. "Fitz, strip the Chinks naked and put them among the exhibits in the museum. When Herr Mayer comes out to count noses, I'll tell him they are monkeys." Fitz and Edge made noises of appalled and amused protest, but Florian overrode them. "If he refuses to believe that, I'll convince him that they don't weigh as much all together as Madame Alp did."

So Fitzfarris rounded up the Chinese and led them to the museum wagon. He let down one of its hinged side panels, undid the enclosing wire nettings and pointed to indicate that that was where they were to ride. Then he began, with some repugnance, to disrobe one of the men, and gestured to the others to do the same. The Chinese looked briefly puzzled by this, but seemed to accept it as just another California custom, and complied. Naked, they clambered in among the stuffed animals. Fitz reattached the netting, closed up the side panel and left them in the darkness.

The undressing of them turned out to have been unnecessary. Herr Mayer did emerge from his office to tally the passengers, wagons, animals and other items against the list Florian had given him. But when Florian hurried him past the museum wagon, saying, "In there are the taxidermische specimens I mentioned," Herr Mayer did not bid him open it. Neither did he volunteer to refund any money when the passenger count came out one short. Florian decided not to press his luck; he did not mention it, either.

The loading of coal sacks was finally done, so the collier's derricks were put to work to hoist the circus aboard. Edge and Yount took the job of driving the wagons one by one to the ship's side and there unhitching the horses, while the dockhands attached grapple cables between wagon and boom, and the donkeymen on deck worked a steam capstan to haul each wagon up and swing it inboard.

There was one anxious moment. When it came the museum wagon's turn, it transpired that Fitzfarris had only insecurely latched the side panel. The wagon was just at the ship's gunwale, rocking in the air, when that panel flopped open. The watching troupers held their breath, as a number of deckhands stood gaping with disbelief at the three small, wizened, yellowish, naked creatures clinging terrified to the inside of the wire netting. But all that happened was that one old seaman spat tobacco juice, imperturbably remarked to a younger, "I told ye, lad. Some quair things come in on the tide," and reclosed the panel securely.

Maximus made vociferous complaint and made the seamen look uneasy as his cage wagon was hoisted. But when a belly sling took the elephant aboard, Hannibal clung to it, too—murmuring assuringly, "Steady, ol' Peggy, steady"— and she actually seemed to enjoy the brief ride, with her ponderous weight off her legs for a change. The elephant, with the caged Maximus for company, and two other wagons were positioned along the starboard side of the open foredeck, the rockaway and the remaining three wagons on the port side. The vehicles were all tied down and their wheels chocked, the elephant was tethered to the gunwale cleats by chains on her two right legs. Then the activity shifted to the afterdeck's derrick. The eight horses came aboard there in belly slings, but not as placidly as Peggy had. They whinnied, walled their eyes and kicked, nearly braining a couple of deckhands before they could be haltered to the gunwale.

Mullenax let his three pigs climb the gangway ladder on their own, which they did with gusto and much to the amusement of the workers and idlers looking on. Mullenax herded them to the afterdeck and left them to make their own beds in the straw spread for the horses, only taking care to caution the seamen that the porkers were *not* portable provisions for the galley. The other troupers also came aboard by way of the ladder, carrying various pieces of hand luggage. Rouleau, on his bedroll, firmed by planks under it, had been carefully removed by his fellows from the property wagon before that was hoisted. Now his sickbed was gently laid on one of the coal-loading pallets, and even the rough-handed crewmen took great care in fetching him on board and carrying him to a cabin.

The passengers had been allotted five of the four-bunk cabins in the superstructure "island" between the fore and after masts. Only Florian and Fitzfarris moved into Rouleau's, to give him as much air to breathe as possible. Hannibal insisted on sleeping on deck with his Peggy, and Quincy shared a cabin with his three sisters. That left one cabin for the four other white men, and the five white women were delighted to have two whole cabins to share among them. Fitzfarris, as soon as he could do so unobserved, sneaked to the foredeck to drop the offside flap of the museum wagon, so the three Chinese had light and air and an outboard view, and he even rearranged the stuffed occupants of the museum so the living ones had floor room to lie upon.

All the troupers, as soon as they had stowed their gear, crowded together on the afterdeck to observe the *Pflichttreu's* getting under way. The idlers on shore ceased their loafing long enough to cast off the ship's hawsers from the wharf bollards, and the hands on deck hauled them in and coiled them. There was a clamorous ringing of bells and tooting of whistles and shrieking of piped steam. The stack amidships belched a storm cloud of black smoke, out of which fell a black snowstorm of oily soot, and the gritty iron deck underfoot began to throb as the engines were put in gear. The strip of fetid and trashy water between the ship's side and the wharf began slowly to widen. Then the deck settled to a steadier vibration that made everybody jitter lightly where he stood. Pepper nudged Paprika and whispered, "Look yonder," indicating Monday Simms. Her face was blissful and her thighs rubbing together. "That gal is grinding mustard again."

Nobody else noticed. They were watching the dockside clutter of Locust Point slide away from them—then all of Baltimore, the city seeming to cluster itself around the Shot Tower as it dwindled. There were various changes in the rhythm of the vibration underfoot, and varying densities of black snowfall, as the collier made various small changes of course to get into the channel. Then Fort McHenry was close on the ship's starboard side, the city lazaretto on the port. Then, almost with a rush, the land swerved away on either side, and the *Pflicht-treu* was out of the inner harbor, in the broad Patapsco River, and everybody on deck gave a loud hurrah. There would be a brief delay when the harbor pilot was dropped, and there would still be land visible, near or distant, on both sides, as the collier made its heavy, slow progress down the long reach of Chesapeake Bay. But they were on their way to Europe.

A SEA

I

WHEN the passengers came on deck the next morning to see to the animals before breakfast, there was still land visible on either side of the *Pflichttreu*. Its engines were vigorously churning and its twirling screw left a foamy wake on the water behind. But, like a fat woman who walks with busy, twinkling feet but moves forward only slowly, the ship seemed to be making little progress for all its effort. Captain Schilz was on deck, watching the crew hosing water to clear at least some of the night's accumulation of grit from the plating. However, since the ship was moving at a pace so slow that it never outran its own exhalations, the soot continued to collect almost as rapidly as it was cleared.

"Guten Morgen, pill-grumps," the captain said, amiably enough. Tim Trimm immediately said, in a peevish voice, "That ain't Europe out yonder. Is this crummy bucket traveling at all?"

Captain Schilz gave him a haughty look. "Herr Miniatur, are you calling my ship slow? Not slow it is. Moderate it is."

"It also has rats," said Sarah. She turned to Edge. "Back on shore, Jules got used to the mice crawling into that box you put on him. But last night, when I went to change his dressings, he was in a state of nerves. Big, ugly *rats* were getting into the box."

The captain said, with heavy Teutonic humor, "Gnädige Frau, would you really wish to be traveling on a ship the rats had *abandoned*?"

"What I'm wishing, captain dear," said Pepper, "is that your moderate ship would at least move moderately faster than its own bad breath. Are we to be filthy and smelly all the way beyant the pond?"

"Damen und Herren," said the captain, turning pink with the effort of controlling himself. "By profession a sailing officer I was until—against my better judgment—master of this steam boiler I was made. On board a decent sailing ship, such an abomination as ein Zirkus I would not accept." His voice got louder and angrier. "You are here only because I am now a mere Mechaniker, and what miserable cargo I carry in this verdammt kitchen kettle *I do not care!*"

The artistes looked properly indignant, but dared not interrupt, as Captain Schilz went on, in a contained fury:

"To this Schmutzfink I am condemned until such day as the owners realize that no ship by steam alone to cross the Atlantic will ever be able. Ja, a collier like this—carrying four and a half thousand tons of coal—could do that, ja. But it consumes twenty-five tons each day. If all the way the engines I used, I would empty of cargo arrive in port. So no more coal will I burn than I have to. As soon as on the wide open sea we are, and whenever a fair wind we have, I promise you, I shall shut off the stinking engines and hoist good clean sail."

"We are sorry we presumed to criticize your ship," Florian said diplomatically. "You do it so much better yourself."

The captain, having let off his own steam, simmered down. "Come now, all of you, to Frühstück."

As might have been expected on a vessel under a Prussian master, breakfast was good and rich and plentiful. The Rhenish cook was known as Doc—according to Florian, all ships' cooks were so called—and he had a vile temper—also, said Florian, common to all ships' cooks. He seldom emerged from his cramped galley, where he kept up a continuous conversation with himself, consisting mainly of imprecations at his larder and equipment and wages and working hours and the unappreciative palate of the average seaman. The cabin steward, Quashee, was different. A big, black West Indian, he spoke an almost Oxonian English and served at table with the courtly manner of a professional butler.

The first and second officers and the chief engineer also dined at the captain's table when they were not on watch. They were respectively a Hessian, a Saxon and a Bavarian, but they all spoke English about as well as the captain did. Indeed, despite the fact that the ship's company included almost every nationality of western Europe, English was practically the working language of the whole vessel. Probably because Britain was the chief builder of maritime engines, almost all the ship's "black gang" and a goodly number of the deckhands were Limeys and Jocks and Taffies and Paddies. So every command, instruction, inquiry and revilement, whatever language it might be uttered in, had to be repeated in English for the comprehension of all.

Only the white folk of the circus, then or afterward, dined at the captain's table. But the urbane Quashee did not mind taking trays to the Simmses in their cabin and to Hannibal on deck, any more than he minded taking trays to Rouleau. Also, that first morning, the men of the troupe managed to pocket some rolls and pickles and cuts of cold meat from the breakfast table, and afterward to slip them to the grateful Chinese in the museum wagon. But it later became apparent that Captain Schilz regarded Chinese as no more or less detestable than anyone else connected with a Zirkus, and was uncaring whether or not their fare had been paid. So, after some days, when Magpie Maggie Hag had cut and sewn acrobat outfits for the three and they were decently covered, they were allowed out of the wagon to mingle with their new colleagues, and Quashee fed them when he fed Hannibal, and they returned to the museum only to sleep.

On the second or third day out, the circus folk who had complained about the slowness of the ship's coming south down Chesapeake Bay were given reason to wish that they had more fully enjoyed that time and had complained about it less. For when the *Pflichttreu* at last rounded Cape Charles and turned east into the Atlantic, Captain Schilz gave an order in German and the first mate passed it on to the crew in a bellow of English: "Hang out the washing, lads!"

Men scurried up the mast shrouds to unfurl the sails from the yards. When the canvas was spread and set, the captain gave another order, and there was a sudden, almost eerie silence as the engines were shut down. The passengers had got so accustomed to the continuous mechanical chuntering that to hear nothing but the normal shipboard sounds and the wind in the rigging was as startling as if they had been abruptly deafened.

Meanwhile, Florian was calling, "Abdullah, quick, go and stand ready to comfort Brutus! Barnacle Bill, run to the cage wagon to reassure Maximus! Sir John, Quakemaker, Colonel, come aft with me to hold the horses! Hurry!"

Some of them regarded him in surprise, but they did as bidden, and soon saw why. Only Florian, of the male passengers, had ever been at sea under sail, so he was the only one of them to realize what was about to occur. All the way down the bay, the heavy-laden collier had cruised as level and stable as a circus ring. But now, under canvas and in the open ocean, the *Pflichttreu,* for all its bulk and weight, gave a long, creaking lurch and leaned steeply to port. The animals had to dance to keep their footing on the slanted deck—so did the men, as they patted the animals and murmured soothingly to them—and they all had to continue fidgeting for a while to find a steady balance, for the deck stayed at that steep slope.

When the horses and pigs appeared to have adapted themselves to their side-hill posture, Edge hurried to Rouleau's cabin to make sure the man's leg had not been jarred from its immobility.

"It hasn't, thank goodness," Edge said. "And as long as it doesn't, the ship's motion ought to be good for it. Keep the blood circulating. How are you feeling, Jules?"

"I hurt," Rouleau said wearily. "But merde alors, I am in more boredom than pain. Maggie says the flesh wounds are healing. I hope the bones are, too."

"I think you're doing fine. Another week or so, we'll carry your bedroll out on deck, give you some sunshine for a while each day."

"Then let me, in the meantime, laisser pisser les mérinos. Tell Clover Lee to bring her books each day—and the other children—and we will carry on with their lessons."

The ship remained at its left-leaning cant for about the next four hours, by which time the passengers—and probably the animals—thought they had found their sea legs. But then they heard another shout, "Ha-a-ard a-lee!" which occasioned more shouting back and forth from bridge to deck:

"'Bout ship!"

"Mains'ls hau-au-aul!"

"Jacks and sheets!"

"Let go and hau-au-aul!"

Canvas flapped and blocks rattled and spars clattered and the whole ship groaned, lurched and leaned steeply over the other way, to starboard, and all the passengers, human and animal, had to find new footing. From then on, during every stretch of the crossing when Captain Schilz was able to keep the *Pflicht-treu* under canvas, he would hold one tack for some four hours, then come about to the opposite tack for the next four. Over the first several days, whenever that occurred, the troupers had to endure the jeers of any seamen observing them—"Look at 'em do the cuddy-jig!"—but eventually all of them, even the heavyweight Peggy and the Chinese inside their cage and Rouleau flat on his back, learned to adjust to the lurch without giving it a thought, and could do so even in their sleep.

Nonetheless, they had to develop not only sea legs, but also sea stomachs. The first day or two on the open ocean was a wretched time for practically everybody who had not been at sea before. When at one point the gunwales were draped with Mullenax, Trimm, Hannibal, Sarah and Clover Lee, Fitzfarris, Sunday, Monday, Tuesday and Quincy—all jettisoning the good food Doc and Quashee had fed them—Florian expressed some surprise at not seeing Edge and Yount in the same position and condition.

"Oh, we been vaccinated," said Yount. "The U.S. Army was kind enough to charter a steamboat to take us from N'Awleans to Mexico. The *Portland* was a sidewheeler, and pretty steady, until we run into a storm in the Gulf. We all fetched up our toenails then, I can tell you."

Florian said, "Well, it is true that one attack of mal-de-mer usually makes a person immune. You'd be doing a mercy if you went around and told the sick ones that."

By the next day, most of them had recovered and, by the day after that, all had except Tim Trimm. He turned out to be one of the unhappy few who apparently never can acquire a sea stomach. He was at the gunwale almost all of every day, and would have to bolt from his cabin at unpredictable intervals every night. He never came to the dining table any more, subsisting on ship's biscuits and water, the only nutriments he could keep down, and his dead-fish eyes began to look dead indeed.

"It's bad enough, bein' so miserable," Tim whimpered to his colleagues. "But what's worse is that sauerkraut captain comin' by every mornin' *askin'* if I'm seasick. Can't the sumbitch *see* I am?"

Paprika laughed mockingly. "If you spoke German, little man, you would realize that Captain Schilz is making a joke. He is asking only 'how are you?' but in a waggish way. 'Wie befinden Sie sich?' You see? A pun between the languages."

"The skipper is really a decent old skin," said Pepper. "'Tis plain he despises landlubbers, but he's gallant enough to us ladies."

"And he keeps the lesser swabbies from getting *too* gallant," said Sarah. "The worst they do is ogle and leer when we show a leg."

"Shit, I hope the gallant skipper falls overboard and drowns," growled Tim, and he continued to pass the days at the gunwale. But now, whenever possible, he chose the one to which Peggy was tethered, so that the elephant stood between his misery and any gloating onlookers.

The other troupers, as soon as the novelty of being at sea had given way to the monotony of being at sea, occupied themselves at their various specialties. Magpie Maggie Hag, after making the acrobats' short-legged fleshings for the three Chinese, resewed the rip panel in the *Saratoga,* then turned out extra

costumes for the other performers—much better made and more bedizened
with spangles than their old ones—including, for Colonel Ramrod and Barnacle
Bill, new ring uniforms positively stiff with gold-braid frogs and brandenburgs
and epaulettes. The circus women, more than the men, were pleased that everybody should have extra changes of clothing, because it would enable them to
spend less time at the washtub. Or it would when they got ashore; there was no
keeping clean aboard a collier.

The ship was a lot less besooted when the engines were shut down and the
wind blowing, but even then the hold seemed somehow to exhale coal dust, and
there was always at least a trickle of smoke from the stack. The deckhands who,
on any other kind of ship, would have passed their free time chipping rust or
laying paint, on this *Pflichttreu* had to keep up the Sisyphean task of endlessly
sweeping and swabbing. So the circus costumes, old and new, were kept tight
shut in the cabin trunks, and the troupers wore only derelict overalls or old and
threadbare frocks. And when those got unwearably filthy, the women would
launder them in the manner called by the seamen Maggie-Millering—tying
them in a bundle to a rope, throwing the bundle overside and towing it through
the seawater.

Some of the company were able to rehearse their routines, and work on new
ones, even when the ship was under sail and therefore riding at a steep slant.
Hannibal could juggle anything that came to hand, from marlinspikes to the
dining cabin's best glassware, no matter how the ship was cavorting, and the
Chinese could do almost as well, using their feet and toes, and Yount could do
his walkabout exercises with a cannonball on the back of his bent neck. Edge,
using one of the Henry repeater carbines, shot the scavenger birds that congregated whenever Doc emptied the galley slops overside.

"Why waste ammunition on fowl we can't eat?" Sarah asked him.

"Got to learn the carbine's quirks," said Edge. "The world's best sharpshooter
could hardly hit Peggy with an unfamiliar weapon, even if he's always shot the
same make and model. Every single firearm out of the same gunsmithy has its
particular peculiarities. This one bears a tad high and to the left, but I think I've
got it figured now." And to prove that, he lifted the Henry to his shoulder and
neatly bagged a hovering petrel.

Under the tutelage of Pepper and Paprika, Sunday and Quincy Simms continued their calisthenics. Whatever other and more complex contortions they
did, each of them was made every day to bring on deck a dining-cabin chair and,
holding to its back, do the "side practice"—extending the left, then the right leg
straight sideways, then forward, then backward, and holding each position for
five minutes without a tremor. And they would have to do that all their working
lives, said Pepper—as she and Paprika did—to assure maintaining their "poise
and balance." Quincy had become, as planned, the most limber of the Simmses.
He was now able to stand on even a slanted deck, do an unsupported body bend
backward, and not just put his hands on the deck but clutch them to his ankles
and bring his head, face forward, between his knees.

Mullenax was wise enough not to get into the lion cage to rehearse Maximus
in his old tricks or try any new ones, and Pepper would not heft the perchpole
with or without Paprika on it, except when the ship rode perfectly level. But it
did that frequently enough. The squat, heavy and sparsely canvased *Pflichttreu*
required a brisk wind, even from dead astern, to move at all, and was incapable

of sailing close-hauled. So there was always a low fire kept burning under the boilers, and the watch officers and engineers had a finely developed sense of when the engines were likely to be needed and ought to be stoked. Thus, whenever a fair wind began to fade, or veered anywhere forward of the ship's beam, and the bridge officer signaled for engines, the black gang could have them going before the ship lost way.

Monday Simms was equally sensitive where the engines were concerned. After the first day aboard, she had ceased chafing her thighs together *continuously* in rhythm with the deck's tremors. Now she went into her peculiar trance only when, for navigational reasons, the bridge signaled a change in engine speed or when, for mechanical reasons, the gang below made some adjustment in the engines' workings. Whatever she was doing—harness polishing or Maggie-Millering or helping Quincy shovel animal droppings overside—Monday would sense the change in rhythm before anyone else could, and her eyes would glaze and her thighs begin going rub-rub-rub.

Mullenax was also beguiled by the ship's engines, but in a different way. As he had demonstrated by his treasuring of the apparatus that turned out to be the balloon *Saratoga,* Abner was a man interested in paraphernalia, novel inventions and contraptions in general. So, out of curiosity, he descended into the bowels of the ship whenever he had an opportunity. For some time, he never ventured lower than the catwalk, where hung the engineer's blackboard and some green-glass gauges in which the water level minutely surged and ebbed to the ship's motion. From there, Mullenax could gaze down into the long, narrow room between the coal bunkers, a place crammed with machinery—black iron, shining steel, walking-beams jerking like the legs of giant grasshoppers, convoluted and intertwined pipes and tubes encrusted with salt and furred with fungus. The room was only gloomily lamplighted except when an opened firebox door lit up the place like a glimpse of Hell. The workers in it might have been demons—half-naked, coal-blackened, sweat-glossy—as they moved up and down the walkway between the high flywheel and the spinning horizontal shaft, perpetually greasing things with their long-beaked oil cans.

Eventually Mullenax got to be such a frequent fixture that the chief engineer—a short, rotund, red-faced, balding, middle-aged Münchner named Carl Beck—warmed to him and took him down among the machinery and showed him things and explained them. "The men always greasing are, because always well lubricated the thrust block, the tunnel shaft and the stern gland must be." Chief Beck was also given to grousing about the attitude toward engineers manifested by Captain Schilz and the upper hierarchy of the merchant marine:

"The old-line officers, all once stick-and-string men were—sailing men—so nothing but poker-pushers they call us. They resent that officer rank and privileges we have. Scheisse! So masters of all the ships they still are, all the rules they make. But of the skills we must have they know nothing—the vigilance of us required—the wicked compound engines and lethal live steam to control."

"Looks to me like you do real good at it," Mullenax said sincerely. "I don't reckon steam would run a balloon, would it?"

"Wie bitte?" said Chief Beck, taken aback. "You mean Luftballon? Nein, nein. For balloon Wasserstoff you need—hydrogen gas."

"Somebody said we'd need a generator."

"Ja. The hydrogen to make. Ein Gasentwickler."

"Could you make one of them things?"

"Ich denke... well, different types there are. To generate by decomposition of water, ein Apparat as big as this ship you would need. A mobile generator you would wish. The action of oil of vitriol upon iron filings to employ. Ja, that I could build. Let me see..." He took down his blackboard that recorded steam pressure, vacuum pressure, feed-water temperature and so on. He wiped a clean spot on it and took a bit of chalk. "Zunächst... your balloon how much gas requires?"

"Twenty-five thousand cubic feet. I remember that."

Beck scribbled, then mumbled, "Sagen wir... seven hundred kiloliters."

"Put that way, it sounds a sight smaller."

But Beck was no longer listening; he was calculating and muttering to himself. So Mullenax went topside and sought out Florian.

"The man ought to be a prime recruit, Mr. Florian. He's purely fed up with being a lowly ship's engineer. I bet, if you offered him the job of being our balloon's gasser, he'd jump at it. But besides that, Carl rides a hobbyhorse. In private, he yearns to be a musician. Claims he can play three or four instruments."

"No! A mechanist who is also an amateur windjammer?"

"And you know what else? He's put his trade and his hobby together, and back home in Mernchin, wherever that is, he's done built himself one of them cally-opes you're always saying you'd like to own."

"I'll be damned," said Florian, his eyes shining. "Almost too good to be true. A master engineer *and* a windjammer *and* with his own steam organ. Yes, Chief Beck certainly sounds worth cultivating."

"Well, I got a suggestion about that. Another thing Carl does, he's always frettin' about the state of his liver, and how bald he's gettin', and how unsalubrious it is to work in that heat and stink and noise all the time. Now and again, I give him a dose of tonic out of my jug. But I thought maybe... if old Maggie has some secret recipe for growin' hair..."

"I'll be damned," Florian said again. "For a one-eyed man, Barnacle Bill, you often see a lot more than most of us do with two."

Meanwhile, Pepper had charmed a favor out of Stitches, the ship's sailmaker, a gaunt Welshman who might have been Florian's age, but looked much older. She persuaded him to make, at her direction, a rig for her hair-hang act: a small but sturdy thing of a heavy canvas strap, a metal ring and a metal turnbuckle. She charmed him even further by inviting him to be the one to help her test it. While Stitches freed a block and fall at the forward mast, Pepper braided her long hair into a firm plait, buckled the canvas strap around it, then did some complicated splicing of her braid, so she had a pretty chignon at the back of her head with the apparatus securely fixed in it. Stitches brought the rope end and expertly knotted it to her metal ring. Then, looking apprehensive but obeying her "houp... *là!*" he hauled on the free rope end, smoothly but strongly, and she was lifted off the deck and up among the shrouds.

The troupers and various deckhands and officers had gathered by then, and cheered as Pepper, hanging some twenty feet above the deck, supported only by her own tresses— drawn so tight that she had slant eyes and a masklike grin— did an elaborate series of poses, spins and acrobatic convolutions. When she signaled to the sailmaker to lower her again, and had taken bows to the admiring applause, she undid the chignon, shook out her hair into its customary curly mane and took her new contrivance to stow safely in the women's cabin. Then she, as Mullenax had done, made a confidential report to Florian.

"Dai's a good man with needle and thimble and palm, and he's not leery of tackling new jobs. Seeing as our poor Ignatz is gone, ye might be wanting a replacement canvas boss. I can confide that this old feller hates steam as much as the captain does, because he has so little to do nowadays. His trade is being abolished. Ye might just want to see how he'd feel about joining out."

"I will," said Florian. "What did you say his name is?"

"Dai Goesle. One of them frightful Taffy names that looks worse than it sounds. She spelled it. "But 'tis pronounced Gwell.""

Of all the troupers, Fitzfarris, with no act to rehearse or improve upon, was worst beset by boredom. So, to give both himself and Rouleau something to occupy them, he went to the convalescent's cabin and asked for instruction in the art of voice projection.

"Bien. To begin with," said Rouleau, "engastrimythism, ventriloquism— whichever word you prefer—they both mean 'talking from the belly.' But the Greeks and Romans called it that merely to impress the ancient rubes. The belly is no way involved and there is really nothing to learn, only to practice. All you do is employ a voice not your own, and keep your lips unmoving while you do it. The rest is simple misdirection of the audience's attention, by your gestures and facial expressions."

"Peter Piper picked a peck..." Fitz tried, and gave up. "Come on, Jules. It's impossible to say that without moving your lips."

"C'est vrai. So you do not say that. You do not say any word that has labial consonants in it. If you absolutely must utter such words, however, there is a way to fake. Say Feeter Fifer instead of Peter Piper. For big say dig. For mice say nice. No lip movement. Drop such a word into a sentence, nobody will notice. People always hear what they expect to hear. From *where* they hear it depends on your good playacting. Since you will be doing the act on the midway, you will be working closer to your audience than I did in the ring, and you should have better success. I hope so."

"Thank you, Jules," said Fitz, keeping his lips slightly apart and unmoving. "I'll go off and practice—uh—fractice."

"Oh, one other thing. Don't have animals around when you're working the act. You can persuade the rubes that you've trapped a baby under a tub, but the animals are smarter. They'll stare at you, where the baby's cry really comes from. Ruin the whole effect."

Fitzfarris went and sat in the shade of the lifeboats slung outboard of the cabins, and practiced. When a deckhand came along the row of boats, checking their davit falls, Fitz pointed and said with great concern, "Mate, I believe there's some stowaway *in* that boat." The seaman gave him a dull look, but then looked more keenly at the boat toward which Fitz was cupping an ear and staring intently—as a disembodied, thickly muffled voice gave a bleat of, "Oo-oo-oh, do let us out!" It took a little while, and several repetitions of pleas such as "Dying in here!" and "Good sir, fetch water!" But when the flabbergasted deckhand began hurriedly unlashing and flinging off the boat's tarpaulin cover, Fitz sauntered away, smiling.

He next happened upon Chips, the ship's carpenter, who was tacking a new tin sheathing around a hatch cover, and Fitz's eye fell speculatively on the tin scraps that fell from the man's shears.

"To make a long story short," Fitz afterward told Florian, "I convinced him that some poor soul had got shut in the hold, back in Baltimore when the hatch was closed. After Chips fell for it, and wanted to kill me, I told him he could pull the same trick on other people. To cast his voice, all he'd have to do is put under his tongue a bit of tin shaped just so." Fitz held out his palm, in which lay a piece of tin, cut in a disk the size of a fifty-cent coin and then bent not quite double, so it vaguely resembled a partly opened clamshell. "I instructed him in shaping it, and he was so grateful that at my request he cut me a whole bushel of the things. Chips is off somewhere now, practicing, and I've got a supply of goods for sale. During the sideshow, I'll do my engastrimyth act, then tell the rubes they can do the same, with one of these voice projectors—"

"Swazzles," Florian said admiringly. "In circus parlance, any such bogus gadget for sale is a swazzle."

"If you say so. Anyhow, they're worth money to us. And meanwhile, Chips is our friend for life—or until he gives up on the swazzle. You got any carpentry work you want done?"

"Hm," said Florian. "I wonder if he has any spare paint..."

Chips did, or at any rate pretended that the blue paint he provided was dispensable stock. The men of the troupe all pitched in to patch and caulk and paint the older wagons, and they came out a near match to the two newer ones. Then Chips contributed his own spare-time labor, to paint again the legends on the wagons' sides. Some of the words stayed the same, but others Florian wanted changed. Chips proved to have considerable artistic talent, giving the red-and-yellow, black-outlined letters wondrous swashes and curlicues. He even painted the circus's name, in place of the U.S. Army's, on Hannibal's big drum. When Edge saw the neatly done and newly sparkling titles on the wagons, he looked with approval at FLORIAN'S FLOURISHING FLORILEGIUM, but looked with some surprise at the lines beneath:

> Combined CONFEDERATE American Circus,
> Menagerie & Educational Exhibition!

"I thought you liked to brag and look prosperous," he said to Florian. "Putting 'Confederate' in there, it'll look more like we're desperate and refugeeing."

"Not at all, Zachary. You are evidently unaware of the climate of European opinion these past years. Practically every nation and native over there was hoping the Confederacy would win the war. This will gain us sympathy and warmth and welcome. You'll see."

"You're the main guy. I'll take your word for it."

"That's another thing. I must inform the whole company. I am no longer the main guy. In Europe, I shall more properly be referred to and addressed as the Governor. And the pavilion will be called the chapiteau, not the Big Top. There are various other differences in terminology. The pitch is the tober, the rubes are flatties or jossers. The rope-fall is a lungia. The ring is the pista. A straw house is a sfondone and a bloomer house is a bianca..."

"It sounds like Europe got most of its circus jargon from Italy."

"And why not? It was the ancient Romans who *invented* the circus." Florian

sighed slightly. "Rather a pity, that the Italians will not again found a Roman
Empire. In fact, Rome—the Papal State—remains the only holdout, now that
the rest of the peninsula has so recently united into one kingdom. Still... Italy
... birthplace of the circus. It is only a coincidence of circumstances that is
taking us first to that country. But might it not be a happy augury?"

"Hell, I'll be happy to get anywhere. Sea travel is as boring as garrison duty in
flat old Kansas."

"Pray, do not say such things. At sea, the alternative to boredom is disaster.
Try not to call it down upon us. I've warned Maggie, too. She has lately been
glooming and fidgeting, and mumbling something about an ominous waterwheel."

"I think she's got wheels on the brain," said Edge. "Wheels are all she's
dukkered recently. And we sure won't see anything like a waterwheel until we're
safe on land again." He looked past Florian and frowned. "What are those Chinks
up to?"

The three Chinese had discerned that Florian had no more chores to ask of
the ship's carpenter, so they were presenting him with a request of their own.
Chips looked alarmed as he was surrounded by the gibbering and gesticulating
little men, but he relaxed and smiled when one of them pressed upon him a
piece of paper and they all jabbed their fingers at the pencil drawing on it.

"Oh, aye. You want a thing like that, mates?" He brought the paper to show
to Florian and Edge. "Your John Chinee fellers are askin' me to build this for 'em.
But you're the pilots."

The drawing was elegant and instantly recognizable. "A teeterboard," said
Florian. "For their act. Well, it's certainly all right with me, Chips, if you want to
go to the trouble."

"Depends on how big they want it." He consulted with the Chinese, meaning
that they gabbled excitedly, took Chips's hands and held them at various measures while they pointed to the drawing's various features. Finally Chips called to
Florian, "Only a wee one. I can do it," and went off to the stores hold to seek
materials.

Two days later, he had the thing finished and brought it on deck for the
antipodists' approval. It was a broad plank, about four feet long, on a heavy base
no more than eighteen inches high, and Chips had put a padded leather cushion
on either end of the teeter. The Chinese were vociferous at sight of it and, two at
a time, stood on the board and seesawed it. Then they vociferated some more at
Chips.

"Want it made heavier, as I understand 'em," he said. "With beefier hardware
and hinges."

"Damned if I can see why," said Florian. "They're all featherweights. If it's
troublesome, friend..."

"No, no," muttered Chips. "I want to get it right."

He brought it back the next day and the Chinese put it through a rigorous
test. One man stood on one end of the teeter, a second jumped heavily on the
other end and bounced the first, twirling and somersaulting, through the air to
land standing upright on the third man's shoulders. Then that top man plunged
feet first to the board, to send the man on the other end soaring even higher,
with many more midair flips and contortions, to land on the third man's
shoulders. Then they all became a sort of flickering blur, as they variously

jumped on the board, flew through the air, landed on one another and jumped again, until all three seemed to be doing everything simultaneously.

When they finally slowed, and became three distinct persons, and the teeter-board ceased to rock and thump, and the watchers cheered, the Chinese stood side by side, bowed politely, then dragged the teeterboard to where Peggy was tethered, and began to jabber at Hannibal. After a moment, he announced to the watchers in an incredulous voice:

"Dey wants ol' Peggy t' git on dis rocker perch."

"Well," said Florian, after brief deliberation, "she can stand on a pedestal, Abdullah, so let's see if she can do this. The Chinamen seem to have encountered some such bull act before."

Hannibal made a face of disassociating himself from the consequences, but obediently prodded and spoke to Peggy. The elephant's chains were long enough for her to lift all four feet and move a step or two. When she lurched away from the gunwale, she revealed the wretched and retching Tim Trimm, draped there as usual. With great care but without hesitation, Peggy shuffled slowly up the inclined board. She looked a trifle surprised when the weight of her forebody made the board rock and gently tilt her forward, but it did not frighten her. After a pensive moment, and without moving her big feet, the bull shifted her weight slightly and the board gently rocked backward again. Turning her head, Peggy favored the company with bright eyes, uplifted trunk and what was almost a human grin of pride and pleasure. Then, without command, she continued shifting her weight and seesawing forward and backward.

"I'll be damned to Davy's locker," said the admiring Chips, and he was the first to break into applause.

Thereafter, when the Chinese spent almost every day doing their own practices on the teeterboard and evolving ever more spectacular flying acrobatics, they would allow a certain while for Peggy to enjoy the thing, too—but only on days when the *Pflichttreu* was under steam and riding level. After the elephant had got used to seesawing by herself, she was gradually persuaded to do the same with one and another of the Chinese on her back, until all three of them were up there, doing poses and pyramids, and eventually with Monday and Tuesday also up there joining in the posturing, while the great beast happily teetered and occasionally trumpeted with joy.

2

ON THE FOURTEENTH DAY out from Cape Charles, when the ship was somewhere in the featureless vastness between the Azores and the Madeiras, steaming across a sunlit sea of only frolicsome choppiness, the voyage ceased to be boring.

That day began ordinarily enough. The wind was out of the east, so the *Pflichttreu* was proceeding on engines, but the headwind dispersed most of the stack's smoke and soot. Rouleau had been brought out on the foredeck, still supine on his pallet and still rigidly fixed in his bran box, but looking cheerful as he watched the doings of the other troupers. The Chinese were rehearsing with the teeterboard and Peggy, while Monday and Tuesday Simms waited to join in. The Quakemaker was up in the very prow of the ship, trying mightily to see if he could lift the massive anchor all by himself, but not doing very well at it. Near Rouleau's pallet, Florian and Fitzfarris sat playing blackjack for matchsticks. When Florian took several hands in a row, Fitz cursed mildly, shoved over his matchsticks and cards, and said:

"A man of your talents ought to be in the confidence game full time. How is it you got into the circus business instead?"

Florian shrugged. "Apprenticeship, the same as any other art or profession." He shuffled the cards and looked dreamily off toward the horizon. "The Donnert Circus came to my hometown when I was fourteen years old. When it departed, I went with it. Maggie Hag was on that show then, and she took me under her wing."

"The classic runaway story. Your folks didn't chase after you?"

"No. My mother was dead. My father surely realized where I'd gone, but he may even have approved of my venturesomeness. He had always wanted me to be something better than the millhand he was, and God knows the circus was a good many cuts above that."

"Anything is. But how did you persuade the circus to hire you? Just a kid."

Florian smiled. "If by 'hire' you mean 'pay,' there was no pay. I might not even have got peck—might have had to forage for myself—if I hadn't had Mag plugging for me. As it was, I had to sleep on the folded canvas in the tent wagon. *Among* the folds, when the weather got cold. Until I took up with my first—wife, to put it euphemistically. An équestrienne, twice my age. She was not at all attractive, but her caravan was."

"I take it this was a mud show, then."

"Lord, no. Donnert's was a fair-sized and reputable circus. Still is, as far as I know."

"Did you do an act? Roustabout? What?"

"Hell, it was a long time before I could even dignify myself with the title of roustabout. I swamped out cages, I carried water buckets, I posted paper, I did every least and dirtiest job there was to do. And there were plenty of them, on a show the size of Donnert's. Oh, eventually I worked my way up to a meanly paid position on the crew, and later I did some juggling. But I thank heaven that I never had to depend for a career on either my muscularity or my performing graces. As you have remarked, my talents tended more to the, ahem, acquisitive and the annunciatory. As I moved from circus to circus—from the Donnert to the Renz to the Busch, back to the Donnert again—I was variously a talker for the midway joints, and for the sideshow, and I worked advance and patch, and I became quite proficient at horsetrading. First for mere road stock, but then for ring stock, and finally I was entrusted even with buying the exotic animals. Along the way, also, I acquired various other wives, so-called, of various nationalities. Acquired and discarded or lost them. Happily, I did not lose the languages I learned from them."

"Classic success story, too, I guess. When did you strike out on your own?"

"After my second stint with the Donnert. Maggie Hag was still on that show, and it was she who prodded me to such overweening ambition. She even came with me, which was a real act of faith. It was she and I, and what small menagerie I could afford."

Still absentmindedly shuffling the cards, Florian went silent, evidently into reverie. After a minute, Fitz asked, "Well? How did you do at it?"

"We kept a step or two ahead of starvation. And what profits there were, I plowed back into the business. We gathered unto us a few more exotics, a few wagons, a few boozy or antiquated or otherwise next-to-unemployable troupers and crewmen. The one and only really good act I managed to hire, toward the end, was the perchpole. Pepper and Paprika. I might not have got *them* if they had not also just been starting their careers. They were only about fifteen or sixteen years old."

"You said 'toward the end.' Did you go bust?"

"I, sir, have *never* gone bust," Florian said, a little stiffly. "I meant toward the end of my stay in Europe. Maybe you wouldn't know, but, after all the revolutions, rebellions and other uproars of 1848, there had begun the great migration of Europeans to the United States. Well, this was ten years later, and both Pepper and Paprika were getting letters from relatives, friends, other troupers who had gone to America. The usual—streets paved with gold, opportunity unlimited, come make your fortune in the New World. So we decided we would try. It didn't require anything like this *Pflichttreu* to bring my Florilegium across the pond that time; we could have come in a rowboat. It was only Maggie, Pepper, Paprika and me."

"I gather you *did* do well in the States."

"Oh, passably... passably. Monsieur Roulette there will verify it. He was one of the first Americans to join out with me. But then, damn it, along came *your* rebellion and knocked everything to flinders."

"Christ knows it did," Fitz said feelingly. "Do you think you'd have done better to stay in Europe?"

Florian sighed. "Well, that's what we'll soon find out, won't we?" He looked dreamily off toward the horizon again. "I had one ambition in those days that I never got to achieve. *The* ambition of every circus man. I have been to Paris many times, but never—neither with my little tramp show nor with any of the more respectable ones—never did I go with a *circus* to Paris...."

"Arrah!" exclaimed Pepper, as she walked unannounced into the Simms children's cabin. "I swan, all you pickanins are queer in the attic." Sunday Simms guiltily spun away from the washstand mirror, where she had been studying her reflection. "The injines just changed tempo, so your sister is doing that stand-up kerfuffle of hers. And *you*—what in bejasus have ye *done* to yourself?"

"Improvements," Sunday said sheepishly.

"Im*prove*ments? Just look how you look!" Now Pepper espied the bottles and jars Sunday had laid out on her bunk. "What the divvil *is* all this muck?"

Sunday said defensively, "I heard the captain mention that we'll sight the first land in maybe five days. I thought I'd practice making myself pretty, for when we finally get to port."

"Crown Princess Hair-Straightening Pomade?" Pepper was officiously examining the labels. "Dixie Moonglow Complexion-Lightening Cream? Where did you get all these nigger-swindling quack physics?"

"They're mine! I bought them, that last day in Baltimore. Clover Lee helped me pick them out."

"But whatever for, girl?"

"To make me look less like a *nigger,* that's what for!" Sunday's language lost some of its acquired precision. "Less like a *pickaninny*—that just anybody can walk in on her without knocking, and paw through her belongings!"

"Whisht, darlin'... easy, easy..." said Pepper, raising her hands in placation. "Ye're right. I had no call to do that. 'Twas only looking for Pap I was, but I had no right to barge in. And now that I've apologized, alannah, let me tell ye something. Ye've no need for that muck on your face and hair. Ye're as pretty a colleen as any white girl, only a different color."

"That's right," Sunday said bitterly. "I'm a yellow rose, a mulatto, a high-yaller, a buffalo gal, a nigger. So tell me, what would a pretty *nigger* girl look like?"

"Be blessed if I know. I never laid eyes on any such thing amongst the real black ones. But instead of trying to cover up your tan color, ye ought to play up the prettiness. Ye've got a plenty of it." Pepper again scornfully scanned the array of cosmetics. "Dixie Moonglow, bedad! Dixie Blaflum is what it is! Throw away that paleface ointment. The three of yez Simms gals have got the complexion of doe fawns, and yez ought to glory in it. Forget the hair straightener, too. Ye've not got Uncle Tom wool nor kinks, but nice wavy hair."

"Only on top," said Sunday, sniffling. "Do you remember, Pep, how you and Pap told Clover Lee about the—the other hair—down here? How men go wild about it? Well, mine—down here—it *is* kinky. Just little knots of hair. Like a sprinkle of peppercorns. They don't even begin to hide my... my... you know."

Pepper laughed heartily. "But why hide it, minikin? 'Tis the mother of all the saints, as we say. Anyhow, as I can tell you who shouldn't, there's them that *prefer* a woman's periwinkle-flower not to have foliage on it. So it's plain visible and easily accessible. For very par-ti-cu-lar attentions, which no doubt ye'll learn about in time. Now, wipe your face and wash your hair and throw all this blaflum out the porthole. Where is that Clover Lee? I've a mind to give her the father and mother of a cussing for her letting you buy these humbug things."

"Well, she bought some things, too. And she's practicing with hers, just like I was. Pap is helping her."

"Is she indeed?" Pepper said frostily. "Where?"

"One of the lifeboats is uncovered, but it's slung up too high off the deck for anybody to see into it. In there they can take off some of their clothes and have a sunbath. I don't know why anybody would *want* her skin tan-colored, but—"

But Pepper was already out the door. Fuming, she went and stood below the one lifeboat that did not have a tarpaulin over it, and listened. It sounded as if Paprika was giving Clover Lee much the same advice she herself had just given Sunday. But the white girl seemed to be taking it more submissively than the mulatto had done. Anyway, the only voice audible was Paprika's.

"Angyal, these are semmiség—silly things. Such garbage! Mrs. Mill's Mammarial Balm and Bust Elevator! Cadmium ointment and a funny glass-and-rubber bowl." Paprika laughed. "I see. The ointment is to stimulate the titties and the vacuum globe is to suck them outwards. What foolish badarság. Clover Lee, the only way to develop yourself there is to grow normally, and you are doing nicely in that regard. Here, let me show you what an artist once showed me in Pest. What artists consider the ideal proportions for a woman's breasts. Allow me to touch you..."

There came a faint noise of their bodies shifting position inside the boat. Pepper ground her teeth.

"Here, regard the distance between my two fingertips—one on your nipple, the other on your collarbone above. That distance should exactly equal the distance from one nipple to the other. It does, you see. Also, the distance between those two darling little buds should be precisely one-fourth of the circumference of your whole chest at the level of your nipples. Allow me..."

There was another sound of movement.

"As nearly as I can measure with a mere embrace, angyal, you are of the ideal female dimensions. And as you grow, those dimensions will keep pace. Meanwhile, it is obvious that the nipples are already most femininely sensitive. See? How they reach out to be touched some more?"

Pepper started to make her presence known, but desisted when the next sound was only the clink of glass, and Paprika went on:

"Regard this other awful ürülek you bought. Dixie Belle Extract of White Heliotrope. Jaj! It is a waste of money, Clover Lee, ever to buy manufactured perfume. I will tell you a Magyar secret, long known only to us women of Hungary. The most seductive and irresistible scent a woman can wear is her own. The aroma of her own most private and most precious fluid, the nemi redv, her juices of joy. What you do is take some with your finger, like this—allow me, angyal—and dab it behind your ears, at your wrists, between your breasts..."

Clover Lee finally and suddenly spoke. Her voice was low and tremulous, but determined. "P-please...don't d-do any more of that." There was a slight scuffling noise, and the boat rocked a bit. "I th-thank you...for teaching me things. But I think I want to get dressed now. *Please* stop that."

Pepper snarled silently and bent to jump for the lifeboat's gunwale. But, at the same instant, the whole ship under her made a sudden movement of its own, and she was thrown headlong on the iron deck. The *Pflichttreu* had slowed as violently as if the Quakemaker had flung the anchor overboard and snubbed it. Simultaneously, there came a terrific mechanical howl and clatter from the ship's bowels, and shouts from officers and crewmen everywhere: "Belay that!" and "Scaldings!" and "Shake a leg!"

Peggy had been standing on the teeterboard, tilted aft. When the ship gave that jerk, it tilted the board and the elephant abruptly the other way. Though Peggy managed to keep her feet, the acrobats on her back were spilled to the deck. Even those people simply standing about went sprawling, as well. For a few seconds, there was confusion and shouting, and men running, and the deck —the whole ship—was juddering like a coffee grinder, and the masts and derricks flailed in all directions. The tall smokestack toppled with a ringing crash and a twanging of guy wires and a voluminous eructation of smuts, rust, scales and scurfs that enveloped the ship's entire upper works in a suffocating black cloud. The vibration increased to spasm and the grating howl from the engine room rose to a roar, before it abruptly went silent and the whole ship went still, and the fallen people began picking themselves up and brushing at the grime all over them.

Then the officers and men were shouting again, even louder in the silence. Some deckhands leapt for the shrouds and climbed to the yards, others clambered to the island top to secure the smokestack before it could roll overboard, others took precautionary stations at the lifeboat davits. Before any of the passengers could begin asking what had happened, Mullenax came popping up from the companion leading below, and shouted to tell them.

"Threw its propeller, it did! Shaft runnin' free, rods all jumpin'! Everybody grabbin' levers and valves to shut down. I got the hell out of the way."

"Is anybody injured?" asked Florian, his voice shaky. "Is everybody all right?"

He swept his gaze around the troupers on the foredeck. Yount was approaching from the bow, looking dazed and rubbing a bump on his bald head. Pepper and a couple of seamen were helping Clover Lee and Paprika down from their lifeboat. Those two, having been directly under the cabin eaves where the falling stack landed, were filthy with soot from head to toe. They were hastily fumbling to do up the buttons of their frocks, and were misbuttoning most of them. The scattered and hard-fallen acrobats were the last to pick themselves up, but get up they did, apparently unimpaired. Peggy remained in the position the jolt had put her in. Her four big feet were still on the teeterboard, but her bulk leaned outward against the gunwale alongside her.

"I thought I'd really made a quake," said Yount. "What happened?"

Pepper took Paprika aside and, while maternally dusting her off and buttoning her properly, was also giving her a most peppery scolding, to which Paprika replied with equal heat. But they kept their voices low:

"... Shimmy-lifting... scunging like an old fairy in a schoolyard..."

"Jealous are we, Pep? Did you have *your* eye on that one of the little tea cakes?"

"Don't come the lardy-dardy with me! The totty clearly wants none of your playing at up-tails. Instead of cherry picking, ye could at least have the decency to try it on with somebody your own age."

"Oh, shut up! They'll hear."

But everyone else was listening to Mullenax's report on the chaotic state of affairs below and, when he had finished, Edge asked him, "What happens now?"

"Well, I know there's a spare propeller. I seen it. But how they'll go about puttin' it on, underneath the water, I'm damned if I—hey, is Jules hurt?"

They had completely overlooked Rouleau, where he lay, and only now became aware that he was frantically waving his arms and shouting weakly, "Nom de dieu, go back! Turn around! Man overboard!"

"What? Where? Who?"

Out of breath and hoarse from yelling unheard, Rouleau gasped to Edge, the first to bend over him, "Peggy... bumped... I saw... Tiny Tim..."

Edge dashed to the side, looked aft and said, "Jesus." Far astern, there was a dark speck among the choppy waves and—it was hard for him to tell—it might have been thrashing to stay afloat. The ship had seemed to come to a full stop when it lost its screw, but it actually had glided for quite some distance. Now it wallowed and yawed heavily, dead in the water, all momentum gone, while the officers bawled for the spreading of canvas.

Rouleau told the others, "Tim was leaning over, as usual. When Peggy lurched, she bumped him and he went right over."

Florian reached to seize the sleeve of Captain Schilz, who was hurrying past just then, alternately muttering curses and bellowing orders. "Captain, we must turn back. One of our—"

"Dummkopf!" barked the master, jerking out of his grasp. "We have no headway, no power, the rudder loose it flaps. Until unfurled the sails are, we go no—"

"But there's a man overboard!" several people cried.

"*Was?*" The captain was immediately galvanized, and shouted to the men at the davits to lower a boat.

That was done as swiftly as possible, and the boat began to beat back along the ship's track. Most of the troupe stood at the gunwale, watching its progress and trying to see the speck Edge had spotted, but even he could no longer see it. Sarah spared a look at the elephant, still leaning where she had been lodged, and wearing a most mournful expression.

"Poor Peg looks as guilty as if she had done it on purpose."

"Abdullah," said Florian. "Go and attend your bull. Get her down off that teeter. Make her comfortable and console her."

Peggy seemed reluctant to move, or even to be touched by her keeper, but Hannibal eventually coaxed her to step off the board and stand upright. So, at just about the same time that the seamen in the distant lifeboat were wagging their oars aloft—signaling that there was no sign of Tim Trimm to be found—the other casualty of the accident was revealed. When the elephant heaved her bulk away from the gunwale, Tuesday Simms flopped to the deck in a position impossible to a living body. Obviously she had fallen when the other acrobats did, but on the far side of Peggy. The elephant's leaning weight had crushed her against the rail, pinched and broken her in the middle, and she lay now like a puppet come unstrung, except that she was dripping substances no puppet contains.

Hannibal had to go away and vomit over the side, but, when he was done, he dolefully said to the others, "Ol' Peggy, she was holdin' Tuesday dere a-purpose. Peggy b'lieve anybody still alive, long as dey standin' up. She di'nt want let li'l Tuesday drop an' be dead."

The double funeral, for the dead and the gone, had to wait until the *Pflichttreu* got under way again, for no seaman would willingly drop a dead body directly under his immobile ship. It meant waiting until the spare screw could be put in place, and that operation occupied the rest of this day and all of the next.

The helmsman used the rudder, and the men at the sheets used the set of the sails, to keep the ship as much as possible in one place and on an even keel. The officers directed the moving of every heavy thing in the ship's upper works as far forward as possible, and the black gang below shifted as much coal as possible into the hold's forward bunkers. Even the circus horses were led from the after-deck and tethered with Peggy on the foredeck. The lifeboats were all unslung from their davits, hauled to the bows and pumped full of water. By sundown, the *Pflichttreu,* with every possible weight laid on its fore end, had assumed a new slant, stern up, stem down. A man at the taffrail could look down the transom and see the rudder standing half above the water, with the stub of the propellerless shaft just awash.

Next morning, while deckhands knotted ropes to the stern rail and let them trail down the transom, stokers came hauling the huge brass spare screw topside. Captain Schilz was growling to himself in German that if the verdammt shipowners of the world *must* have steamships, they could at least go back to sidewheels or sternwheels which, if they broke a blade, could be rotated above water for repair.

"Have you had to do this before?" Florian asked him.

"Nein, Gott sei Dank. But I once watched it on another ship done. Simple enough in theory it is. However, in practice...down the ship's stern on a rope going, work for an Alpinist that is...and placing the propeller, the setscrews underwater tightening, work for a Perlenfischer that is. No man of this crew has ever had to do it."

Florian felt a tug on his coattails. He turned to find the three Chinese—all stripped naked—again jabbering and gesticulating, pointing variously to the big screw, to themselves and down to the water. Before Florian or Schilz could express astonishment or anything else, one of the antipodists leapt lithely to the taffrail. He seized a rope and, bracing himself between rope and stern plates, walked himself backward, barefooted and surefooted, down to the water. Once there, he simply kept going backward, right through the surface chop, under the water and out of sight, until only the rope's tautness indicated that he was still in the vicinity. Florian felt another tug, this time at his vest front. One of the other Chinese had pulled his big tin watch from his vest pocket and was jabbing a finger at its dial.

Schilz, peering down at the dark water, murmured more in wonderment than in anger, "Another beschisse Dunkel has himself drowned."

"No . . . these two are wanting me to time him," said Florian, looking from the watch to the spot where the rope went underwater, and after a little he said, "By damn, the man's good at it. At least a minute already." When the water heaved, splashed, and the man grinned up at them, Florian repocketed his watch and said, "A minute and a half, if not nearly two. Maybe these lads *have* been pearl fishers. Anyway, I gather that they are volunteering to do the job for you."

"Du lieber Himmel! To three naked apes I should trust that?"

"Monkey see, monkey do. I'll wager that your men would rather show them how, than have to do it themselves."

The captain grumbled and swore, but finally acceded. And the crewmen were only too happy to relinquish the chore. All that was required was for Chief Beck—doing much sign language and occasionally drawing with a piece of charcoal on the deck—to acquaint the Chinese with the very basic facts that the propeller had on one side a square opening to fit the shaft, and on the other a fairwater that had to point astern, and around its collar four big setscrews that had to be made immovably tight. Then the deckhands lowered the big brass thing on ropes while the Chinese went down another, one of them carrying the setscrew wrench in his teeth.

Actually, the captain's part of the job was the more ticklish. Since the rudder could not be moved while the Chinese were working about it, the *Pflichttreu* had to be held as still as possible by using only the sails. So seamen were on every yard and at every sheet and halyard, and Captain Schilz masterfully orchestrated their hauling in and letting out of canvas. He and the crew and the ship performed well enough that the Chinese manhandled the new screw onto the shaft and secured it there in no more than two hours—during which they took turns at surfacing to breathe: only one at a time and taking only a gulp of air before going under again.

When they climbed back aboard, rather less nimbly than they had gone down, they were given a rousing cheer by the ship's company. Chief Beck went down the companion and Captain Schilz up to the bridge, whence he telegraphed for engines start. The deck began to tremble, and everyone held his breath, and then the captain signaled for slow ahead. The water beneath the transom bubbled and burbled, and the deck's vibration increased, but it was regular, not eccentric—and men who had thrown wood chips overside saw them move astern. Another cheer went up. The captain had the engines stopped and gave orders for all the heavy movables to be rearranged and the ship trimmed to its proper stance again. Not until that long job had been done—at nightfall—did he order the sails refurled and the engines full ahead, and the *Pflichttreu* resumed its voyage.

Stitches the sailmaker provided a sheet of canvas and the big curved needles with which, after Magpie Maggie Hag had prepared Tuesday's body, he helped her sew a shroud. Once enclosed, Tuesday's small remains looked larger than adult size, for she had at her feet a quintal sack of pea coal to weight the pall. Then Stitches disclosed that he was a lay minister of the Dissenter Methodist persuasion—so Captain Schilz was pleased to let him officiate at the next morning's funeral service.

"Lord, we send Thee two small souls that have slipped their cables," he told the sky, as the whole remaining circus troupe and all the off-duty ship's company bowed their heads. "Jacob Brady Russum is already on Thy crew roster, Lord, and the other is about to trudge up Thy gangplank, now just." The canvas containing Tuesday Simms lay, secured by a single rope, on a hatch cover that had been raised and fixed to make an inclined ramp, and at its foot the deck rail had been removed. "We humbly ask Thee to pipe our shipmates aboard with all fitting ceremony, and to kit them out in proper slops, and to mess them always on dandy duff, and to give them only easy duty and daytime watches, and to cuss or cat them only seldom."

Sunday Simms was weeping, making no noise, just letting the tears run down her face. Edge, standing beside her, put an arm down around her shoulders and gave her a compassionate hug. Sunday looked her gratitude up at him and her tears ceased. She even exchanged a small smile with him, from time to time, as Stitches continued to elaborate on his salty tropes.

"We beseech of Thee, Lord, that Thy hand rest soft on these two souls. Grant them fair weather and a clock-dial sea and a following wind, Lord, as they crack their canvas and set sail for Eternity."

After only a few more nautical references, Stitches bent to the book and its far less eloquent standard service. "We therefore commit the body of Tuesday Simms to the deep, to be turned into corruption..."

When everyone had said "Amen," some of them making the sign of the cross, and Florian had murmured the old Roman epitaph—this time in the plural: "Saltaverunt. Placuerunt. Mortui sunt"—a deckhand cut the single line, and Tuesday, with no more sound or fuss than anyone had ever heard her make in life, slid down the hatch cover and over the side and into the sea, and in that creased and crinkled and ruffled water she left not even a briefly visible ripple.

Edge and Yount carried Rouleau back to his cabin, and Edge stayed to comment, "You look like a wet winter, Jules. Is the leg giving you trouble?"

"Non, non, ça marche—or it will eventually, I trust."

"What, then? Grief? None of us got even barely acquainted with that one of the Simms girls. And I can hardly believe you're more broken up about Tim Trimm than you were when Ignatz got killed."

Rouleau sighed. "Non...I do not miss Tim *as* Tim. But he occasionally afforded me a certain relief. I do not mean comical."

"Oh? What, then?"

Rouleau shook his head, but Edge continued to regard him with concern, so he finally sighed again and said, "Ami, on a male midget there are just two things of normal size. Les orifices des deux bouts." There was another long silence. "The reason why I had to leave New Orleans was small boys. Comprenez? As long as Tim was around, repulsive though he was, he enabled me to avoid temptations and embarrassments. Are you scandalized?"

"No," Edge said, after a moment. "No, just sorry for you."

Edge said nothing of that to anyone, but he did go looking for Florian to tell him, "Foursquare John is mumbling that he's going to land in Italy unemployed. He's got a point. First his sideshow lost its Fat Lady and now one of its White African Pygmies. When you subtract one-third from a set of triplets, you're not left with much of a curiosity to show."

"Tut tut, he mustn't worry," Florian said airily. "There are plenty of freaks to be found in Europe. Hell, some of them are wearing crowns and coronets. We'll just have to work things out as we go along. What we'll have the hardest time replacing is Tiny Tim."

"Why? There must be more midgets and dwarfs in the world than any other kind of freaks."

"Oh, yes, quite. But I meant we'll miss Tim *as* Tim."

Edge gave Florian much the same look he had earlier given Rouleau, and said, "All right, nil nisi bonum and all that. On a funeral day, I can be as properly hypocritical as anybody. Still, that Russum was nothing but a little blister."

"And a great loss *because* he was a little blister. We must try to get another one."

"Another loathsome midget?"

"It doesn't even have to be a midget. Any kind of new performer, as long as he or she is loathsome."

"Have you gone crazy?"

"Zachary, you do not yet have long experience of managing a company of temperamental artistes. But you must have noticed that, in the main, we've all got along together quite well. Very little friction, very few quarrels. It was because we *all* detested Tiny Tim. In him, we had a focus for all our ill feelings and animosities. We could concentrate them on him, and thereby dissipate them, and therefore more easily endure the foibles and crotchets of our other companions, the slings and arrows of everyday life."

Edge considered, then nodded. "Now that I think about it, I have to concede that you're right. So... as soon as we land, we've got to start scouting for another despicable dwarf?"

"We need a little person, yes. And we need a clown. That's a must for any circus. And we need another abominable toad like Tim. If we can find all three in one skin, at one salary, so much the better. Better yet if he or she can also play the cornet."

Four days later, they raised the Strait of Gibraltar, and that raised the spirits of all the troupers and all but the mossiest shellbacks among the crew. As a sort of celebratory gesture, chief engineer Carl Beck came topside with a small gift he had made for the circus ladies.

"Watching you practice the other day I was," he said. "And to me it occurred:

when a pretty lady does a pretty movement, up or down going, it would be good if a little musical accompaniment she had, at the same time up or down trilling."

He had collected, from his engine-room stores, eight tin oil-vent caps, all different sizes, and had strung them on a two-foot length of fishing line, graded from large cap down to small. Holding the line dangling from one hand, he could run a metal dipstick along the bits of tin, up or down, and make them give a melodious ripple of ringing. He demonstrated how they could play a slow octave, say, when Sarah unfolded swanlike in one of her bareback postures, or a quick tinkling arpeggio as Sunday spun through a fast one-hand walkover.

"Bedad, and a sweet ascending trill when I get h'isted by me hair," said Pepper, "or a descending one as Paprika comes down from the perch."

Beck said, "Aber natürlich, for more dramatic movements, big dramatic band music you should have. However, these little Kinkerlitzchen, even one who is no musician can play."

"It takes a real musician, though," said Florian, "to *invent* something like that. Ahem. I should think such a musician would seek avenues in which to explore such talents."

"Ja..." Beck said uncertainly. "I have been thinking so... but I must think more." Then he spied Mullenax, and seized on him. "Herr Einäugig! I have some reading in my technical manuals done, regarding your Gasentwickler."

"Huh?"

"The Handbücher says one kiloliter of hydrogen gas it takes to lift half a kilo of weight. Therefore, I think the generator—"

"Oh, yeah. The generator. But before we discuss that, Chief, I want you to meet another little lady. Our company apothecary. I was tellin' her about your— uh—your concern for your hair. And I do believe she's concocted a remedy for that."

"Im Ernst? Wunderbar! With embraces I shall meet her."

As Mullenax swept Beck off to meet Magpie Maggie Hag, Florian smiled after them and rubbed his hands together, then went off himself to find the sailmaker. Stitches Goesle was, as usual—except when he had preached the funeral—wearing the heavy leather belt that jingled with its array of knives, awls, fids and spikes.

"Mr. Goesle, the captain was kind enough to give me some blank paper. Could you cut it into pieces small enough—and sew them into pages—to make eighteen little conduct books?"

"To be sure. But what the deuce are conduct books?"

"To show to the authorities on demand. European magistrates and constables and hotelkeepers are exceedingly suspicious of traveling show folk. Each of us must carry such a book, and put down in it our occupation and age and description and all that. Then, whenever we engage a lot or take lodgings, on our departure we must have the mayor, the landlord, whoever, write in the book that we caused no trouble or breakage, did not get offensively drunk, things of that nature. In fact, I shall ask Captain Schilz to make the first entries in our books. I trust he will give us all a good character."

It soon became evident even to the lubberly passengers that the early-autumn winds of the Mediterranean, though mild and pleasant, were maddeningly contrary, shifting from point to point of the compass. The captain, still determined to burn no more of his cargo than was absolutely necessary, called for so many and such frequent changes from steam to sail and back again that the *Pflichttreu*, which had crossed the whole Atlantic—even with the mid-ocean delay—in twenty days, took another nine to cross a mere half of the Mediterranean, from the Gibraltar Strait to the Ligurian Sea. There, on a late afternoon, Quincy Simms was the first to sight the white Livorno lighthouse, and he gave a yell, and all the passengers excitedly milled about the deck, looking at the other ships around them in the harbor roads. But then a steam launch chugged fussily out from around the breakwater, and the uniformed men aboard it waved "stay away!" gestures. When the launch was close enough, one of its crew shouted through a megaphone, in several languages, for the *Pflichttreu* to stand off.

On the bridge, Captain Schilz cursed and said, "I want to be berthed before dark. What is wrong here?" He grabbed his bridge trumpet and bawled down, "Was gibt es? Che cosa c'e?"

The launch officers conveyed that they were asking the *Pflichttreu* to delay only briefly its entry into the harbor, and they pointed to something that was occurring about a thousand yards away across the water. Captain Schilz used his spyglass to look at it, but it was easily visible, even in the waning light, to the circus folk lining the port gunwale. On the sea between them and the squat, crumbling, red Fortezza Vecchia, there sailed an immaculate three-masted man-of-war under a full cloud of canvas.

"Look you at her hard and well, mates," said Stitches, joining them. "You'll never see the like of her again. An old line-of-battle ship, vintage of Villeneuve and Nelson, two-decker, seventy-four guns. Wearing every thread she's got, from flying jib to skys'ls to spanker."

The ship also was wearing a flag, and it was not the red-white-and-green of the lately united Italy, nor the flag of any of the preunification nations. It was a pure white field with a broad, dark-blue X slashed from corner to corner.

"Russian Imperial Navy!" Florian exclaimed. "What in the world...?"

"The Russian Navy does often come here on maneuvers," said Goesle. "Mainly to shake a fist across the water at the Turks, I think. But it's all modern ships. I can't imagine why it has trotted out a lovely old museum piece like her yonder."

Some other curious things about that ship were noticeable when they had watched for a while. There was not a man to be seen on her decks or in her rigging, and evidently not even a man at her helm: she moved indecisively in the capricious evening wind. The watchers realized that she was totally abandoned, flotsam adrift, and then they saw why. Smoke trailed out, then billowed out, from the open gunports all along her lower deck, and then flames belched after it, brilliant orange in the twilight.

"The thing is afire!"

"And no one is even trying to put it out!"

All around the beautiful, stricken old warship, but at a respectfully far distance, stood a flotilla of smaller craft—everything from steam launches and smart sporting sailboats to grubby fishing smacks—everything except a water-pumper steam fireboat.

"Ach y fi!" Dai Goesle gave a cry of real pain as the fire leapt from the warship's woodwork to her magnificent plumage of sail. In a minute, the whole ship was a torch, burning far more brightly than the lighthouse lamp, which had just been lit and begun revolving. Fitzfarris was suddenly jolted as Monday Simms ran to fling her arms around his waist. She kept her blissful face turned toward the scene at sea, but rubbed the rest of herself against his leg.

In a few more minutes, the fire consuming the warship reached its magazine, and plainly that had been full loaded, for there was a tremendous booming, flaring explosion, and planks and spars flew like twigs out of the fireball. The whole air trembled, and the *Pflichttreu* rocked slightly, and the watching people's hair was stirred. Monday gave a last, hard rub against Fitz's leg, and a low moan. He reached down to disentangle her and, when she turned drowsy eyes up to him, he said sternly, "Don't do that any more, kid. There are better games to play. Go away and learn them." Her eyes came awake, and she gave him a sad look, but went away.

From the wreckage of the warship, still afloat, came several subsequent smaller explosions, probably of powder in the cannons as they heated up. But the officials in the launch alongside evidently judged that the main spectacle was concluded, for they signaled to Captain Schilz that he could proceed.

When the *Pflichttreu* rounded the breakwater and another launch brought out the harbor pilot, Florian was the first to meet him as he came on board. A pilot, by tradition too toploftical to speak to any lesser rating than a ship's master, could have been expected to rebuff such a thing as a mere passenger, but this pilot seemed surprised and pleased to be accosted in his native language by a foreigner. He paused to reply civilly and at some length before climbing to the bridge, and Florian came to report to the others.

"I asked him what that show was all about. Damndest thing I ever heard. It seems that Tsar Alexander recently commissioned an artist to paint a picture for him—a panorama of a sea battle a century or so ago—and one of the sensational events of that battle was the explosion of a munitions ship. Well, the artist said that he had no notion of what such a catastrophe would look like. So the Tsar arranged this demonstration *just for the artist's edification.* The painter is in one of those small craft out there. He was sent down here, where that old ship has been docked, and the Russian Navy boys loaded her and fired her and blew her all to hell—all that, so the artist will get the details correct in his painting. I'll be damned if that is not *style!*"

Stitches Goesle sniffled mournfully and shuffled off to his cubby below. The troupers and a number of idling crewmen stayed on deck, looking about them with keen anticipation or old-acquaintance ennui, as the *Pflichttreu* slowly chuff-chuffed along the Molo Mediceo. That was a curving quay a couple of miles long—like an interminable high wall to those seeing it from deck level— of sea-eroded stone blocks splotched with weeds and lichens. But it was solidly built and handsomely lighted by standing lamps at regular intervals. The lamplight cast bright squiggles on the dark-green harbor water and gave hulking immensity to the dark shapes that were moored or anchored ships. Besides the lamps and the lighthouse and the many ships' riding lights, there were numerous moving points of light, for the night fishers were just then putting out to sea, and each boat carried a big, mushroom-shaped lantern bobbing at its stern. There was also noise all about—steam winches and windlasses huffing and grinding, derricks rattling, oarlocks creaking, berth and channel buoys ringing o hooting. And from the town streets at the still-distant inner bend of the harbor came an occasional trill of music or of singing or of women's laughter.

"I think I'm going to like Italy," said Edge.

"Yes, it will be a pleasant place to winter," said Florian. "Lots of people come from the chill north to do just that—including numerous circus and music-hall artistes who happen to be between engagements. So we ought to be able soon to augment our troupe."

"Abner has been grumbling that one lion and one elephant don't make much of a menagerie. He'd like to augment the animals, too."

"Hell, so would I. What circus proprietor wouldn't? But if we're to get to the rest of Europe, beyond Italy, we've got to cross the Alps. And the Hannibal we have in our company is not *the* Hannibal. Until we cross those mountain passes I'll forgo acquiring any more creatures that can't walk over them on their own feet."

"Well, you're the main—no; sorry—you're the Governor. But you never have confided what your traveling plans are, from here on."

"Simple. We'll work Italy for all it's worth, then move along. We shall aim eventually for Paris. That is the Mecca of all circus folk in Europe—in the world. Nowhere else, these days, is the art of circus so aesthetically appreciated. Mediocre shows, of course, are hooted out of there, or prudently stay away. But a good one—it can win accolades, kudos, royal command performances, even medals personally presented by Louis Napoléon and Eugénie. When that happens, the circus so blessed can pick and choose among the gilt-edged invitations it will receive from every other palace on the planet. It is an attainment more to be desired than any amount of wealth. A circus that can win acclaim in Paris can rightly take pride in standing at the acme of the profession."

"Then we don't go there until we *are* the crème de la crème."

"Right. Along the way, we must add to our troupe and our train and our menagerie and our equipment and our program."

"Along the way. You still haven't specified the way."

"I originally planned to travel from Italy across the border into Austria-Hungary—Vienna, Budapest—then up through the intervening states to France, and meander through that land to Paris. But now...this very day... I have decided not to limit our travels only to western Europe."

"Today? Why today?"

"I decided when that pilot came aboard and told me the reason for that spectacle yonder." Florian pointed astern. Beyond the bobbing lanterns of the outbound fishing boats, the horizon was still ruddy with the glow of the still-burning warship. "The pilot said—I quote his very words—the tsars of the Russias have always been splendidly prodigal in their support of the arts."

"I can believe it now. But how did that change your mind about—?"

"Zachary, *we* are of the arts. We must go to Russia. Soon or later, we must make our way to the Court of Saint Petersburg."

"You'll need these, then," said another voice. It was Stitches, returned from below, and he handed Florian a stack of paper folders.

"Ah, the conduct books, yes. Thank you ever so much, Mr. Goesle. I will have Madame Solitaire start setting down our particulars in them. But what's this? I asked you only for one apiece, and at latest count there are eighteen of us. You have made twenty."

"Two of 'em's already got writing in," said Stitches.

"Eh?" Florian riffled through them, found one that bore inked words on its first page, and leaned to read it in the light of a quay lamp the ship was just then passing. "Dai Goesle, age sixty-two, born Dinbych-y-pysgod, Wales... *circus canvasmaster*... bless my soul!"

"You're coming with us, Dai?" Edge said warmly, and reached to shake his hand.

"*And*," said Florian, opening another book, "Carl Beck, born München, Bayern, engineer and ... and *rigger and bandmaster!*"

"Aye," said Stitches. "We'll both come if you'll have us, Guv. We'll swallow the anchor and try a new life ashore. Him and me, we're tired of farting against the thunder. Chief Beck, he complains that his trade is too much scorned at sea; he'll never get his master's ticket. And me... well, yonder goes my trade." He waved toward the red glow on the horizon. "Dead as Owen Glendower."

"Why, this is tremendous!" Florian exulted. "Of course we'll have you."

"Well, there'll be no debarking nor unloading 'til morning," said Stitches. "If you will take a word of advice from a new hand, you will give those books to Captain Schilz tonight, for him to write your good conduct in. I suspect tomorrow, when his kettle-keeper *and* his sailmaker collect their pay, and he sees you make off with the both of us, the captain will be snorting fire like that man-of-war back yonder."

*I*TALIA

I

WHEN the troupe was on shore and out of earshot of Captain Schilz's fulminations about "betrayal by a Bruder of the craft," Florian went alone into the wharfside building marked DOGANA ED IMMIGRAZIONE. He carried all the conduct books, bearing every person's personal particulars, plus the brief laudatory comments added by the captain before he was disillusioned. Sarah had had to invent the data for the three Chinese, but they had at least been able to put down their signatures — very elegant little scribbles of ink — which was more than some of the company could do. Abner Mullenax, Hannibal Tyree and Quincy Simms signed only with an X and a thumbprint. Sunday and Monday, thanks to Rouleau's tutelage, were able to write legibly, if childishly.

They all waited, with the wagons, animals and stacked luggage, on the vast, cobbled lungomare that stretched from the harborside to where the streets of Livorno city began. Around them, the cobbles were overlaid with tarpaulins spread by the come-home fishermen, selling the night's fresh catch to housewives, domestics and even grandly attired ladies who pointed, beckoned, inspected and bargained without getting down from their carriages. Some of the troupers passed the time by walking about in small circles, awkwardly and tentatively, and occasionally stamping their feet.

"Feels funny, walking here," Yount grunted.

"You are a tenderfoot," explained Stitches. "Look you, after a long time on a smooth and springy deck, you step on the hard, unyielding land, you'll walk like on eggs for a while. Anybody newly come ashore is a tenderfoot."

They had not long to wait there. Florian emerged from the customs house looking most satisfied, and saying, "No problems at all. They may have been a little amused to find among our company three persons named A. Chink, but they made no issue of it. We are cleared to land."

"They don't even want to count our armaments?" asked Fitzfarris. "Examine the animals for disease?"

"No. And no quarantine. Not even a tariff to pay. I think Italy is simply too new and inexperienced at being a wholly unified nation to have had time yet to promulgate a welter of rules and red tape and tiresome petty clerks."

"All right. What now?" asked Edge.

"First, tov!" Magpie Maggie Hag said firmly.

"Yes, first a good bath," Florian agreed. "And not in a tub of salt water, for a change. Ladies and gentlemen, I shall make an extravagant gesture, perhaps my last for some time. Follow me to yonder hostelry."

He pointed. The Hotel Gran Duca, on the inland side of the lungomare, was an imposing three-story structure, built of stones to match the other harbor-works architecture. It had the appearance of being able to cater to any kind of traveler, by land or sea, for on one side of the main building was an extensive stable, coach house and yard, on the other a ship's chandlery and seamen's slops shop.

"I shall engage rooms for us," said Florian, "and order baths drawn and command that the dining room be laid for a noontime colazione. We will spend our first night in Europe in sybaritic luxury." All the women gave little cries of pleasure. "Meanwhile, Zachary, would you apply to the hotel stalliere and have his men run our animals and wagons into the stable yard? Arrange for feed and cat's meat—and a place for Abdullah and Ali Baba and the Chinks to bed down nearby."

It was with some hesitancy that Edge went to the task of accosting his first Italian. But he found the hostler to be fluent in numerous languages, and so worldly that he evinced no least surprise at being asked to tend—besides eight horses—an elephant, a lion, three pigs, two black men and three yellow. When those arrangements were made, Edge went around to enter the hotel by its front door. The Gran Duca's lobby was an immense hall of rather gloomy magnificence, all dark mahogany furniture, wine-velvet draperies and upholstery. Besides the people being loudly convivial in the adjoining taproom, there were more sober ones occupying the lobby's armchairs and divans: well-dressed women chatting over teacups, well-dressed men perusing newspapers, smoking enormous cigars or just snoozing. Since Edge was wearing his only passable street attire—his old army tunic and trousers, boots and cocked-brim hat—he felt very much the country hick in these surroundings.

Then he heard a call: "Signore, per favore. Monsieur, s'il vous plaît," and he turned to see a small, very shapely young female stranger waving to him.

She was dressed all in pale yellow—full crinolined skirt, an almost naughtily low-cut bodice, pert little kiss-me-quick hat, and she was just lowering a pale-yellow parasol as she came toward him—so she gleamed like a sunbeam in the dark hall, and the bright shine of her attracted the admiring gaze of every male idler, the stony stare of every woman. She had long, wavy hair the red-brown color of polished chestnuts. The brown irises of her eyes were so flecked with gold that they looked petaled, like flowers, and there were dimples about her mouth that made it appear ready to smile at the least excuse. She came up to

Edge—and she came up only to his chest in height. Also, she had the tiniest waist of any woman he had ever seen, but it obviously was not made so by any kind of corset; she moved too lithely and her breasts moved too naturally. She looked up at him with that barely contained smile lurking on her lips, and she cocked her pretty head as if debating what language to employ. When Edge doffed his hat and inquiringly raised his eyebrows, she said:

"You are Zachary Edge."

"Thank you, ma'am," he said solemnly, with a nod of acknowledgment. "But I already knew that."

She looked a trifle disconcerted at his not having said, "At your service," or some such stock rejoinder. The dimples around her mouth wavered slightly and she tried a different language.

"Je suis Automne Auburn, monsieur. Du métier danseuse de corde. Entendez-vous français?"

"Well enough, yes, but why don't we stick to English?"

She reestablished the dimples, gave her bronze curls a brazen toss, twirled her parasol in a wanton way and said in broadest cockney, "Ow, orright, guv'nor. Oy'm an equilibrist, nyme of Autumn Auburn, and—"

"I don't believe it."

"Why, 'ere 'tis in print!" she cried, and whipped a folded newspaper from under one arm. "The *Era*, see? The circus tryde-sheet. Sixp'nce a copy, but oy'll give yer a free dekko. Look there in the h'adverts. *That* cost me five bleedin' bob."

She pointed to a column, and Edge read aloud, "'A FATHER OFFERS to managers: his young daughter, fourteen years old'..."

"Nar! Not that 'un." She tugged at the paper, but he kept reading, and kept a straight face:

"...'Fourteen years old, who has only one eye, placed above the nose, and one ear on the shoulder. Interested parties apply this paper.'" He handed the *Era* back to her. "I'd have taken you for older than fourteen. But then, you freaks often do look—"

"*Will* 'ave yer jollies, wontcher? 'Ere. This 'un's moyn." She pushed the paper at him again, and he obligingly read:

"'MISS AUTUMN AUBURN, la plus grande équilibriste aérienne de l'époque—ne plus ultra—affatto senza rivale. Frei ab August, this year.' Well, miss, I admire the linguistics. I count five languages in just those few words. But I still refuse to believe that anybody ever got christened Autumn Auburn."

She coyly ducked her head, and let her smile become a confiding laugh. "Ow, it ayn't me real nyme, o' course." She looked up at him through her luxuriant eyelashes. "But if Cora Pearl—'er wot was plyne Emma Crouch back in Cheapside—if she could myke 'er forchune in gye Paree by callin' 'erself Cora Pearl..." She twirled her parasol. "...I sez to meself, 'ow come little Nellie Cubbidge carn't do th' syme wiv a nice nom-dee-chamber like Autumn Auburn?"

"I don't believe that atrocious dialect, either. I heard enough genuine limejuicers on the boat."

She laughed again, and said, in an English accent that was merely melodious, "Are you armor-plated against teasing, Mr. Edge? You don't even smile."

"You do it so much better, miss. I'd like you to do the smiling for both of us, the rest of our lives."

For a moment that was silent but richly reverberant, they looked at one another. Then she gave a small, come-awake shake of her head and turned hoyden again.

"Give us a job, guv, and oy'll larf me fool 'ead orf."

"How did you know who I am?"

She resumed her normal voice, but still sounded mischievous. "I know everything about you. I saw the circus carrozzoni come in, and I ran to question the portinaio. He said everybody in the troupe had gone to the baths, except the Signor Zaccaria Ayd-zhay, who apparently does not bathe. I refused to believe that anybody ever got christened Zaccaria Ayd-zhay, so I made him let me look at your conduct book. You are an American, and you will have your thirty-seventh birthday on the twentieth of September, and you are the equestrian director of Florian's Flourishing Florilegium et cetera. And all those particulars were written in a feminine hand, so you have a wife... or a lady friend..." She paused, as if waiting for him to say something, then added lightly, "I cannot imagine how you got one, if you are averse to bathing."

"Is your name really Nellie Cubbidge?"

"Crikey, would I invent *that*?"

"Then I'll call you Autumn, if I may. And if I'm not mistaken, an équilibriste is a ropewalker...?"

"Rope or wire. Slack or tight. And I have my own rigging."

"It's Mr. Florian who does the hiring, but I'll break his neck if he doesn't hire you. Now that that's settled, may I offer you a drink of something, in the bar yonder, to seal the contract?"

"To be honest, I'd rather you offered me a bite of something."

"Well, we're all convening in the dining room for a colazione, which I take to mean a meal."

"Ooh, lovely."

"Come and help me, in case I need Italian spoken, to tell the desk clerk to add you to the dining roster. Then, if you'll excuse me just briefly, I'll abandon my lifelong aversion and go take a bath."

"Ooh, lovelier yet."

"And I'll join you at the table, to introduce you to your new colleagues."

When the company assembled, the dining-room servants shoved together several tables to accommodate them. Everyone was in Sunday-best clothes, such as those might be, and Clover Lee was redolent of Dixie Belle Extract of White Heliotrope, and Carl Beck was redolent of the unidentifiable odors of the hair-raising lotion Magpie Maggie Hag had compounded for him. Hannibal, Quincy and the Chinese, of course, were eating with the stable hands. And Monsieur Roulette was being served in his room, said Florian, adding that, after the meal, the hotel's physician would be giving him an examination. So there were fourteen at table, but Edge fetched an extra chair to set between himself and Florian, then went to escort Autumn Auburn from where she waited in an alcove.

He presented her to the troupe with the prideful air of a connoisseur who had discovered an unrecognized objet d'art in a shop of common trinkets, and Autumn good-humoredly did her best to look maidenly grateful for that deliverance. Every man in the company beamed admiringly at her. And, although Autumn was better dressed than any of them, so did the women—all but two. Sarah

Coverley and little Sunday Simms had instantly read Edge's glowing face, and they regarded the newcomer with a certain melancholy. Florian greeted her warmly, and so did most of the others. Carl Beck, when he was introduced, gazed at Autumn intently. "Fräulein Auburn, the very image you are of some other beauty I have met, or seen a picture of, but who it was I cannot think."

Sunday, on shaking Autumn's hand, merely murmured, "Enchantée." But Sarah, in her turn, lightly remarked, "Zachary, I congratulate you, but I am disappointed. Miss Auburn is not a klischnigg."

Edge said gruffly, "I decided I ought to step aside from your stampede of dukes and counts."

"A gentleman would have waited," she said, but still lightly, "until he was trampled by at least the first of them."

Autumn, whose brown-gold gaze had gone back and forth between them during that exchange, said, "Madame Solitaire, it must have been you who did the writing of his conduct book."

"Yes. And I can assure you, my dear, that he will conduct himself to your utmost satisfaction."

"Oh, my dear, you should have written that in the book. Now I shall have to judge for myself."

"Touché," said Florian. "Now, down swords, ladies. A man of any manhood abhors being discussed in the third person, as if he were a mute or a ninny or a dear departed, and Colonel Edge is none of those."

"Coo! You're a real colonel?" Autumn said to Edge, with exaggerated chagrin. "And I only called you mister."

"Sit down, everybody," said Florian. "Here is our antipasto and—not champagne, not yet—but a decent vino bianco. No doubt you are acquainted with the local provender, Miss Auburn. Are you lodging at this same hotel?"

"Not exactly," she said, as she eagerly helped herself from a platter. "In the hotel's coach house, in my own caravan. So I've been staying here at stable rates. On stable rations, come to that."

"Well, we ought to inform you, before you decide to join out," said Florian. "This is our first lodging under roof in a long time, and perhaps our last. But let us not talk business until we are well nourished. Tell us how you came to be here."

Between voracious partakings of the cold meats, pickled mushrooms and artichoke hearts, Autumn replied with staccato economy, "Old story. Goat show. Circo Spettacoloso Cisalpino. Folded on the tober here. Governor did a Johnny Scaparey. Stranded us all. Some of us stayed. Not much choice. Played to the summer seasiders. Passed the hat. Hat usually came back empty. Now the season is over. Still stranded."

The waiters brought the soup course, tureens of fragrantly steaming cacciucco, and started to remove the platters of antipasto. Autumn hastily said, "Prego, lasciate," to halt them, then said to the table at large. "Please, you have paid for all these tidbits. If you are not going to finish them, might I . . . ?"

"Wait you, missy," said Stitches. "There is plenty more will come, now just. You need not fill up on the preliminaries."

"I didn't mean for me. I thought—if I could have them wrapped—there are some other hungry kinkers, castaways from the Cisalpino, who'd be thankful to you all."

Florian instantly gave orders in Italian and the waiters bowed in acknowledgment. Autumn went on:

"I'm luckier than the others. I've my own rigging and my own transport. Actually, I had an offer to come on the Circo Orfei, but they're away up in the Piemonte somewhere. The hotel people here have been noble about my stable bill, but they won't let me hitch my nag to my van until it's paid up. So I was simply hoping to survive until the Orfei gets to this neighborhood, if it ever does."

"Orfei good show," said Magpie Maggie Hag. "Famous all over. Also prosperous. They no scarper. Better you go with them."

Edge frowned at her. Florian gave her a pained look and said, "Confound it, Maggie. I wanted to defer any shop talk, but..." He turned again to Autumn. "I'll concede that the Orfei family would probably pay you more, and more regularly. We can offer only part pay and promises."

"We should also confess that we don't always eat this well," said Edge, indicating the platters of red mullet and bowls of spaghetti that the waiters were just setting on the table.

"I am free, white and twenty-one," said Autumn. "Isn't that how it is phrased in your country, Colonel Edge?"

"Twenty-one," Sarah echoed faintly into her glass of wine.

"And I can make up my own mind," said Autumn. "If there's a place for me, Mr. Florian, I'll be glad to accept it."

Pepper exclaimed, "That's talkin' Irish, alannah, even if ye be a Sassenach. Hitch your wagon to a rising star." She lifted her wine glass and broadened her brogue. "In Paris we'll be toastin' ye in fine shampanny, whilst we sashay in carriages up and down the Chumps Elizas! Won't we, Pap?" When there was no immediate answer, she said sharply, "Won't we, Paprika mavourneen?"

"Oh," said Paprika, startled out of her contemplation of Sarah's wistful face. "Yes. Yes, indeed, Pep."

"Also, Mr. Florian," said Autumn, "if you're the only one of the troupe who speaks Italian, I might be of help in that regard, too."

"Are you fluent?" He held up a cruet from the table—a double cruet, of oil and vinegar, its two necks bent in opposite directions. "In dictionary Italian, this is an ampollina. Do you know the idiomatic name?"

Autumn smiled her dimpled smile and said, "It's the suocera e nuora, the mother-in-law and daughter-in-law. Because both the spouts cannot pour at the same time."

Florian smiled approvingly back at her. "Zachary, you have indeed found us a treasure." He turned to Fitzfarris. "Sir John, until you acquire some languages, I shall have to do all the dealing with authorities, and every necessary patchwork, and all the talking on the show."

"I'll start learning as fast as I can," Fitz promised.

"Meanwhile," Florian went on, "this afternoon I shall visit a printing shop and order plenty of new paper. Zachary, you and I must also work out a new program, to accommodate the addition of Miss Auburn and the Chinamen. Also, before anything else, I must visit the Livorno municipio, to arrange a tober for tomorrow. How long we will show here—before we move on inland—that depends, of course, on how well we do here."

He looked around the room, at the well-dressed, heartily eating and comfortably chatting other diners, as if estimating their eagerness to be entertained and their ability to pay for it.

"If I might suggest something," said Autumn, and waited for Florian's nod. "Ask the municipio for permission to pitch in the park of the Villa Fabbricotti. Our ragtag dog-and-pony Cisalpino couldn't get it, but that park is in the most fashionable part of town."

"Thank you, my dear. You are proving more valuable every minute. Can you by any chance play a cornet?"

She laughed and said no, and Carl Beck spoke up. "Your Kapellmeister I am. A band of musicians I require, nein?"

Florian raised his hands helplessly. "We have an energetic drummer, a neophyte accordionist and a spare cornet. Im Kleinen beginnen, Herr Beck, but we shall hope to build—"

Stitches Goesle waved his fork around the room and said, "Deuce, there is all these dagos can sing like Welshmen just, and can play any instrument you put in their hands."

"True enough," said Florian. "But most Italians, except the upper classes, have a dread of traveling any distance from home. No, here in Europe... well... Paprika, Pepper, Maggie, I'm sure any of you can tell the canvasmaster."

The younger women deferred to Magpie Maggie Hag, and she said, "Slovaks you want. Slovaks the niggers of Europe. Every circus uses. They work roustabout—teardown, driving, setup—then they play band music. So poor their country is, they leave there, work circuses all over Europe. Get money in pocket, take it home to families, come out to work circuses again."

"Upon my Sam!" said Goesle. "So much the better. Let us hire Slovaks, Carl, to be your band *and* to be my crew. Looking at your canvas I was, Mr. Florian, and I have an idea that will double your tent's capacity."

"Well, until we know what kind of crowds we'll draw..." Florian began, but Carl Beck spoke up again.

"Also, I wish the Gasentwickler for the Luftballon to get started. Extra hands for the making of it I will need."

"Gentlemen, gentlemen," pleaded Florian. "I thought I had made it plain to you both, that we are starting this tour with pitifully small capital. Until it is replenished—"

"What can cost the Gasentwickler?" said Beck. "Some metal, some wheels, some gum hoses. No great expense. For working it, the iron filings from any smithy we can get. Only will cost much the carboys of vitriol."

"Herr Kapellmeister, right now, *any* expense is too much expense."

Beck looked at Goesle and said, "Our sea pay we have." They nodded at one another, and Beck looked to Florian again. "Ein Abkommen. Slovaks you provide, Dai and I investment make in canvas, sheet metal, Musikinstrumente, all necessary. The quicker we have good show, good band, good chapiteau, the quicker we all prosper, nicht wahr?"

"Indubitably," said Florian. "And I thank you both for your gesture of good faith. But I fear such a gentlemen's accord would not persuade any Slovaks to join in it. They are a laborer class, and thinking is the one labor they cannot do. The notion of working for shares would be too subtle for their simple intellects. They comprehend only coin in the hand."

"But they're also accustomed to the holdback," said Autumn. "Don't you pay that way in the States?" She blushed slightly and said, "I seem to be sticking in my oar frightfully often. But our Johnny Scaparey left a crew of Slovaks also marooned here."

"The holdback, yes," murmured Florian, regarding her appreciatively. "Circuses everywhere do it, and so did I, in the solvent years of weekly salary days." For the benefit of the inexperienced, he explained, "Every new hand always had his first three weeks' wages withheld, not to be paid until the end of the season. It's an old custom, partly to discourage the good hands from defecting to some better-paying outfit, but partly also a philanthropy—to ensure that the drunkards and wastrels among the crew have at least money to get home on when the show closes."

"There you are, then," said Pepper. "The Slovaks will cost you only their keep, and glad they'll be to get that. They won't know we *can't* pay 'em. They'll suppose it's merely the old holdback. And if, after three weeks, we still can't pay 'em ... well, we'll have worse worries than that, me boyos."

"True, true," said Florian. "And we do have funds enough for sustenance. Very well. Herr Beck, Mr. Goesle, you shall have your Slovak crew and bandsmen. You may proceed with your plans." Those two immediately put their heads together, while Florian again addressed Autumn. "You mentioned that some other kinkers had got the shove. What acts? And are they equally hard up that they might join out on a holdback basis?"

"Well..." Autumn said. "Now you'll think me a dog in the manger. Finding a place for myself and leaving them out. But I truly don't know that you'd want the others."

"Try me."

"The only ones who are still in town are the Smodlakas. Yugoslavs. A family act. Slanging buffers."

At least half the people at the table looked blank. Florian translated for them, "A performing dog act."

"Three mongrel terriers," said Autumn. "Nothing to look at, but jolly good they are. The Smodlakas had Yugo names for them—unpronounceable, of course—so I always called the tykes Terry, Terrier and Terriest, and now those are the only names they'll answer to."

Florian laughed, and asked, "And what is the drawback to our hiring these Yugoslavs?"

"Well, they include two children, younger than any on your show. A six-year-old girl and a boy seven or so. It was for the Smodlaka family that I wanted the table leavings."

"Are the brats mere appendages, or do they work their way?"

"They do. As exhibits. They're both albinos. White hair, white skin, pink eyes."

"True albinos? Why, there's the beginning of a sideshow for us again, Sir John! A pair of Night People to present alongside our pair of White Pygmies. Why in the world, Miss Auburn, would I *not* want such a family?"

"Because Pavlo, the father, is such an absolute bastard. Everyone on the other show detested him."

"Aha," said Florian softly, and flicked a collusive glance at Edge. "How does his bastardy manifest itself?"

"He mistreats his family. He never even speaks to the children, and when he addresses his wife he always barks, just like one of his terriers. He's been known to hit her, too. And Gavrila is such a sweet, soft person that everyone hated Pavlo for that."

"Zachary?" said Florian. "Our replacement focus?"

"If you say so, Governor. When he gets totally insufferable, we can always feed him to his own dogs. We may have to. For somebody who can't pay wages, you're fixing to take on one almighty expense just for sustenance."

"Speaking of sustenance," said Florian. "Here are the sweet and the bitter to top off our meal. Zabaglione and espresso. Miss Auburn, can you find all those people for us? The Slovaks and the Smodlakas?"

"They're scattered around the city. If I might have an escort..."

"I'll go with you," Edge said, before any other man could volunteer. "But let me take you to meet Jules Rouleau before we go. I want to hear what the doctor says about his recuperation."

When the meal was concluded, Florian left a heap of paper money for the waiters. Mullenax and Yount raised their eyebrows at that, so he admonished them, "Being poor is a disgrace only if it makes you *act* poor. Anyway, that mancia is not as lavish as it appears. A lira is worth just twenty Yankee cents. Which reminds me. All of you new arrivals ought to change your American money and begin to practice at calculating in lire."

The whole troupe went to the hotel desk to do that. The Gran Duca's resident physician was waiting there, a Dottore Puccio, so Florian led him to Rouleau's room, accompanied by Edge and Autumn, and Carl Beck and Magpie Maggie Hag trailed along.

"Madonna puttana," muttered the doctor, when he lifted the sheet of the invalid's bed and saw the bran box. "È una bella cacata." Autumn tittered at that, but did not translate for Edge.

Dr. Puccio had reason to exclaim. The bran in the box had been replenished from time to time, as the marauding mice or rats or both had eaten at it. But the grain was intermingled with the rodents' droppings and a goodly admixture of coal-fire soot. Toward the bottom of the box, where the bran had got matted by the drizzle of the various medicaments applied to the leg's flesh wounds, it had also gone quite green with mold.

The leg was likewise a ghastly-looking object when he lifted it from the box: shrunken, discolored by the bran and wrinkled like a twig. The doctor continued to mutter—"Sono rimasto...cose da pazzi...mannaggia!"—as he swabbed the leg clean and then prodded and manipulated and scrutinized it. Still, the leg was whole, and it bent only in the places where it should, and its flesh wounds were now only scars.

Dr. Puccio looked around at the others in the room, with a threatening scowl, and in perfect English demanded, "Who prescribed this lunatic treatment for the injuries? No physician, surely."

"The bran box was my doing," Edge confessed. "It worked once for a horse I was reluctant to shoot."

The doctor snorted at him, then glared at Florian. "Signore, you did not inform me that I was being called to examine a veterinary patient." He raked his gaze around the others again. "Aside from this merdoso box, what attentions were given?"

"Cleaned wounds with carbolic," said Magpie Maggie Hag. "After, used basilicon ointment, Dutch drops, cataplasms of emollient herbs."

"Gesù, matto da legare," said the doctor to himself. Then he announced angrily, "None of this should have been done. Utter stupidity, peasant remedies, horse cures, unforgivable meddling." The troupers looked contrite and Rouleau looked worried. But the doctor gave an Italianate shrug of shoulders, arms, hands and eyebrows, and continued:

"Nevertheless, it all worked. You people could not possibly know why, so I shall tell you. None of those ridiculous old-wife nostrums of yours, signora, could have prevented the fomites and miasms of corruption from getting into the wounds. This patient should rightly have died of the frenzy fever. As for this—this merda—these recrementitious husks of grain"—he disgustedly sifted a hand through the bran—"you might as well have packed the limb in sawdust. *Except.* Surely you were all too ignorant to expect it, but the bran spontaneously generated these aspergillus fungi." He fingered the nasty mold in the box. "It is known to physicians—*but only to physicians,* not to dilettanti lay persons like yourselves—that certain of the aspergilli have a subjugating effect on the fomites of disease. This green mold, this particular green mold, this alone, healed the patient's limb and preserved his life."

"We did good, then, hey?" said Magpie Maggie Hag, and she cackled.

Dr. Puccio gave her a sour look. "Good is the prognosis, at least. The leg will require frequent massage with olive oil to restore its muscularity and flexibility. It will be two or three centimeters shorter than the other leg. You will walk with a limp, signore, but you will walk."

"I am by trade an acrobat, Dottore. Will I leap again? Jump, bound, vault?"

"I doubt it, and I disencourage it. After all, the limb was not set and mended by a professional, but by ignorantes, however well-meaning." He gave another daunting look around at them.

"But you have a whole new career, Monsieur Roulette," said Florian. "As an aéronaute extraordinaire. Chief Beck here is about to commence the construction of a gas generator for the *Saratoga.*"

"Zut alors! Then my accident has liberated me forever from the dull, flat ground. I must be grateful to it. And to you, Zachary and Mag, my ignorant, meddling amis."

The visitors left the room and, in the hall, Carl Beck said, "Bitte, Herr Doktor. A word of advice, if I may request? You shall already be perceiving that my hair is thinning."

"Yes. What of it? So is mine."

"Your professional opinion of this medication I merely wish to ask." Beck pulled from a pocket the bottle of potion Magpie Maggie Hag had given him.

"Is *that* what I have been smelling on you?" The doctor turned to the gypsy. "What is it?"

With a good imitation of his own supercilious air, she said loftily, "Old-wife nostrum."

For the first time, the doctor's eyes twinkled. He uncorked Beck's bottle and sniffed at it. "Aha! Yes! Per certo. I can distinguish the secret ingredients. But fear not, signora, I will not divulge them. Ja, mein Herr, this therapeutant should serve the purpose as admirably as anything known to medical science."

"Danke, Herr Doktor." Beck bowed to him, then to Magpie Maggie Hag. "I was not disbelieving, I assure you, gnädige Frau. But it is a comfort from a professional an expertise to have."

Trying not to laugh aloud, the others departed. Edge and Autumn went on, out of the hotel, he carrying for her the ample paper sack of leftovers from the meal. Florian and Magpie Maggie Hag watched them go, and Florian asked idly, "What do your gypsy instincts say, Mag? About the hiring of the new people?"

"I dukker yes, hire them all. All except that rakli."

"The girl?" Florian blinked. "Surely you can't see any danger in Autumn Auburn."

"No. Beautiful, loving rakli, her. Make fine artiste. For Zachary, make fine romeri."

"Wife? Well, well. Do you foresee jealousy from—?"

"No. Even Sarah be not jealous of so good a rakli. In Autumn Auburn, no danger, only hurt."

"Oh, damnation, Mag! Save the mystic ambiguity for the jossers. How am I supposed to interpret that?"

She shrugged. "I dukker no more than that. No danger, only hurt."

In the piazza, when Autumn put up her pale-yellow parasol, and the late afternoon sun shone even more sunnily through it onto her auburn hair and piquant face, Edge could not help exclaiming, "You are the prettiest thing I have ever seen."

"Grazie, signore. But you've been in Italy less than a day. Wait until you've seen a sampling of the signorine in these streets."

"I'll never see them. Your dazzle is too bright. Will you marry me?"

She pretended to ponder the question, and finally said, "Mrs. Edge. It sounds like a female sword swallower."

"Anything is an improvement on Miss Cubbidge. But if you insist, I'll become Mr. Auburn."

"I don't insist on anything, Zachary, including marriage. Why don't we, for a while, do what the common folk call 'practice to marry'?"

He gulped and groped for words. "Well . . . fine. But that's an even blunter proposal than mine was."

"I hope it doesn't frighten you off. I am not a wanton, but neither am I achingly respectable. I wanted you the moment I met you, despite the grumpy greeting you gave me."

"That was self-defense. The sight of you nearly knocked me over."

"Then we both knew from the start. Would it not be foolish of us to delay through all the trivia of flirtation and courtship and being teased by our friends and the publishing of banns and . . ."

"Yes. Why don't we go back to the hotel right now and—"

"No. I may not be righteous, but I will be fair. I will make you look at what you could be wooing instead. There—look at that lissome lass. Is she not gorgeous?"

"She's no trial to look at, no, ma'am. But I'd lay money that she'll be fat before she's forty."

"How do you know I won't? Very well—that one. You cannot fault her. The girl with flowers in her hair."

"Autumn, you have flowers in your eyes. Stop pointing out prospects. I've got the one I want."

"Ah, lackaday. Impetuous man."

"Can we turn back now?"

"Certainly not. We are on a mission for the Governor. Meanwhile, Zachary, leave off staring at me and look about you. This is your first day in a new country, on a new continent. You should be devouring the sights like any Cook's tourist."

Now that Edge and Autumn had come a considerable way inland from the harborside smells of coal smoke, steam, salt and fish, Livorno was more of a treat for the nose than for the eyes. The advancing twilight was made misty and sweet by the wood smoke that drifted from kitchen doorways. From every front garden and window box came the tart, pungent, no-perfume-nonsense smells of old-fashioned flowers: zinnias, marigolds, chrysanthemums. Autumn even showed Edge a little city park that was pure fragrance: a cool-smelling fountain in a grove consisting entirely of aromatic lemon trees. Even now in the early fall they were all still laden with fruit that was evidently public property. Numerous urchins were climbing the trees to pick the lemons, filling cans and jars with water from the clear fountain, mixing the fruit juice and the water to make lemonade to peddle on the streets.

There were beggars everywhere, even in the most elegant neighborhoods, and not all were as enterprising as the lemonade children. Most of them merely squatted or lay about on the sidewalks, their sleeves or trousers or skirts pulled up to exhibit awful sores. They plucked at the passing Edge and Autumn, and uniformly, monotonously whined, "Muoio di fame..."

"I perish of hunger," Autumn translated. "Don't feel sorry for them. More than half are ablebodied humbugs, and even the real cripples could find work mending nets on the docks."

So Edge gave alms to only one beggar, because that one looked genuine and because he did not pester them. In fact, he was identifiable as a beggar only by the card hung around his neck: CIECO. He wore opaque eye goggles and he was being hauled along the street by a dog straining at its leash, trotting its master too rapidly to give him much opportunity to accost anybody. Edge almost forcibly had to stop them to put a copper into the man's hand. The blind man breathlessly gasped, "Dio vi benedica," shook his head despairingly, pointed to the dog that still scrabbled to keep going, and told Edge something.

Autumn listened, laughed and said, "Give him a bit more, Zachary. He says he used to have a well-trained lead dog. It would stop of its own accord whenever it saw a good prospect for a handout, and it would wait patiently while he unfolded the sad history of how he used to be a prosperous tanner, until he fell into one of his vats and was blinded by the acid. But that dog died, and this new one is hopeless. He says, 'Now, when this dog stops, I often find myself telling my life story to just another dog.'" She laughed again, and so did the blind man, ruefully. "Do give him more, Zachary. Those coins are only centesimi. Give him a whole lira."

As they walked on, Edge remarked to Autumn that the Yugoslavs were residing in quite a fancy district for troupers out of work. But then she led him around behind one of the mansions, and he saw that the Smodlakas were inhabiting only one end of a woodshed on the property. The head of the family, a man about

Edge's age, with a great deal of blond hair and beard, was sitting on the shed's doorless doorstep, moodily whittling at a stick.

He looked up at Autumn's approach, gave no greeting, but made a wry face, hacked gloomily at his stick and said in English, "One must have something to do when one is doing nothing."

"Instead of splinters, you could at least carve a doll for the children. Pavlo, this is Zachary Edge, equestrian director of a new show that just landed from abroad. He is here to offer you a try at a place on the show."

"Svetog Vlaha!" the man exclaimed. He bounded to his feet, pumped Edge's hand and bawled greetings at him in a number of languages. Edge replied, "Pleased to meet you," so Smodlaka spoke mostly English from then on, including the command he bellowed into the shed's dark interior, "My darlings, come! Come and give welcome!"

Edge was really looking forward to meeting the albino children and even the downtrodden wife, but what came hurtling out of the dark, making joyful noises, were three small, scruffy mongrel dogs. Smodlaka immediately gave orders—"Gospodín Terry, pravo! Gospodja Terrier, stojim! Gospodjica Terriest, igram!"—and the dogs began skipping around Edge, one upright on its hind legs, one walking upside down on its forefeet, the other merrily turning head over heels.

Autumn gave Pavlo a look of vexation, leaned into the shed and called, "Gavrila, children, you may come out, too."

When the first of those ventured shyly to the doorway, twisting her hands in a patchwork apron, Pavlo interrupted his commands to the capering dogs—"Woman, fetch wine!"—and she whisked back out of sight as if he had tripped a spring.

Pavlo continued to bark like a dog at the dogs, while they, as silently and efficiently as the Florilegium's three Chinese, went on with their frantic cavorting. The woman appeared again after a minute, bearing a leather wineskin and three painted wooden cups. Without command, she filled and handed the cups to Autumn, Edge and her husband, then resumed twisting her apron. From behind the breadth of that apron, one on either side, peered out faces like wax topped by hair like flax.

"My woman," grunted Smodlaka, barely inclining his head in her direction. "Her hatchlings." He clashed his cup against Edge's and took a slurp from it.

"They have names," said Autumn. "Gavrila, this is Zachary Edge. Zachary, the little ones are Velja and Sava."

"Zdravo," they all said, and shyly shook his hand.

The mother was as Slavic blonde, fair-skinned and blue-eyed as the father, and she was quite a pretty woman, in a broad-faced and chunky-bodied way. But the two children were so extremely bleached as to be indistinguishable of sex, and their waxen faces appeared almost featureless—pale nostrils, pale lips, pale brows and lashes—except for their startling eyes: red pupils centering silvery-gray irises that flashed bright pink when they caught a ray of light.

Gavrila warily eyed her husband before asking the visitors, "Have you yet eaten, gospodín, gospodjica? We have bread, cheese. We have wine. We have everything."

"We have dined, thank you," said Autumn, and handed her the paper bag.

"Here are some more goodies to supplement your everything, dear. Now we have other errands."

"But you have not yet seen my darlings' entire routine," Pavlo protested. The dogs were still frenetically doing their act, now leaping over one another in a complicated dancelike sequence.

"Take your *darlings*," said Autumn, "and your family, and show them to Monsieur Florian at the Hotel Gran Duca. I'm sure he will like them and engage them. Do you know where I can find the Slovaks?"

"Prljav," Smodlaka said contemptuously. "They are all doing beggar work at the railroad depot. Carrying bags, hoping for mancia. Debasing themselves."

"While you sit and whittle in unblemished prestige," said Autumn. To Gavrila she said, "I'll hope to see you and the children on the show tomorrow. Come, Zachary, I know where the station is."

It was not far away. Like most railroad depots, it was fairly new and—because a railroad, for all its noise and dirt, was a proud acquisition for any community—had been erected in the very heart of the city, built big and ornate, faced with Carrara marble. It overvaulted two immense marble platforms, alongside two sets of tracks, one incoming, one outgoing, and that area of the station looked neither new nor proud: already begrimed with soot and shadowed by a permanent pall of smoke hanging under the girdered glass roof.

One train had just come in from Pisa, and the passengers were elbowing, pushing, all but fighting each other to get out of the compartments and dash to relieve themselves in the depot's toilets. Edge was interested to notice that the European locomotives were coal-fired, like the steamship *Pflichttreu*. The engines puffed out less voluminous smoke clouds than did the wood-fired American trains Edge was used to seeing—and evidently fewer sparks; these locomotives did not wear the big, bulging spark catchers atop their smokestacks. But their effluent of smoke and ash was greasier, filthier and more inclined to befoul the train's coaches, passengers, station surroundings and even the countryside along the right of way.

After the desperate egress of its passengers, the train disgorged an astonishing quantity of luggage they had brought: satchels, trunks, carpetbags, portmanteaux and a great number of huge, flat wooden crates. Each was of a size to contain a sizable tabletop, but evidently did not, for it required only a single porter to lift it from the luggage van to the platform. Edge looked more closely at one of the boxes and saw that it was stenciled CRINOLINA.

"Does that mean what I think it means?" he asked Autumn. "There's nothing in that big crate but hoopskirts?"

"Just one," she said. "One gown's collapsible hoop. One to each crate. How else would you expect a woman to transport her wardrobe's understructures? Ah, look. One of those porters is Aleksandr Banat."

She beckoned to a short, squat, shabby man, who instantly came to her, doffing his shapeless cap so he could tug his forelock. Autumn spoke to him in Italian, and he replied with grunts and an occasional word in the same language. Then he tugged his front hair so hard that he bowed. Then he motioned for Autumn and Edge to follow him, along the depot platform to where the tracks emerged into daylight.

"He says he and all his fellow Slovaks are living in squatters' shacks beyond the freight yard," Autumn explained. "Pana Banat is sort of the chief of them. You may have noticed that he has a whole inch and a *half* of forehead. He also has some Italian and even some grasp of English."

They picked their way over tracks and sleepers and switches and between sidelined coaches and goods wagons. On the outskirts of the rail yards, they came to a veritable township of shacks built of cast-off materials—rusty old corrugated metal, pasteboard, canvas, but mostly leaned-together CRINOLINA crates. The populace of ragged, dirty men and a few ragged, dirty women either sat about in listless boredom or stirred tin cans hung over scrap fires or picked vermin from the seams of their rags or sullenly regarded the newcomers. Banat went among the shanties and came back with half a dozen men. They could have been his blood kin, they so closely resembled him—dark, hairy, barrel-built. Banat, with flourishes, introduced them individually and effusively, but Edge could grasp only that all their names were prefixed with Pana, and all their names sounded like gargles.

"He says Pana Hrvat can play the cornet," Autumn translated. "And he himself can play the accordion, and Pana Srpen even *owns* a trombone, and Pana Galgoc and Pana Chytil can play various other instruments. Anyway, they're all eager to work. Crew or band or both." She gave Banat instructions. "Pana Banat will round up all of them—there are five or six more—and take them straightaway to meet Pana Florian."

But first Banat led Autumn and Edge out of the shanty warren, back to the city proper, so they would not have to retrace their way through the rail yard, for darkness was coming on. They found themselves in a mercantile, working-class part of Livorno, where the night and the nighttime sea fog were oozing together through the narrow, crooked streets. The municipal lamplighters were hurrying at their work, to keep apace of the darkness. The lamps they kindled shone blurrily through the mist, lighting the shopfronts and street stalls and pushcarts of knife grinders, pasta makers, coral carvers, cheesemongers, mallow gatherers, birdseed sellers, porcelain menders, all still crying their wares and services to the passersby hurrying home for the night.

Then there came down the street a considerable number of people walking together in a clump. As they passed a lamp standard they became recognizable as a crowd of beggars—all ragged and filthy, some covered with sores, others crippled and hobbling, a few actually shuffling on all fours—but there was something even more odd about the man leading the bunch and walking normally.

"It's Foursquare John Fitzfarris," said Edge, and hailed him. "We've been out collecting new troupers, Fitz. What in God's name are these you've been collecting?"

"Damned barnacles," said Fitz. "I came out for a walk, because in every new town I like to find out some of the best places"—he grinned—"and all of the worst ones. Instead, I found myself leading this scurvy beggars' parade." He glared at the mob of old and young, male and female. They were not plucking at his clothes or whining "Muoio di fame"; they were simply studying him in a sort of dumb wonderment. "I've thrown them every copper I possess, but I can't get rid of them. I think they think I'm one of their own."

Autumn made inquiry in Italian, and a couple of the beggars muttered replies. She said to Fitz, "They're hoping to discover how you got your face half-blue like that. It seems you're unique among the profession. No doubt they want to try it themselves."

"Goddamn," growled Fitz. "I'd like to *show* them how it was done. Serve them right. I never saw such an assembly of frauds. At times in my life, I've been on the cringe myself, so I know the real from the fake. See that one there? With all those revolting ulcers and scabs on his face and arms?"

"They look real to me," said Edge. "And horrible."

"That's the scaldrum dodge. You slap a thick layer of soap on your skin, then sprinkle it with vinegar. It blisters up, looks gruesome as hell, like advanced leprosy or something. Now, that fellow yonder, he's a bogus epilept. Falls down in the gutter, throws a fit of flailing and foaming, draws a sympathetic crowd of good Samaritans. Then that skinny woman—his wife, maybe—she slithers among the Samaritans and picks all their pockets. I'd like to hope I'm not going to have this rabble trailing me all through Italy."

Autumn immediately gave the crowd a blistering of Italian invective. They quailed and dispersed and trickled away down various alleys. Fitzfarris thanked her wholeheartedly and said from now on he wouldn't come outdoors without his cosmetic mask, and he accompanied Edge and Autumn back to the Gran Duca. When the three made their way through the front door, they found the lobby full of people who were not the usual well-dressed lobby loungers.

"Florian's holding court," explained Mullenax, who was looking on and smoking a twisty black Italian cigar. Its rank aroma did not quite disguise Mullenax's own ripe breath, which suggested that he had early found the hotel's barroom and well availed himself of it. "He's been lookin' at the conduct books of all them new folks you sent, Miss Auburn. He's already done hired the dog people, and got 'em a room here. Now he's talkin' to all them workmen."

Edge asked Autumn, "Reckon I ought to help him with the sizing up of them? You can interpret for me."

"No," she said firmly. "We have practicing to do, remember?"

So, early though it was, they said good night to Fitzfarris and Mullenax and retired forthwith. Edge had been allotted a room to himself, and they went there instead of to Autumn's caravan, because she wanted to take advantage of the hotel's bathing facilities. A maid was sent running to draw the bath, and she shortly came back to lead Autumn there and assist in the ablutions. Autumn went fully dressed, except for her hat and parasol, because she had no dressing wrapper and the bath was a considerable journey distant through the halls. For the same reason, she returned to Edge's room completely dressed.

"Not to provoke any scandal," she said to him, "I have just now had to undo all my buttons and laces and things, and then, after the bath, to do them all up again. A tiresome business, being modest."

"Then let us be immodest," he suggested, "and really scandalous. Allow me to do the next undoing for you."

For the first time in his life, Edge had the ineffable delight of undressing with his own hands a delectable woman clad in the numerous layers and elaborations of European street attire. For the rest of his life, he would never forget the novelty, the nuances, the intricacies of that night's particular preliminary to the making of love. It was like a chaste defloration to be enjoyed before the actual union—like gently loosing the petals, one by one, from a peony or a camellia or some such many-petaled flower.

While Autumn submitted to his ministrations, she wore—in addition to everything else she was wearing—that mischievous about-to-smile expression of hers, complete with dimples. She stood patiently in the middle of the lamplit room like a child being readied for bed by her nanny. Edge being no nanny, his denuding of her took quite a long time, but it was for him a deliciously anticipatory time. And, as he went about it, his combination of painstaking carefulness and fumbling eagerness seemed to excite Autumn as well. She trembled, slightly but perceptibly, whenever she felt his touch on her body.

Edge began, after some study and deliberation, by unhooking and lifting away the amber bead garniture that edged her costume's low neckline. When that decoration was removed, the pale-yellow percale beneath was loose enough to reveal the shadowed cleft between the upper rounds of her breasts. That made Edge pause and gaze in pure appreciation for a minute, and *that* made Autumn take a deep, tremulous breath, and *that* made her breasts all the more interesting to observe. Then Edge collected himself and considered the next step, and decided it was to undo the extremely tiny imitation-smoked pearl buttons of her sleeves' embroidered cuffs. They were maddeningly difficult for his man-sized and inexpert fingers, but next were the larger buttons that closed the percale blouse at the back, and they were easier. However, when they were undone, something was still holding the two halves of the blouse together between Autumn's shoulderblades. She had to assist for the first time—reaching her hands behind her to show him how a hook-and-eye worked. Then, to help further, she shrugged loose of the blouse and peeled it down her arms and threw it onto the bed.

The next layer under the blouse was a complex of sateen-and-elastic straps running over her shoulders, crisscrossing her white cambric chemise to attach to her yellow percale skirt. Edge investigated and discovered that the loops could be unbuttoned from the skirt's waistband. Then the lacings of that band around her waist had to be untied. Then another lacing all the way down the back of the skirt had to be unthreaded from the eyelets of seams concealed by a ruffle. When those things had been attended to, Autumn unwound the yellow skirt from around her and tossed it, too, onto the bed. She was still enveloped from waist to ankle by the contraption that had supported the bell skirt—horizontal hoops of stiff wire hung from each other on tapes, graduated in size from small at her hip level to extravagant at ankle level. But only another unbuttoning from the arrangement of straps was required, and the hoops collapsed around her feet in a ring of concentric circles. She stepped out of that enclosure, kicked it to one side and kicked off her little yellow kid slippers at the same time.

Autumn was still by no means naked, but she was rather more naked than most women would have been at that stage of the proceedings. She wore no corset cover, and no boned corset under it to pinch her waist smaller, and no padded "dress form" to lend her a false bosom. She did not require any such artificial enhancements. Though she continued to stand like an obedient child being readied for bed—and stood perhaps no taller than one of the Simms girls —Autumn Auburn could not have been mistaken for a child. Above and below the waist that Edge could almost span with his two hands, her breasts and hips and buttocks were beautifully of woman proportions.

The next visible layer of dress was the sleeveless, waist-length white cambric chemise held up by narrow shoulder strings, and a full underskirt of tiered Valenciennes lace, the cheap machine-made sort. When Edge untied the ribbons that bound the skirt about her waist and it crumpled to the floor, it revealed another layer of apparel underneath. Autumn still wore a pair of drawers—finely pleated, edged with Hamburg lace—and garter-supported stockings of Richelieu-ribbed lisle, rather gaudily striped blue and white at the thigh tops, but of pale yellow the length of her legs, and with vandyke work ornamenting the ankles.

Edge did the rolling down of the stockings one at a time and very slowly— both to enjoy the gradual, exceedingly provocative revelation of her bare legs and to enjoy the tremor his slow motion induced in Autumn herself. She was hardly trembling for shame; her legs were not anything to be ashamed of; they would have graced any classical statue of a dancing nymph. They were firm with muscle, but not muscular, most delicately molded, sheathed in peach-colored skin that was as inviting of caress as real peaches are. Edge would have expected the soles of a ropewalker's feet to be tough and callused, but Autumn's were as velvety to his touch as were her calves and thighs, and he realized they probably *had* to be kept soft—sensitive to every quiver of the tightrope.

When the stockings were off, he rose to his feet and looked her over, with both satisfaction and calculation: the next layer had to be the ultimate. She now wore only the scanty chemise on her upper body and the drawers below. When he lifted the chemise up over her head, that brought her arms up, too. So he observed that Autumn did not subscribe to the practice of Pepper and Paprika: retaining the tufts of hair under their arms to excite the male rubes. Autumn was clean-shaven and smooth there, and in each armpit was a minor constellation of auburn freckles. That seemed a trifle odd, since she had not a single freckle on her face or throat or shoulders or—as was obvious when the chemise came off—anywhere else on her upper body. Edge would later deem it an appealing feature of Autumn's, and one known only to him: that all of her few small brown freckles were neatly tucked under her arms, and no others interrupted the pearly perfection of her body. But right now he was too pleased contemplating the more evident and even more appealing features of her.

The lifting off of her chemise made her breasts bounce merrily, as if they rejoiced to be free of even that light confinement, and they were a sight to make a man rejoice along with them. But Edge devoted only a moment to that. As he bent to take hold of the elastic waistband of the girl's last concealing garment, he bestowed a quick passing kiss on each of the auburn buds perkily upraised from its auburn halo. Then he slid the skimpy garment down past the triangle of auburn curls, still damp from Autumn's bath—and he kissed there, too, on the way—down to her pretty feet, and he kissed each of those as she stepped out of that final bit of cloth goods.

Kneeling where he was, Edge could now observe that Autumn was delightfully flower-petaled in her most secret part, as well as in her eyes. Her thighs were slightly apart, and she was aroused and invitingly open down there, and there peeked out dainty, glistening ruffles of soft pink, like the fluted edges of dew-damp petunia blossoms. After a minute or so of his simply gazing adoringly at that part of her, Autumn said in a shaky voice, but teasingly, "You did not quite finish the job. I am still not *entirely* naked." She lifted up her waves of auburn hair to show him the tiny imitation smoked pearls clipped to her earlobes.

"You can leave those on, if you want," said Edge. "If you don't want to be *entirely* immodest and shameless and scandalous."

"Oh, but I do!" she cried, unclipping the eardrops and tossing them away. "I do!" she sang, flinging herself on the bed. "I do, I do!"

2

AS AUTUMN SMILED and slowly spread her legs, the crowd roared *"Brava!"*—and then *"Bravissima!"* as she gracefully slid down to a stride split on the tightrope, and Bandmaster Beck tinkled a sweet descending arpeggio on his string of little tin bells.

It was a straw house—a "sfondone!" Florian had declared it, with some astonishment but with great satisfaction. He *had* got the Livorno authorities' permission to pitch in the park of the Villa Fabbricotti—"and for a trifling five percent of the ticket receipts," he reported. "They'll even trust me to do the calculations. I begin to believe that *all* the officeholders in this young Kingdom of Italy are still too new at their posts to have learned the clerkly delights of obfuscation and extortion."

Early in the morning, Florian and Canvasmaster Goesle and Crew Chief Banat and the dozen other Slovaks had driven the animals and wagons to the ungrassed athletic field in the park, and set up the chapiteau and the seats and tamped the ring curb. The roustabouts knew their business—they even chanted a Slovak version of the heeby-weeby as they worked—and the only helper they needed was elephant Peggy. Florian did not lay hand to a mallet or a rope; he participated only to the extent of pointing and suggesting and approving. He smiled broadly, in fact, watching the Slovaks hammer two stakes at a time into the ground, six men to each, all swinging the sledges in a rhythmic blur that made a burst of noise like a fast drum tattoo.

The artistes of the company ambled out of the Hotel Gran Duca after a leisurely breakfast and took their time about arriving at the tober and getting into costume. Meanwhile, there was yet no paper to post about town, and no time to get a notice into any local newssheet. So, as soon as Peggy had finished her part in erecting the pavilion, she was attired in the red blanket and became Brutus. Hannibal got arrayed as Abdullah, and Florian rehearsed him in a few simple words of Italian. Abdullah set out proudly—"speakin' furrin, fust time ever," as he put it—beating his drum and bawling, "Segue al circo! Al parco! Al spettacolo!"

And by show time that afternoon, the city folk had come swarming—well-dressed gentry from the Fabbricotti neighborhood roundabout; middle-class merchants and their families from downtown; seamen, naval cadets, fishermen and dockworkers from the harborside—and all paying in lire, not in barter goods.

Gavrila Smodlaka said shyly to her new colleagues, "Gospodín Florian must possess some magic. The other show never drew like this. Gospodja Hag, did you work some gypsy enchantment?"

"No," said Magpie Maggie Hag. "But if there be ever any magic anywhere around, Florian he will grab onto it."

There had been warm applause for the come-in spec, even though the "All hail, you ladies, gentlemen" was sung in English; and for the violent voltige of Buckskin Billy, Dauntless Reinsman of the Plains; and for Barnacle Bill and his talented pigs; and for the Smodlakas and their even more talented dogs; and for the Chinese antipodists performing first in trio, then with Brutus and the teeterboard and the surviving Simms children; and for Pepper and Paprika on the perchpole—and quite hysterical acclaim when the little old birthday lady, "Signora Filomena Fioretto, bisnonna di settenta anni," turned out to be the vivacious Madame Solitaire. But not until Autumn Auburn danced out upon her tightrope did the audience so boisterously proclaim its enthusiasm.

Now she was stretched in her stride split, one leg forward along the rope, the other backward, balanced there with no assisting prop except the pale yellow parasol. Her ring dress was very simple: a low-cut and sleeveless blue léotard, flesh-colored tights on her legs, flesh-colored soft slippers on her feet. And the costume was unusual in being not spangled at all. Instead, Autumn had lightly oiled her bare shoulders and arms and bosom, and on the oil had sprinkled random dustings of a gold and silver glitter powder. "It is called diamanté," she told Edge, when he admired the effect. The effect was that, when she moved, she gave off no sharp slivers of light, but the exposed portions of her own flesh gleamed and glinted in a manner even more provocative.

Bandmaster Beck rang several upward-lilting arpeggios on his little bells as Autumn levitated from her split, slowly scissoring her legs together again and levering herself upright on the rope. She did a pirouette there, then twinkled along the rope to its platform end and threw up her arms in an exuberant V. The Slovak who had provided his own trombone and the Slovak who had been assigned the cornet blared some kind of Slovak hurrah. For the first time since Edge had been on the show, he not only heard, he *felt* the concussion of the massed clapping and shouts and whistles and cheers.

Every female of the company had been watching Autumn's début performance with the eyes of cats. Paprika murmured, half in admiration, half in envy, "But she is magnificent, that one. And she is beautiful." She turned to Pepper. "You and I got no such applause."

"We might do," her partner replied through her teeth, "if our act wasn't going all to ballyhack. I wish you'd put your mind again on your under-stander, and not up every other woman's winkle."

"Vulgar cow," said Paprika, and strode away. She went to the other side of the ring, where she engaged Sarah in close converse. Clover Lee had been standing with her mother, but she gave Paprika a chilly look and sidled away from them.

Edge had run into the ring to take Autumn's hand as she came down her ladder, and they both threw up their arms, to a renewed burst of clapping. Then Equestrian Director Edge blew a shrill blast on his whistle, and that brought four canvas-trousered Slovaks trotting into the ring. Two of them began dismantling the tightrope apparatus, two began working the ropes at the center pole to prepare the hoist for Pepper's solo hair-hang. Meanwhile, the meager band began a stately passamezzo, and Sunday, Ali Baba and Florian also entered the ring. While Florian commenced the next introduction—"Adesso, signore e signori!"—the Simmses went into their capers, intended to keep the audience entertained during the few minutes of working confusion. Ali Baba collapsed onto the ground, his body in a knot, his chin incredibly propped on his buttocks, his hands and feet sticking out from impossible places, while Sunday did flying flip-flops back and forth over him.

"I surely do like that diamanté costume of yours," Edge said to Autumn, when they were out of the ring. "You looked like a fairy sprite up there. Also, I owe you a deep bow. I truly had not expected you to be such an absolute marvel of an artiste."

"Oh, I have done better performances," she said, professionally self-critical, but then she laughed. "The fact is, damn it, I'm *sore*. You and I are going to have to moderate our enjoyments, Zachary, at least on the nights before a show."

"I was worried we might not *have* any more nights. I was biting my knuckles the whole time you were up there. My God—splits and jumps and somersaults —landing on a half inch of hemp..."

Autumn flicked a drop of perspiration from her forehead and said disparagingly, "Zachary, that rope is only a scant eight feet off the ground. I want Stitches to put my rope right up under the roof."

Edge looked back at the rig. It was like a very tall sawbuck, only with a rope substituting for the buck rail. A long-legged X of wooden beams on either side of the ring held the rope taut between them, and those X's were braced by a cadrolle of pulleys and guy ropes pegged outside the ring curbs. One of the croisé supports was built taller than the other, and provided a bit of platform, so Autumn could stand and lean there to rest between exertions. Behind it was the ladder for her ascent and descent. The shorter X support on the other end of the rope was her "croisé de face," painted white just above the rope, to give her, even in poor light, a distinct guidon on which to fix her eyes and concentration.

"You listen, lady," Edge said sternly to Autumn. "You want to ask *Stitches* to put you up higher? The equestrian director also gets consulted on projects involving any danger."

"Then regard it, my dear, like a director, not like an anxious papa. If I ever fell, I assure you, even eight *inches* off the ground, I should be irredeemably disgraced... Pepper, you lunatic mick, what in the world are you doing?"

"Yours is a difficult act to follow, Sassenach woman," growled Pepper. She was waiting for Florian to conclude her lengthy introduction. Meanwhile, she was doubled over, had got one hand inside her tights, and was groping at a rather intimate area of herself. "But one thing I know—dagos have an appetite for spice." She got hold of what she was after, the cache-sexe at the crotch of her fleshings, and yanked it out, then hastily rearranged her costume and grinned wickedly. "So, begod, I'm going to flash them the upright grin."

"Ecco! L'audace Signorina Pepe!" Florian finally announced, and the music blared into a fanfare, and Pepper casually tossed the cache-sexe to Edge and danced blithely into the pista.

Yount the Quakemaker, who would go on next, came to stand with Edge and Autumn. They watched as two of the Slovaks hauled on the rope that lifted Pepper by her chignon, and the two musician Slovaks played the music she had earlier sung to them. At that, Yount said in amazement, "Miss Autumn, how come them foreigners of yours know that song? It's 'The Bonnie Blue Flag.'"

"It's 'The Irish Jaunting Car,'" Autumn corrected him. "And that Irisher is jaunting, right enough."

Pepper had extended her arms and legs sideways as soon as she was raised from the ground, and she stayed in that cruciform position all the way up to the lungia boom from which she hung. Then, before starting her acrobatics, she clapped her legs together, and her tights of course creased in the cleft between them. Since her tights were flesh-colored all over, except for their tracery of green sequins, she looked quite unabashedly nude up there. The women in the audience made sotto voce comments and the men made rather loud ones. But the remarks were all admiring, not appalled or denunciatory, as they would have been in the part of the world Pepper had recently come from.

Clover Lee grumbled, "Florian would give *me* Hail Columbia if I went on without my cache-sexe. And her, he's not even watching. Where did he go?"

"The king is in his countinghouse," said Fitzfarris, beside her. "I think he's been running to the red wagon between every two acts, just to finger the heaps of lire. But here he comes again."

"Sir John," Florian said immediately, without even looking up at the focus of everyone else's attention, "we'll break for intermission right after the Quake-maker, so you can start getting your sideshow ready. Let's see... you won't need Ali Baba. I want to send a message back to the hotel, and the lad can run a note to—"

"Send my woman," said Pavlo Smodlaka. "She speaks Italian, needs no note. And I have already commanded her to change into street dress. Woman! Come here!"

"Very well," said Florian. "Gavrila, I told the Gran Duca that only Monsieur Roulette would be staying there tonight. But happily we can now afford to keep all our rooms, and I see no reason to deny ourselves that comfort. Will you tell the management to expect our whole troupe back tonight? And for some nights to come. Only the stable facilities we will no longer require. The colored gentlemen and the Slovaks, they will bed down here on the tober to attend all the animals."

"You have the message, woman," said Pavlo. "Go." And she went, like a shot.

Florian took out his mason's pencil and his pocket notebook, and began intently scribbling and muttering to himself, "Item—translate all songs from English. Item—have Mag make ruffs for dogs..." From time to time, he distractedly scribbled the pencil in his beard, marring its silveriness.

Sarah slipped close to him and said quietly, "Since we're keeping the rooms, might I drop into yours tonight? I would like—"

"Oh, not tonight, not tonight," Florian said, without interrupting his memoranda, apparently even unaware of who had spoken. "Consultation tonight. All our executive people. Into the wee hours, most likely."

Sarah looked crushed. Fitzfarris shook his head and glanced about at the others nearby. Paprika was smirking in a smug sort of way. Clover Lee was frowning, but Fitz could not tell whether she was annoyed by Florian's rebuff of her mother or his not noticing and raising hell about Pepper's flagrantly revealing attire.

Anyway, by now, the audience was more enthralled by Pepper's daredevil performance than by her brazen self-exposure. As she spun and twisted up there, thirty perilous feet above the pista, the crowd was ooh-ing and aah-ing. So was Monday Simms, in her own way. Fitzfarris, going out the back door to ready his sideshow, found Monday peeking in, from behind a fold of the canvas, and ardently rubbing her thighs together.

"I told you not to do that, kid," he snapped.

Monday started and gave him a shamefaced look. Then that turned to a look of genuine appeal, and she said, in a slurred voice, "Yes, and you told me there's better games to play. So show me 'em."

"You keep that up and somebody will, I guarantee it."

"You," she urged.

"Be damned if I'll take advantage of a little tan puppy. I prefer my women older and more experienced. Come see me when you're grown, kid. Right now, get your sister and get set to play pygmy."

She burst out, "How'm I s'posed to get experience if you won't give me it?" But then she clamped her mouth shut—Autumn had emerged from the back door, regarding them with some surprise—and the girl ran off around the side of the tent.

Fitzfarris shrugged and said to Autumn, "Every female in the company seems to be suddenly in heat."

"Oh?"

"And it's your fault."

"Oh?"

"I don't know why it happens, but I've observed it everywhere I've been. As soon as there's a striking new girl in town, so to speak, every other one starts stoking up her biological urges."

"Wha's all this about urges?" Mullenax said jovially, as he lumbered up to them, wearing his new lion-trainer uniform.

Autumn only said, "I'd have thought Monday Simms was too young to have any kind of urges at all."

"It's the black blood in her," Fitzfarris said. "The tropical races mature early." And he went on his way.

"He's right, y'know," said Mullenax. "A doctor told me once, it's the niggers all the time eatin' watermelon that does it. He said watermelon is a powerful inspirer of them urges."

"What utter nonsense," said Autumn.

"You think so? You got niggers in that England where you come from? You got watermelons?"

"Negroes, not many. Watermelons, very seldom."

"Then who're you to say nonsense? You watch that other high-yaller gal—that Sunday Simms—watch the way she yearns at your man. Awright, to git Zack Edge you cut out Ma'am Solitaire, but niggers can cut, too. Lemme tell you, niggers cut with *razors*."

"Abner, are you drunk?"

"Miss Auburn, I'm goin' in the lion's cage this afternoon. And I've decided it's time I try that head-in-his-mouth business. You think I'm go' do that *sober*?"

There came a tumult from inside the chapiteau, as Pepper finished her performance. But her applause was not quite the tumult Autumn had been accorded, and Pepper wore a disgruntled look when she was wafted down to the ground and the Slovaks helped her unhook her chignon from the rig. She gave the crowd only a cursory couple of bows, then ran out, so the musicians awkwardly let her music trail off, and Florian had to pounce into the ring to commence his introduction of Obie Yount, "il Creatore del Terremoto."

On her way to change her clothes, Pepper encountered Quincy Simms. She stopped short, and speculatively looked him over, and said, "Hey, gossoon, what do you weigh?"

He studied, as if she had set him a deep philosophical question, and finally said, "Law', mistis, I dunno."

"Well, can't be much. Do you think you could do them contortions of yours while holding to a bar, up in the air?"

He studied again, and finally said he "specked" he could.

"We'll see. Meet me after the night show, and don't change out of your tights. We'll practice."

The Quakemaker, when he had gruntingly lifted and rolled and tossed cannonballs, and had gruntingly had one dropped on his neck—*two* Slovaks, for the effect, gruntingly doing the lifting of it up the ladder—and had lain grunting and grimacing while Lightning the Percheron walked the boards across his chest, got a respectable roar of acclaim, mixed with cries of *"Bravo!"* and *"Bravissimo!"* and here and there *"Fusto!"*

While he took his bows, he said sidelong to Florian at his elbow, "I know what 'bravo' means. But what is 'fusto'?"

"Literally, it means a tree trunk. But it also means 'bravo,' only, um, more so. Surely, when you were in Mexico, you heard the word 'macho.' Same thing. A 'fusto' is a real man's man."

"No fooling?" Yount said in wonderment. And as soon as he could make a graceful exit from the chapiteau, he went directly, manfully, man's-manfully to Paprika Makkai, and inflated his chest and bulged his biceps and said without a trace of timidity, "Mam'selle, would you walk out with me?"

"Miért?" she said, startled out of her other languages.

"My chum Zack says Livorno is a nice town to walk around in. I thought you and me might take a stroll after the show. Maybe have supper together somewhere."

Paprika eyed him thoughtfully, while she recovered her aplomb—and while he manfully maintained the fusto inflation of his chest—then let her eyes go to Sarah, who was hiding a smile. "Why, you are most gracious, Sergeant. I think that would be a pleasant thing to do. But of course we must have a gardedám... a chaperon."

"Oh. We must?" His chest deflated a bit. "Well, all right."

"If Madame Solitaire might be persuaded to accompany us? I believe, madame, you have no other engagements..."

The musicians were playing a thin but lively march as Florian proclaimed the interval—and the availability of Magpie Maggie Hag's divinatory services. The people chattered and laughed among themselves as they evacuated the pavilion. But quite a few stayed inside and moved down to the front benches to consult the gypsy. Edge observed that, as usual, they were all women. But most of these appeared to be in advanced states of pregnancy, so they could hardly be wanting advice on how to snare a man. Even more unusual, Magpie Maggie Hag was now carrying a little notebook, like Florian's, and she wrote something in it each time she and a woman had their heads together. Edge took an opportunity, when one big-bellied woman had departed and another was ponderously approaching the gypsy, to ask her what all these imminent mothers wanted to consult her about.

"What you think? They ask if they going to have boy or girl."

"And how do you make your guess?"

"What you mean, *guess?*" she said, indignant. "I am Magpie Maggie Hag! I no guess. Of ten women, nine want boy."

"And they want to see it in writing?"

"No, no. That is for later, just in case. Here in Europe, circus often stay long enough one place that baby *comes*. If it what I said, boy or girl, mama and papa have such joy, maybe come give me gift. If it not, they maybe come angry at me. So I show them writing, say I no dukkered wrong, you *listened* wrong. Always, see, if I tell woman is boy coming, I write girl. If I tell her girl, I write boy. Now go away. No pester. I making much money."

Edge chuckled, patted her on the head, and went away. Out in the front yard, Florian was just finishing his oration on the contents of the museum wagon— and these Europeans *did* seem fascinated, as he had said they would be, by the moth-eaten mummies, simply because they were the relics of creatures mostly foreign to these shores. Next, Florian pointed to Fitzfarris, standing nonchalantly on an upended fruit crate—"Un' uomo bizzarro, Sir John il Afflitto Inglese"—and at the sight of the Afflicted Englishman several of the working-class folk in the crowd muttered and made the sign of the cross over themselves. But Edge's attention was taken by a different sight, to him equally bizarre. He went to find Autumn, to ask her, "Do the Italian people smoke *paper?*" and waved a hand around to indicate the many men and women who were apparently doing just that.

She looked faintly surprised that he was so surprised, and said, "You don't have the sigaretta in the States?"

She explained that it was really nothing but a short, thin, mild cigar, only wrapped in paper instead of a tobacco leaf. The sigaretta was becoming popular for occasions like this, or between the acts at the theater, when there was time for only a short smoke, and a whole cigar or a full pipe would be wasted. Women especially liked them, said Autumn, because they were not so odorous as cigars and were more graceful to hold in the hand.

"And now, good people," said Fitzfarris, when the crowd had got its fill of studying his affliction, "allow me to present my fellow monsters. First—here, step up, girls—behold! The world's only pair of genuine White African Pygmies in captivity!"

"I Pigmei Bianchi!" Florian translated, and kept on doing so, as Fitzfarris spun his fancies:

"And now, observe the exact and diametrical opposites in the catalogue of human races—heads up, kids—the Night Children!"

"I Figli della Notte!"

"Born in a cavern, reared in a cavern, never seeing God's sunshine until just a few months ago, when they were by chance discovered and brought forth from their immurement. Regard them well, for their delicate pale skin and sensitive pink eyes cannot long bear this daylight, and they must quickly retire to their accustomed darkness, or suffer most cruelly..."

When the wispy little Smodlakas had scampered off, presumably to shelter in darkness, Fitzfarris trumpeted, "And now, let me introduce to you, ladies and gentlemen, *Little Miss Mitten!*"

This caught Florian unprepared, and he stumbled for a translation, "La Fanciulla Guanto...er...Mezzoguanto..."

But the crowd was already laughing, for Fitzfarris had yanked a hand from his side pocket, and the hand was wearing a mitten, brightly painted with eyes, nose and an upper lip on the hand part, a lower lip on the thumb part. He immediately started wiggling his thumb to make the glove appear to talk, meanwhile himself saying—but not moving his own lips—in a high-pitched, shrewish-female voice, "Kept me waiting long enough you did, cuss you, John!"

In his own voice, lips frankly moving, Fitz apologized, "Only saving the best for last, my dear." He then embarked on a few minutes of quarreling with his own hand, in those two voices, and bantering antique jokes, and letting himself be the butt of them all, and giving Miss Mitten all the snappy "Punchinello lines." But the effect was unfortunately diminished by Florian's having to translate both ends of the duologue, and in one voice. Thus, when Fitzfarris plunged the obstreperous mitten back into his pocket (it crying from there in muffled bleats), then brought out his tin swazzles—"Any of you folks can perform the same trick! Amaze your friends! Be the life of every party!"—he sold disappointingly few of them.

So Florian waved a signal to the Slovaks and Hannibal at the tent's front door, and they began playing "Wait for the Wagon" and the jossers threw away their cigarettes and surged back inside the chapiteau.

The second half of the afternoon's program went off without the crowd's enthusiasm waning in the least. Barnacle Bill may have been a bit tottery in his swagger, and his German commands a bit blurry, but he got in and out of Maximus's cage—and in and out of Maximus's jaws—unscathed, and not even pretending to be scratched, for Florian had decided against reinstituting in the act the late Captain Hotspur's "bloody arm" trick. Brutus the elephant dragged a dozen burly and humiliated stevedores around the ring. Abdullah the Hindu juggled, among his many other items, several live and wriggling mullets from Livorno's own waters.

Colonel Ramrod now used one of the Henry repeating carbines for his first trick, and used Sunday and Monday Simms for assistants. He had been pleased to find, in the Gran Duca's amply stocked chandlery store, the cartridge ammunition the Henry required. He had pulled the bullets, poured out some of the powder to make a less powerful propellant, and replaced the bullets in the shells. Also, Abdullah had taught the Simms girls to do a rudimentary juggling act, standing well apart and flipping saucers from one to the other so there were always one or two in the air between them. As they tossed the saucers, they stood so that Colonel Ramrod's spent bullets would land harmlessly in the back yard. Across the ring, he worked the carbine's lever and trigger, with indolent ease, and blasted the flying saucers to powder until the girls had no more to throw.

Then, using his familiar old Remington revolver, he shot, from various positions, the five gourds the girls propped up on the ring curb (dried gourds were plentiful and cheap in the Livorno markets), demolishing the fifth one, as he always did now, by aiming with his little mirror and firing bird shot backward over his shoulder. Meanwhile, Clover Lee had taught Sunday how to snatch up surreptitiously one of the spent balls and to stand firm and wear an apprehensive expression and flinch backward when Colonel Ramrod fired the sixth shot "into her teeth." And the audience broke its enjoined breathless silence with a crash of applause.

"All right, I owe a bow, too," said Autumn, when he came out of the ring. "I had no notion that *you* were such an accomplished artiste. I should have suspected, though, when I learned you had the closing spot."

"Florian and I have already decided that you should have it from now on."

"Zachary! I didn't mean to sound bitchy-hinting. I'm *glad* you are as good at your work as I am at mine. I would not want to be billed above my man—or even to feel in secret that I deserve to be. Equal talents but different talents, that's us."

"And I say vive la différence."

"Coo! And 'e's a cultured gent, as well!"

During the grand-walkaround finale, the Slovaks played the music well enough, but fewer than half of the performers now constituting the troupe could sing the words—"We loved each other then, Lorena"—so most only hummed or mouthed along. The people of the audience did not seem to feel cheated by that. They departed still in good humor, dispersing into the park or climbing into waiting carriages or hailing vetture on the parkside streets or simply sauntering off along the pavements. Magpie Maggie Hag left at the same time, returning to the Gran Duca to see that Rouleau got fed and then to give him his olive oil massage. Yount and Paprika and Sarah hurried away to the wagons to change into street clothes, and then they also strolled off the tober, Yount looking inordinately proud and fusto in the company of two pretty women.

The three of them almost immediately got lost in some of Livorno's more intestinal alleys, but the women did not mind. They dawdled along the narrow and twisty streets, stopping to examine the produce for sale in stalls and on pushcarts, and counting on their fingers to convert the prices of those things into currencies they were better acquainted with.

"Five centesimi!" Sarah exclaimed, at a greengrocer's cart. "That's—let's see —one cent. Look, Paprika, a *whole basket* of grapes for *one penny!* And here... greens enough to make a salad for an entire family, only a penny!"

"And here," said Paprika, at a poulterer's. "A pair of plump chickens, only seventy-five centesimi for the two. That's... hetvenöt heller... fifteen cents in your money, Sarah."

"No wonder Florian was so eager to get here. Why, we can live like royalty on a beggar's income."

After a while, Yount made bold to remind them that they had to be back at the park in time for the evening show. So they went into the first place they found with a TRATTORIA signboard. The proprietor managed to convey to them that he served nothing but a selection of pasta dishes, and they accepted his recommendation of fettuccine alle vongole. The trattore also, without being asked, set down a straw-clad bottle. Yount poured some of its contents into their glasses, and took a taste, and made a face.

"What is this stuff?"

"Chianti," said Paprika, sipping hers with enjoyment.

"What's it good for?"

"Whatever do you mean?"

"Something that tastes this sour ought to be good for curing some ailment."

"Idiota. It is a Tuscan wine."

"It sure ain't elderberry."

"Tuscany is this region of Italy we are now in. Chianti is one of its proudest products. The tartness of the wine is to make you better appreciate the buttery and salty taste of the pasta and the clams."

"Oh." Instructed, now, he attacked his meal as two-fistedly as a strongman ought to do, and Sarah was not far off his pace. But Paprika only picked at her food, evidently preferring to take this opportunity for serious conversation—or rather, to deliver a homily. And Yount gradually found his own gustatory pleasure dwindling, for what Paprika had chosen for a subject was the inadequacy of males as lovers. Perhaps Paprika was being kind, Sarah thought—talking in generalities about "men," rather than saying straight out that she wanted to discourage Yount's oafish wooing. Even if that was so, Obie Yount found it an uncomfortable experience, to hear his whole sex systematically denigrated.

"Men," said Paprika, "are clumsy in courtship, selfish and insensitive in the art of love. They neglect the infinity of subtleties that a woman best enjoys."

Through a mouthful, Yount said, "This sure is good macaroni, ain't it?"

"A man thinks of a woman as nothing more than a receptacle, to be filled with himself. She is expected to be thrilled just to be penetrated. But a woman can be immeasurably more thrilled by attentions to the outside of her, rather than the inside."

"Can I pour you some more of this Canty, Miss Paprika?"

"Not any man can ever know all the wonderfully excitable little places on the outside of a woman's body. Only another woman can."

Sarah, eating with gusto, had been only amusedly glancing from one to the other of them. But her look became thoughtful, and stayed on Paprika, as she realized that she as well as Yount was being lectured. And Yount, for his part, began to find the experience more than uncomfortable; he was getting excruciatingly embarrassed. His two hands ceased shoveling fettuccine and found other occupations—one hand twining nervously in his beard, the other wiping sweat from his bald pate—when Paprika began to dwell on specific techniques and technicalities.

"Obie, have you ever, when making love to a woman, taken the time and trouble to admire the woman's . . . her chelidon, say, for instance?" She smiled salaciously. "Or her philtrum, perhaps?"

Yount looked warily about the restaurant. "Please, Miss Paprika. Some of these other folks might recognize low language, even in English."

"Don't be an ass. Answer me. When you make love to a woman, do you ever think to caress her chelidon? To stroke her philtrum?" Paprika's pink tongue came out and lasciviously touched her upper lip. "Have you ever *kissed* those places on a woman?"

Yount squirmed and said wretchedly, "Ma'am, I couldn't let myself say such *words* to a woman, let alone—"

"There. You see what I mean about males being dense? Would you be this much shocked, Obie, if the woman paid loving attention to *your* philtrum or chelidon? You have such places, too."

Yount wrung his beard and squeegeed his scalp. "Ma'am, please, could we change the sub—?"

"However, your own philtrum," she said, scrutinizing him mischievously, "is covered with hair."

"And decently clothed, too!" he burst out. "Why, I never heard such talk from a woman. Even in stag company, even in barracks, I wouldn't talk like you do about such things."

"Imbecile man, you do not even know what I am talking *about*. Here, I will show you those things."

Before Yount could leap up and flee, she was already showing them—not her own, or his, but Sarah's.

"This is the chelidon." Paprika reached over—making Sarah start slightly— to stroke her slim forefinger across the bend of Sarah's unsleeved arm. "The chelidon is the inside hollow of the elbow." Sarah quivered all over, as if she had been intimately fondled. "And this is the philtrum," added Paprika, stroking her fingertip down that little crease of Sarah's, and giving Sarah another frisson. "It is the indentation between the nose and upper lip."

"Oh," said Yount, settling onto his chair again.

"Do you honestly think that such anatomical terms—such innocuous words —are somehow lewd and nasty?"

"I reckon not," he mumbled, feeling foolish, not mollified. "But the way you talk about 'em is. Like you're lickin' the words as they come out."

"Sometime you should try licking the chelidons and the philtrum of a woman. She will probably be surprised. She will most certainly be pleased. And aroused. And responsive. She will account you an exceptional man. Nevertheless, no man has ever *been* a woman. So there is no way he can know all the delicate nooks and crannies, the delicious places and things that yearn to be played with."

Yount said, "Hey." He had recovered sufficiently to be scandalized all over again. "Are you suggesting that a woman could be pleasured better by another *woman*? Than by a *man*?"

"I am not suggesting. It is a fact. It stands to reason. When a woman wants that sort of pleasure, why should she not seek it from one who knows best how to give it?"

"Why... but...." Yount groped for an adequate but inoffensive simile. "That would be like her buying a teapot without any spout."

"Ah, kedvesem, you men are so proud of that spout. You forget, the inside of a woman is only a place for childbearing, exactly like the inside of any sow or ewe, and a woman is no more humanly feminine or sensitive in there than those animals are."

"Now, that's got to be a lie," said Yount in horror. "I ain't gonna talk as blunt as you do, but I will aver that I'm no virgin myself, and no woman ever *not* enjoyed my—my masculine apparatus. Miss Paprika, you are flat telling a lie."

"I am flat telling the truth. A woman is sensitive only a finger's length or less"—she smiled—"inside her feminine apparatus. Sarah here will confirm that that is so."

But Sarah only said faintly, "I—I never thought about it," and Yount, appalled, made no further protest, so Paprika implacably went on at him:

"Even if you, teapot, have a spout like an elephant's trunk, its only real function is to deposit babies inside a woman. For sensation, for pleasure, for ecstasy, a finger in there is sufficient—or a tongue—and far more nimble, and far more capable of driving her nearly mad with—"

Yount abruptly stood up and waved for the proprietor. "I reckon it's time we got back to the..." He paused and said brutally, "Back to the other circus freaks. Miss Makkai, if you intended to rid yourself of me, you have surely done that. I only hope you haven't curdled my feelings for every other woman in Creation."

Thus it was that, immediately after the night show, Yount again dressed in civilian clothes and left the tober. He made his way to the nearest cab rank, where he managed, with vivid gestures, to inform a vetturino that he required a whorehouse. Arriving at such an establishment, he managed to inform the madam that he required a whore, whereupon he was ushered to a tawdry room containing Teresa Ferraiuolo. If Teresa Ferraiuolo shared Cécile Makkai's low opinion of the male half of humankind, she had sense enough not to make untimely pronouncements on the subject, and in any case could not have aired her opinions in English. However, after Obie Yount had departed—satisfied, gratified and to some degree reassured—Teresa Ferraiuolo went around to her sister inmates of the house, to warn them that those notorious perverts, "gli Inglesi," were getting queerer all the time. This one, she told them, had insisted, between more routine and normal diversions, on being allowed to lick her elbows and her mustache.

At about the same hour, the Gran Duca's dining room was emptying of its late-dinner occupants, including most of the circus people. But Florian commanded the waiters to clear one large round table for his conference with his Equestrian Director Edge, his Canvasmaster Goesle, his Bandmaster Beck and his Sideshow Director Fitzfarris. He also, when the other women of the troupe dispersed, asked Autumn Auburn to stay. So the six of them sat down around the table and the waiters took their orders for conferential lubricants.

Florian took out his little notebook and began ticking off items. "I will not bore you, lady and gentlemen, with a detailed treasurer's report. Suffice it to say that today's attendance was far better than I could have anticipated. I imagine we can mainly ascribe that not to our being the greatest circus ever to show here, but to our being foreign, hence a novelty. Whatever the reason, I believe we can profitably go on showing here in Livorno for another two weeks at least, before the receipts begin to tail off. Not to deplete our treasury too much, I shall continue the holdback on those firsts-of-May who have newly joined out, but I *will* be able to institute regular salary days for all the lifers. Meanwhile, Messieurs Goesle and Beck, you may proceed with those purchases we discussed... and with every expectation of being soon repaid for your out-of-pocket expenses."

"Already the drawings for the Gasentwickler I have prepared," said Carl Beck. "Tomorrow the buying of the materials I shall commence."

"Good," said Edge. "Maggie tells me that Jules ought to be moving to a wheelchair in a day or two, and at least hobbling with a cane not long after. It would be nice if we could have his balloon ready for tryout as soon as he's on his feet."

"Tomorrow also," said Beck, "additional Musikinstrumente for the otherwise unoccupied Slovaks I will buy, so they can be bandsmen—windjammers, as you say—during performances. For a start, I am adding only brass. I can buy them cheap at a monte di pietà pawnshop. Maybe later add woodwinds, more percussion."

"I leave that in your competent hands, Kapellmeister," said Florian. He went on, "Tomorrow our attendance should easily equal today's and perhaps exceed it. The printers delivered our posters and throwaways this evening. I will have some of our men out papering the city at dawn." From under his chair, he got samples of the posters and handed them around the table for all to admire.

"Wait you, Governor," said Goesle. "Better business we *cannot* do. If we had had any straw on the ground today, the jossers would have been sitting on it."

"Straw, yes. I have not yet been able to procure any, Dai. But I have already contracted with a local mill for sawdust. Very cheap. They'll deliver before show time tomorrow. Have your roustabouts spread it over the pista and the seating areas alike."

"Seven and seven times welcome it is," said Goesle. "But Governor, if more people come tomorrow, Maggie the Hag will be turning them away at the red wagon."

"No bad thing," said Florian. "Success breeds success. If the town hears we are turning folks away, they'll be all the more eager to see us."

"This poster," said Edge, "as well as I can make it out—it seems uncommonly restrained. No strings of superlative adjectives. What has happened to your usual blowhard bombast, Governor?"

"Ah, my boy, once you have the real goods, you no longer have to do empty bragging. Leave the flummery to the would-bes and the has-beens and the never-will-bes."

"Then it's a good poster, I reckon, for our classy show."

"Nevertheless, we will always find room for improvement," said Florian, and he consulted his notebook. "We must work things out as we go along. For one thing, those songs we sing. We could, of course, do local folk music. But that would mean everybody's having to learn new tunes in every country. I'd prefer to keep the old tunes and substitute new words as necessary. Miss Auburn, could you spare me the task, and do the rendering of them first into Italian?"

"Well... I'll try..."

"The words need not *say* anything, actually. What the hell, they don't now. Just make sure that the opening chorus sounds brash and sprightly, and Madame Solitaire's accompaniment is romantically sweet, and the closing chorus is a lingering farewell."

"Crikey. You don't ask much, do you?"

"Now..." Florian consulted his notes again. "Today's performances were necessarily inchoate, because we were in a hurry to put the show before the public. But we should be a *circus,* not a vaudeville of skits and tricks in helter-skelter sequence. A circus should open with a flourish and close with a flourish. In between, it should be a well-considered alternation of the acts that entertain and the acts that thrill. Intervals of jollity relieving the spells of suspense and nail biting. So I have drafted a new program. See if any of you have any comments on it."

He tore the page from his notebook and started it around the table, while he went on:

"Miss Auburn, yours is so clearly the most popular turn of all that it will henceforth close the show. The jossers will go home with pleasant memories of us, and will spread the good word. Colonel Ramrod, I am moving you up to close the first half of the program with your shootist exhibition. That will empty the crowd from the chapiteau at intermission in an excited mood, receptive to exploitation, ready to buy."

"Buy what?" asked Fitzfarris.

"For now, Maggie's services, your swazzles and your mouse-and-board game. Let us reinstitute that after the sideshow presentation. The Italians are not simpering ninnies who will protest at a mouse's being put to worthwhile employment. Speaking of animals, Mag is already making ruffs for the Smodlakas' dogs, and new costumes for the Smodlakas themselves. When our wardrobe mistress is done with that, I will have her start on uniforms for your windjammers, Carl."

"Still speaking of animals," said Edge, "I'd like to put the liberty act in the program before long. A couple of the horses are still wobbly from the sea voyage, but I'll get on with the training as soon as they've got their land legs."

"And both Sunday and Monday," said Autumn, "have asked me to teach them wire-walking. If you're agreeable, Governor, I thought I'd give them a slant climb for a start. If they're any good, they can go on to do a crossover."

"All right. Let me know if either shows any aptitude."

"Well," Autumn went on, "a slant climb should go up high and scary, so it can close with a slide-for-life. Come to that, I want to get my own rig up high, too."

"Confound it, Autumn—" Edge began, but Florian interrupted:

"My dear, I am in total accord. A thrill act should evoke as much thrill as possible. However, to point out the obvious, our chapiteau has only a single center pole. There is nothing up there to string your tightrope *between*. Until we have more room..."

Carl Beck interjected, "Ja! And my windjammers will a bandstand in the tent be needing. What we have now, richtig, they can from the back door lean in and play. But a proper band—"

Without force but with authority, Goesle said, "We are needing more room, Governor, for more than a bandstand and the missy's rope rig. There is no profit to having popularity if we have no place to put the crowds. Here is my thinking. At inconsiderable expense—one more center pole and some extra canvas—we can double the chapiteau's capacity. You have now a round tent. We simply split the round in half, move the two semicircles apart, each held up by a pole, and lace between them a sufficient rectangle of canvas, from peak to ground on either side..."

"You need not elaborate, Dai," said Florian. "A tent of middle and rounds is no novelty."

"I am not pretending that I invented it. I only say that I can do it, and cheap. I can give you an oval-shaped pavilion, plenty of seating room. And putting the poles at either side of the ring means much more freedom for the performers— no impediment sticking up in the middle of their ring—and between the two poles can be slung Miss Auburn's tightrope. All sorts of capabilities. Also, I can arrange to incorporate in the tent a bandstand. Over the front door entrance, in the European style."

"Sehr gut!" Beck said approvingly. Autumn nodded and looked triumphantly pleased, and Edge scowled at her.

"I am well aware," Florian said patiently, "that a tent can be expanded. And naturally I have wanted to do exactly that. But we are talking more than one extra pole and some extra canvas. We are talking a considerable amount of additional seating."

"You will have to have it, soon or later," Goesle persisted. "Look you, what you have now—boards laid on boards, held together by the grace of God. That may have been necessary in America, where the seats had to be put up and taken down every day. But here in Europe, where they will stay in place for a week or more at a time, they must be more secure. I shall procure real metal jacks instead of your puny saplings, and the boards will be nailed to the stringers. The Slovaks tell me they can get me lumber, free gratis. I think they mean they will steal the railroad passengers' wooden crates, but I am careful not to inquire too close. Gratis is gratis."

"Nevertheless..." Florian muttered.

"Also," Goesle pressed on, "that piled-earth ring may have sufficed for your one-day American stands. Here it will have to be made and remade. From the gratis lumber I can also cut and shape the pieces for a permanent but portable ring curb. Brightly painted, padded on top. All these things I can do."

"Canvasmaster," Florian said earnestly, "these are all things I devoutly want done. However, consider. You can get canvas and lumber and jacks and everything else required. But then *they* require transport. We are also talking of more wagons and more draft animals. More harness, more feed, more animal tending, a bigger tober required everywhere we go..."

"Allow me to say a thing," Edge put in. "As you predicted, Governor, goods *are* cheap in this part of the world, at least compared to back home. I haven't priced big things like wagons, but if they're on a par with stuff like oats and hay and cat's meat, they shouldn't be out of our reach. As for the actual transport and tending, I might mention that Hannibal and Quincy give promise of becoming as good as Roozeboom was at hostling and wagonmastering."

"Yes," said Florian, nodding thoughtfully. "I don't know how Abdullah did it, without a word of the local lingo—all I did was give him money—but he laid in good provender for the horses and the bull and the cat. And little Ali Baba, even with his atrocious *English*, somehow does a good job of supervising the Slovaks in their feeding and cleaning and care of the animals."

"Well, there you are," said Autumn. "If the crew are adequate and capable, Governor, you can't worry about the circus train or the tober being unmanageable."

"It is managing the money outlay that mainly worries me. Zachary, do I take it that you, as equestrian director, support Dai's grandiose schemes for immediate expansion?"

"I think what I'd recommend is hedging our bets. Let Stitches go ahead with all those extras. At the end of our stand here, if it has paid us well enough to afford the new wagons and draft stock and other equipment, then we'll get them. If not, we'll probably have to dump all the new goodies and go on without them."

"Satisfactory!" said Goesle. "Chance it I will. Because I am so sure of our success that I already have further plans for down the road. Our night-show lights are pathetic, and very soon I want—"

"Oh, lordy, lordy..." Florian moaned.

"Hear you now!" Goesle insisted. "That Missy Pepper is complaining and rightly. The mere ground performers only get sprinkled with pellets of candle drippings. But *she* hangs by her hair close up to the chandelier, and she gets the drops of *hot* melted wax."

Edge laughed and stood up. "Well, you fellows can get on with the planning and arguing, but Autumn and I have to be clear-eyed and steady to perform tomorrow. We're off to sleep."

As he and she left the dining hall, they could hear Carl Beck bringing up the matter of music again. "... Not one of the dumb Slovaks can read notes, and anyway we have no notes to read. But at them *anything* besingen or brummen they can play. So, for the slow and graceful acts, I think Strauss. For the brisk and lively acts, Offenbach or Gottschalk..."

"You know something?" Edge said to Autumn, as they climbed the stairs. "All that hesitating and fussing and raising of objections that Florian does? It's nothing but humbug. He's the greatest risk taker on this planet. He just wants us all to crank up our own enthusiasm for the outrageous ideas. And we always do."

"Oh, but I hope you have some enthusiasm left over," Autumn said seductively, "for other outrageous ideas."

She did her own disrobing this time, to save delay. And when she had peeled off all the concealed petals of fabric, she disclosed for Edge a small and sweet surprise. He stared—admiring, amused—and she said, "Well? You told me you liked the diamanté."

3

IT APPEARED that Livorno would not soon tire of the Florilegium. The next day was another turnaway day, and so was the one after that, and the one after that. The Livornese were cheerful folk; whenever they were told there was simply no more room even for standing in the chapiteau, they shrugged and grimaced humorously and went away, to come again another day. Also, Aleksandr Banat reported that he recognized many repeat and re-repeat visitors among the crowds. Banat had appointed himself ticket taker and keeper of the front door at each performance, and he did that job so assiduously that Florian instructed the wardrobe mistress to dress him for the post—"as a merry-andrew, I think"—but Banat deemed that inelegant.

He pointed to the sign on a wagon and said, "Is Circo Confederato, no? Ought to be Confederato doorman."

"You have a point," said Florian. They went to the Quakemaker and asked if he still had his old Rebel sergeant's uniform.

"Uh huh," said Yount, surveying the short, stout Banat. "It'll go around him all right, I reckon, but you'll have a helluva lot left over at each end."

However, Magpie Maggie Hag was able to alter the uniform to fit and, when Yount showed Banat how to wear the forage cap properly atilt, it even disguised the man's lack of forehead. Later, Banat went downtown to a monte di pietà and bought some old, tarnished medals, polished them and pinned them to the breast of his gray uniform. Thereafter, at the chapiteau's front door, he greeted the incoming patrons with soldierly dignity, and none of those ever remarked on the anomaly of a Johnny Reb speaking an Italo-Anglo-Slovak jargon and wearing the Order of the Netherlands Lion, the Médaille Militaire and the Order of Guissam Alaouite.

Since the Florilegium was now far from what Florian had once called Biblethumping-bumpkin land, there was no obstacle to its giving performances on Sundays. So the troupers and crew alike worked two shows every day, seven days a week. The weather stayed fine during their time in Livorno, and the one rain that fell during that period fell in the middle of the night. It waked Canvasmaster Goesle in his Gran Duca room. He hastily dressed, strapped on his jingling belt of knives, fids, awls and other implements, ran downstairs, woke a vetturino at the hotel's cab rank and had himself galloped out to the park. But he found, when he got there, that Banat had already rousted out his crewmen to loosen the tent's guy ropes and to spread tarpaulins wherever the rain threatened to dampen the sawdust.

"That man Banat is quite competent," Goesle reported to Florian next day, "and glad of it I am, by Dafydd. He even knows to make the roustabouts halfhitch the end of every rope back upon itself, so the ends won't trip anybody or get frayed from being trodden on. Not much misses Banat, and the other Slovaks readily obey him. Only one of the dozen—lout named Sandov—is a slacker and a whiner and an absolute blockhead. But Banat says, if you will allow it, he will get rid of the misfit."

"I hope this Sandov is not one of the bandsmen."

Goesle shook his head. "There is singing he does sometimes. Bawdy songs, I judge, from the way the others giggle. But he has no voice at all. It grates on a Welshman's ear."

"Very well, then. Banat has my permission to get rid of him."

Meanwhile, whenever the roustabouts were not patching the chapiteau's old canvas or doing routine yard tidying or attending the animals or, during performances, playing music or shifting rigging or running props in and out of the pista, they were being worked even harder in their "off time." They did fetch the free lumber, as they had promised (much of it was stenciled CRINOLINA), and Goesle set them first to sawing curved sections from it and nailing the pieces together, while he himself, with palm and big needles and waxed twine, sewed heavy leather into cushions and stuffed them with rags. The wood became twenty sturdy curved boxes, each a foot high and deep, and some six and a half feet long. Goesle had the men paint them in gaudy Italianate stripes of red, white and green, then affixed his padding to their upper sides. The boxes, laid end to end, made a handsome circular curb enclosing the forty-two-foot pista, except for a four-foot gap facing the tent's back door, for the entrance and exit of horses, the elephant and the cage wagon. Nevermore would anybody of the Florilegium have to dig and heap up and tamp an earthern curb. And nevermore would the Florilegium leave one, when it moved on, for the local children to play circus in.

Next, Goesle turned to the improvement of the chapiteau's rickety seating arrangements. He began by sending the Slovaks out again to liberate more lumber, while he went to the Gran Duca chandlery to look for metal jacks. That well-stocked shop did not disappoint him, because it kept those items in stock for the many aging ships that had to use such underpinnings to prop up sagging decks. So Goesle brought Florian to haggle in the vernacular, and they got a good price by buying more of the things than any one ship's master ever had to have.

During the while that Goesle kept the Slovaks busy at carpentry, he would occasionally spare them to rehearse under Bandmaster Beck, playing the old instruments and learning to play those newly acquired from the various local Mounts of Pity. One bandsman at a time was usually all that Beck required, because, having no sheet music, he had to sing or hum to each separate musician each separate instrument's part of every tune he wanted learned—"Like so it goes: boompty-tiddly-deedly-boomp." Then, after the cornetist and the horn player and the trombonist and the tuba player and the accordionist had each learned his individual part, Beck would beg from Goesle two men at a time, then three, and so on—and call in Hannibal and his drum—and rehearse them gradually at playing in unison. It was a system that might have daunted even such professional conductors as the brothers Strauss, but somehow the amateur aspirant Beck made it serve.

Also, whenever any number of the Slovaks were not working for Goesle or practicing music, Beck would have them shearing sheet metal or bending tubing or riveting and soldering together the fairly intricate bits of his hydrogen generator. That was perhaps an even more ticklish business than his piecework music instruction. Beck himself was proceeding mostly by inspired guesses, and he had to impart those notions to untaught mechanists who could no more read his exquisite drawings than they could read sheet music, and with whom he had no language in common. But here again—"This pipe like so should go: hammer boompty, bend it, boomp again"—he made his impromptu system work, and the generator began to take coherent shape.

In the process of acquiring a Gasentwickler and a passable circus band, Beck also acquired a nickname. One day, one of the Slovaks hailed another—"Hey, Broskev! Pana Boom-Tiddly-Boom wants you!"—and it was not long before everybody on the show knew its Kapellmeister and chief engineer as Boom-Boom Beck.

While all that industrious construction and creation went on, the performing artistes happily enjoyed what was for them comparative indolence. Although they had to work before the public two times a day, and in their spare time practiced to improve their old tricks, and experimented with new ones, and instructed the young apprentices, and saw to the upkeep of their props and animals, they were unburdened of most of the "housekeeping" drudgery that had formerly been their responsibility. They rejoiced in being well fed by the Gran Duca's dining room, at dependable intervals, and in being able to resort to the hotel's hot baths as often as they wished, and in having their laundry done by washerwomen invisible belowstairs, and in being able to call on the hotel maids for clothes mending and pressing and button replacing whenever Magpie Maggie Hag was busy, as she almost always was these days, designing and making new costumes.

Best of all, they found they could count on enjoying a regular weekly salary day. And, since they no longer had to spend their stipend just to keep their acts and the whole Florilegium in existence, they could use the money for personal acquisitions. Few of them, however, squandered their first wages on nonessentials. The benign autumn days were getting shorter, the nights were getting chill and damp and winter was not far off, so most of the purchases were of sensible civilian clothes. Florian advised the women, though, that Livorno's shops and tastes were as provincial as those in Virginia, and recommended that they postpone all expensive indulgences until they got to the fashionable and cultured Firenze.

Abner Mullenax treated himself to a new eye patch. He discarded his old army-issue patch and had one custom-made for him by a local tailor—of fine black silk inset with a little star pattern of rhinestones. He still looked like a pirate, but now a prosperous one, or an eccentric one. The three Chinese managed to buy vast bundles of spaghetti, and at every mealtime they would make their own fire on the lot, first to boil the pasta, then to fry it to greasy crispness. And they ate with gusty sighs of satisfaction, as if they had rediscovered something they had long been yearning for. Several people remarked that the Chinese might more sensibly have bought themselves shoes, but the three men seemed to disdain footwear, and even politely refused offers of hand-me-down shoes from other troupers, and continued to go barefoot, whatever the weather or the conditions underfoot.

For his part, Florian was sufficiently emboldened by Livorno's unabating patronage of the show and the unabating receipts at the red wagon that he did not wait for the close of the stand to make his decision about investing in additional transport equipment. Indeed, he went at it with some extravagance. He bought four new closed-van wagons—not really new but in good condition—one to carry the chapiteau's added canvas and seat planks and stringers and jacks and ring-curb sections; one for the Slovaks to ride and bunk in; one to accommodate the Smodlaka family and dogs, plus Hannibal, Quincy and the Chinese; one to carry wardrobe, musical instruments and props and, on the tober, to give the artistes a real dressing room for the first time. That van he even equipped with a small coal stove to keep them warm this winter while they dressed, and on which Magpie Maggie Hag could cook whenever they were not near a town or an inn at mealtimes.

The already overworked roustabouts now had to devote their every least remaining spare moment, usually late at night, to painting the new wagons to match the rest of the train and to putting a glossy new coat of black on Florian's rockaway. But they did the job stolidly and uncomplainingly—all of them except the already notorious malingerer Sandov. One of the Chinese antipodists turned out to be an accomplished calligrapher and, though he could not at all comprehend the words or letters, he beautifully copied them from one of the old wagons onto each of the new ones, and even onto the wooden panels that enclosed Maximus's cage when it was on the road: FLORIAN'S FLOURISHING FLORILEGIUM, etc., etc.

Because those new-bought wagons would be immensely heavy when they were loaded, Florian bought two horses to draw each one, and he did not stint there, either. Somewhere he found a stable that had for sale eight of the Pinzgauer Tigerschecken horses bred in Austria: white horses spotted with black—not splotched like American pintos, but polka-dotted exactly like Dalmatian dogs. They were horses hefty enough for draft work but gorgeous enough for Edge eventually to work into his liberty act.

The artistes were now performing in a new order-of-appearance that Florian had devised to make for a better alternation of acts amusing and acts thrilling.

Since the revised program gave Autumn Auburn the closing spot, and Pepper
Mayo did her hair-hang several acts earlier, the disparity of applause the two
women received was not so blatantly apparent. Nevertheless, it was apparent
enough to Pepper, and she seethed and sulked—especially when Florian finally
took a good look at her act, saw the scantiness of her dress and commanded her
to resume wearing the cache-sexe under her tights.

"It's not that *I* mind ogling the vertical grin," he said. "And clearly the worldly
Italians do not. But if I let you perform so, Pep, I can hardly refuse anyone else.
Next thing we know, Clover Lee or the Simms girls will be wanting likewise to
wink at the jossers—or the Quakemaker to flaunt his cod—and we can't have
everybody baring everything God gave Adam and Eve."

So Pepper, fuming and fizzing, flounced off to continue her training of
Quincy Simms in secret. They simply went some distance from the tober into
the park, she tied a rope around the boy's waist, threw the rope over a tree limb
and hoisted him a little way off the ground. There he practiced doing the serpentine twinings and knottings of himself without any support under him.

His sisters were also getting extra training, from Autumn, in the rudiments
of ropewalking. Since Sunday and Monday would have had to do that either
barefooted or in their only shoes—the bright yellow spring-heel shoes, which
would have been impossible—Autumn spent her own money to buy them each a
pair of unpadded ballet slippers, and got Goesle to make a long, springy balance
pole weighted with lead at either tip. The training began with each girl's teetering
back and forth along the narrow edge of a two-by-four borrowed from the carpenter Slovaks. Eventually Autumn exchanged that board for a one-by-eight,
and made the girls walk the one-inch strip. When they progressed to a half-inch
rope, pegged only a foot above the ground, both Sunday and Monday had already
become commendably surefooted.

At other times, Monday Simms continued to take riding instruction from
Sarah, who told her, "I have made a decision. Since Clover Lee and I already do
rosinback routines on Snowball and Bubbles, I want you to start riding Zachary's
horse Thunder, and start learning the very ladylike and genteel art of haute
école."

"Ma'am?" Monday said blankly.

"It means 'high school.' In other words, a very well-educated horse and rider.
It's not a thrill act, like our basse école rosinback acrobatics, or Buckskin Billy's
galloping voltige. It's a subtle sort of fancy stepping, and you may think it tame
by comparison. But it will be highly regarded by every spectator who recognizes
fine horsemanship. It is done on this English saddle, which I just bought for that
purpose."

"That's a saddle? Looks more like a pancake."

"I guess it does, compared to one of those cavalry rocking chairs. But you'll
soon realize what freedom its lightness allows the horse, and what excellent
control its smallness allows to your legs. Mount up, and I'll show you some of the
steps Zachary had taught this horse long before he ever saw this circus."

Monday vaulted aboard, and Sarah handed her a light riding crop. "Start him
at a lope—not full run, just a Canterbury gallop—then touch his off shoulder
with the quirt. That's called 'checking' him." Monday cantered halfway around
the pista, touched Thunder and he instantly changed leads, reversing the order
in which he put down left and right feet. "Touch him again," Sarah called. Mon-

day did, and Thunder resumed his original gait. As the girl went past her, Sarah called, "Now check him every fourth step, and then every second step." The horse circled the ring again, changing step so frequently and smoothly that Monday cried delightedly, "He's dancing!"

She added, when she brought the horse to a halt beside Sarah, "O' course, I nearly fall off this-here pancake every time he checks."

"You'll soon learn to ride with the changes. Now, if the band plays a polka, and you put Thunder to a canter, and keep checking him in that order—fourth step, second step, fourth, second—it will look to the audience like Thunder is dancing a perfect polka. As soon as you've learned that one, I'll teach you the other sequences of checks that will make him dance the waltz, the schottische and so on."

"Swine!" roared Pavlo Smodlaka, when one day he came raging to Florian, to report that Mullenax's pigs had viciously attacked his terriers. The children Sava and Velja had first intervened, he said, but they were too frail to separate the combatant animals. Pavlo had had to bestir himself and wade in to break up the fight, "before the filthy swine could maim or kill or eat any of my darlings—or the children—but the dogs' pelts are much scratched and their nerves are in a terrible state! I demand that those prljav pigs be butchered!"

Since Florian was aware that the pigs had also become so corpulent that they could hardly do their own ladder climbing and other tricks, he spent the rest of that day preparing a convincing argument for retiring Hamlet & Co. from show business, then went to confront Mullenax, only to find that the predicament had already been resolved.

"Them pigs? Funny you should mention 'em, Guv'nor. I just this afternoon got rid of 'em. Gettin' rambunctious they was, and too big to be cute any more. Anyhow, all this time, I only been workin' 'em until they was well fatted up for eatin'."

"You *ate* them?"

"Naw. I couldn't eat no old friend. Knowin' who it was, anyway. I gave 'em to the hotel kitchen."

"You simply gave them away?"

"Well, more of a trade." Mullenax winked his one eye, which was quite spectacularly bloodshot. "The management's givin' me unlimited credit in the hotel grogshop as long as we're in town."

Florian cleared his throat. "Er, Barnacle Bill, I sometimes worry..."

"Now, now. Nothin' to worry about, Guv'nor. That act's gone, yes, but I'm workin' up a real special 'nother one with Maximus. It'll outshine old Ignatz's bogus-bloody arm for damn sure. What I'm gonna have the lion do is jump through *a hoop of fire*. With me right there inside the cage holdin' it for him."

"Well, yes, that would be grand. The trick is not unheard of, but not many trainers can accomplish it. Not even the most dedicated and sober ones." Florian slightly stressed the word "sober."

"I can do it. Me and old Maximus. See, he's got a lot livelier now that he's gettin' good vittles regular. And he already knowed to jump over my whip when I yell 'springe!' So what I did—I got a little curved piece of wood from Stitches. Propped it in the cage, made him jump over that. Maximus, I mean, not Stitches. So, after he got used to that, I added two curved pieces on both ends of that first piece. He jumped between 'em, over the older piece, just fine. So every few days I been puttin' him through a wider and higher curve of wood. All of this takes time, but one thing Ignatz taught me was patience. One day soon, I'll have that wood a complete circle around Maximus, and he won't balk at all."

"He might when you set fire to it."

"No, I'll do that slow and cautious, too. Dab just a little bit of coal oil at the top of the hoop, set it afire, have Maximus jump *under* it. When he realizes it don't hurt, I'll gradually bring the fire down and around the circle—everywhere except at the very bottom—because if he ever gets singed, I'll either get chawed to bits or we'll have to start over from the very beginnin'. Anyhow, if it works, it'll look to the crowd like Maximus is jumpin' through *a whole burning hoop of fire*. Nobody'll notice that the bottom of the circle ain't never fired."

"Yes. Well. I shall look forward to it. You will be acclaimed and renowned. As you say, the secret is being patient—and careful—and sober. Above all, sober."

"Guv'nor, I can tell you truthfully. I ain't never seen Maximus anything *but* sober."

The Florilegium's program still lacked what Florian regarded as indispensable to a circus: a clown. But Florian could at least console himself that Pavlo Smodlaka, though neither a clown nor a midget, was Tiny Tim Trimm's veritable replica in loathsomeness and an ideal replacement for Tim, in that the other troupers were all nicer to each other just for having Pavlo Smodlaka around to abhor. The man was dependable. Three shows out of four, the trained-dog act would conclude like this:

As the audience broke into applause, Pavlo and Gavrila would skip from the ring, hand in hand, smiling broadly, their three terriers frisking around them as they bowed their way backward out of the tent. Outside the back door, Pavlo would fiercely slap Gavrila's face, contort his own in a sneer, and snarl at her, "Prljav krava!"—or as often in English, "Filthy cow!" Then they would link hands again, skip smiling inside again, while the still-clapping crowd beamed fondly at the husband-and-wife artistes working so joyfully together. The two would bow their way out again, and outside he might slap her again, or cruelly yank one of her braids so hard that she staggered, and growl something like, "You planted your fat bottom right in the line of view between Terry and the best-dressed people in the seats!" or "Why do you always stand in the posture of a new-dropped turd?" If the applause continued long enough to summon them inside for several bows, the alternating smiles and abuse could go on for quite a while.

Only once did the company have the pleasure of seeing Gavrila openly defy Pavlo. After one evening's performance, when the crowd was clearing out, Florian brought an elegantly attired, high-hatted gentleman around to the backyard. The two approached the new dressing-room wagon, from which all four of the Smodlakas were just emerging in their street clothes, and Florian said:

"I have the honor, my friends, of introducing to you il Conte Ventimiglia. He begs a favor of you. The count's hobby, he tells me, is photography. He has a fully equipped daguerrian studio in his villa, and he is compiling a collection of photographs of, um, curiosities. He would like to borrow your little ones overnight—to add their pictures to his collection."

"Pictures?" Pavlo said delightedly. "But is that possible? To capture a picture of the dogs performing in such rapid motion?"

"No, no," said Florian. "Not the dogs, the Night Children. Sava and Velja."

"Sì!" the count said eagerly. "I figli della notte. Svestito. Tutto nudo. Affine di fare posture—ah—speciale."

"Er—nude?" said Florian, disconcerted. "Special poses? Count, you did not earlier mention—"

"Bah, only the hatchlings," said Pavlo, looking disappointed. But then he looked shrewd and said, "This count will pay? For this borrowing?"

Suddenly and ferociously, Gavrila spat, "He will do no such thing! Let him undress our children? Put them in *special poses*? Oscenità! Not while I live!" She curved her arms around the boy and girl and swept them away to their wagon.

Pavlo scowled darkly as he watched them depart, but then turned back to the count and gave him a shrug of resignation.

"Che peccato," murmured the Conte Ventimiglia. He brooded for a moment, while Pavlo also departed, then said to Florian, "Ebbene, per caso—i pigmei bianchi?"

"Sunday and Monday?" said Florian, now regarding the hobbyist with open distaste. "I had not suspected the nature of your collection. Nevertheless, here comes Sir John, the girls' guardian. I will at least relay the request to him."

He did so, and Fitzfarris said coolly, "As you know, Governor, I'm trying to learn the language. Tell me. How does one say in Italian 'go shit in your fancy hat'?"

Ventimiglia made a face of frustration, brooded some more, then gestured toward the dressing wagon. Its door stood open, and visible inside was Magpie Maggie Hag. With a heavy flatiron she had heated on the stove in there, she was pressing a costume she had just completed.

"Ebbene," said the count, with a wan sort of hope. "Per caso la strega?"

Fitz stared at the man in appalled fascination, and said to Florian, "Old Mag? This bug must really be desperate for perversion."

"Well," Florian chuckled, "just for the hell of it..." He called the gypsy to the van door and, trying not to laugh, solemnly put the proposition to her.

Magpie Maggie Hag still held the flatiron; it was smoking slightly. She came down the wagon steps with surprising speed for an old crone. She was too short to reach the count's face with the iron, but she gave one of his bare hands a sizzling blistering before he had the good sense to turn and run. The last seen of Ventimiglia, he was fleeing the tober and the park with Magpie Maggie Hag in literally hot pursuit.

"Good for Mag," said Florian, laughing. "And good riddance. That one was only a papal count, anyway, not real nobility."

"I'm glad to know it," said Fitz. "I was looking forward to meeting some real nobility over here."

Jules Rouleau was by now making daily visits to the tober in a wicker wheel-chair lent him by the Hotel Gran Duca. His first visits were brief, but, as his long-unused arm and chest muscles strengthened, the visits became day-long, during which he wheeled himself around the lot, in and out of the chapiteau, faster than he could have walked.

"But I *will* be walking, par dieu," he said. "Sarah bought me a fine malacca cane, and in my room each night I take a few more steps. I limp, of course, mais merde alors, I am happy enough to be upright again. Even able to take a real bath, instead of having women sponge at just the accessible parts of me. An acrobat I will never be again, but an aéronaute, oui. I observe, Maître Beck, that you have made laudable progress with the machinery."

"Ja. The Gasentwickler should not too much longer require to complete. But the gas-making chemicals, I think, not until Florenz will we be able to buy. So there in Florenz the Ballonflieger you will become."

"Merci, maître. Grand merci."

"Call me now Boom-Boom," Beck said shyly. "Everybody does. More freund-lich und Familie it sounds."

"Bien, Boom-Boom."

"Now, friend, allow me some ballooning instruction to impart. I know you have before on a tether gone aloft. But when to float free you wish, certain accessories you must employ. Around the basket will be hung many bags of sand ballast. To ascend faster and higher, one after another the bags you will drop. Nein, nein—not *drop*, verstehen—or somebody on the ground you maybe kill. *Empty* from a bag that sand. How much and how often you will learn to judge."

"Bien. And I already know about pulling the cord of the clack valve to release the gas, little by little, to descend."

"Richtig. Then if to ascend again you wish, you empty more sand. By up and down going, various breezes you will find, in various directions blowing. Thus, by choosing your breeze, the Luftballon actually *steered* can be, wherever you wish to go, then back to your starting point. The Zirkusplatz or wherever. Slowly release all the gas and like a feather down you come." Beck smiled and added, "I should say, all these things not from experience or genius I know. I have been reading many Bucher."

"C'est bandant, Boom-Boom. I sincerely thank you for all you have done— and for the masterly instruction also."

But it was Boom-Boom Beck who required some instruction in one of his other vocations, that of bandmaster.

"For the entrance of the elephant a ponderous music I have selected," he told Florian and Edge. "From Liszt's 'Battle of the Huns.' For your horses, Herr Edge —what else?—Strauss's 'Thunder and Lightning.'"

"You may have to play substitutes on short notice," said Florian. "Johann Junior is forever touring all over Europe, and we're likely to meet him anywhere. He's said to be a tight man about money, and he may demand payment for our using his music. But for now, let us rehearse to it."

So one day, in the free time between the afternoon and evening shows, Edge brought into the pista the horses he had already trained to perform without riders or harness—Snowball, Bubbles, his own Thunder, and the three unnamed horses acquired from the bummers back in Virginia. They all wore brilliant blue saddle blankets, liberally sequined and fringed with tassels, and spangled halters that held high blue plumes above their heads: costumes designed by Magpie Maggie Hag and fabricated with the help of Stitches Goesle.

Right now, Goesle had the Slovaks helping him round and taper and smoothe the three sections of a new, second center pole for the soon-to-be-expanded chap-iteau, and making a tall-spiked gumshoe to support the new pole, and forging a bail ring for it—but Florian and Beck persuaded him to part with the musicians among those crewmen. The windjammers fetched their instruments and Bandmaster Boom-Boom conducted them in a rather raucous rendition of the "Thunder and Lightning" polka. Edge stood at ring center and, with loud cracks but only gentle taps of his long whip, conducted the horses as they trotted or cantered around the pista—pranced, danced, pirouetted—formed in rank and reared all together or mingled in intricate patterns of crisscross and figure eights.

But after just a little while of this, Boom-Boom waved his band to silence and called indignantly to Edge, "Herr Direktor, your horses are not at all moving in time to my music! Cannot you train them to listen better? It is a great confusion of rhythms between us and them. Ein Mischmasch."

Florian smiled tolerantly and said, "Excuse me, Herr Kapellmeister, but even the sweetest music means no more to any animal than a concert of jackdaws. It is *you* who must watch the performance and conduct in tempo to *them*. The horses, the bull Brutus, even the human acrobats and aerialists and jugglers. You must also be prepared for frustrations and emergencies. If, say, you have allotted thirty seconds of a cancan for one of the terriers' tricks, and the dog fails or balks at it, you will have to stretch or repeat that music. At all times, it must look to the jossers as if every performer *is* intelligently and skillfully performing in time to your music. In actuality, it is you who must exert that skill. Just the way you ring those little arpeggios on your string of tins in time to Miss Auburn's rope-dancing."

"Herr Gouverneur, those are random notes. This is a Strauss polka. And, mein Gott, a polka is in strict two-quarter meter, with its tempo specified by its composer. Do you expect me to make it drag or race—ritardando, accelerando— from moment to moment?"

"Yes. Rubato—it is no sin. Composers far superior to the Strauss brothers have often marked their scores rubato, to allow the conductor that freedom of varying tempi. You will simply apply rubato to Johann's polka. And to all the other music you play for artistes in motion: Liszt for the elephant, Wagner marches, schottisches, whatever. I told you it takes skill. I am confident that you will provide it."

Beck looked duly flattered, but grumbled nevertheless, "Wagner and Liszt and the Strausses—if them we encounter—for using their music they will not make you *pay*. Into the pista they will leap and with their bare hands *strangle* you they will."

"I doubt it," Florian said calmly. "I have heard Wagner and Rossini operas, and one Strauss operetta, sung by divas who made the conductor and the whole orchestra sweat to keep abreast of them. One other thing, Carl. I mentioned also emergencies. Keep an eye on me or Zachary, as well, whichever of us is in the pista. If we make this signal"—he raised his arms and crossed them in an X above his head—"it means the canvas is on fire or something else baleful has occurred. You will immediately switch from whatever you are playing to Mendelssohn's 'Wedding March.'"

Beck looked horrified. "Not circus music that is! Schwabbelbusen that is! To listen to Mendelssohn is like with warm water being wetted."

"Perhaps. But it will instantly alert all the performers and crew. We can fix whatever is wrong, or hide it, or evacuate the chapiteau if necessary. My long-time associates know what the 'Wedding March' signifies, and I will so inform everyone else on the show."

Florian had told the company to hope for perhaps two weeks' stay in Livorno. It turned out to be more than four weeks of straw houses before they found themselves performing one night before a less than sfondone crowd. When the show commenced, Florian swept his gaze around, saw the two or three upper tiers of planks quite empty and made a decision on the instant. As soon as he had introduced the first act, Abdullah and Brutus, he went to the backyard, found Dai Goesle and said:

"Stitches, we'll strike it tonight. Bust the lacings right after the audience leaves. Pisa is only some fifteen miles northeast of here, an easy overnight run, but I won't ask you to go tonight. Ordinarily, I'd have had an advance man there already and arrangements made."

"Glad I'd be to roll this very night, Governor."

"Thank you, Dai, but no. You wouldn't know where to make the haul from the main road to whatever tober Pisa allots us. It would be senseless for you and the whole crew just to loiter about, unable to unload. No, we'll all get a good night's sleep and depart early in the morning. My rockaway can make better time than the rest of the train. I should have everything arranged with the Pisa municipio before you all arrive, and I'll be at the roadside to guide you in. There may even be time before dark to do the setup."

"Or to start it, anyway," said Goesle. "Mind, I'll be putting the middle between the rounds of the chapiteau for the first time. It may take some few setups and teardowns before we can do it swift like."

"True. So I won't schedule a performance for the next day, either. That will give us extra time for papering the town and stirring up enthusiasm."

During intermission, the whole troupe got the word of their imminent departure from Livorno. When the show resumed, Sarah Coverley was watching her protégée Monday Simms putting Thunder through a passable haute école of cross step, Spanish walk, piaffe and half-passes, when Paprika came up to her to say confidentially, seductively, "Angyal Sarah, this will be our last night in the Gran Duca, and we may not have such luxurious and—private—lodgings again for a while. Let us spend this last night here, you and I, together."

Sarah blushed noticeably, but she kept her eyes on the pista and said indifferently, "Whyever should we do that?"

"Oh, talk girl talk. Shop talk. Perhaps entertain each other."

"Entertain?" Sarah said absently, still watching the haute école.

Paprika said, with a pretense of impatience and scolding, "Kedvesem! Nemi érintkezés."

"You know I don't speak Hungarian."

"Kedvesem means darling. Nemi érintkezés means the sort of mutual entertainment I have in mind. I also know that you are neither stupid nor ignorant. You understand very well what I mean."

Now Sarah's eyes were closed. In a small voice she said, "Yes."

"Then let us cease playing hide-and-seek. Have you ever been kissed, Sarah, or licked or caressed at your philtrum or chelidon?"

"I really don't remember," Sarah said in a firmer voice, and she finally turned to face Paprika. "But I am not a prude, and I was never the typical American wife—'one position, under the covers, lights out.' I have enjoyed those—

caresses—in every other part of me. And I have always been satisfied to have a man do them."

"But you do not have a man at present. You truly *are* Madame Solitaire. Zachary has jilted you. Florian is preoccupied with business. Who, then? Pavlo the Gross?"

Sarah had to smile at that, and grimace. She said, "I grant that you are a coquette who would tempt anybody of either sex..." She let her voice trail off.

"You can pretend that I am a man, if you like," Paprika suggested impishly. "I do not care what goes on in your *mind*. Only in your—"

"No." Sarah shook her head. "You said we have private lodgings. We do not. Clover Lee shares my room. Pepper shares yours."

"Those are your only reasons for saying no?" said Paprika, visibly brightening. "Not sanctimony? Not priggishness? Only lack of privacy?" Sarah blushed even more deeply. "We can easily ask the night porter to rent us another room."

"It's still no, Paprika. Clover Lee might go looking for me. Probably in Florian's room, and God knows what uproar that might cause. Pepper would certainly know why she'd been left to sleep alone. She would probably kill both of us in the morning."

Indeed, Pepper was watching them from the farther side of the pista, watching with the eyes of a viper. When she saw Sarah leave the tent, she went to stand beside the Quakemaker, who was waiting to go on next, and engaged him in conversation, and glanced to make sure that Paprika saw *them*. She chattered only trivialities, but Yount was pleased at this unaccustomed familiarity, and she nestled against him to put their faces close together, and they both smiled a lot. Paprika was still watching them, and now it was she who watched with the eyes of a viper.

Late that night, any passersby in the hotel corridor outside the room of Pepper Mayo and Paprika Makkai could have heard their voices even through the closed and heavy mahogany door.

"Ye cheeky ginger-hackle! The little Clover Lee thistledown would have none of your letch. So now, purely to spite her, ye'll play firkytoodle with her *mother!*"

"It is not for spite, sárkány! Sarah is a beauty, too!"

"Blaflum! Very froncey she may be, but she's half again as old as you are. Mutton dressed as lamb."

"Menj a fenébel! She is anyway a woman. I am at least being true to my nature. You are making moon eyes at a *man!*"

"If ye continue to scunge after that Sarah biddy, then may the fiend ride through the both of yez, booted and spurred. Meantime, I'm working up a new act. I guarantee I'll steal the show and outperform the two of yez into oblivion. Also I'll be showing that Obie boyo more than moon eyes, bedad!"

The eyes they both showed, next morning, were red from anger, weeping and lack of sleep. But the other artistes did not look much more sparkly, for Florian had pounded on their doors at first light, so that they could have a hearty breakfast and still be early on the road. Early as it was, though, they found that Stitches Goesle was already up and had been busy.

"In the ships' chandlery next door, just," he said. "Buying blocks and tackle for the new center pole. Such things may be hard to come by, inland."

Most of the troupers ate sleepily and fumblingly, but Florian bolted his breakfast and hurried to the hotel desk to settle the accounts. When he paid the bill in full—without quibbling about each and every item on the long tally, as any Italian guest would have done—the Gran Duca's manager was pleased to accept from him the now thirty-eight conduct books of troupe and crew. He carried the stack into his office and when he came out each book contained his exquisitely scripted declaration that its bearer had behaved irreproachably during his or her stay in Livorno. He called the names, to hand each book personally, with a deep bow, to its owner.

"Signor Rouleau... Signorina Makkai... Signor Goozle..."

" 'Tis pronounced Gwell," growled Stitches.

"Signorina Mayo... Signor, uh, Cheenk..."

Florian said impatiently, in Italian, that he'd take the rest of the books, their owners all being out at the circus ground.

When the company went out the front door—porters wheeling Rouleau in the wicker chair and carrying out considerably more luggage than these guests had arrived with—there was a sleepy but doughty Aleksandr Banat waiting with the dressing-room wagon. They all, except Edge and Autumn, managed to crowd themselves and their luggage and Goesle's big coils of rope and heavy wire, turnbuckles and pulleys into or on top of that wagon. As the two polka-dot horses hauled it off toward the Fabbricotti park, Autumn and Edge went around to the Gran Duca's stable yard and the stalliere hitched Autumn's ribby old horse to her little van. They stowed their luggage and Edge's armaments inside, then climbed to the driving seat and Edge took the reins.

He commented, "From the glimpse I got inside, this is a dandy little cottage on wheels."

"I bought it from a family of tinkers who had decided, for some reason, to settle and stay in one place. It housed the whole family, so it's more than ample ...for me... alone..." She grinned at him.

"Oh, I don't require any hints, my lady. I can hardly wait to set up housekeeping with you."

Edge headed directly through the city for la Strada Pisa, and reached it simultaneously with the circus train coming from the tober. As it passed from right to left in front of Edge and Autumn, the Florilegium now made quite an impressive parade: eleven vehicles, all of them gaudily painted—except the gleaming black rockaway—four of them drawn by matched and spectacularly handsome two-horse teams. Behind the wagons, the circus's one spare horse towed Beck's not yet completed but at least already wheeled Gasentwickler, and Peggy lumbered last of all, swathed in a new, betasseled, gold-lettered, gloriously scarlet covering. Edge saw with mild surprise that Pepper sat conspicuously beside Obie Yount on the wagon he was driving, and Yount looked mightily pleased about that. Jules Rouleau was stretched out comfortably atop the tarpaulin that covered the balloon in its wagon, where he was best insulated against jolts and jouncing.

Edge turned onto the Strada Pisa behind the elephant, then flicked the reins to urge Autumn's old nag up past the train, and fell in behind Florian. As soon as the train was off Livorno's cobbled part of the strada and onto a hard-packed, smooth dirt surface, Florian put his horse to a brisk trot and his rockaway began to draw away from the rest of the procession. After a couple of miles, the rockaway had gone out of sight in the morning ground mist, and the little cottage on wheels was leading the train.

Riding up front there, with all of Italy before him, feeling very much the professional equestrian director of a circus that was no longer a mud show but a real circus, with his beloved sitting close beside him, with prospects of their seeing new and exotic places, Zachary Edge was more pleased with life and the world than he had been since before the war, or maybe since much longer ago than that.

He took from his frock-coat pocket a box of Sigarette Belvedere—Autumn had given him a quantity of them as his birthday present, a week or so ago— struck a match, lit a cigarette and took a deep, satisfying inhalation. He had earlier considered the Italian men sissified, smoking these little tubes of tobacco, but when he tried one he found it tasty and pleasurable. It was also a safer thing to smoke than a pipe, around the circus's hay and straw and sawdust. When one's leisurely smoke was interrupted by urgent work to do, a cigarette could simply be stepped on, but the emptying of a pipe took time and scattered sparks broadcast. Edge smoked only cigarettes now, and so did almost every other smoker in the company, including Pepper and Paprika. Abner Mullenax and Magpie Maggie Hag smoked the twisty, black, rank Italian cigars. Only Obie Yount, perhaps thinking it better sustained his "fusto" status, stubbornly stuck to his pipe.

The view of Italy that Edge and Autumn were at this moment observing from the Strada Pisa was not much of a view. The road was as straight as Autumn's tightrope, crossing the extensive coastal plain of the Toscana region, and that plain was as flat as Kansas. The road itself was pleasant enough to drive on, lined on both sides and completely overarched by evergreen, flat-crowned umbrella pines. But, when the ground mist finally wisped away in midmorning, there was nothing to be seen beyond the trees but flat farm fields, with the farmhouses so far away that only occasionally could one be glimpsed. Now and again, the circus train met a farm cart headed for Livorno, or was passed by one going toward Pisa, and the occupants gave the troupers cheerful waves. But those were the only people to be seen, for the farm fields had already been harvested of their wheat and barley. Oddly, though, between the bleak, brown expanses of stubble, there was frequently a field of brilliant yellow flowers, so profuse that they made a solid yellow blanket over the ground. Edge asked Autumn if she knew what kind of crop that might be.

"It's what they call here colza. In England we call it rapeseed. You'll see it all over western Europe, winter or summer. Whenever a grainfield gets poor and scanty, the farmer lets it rest for a year and plants only colza on it. Somehow— don't ask me how—that makes the ground rich and fertile again."

"Well, right now, those patches of colza are the only pretty things in this landscape."

"No farmer would plant colza just for its prettiness. He doesn't think of beauty; he knows only fertile and fallow. He is tied to the land; shackled to it." She leaned her head on Edge's shoulder. "Thank goodness we are not. We can just enjoy the prettiness and then move on to the next prettier place. Aren't we lucky?"

"I've begun to think I'm the luckiest man in the world."

"But you shouldn't smile about it. You look much handsomer when you are not smiling."

"Confound it, woman! People are always telling me that. Do I have to go around glooming like Job, just so I won't cause comment?"

"Oh, I can tell when you're happy, Zachary, whatever face you wear. When we first met, you told me I could do the smiling for both of us, for the rest of our lives. And I can, too, because I am the luckiest *woman* in the world."

4

" I CAN scarcely believe our good fortune!" crowed Florian, when he met the train, as promised, just outside Pisa. "The municipio is renting us the city's Campo Sportivo for our tober. Very near to the famous Leaning Campanile. I gather that some visiting Livornese have highly praised our show. And, when I showed the authorities our impeccable conduct books, I did not even have to ask. They *volunteered* that ideal location. Well, let us not waste time. Follow my carriage."

The troupe had not stopped along the road for a noontime meal; they had munched on snacks they carried, so it was now only midafternoon. Edge followed Florian, and the rest of the train followed him, across the bridge over the river Arno and then along a broad road skirting the main city, a road much crowded with other vehicular and pedestrian traffic, most of which came to a stop to gawk at the entry of the Florilegium, while other folk, in a hurry or uninterested in circuses, loudly cursed the jamming of the road.

This part of Pisa could have been the outskirts of Baltimore: all dingy warehouses and industrial buildings. But when the train had turned from the outer road into the city itself, the troupers could see, over the warehouse roofs, the skewed belfry of the Leaning Tower and the dome of the cathedral, almost as high as the Tower. Those tops of the two tallest buildings in Pisa remained in view all the way to the Sports Field, which was an oval racetrack with roofed wooden stands on either side and a neatly mown grass infield ample enough for the circus to spread itself out more than comfortably.

"Smooth as an English manor lawn," said Autumn.

And proudly Florian said, "I told you, Zachary, that we would be a low-grass show in time."

When most of the wagons were ranked in what would be the backyard, with the dressing-room nearest to what would be the back door, Stitches Goesle—sparing not even a glance for the Leaning Tower in the near distance—bawled for the roustabouts to start unloading the tent and baggage wagons, and to unhitch and grain the horses, and to feed the lion and elephant. Florian stayed on the lot to help Goesle supervise the setting up and to get his first look at his expanded chapiteau. So did Carl Beck, to start the internal rigging as soon as he could. But the artistes, being no longer involved in that hard labor, had the afternoon to themselves. And Autumn, though she had worked in Pisa several times before, cheerfully went as guide to Edge and those other troupers—including even Magpie Maggie Hag, Hannibal Tyree and the three Simmses—who were eager to take a look around the city.

They strolled back to the broad road, through a gateway in the ancient city wall, then down a cobbled avenue, across two or three narrower streets, to emerge in the many-acred expanse of the Piazza dei Miracoli. They looked about, and most of them looked dazzled. Tucked off in a far corner of the piazza was the Jewish Cemetery and—in Edge's opinion—the high wall around it was distinctive for its plain simplicity, because the four other structures on the vast green lawn flaunted more pillars and arches and pinnacles than he had ever seen in all the years of his whole life. And surely nobody anywhere could ever see so many at one time as could be seen here simply by swiveling one's gaze from left to right.

The immense cathedral, besides being unstinting of columns and arches, was horizontally striped by alternating courses of black and white marble—rather aptly, thought Edge, like alternate layers of devil's-food and angel cake. Similarly striped was the huge, circular baptistery, a little way distant from the cathedral's façade. Edge told Autumn that it looked to him like a spare dome—complete with ornamental pillars and arches and pinnacles all around it—left over from some other massive church building.

"Not to me," she said, with a smile. "See, it's got that little cupola on top, like a nipple. I always think of the baptistery as the exposed giant breast of some pagan Titan goddess buried under all this holy Christian ground."

The far-famed Leaning Tower was also of black-and-white stripes of marble, pillared and arched around every one of its seven tiers and the belfry on top. Edge had been seeing engravings of it ever since his childhood geography classes, but the tilted campanile was far more impressive in actuality than in any mere picture. Now *that,* he thought, could be a Titan's wedding cake. Some jealous rival Titan had reached down, grabbed it and given a malicious yank, so that now the cake was stretched painfully high and uniformly cylindrical, all the way to where the belfry perched, and it seemed about to topple sideways off the Titans' wedding reception table.

Hannibal asked Autumn, "When it s'posed to fall over, ma'am?"

"Well, it has stood like this for about six hundred years," she said. "I don't think you have to worry about standing beside it this minute. Nevertheless, it goes on leaning a fraction of a millimeter more each year."

"So it's *bound* to fall sometime," said Clover Lee, with awe.

"Sometime, but not today. We people are too lucky." Autumn gave Edge a glance and a smile. "Florian and Zachary and I all say so. Would any of you care to climb to the top? There's a spectacular view. I should warn you, though: there are nearly three hundred steps."

"Hell with that," said Mullenax. "There's a saloon right across that next wide street yonder. I'll wait for y'all there."

Fitzfarris lazily said he would, too, and so did Magpie Maggie Hag, saying she was too old and rickety for mountaineering. The rest paid their admissions —along with a few other tourists, all Italians from elsewhere in the country— and trudged up the stairs. Edge and Yount and some others ascended warily, holding to the wall and going up practically hand over hand, because they had the eerie sensation of being continuously and irresistibly drawn toward the tower's lower side. Only those whose acts and lives depended on an unerring sense of balance went up with agility and assurance.

But the view from the balcony that encircled the belfry was worth the climb. Westward, they could have seen all the way to the sea, and southwest to Livorno, but for the haze of Pisa's multitude of smoking chimneys. To the north and east, mountains were visible, an inspiriting sight after the plain they had just crossed. To the south, the greater part of Pisa lay spread out before them. The city was about twice as big as Livorno, and much more richly studded with ornate palaces and churches and towers and citadels.

An ancient docent was posted on the balcony and, like something run by clockwork, he droned facts and figures about il Torre Pendente, first in Italian, then in English, concluding with the information that "in order to establish the laws of velocity and acceleration of falling objects, Galileo Galilei—from the downward side of this very balcony—dropped cannonballs and lesser weights..."

"Hoy," Quincy said under his breath, looking over the balustrade at the insectlike figures on the lawn below.

"Cannonballs, eh?" boomed Yount, grinning, having at last heard of an Italian with whom he had something in common. "Fetched 'em all the way up here to drop 'em? Where might I meet this Gali-Gali and shake his hand?"

The docent only blinked, and Autumn laughed. "Probably in heaven, Obie. He's been dead for more than two hundred years. Come to think of it, though, you might not even find him there. The Church denies heaven to men who are *too* strong."

"Shucks," said Yount, disappointed.

"Perhaps of more interest to the females among us," Autumn went on, "that widest avenue you see to the east is where you'll find the fanciest and most fashionable shops. It goes right on across the river bridge and farther yet. Plenty of shops. Just don't bankrupt yourselves before we get to Firenze, where—"

Pepper said, "Och, the sun is about to go down, and I'm thinking we'd better get down, too." She looked behind her, warily, at the seven sizable bells in the belfry. "If they ring the Angelus, or whatever these dagos do, it's lifelong deaf we'll be."

"Not to worry, signorina," said the aged docent. "The bells have never been sounded since they were hung here. The vibration might be too much for the Torre Pendente."

They went, anyway, to be back on the tober before dark. Each of them gave the old man a few coppers of mancia, and again many of them negotiated the staircase with caution and queasiness. They found Fitzfarris, Mullenax and Magpie Maggie Hag loitering about the base of the tower, all three of them exceedingly aromatic of breath.

As they approached the Campo Sportivo, Florian came across the racetrack to meet them, saying wearily, "The crew and I will be working for a while yet, so we'll be having a late supper. But I took time out to go and engage rooms at a hotel. You people might want to haul your luggage there, freshen up, take dinner at a decent hour. The hotel is not quite as magnificent as the Gran Duca, but it is convenient. La Contessa Matilde. Go back to the first corner and turn right."

"Well, all our hotels got noble names, by damn," said Yount. "Miz Sarah, you and Clover Lee ought soon to be meeting your counts or jukes at *one* of 'em."

Sarah gave him a wan smile. They and the others just now seeing the transformed chapiteau—much larger and more imposing than it ever had been—took the time to walk completely around it, admiring and marveling. Then most of them piled their personal belongings into an empty wagon.

Edge said to Autumn, "If you'll forgive me for letting you dine unescorted, I'd like to stay and get acquainted with the new setup."

"Of course, my love. I'll take your luggage along with mine."

The pavilion was still the same height as before: some thirty-five feet. But, with the fifty-foot-wide new canvas laced between the parted halves of the old round tent, it was now an oval spanning a splendid hundred and twenty feet from end to end. The old and new center poles protruded above bail rings at either side of the inset panel. Clearly that had required some alterations in both the old and new canvas—and still did. Two roustabouts were atop the tent peak, one clinging to each pole top, both of them busily stitching at the canvas and relacing ropes about the bail rings. From the ground, Dai Goesle was giving rapid-fire instructions which Aleksandr Banat, beside him, translated to them in a bellow.

Goesle saw Edge appraising the work, and paused to say, "When we tear down here, I shall ask Florian and you, lad, for a day's layover. I should like to spread the canvas all on the ground and paint it. Look you now. 'Tis an obvious patchwork, new-canvas-colored and old-canvas-colored. I suggest stripes all over, but we can discuss that. At all events, a thin coating of oil paint will improve the chapiteau's rain resistance and life span. Also, I will have that artistic Chink paint the circus's name—big, *big*—above the marquee. What think you of the marquee, Zachary?"

Instead of having merely left a side panel unlaced so it could be pinned back to make a front door, as had heretofore been the practice, Goesle had made two neatly hemmed slits, ten feet apart, in his new center canvas, from ground level to a height of eight feet. That flap was raised outward and supported on two new, candy-striped poles, like the roof over a front porch: a much more inviting entryway. Edge could look in and see the pavilion's similarly cut back door just opposite, beyond the ring, which now had no center pole in its actual center to impede his view.

To make a sort of avenue leading patrons to the front door, Goesle had erected a four-foot-high plank platform on the left—where Fitzfarris would present his sideshow and mouse game and ventriloquy during intermissions. On the right, the red wagon and the cage wagon were parked end to end. Patrons would first encounter the red wagon's ticket booth, then could view the museum at the rear of that wagon, then move on and regard Maximus, then move on beneath the marquee and into the chapiteau. Both sides of the avenue were lined with Roozeboom's old pole torches, for the nighttime shows.

"Go you along inside, Zachary," said Goesle. "You will hardly recognize it."

He hardly did. The pista looked much bigger than forty-two feet across, with no pole in it. The two center poles stood four feet away from the curbing on either side, leaving ample room for the come-in and the closing specs to parade around the outside of the ring. Canvasmaster Goesle and Chief Rigger Beck had strung guy wires outward and sideways from high on the two poles, to brace them, and those wires disappeared among the seat planking, heavily staked and turnbuckle-tightened at ground level.

Mathematically, the addition of the fifty-foot center canvas should have increased the chapiteau's seating capacity by half again. In reality it nearly doubled the capacity. The old tiers of seats, their stringers now firm on real iron jacks, curved around the semicircular ends of the tent, and Goesle's new, matching tiers of planking covered the straight sidewalls. But there was a good deal of space remaining between the old seats and the center poles, and the canvasmaster had not wasted that. He had made still more plank seats and placed them all at ring-view level, to fill in the space. To all the front seats were attached, at intervals, Roozeboom's tin-reflector oil lamps.

"For the time being," said Florian, who was supervising the interior work still going on, "we'll let the jossers race each other for those front seats, or fight for them. But eventually Stitches wants to build comfortable folding chairs—what a circus calls its 'starback' seats—to occupy that best viewing space. And we can charge a higher ticket price for them than for what we call the 'blues'—the plain planks farther back."

In some awe, Edge looked around, at what appeared to him to rival the pictures he had seen of the vast Roman amphitheaters of old. For a moment, he thought Goesle had extended the seat planking right over and across the tent's front door. But then he realized that the wooden construction up there, braced on jacks, was a stand for the circus band, neatly fenced about and provided with stools.

"Our chief rigger is almost finished with hanging the show," said Florian, gesturing upward.

Edge looked up and remembered how he had once thought that being inside the Big Top was like being inside a *Saratoga* sort of balloon. Now he might be inside a canvas cathedral, the space up there was so immense and airy, and the chapiteau top looked so much higher than it really was. The guy wires glinted where they converged on the center poles. The old pole still wore its lungia boom, canted out at a slight angle over the pista. A roustabout was clinging there, affixing to the boom's end a block and fall for the hoisting of Pepper by her hair. Florian was gesturing to him instructions on how to rig the hoist in such a way that it would not tangle with the chandelier, also hanging up there.

The new pole had, on its ring side, a small wooden platform, with a rod-and-rope ladder dangling from it to the ground, and it took Edge a moment to recognize that the platform was Autumn's resting stand. At this moment, Boom-Boom Beck was kneeling on it, and he and a Slovak on the other center pole were adjusting the turnbuckles and tension of the tightrope that crossed the fifty-foot space between them. On the old pole a bright white spot had been painted at what would be Autumn's eye level, for her guidon. The rope was exactly twenty-seven feet off the ground, but it seemed sky-high to Edge.

"Miss Auburn is a consummate artiste," said Florian, though Edge had not spoken. "As surefooted on a rope as on the pista sawdust. And an artiste wants her work or his work displayed to best advantage. You love the little lady, yes. But Zachary, if you want to have her go on loving you, take my advice. Do not attempt to be her *keeper*."

"You're right," said Edge. "It'll chill my gizzard every time she goes up there, but I'll try not to show it. To change the subject, let me ask you something. Since we don't now have a pole or any such thing in the middle of the ring—excuse me: in the pista—why are those men digging a big hole there?"

"For a grave," said Florian.

Edge stared and said incredulously, "You tell me not to worry about things. And you're expecting somebody to *die?*"

"Someone already has. I hoped you would not notice."

"*What?*"

"An unfortunate accident, but an expendable someone. You recall that useless layabout named Sandov? When we unfurled a bale of canvas during the setup, he rolled out of it, quite stiff. We could have used him for a stringer jack."

"Governor, that doesn't sound to me like any accident."

"Not a mark on the body. He simply got baled up while he was napping, and suffocated."

"That story smells a little tall. How could his chums not notice him napping on the canvas they were furling?"

"Ahem. Let me put it this way, Zachary. The identical accident has happened many times...during many teardowns...at many circuses. That it seems always to happen to an unlovable and worthless person I prefer to ascribe to coincidence. I will ask, though, that you do not mention this incident to anyone else. None of the performers has ever troubled to count the roustabouts, I think, and certainly nobody could tell one of them from another."

Edge somberly shook his head. "Of course I won't say anything. Hell, who am I to make a fuss about men dying, deservedly or otherwise?"

"Please remind me, however, when we get to the hotel, to scrap the man's conduct book," said Florian. "In case some meddlesome authority demands to see a match-up of books and their owners."

So, when Florian, Edge, Beck and Goesle finally trooped to the Hotel Contessa Matilde, and were the only persons eating in the dining room at that hour, and some of the other troupers came just to sit and keep them company, the only subject discussed was that of the circus's come-in music.

"I've tried and tried, Governor," said Autumn, "but I have to confess that I just cannot concoct Italian lyrics to fit your accustomed 'God Rest Ye Merry' tune. Anyway, that's an old English song, and not many continental audiences will even recognize it. So I consulted with Kapellmeister Beck"—Beck nodded gravely—"and, with your permission, we'd like to use 'Greensleeves' instead. It's English too, of course, but it's known and loved all over the world."

"It is," Paprika concurred. "I have heard it played on cimbaloms in Hungary."

"Commendable initiative, my dear Autumn," said Florian. "But isn't it somewhat treacly for a come-in?"

"No, sir. Our talented bandmaster has done a very merry and bouncy arrangement of the melody"—Beck looked modest—"and I did new lyrics, not so soppy and sentimental." She handed a piece of paper across the table. "I don't claim it's *Die Meistersinger,* but it's simple enough that anybody can memorize the words."

Florian, chewing, scanned the little quatrain she had written in Italian, quietly beating the measure of "Greensleeves" with his knife and fork, then put down the utensils to applaud all by himself. "A fine job of work, my dear. We'll assemble the company and the band to rehearse it in the morning. Zachary, I repeat, you found a true jewel when you found this little lady. I bid you: treat her tenderly."

"I try," said Edge, a trifle glumly, thinking of the high rope.

5

THE CHAPITEAU'S PISTA was again a level and unblemished circle of saw-dust by the time the Florilegium prepared to open its first show in Pisa. Magpie Maggie Hag, in a sort of blur of movement, dealt out tickets from the red-wagon booth, and scooped in the lire and centesimi, and shoved out change—or most of it—and the incoming patrons scarcely glanced at the museum or the lion in their rush to claim the best seats, and the pavilion quickly filled, from front benches to those in the uppermost rear. After Banat dropped the marquee flap to close the front door, he reported to Florian, with what he evidently supposed was a snappy Confederate salute, "Almost one thousand tickets I took."

"Glory on us!" said Pepper, overhearing. "Faith, we'll soon be rich as Crazes."

Florian laughed. "Then let's not keep the good people of Pisa waiting, Irisher. Around to the backyard wid ye, for the come-in."

The Grand Entry and Promenade was now led by Brutus, so that Abdullah, on her back, could add his bass drumming to the band's music right from the start. Except for the elephant and the horses and the capering terriers, every-body in the procession sang Autumn's words to Beck's rollicking rendition of "Greensleeves":

> Circo-o è allegro!
> Circo-o è squisito!
> Circo ha cuore d'oro,
> E benvenuto a-al Circo!

As Autumn had said, everyone in the audience knew the tune. By the time the parade was on its third circuit of the pista perimeter, the crowd had got the words as well, and was singing along in a roar that almost overwhelmed the windjammers' utmost efforts.

Florian and Edge had rearranged the program so that now the liberty horses did the come-in already wearing their plumes and spangles and tasseled blan-kets, and Colonel Ramrod could turn them into the pista while the rest of the parade went out the back door. The band swung smoothly into "Thunder and Lightning" and, at the crack of the sjambok, the horses went smoothly into their routine. Edge was exceedingly glad, this first time under the new high rigging, that Autumn was not going up there until the very end of the show. He would doubtless be nervous enough while he watched that, but at least he was not rattled and addled *before* doing this opening liberty act, or his later sharpshooting and his still-later Buckskin Billy voltige.

When the elephant reentered, after the horses' departure, she strode majes-tically and Abdullah boomed his drum doomfully to the "Battle of the Huns." The band went into a brisker music—a medley of von Suppé overtures—while Brutus did some of her solo tricks. The tug-of-war with volunteers had been cut from the act. Instead, Monday, Quincy and the three Chinese cartwheeled into the pista, beckoned Brutus onto the teeterboard and, as she seesawed happily, did their poses and pyramids and leapfrogging on her back. When Brutus carried Abdullah and the Simmses off again, the Chinese stayed in the pista to do their antipodal kicking and twirling of each other, to the incongruous accompaniment of some frantic Russian dances by Glinka. Next, Pepper and Paprika did their perch-pole performance, to one of Liszt's Hungarian rhapsodies.

The band went silent while Florian called and coaxed "Bisnonna Filomena Fioretto" from the stands, and introduced her with all his usual flapdoodle. Sarah had now learned by rote to say her thanks in Italian when the cringing old lady was presented with the little cake and candle, and also to make her astounding request for a birthday horseback ride. She did so, over the soft music of "For He's a Jolly Good Fellow," in a cracked and quavery voice that served to mask any infirmities of her pronunciation.

When the horse ran away with the old lady, the act went over more spectacu-larly than ever before—numerous real old ladies in the seats actually swooned —and the crowd's gasps of relief and gusts of hilarity and thunders of applause were correspondingly greater when Filomena stood up on the horse's rump and shed all her grandmotherly black and stood revealed as Madame Solitaire. For the first time in a long time, Jules Rouleau, seated on the washtub near the back door, again sang, "As I sat in the circus and watched her go round..." After Sarah had taken her bows, she went, toweling herself, to congratulate Rouleau on finally "kicking sawdust" again after his long layoff. The band began "The Irish Jaunting Car" and Pepper went aloft for her hair-hang. Sarah was still chatting with Rouleau when she was suddenly spun around and kissed on the mouth.

"Pompás! Magnificent!" cried Paprika, hugging her tightly.

"It's—it's hardly the first time you've seen the act," Sarah said breathlessly.

"Ah, but your voice, your bit of Italian this time. Almost I believed it all real and true! You are öszintén müvészi. Does one say in English you are a mistress of your art?"

"Well... er..." said Sarah, but then Paprika was kissing her again, long and passionately, while Rouleau looked on with one eyebrow lifted.

They were being watched from aloft, too, as Sarah saw when at last she was loosed from the embrace. Paprika followed her glance, but only mockingly smiled upward. Pepper, still and rigid in midair, was staring down at them with that hair-strained rictus grin and eyes of green ice. Beck was desperately putting all manner of trills and flourishes into "The Irish Jaunting Car," waiting for her to start her performance. Pepper did not, until both Paprika and Sarah had van-ished through the back door. Then she threw herself into her spins and convolu-tions and swing-overs with such frenzy that Beck had to put the "Jaunting Car" to a headlong gallop.

Late that night, in the Contessa Matilde dining room, most of the troupers, at the several tables they occupied, prattled gaily about the success of their various acts, and how much better they could perform in the new, unimpeded pista, and with appropriate band music, and what an appreciative audience the Pisans were. But Pepper and Paprika sat at different tables. Sarah sat at yet another, not saying much and moodily picking at her supper.

Neither did Edge have much appetite, though he sat beside his Autumn, and she was as pleased and excited about the day's triumphs as any of the lesser artistes. Her tightrope act had brought the audience to a standing ovation at both the afternoon and evening shows, and now she was repeatedly trying to convince Edge that his own voltige act was, in fact, much more dangerous than her own. "I have to avert my eyes, Zachary, when you slide from the saddle of a galloping horse, and under its belly, among those churning hoofs, and up the other side into the saddle again." That did not much reassure him. Autumn had looked so tiny and so vulnerable and so fragile away up there under the tent roof, doing feats that had made him gulp even when she was doing them a mere eight feet off the ground. He could only hope that in time he would get over his dry-mouthed, clammy-palmed anxiety whenever she was aloft.

Much later that night, Jules Rouleau was just falling asleep when his hall door quietly opened and someone slipped into his nearly dark room. "Qu'est-ce que c'est?" he mumbled. "Surely not another massage at this hour?"

"It's not Maggie. It's me—Sarah. I need your help, Jules."

"Qu'est-ce que c'est?" he asked again, but now wide awake and startled. In the dim light that reflected into the room from the kitchen courtyard downstairs, where the scullions were still cleaning up, Rouleau could see that Sarah was taking off her clothes.

She said shakily, "You—you watched that girl Paprika kiss me. Not just the quick kiss that show people often give one another, but like a—like a lover."

"Chérie," he said, sitting up in the bed, his own voice a little unsteady as Sarah continued to undress. "You could never have deluded yourself as to the nature of those two flagrant toms."

"No. But P-Paprika has lately been courting *me*. And when she kissed me today, I almost—no, I *did*—I enjoyed it. I was aroused by it."

"That can happen," Rouleau said, with what sangfroid he could muster. "But why come to me? Why are you taking off your—?"

"Jules, I need a man. Just to prove to myself that *I* am not a tom. I beg of you, Jules..." She was naked now, and slid under the covers beside him.

Rouleau shrank away, saying almost in panic, "Chérie, you embarrass me. You have long known that I am—in my way—what Pepper and Paprika are in theirs."

"You have at least a... male body. Please, Jules!"

"To me it would be... not *you*, you understand, dear Sarah... but the act itself would be abhorrent. There are other males on the show, masculine males, who would rejoice in obliging—"

"I have lost Zachary, and Florian is consumed with business, and any other man would swagger and brag and gossip. You are an old friend. Do it just once, for friendship's sake."

"I simply *cannot*, Sarah. You know I would do for you anything in my power. But that, it simply is not."

She pondered for a moment, then said diffidently, "Could you not pretend—pretend that I am a boy?" She turned so her back was to him, and nestled herself close against him. Rouleau groaned slightly, slid down from his pillow to curve his body to hers, and put his arms around her—but only at the waist, being very careful not to touch anything palpably female about her. "Now," Sarah said softly. "Try to imagine that I am... anyone you would prefer." She reached back to take hold of him, but he recoiled.

"Do not do that, please. It is too plainly a woman's hand. Do not even speak. I shall—I shall try..."

Except for the creaking of the bed, there was no sound in the room for a long time, while Sarah tried with little movements of her bottom to entice Rouleau to an arousal of what stubbornly remained flaccid. She could feel him beginning to perspire, but nothing else.

At last he broke the silence. "It is no use, Sarah. I am sorry, very sorry, but..."

"Perhaps if I did this?" she said, and slid downward in the bed. Her voice was muffled under the covers when she said, "Boys do this, don't they?"

Rouleau feebly groaned again, but let her try. And she tried with passion and energy and skill and patience, but to no effect.

"Je suis désolé, Sarah. It is hopeless."

After a moment, still under the covers, she said meekly, "Would you—could you do that? To me?"

"No!" he said, and violently moved away from her. "That, I will not even attempt. I am again sorry, Sarah, but I am certain I should be sick. You would feel more than ever rejetée."

Like a wounded animal, she crept upward in the bed again, and laid her head on the other pillow.

"Would you just hold me, then? Nothing more. Only hold me until we fall asleep."

He did, but still gingerly, touching no place feminine. The room was full dark now, the scullions having finished their late cleanup and put out all lights, but Sarah did not sleep at all. She was still wide-eyed when the darkness lightened slightly toward dawn and the rattle and clash of pots and pans began again, as the cooks came back on duty to prepare for breakfast. Rouleau's arms were still around her, so she considerately did not stir until he awoke, and that was quite late in the morning.

Thus it was that Clover Lee, heaping her breakfast plate at the dining room's luxuriantly provisioned buffet sideboard, naïvely said to Florian, beside her, "Mother didn't sleep in our room last night. Was she with you?"

"Er...no," said Florian. "Not last night, no." The question had caught him unawares, or he might have equivocated, because Pepper and Paprika were next in line at the sideboard.

Pepper rounded on Paprika, her face contorted, but Paprika said, "You *know* where *I* was. In our room and in our bed. Remember? We kissed and made up. Five or six times, and very nicely, too."

Diplomatically, Florian and Clover Lee sidled off to a far table.

In a tight voice, Pepper said, "And *you* know bloody well how deep I always sleep afterward. Ye could have gone anywhere, wench!"

"Don't make a ridiculous scene, kedvesem. I don't go lurking about in the middle of the—"

"Och, ye lurk about her in the clear *daylight!* But let us just ask herself. Here's the hussy now." Sarah came into the dining room, noticeably red-eyed and tousled. Pepper rushed up to her and demanded, "Where *did* ye sleep, then, if not where ye belonged?"

Sarah snapped, "None of your goddamned business!" and walked around her.

Pepper hissed, ground her teeth, turned and threw her plate—whether at Sarah or at Paprika could not be told, because she missed. An innocent Milanese traveling salesman, taking only a continental breakfast of buttered panino, marmellata and coffee, found himself with a lap full of hot salsiccia and scrambled eggs. He sprang up, bellowing, "Fregna! Sono fottuto!"—but Pepper had stomped out of the room.

She was not seen again—and Paprika looked everywhere—until the band was already tuning up for the afternoon show. Then Pepper and Yount, cozily arm in arm, came strolling onto the Sports Field among the crowd that milled about there. Yount was flushed of face and pate, his beard was in some disarray. Pepper no longer looked furious, but serene, and the bodice of her green street gown was misbuttoned here and there.

"Pep!" cried Paprika, in something of a sob. "Hurry! We have another straw house. You've barely time to change for the come-in."

"Lardy-dardy," Pepper said offhandedly. "It's getting in practice I am for undressing and dressing in a twinkle. Ain't that so, ducks?" She gazed at Yount adoringly.

Yount went pinker, and said, "Uh, well, I reckon that's commendable in a woman. Punctuality."

"Whisht, I've always come quickly. And often," said Pepper, while Paprika stared in horror. "Obie, macushla, would ye like to precede me in the dressing room?"

"No need, Miss Pepper. I only got to step out of these clothes. I got my Quakemaker leopard skin undern—"

"Losh, it's forgetting I was." And she giggled lasciviously. "Ah, well. Tooraloo for now, love, 'til next time."

Yount lurched away, looking almost tipsy, and Pepper tripped lightheartedly up the little stair of the dressing wagon. Paprika followed.

"You were just quizzing me and tormenting me, weren't you, Pep? All of that was színlelés—pretending—wasn't it?"

Pepper murmured, but to herself, "Musha, look at me. Did I come all the way from the hotel clad awry?" She began unbuttoning.

"Pep! Tell me none of that was true. You and that dumb ox."

Pepper looked at her, finally. "Nay, instead I'll tell ye an old tale the tinkers do tell. This jackeen comes to Biddy Early, d'ye see, and he asks the witchwoman for a talisman that will keep his pretty wife faithful to him. Biddy tells him he already *has* such a thing. Jackeen says what? She says 'tis a magic ring, boyo. Jackeen says where is it, then? Old Biddy says 'tis 'twixt your woman's legs. As long as ye keep your finger in that ring, never cuckolded can ye be."

"Oh, Pepper, dearest one, I've not been unfaithful. I've no more than flirted. And never with a *man*, never since I've known you."

"Shall I tell ye, then," said Pepper, stepping with sensuous slowness out of her last garment, "what ye've been missing?"

"Pep, you didn't!"

Silence.

"Did you?"

Silence, as Pepper slipped sinuously into her tight fleshings.

"You only teased him," Paprika said hopefully. "Perhaps you let him stroke the velvet..."

Silence, with a dreamily reminiscent smile.

"Please, Pep," Paprika said despairingly. "Don't say that you actually let him thread the needle!"

"Again and again. He ain't called the Quakemaker for nothing."

Paprika was weeping now. "You swore you would never—"

"Arrah, don't go having the sterics. 'Twas not as terrible as the only other time a man took me. I've told ye about that. How me uncle Pete Robie bundled me school frock over me head and skewered me like a chicken—in the wrong hole, even, he was that dim-witted. But with dear Obie, now, I do think I might even learn to *prefer* doing it proper, like." And she swept out of the wagon, leaving Paprika in tears.

So it was Paprika who was truant from the Grand Entry, ashamed to show her puffy face and its ruined makeup and her general air of misery. In consequence, she got a severe scolding from Florian, and another when she went through her perch-pole routine as stiffly as an automaton.

When the afternoon audience had dispersed into the twilight, most of the performers and crew busied themselves with seeing to their equipment, props and animals, and Autumn said to Edge, "Would you come with me, Zachary? Herr Beck is rearranging my rig for a practice session, and I'd like to show you something."

He walked with her inside the chapiteau. Up on the bandstand, Dai Goesle was affixing pole lamps he had bought that morning in a Lungarno shop. None of the windjammers really needed them, since none but Boom-Boom Beck could read music, with or without light. But Magpie Maggie Hag had created for the bandmaster a uniform that made him look as impressive as a Feldmarschall, and he wanted it to be visible. Beck was visible at this moment, but in work clothes. He and a couple of Slovaks had disconnected the farther end of Autumn's tightrope from its guidon-marked center pole, brought it down at an angle across the pista and were securing that end to a heavy stake.

"I'll be rehearsing Sunday and Monday in their slant climb," said Autumn. "They should be ready to make their début at it by the time we get to Florence. But what I wanted to show you... Well, every time I look down when I'm up there on the rope, I see you watching me, all pale and tense. I thought perhaps, if you just climb to the platform with me"—she gestured to the rod-and-rope ladder—"it might relieve you of some of your apprehensions."

"All right. Yes, it might."

"Go ahead. I'll follow you up."

Like the rankest of rubes, Edge started to climb the rope ladder as he would any ordinary wooden one. But as soon as he had both hands and both feet on the rungs, the ladder abruptly slanted outward so that he was hanging almost horizontal. He found himself braced that way, unable to proceed, as if he were climbing the *underside* of an ordinary ladder.

Autumn laughed tolerantly and said, "Not like that. There's a knack to it. Drop down and I'll show you." He did, shamefacedly, and watched her demonstrate. "You actually climb up the side of it. See? The rope against your body, hands and feet around either side of it to the rungs." She went up as swiftly and agilely as a monkey, though she did not at all resemble a monkey in any other respect. "Now you try," she called down from the resting stand.

Edge did it, though slowly and awkwardly, feeling as if he had suddenly doubled in weight. He was so intent on placing his hands and feet alternately on the rungs that not until he stood beside Autumn on the tiny platform did he look down, and he almost reeled. Hands locked on the center pole behind him, he exclaimed:

"Jesus, woman! It's like looking down from Natural Bridge! It looks a damn sight higher from here than it does from down there, and that was fearsome enough."

"Oh dear. I hoped this would cure you of worrying about me."

"And look yonder," he said in awe. "You have to cross that gap between here and the other pole where the white mark is. It looks as wide as the Mississippi!"

"I don't *have* to do it. I do it because I have a talent for it. Because it's what I do best."

"Now that's a flat untruth," said Edge, relaxing slightly. "I can list any number of things you do—"

"Zachary!"

"Well, it's a fact. All right, you've fetched me up here, and I've looked, and I still can't promise I'll ever get case-hardened about your performing up here. It's only because I love you that I worry about you. But, as you say, it's your work and your art."

"And my pleasure. Up here—especially when the crowd and the band go all hushed and suspenseful—I don't think of danger or the altitude or the need for precision and caution. My body goes on performing while I do nothing but *listen*. Up here, everything murmurs so sweetly. You listen, too, Zachary. Do you hear? The canvas just above us quietly ruffling, the guy wires humming, even the center pole vibrating enough to sing gently..."

"Autumn, I love you too much to let my worrying worry you. Too much ever to do anything to hinder or handicap you. So *that* I never will. No conditions, no thou-shalt-not's, no meddling."

"You are a considerate lover. Maybe that's why I love you, too."

"Right this minute, I'm a slightly dizzy lover. Do I go down the same way I came up?"

"Same way. Feet and hands on opposite sides of the rope."

When they were down, and Autumn had skipped off to change into practice clothes, Edge stayed. When there was no one in the chapiteau except Slovaks, he climbed up and down the ladder several more times. He would never get monkey-agile at it, he decided, but at least he could do it now less like a fearful and feeble old codger.

Outside, in the front yard, Paprika found Sarah loitering not far from where Florian was conversing with a well-dressed stranger.

"Sarah, kedvesem," Paprika said. "Pepper and I have come to a final, definite parting of the ways. I have taken a separate room at the hotel. Perhaps now I could persuade you—"

"Hush!" Sarah said irritably. "Florian has a distinguished visitor. I am trying to hear what they say."

The stranger was saying, "... Elder brother is of course il Direttore, but I am the one brother who speaks English. And we assumed, seeing your affisi—'Confederate American Circus'—that you yourself would be American."

"I am honored by the visit, signore. During my earlier days in Europe, I never had the good fortune to encounter your circus or any of your family. We can speak in Italian, if you prefer."

"No, no, sta bene. English is good practice for me. I enjoyed your show, Signor Florian. Small but well organized and pieno di energia—how would one say it? Full of vim?"

"Here is our equestrian director, signore," said Florian, as Edge came to join them. "Also our tiratore and voltige rider, as you have seen. May I introduce you? Signor Orfei, Colonel Edge." The two men bowed and shook hands. Florian went on, "A visit from one of the famed Orfei family is compliment enough. That you speak a compliment, as well, is high praise indeed."

The visitor said, "One likes to pesare—size up, do you say?—size up the competition."

"Now you flatter us," said Florian. "We can hardly be competition for the Circo Orfei. Yours must be the oldest circus in continuous existence in all of Europe."

"We believe so. It was more than a hundred and thirty years ago that an Orfei—he was a monsignore of Holy Church, can you imagine?—fell in love with a gypsy girl, shed his vows and vestments and ran away with her. On the road, he played flauto music and she danced, for coppers thrown. Until they accreted other wandering show folk. But for many decades, Signor Florian, the Circo Orfei was only a gypsy caravan train, much smaller than yours is now."

"An inspiriting story, signore," said Florian. "And I warn you, I hope to emulate the Orfei's growth and success."

"I wish you buona fortuna. Some circus proprietors fear and fight competition. I personally believe that the more and better circuses there are, the more of them the people wish to see and enjoy and compare. I did not come here, I assure you, to dissuade you from competing. We are showing now in Lucca, just nineteen chilometri from here, so I am making a courtesy call on a colleague."

"Perhaps you would like to look around? The colonel and I will be pleased to escort you."

"Grazie, but I have already circulated, sconosciuto. One sees best that way. And of course I observed immediately one thing odd. You have no teloni del giro."

Florian translated for Edge, "High fencing around the whole tober." And to Orfei, "I am familiar with the European practice of fencing to block the view of everyone not a paying patron. Actually, that would be better employed in America, where the natives are incurably nosy. Here in Europe, the people are more polite, and do not go prying into our privacy of the backyard. If and when I find fencing desirable, I shall have it built. But there are a great many other things taking priority."

"Senz'altro. Si capisce." Orfei leaned both hands on the ivory handle of his ebony cane. "While I am here, signori, may I essay one inquiry? Your funambola, the Signorina Autunno, she had made application to join the Circo Orfei. I would certainly not deprive you of your finest act. However, if the signorina still wishes..."

Edge bristled, but Florian spoke first. "I think not, signore. The fact is, she and Colonel Edge here have—ahem—become as close as your apostate ancestor and his gypsy love."

"But I don't own her," said Edge. "You can speak to her yourself, and in private."

"No! Never! Colonello, I am an Italian. I charge you: remember Romeo e Giulietta, Dante e Beatrice, Monsignore Orfei e la zingara. Interfere with a love affair? I could never hold up my head in Italy again!"

"Much obliged," Edge murmured.

"As a matter of plain fact, signori, our program is already somewhat overcrowded. My elder brother is occasionally too enthusiastic in hiring, and too sentimental to dismiss anyone. But one of our best trapeze artistes, his contract is soon to expire, and I think he would like to move elsewhere."

Florian said, "I should be more than pleased to have a trap act, but we have no rigging for it."

"Maurice LeVie—a Frenchman, but he speaks also Italian and English— Maurice owns his own rig. Nickel-plated. Beautiful. Also his own horse and van for transport."

Florian whistled admiringly. "Could I afford him?"

"One hundred fifty lire each week."

Florian whistled again, not so admiringly. "Thirty dollars. That's twice as much as I'm paying my equestrian director here."

Edge said, "Don't concern yourself with that. A good trapeze act ought to be worth that and more to us. And I won't grudge his making a salary bigger than mine. I've been up there in the tent peak once, and I'm damned if I'd *cavort* up there for any amount of money."

Orfei said, "Perhaps you signori—and any others of your company—will honor our show with a visit in Lucca. Maurice closes the first half of our program, before the intervallo. You can see him perform, and judge his worth, and get back here, all in one day."

"Good idea, that," said Florian. "We will have a day's layover here after the close of this stand, to do some furbishing. Thank you for the invitation, Signor Orfei. The colonel and I and our sideshow director will see you in Lucca."

The Florilegium's stand at Pisa lasted only ten days in all, but it was by no means what Florian would have called a bloomer stand back in the States or a bianca here in Europe. It was a succession of well-packed, often turnaway houses. Evidently every person resident in Pisa attended, and every tourist and traveler passing through, but, with the chapiteau's vastly increased capacity, ten days sufficed to entertain them all. During that time, the circus suffered no accidents or internal strife, though everyone noticed how Sarah avoided Paprika's company, and Paprika and Pepper avoided one another, except when necessary at performances.

When, at the night show on the tenth day in Pisa, the chapiteau seats were only two-thirds occupied—mostly, said doorman Banat, by patrons he recognized as repeaters—Florian gave orders for the teardown that very night. Early next morning, all the canvas lay spread out flat on the now brown, trampled and sawdusty oval of grass where it had stood. Stitches was walking, barefoot and bent over, ruling chalk lines on the canvas to guide the barefoot Slovak painters waiting with buckets of the colors chosen: green and white.

"I am using only the thinnest possible wash," Goesle announced to those of the company looking on, "to preserve the canvas's flexibility, and not to diminish the lovely glow of it when it is lighted inside at night. Also, the paint will dry by tomorrow."

Edge hitched Snowball to the rockaway, and he, Florian and Fitzfarris set off at a brisk trot through the morning ground mist on la Strada Lucca. This road was lined on both verges with immense chestnut trees, leafless now, so their limbs meeting above the road resembled the ogive arches and groins of some kind of churchly edifice. Also, the bark of the chestnuts' trunks peeled and curled like a multitude of scrolls. Edge could entertain the illusion that he was riding through a medieval monastery's library. Beyond the trees, the land was still flat, but no longer just fields of stubble and colza. There were orchards of twisted, tormented-looking olive trees, and vineyards of grapevines similarly warped, knotty and contorted.

Fitzfarris said, "If somebody was to ask me right now for a capsule description of Italy, I'd call it a gnarled land."

"Oh, you'll see a variety of landscapes before we leave Italy," said Florian. "Alabama cotton fields, Vermont stone quarries, Minnesota iron mines, Louisiana rice paddies, Virginia timber forests, snow-capped Adirondacks..."

They arrived at the Circo Orfei's tober—on a Campo Sportivo almost identical to Pisa's, set between two projecting bastions of Lucca's high and thick old city walls—just before the afternoon show began. So Florian hurried Edge and Fitz along the circus's midway: a row of booths topped by canvas banners portraying, with unabashed exaggeration and artistic license, the attractions to be found within: La Dama Obesissima, Ercole il Potente, Il Ragazzo Pinguino...

"Very Fat Lady, Hercules, Penguin Boy," Florian translated, as they went by. "He'd be one of those flipper-armed children."

The Orfei's chapiteau was no bigger than the Florilegium's now was, but it was painted all over with varicolored stars, and flew pennons and burgees emblazoned "Orfei" not only from its two center pole tops but also from the points of all its surrounding side poles. And there were numerous other tents around and behind the big one. The two most prominent bore banners: one crowded with pictures of animals around the word Serraglio; the other showed a gauzily veiled dancing girl and the words Ballo del Tabarin.

"Menagerie and Music Hall," said Florian. "The latter being, no doubt, a rawhide girly show for men only."

The smaller tents had only small signs, all the same: È Vietato l'Ingreso. "No admittance," said Florian. "The troupe's dressing rooms, cook tent, smithy, that sort of thing. And look, there are even donnickers for the patrons." He pointed to two privy-sized boxes off to one side of the tober, marked Uomini and Donne. In the circus's backyard, beyond all the no-admittance tents, were ranked and filed numerous tinker-style caravans similar to Autumn's, with little tin chimneys trickling smoke.

"This is some spread," murmured Edge.

"Don't let it daunt you, lads," said Florian. "Ours will be as grand someday. Grander."

At the front door, a haughty Harlequin took their tickets and a haughty Columbine handed each of them a well-printed program of several pages. Fitzfarris examined his with professional interest, noting that it carried advertisements for numerous Lucca merchants and services. As at their own chapiteau, Florian, Fitz and Edge entered this one under the bandstand. It held three times as many musicians as Beck commanded—all of them ornately (and irreverently) uniformed as the Pope's Swiss Guardsmen—and they were thundering a medley of operatic marches for the come-in.

"Just look at that," said Fitzfarris, marveling, when they found their numbered starback chairs. "The back door has velvet curtains and a fancy proscenium arch."

The Grand Entry and Promenade that came through it was even more splendiferous. It was led by the equestrian director, dressed not gaudily but in formal riding dress: glossy top hat, "pink" swallowtail coat, well-cut breeches and gleaming high boots. Besides the multitude of artistes strutting in the procession—spangled and flowing-cloaked and profuse of ostrich plumes—there were four elephants, two camels, twenty or more caparisoned ring horses, a lion and a tiger and a leopard, each in its separate cage wagon.

There were also nonfunctional tableau wagons, richly carved and gilded, bearing painted panoramas and appropriate props, depicting such events as Columbus discovering the New World, Marco Polo discovering China and various other Italianate historical highlights all the way back to Caesar discovering Britannia. To judge from the tableaux, Columbus and Polo and Caesar had been greeted in every new land by numbers of native women only diaphanously clad in gauze and gossamer. Edge stood up and peered to get a better look at those wagons as they made their way around the farther curve of the pista. Their inner sides consisted only of laths and chicken wire and two-by-four buttresses. Edge sat down again and remarked on this.

"Common practice," said Florian. "Every circus promenade goes counterclockwise around the outside of the pista. Why waste work and expense to adorn the left side of the wagons?"

The last of the procession was still trickling out through the back-door proscenium when the first performers erupted inward through it—a violently harum-scarum tumbling act. "I Saltimanchi Turchi!" bellowed the equestrian director before the band bellowed, even more loudly, the overture to Rossini's *Il Turco in Italia*.

Signor Orfei had complimented the Florilegium's "well-organized" show, but this one was much more so. It had to be, there was such an abundance of it. While one act was making its bows to a storm of applause, another performer or troupe would be already going into action. Edge watched enviously but closely, making mental notes, as the equestrian director, ever cool and suave, managed all that teeming cast of characters and animals, plus props and rigging and the roustabouts (every one deft and unobtrusive, wearing black coveralls) who carried and rolled and hauled the varied equipment in and out of the pista.

There was not a fumbled performance in the whole first half of the program, nor a slow-paced one. Even the four elephants came in at a lumbering trot, unaccompanied by any bull man, and went briskly through their strength-and-balance tricks without any evident commands except an occasional snap of the equestrian director's whip. Seemingly of their own accord, they closed with the dramatic "long mount"—the lead elephant rearing on her hind legs, those behind rearing to put their forefeet on each other's rumps, all up-curling their trunks and trumpeting triumphantly.

Meanwhile, the Slovak roustabouts were loosing the ropes to let dangle from the chapiteau's peak the glittery, nickel-plated rigging of "Signor Maurice, il intrepido acrobata *a-e-ro*-batico Francese!" and a small, dark man skipped into the pista. He was enveloped in a scarlet cape, which he doffed with a magnificent, twirling flourish. He was slim almost to skinniness, and his tights were spangled electric-blue all over. He twinkled up the rope ladder as nimbly as Autumn had done.

Edge said to Florian, "He's got *two* trapeze swings up yonder. How can he use them both?"

"When was the last time you saw a trap act, Zachary?"

"Damned if I remember. Sometime well before the war."

"Ah, then you have a treat in store. Since then, Monsieur Léotard in France has revolutionized the art, and every other aerialist in the world is following his lead."

Maurice LeVie's performance was indeed something new to Edge, and to Fitzfarris, too. They had previously seen trapeze artistes do nothing more than the twists and flips and swingovers possible on any gymnasium's horizontal bar —only with the bar suspended high in the air. Maurice likewise did those things first, but then—as the band played Strauss's "Bal de Vienne"—he hung by his knees from his bar and set it swinging, faster and farther and higher with each swing. Suddenly he let go with his legs and launched himself through empty air—the entire audience gasped—to catch the other bar with his hands. The impact started that trapeze swinging, and now the bespangled Maurice literally flashed back and forth, like blue lightning, between the two high-swinging bars, sometimes catching hold with his hands, sometimes with his bent knees, sometimes only by his toes. And in the empty space between the two bars he did daring rolls and twists and tumbles, as if he were absolutely weightless. At the very last, Maurice stood erect, heel to toe, on one of the still perilously swinging bars, held up his arms in the V and continued to swing, balancing there, with no support but centrifugal force, while the audience went wild.

Fitzfarris exclaimed, "We've got to have him, Florian!"

"We will, if he'll have us. Let's get out before the crowd does."

In the front yard, Fitzfarris went off to inspect the midway attractions, while Florian and Edge went to the red wagon and found there the same one of the brothers Orfei that they had already met. He invited them in, set chairs for them beside his desk, gave them each a cigar and a glass of good Barolo wine, and said, "Well? Would you wish to speak to Monsieur LeVie, Signor Florian?"

"I think it unnecessary. His work speaks for itself. And he must be fatigued at this moment; I would not disturb his rest. If I might just see his conduct book?"

"Certo," said Orfei, and opened a desk drawer containing scores of those things, shuffled among them, brought one out and handed it to Florian. "Everything in it is praise and commendation. Nothing whatever in it to discredit the man. Except, of course, that." And he pointed to something on one of the little book's pages.

"Of course, that," said Florian, but he seemed to pay little heed to whatever it was, skimmed quickly through the other pages, and gave the book back to Orfei. "Have you mentioned to him our interest in acquiring his talents?"

"I have, signore, and he was most enthusiastic. It would be a challenge and a delight, he said—his very words—to employ his trapeze in helping to hoist a new, small show to greatness. And he was not being either egotistical or condescending. Maurice really is a gentiluomo—how would you say?—a jolly good fellow."

"Done and done, then," said Florian. "I expect our Florilegium to be in Firenze six or seven days from now, and I shall hope to have a three-week stand there, at the very least. Unless Maurice changes his mind in the meantime, we shall trust in his joining us whenever it is convenient to him."

"Maurice will not disappoint you, signore. He will be there."

"And the Circo Orfei? Whither bound?"

"Siena next, then we move southward for the winter, perhaps as far as Egypt."

"After Siena, Rome, I suppose?"

"Dio guardi, no! At least, we will not go there again until and unless Rome becomes one with the rest of the Kingdom of Italy. The Province of Rome is the last remaining Papal State. Perhaps vindictively, the authorities have become oppressive and censorious. Puritanical, if one may apply that word to Holy Church. The Roman carabinieri nearly jailed me and my brothers for dressing our bandsmen like the Swiss Guard. Believe me, they would make you shroud all your females in shapeless smocks. They would monitor every jest and joke. No, no, I advise you, friend Florian, stay clear of the Holy City and its environs."

"Thank you. We will. A pity, though. Few of our troupe have ever visited there."

"Oh, visit, by all means. No one should miss seeing Rome, and mere visitors are not interfered with. Also, I should tell you that the Roman people are not as sanctimonious as their overlings. If you pitch at Forano, just north of the State border, and if Rome hears good notice of your show—eppur si muove—the people will readily travel the fifty chilometri of railroad to attend."

"I thank you again, Signor Orfei," said Florian, getting to his feet. "You have been most helpful and generous and hospitable. I hope it will be in my power to repay somehow—"

"Only continue to give a good show, signore. Keep the circus, as an institution, in good repute. If we all do that, we all help each other."

When Florian and Edge emerged from the office wagon, the crowd had all gone back into the chapiteau for the second half of the performance, and the midway was empty of every josser except Fitzfarris. He said dismissively, "The freaks are all pretty much standard stuff. And that rawhide hootchy-cootchy is as tame as milk. We've got girls a damn sight handsomer, and I could put on a damn sight racier show . . . if you'd let me, Governor, and if I can talk our ladies into doing it."

"If they have no objection, I have none," said Florian. "But that will have to wait until we've got a separate annex tent, to keep it private and discreet."

The three were mostly silent on the way back to Pisa, each of them mulling over the things he had most admired and envied at the Circo Orfei, and calculating ways and means to adapt those things to his own work, concerns and responsibilities in the Florilegium. It was after dark when they got back, so, since they could not inspect Goesle's canvas paintwork until daylight, Florian drove directly to the hotel. The other troupers, most of whom had spent the free day shopping and sightseeing all over town, were having dinner for a change, instead of a midnight supper. The new arrivals joined them at the tables, and handed around the Orfei programs—Florian called them "Bibles"—for the others to admire, and regaled them with accounts of the wonders they had seen, and with their avowed intentions of making the Florilegium, before much longer, "even bigger and better than the Circo Orfei!"

Next morning, they checked out of the hotel and rode with their luggage to the tober, where they were sincerely thrilled by the great spread of canvas on the ground. It no longer looked like drab, ordinary canvas, but like something fresh from a toy shop—broad green and white stripes from peak to bottom, the stripes converging into points atop the semicircular ends of the tent, and an elaborate cartouche above the marquee entrance flap, within which panel the Chinese artist had painted in vivid black-outlined orange, with frills and garnishes, FLOR-IAN'S FLOURISHING FLORILEGIUM. Everyone made fulsome and congratulatory comments to Goesle—everyone except Magpie Maggie Hag. She looked at it and said, "Red."

"Red?" echoed Dai Goesle. "Are you perchance color-blind, Madame Hag? There is green and white yonder, and a bit of orange and black."

"I see too good," she said. "There is red on it." With which she went and got inside one of the van wagons.

Goesle shook his head, turned to Banat and said, "Order the men to bale it, stow it and get ready to roll, now just."

"If Maggie's dukkering something," Edge muttered to Florian, "oughtn't we to make sure there's nobody asleep on the canvas?"

"Hush," was all that Florian replied.

The troupe's final packing and other preparations for departure were briskly and quickly done. But, once the train was on the Strada Mare-Firenze, Florian's rockaway set a decorous pace. Florence was some sixty miles distant, a three-day run without hurrying. There were other towns along the way, but Florian considered most of them not worth setting up for.

"So we will spend tonight at Pontedera," he told Rouleau, riding with him. "In a hotel or albergo if it has one. If not, we will camp out as we used to do. The next day's run will bring us to Empoli. That town is the junction point of two main railroad lines, so there we will set up and show. The local populace ought to give us two or three days' attendance, and perhaps some of the rail travelers will stop off to see us, besides."

The circus train arrived at Pontedera at twilight, and the town did boast two decent inns which, between them, had food enough to feed the whole company and rooms enough to accommodate all who would not be sleeping in the wagons in the stable yard. Magpie Maggie Hag was one who stayed outside, not even emerging from her seclusion to eat dinner. Autumn and Edge, also, after dining at one of the inns, elected to sleep in her little cottage on wheels, the first time they were occupying it together.

"Compact, cozy and pretty," said Edge, taking a good look around the interior, most of which was painted a cheery sunshine yellow.

"It was rather too cozy," said Autumn, "even for me alone, when I had to carry all my rigging in here. I'm glad Florian gave me wagon room for all that gear."

In one corner was a small coal-oil stove, for heating or cooking, with a tin stovepipe going up through the barrel roof. There were cabinets and cupboards for stores and wardrobe and linens. There was also Autumn's trunk and hand luggage, Edge's dunnage bag, his several weapons and their possibles kit. The one bed, along the van's left wall, was cleverly hinged under its middle. With its outside half folded over the other, toward the wall, it presented its underplanking for a table, and there were two chairs to set at that table. When the tabletop was flipped open again, it revealed a palleted and blanketed bed big enough for two. In both walls of the van and in its entrance door were outward-opening windows curtained with yellow chintz. There were window boxes for them, empty of flowers in this season, with hooks enabling the boxes to be hung inside when the van was on the move and outside when it was stationary. On the wall were two other things: an oval mirror, rather wavery and uncertain of reflection, in a chipped stucco frame; and on the facing wall a much better-framed photograph of the French ropewalker Mme Saqui, autographed "to Mlle Auburn" in English and in a loopy, childish hand, "When this you see—Remember me."

Edge had brought from the albergo a bottle of Capri wine "to toast this blithesome occasion." Autumn fetched two goblets from a cupboard and they did that, happily, clinking their glasses, as they sat at the table. When they had finished the wine, they opened the table into its bed aspect and celebrated the occasion even more intoxicatingly. They were still in one another's arms when, early the next morning, they were awakened by an awful scream.

Edge bounded to a window, threw it open and stuck his head out. Not far away stood the dressing-room wagon, its door open, and Pepper Mayo was running away from it, emitting shrieks like a banshee. Clover Lee was also visible, coming down the steps of that wagon, very slowly and stiffly, as if she were sleepwalking.

"Clover Lee!" Edge called anxiously. "What's going on?" Autumn was now beside him at the window. From various other wagon doorways and windows peeked out bewildered black, yellow and Slovak faces.

Clover Lee continued her trancelike pace until she was close enough to tell Edge, in a voice devoid of any emotion or inflection, "Mother didn't sleep in our room again last night. When none of the others coming down for breakfast knew where she might be, I said I would look in the wagons. Pepper said she would come with me..."

"Well?"

"We found her in there." She waved vaguely toward the wagon.

"Is something wrong with her? Is she ailing? Hurt?"

Clover Lee shook her head, and her eyes filled with tears. She struggled for a less explicit language, and finally managed to say, "We found her... avec Paprika... les deux toutes nues... dorment... en posture de soixante-neuf..."

Edge understood the words, but not the import. When Autumn saw the blank look on his face, she whispered in his ear. Edge colored slightly, but recovered and said to Clover Lee, "You might save yourself some surprises and shocks, girl, if you weren't always snooping and meddling in your mother's private doings."

"Don't call her my mother any more!" said Clover Lee, with a sudden resurgence of spirit. "I won't be daughter to any rotten *tom!*" And she too went running off toward the albergo.

So, when the circus train took to the road again, there were now four females—Sarah, Pepper, Clover Lee and Paprika—riding in vehicles as far apart as possible and avoiding other people's eyes. The rest of the troupers rode in an embarrassed silence, reluctant to talk to their wagon companions because it might look as if they were bandying low gossip or ribald jokes about the morning's incident. When they arrived at Empoli and Florian had visited the municipio, then directed the train to its allotted tober beyond the railroad yards, and the crew began the setup, everybody was still feeling constrained to only necessary remarks, questions and responses. There were not even many cries of wonderment and delight when the tent went up, far more handsome and impressive in its new paint than when it had simply lain on the ground.

The company's stiffness prevailed until show time the next afternoon, when the chapiteau filled to capacity with the local residents, mostly sooty railroad workers and their families. Then all the troupers forced smiles onto their faces for the come-in—and all the subsequent acts were done with seemingly carefree panache, even Pepper's and Paprika's perch-pole act. But then, while Sarah was doing her Pete Jenkins, Pepper went and got Obie Yount, and with him in tow confronted Paprika.

"I want the Quakemaker here to tell ye a thing," Pepper said grimly. "Obie, did you and me ever go to bed together?"

Yount's eyes bulged, and he appeared to have swallowed his tongue.

"Did you and me ever do *any* kind of kerfuffle? Anything more than walk and talk and maybe hold hands once or twice?"

Yount gulped several times before he could say, "Why, no. Never, Miss Pepper."

"Is that the truth, Obie?" Paprika said wretchedly.

"Honest to God, Miss Paprika. After what you once told me, I damn sure wouldn't want to have anything to do with . . . er . . . I wouldn't presume to poach on any private preserves."

Paprika burst into tears. "Oh, Pepper, why did you pretend—?"

"Hoping jealousy would bring ye back and bind ye. Didn't work, did it? Come! Now we'll have a word with your new sweetmeat!"

When Sarah finished taking her bows and acclaim, she found Pepper and Paprika waiting for her near the back door.

"I've told Pap and now I'll tell you, too, ye bawd," said Pepper, almost snarling. "My new act will put the both of yez in the shade. Out on the pavements. Just watch! Yez'll get what the Connaught men shot at!" And she danced out into the pista, where Florian was introducing "l'audace Signorina Pepe!"

She first went through her familiar hair-hang performance, slant-eyed, grin-masked, to the band's "Irish Jaunting Car." But when she had been applauded for that, she held up a hand to the crowd, as if to say, "Wait a bit, and watch what's next." Abdullah commenced a slow, suspenseful, rumbling roll on his drum, while the roustabouts lowered Pepper almost to the ground. There Quincy was waiting. Pepper, with both hands, grasped the loose end of the rope tied around his waist, and the Slovaks again began to haul her aloft.

"No, Pep!" cried Paprika from the sidelines, audible even over the continuing drumroll. "The weight is too much!"

But nothing untoward happened while Pepper and her small black burden were drawn up close to the lungia boom. Nothing happened until Quincy began his contorting and knotting of himself. The strain of that drew Pepper's face into a more than usually broad grin, and the grin was still on her face when, all in one instant, she swung Quincy's rope and slammed him against the center pole —where, surprised and dazed, he clung—and Pepper's whole scalp tore loose from her head and she plummeted to the pista with a deadweight thump and an explosion of sawdust around her, and the entire audience screamed at the sight of what was even more gruesome than her fall: her bright hair still hanging from the lungia rig and drizzling blood.

Abdullah's drumroll was drowned out as Beck immediately set the band to blaring the "Wedding March," and Edge and Florian ran into the pista. While Florian waved for the crowd to be calm and quiet, Edge lifted the limp body in his arms and, as unobtrusively as possible, carried it out the back door. Behind him, the band music subsided enough for Florian to be heard shouting, "All part of the act, signore e signori! Niente paura, the lady will be back in a moment, siano persuasi, amici!..."

Edge and his burden—its loosely lolling, bald and bloody head still grinning, its eyes no longer pulled aslant, but bulging and staring—were intercepted in the backyard by Paprika and Sarah, both of them weeping and wringing their hands.

"Oh, Pep, dearest!" sobbed Paprika. "I never meant—"

"Be quiet!" snapped Edge. "She can't hear you. And don't look at her!"

From the chapiteau came the music from Mozart's *Magic Flute*, meaning that Monday and Thunder were going into their high-school precision paces. Florian burst from the tent's back door, calling, "Zachary! How bad is it?"

"As bad as can be. Her back and neck are broken. Probably a lot of other things, as well."

Paprika let out a louder wail. Florian rounded on her and said brusquely, "Get to the dressing wagon and get out of your tights, quick! Zachary, take Pepper's off her!"

"Don't you dare!" sobbed Paprika, clutching at Edge's arm. "You leave her alone. And leave her with me."

"No, miss!" Florian said severely, while Edge stood, undecided, still cradling the body. "You are going back in there, into the pista, Paprika, to take Pepper's bows for her. Those dago peasants won't know the difference."

"What?" she exclaimed. "Vérszopó! You are a ghoul— a vámpir!"

"No, miss," he said again. "It is the least you can do—and the most you can do—and the last thing you'll ever be able to do for her. Strip, I said!"

Edge took Pepper to the dressing-room wagon and gently laid her on the floor inside. Sarah and Paprika, both still crying, but only softly, climbed in after him. Sarah helped Paprika out of her orange tights, while Edge clumsily peeled off Pepper's green ones. Neither of the girls wore anything underneath, except the little cache-sexe pads. Edge took note, in an abstracted sort of way, that Pepper was exceedingly beautiful—so long as he kept from looking at her terrible face. Paprika was beautiful all over, and he could not help noticing that, for she flung away her cache-sexe and was totally naked.

"Pepper would have wanted it so," she sniffled, seeing the looks Edge and Sarah gave her. She added, trying to smile, "I'll flash the vertical grin at the jossers, sure and I will!" and she began to slip into the green fleshings. Edge brushed the sawdust off her costume, while Sarah did what she could to repair Paprika's smeared makeup.

Florian was outside the wagon, fidgeting. As soon as Paprika emerged, he hustled her again through the chapiteau's back door. When they had gone through the flap of canvas, Sarah and Edge heard a gust of applause for Monday's haute école act. That was succeeded by a greater roar of applause as Florian presented the resurrected artiste—"Ancora una volta, l'audace Signorina Pepe!"—miraculously whole and healthy.

"God, how ghastly," Sarah murmured, between sobs. "The show must go on." She turned to look at Pepper's bare body, shuddered and turned back to Edge again. "And it was all my fault, Zachary. All *my* fault. *All* my fault."

"Get hold of yourself, Sarah," Edge said gruffly. "I'd stay and try to comfort you, but I'm on next."

She was crying forlornly when he dashed for the chapiteau. Florian was beginning the introducion of "il infallible tiratore scelto, Colonello Calcatoio" and everything seemed back to normal in there—except that off beneath the stands, out of sight of the audience, Rouleau was tenderly holding Paprika while she wept against his shoulder. Also under the stands, Sunday was trying to comfort a quivering Quincy, who mumbled, "Hoy..." over and over. His other sister stood nearby, but she was simply looking dreamily up at the lungia and rubbing her thighs together. Edge followed her gaze, but there was nothing to see up there; the roustabouts had made quick work of removing Pepper's last remains.

Colonel Ramrod managed to get through his shootist performance without missing any of his targets and without anyone else getting killed. The intermission followed, and, when Magpie Maggie Hag did not come in to do her stint of palm reading, Edge and Florian went to look for her. They went out the back door, brushing past the Slovaks rolling Maximus's cage into the pista, and found the old gypsy in the dressing-room wagon. She had done the laying out of Pepper: washed her clean of blood, closed her eyes and somehow smoothed the hideous grin off her face, so the dead girl looked pleasantly composed. She had garbed Pepper in one of her street gowns, and had even somehow reaffixed the torn-off hair, and combed it, so it looked quite natural.

"Good work, Mag," said Florian. "Now let me and Zachary put her in one of the other wagons—so the artistes can change in here—and I'll ask Stitches to do up a shroud for her. We'll bury her after the night show."

Edge lifted the limp body, and Florian reached to support the head, but rigor mortis had already begun to set in there, sufficiently that it no longer flopped loosely.

"Do you think we ought to have a show tonight?" Edge asked, as he carried the body to one of the tent wagons. "I don't know if everybody's going to be able to finish this one."

"Yes, everybody will," said Florian. "Just as they went on performing after Captain Hotspur died."

"Ignatz didn't die right in front of them. Or quite as horribly. And he was a middle-aged man, not a pretty young woman."

"We could have lost someone even younger, if not so pretty. Had Pepper fallen on top of Ali Baba, she would probably still be alive and he certainly would not. She swung him to a safe grip on the center pole just as she dropped."

"Yes. I wonder if that was only a convulsive twitch or a deliberate act of heroism. Still, it won't make anybody feel better about her death."

"Nevertheless, circus artistes have remarkable resilience. I grant you, Pepper's partner may be too overwrought to perform for some time, but Paprika has no act now, anyway, with her under-stander gone. So tonight I'll move Clover Lee's rosinback turn to the first half of the program... if that is all right with you, equestrian director."

"You're the Governor. And I can be as resilient as anybody."

"Good. Let's see... I'll spot Clover Lee right after the Chinks' antipody, so she'll lead right into her mother's Pete Jenkins. Maybe move the Quakemaker up, too, to fill the gap where the hair-hang was." He went off, muttering to himself, "Must remember to tear up her conduct book...cancel her room at the albergo..."

When they buried Rosalie Brigid Mayo under the pista late that night, the sometimes-Reverend Dai Goesle conducted the obsequies. This time he gave the funeral no nautical flavor, nor even Dissident Methodist. Somewhere in Empoli he had procured a Roman Catholic missal, and he employed that version of the Order for the Burial of the Dead. He even pronounced the Latin correctly enough to satisfy the other Catholics present—Paprika, Rouleau, the four Smod-lakas and most of the Slovaks—who all crossed themselves in unison at the fitting moments. When each of the company dropped a bit of earth onto Pepper's shroud and it came Florian's turn, he again murmured the Roman epitaph, "Sal-tavit. Placuit. Mortua est." The service was marred by only one circumstance, which not many failed to notice. Sarah, Paprika and Clover Lee stood equidistant around the grave—that is, as far apart as they could get. Sarah wept quietly, but the other two did not. They kept their dry, cold eyes fixed on Sarah, not even lowering their gaze when it was time to bow heads in prayer, regarding her with accusation and disgust.

6

THE NEXT MORNING Clover Lee came to breakfast in the Empoli albergo bearing a piece of paper, and handed it to Florian.

"Again, Mother did not sleep in our room," she said calmly. "This time I was damned if I'd go looking for her. It wasn't until just now that I noticed some of our luggage and gear were gone, too. Then I found this under her pillow."

Florian unfolded the paper, pursed his lips and looked unhappy, tugged at his tuft of beard, then read aloud to the others in the room, "'I am sorry for every-thing. Good-bye, dear child, and good luck. Tell everybody else the same. Your loving mother.'"

"*Should* I go looking for her?" Clover Lee asked, unconcernedly.

Florian shook his head. "Futile. Her grouch bag must have been quite full by now. And, this town being a rail junction, she could have gone north, east, west or south. No, she did as she wished to do, and we shall respect her decision. What about you, Clover Lee? Will you stay on with us?"

"Of course. She may have deserted me, but I won't desert the rest of my family."

So, when the show went on that afternoon, every artiste—including Peggy —stretched his or her performance by a few minutes, to make up for the paucity of acts. During the intermission, Fitzfarris—who by now had memorized his patter in comprehensible Italian—expatiated at greater length on his few freaks, and drew out his ventriloquized banter with Little Miss Mitten and actually sold a good number of his swazzles, while Magpie Maggie Hag had no scarcity of pregnant women's palms to read during that extended interval.

But at the nighttime show, when Florian saw that the chapiteau was not quite full, he said to Edge and Goesle, "Bust the lacings tomorrow, but you can take your time about it. I'll leave early and drive on ahead to arrange for our tober in Firenze. I'll take the Simms and Smodlaka kids with me, to start them posting paper. Then I'll meet you somewhere along the road and we'll camp for the night."

"Florence is only about twenty-five miles from here," said Edge. "We could easily push along—"

"No. This time..." Florian paused dramatically. "This time we are going to *make parade!* Into the city and up and down its main streets, before we haul onto the tober. Not the great Orfei nor any other European circus observes that flamboyant American tradition. It will astound the Fiorentini."

Next day, Edge found that the mere twenty-five miles to Firenze was slow going, for the road became all twists and tight turns and switchbacks as it wound along the tortuous Arno River valley around the foot of Monte Albano.

"Curious climate here in Italy," he remarked to Autumn. "Down in the low-lands the ground mist rose in the morning and burned off before noon. Now that we're in hilly country, the ground mist starts in the afternoon."

The train was still some five miles from Firenze when Edge saw, through the misty twilight, Florian's rockaway at the side of the road.

"This is where we'll spend the night," said Florian. "There's easy access to the river, for watering the stock. And that village you just passed through ought to be able to supply Mag with anything she needs for cooking us a meal."

"Any problems about getting us a stand?" Edge asked.

"And what did you do with the children?" asked Autumn.

"No problems at all," said Florian. "Got permission to pitch in the city's newest and fanciest park. The kids are still posting—it's a big job. After all, Firenze is at least twice the size of Pisa. I booked rooms for the kids in a pensione for the night."

Very early the next day, for the first time in Edge's experience, the train was prepared for "making parade." Florian brushed his frock coat and top hat while he gave the orders. Hannibal was sent to give Peggy a good scrub in the river shallows; then he anointed her all over with neat's-foot oil, polished her toenails and garbed her in her red blanket. All the horses were combed and brushed to a high shine, and the liberty horses were caparisoned in their plumes and spangles. The wooden sides were removed from Maximus's wagon. The Smodlakas' terriers were adorned with their frilly ruff collars. All the artistes—even Rouleau—put on their freshest ring dress, but, because a chill wind was sweeping down the river, those in fleshings donned cloaks over them. Beck and his wind-jammers polished their instruments and put on their band dress, and Banat wore his bemedaled Rebel uniform. Fitzfarris applied the cosmetics to hide his one marketable attribute, and he, Goesle and the roustabouts took over the job of driving the eleven wagons behind Florian's rockaway.

When the train arrived in the outskirts of Firenze, a neighborhood of shacks and shanties, the occupants of which came to their doors with wide eyes and open mouths, Florian halted and called, "Take your places!" Edge mounted one of the saddled horses, threw his cloak back from his shoulders to show his resplendent Colonel Ramrod uniform and moved up to take the lead ahead of the rockaway. Beck and his bandsmen disposed themselves atop the tarpaulin of the balloon wagon. Hannibal, with his drum, climbed up to Peggy's neck. The other performers perched in graceful attitudes on the roofs of various vans and threw off their cloaks. Barnacle Bill stood, legs braced apart and arms akimbo, on the top of Maximus's cage. Terry, Terrier and Terriest were let down to the road and instantly began throwing somersaults and cartwheels. So did the three Chinese.

Beck and his band began blaring the *William Tell* overture, as Colonel Ramrod led the parade along the Via Pisana, a street of rather better residences. From every house window popped out the heads of the adult inhabitants to watch this most novel spectacle, and from every door popped out children to caper and cheer and point—eventually two mobs of them, one dancing backward in front of Colonel Ramrod's horse, the other prancing behind the elephant. As Beck and company went on through their repertoire, Edge kept watch for the lampposts and other objects bearing the Florilegium's posters, leading the way to the Arno's south bank, where a broad, paved thoroughfare ran alongside and well above the green, opaque, swift-flowing water.

"Yonder across the river," Florian yelled to him, "that's the Cascine Park where we'll be setting up. But now we'll keep going along this Lungarno Soderini."

The riverside Lungarni served a dual purpose, Florian later explained. They were embankments only recently piled up and faced with stone, primarily to contain the Arno's frequent floods. But their paved tops had also become favored promenades for strollers, riders and carriages, especially for those people who came in summer to admire the spectacular sunsets reflected in the river beneath the succession of elegantly proportioned bridges.

At any rate, most of the bridges were elegantly proportioned. But Edge gaped in wonderment when the Ponte Vecchio came in sight. The river ran under it, so it was a bridge, all right, but like none other he had ever seen. It might have been a village suspended in a mirage, it was so clumped and clustered all along its length with two-, three- and four-story buildings, arches, tile roofs, chimney pots at crazy angles, lines of laundry, men with fishing poles leaning out of some of the windows. Most of the houses hung out sideways from the bridge, as if just barely clinging there over the water. Only when Edge passed the southern end of the bridge—the crowds strolling onto and off it had stopped in surprise— could he look along its length and see that, though the Ponte Vecchio was crammed with awninged shops and stalls on both sides, it was indeed a passage from one bank of the Arno to the other, unroofed and open to the sky the whole way.

Meanwhile, the Florilegium was somewhat forcibly making a right-of-way for itself along this south side of the river. The ever-increasing throng of children preceding it made other people and vehicles retreat into side streets as the parade passed. All along its route, people peered from the windows and doorways of the very tall and ornately decorated buildings it was now passing. Across the river, as well, the walkers and riders on the Lungarni over there came to a standstill, the people shading their eyes, pointing, calling each other's attention to the phenomenon.

The Florilegium artistes tirelessly smiled and waved from their wagon and van-roof perches. A few of the townsmen closest to the parade doffed their hats and half-bowed, a few of the women half-curtsied, as if uncertain whether they might be seeing some new kind of entourage accompanying the visit of some new kind of royalty. Some of the townswomen, though not many, turned away or pressed their children's faces into their voluminous skirts, to shut out the sight of the skimpily costumed circus females. Jules Rouleau, seated with Paprika atop the dressing-room wagon, laughed when he heard her grumble through her smile. "That's right, hide, Signora Tub-of-Lard there. I'm posturing up here, chilled to the marrow, pimpled with libabör and risking pneumonia, purely to affront your matronly modesty."

The band had twice or thrice repeated every piece of music it knew, when Edge espied a circus poster stuck on the balustrade of a bridge ahead. Having to dodge among the children milling about in front of him, Edge turned his horse onto the Ponte San Nicolò—a wide bridge, with no accretion of buildings on it—and the bandsmen took a breather while the Florilegium crossed the river. They lifted their instruments again, and pitched into *William Tell* when the parade came off the bridge and proceeded up the Viale Amendola directly ahead, where still more gawkers watched from the pavements, from windows, from halted vehicles.

When the viale debouched into a broad, circular piazza, the posters guided Edge half-left and into an avenue that led westward again, more or less parallel-ing the way they had come along the other bank of the Arno. A couple of times, the parade had to thread its way through a street so narrow that the watchers in its windows had to duck inside when the wagons passed. Then Florian's poster-marked route took the procession between two crumbled stumps of ancient stone pillars, the remainder of what had been the Porta di Prato in what had been the city's walls in olden times. Beyond were the young trees, lawns, grav-eled roads and walkways of the Pratone delle Cascine.

"It means the Dairy Farm," said Florian, when the train had gone some way within the park and halted on the grassy oval inside another racetrack. "A dairy farm is what all this area used to be, until the city grew up around it and appro-priated it for a public park."

"I'd like to meet the man who designed those lamps for it," said Edge, point-ing. Every one of the park's countless lamp standards rose from a cast-iron base that consisted of three clawed paws clutching the ground.

"Yes," said Florian, chuckling. "If the man ever encountered some such three-legged beast, I'd like to ask him where, so I could acquire it for the show."

The artistes climbed down from their parade perches—Rouleau requiring some assistance—while the three terriers and the three Chinese collapsed on a grassy bank, panting and cramped from their having flip-flopped and cart-wheeled all the way here. The brass players of the band were gingerly feeling their lips, bruised from the jolting of their band wagon while they played, and a couple complained that they had even suffered some loosened teeth.

"Well, they don't need lips or teeth to do their roustabout work," said Florian. "Goesle, Banat, get the whole crew started on the unloading and setting up. Abdullah, undress the bull and get her ready to pull her weight. Then you and the Chinks keep all those ragamuffins clear of the area. I am going back to town to fetch our own kids and to book hotel rooms for us. You others, who have no chores to do, may wish to change into street dress and amble about the city while it's still daylight."

Several of the artistes did that, including Edge and Autumn. He and she, arm in arm, turned to the right on leaving the park, and walked among the townsfolk promenading along the Lungarno Amerigo Vespucci.

"I know who Vespucci was," said Edge. "America was named after him. But you'll have to explain everything else, my dear. I'm especially intrigued by that peculiar bridge yonder." He gestured past the two intervening bridges to the third, the Ponte Vecchio, a mile away but easily visible, bulking above the others and glowing like red gold in the afternoon light.

"It is reserved to the shops of goldsmiths and silversmiths," said Autumn. "That highest story, on the upstream side of the bridge, used to be a private passage for the royals and nobles to cross from the Uffizi Palace, when it was the government offices. They could get to the royal residence on the other side of the river, the Pitti Palace, without having to elbow their way through the squalid common folk on the bridge and the streets."

Themselves having no great prejudice against mingling with the common folk, Autumn and Edge crossed the bridge, jostled by the crowd, marveling at the gold and silver and vermeil works on show in the row of shop windows or being personally displayed and loudly advertised by the artisans who had created the pieces. Then they recrossed the bridge, along the opposite row of shops, Autumn gasping or sighing at sight of this or that bijou, and Edge wishing he could afford to buy every one of them for her.

When they came off the bridge, and into the Piazza della Signoria, Autumn said, "Over there on the farther side of the square is the spot where two famous fires were lighted."

"Famous fires?"

"Four hundred years ago, a man named Savonarola was jilted by his childhood sweetheart, so he fled to a monastery, but that only increased the bitterness in him. He came here to Florence as a missionary, and preached against lust and vanity and pleasure and wine bibbing and all those good things. He convinced the Florentines that they were damned unless they reformed. So, one Carnival day, they made a tremendous bonfire here in this piazza and threw into it all their more worldly possessions—mirrors, perfumes, wigs, dice, portraits of the most beautiful courtisanes—everything that hinted of dissipation. Florence must have been a bleak city after that orgy. Then, about ten years later, the Florentines had had enough of Savonarola and his perpetual carping. They made another fire here in the piazza and burned *him*. Let that be a lesson to you, Zachary Edge. Don't ever try to reform the Florentines."

"I'd never dream of trying to reform anybody. A reformed rakehell is the most obnoxious of human beings."

"I am so glad you agree. Before Savonarola arrived here, the ruler of Florence was a man affectionately known as Piero the Gouty. One gets gout only from high living. So I like to think that Florence always has been and always will be a place of luxuriant sensuality and hedonism."

There was one memorable thing Edge had already noticed on that first day, and would notice it on every other, and would always remember it as his most enduring impression of Firenze. It was the way the sunlight, even at midday, seemed never to fall direct and harsh down onto the city, but fell always aslant, caressingly, making every crumbled old stone wall as vivid and distinct as the deliberate relievo of palace façades, and making the narrower streets into mysterious, dark crevices from which one emerged into courtyards or piazze or gardens so warm-colored that they seemed preserved for eternity in purest amber.

When Edge and Autumn got back to the Cascine racetrack, just as night fell, the setup was all but completed. Under the work lights of basket torches, sputtering and dripping gobbets of fire, the roustabouts were doing the finishing touches to the chapiteau, going around it adjusting the tension of guy ropes and hammering a stake more securely here and there, and growling throatily every time they made any move.

Edge asked, "Stitches, why are your crewmen growling like that? Do their teeth still hurt?"

"No, 'tis by my order. I am trying to get us all trained, now just. I have told everybody, even the Governor—and now I tell you—whenever any of us feels like uttering a profanity in public, he is to growl instead."

"All right. But why?"

"Look you." Goesle pointed to where two nuns and a crocodile of small children in school uniforms were watching the work. "There'll be more of that—nuns and nannies and schoolmarms bringing their tykes out to watch us set up or tear down. For an educational experience a little out of the ordinary, y'see. And then maybe the bull Peggy acts balky and somebody will let fly—in no telling what language—with something like 'You goddamned two-tailed son of a bitch!' And the schoolmarm will find that a trifle *too* educational for her kiddies, and we'll get a delegation coming by here to complain about morals and suchlike."

Florian came out of the chapiteau, dusting his hands, and said to Goesle, "As soon as your Slovaks are finished here, get them out slapping up more paper—all over town—all night, if it takes that long." To Edge and Autumn he said, "Most of the artistes have already gone to the hotel to dress for dinner. If you two would like your luggage taken over there, pile it in my carriage and follow me. It is in easy walking distance of here. The Hotel Kraft on the Via Solferino."

"Oh, good," said Autumn.

Edge asked, "An English-run hotel? German?"

"No," said Florian, "though there are plenty of foreign-owned hotels. This city's population is only one-third actual Florentines. Another third are expatriate English and a third are other foreigners—Americans, Russians, Germans, Frenchmen. The Kraft is owned and operated by Italians. But its clientèle is mostly of visiting show folk—theatrical, operatic, circus, pantomime..."

At the hotel, when Edge and Autumn had washed and refreshed themselves in their room, they met Florian and Carl Beck in the hall, and the four took a table together in the dining room downstairs, among the several tables at which their fellows were already eating. Edge looked around, to see if he could identify any other show folk on sight. Nobody was actually leaping about or striking attitudes—everyone in the room ate sedately and conversed quietly—but several obviously *were* of some theatrical occupation, for their faces were leathery and dyed almost orange from years of wearing stage makeup.

"I told you this is a cosmopolitan city," said Florian, taking a folded newspaper from his coat pocket. "This afternoon, I was able to buy from a street-corner news vendor the latest issue of *The Era*, imagine that. After dinner, I'll peruse the Situations Wanted, to see if there's anyone at liberty here in Firenze who might be useful to us."

"May I look at it, Governor?" asked Autumn. "I always like to see if there are any names I know."

Florian handed it over, and Autumn began to leaf through the pages. Carl Beck was saying, "... Into town tomorrow morning. For the acid and other chemicals I will go seeking."

"Well, don't make the balloon gas your overriding priority," said Florian. "When that trap artist arrives, you'll have to think about ways to hang his rig so it doesn't interfere with Autumn's. I wish he were here already, so we'd have him on the program right from tomorrow's opening show."

"He is here, Monsieur Florian," said a dandily dressed gentleman sitting alone, with a cup of cappuccino, at the next table. He stood up and bowed. "Maurice LeVie, à vos ordres. I arrived this morning. I watched you make parade in the American style. I was much taken by it."

"We are very, very pleased to meet you," said Florian, beaming, as he and Beck and Edge also stood. "Didn't recognize you out of pista dress, monsieur. Allow me." And he made introductions all around. LeVie shook the men's hands and kissed Autumn's. The trapeze artiste was small and trim, and seemed composed not of quicksilver, as he had looked in performance, but of all sharp points: sharp nose, sharp chin, sharp widow's peak in his glossy hair, and extremely sharp, darting eyes.

"Do join us," said Florian. "Some wine, perhaps?"

"Merci, no wine," said LeVie, sliding his chair over to their table. "My profession, comprenez, forbids me to risk either tipsiness or the morning-after."

"Of course."

"I had the opportunity," LeVie went on, "to admire all of you, especially your so-lovely ladies, when you rode in. Here in the hotel, I have taken the further opportunity—incognito—of observing your Confederate American company at closer range."

"Aha," said Florian, humorously wagging a finger at him. "And if you had observed, say, that we ate our petits pois with a knife, or exhibited other American barbarities, you would have remained incognito and slipped quietly away."

LeVie smiled—his mouth made a sharp V—and shrugged his pointy shoulders. "Say only that I am satisfied. Indeed, that I am happy to join—your expression is 'join out,' I believe. I shall present myself and my appareil at the tober in the morning, to assist you in the hanging of it. Also, Monsieur le Chef de Musique, you will wish to know my motifs d'accompagnement."

"Ja. Ja doch," said Beck, apparently awed by the man's confident professionalism.

"I would like to ask you one thing, Monsieur Maurice," Florian said almost diffidently. "Understand, now, I have no desire to mar the purity of your solo performance. But we have in our troupe a young lady—a beautiful and accomplished young lady—who is temporarily without an act. Her perch-pole understander was incapacitated by an accident. But the young lady can also do a trap turn."

"Old style or Léotard?" LeVie instantly asked.

"Old style only. She has been in the States for some years, and the Americans are woefully behind the times in that regard. But I wondered if perhaps..."

"I could teach her the leaps? Work her into un jeu duel?"

"Only if you think it would enhance your own act. Otherwise..."

"Is the young lady in this room at this moment? Do not call, please, merely indicate."

"That is she," said Florian, nodding toward another table. "Elle des cheveux roux. Cécile Makkai."

"Ah, oui. Une demoiselle charmante. And that orange hair should nicely complement my blue fleshings. Always I wear blue, messieurs."

Edge remarked, "Paprika is partial to orange tights that match her hair."

"Splendide! And what a perfect nom-de-théâtre for her."

"She is Hungarian," said Autumn.

"A delightful race, especially the females of it. I concur in your suggestion, Monsieur le Gouverneur. If La Paprika is willing, I shall take her to be my partner."

"Fine," said Florian. "I will introduce—"

"In the morning, s'il vous plaît, make all the introductions." Maurice stood up again. "For now, avec permission, I am always early to bed, even when—ha ha!—it is a solo turn."

When he had saluted and left the room, Florian murmured, "Brisk little chap, isn't he?"

"He also seems to have an eye for the ladies," said Edge.

"His conduct book recorded nothing disgraceful."

"I only meant—if he's a ladies' man—in fairness, shouldn't you have mentioned Paprika's, uh, proclivities?"

"Why warn him?" Florian said carelessly. "Either he will soon perceive her nature or—who knows?—with a handsome male partner, Paprika may just possibly change her inclination."

"Per piacere, signori, signorina..." said a new voice, a hoarse and husky voice. Another short, slight, but much paler man was addressing them. "You are of the Florilegium, no? I saw you conversing with Monsieur Maurice. He and I once worked at the same time on the Zirkus Ringfedel. I thought... if you are hiring... I happen to be between engagements. I am Zanni Bonvecino."

"A joey, eh?" said Florian, looking him up and down.

"A sad-face, Governatore," the clown said. He had the mournful voice for it, thought Edge.

"A toby, then," said Autumn, regarding him closely.

"Sì, signorina. I notice you have there *The Era*. You will find my inserzione there, inquiring for employment." While he talked, the clown had taken two empty plates and two knives off the table. Now, a knife in either hand, he was spinning a plate on each point, keeping both the dishes horizontal as they twirled. He seemed to be doing this absentmindedly, as another man might twiddle his thumbs while talking. "I also do Harlequin merriment, humpsty-bumpsty, droll patter, impudent repartee, funny songs. I can even do the Lupino mirror."

"Not until we get another joey, you can't," said Florian. "We have none at all, at the moment." The clown was now spinning one of the plates behind his own back, and the other he passed back and forth, still serenely spinning, under one of his legs. "What sort of patter do you do, Signor Bonvecino?"

"Improvviso, or I make it seem so. On arrival in any new town, I go immediately to the local hairdresser. He always knows all the town gossip, and freely tells it. So my patter makes laughingstocks of the local notables and despicables. I deride the scandals, the pomposities, the peccatuccie, whatever offers, in whatever the local language."

"Maraviglioso," said Florian.

"Erfinderisch," said Beck.

Edge asked, "How often do you get shot at, friend?"

"Signore," Autumn said abruptly, and leaned forward. "Are you perhaps related to one Giorgio Bonvecino?"

"No, signorina." He let the plates spin off the knives, and put the utensils back on the table.

"Are you sure? He was a—"

"Quite sure, signorina. I *am* Giorgio Bonvecino."

Autumn's eyes widened, and she said almost reverently, "I heard you sing with La Diva Patti in *Sonnambula* at Covent Garden."

"I had that honor, sì, and others. Unfortunately, I lost my voice when a mistress lost her temper. She kicked me in the throat. Fortunately, I did not lose also the several languages in which I had learned to sing. I told you, I do now funny songs. They are Zanni Bonvecino's parodies—I do not have to exaggerate to make them so—parodies of the arias for which Giorgio Bonvecino was once famous."

"Good heavens," murmured Florian.

"Ah, well," said the clown. "She might have kicked me elsewhere to even worse effect. Here is my conduct book, Governatore. Will you look at it?"

"No hurry," said Florian, tucking it unopened into a pocket. "Are you stopping at this hotel?"

"No, Signor Governatore. I have a cheap pensione."

"I will engage a room for you here with the rest of us. Welcome to the troupe, Signor Bonvecino."

To everyone's delight, the next day's two shows were both turnaways, even with the vastly bigger chapiteau—and the company put on the best show Edge had yet directed or watched. The Florentine audiences, too, were among the best the Florilegium had entertained. As the troupe made its Grand Entry and Promenade, the crowd joined in, at about the second go-round, to sing along with "Circo-o è allegro!" and never let their enthusiam flag from then on.

After Colonel Ramrod's liberty act, the new clown Zanni came on to exchange banter with Florian. That was all in Italian, but Edge recognized some words—"Robert Browning" and "Daniel Dunglas Home" and "medium" and "humbug"—and those particular mentions drew the loudest laughs from the crowd, so Edge assumed Zanni was dealing with local gossip. The whole time the clown was talking back to Florian, he was doing his plate spinning, this time with the two plates atop long, whippy slivers of bamboo, so the feat was even more magical than it had been at the dining table.

In the pista, Zanni looked quite different from the unemployed toby who had humbly approached Florian the night before. He wore a tight-fitting Harlequin costume and a tiny cock-and-pinch hat. Just a few touches of greasepaint had completely altered his face—a dark lining to accentuate his eyelids, his eyebrows redrawn in little quirks like caret marks, his mouth slightly broadened by rouge—and he had combed his hair downward all around, in the style of an old-time knight's page. After his repartee routine with Florian, he repeatedly ran into the pista between other acts, to help acrobat Sunday and contortionist Ali Baba entertain the crowd during those intervals. While Zanni cavorted, flickered and pirouetted, he held his elbows high and seemed to dance weightlessly on his tiptoes. He also appeared to be taking some perverse enjoyment in his antics: his face and graceful movements combined glee and mischief, so he rather resembled a faun or satyr. Then he would contrive to trip over something, and look suddenly graceless and disgraced, and he would fold, kneel, bow his head into his arms, the picture of abject humility and melancholy.

When there had to be a long interval between acts, as for instance when the cage wagon got rolled in, Zanni would cartwheel into the pista, clasp his little hat to his breast and announce loudly, "Il gran tenore Giorgio Bonvecino canta 'M'appari' "—or some other aria. He would proceed to sing it, with no more hand wringing or gesticulation than any stage tenor would have done, but the Florentine patrons were familiar with opera and they remembered the once-great tenor, though they did not now recognize him. When Zanni sang in his gruff, broken, often-cracking voice, the audience took it as a genuine and expert burlesque. They laughed so hard they nearly reeled off the stands, and at the finish they applauded and bravoed for the mimic as appreciatively as they would once have done for the real Giorgio Bonvecino.

Every other act went equally well. For the first time in public, Maximus vaulted through his fire hoop—though Edge had had some apprehensions about that, because Barnacle Bill's breath was so spirituous that he might well have gone up in flames himself when he lighted the hoop. Maurice LeVie was again blue lightning on the trapeze, and sent the patrons out at intermission smiling and chattering excitedly. Sir John took advantage of their happy frame of mind —after showing them his "tattoo," the museum, the Night Children and the White Pygmies—to sell them scores of his ventriloquy swazzles and then to inflict on them his long-unused mouse game. Fitz was getting his mice now from a cage trap the Hotel Kraft had obligingly let him set in its kitchen, and he had memorized enough additional Italian to shout seductive come-ons and congratulatory payoffs.

The Confederate doorman Banat had taken it upon himself to institute a new system of doorkeeping. The jossers had only to show him their tickets on first entering the chapiteau. Not until after intermission, when they swarmed in again, did Banat actually take their tickets—this to ensure that none of the vagrant promenaders attracted by Fitzfarris's shouts sneaked in with the paying customers.

In the program's second half, the Simms girls now did the slant-climb. Holding the long, limber balance pole, Monday stepped tentatively, as if fearfully, onto the tightrope angled down from the center pole to a stake under the first rank of seats. Then, still pretending awkwardness and trepidation, she went slowly, step by tremulous step, while Abdullah rumbled a suspenseful roll on his drum, until she was all the way up to the rope's top turnbuckle. Cautiously, she turned around up there and started down, just as Sunday, with another balance pole, started up from the bottom. The audience whispered and mumbled: what would happen when the two girls met in the middle? When they did, it occasioned a quick twinkle of feet and poles—for one moment during the crossover, each girl was standing on the rope on only one foot, and the two were exchanging poles —then they were past each other, and Monday came trippingly down to the ground while Sunday went to the top.

Then Florian bawled to the audience, "Allora...il scivolo di salvezza! *The slide for life!*" (In private he, Autumn and the girls called it simply the go-down.) Sunday turned to face the descent, let go one hand from her balance pole, let herself suddenly plummet from the rope—to a concerted gasp from the crowd,

and a *boom!* of Abdullah's drum "taking the fall." But somehow her free hand
shot up and grabbed the pole again, from under the rope and on its other side, so
the pole became a supporting bar. Holding to that, dangling under the rope, she
slid down in a rush—to a loud glissando from the band—to be caught by Edge
at the bottom. He gave her a squeeze of reward, and she gave him a glowing,
adoring smile.

The closing spec was done to new music. Autumn had despaired of ever
being able to translate "Lorena" into Italian that would fit the meter—and in fact
declared that, though the music was stirring, the words were not *worth* translating. So Florian decreed that the show would henceforth close with the national
anthem of whatever country they were in. Tonight the final Promenade
marched, with all the artistes waving and smiling, many of them capering, to the
music of "La Marcia Reale."

Twice a day, day after day, the artistes continued to perform before sfondone
houses. Despite that rigorous regimen, most of them were at the tober every
morning to continue their ceaseless practice of old turns, tryouts of new ones,
and the teaching of apprentices. Clover Lee was now essaying every rosinback
posture and spin and leap from horse to horse that both her mother and Captain
Hotspur had ever done. Hannibal Tyree, whenever he was not practicing juggling every sort of object that came to hand and was not rehearsing with the
band, was working with Obie Yount to train Brutus to *lose* in a tug-of-war with
the Quakemaker. The Smodlakas had got Goesle to build them a midget Roman
chariot, and were teaching the dogs to open their act by trotting into the pista
hauling one of the albino children in it.

Edge labored to train the polka-dot Pinzgauer horses to join his liberty act,
meanwhile rehearsing Monday and Thunder in ever more precise refinement of
their haute école two-steps, travers, renvers, courbettes and caprioles. Rouleau,
not yet having anything of his own to do, went on teaching Sunday new acrobatic tricks and Quincy more incredible contortions. Between those sessions,
Monday and Quincy worked on new routines with the three Chinese, the elephant and the teeterboard, and Sunday went doggedly on with her language
lessons. She evidently had determined to rival Florian in multilingual prowess:
she was not only studying French (and good English) with Rouleau, she was
also beginning to learn Italian from Zanni Bonvecino and German from Paprika
—whenever Paprika was not being initiated by Maurice LeVie into the mysteries
of Léotard-style trapeze work.

Besides feeling it the duty of an equestrian director to have some knowledge
of all the acts under his command, Edge was fascinated by the trapeze practice,
and often wandered into the chapiteau of a morning to watch Maurice and Paprika at it.

"But the damned bar is so damned heavy, kedvesem," Paprika complained,
during one of her early lessons. "Mine was never so heavy when I had my own
aerial rig."

"Your bar had only to support you, mam'selle," Maurice said patiently. "And
your weight kept it steady at all times. These two bars are heavy for good reason.
A lightweight trapeze would jiggle and sway when swinging loose. If the bar is
not always perfectly straight, horizontal, parallel to the ground when you or I

lunge for it, you or I or both of us could miss our grip, and fall, and be dead. Hence the heaviness."

Edge already knew, from supervising the hoisting aloft of the rig, that each of the bars—wound along its length with lint bandage fixed by sticking plaster— had a five-pound nickel-plated knob beyond the rope on either end of it. He also knew, from seeing Goesle make the things for Paprika, that both she and Maurice wore tight wristbands for added strength there, and on both hands sailmaker-style "palms" of suéde leather, with holes cut for their fingers.

"No, no, no!" Maurice shouted, on one occasion when Edge was observing. Maurice was on one platform and Paprika on the one opposite. "Do not lean forward to anticipate the bar when it swings to you. Lean *backward* as you seize it, and remain leaning backward as you leave the platform. That way, you are putting your weight on the bar from the start of your swing. You will not feel so much tug of gravity—you will not feel so heavy—at the bottom of your arc."

The chief crewmen of the Florilegium, Goesle and Beck, were also on the Cascine tober every morning, and also hard at work. Carl Beck had procured, from pharmaceutical merchants in the city, the various chemicals he required for his Gasentwickler. Now he spent most of his spare time in empirical tries at determining the proper proportions of those ingredients—and Rouleau could only fidget impatiently, because Beck insisted, "Not until I know what I am doing will I let you try what you can do as a Luftschiffer." Beck also had some of the bandsmen-Slovaks building something for himself, the nature of which he declined to disclose until it was done. Meanwhile, Dai Goesle and some other crewmen were putting planks and hardware together into some object Fitzfarris had requested, but the purpose of which he refused to reveal even to the builders. Magpie Maggie Hag, as usual, was sewing costumes—now for the Simms and Smodlaka children, who had outgrown their older ones.

Only during the three-hour intervals between the afternoon and night shows did the troupers indulge themselves, a few times a week, in dressing in street clothes and wandering through the city. They ogled the local architecture, toured museums and galleries, browsed or bought in the luxury shops or the cheap flea markets, strolled in the Boboli Gardens, or rode in a vettura to see the view that Boccaccio and Lorenzo de Medici and Shelley and other immortals had seen from the hill of Fiesole.

Mullenax spent most of his leisure time in whatever workingmen's Italian bettola he happened to chance upon, because he could count on the other tipplers' standing him free drinks when they learned that he was the lion tamer Barnacle Bill. Edge, Fitzfarris and Yount spent a few hours each week in Doney's Café, the favored watering hole of Americans resident in Firenze. There they would sit over wine or espresso and review with the other expatriates the latest news from the States. American highwaymen had now moved from the roads to the rails; in Ohio a train had been stopped by armed bandits, its baggage car and passengers robbed. The whole South was being overrun and bullied and ransacked by Yankee and Free Negro "carpetbaggers"...

But as a general thing all the circus folk preferred to roam among the native people and native scenes, and even found some scenes that the Baedeker guidebooks neglected to mention. One day, Autumn took Edge to show him the venerable house where the great Dante was "believed to have resided" before his banishment from Firenze. Edge regarded it with due gravity. But then, when they walked along the street behind the house, the Via del Proconsolo, Edge noticed that every single shop was devoted to the display and sale of formidable canvas corsets and belly flatteners, and even uglier abdominal furniture constructed of india rubber, leather and cork—trusses, hernia belts, scrotum supporters—and he mildly suggested that the city fathers might have located Dante's presumed residence in a more high-minded neighborhood.

Maurice and Paprika, even when they were sightseeing with other artistes, never ceased discussing the finer points of trapeze work. When they were out walking with Edge, Autumn and Florian one day, and a drizzle of rain began to fall, Maurice was moved to say, "Mam'selle Paprika, we will never go aloft on a day of really heavy rain. Should the rain seep in through the canvas"—he nodded to Edge—"our equestrian director will not *let* us take the risk, or the Mam'selle Auburn either, for the bars and the platforms and the tightrope will probably be slippery."

The group ducked out of the drizzle into the Uffizi Gallery, where Botticelli's painting of *Spring* inspired Maurice to add, "Pleasant weather can be as hazardous to us, mam'selle, as the rainiest or iciest weather. On a merely balmy day, it can be actually *hot* up there close under the peak. I have known trap artistes to faint and topple during their exertions, and others to sweat through the suéde palms so they lost their grip and fell."

Later, at the Hotel Kraft's dining table, Maurice was reminded of another caveat: "Never eat before a performance, Mam'selle Paprika. It is wise to be as light as possible in the air. But more important—should there occur an accident, an injury, then swift surgery may be necessary. If ever that happens to me, I should dearly hope to be put to sleep while I am cut open. And no physician can administer the mercy of ether or chloroform unless the patient has an empty stomach."

Notwithstanding LeVie's expert tutelage, Paprika never became as proficient as he was at the "flying" part of the trapeze act, but she did not have to be. As eventually worked out, their act commenced with only Paprika being introduced by Florian—"L'ardumentosa acrobata *a-e-ro*-batica, Signorina Paprika!"—and she went lightly up the rope ladder to her platform, untied the trapeze bar, swung it out and—to the band's playing the sprightly Hungarian cigány "There Is But One Girl"—while the bar continued to swing, did every sort of pose, flipover, knee-hang, toe-hang and even a handstand on the bar. She concluded her solo turn by swinging again to the platform and flinging up her arms in the V for applause. At that moment, a ragged, dirty, drunken man came staggering and stumbling from the stands.

He argued profanely with Florian and Edge, and struggled with the roustabouts who dashed into the pista. But the drunk always broke loose of restraint, ran to climb the rope ladder—pretending several times to slip and almost fall—before gaining the platform, releasing Paprika's hooked-back trapeze and launching himself out on it. As he swung back and forth, sometimes by just one hand, sometimes fearfully clutching with both arms and both legs, Paprika looked aghast and the band played a cacophonous hash of Wagner's *Flying Dutchman* overture. But then the drunk began shedding and dropping his ragged clothing, piece by piece.

At the instant Pete Jenkins hung revealed in his electric-blue spangles, and the crowd laughed at its own credulity, and the band rippled smoothly into the "Bal de Vienne," Paprika swung out on her trapeze. Maurice performed acrobatics on one bar while Paprika imitated him on the other. Then she retired to her platform and Maurice did his blue-lightning tumbles and twists and twirls as he hurtled back and forth between the traps. At the climax of the act, both Maurice and Paprika were on the bars, swinging faster and higher, faster and higher—until both let go of their traps (thunder of bass drum), whizzed past each other in a dual midair somersault, caught the opposite bars, hauled themselves up to sit casually on them, waving and smiling, to a frenzy of cheers, clapping, whistles, bravos and bravas.

At one afternoon show's opening, the artistes in the come-in spec were surprised to hear their "Greensleeves" music sounding even louder, bouncier and more jingly than usual. They all peered up at the bandstand every time they promenaded past it, but could discern only that there was one more uniformed Slovak up there than usual. Nobody could see, over the projecting edge of the stand, what instrument that windjammer might be playing, and Bandmaster Beck only smiled smugly down at them. Whatever it was that he had added to the band continued to augment all the music for all the subsequent acts, with jingles, rat-a-tats, hollow clunks, brassy clashes and strange, unearthly shimmers of sound. Not until the crowd emptied out at intermission could Florian and Edge climb up the seats adjoining the bandstand, to investigate.

"An old Bavarian plaything it is," Beck said proudly, as they stared at it. "The Teufel Geige, by name—Devil's Fiddle. My Slovaks I showed how to make it."

The Devil's Fiddle was only an upright pole, five feet tall, at the bottom of which was attached a coiled spring that rested on the bandstand flooring. Fixed here and there along the pole were cow bells and sleigh bells of assorted sizes, a tambourine, some hollowed-out wooden blocks and a brass cymbal.

"Not even a trained musician it requires. Anybody can play it," said Beck. "With a single drumstick, this or that piece of the Teufel Geige he strikes. Extra resonance and reverberation, the spring at the bottom gives. Or, for loudest crescendo and fortissimo, the player simply up and down bangs the whole pole. On the spring, the Apparat bounces, and all the attachments together go bing-bong, tinkle-jangle, tock-tock, boom, crash, clash . . ."

"Ingenious, you Bavarians," Florian murmured. "I'm glad that some of the Florentines got the opportunity to enjoy it."

"Some?" said Beck. "Then closing here in Florenz we are?"

"It is time. We have had more than three good weeks, but no turnaways these last few days, and today even some empty seats. Besides, it's getting damned cold. We will emulate the Orfei and head south."

"Let us, then, with a grand flourish go out," said Beck. "Make posters, please, Gouverneur, announcing a Luftballon ascension for the final day, between the afternoon and nighttime shows. Weather permitting, be sure to add."

"You think you are ready, Carl? And Monsieur Roulette? Very well. I shall have the paper printed overnight and posted tomorrow. The next day will be our last in Firenze."

Ascension Day, as the eager Rouleau irreverently referred to it, dawned clear and cloudless. Early that morning, Beck and five of his Slovaks unloaded the *Saratoga* from its wagon and carefully unfolded the silk bag and its netting and its ropes outward across the grass of the racetrack's infield oval. While four of the men went to fetch the Gasentwickler, the other hung sandbags around the outer rim of the upright wicker gondola. Early though the hour was and much as Beck might have wished to do this first inflation unobserved, in case of embarrassing incident or failure, quite a crowd of Florentines had gathered, including a number of nuns marshaling crocodiles of schoolchildren. So the roustabouts grunted and growled instead of blaspheming while they worked.

"These ascensions you will only in important cities be able to make," Beck warned Rouleau, who stood leaning on his cane beside the bag-hung basket. "And then perhaps only once or twice on opening or closing day, for a special attraction. I had not realized, until I experimented, how much of the chemicals for each inflation are required. So much and so heavy that with us the supplies we cannot carry, but must purchase on the spot. Observe."

The Gasentwickler consisted of two very big, metal-sheathed boxes, each on its own set of four wheels. They were currently connected by a length of six-inch india-rubber hose. Boom-Boom unscrewed and lifted open a sort of hinged iron manhole on top of one of the boxes and bade Rouleau look inside.

"This tank the generator is. Lined with lead, to resist corrosion of the acid. You will also see that random and staggered shelves it has inside, for better distribution of these iron filings."

The five Slovaks came up, each bowed under the weight of a heavy sack. One man at a time hefted his sack to the manhole and poured its contents into the tank, shaking and waggling the mouth of the bag to scatter the filings over the inside shelves. The men made several trips, pouring in—Rouleau lost count —fifteen or twenty sacks of the filings. Then they came again, now with buckets of water, and filled the box to within a couple of feet of its top. Beck closed and screwed down the manhole cover, while the men went away again and began returning with immense glass carboys of what looked like more water.

"Oil of vitriol—sulphuric acid," said Boom-Boom. "Much experimenting this required, to determine the amount and correct procedure of adding it."

Into a copper funnel at one end of the generator tank, the men slowly poured, one by one, five carboys of the acid. Then there was a long wait, timed by Beck with the watch he had borrowed from Florian. Finally he gave a nod and the roustabouts slowly poured in three more carboys. Another long wait, another nod, and the men slowly poured in two more carboys.

"The Wasserstoff—the hydrogen gas—by now is generating," said Beck. "The slow addition of the oil of vitriol prevents too rapid generation, for the tank walls it might strain. Now is passing the gas through this thick hose into the other box. Feel."

Rouleau put a hand to the hose between the two machines, and jerked his hand away again; the rubber was almost burning hot.

"That is why the second Apparat, the cooler and purifier, we must employ. In there, over and around a grid of tubing full of cold water, the hot gas circulates. Then through a second chamber, charged with lime water, it bubbles, losing all impurities and useless gases. Now the connection I make—observe—of this outflow hose to the fitting at the bag's appendix. And in between, a force pump we have, to hasten the pure hydrogen's passage from Gasentwickler to Luftballon." He beckoned, and a Slovak came to start energetically working the pump handle.

By now, the whole Florilegium company had gathered to watch, as avidly as the jossers. But it took a long time before anyone could see that anything was happening inside the *Saratoga,* and it had to be taken on faith that something was noiselessly happening inside the Gasentwickler. But then the limp vermilion-and-white silk stirred gently. A wrinkle unwrinkled here. A small fold unfolded there. After twenty minutes or so—the roustabouts taking turns at the force pump—it was evident that the bag's upper layer of silk was some inches above the ground it had been lying on. In an hour, the silk had formed a dome, still amorphous and earthbound, but higher than a man's head. Two hours after that, the *Saratoga* was fully inflated, towering tall and broad and proud above its gondola, contained by its netting, restrained by its anchor ropes—and all the watching circus folk, city folk, nuns and children were chattering excitedly.

Beck disconnected the hose coupling from the balloon's appendix, then set his men to flushing out the two generator boxes with many, many buckets of water before the machines were rolled off to the circus's backyard, out of sight. Edge noticed that balloonist Rouleau had been buttonholed by Fitzfarris, Monday and Sunday Simms. Fitz was talking and pointing—to the balloon, to the girls, to himself and to Rouleau, who listened with apparent interest. Only the final exchanges of that colloquy were audible to Edge as he passed them.

"... Do it, won't you, girls?" Fitzfarris asked.

"Mais oui," said Sunday. "Il commence à faire une grande aventure."

"Bien," said Rouleau. "Then do it we shall."

By the promised time of the ascension, just before sundown, not only the entire Cascine Park but also the farther bank of the Arno and the balconies, windows and rooftops on both sides of the river were packed with oglers elbow to elbow. All those nearest to the Florilegium's red wagon were waving lire notes and clamoring for tickets to the final show. Edge remarked to Florian that the city appeared to have a suddenly renewed interest in circus entertainment, and maybe it would be profitable to stay here a while longer.

"No," said Florian. "It's always better to depart while you are a novelty, and interesting, rather than after you have become a fixture, and stale. Besides, Firenze would be expecting to see a balloon ascension every day now, and that is impractical."

Now there came a tumultuous band fanfare from inside the tent. Beck and his band emerged, drummer Hannibal and the Devil's Fiddle player included, all marching to the exuberant music of "Camptown Races." Behind the band strode Jules Rouleau, without his cane, subduing his limp as much as possible. Over his yellow-and-green fleshings, he wore Colonel Ramrod's yellow-lined black cloak, and the train of it was carried by Autumn and Paprika, also in their pista costumes. Arriving at the *Saratoga's* gondola, Rouleau shed the cloak with elaborately swirling flourishes, to disguise the fact that the two girls were discreetly assisting his climb into the basket.

The band music muted so that Florian, with a poster rolled into a makeshift megaphone, could bray a long harangue at the crowd—on the perils of aerial journeying, the courage and skill of Monsieur Roulette, his doing this ascent purely to thank the city of Firenze for its generous hospitality, etc., etc. While all other eyes were on Florian and the *Saratoga,* Edge happened to glance toward the chapiteau's front-door marquee. Fitzfarris, wearing his makeup to cover his blueness, was directing a couple of Slovaks in hauling out the object he had had

Goesle construct for him. It was a large wooden cube that looked like nothing more than a furniture crate painted black and ornamented with gilt stars, crescent moons and other cabalistic designs. When the men set it a little way out from under the marquee, Edge could see that there was a narrow, shallow tin gutter tacked around the outer four edges of the crate's top.

Florian finished his introduction, the band blared a theme from Corette's *Le Phénix*, some roustabouts cast off ropes, and the vast crowd let out an "Oo-ooh!" that must have been heard as far away as Fiesole. But the balloon went up only slowly, as it had done in Baltimore, the Slovaks paying out the haul-down rope so that Rouleau, when he was some three hundred feet up, could make the crowd gasp again when he insanely vaulted out of the gondola. Then he did his acrobatics on the rope ladder slung over its side, but—in deference to his fragile leg—he did not prolong that exhibition. When he climbed back inside the basket, the crewmen—not he, this time—let go the haul-down rope, and Rouleau took it up with him, coiling it into the basket, as the *Saratoga* soared free.

Still rather slowly, or so it seemed from the ground, the balloon went higher and drifted off to the northward. The watchers could barely see the distant Rouleau now busy at the gondola rim—emptying one of several sandbags—and the balloon more swiftly dwindled higher, until it caught a breeze from the opposite point of the compass, drifted back over the Cascine Park and southward across the Arno. Evidently Rouleau was determined to test what control he had over the craft, for he took it higher, then lower, then higher again, by alternately dumping sand and opening the clack valve, to float in various directions at various levels of the sky. Boom-Boom Beck conducted without looking at the band, so he could keep an eye on the balloon and nod with admiring approval of Rouleau's maneuvers.

Finally, with the slow, deliberate, inch-and-pinch caution of a sea captain berthing an immense ship, Rouleau brought the *Saratoga* down and sideways, aiming for the tober again. It was hardly to be expected that he would make a pinpoint landing on his first try, but he did get close enough and low enough to drop the free end of the haul-down rope, and the Slovaks rushed to seize it and tow the balloon toward touchdown. The crowd roared and applauded as the *Saratoga* was slowly dragged earthward. Then the band gave another blast of fanfare to attract the people's attention, and Fitzfarris bellowed through the paper megaphone:

"Ebbene, signore e signori!...Attenti!...Un pezzo della arte magica!... Osservate!"

The jossers lowered their gaze from the balloon to ground level and saw Fitzfarris languidly puffing on a large cigar, then gesturing with it to his gilt-and-black platform. On it stood Monday Simms, in a graceful pose, wearing a proud smile and—in her fawn-colored tights—seemingly wearing little else but a few strategically placed patches of sequins.

"Osservate!" Fitz continued. "La fanciulla che sparisce!"

"The girl who vanishes," said Florian, for anybody who needed a translation. "What is Sir John up to now?"

Keeping an eye on the balloon being brought down hand over hand by the roustabouts, Fitzfarris went on bellowing his broken-Italian to hold the people's attention:

"Osservate vigilantemente, signore e signori!... In un istante, la fanciulla... sparirà!" The *Saratoga's* gondola was only a few feet above the ground when Fitzfarris bawled more loudly, "*Signorina... sparisca!*" and waved his cigar toward her.

There was a not loud but concussive noise—*fwoompf!*—and a bright flash of flame, succeeded by a billow of white smoke that rolled upward from the four sides of the platform, briefly hiding the girl, and the front ranks of the surrounding crowd recoiled from the small explosion. The smoke rolled up and off the platform and away into the air... and there was no Monday Simms standing there any more. The crowd made a murmur of marveling disbelief, but Fitz gave them no time to discuss the phenomenon. He was already shouting, "*Ecco!*" and pointing to the gondola just now touching the earth. "Ecco! La fanciulla magica!"—and the people looked and blinked and gasped, for there in the basket, just come down from the sky, standing in a graceful pose beside Monsieur Roulette, stood the very girl they had just seen disappear from the platform on the solid ground.

"Trust Sir John," said Florian admiringly, "to find a new use for pretty twins."

"I'm only surprised," said Edge, as the crowd burst into renewed applause, "that he didn't think of some way to make money from the trick."

In a way, Fitz had, for the nearmost of the jossers clamored even more loudly for tickets to a show that so freely displayed such wonders as they had just seen. When Goesle and his men loosed a section of the rope fencing to let them through, there was a stampede for the red-wagon counter where Magpie Maggie Hag presided. Fitzfarris threaded his way through the throng and, smiling triumphantly, came up to Florian and Edge.

"Found some of that stuff the stage magicians call lakapodum powder," he said. "Thought I'd put it to good purpose."

"Lycopodium," Florian corrected him.

"Whichever it is, what is it?" asked Edge.

"A sort of fungus," said Florian. "Dried and powdered, it is used in fireworks —or for such effects as we have just seen."

"Touched my cigar to it," said Fitz, "and at the same time touched a spring latch that dropped Monday through a trapdoor. I won't do that trick too often, though, because now I can't show the White African Pygmies without giving away the gimmix."

"No matter," said Florian. "You'll have more time at intermission to work your mouse game, and you ought to do a booming business. We have certainly got a turnaway crowd."

Even those folk who were turned away from the ticket counter, though they looked mortally disappointed when the more fortunate ones swarmed inside the chapiteau, loitered about the tober to watch Monsieur Roulette pull the *Saratoga's* ripcord and collapse the balloon. They stayed on to watch him and the Slovaks carefully fold all the silk and net ropes and hoop and basket, and stow the apparatus in its wagon. They stayed on to gamble at the mouse game during intermission. They even stayed on until the show was over—and the come-out audience loitered, as well—to watch wistfully while the roustabouts and the elephant dismantled the entire chapiteau, while the artistes went by ones and twos into the backyard dressing wagon, and emerged in street clothes and went off to the Hotel Kraft for one last supper and one last night's sleep in Firenze.

7

THE JOURNEY south from Firenze might have been plotted on a map with a dash-dot-dash line, the dashes representing the road runs of about twenty miles apiece, and the dots being the villages, towns and cities to which each of those runs brought the circus train. Florian had laid out the route to follow the inter-linking river valleys west of the Apennine mountain chain running the length of the peninsula. This necessitated a sometimes meandering and circuitous prog-ress, but it was preferable to suffering the winter cold and fogs of the mountains, the steep and twisty roads up and down them and the lack of grass or hay up there for the stock to pasture on.

All the circus folk were sorry to leave the beauties and pleasures of Firenze, but, at the end of the very first day's run, when they came to the outskirts of San Giovanni Valdarno, they were heartened by the town's looking promising in a peculiar sort of way. The road ahead was flanked by high mounds that flashed gemlike glints of ruby, emerald and sapphire in the late-afternoon sunlight. "Look at that, by damn," Edge remarked to Autumn. "This place is surrounded by hills of jewels." But as they got closer, the glittery hills proved to be only heaps of many-colored broken bottles—the refuse piles of a grappa distillery. The rest of San Giovanni was likewise all industrial and ugly—the workshops of ceramics makers, gravestone carvers, harness-and-saddleries.

The train's southward route almost regularly alternated colorful and pleasant places with dreary and ugly ones. The troupers were much more taken with their next stop, the city of Arezzo. It was built on a hill rising from lowlands of grainfields, orchards and vineyards. To the eyes of those approaching, it looked as if the city, contained and delimited by an encircling medieval stone wall, had had no place to grow but upward, piling terrace upon terrace of buildings, and thereby lofting its biggest edifice, the Citadel, to the topmost height of all. But the next stop, Cortona, was another disappointment—a grim, silent town, all ramparts and fortifications. And the next stop was another treat for the eyes and spirits, a hamlet beside the lovely lake of Trasimento, shimmering silver in color.

"However, it was not always that color," said Florian, and he addressed Han-nibal Tyree in particular. "This is where your namesake, Hannibal of Carthage, battled against the Roman consul Flaminius. A hundred thousand men died hereabout, and it is said that their blood made the lake red for years afterward."

When, late one afternoon, the train approached the high walls of Perugia, Florian was waiting—he having, as usual, hastened on ahead to deal with the municipal authorities. This time, he called the company together to tell them, "Once again, we will be pitching on the local racetrack, and it is only a little way from here, outside the city ramparts. However, we will be sharing it with a fair already in progress."

"Oh, hell," said Fitzfarris. "Oughtn't we to give this place the go-by, then?"

"Certainly not," said Florian. "The fair will be no competition for us. Rather, it will be an added attraction—part of your midway, so to speak, Sir John. And the fair and circus together will definitely draw good crowds. But I do think we ought to make it clear that we are something more rare and special than a commonplace provincial fair. I propose that we make parade again, all around the city, before we pitch."

So the Florilegium entered Perugia as it had entered Firenze, with flamboyance. The band played numerous times through its repertoire, the women waved and smiled and—though the evening was chilly enough that they wore their cloaks—occasionally bared a glimpse of their fleshings or their real flesh. The procession followed the broad main avenue that circled the city, sometimes outside, sometimes inside the old walls, and the Perugians gathered alongside the avenue or peered down from the ramparts or leaned out the windows, with loud noises of welcome.

The circuit of the city being some two miles in extent, night had fallen by the time the circus got back to its starting point, and Florian's rockaway led it south toward the Hippodromo. There was no trouble in finding that, for one half of the racetrack's infield oval was brilliantly lighted by the fair's lamps and torches set around tents, stalls, booths and one immense wooden construction too big to be under cover. The fair was also loud with voices, noise and music—several different musics being sung or played simultaneously. The circus wagons drew up on the unoccupied half of the infield, the bandsmen changed from uniforms into work garb and joined the other roustabouts in starting the setup, while Florian went back into the city to seek a convenient and suitable hotel or inn.

The artistes next got out of costume into warm street clothes and went sauntering through the fair, for many of them had seen fairs only in America, and those had consisted mostly of the local folks' showing off to each other their champion livestock, homemade quilts, garden produce of the giant-pumpkin sort. This Italian fair seemed more like a vast sideshow, every participant offering some kind of entertainment, or something to eat or drink, or a game to gamble on, or some odd product for sale.

Edge and Autumn went first to inspect the tremendous wooden thing they had noticed on arrival. It was a wheel as high as a house—or, rather, two wheels fixed together side by side with crossbars at intervals, and from those crossbars were hung half a dozen little two-seat gondolas. People sat in those, looking brave or merry or terrified, as the wheel ponderously turned, the gondolas always hanging level while they went up, over and down. The turning was done by a man on a platform at the wheel's hub, profusely sweating even in the chill night air, as he toiled to turn a crank extending from the axle. An accordionist on the ground played a raucous musical accompaniment.

"Those are the new swinging boats," Autumn said. "I first saw one of those machines in Paris. Now they're popular everywhere."

They went on, through the milling, noisily excited crowds, up and down the rows of torchlit tents, stalls and booths, those variously identified by fancily painted or merely scrawled signboards: Museo di Figure di Cera, Sala de Misteri, Tomba della Mummia...

"Wax Museum," Autumn translated. "Hall of Mysteries. The Mummy's Tomb. These are all known in the trade as entresorts—entertainments that the public pays simply to walk through. And their proprietors are called voyageurs forains, meaning they're not much better than gypsies."

She and Edge stopped to buy a hot salsiccia. The charcoal brazier was attended by an old woman who sat on a stool with her feet in a basket to protect them from the cold ground. For a very few centesimi, she handed each of them a greasy, sputtering sausage impaled on a sliver of wood. As they walked and ate, they could see others of their company eyeing and trying the fair's offerings. Fitzfarris was making a particularly close scrutiny of the entresorts, paying to walk through one after another.

"Now what in the world is this?" asked Edge, as they came to a stall that was only a many-slatted wooden rack all covered with hair. There was hair of every human color—including aged gray, white and silver—bunched in swatches like horsetails, some short, some long, some straight, some curly.

"Just what it looks like," said Autumn. "False hair for sale. There's a customer trying some on." She pointed to where, at one side of the stall, a woman was trying to match the rusty color of her own scanty hair, holding to her head one horsetail after another, peering into a cracked small mirror hung there on a nail. "She'll braid it in among her own—a switch or a rat, we women call it—and pay for it by the gram or kilo, depending on how much she needs."

"I'm glad you don't need any such thing," said Edge. The swatches reminded him too much of what Pepper Mayo had left hanging from the circus's lungia. "Where does the hair come from, anyway?"

"From poor women—or dead ones. From streetwalkers who have fallen clear to the gutter. From workhouses, almshouses, hospitals, lunatic asylums, morgues..."

"Jesus, I'm *really* glad you don't need any. But maybe we ought to mention this booth to Boom-Boom Beck."

"You are wicked." She laughed. "Now I think I will go back to the caravan, Zachary. I do believe that sausage has disagreed with me."

Edge looked alarmed. "I'd better walk along with—"

"No, no. I am not ill, dear, only queasy. Bit of a headache, too. You go on and see everything there is to see."

So he did, for he had seen and heard something in one booth that interested him. The booth contained mainly a clutter of what Florian called "slum"—trumpery gimcracks and souvenirs—plaster Madonnas, cheap penknives, chromos of the Last Supper. But among those things, prominent in a place by itself, was a round box of genuine cloisonné, the lid of which the old man in the booth lifted every time someone passed by. And when the box was opened, it played, in a thin, twinkly way, the music of "Greensleeves." Edge went close to look at it, the old man raised the lid and the music pinged and jingled.

"Bella, no, la scatola armonica? Un oggetto di mia nonna..."

He went on at some length and, after he had repeated himself several times, Edge grasped that the box was suitable for snuff or small jewelry, that it was a bequest from the old man's old grandmother, that the music-machinery in the base of the box had been made, very long ago, by an English master of such instruments. When "Greensleeves" slowed to a lugubrious plunk-plunking dirge, the old man showed Edge the winding key on the bottom of the box. Then he named a price indicating that he highly valued either the work or his dear grandmother's memory. Edge named a price quite insulting to both. They haggled until Edge—not wanting to pay *too* cheap a price for a gift for Autumn—finally agreed on a figure and paid it.

On the way back to the tober, Edge fell in with Fitzfarris, who said he had had a stroke of what might be good fortune, but he waited to broach it until they found Florian, busily rounding up all who would be staying in the albergo he had engaged.

"I've found me a tent for my rawhide show," Fitz announced.

"A top for your annex," Florian automatically corrected him.

"There's a fellow here, speaks a little English, and with my little Italian we got to colloguing. He's showing a dismal old mummy, and he wants to sell out and fold up. The top is no bigger than an army hospital tent, but plenty big enough for me to stage a hootchy-cootchy. And it's pretty dingy, but Stitches can paint it up to match the chapiteau. Anyway, I can get it at a reasonable price— and he'll throw in the mummy. What do you say, Governor?"

"What do you want with the mummy, if it's no draw?"

"Oh, hell, this dago doesn't know anything about presentation. He just lets the damned thing lie there. I'll have Mag put some suggestive scanties on her, I'll concoct a history for her..."

"Her? It's a female mummy?"

"Who can tell? It's all shriveled—and I mean *all*. I can bill it as a morphodite, if I want to. It's the tent I mainly want."

"It's fine with me, then, Sir John. Go get it."

So Fitzfarris acquired the tent, and Goesle and his men began darning its canvas and replacing its old ropes with new ones, and at the plains town of Foligno and the hill town of Spoleto, in each of which the Florilegium played for two days, Fitz included his mummy among the phenomena of his sideshow. Magpie Maggie Hag, with her clown paints, plus ointments and powders borrowed from the other women of the troupe, had enlivened and plumped out the mummy's furrowed face so that it looked, if not gorgeously feminine, at least rather more human than tree bark. She had hidden the bald brown skull under a vaguely pharaonic hat and clothed the body in a gauzy gown embroidered with her notion of an Egyptian design. The gown left the withered arms and legs visible to demonstrate that this was indeed a mummy, but the bosom was padded to give some added semblance of its being a female mummy. Meanwhile, Fitz had had Zanni Bonvecino write for him a rigmarole in Italian, and had memorized it.

"La Principessa Egiziana, signore e signori!" He went on to aver that she was six thousand years old and "of royal rank, as indicated by the luxurious linen which still covers her shapely body."

That was *all* he said about the exhibit in those two towns, as if uncaring whether or not the jossers marveled at the exhibit. But, by the time the Florilegium arrived at the sizable industrial city of Terni, Fitz's new top was all painted and set up on the midway. So, at the first show's intermission in Terni, Fitz presented his "Egyptian princess" with a bit of extra patter that Zanni had provided, and spoke it in a confidentially low voice:

"Any gentlemen in the audience who identify themselves as physicians or surgeons, and who might wish to examine more closely the physiological details of this amazingly preserved young female body, may apply at the specially restricted pavilion yonder, after the close of our main performance, and upon the payment of a small additional honorarium..."

A surprisingly large number of the adult males in that audience proved to be physicians or surgeons, willing to spend five lire just to satisfy their professional interest in ancient Egyptian anatomy.

The next town on the route, Rieti, provided another abundance of doctors to patronize the mummy's tent. But they—and their women and children, too—were almost as much beguiled by another addition to the show. For the first time, Colonel Ramrod introduced the eight polka-dot Pinzgauer horses into his liberty act. That meant that he had in the pista, all at one time, a herd of fourteen horses, handsomely blue-blanketed, plumed, spangled and tasseled by Magpie Maggie Hag. There was one difference in their dress now: each horse's blanket bore on its right side a large number, from 1 to 14.

After Colonel Ramrod had put individual horses and teams of them and ensembles of them and all of them through their several tricks and patterns and dances, the close of the act consisted of their cantering counterclockwise in a mixed bunch around the inside of the pista curb. Then, as the equestrian director flicked his whip in signals known only to him and to them, the horses began to fall into single file. The horse bearing the number 1 drew ahead of the others, number 2 moved up, and so on—until the horses composed a complete circle, 1 to 14, cantering around and around their master, and looking properly proud of themselves. The audience paid the supreme compliment of sitting silent for a moment, in stunned admiration, before breaking into a storm of applause. Then the carousel-like circle broke, and the horses—seemingly of their own accord—cantered through the curb opening and out the back door, still in numerical order.

The Florilegium's next run, up the Salto River valley, took three days and nights. There were no towns big enough to pitch in, and the alberghi and locande along the roadside had kitchens and larders sufficient to feed the company, but not beds enough for them. So the artistes and senior crewmen took their meals in the inns, and retired to wagons and pallets afterward. On one of those nights, Fitzfarris put to Paprika a persuasive suggestion, but evidently not persuasive enough, for she was heard to snarl at him:

"You ask me to do rawhide? Csúnya! I have been wondering what to do with my perch pole. I think I will shove it up your végbél."

Whereupon Fitzfarris applied to the younger females: Clover Lee, Sunday and Monday. "It will be a tableau," he pleaded. "You only *pose*. More or less. And it's *biblical*. What could be more praiseworthy than illustrating the Scriptures?"

"Well . . ." said Sunday charily.

"Splendid! You and Monday will portray the daughters. Now, what do you say, Clover Lee, to the very grown-up rôle of a Hittite matron?"

In that time of no performances and no other distractions, Magpie Maggie Hag did the costumes for Fitzfarris's planned biblical tableaux, while he rehearsed in their rôles the three girls, plus two Slovaks he had conscripted besides. With Zanni's help, he also sketched out the lettering for a signboard, and got the Chinese painter to do it "artistically" for him.

When the circus set up in the castle-topped town of Avezzano, Fitz did not immediately display that sign, and during his sideshow presentation at intermission he did not, this time, invite any doctors to an intimate showing of the mummy. Instead, having concluded the sideshow, he announced in words again provided by Zanni:

"After the main show, there will be presented, in the smaller pavilion you see yonder, for the modest entrance fee of just ten lire, a special educational performance for gentlemen only. You will see and be thrilled by a vivid tableau taken directly from the Holy Bible. It unfortunately cannot be performed before women and children. (You gentlemen, I am sure, know the indelicate frankness of certain parts of the Good Book.) This educational show must be discreetly and privately presented *only* to those adult male students of the Bible who will not be shocked or scandalized by seeing the Holy Scriptures . . . ahem . . . laid bare."

Immediately after the closing spec, Clover Lee, Sunday and Monday ran to change in the dressing wagon—the two Slovaks had only to shed their working overalls, as they were wearing the basics of their costumes underneath—and then to Fitz's annex, where they all ducked inside under an unpegged piece of canvas at the back.

Florian and Edge came sauntering out of the chapiteau, and Edge said, "Good God, will you look at that?" He pointed to the mob of men besieging the annex tent, where Fitzfarris was feverishly selling tickets. There evidently were as many Bible students in Avezzano as there had been physicians and surgeons elsewhere. These all were elbowing each other to crowd through the tent's front flap under the now prominently displayed signboard:

SPETTACULI BIBLICHI
E SCOLASTICHI
I - La CONCUPISCENZA di *David* e *Bathsheba*
II - Il *Stuprato* di LOT per sue FIGLIE

When Edge and Florian also squeezed inside the top, Fitzfarris turned away all the other men still clamoring and waving their money—assuring them that tickets for the second tableau would go on sale as soon as the first Bible study session was concluded. The small tent was packed chockablock already, except at its far end, where hung a drab piece of spare canvas for a curtain. Now Fitz pulled a string that slid the curtain aside, disclosing an elevated wooden platform. Behind it, on the inside of the tent canvas itself, the Chinese artist had painted his Oriental notion of the landscape of Israel. At the same moment, one of the conscripted roustabouts invisible "offstage" began playing on the accordion his Slovak notion of what David, King of the Israelites, would have played on his harp.

The first tableau commenced, but it was not really a tableau, for there was some action to it. There climbed upon the platform the other Slovak, clad in a silver-painted pasteboard breastplate and a pleated short skirt, below which his legs were bare and hairy. Next Clover Lee appeared, clad in a short frock of almost transparent gauze. While those two nuzzled and pawed each other, simulating a fond leavetaking, Fitzfarris began reciting in Italian below the platform:

"The men of the city went out to fight against Joab. And, by the treachery of David the King, Uriah the Hittite departed from his wife Bathsheba." The armored Uriah retired from the platform, leaving Bathsheba in throes of exaggerated grief. There was a brief interruption of the music as, out of sight, its player relinquished the accordion to Uriah the Hittite, and himself climbed onto the platform, wearing a short-skirted chiton, hairy legs and a gilt pasteboard crown.

As the music resumed, Bathsheba recovered and began making gestures of scrubbing her blonde-tufted underarms. "And it came to pass," intoned Fitzfarris, "that David, from his roof, saw a woman washing herself." The Slovak David made his eyes bug out at her. "And she came in unto him, and he lay with her." David and Bathsheba lunged together, and embraced, and slavered over one another, as Fitz slowly pulled his string and the canvas curtain slowly obliterated the scene. "But the thing that David had done displeased the Lord."

It had not at all displeased the crowd of Bible students. They all shouted lusty encouragements and bawdy suggestions to the illicit lovers as the curtain closed entirely.

Florian and Edge, at the rear of the audience, threw open the front-door flap of canvas, and they were the first out. Most of the rest of the crowd exited only as far as where Fitz had reappeared, so they could each throw him ten more lire to see the second tableau. That caused some squabbling with the turned-away patrons who had impatiently waited outside, but Edge and Florian left Fitzfarris to deal with that. They went around to the back of the top to intercept Clover Lee as she slid out from under the sidewall.

"Er...Clover Lee, my dear," said Florian. "Since the departure of your mother, I consider myself as being in loco parentis. And I would be remiss in that duty if I did not express my mixed feelings about your appearing in such a *raw* rawhide exhibition."

Clover Lee giggled. "I don't mind showing myself. It's even kind of exciting, to feel all the heavy breathing going on in there, and knowing none of them can get near me. Except that hairy Slovak. You might tell Sir John—no, I'll tell him myself—to make his damned David stop drooling on my boobies."

She skipped blithely off toward the dressing wagon, and Florian and Edge shrugged at one another.

"Well," said Florian. "No hope of squeezing back in there to see what Sir John has put the Simms kids up to. We'll have to wait until tonight."

"Maybe longer than that," said Edge, looking up at the low gray clouds from which snow was beginning softly to fall. "Do you reckon Fitz has offended the Almighty?"

The snow came only in fitful flurries during the rest of the day and did not prevent the people of Avezzano from making the nighttime house another sfondone. But Florian kept sticking his head outside the chapiteau during the first half of the program and finding the snowfall heavier each time. Edge kept a roustabout posted up on the trapeze rig, to alert him if the snow should drift in upon it. It did not, and Maurice and Paprika went through their performance without mishap. Theirs was the closing act before intermission, but Florian informed the audience that, since the snow was quite thick on the ground outside, he would suggest that they keep their seats. So, while Magpie Maggie Hag circulated among the stands, doing her predictions for pregnant women, a disgruntled Fitzfarris had to display his Tattooed Man self, his White African Pygmies, his Night Children and his Egyptian Princess from the middle of the pista—where he could work neither his Little Miss Mitten swazzle sale nor his mouse game.

The second half of the program also went without incident, including— when the lookout crewman reported it safe—Autumn's tightrope performance that closed the show. But before the troupe could complete a single circuit of the "Marcia Reale" closing spec, many of the jossers were already marching for the front door, and all the rest soon followed, and everybody went running for home or for carriages and wagons, not one of them lingering to attend the annex's Spettaculi Biblichi.

"Shit," said Fitzfarris, glaring out from under the marquee.

"No, that's snow," Edge said humorously, and he turned to Dai Goesle. "The body heat of the crowd kept the snow from accumulating on the chapiteau, Canvasmaster. But now that they're gone, what do we do?"

"No problem," said Stitches. "Look you, I will set a couple of Peggy's bales of hay on a slow burn in here, and leave a couple of my men to tend them through the night. That will keep the canvas clean and dry."

There was no snow falling next day, but the town streets and the circus tober were so slushy and muddy that Florian gave orders for immediate teardown. However, the Florilegium—and most particularly Fitzfarris—had no better luck at the next town, Sora. It was bad enough that Sora was a paper-mill town, as nauseously stinking as Baltimore had been, but no sooner had the afternoon show begun than a drenching rain began to fall. Then a wind began to blow. Then both rain and wind got fiercer. Between the noise of the elements and the distressed flapping and booming of the chapiteau canvas, even Florian's bellowed introductions of the acts were overwhelmed.

Edge had again posted a roustabout in the peak and, long before Maurice and Paprika were scheduled to go on, that Slovak descended from his perch to report that the trapeze rig was soaking wet and so was he. Edge put out the word to the company that both the trapeze and tightrope acts were to be canceled, and that everyone else should stretch his, her or their act to fill. Meanwhile, Florian herded half a dozen crewmen out into the howling storm. He directed them in hauling all the heaviest circus wagons to the windward side of the chapiteau, and rigging extra guy lines from the canvas to those wagons.

"At least we won't have to fear a blowdown," he informed Edge when he returned, sodden and dripping. "Not unless the storm gets a lot worse."

"Couldn't make much difference," said Edge. "The people are already pretty damned damp from the water blowing in under the eaves and down from the bail-ring openings."

Damp or not, the audience chose to remain inside during the intermission, as Florian recommended. And so Magpie Maggie Hag and Fitzfarris again had to do their stints indoors. Later, after the closing spec, Florian made another announcement to the crowd: that the storm appeared to be slackening, and that all who wished to wait until it stopped entirely could remain in the chapiteau and be entertained—at no extra charge—by a concert of "canti spirituale" performed by Genuine American Negroes.

"The Happy Hottentots, signore e signori—Gli Ottentotti Felici!"

There came into the pista Sunday, Monday, Ali Baba and Abdullah, all of whom had hastily changed into street clothes. They sang, and quite sweetly, a long medley of "Sometimes I Feel Like a Motherless Chile," "Joshua Fit de Battle ob Jericho" and the like, accompanied pianissimo by the band—pianissimo because Boom-Boom Beck had not much rehearsed his windjammers in this music. Meanwhile, Fitzfarris sulked and fumed at the repeated cancellations of *all* his money-making innovations.

It was not until the Florilegium pitched in Cassino—a town that seemed to cower under the massive, majestic Benedictine abbey on the mountain overlooking it—that Fitzfarris was able to resume his annex show. Florian and Edge were too busy with other matters to attend the tableaux presented after the first circus performance. But after the nighttime show, when just about every man in the audience flocked to the smaller top, Florian and Edge made sure to get themselves standing room for "The Ravishment of Lot by His Daughters."

"And it came to pass," Fitz recited, "when God destroyed the cities of Sodom and Gomorrah, that he sent Lot out of the midst of the overthrow."

The offstage accordion started wailing a Slovak notion of the orgiastic music that would have been a staple in Sodom and Gomorrah. The canvas curtain opened, revealing the other Slovak, wearing a shapeless burlap robe, carrying over one shoulder a burlap bag. "And Lot went up and dwelt in the mountain, and his two daughters with him."

Sunday and Monday appeared on the platform, wearing diaphanous, all but all-revealing frocks, and conspiratorially put their heads together. "The firstborn said unto the younger: Come, let us make our father drink wine." Lot produced from his bag a bottle of grappa, and swigged from it, and reeled about the platform, and fell supine with a crash.

"And the firstborn went in and lay with her father." Sunday lay down only chastely beside Lot, but the fact that Monday looked on with a gloating expression and suggestively chafed her thighs together could have made the jossers imagine that they were watching a most indecent coupling there on the platform floor.

After a moment, Sunday crept away again, Lot awoke and arose and staggered about. Fitzfarris spoke again, "The firstborn said: Let us make him drink wine this night also." Lot brought out his grappa once more, and drank heavily, and fell down. "Go thou in, and lie with him." Sunday gently shoved her sister down beside Lot, and Monday lay not quite so chastely; she was perceptibly writhing and rubbing her legs together. The Sodom-Gomorrah accordion music went crescendo, and the curtain began edging across the scene, as Fitzfarris bawled his last line—"Thus were both the daughters of Lot with child by their father!" The assembled Bible students exploded in hurrahs and shouts of "Ha coglioni duri, questo padre!" and "Lui sì è rizzato!"

But those cries were drowned by a louder, very angry bellow of "Desistiate! Infedeli!" The jossers all turned and craned to see the source of that—and quailed when they did. Two men who had been wearing heavy overcoats, although the evening was mild, now flung those open to display their cassocks underneath, as they went on roaring in outrage, "Scandalo! Dileggio! Putridità!"

"Damnation," growled Florian. "I should have foreseen something like this, right here in Saint Benedict's bailiwick."

The men in the tent, averting their faces, poured fearfully outdoors and away, leaving only the two irate priests, Florian, Edge and the bewildered-looking Fitzfarris.

"What's eating these birds?" he asked, as they continued to shake their fists and shout invective at him.

"I fear, Sir John," said Florian, "that we may be in trouble." He spoke in Italian to the two, and gamely introduced himself as the circus's owner, therefore the party to blame. That did not appear to mollify the padres, still fizzing and sputtering. "It seems," Florian translated to Fitzfarris, "the word of your show spread far and wide since this afternoon. The abbot-bishop delegated these two functionaries to come and investigate. They didn't much like what they found. They predict that the bishop will like it even less."

"Hell," said Fitz. "What can a bunch of preachers do to us?"

"Here in Italy, the Inquisition still wields considerable authority," said Florian. "I might also mention a unique method of execution once practiced here. A condemned man had his abdomen slit, his intestines drawn out and slowly cranked around a wheel, while he still lived and looked on."

Fitzfarris gulped, and said, "Oh, come on, now...Florian, tell them I was only quoting from the Bible. Well, I was, wasn't I? Or did that Zanni pull some kind of dirty trick in his translation?"

"No, you read aright," said Florian, and he conversed briefly with the seething clerics. "Now they're quoting, too—from Shakespeare—that the Devil can cite Scripture to his own purpose."

"This is a lot of balls," said Edge. "These two busybodies waited until they'd seen all there was to see before they started to fuss."

"Hush up, Zachary," said Florian. "The two of you clear out of here. I've taken responsibility, so I'll take any castigation that's coming. Go on, get out."

They went, but they stayed close by, in case Florian needed rescue—or his entrails replaced. After some time, they saw the two priests emerge from the annex into the light of the torches outside it. They clapped on their pileus caps and strode briskly off the tober, their cassocks and overcoats flapping. A moment later, Florian also came out, evidently unscathed.

"Well, what happened?" Fitzfarris asked.

"Oh, I made a contribution to the diocesan charity fund."

"That's *all*?" said Edge. "That got us off the hook? Heresy, blasphemy, whatever the hell it was?"

"The thing is," said Florian, "they spotted the trace of bay in the complexion of the Simms girls, and correctly surmised that they are mulattoes."

Fitz was staggered. "You mean those dago buck-nuns complained about *miscegenation*? Two pretty buffalo gals frolicking with a *Slovak*?"

"Oh, the padres didn't so much mind seeing a white man cavorting with two mulattoes. Their objection was more theological than moral."

"What?"

"You see, those sons that Lot begat on his daughters were Ammon and Moab. Much later, among King Solomon's wives were Ammonite and Moabite women, descendants of that episode on the mountain, and it is established that Saint Joseph was lineally descended from Solomon. The Church theologians are bothered enough by the possibility that Jesus's mother's husband could have been a product of that incestuous coupling ages before. And now—when you introduce a couple of high-yellow girls into your reconstruction of the epic—you appear to be smearing the Holy Family with a tar brush besides."

"I'll be damned."

"Maybe not. If you'll promise not to show the Lot and Daughters tableau again while we're here in Cassino, the good fathers have promised they'll pray for you."

"I'd like to tell the good fathers one thing," Fitz said sourly. "Let them pray into one hand and piss into the other, and see which fills up faster."

As the Florilegium moved on from town to town, Stitches Goesle and Boom-Boom Beck, in their free time, continued to make improvements in their departments of the establishment. Beck somewhere found and purchased a snare drum and a tenor drum, and conscripted another Slovak into the band to play them, for they served better than Hannibal's big bass drum to sound a suspenseful roll during a thrill act or a brisk rataplan during clownish knockabouts. Goesle, for his part, built a pair of what the longtime circus folk called donnickers, and he designed them to be portable—three walls and a hinged door, enclosing a single-hole bench, the whole of which could be collapsed flat for transporting—and had the Chinese artist paint "Uomini" on one door, "Donne" on the other. At every new tober, as soon as the tents were set up, he put roustabouts to digging pits at a suitable distance, over which to set the two privies.

The Florilegium had been only briefly and not seriously incommoded by the mild mid-Italy winter and, as the circus traveled southward from those wintertime latitudes, springtime was moving northward from the Mediterranean. The two met in the town of Caserta, where every flowering plant was in bud, and the plane trees lining the long, broad avenue leading to the old Royal Palace were already in brilliant green leaf. It was there at the avenue that Florian, after his ride on ahead, met the circus, to report:

"The Caserta authorities will have none of us. They decline to grant us a tober in the town."

Edge said, "Do you mean they already got wind of Fitz's hootchy-cootchy? Are we going to be banned everywhere from now on?"

"If that is so," said Autumn, "why are you grinning, Florian?"

"Because King Victor Emmanuel just happens to be temporarily in residence here at La Reggia"—he gestured to the avenue and the vast, colonnaded palace visible at the far end of it—"instead of in Firenze or his palace at San Rossore. And the king's authority supersedes the local. When I called at the municipio, I was referred to a court steward."

"My God," said Edge. "Has even the *king* heard of the rawhide?"

"If he has, he'll want to see it," said Florian. "I won't tease you any longer. I am smiling because we are moving up in the world." He raised his voice to the rest of the train. "Gather around, everybody!" When all the principals of the company had assembled, he explained, "It seems that King Victor Emmanuel has a passion for circuses, but has never seen an American one. His Majesty invites us to pitch in the park of La Reggia here, and to stage a command performance for him and his court."

There were various exclamations, Clover Lee's the loudest: "At last! Counts and dukes!"

"Even a crown prince, my child," said Florian. "The king is accompanied by his son Umberto. Very well, everybody, let us first oblige His Majesty by making parade as we go up the avenue."

So they did, and the day was warm enough for all the troupers to strip down to their pista costumes, and they all did their most graceful postures and movements, and the band played its lustiest. As they got close to the palace, some French doors opened in an upper story, and a number of uniformed, gold-braided and bemedaled figures emerged onto a balcony to watch. At that, Beck broke off whatever music his band was playing, to roar out "La Marcia Reale"—and all the men on the balcony doffed their cockaded hats.

A pair of palace flunkies in antique wigs and knee breeches trotted out of a ground-level door to direct the train into the two-mile-long park. The servants ran on ahead and finally stopped to indicate that the circus was to pitch on a grassy lawn among fountains, fishponds, temples and statuary. As the roustabouts began unloading the wagons and preparing to set up, Florian told Beck:

"The command performance will take place tomorrow, at whatever hour best suits the court's convenience. After tomorrow, His Majesty will graciously allow the local town and country folk into his park for our subsequent performances. Meanwhile, Chief Beck, I don't know if it is possible to find chemicals for the balloon's generator in a town this size. But why don't you hasten into Caserta and see what you can do?"

"Ja wohl," Beck said, and began to bellow at his Slovaks.

"It looks like some nabob is paying us a visit already," said Autumn, drawing Florian's attention to the royally carved and ornamented gold-and-white coach which just then drew up at the edge of the tober area.

Two guardsmen first alighted, then handed down from the coach a short, plump, bluff-featured man in an elegant military uniform, with the big rosette of the Order of Annunziata above rows of medal ribbons. He was bald, even of eyebrows, from his forehead to the caput of his head, but he compensated for that with an imperial beard and thick, upturned mustaches that extended like a frame far on either side of his face.

"Bless my soul, it's His Majesty himself," said Florian. "Clear out, everybody. Colonel Ramrod, you stay to welcome him with me. And you, Miss Auburn, to interpret for Zachary."

The other troupers dispersed about their business—all but Clover Lee, who retired only to a respectful distance, and there began practicing flip-flops and cartwheels to display her legs and under parts to best advantage. His Majesty seemed to appreciate that, for his porcine little eyes were on her even while Florian and Edge were bowing and Autumn curtsying to him, and Florian murmuring, "Benvenuto, Maestà."

The king shifted his connoisseurial gaze to Autumn, as Florian introduced her and Edge. Then the four of them together, followed closely and watchfully by the guardsmen, strolled to where the roustabouts were laying out the tent poles.

"The king says," Autumn translated to Edge in an undertone, "that he is interested in the mechanics of our trade. Because, he says, the King of Prussia has personally observed the methods by which circuses move from place to place, and has applied some of those methods to his Prussian Army. The king thinks his own army might learn something from the technicalities of circus stowage and transport and general efficiency."

When Hannibal commanded the elephant to haul upright the first center pole, Florian waggishly told Victor Emmanuel, "Regard, Your Majesty—that one we call the *king* pole. As Your Majesty is to your kingdom, so is the king pole the mainstay of our chapiteau. Because, when it is erect, it becomes the fulcrum that enables the levering upright of the second center pole..."

The king smiled, making his mustache tips almost meet between his eyes, and spoke at length.

"He is admiring big Peggy's obedience and skill," Autumn told Edge. "He says he is a lover of animals. He is putting together the first zoölogical garden Italy has ever had. And he is especially proud of having acquired a whole herd of Australian kangaroos."

When the chapiteau's roof canvas was hauled up by its bail rings to the peaks of the two center poles—the roustabouts doing the heeby-weeby chant—the king asked something of Florian, who immediately started scribbling with his mason's pencil on a piece of paper.

"His Majesty asked for the words of that chanty," Autumn told Edge, and laughed quietly. "Perhaps he thinks that is the secret of circus and Prussian efficiency. It is amusing to imagine the whole Italian Army marching off to battle in cadence to 'Heeby-weeby-Maggie-*moo*-long...'"

At any rate, the king's curiosity seemed satisfied. He took the paper and parted from Florian, Edge and Autumn, after many mutual bows and compliments, returned to his coach, detailed two liveried attendants to remain on the scene, and was driven away.

"His Majesty requests that our performance be at three o'clock tomorrow afternoon," said Florian, flushed with pride and pleasure. "These equerries are to provide anything we might need. And at every mealtime while we are here, they will escort us to one of the palace's dining rooms, and the Slovaks, Chinks and blacks to the kitchens."

Both of the equerries hovered about until the crew erected the seats in the chapiteau. Then the two men conferred, and one of them set off at a run toward the palace. Shortly afterward, a number of wagons and servants came through the park bearing more suitable seating.

Florian said, "I should have realized that a royal court can't be expected to sit on planks. Chief Goesle, please remove those foremost benches."

That was done, and in their place the servants set a tremendous high-backed thronelike armchair, then, on both sides of and behind it, some dozens of exquisitely gilded and tapestry-upholstered chairs. Meanwhile, the crew and artistes completed what work they had to do, saw to their animals, laid out props for the next day, then washed themselves and dressed in their best civilian clothes. Leaving only Aleksandr Banat, who insisted that a circus needed a watchman even when it was installed in a royal park, the rest of the company rode in the wagons with the servants back to the palace and were shown, according to their station, to either dining room or kitchen.

The dining table provided for the artistes and crew chiefs was ablaze with candlelight from chandeliers and candelabra, shining on porcelain, crystal, silver and damask. There was a footman behind every chair, and a constant procession of other servants—commanded by a maggiordomo—bearing tureens of various soups, platters of many meats, bowls of pasta and vegetables, ice-filled buckets in which reposed bottles of wine, still and sparkling, white, rosé and red.

Zanni Bonvecino exchanged some banter with the servants—they seemed slightly distressed by the familiarity—just long enough to assure himself that none of them except the maggiordomo comprehended the occasional English word he addressed to them. Then, when the maggiordomo was briefly out of the room, Zanni leaned across the table to say confidentially to Clover Lee:

"I would strongly recommend, signorina, that you be careful how you comport yourself when our royal host is about."

"I beg your pardon?" she said stiffly.

"He is a notorious womanizer, and not at all subtle or discreet about it."

"Oh, tut," Paprika put in. "Sheer gossip. They say that about every royal male."

"Well, ten or so years ago," said Zanni, "when he was merely King of Sardinia and came to visit Paris, I was present—only as a singer, of course—at a gala given for him by the emperor and empress. I personally heard him commit two frightful breaches of manners. On being introduced to a certain lady of the French nobility, he announced quite loudly that he already knew her well, having once bedded her in Torino. Later, when we entertainers were preparing to perform, he asked the Empress Eugénie, again in no hushed voice, whether it was true, as he had heard, that in France the female dancers never wore—er—undercoverings. If so, he said, then France would be absolute heaven for him. Needless to say, he has not been invited back to Paris since then."

After dinner, the troupers only slowly made their way to the palace's outside doors. By ones and twos and groups, they idled to traverse and admire as many rooms as possible of the reputed twelve hundred in the palace. They did not venture above the ground floor, but there every room was of museum opulence and preservation: all gold and marble and velvet and monumental staircases and priceless antique furnishings and immense hanging tapestries and ceilings clustered with stucco putti and curlicues. Clover Lee murmured dreamily, "I should not mind living here..."

Back at the tober, they discovered that Beck and his assistants had returned from town—and by some magic or miracle or sheer Bavarian tenacity, he *had* procured sufficient carboys of acid and barrels of iron filings, and was setting everything out in readiness for the balloon's inflation on the morrow.

Well before three o'clock the next afternoon, the *Saratoga* was towering impressively above the highest trees in the Reggia park, the artistes were all in readiness and even the windjammers had finished their interminable tuning up. But the king and court exercised the royal prerogative of being three-quarters of an hour late, arriving in a train of elegant coaches, broughams, clarences and landaus drawn by matched teams of horses. Banat directed his fellow Slovaks in assisting the guests from the carriages and—after they had all exclaimed at the unexpected sight of the *Saratoga*—escorting them to the chapiteau marquee. From there, Florian and Colonel Ramrod ceremoniously ushered them to their seats—the king to the thronelike big chair, and to the others the handsome young Crown Prince Umberto, various elderly or middle-aged duce and conti and marchesi, plus officers of the army and of the royal household, and many of their wives, daughters and consorts, the men and women alike dressed as richly as if for a court ball. There were some forty people in all, the smallest audience the Florilegium had ever played to—but every artiste performed to perfection.

As he did everywhere, Zanni the toby made his verbal clowning suit the place and occasion—*not* referring to any of the present patrons, but to "Sophie's boy." Victor Emmanuel laughed long and loudly, and so did his retinue, for Zanni was poking fun at the king's own bête noire, the Emperor Franz Joseph of Austria and his meddlesome mother, the Dowager Empress Sophia.

The Quakemaker risked rupturing himself, showing his feats of strength with the cannonballs, and of endurance when his Percheron repeatedly plodded over him, but he still managed to "win" in the tug-of-war with Brutus. Even the Chinese antipodists seemed to realize the importance of this occasion, and did upside-down exploits more impossible-seeming than any they had ever done before. Clover Lee did her rosinback act with consummate grace, performing her most spectacular tricks directly in front of the chair of the young, slim, smiling Prince Umberto. Monday and Thunder were picture-perfect in their haute école fancy stepping. The Pete Jenkins flabbergasted this august audience as much as it had done any crowd of yokels, and, after the intrusive drunk became Maurice LeVie, he and Paprika became a faultless dazzle of blue and orange on the trapezes.

For a wonder, thought Edge, as the show proceeded, none of the animals— dogs, horses, lion or elephant—discourteously shat in the pista. It was customary to do what Florian called "rearing" the animals before any major performance, meaning to give them a mild purge and an opportunity to evacuate themselves before the show, but it did not always suffice. On this occasion, however, none of the beasts even made water. At intermission, Magpie Maggie Hag read the palms of several of the court ladies, and they tittered with delight, for she made only the most glowing predictions. Sir John presented himself and his other freaks close to the seats, then entertained the guests with Little Miss Mitten, then let the gentlemen take a fling at his mouse game, punctiliously paying off the winners and, at the end, generously returning all the money of the losers.

During the second half of the program, Barnacle Bill was uncharacteristically untipsy, and Maximus got into the spirit of the occasion, growling and clawing bloodthirstily but performing as tamely and willingly as a dog. When the real dogs came on, Pavlo Smodlaka introduced a new turn. He borrowed the band's accordion and played a simple tune while the terriers singly, in twos, or all three, yapped in various tones to provide a passably harmonious "singing." During the shootist act, Colonel Ramrod missed not a shot, and at the last one, into Sunday's teeth, she did a wonderfully realistic backward jolt.

Abdullah the Hindu juggled an incredible simultaneous assortment of eggs, lighted candles, a bottle of wine and some horseshoes. Then, nonchalantly juggling several of those things with only one hand, he extended his other to the seats, offering to include whatever else he might be given. The *king himself* unsheathed and gave Abdullah his jewel-hilted sword. Unfazed, Abdullah added it to his blur of flying things, making the sword twirl and flash as it flew, finally catching it in his teeth, like a pirate. Buckskin Billy rode a voltige that should have broken every bone in his body, concluding with the "Saint Petersburg Courier," one foot on each of two wide-apart horses, the other horses galloping one by one between his legs. Last, Autumn Auburn gracefully did on the narrow, high tightrope the twirls and pirouettes and splits and back flips that other performers had done on solid, safe ground or on the broad backs of horses. Then the closing Grand Promenade was done with as much pomp as the opening one had been, and as if it were playing to a tent-bulging throng of people.

After their polite and sparse but appreciative applause, the king and his courtiers got up from their chairs to come to the pista and mingle democratically with the players and praise their performances and—with Florian or Zanni or Autumn translating where necessary—ask questions about their art and their way of life. Most of the questioners were eager to know the tricks the artistes *must* employ to do some of the apparently impossible things they did. But most of the artistes answered truthfully that they used no tricks, only experience and practice. However, when Prince Umberto and some other army officers inspected Colonel Ramrod's revolver and carbine, and congratulated him on his awesome marksmanship, Edge said nothing about the use of bird shot or blank charges for some of his effects. Florian watched with amusement as a fat, white-haired duchessa playfully squeezed the Quakemaker's bulging biceps. Then she asked him, in stilted English, what sort of companion he considered the best for the road.

Yount pondered, then said, "A stiff dose of constipation, ma'am. So you don't have to stop and tarry too often."

The dowager rocked, so Florian quickly and loudly inquired if any of the guests would be pleased to visit the annex tent and view Sir John's version of scenes from the Bible—adding that only the gentlemen would be likely to enjoy them to the fullest. King Victor Emmanuel leered and remarked that, while the ladies of his court might have forgotten much of the Bible since their catechism days, he would wager they could quote word for word from such smutty "backstairs books" as *Eveline* and *Schwester Monika*. The ladies, young and old, all tittered and put up their fans before their faces, but did not contradict him. So the whole court trooped outside and into the smaller top, and Fitz boldly launched into his recital.

Some while later, when both tableaux were done and the audience emerged from the tent, the men and women alike were smiling salaciously, and none of the women was being carried in a faint. Fitzfarris came out last, and Florian was waiting, to say, "Well?"

"Well, that fat, white-haired old bat invited me to dine privately with her tonight."

"That old bat is the Duchessa da Brisighella."

"And Clover Lee is invited to do the same with Prince Umberto. If that's all right with you, Governor."

Florian grimaced. "Clover Lee has told me flatly that she needs and wants no protecting. You might, though, Sir John."

"Ah, well. I told you once that I had looked forward to meeting titled Europeans. I can hardly repulse a duchess, however repulsive she is. But even if I'm profaning my chastity, by damn, I've regained my artistic integrity. I'm going to have our Chink artist add an imprimatur to my signboard. 'As presented at the Court of His Majesty Victor Emmanuel II.' I defy any more meddlers to interfere with my Bible studies—at least as long as we're in the Kingdom of Italy."

The balloon ascension was the closing spectacle of the afternoon. It drew awed and admiring cries from the gathered royalty—and from others besides. Though the town of Caserta was some way distant, the people in the park could hear shouts and oaths from that direction, and the hoofbeats and rumbling wheels of at least one runaway horse and wagon. When Rouleau brought the *Saratoga* down again—and again with surprising accuracy, so the ground crew did not have to run far to catch its trailing rope—and was hauled to the ground and took his bows, many of the royal gentlemen pounded him on the back, and many of the ladies caressed him more gently.

Then the courtiers made their adieux personally to each and every member of the company, even to those roustabouts in evidence. Servants now came from the carriages, their arms laden, and the king himself presented every female artiste with a huge bouquet of hothouse carnations and a fine, fringed silk shawl embroidered with a crown. To each man—even Hannibal and the three Chinese—he gave a silver cigarette case engraved with the royal arms. To each of the children—Sava, Velja and Quincy—he gave a small, stuffed velvet kangaroo. Then he wished the Florilegium a capacity crowd of the common folk during its stay, and he and his retinue returned to the palace.

That night, when the troupe went to the palace for dinner, Fitzfarris and Clover Lee were conspicuously absent from the table, and one other—Monday Simms—sat silent and glum. The rest chatted and praised the provender and joked and laughed. Then, when the servants brought in platters of ortolans broiled in black butter and capers, and everybody was silently admiring the dish, Autumn suddenly raised her head and tilted it as if listening to something far off, and said wonderingly into the silence, "A clock just stopped somewhere."

Everybody, including the servants, looked at her—some uncomprehendingly, some in surprise, but Magpie Maggie Hag's look was intent and searching. The dining room's maggiordomo smiled at Autumn, said, "Signorina, it still ticks and tocks," and indicated the priceless ormolu clock on the mantel, its little pendulum busily waggling.

"No," said Autumn. "Not in here. Somewhere else."

"Signorina," the steward said patiently. "There must be two, maybe three hundred clocks in this palace."

"Nevertheless," said Autumn, "one of them stopped. I know it. Just hearing it stop gave me a twinge of earache."

The other troupers made dismissive noises and began to attack their broiled little birds. But Magpie Maggie Hag still gazed at Autumn, while the maggiordomo, to humor that guest's queer whimsy, snapped his fingers to the footmen standing at attention behind all the diners' chairs, rattled instructions in Italian, and the footmen departed the room in quickstep.

Autumn smiled her thanks to the maggiordomo and then, like the others, proceeded to eat. When they had finished the ortolans and were using their finger-bowls in preparation for the next course, Florian leaned over to say privily to Edge:

"I must impart something which His Majesty confided to me. He is preparing to make a military alliance with Prussia. I think it behooves us to turn around and head north again, if we wish to see Rome at all, and I'm sure we all do."

"I'm sure," said Edge. "But what's the hurry? I don't see the connection."

"It is rather complicated to explain," said Florian. "All of the Italian peninsula is now a united kingdom, except for the Papal State around Rome. However, on the mainland is the Italian-speaking region of Venezia, which has been held by Austria for fifty years. Victor Emmanuel—and the Venetians themselves—wish that land to become a part of Italy. Meanwhile, Prussia envisions an equally united federation of all the German-speaking peoples. That will require the conquest of Austria, among other acquisitions. A Prussian-Italian alliance almost certainly presages war against Austria, the Prussians striking from the north, the Italians through Venezia."

"So? Are you afraid they will conscript Hannibal and his elephant?"

"No. But unless we intend to spend years in Italy, we have only two means of egress to the rest of the continent. One is by ship again, God forbid. The other is through the alpine passes, and those of Venezia are the easiest. I want us to get through those passes before they are closed or under fire. If we turn north again, immediately after we close here in Caserta, we should have time to pitch for some while outside Rome—and make visits into the city—before we have to move on to Venezia and through it, in advance of the outbreak of hostilities there."

Edge said, "Well, Governor, I reckon you know best."

"And you of all people, Colonel, know that a battleground is no place for noncombatants." He sighed. "A pity, though. I had hoped to show Naples to all our company. Even more, I wanted us all to taste the sybarite life of the Amalfi coast." He sighed again. "But the old saying is 'Vedi Napoli, e poi mori.' I had rather *not* see Naples and not die. So we must simply work things out as we go along. Now that spring is upon us, we can go north again by a different route—over the highlands instead of the low—so we will at least see different scenery along the way."

When dinner was done, the artistes left the dining hall leisurely, again ambling through the splendid rooms and corridors. Gavrila Smodlaka, wandering by herself into a great, banner-hung hall, was surprised to see Clover Lee there, looking slightly disheveled and very despondent, sitting on a tread of the broad staircase. In her usual self-effacing way, Gavrila said good evening, and diffidently asked if anything was wrong.

Clover Lee looked at her, sniffled and said distantly, "Is that all there is to it?"

"Excuse. My English is not well. Is what to what?"

"Making love. Watching Prince Umberto gobble down the food and wine in a hurry, so he could tumble me onto my back, and then do a lot of shoving and bouncing and poking and sweating and hurting me. Is that all there is to it? I thought it was supposed to be an enjoyment."

"Um...well...the prince is young. Not experienced. Too eager, perhaps. Did *he* appear to enjoy?"

Clover Lee made a mouth. "He said 'grazie mille' and lit a sigaretta. Then he gave me this." She held up a small satin evening purse embroidered with the royal arms; it jingled as she did so. "There are twenty little gold coins in it."

"Scudi, those are. Twenty scudi—one hundred lire—perhaps twenty dollars American. Some men would not even have given you the thousand thanks."

"Twenty dollars. Twenty minutes. That's all it took." Clover Lee added pensively, "I wonder what my mother ever saw in men."

"But she had older men," said Gavrila. "Gospodín Zachary. Gospodín Florian. Perhaps you should, too. It makes better if the man is old and you are new."

"I think you mean young. But if a young man is too eager, an old man wouldn't be eager at all."

"If you think such, gospodjica, you will never know anything about making love. The older man, less greedy for his own pleasure, gives most pleasure to the woman. Believe me or do not, but a man too old even to use his húy—excuse the word—can delight a woman to onesvesti. How would you say? To swooning, to delirium."

"To hell with that," said Clover Lee. "Let the men do the swooning, and let them pay for it. From now on, my female parts will be just a commodity for sale or trade, and on my terms. This time, for just twenty minutes, I got to play Crown Princess Clover Lee..."

"Tikh, little one. Someday you will meet someone to whom you will want to *give* yourself. Come now, walk with me, back to the tober."

Clover Lee got slowly to her feet. "It hurts some—to walk."

"Unfortunate it is," said Gavrila, as if she knew whereof she spoke, "a large part of love is the hurting of it."

"Then you can bet that I'll peddle my love for a higher price than twenty scudi a hurt." Clover Lee laughed a mirthless laugh. "And when I *give* myself, it'll be for a title that lasts longer than twenty minutes."

Meanwhile, the dining hall's maggiordomo had hurried to catch up with the main group of sightseeing troupers. Looking as astonished as his professional dignity would permit, he came to Autumn and announced:

"The signorina has an exceptional sense of hearing. One of the footmen I sent searching has just returned and informed me that a timepiece *had* stopped, sì, just about the time the signorina mentioned that occurrence. A girandole clock in the western Tapestry Room. No mystery about it; evidently the palace orologiaio simply neglected to wind that one." He paused. "What *is* remarkable —the clock is two floors above and a hundred paces west of the dining hall where the signorina was seated."

Autumn laughed, a trifle unsteadily, and said, "Oh, well. I hope I haven't cost the clock man a reprimand."

"We'd all best be careful," Yount said jovially, "how we whisper secrets anywhere around this little lady." And the matter was dismissed, but Magpie Maggie Hag continued to look sidelong at Autumn from time to time.

8

THE FLORILEGIUM proceeded east from Caserta, a two-day run to Benevento. As they came into the town's outskirts, Edge and Autumn, in the lead, were keeping a lookout for Florian, when they found themselves catching up to another, even slower-moving procession.

"It's a funeral cortège," said Autumn. "Don't try to go around it. Decency requires that we trudge along with it. And from the number of carriages and black plumes, I'd say the deceased must have been somebody important. Benevento might look more kindly on us if we pay our respects, as well."

So the circus train, however bizarre an addition it made to the cortège, went along behind it and even turned when it did, into a cemetery. Edge pulled up some distance from where the black hearse and flower carts and mourners' carriages did, outside an impressive mausoleum bedizened with stone angels. Edge and Autumn and all the rest of the company got down from their wagons and vans, and stood with bowed heads while several priests and acolytes went through the lengthy ritual. Then the pallbearers removed a bronze coffin from the hearse and bore it into the mausoleum. After a while, they came out, but the chief pallbearer among them turned and shouted a question in through the open door: "Vostra Altezza non commanda niente?" Not surprisingly, he got no reply from the crypt, so he turned to the clerics and mourners and called, "Tornate a casa. Sua Altezza non commanda niente."

"He says everybody can depart," Autumn translated. "His Highness, whoever he was, has nothing further to command."

So the company hastily climbed back into and onto the circus train, and Edge hurried to lead it out of the cemetery ahead of the cortège, and resumed the road at a brisk trot. They found Florian waiting as usual, but this time with his big tin watch in his hand. "You had me worried," he said. "I'm no Maggie Hag—and *she* hasn't lately dukkered anything bad that I know of—but one could say that this town is replete with omens."

"With a name like Benevento?" said Edge. "I'm lame in Italian, but I'd read that as meaning 'fair wind.'"

"However, that was not always its name. It was first founded, away back in B. C., by a tribe that took refuge here after being trounced by the Romans—so they called it aptly Maleventum, for the ill wind that blew them here. It wasn't until some centuries later that the Romans took over the town and superstitiously changed the name to the exact contrary."

But nothing at all bad happened to the Florilegium in Benevento. And nothing worse than an occasional wheel slipping its rim or a bit of harness breaking happened to the circus train during its subsequent climb up into the Monti del Matese ranges of the Apennines, where it stopped to perform for a day or two in any town along the way that promised a profitable attendance. No real trouble occurred until they were high on a twisty, rutted, rocky road between two mountain towns: Castel di Sangro behind them, Roccaraso somewhere ahead.

"Those names sound ominous to me, Mr. Florian," said Sunday Simms, who was today riding beside him on the rockaway. "Castle of Blood. Razor Rock."

"You are getting your Italian slightly corrupted by your French, my dear," he said. "Sangro is merely the name of that river down in the ravine beside us. Castel di Sangro is just Castle on the Sangro. And Roccaraso means only Cut Rock. Probably a cliff or a mountain cleft—oh, *damn!*"

He reined Snowball to a sudden stop, and the rest of the train behind him had to stop so abruptly that some of the horses reared in protest. Just ahead of the train, the road swerved sharply around a shoulder of the mountain. Out from the shrubbery there, three men had stepped into the road, holding firearms at the ready, and the biggest of the men was holding up a hand, palm outward.

"Alto là!" he shouted. "Siamo briganti!"

They were beefy men, swarthy, bearded, dirty, ill-dressed and generally evil of aspect. Their extremely old flintlock shotguns, however, looked better cared for than the men, and just as wicked.

"Sit still and quiet," Florian told Sunday. "They are bandits."

"Niente affato," said another of the men, looking insulted. "Siamo briganti!"

"All right, they prefer to be called brigands," Florian told Sunday. "Just don't do anything sudden or foolish."

"State e recate!" demanded the biggest man.

"Stand and deliver," Autumn translated for Edge, on the vehicle next in line. "They don't look scholarly, but they must have read a Walter Scott novel at some time."

"This isn't funny, damn it," said Edge. "All my weapons are inside the van."

The three were now shouting: "Abbassate!" "Tutti!" "Mani in alto!"

Florian spoke to Sunday, and they climbed down from the rockaway seat, holding their hands high, as ordered. By ones and twos, all the others of the circus company got down to stand in the road, hands up and empty. The brigands waved their shotguns and barked more orders.

"They want us all to stand where they can see our hands," said Florian. "Banat, please pass that instruction to the other Slovaks." But no one could translate to the three Chinese. Though they imitated the general hands-up pose, they jabbered among themselves, as if discussing what may have looked to them like a new California peculiarity of behavior.

"Che portate?" snarled one brigand. "Togliamo lo tutto—denaro, beni, cavalli, vagoni..."

"They want everything we've got," Autumn translated. "Money, goods, the horses and wagons..."

"Goddamn it," Edge growled again in frustration.

Then everybody heard a sort of mingled whiz and flutter in the ambient air, and all three bandits suddenly fell over backward, rigidly and simultaneously, as if they were some kind of circus act themselves. As their shotguns clattered to the road, so did the fist-size rocks that had hit each of them in the head. The bandits lay still and, for a moment, everybody else stood immobilized by surprise, hands still high. Then they looked about, and there was a chorus of glad exclamations, as they saw the three Chinese each gripping with a prehensile bare foot another rock, in case a second barrage was necessary.

"Well, I *will* be goddamned!" said Edge. He hastily kicked the fallen shotguns away from the fallen bandits, then he and Yount knelt to examine the men.

"One of 'em's turned black in the face," Yount reported to Florian. "I'd reckon his skull is cracked. The other two might recover. Do you want 'em to?"

"Not until we are well along the road," said Florian. "Pitch them all into the river ravine. If any of them survives and can climb out again, maybe he'll repent and reform."

The females all shuddered and turned their backs while the bandits were disposed of. Meanwhile, Florian went and gratefully shook each Chinese by the hand, though Sunday murmured to him, "Properly, sir, you ought to shake them by the foot."

"I just wish I could speak to them. But one thing I promise. From now on, these resourceful lads will no longer be treated as Chinks. They'll have a room in a hotel whenever we do, and dine with us like white men."

Fitzfarris said, "They may have to put on shoes, to be allowed in."

"Damned if they will," Florian said staunchly. "Any hotel that refuses them entry will lose *all* our trade. And, while I'm at it, I will also demand a room and a place at table for Abdullah and Ali Baba from now on."

L'Aquila was the next city interesting enough and populous enough to keep the Florilegium for more than a couple of days. When the troupers first saw, at the city portal, the huge pink and white stone fountain with its ninety-nine faces spouting water into its immense basin and heard Florian tell the story—"It is said that this city came miraculously into being, with ninety-nine piazze, ninety-nine castles, ninety-nine churches and ninety-nine fountains. And at every sundown you will hear a bell in the Law Court tower toll ninety-nine times"—they all clamored to spend time enough in L'Aquila so that they could see all those marvels.

As soon as the circus was set up on its assigned tober there, Beck and Goesle came to Florian with the latest innovation they had produced between them.

"Regard, Herr Gouverneur," said Beck, holding out to him a handful of crumbly, pebbly, gray-white substance. "What would you call that?"

"Plain old lime, isn't it? The same stuff you use in your generator's cooling machine, Carl? What you pour in the donnikers, Dai?"

"Kalk it is, ja," said Beck. "Calcium. But a kind new to me. At a Fabrik in the last town, it was given to me. Carburetted calcium, it is called."

"And why are you showing it to me, gentlemen?"

"Because if water on this karburiert Kalk is poured, a gas it makes. Ethine gas, it is called."

"Boom-Boom has built this tank apparatus," said Goesle, indicating a thing that looked vaguely like a patent washing machine. "Put in that calcium stuff and some water, turn a valve and it feeds the ethine through a hose to a burner. Just by itself, the gas gives as good a light as any coal-oil lamp."

"However, Stitches on that has improved," said Beck. "A lamp he has built in which the gas flame makes incandescent a stick of *ordinary* lime and—"

"*Limelight!*" exclaimed Florian. "By damn, you fellows have been wanting it long enough, and so have I! But I thought it required all kinds of complicated equipment."

"So it does, if you are wanting an oxyhydrogen flame," said Goesle. "Which means a retort contraption that is complex and always eager to explode, besides. This ethine flame does not give quite so brilliant a limelight. But it has the advantage of being easy to produce—and safely—from the carburetted calcium that is cheap and can be procured in any fair-sized city."

"But this is magnificent!" crowed Florian. "Gentlemen, I can't thank you enough for your enterprise and ingenuity."

"We thought first to surprise you," Beck said proudly. "Not to tell you, but tonight to *show* you. However, then we thought, ach, so bright it is, it might frighten the animals or even the artistes."

"Yes," said Florian. "I will inform everyone beforehand."

"And only dim I will start the light," said Beck. "From the bandstand I will the tank and valve operate. Up gradually I will make bright the light during the come-in."

"Splendid. And you, Dai, by all means, get on with making as many more lamps as you think we should have. Including at least one for Sir John's annex."

Goesle did. Before the circus departed from L'Aquila, it was performing its nighttime shows in a blaze of pole lamps and footlights. Shining through the green and white painted canvas, the limelight added a pale-green luminosity to the orange light cast by the outside torches, so the whole tober became a beacon that drew the Aquilani like moths. Meanwhile, in one of the town's reputed ninety-nine squares, Goesle found a maker of eyeglasses, and Autumn went there with him to translate to the ottico his request for a lens much bigger than was ever used in any spectacles. The lensmaker was not taken aback; he only said, "Ah, per una lanterna magica?" and produced the item from his stock.

Goesle worked on his next lighting innovation, by trial and error, whenever he had time, while the Florilegium now moved westward, and he had his new limelight contrivance perfected in time to bedazzle the citizens of Cantalupo. It was a movable spotlight that cast a beam instead of a flood of light, and cast it as far as the very top of the chapiteau. During the performance, Goesle—wearing heavy gloves against the heat of it—could fix that specially brilliant glow on whatever artiste was performing, and thereby make less noticeable any roustabouts or other extraneous persons who had to be in the pista at the same time. He could also make the light follow every move of the galloping horses and riders, and even the hurtling trapeze artistes.

Rome was the circus's next destination. But, when the circus arrived at the nearest practical place outside the Papal State, which was Forano, that proved to be not much of a town. There was a railroad depot alongside two sets of tracks, some tool and equipment sheds, some shacks occupied by the railroad workers, and a bettola in which they drank away their spare time and lire. The station-master said the Florilegium could set up wherever it pleased—there were empty fields all around—so Florian instructed that it be pitched a good distance from the noise, smoke and sparks of passing trains. "However, there is no need to make haste in the setting up," he said. "We have all earned a breathing spell."

He called the whole company together and told them, "The stationmaster says there will be a train to Rome in half an hour, at six o'clock. All who wish— including you, Abdullah, and little Ali Baba—may get your hand luggage and accompany me there. We will take a hotel and spend the next week merely luxuriating and sightseeing about the city. Canvasmaster Goesle, Chief Engineer Beck, Crew Chief Banat, you may also come to Rome whenever you are ready. Let the roustabouts come, too—in shifts, so there will always be some on watch here. Have every man bring paper to post, plenty of it. I want to see it on every one of the seven hills of Rome. Mark on those posters that our first performance will be a week from tomorrow."

So the artistes were all in street dress and waiting on the platform when the train arrived from the north, chugging, chuffing, rattling, spewing smoke, soot and steam. Some of those waiting—the Simms children and the Chinese, who had never before been so close to such a monster—cringed away from it, flat-tening themselves against the depot wall. But the pale little Sava and Velja Smodlaka coolly stayed at the edge of the platform, as did all the others to whom railway trains were no novelty. When the doors swung open, the troupers climbed into the compartments and, when the train clattered into motion again, even the first-time riders soon got over their nervousness. Indeed, they took delight in being whisked across the landscape at such a dizzy speed. The train was making nearly thirty miles an hour—half again more distance in a single hour than the circus train ordinarily accomplished in a whole day.

Jules Rouleau had appointed himself guardian of the children, and had shep-herded them all into one compartment. He took note, with rueful amusement, that Monday Simms enjoyed the trip even more than the others, though she never looked out the window at the countryside blurring past—farmhouses, barns, haycocks, ox-drawn plows, even the occasional glimpse of the brown river Tiber. Monday simply sat with her eyes unfocused and a trembly smile on her lips, clearly because the plush-upholstered seat vibrated more pleasurably than anything she had ever before felt in contact with her phenomenally excitable under parts.

There were no more stations after Forano, and the train did not slacken its breathtaking pace the whole way to its destination. But the houses visible out-side became more numerous, with only yards or garden plots between them. Then they became clusters of houses separated only by streets and alleys. Then they became solid city blocks of soot-blackened stone and brick buildings, and crowded closer to the railway line. Less than an hour and a quarter after the troupe had boarded it, the train slowed but its noise increased, as it rumbled under an echoing, girdered glass roof, then racketed along beside a platform crowded with people dressed for travel, with railway men, porters, baggage carts, vendors hawking every imaginable sort of food, drink and curio. When the train at last juddered and jolted to a halt, Florian went along the passage from compartment to compartment, announcing, "We are here! Roma, La Città Eterna! Everybody out!"

They made their way through the crowded and noisy terminal, and came out at the edge of a piazza that was, by contrast, silent except for the sigh of a sundown breeze, and almost empty except for a waiting line of vetture for hire. Florian commandeered a sufficient number of those to carry all the troupers and their luggage, climbed into the front one and led the way to a hotel called the Eden, near the Borghese Gardens. Rome had about the same number of inhabitants as Florence, but the city was so much more open and sprawling that, to those visiting for the first time, it seemed extremely scant of both people and vehicular traffic on the streets. While the Hotel Eden's porters were carrying in the bags and the desk clerk was leafing through the conduct books, Florian bought a newspaper from the stand in the lobby, took a look at it and said, "Oh, hell."

"Something wrong, Governor?" Edge asked.

"Well, no more than I expected. King Victor Emmanuel did sign that alliance with Prussia. Just a week after Easter."

"Does that mean we cut and run? I'll round up the others before they get settled in."

"No, no. There'll be war, that is certain, but I doubt that it can start instantly. I will not deprive us all of this chance to enjoy Rome. Instead, we will cut short our stand in Forano. Rome would no doubt have given us something like three weeks of sfondone houses. But after our week of holiday, we'll give only a week of circus shows, and then move on toward the frontier. Now, let us get out of these sooty traveling clothes and dress for dinner. The Eden sets a good board."

As the company ate and drank voraciously and happily, there was sitting at another table a slender middle-aged gentleman with a very pretty girl who might have been his daughter. He waited politely until the artistes were on their coffees and liqueurs, then stood up, approached Florian and said in English:

"Forgive the intrusion, sir. But I heard you earlier, in the lobby, mention a circus. And just before dinner I saw a paper on a lamppost in the street."

"Ah, then some of my crewmen have already come to town. Good."

"So I assume, sir, that you are the Florian of that Florilegium. Perhaps I might introduce myself—a fellow showman. I am Gaetano Ricci, balletmaster, choreograph and teacher of the art."

"A pleasure, Signor Ricci. Allow me to introduce the artistes of my troupe." He took Ricci from one table to another, and the balletmaster cordially shook the hands of the men and boys—even those of the Chinese and blacks—and kissed the hands of the women and girls. When Florian presented "the Signorina Autunno Auburn, funambola staordinaria," Ricci was moved to sigh and say:

"Signorina, I only wish my stage were as narrow as your rope."

"Good heavens. Why would you wish that, signore?"

"Because then not so many people would think that dancing and acting are so easy. I should have to endure fewer damned interviews with abysmally untalented hopefuls. But here... allow me to present one who *is* talented." He led forward the young girl. "The Signorina Giuseppina Bozzacchi. Only twelve years old, but she has been training since she was five, and is now in my corps de ballet, and very soon will be una prima di tutto." The girl smiled and curtsied shyly, and a few of the male troupers dared to kiss her hand. Signor Ricci continued, "I invite you all to a rehearsal at any time, and you can see Giuseppina dance. My school is on the Via Palermo, behind the Teatro Eliseo."

"That is kind of you, signore," said Florian. "Our young ladies might well learn something to their advantage by seeing real ballet performed. In return, let me invite you and the signorina, any others of your pupils, to visit our circus next week as our guests."

After breakfast next day, Florian told the troupe, "There is one sight I wish to show you all. Some of you will have seen it before. But humor me. Then you can wander the city at will."

And he called for another train of vetture, and drove everybody to the Colosseum.

"I wanted all of you to see the birthplace of the circus," he said, as they leaned backward and stared up in awe at the three-tiered façade of stone arches. Its dignity was just slightly diminished by the many lines of laundry strung between its columns by housewives of the immediate neighborhood. "Actually, the earliest such shows took place in the Circus Maximus, down there in the valley"—he waved toward the southwest—"but nothing of that remains to be seen. The Circo Massimo had fallen into disuse by the time this Colosseum was built. The Anfiteatro Flaviano, to give it its proper name."

As he led them inside the massive structure, he went on, "Sadly, it has decayed over the past eighteen centuries. There once were slopes of boxes and seats all around this vast ellipse, for perhaps forty or fifty thousand spectators. Away up there, on what is left of the upper cornice, you can see the holes for long poles that supported an awning of cloth—more cloth than would make a hundred *Saratoga* balloons—that protected all the seats from sun or rain."

"Incidentally," added Autumn, "it was only during *circus* performances that the Roman men and women did not have to sit apart in separate sections."

"Try to envision," Florian continued, "the chariot races, the battles between wild beasts, the duels between gladiators, the contests between Christians and lions, the acrobats and jugglers performing by *hundreds*. In those times, this immense arena floor was not just packed earth, as you see it now, but polished marble—sometimes sanded to absorb the blood shed. Underneath the floor, invisible now, were the dressing rooms for the performers, the dens and ramps for the animals, the armories of the gladiators. Perhaps sometime they will be excavated and brought to view."

He gazed around as if he could see all those old-time events occurring again, and the Colosseum thronged with cheering crowds. "Ah, those were the days!" he said, and sighed. "Now that you have indulged me and my nostalgia, friends, go your separate ways. I recommend that you first stroll yonder, westward, and see the remains of the Forum, the center of the Empire, the heart of Rome to which all roads once led."

So that day they roamed about the weedy ruins of the Forum and the Palatine Hill. Over the following days, some or all of them visited most of the famous landmarks of the city. They each threw the traditional two coppers into the Trevi fountain, and squandered a great deal more money in the fashionable shops of the Via Condotti, and some of them rode out to see the view of all of Rome from the Gianicolo.

"But this one is my favorite building in the whole city," said Autumn, leading Edge into the Pantheon as proudly as if she had just bought it. They stood in the middle of its rotunda of majestic emptiness, directly under the round opening at the tip of the coffered dome, nearly two hundred feet above their heads, from which a sunbeam slanted dustily down to lay a tremendous golden oval on the curve of side chapels at floor level. "That dome up there," said Autumn, "is exactly as high as its diameter—a hundred and forty-four feet. It was built more than seventeen hundred years ago, but *still* it is the biggest dome in all the world unsupported by ribs or braces or chains."

Edge asked fondly, "Is that why this is your favorite building?"

"I like things that last," she said simply.

Since the Hotel Eden was situated very near the top of the Spanish Steps, the troupers generally took that route down to the Piazza di Spagna and ambled from there to other quarters of the city. But often they would stop at one of the popular trattorie on or near that piazza, for a bite to eat, or to sip a cappuccino, grappa, wine or the incomparable Tuscan mineral water while they watched the other foreign tourists come and go.

"The staircase is rightly named la Scala della Trinità," said Florian. "There are three landings, you see, and at the top is the Church of the Trinity. But this piazza got *its* name because long ago the Spanish Embassy was here; hence the popular name for the stairs. And this piazza also has another name. It is derisively called by the Romans 'il ghetto degli Inglesi' because it is so constantly full of foreigners."

He and Edge were at that moment having a drink in the Caffè Greco, just off the piazza. But Edge felt out of place there, under the portraits of the great men who had been patrons there before him—Goethe, Leopardi, Stendhal—and he was vaguely uneasy at not having any idea as to which of the many men drinking in his presence might sometime or already be equally famous. Anyway, he found more interesting an old cart horse at the curb just outside the Greco's window. It was having a feed of grain, and it was apparently the Roman custom to provide a horse with an extraordinarily long nose bag with only a little grain in it. This bag, at least, hung almost to the pavement, so, after the horse had munched one mouthful of oats, it had to toss its head and fling the long sack high in the air, to snatch another mouthful as it flopped down again.

Edge and Yount and Fitzfarris more often patronized Lepre's, where they could usually find visiting Americans with whom to discuss the latest news from the States. Similarly Dai Goesle several times squired Autumn Auburn to the Caffè Dalbano, frequented by visiting Britons, to get the news from home.

One afternoon Florian gathered all the females except Magpie Maggie Hag, and as many of the males as showed any interest, and herded them to Signor Ricci's rehearsal studio. The balletmaster seemed genuinely pleased to have them visit, and introduced them to the dancers in the hall—young men and women, younger boys and girls—all handsome, svelte and lithe, all wearing practice costumes.

"We are just now trying a new little story, 'Il Stregone,'" said Ricci. "I have set it to old music by Monteverdi, and it employs every dancer in my company. The principals are the Enchanter, the victim Princess, the wicked Stepmother Queen, and the gallant Prince who comes to the rescue. The girl whom you met the other evening, Signorina Giuseppina, you will see among the corps of Summer Blossoms in the palace garden. You must, of course, imagine the garden and all the costumes. But I believe the music and dance will set the scene for you."

He placed chairs for his visitors around the big bare room, sat down to a pianoforte and began to play, and the numerous ballerini and ballerine began dancing on the polished expanse of floor—pas seul, pas de deux, de trois, and so on. Whenever the principals tired or retired, the bevy of Summer Blossoms came on—variously de suite or tout ensemble.

Obie Yount leaned and muttered to Florian, "Damned if I can make any sense of all this prancing. Does it say anything to you?"

"Well, yes. That chap doing all those flutters with his arms, he is the evil enchanter, putting the princess under a spell, so that—"

"Why?"

"Why? Why what?"

"Why should he? Put her under a spell?"

"Well ... er ... well, it's what evil enchanters *do*."

"Oh."

"He puts her in this spell, you see, and—"

"Knew a fella back in Chattanooga, used to have spells."

"Confound it, Obie! Not *that kind* of spell."

When the performance was concluded, and the visitors had applauded, and the dancers were toweling the sweat off themselves, Florian said to Signor Ricci, "I am sure that all our ladies envy yours their grace and gossamer lightness. Of course, ours—performing on horseback or sawdust or a mechanical rig—do not have so many opportunities to show such qualities."

"A woman should *always* be graceful. Let us see. You circus ladies, stand up!" A little startled at his vehemence, they all complied. "Stand here before me and look feminine." Ricci nodded approvingly at Autumn and Paprika, but barked at the others:

"Regard! The Signorine Auburn and Makkai—how those two girls stand. Have the rest of you never troubled to take notice? Never tried to emulate their stance?" Clover Lee, Gavrila, Sava, Sunday and Monday looked guilty. "Do it now!" he commanded. "Stand with one foot just behind the other, the two pointed away from each other. That gives the best line to your legs. Now put your shoulders back, thrust your titties out. Do as I tell you!"

"Please, sir," whimpered little Sava. "I no have any titties."

"Until you have got them, pretend you do! That is better. All of you remember that posture, practice it, stand so every time you stand anywhere." To Florian he snapped, "For those who work on the ground only, put on them very short skirts and calf-high boots. That will make any girl look taller and willowy, make her legs look longer and slimmer and more shapely."

"Er ... sì, signore."

"Now, all of you, walk!" Ricci commanded the females. "Walk around me in a circle." They did so, trying still to keep their shoulders back and their titties outthrust. "Terrible!" he snarled. "Except for the rope artiste, all of you walk like ordinary women—stamping on the heel bones. Ghastly! Signorina Auburn, why have you never shown these slovens how to walk?" Autumn tried to make some reply, but he overrode her. "Take them away and teach them to walk, before they taint my own girls."

"Please, sir," Sunday said meekly. "When we've learned that, can we come back for other lessons?"

"Aha! One of you at least has the ambition to improve her grace and appearance. Anyone else?" All of them except Monday raised a hand. "Signorina Auburn, you need no improvement. The rest of you, if you are sincere, be here at ten tomorrow morning. Dismissed!"

And the entire circus company found themselves again outdoors, on the Via Palermo, feeling rather as if they had just come through a whirlwind. During the few days that remained to them in Rome, those females who had been invited to attend Signor Ricci's classes conscientiously did so.

When the holiday was over, and the company returned by the railway to Forano, and the circus began giving its performances, Signor Ricci came to every nighttime show. The first time, he brought all his dancers—and Florian gladly, as he had promised, let them attend free of charge. Thereafter, Ricci came accompanied only by little Giuseppina, and he could be seen pointing out to her various aspects of the artistes' performances—because, he explained to Florian, a ballerina could learn something even from Clover Lee's rosinback routine and Zanni's extravagant falldowns. And, after each nighttime show, Ricci stayed on the tober for an hour or more to continue his how-to-be-graceful instruction of the several circus females. Sunday Simms was the most attentive of those, and the most persevering at practice after he had departed.

Meanwhile, Rome provided every one of that week's shows with a straw house. There was daily a noontime train outbound from the city, and another at five in the afternoon, and each came to Forano with its coaches packed full of Romans. The people willingly whiled away the time before the performances—eyeing the museum and the lion and the mummy or gambling at Fitzfarris's mouse game or having their futures foretold by Magpie Maggie Hag. And, after the shows, they just as willingly waited—or the women did; the men spent more of that time attending Fitz's Bible-study sessions—until they could catch the six o'clock and eleven o'clock trains inbound to Rome.

Finally, one noontime, Florian sent a bunch of Slovaks in to plaster the city with posters announcing a balloon ascension at sunset the next day. He also showed one of the posters to the Forano stationmaster and spoke persuasively enough that the man immediately sat down to his telegraph key. The next day's two trains from Rome each had two locomotives in tandem, pulling a double length of passenger coaches, and all of those were crammed with circusgoers. The two shows that day were more than sfondone, and Florian could hardly declare a turnaway of people who had come so far. So he had the roustabouts take down the chapiteau's sidewalls, and the overflow crowd could at least peer in under the seat stands. They did not seem to mind paying full-ticket prices for seeing the performance only distantly and narrowly. At any rate, everybody had a good view of the Saratoga going up, floating back and forth above the Tiber, and finally coming down, and their approving roar at that would have done credit to the Colosseum.

It appeared that the Florilegium could go on enjoying full houses indefinitely, but it was now the first week of May, and Florian was anxious to be starting out of the country. So the teardown was done, the wagons were packed and the train went northward. From now on, Florian announced, the circus would show only in major and populous towns, and for no more than three days in any of them. Viterbo was the next nearest and sizable city, but it was, like Rome, inside the censor-ridden Papal State, hence had to be slighted. So the first run was a long one, three days and two nights on the road, before the circus reached the town of Orvieto.

The troupers could see that place for half a day before they got to it, for Orvieto sat like a town on a table above the floor of the plain they were traversing—the whole of it clustered atop a rock pedestal nearly an eighth of a mile high. When they arrived at the base of that cliff, they saw that there was a brand-new, steam-driven funicular tram to keep the town above supplied with the produce of lowland farmers, vintners and such. But the circus train had to toil its way up a long incline of road that angled back and forth up the cliff face to the city's Porta Romana, where Florian was waiting.

While the roustabouts did the setup on the assigned tober, Florian invited everybody not working to come for a stroll with him and see the truly unique feature of Orvieto. He led them nearly to the drop-off of the rock pedestal on which the town sat, gestured and said, "Il Posso di San Patrizio." The Well of Saint Patrick was unique, indeed: a circular pit dug down through the rock as big across as a circus pista. Its rim was surrounded by men and women leading asses that carried casks, barrels or enormous jars. When the troupers made their way through that waiting crowd and peered over the edge of the well, they nearly reeled with vertigo. The water level was a dizzying two hundred feet below them, and the men and women ascended and descended that chimney along a spiral staircase hewn from the rock walls—or rather, two concentric spiraling staircases arranged in a double helix, so that the trains going down and coming up could do so simultaneously, never having to meet and pass each other. Not only was the well pit a work of staggering dimensions; the men who had dug it had done the extra incredible job of hacking seventy-two "windows" from the pit wall through the rock to the outer cliff face, to provide daylight for those going up and down inside.

"It was dug more than three hundred years ago," said Florian, "to ensure that the city had fresh water whenever it was under siege. Ever since, the Italians have said of any spendthrift that 'he has pockets as deep as the Well of Saint Patrick.'"

As they all turned back toward the tober, Florian added, "Speaking of spending, I have a suggestion to make. I, for one, am getting too old and feeling too prosperous to continue living the vagrant gypsy life when we are between stands. I mean having to put up in seedy roadside inns or to sleep in an even less comfortable circus wagon. All of us now have some money put by. I suggest that we spend some of it to purchase traveling vans like those owned by Miss Auburn and Monsieur LeVie. We need not get one apiece—that would be costly, and make our train inordinately long—but a caravan house-on-wheels can be bought and shared by several people. I personally will be purchasing a van in consortium with Mr. Goesle and Herr Beck and Signor Bonvecino. I submit the idea for the rest of you to think about. And I will say one other thing. Either spend all your lire before we get to the frontier, or exchange them for good gold or gems. The Italian paper and coins will be worthless in Austria."

Among the several discussions of the caravan idea, one took place between Maurice and Paprika. He said to her, "My van is not large, but it could easily accommodate one other. And gladly."

"Merci, mais non," she said.

"Pourquoi non? We are partners in the air. Why not on the ground? I have long wondered why you keep me at a distance. I know you have no other man."

"And I will not have any. You are a worldly person, Maurice, and an understanding one, so I shall tell you. The fact is that I can get—satisfaction—only from a female. I have been that way ever since... well, there was something that happened in my childhood."

"Ah, pauvre petite. Some kindly old uncle, no doubt." Paprika shook her head. "An older brother, peut-être. It happens." She said nothing. "Your father, then? Mon dieu! Que de merdeux—!"

"No, no! My father was a decent man. All he did was die." She looked away. "It was my mother! My istenverte mother!"

"Qu'est-ce qui?" Maurice gasped. "C'est impossible!"

"No, it is not impossible," she said sulkily. "And maybe it was partly my own fault. I was an only child, and willful. When my dear father died, I was just eleven years old, but I was determined to preserve his memory. I insisted that my mother not seek a new husband. So she said, 'Then you must take your father's place.'"

"Surely she meant—"

"She meant in bed. And she made me do exactly that. Of course I could not do everything, but we... we devised substitutes. And in some respects, she said, I was better than my father had been. Better than any man could be. She never did marry again. I was her lover—no, her tool—until I was old enough to leave home and make a life for myself."

"And that..." Maurice had to clear his throat. "And that has influenced you to love only women?"

"Love them?" Paprika laughed like a vixen barking. "I hate them! I loathe and despise women, exactly as I loathed and despised that one. Unfortunately, I remain as warped as she made me. To this day, I can get sexual pleasure no other way. I know. I tried once with a man. And that was such a pathetic farce that I shall never try again."

"But, chérie, consider. Une hirondelle ne fait pas le printemps. There are men and there are men."

"No, Maurice. I will not demean and disgust us both. I know myself too well. I can only couple with another female, even though I feel no affection, nothing but contempt for her. And if, to indulge myself in that way, it requires that I corrupt some innocent girl or woman—why, then, I get even more pleasure from it. You asked. Now I have told you. Think what you will of me, but... can we go on being partners? In the air?"

"In the air," he said sadly. "Ainsi que les hirondelles."

Before the circus left Orvieto, Florian, Goesle, Beck and Zanni had found and bought a very nice caravan for themselves, and a horse to draw it. The journey to the circus's next stand, Siena, took four days and three nights, and after those nights on the road—two spent sleeping in the wagons, one in an extremely dismal locanda—the other circus folk were ready and eager to procure vans of their own.

In Siena they found two more for sale. Pavlo Smodlaka, though he grumbled bitterly about having nobody to share his outlay, bought the better van to carry and house his family. The other vehicle was rather shoddy and smelly—it being the property of a squalid gypsy clan—but it was at least commodious. Hannibal Tyree and Quincy Simms consulted together—"We's got pockets like dat Saint Patrick's well"—then somehow managed to convey a proposal to the antipodists. The Chinese not only cheerfully proffered all their accumulated wages—but they then cheerfully and immediately started sweeping and swabbing the van's interior to make it habitable for its five new owners.

The remaining unhoused troupers had to live and sleep in whatever accommodations offered during the next four-day run, to Pistoia, and in that town they found no such vehicles for sale. When Yount and Mullenax loudly complained about their being "orphans" among the others' opulence, Zanni remarked humorously, "Well, you have arrived in a good place to put yourselves out of your misery. This town of Pistoia is where pistols were first made, and got their name."

However, after the stand there, another four-day run brought the circus to Bologna, and that was a big city where almost anything could be purchased. "A most beautiful and hospitable city," said Florian. "Why, the Palazzo Comunale, where I applied for permission to pitch, has a staircase specially built so horses could climb up to the council chamber in the olden days, when the council members were too haughty to walk up on their own feet."

"And Bologna's university," said Autumn, "has been hospitable enough to engage even *female* professors from time to time. One of them was so beautiful, they say, that she had to stand behind a curtain when she lectured, so the students wouldn't be too distracted to take notes."

"That reminds me," said Maurice. "A student of your own, lovely lady, has asked to study also with me. Your apprentice ropewalker, Sunday Simms. She probably does not realize it, but she is following the classic progression—from parterre acrobat to the rope to the trapeze. I told her I would require your permission."

"You have it, of course. Sunday is eager to learn all she can. Just in those few lessons from Maestro Ricci, she acquired a good deal of new poise and assurance. And she is indefatigable. When she is not practicing in the pista, she is at her books. Let us, by all means, encourage her every ambition."

During the three days the circus showed in Bologna, it found the necessary two more houses-on-wheels. One was bought by the quartet of Yount, Mullenax, Fitzfarris and Rouleau. The other was bought jointly by Paprika, Clover Lee, Sunday and Monday Simms. Florian looked dubious when he heard of that arrangement, but Clover Lee privately assured him, "I agreed to share the cost and the quarters only after I took Paprika aside for a *very* frank conversation, and I laid down some strict rules. Whatever mischief she tries to do outside the caravan, I can't control. But inside those walls, she is not even to *leer*."

Of the artistes and managers, that left only Magpie Maggie Hag without a traveling house, but she did not want one. "I have whole dressing and kitchen wagon now all to myself, all I need. I am gypsy, anyhow. Too much easiness no good for gypsy."

She and others of the company spent their free time in Bologna making other purchases, because Florian told them, "Buy for the road ahead. When the war starts, *everything* is going to get scarce and expensive, in Austria as well as here." So the wagons in which people no longer had to ride to sleep were stocked full of hay and grain for the horses and elephant, smoked meats for the lion, staple groceries for the humans, canisters of calcium carbide for the limelights, coils of rope, cans of paint and tar and coal oil and axle grease, harness and horseshoes and miscellaneous hardware, fabrics and thread and sequins for the wardrobe.

Carl Beck found and bought acid, iron filings and lime to stoke his Gasent-wickler machines this one more time, because Bologna was the last big city the circus would visit in Italy, and he and Rouleau felt it merited a balloon ascension, which might well be the *Saratoga*'s last performance for some while to come.

None of the Bolognese seemed to share Florian's apprehension of impending war. Or, if any did, they did not let it inhibit their appetite for enjoyment. They packed the chapiteau at every show, and all but fought for the divinations of Magpie Maggie Hag and the diversions of the mouse game at every intermission, and the menfolk crammed into the biblical-tableau top after every show, and a vast crowd came to attend the closing-day ascension of the *Saratoga*—and to exclaim both at that and at the accompanying magic of a pretty girl disappearing in a puff of smoke from before them, while the balloon was high aloft, yet reappearing in its gondola when it landed.

In fact, the Bolognese poured into the red wagon's coffers so much Italian coin and paper currency that the circus's departure, on the morning after teardown, had to be delayed while Florian, Zanni and Maurice, each of them carrying in each hand a satchel full of lire and centesimi, scurried about to every money-changing establishment in the city. Unlike the happy-go-lucky circus patrons, the dour and sad-eyed old Jews who ran those establishments had either personal experience or a long racial memory of many a war, pogrom, revolution and financial crisis. Every man of them set a stiff (and identical) price for their alchemy of changing paper and copper to gold. Florian and his assistants accepted what they could get, and get in a hurry. Though they lost on the exchange, they returned to the wagons bearing an estimable cargo of specie that was legal tender anywhere in the world.

The circus train that finally departed from Bologna was now a train of which the tail end—that being literally the tail of the elephant—departed something like half an hour after Florian's rockaway pulled out of the tober. Besides the elephant and the rockaway and the tandem machines of the gas generator, the train comprised seven house-vans and six wagons drawn by one horse apiece, and four heavier wagons drawn by the double teams of polka-dot horses. The vehicles were so numerous that almost every man of the artistes and crew had to drive one. They all had to travel some distance apart, to stay out of each other's churned-up dust, so the train, from Snowball's white nose to Peggy's tufted tail, strung out for nearly a fifth of a mile.

At Modena, Florian said, "All right, everybody, I have already converted our main treasury into bullion. Now let us all get rid of every bit of pocket money we are still carrying." He and his three van mates spent theirs in stocking their caravan with wine, the good local Lambrusco. And most of the women spent their remaining lire to buy bottles of Modena's unique Nocino, a sticky-sweet liqueur made from walnuts.

Even though the troupers were hurrying to outrun a war, and putting on shows as they went, they did not neglect their free-time responsibilities. Goesle and Beck put their Slovaks to painting all the newly acquired caravans to match the rest of the train—blue bodies with white wheels, window shutters and trim. They left the Florilegium's name off those vehicles, however, in case any of their owners should have occasion to decamp to another show. Magpie Maggie Hag had tired of seeing Monday Simms do her stately haute école riding in a mere suit of fleshings, so now she rigged Monday out as a Cordobesa of her own native Spain: black velvet trousers with silvery conchas down the seams, soft boots, a white blouse with wide sleeves and a bright red bolero over that. On Monday's head, she set the low-crowned, flat-brimmed Cordobés hat that was intended for men but has always been one of the most flattering headpieces a woman could wear.

Maurice and Paprika began showing Sunday some of the rudiments of the trapeze art, making her wear at all times the safety lungia rope.

"No, no, no, kedvesem!" Paprika chided her. "Do not reach out with your legs when you prepare to alight on the platform. Always keep your hips forward—*hump it!*—so you alight gracefully."

"If you come feet first," Maurice told her, "you will find the bar dragging you backward off the platform. Clumsy, that, and dangerous. Only when you are swinging free and pumping—to swing faster and higher—only then, never otherwise, do you bend in the middle to bring your legs forward."

And little Quincy Simms was likewise trying to enlarge his ring talents. He had begun following Zanni Bonvecino everywhere except to the donniker, and gamely trying to imitate his every comic turn except the aria singing. Zanni graciously favored the boy with some elementary advice, of which Quincy comprehended perhaps half.

"There are six basics in the clowning art: stupidity, trickery, mimicry, falls, blows and surprises. You should exclude the first from your repertoire, because you are a Negro. Stupidity would merely mark you as a lazy chuckleheaded Jim Crow; leave that to American circuses. Here in Europe—well, for example, in Paris there was a clown called Chocolat. Nobody watching him ever thought, 'There is a Negro clown.' Everybody thought, 'There is a great clown.' Now, if you wish to try the clowning art, you must become no longer *you*. A clown is not a person, not an object, he is what *happens*."

"Yassuh."

"And, damn it, don't open your mouth. For all I know, you are a genius, but you *talk* stupid. Bene, the first thing necessary is what we call avoir l'oeil—to have the eye. Try the basic clown tricks and watch. See which, in your case, best amuses the audience. Joey ribaldry or toby pathos, the horse laugh or the weary smile, joey cunning or toby helplessness, pure pantomime or a pista full of props, joey knockabout or toby melancholy. Thus you find your particular bent, your métier, your magic. Then you *make fun of it*."

"Yassuh."

When the circus train left Modena, it had not gone far along the road to the north before it found itself again a conspicuous and incongruous part of another procession. It had got between two road-filling columns of the Italian Royal Army on the march—infantry soldiers under full field pack and shouldered arms, gaudier-uniformed cavalrymen on war horses slung with a superfluity of equipment, horsedrawn cannon carriages and caissons, supply wagons, ambulance wagons, all the necessaries for waging war. Florian passed the word back along the train for all the women to put on the crown-emblazoned shawls the king had given them, to proclaim the Florilegium's allegiance. Having no choice but to travel along with the army, the circus people were somewhat uncomfortable and embarrassed, especially when various soldiers bawled comic comments at them, and others bawled curses of complaint—because Peggy imperturbably beshat the road, and the soldiers had to break step and break ranks to avoid trudging through it.

But when twilight came, the circus train pulled off into a meadow beside the road for the night. And when it resumed its northward journey next morning, there was no more army in sight. All that day, the train did not catch up to any, and none overtook it. "The troops will all have moved off to east and west from here," Florian guessed. "The river Po, about twenty miles up ahead of us, is the Venezia border. Beyond that will be the Austrian troops. We are right now in a potential battle zone. So let us make haste—and ladies, don't wear those shawls today."

Meeting no further impediment, the train reached the Po at the next twilight, and found a bridge with a barrier and a sentry post at either end of it. On the closer side, the station was candy-striped bright red, white and green, and flew the Italian flag of those same colors, and was manned by a squad of the Alpine Brigade—looking not exactly prepared for alpinism, since they wore high-fronted jackboots, tall shakos and tunics encrusted with braid, frogs and epaulettes. Florian leaned down and spoke to them in Italian, and they raised the barrier without any fuss, except for some you'll-be-sorry comments on the idiocy of leaving sunny Italy for sullen Austria.

The flag and the sentry post on the other end of the bridge were of Austria-Hungary's more somber black and yellow, and the guards—of the Tirolean Rifles—were dressed in trimmer, no-frills uniforms of silver-green. They likewise appeared indisposed to make any fuss about the Florilegium's crossing their border. They did manifest Teutonic efficiency to the extent of demanding the troupe's conduct books, though they gave them only a desultory riffle-through when Florian handed them over. Then they raised the barrier and the circus train plodded past. The word went down the line—"We are now in Venezia"—but nobody could see any immediate difference in the environment. The landscape here looked just as Italian; so did the people, the farmhouses, the vineyards and olive groves; when they bedded down by the roadside again that night, a farm woman who sold them a pail of milk spoke Italian while she did so.

Two days later, the circus pitched just outside the walls of Verona and, while the crew started the setup, Autumn led every female of the troupe into the Old Town—all of them twittering with excitement, even Magpie Maggie Hag—to show them the Capelletti house, from the balcony of which Giulietta had traded compliments and vows with Romeo Mantecchi. Florian chuckled as they trotted off and told the men of the company, "I fear they'll be a little disappointed with that landmark, but they should enjoy the rest of Verona. It is a beautiful city."

It was, the men agreed, as they strolled in through the Porta Nuova and along the broad, flower-bedded Corso. The city was red and gold and pink, except where the occasional house wall was entirely covered with a giant mural—David besting Goliath or St. George besting the Dragon or some such scene.

"I only regret that I cannot take us either east or west," said Florian. "East-ward, of course, there is Venice, and everybody should see Venice at least once in his life. Westward, though, on the other side of Lake Garda, there are two pretty towns that not even many Italians have ever heard of. They are side by side on a little hill, and they're both named Botticino. But one is Botticino Mattina and the other is Botticino Sera—the morning and the evening Botticino—according to when each of them gets the sun on its vineyards."

The circus women did return from their excursion looking a trifle dis-appointed. The Capelletti house had not just a balcony, but *two* balconies, and Autumn confessed that she had no idea which one the visitors should be adoring. Furthermore, when the women asked the whereabouts of Romeo's family mansion, Autumn confided that there were several houses in Ver-ona that claimed that distinction—and anyway, according to Shakespeare's own countrymen, the whole Romeo and Juliet story was nothing but a bitter-sweet fable.

But no one had much time or leisure to pine over that disillusionment. Ver-ona was having its annual Agricultural and Livestock Fair, so the town's popula-tion was swelled with visitors. The fact that many of the visitors were in Austrian uniforms did not dampen the other folks' festive mood. They spilled over from the fairgrounds to the circus grounds and packed the chapiteau at every perfor-mance during the three days it stayed.

"Why can't we stay longer?" Fitzfarris asked at the closing show. "We've been making money hand over fist. Good Austrian kronen. And hell, we're already in Austrian territory, aren't we?"

"The very territory that Italy is preparing to fight for—and to fight on," said Florian. "No, we keep moving."

That he was not being overcautious was demonstrated when, in the after-noon of the circus train's second day outbound from Verona, on a road that was gradually but steadily rising toward the distant highlands, the train found itself again in the midst of an army on the move. This time the Florilegium could not march with it, for the army was coming from the other direction, from the north, and was composed of Austrian infantry, cavalry and artillery. So the circus got entirely off the road to wait while it passed.

"Right around here," said Florian, "we are leaving Venezia and entering the Trentino area. Ninety-nine percent of the people here are Italian, but you'll see differences in the architecture. And every geographical feature has two names. That river alongside the road is the same Adige that it was in Verona, but up here it is also the Etsch. Our next stand will be in the town called Trento in Italian, Trient in German."

When the road was clear of soldiers again and the circus train resumed its journey, climbing all the time, the troupers did remark the change in the farm-houses along the way. They were still painted in passionate Mediterranean colors, but they had the heavy, overhanging roofs of alpine chalets. Whenever some passerby or farm worker stopped to gape at the sight of the train, he or she would shout a greeting in Italian, but he would be wearing lederhosen and she a dirndl. At last, four days' climb from Verona, the train came in sight of Trento/Trient—and a striking sight it was, for the town completely filled the breadth of the Adige/Etsch valley, and over the town towered the great isolated rock called the Dosso Trento. Although there were palaces and loggias of the Venetian style in Trento, most of the buildings had massive roof eaves, balconies set above high-snow level, and belfry caps on their chimneys.

Florian, waiting to guide the train to its tober, greeted the troupe with the news: "It has begun. On June sixteenth, the Prussians invaded the Austro-Hungarian province of Bohemia."

The predominantly Italian populace of Trento might have been undecided whether to cheer for Austria, to which they belonged by treaty, or for the other side, the Prussian ally of Italy. But one thing they could unreservedly cheer for was a circus, so they flocked to the Florilegium and forgot politics. The company enjoyed another well-received and profitable stand—but only for two days, then Florian moved them on.

They climbed higher yet into the mountains, to the town of Bolzano—or Bozen—and during the two days they showed there, they got the news that Italy, as expected, had joined Prussia in declaring war on Austria. When Florian called for the teardown this time, he told all the wagon and van drivers that they would now detour off the main road they had been ascending, and would instead take a secondary road that continued alongside the Adige River and went northeast by way of a town called Merano.

"What for?" asked Edge. "All the way here, I've been assuming we'd cross the Alps at the Brenner Pass. It's directly north of here, the road is good, the pass is not impossibly high and—hell—that's been the classic alpine crossing ever since the Ostrogoths."

"The classic invasion route to the south, yes. Therefore the likeliest route by which the Austrians will continue to pour cavalcades across—as an ex-cavalry officer like yourself must be aware. I don't want to sit on top of an Alp waiting for a whole army to get out of my road. We will go over the Paso de Resia instead. It is only a few feet higher, and a few days farther from here."

Just before nightfall of the first day out of Bolzano, the train reached Merano, a town that seemed to be composed of nothing but inns. Florian announced, "We will not show here. Merano is a resort for consumptives. They come for the rest cure, for the clear air cure, for the whey cure, for the grape cure. Probably they could not wheeze their way up into our seat stands. However, let us find enough inns to accommodate us all. Then everybody eat hearty and get a good night's rest in the feather beds. The road ahead will be hard, and empty of any amenities."

After dinner, Autumn and Edge, before availing themselves of their bed's big, warm but weightless feather quilts, stepped out onto the balcony of their room. The moon was full that night, and its light made especially imposing the snow-capped sharp peaks all around Merano, but high above it. The rim of mountains, luminous blue-white with sharp black valley shadows, looked as hard-edged as a jagged piece of tin against the dark blue sky.

"Lovely," murmured Autumn. She gazed all about the horizon and, when her eyes came back to Edge, he saw that even in moonlight their flower-petal speck-lings of gold were visible. She said, "You know, if you think about it, the moon is *always* a full moon. Only we can't see it."

He said admiringly, "I'd think, with the eyes you've got, you could see it all the time. Now me, I'm not so perceptive. It's only just this minute that I've noticed something. My shadow is black. Everybody else's shadow is black. Yours is rose-colored."

Involuntarily she looked down, then laughed. "Liar. Idiot."

"Well, it looks so to me. Everything about you, my dear, looks flowery to me."

The next stretch of road took five days and nights to negotiate. It got ever steeper and more twisty, making the horses labor and frequently requiring the troupers to get down and walk to lighten the load. It also made for chilly nights, even inside the caravans, even now in high summer, for they were nearing a mile above sea level. But the road at least stayed below the snow line, and nobody and none of the animals got intolerably fatigued, none of the wagons broke down, and—whether or not there were armies crossing the Brenner Pass—no marching columns blocked the way up to this one. In the forenoon of the sixth day, the troupers discovered that they were no longer climbing, but proceeding on a level piece of road. They came abreast of a small chalet, painted Austrian black and yellow, flying the Austrian flag, and a few Tirolean Rifle sentries came out of it—but only to wave a greeting. Florian halted the train there, went to have a few words with the guards and returned to say:

"Ladies and gentlemen, you are at the crest of the Lechtal Alps. This pass is called, behind us, the Paso de Resia—ahead of us the Reschenpass. We are leaving the cisalpine lands for the transalpine. And just in time, from what these good fellows tell me. The Austrians and Italians are furiously battling right now, somewhere in the vicinity of Verona, where we so recently were situated. From here, my friends, the road is all downhill, into the Tirol valleys of Austria—or, as the country prefers to be called in its own language, the Österreich."

Ö STERREICH .

I

T H E R E S T of that day, they descended the mountain valleys down which tumbled the river Inn, young and boisterous up here, a pale jade green in color because of all the oxygen it had absorbed from the snows higher up in the ranges. There were noticeable differences between this transalpine side of the pass and the cisalpine they had just ascended. Back there, they had been climbing through oak, beech and ash trees. On this side, the trees were mostly evergreen: pine, fur and spruce. On that southern side, the wild flowers had been mostly oleanders and verbena; on this northern side they were gentians and saxifrage.

There were a few very small villages sprinkled down the Inn's high valleys, all too small to have any accommodation for strangers. When the train stopped outside a hamlet named Pfunds, to pass the night, Florian said, "Maggie tells me we have just about used up all our provisions over these last days. I shall go and knock on doors and ask if I can buy bread, milk and cheese from some good Hausfrau. Come, Banat, and help me carry whatever I can get."

The two of them returned well laden. Magpie Maggie Hag had made up a campfire, the Slovaks another, around which the artistes and crewmen sat as they ate their bread and cheese. Suddenly they all sat up a lot straighter, startled by a very loud, very weird noise—a sound commingled of rattle, hoot and shriek —from somewhere in the blackness of the pines on the other side of the road.

"Jesus Jumping Christ!" said Yount.

The extraordinary noise sounded again. The elephant uneasily shuffled her feet, Maximus uttered a growl and the terriers could be heard yapping inside the Smodlakas' caravan.

349

"I bet it's a g'nome," said Sunday, shivering.

"A what?" said Fitzfarris.

"A g'nome. A sort of boogey-man. Monsieur Jules lent me a book about the Alps, and it said the Alps are full of g'nomes."

Rouleau sighed. "Your erudition, my dear, sometimes outruns your vocabulary. In English it is pronounced *nome*."

As if answering to the name, the appalling sound came again.

"Well, whatever it is," said Mullenax, "I don't think I can sleep with it squawlin' like that. Zack, you got your carbine loaded with scatter shot? Lend me it."

"You'd go after the thing? One-eyed? In the dark?"

"I'm the animal tamer, right? And in the dark, two eyes ain't much advantage over one."

Edge shrugged, got the carbine for him, and Mullenax went slinking off into the woods.

"I think Abner's fairly well loaded, himself," said Fitzfarris. "If he lets off that weapon in a careless direction, we're all liable to get sprinkled with bird shot."

But the creature, whatever it was, gave its clatter-howl screech again, and no gunshot followed. A few minutes later, the creature sounded off again, but the noise stopped abruptly in mid-yammer. All the people around the fires looked at each other questioningly. After a long silence, Mullenax came into the firelight, carrying a large, untidy black bundle.

"Didn't have to shoot him. Just whacked him off a branch with the gun butt. He's still alive, so I tied him with my belt. I never seen nothin' like this critter, and I'm damned if I want him loose when he wakes up mad at me." He dropped the thing on the ground in the light, and everybody gathered to look. "Big as a turkey—but no turkey ever made such a noise, or ever had such a wicked bill as that."

The bird was mostly bronze-black in color, with shimmers of blue and purple, and its body did resemble that of an American turkey, complete to the fan-feather tail. But it had the head, beak and talons of a raptor. When it began to stir awake, it opened fierce hawkish eyes, over which were bright red-feather "eyebrows," and clacked a viciously hooked yellow beak, and again uttered that shattering noise, and everyone recoiled from it.

"Nothing supernatural or threatening," said Florian. "It's a kind of grouse. In every European language it is called something like cock of the wild or cock of the mountains. Back in Italy it would have been the gallo alpestre. Here, it's the Auerhahn."

"In Scotland it's the capercaillie," said Autumn. "Gaelic for cock of the woods."

"Is it good to eat?" asked Yount.

"Yes, indeed," said Florian. "At this season, anyway, when it has been feeding on berries and such. In the winter it feeds on pine needles, so it tastes like turpentine."

"Hey!" said Mullenax. "Ain't nobody goin' to eat a bird I bothered to take alive. He's for *showing!*"

"You'll never tame and train that thing," said Fitzfarris. "But we could put him in among my stuffed museum birds."

"Yes," said Florian. "Hereabouts, it is not an exotic, like a hummingbird or an opossum. But most city folk will only have seen an Auerhahn dead and stuffed. That's what we'll do: put it alive in the museum."

As the circus train continued on down the valley of the Inn, the scenery sloped up toward the sky on either side, and consisted of dense forests of black-green pines, from which wafted occasional wisps and toots of gray mist, like ghosts standing up to observe the passing procession. Here and there, the ranks of pines gave way to forests of fir trees, as ripply looking as a sea washing upon the mountain flanks. Among all those dark evergreens, the infrequent deciduous tree—a linden or chestnut—flared as bright as a pale green explosion.

Every mile or so, the forest had been cleared for a house and pasture. The houses were of the solid alpine design: the front for the human inhabitants, the rear for stabling the livestock in winter, so their body heat would help warm the humans' quarters. The roof of every house was massive, its eaves overhanging all around, and a balcony encircled the house under the second-story windows —the balcony and every windowsill overflowing with brilliant red geraniums. Over the front door was nailed a great wide rack of deer or elk antlers, and beside every house stood rows of beehives. The pastures behind the houses were so steep that it seemed impossible that any animals could stand on them to graze. But there were herds in plenty—as beautiful as show stock: horses of glossy brown with blond manes and tails, cows of a delicate silvery-dun color. And on these warm summer days, not just the colts and calves but even the full-grown horses and matronly cows bounded and cavorted about. There were sheep, too, but they were not so surefooted on the slanted pastures; the troupers laughed to see one of the sheep lose its purchase and tumble like a barrel downhill.

Since the weather continued fine, the troupe camped along the road every night, but frequently stopped at a Schenke or Gasthaus for a meal. Some of those inns were poor places and served the food of the peasantry, which seemed to consist solely of the Sterz, a cornmeal cake with strips of pork-fat cracklings laid on top. And in one of those taverns, a couple of the newcomers made the mistake of ordering the peasant beverage called Rhum—to discover that it was not even a distant relation of rum, but a vile distillate from potatoes, mixed with brown sugar, almost too awful even for Mullenax to drink. But other houses catered to richer travelers, and in those the viands were superb: jugged hare, roast wild boar, fish fresh from the Inn, immense dumplings, vigorous beer, gentian-flavored liqueur.

Around the campfires at night, the more experienced travelers explained to the newcomers various things about Austria:

"The Habsburgs who have long ruled this land," said Florian, "must be the oldest continuously ruling family in all of history. I'd guess that they have held one throne or another—as dukes, counts, kings, emperors—longer than any Egyptian dynasty ever did. Their family tree goes back to a Count Guntram the Rich, around the year nine hundred, who named the line for his Habichtsburg —Hawk's Castle. In their time, the Habsburgs have ruled everything from little duchies to the entire Holy Roman Empire. Right now, there is a Habsburg trying to rule a rather unruly Mexico."

"That won't last long," said Edge. "Maximilian only managed to sneak in there because the States were distracted by their war."

"And of course he went only because Franz Joseph commanded him to," said Florian. "After all, what does an emperor *do* with a younger brother? Try to find some second-rate job for him abroad. Maximilian had already made a mess of governing Venezia. The man is a simpleton."

"I was once among the singers summoned to entertain at Maximilian's court, when he was in Venice," said Zanni Bonvecino. "His wife is Charlotte of Coburg, and she is quite unbalanced. She is a rabid and perpetual housekeeper, forever dusting tables and things, like a demented chambermaid."

Carl Beck said, "And Franz Joseph to Elisabeth is married. Of our Bavarian Wittelsbachs she is, and for lunacy the Wittelsbachs are long notorious."

"Well, Franz Joseph had *one* damned good reason for marrying Elisabeth," said Florian. "She is said to be the most beautiful woman ever to wear a crown since Nefertiti."

"Nevertheless," said Paprika, "Elisabeth *is* a Wittelsbach—and eccentric at the very least. She is obsessed with her beauty and health. Always exercising, bathing in strange oils, eating strange substances. Also she detests court formality and royal duties, and despises her husband. I hear that she travels now as often as she can, and, even when she returns to her own domains, she spends most of her time in Budapest, leaving Vienna and her own children to Franz Joseph and his iron mother, Sophia."

"Let us say this for her, though," Autumn put in. "The Empress Elisabeth adores circuses, and she herself is a skilled rider. She has even done trick riding, and is said to take every opportunity to indulge her fondness for circuses. Goes about incognito like that sultan—who was he, Florian? The one that was always prowling among his subjects in disguise?"

"A Persian caliph. Harun al-Raschid."

"I have heard that, yes," said Paprika. "Also that she now speaks Magyar to perfection, among all her other languages." Paprika paused to giggle. "Do you know, they say Elisabeth has a pet name for her husband. She calls him 'Megaliotis.' Not just behind his back; to his face as well. And the poor fool *likes* it, because in classical Greek it would mean Majesty. But in Magyar that word would translate as something like 'Dead Standstill.'"

"Well, standing still *we* should not be," said Florian. "Let us get to bed, and be early on the road tomorrow."

He was off earliest of all, because on that afternoon the Florilegium would arrive at its first sizable Austrian city, Landeck, and Florian had to hurry there to arrange for the tober. So Edge and Autumn led the train, with no possibility of losing the way, for there was only the one road following the river Inn down the valley. Edge knew that the Inn eventually in its course became one of the major waterways of Austria, but it was still no more than what in Virginia would have been called a creek. However, the main road now began to be intersected by crossroads at intervals, and those crossed the Inn on high-humped covered bridges, each as solidly wooden-walled and roofed as any mountain house. Then, quite suddenly, another creek joined the Inn and made it more of a respectable river, and there at the meeting of the waters was Landeck, with Florian waiting at the roadside.

"We'll pitch on the Eislaufplatz. In the winter it is a skating rink. While I've been waiting for you, I have been doctoring these Italian-language posters. Let's have all the lads who are not driving start pasting them up while the rest of us go on to the tober."

Landeck was an exceptionally clean city, especially as compared with some of those in Italy. There was not a scrap of litter to be seen, nor a single untidy house or yard, nor an unkempt person. Most noticeable, here as in the villages they had already come through, there were no beggars anywhere in residence. But Autumn told Edge that Austria was not entirely devoid of them; they had all migrated to Vienna, where the pickings were better.

Landeck appeared to have grown rather haphazardly around its centerpiece —an immense, square-towered castle—the buildings having accreted there first, then sprawled out over the valley and then up the surrounding mountainsides. The circus train had to wind a slow, tortuous course through the narrow streets, all the way to the other side of the city. So the crewmen posting the paper could pretty well stay abreast of the train while they worked. To the top of each poster, Florian had added with his mason's pencil, in big black letters: NICHT DENKEN AN KUMMER! When the train pulled up at the sometimes ice rink and everybody piled out, Edge asked about the addition to the posters.

"It means 'Forget Your Worries,'" Florian said. "Come to the circus instead of moping. If we're in the Germanic lands long enough, I'll get those posters entirely reprinted. But the word 'circus' is recognizable enough."

"Does this town have something in particular to mope about?"

"All of Austria does. I have heard the latest war news. Austria's troops down south have soundly trounced the Italians, as expected. But its armies in Bohemia are steadily retreating before the Prussians, with heavy losses. And that was *not* expected. The Austrian soldiers are known to be better trained and disciplined than the Prussians, and they had recent combat experience against the French just seven years ago, while the Prussians have not fought a war in fifty years. But I am told that the Prussians have some terrible new weapons—breech-loading repeater rifles versus the Austrians' old muzzle-loaders, and cannons made of Essen steel instead of cast iron, so they can fire more rapidly and accurately. I gather that courage and experience don't count for much against superior firepower."

"I can guarantee you they don't," Edge said drily.

But the Landeckers, however patriotically preoccupied they may have been, congregated to watch the elephant and the Slovaks erect the chapiteau and the smaller top, and a goodly number of them went to Magpie Maggie Hag in the red wagon to buy tickets for the morrow. Fitzfarris was also at the red wagon, but he was at the back of it—the museum part—and he called Florian over.

"I hope Abner's goddamned turkey bird is worth the showing," Fitz said angrily. "This is the first time I've taken down the side panels since we put the bird in there. And just look what it's done to the rest of the museum!"

The rest of the museum was now quite nonexistent, except for a pile of scraps of fur and hide, wads of stuffing, scattered feathers, and three glass eyes, relics of the two-headed calf. The Auerhahn's wicked beak and talons had demolished every last exhibit—the birds, the animals, even the milk snake. The malefactor spread its fantail and glared out at them defiantly.

"Hell," said Florian. "I should have known. When we heard that bird bellowing in the middle of the night and the middle of summertime, I should have realized it wasn't doing any mating call. It was defying any other birds to trespass on its territory."

"It's sure got *this* territory all to itself now. Good thing the Chinks weren't still living in there. I ought to make Abner eat the confounded thing—raw—feathers and feet and all."

"Well, we did toss the Auerhahn in the cage without any provender. Probably it got hungry."

"All right, then *it* can eat *Abner*. Any creature that could make a meal of a three-eyed embalmed calf ought to really enjoy a one-eyed clodhopper pickled in alcohol."

"Simmer down, Sir John. You have to admit that the museum was a rather shoddy makeshift. I'll have one of the Slovaks scrape the mess out of there, and then I'll work up a gruesome patter about the Killer Bird from the High Crags. Later on, as we go along, maybe we can pick up some more real live museum pieces. Hello... what's this?"

A uniformed, official-looking gentleman strode briskly onto the tober, gave the tents a contemptuous look, then made his way to Florian and superciliously addressed him in German. The two conversed for a minute, then the stranger strode inside the chapiteau.

"Who's he?" asked Fitzfarris.

Florian made a face. "A manifestation of the Teutonic efficiency I have been expecting and dreading. He'll have a title something like the Herr Inspektor of Diminutive Details, from the Department of Obstruction, in the Ministry of Public Meddling. We'll be pestered by another like him in every town big enough to support a typically layabout civil service. I'll deal with him."

He went into the tent, where Stitches Goesle was watching the roustabouts put up the seating. The Landeck inspector was feeling a fold of the sidewall canvas, and looking critical of it. When Florian entered, the inspector officiously snapped his fingers and commanded, "Benehmenbüchern!" Florian went out again, and to his caravan, and brought back all the conduct books. The inspector paged through every one of them—and carefully, reading every entry in every language, or pretending he was doing so. At least one of the words he recognized, for he looked up from that book and said, "Kanevasmeister?"

Florian told him that the canvasmaster was the man in charge of the chapiteau. He pointed to Goesle, and the inspector asked that he be summoned. When Dai came up to them, the man said, "Herr Goosely?"

"'Tis pronounced Gwell," Dai growled. To Florian he said, "And who is this clinchpoop, then?"

"City inspector," said Florian, and he listened as the official went into a lengthy speech. He translated to Goesle, "The inspector says our canvas is highly flammable, and there are no buckets of either sand or water for use in the event of fire."

"Wait you, Governor," Goesle said indignantly. "Why tell me these things? You know them as well as I do."

"Of course. Let us simply seem to be discussing the matter."

"What is to discuss? I know of nothing that will stop canvas catching fire. If you want me to procure buckets, that I can do, given time and opportunity."

"This twit can forbid us to open the show, if he is so minded. Naturally he did not come around until after I had paid the city a fee for the tober, and we are all set up. So we would waste time, effort and money if we were simply to fold on command. That is the way such petty officials operate. Now you say something else, Dai, so I can translate to him."

"Say *what*, Governor? You can tell him from me that he can go from here before I will hit him with a stake mallet."

"Thank you, Dai." Florian turned to the official and delivered a long spate of German, with gestures. The inspector rubbed his chin and looked suspicious.

"What did you tell him, then?" Goesle asked.

"That the wagon carrying the fire buckets is not here yet. It threw a wheel rim on the road. But the buckets will be here—and filled—before we open tomorrow."

"He doesn't appear to believe you."

"He will." Florian took from his pockets a sheaf of tickets, with a number of Austrian gulden notes folded among them. These he presented to the inspector, with a laving of syrupy German compliments. The official took the tickets and money, but regarded them with even more suspicion.

"I think now," said Goesle, "you are going to be charged with bribery."

Just then Autumn came into the chapiteau, wearing street dress. "Dai, one of my rigs's turnbuckles seemed loose, last time I—oh, excuse me. I didn't notice that you were occupied."

The inspector looked over at her, blinked and looked more intently at her. Then he whipped off his hat, bowed deeply to her and began backing out of the tent, meanwhile bowing likewise to both Florian and Goesle, and saying rapidly and obsequiously, "Gut gemacht! Alles in bester Ordnung sein. Verzeihen Sie, mein Herren! Küss die Hand, gnädige Dame . . . " and he was gone.

"What caused all that?" said Goesle, bewildered.

Florian said, "We finally convinced him that he will see the fire buckets here tomorrow."

"But he won't, Governor."

"He will, if he has to close both eyes to do it. I must say, a lovely lady arriving at just the right moment seemed to help convince him. Miss Auburn, he must have mistaken you for his empress in disguise. Remind me to have you around every time I have to deal with officialdom."

"Here is something else to remind you about," she said, producing a piece of paper. "New lyrics for the come-in spec. Boom-Boom and I worked them out together. Still to the tune of 'Greensleeves.'"

"Bless me, I had quite forgotten we'd need that," said Florian. He read and softly sang the words:

> Zirku-us ist Vergnügen!
> Zirkus vor Freude hüpfen!
> Zirkus hat Herz rein golden!
> Und alles zu Zirkus willkommen!

"We can all get together and practice them tonight," said Autumn. "Carl also has to teach the band a new march for the closing spec."

"Yes, that's right. The Austrian anthem. Well, I do thank you and him for these lyrics, my dear. Truly remarkable. To make German words rhyme and scan—even approximately—must put a strain upon the genius of Wagner himself."

By the next day's first performance, Zanni had done his accustomed snooping about the locality. So when, early in the show, he and Florian did their comic exchange, most of Zanni's jokes were topical. He made the audience roar when he poked fun at "die Sechsundsechzig Starken," the sixty-six local merchants who composed Landeck's civic promotion board. Zanni played that for all it was worth, because Starken could be made to mean either "men of big business" or "big fat businessmen."

Zanni also introduced a new element into the act: an assistant joey, in the small person of Quincy-Ali Baba Simms. And Ali Baba got his first-ever laugh just by walking into the pista, for Zanni had done his makeup like that of the Tambo or Bones in an American minstrel show. Ali Baba's face was blacked even blacker with burnt cork, except for a watermelon-slice mouth. He wore a sober suit and white gloves. The effect was of a little Negro exaggeratedly impersonating a white boy exaggeratedly impersonating a Negro, and the crowd thought it hilarious at first sight.

During the comic-patter exchange, Ali Baba had little to do. Only when Florian, pretending fury at Zanni's retorts and insults, tried to chase the clown, Ali Baba would contrive to be hanging onto Florian's frock-coat tails, or just then bending over to adjust a shoe so Florian tripped over him. Ali Baba's real clown début came at the end of the act, when Florian finally got furious at *him* and chased him around the pista. At that, Zanni produced a plug hat from somewhere and set it on his head, but put it there upside down. Ali Baba, fleeing from Florian, did a high leap that took him over Zanni—and he somersaulted there in midair, so that for an instant he and Zanni were head to head—and came down beyond, on his feet, with the plug hat right side up on his own head.

Because he and Zanni had practiced and perfected that trick in strict secrecy, even the watching troupers burst into surprised applause, along with the audience. And the audience produced a kind of uproar that Ali Baba and the other Americans had never heard until now. The people clapped their hands in the ordinary manner, but they augmented that noise by loudly stamping their feet upon the seat planks—and, after a moment, they were all stamping in unison, so the noise was thunderous. It did not abate until Florian, Zanni and Ali Baba—especially Ali Baba, his grin nearly splitting his head in half—had returned again and again for bows.

The Landeckers did that simultaneous hand-and-foot acclaim for every act, but they did it loudest for one turn in particular. The troupers never could divine the reason, but every show in Landeck drew a house full of apparently fanatical dog-lovers. The Smodlakas' terriers got such deafening applause and cries of "noch einmal!" at the first show that Pavlo and Gavrila and the children had to repeat several tricks and then take repeated bows. At that night's show, in the limelight, with Goesle's spotlight following the dogs' antics, the act elicited the same response, and the Smodlakas obliged with even more encores.

When the same thing happened at every subsequent performance, Gavrila began to get almost embarrassed by the unceasing curtain calls. She would have bowed out of the pista after a number of encores, but Pavlo always gave her a black look that kept her, the dogs and the children performing until the pale Velja and Sava were drained almost transparent. And at the Florilegium's very last performance in Landeck, the Smodlaka act went on and on until even the terriers were half dead, and Colonel Ramrod had to shrill his whistle and crack his whip repeatedly before Pavlo would let his family and animals retire, then himself stayed to bask and bow and beam until the equestrian director almost had to drag him off.

"Confound it!" Edge snapped at him. "I've got to fit in five more acts before the closing spec, and then we've got to tear down, and you've hogged the pista for nearly half an hour."

"Cut short the prljav other acts, then!" Pavlo snapped back at him. "Not mine, that these good people like best."

Edge had an inspiration that he thought clever. "Has it occurred to you," he said, "that all that hoorah might have been led by some rival dog trainer? Keeping you on view long enough for him to steal all your signals and tricks for his own act?"

Pavlo started, gasped, "Svetog Vlaha!" and went almost as white as either of his children. He stooped, grabbed up Terry, Terrier and Terriest as if they were in imminent danger of abduction, and hurried them off to their caravan.

There was one other unscheduled incident that night, but it caused no trouble except some missed beats of Edge's heart. Autumn was nearing the end of her act, slowly inching her way upright from her stride split on the tightrope. Every eye was on the tiny, high-up, yellow-clad sprite, and so was the brilliance of Goesle's spotlight. The silence in the chapiteau was such that the hissing of the lights' gas flames could be heard. Then, for no reason anyone could see, Autumn lost hold of her little yellow parasol. It fluttered down out of the limelight, so it seemed to vanish from existence, but Edge was not watching that. He kept his anxious gaze fixed on Autumn, sure that his breathing and his pulse both stopped during the fraction of a second that she was put off balance by the loss of her prop. Autumn only barely wavered—probably no one in the audience even noticed—then she continued to inch her feet together from the split until she was again standing on the rope, and she skipped along it to the platform to take her bows and applause.

"It simply slipped out of my hand, Zachary," she said, when she was down. "Maybe I'm still not accustomed to the spotlight. It does give me a bit of a headache..."

Edge said only that he was happy it had not proved serious. He sternly restrained himself from saying anything critical or cautionary. But he was aware that Autumn's confidence in herself was no longer absolutely unshakable. Her flower-petal eyes had in them a new look. It was not fear or worry or apprehension; it was pure puzzlement. Autumn Auburn had made a mistake she had never made before, and she was wondering why.

However, she had brightened again by the close of the show, when the band was playing "Gott Erhalte Unseren Kaiser," and the troupe was doing its final promenade around the chapiteau. Marching beside Edge, who was leading his liberty horses, she said to him:

"Listen at that chune. Owlwise—"

"Owlwise?"

"Hush. I'm doin' me cockney. Owlwise in Stepney we used ter sing that chune, but wif bawdy words." So she sang along with Haydn's august anthem, for Edge's ears only, all the lyrics of "She Was Poor But She Was Honest," and they both laughed again.

Next day, the circus train went leisurely on down the Inn valley. There were no villages or towns big enough to merit making a stand, and the next sizable one would be Innsbruck, but Florian was in no rush to get there. He explained, "We take our time on the road, and Innsbruck is of a size to give us a good long engagement. Then we take our time going wherever we go from there. By the time winter is upon us, I want us to be in the Danube lowlands, and we will stay in those more clement lowlands until the spring."

The troupers did not mind traveling at a sauntering pace, for the ever-widening valley was ever more beautiful to look at. Every village square and farmhouse yard glowed with garden flowers and the fields between were riotous with wild ones. "The Blumenmeer," said Beck. "So the Österreichers call it. The Blossom Sea. Especially in spring, when in flower all the orchards are: cherry, peach, apricot, almond. Now blooming only the Pappeln are." Those were the poplars, the trees mainly in evidence along the way. In this season, they were shedding such a snowstorm of white fluffs that the road was banked deep with them. The horses' hoofbeats were almost inaudible, but they kicked up clouds of the white down, and the wagon train left a high, long-hanging white trail behind it, like smoke, so that from a distance it could have been mistaken for a steam-propelled railroad train.

One evening, when the troupers camped by the roadside and applied to a nearby farmhouse for fresh food, the victuals they got included a basket of goose eggs. Fitzfarris, unnoticed, purloined one of those eggs and took it off somewhere. The next night, at the next camp, when Magpie Maggie Hag was preparing to fry some of those eggs, Fitzfarris happened to be standing by, and he suddenly said, in a voice of awe, "Good Jesus, Mag! Look at that one you just picked up."

She did, and cried, "Devlesa!" and dropped it, but Fitz nimbly caught it.

Others gathered, and Fitzfarris handed the egg around—"Just look at that!" —and the others all exclaimed or murmured over it. When Florian joined them, he asked lightly, "Have you discovered the goose that lays the golden eggs, Sir John?"

Mullenax said, "Damn near as good as. Look at it, Governor."

Florian turned it over and over in his hand. It was an ordinary goose egg, except that its shell was not quite smooth. It bore an embossed figure: a neatly recognizable Christian cross slightly upraised from the surface.

Yount asked excitedly, "How could we find the one amongst them geese back yonder that laid this egg? If that goose makes a habit of it, we'd sure as hell have some curios to sell!"

"I don't think Sir John needs the goose," said Florian, his eyes twinkling. To Fitzfarris he said, "You figure this would be a good gimmix for the Auerhahn, don't you?"

"Aw, shucks," said Fitz. "You've seen this dodge before."

"Usually in the more backward communities, where the yokels are good game for superstition and miracles. What did you use, Sir John?"

"Drew the cross with wax, dipped the egg in some of Boom-Boom's leftover generator acid for a couple of minutes, then scraped the wax off. Governor, you talked up that bird real well in Landeck—made it sound like Sinbad's roc—but the jossers didn't look very impressed. So I thought: suppose we put a twig nest in that cage, talk up the creature as a miracle layer, peddle the cross-marked eggs..."

"Well, it's certainly worth trying. This is all Catholic country hereabout. But I fear you'll find our next audiences—the folk of Innsbruck—quite civilized and blasé."

"Anybody religious is easy game for religious flimflam," Fitz said confidently. "But if crosses don't sell, I'll do a patriotic flimflam instead. Make the eggs wear the Austrian coat of arms."

However, the circus arrived at Innsbruck to find that its people were feeling rather glum about patriotism and not very hopeful of miracles.

"The war news was slow getting up the valley," said Florian, when he met the train at the city's riverside outskirts. "While we were still at Landeck, the Austrians were so dismally defeated in Bohemia—at some place named Königgrätz —that they have retreated all the way south to the vicinity of Vienna, and Franz Joseph is asking Prussia for an armistice. Austria has lost the war."

"What will this mean to us?" asked Edge.

"Right now, probably scant houses and not very joyous audiences. I have secured a tober for us—in the Hofgarten—but I do not think, at this solemn time, I will be so tasteless as to put up any of those forget-your-worries posters."

He led the train along the river avenue, through the grounds of the university, skirting the constricted area of the Old City, over which gleamed the gold-plated balcony roof of the Schloss Fürstenburg, and on into the public park that stretched beyond the State Theater. While the roustabouts unloaded the wagons and prepared for the setup there, Florian resumed talking to Edge:

"As regards the immediate future, Austria's defeat probably will mean a depression of business, including ours. I hear that Franz Joseph has already agreed to let go of Venezia. That is a large and costly loss, and Prussia's Chancellor Bismarck is likely to demand even more concessions."

Edge said, "So Austria will mean poor pickings for us."

"At least for a while. Not long. Austrians have a faculty for rebounding quickly from adversity, or developing an indifference to it. But I am looking farther down the road, so to speak, and I foresee future political upheavals."

"Affecting us?"

"Affecting all of Europe, I fear. For a long time, Bismarck has been trying to unite all the independent Germanic states into one cohesive and invincible Deutsche Reich. Until now, two other empires—the French and the Austrian— have maintained a fair balance between them. And Louis Napoléon and Franz Joseph, between them, have pretty much managed the destiny of all the rest of the Continent. Now Austria has lost a good deal of power and prestige. Louis Napoléon won't weep over that, but neither will he smile on a Germanic nation getting itself unified and rising to power. Soon or later, France must act to crush Bismarck's ambitions."

"Meaning another war," said Edge. "Where, do you reckon?"

"Ah, I wish I could foresee *that* clearly, Zachary, so we could avoid the place and the occasion. We must simply make our plans as best we can, as we go along."

"Per piacere, Governatore... Direttore..." said Zanni Bonvecino politely, coming up to them. "I heard you mention plans. I wonder if they might be elastic enough to include some new artistes."

"Unfortunately, signore," said Florian, "we were discussing plans gone agley, as a poet once put it. Meaning tutti rotoli."

"Ohimè. Then forgive my being presumptuous. But might I at least introduce some old friends to you? They saw us ride in."

"Oh, by all means. Always pleased to meet fellow showfolk, even if I cannot ...well..."

"Here are the Kyrios and Kyria Vasilakis, which is to say the Signor and Signora Vasilakis." They were a darkly handsome couple, aged perhaps thirty. "Spyros and Meli—originally of Greece."

"Kalispéra," said Florian. The Vasilakises immediately grinned brilliant ivory grins and began jabbering simultaneously. "No, no, please!" said Florian, laughing and making fending-off gestures. "Kalispéra is one of maybe eight Greek words I know, and the other seven are indecent."

"Parakaló," said the male Vasilakis, with a shrug. "We spik some Angliká. Also other. Franks. Talian."

"And this," said Zanni, "is a native Austrian, the Herr Jörg Pfeifer. All of us have worked at one time together on the Zirkus Corty-Althoff. My friends, allow me to present the Florilegium's Governor Florian and Equestrian Director Edge." They shook hands all around, and Zanni went on, "Jörg and Spyros and Meli were engaged to entertain during the annual Trade and Crafts Fair here in Innsbruck. But that fair has just now closed, early and abruptly, because of the bad news from the war front. So they are at liberty."

"Ah...yes..." Florian said uncomfortably. "And tell me, what do you all do?"

"I am a white-face," Pfeifer said proudly. He was a short, broad, gray-haired man of about sixty. "In the pista I am called Fünfünf."

"He and I," said Zanni, "used to do the Lupino mirror together."

"No! Is that a fact?" exclaimed Florian, his face brightening.

"And I," said Spyros, "I it fires, swallow swords." He pronounced the *sw* in both those words. "Wife Meli snake kharmer."

Zanni helpfully translated. "He *eats* fire and swallows *swords*. She is a snake charmer. They have their own equipment and snakes, and their own caravan. Jörg also has his own van, and a splendid wardrobe of the traditional white-face dress."

"Well..." said Florian. "As you all must realize, the war news is distressing to us, too. I don't expect that we will shut down like the Trade Fair. However..."

"I myself," said Pfeifer, "would seriously consider any salary offered, however much less than my usual five hundred francs a week."

Florian calculated, and murmured for Edge's benefit, "A hundred American dollars. I am sure you are worth every centime of that, mein Herr. So I would not demean you or myself by uttering such an offer as I would have to make."

"Utter it. I am a comedian. I can do no worse than laugh."

"One hundred fifty francs, Herr Fünfünf."

"Accepted." He turned to Zanni. "We will try doing the mirror at the very first show. Let us go and see how rusty we have become."

"A moment," Zanni said to him, then to Florian, "What of Spyros and Meli, Governatore?"

"We can hardly doom them to performing on Innsbruck's street corners, can we? But I must consult with our sideshow director regarding their salary. Will you take them along, Signor Bonvecino, and introduce them to Sir John?"

When the four had gone off toward the backyard, Edge said, "We no sooner run into hard times again, but you have to play Lord Bountiful. You're going to pay a joey as much as you pay Maurice LeVie?"

"Not just a joey, a *white-face*. I'd have been stupid to let him get away. The white-face is the most ancient traditional element in a European circus. But it would have been heartless to take him and then refuse the other two. Anyway, I got Fünfünf at such a bargain rate that we can afford the sideshow Greeks."

"What kind of name is Fünfünf? It sounds like a cat sneezing."

"Only a nonsense word. If it translated from the German at all, it would be something like 'five-by-five'—which is approximately the shape he will have in the pista: five feet high, five feet wide. You will see what I—oh, Christ Almighty, here comes another city inspector to poke around and find fault and want his palm greased. Go fetch Autumn for me, Zachary."

"I can't. She's feeling poorly. Of course, she'd never admit to any such thing, but I could see she's been looking not as sprightly as usual. I'm making her stay abed until Maggie Hag can take a look at her."

"I'm sorry to hear it. And sorrier that I'll have to deal with this jack-in-office all by myself. But I hope your dear lady's indisposition is only trivial and temporary."

Florian went to meet and greet the inspector, and strolled along with him as he scrutinized the rising tent, and peered at other things, and scribbled in a notebook. Florian kept up an amiable chatter of German, but the inspector only grunted in response—until Florian had the inspiration to remark that "this whole circus is on the square." The inspector gave him a keen look and asked if it was also "on the level?"

"By the plumb rule," replied Florian.

"Then the builder is smitten," said the inspector, shutting his notebook. When the two had exchanged certain discreet signs, he asked another question: "And if there be no stones for the builder?"

"Then refresh him," said Florian, "with money to bring him to the next lodge." There was a discreet transaction of another kind, and the inspector took his leave.

Edge was sitting on the let-down little steps at the back of the caravan when Magpie Maggie Hag came out the door. He stood up to let her descend the stairs, and said, "Well?"

She beckoned him a short distance from the van. "Has bad headache, says your romeri. Also weakness sometimes in her hands. It comes, goes, one hand, then other. But is not weakness, is numbness. I know. When she not look, I prick with pin, she no feel."

"What's causing it, Mag?"

"Could be many things. Some no matter, some matter much. But tell me. You not notice any difference in her?"

"Why...yes. She's been listless—downcast—ever since the night she dropped her parasol during the Landeck show."

"You not notice any other thing? From before that?"

"Well, how do you mean? Have *you* noticed something? When?"

"Long time ago. In Italy palace. When she heard clock stop."

"Oh, come on, Mag. That was peculiar, yes, but don't use it to start a rube routine on me. If Autumn is ailing, I want to know about the ailment, not listen to any gypsy-jinx talk."

"But that clock she did hear stop. Person's head can do strange things. And when head start doing strange things, should start wondering why."

"Damn, Mag! Are you saying she's sick in the head?"

"You not notice any difference in face... in how she *look?*"

"Well... yes. Her eyes have lost some sparkle. But wouldn't that be natural, if she's feeling puny?"

"Next time you look her eyes, look close. For now, make her rest. Not let her perform tomorrow. I have rub her hands with hot-pepper salve. Now I go mix potion for make strength. We will see."

Edge stood slumped for a minute, thinking, then squared his shoulders and entered the van. Autumn lay on the bed, propped against a pillow, with a pencil and paper in hand, and she was listening to the tinkly music of "Greensleeves" being played by the little music box Edge had given her back in Perugia.

"Rather than just lie here," she said, "I thought I would get a start on composing French words for the come-in—for when we get to Paris. Somebody else will have to put them into Magyar and Russian, for when we go—"

"You stop worrying about the circus," said Edge. "Concentrate on getting yourself well again, my girl." He pulled over one of the two chairs and sat down beside her.

"Oh, Zachary, you know how we women get the mopes and the fanteagues from time to time. If we simply quit work and downed tools every time—"

"I won't risk your having a female swoon thirty feet up in the air. You're not going on tomorrow. Not until Maggie has spooned some of her nostrums into you, and you get your strength back."

"But I am *the close of the show!* Florian will tear out his beard."

"No, he won't. Sunday and Monday can do the slant-climb, and that will satisfy the jossers that they've seen ropewalking. And now Florian has just hired a new joey that he thinks is something special. So we'll have a full program; the audience won't feel cheated."

"I shall not be missed at all?" she said, pretending dismay. "That is a worse prospect than taking a tumble."

"You'll be missed by me. And to hell with everybody else but you and me. I want you well again. I'll tie you to that bed if I have to."

She went on making protestations, but Edge was not listening. He was, as Magpie Maggie Hag had instructed, taking a very close look at Autumn. And there *was* something different about her—about her face—it was noticeable only now when he was seeking something to notice. It looked as if... but that was impossible, he told himself. A face couldn't *do* that. The most beautiful features might get ill, old, wrinkled, coarse, even scarred, but the change he now seemed to see was a physical impossibility for a face. Goddamn it, he thought, that old gypsy has spooked my eyesight.

"You just lie there," he said, "and luxuriate in idleness. I'll be looking in on you, and as soon as I get a chance to go downtown I'll buy some books for you. When Maggie brings her witch's brews, you be a good girl and choke them down, you hear?"

Outside again, Edge found Florian in conference with a gathering of men and women of various ages, the men in dusty-green lederhosen, the women mostly in varicolored dirndls. The conference ended with several of the people handing money to Florian, then they departed. Florian beckoned to Edge and said happily:

"Sir John is going to be in his glory. Not only does he have two new attractions for his sideshow—the sword swallower and the snake handler—he will

also have a full and flourishing midway for the first time. Those people were
seeking what we call faking privileges—permission to set up in our front yard
here. And some even want to come on the road with us afterward. Every kind of
joint and butcher."

"Joint? Butcher?"

"Souvenir joints, slum joints, candy butchers, pastry butchers. Like the stalls
you saw at that fair in Italy. These folks were all peddling edibles, potables,
craftwork, slum, every sort of thing—here at Innsbruck's Trade Fair—and they
all got dispossessed when it folded. Now they are eager to cleave to us. Not much
money in it for us, of course. I asked only a nominal fee from each of them for
the faking privileges. I demanded no rake-off from their take. Still, they'll add
bustle and color and vivacity to our front yard."

"If you say so, Governor."

"Well, surely you saw that some of those female cheapjacks are young and
pretty. I especially admire them in their crisp native dirndls—making their
bosoms so high and perky." He smiled appreciatively. "It used to be that only girl
children wore dirndls, until their older sisters saw how fetching that frock-and-
apron is. Virginal and seductive at the same time. I do believe there's no more
flattering dress a pretty woman can wear."

"You sure are sounding exuberant, Governor. I reckon that civil inspector
wasn't too incivil in his snooping."

"Oh, I got rid of him easily enough. We turned out to have some interests in
common. Also there is an old Austrian custom called Freunderlwirtschaft. What
I believe you Americans call 'you scratch my back and I'll scratch yours.' But
you, Zachary, my boy, you are *not* sounding exuberant. Why?"

"I have to tell you, we've got to rearrange the main program. Autumn can't go
on tomorrow. Maybe not for some while."

"My dear friend, I am sorry to hear that. You and she both have my condolences, and of course my hope that she soon gets better."

"Thank you. But the program?"

Florian considered only briefly. "Instead of Autumn coming on to close after
the Simms girls, we'll bring on Fünfünf and Zanni to do the Lupino mirror.
That's always a guaranteed audience pleaser."

"I thought sure you'd move the trapeze act to the close."

"No. Herr Pfeifer has nobly accepted a comedown in salary. Let us at least
pay him in program status. Let him and Zanni close the show with a slambang,
knockabout spill-and-pelt."

"There'll be slamming and banging, all right, when Maurice and Paprika
hear about this. You said you foresaw another war in the offing. I suspect it's
closer than you think."

"Let us get it over with, then. I believe all the principals concerned are in the
chapiteau right now."

Florian and Edge went in, and found Beck and his roustabouts hanging and
testing the security of several aerial rigs at once. Maurice and Paprika were
closely eyeing the men arranging their trapeze apparatus up near the roof peak,
and Sunday and Monday Simms were just as closely watching other men
tighten the turnbuckles of their rope slanted between peak and ground. In the
middle of the pista's sawdust circle, heedless of all the work going on above and
around them, Zanni and Fünfünf were demonstrating to little Quincy Simms a

nicely carved wooden frame. It was big enough to have contained a grown man's full-length portrait, but it was only an empty and open rectangle.

Florian had to shout, above the noise, to the clowns and the aerialists. They left their several occupations and came over to him. Edge would probably have broached the news with some tergiversation, but Florian said bluntly, "Our show closer, Miss Auburn, is ill and will not appear tomorrow. Misses Sunday and Monday, you will go on as usual, next to closing. Herr Fünfünf, if you and Signor Zanni believe you have sufficiently mastered again the Lupino turn, you will follow the Misses Simms and close the show."

The two clowns said "Ja" and "Sì" together.

Maurice essayed only a mild protest. "Surely, Monsieur le Gouverneur, the show should close with a thrill act. Meaning myself and my partner on the trap."

Florian said, "I usually have a reason for my decisions, Monsieur LeVie. Let that suffice."

Maurice shrugged in Gallic resignation, but Paprika flared in Hungarian high temper. "It does not suffice for me, kedvesem! After all our years of kicking sawdust together, you now deny me the close and give it to this... this first-of-May? Ó jaj, actually he appears more like a first-of-December!" She scathingly looked the newcomer up and down, from his thin gray hair to his shabby attire of civilian suit and shoes. "Do you really expect me to accept second place behind this—this feeble old derelict?"

Before anyone else could speak, Herr Pfeifer quickly knelt, tugged off his heavy shoes and then, without removing any other of his confining clothes or even loosening his cravat, stepped in his stocking feet onto the Simms girls' slanted tightrope. Without balance pole or any other helping prop, he ran surefootedly up the rope to its top, where it was secured near one of the trapeze platforms. He vaulted nimbly onto that platform, unhooked the held-back trapeze bar, swung out on it, did a number of flipovers, knee-hangs and handstands—his incongruous street clothes bunching and coming awry and flapping—then swung back to land lightly on the platform, leapt from there again to the slanted rope and came *cartwheeling* down it. Back on the ground, not even breathing hard, he gave Paprika as haughty a look as she had given him, then sat down on the pista curb to put his shoes on again. Everyone in the chapiteau, from Florian to the least Slovak, was staring at him, stunned and speechless.

Paprika broke the prevailing silence, and she did it graciously. "Verzeiht Sie, Artistenmeister. What I said was inexcusable. I shall be proud to appear anywhere on any program in company with you. I abase myself."

"Never abase yourself, Fräulein," the old fellow said gruffly.

Zanni said, "Jörg also was once an aerialist."

"But then I fell. I broke some bones. And I lost my nerve."

"Ma foi," Maurice said in awe. "I should hate to compete with you whenever you recover it."

"Aber, Herr Fünfünf..." Sunday said timidly. "Aber... warum werden ein Clown?"

"I did not become a *clown*," he said. "I became a white-face. It is a higher calling even than aerialist. You will see tomorrow."

2

THEY ALL SAW a great many new things on the morrow. By noontime, in the tober's front yard, two rows of what Florian had called joints lined the way to the chapiteau. Some of the stalls had bright banners stretched above them to extol their wares, and all had their wares prominently to be seen or smelled: Chinese paper parasols, steaming wurst and kraut, head-and-stick hobbyhorses, fresh-baked hot waffles, tortoiseshell combs, beer straight from the keg, goat's milk straight from the nanny, tin trumpets, layered tortes, decorative little lamps, sugar sticks, toy drums, cuckoo clocks...

Beyond the stalls, nearest to the chapiteau's front-door marquee, was Maximus in his cage, staring out with impassive dignity, except when he caught a scent of cooking sausage and wrinkled his big nose in wistful sniffs. Across the way from him was Fitzfarris's "disappearance" pedestal, now doing duty as a stand for Spyros Vasilakis. He repeatedly took from a bottle a mouthful of naphtha, then blew it forth in a spray ignited by a burning pine splint in his hand, and so spouted a fountain of flame that made an advertisement for the circus visible all over the Hofgarten. Meanwhile, from inside the pavilion could be heard Kapellmeister Beck's entire band—cornet, trombone, tuba, French horn, accordion, Teufel Geige and snare, tenor and bass drums—rendering, with real Tirolean oom-pah-pah, every one of the circus's themes, from "Green-sleeves" to "Bollocky Bill" to "Bal de Vienne."

Next forward of Spyros's stand was the red wagon, with Magpie Maggie Hag at the guichet up front, waiting for ticket buyers. At the museum at the rear of the wagon were Sir John in his tattoo-concealing makeup and Jörg Pfeifer in street clothes, both of them shouting "Kommt! Herein!" and such things. The Innsbruckers attracted by the fire eater's billows and seduced by the museum keepers' bellows into buying tickets then got to see Spyros close up and the lion in his cage and the Auerhahn glaring maniacally out through its museum wire netting. In a corner of the museum, and netted over to be safe from the bird's likely depredations, was its "nest" of woven twigs. Whenever a sufficient crowd of jossers had assembled there, Sir John would cease shouting and start expatiating—Pfeifer translating—on the frequent miraculous eggs to be found among those laid by the Auerhahn, and would take out and display one. The eggs now bore the embossed sentiment "Gott und Kaiser." Occasionally a knowledgeable spectator would sarcastically point out that a miracle even greater than the egg tribute to God and Emperor was its having been laid by a *cock* bird. But occasionally, too, a pious or patriotic onlooker would beg hard enough to persuade Sir John—who made sad grimaces of reluctance and sacrifice—to sell him the egg, and would pay a fancy price for it.

"It's a pity you can't be seeing it all," Edge said to Autumn. "The Florilegium is about as splendiferous as the Orfei now."

"Just as well I can't, I suppose," Autumn said wanly from her sickbed. "Even from a distance, the noise doesn't improve my headache. I *would* like to watch that white-face, though."

"That reminds me," said Edge, elaborately offhand. "Can I borrow your wall mirror? Fünfünf and Zanni are going to do something called the Lupino mirror, which means a fake one of some sort. But to lead into the act they need a real one."

Autumn gestured consent, with one hand, and Edge took the mirror off its hook. Autumn continued to move that hand, clenching and unclenching it, flexing the fingers. She murmured, "It's gone feeble again. What could be the connection between an aching head and a weak hand?"

"Don't worry about it. Maggie will soon have you hale and hearty and bonny again."

Autumn said, with a rueful laugh, "Gorblimey, I think she's making me drink that tincture she had Boom-Boom smearing on his head."

The Florilegium drew only a medium attendance that afternoon, not a scanty bianca, but not a sfondone crowd either. However, at intermission Florian said philosophically, "Well, at least we're making our nut," because the audience that spilled out onto the midway began indulgently spending money. They bought every sort of thing from Sir John's voice-projecting swazzles and the Auerhahn's eggs to the cartes-de-visite of the White African Pygmies, and they kept Magpie Maggie Hag profitably occupied at palm reading and dream dukkering. The people also patronized the midway joints, eating and drinking, buying slum mementos of the occasion. During the sideshow, Sir John, with Florian interpreting where necessary, first showed off his own freakish face, then his old-standby freaks of Night Children, Pygmies, the Egyptian mummy, Little Miss Mitten, and in dramatic conclusion brought on his new pièces de résistance.

"The Gluttonous Greek!" he introduced Spyros, who bounded onto the platform clad in doomfully black fleshings. Inside the chapiteau, Beck took the signal to have his band crash into Wagner's "Magic Fire Music." Sir John went on, "This is a man who will eat anything, Herren und Damen, things that would kill you and me—including blazing fire and razor-sharp steel!"

Spyros took a gulp from what looked like a bottle of water, but was really olive oil to lubricate his innards. Then he unrolled a bundle of chamois skin to reveal a dagger, a short sword and a real cavalry sabre, all brilliantly nickel-plated. He hurled them, one by one, point first into the wooden platform to show that they were not bogus or telescoping blades. He retrieved the dagger first, wrenched it out of the wood, wiped it thoroughly with the chamois skin, threw his head back, opened his mouth and let the dagger slide down inside, to the hilt. Next he did the same, more slowly, with the short sword. Next he did the same with the long sabre, but with grimaces, grunts and eye rollings to proclaim the superhuman difficulty of getting it all the way down his gullet. Sir John had learned from Spyros that there truly was no trickery to this, except for one small and unnoticeable deception: the cavalry sabre's blade had been shortened from its standard length of thirty inches to twenty-six, which Spyros had long ago determined, by experiment, was the distance from his lips to the pit of his stomach.

"And now," announced Sir John, echoed by Florian, "der gefrässig Grieche will do the impossible! He will swallow all three blades at one gulp. Watch closely. You will actually see his Adamsapfel bulge and wriggle as the steel is forced past it." The Greek's Adam's apple did exactly that, and several women in the crowd had to be led away by their escorts. When Spyros extracted his armory, piece by piece, he again carefully wiped all the blades, and Sir John explained, "The Gluttonous Greek must cleanse the steel beforehand, because even a speck of dust could make him retch, and that would make the razor edge slice into his esophagus. He also wipes them afterward, but for the *swords'* protection. Because of the Greek's unorthodox diet, his stomach acids have become so powerful that they could corrode even Essen steel."

Now Spyros took a swig from a bottle of goat's milk, partly to wash down the olive oil, which could have caught fire, and partly just to moisten the lining of his mouth. Then he lit oil-soaked wads of cotton wool on short rods, stuck one in his mouth, closed his lips, brought out the wad extinguished and smoking, stuck another lighted one in his mouth, stuck in the extinguished one and lit it from the other in there. After several repetitions of and variations on the burning wads, he did what he had been doing previously—the less uncomfortable but more spectacular feat of taking a mouthful of naphtha, spewing it out and lighting it as it sprayed, so the great mushroom of fire went *whoompf!* over the heads of the people, making them cringe and duck and turn away from the undeniable furnace heat of the flames.

When they returned their attention to the platform, Spyros was gone and Meli stood there. She wore fleshings that were entirely covered with silvery spangles, like scales, making of her a most fetching, curvaceous, sinuous serpent-woman. She wore her dark hair in two long braids, and there were two large, covered wicker baskets at her feet.

"Meli the Medusa!" shouted Sir John. "The only woman in the history of the world, since our Mother Eve, so beautiful and tempting that snakes come to her of their own accord. Venomous snakes, crushing snakes, no matter. She so charms them that they never do her harm. Or"—he paused impressively—"they have not *yet.*" From inside the chapiteau came the single sound of the cornet, doing a tweedly, Oriental-sounding rendition of Rameau's "Zéphire." Sir John and Florian continued, "Notice, Herren und Damen, the prettily patterned but clearly vicious reptiles Meli the Medusa is now taking from one basket. The country dwellers among you will recognize them as specimens of the adder, the deadliest snake found in Europe."

They were not. If Meli had not earlier confided the truth to Sir John and Florian, they would probably not have been on the same platform with her and her pets at this moment. The snakes indeed were, to the lay observer, well-nigh indistinguishable from the venomous European adder, but in fact they were the harmless smooth snakes of Britain. Meli now had half a dozen of them twining about her arms and shoulders and throat, while she herself did an undulating, serpentine, suggestive dance to the tweedling cornet music. Finally the snakes found her two long braids of hair, slithered up along them, and the dance ended with Meli's head crowned, like Medusa's, with a coiffure of snakes intertwining and coiling about each other.

They were not *trained* to do that, she had explained, but did it naturally. They were arboreal snakes, always seeking to climb upward. The twining they did around her arms and neck during the dance was accomplished by her *preventing* their climbing, and, when she ceased to frustrate them, they simply slithered up to her highest point, the top of her head. Now she reached up and disentangled them, returned them gently to their basket and covered it. From the other basket she lifted a different snake—or, rather, lifted the fore end of it, for it was a rock python eleven or twelve feet long, and heavy, and at midbody as big around as a man's thigh.

So Meli merely dragged out its foremost part and let it curl around one of her legs, and slide the rest of its length from the basket, and up around her—while she went again into her undulating, erotic dance. Part of the dance's eroticism was supplied by the python itself. In its climbing of Meli's body, it brought its big head and phallic length up from between her legs, before coiling around her hips and continuing on up her. Meli's dance necessarily got even slower when she was bearing the python's full weight. When she ceased to dance and threw up her arms in the V-posture and the audience broke into applause, Meli was wearing most of the snake as a massive belt around her middle, its fore length extending up her back so its head looked over her shoulder—the eyes coldly unwinking, the forked tongue flickering in and out. The chief secret about letting a python get you in its clench, she had explained to Florian and Sir John, was to make sure that most of it wound around your belly; any constrictor snake was not so likely to start squeezing in earnest when it was gripping soft flesh as when it was coiled around a bony part like the rib cage.

While Meli let her python pour itself back into its basket, Sir John produced his wooden apparatus and a field mouse and bellowed an invitation for all and sundry to rally around and join in his "Mauserennen." Florian let that game and Magpie Maggie Hag's divinations go on until some of the people not partaking began to look restless. Then he sent word to Beck to strike up the band again, and the crowd hurried back inside the chapiteau.

The second half of the program went well, and Pavlo Smodlaka this time did not prolong his slanging-buffers act—although this audience, too, seemed greatly to enjoy the talented terriers and to applaud them extravagantly. In fact, Pavlo hurried the act along and kept furtively scanning the stands for possible lurking spies. Several times he was so distracted that Gavrila or one of the children would have to give the dogs their next signal. And when the act finished, in record time, Pavlo allowed himself and his family only the briefest of bows before hurrying with them out of the tent.

Finally, when Sunday and Monday were taking the applause for their rope work, Zanni skipped into the pista, bringing with him this time Fünfünf, and Edge got his first look at what Florian said was "one of the oldest, most esteemed, ever-changeless characters of European circusdom." Zanni was attired, as he had been all during the show, in his Harlequin outfit, with just enough makeup to give his face its range of expressions from glee to mischievousness to despair. But Fünfünf was a complete transformation from the man Jörg Pfeifer —or from any mortal being, thought Edge.

He wore a one-piece, loose costume of bright red satin, lavishly adorned with silver sequins. It had tight, wrist-length sleeves that rose in high peaks at his shoulders. From those peaks, the dress hung as straight and waistless as a smock, until it forked into a pair of short, broad pants ending just above his bare knees. The costume did make his torso look almost perfectly square, as the name Fünfünf implied. Below it, he wore white slippers and calf-high white stockings. Above it, his entire face was white with greasepaint, and on that dead-white skin his eyebrows and lashes were blacked, his mouth rouged bright red and both his ears painted bright red as well. He wore a brimless, conical white hat which, blending into the white of his forehead, would have made him rather resemble a bald pinhead, except that the cap was jauntily tilted just a bit to one side.

The white, black and red makeup was both droll and demonic; Fünfünf could have been of any age, or ageless. Throughout the act, when his face was not comically-evilly impassive, it showed only two other expressions: eyebrows raised in disdainful hauteur or red mouth grinning sardonically wide. The bizarre makeup and dress, unvaried through generations of white-faces, seemed —even to Edge—imbued with the tyrannical authority of antiquity. So did Fünfünf's superior and domineering manner, as he ordered Zanni about, and derided him, and humiliated him, and made him grovel—and made the spectators roar with laughter. Like them, Edge had to laugh at the white-face, but he laughed with some unease, and he suspected that those others did the same. Though he had never seen a white-face before, he felt that the seriocomic figure was somehow eerily familiar—like a recognizable memory from childhood of that funny-frightening goblin or spook or bogeyman never encountered but always lurking to "get you if you don't behave."

Edge could understand only an infrequent word of the German the two joeys spoke, but the give-and-take could be inferred from the action—as now, when Fünfünf blindfolded Zanni and gave him instructions to walk, stop, turn left or right in response to whistled commands. With a tiny whistle, the white-face began to blow various numbers of tweets, and Zanni obeyed—only to have the malicious Fünfünf send him walking into a center pole, from which he ricocheted flat on his back (*boom!* from the bass drum). The white-face next sent him across the pista, to trip over the curbing and fall flat on his face (*r-r-rip!* from the snare drum). When Zanni got up, he scratched his head and ponderously cogitated, then smiled slyly. Meanwhile, Fünfünf had beckoned to little Ali Baba, who ran in with a bucket of water to set in the ring. Now, when the white-face whistled, Zanni looked smug and clever, and obeyed the commands in reverse, turning left when directed to the right, and so on—and of course stepped into the pail with a splash (*cr-rash!* from the cymbal).

While the audience roared, Zanni angrily tore off his blindfold and, with the bucket wedged on one foot, stumped over to Fünfünf and kicked the bucket at him. But it remained stuck on his foot, so Zanni was flung on his back again (*boom!*) with that foot in the air, the pail upside down and emptying the rest of its water on him (*cr-rash!*). Fünfünf sent Ali Baba trotting off, then helped Zanni to his feet, pretended solicitude, dusted him off and—when Ali Baba ran in again, bringing Autumn's wall mirror—held that up for Zanni to resettle his little hat, pat his wet hair straight, smooth his eyebrows. Then Zanni bent closer to the mirror, shut his eyes and just stood there.

"Was gibt's?" asked the white-face. Zanni replied, with gestures—so that even Edge could comprehend—that he wanted to see what he looked like when he was asleep.

"*Kretin!*" snarled Fünfünf. He whipped off his own hat and beat Zanni over the head with it. When the white-face put his hat back on, he was dissatisfied with its placement, and bade Zanni hold the mirror for him. Fünfünf looked into it, bent and stooped this way and that, made it plain that he was dissatisfied with the mirror, and demanded a bigger one. Zanni and Ali Baba obediently scampered from the pista and through the back door.

After a moment, there came a loud smash and tinkle of glass from out there. (Goesle had provided a scrap piece for the effect.) The audience began laughing in anticipation of Fünfünf's rage at the mirror's having got broken, but he appeared not to have heard. He merely waited in the pista, still finically adjusting his hat, striking attitudes, humming to himself. Then Ali Baba, looking terrified, crept into the pavilion again, lugging that big, empty, rectangular wooden frame. Crouching on the far side of Ali Baba, hiding, Zanni also came creeping and looking terrified. The white-face noticed nothing until Ali Baba got near him, set the frame upright on the sawdust and stood to one side to hold it there.

"Ah!" said Fünfünf, and stepped in front of the "mirror." At the same instant, Zanni stood up on the other side of the frame.

"Eh?" said Fünfünf, raising his eyebrows and taking a startled step backward. At exactly the same time, Zanni opened his mouth, raised his eyebrows and took a step backward.

Fünfünf shook his head as if to clear it—so did Zanni—stepped forward again—so did Zanni—and bent to scrutinize his reflection—Zanni did the same. Fünfünf/Zanni slowly, very slowly raised a hand, adjusted his/his hat a millimeter to the left/right—then abruptly dropped his/his hand again. Already the jossers were falling about and nearly strangling with laughter, and so were most of the troupers looking on. The mirror effect was appreciable and enjoyable, whatever side of the pista it was viewed from. Since both clowns moved in such perfect synchrony, and both were visible to everybody, it was the viewer's choice: which was the real, which the reflection, which imitating which? After a good deal of this, Fünfünf totally turned his back on the mirror. So did Zanni. There could not possibly have been a signal between them, but, when the white-face slowly, furtively turned his head to look at the mirror over his shoulder, there was Zanni looking just as suspiciously back at him.

Fünfünf's movements and dodges got more and more convulsive and complex—interrupted by sudden freezes of position—but every one of them was faultlessly imitated by Zanni. At last, when the clowns evidently decided that to make the crowd laugh any more was to risk the people's having mass apoplexy —and when even Ali Baba was laughing so hard that the mirror was shaking— they somehow mutually agreed to end the show. Fünfünf suddenly sprang clear to the right of the frame, Zanni sprang to his left, and they were face to face with no pretended glass between. Infuriated, the white-face again began beating Zanni with his hat, but that was not enough; he snatched the frame from Ali Baba and brought it down over Zanni's head, astonishing the whole audience and troupe with the sound of real glass violently smashing. (One of the bandstand Slovaks provided that with another piece of scrap.) Zanni acted as if a genuine mirror had been broken over his head; he reeled and collapsed across the frame. Since the white-face was dragging that as he ran from the pista, he dragged the limp Zanni behind him, flopping and flailing, out of the chapiteau.

The two had to come back again and again to take bows to the people, who were wildly clapping hands and stamping feet, even while they continued to laugh and spill tears down their cheeks. At every other reentry, Fünfünf and Zanni brought Ali Baba with them, to share the acclaim.

"Pure magic!" Edge shouted to Florian beside him. "The Lupino it's named for, was he an Italian like Zanni?"

"No. George Lupino. Englishman," Florian shouted back. "Quick, now. Call the closing spec while the crowd is still on the crest."

Edge's whistle shrilled over the noise, and the noise was immediately increased by the band's thundering into "Gott Erhalte Unseren Kaiser." Edge took his part in the promenade, riding Thunder and, with his sabre, saluting the audience. But, the moment it was over, he flung his reins to a roustabout and hurried to the caravan to see how Autumn was.

She was fine, she said, feeling much better. In fact, she was out of bed and dressed, and pottering about the van's interior, doing little tidying-up chores. "You were right, Zachary. The bit of rest was all I needed." She came and kissed him. "You're a competent physician. The weakness is all gone, and the headache all but."

"Now, let's not hurry things," he cautioned. "That's a sure way to bring on a relapse."

"No, honestly, darling. I think I could be up on the rope for tonight's show. Certainly by tomorrow."

"Well, let's just try you," he said, with a sigh. This would be cruel, but it had to be done. "Come outside, dear."

He led her out of the van and around to the side of it. There he took down the rope slung for their wash and laid it in a straight line on the ground. "All right, walk that."

"Really, Zachary, this is an insult. A rope not an inch aloft?"

"Humor me, dear one. It's only a test."

She made a face of good-natured toleration and stepped onto one end of the rope, and started along it, and wobbled and was off it. "Oops. You see how the least layoff gets one out of practice?" She went back to the rope end, started along it again, squinting narrowly at it, and staggered and was off it again. She looked up at Edge, with an expression of bewilderment and chagrin. "Oh, Zachary, what can be the matter with me? I see *two* ropes... I can't focus... they blur back and forth..."

"We'll try again when your headache is entirely gone," he said gently, as he coiled the rope. "Now, will you humor me some more and get back to bed? I'll go and consult with my colleague, Dr. Hag. If she can't come up with some concoction to cure that headache once and for all... well... I think we ought to take you to a real, honest-to-God physician."

"Zachary, I have never had to go to a doctor in all my life." But she let him assist her, as if she were a fragile and ancient lady, up the steps and into the van. "I've always been as healthy as a horse."

"Then I'll be sure to find a horse doctor," he said, hoping to make her laugh. And she did, but it was not her old laugh.

Of the crowd that had emptied from the chapiteau out into the front yard of the tober, most of the males had made directly for the annex tent where Sir John bawled invitation to his "biblischer Bilder." But one of the men who did not, a very young man, came to where Florian was in conversation with his bandmaster. He said, "Bitte, Herr Florian" and introduced himself as Heinrich Mehrmann.

"From your speech," said Beck, also in German, "I take you to be from the north. Hamburg, perhaps?"

"Hamburg, exactly. I am assistant to the Herren Hagenbeck."

"Du meine Güte!" Florian exclaimed. "It has been years since I have seen the family, or heard word of them. How is my old friend?"

"He is well, Herr Florian. I have often heard the elder Herr Hagenbeck speak of you. So, when I saw your train arrive here, I telegraphed to him. He sends his regards and best wishes for the success of your tour."

"Why, that was thoughtful of you, Herr Mehrmann. Are you traveling on business for him?"

"I was," the young man said, rather dolefully. "The city fathers of Innsbruck had decided they wanted to have a zoölogical garden here, and they asked the advice of Herr Hagenbeck, because his Hamburg Zoo is so famous. He sent here his son Carl to help with the design and planning, and to recommend animals to start the stocking of it."

Florian turned to Beck to say, "In case you do not know, the Hagenbecks, senior and junior, do not believe in caging animals. In the zoos they design, they have areas separated by moats and fences from each other and from the viewing public. And in those areas, they recreate the animals' natural habitats, insofar as possible, where they can live untrammeled."

"Anyway, everything seemed settled," said young Mehrmann. "And I have brought all the way from our Hamburg park and stables the exotics selected. But now, because of the verdammt war, Innsbruck has decided that this is no time to spend city funds on nonessentials."

"I can see their point," said Florian. "But I am sorry for you."

Mehrmann quickly asked, "Are you sorry enough, Herr Florian, to buy the animals yourself?"

"*Eh*? Why, lad, the war has pinched me, too. Of course I am desirous of adding to our menagerie. You saw what a scant few animals we have. But you also saw the empty seats in the chapiteau. Like the Innsbruck city fathers, I feel this may be a time for prudence and conservatism."

"But... if you acquired these exotics at a most bargain price, Herr Florian? In his telegram to me, Herr Hagenbeck der älter himself suggested it. He knows you personally, he knows what it cost to bring the animals here, he knows it will cost more yet to take them home again, so he suggests it is best for all concerned to offer them to you—at any reasonable price you can pay."

"Well!" said Florian. "Well... this *is* a most tempting offer. But, my dear fellow, it involves more than just my purchasing the animals. I should have to hire extra keepers, buy cage wagons, horses to draw them..."

"I am empowered to sell you also the cage wagons and the very good horses which transported the exotics here," said Mehrmann. "Again at a bargain. And they came driven by their Slovak keepers, who are paid trifling Slovak wages, and I am instructed to give you leave to hire them away from us."

"Du meine Güte," Florian said again, this time in a marveling murmur. "Your offer is unbelievably generous, young Herr, and well-nigh irresistible..."

"Nevertheless, Herr Gouverneur," said Beck, with Bavarian practicality, "it must be pointed out that, as soon as you own the animals, this bargain ceases to be a bargain. Every week from then on, the additional wages must be paid. The animals should probably have a tent of their own. The meat markets and feed dealers, now and in perpetuity, will ask no bargain prices for their commodities."

Mehrmann said, "What more can I offer than everything in my keeping? Some things are beyond my capacity."

"Of course, of course, my boy," said Florian. "We are merely trying to make plain our own situation. But at least I could look at what you have—and *wish* I had them. Where are they?"

"Across the river, in the Mariahilf district. The Innsbruck councilmen, embarrassed at having caused so much bother, have made a small gesture of atonement by letting me use some city-owned stables over there."

"Very well, I should like some others of the company to see them, too. Will you wait here, lad, while I round them up?"

Beck remarked, in English, as he walked away with Florian, "Impoverished we are not. As you said at intermission, we are here our nuts employing—"

"I said *making our nut,* Boom-Boom. Circus jargon for earning at least our daily expenses."

"Ja. And before, in Italy, we were well prospering. Natürlich, for the bargaining effect, we can cry poor. But I hope you will not too cruelly of such a Jüngling take advantage."

"I have known and traded with and respected Hagenbeck der älter since before his son was born—the son who is now taking over the family business. I would not dream of mulcting any of them. But first let us determine if they have anything we want."

In the circus's backyard, they found the company cleaning up and relaxing after the show. Magpie Maggie Hag was stitching a tear in somebody's costume. Pavlo Smodlaka was using a heated curling iron on his blond beard and tying up strands of it in his wife's curl papers. Meli Vasilakis was stirring her smaller snakes about in a tub of tepid water, taking them out one at a time, carefully drying each one and then anointing it with warm olive oil. Jules Rouleau was holding Autumn's mirror for Jörg Pfeifer, who was using lard to wipe off his makeup.

Abner Mullenax, watching that process, asked, "Jules, what is that greasepaint made of, anyhow?"

"Call it muck, ami," said Rouleau. "The joeys all do. The white is made by mixing melted lard with oxide of zinc and tincture of benzoin."

"And hard on the skin it is," grumbled the white-face. "I am glad I finally got old enough to deserve this wrinkled face of mine, but I have had it ever since I first started wearing the muck."

"At least hair you have," Carl Beck said wistfully. "Hair makes one not so old look."

"Oh, Zachary," said Florian, as Edge joined the group. "As soon as Fünfünf is finished here with Autumn's mirror, you can return it to her. We're going to town, so we can buy another to use as the prop."

Magpie Maggie Hag looked up from her sewing, and she and Edge exchanged a glance. He said, "Let the fellows use it as long as they want. I'll—I'll buy a really good one for Autumn... when she's up and about again."

"As you like. Anyway, can you leave your lady long enough to accompany us? Boom-Boom and I are off to inspect some exotics that are for sale. Barnacle Bill, I'll want you to come, of course, and—"

"What the hell are exotics?" Mullenax asked.

"Barnacle," Florian said patiently, "your lion Maximus is one. Exotics are show animals that are not native—like that Auerhahn—not familiar to the jossers. Abdullah, you come along, too. And Canvasmaster, will you also? We may have new tent making to discuss."

Florian took young Mehrmann beside him on the rockaway, to direct him. Edge, Beck, Mullenax and Goesle rode in one of the empty canvas wagons, and Hannibal drove. When they had crossed the bridge over the Inn, they proceeded through suburbs that got increasingly rural, and came eventually to a field containing stables, barns and fenced enclosures. Two exceedingly un-Austrian creatures came to one of the fences to peer over at them: a Bactrian camel and an Indian elephant that could have been the twin to Peggy, except that this one had formidable tusks. But when Edge saw what was in one of the other stockades, he breathed, "Godamighty!" At the same time, on the rockaway, Florian said to Mehrmann, "Mein Gott, are those your draft horses, Heinrich? Why, even *they* are splendid enough to rank as exotics."

"Ja, thoroughbred friesisches Vieh. You begin to comprehend the bargain I offer, Herr Florian? For the price of ordinary draft nags, show-quality horses."

They were, indeed. The seven horses were as big as Obie Yount's Percheron, but not so bulky and much more graceful. They were shiny black all over, but the most striking thing about them was the natural waviness of their long manes and ground-sweeping tails, and the little wavy plumes of hair at their fetlocks, like wings on their feet. As soon as Edge got down from the wagon, he went among the Friesians, admiring and caressing and talking to them, and he almost had to be dragged away to see the other animals that the elegant black horses had hauled here.

Young Mehrmann waved toward the two animals peering at the visitors, and said, "Elefant, Trampeltier." Then he led them through a barn where his cage wagons had been lodged under cover. The cages were all much more commodious than the American-standard four by ten feet that Maximus lived and performed in. Mehrmann pointed and identified their occupants. "Tiger und zwei Tigerinen bengalisches," he said at the cage containing those cats, a male and two females, all in prime pelt and alert of eye. "Bär und Bärin syrisch," he said at the cage containing two good-sized bears of unusual color: brown flecked with silver.

"Syrian bears," Florian told the others. "The breed most amenable to training." He asked Mehrmann a question, and translated the reply. "They are three years old. Which means we'd get five or six good years of use out of them before —as is quite common with bears—they go blind, and get difficult to work with."

"Zwei Hyänen," said Mehrmann at the cage containing two specimens as handsome as hyenas could ever be, meaning ugly and scruffy.

"I've heard about them critters," said Mullenax. "How come they ain't laughin'?"

"It's only the spotted hyena that laughs, Barnacle Bill. These are the striped variety. Be glad. If we acquired the spotted ones, none of us would ever get another night's sleep."

At the next cage, Mehrmann said, "Zwei Zebras und ein Zwergpferd sudamerikanische." The one that was not a zebra was clearly an equine, dun-colored, but not much bigger than a large dog.

"Heinrich says it is a dwarf horse from South America," said Florian. "Colonel Ramrod, are you familiar with any such thing?"

"No. But I'd bet the joeys could do a lot with him in their act."

"Schimpansen," said Mehrmann at a cage that was pretty well filled with part of a tree, and the tree was hung with five or six chimpanzees, all of which began shrieking and gibbering at the visitors. "Zwei Strausse," said Mehrmann at the next cage. It had no solid roof, only bars across its top, so the two seven-foot ostriches could stand comfortably erect with their heads poking through.

The next cage was only half floored, the other half of it being a tank slung below the wagon's axles, full of water into and out of which four sleek creatures were frolicking. "Seelöwen," said Mehrmann, but Florian said rather scornfully, "Water dogs," and Edge said, "Me, I'd call them seals."

"Sea lions, to be accurate," said Florian. "Water dogs in circus parlance. Just as a camel is a hump, a zebra is a convict, a hyena is a zeke, apes are the jockos. I can't remember all the other nicknames for other animals. Well, gentlemen, have you any comments you wish me to translate to Herr Mehrmann?"

"Oh, Sahib!" Hannibal said eagerly, and with his best Hindu servility. "Peg—I mean Brutus—she be powerful glad to have 'nother bull for comp'ny. Me too, Sahib."

Mullenax asked apprehensively, "Governor, was you plannin' on just exhibitin' these critters? Or—Jesus!—am I supposed to *tame* them bears and tigers?"

Florian said to Mehrmann, in German, "I did notice that your tom tiger has that bristly, lionlike mane that often betokens a bad cat."

Mehrmann shook his head. "He and his sisters are good ones. Already accustomed to persons entering their cage, soon ready to learn tricks. I would not deceive you, Herr Florian. These are Bengal cats, not the stupid and untrustworthy Siberians. Also they were captured in the wild, and so have a healthy respect for men—not domestically bred, hence contemptuous of their masters."

"Very well, the tigers would be acceptable. My bull man would be thrilled to have the elephant, and my equestrian director, as you noticed, is enamored of those Friesian horses. I personally do not adore a camel. I don't mind it spitting on its Slovak keepers, but it often causes complaint when it spits on paying customers. Nevertheless, it has the advantage of being able to travel on its own feet, and it looks good on parade."

Mehrmann had taken out a notebook and was listing the items mentioned. "Katze, Elefant, friesische Pferde, Trampeltier..."

"However, I definitely do not want the sea lions," said Florian. "It is too often difficult to find fish for feeding them, when on the road. Also their fishy smell permeates the entire train—everything from canvas to costumes—and is impossible to eradicate."

"Scheisse," muttered the young man. "I have to drag that tank wagon all the way back to Hamburg?"

"And the wagon full of chimpanzees," said Florian.

"But, Herr Gouverneur, what is a menagerie without jockos? All circus patrons *love* to watch their antics."

"True enough, lad, but I'm damned if I know why. When the beasts are not plucking nastily at each other's hides, they are playing obscenely with their own privates. Why a chimp is supposed to be intrinsically funny, cute and lovable is a mystery to me. But I once saw a small girl hand a peanut into a chimp cage— and have all her fingers bitten off. The way an ape's teeth are interattached in the jawbone, it is impossible to remove the dangerous eyeteeth without taking out all the others, and then the brute starves to death. No, I will not have any."

Mehrmann muttered some more, about being stuck with the two wagons most troublesome to deal with, but then said philosophically, "Well, it could have been worse. On my next trip, I was supposed to be bringing here a rhino, a hippo, giraffes..."

"Maybe you can still interest the Innsbruck elders in your jockos and water dogs—if the price is right—as a nucleus for their zoo, whenever they do get around to building it. In the meantime, Heinrich, will you calculate your lowest possible price for all those other creatures, and their five wagons, and five of the Friesians to draw them, and the number of your Slovaks we'll be needing as keepers. My colleagues and I will be discussing the pros and contras of buying a menagerie in these precarious times, and what we can afford to pay for it if we do. Come to the tober tomorrow, and we will talk again."

3

F LORIAN asked Edge to ride with him on the way back. And, after some inconsequential remarks about the menagerie prospects, Florian said guardedly, "I dislike to pry, Zachary, but I and the whole troupe miss your lady Autumn. I don't mean as part of the program, I mean the much-loved girl herself. Is there anything any of us can do? Can you tell me what is ailing her?"

"I wish to Christ I knew," Edge said dully. "I only know what it's doing to her. And she's just beginning to realize—to admit to herself that it's no small affliction." He described the ropewalking test she had tried and failed.

"Well, loss of balance, loss of focus," said Florian, "even a light touch of la grippe can sometimes cause that."

"It's something a damned sight worse than the grippe. Florian, will you keep it to yourself if I tell you? Mag is the only other one who knows. Not even Autumn knows yet just *how* bad this is."

"Of course I will. But what could possibly be so—?"

"It's her eyes. Autumn's eyes. I don't know how to say this. It sounds ridiculous. But it's a fact, and it's terrible. Her eyes are... they're shifting."

"Shifting?" Florian puzzled over this for a moment. "Is that why you're not eager for her to have her mirror back? Do you mean her eyes are rolling wildly about?"

"No. They've gone out of alignment. Mag noticed it first. But now I can see it, too, and it's more obvious every time I look at her."

Florian meditated again, then said, "Zachary, I am not trying to make light of this. But you describe the girl as if she has gone cockeyed. Can you be more specific?"

"Yes, I can, goddamn it," Edge said fiercely, wretchedly. "One of her eyes has moved *lower on her face* than the other one. That's why she couldn't focus on the rope. That's why I took away the mirror. I can't let her see what she looks like. Her whole head has somehow begun to change shape. To get lopsided. I reckon that accounts for her persistent headache, but what accounts for the—for the disfigurement, I just don't know. I realize it sounds crazy and impossible, but *that is what is happening.*"

"Sweet Jesus," said Florian. "That gorgeous girl. Zachary, I can't tell you how desolate I... but look here, man. This is clearly beyond Maggie's witcheries. We must get Autumn to a professional doctor."

"I figured to take her tomorrow morning. I was going to ask if you'd help. To find a good one, and then do the talking for us. And, please God, tell him before-hand not to look horrified, not to let Autumn suspect that she is... that she's changing from being beautiful."

"Yonder is the shop of an Apotheker," said Florian, for they were back in the middle of town by now. "Wave the other wagon to go on. We'll stop here and I will inquire about the local physicians and their specialties and their reputations. We shall want only the best."

Edge waited on the rockaway while Florian went in. He was gone for some time, and returned to say, "The apothecary recommends a Herr Doktor Köhn. Not far from here. Let us go and make sure he can see us tomorrow."

Again Edge waited, nervously twiddling Snowball's reins, outside a very ancient-looking, half-timbered house. Florian was absent for an even longer while, but finally emerged, looking rather more cheerful than when he had gone inside.

"We have an appointment for ten tomorrow. I was fortunate enough to have a word with the Herr Doktor himself, not just a servant. He looks about as old as his house here—old enough to be experienced and wise, I judge."

"Did you warn him—?"

"Yes, yes. I told him exactly what you've told me. I don't know if he believed it. I don't know if *I* believe it yet. But he did hazard one optimistic guess. A mild apoplectic attack, he said, certainly will cause a lingering headache and may produce a partial paralysis of the face, but that can be merely temporary."

"Well, I'll hope so," said Edge, not sounding very hopeful.

When they arrived at the Hofgarten, Beck already had his band tuning up, and the outdoor torches were being lighted, and the joints on the midway were setting out their replenished stock, and the snack butchers were firing up their braziers and grills. At a Weissbier stand, Fitzfarris was drinking a seidl of the pale lager with a lemon slice floating in it, while he gallantly and laboriously tried to flirt with the barmaid. That very pretty girl, even prettier for being dressed in the summery freshness of a pink-and-white dirndl, pink stockings and shoes, was laughing at Fitz's inept attempts at German endearments, but looking pleased with them, nonetheless. At a little distance, Monday Simms was watching that byplay and looking sulphurous. When Florian came along the midway, she intercepted him.

"Governor, me 'n' Sunday wants a word with you."

"Certainly, my child. But can we make it a quick one? It is almost show time."

Monday beckoned Sunday from somewhere and went on, "We does like tra-velin' with you-all, and learnin' trades, and earnin' money of our own. But we thinks we *earns* it—and we tired of bein' treated like nigger trash."

Florian looked astounded by her vehemence, but, before he could speak, Sunday said, "Excuse her, Governor. Monday has learned pretty good manners, but she sort of mislays them when she gets excited. What she means to say—"

"I know what I means to say, sister! We done noticed that these Europe people see us like foreigners. But so do they see them Chinamen—even Clover Lee—even you, sir. They see *foreigners*—not black or yeller or white foreigners."

"That is undeniably true," said Florian. "So, if all of us foreigners are equally regarded by the natives, how have you been slighted?"

"By *you-all*. 'Specially that—that high 'n' mighty Sir John." At Fitzfarris and the barmaid she shot a look that should have set their hair aflame.

"Ah," said Florian, trying not to show amusement. "Une fille jalouse."

"Oui," said Sunday. "Still, she is right, you know, Governor. Sometimes we're Hottentots, and all the time we're African Pygmies, which is degrading enough. But Sir John has us doing that rawhide show, which is becoming unendurable. The men who pay to see it *sweat* at us and *pant* at us, and the Slovak playing Lot is forever *feeling* us."

"We tries hard t' be better'n trash," said Monday. "We does the slant-climb, and I does the school horse act and Sunday does her acrobaticals, and she's practicing good on the trap, and I done axed Mr. Pfeifer if he'll teach me *real* ropewalking, and he said yes, and—"

"Whoa. Aspetta. Halte-là," said Florian, raising his hands in surrender. "You are absolutely right. I concede it, and I apologize for my thoughtlessness in letting you be exploited for so long. You are no longer orphan lambs, but estimable young ladies, and you deserve to be treated with more dignity. I will lay down the law to Sir John. No more sideshow for you, no more rawhide show. Would that appease you, mam'selles, and would you accept my contrition?"

They said that it would and that they did. They went off hand in hand, holding their pretty heads high—though Monday turned hers once, to flash a look of black lightning back at Fitzfarris and his pink-and-white charmer. Florian was just then interrupting their tête-à-tête, to lay down the law to Sir John.

And that night, after the show, Florian, Fitz and most of the other chiefs of the Florilegium held council as to its immediate future. All the troupers except Edge and Autumn, who ate supper in their caravan, were taken by Florian to the five-hundred-year-old Hotel Goldener Adler. In an elegant dining room, they feasted on salmon-trout, pheasant, Knödeln dumplings, Inntaler wines and, for the sweet, a dish called Schmarrn. "The word means balderdash or swill," said Florian, "but order it anyway." And it turned out to be delicate crêpes scrambled together with whortleberries. When the others of the company had departed, sated and happy, Florian, Fitzfarris, Beck, Goesle and Mullenax sat on, over coffee and liqueurs.

"I'll repeat, Sir John," said Florian. "I am sorry that I yanked Sunday and Monday away from you so abruptly. But it was a move too long overdue."

"No great hardship," said Fitz. "The sideshow is still ample, and the Bible study group tonight seemed satisfied just to see David and Bathsheba. But I suppose Clover Lee will resign, too. I think she *likes* making the jossers' tongues hang out, but I doubt that she'll go on doing an act that two mulatto girls consider beneath their dignity."

"Quite so," said Florian. "And I have a suggestion. From now on, Sir John, suppose you confine the whole sideshow inside the annex top, and we'll make it an extra-ticket entry at intermission. More than that. After you've displayed the Tattooed Man, the Night Children, the mummy, your Miss Mitten and the Gluttonous Greek, make Madame Vasilakis the blow-off, accessible only to adult males, for another extra fee."

"Have Meli do a biblical tableau? Eve and the serpent, maybe?"

"I'll leave that to you and her. And your fertility of invention. I will only remark that the sight of a toothsome female fondling a snake... well, it excites certain other imaginings in the mind of even a spectator as elderly and jaded as myself."

All the other men around the table smiled and nodded. Fitzfarris looked thoughtful and said, "Um...yes. You don't think Spyros might object to his wife—er—performing for a private audience?"

"I doubt it. He is a Greek."

It was Stitches Goesle who raised a minor objection. "One thing, just. Since the war news, Governor, we have shown to houses only two-thirds of capacity. Yet you are planning now to charge *extra* for the sideshow that was formerly gratis?"

"It seems sensible to me, Dai," said Florian. "The fewer the patrons, the more we ought to get out of them, as long as they're on the tober. But I am not being avaricious. They'll soon be getting more for their money, even if they only pay to see the main show in the chapiteau. Unless young Herr Mehrmann proves impossible to bargain with—and he won't—I expect to acquire those animals of his, and soon to work some of them into the main program."

"That reminds me," said Fitzfarris. "I can arrange another addition to the program, Governor, and it won't cost us a kreuzer. You noticed that tap wench I was cozying up to?"

"Indeed I did."

"Well, there's a lot of girls just as pretty in the other stands and joints. They say they want to tag along with us when we hit the road again. And all those girls like to dance. Have any of you ever seen an Austrian dance called...something like 'the shoe-slapper'?"

"Der Schuhplattler," said Beck. "Not Austrian, *Bavarian* it is."

"Whichever," said Fitzfarris. "Anyhow, it's all jumping around and kicking cross-legged and slapping the thighs. Those girls really look good at it, flouncing their short skirts up and all. See, they don't have any work to do, once the crowd leaves the midway for the seats. So why not—even before the come-in spec— have those eight or ten girls out dancing the shoe-slapper in the pista? I suppose you know the proper music, Boom-Boom. Be especially nice if we could have them all in identical dirndls."

"A very good idea," said Florian. "And it needn't be a burden on our wardrobe seamstress. We'll simply outfit the girls all from the same shop downtown. I'll let you attend to that, Sir John. It ought to be a pleasant excursion for you in such company."

Mullenax said grumpily, "Foursquare, you get to fool around with nicer animals than I do. Mr. Florian, you said you want to work some of them new animals into the show. Hell, I don't know how long it'll take me to train them things. Or even if I can, all by myself."

"There are tricks to every trade, Barnacle Bill, and I happen to know a few pertaining to yours. Here..." He picked up from beneath his chair and handed across the table a toy tin trumpet. "From our own midway. A gift for you and your musical bear."

"Huh?"

"Until we decide what else we'll want your animals to learn, you can start immediately by leading one bear on a leash into the pista and ordering him to play that trumpet."

"Huh?"

"Prepare it beforehand. Stick a cork down the bell of the horn, then fill the tubing with sugar water. The bear will take the horn in his forepaws, tilt it like one of your own jugs and drink from the mouthpiece. I'll wager *you* never had to be taught that trick, and neither will he. Meanwhile, unnoticed, Kapellmeister Beck tootles a simple little tune on his cornet. The audience sees a bear, at your command, playing a trumpet. Q.E.D."

"Well, I'll be damned..."

"Also, gentlemen," Florian went on, "until we decide what else we'll do with them, some of those animals will at least promenade with us in the come-in and closing specs. The new bull, the hump, those superb black horses and the dwarf one. I'm not sure about the convicts; zebras are fractious little beasts. We'll see. Anyway, as soon as we've got the animals here, Canvasmaster, will you and Maggie start making harness and trappings and regalia for the promenaders?"

"Aye, Governor. And when they're *not* in the pista or on the road? I assume they'll require quarters."

"Yes. Can you start sketching a design for a menagerie top that will accommodate them? Make it a walk-through: the animals tethered or caged on either side of an aisle from front door to back, so the jossers can stroll and ogle. Some one of us who speaks the local language—perhaps Fünfünf, while we're in these regions—can do a patter on the creatures' habits and habitats."

Goesle was already doing an imaginary drawing with his fingertip on the tablecloth, and muttering, "I think no center pole... a rectangle of quarter poles ... sidewalls that can furl up for airing it out..."

"To play music for a bear and Schuhplattler girls maybe I am only required," Beck said, a trifle peevishly. "Any of my men can play those things. The men the entire *show* can play without direction from me. Even if I am gone away."

"Gone away?" Florian echoed, with some alarm.

"Here in Österreich to poor houses we are showing. The people all by the war are upshaken. But only thirty kilometers north of here my homeland Bayern is, and Bayern by the war not much affected was. Better business surely, if there we go."

"Yes, I had already thought of moving to Bayern—to Bavaria."

"But I ahead of you go on, alone. Direct to my family's home in München I go. There my Dampforgel on a wagon I put—"

"By the Almighty!" Florian exclaimed. "I had totally forgotten. You own a calliope!"

"Steam organ, ja. It myself I made, and good it plays, but not everybody appreciates. The neighbors always have despaired to see me home from my voyages come. This time, though, the Dampforgel away I will bring, so rejoice they will. You and circus northward go, I southward the steam organ transport, we meet wherever."

"A splendid idea, Carl, and a magnificent contribution it will be. Let me see now, which wagon can we spare?"

"Nein, nein. Only a saddle horse give me. Better time I will make—straight north across the Bayerische Alpen. In München a proper wagon I will purchase."

"All right. Take that nag that draws Miss Auburn's caravan. I've been meaning to buy her a better one, anyway. When you get to your family's place, you can give them the horse, sell it, turn it out to pasture, as you like. Then buy another good one to draw the calliope wagon. When do you plan to depart, Carl?"

"At your convenience, Herr Gouverneur."

"Well... scant attendance or not, as long as we're set up here in Innsbruck, I'll give it at least the three weeks we planned on. Get the new animals accustomed to us, that sort of thing. If you're sure the band can function without you to conduct..."

"Tenez!" Rouleau said suddenly. "I trust I am earning my keep on this show, messieurs, as acrobatics instructor and scholarly tutor to the young folk, but I have few chances to participate as an artiste. Boom-Boom, ami, before you depart, I insist that you send me and the *Saratoga* aloft one time here in Innsbruck."

Beck looked inquiringly at Florian.

"Why not?" said Florian. "Neither the aérostat nor the gallant aéronaut should be let to atrophy from disuse. Unfortunately, we cannot charge the public any extra fee for an exhibition so freely visible—but, yes, do that for Monsieur Roulette, Carl."

"Merci, messieurs," said Rouleau.

"After that," Florian continued, "and whenever you are satisfied with the band's competence, Carl, you may go. Autumn's old jade will serve to carry you over the Scharnitz Pass. But, when *we* leave here, our train will go on following the Inn, keeping to the easy ground through the river valleys. We won't pitch again until we are across the border of Bavaria. In Rosenheim. Yes. That is where we will set up, and we'll stay there until you arrive."

Next morning, Goesle took a number of roustabouts, and Jörg Pfeifer for interpreter, in one of the canvas wagons, to see what the Innsbruck merchants could supply in the way of materials for making a whole new tent, plus fancy tack for the animals. Fitzfarris took the balloon wagon, with eight merrily giggling midway girls riding on its soft bed, to get them costumed for their pista début. Florian and Edge helped Autumn—though she protested that she needed no help—to the seat of the rockaway, and set off for the Herr Doktor Köhn's clinic. If Florian noticed the change in Autumn's appearance, he had steeled himself to give no least sign of it. On the drive into town, he determinedly tried to maintain a cheerful atmosphere. He told the happy news of Carl Beck's imminent journey to Munich to bring a real, ripsnorting calliope for the circus, and of Fitzfarris's having recruited a corps of dancing girls. When he had exhausted those topics, he joshed Autumn on her being the first of the Florilegium's troupe to resist such homegrown treatments as Maggie's gypsy brews and Colonel Ramrod's cavalry cures.

"I *don't* resist them," said Autumn. "It's going to a doctor that *I* resist, but the colonel is ramrodding me into it." She gave a small laugh. "This trip reminds me of an old cockney song they sing on the halls in London:

> Every Saturday afternoon
> We loves to drown our sorrers,
> So we owlwise visits the waxwork show
> And sits in the Chamber of 'Orrors..."

Even the glum-faced Edge had to smile his crooked smile at that, and Florian said, "You have a fine voice for the halls, my dear. Is there more to the ditty?"

She nodded and sang the rest, laughing as she did:

There's a beautiful statue of Mother there,
Wot gives us pleasure rather,
For we likes to think of 'er as she looked
The night she strangled Father.

Two hours later, most of which time Florian and Edge had spent chain-smoking cigarettes in the clinic's waiting room, the door of Dr. Köhn's examining chamber opened and he came to join them. They both respectfully stood up, and the doctor spoke to Florian, who translated: "While your Frau is getting dressed, Zachary, the Herr Doktor would like to put some questions."

Edge asked anxiously, "She's in a dressing room?"

"It's all right. The doctor says he took the precaution of removing the mirror in there."

Köhn looked hard at Edge while he spoke again to Florian.

"The various procedures," said Florian, "of inspection, palpation, percussion and auscultation reveal no organic disturbances. There has been no stroke of apoplexy. There is no paralysis. The Frau has a mildly elevated temperature and a neuralgic tenderness in one hand. The most important sign diagnostic is that one most evident—the asymmetry of Autumn's face. Also, the Herr Doktor remarks on some coffee-colored mottlings on the skin of her thorax. Has she always had those, Zachary? Could they be mere birthmarks?"

Edge shook his head. "I've never seen any such thing. She always had skin like fresh cream. All over. But lately...lately...she has undressed only in the dark..."

Florian relayed that to the doctor, who waggled his bushy eyebrows, meditated, then spoke again.

"To your knowledge, Zachary," said Florian, "has Autumn ever visited the East? Anywhere from, say, Egypt to Japan?"

"No. Has anybody? Autumn's told me how much she looks forward to seeing Russia, because she's never been east of Vienna."

More parley between the doctor and Florian.

"Would you happen to know, Zachary—the other shows Autumn has been on—were there any Oriental artistes?"

"She's never said. But hell, Florian, *we've* got three of them."

"True, true. That had slipped my mind."

He spoke to the doctor, who immediately asked another question, which ended—after a brief hesitation that made it noticeable—with the word Aussatz. Florian recoiled and blurted the more common German word meaning the same thing: *"Lepra?!"* Even Edge could comprehend that one, and he also reeled, aghast. The doctor gave Florian a look of exasperation and hastened to speak some more. Florian sighed with relief and told Edge:

"He says he is only eliminating random possibilities. He wanted to know if those Chinamen showed any signs of that dread disease. He says Autumn's condition exhibits certain superficial similarities, but it *cannot* be leprosy—thank God—because there is one sure and certain symptom of that affliction—what the Herr Doktor calls foot-drop—which she does not have."

The doctor demonstrated. He lifted one foot from the floor and made it dangle from his ankle, toe down, meanwhile saying comfortingly to Edge, "Nein, nein. Nicht das."

"Danke," Edge said huskily. "It's good to know she doesn't have something that horrible. But then, what *does* ail her?"

Now Florian and Köhn engaged in quite a long colloquy, from which Florian emerged to say:

"The Herr Doktor is frank to admit that he simply does not know. There are several possibilities. One is leontiasis ossia, which I take to be some kind of bone disease. Another is heteroplasia, which he says is an abnormal tissue formation. There are still other possibilities, neural in nature."

"Christ. Well, can he help her at all?"

After another bit of conversation, the doctor turned and went back inside his chambers. "He is fetching some medicine," said Florian. "Autumn is to take it, and remain indoors and at rest. No activity, no chills. He says the condition will persist, but she is in no immediate danger."

"No *immediate* danger?"

"He wants her to see a certain specialist when we get to Vienna, and he assures me there is no urgency about her arriving there. Whatever is wrong with her, it is chronic, not acute, not critical."

"Damn it," growled Edge. "Even if she's not dying or not getting any worse, I want her to have some relief from the continuous headache... and the uncertainty and the worrying."

The doctor returned to the room, and Autumn was with him. She was fussing with her auburn hair, and said to Florian a little tartly, "You'd better tell the good doctor that he's going to lose all his female patients unless he puts a looking glass in his dressing alcove."

Florian did so, or pretended he did. After his next exchange with Köhn, the doctor handed Autumn a number of very tiny envelopes and a slip of paper.

"Those powders," said Florian, "are something called Dreser's Compound. A very new drug, still in process of trial and evaluation, but the Herr Doktor deems it miraculous. You are to take one of the powders, my dear, whenever you have a headache or a fever or that neuralgic affliction of your hands. Guaranteed relief."

Autumn said, "Coo, ducks, old Maggie guarantees *hers*."

"Well, these at least come from the Herr Chemiker Dreser's laboratory, not from a witch's caldron."

"Ask him, please, if I can take one now. My head *feels* like a witch's caldron."

The doctor went to draw a glass of water. Autumn tipped one of the little envelopes into her mouth, then drank.

"And the slip of paper," Florian continued, "has the address of the Herr Doktor von Monakow, whom you are to consult at Vienna. He is fluent in English and he is a noted myopathist and neuropathist, I am told, but I am not told what those resounding titles signify in layman's language."

So they thanked Dr. Köhn, and Edge paid him, and the three headed back for the Hofgarten, and Florian again tried to maintain a cheerful air by jollying Autumn:

"Only a woman would contrive an ailment to baffle the most highly recommended physician in Innsbruck. Why, if you were a man, you'd have walked in there with an honest dose of the clap. Do you feel any effect from that medicine yet?"

"You know," she said, with some surprise, "I really do. The headache is going away. Already it is milder than it has been in ever so long."

Edge said, "Well, I'm glad the visit accomplished *something*."

Autumn patted his hand and said blithely, but with a sigh, "There, there, my dear. If the sky falls... well... we shall catch larks."

When they got to the tober, young Herr Mehrmann was waiting, with a sheaf of papers under his arm. "Back to business," said Florian. "Zachary, when you have got Miss Auburn comfortably settled, will you join us in my caravan?"

However, by the time Edge joined them, Florian and Mehrmann obviously had concluded their transaction. Florian was signing, with his old stub of mason's pencil but with grand flourishes, one paper after another, and shoving them across the table to where the young man was scrupulously counting a heap of gold pieces. When the count evidently came out right, he said, "Abgemacht," took the signed papers and gave Florian a handful of booklets.

"The conduct books of the newly hired Slovaks," Florian told Edge. "We are getting one to drive each of the five new wagons, and to be keepers to their occupants, and a sixth to help Abdullah herd the bulls and the Bactrian when we're on the road."

When the young man had shaken hands with each of them and departed, Florian chuckled and said, "We are getting all the exotics for no more, I suspect, than the Hagenbecks paid the foresters and poachers who brought them in as cubs and pups and chicks."

"Still, that looked like a considerable outlay," said Edge. "Can we afford it?"

"We are a circus. We should strive to be better than other circuses. There is an old Austrian saying you ought to know, Zachary, since it is a saying of Austrian *cavalrymen,* who are notorious gamblers. 'You can play cards without money, but you cannot play cards without cards.' Now, would you kindly inform Dai Goesle that he can take any spare roustabouts while this afternoon's show is on, and go across the river to help bring our new men and menagerie over here. Tell him also to get paint for those new cage wagons, to match the rest of our train. And tell Banat that he will now be crew chief over six more of his compatriots. It's up to him to make room for them in the Slovaks' sleeping and traveling wagons. Meanwhile, I will discuss with Abdullah and Ali Baba the logistics of procuring extra hay, grain and cat's meat."

"Right, Governor."

"Oh, one other thing before you go, Zachary. No, two things. That horse drawing your van is getting rather superannuated. And Boom-Boom needs a not too frisky saddle hack to carry him on that errand for us. Let him have Autumn's old nag, and I'll get a replacement horse. However, since I know how much you admire those new Frisian blacks, why don't you hitch one of them to your van?"

"Thank you, Governor. That's a thoughtful gesture. Autumn will be pleased, too." Edge waited. "You said two things...?"

"Er, yes... yes..." Florian twiddled his pencil stub for a moment. "Zachary, you must be aware that you cannot forever keep Autumn ignorant of the—of the changes in herself. Soon or later, she is bound to encounter another mirror. And to see her face."

Edge swallowed, nodded wordlessly, and went out.

4

BY THE TIME that afternoon's show closed, Goesle and his men had led the Hagenbeck animals and their keepers to the Hofgarten. It turned out that the new Slovaks were already acquainted with the Florilegium's Slovaks, all of them having variously, at one time or another, been crew on the same circuses, so there was no problem about their assimilation. As the new men ranked the cage wagons and tethered the uncaged animals in the backyard, Aleksandr Banat bustled about among them, issuing trivial and unnecessary orders, luxuriating in being now the crew chief of fully seventeen underlings.

After the last of the audience had drifted off the tober and the artistes had got out of their ring dress, the troupers and the midway stallkeepers, as well, congregated in the backyard to see the new acquisitions—all of the company but Carl Beck and his bandsmen, whom he was rehearsing at being a band without a conductor.

"I tole you, Sahib Florian, ol' Peggy be happy to see new bull," said Hannibal, grinning at the great beasts as they delicately explored and whuffled over one another with their trunks, occasionally entwining them as in a handclasp. "Ol' Peggy must of thought she was the one and onliest elephant on dis earth. Hey, Mas' Sahib, what dis new one's name?"

Florian consulted the list Mehrmann had given him. "Mitzi. That's how she'll answer to commands, Abdullah. But for billing—well, it's obvious: Brutus and Caesar. Now, this camel—let me see—she is Mustafa, and that'll do for billing, too. We'll have Maggie deck her out in fringed shawls and halter and camel bells. Maybe a tassel on her tail." Mustafa curled her rubbery big lips in a sneer.

"Hey, Governor," called Mullenax, from beside one of the cage wagons. "While you're tellin' names, tell me which one of these critters is Kewwy-dee."

"What?" said Florian, puzzled. He went to look: it was the cage of the two Syrian bears.

"You told me the bear that plays the horn is Kewwy-dee. Which one of 'em is it?"

Florian still looked bewildered for a moment. Then he smiled, shook his head and murmured to himself, "Q.E.D." To Mullenax he said, "You'll just have to try them out, Barnacle Bill, and decide which one is better at the trick."

"All right. And he'll be Kewwy-dee. I'll call the other one Kewwy-dah, so I can tell 'em apart. That suit you, Governor?"

"Of course, Barnacle," said Florian, with amusement. "They're your property, after all."

Hannibal asked, "What we feed dese bears, Sahib?"

"That's one good thing about bears, Abdullah, they'll eat almost anything. But they prefer fresh food, not dried stuff like hay. So, in the manner of your former pigs, Barnacle Bill, they'll be our receptacle for table leftovers and such. But we'll also give them fresh fruits and vegetables whenever possible, throw them the occasional fish we may come across. And, during your training of them, reward each successful accomplishment with a morsel of bread and honey. Bears love honey."

Florian went on along the row of cages, looking at his list, and most of the troupers trailed along to listen.

"The tiger's name is Raja," said Florian, "and the tigresses are Rani and Siva. All good Bengal names, I assume. The ostriches are Hansel and Gretel. After a boy and girl in an old German fairy tale."

Clover Lee asked, "What about these awful-looking hyenas?"

Florian consulted his list and chuckled. "Anwalt and Berater. Both words just mean 'lawyer.' Wonderfully apt, I must say, for carrion-eating scavengers. But you needn't bother remembering the names. Even hyenas wouldn't answer to those." At the next cage, he said, "Now, these two zebras—"

"I'd like to call them Stars and Bars," said Mullenax. "After the bonny old Confederate flag. If that's all right with you, Governor. See, the one's got kind of a star on his forehead, and God knows they both got enough bars."

"Fine with me. That other little horse in there is listed as Rumpelstilzchen."

"Why?" somebody asked. "The name is bigger than he is."

"Rumpelstilzchen was a dwarf in another old folktale."

"A good name," said Jörg Pfeifer. "Let us keep it. Zanni and I can do some funny patter on the name, when we work the animal into our act."

"Also, Fünfünf, may I ask," said Florian, "would you do the patter in the menagerie for the jossers? You know the sort of thing."

"Ja, ja. These tigers are man-eaters, and took the lives of twenty African Schwartzen before they were captured, and—"

"*Hindu* Schwartzen, please. The tigers came from India. And of course Caesar gored a score of elephant hunters with his tusks. And Rumpelstilzchen is the sole surviving specimen of the supposedly mythical leprechaun horse."

"Wie sagt man *leprechaun* auf deutsch?"

"Well... Kobold... Troll..."

"Ach, ja. And the camel is called the ship of the Sahara."

"This one is a Bactrian two-humper. Ship of the Gobi. But what the hell, the jossers won't know the difference. And would you mind wearing a suitable costume, Fünfünf? I'll have Maggie get it together—a pith helmet, bush jacket, boots. You can carry one of Colonel Ramrod's carbines while you're at it."

"Schon gut," said Pfeifer indifferently. "Right now, it is time for me to give Monday her ropewalking lesson."

He went off to the chapiteau and Florian turned again to Mullenax. "While we are discussing ferocity, Barnacle Bill, let me assure you that it is not all humbug, not by any means. Until you and these creatures get well accustomed to each other, treat them with the utmost caution. Be wary of the tigers even if you think they are fast asleep. Because of the striping around the eyes, you can never be sure if they are closed or only watchfully slitted. The bears you will *never* go near, or let out of their cage, unless they are muzzled. A strap muzzle won't impede the trumpet-tootling. Be careful also of the bears' claws, even though they have been blunted. I will have Maggie make a special metal codpiece for you to wear under your clothes from now on. If a bear takes a swipe at a man, it will always rake first at his testicles."

"Jesus," said Mullenax.

"Oh, yes. A bear is more to be feared and distrusted than any of the great cats. A bear can even trample you, and accidentally, because a bear does not see very well straight ahead. When you are working it, stay always just within its peripheral vision."

"Huh?"

"Stay just to its left or right front," Florian patiently explained. "Now, excuse me, I must have a word with Stitches."

He found the canvasmaster supervising a number of non-bandsmen Slovaks in the cutting of canvas for the menagerie tent. Florian thanked Goesle for having so expeditiously delivered the menagerie itself, then asked him, "Dai, while you're doing this canvas work, I wonder if you would oblige me by also making a banner line."

"It is a likelihood, Governor, if you'll tell me what it is."

"A series of colorful canvas banners, slung side by side. Each a rectangle— say, six by eight feet—lapped and hemmed top and bottom so ropes can be reeved through. I'll have our Chink artist paint them, each depicting one of the wonders of our show."

"No problem, Governor. I'll have a plenty of remnants left over. Now, look you, another thing. To save me and my lads a lot of time and laborious work, I am having a lumberyard in town shape the quarter poles and side poles for this new top. I know we've been Irish-prodigal of money lately, and not much coming in, but the locals asked a price so low it would have been a foolishness not to give them the job. What else I've been thinking: wood is plentiful and cheap here in this alpine country, and it might *not* be in other places. While we are here, why don't I have the locals also cut the pieces for folding chairs?"

"Aha! Our starback seats. At last."

"With the backs and seats and legs rough-cut, I can have my lads do the finishing of them, and the putting of them together, as we go along, whenever we have a spare moment."

"Commendable initiative, Dai. The extra prices we can charge for comfortable starbacks will eventually pay for them. Go to it."

Leaving Goesle to his work, Florian ambled in through the back door of the chapiteau to glance about at the rehearsal, practice and instruction going on. The pavilion was practically billowing its roof and sidewalls with all the noise inside it, for the bandmaster was at this moment conducting both the band and the eight midway-girl dancers in their performance of the Schuhplattler. The musicians were doing a blasting oom-pah-pah of brassy Bavarian folk music, and the girls, although they were cavorting on soft sawdust, contributed to the noise with the repeated thigh-slapping that the dance demanded. Florian noted with approval that all the girls *were* pretty, as Fitzfarris had said, and that Fitz had dressed them in dirndls of blue and white. Not only did the costumes match the colors of the Florilegium's wagons, they were also intended to please Kapellmeister Beck, because blue and white were the flag colors of his native Bavaria.

The others in the tent went on with their business, taking no notice of the oom-pah-pah and the thigh-slapping and Boom-Boom's frequent vociferations. High up in the trapeze rig, Sunday, securely belted to the lungia, was being swung to and fro in various postures by Maurice and Paprika. In the pista below, out of the way of the dancing, Jules Rouleau was teaching Ali Baba various new ways to tie his limber body into knots. Outside the pista curbing, the Quakemaker grunted and heaved at some new strongman equipment he was preparing to introduce into his act. Yount had somewhere found four more cannonballs—and these were solid, not hollow, two each of eight-inch and ten-inch diameters. He had also procured two stout iron rods with threaded ends, and screwed each of those into two of the soft lead balls. So now the Quakemaker had two sets of dumbbells, not in any way faked or gaffed, honestly weighing more than a hundred twenty-eight pounds and two hundred fifty-six pounds respectively. He was trying different ways to struggle erect—from flat on his back, from a sitting position, from a squat—while he lifted the lighter, then the heavier, then both dumbbells together.

"Con permesso, Signor Governatore," said the clown Zanni, as he brushed past Florian into the tent, carrying something limp draped over one arm. He went to where Rouleau was working with Ali Baba, and borrowed the boy from him. What Zanni was carrying turned out to be two arm-length tubes of black india rubber, each terminating in a white glove like those Ali Baba wore with his clown costume of minstrel-show blackface. Zanni showed him how to put the gloves-and-tubes on, then pulled down his shirtsleeves so that only his gloved hands showed. Then they went together to where the Quakemaker was taking a rest from his labors. They exchanged some words, and the strongman nodded. So Ali Baba bent over, seized a dumbbell bar with both hands, pretended titanic exertion, did fierce grimaces, and very, very slowly began to stand erect. The Quakemaker burst out laughing, inaudibly in all the ambient noise. Ali Baba's new gloves were wired inside, to stay clasped around the dumbbell bar as he slowly straightened and slipped his hands out of them—so the black rubber tubes slid out of his sleeves, making it appear that his skinny black arms were lengthening. Zanni even picked up the boy and lifted him higher, over his own head, making those black arms stretch impossibly longer and skinnier yet.

"A comic effect, no?" said Zanni.

"Yassuh," Ali Baba said, giggling. Then to Yount, "Kin I do dat, Mr. Quakemaker, eb'ry show, when you is done wid de dumbbells?"

"I reckon," said Yount, still laughing. "Here I'm busting my gut to show the folks a real strongman act. And you'll come along and make fun of it, and prob'ly get twice the applause. But hell yes, it's comical. Don't mind me and my perfessional jealousy. You do it, Quincy."

Between the two center poles, but only a foot off the ground, the tightrope was rigged. Ignoring the dirndled girls dancing and swirling and bouncing on either side of the rope, Monday was mincing along it, and Fünfünf, though he stood close beside her, had to shout above the noise.

"Since the Fräulein Auburn does a classic Seiltänzer ballerina act, and you will not wish to compete with her, you will learn a comic turn on the rope."

Monday shouted back, "I druther be classical and graceful and beautiful. Anybody can act funny."

"Ha! Think you so? I learned rope-dancing in a few weeks. Thirty *years* I have been striving to learn funniness. It will take all your skill, Fräulein—and all your grace and all your beauty—to do it right."

"If you say so," Monday said, not with great enthusiasm.

"On the ground you will practice dancing foolery, as we call it. You will learn the stork step, the chicken walk, the crab glide, the skip shuffle, the hesitation walk, all the others. Then you will translate them to the rope. Step down, now.

Imitate me. This is the stork step. Come! Walk as I am doing."

Monday did so, but complaining. "All these-here pretty white gals flouncin' their pretty shapes all 'round, and I gotta walk all crooked."

"Hush! You are a stork. Protrude your tail more. That is better. Now get onto the rope and do exactly the same."

Three times, Monday tried stork-ropewalking, and slipped off each time. "It's 'cause I can't see my *feet*," she protested, "walkin' this stupid way."

"You are not supposed ever to watch your feet. Keep your eyes fixed on the white guidon daubed on the pole yonder." Monday sighed, but tried again, and was rather surprised that—*not* watching her feet—she could stork-step without falling off the rope. "Much better," said her teacher. "Much, much better. Only stick out your tail more. Remember you are a stork. More tail!"

"Mr. Meister," said Monday, through teeth clenched in her concentration, "could you anyways stop callin' it my *tail?*"

"Your sister," said Paprika, looking down from the trapeze platform, "is doing very well at funambulism."

Sunday also looked down and said, "Yes, she is."

"Like you, she has grown a figure, and quite a good one. Tell me, has she outgrown her habit of doing wichsen to herself?"

Sunday looked puzzled and said honestly, "I don't know." According to her decorous German dictionary, "wichsen" meant only to wax or to polish.

"A pretty girl should not have to resort to bringing herself off." That phrase also meant nothing to Sunday, but she could comprehend Paprika's next remark: "What she needs is a lover."

Sunday laughed and said, "What she *wants* is Foursquare John Fitzfarris."

"And you, Liebling, you want Zachary Edge. Too bad he is already taken."

"He is attached, but he is not married."

"Aha! You bide your time. Yes, you are young enough to wait. But perhaps, when your time comes, you would stand a better chance if you were instructed in more than the arts of trapeze. In the arts and wiles of love. I can be an instructress elsewhere than in the air, you know."

"I have heard," Sunday said coolly. "No, thank you."

"Brrr!" said Paprika, pretending to shiver. "You call that in English the cold shoulder, I believe. However, I can warm the coldest shoulder. And other things—"

But Sunday was swinging across to the other platform, where Maurice was standing and tapping a foot impatiently. He said a few words to Sunday, took her bar from her, swung across to where Paprika stood and said probably the identical words to her: "Kindly keep your girlish babillage for the ground, mam'selle. Up here we work."

"Hard work, indeed," murmured Paprika. Then she shifted her gaze from Sunday to Maurice and said, "Once you invited me to share your van. You never spoke of it again. *You* do not work very hard to attain your ambitions."

"You will recall, chérie, you rather effectually demolished that particular ambition."

"But, as you said then, une hirondelle ne fait pas... Have you ever considered deux hirondelles en même temps?" She looked across the intervening space at

Sunday. "In Magyar we call it rakott kenyér. In your language it would be, I think, un homme en sandwich."

He looked where she was looking, then looked again at her. "I am a Frenchman, Paprika, therefore by nature tolerant of others' differing natures. But do not dream of courting your own partner. That is courting trouble."

"You courted *me, Maurice.*"

"We were only the two of us then. What you now suggest is a triangle, and even in French farce, that is an overworked cliché for trouble. Cannot you direct your ambition outside the chapiteau? At least to the ground? Why not one of those lusty wenches dancing down there?"

"Utálatos! Those beefy trulls?" she said, sneering down at them. "No, Maurice, I sometimes think I must be getting old and wicked—like the old men who lurk around schoolyards. I seem nowadays to have a taste for... for the new and fresh and unawakened."

"Old, you are not. Wicked, perhaps. Perverse, beyond a doubt. If you loved—if you *could* love—mais non. Knowing what I know of you, I expressly forbid you to pursue this course. If we three are to survive up here, we must love each other, oui, but not *love* each other, do you understand me? This air up here is mine to command, and I will have it clean."

Still gazing at Sunday, Paprika murmured, "Forbidden, eh?" and ran the tip of her tongue across her upper lip.

"Not another word now. Take the bar. Show me a passe ventre. You were very slipshod at it this afternoon."

Every night, when Edge came home to the caravan after the show, to help Autumn prepare their meal—they had not accompanied the other troupers to any hotel or Gaststätte for a long time now—she would eagerly inquire into all the details of the performance, and he would dutifully report:

"Well, that nitwit Pavlo is still whisking his dogs and family in and out of the pista, faster and faster every show, like he's working up eventually to a genuine disappearing act. I made a real mistake when I warned him to be leery of rivalizers."

Or another day he would report: "Fitz has got a prime replacement for Clover Lee and the Simms girls in his blow-off. That good-looking Greek woman does 'The Amazon Maiden in the Clutches of the Dragon Fafnir.' And she does it so naked that her, uh, vital parts are only covered by the coils of the python—even though it's moving all the time. I don't know how she and the snake manage that. I do know she'd be arrested for indecent behavior anywhere outside that annex tent. She carries on like she's being ravished by a man. Still, it's pretty to look at, too. The snake literally *dances* up her and down her and around her, in time to the accordion music."

Or another day he would report: "The new animals are marching in the specs just fine. Even the zebras, as long as I keep them close-haltered. And the other night, in the menagerie tent, Abner saw Peggy crawling *under* Mitzi's belly. She was only giving her back a brisk scratching, but Abner has made that into an act. Now he announces 'London Bridge!' and has the elephants do it in the pista. Abner's pretty smart with the animals; he's begun to win the trust of the tigers and bears, even. I do wish he wouldn't guzzle a whole bottle every time he has to get into their cages, but he says damned if he'd *get* in, otherwise."

"I wish," said Autumn, "I could *see* the show. There has been so much added since I took ill. I don't know why I shouldn't be allowed. That medicine has completely relieved me of the headache. Of course, I know I can't go back to performing yet, because I still can't focus my vision on anything as close as the rope. But things at a distance I can see perfectly well."

"What about the—those discolored spots on your chest?"

"Still there, but they haven't spread or multiplied. I am sorry the doctor told you about those."

"Damn it, Autumn, you and I have shared every least thing ever since we've been together. I don't like learning things about you from some third party. I'm still peeved that you took to putting out the lamps, just so I wouldn't notice."

"I was afraid you'd take them for those liverish blotches that old ladies get, and decide I was growing old, and discard me."

That was so patently a lie, and so witless a lie from one of Autumn's intelligence, that Edge did not even bother to suggest that it was also an insult to *his* intelligence, and his love and loyalty, as well. He said only:

"The doctor cautioned you not to risk a chill. But right now it doesn't get chilly until nightfall. I think, if you bundled up good, you could attend any afternoon show without danger. And sit in the stands with the jossers, if you see better from a distance."

"Oh, I could!" she said fervently. *"May* I, Zachary?"

"I reckon so. Do me one favor, though. Wear a hat with a veil. If that demented Pavlo Smodlaka should spot you in the stands, he'd be sure he *was* being spied on, and that I'm responsible for the spying. Let's not drive him totally insane."

"Anything you say, dearest," said Autumn, and kissed him.

But that night again, as had become her practice, she blew out the lamps before undressing for bed. Edge did not complain or even comment. He was gratified to have it so. Making love to Autumn in the dark enabled him to delude himself that he was making love to that radiantly beautiful and unblemished Autumn of other nights that now seemed long ago.

"Oo-ooh, how splendid!" Autumn gasped, the next afternoon, when they stood at the entry end of the circus midway. "Why, Zachary, it has become as grand as just about any other stand I have ever seen!"

Autumn was well and warmly clothed in coat, muffler, gloves and high boots. From her broad-brimmed Leghorn hat depended a riding veil, tucked into her coat collar, and within it her face was only a dim glow. At Edge's request, Florian had earlier gone along the rows of midway stalls, ordering their proprietors— somewhat to their mystification—to hide away any mirrors they had on display among their slum. But Autumn probably would not have noticed them in any case; she was so enthralled by the new additions to the tober.

Besides the banners and placards that proclaimed the wares of the midway joints—sausages, beers, cuckoo clocks and such—the Florilegium now flaunted its own banner line, stretched across the front of the chapiteau above the marquee entrance. The Chinese artist had proved a little uncertain of anatomy, both human and animal, but that had not inhibited either his imagination or his palette. In brilliant and unearthly colors were depicted, on one banner, a flamboyantly fanged and clawed and tangle-maned lion, strewing a jungle with bloody fragments of black Africans; on another Colonel Ramrod, anomalously slant-eyed, firing volcanoes of flame and smoke from a pistol in each hand and strewing a desert with bloodily punctured Red Indians; on another a bejeweled Hindu Indian juggling lighted torches while being upheld upon the meshed tusks of two exceedingly corrugated elephants; on another the three Chinese themselves, vividly yellow, engaged in upside-down and sideways and crosswise tortuosities that even they had not yet attempted... and so on: eight banners all together, almost audibly screeching for attention.

Sir John's annex top, off to one side of the chapiteau, had its own separate banner. That one displayed a very pneumatic-looking naked lady with an inhumanly ponderous bosom—the Oriental artist was clearly overawed by Occidental mammaries—her eyes bulging and her mouth gaping in a scream as she was simultaneously squeezed by the coils and scorched by the fiery breath of a reptilian, avian, leonine, winged and lasciviously leering dragon. It was by far the best-portrayed animal of all on the banners.

On the other side of the chapiteau was the new menagerie tent, striped green and white like the others, and Edge led Autumn there. She happily took a deep breath of the evocative mixture of smells—at once ammoniac and aromatic—of elephants, great cats, horses, warm hay, feed bins, sawdust and new canvas.

"Before each show," said Edge, "any josser that has bought a ticket, and doesn't want to patronize the joints, can come in here for a look-around. When there's enough of a crowd collected, Jörg Pfeifer expounds—mainly on what the menagerie cost in outlay of money, time, labor and loss of life."

"What *did* all this cost?"

"Florian won't tell me. I think he gave a part payment and a promissory note. The Hagenbecks know him and trust him."

He took Autumn down the middle of the tent and introduced to her the caged or tethered newcomers on the other sides of the aisle ropes: Mitzi-Caesar, Kewwy-dee and Kewwy-dah—those names required explanation—Hansel and Gretel, the lawyer hyenas, Raja, Rani and Siva.

"Oh, aren't they sublime, the tigers!" Autumn exclaimed. "We humans think we are nature's masterworks, but they *are*. The jungle cats, the house cat, every kind of cat is superior to all other animals."

"Come, come," Edge said chaffingly. "We humans are made in God's image." Then he was sorry he had said it, remembering what Autumn now looked like. But all she said was:

"The cats don't care about God. They worship nothing, they envy nothing and they fear nothing. If that is not superiority, what is?"

The horses were at the farther end of the tent, and there Clover Lee was brushing her old dapple, Bubbles. She greeted Autumn a little uncertainly, seeing her so muffled in concealment. But when Autumn responded in her usual clear accents, Clover Lee forthrightly asked after her health, then expressed the whole troupe's hope that their stellar colleague would soon be among them again.

"Thank you. I hope so, too," said Autumn. "The menagerie is wonderful, isn't it, Clover Lee? But surely it will be a long time paying for itself."

"Well," said the girl, grinning, "you know Florian. Unless he's perched out on a precarious limb, he just doesn't feel he's alive."

Edge said, "Yes, he's buying yet another big wagon and drayhorses. It turns out we'll need them to carry all the provisions for these animals on the road— and the new starback seats, when we've got them."

"And the European troupers keep telling him," said Clover Lee, "that we ought to have rolls of slat-fencing, like other European circuses, to put up around every tober. We do get a lot of sidewallers sneaking in, and that gripes Banat especially. But Florian says a fence is just *too* much to haul about."

Edge and Autumn left the menagerie and entered the chapiteau through its front door. Above them, inside the marquee, Boom-Boom Beck was just then tuning up his band, and he took up the cornet to play a bar of "Greensleeves" by way of salute, and Autumn waved up to him. She kept her head back, then, gazing wistfully up into the peak of the tent, until Edge gently ushered her onward. Goesle and his men had not yet assembled any of the folding chairs, so the "starbacks" were still only the benches nearest the pista. Edge seated her on one of those and stayed with her until it was time for him to go and cast his directorial eye over the lineup of the come-in spec.

He glanced over frequently and anxiously, during the show, to where Autumn sat among fat Bürgers and their fat Fraus and their pudgy Kinder. She appeared not to be feeling any ill effects of her first venture outside the caravan since the visit to the doctor. She applauded as vigorously as the jossers did, and, though Edge could not see her face, he knew she must be smiling to see so many new acts and so many refinements of the old ones.

Abdullah now did his juggling while dancing a-tiptoe from neck to neck of a dozen upright beer bottles, deliberately kicking over one of them every few minutes, until finally he was balanced on one toe on a single bottle, still imperturbably juggling fragile eggs and iron horseshoes at the same time. Zanni had introduced into his clown turn a balancing ladder, like the one Monsieur Roulette had used to have, except that this one was a breakaway ladder. Zanni stood it up with no support, and kept it standing and teetering while he did various acrobatics on it. Then one after another rung fell away when he stepped on it, so his posturing took him higher up the ever more rickety and wobbling ladder, until he was desperately cavorting on only the uppermost and last remaining rung. When that fell, so did he, but to catch the ladder's two uprights under his armpits, at which point he worked them like stilts to go arm-striding in giant steps around the pista.

Clover Lee had added a flock of white doves to her bareback act. She had bought the dozen birds in the market, then during seven days of training had worn a mantle while she rode, in the folds of which were sprinkled grains of wheat. During that week, the pigeons had learned to chase her as she rode, to get at the wheat, and when, on the eighth day, she discarded the cloak, they followed out of habit. Now, as Clover Lee circled the pista on Bubbles, doing ballet stands, jetés and entrechats, the white birds *were* her mantle, following close as she rode and, when she halted, fluttering to alight on her arms and shoulders.

Brutus did her old act under Abdullah's command, then Barnacle Bill brought on Caesar, and Florian announced in German, "The Bridge Over the Inn!" Brutus and Caesar constructed it by entwining their trunks, and Sunday Simms danced a little ballet up and down that span, while the band played a waltz. Then Florian announced, "London Bridge Is Falling Down!" and the waltz was interrupted by a cymbal clash, and the elephants suddenly parted, and Sunday bounded to stand gracefully on Caesar's head while Brutus crawled back and forth under Caesar's great belly.

Sunday also now particpated in the trapeze act, but mainly to the extent of standing on one platform, in artistic poses, and giving the bar a shove toward Maurice or Paprika whenever they shouted for it, "Houp là!" All three of those artistes were now, by Maurice's recent decision, garbed in tights of varying shades of blue, richly spangled. Maurice was still in electric blue, like lightning; Paprika wore a very dark blue, to show off her orange hair; Sunday was in very pale blue, to contrast with her abundance of jet-black hair. And, near the close of the act, Sunday was allowed one trick that brought all three blues together. Maurice and Paprika, on the separate bars, finished a succession of acrobatics with both of them swinging upside down by their knees. Paprika swung close to Sunday's platform, reaching out her arms. Sunday also reached out, the two girls' hands clung, and Sunday was swung dangling in a swoop to meet Maurice. The audience gasped as she somehow transferred her grip in midair from Paprika to Maurice, and he swung her through another arc to land lightly on her feet on the opposite platform.

"I just wish," Sunday shyly told Autumn, who went to congratulate her during the intermission, "that when we clasp each other's wrists up there, I didn't have to clasp Miss Paprika."

"Oh, dear," said Autumn. "Is she up to her tricks with you, now? Well, I suppose it should be no surprise. You are still an adolescent, but you have grown from a pretty child into a beautiful young girl. I take it you are not, um, inclined toward Paprika?"

Sunday's fawn-colored cheeks were tinged with rose, but she tried to sound worldly. "What she has suggested . . . the particulars . . . she says I'd enjoy them. Maybe I would. She ought to know."

"But?" said Autumn.

"But I'd rather save . . . save all that sort of thing for . . . for a man, when I'm grown up enough to have one. Miss Paprika says I might as well enjoy myself in the meantime, and it won't make any difference later on. To me or to . . . to any man. Would it, Miss Autumn?"

"I can't speak from experience. But I know it to be a common experience in the best boarding schools, even convent schools, yet the girls go on to make good marriages. Why do you ask? Are you thinking of obliging her?"

"She says she will see that I never get any further in trapeze work, if I don't."

"Why, the ruddy bitch! That is far more monstrous than—than anything you and she might willingly do. Private acts are private business, but blackmail is a crime. Shall I speak to Zachary?"

"Oh, no, please," said Sunday, in alarm. "Don't do anything to get that woman angry at me. I'll—I'll give it some more thought. But please, Miss Autumn, don't mention this to anyone else." And she ran off to the dressing wagon.

Autumn rejoined Edge, and said nothing about the conversation. They spent the rest of the intermission in the sideshow, and she was as delighted with that as the Innsbruckers were. Then later, after the conclusion of the main show in the chapiteau, she insisted on seeing also the Amazon Maiden and the Dragon Fafnir. When Fitz's canvas curtain closed on the final throes of that performance, Autumn laughingly said to Edge, "My God, I thought you told me she *pretended* to be ravished."

"Come around back and meet her. You can ask her if she takes it seriously."

Behind the curtain, Meli Vasilakis now had a dressing robe on and was putting the lid on the big snake's basket. When Edge had made the introductions, Autumn said, "I hope Fitz never talks me into any such tableau vivant. I'd be terrified."

"Is not kinthynos. Not danger. Python never hurt me. Also he is old age."

"I wasn't thinking of the python. Maybe you didn't see the eyes of those *men* watching."

"Vlepo," Meli said gaily. "I have good house-band of jealousy."

"House-band?"

"Spyros always watch while I work." Meli beckoned, and he stepped onstage to be introduced to Autumn. "Any man look me too hard, get eye burned out. House-band Spyros *real* dragon."

They went off, carrying the python basket between them, and Autumn said, "They make a refreshing comparison to Pavlo and Gavrila."

"The Vasilakises don't have to be the only happy house-band and wife," said Edge. "I proposed marriage to you when we first met, and a dozen times since."

Autumn playfully put a fingertip to the end of his nose, and said, "You are in Germanic lands now, and I bid you, reflect. The German word trauen means to marry. Almost the same word, trauern, means to grieve. It can't be a coincidence."

"Damn it, be serious."

"All right. May I come to see tomorrow's show, too? Seriously."

"Seriously, no. The doctor warned against too much exertion, remember. I'll untether you again two days from now. That's when Jules is going up in the *Saratoga*."

The Florilegium had, all this while in Innsbruck, continued to draw less than capacity crowds. But the attendance improved suddenly and dramatically after Rouleau went soaring up and down the Inn River.

To that spectacle, Fitzfarris again contributed the magical disappearance from the midway and reappearance from the sky of the seemingly same pretty girl. The Simms sisters did not object to *this* as exploitation of themselves, because they much enjoyed the balloon rides, and alternated in the rôles of disappearee and reappearee. This time, it was Monday who leapt triumphantly from the basket when the *Saratoga* alighted. After she and Monsieur Roulette had taken a score of bows to the applause of the watchers who thronged the Hofgarten, he took her aside and said petulantly, "*Must* you do that thigh-chafing business the whole time we are aloft? Your sister does not do it. Your jiggling of the gondola makes it très difficile for me to gauge my landing on the correct spot."

Sunday was nearby and overheard, and she gave Monday a long look, as of speculation.

It had been Florian's posters announcing the balloon ascension that had brought the hordes of city people to the Hofgarten that day, but the increased circus attendance in subsequent days consisted of people who had had no notice of the spectacle. The unexpected appearance in the sky of something as uniquely beautiful as the *Saratoga*, visible for leagues around, piqued the curiosity of every country family in the whole Inn valley. Their farm harvests were safely in, and winter snows had not yet put them into hibernation, so wagonloads of country folk crowded all the roads leading to Innsbruck from then on, and they made directly for the tober.

"Well, I'm glad we stuck it out," said Florian, with satisfaction. "And I'm glad you stuck with us, Carl, to help provide this bounty. So we will stay on here until the crowds begin to dwindle again. Or until snow falls, which will have the same result. That means there is no need for you to make haste to München, but you may take your leave whenever you like. We will keep to the original plan, and be in Rosenheim awaiting you."

So, after conducting several more band drills and leaving innumerable instructions to be followed in his absence, Beck did depart. His colleagues tried not to laugh when he did. A seaman in a saddle would have been a quaint enough sight, but this one very much resembled Sancho Panza, with the swaybacked old nag under him and his plump legs sticking out sideways and his bald spot gleaming as long as he was in sight.

The Florilegium enjoyed many more weeks of prosperity before the first snow fell. It was a heavy fall that required the slow burning of hay bales in the chapiteau and annex tent all that night. No fire could be allowed in the menagerie top, but the animals' own body heat was enough to keep the snow from collecting on its roof. And next day Florian ordered teardown and preparation to get on the road to Bavaria.

He and Edge made a hurried trip into town that day, to request from the Herr Doktor Köhn an ample road supply of the helpful Dreser's powder. The doctor asked numerous questions about Autumn's condition, and Edge's replies—even his report that "her face gets ever more crooked"—seemed satisfactorily to confirm the doctor's original opinion. Florian translated: "He sees no possibility of accurate diagnosis until Autumn is examined by that Vienna specialist, but he still says there is no urgency."

"I don't know whether to take that as hopefulness or hopelessness," Edge said. "Anyhow, since we're detouring away from Vienna, ask him if he knows a good doctor any place near where we're going, in case we need one. A doctor that speaks English, if possible."

Dr. Köhn obligingly took from a shelf a thick directory, thumbed through it, and wrote on a slip of paper a name and address in Munich. Then he filled a multitude of little envelopes with the headache reliever, and wished Edge and his lady "viel Glück."

When the Florilegium left the snow-blanketed Hofgarten, it was now a train like that of an army battalion on the move. The black rockaway was leading a blue-and-white procession of ten equipment and supply wagons, six cage wagons, nine house caravans, plus the rolling Gasentwickler, two elephants and a camel—and trailing those walking animals came the ragtag, varicolored straggle of caravans and wagons of the midway hangers-on. Fully a third of the train had crossed the bridge over the Inn while a third was still on it and another third was still approaching it.

They were two days and two nights on the road—a snow-covered road, banked high with snow on both sides—going northeast to the border. There, at Kufstein, they crossed from Austria into Bavaria, and again everyone marveled at the way the border guards let them cross without challenge or hindrance. "I think," said Florian, "this time it's because the Bayerischer sentries are pleased to see our wagons wearing their national colors." Rosenheim was another day's journey northward along the Inn, but now Florian put his Snowball to a canter to take him on ahead. So once more Edge led the train, alone on his driver's seat, because Autumn was—not by choice but with resignation—riding inside the caravan, in the bed. Edge did not enjoy being alone any more than she did, but he was grateful for the snow under the wheels that cushioned her ride.

*B*AYERN

———————————————————————

I

ON THE RIGHT SIDE of the road, as the circus train neared Rosenheim, was still the Inn River, very broad here, and on the left side were the flat, dreary, seemingly limitless swamps that the local folk called the Great Moss—but not in disrespect, for that expanse of salt and sulphur mud provided their livelihood. A city whose two chief industries were the export of salt extracted from those marshes and the attraction of clients to its numerous salt-mud and sulphur-mud spas could not be expected to smell too good, but at least it held out promise of a prosperous stand, for not even the recent war would have depressed the market for salt and health cures.

As usual, Florian came back along the road to meet his circus and lead it into town, announcing, "The city fathers have allotted us a good pitch in the Kaiserbad park, and I got some children to post plenty of paper last night."

But, when they were on the smooth-stoned streets of Rosenheim, Florian exclaimed, "What the hell have those brats done?" There were posters everywhere, indeed, but they were not the Florilegium's. He got down to examine one, and so did Edge, who could discern only that the poster advertised DER ZIRKUS RINGFEDEL.

"Isn't that something?" said Florian through gritted teeth. "In just the time it took me to go and meet you, those bastard Fedels have pasted over all our paper."

"Like that pipsqueak back in Maryland?" asked Edge. "Are they going day and date against us?"

"Not even that," said Florian, with a snort. "It says, 'Wait for the BIG ONE!

The Greatest Show in Europe will arrive in *No Time at All!* Save your money for the VERY BEST!'"

"I take it you're not the only sly showman in the business."

"But look at the date!" snarled Florian. "The Ringfedel is not getting here for another six weeks! Oh, those Fedel boys are sly enough, and they're notorious for underhanded tricks like this, and they are loathed throughout the profession. Orfei warned me about them. And theirs is not even a proper tent circus. They've got a railroad train, so they can scoot in a hurry to any place that seems circus-ripe—or to snatch it away from any rival circus. They don't even have any canvas to set up; they simply show in auditoriums and armories and such. You see what it says here: 'Herren und Damen, why trudge through a snowy and muddy lot to endure a hard bench in a drafty tent? Wait to enjoy the GREAT RINGFEDEL in gemütlich comfort and warmth.'"

"How would they have known we were coming here?"

"Oh, hell, the Fedels employ more advance men than artistes, and pay them better. They're forever out spying everywhere. And you can wager that the Fedels will have a spy pretending to be an innocent josser among our first audience. He'll go snooping about with detective designs, so he can report on our every act and innovation and gimmix and piece of rigging, so the Fedel boys will know precisely how we measure up as competition to them. And next a Fedel agent in disguise will be slinking around our backyard trying to hire our stellar performers away from us."

"They sound like Yankees. What do we do about this infestation?"

"Keep a sharp eye out, mainly. First of all, let us get the company settled on the tober, and any who care to do so may repair to the Kaiserbad hotel for a good dinner. Meanwhile, even before we start to set up, I'll have Stitches send every spare roustabout through the city, to tear this paper and post ours. If they should encounter one of the Fedel paperhangers, well, they'll know how to discourage him. And we will repaper every damned day, if we have to."

However, once the Florilegium's posters were restored, they were not again interfered with, and the brief appearance of the Ringfedel's paper seemed not to have persuaded many Rosenheimers to stay at home and hoard their money and wait six weeks for a different circus. Although the opening day was cold and that night more so, and the tent *was* drafty and the tober soon *was* trodden into a morass, both of the first two performances drew sfondone houses, mainly consisting of the proprietors and employees of the local saltworks and spas, and the spas' less debilitated guests, and all their wives and children. Nobody complained of the inconveniences attendant upon seeing a real circus under real canvas, and everybody roundly applauded—with much foot-stamping—every act and attraction. The people of Rosenheim, in fact, took a specially excited interest in Sir John's sideshow Egyptian Mummy and spent a good deal of time huddled about it, speculating on what salts and brines had been used to preserve that cadaver.

"That gives me an idea," Fitzfarris said to Florian and Edge, as they watched the people clustered about the mummy at the night show's intermission. "Governor, you mightily admired what you called the Bible of the Orfei circus. Remember? So why don't we print up a handsome program of our own? Use just a couple of pages to list all our acts. And then, to fill the other pages, sell advertisements."

"Advertise mummifying salts?" asked Edge.

"No. Advertise the healthful spas of Rosenheim. The Kaiserbad here in this park, the Marienbad, the Dianabad, all the others. We could give them a real puff—'Marienbad's waters make sick folks as lively as Zanni the Clown!'—or as strong as the Quakemaker—whatever they'd like to see in print. And charge the bath owners a stiff price, because we'll go on using those German programs all over Bavaria and Austria."

"A very good idea, Sir John," said Florian. "I'll start soliciting the proprietors first thing tomorrow, and—"

He was interrupted by the approach of a man who might have been any random josser from the crowd, but who introduced himself, in German, as an unemployed circus hostler. Florian relayed that to the others. "He says he was working most recently for the Ringfedel, but he quit because he despises the outfit. Colonel Ramrod, could you use an extra horse tender?"

"That man's no Slovak," said Edge. "Why is he working a slop job?"

"The very question that occurred to me," said Florian. "But I'll give him a trial chore, and see how he does at it."

He and the stranger exchanged some words, then Florian took out a piece of paper and his mason's pencil. While he leaned against a midway stall's counter to write, he said, "I asked him if he knows where the local telegraph office is. He says he does."

Fitz asked, "Who do you know in Bavaria to telegraph to?"

Florian did not reply until he had finished composing the message. He gave it to the stranger and gestured for him to run with it. Then he told the others, "I telegraphed to our advance man, to advise him that we will omit showing in Munich, because I have heard news of plague there. I instructed him instead to hurry to other towns and book us good tobers in them—Fürstenfeldbruck, Landsberg, three or four more."

"What advance man?" asked Fitzfarris. "I'm the only one you've ever had, and I haven't worked since we left the States."

"There still is no advance man," said Florian. "But no matter. I would bet my purse on your mouse game before I'd bet on that telegram's getting dispatched. The fellow is almost certainly one of the Fedels' spies. We'll never see him again."

"Hell, we could have just flung him off the lot," said Edge.

Fitz asked, "Did you get word of the plague from Boom-Boom?"

"I have had no such word," Florian patiently explained. "And we *will* show in Munich, because now I am quite confident that the Zirkus Ringfedel will not try to rivalize against us there. You see, lads, there are persons who think themselves ever so clever, to pry into another's business by lurking and eavesdropping. But then they must *believe* the things they ferret out, however improbable, or what was the point of taking so much trouble to learn those things? The Fedels will convince themselves that I am privy to secrets they are not—that Munich is stricken and that those other places are plums for the picking. Preposterous, as any reasonable person could tell by looking at a newspaper and a map. A plague in Munich would be front-page news. The towns I listed are mere map dots, not worth our visiting. But those towns *are* on the railroad. Therefore, if the Fedels are so clever as to be fooled by their own snooping..." Florian smiled and spread his hands. Then he said seriously, "The fact remains, however, that we are traveling across a continent replete with circuses and competition. I *would* like to have a competent advance man out ahead of us."

The succeeding days were as busy and profitable for the Florilegium as the first had been. The good people of Rosenheim not only continued zestfully to patronize the show, they also manifested the famous Bavarian hospitality and Gemütlichkeit. Numbers of them begged leave to introduce themselves to their favorite performers among the troupe, and invited this one or that, or several at once, to parties and balls and restaurants and even meals in their own homes. Florian remained wary of spies and abductors, but he did not forbid the fraternizing; the only condition he set was that the younger artistes not go anywhere without a chaperon in attendance.

So the troupers happily accepted many invitations, although, after their free and easy circus life, they often were rather intimidated by the severely efficient domesticity they found when they visited any local household. Right inside every front door were felt pads upon which a guest was bidden to step and thereafter keep under his feet, not walking but sliding the pads with him, so as not to mar the highly waxed house floors—even to shine them more glossily. And many of the objects in every house, no matter how obvious their use or function, the visitors found tidily labeled: "Handtuche" stitched on bathroom towels, "Topfe" and "Pfannen" lettered on kitchen cupboards, "Guten Appetit" embroidered on the table napkins. Fitzfarris solemnly swore that he had even seen a cuckoo clock in one house identified by name tag, "Kuckucksuhr."

Of course, it was the young, beautiful and unmarried females who got most of the overtures. Paprika declined all the enraptured young men who sent her flowers and sweets and notes, on the ground that she had to chaperon and interpret for the Simms sisters, whose un-Bavarian complexion did not at all repel Bavarian swains. Monday complained that Paprika constantly attended them only "to stick a spoke in our wheels." Sunday took Paprika aside and quite bluntly pointed out that Rosenheim contained as many fetching women as eligible males. But Paprika only gave them a motherly-tolerant smile and continued to hover whenever the girls, Sunday especially, went out to dinner, or to a Varieté theatre, or for a sleigh ride along the Inn.

There *were* women in Rosenheim, and the unattached among them were not bashful about introducing themselves to the unattached Florian, Maurice, the two clowns and, in droves, to the Quakemaker. The blacks, Chinese and one-eyed Mullenax were the only troupers unbesieged. Mullenax, at least, did not seem to mind; he was happy to spend his off-hours in a Beisl or Weinstube, soaking up schnaps. When Obie Yount received his first scented billet-doux, and had Florian translate it, and learned that his admirer was a widow woman, he recoiled. He still retained his Dixie boyhood recollection of widows as elderly women, usually obese, wearing shapeless dresses and singing hymns. But Florian knew better and quickly disabused him of that misapprehension. So Yount accepted the invitation and many thereafter, finding that European widows—anyway, the ones bold enough to accost him—were of quite a different breed, and sang songs sweeter than hymns.

"There's one thing, though, that does gravel me when I'm bedding these hot-blooded widder women," he confided to the wallflowers of the company: the married men and other undesirables. "Every one of 'em has a needlepoint picture on the wall by her bed. It shows a grave with a weeping willow sagging over it, and there's a motto—Florian tells me it says 'Our Darling Departed' or 'Love Eternal' or some such sentiment—and the willow's fronds are wove from the late husband's own real *hair*. It's enough—well, it's almost enough—to make a man's pecker droop like the willow."

One evening between shows, Edge was approached by a man a few years younger than himself, who wore the uniform and insignia of a major in the Prussian Army. He introduced himself informally as Ferdinand, and said, "We have something in common, Colonel. I also participated, in a minor way, in your American War Between the States. On the other side, I must confess. The wrong side."

"No apologies, Major," said Edge. "I am neither a colonel nor a Confederate any more. But why do you say the 'wrong' side? It won, after all."

"Ach, Chancellor Bismarck predicted that from the beginning. But the Union Army was deplorably scant on gentlemen. One of my Yankee fellow officers stole my umbrella. Another stole my fine English barometer."

"You must have gone to war very well equipped."

"I went mainly to observe. And I did learn some useful things. I saw how your American stirrups have leather covers over them, to prevent their tangling in twigs and brush. When I came home, I recommended their adoption in the Prussian Army. All our cavalrymen now have them."

"And are you still observing, here in Bavaria?"

"Occupying. Only temporarily. I was engaged in the recent unpleasantness with Austria. My battalion remains on the border, and I am quartered in the Schloss here."

The Prussian officer and the Virginian ex-officer continued to chat of old war times, trying to fix on some battle they might both have been involved in. Then Ferdinand mentioned that "the literal high point" of his Union service had been his once going aloft in an observation balloon. Edge told him of the Florilegium's *Saratoga,* and regretted not being able at present to offer Ferdinand a ride in this one, but summoned the troupe's aeronaut to join the conversation.

"Monsieur Jules Rouleau, may I present Major—?"

"Ferdinand, Graf von Zeppelin," said the man, with a stiff bow and a click of his boot heels. "I am much, much interested in ballooning, gentlemen. Perhaps you both would do me the honor of taking dinner with me at the castle?"

Edge again expressed regrets, not wanting to leave Autumn unattended, but Rouleau accepted with pleasure. Von Zeppelin raised a hand, and a uniformed orderly drove up with a fine landau, and the Graf and the aeronaut departed the tober.

"That's dandy," said Clover Lee, who had been looking on. "A Graf is a count, but do I get him? No. I've been courted by half a dozen young men here, and they've all turned out to be the sons of bath owners."

"Ferdinand already has a Gräfin back home in Berlin," said Edge. "He mentioned her. Never mind, Clover Lee. I'd bet that a Bad-owning family is wealthier than any of the nobility."

"I wouldn't know. My escorts have talked about nothing but Ella Zoyara."

"Who?"

"The greatest and most beautiful équestrienne in Europe, and she performed here a year or two ago. She wouldn't be flirted with, so I guess the local young blades settle for me as the next best thing."

"Then they're no judges of equitation. Or of beauty. You were as expert as your mother even before she left. Since you had those ballet lessons back in Rome, you have far surpassed her. In beauty, too."

"Well, I hope sometime we cross the track of that Zoyara, so I can get a look at her. Meanwhile, I thank you sincerely, kind sir, for the compliments."

When Rouleau returned from the castle, some hours later, he was accompanied in the landau not by von Zeppelin but by a plump, waxy-skinned, waxen-mustached and extremely well-dressed young man, whom he introduced to Edge as the Herr Wilhelm Lothar.

"Willi was among the distinguished company at dinner," said Rouleau. "Florian has been wanting an advance man, and Herr Lothar is seeking employment congenial to his taste for travel. Will you be so kind as to show him around our establishment, Zachary, while I go to find Monsieur le Gouverneur?"

Edge complied, though he found the pudgy young Wilhelm—"Oh, do call me Willi"—almost amusingly perfumed and pomaded. While they went about the tober, and Edge showed him things and presented him to other troupers, Rouleau was enthusiastically telling Florian:

"...Perfect for the post. Speaks as many languages as you do, and has entrée everywhere. I wished to tell you privately, before you meet him, that Wilhelm and Lothar are but two of his names. He has a string of them, and they conclude with Wittelsbach."

"No! Of the Bavarian royal family? Then what was he doing dining with an enemy Prussian?"

"Willi was only one of many local luminaries present. Von Zeppelin keeps open house, so he probably did not know half of them. Anyway, Willi is apolitical; a dilettante; a social animal."

"Well, the title-hunting Clover Lee, at least, would certainly be delighted to have such a princeling among us."

"Er... I did say, ami, this is a private disclosure. Willi entrusted his identity to me in confidence. He is forbidden by the family to make public his lineage."

"Forbidden! I know that family is famous for its eccentricity, but surely to forbid—"

"Even eccentrics can outcast one of their own. Willi is a remittance man, well provided for, so long as he keeps secret his familial affiliation. He is—que disje?—cashiered, defrocked, whatever it is that a family does with an embarrassing cousin."

"He must be eccentric to the point of lunacy. I should not much care to have a certifiable lunatic representing Florian's Florilegium."

Rouleau sighed and said, "The other Wittelsbachs may be mad; Willi is only queer. Pas plus qu'est un enculé, if I must so vulgarly describe him. Are you being deliberately dense, mon vieux?"

"No, but I am relieved to hear the plain truth. An innocuous Ganymede is not necessarily disqualified from our employment. True, he will scarcely be acceptable to Clover Lee. But his, ahem, predilections need not interfere with the duties of an advance man."

"Au contraire," said Rouleau, "if I am correctly informed as to the numbers of—of his and my persuasion—among the European upper classes. Willi Lothar could be our passe-partout into high society, palaces, command performances..."

"Take me to meet him. I shall first try his fluency in Magyar."

So Edge and Rouleau stood by, Rouleau looking proprietorially pleased, while Florian and Willi conversed as volubly and, to the bystanders, as incomprehensibly as any two genuine Hungarians. Then they switched languages, through Italian and French to some others that Edge could not even name. Finally Florian emerged from the colloquy to announce that Willi would indeed be joining the establishment, that salary terms had been agreed upon, that Willi's first task would be to design a printed program for the Florilegium and sell advertising space in it to the Rosenheim baths. After that, he would do his advance-man traveling in his own calash, driven by his own body servant, and his first trip in that capacity would be to Munich.

"Perhaps," said Rouleau, coloring slightly, "since I am a flightless chicken until Boom-Boom is with us again, I might go along with Herr Lothar—to show him the ropes, so to speak."

"Do so, Monsieur Roulette," said Florian. "The young man seems well experienced in dealing with officialdom, but he has probably never in his life haggled with a feed dealer or a meatmonger."

No more than a week later, Willi Lothar proudly presented Florian with the printers' first proof of an exquisite, stiff-covered program printed in blue and black on several pages of good white paper. The inside two pages listed, with flamboyant descriptions full of superlative adjectives, all the acts and attractions of the circus. The surrounding pages contained almost equally perfervid advertisements for the Kaiserbad, the Ludwigsbad, the Marienbad, the Johannisbad and several others, each attempting to top all the others' claims of miracle resurrections wrought by their mud baths, sulphur baths, chalybeate baths, esoteric methods of massage, water cures, galvanic cures, dietary cures, etc. Willi also handed to Florian the heavy purse of money he had earned from that endeavor.

"Magnificent! A promising beginning to your new career!" said Florian. "Tell the printer to run off two thousand copies of this beautiful Bible. And tell door-keeper Banat that he is to treat these *like* Bibles—hand them out to the jossers as they enter the chapiteau, then collect the programs again as they leave, so we can use them over and over. Then you and Jules may depart for Munich whenever you like."

Another week or so later, and hideously early in the morning, everybody on the tober was awakened, practically jerked bolt upright from bed or pallet or straw, by a great shrieking whoop of noise. Even the circus animals started up with roars, squawks, neighs, barks and trumpetings, expressing the same shock and consternation as did the exclamations of the humans:

"Ach y fi!" cried Dai Goesle, as he leapt from his caravan bunk in his long underwear, colliding with Zanni Bonvecino, also leaping and crying, "Che peto forte!" But the third man in that caravan merely sat up in his bunk, smiled beatifically and said, "Carl Beck has brought my cally-ope."

"On the road, Jules and your new man I met," said Boom-Boom to Florian and all the others who had erupted into the frosty morning, wrapped in robes and blankets and rugs. "Chopped wood, we all did, so to fire up the boiler of the

Dampforgel I could, this last mile, for a nice surprise to give you all."

Most of the company growled a sour opinion of his nice surprise—"Christ, if the two elephants could sing," said Mullenax, "that's what they'd sound like"— and went back inside their warm vans and wagons. But Florian, Edge, Fitzfarris and a few others stayed outdoors, their breath steaming like the calliope, as they voiced their admiration of it. Not that it was very admirable to look at; Beck had built it to be purely functional, so it was only a massive, complex, convoluted heap of machinery bulking above the sides of the farm wagon he had fetched it in. Like a railroad locomotive, it had a firebox under a water boiler, but there its resemblance to a locomotive ended. From the boiler, copper tubes snaked all about, to culminate in a rank of various-sized upright pipes with lipped apertures, like those of a church organ, but there the resemblance to an organ ended. The keyboard was unique to the calliope: not dainty ivory keys but stout wooden ones, each about four inches wide, for they had to be played by hammering on them with the fists. The steam pressure inside the organ pipes was such that their stops were held closed by heavy springs, so the linkage from keys to stops made for a stiff action, to say the least.

The contraption stood up there, billowing clouds of mixed blue smoke and bright white steam, while Beck bent to the keyboard, beat his fists on it and ripped off a few snorting, wailing bars of "Les Patineurs." The entire menagerie tent again let out a bellow to rival the calliope's. And from the direction of the Kaiserbad came running several hotel employees and three Rosenheim policemen. All of them stopped at a safe distance from the smoke and steam, and shouted to inquire whether they should summon the fire brigade. Florian called back some words of reassurance, and they went away, but looking back over their shoulders and muttering among themselves.

"I think," said Florian, "we had better defer any further demonstrations for a more decent hour. Carl, can your Slovak accordionist learn to play this?"

"Anybody with strong arm can learn."

"Very well. Instruct him. I shall have Stitches and his carpenters erect a decorative wooden bower over the machine. As soon as that is done, gentlemen" —his voice rose as it did when he made an announcement in the pista—"we will up stakes here and proceed en grand cortège to *make parade into Munich!*"

2

EDGE returned to the caravan from which he had forbidden Autumn to step, even when they were wakened by what had sounded like the Last Trump. She was now in her dressing gown and had lit the little coal-oil stove to start breakfast.

"I could see the calliope from the window," she said. "I should very much like to get a closer look."

"It's bitter cold out there, dear. The wind is coming right across the river ice."

"And it has been a week since I was last let out to see the show. Zachary, darling, I can't make you realize how damnably boring this captivity has become. I feel like Rapunzel in her prison tower. Even reading has become very difficult. Focusing on the page, I mean. Now I can do it only by closing one eye, and that gets wearisome."

Edge gnawed his lip, but said as brightly as he could, "Tell you what, Rapunzel. As soon as there comes another sunny day, even if it's cold, I'll furlough you again. Goesle has got the new starback chairs in place, so we'll reserve one for you. Wait until all the jossers are in, and the tent's warmed up some, and seat you just before the come-in. By then, we ought to have the calliope in the spec, so you'll get your close look at that, too. All right?"

"Jolly well all right," she said happily. "Rapunzel thanks her kindly captor." She turned to smile at him, and her bleared lower eye gave him a cheerful, ghastly wink that turned him colder than the wind off the Inn had done.

Goesle and his assistants now lavished their spare-time labor on the making of the casing Florian commissioned to go over and around the naked machinery of the calliope. They did such an elaborate job of fret-saw scrollwork that the steam organ—with a leather-padded seat for the organist—eventually was hidden within what could have passed for a flower arbor. Then, after painting the wagon and the enclosure blue and white to match the rest of the train, they pointed up the fancier bits of filigree with gilding. While they worked and the calliope was inaccessible to him, Carl Beck lazed away his free time in the Kaiserbad, easing the road-stiffness of his limbs by sitting for hours in a hot saline bath. But that made his *neck* stiff, for at the same time he was having to balance atop his head a tremendous glob of allegedly hair-encouraging sulphur mud.

What with one thing and another, Beck was not ready to fire up his Dampfforgel again and introduce it into the show until the afternoon performance of the Florilegium's last day in Rosenheim. The day was cold but bright, so Edge helped Autumn bundle up in layers of warm clothing and a veil, then bade her wait in the van until the last minute before the come-in. Rosenheim had continued to give the show mostly straw houses, and this closing day brought a turnaway attendance. So the chapiteau was well crowded and tolerably warm by the time Edge ushered Autumn to her starback chair near ringside. The band oompah'ed into its Schuhplattler overture—again without a conductor, because Beck insisted on being the organist at the calliope's début—and the midway girls went into their boisterous dance.

A few minutes later, the dancing girls all gave an involuntary and excessively high leap—the seated crowds almost did, too—and the band's oom-pah'ing was totally obliterated, when there came a sudden cataclysmic roar-hoot-screech from outside the tent. After that first staggering impact, the noise became recognizable as the drinking song, "Wein, Weib und Gesang," but became no less deafening. A horse plodded in through the back door, hauling the high and glittery new wagon from which emanated both the uproar and the damp, scorchy smell of an immense steam laundry. Beck's wagon horse had had at least a little while of earlier proximity to the clamor to get accustomed to it, and the skittish zebras had been excused from this walkaround. But the other horses, the two elephants and the camel came in leaning backward as if they were being urged down a steep hill, and the caged creatures were all but beating on the bars. Not only the animals' drivers and tenders, but also every other trouper in the parade—except the invisible Beck and the beaming Florian—looked almost equally buffeted and dazed by the tempest of noise.

However—circus folk and fauna alike being infinitely adaptable to circumstances—by the spec's third circuit of the chapiteau, they all had evidently decided to take the noise as nothing more than exceedingly loud applause and were calm in consequence. The artistes waved and bowed and blew kisses to the crowd—which *was* applauding, though unheard—and the animals afoot stepped high and proud, and the caged ones relaxed to enjoy the ride. As Beck finally let the "Wine, Women and Song" wane and wheeze diminuendo, his Slovak driver edged the calliope wagon to one side, and let the rest of the spec precede it out of the tent. When the calliope let go its fierce grip of the music, the band picked up the tune, though sounding Lilliputian by comparison, so the Kapellmeister could step out of his fancy bower and take his bows to the now audible ovation.

"Unfortunately, the applause was not universal," Florian told Autumn, when he and Edge sat down with her during the intermission. "We will have to omit the calliope from tonight's performance, and it is just as well that we are leaving tomorrow. A delegation was waiting outside the back door when our spec emerged—irate Bad-proprietors, their house physicians, masseurs and what-not —to tell me what an astonishing number of their brain-fevered patients had leaped out of the mud baths and into the nearest tree branches when Boom-Boom struck his first chord."

Autumn started laughing, and so did Florian.

"Humorous, yes, but not to Carl. He very peevishly demanded to know how he can possibly train his replacement organist before we get to Munich. I told him they can practice together on the road, whenever we're on an uninhabited stretch of it, but if any cows jump over the moon, he'll have to do the placating of their owners."

After the intermission, Barnacle Bill came on, no drunker than usual, to put Maximus and the horn-playing Kewwy-dee and the bridge-making elephants through their turns. When he and they had taken their bows, Sunday, Zanni and Ali Baba did antics to amuse the crowd while the pista was cleared. Then the band played a polka to introduce the Smodlakas' dog act, and the blond man and woman, the terriers, the albino children, came prancing and cartwheeling in. But when Pavlo took his commanding stance for the first trick, he gave no command. Instead, he turned very red in the face, pointed an accusing finger at part of the audience and bellowed, "Is again here the spy!"

Dumbfounding his family and the equestrian director, he lunged from the pista in among the nearer starback seats, elbowing through the startled spectators and overturning some of them, meanwhile roaring, "I see you, prljav snooper! I have every time seen you! Lady dress and veil don't fool Pavlo!" Edge was angrily cracking his whip and blowing whistle blasts, but Pavlo crashed on until he loomed over the chair where Autumn sat, and with a snarl he snatched off her hat and veil.

Then he recoiled, turned pale, dropped the hat, whimpered, "Svetog Vlaha..." and crossed himself with an unsteady hand. Several of the jossers seated in the vicinity had been watching the madman, but their stares now fixed on Autumn. There were murmurs of "Himmel" and "Schrecklich" and "Mein Gott," and more signs of the cross made. Other people farther off, thinking the interruption was part of the act, stood up and craned to see what was happening.

By now, Edge was at Autumn's side, helping her to her feet, and saying through his teeth to Pavlo, "Get back in the pista, you son of a bitch, and keep the show going." Pavlo backed away, speechless, shaking his head in awe, and stumbled to the ring, where his family regarded him with fearful wonderment.

As Edge helped Autumn through the stands to the back door, the band music resumed, and Gavrila could be heard, instead of Pavlo, giving the dogs their first cue: "Gospodjica Terriest... igram!"

Autumn, shaken and bewildered, kept saying, "What...? What...?" as Edge supported her and bore her along as quickly as possible through the backyard clutter and the inquiring looks of idle roustabouts. In their own caravan, he helped her take off her outdoor garments and then tenderly lowered her onto the bed.

"What...?" she was still saying. "What was all that...?"

"Compose yourself, little girl. I told you the man is demented by professional jealousy. And I'll make him sorry he is. But I've got to go on next—do my shooting. Then I'll have Florian take over as director and I'll skip my voltige act. Will you be all right until I can get back here?"

"Yes... yes," she said distractedly. "Don't neglect your duties. But... what *was* all that...?"

When Edge stepped into the pista a few minutes later as Colonel Ramrod, he found, for the first time since he had borne arms in any capacity, that the weapons were unsteady in his hands and, for the first time since his recruit training days, he had to concentrate hard to take accurate aim. But, by pretending that every target was Pavlo Smodlaka, he got through the turn without mishap. After he and his assistants, Sunday and Monday, had taken their bows, he asked the girls to take charge of the carbine and pistol. Then he gave Florian the whistle and whip, told him that Buckskin Billy would not be performing in this show and left the chapiteau, going first to pound on the door of the Smodlakas' caravan.

A few minutes afterward, when Edge entered his own caravan, Autumn was still on the bed, now with her face pressed into her pillow, but she had put a pan of water on the little stove. Because Edge's knuckles were scraped raw and bloody, he went to wash his hands before he touched her. But he paused there, and looked down into the pan, and went cold again. The window curtains were all open, and the van's interior was bright, so Edge could clearly see his reflection in the water.

"You brought me books and all sorts of other diversions," Autumn said miserably, her voice muffled by the pillow. "I wondered why you never brought another mirror. It occurred to me to look at myself in the water, in daylight."

Edge swallowed the lump in his throat, washed and dried his hands, and came to sit on the bed beside her. She hid her face deeper in the pillow and said something else.

"Turn your head, Autumn. I can't hear you."

She adjusted her position slightly. "You can listen, but don't look at me any more. Please. Dear God, what is happening to me, Zachary? I never knew—you never let me know—how awful it is. How could you bear to... to be near..."

"Autumn, nobody knows what it is. Not Dr. Köhn, Maggie Hag, nobody. But don't talk like you're something to be *tolerated*. Damn it, woman, I love you."

"You can't. I don't. Lying here... since I looked... I've been thinking. I'm in the right place. A circus. I may not be an artiste any more, but all I have to do is move across the pitch to the sideshow tent and..."

"I said don't talk like that." He stroked her cheek, the fraction of the "good side" of her face that she had turned toward him.

"But I am a grotesque! A gargoyle!" Abruptly she forgot her own troubles and exclaimed, "What have you done to your hands?"

"I beat the shit out of Pavlo Smodlaka."

"Oh, that was childish. You said yourself he is deranged. He didn't deliberately reveal—"

"I know. But he deserved a thrashing, if only for disrupting the performance. Anyway, I had to hit out at somebody, somebody atrociously malignant, and I can't reach God. You're worried and scared, but I'm worried and *infuriated.*"

"None of which does any good. But what *can* be done?" Her one visible flower-petaled eye filled with tears.

"There's got to be something, and we'll find it. We'll collar every doctor in Europe, if we have to. I've got the name of another one in Munich, and we'll call on him the minute we get there." He held her until the eye closed and she slept.

Munich was two days' run from Rosenheim, and the Florilegium now at last left the Inn River and took a road toward the northwest. Along the way, Beck and his accordionist rode on the new calliope wagon, driven by another Slovak, and let it straggle well behind not only the circus wagons and animals, but also well behind the midway-joint vehicles. Even so, everybody in the train could hear the whoops and hoots and ululations of the Dampforgel, as Beck rehearsed the organist who would play it from now on. None of the draft horses and none of the livestock in the roadside fields actually stampeded, but cows, sheep and horses —and farm folk—did gaze wonderingly as the calliope smoked and steamed and agonized past them. And, when the troupe gathered around its campfires, Fitzfarris swore that he had seen wild creatures—elk, boar, wolves and Auerhahns —come to peer from the shelter of the roadside woods.

Florian reported to the company, "I happened to tell our new organist that, in the States, a calliope player is always known as the professor. So now he insists on being so called, and Banat is miffed, because it sounds more prestigious than his own title of crew chief. Nevertheless, American tradition accords the honorific, so all of you try to remember to address that Slovak as Professor, if ever you have occasion to speak to him."

"He'll soon be too deaf to hear it, anyway," said someone.

And someone else asked Florian, "Where are we to meet Jules and Willi, to lead us to our tober?"

"We made no arrangement, but I have little doubt that they will find us. *They* are not deaf."

When, about noon of the next day, the spired skyline of the city rose ahead of them, Florian halted the train. "Behold—Munich, München, meaning the Monks, for it was named to honor those excellent friars who perfected the art of making the best beer in the world. Now let us prepare to make fitting parade."

He moved the balloon wagon up to second place behind his rockaway, and all the bandsmen climbed aboard it, so their music could be heard, however briefly, before the calliope came along at the tail of the procession. The cage wagons had their weather panels removed, and the elephants and camel were draped with their fringed and tasseled robes. Magpie Maggie Hag had even made big, fuzzy blue pom-poms to go on the points of Mitzi's tusks. The human artistes arranged themselves in attractive postures on wagon and van tops, but kept their cloaks around them until they should reach the lee of the big buildings that lined the city streets.

Florian blew his whistle, Beck gave the downbeat and the band swung into the "Auf der Heide" army march, and, far behind, the calliope did the same. The Rosenheimerstrasse brought the circus into a district of the city that was all industrial buildings, almost all of them immense, block-square breweries. The air was thick with the cheesy smell of hops and barley fermenting, and seemed to be made even thicker by the music's reverberating between the high brick walls of those buildings. The workers crowded the windows and doors to watch —they could hardly avoid hearing—and to wave aprons and paddles and ladles. The parade then crossed the Ludwig Bridge over the river Isar into the city proper. Now it was on the broad avenue called the Thal, laid with streetcar tracks, so the circus's wagon drivers had to steer with care to keep off the rails. Several drivers of the streetcars themselves, hearing the circus approaching, had to hurry their horses to intersections and steer their "toast-rack" coaches off into side streets, whence they angrily shook their fists at the parade for interrupting their schedules.

But other people crowded the sidewalks to watch the procession, and waved and cheered and clapped. Jules Rouleau and Willi Lothar evidently also heard the circus hit town, for they met it at the big Isar Tower, both of them leaping from the crowd into the cab of Florian's rockaway.

"Willi got us a tober in the Englischer Garten," Rouleau shouted up to Florian. "No one but he could have done that."

Florian waved acknowledgment, but did not turn immediately toward that park. He followed the Thal through the big archway that pierced the Old City Hall—and when the calliope roared through that tunnel, it really roared— which brought the parade into the Marienplatz, Munich's vast central plaza, full of memorial columns and statues, and surrounded by buildings whose façades were all balconies, gables, mural frescos and niches in which stood more statues.

The train went from there up one street and down another, some of them broad, some narrow, all impeccably clean and none without its ample decoration of towers, fountains and statues, in addition to the decorative-enough buildings that flanked it. Every street was likewise crowded with Münchners delightedly waving welcome. The parade circled the massive theatres and museums, and the walls of the palace and its park, before emerging into the wide-open spaces of the Englischer Garten, six hundred acres of immaculate lawns, fine old trees and flower beds—now fallow and snow-dusted—and icicle-fringed cascades. There were not enough strollers in the park on a winter day to make a crowd, so the artistes hastened to wrap themselves in their cloaks again. Beck let his band cease playing, to rest their mashed lips and aching teeth, and also the calliope organist, to rest his bruised fists.

When all the troupers had got down from their parade perches and the roust-abouts were neatly ranking the wagons and vans, Rouleau told Florian, "Willi and I have not yet posted any paper, not knowing exactly when you would arrive."

"Well, get on with that, then. The crew will be busy with the setup, so hire some vagrant Kinder to do it. Have you engaged hotel rooms?"

"On reserve," said Willi. "I trust the Hotel Vier Jahreszeiten is satisfactory?"

"Oh, eminently," said Florian. "The Four Seasons is several-star deluxe, as I recall. You may be dangerously elevating our appetites to champagne, when presently we have but a beer pocketbook."

Willi gave a patrician sniff. "One should never lower one's taste to the level of one's trouser pocket. A person who has not a champagne palate seldom is offered champagne."

"Then go and order the rooms made ready. In the meantime, I shall treat the company to a champagne-palate meal at the Chinese Tower here in the park."

When Florian extended that invitation to the troupe, and most of them hastened to change into civilian garb, Edge said thank you but declined on behalf of himself and Autumn. "We'll just have a bite in the van, and we won't need a hotel room either. As soon as we've eaten, I want to get her to this doctor"—he brought out the slip of paper—"Renate Krauss, on Prinzregetensstrasse. How do I find him?"

"Not him, her. A lady physician, most unusual. Anyway, Prinzregeten is the street from which we entered this park. You'll have no trouble finding her."

The park's Chinese Tower was outwardly a faithful simulation of an immense pagoda, but the restaurant inside regaled the troupe with a most Bavarian meal, and a sumptuous one—liver dumpling soup, grilled Waller fish, Sauerbraten, parsley potatoes, orange-sauced carrots, Spatenbräu beer, Virgin's milk wine and, for the sweet, a marvelously sculptured chocolate chalet, its marzipan roof snowed over with whipped cream. After that meal, the troupers had almost to be helped aboard the wagons for their return to the tober.

There Aleksandr Banat was waiting to tell Florian, "Visitor you have," and to hand him a business card printed in several colors.

"S. Schmied," Florian read aloud. "Chefpublizist, Zirkus Ringfedel. Ha! Fancy title for an advance man. Show him to my caravan."

"Not him, her," said Banat.

"Well, well, two rarities in one day," mused Florian, and, when he greeted her, he said in German, "An advance *woman* I have never met before, gnädige Frau. Or is it Fräulein?"

"Schmied will suffice," she snapped, looking annoyed. Florian studied her and decided that S. Schmied must have been a good-looking woman before middle age and self-importance took their toll. She went on, in a slightly less aggressive manner, "I came to congratulate you, Florian, on the fine lie you fed us."

"Bitte? I have not communicated anything to your organization, neither truth nor falsehood."

"Oh, stop it, Florian. At your sly instigation, the Ringfedel is booked for the next two months into a succession of charming but negligible villages. We *would* neglect them, except that we so admire your cunning—to send us off into the hinterland so you can prosper here in München. So we will be good sports about it. Not only will we honorably fulfill those engagments, but also the Herren Fedel good-humoredly wish to reward their fellow showman for such a show of finesse."

"Now *you* stop it, Schmied. I have just come from my Mittagesen, of which I overate to excess, and another serving of sweets might prove vomitory. Let us talk straight. By way of example, I shall begin. I freely admit that I expected interception of my telegram, and that I devoutly hoped someone would swallow it and choke on it. I do not apologize. It is revenge that makes the world go round."

"Very well. You exacted your revenge. Now the Herren Fedel wish to acknowledge that, and extend their hands in friendship, and even offer you a gift, to avert any future quarrels between—"

"I warn you, Schmied, I may lose my meal into your lap. I know very well what good sports the Fedels are, and how honorable. It was your impetuosity, Chefpublizist Schmied, that made those backwoods bookings, and the Fedels are *bound* to them. Because you also had to arrange with the Bavarian National Railways the schedules of open track from town to town, the necessary shunting and so on—nicht wahr?—and the B.N.R. would not take kindly to your scrapping that schedule. From what I know of the Fedels, they are furious at this costly bungle of yours, and probably have threatened you with dismissal. So you are now here to give me a gift. What, pray? A blade between my ribs?"

She gave him a look that could have been exactly that, but managed to say, not too abrasively, "We offer you the contract of one of our stellar exhibits. Wimper, we call him."

"Eyelash?" said Florian in English, then went back to German. "One of the little people, I assume. Dwarf or midget?"

"Not a malformed noué, a genuine nain, perfectly proportioned, but in miniature. In his forties, and stands only one hundred centimeters tall."

"Hm. About the size of a five- or six-year-old. Not really phenomenal for a midget, Schmied."

"But your Florilegium has none at all, as we are naturally aware. A five-year-old with a mustache, and smoking eine Zigarette, well, is not that better than none at all?"

"And you would simply sign him over?"

"Yes. To make us friends."

"Hogwash. This Wimper is a liability you wish to get rid of. What is his particular defect? Stealing? Concealing himself in the females' dressing room?"

"No." She sighed and shrugged. "Nothing more than the usual defect of his kind. He is a snotty little bastard."

"Hm. Well, perhaps we could use a new snot. Our other one has lately been acting most chastened and virtuous. Describe this snot."

"He pretends to be ein Volksdeutscher, and on his conduct book puts the German name of Samuel Reindorf. Actually, he is only a Polack, with a name like Hujek or something. That should describe him sufficiently. But in the pista or on the annex platform, he does a dancing turn, strutting like a real human being, invites a large woman from the crowd to be his partner, und so weiter, and the contrast with reality is comical. Though with us he travels by rail, he has his own caravan and horse."

"Very well. I shall consider accepting him, Schmied... and accepting a truce between our establishments... if you throw in eine Gratisaktie."

"Lieber Himmel! What else? The Ringfedel has not an unlimited supply of expendables."

"Come. I am sure you can think of something."

"You drive a hard bargain, Florian, for one getting *gifts*. However... well... there is the Terrible Turk..."

"Strongman, no doubt. I have a strongman."

"I can offer nothing more. As it is, my employers are not going to be jubilant.

I might mention that the Turk also has his own van, horse, costumes, props..."

"Then give me a little time to think over your offer, to consult with my equestrian director, und so weiter."

"Let me know, then. I am at the Pension Finkh."

"The Fedels don't exactly pamper you when you are working advance, do they? You'll be there a day or two longer? I shall communicate my decision as soon as I have made it."

"And you will have Wimper and the Turk as soon as you might want them," said Schmied, with the first smile she had allowed herself.

With a very similar smile, Paprika was saying dreamily, "After such a good meal as we just had, I always feel like making love. Don't you *ever* feel like that, little kedvesem?"

"Oh, sometimes, yes," Sunday admitted, but hastened to add, "Not on a full stomach, though."

The two had come to collapse on their caravan bunks after the feast at the Chinese Tower; Clover Lee and Monday had been dragged off for costume fittings by Magpie Maggie Hag. Now Paprika and Sunday lay supine, almost inert, on their opposite sides of the van, sleepily staring up at the curve of the roof overhead.

"When, then, do you feel that way?" asked Paprika. "When you are being entertained by the Johnnies from the seats?"

"No. So far, none of those has much impressed me." Sunday hesitated and slid a sidelong glance at Paprika. "It's odd, I suppose. I only feel—excited—that way—when I come down from a balloon ride."

"Nothing odd about it, angyal. It is quite usual to be titillated by any experience of high adventure or high risk."

"Is it?" Sunday said, with elaborate uninterest.

There was a spell of silence, then Paprika asked, "Will Jules be taking the *Saratoga* aloft here in München?"

"He hopes to, if the weather permits."

"And this time it is your turn to ascend, is it not?"

After another prolonged spell of silence, Sunday said, "Yes."

"Get dressed now, Fräulein Auburn," said the Frau Doktor Krauss, when the lengthy and thorough examination was done. "Join your young man in my office, so I can speak to you both at the same time."

Autumn said, "If—if the news is bad, I should prefer that he not know."

"And *I* prefer that you obey orders," Dr. Krauss said.

When the doctor was seated at her desk and the other two in front of it, she looked over the notes she had taken, then said to Autumn, "According to what I know of British history, you English have some Saxon blood."

"Is that what ails me?" Autumn said with a wan smile.

"If you are part Saxon, I should hope that you have the Teuton virtue of Gelassenheit—composure, imperturbability, even in adversity."

"We English call it phlegm," said Autumn, but her smile wavered.

"Whatever her virtues," Edge said impatiently, "let's hear the adverse part."

The doctor gave him a nod, but continued speaking to Autumn. "It is for that news that I would wish you to be gelassen. I must tell you that you are dying."

Autumn and Edge both rocked visibly, and Edge said, appalled, "Damn it, lady, *you* are sure enough gelassen."

Autumn gestured for him to subside, and said, "Frau Doktor, who among us is not dying?"

"Some sooner than others. I could have honeyed the words, Fräulein, but it would have been cruel. Now that you know the worst, the rest of what I say will seem trivial. Whereas, if I had begun gently, and worked up to that dire prognosis, you would have suffered at every word."

"Then please let me now have every word."

"The medical term fibroid phthisis will not convey much to you. There are tubercles forming and multiplying within your bones, and unnaturally enlarging them—at present in the bones of your skull—and, sad to say, this form of phthisis does not respond to any known treatment."

"You said 'at present,' Frau Doktor. Will it spread elsewhere inside me? I am already a repellent sight. Am I to get uglier yet?"

The doctor dropped her eyes and cleared her throat. "You will think me facetious to say that this disease is cured only by death. And you will think me callous to employ the word 'fortunate,' but that I shall do. If the disease had struck first elsewhere, it would almost certainly have invaded one bone structure after another, making your life a torment of pain and helplessness. However—and by comparison, fortunately—it early attacked the skull. The growth there will continue, but not for long, because it is not only warping your face and head, it is growing also inside. Before much more deformation can be noticed, the bone will have constricted around a vital blood vessel or the vital lobes of your brain. You will be dead. And spared. Dare I employ the word 'grateful'?"

"Sweet Jesus Almighty," muttered Edge, slumping in his chair.

But Autumn still sat erect, her ravaged face calm. "Yes, I shall be grateful for that mercy, at least. Thank you, Frau Doktor. Can you estimate when? And will the headache become intolerable?"

"It should get no worse than can be palliated by the Dreser's Compound. I will give you a supply that will last... long enough. But exactly how long that will be, I could not predict without keeping you under observation, to ascertain how rapidly the tubercles are multiplying. And a stalwart Saxon would not wish to spend her last months—weeks, whatever—languishing in a clinic. Go and enjoy what remains to you of world and time. And go, as we say, mit Kopf hoch. Or as you English say, keeping a stiff upper lip."

As Edge numbly escorted Autumn out the front door to the street, she murmured, "I wonder... why *do* we say that?"

"Eh?" mumbled Edge, from the depths of his daze.

Autumn let down the veil from her hat, to hide her face—and the tears now starting—and said, "It is the lower lip that trembles."

3

"HELL, YES, I'll rejoice to get a midget for the sideshow," said Fitzfarris. "I don't care what kind of putrid character he may be. I've just lost half of my snake-charmer turn and the *whole* of my hootchy-cootchy."

"Is something wrong with Meli?" asked Florian.

"Not with her, no. That python of hers. Right now—when we're in the biggest city we've been in yet—he decides to shed his skin."

"That incapacitates him from working?"

"You bet it does. He stinks to high heaven. Meli says it's a common failing with pythons, especially elderly ones. It'll be a week or two before he's presentable again, and I'm glad I'm not sharing the Vasilakis caravan. Anyhow, Meli can only do the Medusa turn in the meantime, with the small snakes. So yes, I'll take all the new exhibits you can get me."

"And Quakemaker, how do you feel about our hiring the Turk?" Florian asked Yount. "You have only to say no, and I'll cancel him."

"Well, Governor, my first thought *was* no. But I don't want to scotch anything that might improve our show. And I think a double strongman act might do that. Him and me, we can pretend a contest in the pista—see which can out-strong the other. Maybe even do some wrassling. If he's the tetchy type, we can take turns winning."

"No, don't!" said Fitzfarris, brightening. "That'll give me another shakedown besides the mouse game. I'll make book on the outcome each time you wrestle. Only a fool would bet on such a proposition, of course, but there are always plenty of fools. Once I've got the bets down, Obie, I'll give you and that new hefty a secret sign to let you know who's to win."

"Here comes our equestrian director," said Florian. "We must have his consent, too." But first Florian asked Edge about the visit to the physician, and the state of Autumn's health.

"Same old story," Edge lied. "She's to keep on taking those powders. No prospect of her rejoining the show any time soon. But this Dr. Krauss says she doesn't have to stay so sheltered. She can at least come and watch the show when she wants to."

"Ah, that's something. We'll be happy to have her back among us even to that extent." Florian went on to tell Edge about the visit of the Zirkus Ringfedel's Schmied, and the possibility of acquiring two new artistes for the company.

Edge said he had no objection if no one else did, only remarking, "Obie, you sure aren't yet a total professional, if you still don't have any professional jealousy."

"Only thing I'll be jealous about," said Yount, "is if this Turk gets more of them widder women from the seats than I do."

"Then I'll send a messenger to Schmied," said Florian. "But not until tomorrow. Maybe cause her a sleepless night."

Edge made a quick inspection of the tober, found nothing requiring his attention, and went to rejoin Autumn in the caravan, where he found Magpie Maggie Hag keeping her company.

"I've told Maggie the verdict," Autumn said.

"Then why did you forbid me to tell Florian or anybody else?"

"Because there's no reason to make anybody else feel bad. I wish *you* didn't. Maybe it's not fair to Mag, either, but I confided in her because... toward the end, you... may have need of her. In the meantime, I want you to put on a brave face, and I..." She determinedly made a joke of it. "Since nobody could tell if my phiz is brave or not, I'll keep it veiled."

The gypsy grunted, "Not everything beautiful has to be pretty."

"You are a dear to say so, Mag."

"Me, I never pretty. So I not bitter because in old age I am not. Only women who once had beauty get crabbed and sour when it goes. You luckier than them. You die young and sweet, not old and bitch-mean."

Edge burst out, "Well, I'm damned if I can see any luck in this! And no amount of tent-show philosophizing—"

"For shame, Zachary!" said Autumn. "You owe Mag an apology. You know very well she has never humbugged any of us. And when you are thinking clearly again, you will have to admit that you and I have had wonderfully good fortune. It gave us more than a year together, and everything that happened was enjoyable. Partly because we were experiencing those things together for the first time. Nothing ever got repetitious and monotonous. Neither of us got stale and predictable. And now... now things will still be enjoyable, maybe even more so, because we'll know they're happening for the last time."

Edge forcibly suppressed his urge to go about kicking things and breaking things, and instead mumbled, "Yes. All right. I do apologize, Madame Hag."

From opening day onward, the Florilegium was as well attended in Munich as it had been in Rosenheim, and so were the sideshow and all the midway stands. Florian and Beck were inclined to give much of the credit for that success to the calliope, which bellowed jolly music for an hour before the start of every show. Out here in the wide-open spaces of the Englischer Garten, it could be played without deafening or deranging any of the local populace, but it could be heard as far as the Marienplatz in the middle of town, where, Beck said proudly, "Lorelei's music it is to the Münchners."

Even while the Amazon-and-Fafnir rawhide show was temporarily suspended, the red wagon took in silver, copper, paper and the occasional gold maximilian or carolin, in such ample measure that Florian wore a perpetual small smile—it broadened when he paid the company on salary days—and everyone knew that the menagerie and other recent acquisitions were already pretty well paid for. Indeed, Florian encouraged still further outlays during the weeks in Munich. Goesle and Beck put new wheels on the wagons that needed them, and decorated *all* the wagon wheels with fret-sawed and wondrously painted "sunburst" panels, and added to and improved the night-show carbide lighting.

Jules Rouleau repeatedly pestered Carl Beck to take time off from those mundane chores and put his balloon in the air. But Beck very sensibly pointed out that the circus certainly needed no attendance booster at present, that to inflate the *Saratoga* right now would require more chemicals and more of his time than heretofore—cold weather, he explained, thinned the ambient air, so more hydrogen would be needed to lift the balloon—and also, which Monsieur Roulette could easily perceive for himself, that this winter in Munich was being an exceedingly windy one, hence unsafe for ballooning.

One day Florian said to Beck and Goesle, "I have for too long been running the Florilegium out of my hat and my vest pockets. Even the conduct books are now too many for me to keep track of. I need an office."

So Stitches and Boom-Boom redesigned the red-and-museum wagon, and supervised their Slovaks in the rebuilding of it. Since the wagon's only permanent occupant was the Auerhahn, the museum part got diminished into just a wire hutch for the bird, and the ticket end was expanded into a real office on wheels. Magpie Maggie Hag's guichet was still at the wagon's rear, but behind her now was a fair-sized room, with a window on either side, a desk with a coal-oil lamp, a desk chair and another chair for any business visitor, and a file cabinet for the conduct books, the new ledgers and the increasing other stationery the Florilegium was beginning to require for its operations and record keeping.

During all this time, Edge was doing as Autumn had bidden him, hiding his misery and faithfully performing his numerous duties. Because he was loath ever to leave Autumn's presence, he prevailed on her to attend as many performances as possible, where he could keep an eye on her—even if she was only a veiled and anonymous figure among the jossers. There was no recurrence of the earlier ugly scene; Pavlo was now, as Florian had remarked, a much improved and more temperate man, or at least was confining his nastiness to his nearest and dearest. Anyway, he no longer raced to get his act offstage, and had even added to it—dressing the three mongrels in miniature papier-mâché horse heads and false tails for their come-in with the tiny chariot, and putting them through an equine "dressage" before taking off the trappings and letting them do their regular dog act.

The other performers also and as always practiced refinements of their accustomed acts and essayed new ones. Barnacle Bill had got the tigers Raja, Rani and Siva trained to the point where he could snap his whip and they would bound atop three wooden pedestals in their cage. Then he would also get inside that cramped space, bark "Hoch!" and they would sit up on their haunches, pawing the air.

"It ain't much, but it's worth showin,'" he said to Edge. "It took me long enough. Next I hope to teach 'em to mosey back and forth past each other, from one stand to another. Once you got a cat on a pedestal, see, at least he's not likely to take a jump at you, 'cause it's an awkward position to spring from."

"All right, Abner. Put the tigers in at the next show," said Edge, backing away and privately thinking that Mullenax's breath might be his best protection against attack.

The clowns introduced two new bits of business into their act. One consisted of Ali Baba's riding into the pista on the dwarf horse, Rumpelstilzchen—which always got a laugh—but thereafter the animal did nothing except stand patiently while Fünfünf and Zanni made jokes about it. Their other new routine was more active and calculated to appeal to the Münchners' well-known affinity for earthy humor. Zanni and little Ali Baba put on pugilists' big practice gloves and did a ludicrously mismatched, humpsty-bumpsty prizefight, trading innumerable fake but resounding punches, concluding the bout by collapsing "unconscious" together, each man's head to the other's behind. Then Ali Baba would suddenly jerk up his head, look aghast, hold his nose, flap his other hand as if clearing the air and shout in German to the haughty referee, Fünfünf, "I won!"

"How do you know?"

"Zanni just let out his dying breath!"

[Uproar of Münchner laughter and applause and foot-stamping.]

Even Autumn contributed to the circus's increasing variety and quality of acts by helping Jörg Pfeifer in the ropewalking instruction of Monday Simms. In the intervals between afternoon and evening shows, Autumn would come to the chapiteau where numerous artistes were rehearsing and the Slovaks were picking up litter, straightening the planks and chairs for the next show. If any of those people wondered why Autumn came always dressed in a street gown and heavily veiled, they were too circus-polite to inquire why, or even to refer to the oddness.

Pfeifer already had Monday working on the rope high up under the tent peak, and the girl was well accustomed to the altitude. She was costumed as a chimney sweep, in black tights, with her face sooted and her hair tucked up into Florian's oldest cast-off top hat. For a balance pole she carried a long chimney brush. Pfeifer stood on her resting platform and called his instructions out to her—usually an exhortation like "More tail! Stick out more tail!"—because her act, though it required artistic precision, was totally a comic turn, all angular movements, jerks, twitches and pretended near-falls. Autumn could not climb to the platform, and she would not presume to interfere between master and pupil, so, whenever she had a suggestion to make, she would call up to Pfeifer and let him relay it across the air to Monday:

"Herr Pfeifer, would you ask Miss Simms to pause after the crab glide and just stand perfectly still for about four beats before she goes into the skip shuffle?"

Pfeifer repeated it, and Monday stopped where she was, her long brush-tipped pole waggling slightly to maintain her balance.

"Now, while she is still," said Autumn, "would you tell her, Herr Pfeifer, to look all around the chapiteau, at everybody in here?"

Monday carefully did so, though seeming puzzled by the command. Then, no more instructions forthcoming, she went on through the skip shuffle, the hesitation walk and the rest of her turn. Not until she and Pfeifer had descended the rope ladder did Autumn explain:

"During that moment when you paused, Monday, did you take note that all the bystanders were looking at you? Herr Florian, Colonel Ramrod, even the Slovaks stopped working to look at you. Not at Zanni and Ali Baba practicing over there, not at Barnacle Bill in the tigers' cage yonder. They looked at *you.*"

"Yes'm. I seen. How come you told me to notice?"

"You have just learned a subtle device of dramatics. When every other person in a crowded pista or on a crowded stage is in hectic motion, what rivets the attention of the audience is the one figure maintaining perfect stillness. Remember that and, whenever you want to, you can seize the audience for your own—better even than if a spotlight were on you."

Pfeifer nodded in confirmation. "That can make the difference between a mere performer and a real star artiste."

"Aw, that I can't be," said Monday. "Can't nobody but Miss Autumn be the rope star."

Autumn bent and, through her veil, kissed Monday on the cheek, and said, "Make me forgotten."

One day, when the Florilegium had been showing in the Englischer Garten for three weeks or so, two well-traveled and weather-beaten house caravans turned from the park drive onto the tober. A few minutes later, Banat ushered their owners into the office wagon, where Florian sat discussing future routes with Willi Lothar, and Banat announced the newcomers as formally as a door-keeper at a state ball:

"Shadid Sarkioglu the Terrible Turk! Samuel Reindorf the Wimper!"

"Ah, gentlemen, welcome, welcome!" Florian said warmly. "You make an impressive pair."

They did that, the Turk being at least as big and bulky as the Quakemaker, so the Eyelash looked very much like an insect beside him. But they said loudly and at the same time:

"Efendi, a pair we are not! We took the same road, no more."

"Do not couple me with this oversized and stinking Terrible Turd!"

"Well, at least you both speak English," said Florian. "That is a pleasant bonus."

"Had to learn many languages," said Sarkioglu, knuckling his immense black mustache. "Nobody outside Türkiye speaks Türkçe."

"And I learned many languages in boyhood, from my many tutors," said Reindorf, stroking his tiny brown mustache. "Because I am a natural scholar."

"A somewhat larger scholar than I was promised," said Florian, eyeing him. "I might have known Schmied would lie about that, too. She said a hundred centimeters. I estimate that you stand a hundred and seven. Forty-two inches. Also, that is a false mustache you are wearing. If it were not for your thinning hair, you might be only a presumptuous Kindergarten brat."

"Is there anything else you dislike about me?" snarled the midget.

"Yes," Willi Lothar put in. "Your professional name. It has no Mumm to it, Herr Florian. No zest, no spunk."

"You are right, Willi." Florian pondered, then said, "I think, instead of Wimper, we shall call you—yes—Little Major Minim. That is understandable in most languages."

"Only a major? Scheisse! Tom Thumb is a general."

"Be satisfied, Minim. Properly ranked by midget standards, you might not even make corporal."

"Now I will tell you what I do not like," said Minim, with gritted teeth. "This is called Zirkus Confederate, and that means Rebels, nicht wahr? Well, I would this minute still be a rich landowner in my native country"—he refrained from mentioning the country—"but for the Insurrection of '63, which overturned the natural order of society and forced me into exile. Therefore, I do not like Rebels!"

"You are no plantation slave, only a hired hand," Florian opened his new file cabinet. "Here is your contract. Do you wish to take it and go?"

"No," the midget said sulkily. "I need the salary. I am at your mercy. But do not expect me to like it."

"Crew Chief Banat," said Florian, "show our new colleagues where to spot their vans in the backyard. As soon as they are comfortable, introduce them to our equestrian director. Then come and fetch me. I shall want you to do your acts for me, Shadid, Minim."

When they had gone, Florian muttered, "By damn, the midget is a worthy successor to our last one. Or his reincarnation."

"The big fellow seems decent," said Willi. "Big men usually are."

"He seems, yes. But the Fedels would not have let him go if there wasn't *something* wrong with him. We'll just have to wait and find out what."

"Hot damn!" exclaimed Yount in the chapiteau, when Edge summoned him to meet his new co-strongman. "Just *look* at his dumbbells, his cannonballs, his teeterboard—everything *nickel-plated!*" He looked also at the Turk, who topped his own height to the extent of having a wealth of curly black hair; the Turk returned the look with mild brown eyes, and smiled tentatively. "Hell, Zack, you better ask him if he'll stoop to be co-strongman with *me.*"

"Ask him yourself, Obie. He speaks English as well as you do."

"No, is that so?"

"That is so," said Shadid. "I am told you have ideas for us to compete in tests of strength. Shall we discuss?"

They strolled off toward the other side of the pista, chatting like old friends. Edge turned to the other newcomer and said affably, "Now, what is it you do for a turn, Herr Reindorf?"

"It is insulting to have to prove myself, and I will certainly not prove myself twice. Florian said *he* wished to see me perform."

"Suit yourself," said Edge, but no longer affably. "Banat has gone to get him. I can wait."

He watched Yount rolling into the pista his homemade dumbbells and Stonewall's cannonballs—those things looking like Stone Age artifacts by comparison with the Turk's glittering equipment. The two strongmen were joined over there by little Quincy Simms.

"Who is that?" asked the midget, staring in amazement.

"Young Ali Baba," said Edge. "Contortionist, acrobat and apprentice joey. He does a comic capper to the Quakemaker's turn. He tries to lift one of those ungodly heavy dumbbells and—"

"That is no Ali Baba," the midget said with contempt. "That is ein Neger." He turned to grin maliciously at Edge. "I thought you Rebels had lynched all your Neger people."

"Ready, Major Minim?" said Florian, arriving with Fitzfarris in tow. "This is Sir John, director of our educational exhibits. What are you going to show us?"

"Here in the pista? Nothing. I am a danseur. I must click my heels and stamp my feet. I cannot do that on sawdust and tanbark."

"All right. We can step across the midway to the annex, which is where you will be performing on the platform. Exactly what dance do you do, Major?"

"Any dance. Any exhibition dance that can be done solo. Jig, hornpipe, flamenco, mazurka. After my solo, I beckon to the largest woman I can see in the audience. We dance together, and I make her look ungainly, fat, shambling, stupid. Gross."

"Yes, I imagine you would. Sir John, we'll have the accordion player be his accompanist as well as Meli's. Banat, go get that man and have him report to the annex for a first rehearsal."

Fitz said, "Major, your routine sounds nicely comical, but—"

"Comical? I do art!"

"Oh, surely, yes. But I think we might improve on it just a little. Suppose, after you've made a fool of the josser woman, you then do a real artistic turn with a proper dancing partner? Maybe one of our pretty shoe-slapper girls."

Minim scowled, grumbled to himself and finally said, "I do not much care for embracing a pretty woman."

"Oh?" said Florian. "Would you prefer a male dancing partner?"

"Scheisse, no!" Minim said fiercely. "I am no goddamned Schwule. You big persons are as thick in the head as in the body. What I mean is that, with a pretty girl of full size who really knows how to dance, I might compare unfavorably. That I should not like."

"I see," said Florian. "Well, let us go and observe your dance, and then we shall confer. Equestrian Director, do you mind if we borrow the major for a few minutes?"

"Not a bit," said Edge, with feeling.

He spent the next half hour watching the two strongmen trying one another's props and discussing the alternation of their feats of strength, and Edge occasionally tossed in a suggestion of his own. When Florian returned to the chapiteau, alone, Edge told him:

"The hefties have settled on a routine. I like it; see what you think. Obie will be the brute caveman, with his rusty old gear, and Shadid will be a modern dandy, with his shiny apparatus. Obie'll pound his chest, play the rough and tough man's man, all fusto. And Shadid—this surprised me—he doesn't mind the rôle of mincing around and looking coy, even effeminate. For one thing, after Obie lets his big Lightning walk the plank across his chest, the Turk lies down under the plank to do the same—but calls in the little Rumpelstilzchen to prance lightly across him."

Florian said, "That is European artistry for you—compared to the American man's horror of looking unmanly. It sounds as if they will make a good duo."

"Of course, eventually Shadid shows himself as strong as the caveman. Lightning walks over him, too, and both men do the heavy lifts, and so on. And they'll close with one of them outdoing the other. One picks up every weight he can possibly lift, then the other picks him up, with the weights and all. Depending on which one Fitz signals to be the winner."

"Very good. Very good."

"How about Little Maggot Minim? What's his act like?"

Florian laughed. "He is funny as hell, without meaning to be, and without suspecting that he is. When he strikes a flamenco pose—and puts on that tormented scowl that every flamenco dancer seems to think essential—and then starts stamping his tiny feet and snapping his tiny fingers, it's a treat even for jaded old me."

"What about the girl partner?"

"He finally acceded to that, when Sir John suggested a girl of Minim's own size. Our Night Child, Sava Smodlaka. She is quite pleased to have something to do in the sideshow besides just stand around. Sir John is rehearsing them now."

"That sounds fine, too. Now, if we can all restrain ourselves from grinding that little maggot underfoot, I'd say we'll be making good use of the Ringfedel's rejects."

"Minim should be no more of a provocation to murder than Tim Trimm was. But I'm wondering why the Fedels let the Turk go. You've perceived nothing obnoxious about him?"

"Not yet. He's good at his work and he seems to be an obliging sort. I haven't seen any bad side to him at all."

Shadid Sarkioglu's bad side did not show itself until he went about the back-yard, among the caravans and wagons, amiably introducing himself to every trouper and crewman he met. And then the bad side was shown only to the Vasilakises. Meli was doing laundry and Spyros was wringing things out and hanging them up to dry. Both of them were clad in worn dressing robes, because all their clothes were in the washtub. Shadid approached, a smile upcurving his monster mustache as well as his lips, and he stuck out a big, hairy hand and spoke his name.

Spyros said, "Kalispéra," wiped his wet hand on his robe and reached to shake the newcomer's hand.

But Shadid's smile vanished, he yanked his hand back, and his face went almost as dark as his hair and mustache. "Helleni?" he exclaimed.

"Yes, we Grik," said Spyros, his hand still out.

"Enemies! Exterminators!" Since Spyros had spoken in a sort of English, Shadid spoke in the same language. "Know, then, that I am a Muslim Turk of Morea. One Turk whom you infidel revolutionaries did not massacre."

"Ai, Kristos," Meli moaned.

Spyros said placatively, "No, no. Is true—Turkia, Hellas old enemies. But not us, friend."

"Friend? How dare you, chiti?" Shadid's eyes reddened and bulged. He shot out one hand, grabbed Spyros by the front slack of his robe and lifted him off the ground. "Hellene man is one thing only—the enemy to be destroyed by jihad!" He flung Spyros against the side of their caravan, whence he slumped to the ground, the breath slammed out of him. Meli cowered by the washtub as the infuriated Turk turned his red glare on her. "Hellene woman also is one thing only—to belong to the victor of the jihad, *if* the victor is merciful." He spun again and aimed a thick finger at Spyros, who was clutching at the wagon wheel to rise. "You! Stay there! In presence of a Turk, you are never to stand erect. Remember!" And he stalked away.

When he was out of sight, Meli helped Spyros upright and said urgently in Greek, "We must run and tell Kyvernitis Florian, and demand his protection."

Spyros shook his head, struggled for breath and said hoarsely, "No...no." And after a moment, "No one else saw. We must not stir up dissension."

"*We?*"

"If the Kyvernitis hired the Turk, he must want the Turk. Perhaps more than he wants us. Remember, wife, he hired us only because we were stranded. Shall we now demand that he choose between the Turk and us? We cannot afford to lose this employment."

"What do we do, then?"

"We must strive hard to stay out of the Turk's way. If he is not provoked by the sight of us"—he sighed—"perhaps there will be no trouble."

"Perhaps," Meli said, and echoed his sigh.

"Perhaps..." Edge dared to whisper to Autumn, as they lay in bed that night. "Perhaps that Dr. Krauss was wrong? Speaking as a layman, I'd say the last half hour or so proved you just about as healthy as any woman could hope to be."

Autumn laughed. "A layman, yes, you are." Then she said soberly, "Well, I truly am thankful that *that* function of mine hasn't been impaired."

The caravan was curtained and dark, as it always was at bedtime now, so they could not see one another, and, when they made love, Edge obeyed one unspoken rule: he would not stroke her face or hair. Otherwise they were in no way restricted or inhibited. What Edge could touch of Autumn felt as perfect and delightful and exciting as her body always had been, and she responded as passionately and happily as she always had done.

She said, "Maybe the thought that it might be the last time makes us even more eager to make it the best time for both of us."

"But if the doctor was wrong...just think...we could go on having such wonderful times forever. You know, a lady doctor is a rarity. So probably she had a hard time getting her medical education, and maybe she didn't get all of it. So perhaps she *was* wrong."

"Perhaps," Autumn said, with a sigh.

The very next morning, and very early, the caravan of the Vasilakises was shaken as violently as if one of the elephants had hold of it. Meli sat up with a little shriek and Spyros, on the outside of the bunk, was actually tumbled out of it. Cursing in fright and confusion, he staggered across the bucking floor, flung open the door and stuck out his tousled head.

The Turk let go of the caravan corner he had been rocking up and down, and said, "Hey, Greek. I must go into town, buy some things I need."

"Ugh?" Spyros rubbed sleep from his eyes. "Well, go. Why wake us to tell?"

"I have no money. I am on holdback salary. Give me money."

"Ugh? What? We not rich people, friend. Go ask—"

"A *friend*," Shadid said menacingly, "would not deny a friend." His mouth and mustache grinned, and he began rocking the van again.

"For God's sake, Spyros," Meli whispered from the bunk. "give it to him."

The caravan continued to toss, making it difficult for Spyros to open a trunk, find their grouch bag and extract two gold carolins from its not very heavy contents.

"Here," he said, bracing himself in the pitching doorway. "All we can spare."

Shadid let go of the van and roughly snatched the outheld coins. "You will learn, Greek, how much you can spare." And he went away.

Florian one morning assembled the cast of the sideshow: Fitzfarris, Spyros and his swords, Meli and her now-recovered python, the two Night Children and Little Major Minim—everybody but the Egyptian Mummy and the egg-laying Auerhahn cock—and took them to town to be photographed at the Studio Zimmer, so they would all have fine cartes-de-visite to peddle to the jossers. While they were thus engaged, Florian went to a printer and ordered new posters and new insert pages for the programs, listing the Florilegium's now considerably expanded roster of acts and attractions.

Sunday, Monday and Clover Lee finally got Florian's permission to go out with young men unchaperoned, provided they and their inviters all went out in a bunch. And, since none of the young men ever turned out to be of royal or noble lineage, Clover Lee made sure that nothing compromising happened on those outings. Anyway, the gallants took the girls only to chaste entertainments like plays and operas and ballets in Munich's great theatres. And there the young men were perceptibly disgruntled because the girls paid no attention to them, but only to the performances, continuously whispering among themselves remarks like, "See that ballerina's fluttery little gesture—I could do that right in the middle of a one-hand walkover" and "See how the heroine goes all the way upstage before she turns to give the hero that look—very effective touch—must remember that."

One evening at dinner, Florian announced to those of the company present, "In this land, the whole of this month of December, even part of the next, is devoted to Christmas celebrations. Today, for instance, is the Feast of Saint Barbara and day after tomorrow will be the Feast of Saint Nicholas. I suggest that we all enjoy our own Christmases early and vicariously, because during the final traditional twelve days of Christmas we will have our biggest crowds ever on the tober."

So the troupers made even more frequent visits into town, simply as tourists and sightseers. They strolled the streets and ogled the enticingly stocked shop windows and bought things. They admired the public buildings' adornments of banners, ribbons, candles and torches, the multitudes of crèches and tableaux of costumed children in Nativity scenes, the carolers on street corners and the trumpeters on church towers playing accompaniment to the bells.

During all of that season, when the Florilegium's "professor" let loose on the calliope before performances, he played medleys of old German carols and hymns, and did them very well, though it may have been the first time in history that "Silent Night" was audible for five miles around its source. On the December 13 Feast of Saint Lucia, the circus offered only an afternoon show, because Florian knew that the entire population of Munich would be lining the city streets that night to watch their children do the Lichterzug, and the circus folk also went into town to watch. The children were all dressed in their best, and on high poles carried candle lanterns they had made of paper in the shapes of stars, cradles, snowflakes, little houses. Shyly but sweetly singing carols, they marched all about the central city, to come at last to the Maximilian Bridge. There, rank by marching rank, they dropped their lighted lanterns into the Isar River. Some of the paper things instantly dissolved and sank, but a whole flotilla of them survived to go bobbing, whirling or sedately cruising downstream, bright motes in the darkness.

On Christmas Eve the circus did not show at all, because on that day every Bavarian family stayed at home, trimmed the Christmas tree, sang carols, exchanged gifts and feasted. Florian reserved for that afternoon two of the splendid rooms of the Eberlsbräu restaurant in the Karls Tower—one room for the artistes, one for the crewmen—and treated them all to a lavish holiday spread. Edge and Autumn attended that party, but took a table a little apart from the others, so Autumn could lift her veil whenever she took a bite of food or a sip of wine.

From Christmas Day through the succeeding twelve days, as Florian had promised, the Florilegium enjoyed turnaway crowds, and even the people turned away at the ticket booth remained on the tober to squander money on the midway joints and Fitzfarris's mouse game. For these days, which would be the circus's last in Munich, Florian made a change in the show program. Pfeifer and Autumn had declared Monday Simms ready to make her début on the tightrope, so Florian decided to give her the coveted closing spot. Since Pfeifer had trained her, he could hardly complain because the Lupino mirror act was thus relegated to next-to-close, and neither did Zanni protest.

Only Sunday Simms may have felt some resentment and envy of her sister, because Florian canceled their preceding slant-climb as being "anticlimactic" to Monday's new solo turn. Sunday being still only a minor figure in the trapeze performance, she now had no act at all, except her function as a fill-in acrobat. But she did not let any unsisterly feelings show on her face when she watched the sooty and ragged little chimney sweep do her rope clowning—to the band's fitting music from Strauss's "Cinderella"—and then heard the crowd applauding and cheering and stamping their feet as they had done for no previous act that day.

Monday, up there on the platform, swept off her battered top hat to let her glossy hair tumble free, and took bow after bow, and smiled broadly and whitely through her soot. Only a few knowing eyes on the pista level could have perceived that she was also briskly chafing her thighs together, quite ecstatic from the combined effects of loud acclamation and femoral frication.

Paprika, standing beside Sunday, said with amusement, "She is doing wichsen again." Sunday said nothing and continued to clap as vigorously as the crowd and the other troupers were doing. "Don't feel bad, kedvesem," Paprika added. "You will outshine your sister when you are ready to take full part on the trapeze."

Sunday grumbled, "If I ever get the chance."

"You will get your chance. When I decide you are ready to realize *all* your capabilities. Ready for... anything." Sunday turned, then, and looked at her long and thoroughly. Paprika returned the look and asked, very businesslike, "Perhaps after the next balloon ascension?"

Sunday studied her for a while longer and finally said, "Perhaps."

When Monday came down from her platform, flushed and bright-eyed, Florian and Edge were waiting to congratulate her on her smashingly successful début, and Edge handed her an immense bouquet of flowers.

"Ooh," she said. "One of them Johnnies from the seats?"

"No," said Edge. "From somebody who really knows and appreciates good rope work."

Monday opened the little envelope pinned to the bouquet, took out the card and, when she read it, her eyes got even brighter, because now they had tears in them. She gave the card to Florian, stood on tiptoe to kiss Edge on the cheek and told him, "Pass that-there on for me." Then, carrying the flowers, she danced away to take her place for the Grand Promenade forming around the pista.

Florian read the card aloud. "'To Mademoiselle Monday. Make me forgotten. Do not forget me.' Signed... 'Autumn.'" And he turned away so Edge would not see his own misted eyes.

On the ninth or tenth day of Christmas, Chefpublizist Willi returned from his advance run, to report that he had booked tobers in every appreciable community to the northeastward, clear to Regensburg, and had engaged a team to start posting paper in Freising, the first stop on the route. So now Carl Beck, although he still maintained that a balloon ascension would be unlikely before spring, at least acceded to Rouleu's entreaties to purchase in Munich all the iron filings, acid and other generator supplies that would probably be unobtainable in lesser cities.

The countryside was heavily snowbound when the circus train filed out of Munich, but the meticulously efficient Bavarians had plowed and swept clear all the major roads. The troupers and crewmen who had to drive the vehicles sat bundled in coats and blankets and every other covering they could devise. Those who did not have to ride outside stayed in their caravans most of the way and kept their little stoves burning, so the wagon train left hanging in the cold blue air a trail of bluer smoke. The camel uncomplainingly walked barefoot all the way, as it would have done in its cold native land. So did the three Chinese scorn shoes, as always, even when they had to get down on the frozen ground for some reason. But Hannibal and the Slovak bull man had thoughtfully provided sheep-skin boots, the wool inside, to strap and buckle onto the elephants' big feet. One trouper who did not have to ride in the wind and cold was Autumn Auburn, but she insisted on resuming her seat beside Edge. And she clearly took delight in riding there, as if even a featureless desert of snow was worth seeing by one who probably was seeing it for the last time.

Of course, the land was not entirely featureless. Frequently a family of red deer would stand bright against the snow, or there would loom up from the white fields a multicolored and onion-domed church or a sprawling abbey or the jagged ruins of an ancient castle. The towns the circus stopped in, whether just to spend a night or to set up and show, were medievally picturesque — gabled houses with half-timbered or weathered stone fronts and steep roofs dotted all over with dormer windows. The smaller towns booked by Willi were good for only a week's stand apiece, but Freising provided a profitable two weeks and Landshut three. None of those places, however, did Beck regard as worth the effort of sending the *Saratoga* aloft, nor did Rouleau even suggest it.

During that remainder of the winter, the Florilegium experienced no overt misadventures, problems or troubles of any significance, though some occurred covertly. Shadid Sarkioglu continued to molest the Greeks; he particularly enjoyed waking them early and shockingly by making their caravan bounce and, when Spyros came to the door, demanding money.

"But you on salary now," Spyros protested, when it happened in Freising.

"All spent, and I must entertain a lovely lady from the seats. Give me money."

Spyros did so and continued to do so. But his repeated compliance in no way lessened the Turk's enmity and malice. On the street or on the tober, whenever Shadid and the Vasilakises met, he would snarl — or, after a while, a mere glare from him would suffice — to make Spyros and Meli hasten to sit down somewhere or kneel and pretend to adjust a shoe, until he had passed. The Turk somehow managed to time all these occurrences when no other trouper was near to notice, and the Greeks meekly refrained from mentioning their persecution to Florian or anyone else.

One other peculiar circumstance did get reported to Equestrian Director Edge, but he was inclined to dismiss it as trivial. Doorman Aleksandr Banat came to complain — as well as Edge could grasp from his hash of languages — that the circus was being cheated by an epidemic of sidewalling: children sneaking into the show without buying tickets.

"That doesn't sound like the scrupulously honest Bavarians," said Edge. "Even their kids are unnaturally honest."

"Almost every town, every tober, after every daytime show, I see him, chase him, never catch him."

"Them, I reckon you mean. And only at the afternoon shows, eh?"

"*After* afternoon show, Pana Edge. Always little boy."

"Little boys, Banat. Plural. But after the show? Do you mean they sneak in and hide somewhere to wait for the evening show?"

This was too much for Banat's comprehension. He could only shrug and repeat, "Always little boy come, I see, I chase, I no see no more."

"Well, usually it *is* little boys, seldom little girls. Catch them if you can, Chief, but we won't thrash you if you don't."

Banat again shrugged helplessly and went away, muttering.

4

BY THE TIME the Florilegium finally approached the lovely old city of Regensburg, it was early springtime and no longer too cold for the troupers to peel down to their performing costumes. So they did that and made parade into the city, again preceded by the band and trailed by the hooting calliope. The streets were tortuous and so narrow that the buildings seemed to lean and almost touch rooftops high above the cobbles, but Florian led the way through every passable one of them, even when that left no room on either side for spectators, except in doorways and windows. The parade continued on across the Stone Bridge— where the Regensburgers crowded the parapets to watch and wave and cheer— to the more open suburbs beyond the Danube, then back across the bridge to the city.

"Is this town particularly fond of chickens?" Edge asked Autumn and Magpie Maggie Hag, who was riding with them. "There's a plaque right in the middle of the bridge with what looks like chickens engraved on it."

"In memory of an old legend," said Autumn. "Do you see the cathedral towers sticking up above the roofs ahead? Well, centuries ago, the two architects building that cathedral and this bridge were competing to see who could finish first. The devil came to the bridge builder and offered a bargain. If the architect would promise him the souls of the first three to cross the Danube on this Steinernebrücke, the devil would see that it was finished before the cathedral was. So they struck the bargain, and the bridge *was* finished first. The architect of the cathedral was so chagrined that he killed himself by jumping off one of its unfinished towers. If you look close, among the gargoyles on those towers you'll see the stone effigy of the man falling headfirst down it. But meanwhile, when the bridge was dedicated, its architect cheated the devil by sending first across it only three cocks. So that event is still memorialized in the plaque."

Magpie Maggie Hag asked, "The chickens maybe white and blue?"

"Heavens, I've no idea," said Autumn in surprise. "*Is* there such a thing?"

The gypsy said, "Never see such. But I dukker now white and blue birds. I dukker no good from them."

"Well," said Edge, "we've got quite a few birds now. The Auerhahn, the ostriches, Clover Lee's doves. None of them blue and white. We'll keep a wary eye out, but I must say birds don't sound very menacing."

When the circus reached its tober in the Dörnberg-Garten, most of the troupers hurried to change clothes and proceed to the nearby Goldenes Kreuz Hotel, where Willi had engaged rooms. One who did not hurry there was Jules Rouleau. Instead, he went to interrupt Carl Beck's directing of the Slovaks who were starting to unload the wagons.

"I have soared now, ami, over many waters great and small. The Baltimore harbor, the Arno, the Volturno, the Inn. Surely you will allow me to ascend above the mighty Danube."

"Ja, ja, ja," said Beck. "I will no longer postpone. In complicity with your desire, even Johann Strauss you now have. A new waltz dedicated to the Danube he has recently composed, and already the most popular of all his works it is. As soon as the sheet music I can acquire, and my Kapell can rehearse, the ascension will be made. Tell Herr Florian the poster announcements to prepare."

And so, although the circus did a thriving business right from opening day and had no need to promote attendance, Regensburg was soon plastered with new-printed posters. They proclaimed that, on Easter Sunday, the twenty-first of April, when of course there would be no circus performance, the city would instead be treated (weather permitting) to a spectacle never before seen by its citizens. Fitzfarris immediately began canvassing the Apotheken of the city until he found one that stocked the lycopodium flash powder, so he could add his vanishing-girl fillip to the occasion. And Zanni Bonvecino proposed yet another side attraction for that special day.

"All I need is that tub," he said to Florian and Edge, indicating the old wooden washtub that had served the circus for so long and in so many capacities. At this moment, it was serving its basic function; Clover Lee was rinsing out a set of her fleshings in it. "And I shall purchase some geese."

"Eh?" said Florian, and Clover Lee looked up from her work with equal puzzlement.

Zanni said, "This Dörnberg park will not accommodate the entire city populace to see the balloon lift away. The Stone Bridge is the next-best vantage for watching the ascension, so it will be crowded also with spectators. When those onlookers get stiff necks from gazing upward at the *Saratoga,* they can relax by looking down at the Danube. And there they will see me in my tub, being towed along the river by my geese."

Clover Lee laughed, and Florian said, "A comical turn, indeed, signore. But the Danube is a swift and turbulent river, and still bloody cold even now."

"No fear, Governatore, I have no wish for a dunking. I shall keep to the shallows close in to shore."

"And hey, Zanni, buy *white* geese," said Clover Lee. She turned to Florian. "I can do a rosinback turn at the same time, along that broad street that runs beside the river, with my white doves all trailing along."

"Why not?" said Zanni. "Che sarà, sarà maraviglioso. All of us together—myself, Monsieur Roulette, Sir John, Clover Lee, the Mademoiselles Simms—we shall make that a day, Signor Florian, to be remembered in the annals of the circus."

"Oh, and Zanni," said Edge, reminded of something. "Make sure there's not a blue feather on any of those geese."

During the couple of weeks remaining before that epochal day, the circus folk passed their free time in strolling through Regensburg's narrow streets and teeming market squares and along the riverside promenades and onto the Stein-ernebrücke to look down on the midstream Danube islands. More than one of them, on returning to the tober, made sure to go to Carl Beck—who was daily rehearsing both his band and the calliope professor in "The Beautiful Blue Danube" waltz—to tell him that the Danube was actually a muddy brown color and not notably beautiful, with chunks of winter's ice still careening down it. After hearing that six or seven times, Beck began snarling at his informants, "Until Vienna wait and to Meister Strauss himself tell it!"

On several occasions, Florian took three or four troupers to the riverside Wurstküche for its famous sausages and beer. He had to make several trips, taking just a few guests each time, because that restaurant was so tiny and so perpetually crowded with local folk. Each time, before entering, Florian would direct the guests' attention to the date chiseled in the little building's stone wall: 1320.

"I'll be damned," said Fitzfarris. "In America we revere anything that dates back even to George Washington's day. But this place was feeding people when Dante and Robert the Bruce and Marco Polo were still alive."

"And I'll bet," said Mullenax, when they went inside, "that they got stifled by this identical same smoke, 'way back then.'" The single, soot-encrusted room had its stone cooking hearths on one side, rude trestle tables on the other, and under its low beams hung a dense, oily and aromatic gray smoke, so a patron had to stoop to see beneath it. "But, by Jesus, the provender can't be beat!" Mullenax added, when he tucked into the Weisswurst and Sauerkohl and quaffed the amber Bischofsbräu.

Zanni procured his white geese, eight of them, and Stitches made little harnesses for them. Zanni took the birds and the tub to the small pond in the center of the Dörnberg-Garten and began rehearsals. After enduring a painful number of pecks and pinches, he got them all tied to the tub with thongs of varying lengths, and then, carrying Mullenax's heavy sjambok, folded and wedged himself with considerable effort into the wooden vessel. It took him a while of snapping the long whip at the geese to accustom them to going all in the same direction. Even then, some of the geese paddled properly while others beat their wings and tried to take off, but the overall result was to haul the tub at least slowly across the water in the direction Zanni aimed for, and the several watchers cheered from the pond bank.

"We will go better on the river, with the current helping," said Zanni. "And that confusion—some birds swimming while others try to fly—well, that only adds to the comic effect I desire."

Holy Saturday came, fair and windless, giving promise that Easter Day would be as clement. And Paprika's eyes sparkled as brightly as the day when she said softly to Sunday, "After the Saratoga's descent tomorrow, everyone else will repair to the hotel to while away the holiday. So you and I can have the caravan to ourselves."

"Yes," said Sunday, returning the woman's smile so boldly that Paprika gasped with delight.

But then Sunday went to find her sister, and said, "How would you like to go up tomorrow, instead of me?"

Monday blinked and grinned, but then said with a tinge of suspicion, "You ain't go' miss that ride just out of sisterly love. What's it go' cost me?"

"Nothing. It will earn you something," said Sunday. "Another sort of sisterly love." She explained, as well as she could from mere hearsay.

Monday looked surprised, but not greatly shocked. After only a brief consideration of the prospect, she shrugged indifferently. "Don't sound too hard to take. And maybe I'll learn some tricks to bait John Fitz with. Anyhow, it's worth it, I reckon, just for the extry balloon ride."

"And remember not to talk at all," said Sunday. "Don't say a word the whole time, whatever happens. She'll never know us apart except by... well..."

"I know, I know. I can't talk as prissy nice as you do. Awright, I'll keep mum. Unless you lying to me, and I find out this kind of frolic *hurts*."

Carl Beck stoked up his generator early on Easter morning, and by noon the *Saratoga* stood brilliantly red and white and gigantic above its anchor ropes. By that hour, too, it seemed as if every Regensburger of every age and sex and condition was outdoors. The people earliest out had crammed onto the Florilegium tober and throughout the Dörnberg park roundabout, and so got to enjoy the band's repeated rendition of "The Beautiful Blue Danube," interspersed with other spirited tunes, while the balloon preparations went forward. The rest of the population packed into every other open space that gave an unimpeded view of the sky—the several other city parks, the squares, the whole length of the Steinernebrücke and the Oberer and Unterer islands upstream and downstream of the bridge. So, when the band hit a caesura and dramatically stopped playing and the balloon soared aloft, it seemed to be impelled by the breath of the city itself, exhaled in one concerted and prolonged sigh from some forty thousand throats. Then the band resumed, louder than ever, the "Blue Danube" waltz, and the city gave a thunderous cheer.

Clover Lee, in provocatively nude-looking fleshings and a gold-spangled léotard as bright yellow as her flowing hair, and Zanni, in his tight Harlequin costume, and the calliope in its gaudy wagon, with steam up but sitting silent, were at the riverside ferry slip well upstream of the city's center. The équestrienne, the joey and the professor waited until the *Saratoga* had been up for half an hour or so, letting it have the undivided admiration of the Regensburgers as it variously dipped lower, rose higher, moved up and down the Danube, back and forth from city to suburbs.

Then Zanni, with the assistance of the ferrymen, put his tub and geese overside from the riverbank, and the men helped him squeeze himself tightly into the tub, while the geese honked and squawked and beat their wings and churned their feet against the current. Zanni uncoiled his incongruously big whip, gave it a brisk snap, the ferrymen let go—and the geese, willy-nilly, went off in an impetuous swoop downriver, having to hurry to keep the tub from running over them. With a similar sudden swoop, the calliope launched into

"The Beautiful Blue Danube," loud enough to be heard above the circus band by the spectators away inland in the park.

At the same moment, Clover Lee put Bubbles to a lope, then to a canter, just to keep pace with Zanni. The helpful ferrymen then unlatched the coop of doves she had left with them. The birds burst out in a white explosion that resolved itself into a white cloud fluttering and trailing behind the girl. From the ferry slip, the promenade sloped upward from the water level, so Clover Lee quickly lost sight of Zanni down there. But she was too busy to look at him, anyway, beginning her ballet stands and steps and acrobatic postures and somersaults.

At the circus tober, the bandsmen gratefully ceased playing when the distant calliope outbellowed them. Simultaneously, Florian yelled—he now had a proper tin megaphone to yell through—"Achtung, Herren und Damen!" directing their gaze to the platform on which stood a pretty and smiling fawn-colored girl. While he bawled the patter about magic and mystery and vanishment, Fitz leaned against the platform, negligently holding a lighted cigar. Sunday had to keep her smile from widening into a grin when she saw Paprika, not looking in her direction at all, but with her rapt eyes on the gondola in the sky. Then Florian concluded, "Schau mal!" and Fitz languidly moved, and there was the *poof!* of flash and smoke, and the panel dropped from under Sunday's feet. She lit lightly on the ground and hunched down so the panel could slip shut again. Then she snaked through the open back of the platform and under the chapiteau sidewall. She hurried to the caravan she shared with the other females, and there changed into a calico gown belonging to Monday, before she appeared again among the troupers outside.

Meanwhile, the people lining the riverside promenade had brought their gaze down from the vermilion-and-white balloon to the gold-and-white spectacle of Clover Lee gracefully cavorting as she was borne along at the head of her flock of doves. And the people packed elbow-to-elbow on the Stone Bridge brought their gaze down to the comical spectacle of Zanni, already soaking wet from the river spray, flailing his tremendous sjambok, his tub bobbing and pitching and yawing close behind the frantically paddling geese, and all of them together bearing down headlong toward the bridge pillars. Those spectators on the promenade and the bridge had their mouths wide open, but their cheers—or whatever else they might have been shouting—could not possibly be heard over the tumult of the calliope, even by their closely pressed neighbors.

Zanni and his geese sluiced between two of the bridge pillars like wood chips sucked down a drain. The people lining the downstream parapet leaned over to see them squirt out the other side. To Clover Lee, who was also past the bridge by now, Zanni's swift progress was discernible from the fact that the watchers' heads slowly lifted as their gaze followed him down toward the Unterer island, where he had planned to steer to shore. So Clover Lee turned Bubbles, during which slowdown the doves clustered and buffeted each other to find space to land on her head, shoulders and arms. Then Clover Lee cantered back the way she had come—shaking off the doves into a trailing cloud again—and repeated her bareback performance, with variations. She continued to do that, up and down the promenade, until the balloon's shadow swept over her as it softly descended and wavered toward touchdown on the tober.

The city cheered as the *Saratoga* came down and disappeared from the view of most of the watchers, sinking beneath the city's rooflines. The people crowd-

ing the Dörnberg-Garten went on cheering as it settled among them. The roustabouts were right there, to seize the rope Rouleau threw out, and Paprika was
also there, extending a hand as Monday suddenly stood up in the basket—elicit-
ing noises of amazement and delight from the onlookers—and Paprika gently
assisted her to step out. The people enthusiastically kept clapping their hands
and stamping their feet on the ground, but Paprika murmured, "Now don't detract from Jules's applause, kedvesem. Let him take his bows, too. Here, I have
brought a cloak. You must be chilled." And she wrapped it about the girl and
hustled her off toward their caravan, while Jules proudly preened in the crowd's
unabating loud acclamation.

"Ó jaj, you *are* cold," said Paprika, when Monday shed the cloak in the caravan. "Your skin is libabör all over, and it is usually satin. But I will massage you
back to warmth." She continued to chatter, as if she were far more nervous than
the girl about what might happen next. "Quick, take off your tights and lie down.
I shall strip also. Bare bodies are warmer than anything... *Ó jaj de szép!*" She
made that exclamation on an in-caught breath of admiration, as Monday peeled
off her fleshings, then discarded the only other thing she wore, the little cache-
sexe pad.

Paprika said "ó jaj de szép" over and over as she stared with wide and shining
eyes. Monday stood somewhat uncomfortably, one moment covering herself with
her hands, then hesitantly baring her body again. Paprika shook herself and said,
"Ó jaj de szép means simply 'Oh, my, how beautiful!'—but I should not speak
Magyar words you do not know. Since you have some German, I should use for
the endearments—for the intimacies—only German words, ja? But lie down, lie
down, I shall be right there."

Monday slowly stretched out atop the bunk's covers, herself still uncovered,
and her eyes stayed on the woman, just as Paprika's stayed on her. Paprika kept
on distractedly talking, while her fingers trembled and fumbled at her own
clothing.

"I remember from a long time ago that you told my former partner that you
were ashamed of your—your Flaumhaar down there between your legs. Do you
recall, Sunday? You told her it was like a scattering of little peppercorns. And it
is, it is, but it is *enchanting*. It conceals nothing, it leaves your Schamlippen
beautifully visible. Vulnerable. Oh, dearest Süsse, you should never be ashamed
of it." She laughed shakily and said, "For contrast, look at mine."

Monday looked, for Paprika had now shed all her lower garments and wore
only her blouse, at the buttons of which her fingers fluttered. Monday looked
with genuine curiosity and interest, because one of Clover Lee's rules for the
caravan prohibited any occupant's baring herself completely in the presence of
another.

"You see? My pink Flaumhaar is *all* you see there. It might as well be a
cache-sexe, so little it reveals. Ah, but within it... I am almost ashamed to
admit... my little ruby Kitzler has become as hard as a man's Ständer, just from
gazing at you." Again she laughed shakily, but merrily. "And you too, Liebchen
—ha-*ha!*—look down at your breasts. Your darling dark Brustwarzen have also
pushed out stiff, and that is from gazing at *me*, nicht wahr?"

Monday hesitated, then nodded, then swallowed audibly.

"We are much alike, you see? Why did you wait such a stubborn long while to find out? Ach, this verdammt thing!" Paprika impatiently yanked her blouse apart, its buttons flying, and ripped it off. Breathing as if she had been running, she lay down close beside Monday, as close as the whole length of their bare bodies could get. "Oh, Sunday Süsse, we will be so good for each other!" She took Monday's face between her two trembling hands and opened Monday's quivering lips with the passionate pressure of her own.

Clover Lee, carrying the coop of recaged pigeons, took care to ride from the ferry slip the long way around the fringes of the city to get back to the Dörn-berg-Garten. But it was slow going, for even the back streets were jammed with people dispersing after the show, going home or to church or just leisurely saun-tering. When she arrived at the tober and gave Bubbles to a roustabout, Florian asked how her part of the spectacle had been received.

"Couldn't have been better," she said. "Everybody that wasn't watching Zanni was watching me. All the applause we could want, even if we couldn't hear it over the calliope."

"I suppose the professor will be a while, getting that machine back here," said Florian, looking at the jossers still in the park. "What about Signor Bonve-cino?"

"It'll take him even longer, I bet, having to come through the middle of town. He said he was going to give the geese their liberty after their performance, but I hope he'll remember to bring back our washtub."

"Well, small loss if he doesn't. It has been a glorious day. Come along, now. We're all off to the hotel, to change into our best dress and then convene for a sumptuous Easter dinner."

"Usually," said Paprika, "one of a woman's Brustwarzen affords her more pleasurable feelings than the other." With her fingertips she tenderly tweaked each of Monday's, and the girl's body twitched. "I shall kiss and lick and suck them alternately, so we can know which one pleasures you the more." After a little while, during which Monday gasped and wriggled, Paprika lifted her head, smiled maternally and said, "The left one. Deliciously sensitive, ja?" Monday bashfully returned the smile and nodded. "Very well, now you do the same to me, Sunday dear, and guess—from my responses—which of mine."

When Florian, in new-bought clawhammer coat, ruffled shirt and well-cut trousers, descended from his hotel room to the dining chambers he had reserved, he looked about, then commented to Jörg Pfeifer, "I am wondering what became of your fellow comic. Seeing how crowded the streets still are, I'd have thought he would come directly here to the hotel."

"Probably went to return his props to the tober," said Pfeifer. "He's a consci-entious sort."

"Well," Florian said, "there's no hurry about sitting down to table. I notice some others are not here yet. Mademoiselle Paprika, Barnacle Bill, one of the Simms girls..."

"Enough," Paprika said breathlessly, breaking the long and mutually probing kiss they had been exchanging. "Enough of these preliminaries, or I shall go crazy. Feel here, how my Kitzler is standing to salute you. Put your hand here, so. Ah-h. Now open that place with your fingers, gently, like the wings of a butterfly. Ja. And within... ah, there!" Paprika writhed in delight, but was conscious that Monday was also vibrating. "Ah, it excites *you*, does it, merely to touch me there? But, my dear one, you are doing wichsen to yourself, like that dolt of a sister of yours. Let me do it for you, while you do for me. Open your legs just a little. Ja, yours is as pert and juicy and eager as my own. Let us together ...ja, ja, like that... Ach, Gott!"

Florian rapped a spoon on a wine decanter until he had the attention of the assemblage, and announced, "Some of us are still tardy, but there's no sense in our letting the viands get cold. Be seated, ladies and gentlemen. And Dai, perhaps you'd invoke an Easter grace upon the board."

While lay preacher Goesle was doing that, Florian went to the adjoining room where the roustabouts were dining, and called Aleksandr Banat away from the table. "I hate to interrupt your meal, Crew Chief, but I need a trustworthy messenger."

Banat, chewing a mouthful of something, nodded trustworthily.

"Several troupers have yet to arrive, but I am mainly concerned about Zanni. No one seems to have seen him since he went to the river. Would you run to the tober, Banat? The equestrian director and his lady remained there in their caravan. Inquire of Zachary whether Zanni has returned. If he is not to be found, hurry back here and tell me."

"Du lieber Himmel," gasped Paprika. "We have each reached the Höhepunkt half a dozen times, and never yet moved from lying side by side. Let us do Mundvögeln. Do you know Mundvögeln?" Monday shook her head, only slowly, because her tousled hair was heavy with perspiration. "I shall show you." Paprika changed position on the bunk. Monday jerked convulsively at the first warm, moist sensation, and cried out. "Put your arms around my hips," said Paprika, her voice muffled, "and rest your head between my thighs. This will drive you wild, so hold me tight." Monday kept on convulsing—and crying out—until, burying her face in Paprika's pink fluff, she discovered for herself a new use for her mouth. Thereafter, they both thrashed and rolled about, but quietly, all their noises cried inside each other.

After searching everywhere on the tober, in the chapiteau and the annex, even in the midway stalls and booths, Edge and Banat ran to the backyard and flung open every closed wagon. At the caravans, they knocked on each door before throwing it open. At one, Edge's knock elicited a startled response. "*Pokol! Ki a csuda?*"

"Is that you, Paprika?" Edge called urgently. "Is Zanni in there, by any chance?"

There was a moment of stunned silence, then what sounded to Edge like two voices giggling, but only Paprika's voice answered, and angrily, "Certainly not! What kind of question—?"

"Sorry to bother you. It's just that Zanni's missing. Never showed up for dinner."

Paprika called something else, but Edge had turned away. Banat was saying, "Not in other vans, Pana Edge. Nowhere is he."

"You run and tell Florian to turn out all the other men. I'll start for the river right now. It'll be getting dark before too long."

"I suppose," Paprika said lazily, "we ought to show ourselves at the dinner. And I suppose we ought to arrive separately, not to cause comment. But not just yet. Let us lie here and rest together a little while. All this time, I have done all the talking, spoken all the endearments, never let you say anything. And I shall frankly tell you why. It was nervousness, as if I were some sheltered maiden and this were my very first time. In a way, it was. Always before, for me, it meant no more than taking a drink of water when one is thirsty. This is the first time ever that I have felt... You know, someone said to me, some while ago, that if I could ever know *love*—and I only laughed and made some jocular reply. I did not believe I *could*, ever. But now, with you... oh, Sunday, Sunday Süsse! Still, I must not too boldly declare myself. Perhaps you have only casually indulged, and it may take you some time to decide whether you, too... Anyway, at least we have now let down the barrier. There can be many more such times, Sunday dear—opportunities for us to learn every secret part of each other, and where and how best to do what, so we pleasure each other in the highest degree." She laughed happily and hugged Monday more warmly. "But right now... what we have done already... nothing nicer I could conceive."

Monday started and raised her head, to say dazedly, "Conceive? Miss Paprika, ma'am, do that mean one of us done *made a baby*?"

Paprika's whole body jerked, as if the tangled bedclothes had suddenly discharged an electric shock. She flailed away from Monday and leapt from the bunk. She stood beside it, rigid, trembling, staring down at the girl.

"You are not—" she said, in a voice choked with astonishment and rage. "Not—"

"You wasn't s'posed to know," Monday said contritely.

"Isten Jézus!" Paprika's face flushed to the exact color of red paprika.

"I traded. For the balloon ride."

Paprika's flush spread, all the way down her breasts, and she said in a terrible low voice, "Never in all my life have I been so insulted, so humiliated, so demeaned."

"And you *didn't* know, Miss Paprika, so why you get mad? Sunday and me is triplets, not no bit different nowhere on our bodies. Wasn't it just as much fun as it would of been with—?"

Paprika snarled wordlessly and, as if Monday had been a sudden intruding stranger, she seized up a pillow to cover her slick-shiny belly and its matted pink fluff. With her free hand, she gestured violently for Monday to go.

"But—Miss Paprika," the girl beseeched. "*Is* I go' have a baby from doing what we done?"

"You *stupid* néger bitch! Get... out... of my *sight!*"

Monday slid off the bunk, as far from Paprika as she could get, and grabbed the nearest street frock at hand, one of her sister's, and hastily pulled it over her head, stepped without stockings into her shoes, and fled the caravan, buttoning the dress as she ran.

5

E DG E had not gone far from the park when he met Mullenax ambling toward it, and asked him, "Are you coming from the hotel, Abner? Has Zanni shown up there?"

"Aw . . . the hotel. The dinner. I knowed I was forgettin' somethin'," drawled Mullenax. The local grogshops had not closed for the holiday. "You lookin' for Zanni? Hell, he must be in Vienner by now, or wherever that river goes."

"You saw him? Where?"

"Like I said, whizzin' downriver. I watched from the bridge, with the rubes. Wherever that joey ends up, he'll end up mighty bedraggled. Last I seen, that tub was rollin' over 'n' over, dunkin' him under every time. He wanted to make them folks laugh, and by damn he *did*. Say, is there any of that-there dinner left?"

But Edge had already hurried away. When he emerged from the narrow streets at the old Wurstküche, at the near end of the Stone Bridge, he turned right and trotted down the riverside promenade, peering anxiously over the water. But water was all he saw, with still some chunks of dirty ice ripping along in the brown turbulence, and beyond the water the tangled underbrush of the Unterer island. He tried stopping some of the people still peaceably promenading, but his few words of German and his gesticulations produced only uncomprehending shrugs and apologies. So he trotted on and kept peering until he was past the island's end, and the Danube's farther shore was dim in the fading daylight. If Zanni had made that bank, he was too far away to be seen. So Edge turned and retraced his steps, and about halfway back to the bridge he met Florian, who said:

"Almost everybody, male and female, is out searching. I left Sir John posted at the hotel, to send us word in case Zanni does get there. The Quakemaker and the Terrible Turk have climbed down from the bridge onto that island, to comb it from stem to stern."

"I tried asking the passersby," said Edge. "Not with much luck."

"I have asked, too. A few who watched Zanni's performance said they tried to shout and wave warnings to him. They thought him foolhardy—or suicidal."

"So do I, now that I've had a close look at that river. He only practiced in a quiet pond. If he'd tried it here first, he'd have changed his mind in a hurry."

"My fault, mainly," Florian said gloomily. "I really should have paid more attention. I did have qualms, when I saw how tightly he had to stuff himself into that vessel . . ."

"And Maggie dukkered something about birds. But white and *blue*."

"Eh?"

"Never mind. Let's get back to the bridge and see if Obie and Shadid found any sign of him."

As they went, Florian said, "Fünfünf is taking it hardest. So, to give him something to occupy him, I sent him to inform the Polizei. They have a river patrol—a steam launch, and good lanterns, if a night search is necessary."

When they reached the bridge, they hastened out onto it, for they could see

Yount and the Turk laboriously climbing one of the high center pillars, and carrying something from the island up to the parapet, where several other troupers and a knot of city folk had gathered.

"All we found was this," said Yount, panting. He and Shadid were muddy to the waist, and much scratched elsewhere. What they had found was the wooden tub, its staves now loose and clattery. "It don't look good for Zanni, Governor. There was only three of the geese still tethered to this thing, and dead. Pretty near stripped of all their feathers, besides. Any water that can drown something as feisty as a goose ain't going to be very easy on a mere man."

They were all silent for a minute. Then Edge asked Florian, "Should I spread the word that we'll stay shut tomorrow?"

"No, no," said Florian. "Alive or injured or dead, Zanni would not want that. The news is bound to get around the city, but we can't have the people *pitying* us. No, spread the word to the company that they're all to strain to look as jovial as possible. To prepare to perform at their tiptop best—and maybe at length, to make up the slack if Zanni is still missing tomorrow."

"Have *you* seen Zanni, sis?" demanded Fitzfarris, springing up from his armchair in the hotel lobby as Monday moped in through the front door, her dress unkempt and her hair a mare's nest.

"No," she said dully. "Somebody else was lookin' for him, a while ago. Is he lost? It's my sister I'm lookin' for."

"Yes, he's lost. And Monday is out with the others, hunting—"

She almost shouted, "*I'm* Monday, cuss you, John Fitz!" and heads turned in the lobby.

"Well, excuse me all to hell. But that's Sunday's dress you're wearing, unless I'm mistaken about that, too. And you're not wearing it very securely. Kid, you look like you got dragged through a knothole backwards. What've you been up to?"

She wailed, "Oh, John Fitz, I'm scared I'm go' *have a baby!*" Several of the lobby loungers and desk clerks stood up or leaned around columns to see better.

"Hey, now..." said Fitzfarris, embarrassed, glancing about at the spectators. "Try not to have it here. Get on upstairs."

"*You* don't care!" she wailed, even louder, then burst into tears and flung herself upon him, clutching his shirt front.

"Hey, now..." Fitz said again, helplessly patting her back and giving a gruesome grin to all the people staring. "Sis, I sure do thank you. You've made my reputation in Regensburg. Come on. Let me help you to your room."

She subsided to sobs and sniffles as he half-supported her up the stairs and asked solicitously, "Who—I mean, what makes you think you're in the family way?"

Monday hiccuped and said. "I ain't sure why. But ain't that what 'conceive' means?"

"Yes. But you're not sure *why*? Well, I've heard that that happened once before. Only I hope the Holy Ghost didn't leave the Virgin Mary looking as scraggly as—"

"I ain't no virgin no more!" she wailed. A passing hotel maid shrank against the banister to let them by, giving Fitzfarris a scathing glare as she did so.

"Je-sus..." he muttered. When they got to the upper floor, he asked which way her room was, took her there and led her to the bed. "Kick off your shoes and lie down." She threw herself supine, threw one arm across her eyes and lay there, still sobbing. "Wouldn't you be more comfortable if you buttoned that dress less crooked?"

Without looking, she used her free hand to work at the buttons, and mumbled, "What happened?"

"You tell me."

"I mean to him. What happened to Zanni?"

"I'm sorry to say that he hasn't come back from his ride on the river. We're afraid he's drowned. But don't you trouble about that right now. I gather you've got troubles of your own. *Did* somebody take advantage of you, Monday?"

She sniffled and said faintly, "Yes."

"Some stranger? Or one of your Johnnies from the seats? Or somebody from the show?"

More faintly, "Show."

"Damn. Then I think I'd really rather not know who..."

She moved the arm so she could look at him, and said, not so faintly now, "You're jealous?"

"Well, more concerned than jeal—"

She flung the arm across her face again, wailed, "Oh, you don't care one bit!" and resumed weeping.

"All right, all right, I'm jealous, I'm jealous. And I guess you'd better tell me who he was, so I can—I suppose *something* will have to be done."

She peeked out at him again. "Awright. It was—it was him. It was Zanni."

Fitzfarris looked at her long and hard. "Come on, sis. The truth."

"It *was*. That's why I axed what become of him."

"You stumbled into the hotel just a minute ago. Zanni's been gone since noontime."

"It was afore he went. I just been layin' and cryin' all these hours. But it was *lots* of times afore that."

"Now, Monday, it's convenient to accuse somebody who maybe never can deny it, but that's a mighty scurvy thing to do. If you want to protect the real culprit, then I wash my hands of—"

"It *was* him. Ain't you never wondered how come Quincy got took into the clown act with the real joeys? I *axed* Zanni to give my li'l brother a real act to do. And he said awright, he would, if I would...if I would...and he's been doin' it to me ever since."

"Son of a bitch," said Fitz, but still uncertainly. "Zanni's always been such a courtly fellow. Are you sure you didn't dream all this, kid?"

"I can show you," Monday said simply. Her dress was unbuttoned all down the front, and now she flipped the two halves open, so he could see her entire: the fawn-colored flesh, the dark-brown nipples, the black peppercorn tufts and the dried white flakes clinging there.

Downstairs, Florian said to the several troupers and crewmen who had returned to the hotel with him, "Well, I don't know where Sir John has got to, but the desk porter says Zanni never arrived. Anyhow, I've instructed the porter to send everybody to the dining room as they come in. Since our dinner was so tragically interrupted, we'd all better have a bite now to sustain us."

"I don't have much appetite," said Edge. "And I want to get back to Autumn."

"I ain't hungry neither," said Yount. "But I could sure use a stiff drink, and I bet Terrible could, too. We're both pretty chilled and sore."

So Edge departed, and the others went to the dining hall, and still others did, too, as they came back from the several fruitless searches.

"You little liar," said Fitzfarris, rolling away from Monday and showing her the red stain on the sheet. "Taken advantage of, were you? Scared you were pregnant, eh? Well, now you *can* worry."

She looked anything but worried, smiling with satisfaction and triumph. But she tried to put on a solemn face as she said, "We never done it that way. We done what Miss—what Mr. Zanni called mumfergle. Do you know that way?"

"I never learned much Italian," he said drily.

She said, with some hesitation, "Well, I reckon it would work on you, too. On that."

Fitz said skeptically, "Was Zanni built different some way?"

"Uh, no. No. It's just... well, let me try..."

She changed position on the bed and, after a moment, Fitzfarris murmured in wonderment, "I'll be damned." Some while later, when he was breathing normally again, he said, "Did you really think you could have got pregnant, doing that? Didn't your mother ever tell you girls how you *do* get pregnant?"

"Uh huh. I reckon Mammy told us everything she knowed to tell. But surely no woman in Virginny ever even *heard* of mumfergle. I never did, until just... so how was I to know any different? I didn't mean to trick you with no lie."

"Well, one thing is certain. I can't call you kid any more."

"No. I'm a woman. *Your* woman, now."

"Are you sure you'd want to be? Obviously I'm no better a man than that Zanni. Letting you—"

"But you're *my* man. Whatever I do with you, it's on account of I want to. Could we maybe, from now on, be a real pair, you and me? Out in the open, like Colonel Zack and Miss Autumn? Even if I'm a nigger?"

"If ever you call yourself that again, I'll slap you around, like a real husband." He sighed, but not unhappily. "I never thought I'd take me a child bride. But I won't skulk to do it, like Zanni. Yes, Monday, from now on..." She squealed and hugged him. "You'd better break the news to your sister. I'll tell the others. It'll mean some changes in traveling arrangements. Let me get dressed and get back downstairs."

"So it's up to the Strompolizei now," Florian said resignedly. The pickup meal finished, he and a number of the men of the troupe were drowning their sorrow in schnaps, wine and beer. Several of the women had also taken a bracer of strong drink, then had retired to their hotel rooms or caravans to mourn in seclusion. "Ah, here comes Sir John. Man, we were a little worried that we'd lost you, too."

"No, I was—uh—doing my good deed for the day. Monday Simms came in all fagged out, and I helped her to bed. Hand me that bottle, will you, Maurice?"

"If, as you say, Florian, the show must go on," said Rouleau, "the *Saratoga* is still almost fully inflated. Boom-Boom would have to give it only a small recharge. But we can have another ascension tomorrow."

"Good idea. Show the flag, so to speak. Fünfünf, have you any routine you can substitute for the Lupino mirror on such short notice?"

"Nothing as good. But Major Minim..." Pfeifer turned to the midget, whose head barely topped the table. "You could take Zanni's place in the farcical prizefight with Ali Baba."

Minim snapped, "I will not be made fun of!"

"You'll do as you're told!" said Florian, just as snappishly. "In this extremity, we will not coddle your precious artistic pretensions. We must all work things out as we go along, and that includes you."

Minim snarled viciously into his glass, but made no more demur.

"Tell you what else, Governor," said Yount. "Me and Terrible can string out our wrassling with a new touch we've practiced. Just leave the lungia boom angled out from its center pole, dangling its rope where we can get at it. What we do, we take turns swinging across the ring, like jungle apes, and kicking each other all to hell."

"Good, good. Every little bit helps. But that rope will still be hanging there, Maurice, when your trap act starts. It won't be in your way?"

"It should not be any bother," said LeVie. "Come to think of it, that can add a touch to my Pete Jenkins. When my drunken pignouf is struggling with the roustabouts, Paprika will look down disdainfully and even haul up the rope ladder. Then my pignouf will have to do a comic climb up that extra rope, to get to the platform."

"Good, good."

"If you have no more instructions for me, Efendi Florian," said the Turk, "I must go and clean up. I have a rendezvous tonight with a lady who admired the way I climbed the bridge." He and his mustache grinned. "For that, I must go and get money, also."

"Say, Shadid," Fitzfarris said. "To entertain ladies as often as you do costs like hell. I know. If you don't want to plunder your grouch bag all the time, maybe you'd like to make some money real easy. How about selling me your caravan and horse?" The Turk looked interested, and the other men looked curiously at Fitzfarris. "I'd deduct the price of my present caravan share, and you could move in there with Obie and Abner and Jules."

"Make an offer," said the Turk. "I do not need a whole house to myself. Quakemaker? Roulette? You would not object?"

They both said, "No, not at all," and gave it as their opinion that the absent Mullenax would not mind, either, since he was usually too drunk when he came to bed to notice who else was in the van. So Fitzfarris and Sarkioglu did only a brief dicker, and Fitz paid over the money, and the Turk went off to his assignation.

"I'll tell you fellows why I'm moving out," said Fitz.

"None of our business," said Rouleau. "No need to explain."

"It's your business then, Florian," said Fitz. "Since you're sort of the Simms kids' guardian, I probably ought to have your blessing. Monday and I—"

"Say no more. That girl has been mooning after you for ever so long. If she's finally caught you, I will only say that congratulations are in order, and that this news does much to brighten an otherwise dark day." Florian raised his glass and gave Fitz the traditional German toast, "Hoch soll'n Sie Leben, dreimal hoch!" And the other men followed suit, with comments not so dignified:

"No wonder you looked wistful when Terrible left, Fitz," said Yount. "A woman of your own will stop *you* bucking the tiger."

"Well, here is hoping she can tame him," said Pfeifer. "I would not wager on it."

LeVie said, "Ah, but love, like religion, can accommodate every sort of eccentricity."

"Ach, Mumpitz," said Beck. "With his tall tales, Sir John always her can subdue."

"C'est vrai," said Rouleau. "I overheard Fitz saying his prayers before bed the other night. And you know what? He was lying!"

Monday was still supine, still wearing nothing but a beatific smile, when Sunday entered the room, sat down beside her and said wearily, "So many things have been happening that I forgot to worry about you and your adventure. Have you heard about Zanni?"

"Uh huh," Monday said dreamily, still smiling.

"I've been out tramping the streets, trying my German on everybody I met, but nobody knows anything." Sunday blew out a long breath. "Well." She cast a sidelong glance at her naked sister and said, "Well, from the look of you, the adventure wasn't intolerable."

"No, ma'am!" Monday said emphatically. She sat up, clasped her arms around her knees and beamed even more radiantly. "Every bit of this whole day's been downright nice. And I got you to thank for it."

A trifle uncomfortably, Sunday said, "Well, I just came up to make sure you were all right. You seem to be. Don't you want to come downstairs and get something to eat?"

Monday giggled. "Sister Sunday, you wouldn't believe how full I is. And all I've done *learnt* today."

"Oh, my. From her? I hope it hasn't made you what she is."

"Not nohow! You told me true, and I'm obliged to you. It got me John Fitz. How 'bout that?"

"What got you John Fitz?" asked Sunday, bewildered.

"What-all I learnt. Things that might get *you* your Mr. Zack. Listen here." And Monday, with relish, told everything that had happened since she stepped out of the balloon gondola, and Sunday's eyes went wide with amazement as the tale unfolded.

Only once did she interrupt: "So you gave the game away."

"I'm sorry, sister. I truly did mean to keep quiet."

"It doesn't matter. Soon or later, she'd have found out. I figured she'd have a fit, then."

"Did she ever. Well, after I skedaddled out of there..." and the tale went on, and Sunday's eyes got ever wider.

The next day, there was still no sign of Zanni Bonvecino and no word from the river police, and most of the artistes were frantically busy, rehearsing new bits to prolong their acts, and Beck and his roustabouts were pumping additional gas into the *Saratoga,* and the tober was overrun with jossers waiting, well before noon, to buy tickets to the two o'clock show. Clearly, the whole town had heard of the circus's presumed tragedy and, apparently, everybody in town had come to see how the circus was bearing up under it. What with the troupers' busy doings and their attempt to show only smiling faces to the jossers, they took no notice of the one face so implacably furious that nothing would ever make it smile again.

There was a turnaway house, of course, and the crowd that managed to get in seemed to find nothing lacking in the performance. Perhaps their applause for each act was done even more vigorously, out of sympathy as well as appreciation. Everything in the show went well until the closing act of the first half. Paprika had neither looked at nor spoken to Sunday all day long—they had both taken care to go separately to the dressing wagon to get into their blue fleshings—and Sunday was just as pleased to have Paprika silent, instead of in a Hungarian rage. The two still did not speak when they were up on the platform, and Sunday dutifully swung out or hooked back the trapeze bars, as Paprika went through her solo turn to the band's playing of "There Is But One Girl."

Then, when Paprika took her bows and the band went into "The Flying Dutchman," there emerged from the crowd the drunken Pete Jenkins, with all the attendant hullaballoo before he got up to the trap and revealed himself as Maurice and turned into blue lightning. After his dazzling solo, he and Paprika went into their duet to the "Bal de Vienne," and Sunday continued to monitor the bars according to their "houp là!" commands.

The audience's attention was abruptly distracted from the act by some obtrusive activity at the chapiteau's front door. Several uniformed policemen had entered, and Banat was officiously trying to bar them because they had no tickets, so Florian trotted over to intervene. After a moment, he beckoned for Edge to leave his post in the pista and join them. The jossers got so intent on that business—knowing it must pertain to yesterday's tragedy—that not many of them saw what now occurred on the trapeze rig high above.

It was time for Sunday's brief participation in the act. Paprika came swinging toward the platform on her bar, hanging by her knees, her arms extended. Sunday reached out and leaped, their hands seized one another's wrists, and Sunday was swung in a swoop and, just at the bottom of the arc, Paprika bared her teeth at Sunday and let go of her wrists. The smaller girl was strong enough to hold on for only another fraction of a second, not time enough to gain the altitude or momentum to reach Maurice as he swung in approach. Her grip broke and Sunday went flying, passing close enough under Maurice to see the horrified look on his face.

Florian was saying to Edge, "The Polizei found a body far downstream, and have fetched it back to Regensburg. They say it is waterlogged, bloated, much ravaged by the river fish. It could be someone else. They want us, as the circus's chief authorities, to come at once and see if we can identify it."

Only about half of the more than one thousand people in the chapiteau were watching what happened aloft, and only a few of those gasped in realization that Sunday's free flight was unintended, that she had been hurtled toward a plunging crash into the farthest tiers of seats. But Bandmaster Beck was observing, as always, to keep his music matched to the act. Almost before Sunday's brief flight ended, he had wigwagged the band to break off and blast into Mendelssohn's "Wedding March" at an emergency jog-trot tempo.

Edge was saying to Florian, "What's the damned hurry? Tell the police to curb their damned efficiency and wait. Tell them we'll break for intermission right after—Jesus Christ!"

Hearing the disaster music, he and Florian whirled to look. The whole audience was now clamoring in distress and disbelief. Sunday was still aloft, and her slim blue body was jerking wildly about. In midflight, she had caught the rope left dangling for the strongmen's act, and she had hit it with such force that it and the lungia boom were flailing, the rope's lower end cracking like a whip over the nearer jossers' heads—but Sunday was holding fast. Maurice had alighted on the platform above her, and dropped the rope ladder, and was rapidly descending it. Paprika still hung by her knees from her bar, and swung almost placidly back and forth, watching, and no one could see what expression her face now wore.

"*Blue . . . birds . . .*" Edge said to himself, as he and Florian went running.

Maurice got to a rung of the ladder on a level with Sunday and, though she was still dizzily oscillating, managed to reach out and grab the rope and gentle it to steadiness. Then he helped Sunday shakily put out one leg, then her other, to the ladder's rungs, and finally clutch it with her hands. Maurice keeping close, Sunday weakly descended, and her legs nearly gave way beneath her when she touched the pista ground. Florian and Edge were waiting there—and the police as well. Sunday pointed up at Paprika, but had to pant and gasp and sob for a minute before she could get the words out: "She tried to kill me. She deliberately let go of me."

The crowd did not hear the words, and the policemen did not comprehend them, but every face in the chapiteau followed Sunday's arm and stared accusingly up at Paprika. Away up there, she was now pumping her body, swinging in longer, swifter swoops and going higher each time—and, incongruously, the band kept the "Wedding March" in perfect rhythm with her. Then, at the top of a swoop, Paprika relaxed her bent legs and swan-dived into space. Her parabola kept her airborne for only a moment, then she hit the sloping underside of the tent roof—with a *splat!* audible above the band music—and there she turned from a swan into, briefly, a blue star suspended and glittering, her arms and legs outstretched. But the canvas bounced her off and inward, and she fell in another parabola to hit full-length on the pista curb with another audible noise—this one of sickening finality.

Florian was immediately at pista center, with the megaphone, and Beck hurried his band into the come-out anthem. As Yount and the Turk ran to lift Paprika and pretended to help her "walk" between them out the back door, Florian bawled to the crowd that they had just witnessed a specially staged scene of daredevilry, that no mischance had occurred, that it was all part of the show. He signaled urgently to Sunday, and LeVie and Edge supported her while somehow she smiled and even threw up her trembling arms in the V. Now, Florian bellowed, it was intermission time, time for all to adjourn and enjoy themselves on the midway, and the whole troupe would return afterward, safe and sound, with the second thrilling half of the program.

The next morning, Regensburg was treated to a spectacle as never-seen-before as the two balloon ascensions had been: a circus funeral, and a double funeral, at that. Led by Florian's black rockaway and the steaming but silent calliope, a few of the circus wagons, draped with black bunting, carried all the circus folk. The balloon wagon, its bed covered with a black pall, bore the coffins of Zanni and Paprika. With the bandsmen in their wagon playing the theme from Chopin's "Sonata Funèbre," the train plodded at the dead march from the Dörnberg-Garten to the Katholik-Friedhof.

Although the civic authorities still wanted to ask many questions—and to fill out innumerable forms—concerning the "irregularities" occurring over the preceding two days, there had been no problem about the bodies' getting proper and public burial. Florian had merely shown their conduct books to attest that both Giorgio Bonvecino and Cécile Makkai had been Roman Catholics in life, and the ecclesiastic authorities graciously gave permission.

Nevertheless, the officiating priest looked uneasy at this particular ceremony, and frequently flicked glances up from his missal at the motley crowd of mourners standing about him and his acolytes. Besides the bandsmen in uniform and the crewmen in canvas and denim work clothes, Pater Frederick could count three unmistakable Orientals, two blacks, two albinos, a midget, a cloaked and hooded person of indeterminate sex, a giant in a leopard skin and another in a skimpy breechclout, one man wearing as white a face as any corpse in the cemetery and another with a face half-blue, one man in fringed buckskins, five young women in decidedly unsolemn near-nudity. Pater Frederick could approve of only two men—Florian and Goesle—respectably attired, and only one woman—Autumn—who wore a decent dress and veil.

After the spoken service and prayers, and the numerous signs of the cross, and the several aspersings with holy water and censer smoke, and the sprinklings of earth into the two graves, Florian spoke the last words over them—once again in the plural: the Latin for "They danced about. They gave pleasure. They are dead." Then, at Florian's signal, the prevailing decorum was riven and shattered and abolished, and Pater Frederick was all but blown out of his vestments, by the calliope's earthquake-volume blast of "Auld Lang Syne."

6

T H E   F L O R I L E G I U M and its raggle-taggle tail of midway vehicles followed the Danube downstream, toward Austria again, stopping to show for a week or two in each of the larger towns along the river. Sunday had required only brief rehearsal to take Paprika's place as Maurice's partner, and to do the act exquisitely. Now that she and Monday were star turns, Florian accorded them noms-de-théâtre. For the trapeze act, Sunday became Mademoiselle Butterfly, and Monday, as the ropewalking chimney sweep, of course became Cinderella. (In the backyard, Monday liked to be addressed as Mrs. Fitzfarris, though that union had yet to be endowed with any certificate of marriage.) Major Minim remained in the pugilistic comedy act with Ali Baba, though still grumbling and even, during the performance, trying really to pummel the boy. The circus's new audi-

ences seemed to perceive no scantiness in the program, but Florian did, and
yearned to discover new artistes.

On the road between towns, the travelers now found the Bavarian landscape
lush to look at. Autumn, in particular, could not get enough of looking at it. Here,
as in Italy, the fields of grain and vegetables were interspersed with fields of the
bright-yellow colza—here called Raps, said Jörg Pfeifer. But the Bavarian
farmers did not till their earth as the Italians had done—with a crude plow
drawn by horse or mule or ox; the Bavarians used modern machinery. The entire
circus company stopped to watch, in wonder and admiration, the first time they
saw a field thus being plowed.

On either side of the expanse of bare ground stood an immense, high-
wheeled steam traction engine. Both machines smoked and steamed like the
circus's calliope, and made almost as much noise, though not at all musically. A
cable was stretched between the two engines, and from it depended a plow more
massive and heavy than any man could handle, being hauled by the cable back
and forth across the field. The engine tenders moved their machines a couple of
feet every time the plow finished one long furrow, to start another, perfectly
parallel.

"Just look at that!" said Mullenax, the most impressed of those watching,
because he had once been a farmer himself. "Not a single animal doin' none of
that work. How can any dirt farmer afford such a rig?"

"The farmer does not own it," said Pfeifer. "The engine men are entrepreneurs. They travel from farm to farm and rent their services."

Another novelty noticed by the travelers was mainly evident in the towns—or
rather, on the outskirts of the towns: every garbage dump was piled high with
tangles and thickets of looped wire. These, when seen close, proved to be great
heaps of women's dress hoops. And it was Sunday Simms who was able to explain this curiosity, because she assiduously read every town newspaper, to improve her German, and always translated the society news items for Clover Lee,
who liked to keep abreast of the doings of counts and dukes and such.

"The stylish women all over Europe are throwing away their hoops," said
Sunday. "I don't know why, but the big crinoline skirts have suddenly gone out of
fashion. Look at the women on the streets now. Their skirts are all flat in front,
and they use only a sort of little half-hoop to make what they call a crinolette, a
flaring, trailing train behind."

Some of the other newspaper reports were of more interest to the older
members of the troupe, as when there came the news of the Ausgleich. This
political compromise had, after Hungary's years of agitating for independence, at
last given that country some measure of separation from the Austrian Empire.
By the terms of the Ausgleich, Franz Joseph and Elisabeth would remain emperor and empress of Austria, but now were being crowned a second time—as
mere king and queen of Hungary—and that nation, under this new dual monarchy, would henceforward make and administer its own laws, courts and civil
statutes.

"Well, it will calm the longtime rumblings of rebellion in Hungary," said Florian. "But Elisabeth will be particularly pleased with the arrangement. She will
have more excuse than ever to stay apart from Franz Joseph and spend most of
her time being queen in Budapest instead of empress in Vienna."

Just a week or so later, the front-page news in the Deggendorf *Zeitung* was that the tottery French-supported régime in Mexico had completely disintegrated and its Emperor Maximilian—brother of Franz Joseph—had been shot by a Mexican firing squad. A boxed item in that story added that, to express their displeasure at Louis Napoléon's having let such a calamity happen, Franz Joseph and Elisabeth would be the only two European monarchs *not* attending the great World's Fair opening in Paris.

And another news item that Sunday translated from the paper, though it had nothing to do with a royal, a noble or even a man, so excited Clover Lee that she ran to Florian and requested a day off from work.

"The Great Zoyara," she told him, almost dancing, "is giving an exhibition of her equitation in Plattling, and that's only a few miles the other side of the river. Imagine! Ella Zoyara, the greatest équestrienne of the age. My heroine ever since I first got onto a rosinback. Please, Florian, may I go and see her perform? I'll only miss two shows. And I might learn all kinds of new tricks to make it worthwhile. Please, may I go?"

Florian plucked at his beard. "I do hate to lose, even temporarily, another principal from our already depleted program. But I can hardly say no. The fact is, I wish I could play truant and see that splendid lady myself. It wasn't until after I went to America that she made her first reputation with the Zirkus Renz."

"They say she does things no other female rider has ever attempted," said Clover Lee. "Jumps over five flags held horizontally. Somersaults through fifty paper hoops in succession..."

"Yes," said Florian. "If we weren't already so well supplied with good riders, I might even go and make La Zoyara an offer. But she would refuse. She must be making a fortune with her solo tours. Very well, my dear. Saddle up Bubbles and go. Only one day, mind. And ride carefully on the way."

But Clover Lee was gone for three days, and Florian was alternately irate and worried. He was about to send someone on her trail when she returned, about midnight of the third day, riding indolently, smiling in a knowing way. Florian and Edge both began to berate her the minute she dismounted, but she went on smiling and, when they paused for breath, she said:

"I know. I overstayed my leave. But I think you'll agree that it was worth it, when I tell you why. Ella Zoyara is not Spanish, as the posters all say. Ella Zoyara is as American as I am. Omar Kingsley-Stokes by name, and even that is probably fancified. I bet it's only Homer Stokes."

"Omar?" said Florian.

"Homer?" said Edge.

Clover Lee nodded. "Small wonder the Great Zoyara can do riding tricks no woman can. It's because no woman has the strength. She is really a man. The secret is closely kept. He even wears female clothes on the street and in private. Wears his hair long, shaves and powders his arms and legs, as well as his face..."

Florian said, "It is inconceivable. If no one else in all of Europe has even suspected such a masquerade, how could you possibly know—?"

"Now, Florian," Clover Lee said sweetly. "How would you *suppose* I know?" The two men looked faintly shocked at such blithe shamelessness. "Anyway, this time, I was given more than an embroidered purse and twenty scudi. Maybe my virtue is going up in value." She took from behind Bubbles's saddle a paper-wrapped bundle, large but evidently light of weight. "As soon as I've had Maggie do some seamstress work for me, I'll show you what Homer Stokes gave me and taught me."

She had the new turn ready to add to her act by the time the Florilegium reached the last town in Bavaria in which Willi had booked a tober—Passau, on the Austrian border—and Clover Lee's act was so warmly received there that Florian had to concede that she had made up for her delinquency. While she could not imitate the Ella Zoyara feats that required masculine muscularity, she *could* commence her act the same way La Zoyara did. She told Boom-Boom what new music she would require—quite a variety, and changing in rapid succession—and told Florian how to introduce her entrance, and what to say thereafter. So, the afternoon of her new turn's début, Florian bellowed through his megaphone, "Die Nationen im Prozession!"

The band let loose with oom-pah music and Clover Lee rode into the chapiteau erect on the cantering Bubbles, dancing there a lively Schuhplattler and wearing a Bavarian woman's dirndl and bonnet, and Florian announced, "Beglücken Bayern!" and the jossers loudly applauded the salute to their homeland. After one circuit of the tent, Clover Lee deftly doffed that garb, but was still costumed. When Edge ran to get the discarded garments out of the way, he discovered that they were made of such fine-denier silk that, though opaque, they had almost no bulk.

Clover Lee was now wearing the next layer: a kerchief and a Colombina skirt of red, white and green. The band now played a saltarello, and she danced it on Bubbles's back, and Florian cried, "Innig Italien!" Next she was wearing a flat blue cap and a jack-tar's flap-collared blouse, and she danced a hornpipe—"Blühend Britannien!" Then she wore a tartan kilt and a fuzzy sporran, and danced a fling—"Schottland das Schöne!" Then she was wearing a small round cap and a toreador's suit of lights, and she was dancing a fandango—"Sonnig Spanien!" And finally, under all, she wore only her gold-spangled fleshings and her own golden hair, and—"Die amerikanische Artistin, Fräulein Clover Lee!"—went into her accustomed routine of ballet steps, acrobatic poses, the leaping of garters and garlands. From the back door, a roustabout opened the cage so her doves flew after her and did their participation in the act.

Her routine was so popular there in Passau, and everywhere thereafter, that the Mademoiselles Cinderella and Butterfly were a trifle annoyed—also amused —that a mere showy embellishment should have made Clover Lee as much of a star attraction as they with their more hazardous thrill acts. However, no real rivalry or estrangement developed among the girls, and Clover Lee refused to let Florian invent any flamboyant new "star name" for her.

"Let Homer Stokes hide his homely name and his sex and his nationality if he wants to," she said. "But I'm quite content to be billed as plain American Clover Lee. At least until I marry a real title to go with the name."

Passau was a busy crossroads of commerce, situated as it was at the confluence of the rivers Ilz, Danube and Inn. Passau was also currently being host to a citywide trade fair, nearly doubling its normal population. The troupers, in their free time, enjoyed wandering through the pavilions exhibiting the latest inventions, machinery, tools and products—and through the streets crowded with entresorts: slum joints, mountebanks' stands, waxworks stalls, puppet-show tents and the like.

Florian was especially interested in prowling those streets, and hauled Edge along with him, in search of new talent. At one grubby tent, where the proprietor was halfheartedly proclaiming his exhibit in German, though his banner was in some other language, Florian said, "This might be edifying."

Edge looked at the banner—the most prominent words on it were FRØKEN ÅL—and hazarded a translation: "Freaks all?"

"No. It's her name: Miss Eel. Danish. A lady klischnigg. A contortionist. Let us buy tickets and see what she is like."

She was good, and she worked hard at being good, although her audience consisted of no more than ten or twelve bored-looking idlers. She was as flexible and fluid as any real eel, but incomparably prettier, and she had delicate curves and shapely limbs that an eel does not, and what she could do with those was simultaneously admirable, amazing and erotic. However, her costume—what there was of it: merely a skintight léotard—was colorless and much darned. She performed on a bare-board platform with no accompaniment but the manager's languid tweedling on a flute. When the act was concluded and the other people drifted out of the tent, Florian stayed to accost the girl and say:

"Jeg vil gerne, Frøken Ål, De har noget bedre. Er De ledig?"

With a glance of contempt, and in English, Miss Eel said, "Piss off, squire."

Edge laughed, which made her give him a look more surprised than contemptuous.

"Er... ahem," said Florian. "When I suggested 'something better,' perhaps I phrased it ambiguously, but—"

"If I took every better position suggested by every gawk, I should have to know a hell of a lot more twists than I do. What position do you want me in? Talk to my manager there. For enough money, the damned pimp will probably make me turn inside out."

"Please, Miss Eel, desist. I am not a gawk or a voyeur, and I am not a voyageur forain, like your—er—manager. I am the owner of Florian's Flourishing Florilegium, a highly reputable traveling circus. I come with a legitimate offer of lucrative employment."

"Oh." She looked abashed, and apologized, "Det gør mig ondt. I should have realized, when you spoke in dansk, that you were not the usual dirty-minded slet menneske."

"Are you under contract or are you free to negotiate, Miss Eel?"

"Please call me Agnete, Herr Florian. My name is Agnete Knudsdatter. And I can be free in three minutes, if you wish to purchase the banner. That is all the pimp owns of me."

"We will provide for you a much better banner."

"Two minutes, then. I have little else to pack."

When Frøken Knudsdatter emerged from the tent in street clothes, she was followed by the manager, beating his breast, bleating and imploring in several languages. But she paid him no heed, so neither did Florian nor Edge. Carrying her meager luggage—two worn carpetbags—they escorted her to the tober and to the caravan now occupied by only Clover Lee and Sunday Simms.

"I am sure the other girls will not mind your sharing these quarters," said Florian, "until you can afford to pay your way. Now come with me to our wardrobe mistress. I think, since you are one of the few dark-haired Danes, we will maintain the persona of Miss Eel and dress you in dark, shiny, eel-like tights. We have also on the show a very young and small black boy who is himself no mean posture-master. Not so talented as you, of course. But, since he is already eel-colored, you might wish to work him into your act. Eel and elver, so to speak."

"I am at your command, Herr Florian," said Agnete, looking dazed at the sudden change in her fortunes.

On another foray among the streets of entresorts, Florian and Edge came upon three performers—two middle-aged men and a young girl—working literally in the street, without tent, stall, talker or banner. They were garbed, rather raggedly, as clowns: the girl as an Italian serving wench, the men as loutish Bavarian or Austrian peasants. At the moment they were performing, to a sizable crowd of strollers who had stopped to watch, an act that was acrobatic as well as clownish. The men each held an end of a long bamboo pole that they were whipping and twanging up and down, while the girl used it very like a tightrope, and almost as skillfully as Autumn Auburn or Monday Simms, letting it toss her into leaps and flips and somersaults, but always landing again on the bamboo.

"The sky pole," Florian told Edge. "These are casse-cou clowns. The daredevil, breakneck variety."

After a while of that, the three abandoned the acrobatics, and the older man and the girl began a loud-voiced repartee routine. He was a seedy figure—wearing knee-length Leder-Bundhosen, but without stockings, so his pale and scrawny calves were bare all the way down to his battered boots—and he conveyed an old man's impotent and envious lechery. During the colloquy, the girl simpered and looked coy and threw flirtatious looks at all the other men nearby. Florian translated the patter for Edge:

"He twits her about her multitude of beaux and lovers and suitors, and inquires how she handles so many. She says, 'Ah, sir, they pass away like the waters.' He leers lasciviously and asks, 'Pray, Fräulein, do they pass by *the same route?*'"

The crowd laughed heartily as the bawdry went on, and tossed coppers into a hat being passed by the other man. He had put an idiotically vacant look on his face and was awkwardly jostling through the onlookers, occasionally stumbling deliberately off the pavement into the street and nearly getting run over by passing vehicles.

"These joeys are almost certainly from Vienna," said Florian. "When we get there, Zachary, you will see what a mixture of nationalities that city is. So this kind of clown trio is something of a fixture there. The evil old man is the Hanswurst—Jack Sausage—a traditional joker in Viennese folklore. The Emeraldina, the comedy wench, appeals to the Italian population. The other is clearly the dumb yokel Kesperle, a standard comic figure among the Czechs."

The crowd had begun to straggle away, so Florian approached the clowns and, for Edge's benefit, first addressed them in English. The girl—who, at closer sight, was somewhat pudgy, but very pretty—turned out to be the only competent English-speaker of the three.

"From Wien we are, yes, ja, sì. We came only to work this Passau fair, then to Wien we are returning. We work anywhere we can draw a crowd. I am Nella Cornella. The troublemaker Hanswurst is Bernhard Notkin. The village-idiot Kesperle is Ferdi Spenz."

"I am pleased to meet all of you. I am the proprietor and this is the equestrian director of Florian's Florilegium."

"What, the grand circus showing here?" she exclaimed.

"Yes. We are also on our way to Wien, and I am seeking to augment my corps of clowns."

"You think to engage *us*?" she asked, in an unbelieving squeak.

"Perhaps. Your ensemble work is passable, and a female joey I have never had. Do you people possess transport?"

"We travel in caravan together. But not *together*, you understand. I am not the süsse Mädel—not the amante—of either old man."

"That does not concern me in the least. However, one thing I would like. Can either of these gentlemen do the Lupino mirror?"

The question did not have to be repeated in any other language. The man named Ferdi Spenz caught at least the one word and exclaimed, "Rozumím! Lupino zrcadlo! Ano! Vim! Dobrý jsem!"

"He says yes," the girl translated.

"Thank goodness that mirror act is done without words," said Edge, as he and Florian walked back toward the tober. They were trailed by the clowns' extremely dilapidated caravan, drawn by an extremely emaciated horse. "If we add many more nationalities and lingos, we're also going to have to hire a corps of interpreters. Hell, I'll have to start carrying a little notebook like yours, just so I can remember all our people's *names*."

The three new hirelings looked as dazed as Agnete the Eel had been when, immediately on arrival at the tober, they began getting "improved." Their ruin of a caravan was turned over to the Slovaks, to be put in good repair and painted. Their ruin of a horse was turned over to Hannibal and Quincy, to be fattened up and revitalized insofar as possible. The clowns themselves were first turned over to Magpie Maggie Hag, to be measured for new costumes, and then to Jörg Pfeifer. He immediately started Lupino-mirror practice with the Kesperle, and meanwhile began rehearsing the Hanswurst to replace little Major Minim in the pugilist act with Ali Baba—and, between times, began introducing refinements into the Emeraldina's casse-cou performance.

"It is all very well, Nella, to be a breakneck joey, but any *man* can do that. I wish you to show off your undeniably saftig femininity at the same time. Now, try it like so..."

He worked the newcomers with drill-sergeant rigor and discipline, and worked them late into the night after every evening's show, so passersby would often hear shouting from inside the chapiteau:

"Yes, Nella, do as I just showed you! And no, Nella, do not attempt to improve on my improvements!"

"Madonna puttana! All these yesses and noses!"

When the Florilegium again crossed the border into Austria, continuing on down the Danube, it was apparent that that nation had recovered from its postwar gloom and depression. The Austrians were once more hard at work, looked prosperous and cheerful, and seemed eager for entertainment. When the circus set up in the substantial city of Linz, the very first show drew a sfondone house. By that time, too, the new acts were ready for presentation.

Besides Ferdi Spenz's doing with Fünfünf the Lupino mirror act, and doing it almost as well as the late Zanni had, the three new joeys also did together a King-of-the-Mountain knockabout routine—fighting for possession of a pedestal Carl Beck had built for them. First the Emeraldina would stand atop it, then she would be flung off by the Kesperle, who would be frightened off by the Hanswurst flailing a long sausage, who would in turn be chased off by the Emeraldina wielding a brick. The comic struggle and its weapons escalated: to a stick, to a club, to a ridiculously giant slingshot, to one of Edge's spare pistols, to one of his spare carbines. Finally, when the contest was an anarchic mêlée—and the audience convulsing in hilarity—the contested pedestal itself suddenly became the victor, by sprouting a giant and thorny cactus. This was another Beck contrivance, of canvas and india rubber and spikes, inflated by a hidden roustabout working the *Saratoga*'s force pump. When the formidable cactus became King of its own mountain, the Hanswurst, the Kesperle and the Emeraldina all shrugged, threw away their weapons and went off amicably arm in arm.

Miss Eel, in the eel-slinky and even eel-*wet*-looking tights that Magpie Maggie Hag had fashioned for her, became the newest exhibit in Fitzfarris's sideshow. The accordionist played during her serpentine performance on the platform, and Fitz talked all during it—with Florian interpreting in German—"Yessir, ladies and gentlemen, Miss Eel is a good girl, for the shape she's in, and just *look* at the shape she's in! Why, do you know, folks, on salary day she sometimes collects her salary two or three times? Keeps coming to the pay wagon in a different shape..."

Many of the other artistes had joined the jossers to watch Agnete Knudsdatter's début, and afterward Mullenax remarked, "Say, Fitz, ain't your part of the show getting a little heavy on the reptiles? You got a snake woman in the annex and an eel woman on the platform, not to mention that maggot, the midget. What next?"

"Well, Abner," Fitzfarris said, mock-seriously, "you haven't done the Crocodile Man for a long time." And Mullenax fled in a hurry.

Another onlooker, Obie Yount, kept coming back to watch Miss Eel's every performance. After a week or so, he got up the courage to go to where she was toweling herself and catching her breath, and to say diffidently, "Miss Eel... oh, hell, I can't call a woman that. Miss Kanoods—oh, damn, I'll never get *that* right, neither."

"Can you manage 'Agnete'? What do you wish to say, Herr Quakemaker?"

"Call me Obie. I wanted to say that your act is purely perfect."

"Thank you, Obie."

"But I think Fitz don't talk it up with the dignity it deserves. I've got an idea, if you'll let me put it to you."

"Havd ønsker De?" She sighed. "Another new position?"

"Well, sort of. I think you ought to be a showpiece in the main ring, not out there with freaks and fire-eaters. So my idea—see, I used to do a pyramid—me supporting a bunch of girls. And, why, you alone, I could hold you over my head with one hand. Could you do your contortions like that, up there?"

She looked surprised and amused, and even pleased. "With some practice, Obie, I imagine so."

"And then, if you want to put the Simms boy into the act, I could hold him up on the *other* hand."

"Are you really so strong? To hold us over your head for so many long minutes?"

Yount did some chest-expanding and muscle-bulging. "Miss Agnete, I'm the *Quakemaker*. I'll go right now and talk to Zack and Florian."

He found them in the red wagon, and they gave him permission to try the act, but they gave it somewhat distractedly, because the office was full of other petitioners. Carl Beck and Jules Rouleau were arguing to Florian that Linz was a city important enough to merit sending up the *Saratoga*, while a delegation of elders from the city of Linz itself waited to speak to him. Florian said, "Very well, Monsieur Roulette, start the preparations and I will get paper printed," and shooed those two out. Meanwhile, Edge was being harangued by doorman Banat:

"Must have tober fencing, Pana Edge, like other Europe circuses. Too much now I see child boy sneak in every afternoon."

"Look, Chief. You know how much those rolls of fencing would cost. I reckon it hurts your professional pride, but how much do we lose in half-ticket sales to the few boys sneaking in?"

"Not boys. Boy."

"All right. One at a time, then. On each one, maybe we lose—"

"Not one boy at a time. Same boy."

Edge gave him a long look. "Alex, you first complained about this somewhere back around Landshut, in another country. Are you claiming that the same boy is still sneaking in and out?"

Banat shrugged.

"Well, it can't be one of our own, doing mischief just to plague you. We've got only two small boys on the show. One is black as midnight and the other is pale as the moon. You'd have recognized them. So are you telling me that for more than a hundred and fifty miles we've been dogged by a kid—the same kid—that keeps sneaking onto and off the tober? You can't catch him, and nobody else has even seen him. If you're not crazy, Alex, the kid has to be a ghost. Now, I've got problems enough with the solid bodies in this company. You either catch that spook or shut up about him."

Banat departed, looking chastened but unconvinced. Edge gave his attention to the delegation of city elders, who were all talking in German. Florian translated for Edge, because the import of their visit was so utterly astonishing.

"I told the gentlemen that we were going to favor their fair city with a balloon ascension, but they would rather that we do not. They would prefer to see us pack up and clear out entirely."

"What?"

"I have never in my professional life been thrown out of a city before. But these men are serious. One of them is the Bürgermeister, the other is a high magistrate and the third is the chief of police. They are not at all jesting."

"But, in God's name, what's the reason?"

"They appear strangely reluctant to be specific, but it has something to do with the local children."

"Is our show supposed to be corrupting them? There's been no complaint from any audience. Or—wait a minute—Banat was bellyaching about boys sidewalling the show. Are we suspected of abducting small boys? Of playing the Pied Piper?"

Florian put the question to the city elders. They replied only curtly, and with some evident embarrassment, but forcefully.

"No," Florian told Edge. "It involves little *girls,* but they decline—on grounds of delicacy—to say exactly *what* it involves. They merely keep repeating that no such thing ever happened in Linz before our circus came to town."

"Well, I'm no lawyer, but this sounds like a pretty thin case to me, Governor. Purely on the basis of coincidence, they're accusing us of some crime they won't even put a name to."

Florian talked to them some more, and again their response was brief, frigid, adamant.

"To judge from their mood," Florian told Edge, "I'd rather not inquire further into the details. Something atrocious has been happening to girl children in this city. Whether or not the coincidence of our being here at the same time makes us culpable, they would prefer that we be gone. I believe discretion dictates that we obey. They could easily make more trouble for us than mere eviction."

"We've been doing damn good business, this while we've been here, but I personally won't be sorry to move on. I'm anxious to get Autumn to Vienna and that specialist doctor there. Do we tear down right this minute?"

Florian again consulted with the men. "They will, albeit grudgingly, let us proceed with tonight's show. Tell the crew to bust the lacings immediately afterward, and we'll hit the road in the morning."

Edge went to convey that message to the company, and an additional one to Aleksandr Banat: "I still don't believe in ghosts, Crew Chief, but there's a sudden rash of coincidences going around. Too damned much of it to suit me. I want that sidewalling kid caught. You tell your roustabouts and I'll tell the artistes and the midway folks. Every last man, when he's not on working duty, is to be on the lookout."

Then Edge heard his name called, and turned. It was Major Minim, and he spoke in his customary voice of snarl, but, for him, almost in a humble manner.

"Colonel, I want to apologize for something." He fingered his little false mustache. "When I got shoved into the pista as a cheap clown, and with a Neger besides, I did not like it, and I know I showed it. So now you have a whole chapiteau full of joeys, and I am back on the midway. But I have to confess, during that time I got a taste for performing in the pista. And now I have an idea for a whole new act, and I would like your permission—"

"I don't particularly give a damn what you do, Reindorf. But if it's a good act, I'll work it into the program."

"I am thinking of a comedy lion tamer turn. Midget tamer, midget lions. You will like it. But I need a prop cage built."

"Then talk to Stitches or Boom-Boom. If they've got the time and the materials, and they're willing, then you've got my permission."

Two other things happened in Linz that night before the circus pulled out in the morning, but they were of concern only to the parties involved. After the come-out of the closing show, the Terrible Turk, for the first time in quite a while, had no local widows applying for his attentions. So he wandered into Fitzfarris's blow-off to watch, for the first time, the Amazon Maiden in the toils of the Dragon Fafnir, and he was impressed by what he saw. He gave her time to go and get out of her scale-spangled fleshings, then went to the Vasilakises' caravan and did his usual bouncing of it. Meli came to the door, groaned and said wearily:

"You want money. You must come other time. Sypros went town for buy olive oil and other things."

"How convenient for me," said Shadid, quite good-humoredly. "But I do not want money. This time I come to ask what do *you* want?"

"What I want? I want you leave us in peace. You trouble enough, but what I fear is soon Spyros kill you. Then there be trouble in plenty."

"Bosh! That bull canary kill me? I have no fear, but I do have a proposal. You want me to leave him alone? I will. I promise that. If you oblige me with a fair exchange."

Meli looked wary and clutched her robe closer around her. "What exchange?"

"So simple. You are the Amazon maiden. I shall be the dragon."

She recoiled. "I am married woman and decent woman. You not just greedy and bully. You are vile."

"No doubt," Shadid said indifferently. "But I believe you will find me superior, in many respects, to either a limp snake or that flabby husband of yours. And in return, your flabby husband gets molested no more. Now, none of your Greek haggling, woman. You invite me inside or I come uninvited."

A few moments later, weeping silently, she got out of the robe and he commented approvingly, "Ah, good. You are as bushy there as any Turkçe woman..."

Like the Turk, the Quakemaker had no ladies from the seats seeking his services that night, nor had he flirted with any. He and Agnete Knudsdatter were at this moment lying together, naked, under the stars of the balmy night, on the cushiony tarpaulin covering the balloon in its wagon. Agnete ran her hand through his dense beard and then down the almost-furry rest of him, and laughed and said:

"A bear and an eel, making love. Is it a violation of natural law, or is it a fable by Andersen?"

"I don't know who Andersen might be, but I wish you'd stop calling yourself an eel. I never liked the damned things. Always fouling my fishing line."

"But observe my eeliness, Obie. Feel. Here. I am almost as flat as a boy. I do not know why you should be attracted to me. You have many more curves and bulges than I do."

"You feel good to me. I ain't never been attracted to cows just because they've got big udders."

"Do you know something?" She laughed again. "When I was a schoolgirl, and all the other girls were beginning to—bulge there—and I was not, I saw a newspaper advertisement. A guaranteed bosom developer, for just twenty öre. So, like a simpleton, I put twenty öre in the post, and guess what I received in return. *A pasteboard cutout of a man's hand*. Never did I feel so foolish." Yount laughed indulgently. "But, of course, now I am glad I never grew much brystet, as most women do, or got fat, as most Danish women do, for I could not have taken up my contortionist career."

"And you wouldn't be here this minute. And you wouldn't be mine. And now you are."

She nestled close against him and murmured, "Jeg elsker dig," and then translated it into English for him.

When Spyros returned from town to the Vasilakis caravan, carrying the supplies he had bought, he found Meli in bed, but sitting up awake, and looking morose.

"What is it?" he asked. "Has that ekithiros been pestering again?"

With an effort, she said, "He was here, yes, but this time we came to an understanding. He will not be demanding money any more, or making us dodge him when we meet, or in any other way making your—making our lives miserable."

"Indeed? And you took this upon yourself?" Spyros sounded more offended than pleased. "How did you do it? A bribe, I assume."

She hesitated, then said, "Yes."

Still sounding hurt and annoyed, he said, "You might have consulted your husband before declaring any such truce. After all, I am the head of this household and the keeper of its finances. This bribe, did it cost me a great deal?"

Meli looked at him for quite a long while before she said, "It cost you not a great deal."

WIEN

I

THE FLORILEGIUM stopped to show for some days in the small town of Amstetten, then left the meandering Danube to head directly east toward Vienna, and stopped again to show in the town of St. Pölten. As early as the Amstetten stand, Miss Eel had moved from Fitzfarris's sideshow inside the chapiteau, to do her entire performance uplifted by the sturdy arm of the Quakemaker. Even for a practiced strongman, it was clearly a strain to hold the slender Agnete aloft for the exactly seven minutes it took her to do her amazing convolutions. Though Yount perspired copiously and sometimes trembled slightly, he maintained a stable support for her, and he obviously enjoyed doing it. Those jossers who occasionally took their fascinated gaze off the pretty and infinitely lissome woman could see the Quakemaker's proud smile and the loving glances he gave her from time to time.

Because of that, the circus again had some trouble with the citizenry. After the second night's show in St. Pölten, when the audience was dispersing from the chapiteau onto the torch-lit midway—many of the males heading for the Amazon-and-Fafnir tent—a sudden hubbub broke out in the crowd. There were shouts and curses, and several women shrieked, and the people milled away from the disturbance, leaving an empty space in which two men were wrestling, and not playfully. Clover Lee happened to be close enough to see them, and she immediately began yelling at the top of her voice, loud enough to be heard over the commotion, "Hey, rube! Hey, rube!"

Edge came running to her. "What the hell goes on, girl?"

"It's a clem! Look! Some fellow is mixing it up with Obie. I don't know what you yell in Europe, but when there's trouble back home you yell 'Hey, rube!' to fetch help."

"Then keep on yelling it," said Edge, and began to force his way through the crowd, for he had seen that Yount was now fighting several men at once.

"Hey, rube! Hey, rube!" Clover Lee continued to shout, and someone somewhere shrilly blew a whistle, and Florian and Banat and numerous roustabouts poured out of the chapiteau, each with a tent stake.

But, before they or Edge could join in the fracas, it was being brought to a quick conclusion. The Terrible Turk had already got there, and, though he and the Quakemaker were embroiled with about a dozen burly locals, the locals were losing badly. In fact, those not being actually flung through the air were limping and crawling desperately from the scene, their clothes torn and some of them bloodied. In another couple of minutes, the fight was over, the losers had fled, and the rest of the crowd quieted down and drifted away. Yount had suffered only a black eye and some damage to his leopard-spotted léotard. He was gratefully shaking hands with Shadid, neither of them even out of breath, when Edge got there to ask:

"What started this ruckus, Obie?"

"Just the one gallinipper at first. I thought he must be crazy to tangle with a circus strongman, but then it turned out he had a whole bunch of toughs to back him up."

"Good thing it was short and sweet," said Florian, joining them. "Before somebody called for the police."

"Hell, me and Terrible could of handled them *and* the police. Between us, we could take on the devil, and give him an underhold."

Edge persisted, "You mean some bully actually came up to you just to pick a fight?"

"Well, no. *I* started the fight. He came up and insulted me."

"Insulted you how?"

"Never mind. Let me get these duds off so Mag can patch 'em. Then I think I'll go downtown and have a drink."

When Yount went into St. Pölten to seek a Biergarten, Fitzfarris went with him. After they had ingested several seidls apiece, Fitz felt emboldened to say, "About that clem and the rube who insulted you—well, it's none of my business. But I've known you for a long time, and I know it takes a jesusly lot to perturb your temper. It wasn't you he insulted, was it?"

"No," Yount admitted, and belched. "Son of a bitch comes up to me—spoke English, he did. Gives me this oily grin and says something like, 'You and that twister lady are partners, right? In the tent and in bed, too, right? So what's it like—bedding a female as bendable as that?'" Yount belched again. "So I did my best to show him what bendable *is*."

"Don't blame you." After a period of companionable silence, Fitz said, "Still none of my business, and I'm not eager to get bent. But, Obie, what *is* it like?"

Yount chuckled, shook his head in marvelment and said, "Man, it's *something*."

There was another silence, and the two drank beer and, since it appeared that Yount was not going to elaborate, Fitzfarris said, "You and me, Obie, we've both got—sort of exceptional ladies."

"Well, that Simms kid of yours, young as she is, she's got more in her upstairs structure than Agnete does. Not that I'd want Agnete any different, mind, but a fellow can't help noticing."

"I wish I could tell you what Monday's got in her *basement*. After she's worn me down to a nub, even that's not enough for her. If she watches the lion act, or the elephants clumping around, or anything else exciting, she goes into that spasm of enjoying herself all by herself. I swear, I'm getting fatigued."

"Reckon it is rough on us men," said Yount, with a boozy smile. "But, hell, what else is there *besides* women?"

"It's a pity," said Autumn. She was at the caravan stove, frying sausages for dinner. "Obie and Agnete seem so genuinely fond of each other."

"They're even buying a caravan to move into together," said Edge. "But what's the pity about it?"

"That they won't grow old together."

"Why in the world do you say that?"

"The india rubber artistes never have a very long life span. They know it, too. It's one of les risques du métier. All that bending and twisting puts such a pressure on the rib cage that their lungs have no chance to develop; they never get bigger than the lungs of a child, so they're easy prey to the consumption. Maybe you haven't seen how Agnete pants and wheezes and coughs after every performance. She hurries off to some private place, so Obie won't notice, and of course she won't tell him, but she's already got the consumption. And don't you say anything either, Zachary."

"I won't." He added, gloomily, "But I will say that I'm getting almighty weary of hearing about people dying young. In wartime is one thing, but—"

"Now you hush," she said. "I was told that I'd be one of those people, but it's been months now, and I'm not dead yet. Probably Agnete is like me—enjoying every day simply because it *is* an extra day. And me, I feel just fine. I only wish I looked as good as I feel."

"Well, let's pin our hopes on that doctor in Vienna. And Vienna is our next stop."

"Then you'd better start pronouncing it the way they do there. Wien. These are Wiener sausages we're going to have for dinner."

"Wien. All right." Edge idly lifted the lid of Autumn's music box. It emitted a few notes of "Greensleeves," in a dolorous, run-down jingle and tinkle. "You don't play this very often any more."

"I'm sorry. I do neglect your sweet gift. Here, let me wind it up again. It's just—sort of a painful reminder—that I'm not out there prancing and strutting in the spec when that music plays."

"Would you like to get out for a little while, at least? Dump the sausages. We can join the others at the hotel for dinner."

"Let's not, dear. It's such a chore for me to eat in public, with the veil on. Besides, haven't you heard enough of hotel music? All through Austria, in every dining room, those poor, pathetic, imitation Strausses, with accordions and harmonicas and zithers, playing their poor, pathetic renditions of Strauss."

"True," said Edge. "If there are two things Austria doesn't lack, it's music and clocks. And musical clocks. Even wind harps that play themselves on the house porches. But downtown, a while ago, I came across something I thought unusual, and...well, I bought it for you. Today is Saint Anne's Day, they tell me, and here in Austria, they tell me, it's the same as Saint Valentine's Day else-where—when a man gets his sweetheart a gift. If you don't mind another gift."

"Oh, Zachary. Mind?"

"I have to confess that it's musical, too, in a curious kind of way. I can always take it back."

"Oh, Zachary."

So he reached outside the caravan door and brought it in. It was a bird cage made of brass wires, with a live canary teetering on a little trapeze inside. It looked like nothing more extraordinary than a canary in a cage, but Edge said, "Wait until he finishes flustering and settles down."

The tiny yellow bird, cocking its head and turning about on its perch, took some while to inspect the two hovering humans and the other visible surround-ings. Then, evidently approving of its new home, it serenely preened down a ruffled feather or two, took a sip of water from its little dish, and hopped onto the brass strap that encircled and held together the cage. There it began to hone its beak on one and another of the cage's vertical brass wires, making them twang and vibrate.

"Why, the wires are *tuned!*" Autumn exclaimed in wonder.

"And he'll hop and peck on them all around. He can't play music, of course, but it's nice and harmonious. I thought it was nice."

"Oh, Zachary, it's like something out of the Arabian Nights!" She gave him a loving hug.

"Anyhow, it's not hotel-imitation Strauss."

"Ah, my dear"—she hugged him more tightly—"when we get to Wien, we shall hear the *real* Strauss. One brother after another, conducting hundred-piece orchestras in palatial ballrooms. And there never has been, nor ever will be, any dance devised that is as lovely to hear and watch as the waltz. Perhaps, if the doctor allows, you and I could even go and *dance* it."

"Whoa, woman. I never learned how to dance. I could teach old Thunder his fancy stepping, yes, but I can't do so much as a squaw wrestle."

"But the waltz is so easy." She took the sausages off the fire, came to hold his hand and his waist and began to hum "Light of Heart." Edge, staring down at their feet, tried to match her movements. Autumn said, "Like you're standing in a square box. Step—draw—forward. Step—draw—back. Then we both turn a bit and do it again." She continued humming while they practiced, and the canary plinked and plunked its wires, as if trying to harmonize. "And even more graceful is the Linkswalz—the valse renversée. You simply do that same step, only leading with the right foot instead of the left. It makes for a more gliding movement and less pumping of the arms."

So Edge wore a face of concentrated studiousness, while he lumbered awk-wardly about the confines of the caravan, and Autumn wore that lopsided and repellent face, incapable of expression, while her young and shapely body swayed and twirled as liltingly as a flower in a breeze, to her humming of "Light of Heart."

Then there came a knock at the van door, and they parted abruptly, and Autumn went back to the stove, where she was concealed in shadow. It was Banat on the doorstep, holding a small person by the scruff of the neck. The usually dour doorkeeper was looking almost amused as he announced, "Finally catch our sidewall sneak, Pana Edge. And behold! All time, it was joke."

Edge actually had to look twice at the small person—wearing a boy's school-uniform cap, lederhosen and stockings, carrying some books secured by a strap—to perceive that it was Little Major Minim. He was without his false mustache, and had combed his scanty hair down into boyish bangs across his forehead, and had powdered his face to almost babyish smoothness.

"A joke, ja," the midget said, grinning foolishly. "Wanted to see how long I could run on and off the tober before this dumb Slovak went out of his so-called mind."

Edge, also amused by the little man's grotesquerie, almost said something like "go and sin no more." But then he remembered what he himself had called a rash of coincidences. He said, "Let's you and me go to the red wagon and discuss this *joke* in private. Banat, you find Florian and fetch him there."

In the office, Edge plunked Major Minim into one chair and sat in another, facing him, saying nothing, only eyeing him levelly. The midget fidgeted for some minutes, until he could no longer stand the silent scrutiny, and finally blurted, "Let me put it to you like this, Edge—"

"Herr Direktor to you, Reindorf."

"Ja wohl, Herr Direktor. Every other man on this show has got a woman, even if it's only one of the midway trulls or some trifler from the seats. You've got a steady woman, the Quakemaker has the Eel, the Tattooed Man has got that Neger. Even the plump new girl, Nella—did you know?—she is flirting with that skinny LeVie. She would make two of him. Scheisse! But look at me. What chance do I have? Ach, ja, sometimes a woman has solicited my attentions just out of perverse curiosity. But then, when I undress, and she sees my pale little worm of a hujek, she shrieks with laughter, and that's an end of the episode. True, I have rented a whore now and then, and paid her enough that she does not laugh. But a fully-grown woman, why, I just wobble around inside her. And what did I ever get out of it? From some one of those whores, I got a dose of the Tripper. So I had to invent my own way to get my—to get some satisfaction. Am I to be despised for that?"

Edge said nothing.

"I thought maybe," the midget went on desperately, "if I tell you the whole truth—throw myself on your mercy—promise to mend my ways—you might square it with the Herr Gouverneur...?"

Edge said nothing.

"I am begging you, Herr Direktor. He would throw me off the stand, make my name a stink with *every* Zirkus, maybe even hand me over to the Polizei. And—and I told you—I am working up a splendid new pista act. You would not wish to lose that..."

Florian entered the office just then, glanced at the stony-faced Edge, stared at the ludicrous other figure and said, "What in the name of all that's holy is going on here?"

"Nothing very holy," said Edge. The midget gave him another frantically imploring look, but Edge went on, "Take a look at those books he's carrying, Governor."

Minim numbly let Florian take the strap bundle from him and undo it. In some stupefaction, Florian said, "A spelling primer, a hornbook, a school slate. And—and a damp soapy rag? Zachary, will you tell me what this is all about?"

"It's about our getting thrown out of Linz."

"What?"

"It's a wonder we haven't got the shove from other places. Or been tarred and feathered, maybe even lynched. Go on with your life story, Reindorf." The little man looked sullen, miserable and disinclined to say more. "*Go on*, or I'll take you over to the lungia and lynch you myself."

Minim slumped in total despair and commenced a full confession. "I already told the Herr Direktor: once I acquired a venereal infection. Then I read somewhere that a man could easily cure himself by—by making sex with a virgin small girl child. So I found a beggar brat—this was in Krakow—who would have done anything for two coppers, and with me she did that. By the way, I can tell you in confidence, mein Herren, the cure is a myth. Do not try it. I still suffer from the Tripper. But the attempt did do me *some* good. It made me realize how delectable are the little girls. The silky skin...why, grown women are like leather by comparison. The bare and tight-shut little coin purse..."

"Spare us the slavering," said Florian. "Get on with it."

Minim bowed his head and lowered his voice to a mumble that they had to strain to hear. "After the walkaround of the afternoon show, I make haste. I have just time to go and get—dressed like this—and get into town at the hour the schools are dismissing their classes. I mingle. I look just like one of the Schülers. I choose a pretty little girl, ask if I can carry her books for her—"

"But you *don't* look like a schoolboy," said Florian, with revulsion. "Not when you're seen close. You look like a ventriloquist's painted prop manikin."

"Ach, ja, sometimes a little girl might say, 'Hotte'hü, you have bushy eyebrows for a boy your age.' But usually they come along with no suspicion. And then...well...I walk her into some alley or some park bushes and..." He shrugged his little shoulders.

Florian said, still unbelievingly, "But surely, a child that age, she must object ...struggle..."

"*She* does not know what is happening—not a child that young—not until it is well along. And afterward she is always crying and trembling, so it takes her a while to put her clothes on again. It gives me time to get clean away, and back here to the tober."

Florian and Edge sat and regarded him with a look colder than loathing, so Minim raised his voice, as if to propound the most reasonable of arguments. "Herr Gouverneur, Herr Direktor, for a miniature hujek like mine, a girl of five or six years, she is of exactly the proper and enjoyable tightness, and my hujek is for her the right size. Perhaps sometimes even *she* enjoys it. Anyway, I think the little girls seldom complain when they finally get home. They do not know what to complain *about*, except that they got undressed by a schoolmate, and poked in their peeing place."

Florian muttered, "My experience of life has been long and checkered. But this is unprecedented. Reindorf, how long have you been—how *many* have there been?"

"Since Poland?" the midget said indifferently. "I long ago lost count. Whenever one was required."

"So you have violated innumerable female infants, and probably infected most of them with gonorrhea, or worse. And I was fool enough to pair you with little Sava Smodlaka in your dancing turn."

"Ach, nein, Herr Gouverneur!" Minim exclaimed, with such genuine terror in his voice that he had to be speaking the truth. "I would not dare. She is pretty, ja, desirable, even unique. But her father Pavlo is a madman. To little Sava, I have been nothing but the perfect gentleman and partner."

"Perfect gentleman," Florian repeated.

"I shall so continue to be, if you will please not dismiss me. I tell you this sincerely. On and off the tober, I shall behave myself. No more little girls, no more trouble. Only give me this chance, Herr Gouverneur, I beseech you. Also, as I have told the Herr Direktor, I am preparing a whole new pista act. You will find it irresistible. I dress as a midget lion tamer, you see. Drive in, with the dwarf horse drawing a midget cage wagon, full of wild midget animals. Only alley cats, you see, but I get into it and crack a whip and posture like a midget Barnacle Bill. The audience will wet themselves with laughing. By Wien, I shall be ready. Keep me on the show only until Wein, and then, if I have not redeemed myself"—he made a doleful face—"discharge me, blacken my name, send me to prison, do what you will. I ask only until Wien."

Florian said, "One thing still baffles me, Reindorf. The schoolbooks were part of your vile disguise. But the soapy wet rag?"

Minim smiled tolerantly. "Ach, I am an artiste off the tober as well as on. And art means attention to details. Always, afterward, there is some small blood. So always I wash myself. And her, so she does not go home staining her little—"

"Florian," said Edge. "In my whole life, I have been acquainted with only two midgets. But if every damned one of them is like Russum or Reindorf, I'd say our show can do without any. I suggest we bury this son of a bitch under the pista *alive.*"

"Ostrożnie!" Minim snarled at him. "Remember, the Fräulein Eel has left the sideshow. Take me and my dancing act away, and how much of a sideshow does Sir John have? Also, consider *all* the aptitudes of midgets, Herr Edge. I can pry into other places than school yards. I have peeked in a caravan window and seen your Fräulein Autumn unveiled and in full light. Will you display that monstrosity in the sideshow instead of—?"

Edge came across the room like a projectile, but Florian, with almost equal speed, interposed his body between them.

"Zachary, Zachary, there has been killing enough!" He turned to the midget. "Reindorf, get out of my sight and stay out of my sight. Stay out of trouble, too. As you request, I give you until Vienna. Now get out of here!"

Minim did, and Edge stood and glowered at Florian. "We haven't had many disagreements, Governor, ever since we've been traveling together. But now we're butting horns. That runt swine could ruin this whole establishment, and you must be totally insane to let—"

"Zachary, Zachary," Florian said again. "We have only to wait a little, and let him do away with himself, in such a way as to bring no onus on our show, no blot on its reputation."

"How, goddamn it? Wait for him to die of the clap?"

"No. A minute ago, I would readily have killed him myself. But then he mentioned the act he is preparing. You have studied history, Zachary. Go and ponder on what you may remember of Europe's medieval history, especially the most popular entertainments of those times. In the meanwhile, calm yourself, do nothing but your job, give loving attention to your dear lady, and trust that Major Maggot will get what he deserves." Florian added, as a practical afterthought,

"Also, we have some dozens of his cartes-de-visite that I bought in Munich, still to be peddled."

2

O N A H I L L T O P at a wide place in the road, the circus train found advance man Willi Lothar and his companion Jules Rouleau waiting in their calash. Rouleau waved a hand expansively around and said, "I know some of you have seen this before, but I never had. Voilà. Here, mes amis, you are on the heights of the Wienerwald. The world-famous Vienna Woods."

"I was just remarking to Autumn," said Edge, "it looks to me more like rolling farmland and vineyards."

"But there are parts of it," said Jörg Pfeifer, "that are more blackly wooded even than Baden's Black Forest."

Edge said, "And I assume that's Vienna—Wien—sprawled out down ahead yonder. Damned big city. Do we make parade, Florian?"

"No, not this time. Too much trouble, what with the emperor's grandiose rebuilding of his capital."

Willi explained, "The work has been going on for ten years now, but the city is still a frightful mess. Streets torn up, excavations everywhere, new buildings half finished, piles of masonry and cobbles and tramway rails, rude laborers, all manner of litter and clutter. But that is all within the Innere Stadt, inside the new Ringstrasse. So our train can detour around through the outer streets. We will cross the river branch to set up in the Prater."

Even in the merely residential and mercantile, not monumental, parts of the city that the circus train plodded through, there was much for the newcomers to see and marvel at—splendid palaces and mansions, triumphal arches, statuary, plazas, fountains. Edge's own first impression of Wien he could have put in one word: "squirminess"—because every bit of stone and gesso and terracotta ornamentation was so tortuously convoluted and filigreed, every building's columns and caryatids and friezes so festooned with carved acanthus leaves and grape clusters and cartouches, every nude statue of a muscular god or voluptuous goddess so very nearly klischnigg in its petrified contortion—and the nudes' nudity not minified but somehow emphasized by a scrap of carved cloth fortuitously "windblown" over nipples or crotch.

The Prater, when the circus crossed the Rotunden Bridge to it, was the most pleasant place the Florilegium had ever yet been assigned for a tober. It was an island parkland of some eight square miles, with the Danube River on the far side and a narrow oxbow branch of the river on the inner. Part of its vastness was still primal wildwood and wild-flowered meadows; other parts were more tailored, with trim flower beds, hedge mazes, strollers' paths and bridle paths and gas lamps. There were numerous edifices here and there, expansive distances apart—a trotting-race track, a huge sports stadium, a gymnastics arena, band shells and benches for open-air concerts, immense and ornate pavilions for indoor musicales and dancing. There was every kind of eating place, from small taverns and coffeehouses tucked among shrubbery to commodious garden restaurants under flower-draped arbors.

The portion of the park near which the Florilegium pitched was the Wurstel-prater, the all-summer pleasure resort that was almost a small village in itself, of shops, booths and stalls—well-built ones, not gypsily impermanent—advertising entresort attractions, exhibits, games of chance, every kind of slum for sale. There was a children's playground, a pony-riding ring, a gaily painted carousel, one of the "swinging-boat" vertical wheels, a target-shooting alley...

"And after dark," said Willi, "you will see the red lamps of those establishments which are whorehouses. Even during the day, you will see the brothels' Strizzis—their pimps—on the prowl. Not to solicit customers, but hoping to find and entice, among the maidens strolling in the Wurstelprater, new talent for their houses."

"This sure is as up-to-date as any resort I've ever seen," said Fitzfarris. "Every modern convenience."

"Yes, indeed," said Florian. "Still, some of the old-time fixtures remain. There goes a Buttenfrau, for example."

It was an aged woman, bent and shuffling along in a sort of crouch, almost totally enveloped in a canvas cloak that bulged behind her as if she bore the world's most extreme affliction of hunchback. Even though she was some distance away, she was noticeably smelly.

"What the hell is a Buttenfrau?"

"On her back she carries a Butte, a wooden tub. Should you feel a sudden need to relieve yourself—and not be near any of the park's public donnickers, or even a handy patch of shrubbery—you yell for a Buttenfrau. Give her two copper kreuzers, she sets down the tub, you sit on it, she covers you with the canvas from the view of passersby, and you do your business."

"All right, then," Fitz said, smiling. "The Prater has every modern convenience, and at least one old one that other resorts might do well to imitate."

The first thing Edge did, next day, was to hail a Fiaker—there were always many of those hire cabs cruising in the park—and help Autumn into it, and hand to the cabman the paper bearing the address of the Herr Doktor von Monakow. They were taken back across the bridge, and then for quite a long ride, because the Fiaker also circled around the construction clutter of the central city.

"You wait here," Edge told Autumn, when they arrived at the house. "I'll ask if he'll see us right away. He's supposed to speak English."

At a desk in the entry hall was a stern and starchy woman who also spoke English. "Three weeks from Tuesday, Herr Edge."

"Er, ma'am—I mean gnädige Frau—we've come a lot of miles and months to consult this particular doctor."

"Then it can scarcely be an emergency call."

"As far as I'm concerned, lady, it's been an emergency the whole time."

"Young Herr," she said, still crisply but not unsympathetically, "there are many others, as worried as you are, anxious for appointments. There is a long list. Meanwhile, the Herr Doktor has patients to attend and operations to perform in the Krankenhaus. Three weeks from Tuesday, Herr Edge, at ten o'clock."

Edge resignedly went and reported that to Autumn, who seemed unperturbed. She said, "Then let us have the Fiaker take us back only as far as the

Ringstrasse, and walk for a while. On foot, we will have no trouble making our way through the inner streets. And we've plenty of time before you have to report for duty."

They had only occasionally to sidle around piles of rubble from old structures being torn down, or piles of material for new structures being erected. And plenty of other Viennese—afoot or on horseback, not in wheeled vehicles—were doing the same.

"Everybody comes, almost every day, to admire the improvements," said Autumn. "This used to be the old city's fortification embankment, but Franz Joseph determined to make it a grand boulevard encircling the whole central city, lined with incomparable examples of architecture. Those two tremendous buildings going up over there"—she pointed—"are intended to be the world's most magnificent museums: one of art and the other of natural history. And the people *are* much impressed with all this new splendor. Look yonder. That old country peasant reverently removes his hat before he presumes to cross the Ringstrasse."

"So he did. But a peasant from what country? I've never seen so many different-looking people in any one place we've been."

"Franz Joseph probably rules over more different races and nationalities and religions than Queen Victoria does. Austrians, Hungarians, Czechs, Trentino Italians, Poles, Serbs—I couldn't begin to name them all. And a lot of them congregate here in the capital, if only to market their native wares. That chap there, hawking the fancy silver teakettles—he's wearing a red fez and curly-toed slippers, so I'd guess him to be a Muslim from Bosnia. Those two old gentlemen with the long black robes and big-brimmed black hats, they are Hasidic rabbis. Those other two yonder, with the dark green gowns and the miters, they are Coptic priests."

"It's a cosmopolitan city, all right," said Edge. "Mighty overwhelming for a Virginia hillbilly."

"Ah, and there's the new Opera House," said Autumn approvingly. "The centerpiece of the whole Ring. It wasn't finished, last time I was here, but now at least the outside is."

"Handsome, sure enough," said Edge.

"Franz Joseph wanted it to be, and it is. But poor, dull man, he has absolutely no tact. When he first came to look at the façade, he mumbled something about its seeming too *low* for its surroundings. The architect immediately went off and committed suicide. Ever since then, the emperor hasn't dared to make any controversial comment on *anything*. Whether he attends a ballet or a concert or a monument being unveiled—whatever—he has a stock remark. 'Es war schön. Es hat mich sehr gefreut.' It has been nice; I have enjoyed it."

"What *I'd* enjoy right now is a morning snack," said Edge. "Every single person we've passed on the street is walking along eating a pretzel or an ice or a hunk of wurst. It's made me a little peckish, too." And he steered Autumn into the street-floor coffeehouse of a hotel right behind the Opera House.

"Well, you're a good chooser," Autumn said. "This is the Sacher, probably the most famous hotel in Europe."

They were seated by an urbane waiter, impeccably attired in white tie and tails even at that hour of the forenoon, who asked in several different languages what he might be honored to serve them. Autumn said, "Zwei Mokka, Herr Ober. Und die Konditorwaren, bitte."

So, when he brought their two coffees, he also rolled to their table the sumptuously stocked pastry cart.

"The many-layered dark chocolate thing there," said Autumn, "is the inimitable Sachertorte. You must have that, Zachary. I think I'll have a slice of that walnut strudel."

"Mit Schlagober?" asked the waiter.

"Bitte."

At which, the waiter slathered and smothered her pastry with a mound of whipped cream, artistically swirling and peaking it.

Edge said, "Girl, if you eat all that whipped cream, you won't be able to walk out of here."

"I'll manage," she said, and laughed, for she had got a dab of it smeared onto her concealing veil. "You'll learn to, too. Other cities fly flags bearing their civic escutcheons. If Wien has any such insigne, it must be a flying plume of Schlagober."

Edge looked about at the other tables, where extremely well-dressed men and women were having their midmorning confections. True enough, there seemed to be enough whipped cream in sight to have filled the circus pista. He said, "When we first rode in, I thought the local architecture and ornamentation looked—squirmy, you might say. I was wrong. Obviously, it's all designed to be just as puffy and rich and creamy as the Schlagober."

Autumn laughed again. "For a Virginia hillbilly, you are perceptive. Someone else once remarked that every view in Wien looks like the artwork on a chocolate-box lid."

"This hotel is a pretty place, too. But why is it so famous?"

"Oh, my dear, we are merely in the coffeehouse. There are half a dozen other dining rooms inside, and private cubicles where a young man can wine and dine his süsse Mädel. And upstairs is the vast marble-paneled séparée, where rich men have often entertained the entire corps of the Opera ballet. There is even a branch restaurant—Sacher's in the Prater—out there near our tober. Speaking of which, we've time for me to show you one more thing before we have to return. The center and pivot and pride of all Wien."

She led him along the Kärntnerstrasse, a broad avenue restricted to pedestrians only, and blocked to vehicular traffic by immense stone basins placed at intervals and angles, each basin overflowing with petunias or geraniums. On both sides, the avenue was lined with Wien's most exclusive and expensive shops, flaunting in their polished bay windows every kind of rich apparel, haberdashery, millinery and jewelry. At one point along the way, Autumn gestured to a side street and said, "Down there you'll find Auntie Dorothy."

"What?"

"The Dorotheum. It was started as a civic pawnshop for the benefit of the poor, like the Mounts of Pity in Italy. But it very soon became nothing but a fence shop where thieves and burglars sell their plunder. So, if anything of ours gets stolen while we're here, don't even bother complaining to the police. Just go to Tante Dorothee and buy it back. I've always been struck by the coincidence of the name. In London, the same sort of fence houses are all called Dolly Shops."

The Kärntnerstrasse brought them out into the grand expanse of the Stephansplatz, in the center of which square towered the exceedingly tall, vertical, spiky-steepled and gaudily roof-tiled cathedral of St. Stephan.

"One of these days, Zachary," said Autumn, "we'll go up into the Stephansdom tower—if we don't get blown off by the perpetual wind here. The view is sublime. Stay all day and you can see the sun rise from over the Danube plain and set behind the foothills of the Alps. But we'd better be getting back to the Prater now. There's a Fiaker rank right here beside the cathedral."

They arrived at the tober to find Florian conversing with a young man and woman in spangled bright-red fleshings.

"Compatriots of yours, my dear!" Florian called ebulliently to Autumn. "Cecil and Daphne Wheeler, who—believe it or not—actually do a *wheel act*. Mr. and Mrs. Wheeler, allow me to present Miss Autumn Auburn, expatriate of your own England, who is our principal équilibriste aérienne, though temporarily on leave. And Colonel Zachary Edge, of your American colonies, who is our capable equestrian director, and wears many other hats besides."

"How do you do?" said Daphne, smiling—her smile wavering when Edge smiled back. Daphne was a very pretty young woman, ash blonde, peach-skinned, with a somewhat subdued air about her.

"D'y'do?" said Cecil. He was handsome, sandy-haired, ruddy of complexion and not at all subdued. "Truly, Wheeler is the name—though one might wonder which came first, what?—one's name or one's game. Back in Merrie Olde, Daf and I did a velocipede turn. Then, in Paris, we got our first look at the new skating without ice. So now we do that, as well. Just different wheels, ennit? And one must constantly aspire and improve, mustn't one?"

Florian interrupted to say, "Forgive me, Zachary, Autumn, but I completely neglected to inquire about your consultation in town."

"We didn't have any," said Edge. "But he must be a good doctor. He's got so much business that we can't even get to see him for more than three weeks."

"Ah, well, a heartening commendation, that, though I know you must be impatient."

Edge said, "Right this minute, speaking as your equestrian director from the backward colonies, I wish somebody would please tell me what is a velocipede turn. And skating without ice."

"Spectacular. Sensational," said Florian. "They've just been demonstrating for me. We'll bill them as *The Wheeling Wheelers!* But go ahead, Cecil, you tell the colonel what it is you do."

"Well, old boy, a long time ago there was a machine called the dandy-horse, with two wheels, fore and aft. One straddled a bar between, and scooted it along with one's feet. Then somebody thought to put crank pedals on the front wheel and—"

"Yes," said Edge. "The bone-shaker we call it in the colonies. High wheel up front, small one in the rear."

"Right you are, old boy. The penny-farthing we call it in Merrie Olde. More correctly, the velocipede."

"Since we've been in Europe, I've seen several men riding the things in the parks. It looks damned uncomfortable."

"Dunnit, though. But it's capable of some dashing tricks. I do the pedaling and Daf does postures on my shoulders. Then I close by riding the bloody thing solo, at breakneck speed, stop short and take a header into a vat of flame. Meaning a vat of water with a skim of oil burning on top, don't y' know."

"Bloody hair-raising it is, too," said Florian, as if unconsciously adopting Cecil's mode of speech.

Daphne Wheeler and Autumn had moved off apart, and the new girl hesitantly asked, "On leave you are, Miss Auburn? And seeing a doctor? Excuse the presumption, but are you—would it be a blessed event?"

"Oh, dear, no," said Autumn. "Merely an ailment that has me out of action and all bundled up for a while."

"Ah, one of our notorious female complaints, then. Isn't it bleeding hell, being a female?"

"And you and Mr. Wheeler? Have you a family?"

"No. Ceece isn't much of one for—well, he likes to get about. That's why he applied to Mr. Florian. We've been here in the Prater for two summers now. Doing our wheel acts as fill-ins between the contests in the gymnastics arena. So Ceece is itching to get on a show that will take us moving again."

"Well, while the men are talking, Daphne, come and I'll introduce you around among our female contingent."

Cecil was now explaining to Edge: "When we visited the Hippodrome in Paris, they were putting on this Jolly-Old-Winter spectacle—'Happy Holland' or 'Sweet Sweden' or some such bloody thing—sleighs and cutters and fur costumes and all." Cecil laughed; he had a laugh that was a sort of well-bred snuffle: hnoof-hnoof-hnoof. "But they didn't care to flood and freeze their fine parquet floor, don't y' know. So the whole corps of skater-dancers wore Plimptons instead of blades. Do you know Plimptons, old boy? They're a Yank invention, after all."

"I'm afraid I don't, old boy. I'm not a very good Yank."

"Well, instead of strapping skate blades on one's boots, one straps on these little clogs, each with four tiny boxwood wheels. One simply *rolls* about, as smoothly as on ice. And, with practice, one can cut any caper that can be done on real skates."

"Surely not in the sawdust of a circus pista."

"No, no, old boy. We carry on top of our caravan, in addition to the vat for the flaming-water trick, a collapsible board affair. In the pista it unfolds to a circle. On that, we whirl and glide and figure skate and dance together."

Edge said, and sincerely, "I'm eager to see it."

"Yes," said Florian. "But the Wheelers must give notice to their present employer, so we have plenty of time to decide where to spot them in the program. Now, Cecil, come and meet some others of your soon-to-be colleagues. Right here, for starters, the Quakemaker, Miss Eel and young Ali Baba."

Yount could only nod and grunt, for he was practicing holding aloft both Agnete and Quincy while they contorted. Agnete, lying prone on Yount's right hand, brought her head out of a tangle of her own limbs to smile and say, "Welcome." Quincy, his rump on Yount's left hand, had his legs straight up in the air, but parted them enough to put his head in his own crotch and shyly say, "Hoy."

Cecil said, "Monkey-boy, you must be a source of great satisfaction to yourself. Just be careful not to bite it off"—which left Quincy staring after him, looking puzzled and concerned.

When Cecil was introduced to the Smodlakas, he spoke amiably to Pavlo and

Gavrila, and dutifully patted the terriers that Pavlo proudly brought to show him. But he stared in open admiration at the albino Sava and Velja, whom Gavrila was bathing in a zinc tub.

"By Jove, Florian," Cecil said. "You ought to exhibit them just like that: totally nude. Pure porcelain they are—Sèvres biscuit. Never saw any human bodies so porcelain white all over. The little girl's nipples, even the little boy's knob end..."

"Stvarno ne," muttered Gavrila, giving him a wary look and covering each of the children with a towel.

After meeting Willi and Rouleau, Cecil at least waited until he was out of their hearing before making another crass remark: "Couple of queans, what?"

Florian said coldly, "Let's go back, and you can ask them."

"Oh, I've nothing against queans, old boy," Cecil said hastily. "As artistes, all well and good. But I say, is it the best policy to have a nancy representing you as advance man? I mean, what sort of impression—?"

"Herr Lothar has done an excellent job for us, so far. And Monsieur Roulette is indispensable. Their private lives are *nobody's* business."

"Quite, quite. They're two full-grown men, after all. Or two full-grown some-things, what? Hnoof-hnoof!"

The tober was thronged with people waiting to buy tickets for the opening show and meanwhile crowding to every booth and stall and joint on the midway. The tap wenches were handing out seidls of beer, the lemonade and Eis butchers were handing out paper cones of their products, the wurst braziers were fogging the air blue—and the few Viennese not eating something were busily buying gimcracks from the slum stalls. They were buying exactly the same sort of food and drink and cheap souvenirs that the whole Wurstelprater had been selling all summer long, but evidently the Florilegium's being itself something new must have lent a newness to everything about it.

At the entrance end of the midway, the calliope was steaming and smoking and roaring Strauss's "Delirium Waltz" loudly enough for its own composer to hear, wherever he might be in the city. Over the front door of the chapiteau, the florid banners were flapping and thwacking in the wind. At one side of it, the Gluttonous Greek was erupting plume after plume of fire; on the other, Fitzfarris was touting his mouse game, and hordes were elbowing to wager on it. Edge was making his way toward the marquee when he was intercepted by Florian and Lothar. "For your information, Colonel Ramrod," said Florian, "a week from today, we will close the tober to the public for the nighttime show. Willi has engaged for us a private audience, and sold out the entire pavilion."

"Well, dandy," said Edge. "A command performance for the swells?"

"Er, no," said Willi. "I am working on that, and I expect to arrange it. But no, this private showing will be to celebrate a beggars' wedding."

Dumbfounded, Edge said, "Since I've been on this show, we have reserved the whole works just twice. Once for the King of Italy. Once for a hive of stump preachers back in Virginia. Won't beggars be kind of a comedown even from *that* one?"

"By no means," said Florian. "Viennese beggars stand considerably higher on the social scale than any backwoods gospel-grinders."

"You see, Herr Edge," said Willi. "Wien is such a very wealthy city that even cripples do not *need* to beg, but it is an accepted vocation. In this case, the father of the bride has his recognized post at the Stone Bridge, his wife at the Burgtor —as did their parents and grandparents before them. And their daughter is marrying a very up-and-coming young beggar with a stand of his own near the Albertina. The profession is so profitable that these proud parents wish to lavish thousands of kronen on the wedding. The ceremony at Saint Stephan's, the entertainment here at the Zirkus, afterward a gala reception and dinner in the chapiteau—Sacher's will cater the meal—and to that, incidentally, all of *us* are invited."

"Well, it quizzes me, I'll have to admit," said Edge, "but I can hardly complain. If ever I'm in Virginia again, I'll suggest to the preachers that they contemplate a different calling." He broke off to say, "Hey, Maggot!" and reached out to collar the midget, who was trotting past, dressed in his sideshow full-dress dancing suit. "This is Wien. When do we see this great new act of yours?"

The little man snarled, "Ach, come on, Edge—"

"*Herr Direktor!*"

The snarl changed to a whine. "Have a heart, Herr Direktor. Stitches and Boom-Boom have built the cage, but I've got to collect the cats—catch them one by one."

Florian said drily, "I imagine alley cats are harder to catch than jüngferlich little girls."

Major Minim scowled, but said only, "I want a score of cats, and so far I've got only four, and already my caravan smells like a sewer." He snatched himself out of Edge's grasp and scurried away.

"We'll give him time," said Florian. "I'm as eager to be rid of him as you are, Colonel Ramrod, but I do hate losing a trouper until we have a replacement. I figure we'll be losing him just about the time the Wheelers join out."

"Are you still letting little Sava do the dance turn with him?"

"Yes. I think he spoke truly about being afraid to molest *her*. But I've cautioned Gavrila: never to let Sava near him except during the dance act. Or Velja either. The Night Children have permission to fraternize with anybody else in the world except Major Minim."

After the come-out of that afternoon's show, when the blow-off tent filled with its customary male audience to see the Amazon Maiden's ravishment by the Dragon Fafnir, Fitzfarris was surprised to see that the audience was, for once, *not* all male. Among the men, a pretty girl, in chic bonnet and crinolette, stood holding a sketch pad and busily working on it with a stick of charcoal while she watched intently. When the performance was over and the men went out snickering and exchanging ribaldries, as usual, the girl remained. She approached Fitzfarris at the platform, and got prettier at every step. She was in her early twenties, had black hair, violet eyes and an exquisite figure. Then Fitz noticed that she was accompanied by another female, about her own age, but not at all pretty. She had a hanging bush of kinky hair like Spanish moss, and she looked extremely disgusted at finding herself in such surroundings.

"Bitte, mein Herr," the pretty one said. "You are the Herr Direktor of this spectacle?"

"I am, gnädiges Fräulein. Can I do something for you?"

"I should like your permission to speak to the—to the Amazon Maiden."

"Give her a minute to cram the dragon back in his lair, then I'll call her. May I inquire . . . ?"

She showed him the sketch pad on which, with quick, minimal and expert strokes, she had limned Meli and the python in several of their erotic intertwinings. "My name is Tina Blau. I should like to ask the lady if she would consent to sit to me for a painting."

"Ah, you draw," Fitz said approvingly. "A most ladylike avocation. And paint, too? Watercolors, I daresay."

"You *daresay!*" the other female snapped at him. "What a typically masculine condescension. Why do you not pat her on the head? I would have you know that Tina Blau is no wilting hothouse damsel who occupies empty hours doing dainty watercolors. Tina Blau is a *professional* painter, and of growing renown."

"And you? Who are you?" Fitz asked, not cordially.

"Please," said Tina Blau. "You must excuse my friend. She is Bertha Kinsky, a leading figure in the Peace Society, in the Young Liberals and in the Anti-Suppression of Women Society."

"And is she your manager, Fräulein Blau? Your keeper?"

"No, no. A friend and patroness. Sometimes Bertha's enthusiasms tend to vehemence, but—"

"I can speak for myself!" said the other. "This whole exhibition is a disgraceful debasement of that poor woman on the platform. But, Tina, if you wish to paint her, I simply want this—this exploiter—to know that you are *capable* of painting her." To Fitzfarris she said, "The Fräulein Tina Blau is a far more accomplished artist than a schmud'l candy-box decorator like the so-famous Herr Makart."

"All right, all right, I'll believe it." Fitz added a wry pun: "I paint myself," then took out a handkerchief and swiped it down his face, revealing the blue half. Tina Blau's violet eyes widened, and the redoubtable Kinsky gasped, then shut up. Fitz said, "I'll fetch the Amazon Maiden for you."

Meli Vasilakis came back into the tent, wrapped in a dressing gown and looking not very happy. Given the language difficulties, it took a while for Tina Blau to convey her request that Meli and the python pose for a portrait.

"Ah, you want dirty picture. Me making zefyos with snake. How you like *real* dirty picture? Me making zefyos with *real* snake. Two, three times a week I must do. Come any time, watch, paint." And she abruptly departed.

"I don't quite understand," said Tina.

"Frankly, I don't know what she's talking about, either," Fitz confessed. "But we'll be here in Vienna for quite a while, Fräulein. Come again, come often, gain her confidence, she'll warm up to you. Anybody would. As for me, I've never met a genuine artist before, and I don't think I ever even *heard* of a female one. I'd be most pleased to see some of your work."

She gave him a long and thoughtful look, then handed him a card. "My studio address. Feel free to call, mein Herr." The Fräulein Kinsky almost yanked at her elbow, to lead her from the tent. Fitz's gaze, following her, collided against the stare of Monday Simms, who stood in the front door opening, regarding him with eyes of anthracite.

That afternoon's show had been so well attended—and so was that night's, and so were the several subsequent shows—that Florian convoked a meeting of his executive managers in the office wagon, to announce:

"This, gentlemen, will be our longest stand yet. We shall stay throughout the autumn and winter and perhaps well into the spring. Much of the Wurstelprater —the entresorts and such—closes down for the winter, and so do the sports stadia and the open-air restaurants in the rest of the Prater. But plenty of people still come out from the city, even on the snowiest days, to sleigh ride or to skate on the river and the ponds, and I trust that some will come to see us. Even if we have only a scant attendance during the winter, I believe we shall still prosper better than by going to the expense and trouble of traveling, setting up and tearing down in smaller communities. Also, Wien offers a wealth of diversions for *us*. We might as well enjoy them. It offers, as well, every kind of supplies and equipment we might desire, in the way of improving our establishment and our program. For example, Carl, you can acquire all the chemicals necessary to send up the *Saratoga* as often as you and Monsieur Roulette may wish."

"Dankes," said Beck. "Might I also some more instruments for the band procure? Woodwinds I should like to add, the band's brassiness to temper somewhat. Also strings, for the more gentle acts, like that of the Fräulein Eel."

"Yes, go and buy as you will. I would suggest that you'll find the best bargains at Auntie Dorothy's thief shop."

"There will be need, then, for more crewmen, Governor," said Dai Goesle. "What with band work and balloon work and routine work and special jobs like that cage for the midget, Banat and the other Slovaks are spreading themselves fair thin. And when we are getting those wheel people, mind you, with their vasty props to handle..."

"Quite right, Canvasmaster. Tell Banat to go and recruit. He probably knows the haunts of any Slovaks resident here."

"Speaking of the midget," said Edge, "he now tells me that he'll have enough cats by the time we put on that special show for the beggars' wedding, and he'd like to introduce his parody lion-taming act then."

"No," Florian said firmly. "A wedding should be a happy occasion. We'll save the major's début for some weekday afternoon performance, when the city children will be mostly in school, and the audience will be predominantly adult."

"You want to protect the children from him?" said Edge, a little puzzled. "Hell, he'll be in a cage. But whatever you say, Governor."

At that moment, in the circus's backyard, Major Minim *was* inside the cage, with one of his collection of cats. Abner Mullenax was looking in at them with a mixture of amusement, amazement and skepticism. The cage was a perfect copy of Maximus's wagon, complete to the sunburst wheels, but scaled down to the midget's stature. Right now, Minim was struggling to paint his cat with stripes of black and yellow to simulate a tiger. The cat was understandably flailing and biting and scratching and screaming bloody murder. Minim was cursing almost as loudly, and getting almost as much of the paints all over himself.

"Little man," said Mullenax, "if you think you're goin' to train a bunch of tough old alley cats to do any kind of an act, you're crazy. Me, I'd sooner try trainin' the savagest lion in any jungle."

"Then go do it!" snarled Minim. "I had rather be doing that myself, than having to paint these cursed beasts one by one. Scheisse! I am worse clawed and chewed than I could be in any jungle. But I only want them colorful, not talented. Of this act, *I* am to be the star!"

3

AUTUMN said, a little wistfully, "This is the last place, Zachary, that I will be able to strut and swagger as your knowledgeable tour guide." They were standing atop the wind-buffeted north tower of the Stephansdom. "Prince Metternich once said that east of the Landstrasse begin the Balkans. The Landstrasse is that street you can see down there by the Stadtpark. Some people claim that he said 'There begins *Asia*.' In any case, I've never been east of Wien, so wherever we go next will be as new and foreign to me as to you."

"Well, you've done fine, so far, and taught me a lot," said Edge. "So go ahead. Strut. Swagger. Show me things."

As they circled the tower balcony, she pointed out the distant Belvedere palace, and the Bösendorfer piano factory, and the old monument raised in gratitude for the end of the Great Plague, and the cluster of grand palaces that centered on the Hofburg, the emperor's own palace.

Edge said, "There's one Viennese landmark that even hillbilly horse soldiers have heard of. Can we spot it from here? The Spanish Riding School. I'd sure like to visit there."

"It's one of the buildings among those of the Hofburg. Properly, it's the Royal Winter Riding Academy. People call it Spanish only because its special breed of horses originally came from Spain. See, your tour guide is showing off again. But actually I've never been in there. Very few commoners have. I'm sorry, my dear, but the horses are ridden only by titled officers of the Imperial Army. And even the spectators' gallery is reserved to royals and nobles—or to the emperor's special guests by invitation only."

"Damn," said Edge, looking disappointed. Then he brightened. "Aha, I was forgetting. We have our *own* resident noble."

So, when he and Autumn returned to the tober, he sought out Willi Lothar and put a request to him.

"Well," said Willi, "getting you Eintritt there ought to be easier than what I am presently trying to arrange—that royal command performance. I shall see what I can do."

"Five tickets, if you can," said Edge. "For me, Autumn, Obie Yount, Clover Lee and Monday Simms."

That evening was the special show for the beggars' wedding party, and, contrary to most of the artistes' expectations, it was by no means a ragamuffin audience. The people who came into the chapiteau—merrily but not riotously—were as well dressed as any crowd of bourgeoisie attending an opera. Among the principal figures, the bridegroom did have a peg leg, but the bride was whole and even rather handsome, and so were the parents, and the best man and maid of honor. So were most of the approximately two hundred beggar guests, only a comparative few of them deformed or mutilated in some way. A number of leg-less men wheeled themselves in on little platforms, and some lepers had to be carried by other people; but even those wore fine clothes on what bodies they had, and seemed to be enjoying the occasion as much as did all their colleagues.

"Hell," said Fitzfarris. "I figured there'd be more freaks in here tonight than there are in the whole Wurstelprater, and maybe some I could recruit. Not any of these look like exhibit material to me."

"The bridegroom, I understand, lost his leg in the recent war," said Florian, "and was awarded his begging station at the Albertina Museum by a grateful government, in lieu of a pension. Most of the long-ago original beggars probably got their permanent posts in much the same way, but you are looking at their heirs—children, grandchildren—who are mostly hale and hearty professional beggars. The few real cripples are, like the bridegroom, presumably new in the profession."

Kapellmeister Beck and his now much augmented band gave a lyrical rendi-tion of the "Wedding March"—this time not to signal calamity—while the guests seated themselves, or, if they could not sit, found advantageous places in which to squat or recline. Then the band went into the Schuhplattler overture and Sir John's corps of midway wenches did their energetic thigh-slapping dance—and all the beggars who had hands happily clapped them in time to the beat. At last, Beck thundered into his rollicking version of "Greensleeves" and the Grand Promenade began.

The night's crowd filled hardly a fifth of the chapiteau, but, perhaps because they themselves were also professional performers of a sort, they applauded every act as lustily as a sfondone house could have done—and those spectators who had feet stamped them as loudly. At intermission, to spare the cripples the bother of getting outside to the midway, Florian bade everyone remain seated, and the sideshow was presented in the pista. Then, after the closing Grand Promenade, Florian again bade the audience wait, and Sir John brought Meli and her python to do their tableau vivant inside the chapiteau for the first time. This was also the first time it had ever been performed before an audience fully fifty percent female, but there were no complaints; the women whistled and yelled as bawdily as the men.

Next there arrived on the tober the variously stove-heated or ice-cooled wagons from Sacher's Garden. A multitude of tail-coated waiters brought and assembled immense trestle tables in and around the pista, and covered them with snowy linens, stacks of bone-china dishes and heaps of silver tableware. Then they began spreading the trays and platters of food, buffet style, for the guests to help themselves, but there was so much food that the waiters laid it out by courses, the first being oysters on beds of ice. The circus people of course stayed apart until the beggars had heaped their own plates and the plates of their colleagues who could not reach the tables—but there was plenty left over for everybody in both troupe and crew. While the oysters were being consumed, the waiters brought to the tables great tureens of hot turtle soup.

"Christamighty," said Mullenax, as the courses kept coming—lobster à l'Ar-moricaine, truite au bleu with Venetian sauce—"if the local cadgers eat like this, what do the gentry folks eat?"

"Ach, this is probably a once-in-a-lifetime thing for the mendicants," said

Jörg Pfeifer. "Ordinarily, if they dine out at all, it is at the Schmauswaberl."

"The garbage dump?"

"Well, not quite. It is a back-street restaurant—a warehouse, really—originally established to provide the cheapest possible meals for the local students, and its bill of fare consists entirely of leftovers from the emperor's Hofburg kitchens."

But here and now, the superb viands kept coming: quail stew, chicken à la française, salads, four different wines—Chablis, Lafite-Rothschild, Röderer champagne, Sherry Supérieure—and compôtes, ices, chestnut purée, Sachertorten, other pastries piled with Schlagober, coffee, a variety of cheeses and fruits...

When everyone—literally, every one of the circus people and their audience —had eaten to satiety, one of the sturdier male beggars waddled heavily into the center of the pista. He belched, then raised his arms, gave a downbeat, and the tentful of beggars began to sing. The song was clearly a thank-you to their hosts, and clearly had been chosen to appeal to "Confederate Americans":

> Oh, Susannah! O weine nicht um mich!

Boom-Boom Beck sent his bandsmen scrambling up to the bandstand to seize their instruments and, after a moment, they were briskly accompanying the tumult of voices:

> Denn ich komm von Alabama,
> Bring meine Banjo nur für mich...

"That is the prettiest tribute we have ever had," said Florian, as the beggars came—those who could come, and those who had hands—to shake hands with every available individual of the Florilegium, and to express fulsomely fervent thanks for the entertainment. "Probably," Florian added, "a tribute more genuinely heartfelt than we shall ever get from the high and mighty."

The next day, Willi Lothar presented to Edge five gilt-and-deckle-edged cards, dense with Gothic engraving. "Your Eintritt to the Riding Academy's Exhibition Hall," he said. "I got them from the Graf von Welden, but not so easily as I had thought. After I sent in my card, the damned snob kept me waiting like a peasant petitioner in his reception hall for two hours before condescending to admit me."

"Well, I thank you for going to so much trouble."

Willi laughed archly. "Oh, I took my revenge for the affront. There was in the hall a parrot in a cage. So I occupied my time by teaching it to repeat every filthy word I know in every language I know. Anyway, enjoy yourselves."

So that afternoon Edge, Autumn, ex-Troop Sergeant Yount and équestriennes Clover Lee and Monday sat, among a number of other and presumably noble spectators, in the pillared gallery above the acre of tanbark riding area, while a string orchestra in the loggia played and eight gorgeously uniformed officers put their eight extraordinary stallions through their extraordinary paces.

Immediately on entry, the riders reverently lifted their bicorn hats to the loggia's unoccupied imperial box. "They are not saluting the present emperor," Autumn whispered to the others. "They are paying homage to the Emperor Karl, who founded the academy some hundred and fifty years ago. Now... I have told you exactly *everything* I know about the spectacle. You cavalrymen and horse-women must explain to me from now on. For one thing, I thought all the Lippizaner horses were white. Some of these are silvery or pale gray."

"There's not many horses *born* white, Miss Autumn," Yount whispered. "From what I've heard tell, these-here are born charcoal color, and it takes 'em six or eight years to grow through smoke color to pure white. So the darker ones are the younger ones."

While the orchestra played waltzes, minuets, rosse-ballets, gavottes and karussells, the eight horses walked or trotted or cantered through intricate interweavings, with such ballroom perfection that every horse and rider seemed mirror image of the others. Sometimes the horses would cross legs and dance sideways; sometimes they did an almost pouncing sort of high step. Whatever the dance, whenever any two or four or all eight of the horses met and crossed paths, it was always at some geometrically precise point in the rectangular arena.

"Just *look* how they step," Clover Lee murmured in awe. "If you watch close, it's a kind of soft double action. Each hoof is first placed, *then* stepped on with the stallion's full weight. And they do it at any gait, slow or fast, where an ordinary horse would just go clump-clump. Monday, are you watching?"

"I watchin'," Monday said sullenly. She looked so glum that Edge refrained from asking her what was wrong.

In a high-ceilinged, many-windowed, light and airy studio loft on the Marxergasse, Fitzfarris was saying, "Your paintings *are* truly beautiful, Fräulein Blau. I don't speak as any expert, but I concede that your tom lady-friend was right."

"Tom? She is not a viragint, if that is what you mean. Bertha merely tries to be as gruff and surly and unfeminine as a man, so her ideas and opinions will be taken as seriously as a man's."

"Well, her opinion of your work can't be faulted. I wish I could buy one of these paintings—except they're kind of, uh, huge. And I live in just a small caravan. What do you get for them, anyway?"

"For that one you are looking at—*Nachthimmel*—one hundred gold kronen."

Fitz gulped and stared. "That's more than the *caravan* cost."

"Here," she said kindly, her violet eyes soft as velvet. "This little crayon of a single carnation, life-size. It is small enough that it should fit in your house wagon. And it is not expensive."

"It's a lovely thing, Fräulein Blau, but—"

"Call me Tina."

"Uh, Tina... the drawing... how *not* expensive is it?"

"Whatever you wish to give me." She smiled deliciously. "Anything."

"Anything?"

"Anything."

"Are you paying attention, Monday?" demanded Clover Lee. "What that one stallion is doing now is called the 'airs above the ground.' My mother told me all about—" She stopped herself. "Well, look there. That's the levade. The horse squats back on his haunches, lifts his forelegs and holds the position. He probably could stand like that all day, with the rider on his back. I wish some of our nags were as—"

"*Now* look at him!" exclaimed Yount. "I've never in my life seen a horse do anything like that!"

"The courbette," said Clover Lee. "Starting from the levade, without putting his front feet down, he hops on his hind legs like a kangaroo. Only he's much more beautiful than any kangaroo."

That particular stallion, after graciously nodding to the spectators' genteel applause, was led out of the arena and another brought in. This one, after some warm-up prancing and curvetting, did something even more seemingly impossible for any animal heavier than a goat. At a run, it repeatedly leapt high aloft, and there, with all four feet off the ground, kicked its hind legs violently straight backward. Each time, it appeared to hang magically there in the air, in that graceful pose, like a heraldic horse on an old coin or shield.

"Jesus!" said Yount.

"The capriole," Clover Lee said breathlessly.

Even the glum Monday said, "Oh, my!"

"I can tell you something about that capriole jump," said Edge. "It wasn't thought up just to look pretty. Unless it's only a legend, that trick dates back to the knights of olden times. If a knight was being chased by an enemy, he would command his horse, at full gallop, to give that capriole kick backward at his pursuer."

The program concluded with the arena again full of stallions doing another ensemble ballet to the "Österreichischer Grenadiersmarsch." Then the spectators filed downstairs and outdoors, emerging among the vaulted arches of one of the Hofburg's carriage driveways.

Autumn said, "We've time before you have to get back for the night show. Let us go to Griensteidl's for a coffee."

When they got there and seated themselves in a plush-upholstered banquette, an ancient waiter, without being asked, silently set in front of each of them a glass of water, a thick mug of black coffee, a dish of cube cugar and a spoon. He also laid on the table a sheaf of newspapers, each clamped in a split wooden rod, then he silently shuffled away.

Edge commented, "Not exactly as solicitous as the waiters at Sacher's, is he?"

"Oh, much more so," said Autumn. "We could sit here all the rest of the day and night, until closing time, and the Herr Ober would come at intervals to renew our glasses of water—and the coffee, if we ask, or bring anything else we might care to order—and bring other newspapers, when we'd finished these, but he would never *press* us to buy anything. Of all the traditional fixtures of Wien, the Viennese café is the most gemütlich. And each café has its traditional clientèle. Dunel's is for the rich and famous, Landtmann's is for the intellectuals, this one is mainly patronized by young would-be authors, artists and musicians."

Edge looked around and saw that that was so. At any rate, the café's walls were nearly hidden by unframed paintings and drawings, unmistakably the work of not-yet artists, for even he could see the ineptitude of them. There were posters announcing art exhibitions, poetry readings and such, and there was a corkboard covered with pinned-up handwritten cards and papers. Edge went to look at those. As well as he could make out, most advertised the availability of various students as tutors of music, drawing, dance, essay composition, even penmanship. But some of the notices were merely scrawled communications, done in various languages, including English: "Has anyone a #00 sable brush for sale cheap?" and "Gertrud, when *will* you return my Schiller?" The patrons seated in banquettes or at marble-topped tables were mostly young men and girls, and looked rather seedy, but Edge could not have guessed which of them were would-be whats. Some sat alone, reading the newspapers and magazines that the café provided free, but the majority of them sat in clusters, deep in conversation on topics evidently weighty and earnest. And so many of them were puffing away at pipes or cigarettes that a blue layer of smoke hung midway between the room's ceiling and floor.

When Edge returned to his place, Autumn was saying "...Almost all of Wien's cafés—and this is a rarity among European gathering places—are hospitable even to women without escorts."

"Good," said Clover Lee, who was examining the newspaper on the table. "I'll come with Sunday, and she can translate these 'personal notices' to me. Maybe some duke is advertising for a wife."

"Well, me, I ain't go' sit here 'til no closin' time," said Monday. "I got things to see to."

So they took a Fiaker back to the Prater, where Edge was immediately hailed by Florian.

"Cecil and Daphne Wheeler have finished their stint at the arena, and have just brought their caravan to our backyard. We'll put them in the program at tomorrow's afternoon show. If you concur, Colonel Ramrod, I should like them to have the start of the second half. That will give the roustabouts ample time during intermission to set up the Wheelers' skating board and flaming vat. Then, just for this one show, move Barnacle Bill and his animals to the end of the show, with Little Major Minim coming on right afterward to do his parody of that act."

"You'd snub Monday's 'Cinderella' to give the *maggot* the close? The star spot?"

"This once only. Indulge me."

The next day being a school day, the afternoon show's audience was, as Florian had predicted, composed almost entirely of grown men and women. There were only a few children of school age; the others were toddlers or babes in arms.

The Wheelers' rolling skates were something unique in a circus, and even those spectators who might previously have seen the couple perform in the Prater's gymnastics arena clearly had not tired of admiring and applauding them. One at a time or both together, Cecil and Daphne did every "turn and change" known to real figure skating on ice—and did them in the constricted space of their circular board—spread-eagles, sitting pirouettes, four-cross stars. Then, face to face, joining hands, leaning back from one another, they whirled so rapidly as to become a sequin-sparkling red blur. And then Cecil was holding Daphne by one wrist and one ankle, continuing the whirl while she levitated from the board to fly around him like a red bird at that dazzling speed.

Earlier, Cecil had given the bandmaster the sheet music for that act's accompaniment, and Beck had read its title aloud, with a sort of horror: "'Oh, Emma! Whoa, Emma!'—?"

"Don't be distressed, old boy. The lyrics are indeed atrocious—'Emma, you put me in quite a dilemma'—but we don't sing them, after all. The music is cheerful and loud. It *must* be loud, to drown out the rumble of our wooden wheels on the wooden board. And with your chaps making all the noise, so that we seem to skate in silence, well, it makes our skating look the more aesthetic, don't y' know."

The Wheelers' velocipede turn was done to less vulgar music, more to Beck's taste: the bourrée from Handel's "Royal Fireworks." The velocipede itself was not such a novelty to the spectators as the skates had been. Still, no one—until now—had seen it ridden otherwise than sedately by even the brashest young sports showing off on park drives and bridle paths. What Cecil did with it was considerably different. He did not just ride around and around the chapiteau; he made the high, cumbersome velocipede do tight turns in its own length, and frequently roll backward, and sometimes rear up on its small hind wheel—while Daphne stood on his shoulders and struck artistic poses, then inverted herself to do a handstand away up there, never wavering during Cecil's most violent maneuvers.

When she hopped lightly down to the ground to take her bows, a roustabout put a torch to the oil-filmed vat of water, six feet in diameter, that had been positioned for best audience visibility. Cecil pedaled furiously several times around the tent, faster all the time, until at last he steered for a wooden block he had previously spiked to the ground. The velocipede's tall, iron-rimmed front wheel struck it at full speed, with a crash that hardly needed the bass drum's *boom!* for emphasis, and stopped dead. As if from a catapult, Cecil flew over the steering bar and into the flaming and smoking vat, his splash making the flames surge even higher, and there he disappeared—for he stayed underwater during the brief time it took the fire to subside. Meanwhile, Daphne had caught the velocipede when it toppled, so she was beside the vat when Cecil stood up—and the audience nearly raised the roof.

Edge rather wished that the roof *could* be raised, for the tent was left full of acrid smoke, and people were coughing and rubbing their eyes. So he whistled in the Hanswurst, the Kesperle and the Emeraldina to do their bouncy sky-pole turn as a fill-in until the Slovaks could get the Wheelers' props out and the smoke could clear. When it did disperse, Edge noticed that Florian, near the front door, was standing with a uniformed policeman. Since they appeared to be conversing amiably, Edge assumed that the officer had been posted there by "the authorities" to see that the flaming vat posed no menace to public safety. Edge whistled to bring on the next act—the Smodlakas and their dogs—but the policeman did not depart.

After the last real act had been applauded—Barnacle Bill with his lion, tigers, trumpeting bear and bridge-making elephants—and their wagons were being rolled out by the roustabouts, the band struck up Gottschalk's "Grand Scherzo," and Little Major Minim made his grand entrance. He wore his usual natty full dress and his pasted-on mustache, but had added a patch like Mullenax's over one eye. He sat atop his miniature cage wagon, being pulled by the dwarf horse, and was flailing Rumpelstilzchen with a toy whip from one of the midway slum joints.

The cage seemed veritably full of cats, because they all were clinging frantically to the bars, mouths wide open, probably yowling, but unheard over the music and the gale of laughter that greeted them. Every cat's pelt was matted and spiky with the paints that smudgily striped it black and yellow. Minim made a circuit of the whole chapiteau, then turned into the pista and stopped in the center of it. He hopped down from the wagon, gave several sweeping bows, then went to the door at the rear of his cage, slashing with the whip to beat back the cats clinging to it.

The three casse-cou clowns were standing beside Edge, and they exclaimed in their several languages: "Pozor!" from Spenz; "Oy gevalt!" from Notkin; "Porco dio!" from the female joey, and she seized Edge's sleeve. "He will get inside? Signor Direttore, you must not allow."

"It's his own notion, Nella," said Edge. "And he took a lot of trouble over it. Why should I stop him? Florian said something about this act being popular back in medieval times."

She said, so urgently that her English faltered, "In medium-evil times, sì, most popular entertainment was *public execution*. One way of executing was that the criminal be tied inside sack full of cats, and the cats would fight to get out, and—ohimè, too late! He has gone in."

So he had, and Minim clanged the door shut behind himself. He could dimly be seen, whipping the cats down from the cage bars to the floor, so that he could be better seen. When he had the score of cats all cowering about his feet, he flung up his arms in the V, and the band music stopped on a victorious chord. Then one of the cats sprang high from the pack, raking at Minim's face as it flew past him. With the single slash, it tore off his eye patch and his mustache and left a red scratch across his cheek.

The audience laughed at that, but, over the laughter, a child's voice could be heard shouting clearly, "Papa! Ist der Knabe! Er brachten mir zum Nacktheit!" The crowd's laughter became murmurs of puzzlement. Minim stood uncertainly among the snarling and spitting alley cats, his disguise gone, and his face suddenly so pale that the scratch across it gleamed vividly.

"Che cosa c'e?" said Nella. "Some little girl cries here is the boy who made her naked. Can she mean—?"

"Goddamn," growled Edge. "The son of a bitch has been at it here, too."

The child was still excitedly piping, and a louder voice—presumably her papa's—was also audible, and the whole audience was abuzz. Inside the cage, Minim went into a spasm of fury. As if he were beating off his small accuser, he whipped desperately and viciously at the cats. But not for long. No one cat sprang now, all of them did. Minim stayed upright for a time, but invisible inside a seething, writhing, caterwauling mound of black and yellow, and his own screams were muffled. Then the mound collapsed to the cage floor, but continued to wriggle and scream and yowl. The dwarf horse began piteously to whinny and buck in the wagon traces. The crowd noise became shouts and cries, and many people started shoving to get down from the stands and away from the scene. Then the pandemonium was overridden by the band's booming into the "Wedding March."

The policeman came running into the pista and stuck his truncheon between the bars of the cage to beat ineffectually at the furry, heaving heap. Several roustabouts came running with sticks to do the same. Florian and Edge ran, too, to unhitch Rumpelstilzchen before he could run away with the wagon. One Slovak brought a bucket of water and dashed it into the cage, but even that did not deter the maddened cats. They went on with their clawing and rending, and to their black and yellow coloring was now added blood red.

It was some while, in all that confusion, before one of the men milling about the little wagon thought to unlatch the cage door and fling it open. That was evidently all that the cats had wanted; they poured out in a single surge of black and yellow and red, then became separate streaks darting in all directions. Those spectators who had not already been struggling to get out of the tent did so now, when the bloodied cats exploded among them.

The men at the cage looked in at what was left on the blood-puddled floor: Major Minim's toy whip, his mustache and eye patch, fragments of his clothing —few of the scraps bigger than the eye patch—and a raw, ragged, pulpy, blue-red slab that might have been freshly delivered cat's meat, except that it still wore polished black dancing shoes.

When the chapiteau was empty of jossers, and the band was silent, and most of the circus folk, nauseated, also had departed, Florian and the policeman conversed solemnly in German.

"You realize, Brother," the officer said, taking out a notebook, "that I must make a report of this occurrence."

"Of course, Brother," Florian said calmly. "Render the circle of your duties complete."

"The deceased. Was he of the craft?"

"No. An unhewn stone."

"Has he next of kin?"

"Not to my knowledge. I cannot even say, for certain, who he *was*. See, here is his conduct book. He went by many names—Minim, Wimper, Reindorf, another name in an unreadable language."

"Hm. With so many aliases, it is possible that he was a fugitive from justice. In which case, Brother, there could be many official questions asked. However, the children of the widow must stand firmly together. Also, since you did invite me to the performance, and I did witness the unfortunate episode with my own eyes, I can report—on the level, by the rule—the purely accidental death of a person unknown. That will make unnecessary an inquest."

"Then the tenon is mortised, and the mortise tenoned. I thank you, Brother."

"Unhappily, it will also mean that the deceased must be buried as are the unidentified suicides found floating in the Danube. Without priest or rabbi— whatever his religion—without service or sacrament, without tombstone or even the professional mourner hags, in the city's Cemetery of the Nameless."

"Nameless he was. We cannot repine."

"I will send men from the Bureau of the Coroner. Would you wish to donate a coffin, Brother, or shall he be toppled into the common ditch with the day's others?"

"I herewith donate the cage wagon for his coffin. The coroner's men may simply wheel him away in it."

"Sehr gut. The sign is made, the sign is cut," said the policeman. "With your permission, I go now to make the arrangements."

Florian repeated to Edge in English the relevant parts of that conversation, then called some Slovaks to roll the wagon and its contents to some place in the backyard out of anybody's sight.

Edge said, "Stitches and Boom-Boom aren't going to be too happy. They put a lot of work into that thing."

"They'd be much unhappier if we all got accused of harboring a criminal.

Fortunately, I had the officer occupied when that child cried out. And she and her papa decamped with the rest of the jossers, and now there is no criminal to be accused. Pass the word, please, Zachary, that all who care to—troupers and crewmen alike—may dress and join me for a repast before the night show. A good one, at the Café Heinrichshof. To take the bad taste from our mouths."

"To celebrate, you mean. You can be cold-blooded, can't you?"

"It sounds better in French, my boy. Sang-froid. All I did was to stand coolly aside and let fate do its work."

Not everyone accompanied Florian to the restaurant. Autumn and Edge ate in their caravan, as usual; others had quite lost their appetites; others had already left the tober. In a cheap and dirty Beisl on the Rotenthurmstrasse, Mullenax sat at a table with an obese, pink young woman on his lap. One of his hands was under her skirts, the other was repeatedly tossing schnaps down his gullet, and his one eye was rapidly getting red, while he mumbled things she could not possibly comprehend.

"Jesus, them was only alley cats, and look what they done. My cats are a damn sight bigger alongside me than them was to him. Think what *mine* could do. And folks keep sayin', 'Abner, how-come you gotta get drunk afore every show?' Jesus."

"Ja, ja, Gigerl," the woman said soothingly, and suggested, "Du hast etwas Fotze nötig." She pointed upstairs.

"And now that damned Limey has come on the show with a flame-jumpin' act that puts Maximus's in the shade. I gotta invent somethin' better yet."

The woman wiggled her vast bottom and wheedled, "Bumsen-bumsen?" She lasciviously pursed her thick lips. "Pussl-pussl geblassen?" She tried to tug him up from the table. "Kommst du und *kommst*."

Tina Blau leaned her tousled head on her hand, letting the sheet drop away from her ivory breasts, and asked mischievously, "Do blue men make love only in the afternoons?"

Fitzfarris, lying beside her on the studio bed, asked lazily, "Do lady painters make love only to freaks?"

"Only to blue ones. My name *means* blue. We were destined for each other. But you might sometimes visit after the daylight has gone, so my work is not interrupted."

"I'm sorry, Tina. Between shows is my only free time. After the night show I have . . . duties, responsibilities . . . that I can't get away from."

One of those responsibilities of his was at that moment among Florian's other guests at the tables in the Heinrichshof, and she was the only one silent while all the other circus folk talked about the sensational finale to that afternoon's performance. Monday sat a little apart, looking like a small storm cloud, and drizzled an occasional tear into her plate.

When the artistes and crewmen reassembled on the tober, Banat, who had staunchly stayed there as watchman, took Florian aside to report that "the men of the Leichenbeschauer" had already come and taken away Minim's remains.

"Very good. We have still his horse and caravan—and that probably smells abominably of cat piss by now. Will you and your lads clear all his belongings out of it, Banat, and burn them? Give the van a good cleaning, paint it in our colors, and I shall decide what use to make of it."

4

THE HERR DOKTOR VON MONAKOW received Autumn and Edge with a welcoming and solicitous small smile. He gestured for them to take the two chairs before his desk, and his expression did not change when Autumn raised the veil from her face. He merely asked, "Gnädige Frau, have you had any previous physician make pronouncement on this condition of yours?"

"Yes, two. One seemed uncertain, and referred me to you, Herr Doktor. The other identified it as a fibroid something-or-other, and told me to expect soon to die. But that was months ago."

Von Monakow shook his head. "You will not die, I think, until sometime in ripe old age." Edge perceptibly brightened; Autumn blinked. The doctor went on, "Tell me. Long before this affliction came upon you—in your earliest youth, did you have much Sommersprosse? Um . . . freckles. Did you have upon your skin many freckles?"

"Why . . . I don't . . ." said Autumn, in some bewilderment. "I never really paid much attention . . ."

"Excuse me, Herr Doktor," said Edge. "*I* paid attention. She never had but a very few freckles, and they were—well—in places where they were no blemish. Hardly noticeable."

"Only in her armpits, ja?"

Edge and Autumn stared at him as if he had been Magpie Maggie Hag making one of her more thunderclap divinations. He continued:

"I do not pretend to be a wizard. I deal merely with signs diagnostic. Had you come to me in your girlhood, Frau Edge, I could have predicted the onset of this affliction—though I could in no way have prevented it—simply from that unusual distribution of the few freckles."

"It *sounds* like wizardry," Autumn said, with awe.

"Nein. This is not even among my particular specialties of myopathy. It is a very rare disease, and only one young physician—von Recklinghausen, of Berlin—has studied it intently. But I do keep up with his monographs and his articles in the medical journals. Perhaps someday he will publish the glad news of a cure. Or prevention. Or reversal."

"Cure of *what*?" Edge blurted. "What *is* it?"

"At present, it has not even a name. In time, no doubt, in the medical tradition, it will be called von Recklinghausen's disease. As of now, all we know is that it is a neural affection, and incurable, and evidently congenital. It is oftenest apparent in the newborn child, but it can lie dormant until the victim is your age, Frau Edge. The nerve sheaths begin to thicken and accrete about them tumorous tissues of both flesh and bone . . . Ach, not to get too technical, it is no mortal disease. You will not die. Not of that, anyway."

"Then what *will* happen to me?"

The doctor took off his pince-nez and rubbed his eyes. "Unfortunately, the cranial and facial deformity will not go away, but intensify. Eventually, similar distortion will be apparent in other parts of your body—arms, legs, torso, wherever there are affectable nerves—and one's entire body is laced with nerves."

"And there's *nothing* that can be done?" Edge almost implored.

"Very little, I am sorry to say." The doctor turned again to Autumn. "Continue to wear concealing clothing. If and when that becomes inadequate to hide the deformities—the bulges and distortions—we *can* resort to surgical excision of the lesions. To pare away the more obtrusive excrescences. But that would be only a temporary amelioration, you understand, and it would probably have to be done many times during your life."

Autumn said wretchedly, "The last physician I consulted promised me at least an early and merciful death. Dear God, you are telling me that I might live another forty, fifty years? Like this? And getting *worse*? And every so often, like a tree growing askew, I will have to be *pruned*? And all that time, poor Zachary must—"

"Poor Zachary be damned," Edge said firmly. "I've just been made rich." He leaned over, laid an affectionate hand on her knee and looked unflinchingly into her terrible face. "You're alive, Autumn, and you'll stay alive. I won't be losing you. We'll go straight from here to Sacher's and order the biggest celebration Vienna ever saw. I'll even learn to waltz properly with you."

She said nothing, but returned his look. Whether her expression was woeful or grateful was impossible to tell. Then she dropped the veil to hide it.

"If now I might examine you, Frau Edge?" said the doctor. "To assure that there are no collateral complications...?"

"Please, Herr Doktor," she said, in a small voice. "Could I—could we postpone that to another day? I have...you have already given me quite a lot to digest. To adjust to."

"Of course. I understand. The Fräulein Voss will give you another appointment. Auf Wiedersehen."

In the Fiaker returning them to the Prater, Autumn said very little, responding mainly in murmurs to Edge's attempts at cheery conversation: "I might even learn to dance before we throw our shindig"—and optimistic suggestions: "Later on, maybe we could go to Berlin, and see that other specialist..."

When they got down from the carriage in the circus's backyard, several troupers and crewmen loudly called and beckoned to Edge from the back door of the menagerie top.

"Here, I'll help you inside, then go see what they want," he said to Autumn, and kissed her through the veil. "You lie down and rest, and I'll be right back."

There was quite a crowd of people in the horses' end of the tent, and Florian, Hannibal and Yount were kneeling in the straw, examining one ribby horse that lay on its side, breathing stertorously.

"It's the old bonerack that draws the caravan of the casse-cou joeys," said Florian, standing up and dusting his knees. "But first, what news about Autumn?"

"She won't get better, I'm afraid. But she'll live, and that's all that matters." Edge bent to look at the horse. "This poor beast won't, I'm sorry to say."

"What you reckon wrong, Mas' Edge?" asked Hannibal.

"I sure hope it ain't glanders," said Yount. "We could lose every animal we got. Maybe one or two of us, besides."

"No. Look at its teeth—what teeth it's got. I'd reckon it's dying of simple old age. What'll get us all, after a while."

Florian said to the clowns, "My regrets, Nella... Bernhard... Ferdi. Of course we'll get you a replacement horse. But while we're on the subject, Nella, wouldn't you like to move out of that crowded threesome? We now possess a spare caravan."

"Grazie. Danke. Thank you," she said, and blushed. "But I already have moved out. Into the carovana of Signor LeVie."

"Ah... well... forgive me for butting in. And my best wishes to you both. Zachary, can you do anything to ease the horse's misery?"

"Put him out of it, quick, is the best thing," said Edge, standing up. "My weapons are all in the van. I'll go fetch one."

He was just starting in that direction when they heard the single gunshot from there. Edge stood paralyzed for an instant, then said, "Oh, Jesus!" and would have sprinted, but Florian stepped in his way.

"Best let me go. Obie, Shadid, see that Zachary stays here. That's an order."

Yount wrapped his big arms around Edge, and the Turk stood by, while Florian departed at a run.

"Goddamn it, let me loose!" snarled Edge, struggling fiercely. "And that *is* an order, Sergeant."

"I'm sorry, Colonel," Obie said, "but army orders don't apply no more. Terrible, you better help me."

Edge fought and cursed, and it did require both of the strongmen to hold him, and all the others in the tent looked on wide-eyed while, unnoticed by anyone but Hannibal, the ancient horse lying on the straw quietly expired.

Florian arrived at the caravan to find Magpie Maggie Hag already entering it. "You knew?" he asked, panting a little.

"I dukkered long time ago, but you never believed. Now you stay out. I see what need doing."

She was inside for only a minute, then emerged carrying Edge's old single-shot Cook carbine, still smoking slightly and reeking of burned black powder.

"This gun short enough, even small girl like her could hold muzzle to head and reach trigger."

"Christ. And Zachary always kept it loaded with bird shot," said Florian, taking it from her. "There must be an unholy mess in there."

"She wanted nothing remain of what she looked like. I attend to her. You send me Slovak—Slovak with strong stomach—to clean walls and all. Also she leave note and sealed envelope. Here."

Florian took them and did not open either. He tucked the carbine under the caravan steps, called to one of the several roustabouts gawking from a distance, told him to fetch water, mops and rags, and returned to the menagerie. Edge's struggling had subsided, but he and the other two men were much disheveled. Yount and Shadid let go of him when Florian entered and wordlessly held out the note and envelope. He also jerked his head curtly at the others in the tent, so they all cleared out.

Edge opened the folded paper; it had obviously been written hurriedly, but without any evidence of tremor. He read it, stony-faced, then said, "There's nothing in it too private for you to hear," and read it aloud:

"'Darling. You have been everything to me, and I refuse to be a burden to you. No—that sounds like heroic unselfishness, and it is not. Such a life I would find intolerable, as well. Not long ago I told you—wherever we go from here will be as new and foreign to me as to you. I pray that you will be a long time arriving there, but I shall be waiting. Au revoir, my dearest.'" He paused, cleared his throat and said, "Signed with no name, just a little drawing of a heart."

He tore open the envelope, took out another paper and read the beginning of it: "'Darling. I am told that I will soon die...' She must have written this one back in Munich, after we saw that other doctor. 'But you have all of life ahead of you, and I want...'" Edge's voice trailed off, and he read the rest of it silently to himself. Then he tucked the papers in a pocket and said huskily to Florian, "Now... if I could go and see her one last—"

"You would not want to," said Florian. "She would not want you to. Maggie is taking care of her. Please, Zachary, do not make me call for restraints again. Come, get onto my rockaway. I will take you to a good hotel, then proceed with all the proper arrangements."

Edge nodded numbly and let himself be led to the rockaway. As they drove off the tober, Florian called to Fitzfarris, "Sir John, you and everyone else who can write, make posters announcing that there will be no show until further notice. Have Banat and his men plaster them all over the Prater."

A couple of hours later, when Florian returned, he had a different passenger on the seat beside him—that same uniformed officer who had helped dispose of Major Minim—and the rockaway was followed by a hearse, not the city coroner's, but from a private undertaking establishment. As the two vehicles crossed the tober to the backyard, they were trailed by numerous sad-faced or openly weeping troupers.

Magpie Maggie Hag was sitting on the steps of Autumn's caravan while the cleaning-up continued inside. "Third Slovak working now," she reported. "First one, then another got sick, I had to excuse."

Florian asked, "Is she—is everything presentable enough for this gentleman to examine the scene of the accident?"

The gypsy shrugged and got up to let the policeman go in. He came out again very quickly, with a shudder, took a deep breath of the outside air, and said to Florian in German, "I am sympathetic to your great loss, and to your Herr Edge's even greater bereavement. And of course I am sworn to give aid to any needful brother within the length of my cable tow. But, please, how many more times will you be asking me to bend the rules of my professional office?"

"Brother, you need only certify that it was an accident, so the undertaker can assume charge of the remains. And an accident you can plainly see that it was. As I told you, the young lady was our shootist's partner, and while cleaning his tools of the trade, during his absence..."

"A marksman's partner," the policeman said drily, "ought to know better than to try cleaning a carbine already loaded." However, he scribbled on an official-looking certificate, said, "Alles in Ordnung," gave the paper to the undertaker, exchanged a few more arcane remarks and discreet signs with Florian, then again took his leave.

The undertaker directed his men in unloading an extremely ornate mahogany coffin from the hearse, but they were interrupted. Jörg Pfeifer was among the onlookers, and he suddenly cried:

"Nein! Nein! Nichts da!"

Everyone stopped in surprise, and Florian said, "Why, Fünfünf, whatever is the matter?"

"That is but an ordinary civilian coffin, Herr Gouverneur."

"I selected the finest and most expensive in the establishment's stock. What more—?"

"In an ordinary coffin, the Fräulein Auburn can be placed only with her feet side by side. But she was a peerless rope-dancer. I will not allow her to be buried except with her feet placed heel to toe." Without waiting for the stunned Florian to comment, Pfeifer turned and repeated his demand in German to the undertaker.

That gentleman reeled slightly. "Beispiellos! Schändung!"

Florian shook his head. "Unheard of, perhaps, but no desecration. I am in complete accord. You will oblige us with a coffin so constructed."

"Herr Florian, it will have to be custom built," the undertaker protested. "And never in all my experience—"

"Then go and build it."

The undertaker ceased to argue, but kept on muttering remarks about scandalous unorthodoxy. His men brought Autumn's sheet-covered small body from the caravan on a stretcher, gently laid it in the temporary coffin, hoisted that into the hearse and drove away.

During the following day, various members of the company went into town, to the small but elegant Staatsoper Hotel, to give what condolence and comfort they could to Zachary Edge. One of them was Magpie Maggie Hag, who so seldom left the circus tober in even the most enticing cities. She said:

"I know you not believe this, pralo, but you have reason be glad. Long time you already know you losing Autumn. You had time, opportunity for be only kind and caring. No need reproach self now for things done, not done. Others have lost loves, after their last little time came and went unguessed. Que en tranquilidad esté."

"Gracias para decirlo, madama," Edge said sincerely. "Que besa su mano." And he did kiss her withered old hand.

Yount and Mullenax came calling together, and Mullenax brought an armload of bottles of Asbach brandy, saying, "Likker's one of the best things I know for gettin' through bad times."

"Thanks, Abner," said Edge. "But if I wanted just to get fuddled and stay that way, this hotel is amply supplied with the ways and means." He went on, somewhat absently, "It's a very accommodating hotel. Autumn would have liked it. In the morning, the hall porter brings up the day's newspaper, freshly pressed with a hot iron. I can't read it, but it's perfectly flat and uncreased, and nice and warm. Even the donnicker here is warm." He opened the bathroom door. "See, that flooring can be raised, and there are stone channels underneath. When you want to take a bath, or just sit on the chamber commode, you pull this bell rope and a hotel maid comes with a shovelful of hot coals and puts them under the floor, so your feet don't get cold."

"One thing about these maidservants here in Vienna," said Yount, "they're prettier than anywhere we've been yet. And they all *smell* so pretty. They smell of bread and butter."

"I hadn't noticed," Edge said abstractedly.

"You didn't have no reason to, before," said Mullenax. "But in time you will. And that's a better way, even, than the jug, for puttin' pain and grief to rest."

Clover Lee came to tell Edge that she was taking care of Autumn's canary, along with her own pigeons. Jules Rouleau and Willi Lothar came to say that they were occupying his van during his absence, to prevent the theft of anything in it. Willi added, "The emperor is abroad during this month. When he returns, maybe then I can arrange the command performance we have wanted. I mention this because I wish to give you something to look forward to, friend Zachary."

"I'll be relieved enough just to get the funeral over with," sighed Edge, "and get back to work. I don't think Autumn would have wanted us all to stand around and gloom and mourn."

Since no one, not even Edge, knew what Autumn's religion had been—if any—there was no church service. The circus company simply gathered in Vienna's Central Cemetery for another graveside ceremony. Despite the chill of the bright blue autumn day, the artistes again wore their pista costumes—léotards, fleshings, spangles, leopard skin, clown dress—and quaked and shivered rather than hide them under warm cloaks. Edge was somewhat taken aback at first sight of Autumn's coffin, which looked very much like a museum's mummy case. But when the reason for it was explained to him, he warmly thanked Jörg Pfeifer for having thought of it. Then Dai Goesle conducted the service, and he kept it brief and simple, only once indulging in imagery:

"We commonplace creatures stay on the ground, and walk. This lass took to the air, and danced. Now she is dancing somewhere higher yet, on a cloud mayhap, and all the angels are applauding..."

At the close, it was Edge instead of Florian who pronounced the old epitaph: "Saltavit. Placuit"—but he stopped there, not adding the final phrase, refusing to say out loud that she was dead.

When the Florilegium resumed showing the next afternoon, Edge resumed his several rôles of equestrian director, Colonel Ramrod and Buckskin Billy. If perhaps his colleagues perceived that he performed with less zest than formerly, they could not remark that he performed any less than capably. If he seemed somewhat distant, he was certainly not oblivious to anything that went on. At the first opportunity, he called up to Boom-Boom Beck on the bandstand, "What the hell was that new music you played for the come-in? Nobody sang. Why aren't we promenading and singing to 'Greensleeves' as usual?"

"Forgive me, Herr Direktor, for upon myself taking the decision. But I thought—since your Liebchen's music that was—perhaps painful it would be, and to retire it we ought."

"No, sir. We buried Autumn, but we won't bury every memory of her. You put that music back in your repertoire, and keep it there."

Edge was again surprised by an unexpected change in the program when it came time for Monday's tightrope turn and he whistled for her to enter. Monday did not appear, and the band did not go into her "Cinderella" music, or any other. The only sound to be heard was a sudden small hissing as Goesle ignited his carbide spotlight—although this was late afternoon and the chapiteau sufficiently aglow with sunlight diffused through the canvas. Puzzled, Edge started to whistle again, but desisted when he looked where the spotlight beam was pointed. It shone on the rope-dancer's resting platform, now occupied, Edge could see in the limelight brilliance, by a tremendous bouquet of autumn flowers—chrysanthemums and asters—tied with a wide black ribbon and flowing black bow.

Now from the bandstand there commenced a quiet music—what Beck had first played for Autumn's performance—arpeggios on the simple string of tins he had contrived aboard ship so long ago. As that gentle tinkling went on, Goesle's spotlight very, very slowly traveled the length of the empty tightrope, following the remembered antics and graces of an imagined yellow-clad sprite. Most of the people in the audience probably had heard of Autumn's demise, during the time the circus had been closed, but few of them could ever have seen her perform. Nevertheless, they burst into as much applause as if Autumn were really there aloft, and respectfully stood up as they did so.

When the spotlight went off and the applause dwindled and the last arpeggio diminished to silence, there was a pause. Then the band, to end the show in a merrier mood, loudly launched into the clowns' music, and Fünfünf, the Kesperle and Ali Baba ran into the pista to do their Lupino mirror act for the close. But Edge did not see them; his eyes had misted over. He slipped out the back door and away, to be by himself. Then he wondered why. From now on, he thought, even amidst the most teeming and busy company, he would be always alone.

5

GRADUALLY, over the winter, Edge cleared his caravan of what property Autumn had left. He let Clover Lee keep the canary and its tuned cage, and gave to Sunday Simms the "Greensleeves" music box, and to Monday Simms-Fitzfarris the framed and autographed picture of Mme Saqui—"She was before your time, Monday, but she was a rope-dancer, too, and a famous one"—and told them and the other women to divide among themselves Autumn's wardrobe and trinkets. Thereafter, Edge lived alone in the caravan, declining any blandishments of the ladies from the seats and the invitations from Mullenax to join him in "bucking the tiger" in town.

One day, in the backyard, the Smodlaka children came dancing up to their mother, and the boy said teasingly, "Mati, can you open your mouth without showing your teeth?"

"Ne znam," Gavrila said offhandedly, occupied with sewing something. "Why do you ask such a question?"

"Man asked *us* it." Gavrila put down her sewing and looked at Velja with concern. "And Mati, I can do it. So can Sava. See?" The boy made a small circle of his pale lips.

His sister chirped, "Then the man said 'just the right size' and he laughed and he gave us each a gulden."

Gavrila snapped, "Velja, stop making that face. Whoever put you up to that was being naughty. The late Major Minim, no doubt."

"No, Mati, he is long gone. It was just now—"

"Then do not tell me who. I do not wish to know. I wish only that you stay away from this bad man, too. See that you do."

Velja muttered rebelliously, "The Gospodín Florian said we could play with anybody except the Major Minim," as he and his sister shuffled off, chastened and disconsolate.

The artist Tina Blau came from her studio to the tober and, over a span of about a week's work during the intervals between shows, put Meli and her python onto a canvas that she said she would entitle *Andromeda.* To Fitzfarris, who hovered about her easel during most of that time, the artist made one complaint: "I cannot get Meli ever to smile."

"She never does seem to smile any more," Fitz acknowledged. "I don't know why. She used to, a lot. But what the hell, Tina, as far as your painting is concerned, would a woman *be* smiling when she's getting rogered by a dragon?"

"Oh, I think *I* might," Tina said, her violet eyes roguish. "Don't I always smile when I am being rogered by a Tattooed Man?"

That and other such lightsome exchanges were overheard by Monday, who also hovered, unseen, and smoldered at them from behind wagon corners and tent flaps and other concealments. Her smoldering might have flared into flame, but for the cautionary counsel of her sister.

"Don't act ugly," said Sunday. "It'll only make her—or any other woman— seem nicer in comparison to you, and more desirable. But we'll be leaving Vienna sometime, and that woman won't. You'll have John Fitz all to yourself again before too much longer."

Monday said sullenly, "And then what? You got your Mr. Zack all to yourself now, but what good's that doin' *you?*"

"Well... he has his grieving and forgetting to get through."

Monday snorted. "Man might remember one woman, up top in his head, but he got a prong down below that forgets her real quick. I ought to know."

"Why do you flinch away when I undo your breeches, lad?" the man asked. They lay on a pallet improvised of spare canvas, inside one of the tent wagons tucked away in a remote corner of the tober. "See, I undo mine also. I merely expose our different selves, so we may compare and admire each other. And now you stare, as if you had never seen this part of a man before, but you have one of your own."

"Not big. Not red."

"Because you are a unique color all over, my boy. However, our different complexions do not make our private parts behave any differently. Yours is growing in my hand. And look—so does mine, even untouched. We are precisely alike in our responses, so what is there for you to be shy about? There... does not that feel good?"

With a bashful nod, "Um-hm."

"Then come, you must do the same to mine. That's right. Ah-h, yes, it does feel good. Be grateful that I am teaching you something so useful. You *can* do this alone, you realize. And I am sure you often will, from now on. But I am delighted to know that I am the first to pluck such an unusually colored cherry. Now, do just as I do. Tighter. Faster. Yes... yes..." After a time, "There. Wasn't that divinely pleasant?"

"Um-*hm!*"

"Until next time, then, you may enjoy your new prowess on your own. Or with some other lad. Or—oh, but I do hope not. I sincerely caution you against spending your energies on any female—even one as close as a sister. I will explain another day. Go now. And remember, not a word to anyone."

On a Wednesday, which was salary day for the crewmen, Edge went to the red wagon, as usual, to help Florian check off the roster of names and count out the cash. As the men filed through the office, doffed their caps, took their pay and grunted respectful thanks or tugged at their low-growing forelocks, Edge muttered, "Every time we do this I find more new names on the rolls, and faces I don't recognize. For instance, who are Herman Begega and Bill Jensen? Those don't sound like Slovaks."

"No," said Florian. "A Spaniard and a Swede. One is a carpenter that Stitches hired. The other is Boom-Boom's new contrabass tuba. They won't be in to get paid today; they are still on holdback."

"Where are all these new hands sleeping?"

"I told Banat he could have Major Minim's caravan to house the overflow. Our Florilegium is becoming quite a populous community. I only wish we could add to our company of artistes as easily as to the crew. I think I shall send an advertisement to the *Era,* soliciting applications, when we get to Budapest."

In the tent wagon, the boy lay spoon fashion against the man's back, but moving convulsively. When he gave a last heave, he groaned in rapture and shuddered all over. Then he sighed tremulously and began to withdraw, but the man reached backward to hold him there.

"Stay a while, lad. I like the sensation of it dwindling inside me. And while you rest, let me instruct you further. Some will tell you that a woman is better equipped to give a man that kind of pleasure. Do not believe them. Down there, a woman has only great, slack, slobbering lips at the portal of a loose, wet, uninviting cavity. None of the firm, warm, clasping *tightness* you have just enjoyed so much. As for the rest of a woman, what is she? Nothing but a bosom of blubber that exudes ogress milk. Are you paying attention?"

Sleepily, "Um-hm."

"If you are quite relaxed...well, turnabout is only fair play. Turn over, my boy. And remain relaxed...unresisting..."

Clover Lee and Sunday sat in Griensteidl's café—of which they had become frequent patrons—with coffee, tortes and the *Neue Freie Presse,* which Sunday had folded to its "personals" columns.

"Anything interesting today?" asked Clover Lee.

"Well, here's one that says something about 'artistic'..." Sunday studied it, then translated aloud: "'Will the charming Fräulein D. M., who once displayed in my office chambers her artistic Aktentasche, please know that I forever remember her with adoration?'"

"I just bet," said Clover Lee. "I assume a woman's Aktentasche is something, uh—intimate?"

"I have no idea. And I didn't bring my dictionary."

"Anyhow, you know that my initials are C. L. C. If you don't see them anywhere, look for something that *might* apply to me. Preferably signed with a coronet."

"Hm. 'Will the charming Fräulein'—it looks like you've *got* to be charming—'who walked with me through the empty midnight city in a soft snowfall...?'"

"It wasn't me. Damn. Maybe I'll have to put in an advertisement of my own. 'Will some charming and wealthy Graf...?'"

"This time," said the man, "I will teach you how to smoke a cigar."

"Too young to smoke," mumbled the boy.

"Oh, we will not set it alight." The man was much amused. "Dear me—hnoof-hnoof—that would not do at all. No, you will merely learn to take it in your mouth and draw on it properly. I shall demonstrate first on this eager little cheroot of yours. Now, first, one always licks a cigar from end to end..."

After some time and some contortions and some muffled exclamations from both of them, Cecil said, "Jolly well learned, my boy, and well accomplished. Now swallow, as I just did. You see, this is another reason for preferring a fellow male to an alien female. A man has only so much of that precious juice to expend in his lifetime. So, if you enjoy these gamahuche games and want to go on enjoying them, you do not wish to waste what makes them possible."

"No," said the boy, with real anxiety.

"Well, there you are. A woman would simply take your dear juice and give you none back in return. But you and I can keep on absorbing each other's—in one aperture or another—and thereby keep replenishing our mutual supply, and never have to fear running dry."

On a Sunday, some of the circus company went to St. Stephan's Cathedral—along with half the city population, it seemed, from the crush—to hear the renowned Vienna Boys' Choir sing. Afterward, Florian said to Willi Lothar, "Well, that choirmaster Bruckner is also the emperor's organist at the Hofburg. Is this as close as *we* are ever going to get to that Hofburg?"

"Herr Gouverneur, you know that I am constantly importuning my every remotest relative and least acquaintance in court circles. But, if I may suggest—I think also it would help our cause if we volunteered the Florilegium to perform at some civic benefit function."

"Why not? What had you in mind?"

"Ach, there is the Innkeepers' Ball, the Artists' *Gschnastfest,* the Street-Sweepers' Ball, any number of others. But I thought particularly of the gala at the Brünlfeld Irrenanstalt."

"The lunatic asylum!?" Edge exclaimed, when Florian told him. "Willi has talked a lot about a command performance, but what have we had? First beggars and now zanies. Does it occur to you, Governor, that maybe we're going downhill, not up?"

"This is one of Wien's most cherished traditions," Florian said. "On Carnival Tuesday each year, a gala is always held at the Irrenanstalt. The, er, milder inmates are even allowed to participate, in costumes they make themselves. It is not so much an occasion for *their* diversion, of course, as of the spectators—who include royals and nobles and other worthies—to amuse themselves by watching the poor loonies cavort. It will not hurt our prospects if such folk see us cavort, as well."

"All right. I reckon we're all game if you are. Do we tear down here and set up in the asylum grounds?"

"No, no. There is a capacious indoor hall between the asylum building and the adjacent hospital. We will suspend showing here that day, and take to the Irrenanstalt only what we can show to best effect. The artistes, the pista curbing, the band, whatever rigs and props do not require elaborate handling. Brutus, Maximus, the dwarf horse. No more. We will not risk frightening the inmates with the calliope or the more rambunctious acts."

Other things occurred on the Carnival Tuesday before that special performance.

"Ah, you are cheating, lad," said Cecil, but with good humor, as he entered the tent wagon at dusk. "You did not wait for me. But how I do envy you that ability—being able to double over and smoke your own little black cigar. No, no, do not uncoil. Go ahead and satisfy yourself. I can wait, and the sight is ineffably stimulating."

When Quincy had finished and swallowed and caught his breath, he muttered, "Druther do it with you."

"Very well. Let us both take advantage of your elasticity. See if you can manage this. Insert yourself as usual, but upside down, then bend to bring your head—so. Give *my* cigar a good smoking while your own enjoys itself back there. Can you do that?" After only a little experimenting, the boy achieved that contortion and began enthusiastically to work in and on the man, who cooed and crooned, "That's right. Oh, that is *ever* so right!"

The wagon door suddenly opened, and a dark silhouette stood there against the twilight outside.

"Confound it!" exclaimed Cecil, and he urgently shoved at Quincy, who was still working, oblivious of the interruption.

"So this is where you keep disappearing to," said the intruder, sounding puzzled.

"Daphne!" said Cecil, aghast.

"We are all about to depart for the asylum at—" By now, she could see the two naked bodies in the wagon's dim interior and realize what they were doing, and she said hollowly, "Oh, dear God..."

"Get off me, boy, *get away!*" Cecil jerked free of Quincy so abruptly that the disengagement made two distinct noises, as of two bottles being unstoppered. Quincy softly said "Hoy!" in bewilderment and disappointment. But Cecil was hastily getting dressed and Daphne had fled from the doorway.

"The people in the boxes and loges draped with bunting are the nobles and notables," said Florian. "Those in the ordinary seats are the lunatics."

He was not being entirely facetious, for there was not a great deal of other distinction to be seen between the asylum inmates and the visitors, except that the costumes worn by the former were perhaps a trifle more haphazardly put together, and of less rich fabrics, but were no more eccentric or bizarre. In both sections of the audience there were numerous identifiable Napoléon Bonapartes and Pallas Athenes, winged angels, horned demons, several apparent Lord Gods and Jesuses, Saint Brigittes and Saint Annes, and all manner of invented nightmare grotesqueries. Florian had said that the lunatics allowed outside the asylum to attend the party were the less seriously afflicted. Still, there was a multitude of uniformed guards and white-garbed nursing sisters scattered about the hall, unobtrusive but watchful.

The circus was minus several of its acts on this occasion, some of them—like the several horse turns—because they would have been unwieldy or too noisy indoors, some others at the tactful suggestion of the asylum's resident physicians. For example, Spyros Vasilakis marched in the opening promenade, but thereafter sat out the show on the sidelines. To see the Gluttonous Greek swallow swords and eat fire, said the doctors, might give their patients unwholesome ideas. They evidently feared nothing unwholesome in any ideas those onlookers might have got from watching Meli Vasilakis and her serpents do the provocative Medusa-twining and ravished-Maiden routines, or from watching Colonel Ramrod do his fancy shooting. Edge did, however, on his own initiative, reduce his powder loads so the weapons made only muted bangs, and entirely omitted the shooting of a ball into his assistant Sunday's teeth.

To make up for the abbreviated program, Florian informed the asylum attendants that at intermission their wards might descend to the pista and take rides around it on the elephant or the dwarf horse, and he left it to those attendants to select suitable candidates. As it turned out, quite as many of the outside guests came to enjoy that privilege as did members of the asylum population. And one man, dressed and periwigged and beruffled as Louis XIV, after circling the hall first on Brutus's neck and then on Rumpelstilzchen's back, engaged Florian and Willi in an animated, arm-waving conversation.

"Bless me, that little notion of mine proved a profitable one," Florian told Edge. "You saw the Louis Fourteenth who spoke to us? He was so excited at having participated in our circus that *he* has promised to secure our invitation to the palace. And he can do it, too. That was Count Wilczek, a particular favorite of Franz Joseph."

"Are you sure?" Edge said skeptically. "I didn't notice whether he came from the deluxe boxes or the guarded seats."

"Oh, it was he," said Willi. "And I am chagrined. After all my efforts, it is an elephant and a pony that may finally promote us into the Erste Gesellschaft."

The show was to resume with Cecil and Daphne on their velocipede—Florian had decided to delete the skating turn as too noisy—so the band thumped into the "Royal Fireworks" bourrée, and Florian announced "the Wheeling Wheelers!" and the equestrian director whistled for their entrance. The velocipede came in, all right, and with Cecil pedaling it, but with no Daphne on his shoulders.

Edge said with annoyance, "What the hell?"

"He and his woman fought una battaglia," confided Nella Cornella, beside him. "So now he is only playing with himself."

"Uh... *by* himself, Nella," Edge corrected her. "They had a fight? When?"

"Just before we all departed the tober. I was passing their carovana. I heard her shout, 'You will not ever put that thing in me again. Not after where it has been. You will not ever *touch* me again. Now get out of here.' And out he came, scompigliatamente—in haste and disorder. And alone."

"I wonder what that was about," said Edge. "Well, I see he's got at least a temporary replacement. Not anywhere near as pretty as his wife, though."

Ali Baba had come running, in his minstrel-show costume, and Cecil, as he wheeled around the hall between the pista and the front row of boxes, reached down one hand to sweep the boy up and onto his shoulders. Even without practice, Ali Baba did a commendable job of imitating Daphne's poses and handstands and upside-down splits. Since the vat of flames would not cap the act on this occasion, Cecil concentrated on fancy riding—intricate turns, backward pedaling, rearing up the tall machine onto its tiny hind wheel. And one of those sudden rearings caught Ali Baba off balance. He pitched off his perch and tried to twist in the air to make a safe landing, but managed only to turn enough to fall on his head—with a loud crack, for there was no soft ground or straw or sawdust in this hall, but hardwood flooring. The inmate half of the audience immediately began laughing and pounding their fists on their knees in appreciation.

Cecil stopped his velocipede and heeled it over sideways, to dismount and run back. The two other troupers nearest the scene also went running—Florian and Mullenax, who was just then directing the Slovaks in rolling Maximus's cage wagon into the hall. But Ali Baba bounded unaided and spryly to his feet, and threw up his arms in the V. So did Cecil, taking one of the boy's hands in his, to pretend that the spill had been the intended conclusion of the act. So the visitor half of the audience joined the inmates in laughing and applauding.

"Are you all right, Ali Baba?" said Florian.

"Yassuh. Awright."

"Hell, he only lit on his head," Mullenax drawled drunkenly. "Niggers all got heads like cannonballs, ain't that right, kid?" And he playfully ruffled Ali Baba's kinky wool.

"Reckon so, suh."

Florian said frostily to Cecil, "Why this unannounced and unrehearsed substitution, Mr. Wheeler?"

Cecil tried to laugh it off. "Had a little tiff with my storm-and-strife, Governor. Hnoof-hnoof-hnoof. So she played truant, and Ali Baba very kindly volunteered."

Still frostily, Florian said, "I shall have a word with her when we get back to the tober."

The band was beginning to play "Bollocky Bill," so Mullenax whipped a tin flask from his pocket and drained it. Edge, who had joined the group, said, "Let's not have any more surprises. Abner, are you too drunk to go on?"

Mullenax stopped swaying, stood to stiff attention, blinked his lurid eye and said with great precision, "No, sir, Colonel. Just now primed exactly right."

The roustabouts had the cage wagon at pista center by now, so Edge hesitated only a moment, then waved him on, and Florian went ahead with the megaphone to bellow his introduction.

Edge kept a wary watch and kept his whistle at his mouth, ready to terminate the act at any time. But it proceeded well enough, though Barnacle Bill conducted the lion through most of it—*platz* and *hoch* and *krank* and *schön'machen* and several more *hochs*—while leaning, as if nonchalantly, against the cage bars and only flubbily snapping his whip. Then the Slovaks brought the oil-daubed wooden hoop and handed it in to him through the bars. Maximus backed to the farther wall and crouched low in preparation for his leap. The smallness of the cage always required Barnacle Bill at this point to go down on his knees, while he held the hoop with a long-handled pair of pliers and a roustabout ignited it from outside and hastily fled the heat.

But this time, when the hoop flared up, Barnacle Bill uttered no command.

Instead, he slowly toppled forward from his kneeling position, wearily rolled over, stretched out full length on the cage floor and went to sleep. The hoop rolled out through the bars and, flaming merrily, bounced a few times and rolled on across the pista.

"Damnation! Catch that thing!" Edge shouted. Then, "Bring poles! Hold the cat where he is!"

The audience of inmates again briskly applauded—either the impromptu fireworks or Barnacle Bill's insouciant display of bravery. But all the Slovaks had instinctively run to intercept the hoop before it could jump the pista curb and perhaps bound among the onlookers, so no crewman was close to the wagon to fence in or fend off Maximus from moving. And moving he was, now, still in his low crouch, slinking menacingly toward his unconscious master, and licking his lips in apparent anticipation of an unexpected but welcome meal.

Edge himself went running, uncoiling his own whip, as the band struck up the "Wedding March." However, by then, the lion was standing astraddle the supine Barnacle Bill, staring down at him and apparently considering where to taste him first. The animal flicked a sidelong glance out at Edge, curled a lip and gave a low snarl of warning. So Edge still refrained from using his whip, uncertain whether it might infuriate Maximus to an instant attack instead of driving him off. The lion gazed down at his master again, lowered his muzzle to sniff at him and then did something contrary to everything Edge had ever heard about the vengeful ferocity of a great cat with a helpless human at its mercy. Maximus began—it might have been sorrowfully, compassionately—to lick the unconscious man's face.

Edge heard someone behind him shout, "Christ! One of the loonies is loose!" But he did not turn; he watched in mixed amazement and apprehension the lion's ministrations to Barnacle Bill. There was the noise of running feet, then many of them, pounding across the wooden floor, and a hubbub of more shouts, but Edge stayed where he was, ready to wield his whip. The rasping of the lion's rough tongue brought Mullenax awake again. His one eye opened and, fortunately, what he saw with it paralyzed him instead of making him scramble for escape. He stared with horror up at the cat's great jaws and teeth and tongue, and Edge started murmuring—to him as well as the animal—"Steady...platz, now...platz..."

Then, not from either Mullenax or Maximus, there was a sudden flurry of movement in the cage. Its door quickly opened and shut, and there was another person inside—a devil all in bright red, with horns, arrow-ended tail, a domino face mask and, in one hand, a devilish, long trident. Maximus raised his massive head, regarded the newcomer and snarled once more. Edge also snarled: "Get out of there, you maniac. *Raus!* He's protecting his master!" But the intruder ignored them both, coolly touched the points of his trident to the lion's broad chest and told him in a quiet voice, "Zurück...zurück, Kätzchen..." After mulling the suggestion for a moment, Maximus obediently began to back off.

Well, Edge decided, the man might be a lunatic on the loose, but he at least knew the German commands. So Edge also moved from where he stood, slipped around to the rear of the wagon and, when the red devil had stepped over Mullenax, impelling Maximus farther down the cage, Edge growled, "Abner, wiggle your way here, not too fast." Mullenax did so, snakewise, and Edge opened the door just enough to let him slither out headfirst from the wagon sill to the floor.

He lay there quivering and breathing heavily. Florian came to stand over him and say, more in pity than anger, "I hope you're ashamed of yourself. The big, bold lion tamer, having to get rescued by a crazy man."

There were also a number of the asylum guards standing by, one of them holding ready a stout canvas strait-waistcoat dangling many straps and buckles. The man in the cage now told Maximus to "platz!" and the cat sat down, yawning as if he had got bored with all the unusual human behavior. The man backed slowly away from the cat, and Edge cracked the door again to let him out. The band immediately ceased its repetitions of the "Wedding March" and swung into the music for the dog act. The Smodlakas and their terriers ran into the pista and the show resumed.

The asylum guards advanced on the red devil, as cautiously as if it had been Maximus that had emerged. But the man reached up and removed his domino, and the guards stopped and gaped. One of them laughed in relief and said to Florian, "Es ist nicht ein Kranke von uns."

"Non," said the devil, also laughing. "No lunatic, messieurs. Jean-François Pemjean, à votre service." He was a handsome man, with a swarthy complexion and merry eyes that went well with his devil garb. "I was but visiting the *medical* hospital, for a minor complaint, when I learned of the gala in preparation. So I borrowed from a cupboard this spare déguisement, in order to attend."

"Fortuitement," said Florian. "Merci, Monsieur Pemjean, merci infiniment. Tell me, are you merely cavalier by nature, or are you a lion tamer by profession?"

"Oui, c'est de mon resort. Of course, I know the old circus saying: that Frenchmen are too temperamental for such work—not Teutonic-stolid enough." He cast a disparaging look at Barnacle Bill, whom some of the Slovaks were assisting from the pista, while others trundled the cage wagon out. "Nevertheless, that is what I am. Pemjean l'Intrépide, most recently of the Donnert Circus in Prague, formerly of the Cirque d'Été in Paris and now making my way thither again."

"Perhaps Monsieur l'Intrépide," said Florian, "you would further oblige me with a few words in private."

Those two went off together, and the show went on without any more interruptions or mishaps. It even included Mademoiselle Cinderella's rope-dancing and Maurice and Mademoiselle Butterfly's trapeze act, for Beck and Goesle had earlier in the day contrived to hang those rigs from the hall's upper beams and columns.

After the closing promenade, the Slovaks swarmed in to dismantle or remove what equipment and props remained, and to give the floor a good cleaning. When Beck and his windjammers left the bandstand, the asylum guards led a number of their wards up there—all harmless, shambling, vacantly smiling idiots, and all carrying musical instruments. But those were clearly not idiots savants; when they settled themselves and raised their horns and fiddles and woods, the music came not from them but from elsewhere. Curious, Edge went closer to look at the band, and discovered that their instruments were made of papier-maĉhé, the music being provided by a volunteer orchestra—perhaps one of the Strausses', since it was playing Papa Johann's "In the Little Jelly-Doughnut Woods," from concealment in a curtained alcove. Now the audience came down from the seats and boxes to the floor and took partners for the dancing, so commingling that the outside guests and the inmates were more than ever indistinguishable.

Fitzfarris, watching the scene, remarked to Florian, "Isn't it possible that after one of these jamborees some counts and dukes get carried off to the padded cells, and maybe some cuckoos take their places in the seats of the mighty?"

"I daresay. I also daresay that any such exchange might never be detected, either in here or outside. Please pass the word, Sir John, that our artistes are welcome to stay for the dancing and the food and drink, if they wish. They are already adequately costumed. I hope none will end up in a quilted cell."

Florian instructed only Abner Mullenax to accompany him back to the tober, though Edge and some other troupers came along of their own accord—Cecil Wheeler and Ali Baba among them—and so did the fortuitously encountered Jean-François Pemjean, now in street dress. When Florian and Edge led Mullenax into the office wagon and sat him down, he had sobered considerably.

"Barnacle Bill," said Florian, "you could easily have got yourself killed tonight. Worse yet, if you had behaved so in our chapiteau here, with its floor of sawdust and tanbark and straw, you could have burned the whole Florilegium to the ground, and killed numberless innocent people."

"Yessir," mumbled Mullenax. "Reckon you're right."

"What do you think I ought to do with you?"

"Well, you don't have to fire me, Governor. I already decided to quit the trade. I got the nerve scared out of me tonight for good and all. After lookin' that lion in the teeth and smellin' his breath, I couldn't never get in no cage with no wild animal again. Not ever again." He shivered.

"By good fortune, we do have a man willing and able to take your place. But surely you do not wish us to abandon you here in the middle of Europe."

"Nossir. If you could just keep me on as a kind of Slovak, I can nerve myself to swamp out the cages, feed the critters, work like that. Pay me just enough to keep me lubricated, that's all I'd ask, and I'd be grateful for it."

"Very well. Granted. Go now and get some sleep. On your way, please knock at the Wheelers' caravan and ask Mrs. Wheeler to come here."

"A sad thing," said Edge, when Mullenax had shuffled out. "To see a man come all to pieces like that."

"I have seen it too often," said Florian, with a sigh. "Some do it as he did. Others don't hit the skids until *after* they've lost their nerve. But I must unhappily predict, based on those many I have known, that Barnacle Bill will disintegrate further. Somewhere along the road, he will be sodden and comatose when the troupe moves on from one stand to the next. A time or two, he may recover and manage to catch up. But there'll come the time that he won't, and we'll never see him again."

Florian next called in Pemjean, who was idly chatting with Cecil Wheeler outside, to tell him, "The unfortunate dompteur whose place you took tonight has willingly relinquished that place permanently to you. He will, however, remain available—at least for a while—to assist you in caring for the animals. As I told you, we have also three Bengal tigers and two Syrian bears, whose training is not yet very far advanced."

Pemjean said confidently, "I will bring them along with utmost dispatch."

"Good. Now, as to the matter of your persona in the program. I rather liked the effect of that red devil in the cage."

"Aussi moi-même," said Pemjean, grinning. "To my knowledge, no other dompteur has ever worked animals with a trident spear instead of a whip. Therefore, having already pilfered the costume, I took the further liberty of keeping it and bringing it along."

"I commend your foresight. We shall make only one change in it—have our seamstress shorten the devil's tail. It could prove an encumbrance in the cage. And we will bill you as...let me see...yes! *Le Démon Débonnaire!*"

"Excellentissime!" exclaimed Pemjean.

Edge was studying the company roster, and said, "There's an empty bunk in Notkin and Spenz's caravan, since Nella moved out of there."

"I will speak to them," said Florian. "So, monsieur, you can lodge and travel with our Hanswurst and Kesperle, until we or you can afford better quarters on the tober and the road. Fetch your belongings whenever you like. And welcome to the Florilegium. We hope you will be happy in our company."

"Merci, Monsieur Florian. I like it better the more I see of it," said Pemjean, for Daphne Wheeler had just knocked and opened the door, and to the pretty blonde woman he made the elaborate, deep, sweeping bow of a dancing master before he departed.

She did not smile at that, or speak, but stood alternately wringing her hands and clenching them into fists.

"Be seated, Mrs. Wheeler," said Florian and, not too severely, "You missed an important performance tonight, without giving prior notice. A—tiff—with your husband, I understand. I do not customarily meddle in domestic matters, but when they affect the whole establishment, I do like to know—"

"Why don't you ask *him?* He's lurking just outside, fearful that I'm going to peach on him."

"Another thing I don't customarily do is denigrate one partner in the hearing of the other. But I will say frankly that I distrust men who laugh through their noses. I invite equal frankness from you. Go ahead. Peach on him."

Daphne wrung and clenched her hands some more, then blurted a brief but vivid description of what she had seen in the tent wagon.

"Goddamn," grunted Edge. "I thought we'd got rid of that kind of thing when we got rid of Major Maggot."

"This is indeed distressing," said Florian, frowning. "Er, Mrs. Wheeler, is this the first—uh—disillusionment you have suffered?"

"No," she said miserably. "There were plenty of young athletes around the gymnastics arena. But this is the first time he has defiled himself with a...with a *tar bucket.*" She made a face of disgust. "It is the final straw."

Still frowning, Florian said, "Naturally, my first impulse is to horsewhip your husband off the tober, Mrs. Wheeler, but that means discharging you, too—an innocent victim of my outrage. Also, if I dismiss one pederast, do I in fairness throw the boy into the street, as well? It is a dilemma."

"Oh, hell, Florian," said Edge. "Quincy doesn't have the sense—or the looks —to have seduced anybody. He's a victim, too."

"And don't concern yourself about me, Mr. Florian," Daphne said mournfully.

"In the wedding ceremony, Ceece and I pledged to love one another until death. I have ceased to love him. So one or both of us should die."

"Come now," Florian chided. "This is the nineteenth century, not biblical times. There are modern conveniences like divorce, instead of either homicide or suicide."

"I suppose so. I have already turned him out of our caravan. Because it isn't ours, it is *mine*. Bought with the dowry I brought to the marriage." Tears began to trickle down her cheeks.

"At least you have a roof over your head, and transport."

"Transport to where?" she said, weeping more copiously. "I have nowhere to go. I might as well let one of the Wurstelprater's brute Strizzis put me to whoring."

"Come now," Florian said again. "Who owns the act's props? The velocipede and rolling skates and vat and board?"

"We bought them together," she said, and sobbed.

"Then divide them," Florian said decisively. "If you keep only your pair of Plimptons and the skating board, you could work up a solo skating act, could you not?"

Daphne sniffled, stopped weeping and said she thought she could.

"And if later we procure another pair of the skates," Florian continued, "perhaps one of the joeys could be your partner. Very well, madame, your husband must go, but you may stay if you choose."

"Oh, I do choose!" she said gratefully.

"Colonel Ramrod, will you see if that degenerate is still loitering outside? Conduct him to the Wheeler ménage, stand by while he collects his belongings —only *his* belongings—and then see that he departs. Tonight. I will keep the lady safe here until he is gone."

Cecil was now at a little distance from the wagon, but keeping an anxious eye on it, while again conversing with Pemjean. Edge, approaching them, could hear Cecil telling the newcomer, ". . . Do it with the bald-headed end of a broom, that one. Hnoof-hnoof. Yes, indeed, fair game, old boy. Une sacrée baiseuse, as you frogs would say. Let me tell you one particularly favored way. . ." He dropped his voice to a confidential murmur, and Pemjean's eyes opened very wide. But when Edge stopped and stood regarding them stonily, Cecil broke off to ask, "Am I wanted, Zachary, old chap?"

"Not by anybody at all," said Edge. "Come to the caravan and clear out your goods and get off this lot."

"I say, now! You're being a bit brusque, old—"

"I can be a damned sight more so. With a tent stake, if you don't step lively. I'm only surprised that you haven't hit for the tall timber already. You must have known that your wife would tell us the dirty truth about you. Now move!"

Pemjean, appalled, said, "Sacré bleu! That woman is *your wife?*" But the other two men were moving off, Cecil plodding with shoulders slumped, Edge walking behind him like a warder.

Edge came back alone, to tell Florian and Daphne, "He's gone, Mrs. Wheeler. The caravan is yours again. All he took was his clothes and costumes and his personal props—what he could pack in panniers on the velocipede."

"You didn't hurt him?"

"No, ma'am. He didn't require any rough persuasion. And I wasn't eager to touch him if I didn't have to."

"Did he say anything? Any parting message?"

"Well... he said he was leaving the big fire-water vat. No way to carry it. And besides, he said, he hoped you'd drown in it."

"Oh," said Daphne.

"Good night, sweet prince," muttered Florian, and, after Daphne had taken her leave, "Now... about Quincy Simms. I agree that he must have had no notion that he was doing wrong. But he may have acquired a taste for the practice, and we don't want him, in his ignorance, importuning anyone else. I suggest that he be taken off in private and, in a very fatherly way, be told the facts of life."

"Don't look at me, Governor. No father ever told them to me, and I haven't fathered anybody to tell them to."

"Nor I. Hm. Grumpf. As far as I'm aware, the only current or former fathers we have on the show are Pavlo Smodlaka and Abner Mullenax. I'd hesitate to inflict either of those on a confused small boy."

"I know who," said Edge. "Foursquare John Fitzfarris. He's a man of the world, and he once ran a dodge on the solitary vice. At the very least, he'll know how to put the lecture in high-toned medical lingo."

So Fitzfarris, the next day, without too much recalcitrance, accepted the assignment of reeducating Quincy in the ways of a manly man. He came afterward to report to Florian:

"Well, I took the lad off to a secluded, quiet spot in a grove of trees, and I pulled up a pulpit and sat down and sermonized at him, and he said 'yassuh' every few minutes. At one point he told me he'd only played Wheeler's game because Wheeler said his juices would *dry up* otherwise. I think I set him straight on that, and I think he understood everything else I told him, and I think I've got him turned onto the path of virtue again. But—it's curious—after I'd pumped him brimful of What a Young Man Should Know, I asked if he had any questions. He said 'yes.' I said 'what?' He said, 'Mas' Fitz, does you hear that singin'? All day I been hearin' singin'.'"

"So?"

"I told you it was a quiet spot. There was nobody singing. Not even a bird, this early in the spring. Do you reckon the kid's bad experience with that buggerous Wheeler has sent him a little bit daft?"

6

ABOUT A MONTH LATER, there arrived on the tober a grand, gilded, four-horse coach with the imperial arms emblazoned on its doors, from one of which emerged a splendidly liveried steward bearing an ornate staff of office. He wielded that staff to part the crowd of people on the midway as, looking much offended by the sights, noises and smells about him, he made his way to the Florilegium's office wagon, where he rapped the staff on the door. Happily for the man's evident sensibilities, it was Florian who stuck his head out, not Magpie Maggie Hag. The steward handed him an immense envelope and, with an expression of strained politeness, waited while Florian broke the elaborate seal, read the large card it contained and asked of him a few questions.

When the steward was fastidiously edging through the crowd again to return to his coach, Florian was already dashing about to show the card to everybody of the troupe, and to translate for them its elegantly hand-inscribed message:

"'His K. K. Apostolic Majesty has condescended—'"

"What's kay-kay?" asked Clover Lee.

"Kaiserlich-Königlich. Imperial and Royal," Florian said impatiently. "I'll begin again. 'His Imperial and Royal Apostolic Majesty has condescended, in accordance with his All Highest decision, and in amiable consideration of your contribution to the public welfare in entertaining the unfortunates of the Brünlfeld Insane Asylum'"—he had to pause to take breath—"'most graciously to invite you to present a performance of your company at the palace of Schönbrunn at three o'clock in the afternoon of May third.'"

"That is all one sentence?" asked Maurice. "He is longer-winded even than you are, Monsieur le Gouverneur."

"Well, you know bureaucrats. Franz Joseph is popularly known as the Premier Bureaucrat of Europe."

"And what is Schönbrunn?" asked Edge. "I thought the royal family lived in the Hofburg."

"Schönbrunn is Their Majesties' summer palace and estate, on the farther side of the city. I am glad, now, that he waited to invite us until the family moved from the Hofburg. There we should have had to perform indoors or in a courtyard. On the vast grounds of Schönbrunn we can set up all three of our tops, and also include in the show a balloon ascension. Note, too, the thoughtfulness of the emperor. He invites us on the third of May."

"Why is that thoughtful?" asked Fitzfarris. "It'll be just another Sunday."

"His Majesty is clearly aware that we would not want to leave the Prater until after the first of May, for that is Saint Brigitte's Day. It should be the most crowded and profitable occasion of our whole long stand here. Saint Brigitte's Day begins the Blumenkorso, the festival of flowers, and all the Viennese come to parade in their finery through the Prater. Even folk who never leave the city during the rest of the year would feel mean and disgraced if they did not come out here on that holiday. It is also the day on which all the joints and entresorts of the Wurstelprater reopen for the summer. So we shall do a booming business on the first of May, and the emperor considerately allows the next day for our preparations to set up at Schönbrunn on the day following." Florian gazed fondly at the card he held, and added, "I believe I shall eventually have this billet d'invitation framed, to hang in my office."

"Surely the emperor did not write that himself," said Pfeifer.

"No, of course not. It is written and signed on his behalf by some court chamberlain. But below the message the scribe has appended all fifty-six of Franz Joseph's titles. Emperor of Austria, Apostolic King of Hungary, King of Jerusalem, of Bohemia, of Dalmatia, and so on. A thing worth keeping and treasuring, I think. Now then. We have four weeks to prepare for this command performance. Monsieur Roulette, do any varnishing or polishing the *Saratoga* may require to put it in tiptop shape. The rest of you work on any new acts you may have in mind, and do the ultimate refining of all your old ones."

The Florilegium had already, and recently, added several new turns to its pista program. Finding and buying another velocipede had been no problem, and

Shadid Sarkioglu had volunteered to be the one to learn to ride it. He had soon done that and, though the Turk was too big and bulky to be as nimble as Cecil had been in the trick riding of it, he was easily able to support Daphne while she did her acrobatics on his shoulders—and he just as fearlessly closed the act by hurtling over the high steering bar into the flaming vat. Daphne also did a solo skating-without-ice exhibition, until Goesle found, somewhere in the city, another pair of the wooden-wheel skates. Florian would have given them to the Hanswurst or the Kesperle, to learn to accompany Daphne, but the newest member of the company, Jean-François Pemjean, begged to be allowed to use them to create an entirely novel kind of act.

It was Pemjean, le Démon Débonnaire, who had contrived most of the show's new turns—with some small assistance, not grudging but wistful, from the demoted Barnacle Bill, whenever he was sober enough to assist. Pemjean decreed that Maximus was too old to learn any additional tricks, but he almost magically quickly taught the three tigers to do all the sits and stands and leaps and playing-dead that the old lion had always done. So, in performance, Maximus would be brought on first to do his solo stint—much appreciated by the jossers, as always. Then the jossers would be even more thrilled when Raja, Rani and Siva were brought on to do those same tricks in simultaneous trio—concluding with a leap in sequence, one right behind another, through the fiery hoop.

Further, Pemjean managed to make useful even the two stupid and irascible ostriches. He designed light harnesses for them and somehow got Hansel and Gretel accustomed to wearing them. Thereafter, at the opening and close of every show, the big birds were liberated from their cage and hitched to the menagerie's lightest wagon—the one containing the hyenas—and made to draw it around the chapiteau during the Grand Promenades. Though gawky and graceless, they were definitely eye-catching additions to the spectacles.

But le Démon Débonnaire achieved his greatest success with the two Syrian bears. Barnacle Bill had never got beyond teaching Kewwy-dee to stand on his hind legs and suck sugar water from his toy trumpet while a real windjammer provided his "playing." Pemjean taught Kewwy-dah, the she-bear, to stand on her hind legs *and* on the new-bought pair of Plimpton rolling skates, for which Goesle made and attached special canvas boots. Then Pemjean proposed to Daphne that Kewwy-dah take her departed husband's place as her partner on the skating board.

"Monsieur le Démon!" she exclaimed, aghast. "You must think me feebleminded. Isn't it bad enough that I am a grass widow? I don't yearn to hurry into a grave *beneath* the grass."

"Fear not, fair lady. Kewwy-dah will be much too occupied with keeping her balance to think of giving you a bear hug. Also, she is muzzled, her claws are blunted, and I will be always standing close by. You simply take her by the paws, as if she were a dancing partner, and yourself do the impulsion to make her wheel about in concert with you."

It took a good deal more of his persuasion, but finally, bravely, apprehensively, Daphne made the attempt—and was reassured and surprised and delighted with the result. Though she had to exert all the effort and skill, it looked to the bystanders as if Kewwy-dah really was doing her own skating back and forth and sideways and roundabout. Meanwhile, off to one side, Kewwy-dee with his trumpet apparently helped the band provide the "Oh, Emma! Whoa, Emma!"

countess and I both speak English, besides other languages, if needed. You and your Baron Lothar von Wittelsbach and your four chief subordinates will dine with the emperor himself in the Konspirationstafelstube. You will be seated on His Majesty's right, Wittelsbach to his left. The Princess Caroline von und zu Liechtenstein will be your vis-à-vis. The Countess Marie Larisch will be the baron's. All very informal, of course."

"Of course," Florian said, somewhat faintly.

"You will none of you be expected to dress, on such short notice."

"We are inestimably honored by His Majesty's favor and regard, Eure Hoheit."

When the royals and nobles emerged from the palace to cross the lawn to the chapiteau, the emperor exemplified the "informality" of the occasion. Though he was now garbed in a crisp, well-tailored uniform of white tunic and red trousers, with an abundance of gold braid on it, he wore only one of his decorations: the red and green band of the Order of St. Stephan. And the little Crown Prince Rudolf wore a miniature version of his father's uniform, with only the chain of the Order of the Golden Fleece. But the other male courtiers and high army officers who streamed out of the palace were impeccably full-dressed in brilliant uniforms—Hussar pink and sky blue, Tirolean Rifle silver green, Arciere Guard crimson and gold—and were very nearly armor-plated with the quantities of medals overlapping on their breasts. The ladies were equally resplendent in modish crinolette gowns of silk and taffeta and brocade. The numerous court children wore not boyish short hosen or girlish pantalettes but scaled-down facsimiles of their parents' full-length finery. When the audience had assembled in the chapiteau—and they were so many that they almost half-filled it, the lesser ranks uncomplainingly taking the tiers of plain board seats—they quite outglittered even the spangled costumes of the artistes.

Everyone stood, the officers at the salute, Franz Joseph and Rudolf with humbly bowed heads, while Beck's band opened the program by playing the "God Preserve Our Emperor" anthem, accompanied distantly but more than audibly by the calliope up on the hill. Abdullah had earlier brought the two elephants into the pista, so, with up-curled trunks, they also saluted the man and boy in the seats of honor. But thereafter, everyone relaxed, and the august audience applauded the dancing girls and the come-in spec and every subsequent act as boisterously as any tentful of commoners had ever done.

The show went with clockwork precision and smoothness and never a mishap. At intermission, the *Saratoga* wafted beautifully from the Gloriette, and dreamily waltzed about the sky. After vanishing "the Fräulein Simms," Fitzfarris presented his sideshow and then, to many of the men and not a few women, his Amazon-and-Fafnir tableau vivant. Magpie Maggie Hag went about, reading the palms of Prinzessinnen and Grafinnen and Baroninnen, promising every lady a life of joy and romance and riches. The balloon descended as lightly as a dandelion fluff on the tober, and revealed the reappeared "Fräulein Simms" to general astonishment and acclaim. The pista program resumed, and again went perfectly, and closed with a reprise of the anthem. Then, while the audience returned to the palace, chattering and laughing, there was quite a crush of the troupers at the dressing-room wagon, all eager to get into their best civilian clothes. Florian was prompted to tell Dai Goesle, "Make a note, Canvasmaster. We must soon procure two new tops, a dressing tent each for men and women."

When all were clad in their best—though a poor second-best to their hosts—
the deputy marshal of ceremonies came to escort them into the palace. They
went, most of them craning and gawking like jossers, through the great Spiegelsaal, where the entirely mirrored, high, long wall opposite the window wall made
the hall look twice as enormous as it already was, and twice as full of crystal-cascade chandeliers and golden nymphs holding candelabra. Carl Beck traversed
the chamber practically genuflecting at every step and in a hushed voice explained why: "Here it was that the young Mozart his very first court recital
gave."

Quincy Simms said, more pragmatically, to nobody in particular, "What dey
go' give us to eat? I smells sowbelly fryin'."

"Sowbelly?" said Pemjean. "Qu'est-ce que c'est?"

"Salt pork fat," Rouleau translated. "Darky food."

"Ali Baba, you couldn't possibly smell any such thing," said Florian. "For one
reason, the kitchens of every palace in Europe are in a separate building—just
so the smells and the smoke are kept well away. Also the flies and any hazard of
fire."

Every room of the palace was replete with works of art—statues, busts, tapestries, paintings—the greater number of them portraying members of the royal
family, from Maria Theresa to the current occupants. Zachary Edge was not at
all knowledgeable about art, and not particularly susceptible to it, but there was
something about a number of the portraits and busts that gave him a spooky
feeling of having seen them somewhere before. He would have made inquiry of
their escort, but the count was courteously giving a commentary on the rooms
into which he shepherded the separate groups of artistes.

"Meine Damen, you will dine here in the Blue Chinese Room. I invite your
attention to the scenes of Chinese life inset in the wallpaper panels. The figures
of the men and women are painted with a phosphor paint. When the room
darkens and the attendants bring in candles, you will see those figures glow and
seem to move."

Ushering the male artistes into a room of panels so glossy that they reflected
almost as brightly as the Hall of Mirrors, he said, "Meine Herren, please to
observe the perfection of this Vieux-Laque Room. Every one of those panels was
done aboard a ship, well out at sea, so that not a speck of dust could mar the
immaculacy of the lacquer."

The last room—the one to which he escorted Florian, Willi, Edge, Beck,
Goesle and Fitzfarris—was the smallest they had yet seen, though by no means
small, and it was oval, and on that room the count seemed to have no comment
to make. But Fitzfarris did, when Stockau had left them: "The other rooms each
had a dining table. This one's only got chairs. Do we eat off our laps?"

"Only wait," said Beck. "Of this room I have heard. In it Maria Theresa in
secret with her counselors dined. So not even servants should enter."

Just then, Franz Joseph came in, with half a dozen women, most of them
young and handsome. As the Countess Larisch introduced herself and the other
ladies, in English, the emperor gravely pulled a bell rope. The introductions were
interrupted by a grinding and grating noise. A section of the parquet floor slowly
began to slide—nearly taking Dai Goesle with it, before he stepped to one side.

From the considerable gap revealed in the floor, there slowly and majestically rose into sight a damask-covered and fully laid table, complete with its steaming and savory dinner, with napery, porcelain, crystal and plate. There were exclamations and general applause, and Franz Joseph's usually impassive face allowed itself a small smile.

The men brought chairs from against the wall and seated the ladies and themselves in the order Count Stockau had specified, and everyone began immediately to eat, because, the several courses having been served all at once, the soup had to be ingested in a hurry before the rest of the meal got cold. In truth, as the six circus men agreed later, it was neither a very memorable meal nor a very stimulating gathering. The only wine provided was the cheap Heuriger which any least tramp might be drinking in a Wienerwald tavern. And, since the emperor drank only iced water, the others felt constrained to limit their intake even of the mild wine. The meal's pièce de résistance was the common Backhendl, the roast chicken that was certainly on every Austrian bürger's table this Sunday, as it was every Sunday of the year.

The table talk was similarly rather dreary. Florian, Willi and Beck were able to converse in German, and Edge found that he and his vis-à-vis, a young and fairly pretty Baronin Helene Vetsera, had enough French between them to murmur banalities back and forth. But Goesle and Fitzfarris had only English, and their feminine counterparts had little. Anyway, the table talk was much dampened by His Imperial Majesty's taciturnity. On the occasions when he did bestir himself to speak, he did so almost by ventriloquy, directing his remarks to the Princess of Liechtenstein to be passed along.

The first thing he said was, "Wie gesagt—es war schön, der Zirkus. Es hat mich sehr gefreut."

The princess told the others, "His Majesty wishes you all to know that your circus was nice. He liked it very much."

"Besten Dankes, Eure Majestät," said Florian.

Some while later, the emperor told the princess, "Dieser Herr Florian wird Zukunft haben."

"Schönen Dankes, Eure Majestät," said Florian, without waiting for the relay. And later he told his colleagues, "I *assume* it was a compliment—to be told at my advanced age that I 'have a future.' The emperor possesses absolutely no wit or humor, so I doubt that he was being sarcastic. But I swear, I can't remember his making a single other remark during the whole dinner."

Well, anyhow, thought Edge—when the boredom finally ended, and everyone rose, and Franz Joseph again pulled the bell rope, and the table full of litter and picked bones descended into the depths, and the floor returned—if I ever go back to Hart's Bottom, I'll be the only one there who can brag of once eating dinner with an emperor. But nobody will believe it. Hell, probably nobody in Hart's Bottom would know what an emperor is.

The mixed company convened in the Spiegelsaal, and a liveried flunky brought a high-heaped tray, from which Franz Joseph dispensed to each of the troupers a keepsake of the occasion: to the females tiny evening handbags and to the males pocket wallets, all embroidered with the imperial arms in the exquisite Viennese petit point. Thanking him in their various languages, the men bowed and the women curtsied—some of them teetering in the process, for those who had dined with lesser personages had clearly not been discouraged from partaking freely of the wine and even more ardent spirits. Then Count Stockau escorted the troupe out to their tober.

They found the Slovaks even more forthrightly drunk; the dinner in the kitchens must really have been festive. Nevertheless, Florian left those men to do the tearing down, as and when they were capable, under the supervision of glum-sober Goesle and Beck. He appropriated only his rockaway and three wagons to transport the artistes back through the midnight city streets. As if the trip had been a sleigh-ride outing, a number of the passengers sang as they rode, and a few snored, and some—Maurice and Nella, Obie and Agnete—gently wrestled and tipsily giggled, and Monday tried hard to make Fitzfarris do so, and Jean-François Pemjean tried the same with Daphne Wheeler, and with better success.

Florian told Edge, who was riding with him now, "The barges from Budapest are unloading their cargo at the riverfront, and will be ready to load us on the morning after tomorrow."

"How long will this voyage take, Governor?"

"Um... the rest of that day, that night and the next day, I should estimate."

"That's all?" said Edge, with some surprise.

"Well, we will be going downstream with the current helping, and with a steam tugboat pulling. It is only about a hundred and fifty miles from here to Budapest."

Edge said thoughtfully, "No more than maybe the distance from Hart's Bottom to Winchester in Virginia. I reckon I'm a country bumpkin, yet. I still think of the capitals of Europe as all being tremendously far apart."

The rockaway and the first of the wagons arrived at the Wurstelprater somewhat in advance of the other two. Those who climbed down from the bed of that wagon, some of them unsteadily, were Magpie Maggie Hag, the Smodlaka family, the Schuhplattler girls, Jean-François Pemjean and Daphne Wheeler. Pavlo Smodlaka was not too intoxicated to take note that Pemjean accompanied Daphne to her caravan, where, after they had done some mutual giggling at the door of it, they went inside together. Pavlo said, under his brandied breath, "Aha."

He left his wife and children to make their own way in the dark to their home caravan, and himself scuttled off to the one shared by Pemjean and the clowns Notkin and Spenz, not yet arrived. There was a lantern left alight, hanging on a nail over its door, so Pavlo took that inside with him, and did not have to hunt very hard for the book he sought; it was lying open on one of the bunks, as if Pemjean had lately been reading in it. Pavlo took it up and peered at its cover, having to close one eye so as not to see it double. Even then, he managed only with difficulty to spell out the title, for it was in English. He said again, this time triumphantly aloud, "Aha!"—and ran out with the book.

In Daphne's caravan—in the dark, for they had not wasted any time in lighting lamp or candle—she and Pemjean were already undressed and entwined. For some while, there was mostly silence, except for soft rustling noises and the soft applosions of kisses. But then suddenly the bunk jerked and thumped and Daphne gave a small shriek.

"Eeek! My God, Jean, what are you doing?"

"Aïe, ma chère, am I doing it wrong?"

"Wrong!? What a question! What you are doing is horrid!"

"Hélas. Let me then try it from this direc—"

"Stop that!" There was a noise of her scrambling to cover herself with the bedclothes. "What you are doing is disgusting! Immoral! Unheard of! Obscene! It must be Greek!"

"Ma foi, I only wish to do what—"

"I never suspected you were a pervert!" Half to herself, she said, "I must ask Madame Hag—under what sorry star was I born, that I attract only degenerates?"

"Mais, chérie, I thought you *liked*... well, that sort of thing."

"Horrors upon horrors! Do you take *me* for a pervert? Whatever gave you such a nasty idea?"

"Eh bien... your husband did."

"*What!?*" The whole caravan rocked and creaked as she violently shoved at him. "Get out of here, you filthy frog!"

"I only sought to please. De bonne foi, chérie."

"Get your clothes on and *get out of here!*"

"You see, Gospodja Hag?" said Pavlo excitedly, breathing fumes at her and waving the book at her. "What I said: the Frenchman is a koldunya, a wizard, perhaps a Vampir. Regard, his book of zabranjeno sorcery. I, even I, can read the terrible name of it. *The Book of... Pri-vate... K'now-ledge.* You see? I was right to suspect."

The gypsy grunted and took the volume from him. She held it close to her candle and more fluently read aloud the title, all of it: *"The Book of Private Knowledge and Advice, of the Highest Importance to Individuals in the Detection and Cure of 'A Certain Disease' Which, if Neglected or Improperly Treated, Produces the Most Ruinous Consequences to the Human Constitution.* Charva! You stupid dalmatinski, this not anything of sorcery. This only... medical book."

But Pavlo had comprehended one phrase, and now repeated, with relish, "Certain disease, eh? Aha!"

"Here, imbecile. Put book back before he miss it. And stop sneaking, prying, pilfering where you got no business."

"Da, Gospodja Hag," Pavlo said sweetly. "Forgive me for trouble you." He got the book back where it belonged and got himself away from there, just minutes before the disheveled and disgruntled Pemjean came, muttering, to his own bed.

MAGYARORSZÁG

I

"AN AUSPICIOUS COINCIDENCE, I hope," said Florian, referring to the doughty little sidewheel tugboat that towed their string of barges downriver. "Its name, *Kitartó*, means approximately the same as did that of our previous vessel, the *Pflichttreu*—steadfast, loyal."

"I hope it doesn't mean as many misadventures on the way," said Edge.

He and the other circus chiefs were riding with Florian on the first barge in line. The others of the company were distributed in groups on the following barges, riding with their personal caravans or the wagons or animals they were responsible for. Since there could be no visiting back and forth among the tow-roped flatboats, and no communal cooking, Florian had laid out a good deal of money to have Sacher's in the Prater put up a quantity of "Picknick" baskets for their sustenance on the trip.

So the voyagers were more than merely well wined and dined during the two days and a night that they were afloat, and there were no misadventures, and the river trip was, in still other ways, a very pleasant change from road travel. For one thing, the traffic sharing the Danube was much more various than could be seen on a road—sailboats, rowboats, sidewheel and sternwheel passenger-and-mail boats, fishing skiffs, houseboats, barges and broadhorns laden with every kind of cargo from logs and coal to market produce and even flowers. Also, the surrounding scenery changed more rapidly on the river than on a road. For a while, downstream of Vienna, the river flowed at a good clip between reedy banks backed by forests. But then it widened and slowed, and on both sides were farm fields, in which all the workers seemed to be women—heavy, squat, broad-beamed women in kerchiefs and smocks—wielding hoes and spades and scythes and flails. The farmhouses were as dumpy as the women, mere hovels of mud, sometimes whitewashed. Because every house had a thatched roof and was backed by a haystack as wide as the house and three or four times as high, the houses looked from midstream as if they all wore straw roofs preposterously too big for them.

Then, on the left bank, the farms gave way to vineyards, interspersed with winery sheds and vats and mountains of barrels. Those in turn gave way to scattered workshops and forges that multiplied and got bigger and more crowded together until they were the industrial outskirts of a city. Then the city itself slid into view, quite a big one, of medieval stone and half-timbered buildings with steep-pitched slate roofs, many turrets and spires, innumerable tall chimneys topped with storks on nests. Behind and above the riverside city towered a splendid old castle on a plateau.

"The city of Pózsony," said Florian.

"Called Pressburg in German," said Willi.

"Bratislava," Banat said firmly. "Capital city of my home province, Slovakia. Once was capital of all Hungary."

"In any event," said Florian, "we are here crossing a border of the Dual Monarchy. Behind us, the Österreich—Austria proper. On our left, Austria's province of die Slowakei. On our right, Hungary—or Magyarország. It is spelled M-A-G, but pronounced as if it were M-A-D. *Madyar*. You will find other linguistic curiosities in Hungary. For example, Bandmaster, you are now Beck Carl. Or Beck Boom-Boom, if you prefer."

And I'm Fitzfarris John Foursquare?" said that one. "Christ. What kind of a country is it that can't spell its own name and flip-flops everybody else's?"

"You will not encounter many problems," said Willi. "The second language here is German. Except for peasants, everybody speaks it. If you could make your way in Bavaria and Austria, you will do as well in Hungary."

"And there are as many delights as curiosities," Florian assured them all. "But what is the matter, Zachary? Are you not looking forward to our next adventures? You appear slightly doleful."

"Not really. I was just thinking: I'm farther east now than Autumn ever got. And her name here would have been Auburn Autumn. Just as melodious either way."

Three or four barges behind, Monday Simms sat on the steps of her and Fitz's caravan, gloomily and unappreciatively watching Slovakia slide past. Nearby stood Jean-François Pemjean, who had likewise been less than effervescent since the night of the Schönbrunn show. Perhaps seeking to cheer them both up, he made bold to ask Monday why she seemed not to be enjoying the voyage.

Without even looking at him, she muttered ungraciously, "Nobody's bizness."

"Eh bien, if it is nobody's, then I am not butting into anybody's. So tell me."

Monday blinked and turned to gaze at him, trying to grasp the logic of that remark, if it had any. Finally she said, "What's gravelin' me is I'm losin' my man."

"Ah. That would be le bleu Sir John?"

She looked away and nodded forlornly. "He found hisself a white hussy in Vienna. And last night, our very last night there, he spent it with her. And now he's not even ridin' on the same boat with me."

"I am not yet too well acquainted with all the—arrangements among the troupe. Are you and he married?"

"No, cuss it. He never got around to that, neither."

"Alors, it is obvious what you must do. En revanche, find yourself a white man."

She said morosely, "I thought I had."

"He is half-*blue*. It wonders me how a jolie fille like yourself could ever have been attracted to him. Also, he is rather older than you . . . and me."

Monday turned again, very slowly, and regarded Pemjean with some calcula-tion. "Fact is . . ." she said, "I wasn't."

"Comment?"

"Attracted to him. I wasn't. He made me take up with him."

"Comment?"

"See, when I first come on the show, Mr. Demon, I was just a White Pygmy in his sideshow. I wanted to learn the high school ridin'—and to be Mam'selle Cinderella on the rope. But he wouldn't let me loose of the sideshow unless I'd . . . well . . ."

"Scandaleux!" exclaimed Pemjean. "I took Sir John to be a gentleman. But what a bestial, what an *unsubtle* way to seduce." He reached out to stroke her hair. "Pauvre Cendrillon."

"So . . . now that I done been ruined for any other man . . ."

"Mademoiselle!" he said sharply. "Do not speak such prehistoric pruderies to a Frenchman! I, Pemjean, do not regard you as ruined. Only awakened to life's pleasures and possibilities."

"Well, anyhow, I ain't like John Fitz. I can't just hop from one possibility to—"

"Mais oui, you can. It takes but a little imagination, a little daring, a little *French*ness. The which I can very easily teach you."

She regarded him now with open speculation, and murmured, "You a lot handsomer'n he is, too."

"Perhaps also less fickle." He added, more to himself than to her, "I have never before enjoyed une amourette avec une mulâtresse."

The tugboat *Kitartó* now was leading the barge string in a slow dance through the channels winding among numerous midriver islands, and it may have been the perceptible weaving motion that made Monday begin very slightly to chafe her thighs together. Pemjean noticed that, but made no reference to it. Instead, as if changing the subject altogether, he pointed across the darkening fields of Slovakia and said:

"The sun is down, the night draws on. Hélas, I do dread going to bed, for I must share quarters with the Hanswurst who smells like *wurst* and the Kesperle who smells even *worse*. Voilà, how is that for a joke employing two different languages? Mademoiselle Cendrillon, I am trying to make you smile."

She did. She even laughed. Then she stood up on the little steps and opened the caravan door. "Well, Mr. Demon—tonight, anyway—there's a place empty in this-here house wagon."

All night long, the barge string waltzed its way among the river islands, so all the people in their bunks had their sleep or other activity pleasantly enhanced by that gentle rocking. When they arose the next morning, the islands were behind and the Danube was again unimpeded, taking them directly eastward and between the twin cities of Hungary's Komárom on the right bank and Slovakia's Komárno on the left, both consisting mainly of immense, noisy, steaming and smoking shipyards. After that, there was nothing more to see on the left side except the rolling farm fields dotted with kerchiefed peasant drabs. But on the right there were frequent small but brightly painted and sparkling villages, and then the cathedral-dominated town of Esztergom.

There Florian announced, "We have left Slovakia behind. Now it is Hungary on both sides of the river."

As if to emphasize that fact, the land on both banks now rose into high and handsomely forested hills. And the river, as if to show as much as possible of that scenic landscape, curved back and forth—south, east, north, east again—then made a decided bend to the south and continued in that direction, past several more picturesque villages perched on the heights, and two sizable hilltop towns: the many-castle-towered Visegrad and the many-church-towered Szentendre. But south of Szentendre, the greenery began to be interrupted and blemished again by riverside workshops and forges, and then by big industrial buildings, and the sweet-green-scented air got more and more heavily tainted with the yeasty smell of breweries and the moldy stench of tanneries.

"Ah, the signs of civilization," said Florian. "But give the Hungarians credit. They at least locate their manufactories well away from the city and downwind of it."

"Are we there, then?" asked Goesle. "Budapest?"

"In a sense. There are actually three cities. We are now passing Óbuda—Old Buda—on the right. Shortly we shall come to Buda itself, also on the right bank, and we shall have to land there briefly for the immigration formalities. But Buda is so hilly that we should be hard put to find a flat place to pitch. So the *Kotartó* will next tow us across the river to the plains city of Pest, and there we will disembark and make parade to our tober."

The Danube suddenly parted around an island as sharp-prowed as a ship and, like a ship churning upstream, throwing a white bow wave. The tug took the river fork to the right of it and chugged along past the island, which was many times longer than any ship ever built. It was mostly wooded, but here and there a spindly derrick stood higher than the trees, and there were also visible scaffolded big buildings under construction.

"Margit's Island," said Willi. "Saint Margit is buried there. That was the island's chief distinction until just two years ago, when drillers discovered hot and mineral springs. So now there will be grand hotels offering baths to cure every mortal ill. As if there were not already enough spas here."

"Ah?" said Carl Beck, with interest.

The pointed lower end of Margit's Island slid behind, to reveal the great flat city of Pest on the farther shore. And the tiered hillside streets and roads of Buda now loomed on the nearer right bank. The tugboat sidled from midchannel to that shore, lost way and glided up against a tremendously long stone pier, skillfully nestling every following barge alongside it as well. The tug's crewmen jumped ashore to run and do the hitching of all the craft to the pier bollards. Then the circus folk stepped ashore—Pemjean gallantly assisting Monday—to stretch their legs and wait for instructions.

The pier was the river edge of the even more immense, flagstoned Bomba Square, with a church and its appurtenances at one end, government buildings at the other. The landward length of the square was entirely occupied by a great, long, three-story inn, its outbuildings and stables and barns. The main edifice was wavy-roofed, with tiles undulating over its dormer windows, and there was a big, white-painted wooden cross hung for a sign above its central door.

"The venerable and far-famed White Cross Inn," said Florian. "Terminus of the stage line from Vienna, as well as the destination of river travelers. I must report our arrival to the customs and immigration officers in there."

So he went across the square to the inn, carrying the considerable stack of conduct books. All the other circus folk strolled about, taking in what sights they could see from river level. On the other shore, Pest looked to be only ranks and files of ordinary city buildings, except where the occasional dome or spire broke the monotony. But on this Buda side of the Danube, above them and a little to the south, rose an immense hill, with stone stairs and bastion walls zigzagging from the bottom to the walls of a massive castle on top. From somewhere near the base of that hill, a graceful suspension bridge arced across the river to Pest. Beyond the bridge, on this side of the river, rose another high hill, topped with a sprawling walled fort.

"This closer height is Castle Hill," said Willi Lothar. "That is the celebrated Chain Bridge spanning the river, a masterpiece of engineering. You will note that it is suspended by chains, not cables. And beyond it is Saint Gellért's Hill, with the Citadel on top."

"As well as I can see from here," said Yount, "that bridge ends right up *against* this Castle Hill."

"It doesn't end," said Willi. "Its roadbed enters a tunnel on this side, whence the road winds upward to the summit and the castle. The locals have a joke. They will tell you that they treasure their Chain Bridge so much that, when rain falls, they draw it inside the tunnel to save it from rusting."

Florian emerged from the inn and trudged across the square, looking somewhat discomfited, to rejoin the troupe.

"Alas," he said. "Unlike the easygoing new nation of Italy, Hungary appears eager to assert its newly granted measure of sovereignty. It is doing that with a show of fussy officiousness. For one thing, you must each go separately to show your conduct book, answer any questions, radiate good character and so forth. For another thing, these officials are stubbornly speaking only Magyar. So I shall stand by to interpret."

The troupers and crewmen filed through the room off the inn's vestibule that was doing duty as an immigration office. The questioning was not really rigorous or searching, mostly a perfunctory verification of the particulars already set forth in the conduct books: name, age, occupation and the like. For most of the new arrivals, the only thing that momentarily caught them off guard was their being addressed hind-name-first. But one of the men had to cope with a little more than that.

"Geezle Dai?" barked the uniformed official.

"Jesus," growled Stitches. "Dai *Gwell*. I mean, excuse me, sir, Goesle Dai."

"Ejha, *Gwell*. Goesle úr, vallás Dissenting Methodist. Mi az?"

Florian stepped in to say, "Ah ... Methodist jelent metodista."

"És *dissenting*? Elszakadás?"

Florian pretended to hold a quick conference with Goesle. Then he told the officials, in Magyar, "Dissenting means that Goesle Dai is breaking away from the vile Protestant Methodism to return to the forgiving arms of Mother Church."

"Éljen!" all the uniformed men cried enthusiastically, and stood up to pump the mystified Dai's hand and beam at him and wish him "isten hozott!" And they gave barely a glance at the books of the remaining troupers, but waved them cordially past.

Florian consulted his old tin watch and said, "As long as we are here in the inn, and it is getting on for dinnertime, let us dine. Abdullah, run back to the *Kotartó* and ask the captain—you can do it with gestures—if he and his men would care to join us before they take us across the river."

The tugboat crew came with alacrity and appetite. In the vast, smoky, low-beamed dining hall, they and Willi and Florian, who could converse with them, took one of the long trestle tables. The rest of the company disposed themselves around other tables and had their first taste of Magyar cuisine. There was no carte to order from; the handsomely plump waiter girls simply fetched the meal of the day. And the White Cross Inn was accustomed to resuscitating weary travelers, so the meal was rich and ample. It began with Drunkard's Soup, a concoction intended to counter the traveler's long overreliance on his pocket flask.

Quincy Simms took a wary taste of the pale green substance, made a face and said, "Ugh. Fish soup."

"You must be crazy, Quince," said his sister Sunday. "It's made of sauerkraut. You've had sauerkraut often enough to recognize it. And it's good."

Quincy looked puzzled, but mumbled, "Tas' like fish to me," and pushed his bowl away.

Next came Robber's Meat, chunks of lamb, onions, mushrooms, tomatoes and green peppers alternated on a skewer and cooked over an open fire. That was served with little pinched dumplings and potatoes stewed in a paprikás sauce. The meal was accompanied by jugs of black coffee and bottles of assorted wines, from yellow Tokaji to the dark red Bull's Blood. The sweet was Friar's Ears, half-moon tarts filled with plum jam. And afterward more coffee was set on the tables, and more bottles: apricot, apple and pear brandies.

When the company all lurched heavily out of the inn to return to the barges, LeVie remarked to Florian, "I hope, Monsieur le Gouverneur, that we are not now going to make parade. I believe I could not even lift an arm to wave."

"No fear," said Florian. "We shall roll the wagons and vans ashore, attend to the animals, then get a night's sleep and make parade in the morning."

It was full dark now, so the tug's crewmen hung riding lanterns on their own boat and on every barge, and the tugboat's steam horn repeatedly hooted as it towed its string across the broad river on a downstream slant, somehow never colliding with any of the other vessels going up and down and across the Danube. The diagonal course took the circus flotilla under the Chain Bridge, which had become a magically suspended chain of peach-tinted white gas lamps. The long bridge was so high above the water, and so well constructed, that the circus folk gawking up at it could not hear a sound of the horse-drawn carts, carriages and wagons continuously going to and fro along it.

But not everybody of the troupe was admiring the view. Fitzfarris was now riding on the same barge with Monday, and she sat him down on the steps of their caravan and talked to him very earnestly, with many dramatic gesticulations. Then she beckoned for Pemjean to join them, and he also talked very earnestly, with many Gallic gesticulations. Fitzfarris sat and listened, looking slightly stunned but perhaps a little relieved and even a little amused. Only once did he frown, when Pemjean wound up his persuasive argument by saying:

"I think you will agree, ami, that you have no real claim on the young lady— you having employed contrainte to bend her to your will in the first place."

"What exactly is contrainte?" Fitz asked coldly. "Wait, don't tell me, let me guess. Blackmail?"

"Er... oui. Duress. Coercion. Denying her the chance to advance her career unless she submitted to—"

Fitzfarris laughed, but mirthlessly. "Yes, that would have been ungentlemanly of me, wouldn't it? That would have been almost Zanni-like, wouldn't it, Monday?"

But Monday was suddenly absorbed in studying the constellations of the night sky, and apparently did not hear.

"Il n'importe pas," said Pemjean, a trifle uncertainly. "It will be overlooked. Forgotten. I trust we shall all three remain bon amis and—"

"Oh, I wouldn't entirely forget it, if I were you, friend. But I wish you joy of her."

So, before the farther riverbank was reached, Fitzfarris and Pemjean were going back and forth between their two living quarters, shifting their personal belongings.

On a barge farther back in the string, Spyros Vasilakis was urinating over the low gunwale. He would not have done it so publicly, but he had drunk deep of the good Tokaji. And now he was doing it with much groaning and writhing, holding onto the barge's riding-lamp pole for support, and nearly wrenching it from its socket in his agonies.

"Ah, there, Spyros!" boomed Pavlo Smodlaka, abruptly appearing out of the darkness and grinning sympathetically. "You have pain in pissing, da?" Spyros nodded, embarrassed. "Do you not know what that means? You have caught der Tripper, the nasmork, the Parisian head cold."

"Eh?" said Spyros.

"I believe it is called in your language the khonorrein."

"Eh?" exclaimed Spyros, galvanized.

"Have you been doing yébla with one of Monsieur le Démon's women?"

"Eh?" said Spyros, horrified.

Pavlo, helpfully, friendlily told him about Pemjean's secret book dealing with "a certain disease." Pavlo went on to expatiate on the filthiness of Frenchmen, and to commiserate with Spyros on his having somehow contracted the demon's shameful disease. But Spyros, with a grimace and an effort, interrupted his painful dribbling and went hastily off, still buttoning his trousers, in search of his wife.

However, just then, the tug and its string of barges glided alongside another long stone pier at Pest, and much bustle and commotion ensued. The crewmen tied up all the craft, then willingly joined the circus roustabouts to roll the wagons and vans off the barges, and to lead off the horses, camel and elephants. It took two hours or so for everything and everybody to disembark and move inland from the pier to the Corso, the big square fronting on it. The vehicles were neatly ranked there, and the uncaged animals tethered, and all the animals fed and watered. Then most of the troupers and roustabouts fell gratefully onto their beds or pallets—Fitzfarris causing Notkin and Spenz to grunt with surprise when he entered their caravan and, without explanation, flopped onto what had been Pemjean's bunk.

The lamp burned long in only one caravan, that of the Vasilakises, and the occupants of other vans nearby were kept awake for some while by the noise in there. Most of the noise was Spyros's rabid shouting, but some of it was Meli's loud weeping, and that was interspersed with violent slaps when he hit her. Spyros was wielding one of his swords, but considerately using only the flat of it, and hitting Meli only between long spates of Greek imprecations, and only in places that would not show when she donned her parade costume.

But finally she stopped him by pleading, "If I confess my guilt, will you please not hit me again? Then I confess it. Yes, I *did* what you accuse me of doing, but—"

"You whore! When I come back I will use the edge of the blade! It cannot hurt you worse than my poor peos hurts me. But first I kill him!"

"No, no! It was *not* Monsieur Pemjean!"

If Spyros heard that, he did not heed it, but bolted out into the night. It took him a minute or two to find the caravan he sought, and he smashed through the door, felt for Pemjean's bunk, jabbed with the point of his sword and bellowed, "Get up, French! I bring death!"

"*Ow! Je-SUS!*" roared Fitzfarris, scrambling to flatten himself against the back wall of the bunk. There was also scrambling on the other side of the van, and one of the clowns struck a match.

"Sir John?" said Spyros, nonplussed. "It was you betray me?"

"What? You crazy son of a bitch! Somebody light a lamp!"

Notkin did that, while Spyros persisted, "Sir John, it was you beds my wife behind my back?"

"Are you sleepwalking, you dumb Greek? And with a sword? Look, my rump is *bleeding*. One of you joeys take that weapon away from him."

Neither of the clowns made a move, but watched in terror. Fitz edged out of his bunk—his long underwear now wet red at the back flap—and said, as reasonably as he could, "Spyros, wake up. You're having a nightmare. This is me, your friend Foursquare John."

"Yes...you friend," Spyros said stupidly. "You no touch Meli. 'Scuse, Sir John. I go find Pemjean and kill him."

He turned to leave. Fitzfarris made a dive, wrested the sword from his hand and held onto him. "You're still dreaming, man. Wake up and tell me—what's all this about Meli? You haven't stuck *her*, have you?"

"Not yet. Later. Pemjean first."

"Have you got some notion that Meli and Pemjean have been...carrying on?" Spyros nodded numbly and began to cry. "Well, I'm here to tell you that it just plain is not so. Pemjean's been too busy courting somebody else. I can prove it. He and I made a gentleman's agreement this very night. He's moved in with Monday that used to be my woman."

"Is true, Sir John?" said Spyros, sniffling.

"Is true. If Meli's been cheating on you—which I doubt—you'd better get her to identify the proper party, instead of you running around in the dark sticking innocent people. Here, I'll walk you back and we'll have a word with her. Let me get some pants on."

Meli was standing in the lamplit doorway of the caravan, unkempt, distraught, wringing her hands, looking searchingly out over the Corso, and she leapt for joy as they approached. "Oh, Sir John, you caught him," she wailed. "Has my poor dear Spyros made murder? Please God, say no."

"No, ma'am. Only mayhem," Fitzfarris said. "Let's all go inside and not keep the whole troupe awake and interested."

"I tried tell him," she moaned, as Fitz shoved the now wilted and penitent Spyros in and shut the door. "Was not the Monsieur Pemjean."

"I think I've convinced him of that," said Fitz, tossing the sword into a corner. "And I know, Meli, that you'd never—"

"Was the Terrible Turk," she said, with a sob.

"Meli!" Fitz exclaimed, thunderstruck.

"Woman!" bawled her husband, rekindled. "You did such thing with sworn *enemy?*"

"Oh, Spyros, Spyros . . . so he not *be* our enemy."

"What the hell do you mean, enemy?" Fitzfarris demanded. "Are you both still asleep and dreaming, or am I?"

Meli explained. It took her quite a time, and Spyros erupted at intervals, but Fitz effectively shushed him. Meli concluded, "I thought I did for the best—for us both, husband." And they were all three silent for a minute.

Then Fitzfarris cleared his throat and said, "You must realize, Meli, Spyros— if the rest of us had suspected that Shadid was a menace to you, we sure would have got rid of him in a hurry. Hell, I didn't even know that the Greeks and Turks had been at war. None of this need have happened, or gone on for so long." He cleared his throat again. "But what's done is done. As soon as I get a chance tomorrow, I'll have a word with Florian. Shadid will never pester you again, Meli, I guarantee that. And Spyros, I hope you can find it in your heart to forgive Meli—and thank her—for all she went through on your behalf."

Fitz stood up from where he sat, trying to look the staunch and noble family friend, but that fine effect was spoiled when the chair got up with him. Then his bloody seat unstuck and the chair fell back to the floor.

"Idoú!" cried Meli. "You are wounded! Let me fix."

So Fitz had to wait and take down his pants and unflap his underwear and be doctored and bandaged before he could return to his quarters. Notkin and Spenz were waiting awake, with the lamp still lit, and they made inquisitive noises when he came in, but he ignored them and toppled asleep on his messy bunk.

The first circus people to get up next morning were Willi Lothar, Dai Goesle, Aleksandr Banat, the roustabouts and the midway entrepreneurs, so Willi could lead them, and all the vehicles not wanted in the parade, to the tober he had secured in Pest's City Park, a couple of miles inland from the Corso. When the others of the company arose, they breakfasted on what food and wine remained in their traveling baskets, and Florian waited to form the parade until the streets were full of people. When the parade did leave the Corso, it went through some narrow river-district streets until it came to the broad Avenue Sugár where the fast-gathering throngs could really see and appreciate it. As usual, Florian led the procession, with the band in a wagon just behind him, playing lustily, and the calliope bringing up the very rear of the train, playing more than lustily. But this time the parade had a new component, and that one did not stay in line.

It was the Terrible Turk, riding the velocipede, and he was everywhere. Maniacally clowning and making faces, he wheeled back and forth along the line of march, sometimes ahead, sometimes behind, often weaving in and out among the vehicles and the flip-flopping three Chinese and the plodding elephants and camel. He made darts at the watching crowds, sending people fleeing and squealing in delighted terror. He sometimes pedaled backwards, frequently rolled along tilted up on his rear wheel, and sometimes rode without holding the steering bar, his arms carelessly folded. He rode in and out of shop doorways and, wherever a building was fronted with streetside low stairs, he bounced the velocipede up and down them.

"He was a tremendous success!" Florian exulted, when the parade disbanded at the tober, and all the city folk who had trailed it there converged on the red wagon to clamor for tickets to the first show. "Shadid must be a regular fixture of the parade from now on."

Fitzfarris said, "I'd like to speak to you about him, Governor."

"Later, please, Sir John. We've already got a straw crowd here. Let's hold them. The midway joints are pretty well ready for business. So get your fire-eater spouting under the banner line, and you spout your German patter. That'll serve to keep the jossers spending until show time."

"You're the governor, Governor," said Fitz, and went off to find his fire-eater.

All three tops were already up, and their banners flapping, and most of the Slovaks were working on the seats inside the chapiteau. The stallkeepers were firing their braziers, setting up their kegs of beer and tubs of lemonade, setting out their slum for sale. The calliope had stopped at the entrance to the midway and was continuing to hoot and shriek until the chapiteau's bandstand should be ready for Beck and his windjammers to climb into it and commence more musical music. The other parade wagons were being maneuvered by their drivers around behind the chapiteau to take their accustomed places in the backyard. The artistes had all scattered to unload their props, rigs, animals, whatever, from where they had been stowed during the river voyage. Fitzfarris assumed that Spyros was unpacking his bottles of naphtha and olive oil and his other implements, and so wandered among the backyard confusion, looking for him.

But Spyros had gone directly to the Turk's caravan, outside which Shadid stood, toweling off the sweat after his long and active velocipede ride. Spyros there confronted him: "Hey, Turk!"

Shadid looked mildly surprised at the brusqueness of address, but only said contemptuously, "Hey, worm."

"You got der Tripper disease, I think."

"Probably," said the Turk, unruffled. "I usually do. So what?" Then he gave a hearty laugh. "Aha! She got it, too? And gave it to you? How terrible. And a puny man like you, it hurts so you weep, I wager."

"Yes, I weep," said Spyros, plucking his dagger from the back of his belt.

Shadid looked at the shiny blade pointing at him. He could probably have snapped off Spyros's whole arm at the shoulder, and then rammed knife, hand and arm right through the man, but he merely said, with scorn, "You will not stab me."

The blade quivered as Spyros tensed for the thrust. But then, ridiculously, he hiccuped. Shamefaced, he let his arm fall to his side. "You are right, Turk. I am not like you." And he turned and went away, hearing Shadid laugh again behind him.

"Spyros! Where have you been?" Meli asked anxiously, when he returned to their caravan. "Sir John is looking everywhere for you."

"I went again to kill the Turk," he said mournfully. "But I could do no more than tremble at him. The very sight of him makes me sweat, gives me shameful hiccups of fear. I could not kill him."

"Of course not. You are a good man, my husband. A good man does not avenge himself, but forgives his enemies."

"I wanted not to avenge myself, wife Meli, but you."

"Only forgive me, too, Spyros. That will suffice for me. I was not really unfaithful to you, and I will not be, ever."

"I know. I know. You are a better woman than I am a man."

"Be only my loving husband. I ask no more. And Sir John has promised that we need not fear or hide, ever again. Idoú—Sir John! He wants you to hurry and start the fire-blowing at the marquee."

"Yes. I go." Spyros started gathering up his gear. "When I come back, Meli, we start all new again. Everything behind us will be left behind us." He hiccuped again, then kissed her, as shyly as a newlywed. She kissed him back. "Go now and give a fine show."

"Where've you been, Spyros?" said Fitzfarris. "Even through a megaphone, my German isn't much of an attraction. Get up there and give me some volcanoes."

"Better than you never see before, Sir John," Spyros said happily. He vaulted to the platform, set out his bottles and lighted his little pine splints, while Fitz began trumpeting toward the midway:

"Meine Herren und Damen! Hersehen der gefrässig Grieche!"

Only a few people had turned to look when Spyros took his first mouthful of naphtha, tilted his head back, pursed his lips and lifted the burning splint. But Fitzfarris was looking, and he did see an eruption unlike any the Gluttonous Greek had ever previously done. Just before Spyros was to blow the mist of naphtha past the splint's flame, he appeared to gulp, and his bulging cheeks ceased for a moment to bulge. Then there came from his mouth only a small puff of flame and a muffled *whoompf!* and not only did his cheeks bulge, but so did much of the rest of him. What the balloon *Saratoga* required hours to do, Spyros did in a split second, as if he had been attached to the generator's force pump and it had instantaneously inflated him. His chest and belly expanded so suddenly and unnaturally that his black fleshings ripped open at a seam. His whole face got bigger, his mouth gaping, his nostrils flaring and his eyes bulging out of his head. After that one meager eructation of flame, smoke gushed from his mouth and nostrils and from behind his eyeballs. Then he fell down, but went on smoking for a long time.

Once more, Fitzfarris visited the Vasilakis caravan. Meli was sitting on the steps, stitching something, and she hailed him gaily: "Where you leave my husband, Sir John?"

"He won't be coming home, Meli," Fitz said gently, and he told her what had happened. "Florian called it a backfire. Like Spyros must have swallowed or inhaled the naphtha somehow."

Meli stared at the ground and murmured, "He say he got hiccups from see the Turk..."

"Well, I suspected that the quarrel with Shadid might have had something to do with it, and I told the Governor so. I told him the whole story. And the Turk is gone. Florian paid him off like that"—Fitz snapped his fingers—"and Shadid was leaving, cussing fit to turn the air blue, when I came over here. You'll never see him again, Meli. Now...if you'd like to see Spyros one last time...Maggie Hag has, uh, tidied him up, and he's laid out in the red wagon until arrangements can be made. Maggie'll come back here with you, to keep you company while—"

"No," Meli said firmly. "You lost much of sideshow, Sir John. You kind to us. I not fail you also. Spyros not want that. Like usual, I be Medusa at intermission, and after show I do Maiden-and-Dragon."

"That's brave of you, but it's not necessary. I'm sure Clover Lee would agree to go on as Bathsheba again, and—"

"I Greek woman," Meli said, holding her head high. "Always since Troy, Greek women know how best mourn death. Go on with life."

2

So, from the Florilegium's opening day in Pest, its program was again diminished. During the main show, Yount had to resume his old Quakemaker solo act, and he resumed doing the tug-of-war with Brutus to replace his contest of strength with the Terrible Turk. During the sideshow, Sir John had only two real acts to present—his own ventriloquy with Little Miss Mitten and Medusa with her snakes—all his other attractions being merely inert exhibits: the Night Children, the Egyptian Princess mummy, his own tattooed self, and the Auerhahn, or the siketfajd, as he learned it was called here in Hungary.

Yount volunteered to spend his spare time learning to pedal the velocipede—and he did, and got at least as good as Shadid had been, though never so nimble as Cecil Wheeler—and soon he was doing the trick riding on it with Daphne, and before long was even doing the stop-short headlong plunge into the flaming vat. "Not too much different from riding horseback into Custer's guns at Tom's Brook," he said, after his first and, happily, successful try at it.

On that ill-starred opening day, Florian had gone to the nearest police station to report the demise of Spyros Vasilakis, and his report had been received with none of the instant, intense interest and suspicion and investigation it might have aroused back in Austria or Bavaria. The police only languidly made a note of the occurrence and suggested that Florian might tear up the dead man's conduct book, please, when he got around to it. Then Florian was let depart without any questions or any demand for an inquest or even any official person's taking a look at the corpse to ascertain that Spyros was in fact dead. Next, Florian had gone to arrange for the burial in the local Greek-Macedonian cemetery. And, with Meli's permission, the funeral had been conducted without any colorful or noisy circus pomp, so as not to attract public attention and perhaps cast a superstitious pall over the Florilegium's whole stay in Budapest.

Neither that tragedy nor the resultant abbreviation of the show kept anybody away; the local folk continued to attend in sfondone numbers, and applauded unreservedly. The troupers noticed one interesting thing about these audiences: there seemed to be a tradition in Hungary that pretzels were the only approved, accepted and fashionable snack to eat at intermissions of an entertainment. Every time the chapiteau emptied out for the interval between halves, everybody in the audience, young and old, swarmed to the midway stalls selling those big, coarse-salted, brittle twists. Then they all, even the most dignified and best-dressed dowagers, walked about munching the pretzels while they shopped at the other midway joints or watched the sideshow or sat down to have their salty palms read by Magpie Maggie Hag. The males, including the smallest boys, also smoked czigaretta while they ate their pretzels.

The circus people were as pleased with Budapest as Budapest clearly was with them. Pest's City Park made a delightful tober. It was smaller than the Prater in Vienna, but contained every kind of landscape from bosky wildwoods to velvet lawns, brilliant flower beds, ponds with swans, fountains and cascades, bridle paths and walkways. This park, too, had at one end a small amusement area of carousel, swinging-boat wheel, children's playground and numerous entresort booths. At an aloof distance from all that activity stood the elegant and gracious Gundel's Restaurant. Its several dining rooms were rich with paneled walls, leather and plush, chandeliers above and candelabra on the tables; its waiters were tailcoated and unobtrusively efficient; in its kitchens were the best chefs cooking the finest viands to be had in either Pest or Buda. The circus troupers dined there as often as they could take the time to dress as handsomely as those surroundings deserved.

"The Hungarians have a saying," mused Florian on one visit, after a meal that began with Bugac almond apéritif and cold sour-cherry soup, proceeding through pike-perch in cucumber sauce, a gypsy gulyás of chunks of many meats, layered asparagus and mushrooms, noodles in cream with caraway and green paprika, and Aszú Tokaji to wash it all down, concluding with Indianer chocolate-covered cream puffs, Turkey coffee brewed with rose water and finally apricot brandy. "The Hungarians say, 'If we could afford to live as well as we live, ah! how well we should live!'"

The circus folk often entertained themselves with the city folk's own favorite diversion: simply strolling about the streets and squares and boulevards. The men of the company did that mainly to admire the many local females strolling to *be* admired. More than anywhere the Florilegium had yet been, there were here to be seen ravishingly beautiful, high-breasted, long-legged women and girls. Even the barely pubescent girl children were as pretty as filly foals. And none of those females, from budding nymphet to full-ripe matron, wore under her summer blouse anything like a corset cover or bandeau.

"Good heavens!" said Daphne, when she first went downtown. "You can make out their very nipples. Not even in Paris have I ever seen *respectable* women dress so."

Her companion, Florian, said indulgently, "Why should the unrespectable women be the only free spirits?"

Daphne sniffed. "Well, the Budapest women may be gorgeous and shapely from girlhood to maturity. But they must fade quickly after that. See, the old ones are either withered crones or grossly obese."

"Those are peasant women, in from the countryside. You would see the same, my dear, around your Covent Garden market stalls. But do the soignée ladies of London's Mayfair let themselves go to seed or to fat like that? No, and neither do the ladies of civilized Budapest. They grow old gracefully and, after a certain age, do not stroll abroad to be admired, but hold levees at home—well attended by admirers, I assure you."

There were other things to be seen and admired besides the lovely women. Though Pest was a frankly, even flagrantly, commercial city, it was also, as Willi Lothar described it, "a city very livable-in." Almost all the streets were cobbled with stones laid in intricate patterns, and were well lighted at night by decorative multiple gas-lamp standards. There were few tram lines as yet, but there was a brisk traffic of other vehicles, from ox-drawn country drays to imposing four-in-hand coaches. Almost every city square was, by day, a bustling open-air market. From a distance those markets all looked alike—ranks of stalls and carts under bright umbrellas or painted muslin canopies. But they could also be smelled from a distance, and from that distance differentiated as to the wares they sold. One square would waft afar the perfume of flowers brought from the nursery gardens of Margit's Island upstream, and another the fresh aroma of vegetables from the truck gardens of the Csepet Island downstream, and another the less appealing odor of fish hooked and netted from the stream itself.

The numerous cultural attractions of Pest—museums, theatres, art galleries, the Opera—were housed in edifices of magnificently dignified design, and those buildings' walls, columns, arches, cupolas and domes were unadorned by excrescent additions. But the city's far more numerous commercial buildings, though many of those were also architecturally splendid, were much bedizened with flamboyant advertising signs. Every flat wall, even if it was six stories above the street, was a hoarding for ornately lettered, multicolored messages, some of those illustrated with a picture of the product being advertised, or of an eye-catchingly nude female, a winsome baby or a before-and-after bald man and thick-thatched man. Many a building had signs encircling it like ribbons wrapped between every two rows of windows, all the way up its height. And most of the signs were done in duplicate, the Magyar message repeated in German, thus:

OLMOSY FERENC
Gyára
FRANZ OLMOSY
Fabrik

Some of the signboards over the streetside establishments, even if they were written only in Magyar—KAVEHAZ, CZIGARETTA—were comprehensible enough to the newcomers that they could recognize coffeehouses and tobacconists and such, and patronize them. The Kavehaz New-York, actually too palatial and luxurious a place to be calling itself merely a coffeehouse, became the troupe's favorite stop for light refreshment before or after a long stroll through the city. The artistes became known by name to the waiters there, and eventually got used to being addressed in the Magyar style—for example, Maurice was LeVie úr, Gavrila was Smodlaka né, Sunday was Simms kisasszony. The thing they had the most trouble with, for a time, was the local currency. Hungary still honored and used the Austrian Empire's kronen, gulden and kreuzers, but the nation was introducing its own coinage of koronas, forints and fillérs, so the newcomers—and the Hungarians themselves—endured some confusion until they learned to carry the two moneys in separate pockets or purses, and to do quick calculations back and forth between them.

Several of the troupers found other favorite places and things in the city. Down near the Danube quays, Dai Goesle found a raktároz tengerészeti. That was a marine chandlery, and he could no more pronounce the Magyar name than the storekeepers in there could pronounce his, but he and they managed to communicate in some manner. So there he bought the canvas, poles, rope and hardware for making the two new dressing tents Florian wanted. And Dai visited there frequently afterwards, whenever the circus needed some item like a shackle, a turnbuckle, varnish, whatever, and he somehow always came out with the exact item he wanted, in the exactly right size, strength, color or whatever.

The circus women soon discovered the Nagyáruhaz Párizsi, or Warenhaus Pariser, a kind of emporium that those women who had not yet been in Paris had never encountered before. It comprised every kind of shop imaginable, all under one roof and one management, not divided into separate stores but into "departments" ranged over the several floors and mezzanines and interior balconies of the one immense building. There one could buy Scotch whisky, a Turkish rug, a Romanian crucifix, Sicilian silks—anything from a single button to the furnishings for a whole house—so almost all the women of the company found excuse to browse in there at least once a week. When Agnete bought there some of Hungary's own matchless Halas bone lace, Yount was heard to say facetiously, "I don't grudge the money, Lord, no, but it does seem a lot to pay for a cloth full of holes."

Carl Beck spent most of his spare time trying one after another of the huge and stately health spas in the locality. When he was not immersed in some miracle water or mud—in a natural-rock grotto or a Babylonian alabaster pool or a balneo-thermo-magnetic vat—he was either swallowing some patent nostrum or anointing himself with it. He never left or entered the City Park without pausing for a long drink from the public tap at the park gate's marble fountain, fed by a natural hot spring. He forever reeked of the Bánfi Capillary Lotion or the Kneippkura or the Sámson-balzsam smeared on his bald head, and, even at Gundel's or the New-York, he dosed his rose-water coffee with drops from his ever-present phial of Béres Enlivening Elixir.

Groups of the circus folk also went, now and then, down to the riverside

Franz Joseph Square and from there climbed the cobbled incline that led between two gigantic stone lions onto the Chain Bridge. Vehicles using the bridge to cross to or from the lesser city of Buda had to pay a few fillérs for the privilege. The tollkeepers could have taken in a lot more money if they had charged the pedestrians instead, for this was another favored promenade of all the citizens, but those were allowed gratis to indulge their pride in the wondrous structure. Almost all the people crossing it paused for a while midway between the bridge's high stone towers, and there leaned on the railing among the suspension chains to watch the riverboats, far below, going up and down and across the stream. On the Buda side of the bridge, the vehicular traffic had to continue on into the hillside tunnel, but walkers could descend directly onto the riverside quays and streets.

Only in that area was Buda flat enough to provide ground space for buildings purveying goods and services. But the big White Cross Inn was the only sizable enterprise. All the other inns and the shops and markets were small things, compared to those in Pest, and were patronized mainly by residents of the neighborhood, meaning the river workers. Mullenax soon found the Tabán district, where lived all the Danube ferrymen and assorted other hard characters. He thereafter passed most of his spare time—and what should have been working time, as well—sharing with them their preferred potation, a laughably cheap and horrendously noxious Bulgarian gin.

The slopes of Buda were dotted with peasant cottages, and they were pretty, with flower bushes growing from their roof thatch, garlands of red and green paprika looped to dry along their whitewashed walls, and every cottage garden sweetly redolent of basil. The heights of Buda were reserved to monuments and monumental edifices: bronze and stone statues, the royal castle, the Citadel, the Coronation Church. Every visiting group from the circus at least once hired a kocsi to carry them to the top of Gellért's Hill and Castle Hill. But the grim Citadel was a working fortress, and the castle was the seat of government, so sightseers were not allowed inside either of them. The visitors had to be satisfied with leaning on the Fisher's Bastion below the castle, or sitting under the walls of the Citadel, and enjoying the view of Buda below, Pest across the river and the long, shining reach of the Danube.

"This Gellért's Hill," said Florian up there one day, "was named for the missionary bishop who first tried to bring Christianity to the pagans of this place. They did not take to it, or to him, anyway. They drove spikes into all sides of a barrel, stuffed the bishop into it, and rolled him down this hillside to his death and sainthood."

"That sounds like a circus act," Edge commented.

"Then I wish we could resurrect Saint Gellért and his barrel," said Florian. "Do you realize, Zachary—counting the eight Schuhplattler dancers, and not counting the men of the band, we now have more females than males performing?"

"Who's complaining? The females or the males? For the first time since I can remember, they all seem at least to have got their private lives straightened out. No triangles or adulteries going on, no secret seductions or simmering jealousies that I know of."

Edge ticked them off on his fingers. Pemjean and Monday seemed satisfied with each other, and so did Maurice and Nella. Obie and Agnete were clearly happy together; so were Jules and Willi. Fitzfarris had begun courting the Widow Vasilakis, to console her in her bereavement. The Schuhplattler girls impartially distributed their favors among the unattached men, including even Hannibal Tyree, the three Chinese and Kesperle Spenz. Most remarkable, even incredible, the old Hanswurst Notkin had lately been making eyes at Magpie Maggie Hag, and she was not noticeably repulsing him.

"And if I'm not mistaken," Edge concluded, "I've seen you squiring the Widow Wheeler to dinner at Gundel's a time or three."

"Purely platonic," muttered Florian. "Paternal."

"Of course," Edge went on, "Clover Lee is still on the lookout for a noble suitor, but in the meantime she makes do with Johnnies from the seats. Sunday, too, I reckon. So who's complaining about the ratio of males to females?"

"Nobody is complaining," said Florian. "I merely say that it is unusual, perhaps unnatural. I have never known a circus where the female artistes outnumbered the male. Also, among all those happy men you mentioned, I noticed you did not include yourself."

"I'm content. That'll do."

Edge was lying. He was not entirely content. In fact, he wondered privately if he might be going crazy. A month or so ago, he had been vaguely disturbed by the apparent but impossible familiarity of some of the portrait paintings and busts in the palace of Schönbrunn. Now, here, in a totally different country, during two nighttime shows of the circus, he had glimpsed an impossibly familiar face among the audience. Was it conceivable, he wondered, that a man's loss and grief and longing, consciously and diligently suppressed by the man's mind, could yet somehow find crevices in that man's mind to leak through and afflict him with hallucinations?

When it happened again, at another night's show, Edge determined to confront whichever it was: his own lunacy or a verifiable phantom. As before, the woman came with another woman, and both were veiled, and both came in late—during the opening spec, when all the rest of the audience was intent on the spectacle—and took their reserved starback seats, and only then lifted their veils. The companion was a plain-faced, middle-aged woman; the other was—

"Autumn?" Edge said diffidently, imbecilically, but unable to do otherwise, when he walked over to them at intermission. They always remained inside the chapiteau during the interval, not mingling with the midway crowd, not beckoning Magpie Maggie Hag to attend them, and they always had been among the first persons to depart at the show's close. Now both the women started with surprise and immediately dropped their veils over their faces. The one he had addressed asked warily:

"Beszél ön magyar?"

Edge simply stared.

"Sprechen Sie deutsche?"

Edge continued to peer, trying to see through the veil. With it down, she could be the Autumn of the final days. But without the veil, she had been Autumn at first meeting.

"Tiens, parlez-vous français?"

Edge shook himself awake, and mumbled, "Un petit peu."

She laughed, and her laugh was Autumn's. "Oon petty pew? Well, here is *one*

American with this American circus. I had never heard you speak before, sir, only blowing the whistle."

She raised her veil, and so stunned Edge that he stammered, "I don't. Talk much. Ma'am." No, this woman's hair was more bronze than auburn. But her eyes were the same: brown, flower-petaled with gold flecks. Her always-about-to-smile mouth was the same...

"Why did you say that one word at me?"

Edge shook himself again. "It's a name, ma'am. Autumn. Someone I used to know."

She cocked her head, and her mouth did smile, dazzlingly. "Would that someone approve of your accosting other women?"

"I'm sorry. You look so much like her. She was beautiful, too."

"Thank you. If we are going to exchange compliments, we should introduce ourselves. As it happened, you nearly had my name right. I am not Autumn but Amelie, Gräfin von Hohenembs."

"Then I'm even more sorry for my brashness, Your Grace," said Edge, with a bow. "You probably prefer to be incognito in these surroundings. I am Zachary Edge, the—"

"The equestrian director, of course. My companion is the Bárónö Festetics Marie. We are pleased to meet you, Edge úr." She gave him her gloved hand, and Edge bowed again to brush it with his lips. "I myself," she went on, "am an amateur of equitation, and a lifelong circus fancier. But I must indulge my dilettante fancies unrecognized. The common folk might be scandalized or distressed to see their—to see one of us *pompous* folk taking pleasure in something as free and easy as a circus."

"Countess, if you know enough about circuses to call me the equestrian director instead of ringmaster"—he smiled—"then you are no mere dilettante."

"Please do not smile, Edge úr."

"I meant that remark as praise, Your Grace, not impudence."

"I know you did. But you should not ever smile. You are less ugly when you do not smile. Did your Autumn never tell you that?"

"Well, yes. Maybe not quite so frankly."

"A title gives a woman the privilege of frankness. I often tell Ferenc—my husband, that is—I often tell him just the opposite. That he *ought* to smile once in a while."

"The privilege is the count's," said Edge. "To be instructed by so charming a countess."

"My, my!" she said, studying him. "As long as you do not ever try to do it in your Fräuleiny French, you can evidently be gallant. For an American."

"I do my best," he said humbly. "Your Grace, if you would care to linger until all the—the common folk have gone, after the come-out, maybe you would give me the honor of showing you and the baroness the backstage workings of our show?"

She considered, but said, "That might be...imprudent. See how Marie frowns at the idea."

"Some other time?" said Edge, almost urging, not wanting to let her go. Go *again,* he thought.

She said brightly, "Un prété pour un rendu. Why do I not show you my circus?" The Baroness Festetics gave her an even more cautionary frown, but she ignored this one. "Can you take a few days of holiday, Edge úr?"

"Why... I imagine so. *Yes.* Yes, I certainly can, and will. But... your circus, Your Grace?"

"Oh, an ill-favored thing, sir, but mine own. It will probably make you smile your ugly smile. Do you know the town of Gödöllö? I am residing at present in my country house near there. It is only a few hours' fast drive from here. I will send a carriage for you. Dress is casual, except at dinner. Shall we say this day week?"

Edge said that would be fine, and he would look forward to it. Then he remained chatting with them—even the baroness unfroze enough to contribute a few sociable words in English—until the band began playing "Wait for the Wagon" and the common folk came hurrying back into the chapiteau.

Edge resumed his directorial duties with a verve he had not shown for a long time, and he did his Colonel Ramrod shooting with unaccustomed flourishes, and he rode his Buckskin Billy voltige with near neck-breaking recklessness. Each time he took a bow, he bowed directly to Countess Amelie. She applauded with her hands held high so he could see them—noblewomen did not stamp their feet—and Edge had to remind himself not to grin at her. When the performance concluded, the two women did not this time slip out during the spec, so Edge had the chance to say good-bye to them. And when the countess stood up to go, Edge noted that she was also different from his tiny Autumn in being quite a bit taller. But she had just as curvaceous a figure and just as unbelievably slender a waist.

Edge had never mentioned to anyone else what he supposed to be his hallucinations of Autumn encore-vu, and evidently none of the other troupers had noticed the woman, and none of them had noticed him in conversation with her tonight. But all the artistes had observed his sudden new access of gusto, and were pleased but bewildered by it. After the last jossers had departed, Florian approached Edge to say tentatively, almost worriedly, "Did something happen during the interval tonight, Zachary? To make you so, er, unwontedly vivacious?"

"Something sure did, Governor. I'd like to beg a few days off next week."

"Mercy me! Are you ailing, lad?"

"I thought I was, but I just discovered I'm not. She wasn't Autumn, after all. She's the Countess von Something-or-other."

"Oh?" said Florian, taking a step back from him. "Maybe you do need a rest, old friend."

"I'm not loco, Governor. Far from it. Never felt better. I've been invited to visit the country house of this countess I met tonight. Amelie—I remember that much of her name. And you're always encouraging everybody to make friends in high places, right? In case they can be useful to the show?"

"By all means, go, my boy. You've seldom had a break from your work since you first joined out. If even the prospect so vivifies you, the actual visit ought to do you a world of good."

For the next week, Edge spent much of his free time in visits to a tailor Willi found for him, having fittings for a suit of dress clothes. During that time, Clover Lee groused some more about "everybody else finds a prime titled catch except me." And Sunday summoned up courage to come to Edge and say:

"The whole troupe is gossiping that you're going to a rendezvous with a mysterious countess. Is that true, Zachary?"

"Hardly a rendezvous, girl. That sounds furtive. Only a holiday in the country. And there's nothing mysterious about the lady, except that she looks uncannily like Autumn. If you remember the way Autumn used to look."

"Yes," said Sunday, downcast. "She was a beautiful woman."

"It takes one to know one," Edge said blithely. "You're just as beautiful, Sunday. Only in a different way."

"Thank you. Are you going to fall in love with this one, the way you did with Autumn?"

"I'd better not. This one's got a husband."

That encouraged Sunday to say, "Then maybe sometime—if you take another holiday—you'd take me along? For company?"

"Why, sure thing, Sunday. If the countess asks me back again, you come along and use your good looks to lure the count off somewhere, so I can have her to myself for a while."

After a moment of hurt silence, she said, "If you want me to. But Clover Lee could do it better. She'd take the count and keep him. So you could keep the countess forever."

Scarcely hearing, he said, "Reckon that's right." And Sunday went sadly away.

On the appointed day, the promised carriage came: a luxurious, high-sprung, leather-upholstered brougham drawn by matched bay hackneys. There was a liveried coachman on the driving seat and a liveried lackey perched on the rumble. Most of the circus troupe gathered to watch, in some awe, as the lackey leapt down to take Edge's new-bought portmanteau and stow it in the boot, then showed Edge the traveling hamper under the coach seat, full of fresh-prepared food, fruit, sweets, wines and brandies.

"Those are the Festetics arms on the door," said Florian, clearly impressed. "So that's the name you couldn't remember. One of the most distinguished in Magyarország."

"No," said Edge, after consideration. "She was *von* something. I believe Festetics was the woman with her. Well, good-bye, all." He tipped his new gray beaver traveling hat. "I won't be gone long."

3

ONCE out of the park gate, the brougham turned northwestward and soon the last suburbs of Pest were left behind. Edge sat back to enjoy the scenery, but the land was so flat and uninteresting along this road—nothing but Kansas-like prairies of high grass, except for the occasional farm of rye or wheat—that he dozed most of the way. Now and then, when a bad patch of the road jounced him awake, he delved in the hamper for a piece of chicken or a dobostorta or a drink of wine, then dozed again.

He was awakened the last time, just about sundown, by the carriage's sudden brisk vibration of rolling over cobblestones, and he looked out to see that it was on the winding driveway of a good-sized park, but not a landscaped one.

This was all natural woods and meadows, and twice the horses tried to check when a broad-antlered stag went bounding across the drive in front of them. "Her country house," Edge murmured ironically, as it loomed in sight: a handsome castle of fretted stonework and turrets and diamond-paned windows and carved doors, with roses and wistaria climbing all over the high walls.

But, curiously, the brougham did not set him down at the front entrance of that impressive pile; it went through a porte-cochère and around behind the castle. "Servants' entrance? Tradesmen's entrance?" Edge wondered. But he truly was perplexed when the carriage kept on going past outbuildings—handsome ones, but obviously the estate's kitchens, servants' quarters, smithy, storehouses. At last, the brougham drew up before the stables, and the lackey opened the door to bow him out. True, the stables were not a great deal less grand than the castle—but did she *live* here? Had she been putting on airs with that talk of titles and privilege? Was she merely a poor relation of the von Whoevers, or even a scullion of theirs?

Then he heard music. Beside a circular paddock, a man who clearly was a stable hand was playing wheezy but lively cigány music on an accordion. And inside the paddock two graceful Arabian horses, bareback, were going around and around at an easy canter. On the back of each was a slim figure in white shirt and black trousers; in the gathering twilight, Edge could not at first make out whether they were men or women. They were doing an acrobatic and ballet routine almost as good as Clover Lee's: striking postures, standing on one leg, occasionally skipping lightly off the horses onto the paddock fence's top rail and balancing there until the mounts came around again, then skipping back on.

Edge watched with pleasure, and finally one of the riders vaulted to the ground, slithered between the fence rails and came up to him, drawing on a black bolero jacket over her white shirt. Her face was prettily flushed from her exertions, but she was not breathing hard. Amelie wore no cosmetics—she needed none—and her bronze-colored hair was tied back in simple peasant style, hanging in waves to her waist. She could have been just a stable girl, an exceedingly lovely one, except that her shirt was of the finest white silk and the jacket and trousers were of black velvet.

She said chidingly, "As I foretold, you are smiling, Edge úr. Kindly desist."

"Sorry. I was admiring." He bowed and she gave him her hand to kiss. It was ungloved this time, and it was neither the hard hand of a professional rider nor the rough red hand of a servant. He hastened to add, "Your Grace."

"Berni!" she called to the stable hand, and motioned for him to stop playing. She called "Elise!" and beckoned to the other rider.

"Is this your circus, Countess?" Edge asked.

"A very small part of it. Just us two. I must apologize. When I invited you, I quite forgot that I had ordered all my tumblers and clowns to Achilleion. But here—I wish you to meet the Fräulein Elise Renz."

Miss Renz was as young and almost as beauteous as the countess. She forthrightly stuck out a hand to be shaken, not kissed, and this was the muscular hand of a real équestrienne.

"Guten Abend, Herr Edge," she said.

"Elise is the daughter of Ernst Jakob Renz," said the countess. "Of the Zirkus Renz, of which you may have heard. Elise is good enough to play truant from her father's troupe, now and again, to come and instruct me in new bareback routines."

The Fräulein Renz, with a pretty pout, said something in German.

The countess translated, "Elise says, 'But we have no equestrian director to command us,' and it is true. We lack a stern disciplinarian. Perhaps tomorrow, Edge úr, you would crack the whip for us? We much enjoy having a strong hand to direct us—and chastise us, when necessary."

"Ja, Strafe!" breathed the other, her eyes shining.

"I would be delighted," said Edge.

"Good." The countess spoke a few words in German to Elise, who giggled happily. "But now, come, my guest. You will wish to refresh yourself after the journey. Elise and Berni will see to the horses." She called once more—"Schatten!"—and an immense, shaggy dog stalked from a stable doorway. As Edge and the countess strolled toward the castle, it paced solemnly along beside them.

"That dog," said Edge "makes a fair piece of circus all by itself. It's as big as our Rumpelstilzchen. Our dwarf horse."

"Yes. My Schatten is an Irish wolfhound. My faithful companion and bodyguard. His name means Shadow."

"Lucky dog," Edge said involuntarily. Then, to cover the gaucherie, he said quickly, "So it was Miss Renz who taught you equitation?"

"Oh, no. She merely helps me to keep in practice. It was my father who first taught me. He turned his riding school into a miniature zoo and circus, and started me doing fancy riding when I was very small."

"Your father ran a riding school? My father worked in an iron foundry. When there was work."

"You mistake me. The stables and rings and jumps and racecourse of a palace are always called, for the sake of modesty, merely the riding school. My father was Maximilian Josef von Wittelsbach, Duke of Bavaria."

"Oh."

"You have heard of the madness of the family Wittelsbach? Well, my father was mad only in that mild way. He had a passion for the circus life. Once, when I was very young, he and I dressed as vagabonds and wandered on horseback through Bavaria, unrecognized. Whenever we came to an innyard, he played a zither while I did my bareback tricks. Then I would pass my hat among the onlookers." She paused, smiled reminiscently and said, "That was the only money I ever earned in my life. My father, too, I daresay."

Edge chuckled, a little hollowly.

"However, I inherited my father's madness, and some of his circus—the animals, the dwarfs—and I have had them ever since. When my own child was six years old, he was very nervous and shy. So, to teach him fearlessness, I locked him overnight in the zoo full of wild animals. Oh, I left Rudi's tutor hidden nearby, just in case. I would not expose my son to risk, of course."

"Of course. Even so, I expect he had a night to remember."

"He is still very nervous," she said offhandedly. "I am so sorry I did not keep the animals and the rest of my circus here to show you."

"If I had just wanted to see a circus, Your Grace, I could have stayed in Pest with my own."

She gave him a warm look of appreciating that remark, but went on with her small talk. "As I say, I sent them on to Achilleion, where I usually spend my winters. That is my estate on Corfu. I designed it myself, in the Greek style."

They had come around the lawn's white-gravel paths, by now, to the great flagged terrace that fronted the castle, set all about with man-high bronze urns overbrimming with flowers. In each of the weathered stone pillars that flanked the terrace balustrade, a new stone had been set, carved with heraldic arms. Edge noted that the device was different from that on the Festetics brougham, but—again the sense of déjà-vu—he was sure that he had seen the arms somewhere before.

"Ah, you remark that those are recent additions," said the countess. "Yes, this castle was only given to me last year. I am very fond of it, fonder than I am of any of the others. Except in winter. Then I flee to the sunshine."

Edge wondered who had castles to give away, and how many others she had, but said nothing. Footmen swung wide the entrance doors, and they went into a vaulted hall hung with banners and shields and ancient weapons. The Baroness Festetics was waiting to attend the countess and, after curtsying to her, even dropped a small dip in Edge's direction.

"You remember Marie, of course," said the countess. "And this is my chamberlain, the Baron Nopsca." That courtly gentleman bowed and clicked his well-shod heels. "This is Hirschfeld, who will be your valet. I must tell you that the household domestics speak nothing but Magyar." She dropped her voice to a murmur. "That is so I can speak in other languages with confidence. Even with intimacy." Then she resumed, "However, you will find that Hirschfeld knows his duties, and should require no instruction. He will show you now to your suite. Dinner tonight will be at eight, but not in the big dining hall, in the more cozy Ivory Room. Hirschfeld will also show you how to find that."

In something of a daze, Edge let himself be guided up the swooping staircase, abstractedly noticing that even his valet had servants: a footman carrying the portmanteau and another bearing a tray with a ewer of hot water, a basin, various toilet sundries. The suite—a bedroom with a four-poster bed, a breakfast room and a bathroom—was of a baronial splendor to daze Edge even further. But he did not immediately succumb to sybaritic sloth; he insisted on doing his own washing and shaving of himself, though he almost had to fight off Hirschfeld to do it. The valet went to unpack the portmanteau, sniffing occasionally as if contemptuous of the quality of its contents. Then Edge let the man help him don his dinner dress, for he was unfamiliar with the complexities of false shirt front, collar and studs and such, and never would he be capable of tying his own white tie.

The cozy Ivory Room, when Edge got there, turned out to be rather bigger than the house he had been born in. The countess was seated at an ivory-colored—or maybe pure ivory—grand piano in one corner, idly rippling something by Schumann. She stood up and relinquished her place to an unidentified young lady wearing spectacles, who would play, but very softly and sweetly, all through the ensuing dinner.

The countess no longer looked remotely like a stable girl or an équestrienne; she looked like the heroine of some romantic fairy tale. She also still, in the face, looked so startlingly like Autumn Auburn that Edge could not help thinking, "How I wish she were. And how I wish I could have given Autumn such a setting for her beauty." But the Countess Amelie was alive and present, and a gorgeous woman in her own right, and Edge was neither dead nor immune to her undeniable allure. Now her hair was done up in an intricate chignon, and topped with an emerald tiara. There were emeralds about her neck and on her fingers, too. Her dress of dark-green brocade and ivory lace was cut low to bare her fine shoulders—and her breasts, very nearly to the point of indiscretion. Their luster made all the ivory of the Ivory Room look dusty and dull by comparison. Her waist was so slender, above the flare of the crinolette skirt, that she seemed literally breakable there.

"Seventeen inches," she said, as if Edge had spoken that thought. But she spoke a little regretfully, adding, "My waist was fifteen and a half inches before I married."

Yes, she was married, Edge reminded himself. He said, "Won't the count be dining with us, Your Grace?" There were only two places set at the not-very-cozy table that could have accommodated twelve. "I had"—he could not say "hoped" —"I had expected to have the pleasure of meeting him. And your son."

"My husband is abroad, and the children with him. And Zachary, you need address me formally only when we are in company. En tête-à-tête, I give you leave to call me Sissi. All my friends do."

"An odd nickname for Amelie, ma'am. And I don't believe I could call any woman by a diminutive nickname."

"Amelie, then, if you insist on even semiformality." She touched a bell rope. "Will you take an apéritif? Amontillado? Bugac?" A footman entered and poised himself over the decanters and crystal ware on an ivory sideboard. Both Edge and Amelie took sherry and, when the man had gone, Edge said:

"You mentioned children. I was surprised to hear that you had even one, as old as six. *You* don't look old enough..."

"Rudi is now ten. His sister is almost thirteen. There was another daughter before her, but she did not survive infancy. How old is the Autumn you have compared me to?"

"Not quite twenty-four. When she died."

"Oh, dear, so young! And she is dead? I am sorry. A younger woman is a rival formidable enough. A dead one is almost invincible."

"Rival?"

"All women are rivals of each other, Zachary. I might even say enemies. Especially when they are of much different ages. Alas, on Christmas Eve, I will turn thirty-one. Into my fourth decade."

"From the perspective of nearly forty, I can't see that twenty-four and thirty-one are *much* different ages. Particularly when you don't look a year older than Autumn's twenty-four. And you don't."

"Ah, well preserved, am I? That is a compliment that fails of gallantry, Zachary."

"I didn't say any such—"

"Also, I commiserate in your bereavement, but need we talk *all* evening about your lady Autumn?"

"Why, it was you who mentioned—"

"Let us be seated and begin." She touched the bell rope again. Flustered and not a little exasperated, Edge was tardy in drawing out her chair for her, and she looked mildly annoyed at that. But, when the first course was set before them, they managed amiably enough to turn to talk of circus matters, with the pianissimo tinkle of music for background. Amelie just once more made a reproving remark: "Do be at ease, Zachary. You sit as ramrod-erect as—as the Count Hohenembs. I am always having to rebuke him, too."

"I learned my table manners at a strict school." He was also being very careful to choose the correct implements from among the array of silver on either side of his plate.

Edge had already partaken of cold prawns in a spicy sauce and now was having hot leek soup, but Amelie had so far only nibbled at a bit of lettuce salad. It became evident, as the dinner progressed, that the castle kitchens had prepared two entirely different meals. His was hearty and varied, but the only substantial thing served to her was a small portion of some kind of pale fish. No wonder she keeps that wasp waist, he thought.

When the footman brought in the sweets—golden dumpling cake for Edge, a few ripe cherries for her—the servants were accompanied by the Baroness Festetics, bearing a silver salver on which lay a yellow envelope. She murmured something in Magyar. Amelie tore open the envelope, read the flimsy enclosure, laughed and said:

"A telegram. In our private cipher. Shall I read to you, Zachary, what it says?" She did not wait for him to answer. "'Darling. Arriving tomorrow evening. Wear nothing but your jewels.'"

The baroness looked pained and closed her eyes. Edge, embarrassed, made a few incoherent noises before he was able to say, "So the count is coming back from abroad, Your Grace? Then he won't want to find a houseguest in—"

"My husband? Good heavens! Ferenc never had such wit—or such arrogant impetuosity. This is from my lover."

The baroness now looked about to swoon. Edge choked out, "Well. Then *he* damned sure won't want to find a stranger in—"

"But here you are, are you not?" She looked at him long and levelly. "Do you wish to be evicted? To make room for him?"

He returned the look. "No."

"I hoped not. Marie, please reply by telegraph to Count Andrássy. Tell him I will be indisposed tomorrow. And perhaps for a day or two beyond tomorrow. Also, as you go, Marie, please send word to the kitchens to serve our coffee and brandy in my chambers."

The countess herself, not a servant, led Edge up there, and they sat down on opposite sides of a low table. "Plus intime, n'est-ce pas?" she said. The huge Irish wolfhound padded in from some other room, nuzzled his mistress, gave Edge the merest look and, with a grunt, lay down close beside Amelie's chair. After a minute, footmen came with a silver coffee service, Sèvres cups and saucers, decanters of cordials and fragile pony glasses. The countess dismissed the men, and herself poured.

What Edge could see of her chambers—the foyer they had entered through and the sitting room they were in—made his own suite, which he had thought baronial, seem fusty and cramped. Her sitting room alone occupied the entire breadth of a castle wing, so that it had at either end a wall all French windows with a spacious balcony beyond. The windows were open, so their gossamer curtains waved lazily in the balmy night wind and let in gusts of fragrance from the roses and wistaria outside. Edge was looking about, not to compare living quarters, but to avoid staring like a lecher at the smooth, billowy, inviting expanse of ivory flesh that Amelie presented to his gaze as she bent forward over the low table to do the pouring.

"You seemed unduly shocked, Zachary," she said, "even for an American, when you heard that I have a lover. No doubt, before you joined a circus, you did suffer from the provincial American puritanism, but surely not afterward. I know circuses." She smiled, as if she might know some things about them better than he did. "But perhaps you still cling to that belief so treasured by ignorant prudes: that we of the upper classes lead purer lives." She touched the emeralds in her hair. "We wear tiaras and crowns and coronets, yes, but only a peasant or a fool would mistake them for halos. Or perhaps you thought—perhaps you flattered yourself—that you would be my first and only lover."

"All evening long," Edge said mildly, "you have been putting words in my mouth and telling me what I must be thinking. If you ever *asked* me what I've been thinking, I would be happy to tell you."

"What, then?"

"I keep thinking that you are a lovely, desirable woman and, underneath those jewels and laces and brocades, you are absolutely . . . stark . . . naked . . ."

"Oh!" She blushed all the way from her bronze hair to her dress top. "You are as audacious as Andrássy!"

"Another thing I think is that you have mice."

"I *beg* your pardon!" she gasped, quite off balance now.

"The castle, I mean. I hear rustlings inside the walls."

"Have you lived only in a tent all your life?" she asked, recovering. "Never in a proper house? There are passages inside the walls, naturally, so in winter the servants can stoke those great tile stoves from behind, without disturbing the rooms' occupants. Right now, you hear my maids bringing milk for my first bath."

"First bath? Milk?"

"And none but Jersey milk. Wherever I travel, I take with me two Jersey cows. Always before I go to bed I bathe in warm milk. You will find that it makes me wonderfully satiny of skin. Afterward, you will hear the maids scurrying about in the walls again, bringing the warm olive oil for the second bath I always take after I have lain with a man. That, of course, is for preventive purposes. I truly do not crave any more children. Afterward, also, you will go to your own suite by way of the wall passages. My servants are loyal and untalkative, but propriety—"

"I'll be damned if I will." Edge got to his feet. "Not even a countess is going to *command* me to stud and then make me sneak—"

"I do not speak as a countess!" she flared. "I—" She curbed her temper. "I speak as a woman, but not the coy and simpering and swooning sort of woman."

"Then let me be a man, not a flunky. Does your audacious and impetuous Andrássy have to scuttle out of here through a rathole?"

"How dare you! He is noble born, and the premier minister of all Hungary. You are a *commoner*."

Edge bowed and said coolly, "Has this commoner Your Grace's permission to take his leave?"

"No. Sit down." He remained standing. She darkly regarded him and said musingly, "There was a time—and here in Hungary it was not so long ago—if a commoner had spoken to a noble as you have spoken to me... I would have had you set on a red-hot iron throne, with a red-hot crown on your head and a red-hot scepter in your hand. When you were well cooked, but still alive"—she dropped a jeweled hand to touch the dog at her side, and he alertly lifted his head, ready for action—"I would have fed you to Schatten."

Edge did not doubt that she would be capable of it, then or now, but he simply stood and waited. She stood up beside him and suddenly, amazingly, she no longer looked angry. There was a hint of mischief in her flower-petaled eyes when she said, "Now I do not command, I only ask that you stay in this room until I return. If then you still wish to go, you have my leave."

"Your Grace," he said, and bowed again. She swept out of the room, in an electric sibilance of silks.

Edge sat down, took a cigarette from a lapis-lazuli box on the table and poured himself a pony of Bénédictine. He reflected again on the obvious fact that Amelie was not Autumn and, except superficially, was not anything like her. Amelie was herself, but what that might be, he could not make out, because her moods changed so frequently and so extremely. She was imperious one moment, playful the next; frank and free one moment, frozen and haughty the next.

She was gone long enough that he began to wonder, and not entirely idly, if she were having her minions heat an iron throne for him. But evidently she had only been leisurely taking her milk bath, for, when she returned, she had let down her hair, and its tumbling waves of spun bronze were all she wore. She stood regally proud and not the least bashful, and let him look at her. The lovely face, the ivory glow of her, the tiny waist, the high-carried breasts, their gener- ous dark areoles and already excited nipples, those could have been Autumn's. Below the waist, though, she was different in one small detail. She watched Edge's gaze go all over her, and at last smiled and asked, confident of the reply, "Now, Zachary, do you still wish to go away?"

Edge would never again smell the scent of roses or wistaria, or taste milk, without vividly remembering that night. He had first heard in Mexico, when he was a very young man, the hoary old Spanish proverb, "Por la noche todos los gatos son gris," and even then he had laughed at it, already knowing it to be untrue, knowing that no two women were really alike, even in the dark. But Amelie proved to be truly unique in the act of love, as she was in everything else. She did not, like most other passionate women of Edge's experience, sigh or whimper or moan with pleasure. Instead, from his very first ministrations of lips and tongue and fingers, she began to chuckle with delight, like a little girl being affectionately tickled.

As Edge had already noticed, she was like a little girl in another respect. He said. "You are as smooth as a baby... here."

Breathlessly she told him, "The maid who does my hair... I have her shave me in that place. I believe it to be hygienic. Now hush. You have already a red-hot scepter. Let me enjoy. Let me laugh."

And that she did. As Edge made her excitement mount, the low chuckle became a merry trill, getting louder and more joyful until, at her convulsive and writhing climax, she erupted in a peal of full-throated, whole-hearted laughter. Then, as she subsided from the peak of ecstasy, so did her laughter, gradually rippling down the scale again, from exultation to jubilation to merriment and at last to the small chuckle of happy satisfaction. That went on for some while, until she ceased it to say urgently:

"No, no, do not slip out. Stay there. I will...mine will make yours aroused again very quickly."

And she did indeed use only that part of herself, tweaking and squeezing and inwardly pulsating, to revive that part of himself.

"How in the world do you do that?" Edge asked, with admiration.

"Exercise. I exercise *all* my muscles. Including that one...or those...or however many are down there. Now hush again. I am...I am...oh, *yes!*"

More swiftly now, she went from the quiet chuckle up through the gladsome trill until, at the crest, when Edge could feel down there her rapturous spasm, clenched and drenched, she laughed so infectiously that he did, too.

A long time—many times—later, when they lay resting side by side, she was still and quiet for a while, but then she shook with silent laughter.

"I'm not even touching you," Edge said lazily. "What's tickling you now?"

"I was remembering your circus. The joeys' act. You know, that part when the pretty Emeraldina is supposedly the wife of the wrinkled old Hanswurst, and the Kesperle makes lewd advances to her, and she says, 'My husband will not thank you, sir, for making him a cuckold.'"

"And the Kesperle says, 'But I hope, madame, *you* will.'" Edge again laughed with her.

"I do thank you, sir," said Amelie. "Perhaps now you are not so disapproving of this faithless wife."

He said, "And perhaps now I've convinced you that I am not a puritan. No, I wasn't shocked when you said at dinner that you have a lover. I was just surprised that you *said* it."

"What harm? Only in Marie's presence."

"And mine."

"Fatzke!" she said airily. "Even if you were to tell of that—or of anything else—no one would believe you."

Edge grunted, resentful and a little hurt by her unconscious or uncaring disparagement.

She added, "And from Marie I have no secrets."

"And from your husband?"

"I will tell you, Zachary. He is un mari commode. He has to be, for fear that *I* might tell secrets. Seven years ago, and I do not know from whom he contracted it, Ferenc gave to me a...a shameful disease."

Edge grunted again, this time in sympathy.

"You see why I say we people wear crowns—or coronets—but not halos. Anyway, that was when I first traveled incognito and without retinue. To Berlin, under an assumed name, accompanied only by Marie, to have myself cured. And when I was cured, I found that I could be blissfully and unashamedly unfaithful to Ferenc. In fact, I have never slept with him since then, and I avoid his company except on inescapable occasions of state, when we must pretend to be the happy and loving Count and Countess Hohenembs. Now I travel as I please, I have my own estates apart from his, I live my own life. But I do not openly dishonor him or my own high station. I am discreet in my infidelities and I make certain that they do not develop into attachments or entanglements. The Count Andrássy, for example, has a wife and two sons and a reputation to protect, so there is no risk of his wanting more of me than the occasional liaison. Just as you and I, Zachary, will savor this little time together, and then part. Oh, we may meet again somewhere, sometime. But never for long."

Edge sighed. "They say that all is fair in love and war. I've been in love and I've been in war, and I've learned that those have another thing in common. You don't expect any tomorrows. You enjoy, just as much as you can, what is here and now."

"You are wise."

"For a mere commoner?"

"And now you must go. I require my beauty sleep, and first I must have my olive-oil douche and bath. The maids have been long gone from the wall passages; I hope the oil is still warm. Meanwhile, since you were so insistent, I give you permission to depart by way of the door and the corridors. They should be empty at this hour."

"I imagine so. It's nearly dawn. Why don't we sleep a little and then—?"

"No." She sat up in the bed and reached for something from the bedside table. "I sleep in this silken mask—see?—with slices of raw veal inside it. You would not much desire me, seeing me so."

"Good God, Amelie. What's that for?"

"To keep me looking as young as your Autumn. You do not object to *that,* so do not be so appalled at the means I employ."

"I suppose you use only Jersey veal?"

"And do not be impertinent. If this were springtime, now, I would let you remain the night. In the spring, you see, before I retire, all over my face and breasts I crush the ripe wild strawberries fresh with dew. You would find me tasty then."

"I find you tasty right now. I believe I could even ignore the mask and the, uh..."

"No. Not again until tomorrow night. Go now." She kissed him and smiled contentedly. "Es hat mich sehr gefreut."

Edge slept well into the morning, and no one disturbed him. When he awoke, he pulled the bell rope and had not even time to step out of bed before Hirschfeld was there, holding a robe for him, but suggesting by gestures that he remain abed. So Edge complied, and next moment a footman entered with a bed tray of breakfast and coffee, and another brought a freshly ironed copy of the *Pest Világ*. While Edge ate and scanned the smudgy woodcuts, all he could comprehend of the newspaper, his valet and a whole parade of footmen bearing steaming ewers prepared his bath. While he bathed, the valet clucked fussily over the condition of Edge's dress suit—he had removed it in considerable haste the night before, and redonned it only carelessly, and then doffed it again half asleep. So Hirschfeld took it away for some mending and sponging and pressing, but was back in time to help Edge towel himself and dress in walking boots, loden trousers and a hunting jacket that Magpie Maggie Hag had made for him by retailoring and sewing leather elbow and gun-butt patches on his old army tunic.

Edge wended his way down to the great entry hall, and there encountered the Baroness Festetics. She said affably, "You must entertain yourself for a while,

Edge úr. Sissi—I mean the Countess Amelie—will not appear before noon."

"She always sleeps so late?"

"Ó jaj, no! She will have been up and about since half past six. But my lady has a strict and crowded morning schedule." The baroness recited it—as reverently, thought Edge, as Homer sang of heroes, and he had to admit that it was a heroic if not Homeric program.

"First, she has her scented bath, and the application to her face of a cream made of Dutch tulip bulbs, and perhaps the washing of her hair in raw egg and brandy. Then arrives the masseur she conscripted from a spa at Wiesbaden. Then, after breaking her fast with herb tea and toast, she dons a léotard and goes to exercise for an hour on the various apparatuses in her gymnastics room. Next comes there her fencing master, to put her through an hour's practice. After those exertions, of course, another bath. When her hair maid has combed and brushed and done up her tresses, the countess selects from her wardrobe and puts on a costume befitting whatever activity is first on her calendar for the day. Then she sits down for another hour to study, with her books and the professor who is teaching her Greek. Then she takes a light luncheon in her rooms. And it is noon, and her public day begins."

Edge said, "I feel like going back to bed, after just listening to it all."

"Ó jaj, do not do that, Edge úr," the baroness said, in earnest. "Come, I will show you about the castle."

So they wandered through one splendid room and hall and gallery after another, with the baroness explaining the history and rarity and value and mode of acquisition of every last object of art or antiquity. Edge enjoyed best, however, the view of outdoors when they climbed to the top of the castle's highest tower. They could see over much of the surrounding parkland; in one meadow browsed a family of red deer, in another was rooting a sizable herd of extremely sizable and savage-looking black boar.

"Edge úr, have you ever ridden to staghounds?"

"No, ma'am, I haven't. But I've done pigsticking. In Mexico."

"Ah, then you must do that here, with Her Grace. And perhaps she will initiate you in the chase, as well. She is a magnificent rider, as you know, and a veritable Diana in the hunt."

When Amelie did make her appearance, riding was obviously the first thing on her day's calendar, for she was accompanied by Elise Renz, and both the young women were again in bolero jackets and slim trousers, this time of dark blue velvet. They and Edge exchanged greetings and some small talk, Amelie translating for Elise, then the three went to the stables and Elise whistled up the stable hand. He led into the paddock the two superb Arabian horses. The girls mounted them, bareback, and began warming them up while the man went back into the stable to bring out his accordion and a long, wicked, braided-leather whip with a tassel like a cat-o'-nine-tails. That was the korbács, Edge learned later, the whip used by the range riders and cattle herders of the Hungarian plains. The man handed it to Edge, and puzzled him by winking broadly when he did so. Then he started playing his rollicking cigány music.

Edge was not puzzled for long. He cracked the whip to start the women and horses circling in their équestrienne routine and, after he had several times cracked it to direct the women to assume one pose after another, and several times gently flicked the horses to make them change pace, Elise shouted something in German. The countess, riding at a stand, called to Edge, "She says do not tap the horses. Tap *us* with the korbács."

"I'm not going to whip any woman," Edge called back. "Damn it, this is a brute of a whip."

"Do as she says! That is my command also!"

"Command, is it?" Edge growled to himself. He gave a smart snap of the whip's tassel directly to Amelie's shapely buttocks.

It made her shriek and start, so she almost lost her footing on the horse. Edge was instantly dismayed at having stung her more sharply than he really had intended. He sincerely hoped he had not marred that perfect little backside, and he half expected the countess to summon the dog Schatten or an iron throne to punish his presumption. But, when she regained her balance, she only called cheerfully, "That is the way! More!"

So Edge shrugged and continued to do as they wished, snapping the tassel first at one woman, then the other, stinging them on their bottoms, on the backs of their thighs and occasionally, when they rode en arabesque, on the thin soles of the upraised riding slippers. After a time, even that was not sufficient to satisfy them. Elise, while riding easily erect, peeled off her bolero jacket and threw it away. The countess likewise doffed her bolero, and both women were riding in the bright white blouses, their unconfined breasts bouncing merrily. Amelie called to Edge, "Now, see if you can do something very delicate. Try to flick our backs hard enough to hurt—hard enough even to make red welts—but not tearing the silk or our skin."

That was tricky, with an unfamiliar whip, and Edge was reluctant, but he cautiously obeyed. And, after he had given them a few strokes, Elise shouted, and Amelie passed it on: "Harder, Zachary! It scarcely hurts at all! Make it sting!" He shrugged again, and laid on the whip a bit more briskly. That brought squeals and whoops from them, but they never bade him stop. Then Elise, carefully watching each time he flung the lash, waited until it was her turn and did a quick pirouette atop her horse, deliberately causing the tassel to catch her right on the tip of one breast.

She let out a long, warbling cry—and Edge, aghast, let the whip end fall—but Elise's was not a cry of anguish. It went on and on, as she spun again, dropped to straddle the cantering horse, flung herself full length along its back, her arms around its neck, and she rode that way, rubbing herself upon it, still uttering that exuberant cry of bliss. Amelie dismounted from her horse, led it out of the way and watched with a smile while Elise went around and around, until —as Edge perceived it—her perversely whipped-up excitement gradually ran down. Meantime, the stable hand grinned knowingly and lasciviously, and went on playing his gypsy music. The Fräulein Renz at last brought her horse to a halt and got down from it, visibly weak and perspiring and trembling. Amelie supported her until she recovered, the two talking quietly and then laughing gaily, and after a moment the countess crossed the paddock to where Edge stood, his whip at trail.

He said, "Your friend is just a trifle strange, isn't she?"

"Then so am I, n'est-ce pas? But you can judge us both for yourself. Elise will be joining you and me in my chambers tonight. The whip is too long to use there. The stable man will find for you a short quirt to bring instead."

And that night, after some initial reserve and modesty on the part of all three—a good deal of it, in Edge's case—their shyness and reticence gave way to familiarity and then to intimacy. Edge, half wondering, half amused, and feeling totally foolish, obliged the women by plying the quirt, but only gently, and they required only enough of that to make their bare backsides rosy and warm— and their insides a lot warmer, he reckoned, from the way the women squirmed against one another. He put the quirt aside, then, and watched them play. When they tired of pleasuring only each other, they enfolded him, too, and after a while Edge was the only one silent in the bedroom. Elise did her wildly exuberant crying and Amelie did her wildly exultant laughing, and they went on doing so, loud and long and madly, madly. Quite madly.

4

WHEN Edge descended from the brougham at the Florilegium midway in a late afternoon, the several artistes, roustabouts and stallkeepers loitering about called to him, "Welcome back!"—or the equivalent in other languages. By the time Edge's portmanteau was taken down from the boot, Florian had popped out of the red wagon and bustled over to say also, "Welcome, my boy. We have missed you."

"Hell, I've only been gone five days. But it's good to know I'm not expendable. I see Stitches has got the new dressing tents up. Our tober is looking like quite a town now."

"And you are looking nicely tanned and fit after your sojourn among the swells."

"Well, we were out afield for three of those days. Hunting stag one day, then coursing hares, then sticking boar. The countess's larder is well supplied with venison for a while."

"Come over to the red wagon and wash the road dust off your tonsils. Banat, take Zachary's bag to his caravan. And on the way, ask Tücsök to report to me, please."

In the office, Florian poured glasses of Csopaki wine, and they both lit cigarettes, and Edge asked, "Anything happen while I was away that I ought to know about?"

"Why, yes. Several bits of quite good news. Perhaps you were aware that Maggie Hag has been treating Meli Vasilakis for her unfortunate malady, with a regimen of camphor and bromides and calomel ointment. Well, Maggie finally prounounced Meli cured, so she and Sir John have consummated their courtship. At least I assume so; he has moved into her caravan."

"I'm glad to hear it."

"And Boom-Boom has hired for his band a talented new windjammer—I should say a string-banger. Gombocz Elemér, a cimbalom player. We had to reinforce the bandstand to hold the instrument, but the melodious music it makes is worth the trouble."

Edge nodded approvingly.

"And we've added a new trouper. During your absence, I took over the directing duties and the liberty horse act, but of course we had no substitute shootist or voltige rider, so the other artistes were simply given more time in the pista to pad out the program. But on the second or third day, this unique artiste showed up, in response to my advertisement in the *Era*. I shall not even describe the act to you. I'll let you be as astounded at first sight of it as the jossers are. But this Tücsök is no first-of-May. A seasoned performer, and a fantastic one."

"I heard you say that name to Banat. I thought it must be one of our Slovaks."

"No, a nom-de-théâtre. A Magyar word meaning Cricket."

"Cricket? If that signifies what I'm afraid it does—"

"Yes. A midget."

"Christ, you said you had *good* news. Another damned dwarf? After all the trouble we had with the other little sons of bitches—?"

"A female this time, and she will not be a bitch. I have quartered her with Clover Lee and Sunday, and they are as delighted as if I'd presented them with a dear little sister, although Cricket is as old as both of them put together. She is a darling little creature and—well, here she is now. Szábo Katalin kisasszony, may I present Edge Zachary úr? Our equestrian director, of whom you have heard much praise. Zachary, this is Katalin Szábo, known professionally as Tücsök—Cricket."

She said, in a small but not squeaky voice, and in excellent English, "I am pleased to meet you, Colonel Edge."

"Miss Cricket," he said.

He had stood up when the little lady entered. Now he had to bow, deeper than he had ever bowed to anyone royal or noble, to reach down and take Cricket's tiny hand. He had to concede that she was something new and improved in the line of midgets. Except that she was a trifle plump for her height, which was only about thirty inches, she was not misshapen or misproportioned in any way. She was simply a perfect miniature of a very pretty young lady with curly brown hair and bright blue eyes—though she was not so young as her girlish face made her appear at first glance—and she was smoking a cigarette in a long jade holder.

Florian told Edge, "Katalin does her pista act in the first half of the program and I guarantee you it's pure magic. Then, at intermission, she joins Sir John's sideshow. She rides into the annex on Rumpelstilzchen—bareback at present, but Stitches is making her a miniature saddle and bridle. She wears the rough garb of a csikos, a Hungarian plainsman, while she sings some of the bawdy plains songs. Then she doffs the masculine garments, reveals herself in dainty, colorful village-girl dress and does some bewitching csárdás dances."

"I'm eager to see your mysterious pista act," Edge said to the little woman. "And I'm sure Sir John is pleased to have a real artiste in his sideshow, not just another exhibit."

"I hope to make everyone pleased, Colonel," she said. "Monsieur Pemjean and I are already starting to teach the small horse some tricks—head-tossing, rearing, bowing—that I can put him through. A bantam liberty act right up there on the sideshow platform."

"It sounds appealing," said Edge. "And I welcome you to the company." Katalin gave him an elfin smile and blew a Lilliputian smoke ring.

"As soon as I have a free moment," said Florian, "I will take you to a daguerrian artist downtown, Tücsök, and have cartes-de-visite made for you to sell. They ought to sell better even than pretzels."

Katalin thanked him graciously and took her leave.

"I *reckon* I welcome her to the company," Edge said. "But I remember Major Maggot and his little playmates. Governor, this Cricket is delectable enough to tempt full-grown lechers into lusting for such a novelty."

"I am quite sure that she will repulse any advances," said Florian. "I will impart to you, and you only, a confidence she imparted to me. Tücsök has but recently recovered from giving birth to a baby. Paternity unspecified, but no matter. It was a normal-sized baby, as frequently happens among the little people, so she straightaway put it out for adoption, to be brought up in a nice, normal, commonplace family. And she is frank to say that that experience of childbirth was so hideously painful—well, you can imagine—that she will never risk it occurring again. No, I think we need not worry about anything like the Reindorf unpleasantness."

From outside there came a sudden whoop and squeal of music.

"There goes the calliope, to herald the night performance," said Florian. "I must go. But first, tell me. How did you find your countess? Was she still as exquisite as you first thought?"

"Well, I'm no authority on what high-ranking ladies are supposed to be like. But I met Mrs. Jeff Davis once, and she was sure no patch on this Countess Hohenembs."

"Ah, that's her title, is it?" Then Florian repeated, musingly, "Hohenembs... Hohenembs. I was there once. Place with a great rock mountain brooding over it. Very near the border of Liechtenstein. And, if I remember rightly, Hohenembs is a baronetcy. If so, your lady's title would be only baroness. I fear, Zachary, that you may have been imposed upon."

"It didn't cost *me* anything. Quite the contrary."

"Oh, I could be mistaken. It was a long time ago that I was in Hohenembs." Florian put on his best frock coat and top hat. "Are you too road-weary to participate in the show tonight?"

"No. Let me just finish my wine, and I'll go and dress."

Florian went out and left Edge alone in the office, which was what he had wanted. So many of Amelie's remarks had given him the feeling of déjà-entendu that now he wanted to verify something he vaguely remembered. Muttering under his breath, "Ferenc, Franz... Franz, Ferenc," he went to the wall where Florian had hung the framed invitation to Schönbrunn from Franz Joseph, and peered at its long list of that emperor's other titles. Halfway down it, after the several kingships and dukedoms, he found "...Landgraf von Habsburg und Tirol, Grossvoivode von Serbien, Graf von Hohenembs..."

Edge murmured, "Florian, you *are* mistaken about Hohenembs." He tossed off his wine and went to the caravan. He opened his trunk and rummaged among his souvenirs—mostly the few small things of Autumn's that he had kept—found the wallet he had been given at Schönbrunn and took it out to look at its embroidered arms of the Empire of Austria. The double-headed eagle emblem was the same as that on the terrace pillars of Amelie's palace. Still talking to himself, Edge said, "But you're right, Florian. She's not a countess. Or not *just* a countess." Then he laughed. "Hell, I thought for a while she might be a stable maid." He stood up, took from its hanger his Colonel Ramrod uniform and began dressing for the show.

By the time he got to the chapiteau, the calliope had hushed and Boom-Boom's band was playing instead, and the first jossers were taking their seats. Edge climbed to the bandstand for a look at the new cimbalom. It was a big and fancily carved wooden box on carved legs, rather like an old-fashioned square piano, except that it had no keys and no lid, so the innumerable wire strings inside were exposed, to be played on directly with soft little mallets, of which cimbalist Elemér dexterously held two between the fingers of each hand. But the cimbalom was no meek and modest dulcimer, to be overwhelmed by the rest of the band. Though Elemér could, in deliberately quiet passages, make his music merely tinkle and twinkle, he could also make it twang and jangle boldly or even thunder loud enough to be heard above the massed brasses and drums. He obviously enjoyed his work; he grinned all the time he played, and proudly tossed his mane of black hair, and grinned even more broadly whenever he produced an especially tricky and pleasing musical effect. Edge did not interrupt to introduce himself by name, but Elemér, without once ceasing to play—and play well—with his left hand, extended his right for a handshake.

The show commenced, and went smoothly through its usual first-half program. Then, when Monday and Thunder had finished their haute école riding act and taken their bows, Edge got his first look at the other new addition to the company. Florian bounded into the pista with his megaphone to proclaim grandiloquently—in Magyar, in German and, possibly for Edge's comprehension, in English—"A Büvös Gömb! Die Verzaubert Kugel! The Enchanted Globe!" Meanwhile, several Slovaks hauled into the center of the pista a very large apparatus that Edge had never seen before. It was rather like a combination of a circular staircase and a very narrow-gauge tramway. It had two parallel nickel-plated rails that ascended at a gentle angle from ground level, then spiraled upward in easy curves to end at a platform some fifteen feet above the pista sawdust.

The crowd went silent in contemplation of that thing, and in the silence only one band instrument, Elemér's cimbalom, began to play—very softly—the other-worldly opening measures of Josef Strauss's "Music of the Spheres." Then there entered through the chapiteau's back door, rolling between the stands and into the pista, a wooden ball about a yard in diameter, brightly painted in multicolor zigzags. No roustabout had shoved it in and none was pushing it now. The globe was rolling only slowly and sedately, but it was rolling entirely of its own volition. And it did not slow to a stop; it kept on rolling, to make three circuits of the pista. The audience regarded it in silent awe, and the cimbalom kept repeating—quietly, almost eerily—variations on those ethereal opening bars of "Music of the Spheres."

The atmosphere in the chapiteau got even more unearthly as, incredibly, the wooden ball now made a deliberate turn to the nickel-plated tramway, rolled itself between the close-set twin rails and, still slowly but without hesitation, rolled *up* that incline. As it climbed, so did the volume of the cimbalom music, Elemér going on to the crescendo measures of the "Spheres," and playing ever louder and livelier as the ball serenely circled the upward-spiraling rails. When the Enchanted Globe reached the platform at the top, the whole band joined the cimbalom to blare a rousing climax and bring the audience out of its stupefaction to a clamor of applause.

Up there, the gaudy ball did several gyrations in time to the music, and even gave a couple of sluggish hops. Then it opened. Edge had of course early realized the secret of its mysterious locomotion, so he was not surprised when the thing opened like a clamshell, revealing itself to be two hollow hemispheres hinged and with a clasp to hold them together. The zigzag paint pattern served to hide the hardware and also, Edge supposed, some slits to see through. Nevertheless, when it opened and little Tücsök stood up, wearing only a vividly orange-spangled léotard—and smiled and threw up her arms in a V—she was visibly perspiring. Even one as small as she would have been cramped inside that shell, and would have had to walk or crawl laboriously and skillfully to make the globe do all the things it had done. At Cricket's emergence, the band music rose to explosion volume, and so did the audience's cheering, clapping and stamping of feet.

Cricket merrily slid down the spiral tramway like a child on a playground slide, to take her bows in the pista. While the roustabouts removed the props, Edge said admiringly to her, "Florian spoke truly. That was pure magic. And you must be a damn sight stronger than you look for your size."

"Well, I can trundle the ball *up* there all right. But I always conclude the act at the top. Just one time did I try to roll it *down* again. I lost control and it came twirling and bounding down like a boulder in an avalanche, and when I got out of it I looked like a scrambled egg. I won't do that again."

"I hope not. You're too pretty to get scrambled."

"Thank you, Colonel. And thank you, too, for liking the act."

Some of the longtime troupers had added refinements to their routines during Edge's brief absence. Sunday Simms, for instance, had somewhere procured a soccer ball and used it in her act in a breathtaking way. Maurice LeVie had unselfishly helped her learn the trick, declaring himself too heavy and angular to manage it as gracefully as she could. Mademoiselle Butterfly concluded her solo turn by swinging out, seated on the bar, carrying the soccer ball. Then, swooping in long but slow arcs, she stood up, balanced the ball on the bar, then upended herself and *stood on her head* on the teetering ball, her arms and legs extended starfishlike, holding onto nothing at all while she continued to swoop back and forth. Some people in the audience, even grown men, had to avert their eyes in sheer dread of her falling. But Sunday never came to grief, and even told Edge that she found the trick—the taunting of the gods of accident—almost euphorically exhilarating.

Quincy Simms had invented a new contortion. After he and Miss Eel finished their duo act, he provided a nicely horrid coda. In his boneless way he slowly folded to the ground so that his body and arms seemed to disappear, leaving only his crossed legs visible, and between them he propped his chin. Then he grinned a ghastly white grin and bulged his eyeballs. With the grimace, his black face and his angled skinny legs, he exactly resembled the skull-and-crossbones on a pirate flag or on the label of a bottle of poison. Some watchers had to avert their eyes from *that*, too, but most laughed and applauded in appreciation.

"Well, it certainly is gruesome, Ali Baba," Edge told him. "But it's ingenious, and it seems to be generally well received."

"Mebbe dem jossers like it, Mas' Zack," Quincy said, rather grumpily, "but dey don' like *me*. I kin hear 'em in de seats, sayin', 'Dat ain't no Ali Baba. Dat's jist a dirty li'l nigger what got hisself in disgrace wid a white man.'"

"Why, Quincy!" said Edge, in surprise and puzzlement. "I've never heard anybody make any such remark. Hell, they *couldn't*. None of these jossers speaks English. You must be imagining things."

At his first opportunity, Edge went to watch Cricket's performance in Fitzfarris's sideshow. Fitz was clearly delighted to have her among his company, and the audience in the annex tent clearly enjoyed her act there almost as much as her Enchanted Globe. When, dressed as a herdsman and assuming a ludicrously deep voice, Tücsök sang the herdsmen's coarse and indecent songs, the men in the crowd roared hilariously and slapped their thighs, while the women pretended to be scandalized and embarrassed. But the women as well as the men beamed at her and clapped in rhythm when, dressed in a colorfully beaded blouse and a skirt of innumerable tiny pleats, to the music of Fitz's accordionist, Tücsök did the age-old, energetic, coquettish dances of the country inns called csárdás.

"She's a jim-dandy, sure enough," Edge said to Florian. "And either she's an exception among midgets or I was ignorant and wrong to condemn the whole tribe in general. But Governor, before I went on holiday, you were complaining about the company ratio of women to men, and the next thing you do is hire another female."

"Well, I can hardly go out and beat the bushes for male artistes. I'll just have to hope that some men come applying, even if they're first-of-Mays, to start correcting the imbalance."

But the imbalance was not soon improved; a week later it got even more lopsided. At an afternoon performance, Miss Eel's and Ali Baba's contortionist act ended, as it always did now, with the boy sinking down into his skull-and-cross-bones pose. And today he seemed particularly pleased with the jossers' combined gasps and giggles and applause, for he stayed there like that for so long that the equestrian director finally had to whistle for him to get up, take his bows and make way for the trapeze act. Ali Baba ignored him and sat where he was. Colonel Ramrod whistled more loudly and, when the boy still did not budge, crossed the pista to give him an angry shake. Tightly folded as he was, Ali Baba was rather impervious to shaking, but he would have been in any case, for he was dead. The equestrian director beckoned two Slovaks to come and carry him out, just as he was, still fixed in his now sadly appropriate skull-and-crossbones position. The audience laughed and cheered, taking it to be just a farcical conclusion to the act.

The Budapest authorities would have treated Quincy's demise as lackadaisically as they had that of Spyros Vasilakis. But Florian himself was concerned and curious enough to summon a physician to ascertain the cause of this death. After examining the small body, the doctor reported his findings to Florian, and Florian reported to Edge:

"It appears that, in a manner of speaking, Ali Baba's former gentleman friend, Cecil Wheeler, killed him."

"What?"

"Do you recall how, for some time, Quincy had been smelling odors that no one else did, and hearing odd noises, and remarking on strange flavors in quite ordinary foods?"

"Are you saying he was poisoned?"

"No. You'll also remember that, at Cecil's last performance, Quincy fell head-first off the velocipede. He has been walking around ever since—and heroically performing—with a fractured skull. If we had known and immobilized him in bed, he might have recovered. But today his poor head simply, finally succumbed to the injury."

Edge went to say a word of condolence and give a comforting hug to Sunday.

She smiled sadly and said, "We Simmses are sort of dwindling away. Maybe Tuesday and Quincy would have done better to stay with the Furfews, barefoot and poor and ignorant. Maybe we all would."

"Don't talk such nonsense. You know damned well that they both saw more of life, even in their short lives, than if they'd grown old and gray in Virginia. And you are Mademoiselle Butterfly. There is no limit to how high and far you can fly."

When Edge went to condole with Monday, she scarcely seemed overwhelmed with grief. She said, "Lemme ax you somethin', Mr. Zack, that I can't ax my Mr. Demon. He ain't no Southerner, so he wouldn't know. What it is is this. Now that I ain't got no brother Quincy always in plain sight, do you expect folks might raise their opinion of *me*?"

"Why, Monday, I doubt that anybody ever judged you on the basis of your brother. Not your qualities or your talents or—"

"I'm talkin' *color*. Long as Quince was around, I couldn't be nothin' but kin to a black boy. My Mr. Demon calls me his—some French word, means high-yaller. But s'pose some different man never knowed I ever had a blue-gum brother. Mightn't that man take me to be somethin' better'n a half nigger?"

Edge said drily, "You don't mean something better, you mean something *easier* to be." He regarded her, estimating. "Well, I reckon you could pass for an unusually handsome Mexican girl. Or some kind of tropical-island girl."

"Hey, now!" She grinned. "Tell me the names of some."

"Hell, you could *claim* to be the Queen of Sheba. But don't expect people just to take your word for it. The Queen of Sheba was a smart woman, and you'd have to work at getting educated and refined and polished. Like saying ask instead of ax." Monday stopped grinning and looked put upon. "Your sister Sunday, now, she—"

"Yeah, her!" Monday said darkly. "She don't mind bein' a buffalo gal, long as she can talk fancy and show off her fine manners. Damn! And any new man could see I'm her sister, just another high-yaller, couldn't he? I can't better myself unless she does, too. Damn!"

Edge sighed, gave it up and went off to help Florian with the arrangements for Quincy-Ali Baba's funeral.

5

"AUGUST TWENTIETH is Saint Istvan's Day," Florian told his chief subordinates at a meeting called in the red wagon. "Or Saint Stephen's Day, if you prefer. Anyway, it is Hungary's highest holiday of the summer, and we will enjoy our most teeming attendance since we've been here. I shall canvass the troupe and, unless there are cries of rebellion, I intend that day to give *three* shows— one in the morning besides the usual afternoon and night performances."

"Nobody object, I think," said Carl Beck. "We circus people. We rather show, get applause, than on our Arsche sit. And Slovaks all day working, anyhow."

"Very well. Plan for three shows that day. Now, after that day, I am sure we would continue to do the same good business that we've been doing all along, and probably would continue to do at least until winter comes. However, after Saint Istvan's Day, I wish to hit the road again. There is one other particularly beautiful place in Hungary—Lake Balaton—or the Platten See, as Franz Joseph would call it. I think no one should miss seeing that, and the lakeside resorts there ought to provide us with as much patronage as we'd have here."

"Ano, pojd'me na Balaton Jezero!" Alexsandr Banat exclaimed with enthusiasm, he evidently having been there before.

Florian went on, "Then, after a month or so at the lake, when the leaves begin to turn, we will move eastward. We have to cross some four hundred miles of the puszta—the flat, dreary, featureless sea of grass—where there is not even a village big enough to warrant our stopping to show. I want to get to the Russian border before snow flies. I am not eager to make Napoléon's mistake of braving a Russian winter on the road."

"Come you, Governor," Dai Goesle said skeptically. "Russia is one dammo big country, and we will be crossing it as slow as moss. Winter is bound to catch us somewhere there."

"But not on the road and in the open. Although with considerable distaste, I have decided, after long deliberation, to emulate the contemptible Zirkus Ringfedel. From the Russian border, we will travel by railroad train, pausing to show only in Kiev and Moscow before arriving at the destination I have long looked forward to and lusted for—the tsar's grand and shining capital city of Saint Petersburg—where I trust we shall have a long and happy and prosperous stay."

Willi Lothar spoke up. "When all of you leave for Lake Balaton, I shall leave for Russia and arrange to charter a train and engage the first tober in Kiev." He turned to Florian. "Jules will not be accompanying me. I know he will wish to go aloft in the *Saratoga* at the lake. It is a splendid place for a beautiful balloon ascension."

"Hold on," said Edge. "I've had a glimpse of Hungary's prairies—you say they're called the puszta?—when I went to visit the countess. That puszta is dreary, all right. Why should we take the trouble to trudge across four hundred miles of nothingness? Hungary has railroads, too. Why not charter a train here and take it all the way to and through Russia?"

"Because that would be even more trouble," said Florian. "The railroads here in western Europe are what is called standard gauge, if you know what that means. The railroads in Russia are broad gauge, the rails set much wider apart, so the trains are built quite different. We would have to do all our packing and loading and stocking of feed and supplies here, then at the border unpack and unload it all, then repack and reload on a Russian train. It would be more of an inconvenience—and probably take more time—than our going there by road. No, we will head for Czernowitz on the Hungarian border, cross the river Prut and on the Russian side of the river, at Novosielitza, our train will be waiting."

Edge shrugged. "You know best, Governor."

"And, incidentally, we will be leaving behind our midway joints and entresorts and their population. They can continue to do a good trade at Lake Balaton—it has winter as well as summer resorts—and God knows they'd do no trade at all on the pustza. Also, the Russian immigration authorities are notoriously suspicious and unobliging; they probably would not even allow entry to such a gaggle of gypsies. Also, and most important, our chartered train will cost me enough. I am disinclined to hire two or three extra cars to transport the hangers-on."

"Damn," said Fitzfarris. "I guess, like Zack says, you know best, Governor. But I sure will be sorry to abandon my pretty Schuhplattler girls."

"Then start planning and preparing, gentlemen. Canvasmaster, before we leave Pest, lay in any hardware, spare parts, extra canvas and harness, whatever else you might conceivably need in the future. Such things are hard to come by in a country as primitive as Russia, and we won't find them at Lake Balaton either. Kapellmeister, you do the same—sheet music, horn valves, drumheads, whatever —and, in particular, procure an ample supply of the chemicals for the *Saratoga*'s generator. Crew Chief, you confer with Abdullah and that Slovak assistant of his, regarding the quantities of feed and cats' meat we'll need to get the animals across the puszta. Once we're in Russia, that sort of thing, at least, we *can* always replenish." Florian stood up. "In the meantime, I will be buying yet another wagon and span of horses. We will need them, and not just for those extra supplies we'll be carrying. We have recently acquired quite a stock of new and heavy appurtenances: the dressing tents, the cimbalom, Tücsök's globe and ramp. Well, anything else to discuss, gentlemen? Then I declare this meeting adjourned."

On St. Istvan's Day, for the first time ever, the circus presented three shows, and every show was not just a sfondone but a turnaway. Even toward the end of the night performance, no artiste let himself or herself look anything but sparkling and vivacious to the audience, and none of them bungled a single trick in any act. Even the animals seemed imbued with the same spirit, and never once balked or sulked at being overworked. In the night show's closing Grand Promenade, the troupers waved warmly to the crowd and smiled especially brilliantly, proud and pleased at having participated in the best-attended and most profitable day the Florilegium had ever enjoyed. But when the last of the jossers had gone, the troupers and crewmen and bandsmen unashamedly went limp with fatigue, and some did not even take off their pista costumes before falling comatose on their bunks and pallets.

The circus suspended all operations the next day, so the whole company—even the Slovaks, after they had attended to the animals' needs—could relax or rest as they chose. Several of them took this last opportunity to visit their favorite places in the city. Clover Lee, Gavrila and Agnete went for a browse through the Párizsi department store. Carl Beck went to a spa for a final curative soaking and then bought a couple of crates each of the Bánfi hair restorer and Béres invigorator. Abner Mullenax went across the river to Buda to bring back a crate of the ghastly Bulgarian gin, and a quantity of it inside him. Edge, Pemjean, Yount and LeVie went to laze away the afternoon in the New-York coffeehouse. Magpie Maggie Hag and Bernhard Notkin went together to where mostly old people congregated, the checkered concrete tables thoughtfully provided by the City Park, to play a game of chess. Florian spent most of the day in his office, gleefully totting up the previous day's receipts and bringing his ledgers up to date.

The next day was devoted to teardown, cleanup of the tober and loading the circus aboard the wagons. After the loading, every wagon, including the newly bought one, was almost visibly bulging, what with all the extra supplies, feed and bits of equipment Dai and Carl and Hannibal had acquired. Some of the smaller things even had to be stowed in the troupers' living-quarters caravans. Then Florian commanded a number of the Slovaks and the lightest wagon to depart immediately and go on ahead, with a hefty stack of Florilegium posters, to circle the entire extent of Lake Balaton and post paper in every least village and hamlet around its shores.

The rest of the circus train left Pest early the next morning, crossed the Chain Bridge for the last time, climbed over Saint Gellért's Hill, past the gloomy Citadel, and took a road going southwest. Their destination at Lake Balaton was sixty miles and two long days away, so they camped on the roadside that night, near the only building they had seen in several miles: a modest-sized csárda with the signboard Szep Juhászne. "The Fair Shepherdess," said Florian. "With a pleasant name like that, it can't be *too* bad an inn. We will dine there before bedding down."

The innkeeper was delighted to see them; he had doubtless never before had such a mob of patrons squeeze into his establishment. There were not even enough tables for all; they had to eat in shifts. When the first contingent sat down, the landlord immediately, unbidden, set before them immense pewter pitchers of cool dark beer, plus hearth cakes, hot from the fireplace, to munch with it. There was no choosing and ordering of the meal. The diners were simply served huge bowls of what was every Hungarian country inn's standard fare.

"Bográcsgulyás," said Florian. "Kettle stew. What you would call a pot-au-feu, Maurice, or you, Maggie, an olla podrida. Simply a vast iron kettle kept perpetually simmering on the hearth, perpetually being topped up with whatever meat and vegetables come to hand." Whatever it presently consisted of, they all proclaimed it singularly delicious and invigorating.

The happy innkeeper hovered about them during the meal, delighted to be able to converse with at least two of them: Florian and little Katalin.

She told the others, "The fogados—the landlord—says this csárda has been here for ages, and long ago it was the favorite hiding place of the great highwayman Sobri Jóska. He was Hungary's Robin Hood, forever plundering the rich and sharing with the poor."

"No, is that a fact?" said Yount. "And he holed up right here where we're eating?"

"I doubt it," said Cricket. "Every fogados in Hungary will tell you that his csárda once played host to the bandit Sobri, or to the Fair Ilonka, the secret sweetheart of King Mátyás, or to Pál Kinizsi, the Samson of Hungary. In a war against the Turks, Pál killed one of them and then wielded the body like a club to kill a hundred more."

"Well, such stories make for good advertising," said Fitzfarris. "Like some of Florian's flummeries. I think it's clever of the innkeepers."

"Oh, we Magyars are clever, all right," said Cricket, smiling. "I like best the story about the puszta farmer who owed twenty kronen to the local Jew, and couldn't pay. When Uncle Isaac kept dunning him, the farmer offered to sell his cow and hand over the proceeds in full settlement. The cow was easily worth twenty kronen, so the Jew agreed. They went together to the market, and the farmer took along a chicken, as well. A man came up and asked, 'How much for the chicken?' The farmer said, 'Twenty kronen.' The man said, 'Good God! I could buy the cow for that much!' The farmer said, 'Tell you what. Give me twenty kronen for the chicken and I'll let you have the cow for just two copper kreuzers.' So the deal was struck, the farmer pocketed the twenty kronen and paid off the Jew with the two coppers he'd got for the cow. Just as agreed."

All laughing, they got up from the table to make way for the next group waiting to eat.

The next day, as the train got within a dozen or so miles of Lake Balaton, the travelers noticed that the road was bordered by meadows of strange, limp, wild grasses that writhed and whipped like seaweed in just the mild stirring of the air that the passing wagons made. But then, as the train got even nearer the lake, they began to feel a genuine breeze. They were now passing vineyards in which, instead of the mock-human scarecrows common to most countries, long ribbons of bright-colored cloth were hung to flaff and snap in the wind. And they passed haystacks that had originally been cone-shaped, rather like Red Indian tepees, but had been swiveled and swirled by the wind into freer and more graceful shapes, like girl dancers frozen in the middle of a skirt twirl.

"There is always a wind around Lake Balaton," Florian told Daphne, who was riding on the rockaway with him. "I'm inclined to believe that the lake's own configuration must have something to do with it. Lake Balaton is a curiosity in several respects. It's the biggest lake in all central Europe, and not only is it oddly shaped—fifty miles long but only about six miles wide on average—the very lake bed is peculiar. Down at Balaton's southern end, the bottom shelves so very gradually that you can wade out for half a mile before the water reaches your chin. But it keeps on shelving downward, like a fifty-mile ramp, until, at the north end, it is some forty feet deep. I don't know why Balaton's unique characteristics should create a wind, but there always is a wind, and the water is always choppy. When a real storm comes up—and it generally comes from the south—it acts like a squeegee. It scrapes that shallow water up from the southern end of the lake and tries to pile it on top of the deep water to the north. You'll see waves and billows and breakers on Balaton as impressive as any ocean could offer."

"It sounds frightening," said Daphne.

"Well, there have been fishermen and ferrymen here for generations, and they've developed an uncanny knack for sensing any big blow in the offing. When they do, they fire off rockets that can be seen or heard all around the lake. The boatmen and holidaymakers get off the water and out of it, and everybody runs for cover."

The company finally topped a height in the road from which they could see the lake. Its color was a distinctive milky turquoise, polka-dotted with the little whitecaps of chop. Everywhere about it were bright green reed beds, and everywhere above it flew steel-blue swallows and black-headed gulls, and leaning over it from every bank were the ever-present poplar trees, even this late in the summer still shedding their snowfall of white fluffs, and now and then there would be a visible splash in the water as a fish lunged for one of them. Some sporting sailboats were on the lake, but most of the water traffic consisted of fishing dories and the ferrymen's unwieldy big rowboats. At intervals all around the lake were tightly clustered communities ranging from hamlet to small town in size, but there were long reaches of uninhabited shoreline between them.

The two biggest, most popular and most populous resort towns, Siófok and Földvár, were on this southeastern shore that the circus train was approaching, and the resorts were only seven miles apart, so Florian had already told the crew to pitch exactly midway between them. Darkness was coming down, but the travelers could see their Florilegium posters tacked to trees here and there. And when they arrived at their designated tober-to-be, the earlier dispatched roustabouts who had posted the paper were waiting for them. The Slovaks had, on their own initiative, already lighted two cooking fires, fetched kettles of the clean lake water, and had even bought from the local fishermen a basketful of fogas, the Lake Balaton pike-perch. So Magpie Maggie Hag, with the help of Gavrila, Meli and Agnete—and using also the wood stove in the onetime dressing wagon in which she still rode and slept—pitched in to prepare the first outdoor country meal that the company had enjoyed in many months.

Early next morning, Canvasmaster Goesle, Crew Chief Banat, the roust-abouts and the elephants began the setup. Because the lake shore here was all pebbles, they had to move a couple of hundred yards inland to find ground that would hold the tent stakes. And Florian told them to double the number of stakes and guy ropes on the southern side of every tent, as security against the ever-blowing wind. Even that early in the day, quite a crowd of holidaymakers from Siófok and Földvár, having seen the poster announcements of the Florile-gium's imminent arrival, came to watch and admire the setting up and to buy tickets for the afternoon's first performance. That show was a sellout long before the calliope's overture hooted and squealed and echoed up and down the lake. And all the shows thereafter were, as Florian had been confident they would be, as well attended as they had been in Pest. The jossers came not just from the two nearby resorts; many made two-day journeys from the farthest fringes of Balaton and the surrounding countryside.

Jules Rouleau had been hoping to make numerous ascensions over that lovely blue lake and the greenery around it, with which the vermilion-and-white *Sara-toga* would make a striking contrast, but the constant wind kept Carl Beck saying firmly, "Nein! Nein!" However, the wind did tend to gentle down to merely a brisk breeze about sundown, so finally Rouleau persuaded Boom-Boom to let him chance it at that hour. The Slovaks were sent all around Balaton to post paper proclaiming the event, and the tober overflowed with spectators that day.

When the balloon was inflated, it flailed cumbersomely about, as if in distress, alternately slacking and straining and yanking at its anchor ropes. So Florian cut short his usual magniloquent discourse about Monsieur Roulette's bravery and the hazards of challenging the heavens. Rouleau clambered hastily into the gondola— and alone; he refused to risk taking one of the Simms girls—and the roustabouts immediately loosed the tie-downs. The *Saratoga* went up like a rocket, but on a slant, going northward faster than it was going upward, and only narrowly clearing some treetops in its way. However, when it had gained some altitude above the lake, Rouleau found that the breeze lessened—evidently Balaton's eternal winds blew only close to the surface—and at a yet higher altitude he encountered a breeze blowing southward. So he was able, in his accustomed way of letting the balloon rise and fall, to cavort about the sky in various directions.

Then, finally to descend, he took the *Saratoga* toward the south end of the lake and tripped the clack valve to release enough gas so that the balloon dropped to where the surface wind blew. He came whizzing up the lake, adroitly opening and shutting the valve so that he came in on a long downward slant. He was good enough at the job by now that he did touch down just outside the circus midway—a considerable portion of the watching crowd had to scatter in a hurry—but even though he pulled the ripcord to empty the bag in that same instant, his gondola hit the ground with a mighty thump, and bounced several times before it and the deflated bag both fell over sideways. Rouleau was unhurt, but had to scramble rather undignifiedly out of the toppled basket and the tangle of ropes before he could leap to his feet, triumphantly throw up his arms and receive the roar of the crowd.

He didn't try again; that was his only ascension at Balaton. Nevertheless, the village and country folk for miles around the lake talked for months, admiringly, about that event. They were overjoyed that it had happened in their lifetime, for such a marvel had never before been seen hereabouts, and probably never would be again. From that ascension day on, Rouleau found it impossible to buy a beer, a meal or even a pretzel in Siófok or Földvár; the other customers always recognized Monsieur Roulette, praised him, pounded him on the back and insisted on paying for whatever he was eating or drinking.

At one afternoon show, when Edge rode Thunder into the chapiteau in the "Greensleeves" opening spec, his heart gave a little jump. In the starback seats sat two veiled ladies who looked familiar. When they raised and pinned back their veils, they were indeed the "Countess Amelie Hohenembs" and the Baroness Marie Festetics. At intermission, when the rest of the audience departed for the midway, they remained inside as usual, and Edge went eagerly to greet them.

He bowed extravagantly deeply and said, "Welcome, Your Imperial Majesty."

Elisabeth, Empress of Austria, Queen of Hungary, said, in mock dismay, "Ó jaj! You penetrated my modest masquerade. How?"

"I reckon I first got to pondering when you used the emperor's stock phrase to say you had enjoyed yourself."

"Ah, well. I will only remark, Edge úr, that I did not at all *lie* to you. Amelie is my middle name, and I *am* the Countess Hohenembs. And the Duchess of Salzburg and Auschwitz, and the Margravine of Moravia, and all sorts of other things. I could have told you I was something as lowly as the Voivodine of Serbia, and still have been telling the truth. But please, for old times' sake, go on calling me Amelie. I like the tender way you say it—almost as tenderly as you say Autumn."

"What are you doing 'way out here?"

"I am a houseguest at the Festetics palace. I shall be there until the first hint of winter. Then I scurry off to my sunny and balmy and flowery Achilleion."

The Baroness Marie said, "I hasten to tell you, Edge úr, that the Festetics palace is not mine. I have none. It belongs to a cousin, the *Count* Festetics. It is at Keszthely, down at the very southern tip of the lake. Forty miles from here. Even in a coach-and-four, at a canter, we were a whole day getting here. So we put up in a hotel at Siófok last night, and we will do that again before we go back to Keszthely tomorrow."

Elisabeth Amelie said, "I should like to invite you, Zachary, to join us for another holiday stay—"

"Well, I'll feel like a bummer, taking two vacations in one year, but I'm damned if I'll refuse. I'm my own man, and Florian's a decent sort. If it's all right with you, a few short visits would be better than one long one. I could take a day to ride out there, you and I could spend the next day together, then I'd ride back here on the third day. So I'd miss only six shows all together. But, in fairness to the troupe and the audiences, I could do that only, say, at two-week intervals. And I don't know how many times. It'll depend on how long we stay here."

"I am sorry, Zachary. I was about to say that I should *like* to invite you, but Count Andrássy is one of the other houseguests."

"Oh," said Edge, and his face fell. He thought for a few moments, then said, "Could I make an outrageous suggestion? First, tell me, does the Count Andrássy ride?"

"Why, of course. What gentleman does not?"

"But I don't suppose he does any trick riding like yours."

"No. Except dressage, steeplechase, riding to hounds…"

"Maybe he'd like to learn some flourishes. You just saw our équestrienne. Not the dark girl doing haute école. The blonde—she's wearing a scarlet léotard today—who jumped over the banners and through the hoops."

"*Really*, Zachary. The garters and garlands. You forget that I know some of the circus language."

"Well, that's Clover Lee Coverley, and she has a great yearning to get acquainted with noblemen. If you invited both her and me, she might talk your count into letting her give him some lessons in really fancy riding. And meanwhile, you and I could be—doing other things. Clover Lee's only about seventeen, but she's precociously mature for her age, and—"

"Gyula is much attracted to youth," Elisabeth Amelie said pensively. "Even I am fourteen years younger than he is. A girl fourteen years younger than *I* am ought to make him glow like your limelights." She laughed mischievously. "Yes, you truly are outrageous, Zachary. Very well, both of you are most cordially invited." Then she was serious. "Mind you, I should not wish your Clover Lee to displace me permanently in Gyula's affections."

"Affections? That makes me sound like a pimp. I only meant for her to keep him entertained on horseback, and for her to bask in the presence of nobility. Anyway, I'd imagine that a count married to a countess and in love with an empress wouldn't amuse himself for long in the company of a circus bareback rider."

"Be sure you tell *her* that. And for you, dear Zachary, I shall disrupt my regular daily program. Since we will have only one day at a time together, I shall forgo my morning exercises and studies, so we can share the forenoons as well as the afternoons and evenings."

"Thank you, Amelie. Your Majesty."

"Count Festetics, Count Andrássy and I will look forward to seeing you and Clover Lee, as soon and as often as you can come."

Edge went back to work as Colonel Ramrod, highly elated, but at the same time feeling that he was becoming a drone and a deserter. When he and Florian occasionally stood together on the sidelines while an act was in progress, he did not broach the subject. Even after the closing spec, as they stood together watching the audience empty out of the chapiteau, he still hesitated to speak up. But then occurred something marvelously fortuitous. Three jossers lingered behind those departing, conferred briefly among themselves, then came over to Florian and spoke to him in Magyar.

The three were men, and they looked very much alike: brute-ugly, tall, burly, sunburnt almost to bronze, with curly black hair and enormous black walrus mustaches. They were also identically dressed: a leather vest over a bright red shirt, much-scuffed leather trousers so broad that they flapped like skirts, heavy leather boots and, atop all, a black hat that looked like a plum pudding set in a wide soup bowl. Most curious, each of the three carried a korbács whip coiled on one shoulder.

After conversing with them for some minutes, Florian turned to Edge. "These are the brothers Jászi. Arpád, Zoltán and Gusztáv. They are csikosok— herdsmen, range riders of the puszta. They recently lost their jobs when their employer's ranch went bankrupt, so they entrained for the west to have some civilized and cultured diversion in Budapest and here at Balaton before returning to the puszta to seek new positions. Right now, they would like us to lend them three horses so they can give us a demonstration of the csikos riding style. I should like to see it."

"So would I," said Edge. He whistled for a Slovak and sent him to saddle and fetch the three horses acquired so long ago from the ambushing Virginia bummers.

When the horses arrived, the brothers Jászi did not even step on the stirrups, but vaulted from the sawdust to the saddles and had the horses instantly in a furious gallop from a standing start. Then they did amazing things. They performed every trick that Buckskin Billy did, such as sliding under the horses' bellies and up their other sides to the saddles again, at full gallop. But they also turned and rode backward in the saddles, steering the horses by twisting their tails. Then, holding the tails, they slipped off the horses' croups and galloped on foot behind them, going as fast as the horses did. Then they hauled themselves up the tails, leapt onto the croups and bounced forward to the saddles again, and rode standing on them, and then, incredibly, standing on their heads—the horses still going at stretch-out gallop.

Next they resumed their proper saddle seats and uncoiled their korbácsek. First they employed them as whips. Thundering past the front row of starback seats, the first Jászi lashed out and toppled the first chair in the row, the man behind overturned the second chair, the last man the third, while the first man was already toppling the fourth chair, and so on, until the whole row of seats was upended. One of the brothers, careering past Edge, flicked his cigarette from his lips, so deftly that all Edge felt was the swish of wind.

Then they used the korbácsek as lariats. One brother swung at another, not to sting or slash, but to coil the whip around his waist and playfully yank him from his saddle. Another flung his korbács straight upward, at just the right instant to coil its end around a center-pole guy rope. He let that drag him from his saddle and, clinging to the korbács butt, swung back and forth in the air.

After a moment, the whip end loosened from the guy rope, unwound and dropped the man—but at the precise moment his horse had galloped around the pista and was under him, so he dropped neatly into the saddle again.

"Jesus Christ," said Edge. "These boys make my voltige look like a kid on a rocking horse."

"Well, they are seeking employment," said Florian, "and we have been seeking male artistes." He hesitated, cleared his throat and went on, "Also, for a long time, Zachary, I have felt that you give too much of yourself to our Florilegium —equestrian director, liberty act, shootist, voltige rider, general pacificier when there's trouble. It has somewhat distressed me to feel that we were taking undue advantage of your good nature. Now, I am fairly sure that you possess no professional jealousy, but I will ask this. Would you feel you had been demoted or rebuffed if I hired the Jászi brothers to replace you in the voltige?"

"Not at all," Edge said cheerfully, and almost exultantly repeated it, "Not at all!" The brothers had now dismounted and come over to them. Edge exclaimed,

"Welcome, boys, welcome!" and pumped the hands of Zoltán, Arpád and Gusztáv, grinning so broadly that he was almost as ugly as they were.

Florian looked a little puzzled at Edge's ardency, but said, "I'll take them to the office to talk terms, and call in Maggie Hag to talk costumes."

"Before you go, Governor..." said Edge. "Now that you've got such a spectacular replacement for at least one of my acts, I'd like to ask a favor..."

He told of the new invitation from the "Countess Hohenembs," this one including Clover Lee, and his notion of their taking only three days off each time, and not too often, maybe every two or three weeks. He wished he could really stagger Florian by revealing Amelie's true identity, but decided he had not the right to do that.

"You'll still have the liberty act that you can handle yourself, and Monday's high school riding, and now these prodigious Jászi brothers. Three good equestrian turns. So the jossers are not likely to miss one lone bareback rider. And one sharpshooter. Anyway, we'll only be absent from six performances each time we go to the palace."

"Well, I can hardly say no to your consorting with such exalted beings," said Florian, who was, however needlessly, feeling guilty at having taken Buckskin Billy's voltige away from him. "Just please try not to marry off Clover Lee to one of your titled friends. I'd hate to lose her permanently."

So Edge went and found Clover Lee and told her of the invitation, and the limitations on their visits, and his hope that she could keep the Count Gyula Andrássy distracted with horsemanship while he enjoyed the company of the Countess Amelie. Last of all, he thought to ask if she'd *like* to go.

Clover Lee, whose cobalt eyes had been getting bigger and bigger all through his recital, gave a whoop like the calliope and cried, "Hell, yes, I'd like to go! Let's go tomorrow!"

"No. I'll be taking Thunder, meaning I've got to give some other horse a double-quick course in fancy stepping, so Monday can go on with her haute école. Meanwhile, I suggest that you go in to Siófok and buy yourself a dinner gown—we high-toned folk dress up to the nines for dinner. Also let me point out that these will be rigorous journeys. Thunder is an old cavalry veteran; he'll do the trips with no strain; but your Snowball or Bubbles won't. I'd recommend that you try out all eight of those polka-dot horses and pick the staunchest and speediest."

"All right. Oh, Zack, I can hardly wait!"

"Yes, I can see you already putting Countess in front of your name. But this Andrássy is forty-five years old and he has a wife and kids. I don't know what other houseguests may be there. There could well be some bachelor noble closer to your age. I don't care how much flirting you do, but, whenever the countess and I aren't around, you're to *stick with Count Andrássy* and keep him occupied. Is that clear?"

"Yessir, Colonel," she said, smiling and glowing and giving him a snappy salute.

Then she went immediately, bubbling with pride and delight, to tell all the other circus women of her imminent foray into the world of the high and mighty, and of her almost-*certainly* auspicious prospects there. The women lavished congratulations and good wishes on her, and assured her that she would enrapture every Prince Charming in that fairy-tale milieu. Several of them, with affectionate amusement, pretended to be bitterly envious of her. Only one, Sunday Simms, said not much at all.

And she did not say anything when, later, she and Edge chanced to pass on the midway and he gave her a genial greeting. Sunday petulantly tossed her hair and, head high, walked on. Edge turned and caught up to her and said, "Whoa, Butterfly. Why the frost?"

She glared at him and hissed, "So your countess has already got a husband, has she? So what? It doesn't stop her teasing you on, every time she's in your vicinity. It doesn't stop you chasing her like a coon hound after a bitch in heat."

"What is this? Why on earth are you concerned about what I do? I don't think a kid should appoint herself the overseer of a grown man's behavior. This is the first time I've ever seen you show a bad temper, Sunday, and for absolutely no reason to do with you."

"You're falling in love with this one, too, that's why."

Genuinely bewildered, Edge said, "If I fell in love with Maggie Hag—or Cricket the midget—or Willi Lothar—why would you *care?* Anyway, all I'm doing is going for another little holiday in the country. I'm even taking along a chaperon."

Now she spat like a cat. "You're taking Clover Lee to hoodwink her husband while you and the countess frolic in secret!"

"Well, confound it, girl, even if that's so, it was *your idea.*"

"Yes," she said miserably. "*Damn* me and my ideas!" And she burst into tears and ran away, leaving Edge shaking his head in perplexity.

6

THE STREETS of Keszthely were empty at eleven o'clock at night, but Edge finally spotted a man, perhaps an insomniac, out walking. He asked the man for directions in the only way he could—repeating "Festetics?" several times—and the man replied in a way Edge could comprehend—by pointing. Edge and Clover Lee took the road he indicated and, three miles outside town, arrived at the palace. It was a grand edifice, though not so grand as Amelie's—more like a tremendous city mansion removed from the city and set among acres of lawns and flower beds. A butler answered the front door when Edge banged the gold-plated knocker. Edge introduced himself and Clover Lee, but the butler evidently knew no English. He looked haughtily and contemptuously at the man and girl in dusty riding garb, and at the sweat-matted, head-drooping two horses on the drive. So Clover Lee tried her Rouleau-taught French to tell him that they were guests invited by the Countess Hohenembs.

The butler understood that, but said only, "Attendez ici," and shut the door in their faces.

It was opened again by the Baroness Marie Festetics, who welcomed them most warmly and apologized for the butler's not having been told to expect them, if ever and whenever they might arrive. She and the now obsequiously fawning butler led them to the dining room, the baroness saying, more to Clover Lee than to Edge, "The rest of us are in the drawing room, having a brandy before bed. But I am sure you will not wish to be introduced until the morning, when you are rested and refreshed and presentably dressed. Right now, you must be hungry, so I will have the kitchen prepare a hot meal, and meanwhile have your valet and maid draw baths for you. Where is your luggage?"

"On the horses, Baroness."

"I will have it taken up to your rooms, and have the horses taken to the stables, fed and groomed. As soon as you have had a quick wash, Burkhalter will serve you any drink you might like to have."

"Csopaki," said Edge, and the butler poured them each a large goblet of the wine, then bowed himself backward out of the room.

The baroness must have galvanized the cooks and scullions, or they were paragons of efficiency, for Edge and Clover Lee had barely finished their drinks when footmen were laying their places at the table and setting down steaming platters of mixed grill, hot rolls, silver pots of both coffee and tea, and Burkhalter was refilling their wine glasses.

"Golly," said Clover, her eyes shining. "You take this all so nonchalantly, Zack. Butler and footmen and valet and maid and all." She ravenously attacked her meal. "Well, this *is* the south end of the lake, so would you call this 'southern hospitality'?"

"Just the natural Hungarian generosity and the good manners of highborn folk," said Edge. "I'd better warn you that your maid probably doesn't speak either English or French. But she'll know her job; you won't have to lift a finger or give a single command."

When they had finished, Burkhalter led them upstairs to their rooms, where their personal servants were waiting. Edge and Clover Lee had of course not brought their clothes and other effects in portmanteaux, but in ordinary saddle-bags and cavalry-style saddle rolls. So both the valet and the maid were clucking over the wrinkled and rumpled garments. They took them away, indicating by gestures that they would be set to rights overnight and ready for wear in the morning. Edge took his bath unassisted, but Clover Lee was only too happy to have her maid fuss over her, do the soaping and sponging of her, shampoo her golden hair, slip a nightdress onto her and even tuck her into bed.

As she had promised Edge, Amelie shirked her usual morning health-and-strength routine and, like any ordinary empress, came down to breakfast with the others. Introductions were made all around—in English, which everyone present spoke fluently. At Edge's whispered suggestion, and to the amusement of the other guests, the Empress Elisabeth introduced herself as the Countess Hohenembs; Edge did not want an overawed Clover Lee blurting the truth all over the Florile-gium. Their host, the Count Festetics, was a widower, an elderly and portly gentleman, but spry, good-humored and given to long-winded orations; he went on at extravagant length in welcoming his new guests and praising Clover Lee's beauty and grace. Count Andrássy Gyula, first Premier of the new Kingdom of Hungary, Minister of War and Minister of Foreign Affairs, was tall and lean and handsomely hawk-faced, with a sprinkle of silver in his side-whiskers. Besides the Baroness Marie, Clover Lee and Edge, there were no other guests.

Clover Lee and Edge being the newest comers, the others insisted that they go first to the sideboard to choose from among the salvers of various kinds of omelettes, soft- and hard-boiled eggs, bacon, ham, sausage, kippers, calf's brains au beurre noir, racks of toast, bowls of gruel, pitchers of various juices, urns of coffee and tea. They did not serve themselves; they merely pointed, and footmen heaped their plates and filled their glasses and cups.

So Clover Lee and Edge were the first to sit down at the table and, while the others were still at the sideboard, Clover Lee had the opportunity to murmur, "You were right, Zack. It's almost spooky how much the Countess Amelie looks like dear Autumn. *Beautiful!* I'm disappointed that there are no young men visiting, but I can't complain. It'll be no hard task, playing companion to such a distinguished man as the count. He's quite handsome for his age. And he must think the same of me. When he kissed my hand, he practically undressed me with his eyes."

Indeed, when everybody was at table, Count Gyula's interest in the girl gave him the arrogance to interrupt an interminable anecdote his host was telling: "...Though clearly guilty, the man was never prosecuted because, you see, he was a mágnás, an aristocratic landowner. And incidentally, friend Edge úr, from that word comes your English word magnate—"

"They tell me," Andrássy rudely overrode him, addressing Clover Lee, "that, in addition to your beguiling blonde beauty, you have a great talent as an équestrienne, Coverley kisasszony."

"Oh, do call me Clover Lee, Your Grace," she said, coyly blinking her eyelashes at him.

"And you may call me Gyula. Or Julius, if you prefer the English rendition. I should like to ask—after breakfast, would you perhaps favor us with an exhibition of your bareback dancing and acrobatics?"

She said modestly, "I should be flattered and honored to perform for such an eminent audience."

"Better than that," said Amelie. "Miss Coverley has graciously offered to teach *you,* Gyula, some manly nuances of trick riding that will astound your steeplechasing friends. I think you should accept her offer." She laughed. "And imagine how thunderstuck your fellow ministers would be if you rode a horse right into the council chamber and began doing csikos leaps and capers. They'd never dare oppose you again on any measure you might introduce."

"Pompás!" Andrássy shouted, laughing and slapping the table. "Very well, Clover Lee. We will all attend your performance and then, when the others go about their other diversions, you and I will practice in private."

Both Clover Lee and Amelie smiled radiantly, and Edge would have, too, except that Amelie had forbidden him to.

While most of the company leaned lazily against the fence around the palace's riding ring, Clover Lee went with a boy into the stables to pick out a suitable horse—not Thunder or her Pinzgauer; they had to rest for the long ride on the morrow. Meanwhile, Amelie announced:

"I have already and frequently enjoyed Miss Coverley's performances, and Zachary must frankly be weary of seeing them. So I shall take him off and show him some of the local sights." And she sent another stable boy to saddle her two Arabians.

As they rode out of the palace grounds, the huge wolfhound Schatten appeared from somewhere and paced along with them. Amelie first led Edge down to Keszthely and the lakeshore, where many family groups were having "piknikek," wading, swimming, rowing or sailing. They halted their horses in a grove of shrubs—the sweet-scented olive, which lived up to its name by being most powerfully and deliciously fragrant—to watch the children wading so far out in the water that their features were indistinguishable, though they were walking on the lake bottom. The swimmers had to go so far out that they were mere dots.

Then Amelie led Edge around the north shore for a few miles, turned inland for a few miles more, to Szent György, to show him the famous lava rock "organ-pipe" formation there. It was a curving and recurving cliff of massive, round, vertical columns; it looked very like a calliope for Titans. They tethered their horses at the bottom and Schatten lay down to guard them. Then Edge and Amelie climbed up and around and among the columns until they found one with a flat and commodious top carpeted with soft grass and mosses. There, undisturbed except by a couple of goats bounding by, they made love, and Amelie's now-familiar crescendo and climax and diminuendo of musical laughter resounded among the rocks as if the columns really *were* organ pipes.

At dinner that night, Edge wore his white tie and tails, and Clover Lee said, admiringly, almost in surprise, that he had never looked handsomer. The two counts, of course, also wore full dress and Andrássy even wore his ministerial sash across his breast. Clover Lee looked angelic in pale-green taffeta with her golden hair streaming down the back of it, and Amelie looked undisguisably imperial in silk the exact color of her ruby tiara, necklace, rings and bracelet. Throughout dinner, Amelie and Edge exchanged looks that Andrássy would have had to be blind not to notice and interpret. However, he *was* temporarily blinded, for he and Clover Lee were exchanging the very same sort of looks. Only the Baroness Marie was aware of both sets of silent communion, and she evinced neither acceptance nor amusement nor disapproval.

Count Festetics was oblivious to any of that byplay, and equally oblivious to the fact that the others at table were quite oblivious of him. He told anecdotes and reminiscences of exceptional prolixity and dullness, untroubled when they elicited little or no comment or response from his listeners. In the infrequent intervals when he had to stop and catch his breath, the guests traded small talk heavily freighted with mots à double entente.

Amelie asked, "How did your lessons go today, Gyula?"

"Oh—ah—very well, indeed. I learned several new things. Unique ways to check. To change gait. To assume various artistic positions."

"And he taught me some things, too," said Clover Lee. She paused for an exquisitely timed beat or two, then added, "To be more graceful at taking the hurdles, for instance."

Andrássy said, "I hope you will soon return for further practice."

Amelie said, "Surely you did not practice riding all day."

"No, no. I am ashamed to admit it, but I took some amateurish falls and eventually got quite sore. So I walked with Clover Lee down to the deer park to show her this year's fawns. Alas, they have lost their dapples, but they were friendly and not at all timid of us."

"That is because so few people ever go into the deer park," Amelie said roguishly. "It is a private and cozy place."

Count Festetics, having breathed enough to recharge his soliloquy machinery, launched into another anecdote. However, this one did rouse his guests and make them respond with merriment. Count Festetics was evidently among the many who knew that the Empress Elisabeth seldom took offense when people made fun of her emperor husband. For this particular story concluded, according to the count: "Well, Franz Joseph told the poor, pleading supplicant, 'I will have it thought about.' Then he turned to his equerry and commanded, 'Think about it, Klaus.'"

Amelie joined the others in appreciative laughter, and said, "Ó jaj, that is Megaliotis to the life!" and the other Hungarians at the table, though they had heard her use the word often before, laughed even louder at the Magyar pun implied in the Greek.

After coffee and Blood Brandy, a cherry liqueur, Edge and Clover Lee said their warm thanks and good-byes to the company, for they were going early to bed and would be leaving at dawn, before any of the others were up.

"Oh, but not *good-bye*," said Amelie, looking at Edge.

"Let us hope not," said Andrássy, looking at Clover Lee.

Edge rode cavalry style: run a mile, walk a mile—so he and Clover Lee left the palace stable yard at a gallop next morning. When, a mile later, they slowed to an easier gait and could converse, Clover Lee said boldly, "I hope you and Countess Amelie had as much fun as Count Gyula and I did. When you told me he was getting on in years, I expected him to be all paunchy and wrinkled and withered." She laughed. "*Withered* he is not."

"I'd be surprised if he was. He's only five years older than I am."

"Well, I hope the countess properly appreciates *you*. Gavrila Smodlaka once told me that young women and older men make the best combination."

Edge rode in silence for a minute, then said, "You and I have come a long way from that pitiful mud show at Beaver Creek, haven't we?"

"All of us have. Except those we've lost along the way." Clover Lee hesitated and then said, almost inaudibly, "I wonder what ever became of Mother..."

Edge and Clover Lee were back at work in the pista the next afternoon, and Clover Lee had already regaled all her sister troupers with a detailed description of the Festetics palace—"A hundred and one rooms, a library two stories high, and fifty-two thousand books on shelves from floor to ceiling. The fanciest stables you ever saw. A deer park with tame deer..." She had also given a detailed account—perhaps not *too* detailed—of her entertainment by the nobility, her having a personal maid to dress and undress and even bathe her, plus the particulars of every meal she had eaten there. The other women ooh-ed and aah-ed, and when they expressed envy this time they may not have been entirely pretending.

Clover Lee would blissfully have made the rugged journey again within a few days, and doubtless had the stamina to do it, but Edge said a firm no. "We've got responsibilities, girl. We can't desert the Governor and the rest of the troupe and the paying public whenever we take the notion."

"Damn. How many chances in a lifetime does a girl—?"

"However," Edge interrupted, "two weeks from now, so I'm told, there's to be a four-day festival and church doings and street fairs in Siófok. It's to celebrate the birthday of some old fellow named Kossuth, who is a longtime national hero of some sort. So our show will surely draw only scant houses then, and that's when we'll go back to the palace. We'll be able to stay two days this time."

And they did go—only to find, to Clover Lee's dismay, that Count Andrássy had been recalled to Budapest on urgent government business.

"Some kind of tiresome debate about trade agreements," Amelie said indifferently. "Probably not at all important, but Gyula *will* do his duty. The message came by telegraph and he departed immediately. I regret to tell you also, my dear, that he will not be coming back to Balaton this year."

Edge, knowing Amelie's conviction that every younger female was her "rival," privately wondered if she might just perhaps have engineered that urgent summons herself. But he said nothing.

Anyway, Clover Lee was not dismayed for long. It turned out that the palace was now inhabited by a considerable number of new guests: eight young men who were all barons, margraves or counts—or at least were viscounts who would assume those nobler titles when their fathers died—and the wives of six of them. But two of the young men, a Baron-to-be Horvát Imre and a Count-to-be Puskás Frigyes, had no wives, here or elsewhere, and their faces brightened when they were introduced to Clover Lee next morning.

Over breakfast, after the Count Festetics had taken a quarter of an hour to tell of his once having shaken hands with the hero Kossuth Lajos, Amelie announced:

"Zachary and Clover Lee, since you have an extra day to spend with us on this visit, I am preparing a special treat. We shall go to Almádi. Those south-shore resorts of Siófok and Földvár, where your circus is pitched, are the most popular on the lake. Everyone flocks to them. But those of knowledge and taste go to Almádi on the north shore. It is quiet, quaint, little frequented by the vulgar city folk, and it has many delights, as you will see."

"Is it far from here?" asked Edge.

"Yes, nearly as far as it is from here back to your circus. What I plan is that we leave early tomorrow morning and arrive there sometime after dark. Take rooms in an inn, then spend the next day letting me show you about."

"But that will be our fourth day, Countess. We have to be back at the tober that night."

"And so you shall. It is just twelve miles diagonally across the lake from Almádi to your circus ground. The big ferry rowboats can each carry a horse and its owner. With four men at the oars, they make that crossing in only about three hours. So you can leave me and return to the tober as early or as late as you please. Even the next morning, and still be there in time for your show."

"Oh. Well. That sounds fine."

"I assumed it would, so I have already sent the Baroness Marie on ahead to engage rooms for us. The inn I have chosen—for a reason I will tell when we get there—is the Torgyöpi. It is quite a respectable inn, not just a country csárda, but it has only five rooms for overnight guests. For me, for Clover Lee, for you, Zachary, for Marie—and one extra. So, Clover Lee, you may wish to invite an escort for yourself."

"Um-m..." said Clover Lee. Young Horvát and young Puskás immediately put on looks of deep yearning. "Yes, I probably will."

Amelie went on, "I assumed that, too, so I have sent three maids and two valets along with Marie. I dislike being attended by strangers, and even the best inn's domestics are always unreliable. Ours will sleep in the inn servants' quarters, or in its barn, if necessary."

"And what about us," asked Edge, "if those five rooms are already occupied?"

Amelie flicked him a glance of tolerant amusement. "Marie will have only to mention my name. Now then. Let us divert ourselves about the palace and the grounds today, and not too strenuously, so we are fit for the long ride tomorrow."

Clover Lee disobeyed, to the extent of donning her léotard and fleshings and giving another exhibition of her équestrienne skills to the assemblage of new guests, at which the young viscounts Horvát and Puskás cheered and clapped louder than all the others together. When she was dressed again, Clover Lee did spend the rest of the day in leisurely activities. Puskás and Horvát simultaneously requested the honor of showing her the statuary on the grounds, the exotic-fish pond, the lily pond, the deer park. Clover Lee accepted them both, so she was flanked by them as they wandered about the estate, and she flashed coquettish looks at them impartially, and impartially bandied flirtatious small talk. At intervals, the two swains glared go-away looks at each other over Clover Lee's blonde head, while she was wickedly wishing that—like a genuine femme fatale—she could provoke them to a duel for her favor. But they were still a threesome when the company sat down to dinner that night.

Edge did his host the courtesy of spending some of the morning in his company, with the twelve other men and women, and listening, with an assumed air of rapt interest, while old Count Festetics related at tedious length—and sometimes stood up to act out—incidents in his life from boyhood to date. It took him half an hour to get to his thirteenth year, in 1809, when he was initiated by a governess into the Great Mystery. He did not act out that event, but he made it seem as boring and wearisome as his droned account of it; Edge decided that the governess must have been a patient and a desperate woman.

The guest couples, one after another, began to remember errands they had to do elsewhere. Edge stayed long enough to hear about the failed but heroic 1848 revolution against Austria's rule of Hungary, expecting an account of strategies and tactics and battles. But it developed that the count's only heroic revolutionary service had consisted entirely of distributing "Down With the Emperor" manifestos. At which, Edge said he had to go and see how his horses were bearing up after yesterday's long ride.

"God, but that old man is a jawsmith," he said, when he found Amelie cutting long-stemmed roses in one of the gardens.

"That is why you will almost always find a new and different group of guests every time you come here." She added, with a provocative smile, "And there are so many things nicer to do than either talk or listen. Here, help me carry these roses up to my suite."

And there, during most of the rest of the day, Amelie did very little talking but a great deal of her distinctive laughing, soft to loud to soft again, and did it repeatedly, and evidently would have been pleased to go on doing it indefinitely. But they eventually had to pause, to dress for dinner and listen to Count Festetics some more.

Early next morning, the two couples—Clover Lee had chosen Puskás to be her escort; he was handsomer than Horvát—set out in an elegant but fairly lightweight clarence with a four-horse hitch. The great dog Schatten cantered alongside and occasionally leapt up on the seat beside the coachman for a riding rest. The clarence was followed by another four-in-hand carrying hampers of wine and luncheon victuals, the considerable traveling luggage of Countess Amelie and Viscount Puskás, the considerably less luggage of Edge and Clover Lee, and their saddles. On lead reins behind that coach, Thunder and the Pinzgauer ran unencumbered and easily.

They did not eat their luncheon until quite late in the afternoon, because Amelie insisted on waiting until they could detour southward onto the Tihany peninsula. There the coachmen spread linen tablecloths piknik style, and set out the food and wine, in the middle of eighty-five acres of lavender. Tihany, said Amelie, was the supplier of oil of lavender to every parfumerie in Europe. The gardeners were just then harvesting the blossoms, and it seemed to Edge and Clover Lee that the fragrance must be detectable as far away as Budapest.

They reached Almádi about nine o'clock that night, and that town also was perfumed, but by a more subtle citric aroma. The proprietor of the Torgyöpi Inn, bowing and scraping, and the Baroness Marie met them and led them up an outside staircase, so they need not elbow through the taproom full of tipplers, to their rooms on the upper floor. The innkeeper spoke to Amelie in Magyar, but she repeated his message in English to Edge and Clover Lee. He said that the baroness and his local clientele had already dined, but he was holding the kitchen staff in readiness to prepare a superb meal for the new arrivals—and what would it be Her Imperial Majesty's pleasure to eat?

"On this visit I am the Countess Hohenembs, Juhasz úr. And what else would one eat at a lakeside inn but the delicious fogas in that secret caper sauce of yours? Asparagus. Potatoes stewed with paprika. And to start, I think, a cold parsley soup. And, of course, Somlyó."

"It will be on the table, Your Grace, as soon as you and your guests have refreshed yourselves."

A maid or a valet was waiting in each of the guests' rooms, and had, with mysteriously prescient timing, already filled the plunge baths with hot and fizzy mineral water—and Amelie's with hot Jersey milk. The Baroness Marie joined Amelie's maid to help attend her. No one dressed for dinner here, but they all changed from their travel-worn clothes into fresh garments.

They convened again downstairs in the big taproom. Its many tables were all chockablock with men, and a few women, convivially drinking, loudly talking and laughing. In one corner, the wife of innkeeper Juhasz was playing a cimbalom. She played nowhere so well as Elemér Gombocz, but none of the patrons seemed to be listening, anyway. Juhasz led the new guests to an alcove off the room, distant enough that the ambient noise was not overpowering, and curtained for privacy, but Amelie told him to leave the curtain open.

"So I can show you something," she said to Clover Lee and Edge and Puskás. "I always come to this inn because it is unique. It is built on the border between the megye—the county—of Veszprém and that of Fejep. Therefore, what you would call the county line runs through the middle of that vast taproom out there. In consequence, this inn is much frequented by highwaymen and other kinds of outlaws and fugitives. If, as often happens, the police of one county come in to take a look around, or just to have a drink, the rogues simply move to the other side of the room. That longest table in the center actually straddles the megye line. It may be that the men you see sitting at it are detective policemen on one side and bandits on the other, all drinking amicably together."

As they ate their delicate, flaky, melt-in-the-mouth fogas pike-perch, Amelie told of another curiosity unique to Almádi:

"This wine we are drinking is the local Somlyó, which the Almádi folk claim to be the best wine in Hungary, and I am inclined to agree. The vintners say it is so good because the vines eternally 'see their own reflection in the Balaton.' That is to say, the sunlight reflects off the lake waters, so the vines get the sun on the underside of their leaves as well as the upper."

When they finished dinner and went to their chambers, it became evident that they really need not have engaged *all* of the Torgyöpi's rooms, because, after the servants had been dismissed, neither Edge nor young Puskás spent that night in his own assigned quarters. Edge did, however, get up early and return to his room, so Amelie's maid could be summoned to prepare her olive-oil bath.

The day was disappointingly overcast and gray, but the lakeside vineyards were turning red and gold and seemed to radiate a sunshine of their own, and the air was still scented with that clean, tart citric aroma.

"Lime trees," said the Baroness Marie. "Almádi is planted with sixteen different varieties of them, and they bloom at different times, in sequence. So the air here, except in winter, is *always* perfumed."

The town was set within a semicircle of hills, so the two couples went to wander among them, admiring the peasants' cottages—only modest things of whitewashed logs or wattle-and-daub, but every one entwined all about with climbing roses or wearing rose bushes growing all over its thatch roof. Amelie pointed to the highest of the hills in the vicinity, a sort of lopsided cone in shape, which they were approaching.

"This is the Great Nose," she said. "According to Almádi legend, the very last remaining giant of the fairy tales died here. The people respectfully buried him, but they could not scrape up enough soil to cover his nose."

When they arrived there, they found it was a protrusion of solid rock, with no trace of vegetation anywhere on it except for splotches of varicolored lichen. Amelie showed them the numerous but far-apart cells that hermit monks had laboriously chipped out and inhabited, some eight hundred years ago.

"The Nose has always served another function, too," she said. "Perhaps you noticed the boy sitting on its very top. He would be the youngest child of some fisher family. From up there, he can see down through the surface glare on the water, into the lake's depths. When he sees a shoal of fish, he signals its location to the men in the dories."

The atmosphere was getting warmer, grayer and more muggy when they returned to the lakeside. They settled themselves on a beach of reddish sand and, as Amelie had earlier arranged, their coachmen came from the inn bringing hampers of hot food, wine, table silver, linen cloths and serviettes, plus a tremendous beef bone for Schatten. The four were just finishing the last bottle of Somlyó when they were startled by a loud *boom!* overhead, and looked up to see a puff of white smoke hanging below the gray sky. Another puff blossomed near it and, after a moment, came the *boom!* of that one.

Clover Lee said, "They must be shooting off fireworks at that Kossuth festival over at Siófok."

"No," said Amelie, frowning. "Those are the storm-warning rockets."

Indeed, the sky, which had been a featureless lead-colored dome, was now bulging into pouches of bruise-colored cloud.

"Is it likely to be a bad one?" asked Edge, as more rockets burst up and down the lake.

"The storms are always bad on Balaton."

"Then I'm sorry, Amelie, but I'll have to leave you. This could be big trouble for our circus tops. I've got to get over there before it breaks, if I can. Where do the ferries dock?"

Amelie took him and Clover Lee there, while the coachmen ran to the Torgyöpi to fetch their luggage, saddles and horses. Amelie spoke to one of the ferrymen—who, recognizing her, tugged his forelock and bowed repeatedly—but when he replied, even Edge could comprehend that he was being apologetically reluctant.

"He says," Amelie translated, "that every other boat is coming in off the water, and you'd be a fool—so would he—to go out upon it now for a three-hour crossing. He also says that he certainly would not chance the crossing with a horse in the boat. At the best of times, a horse is always nervous, moving about and shifting the boat's balance. If the storm hits, the panicked horse might kick the boat to fragments. Now, if you wish, I can *command* him, and he will not dare disobey. . . ."

"No. Don't call for your red-hot irons. See if you can persuade him to take only me. Clover Lee can stay here overnight—the storm surely will be over by then—and arrange to bring over the horses and our gear in the morning."

So Amelie spoke again, and rather forcefully. The ferryman looked still reluctant, but cowed. He called his three rowing mates and gave them instructions. They looked frankly apprehensive, but also gave the empress a forelock salute, went and piled oars in the boat and undid its painter from the dock. While they were occupied, Edge gave Amelie a quick embrace and a kiss and said:

"These have been two days to treasure among the best memories of my whole life. If that barge doesn't founder out there, I'll try to see you at least once more before the circus moves on. Or, if the whole Florilegium gets blown away, I may have to settle here permanently."

"Isten vele," she murmured, smiling a little forlornly. "God keep you safe."

With the four oarsmen pulling their hardest, even the big and clumsy hulk of a ferry moved away southward at a goodly speed. Incoming boatmen shouted at them in tones of questioning amazement, or warningly, or derisively, but Edge's ferrymen saved their breath and did not shout retorts. The storm held off for two hours, until they were only four miles from their destination. Then it hit—a fierce south wind, into which and against which the oarsmen had to struggle. It was really less wind than water, what with its deluge content of rain. The lake surface changed from chop to waves, then heaved into billows, then the billows became high, curling combers, which the wind instantly decapitated into blasts of spindrift.

Within minutes, Edge and the other men were ankle deep in water. One of them shouted to him and jabbed a finger. Edge looked where he pointed and saw a bucket tucked under a thwart, so he quickly began bailing. No storm could have dumped enough water into that big boat to swamp it, but the oarsmen certainly did not want the extra weight of the water, battling as they were directly into the onrushing waves and the battering-ram wind. Though Edge bailed as rapidly and efficiently as he could, he barely managed to keep the water where it had been when he started, at ankle level, because the driving rain and blown spray came into the boat as fast as he threw it out.

The ferry was tossing and lunging and yawing so, and the air was so thick with water, that Edge wondered how the men could possibly be keeping on course, or if they were. Nothing could be seen anywhere beyond a four- or five-yard radius from the boat, except the forks and jags and writhings of blue-white lightning. They lit up the dense air every few seconds, so the bone-shaking, mind-numbing thunder was like a continuous cannonade.

It took fully two more hours to go that remaining third of the crossing, but they did it and almost perfectly accurately. Something suddenly slashed at Edge's neck, and he looked up from his bucket to see that they were entering the lakeside reed beds. Though the reeds thrashed and whipped at the oarsmen on the windward side of the boat, they did palliate the force of wind and waves to some degree. In just a few minutes more, the ferry's blunt bow grated on pebbles. All the men, including Edge, leapt overside and wrestled the big craft up the bank to where it was securely beached. The four oarsmen then collapsed on the pebble beach, so exhausted and already so drenched that they cared not at all that the rain still scoured at them. Edge left them to follow him and collect their fare when they recovered, and plodded on inland against the wind and rain.

Twilight was coming on, but here, where the roiled and thrown-about lake water was not contributing to the murkiness, Edge could see farther. He soon espied the Florilegium some distance off to his left, but its skyline was different from what it had been when he last saw it. He arrived there, and saw why: the chapiteau's canvas and poles and contents were all on the ground. And the ground, having been denuded by the thousands of trampling feet over the past weeks, was now a morass of glutinous mud. Almost every one of the pavilion's roof and side panels had been ripped from its lacings, and the pieces blown far and wide. The roustabouts and most of the other men of the circus were chasing them and trying to roll or fold them to prevent their being blown away entirely.

The two center poles lay on the ground, pointing in opposite directions. The many side poles, the starback chairs, the seating planks, their stringers and jacks were strewn all over the tober. The bandstand had collapsed into an untidy heap of boards, and the cimbalom stood on its legs, but they were slowly sinking into the mud. The tangle that had been the trapeze rigging gleamed from the middle of a puddle. Snarls and knots and snakes of ropes were everywhere. Of the whole chapiteau, only the tent stakes still stood firm in the ground, outlining the immense oval where the pavilion had been, and the pista curbing in the middle of that oval had not budged.

"Blowdown!" shouted Florian, coming up to Edge. He was red-eyed, his hair and little beard disheveled, and his fancy frock coat and stirrup trousers were plastered with mud, but he did not seem unduly downcast. "Could have been worse. Hell, I've *had* worse ones."

"Anybody hurt?" Edge shouted back, to be heard above the roar of wind and the explosions of thunder.

"Nobody important. A Slovak got his collarbone broken."

They put their heads close together, so as not to have to go on bellowing.

"No jossers injured?" Edge asked. "To hold us to blame?"

"No. Only a sparse bianca house—because of the festival, you know. When the rockets went up, soon after intermission, I ordered the top evacuated—the people were sensibly already going, anyway—and Maggie refunded their ticket money. Meanwhile, we rolled all the wagons to the windward of all the tops, beginning with the menagerie, and running extra guy ropes from them to the side poles. The more skittish animals, the camel and the zebras, we tethered in the woods. Carl got all his instruments inside the wagons, except the cimbalom; we couldn't spare men to move it."

"Sounds like you did all you could."

"Well, the menagerie, the dressing tents, the annex, they are all fairly low to the ground—they merely split some lacings here and there. But, even with all our precautions, the high chapiteau could not buck a storm like this one. And a few of the flimsier midway joints and tents got blown to Kingdom Come."

"Can the chapiteau be repaired?"

"Oh, yes. Have to be dried out and cleaned of mud. Some grommets tore loose and one of the gumshoe spikes snapped off. The lungia boom's yoke tore loose from its center pole. But nothing Stitches can't fix. And we'll need a few miles of new rope."

Edge's four ferrymen appeared just then, looking weary and bedraggled, but also looking proud of their having bested the storm.

"These are the men who rowed me over here," said Edge. "Ask how much I owe them."

Florian did, and they named a price that Edge thought so ridiculously little, after what they had endured, that he voluntarily tripled it. Florian spoke to the men again and pointed, and they went off to the wagon he had indicated.

"Mag has made sandwiches and cooked up a huge vat of soup on her kitchen-wagon stove, so the workers can snatch some nourishment on the run. I invited your ferrymen to partake."

"Well, where can I pitch in to help here?" Edge asked. "I'm just standing around like a rube rubberneck."

"At ease, soldier. The other lads are sufficient. Any more would just get in the way. Besides, when we've got all the fragments retrieved and collected, we'll want one clear-headed and unfatigued boss to oversee the further operations."

"What operations? We'll be out of action for a good long while. Even if we got the chapiteau up again tomorrow, this sea of mud will take a week to dry out. Nobody would wade through this to see the best show on the planet."

"I am talking of teardown. As always, Zachary, we must work things out as we go along, and now the Storm God or Mother Nature or something has told us that it's time to take our leave. You just now came through the lakeside reed beds; they were green when we arrived; they are golden yellow now. Autumn is upon us. Since a good part of the teardown has already been accomplished, willy-nilly, I intend that we do the rest of it, pack up and head east. We'll tarry here until Stitches and his men have done the major repairs. Then they can do the lesser work on the road, whenever we stop for the night."

"Ah, well," said Edge, with a sigh inaudible in the storm. "I sure have got fond of Balaton, but of course you're right. In which case, Governor, I'd like your permission to extend my malingering for a few hours more. I'd like to say a last good-bye to the countess. She's just across the lake in Almádi. As soon as the storm clears, I can go over and back in about seven hours. I'll be here before our men are rested up enough to tackle the teardown or need any clear-headed boss."

"Of course, my boy. Permission granted."

The rain stopped shortly before dawn, as abruptly as if a valve had been turned off. The wind dropped to no more than its usual brisk velocity. The lake subsided to its normal chop, and the last clouds trailed off northward in time for there really to be a dawn. The sun came up and set the whole wet world a-sparkle, striking little rainbows from every raindrop on every tree leaf and on every surface of the battered Florilegium. Edge was again aboard when the ferrymen went back across Balaton. They had been much invigorated by the night's rest and Magpie Maggie Hag's provender. They pulled with a will and chattered among themselves—probably, thought Edge, about the devastation they had seen at the tober.

About halfway across, Edge's boat met two others. In one, the polka-dot Pinzgauer horse rocked and swayed and uneasily shifted its feet and walled its eyes. In the other, Thunder rode more serenely, and Clover Lee was with him. She and Edge both managed to tell their oarsmen to stop, and the men let Edge's boat and Clover Lee's drift close enough together that they could converse.

"What are you coming back for?" she cried, with distress in her voice. "Dear God, is it all gone?"

"No, no. Chapiteau blew down is all. Nobody hurt. It looks pretty chaotic to me, but Florian is taking it in stride. Is the countess still at the inn?"

"Yes. She'll stay until the roads dry out some."

"Florian is going to tear down and move on, so I want to say good-bye to her. You go on, and I'll be back in a little while. And thanks, Clover Lee, for bringing the horses and our gear. I'm only surprised you're not bringing the viscount."

She grinned. "He never got around to proposing. Maybe I kept him too busy to propose. Anyway, if he had, I don't think I could *bear* to have the name of Mrs. Frigyes Puskás. Not even with Countess in front of it."

Amelie, from her upstairs window, saw Edge trudging up the path to the inn and instantly guessed why he had returned. She went down to the taproom and found it empty except for landlord Juhasz and his wife, rearranging bottles behind the serving bar. Everybody else in Almádi was out inspecting the storm damage to his boat or nets or vines. Amelie asked Juhasz úr and né if they would please absent themselves for a little while, and they obligingly did so, as Edge walked in.

He and Amelie embraced and held each other tightly, in silence for some time. Edge did not love this woman and had never entertained any aspirations of ever being anything more to her than an occasional diversion. But he was truly fond of her—and, he would admit it, secretly more than a bit awed and smug and conceited at having been the lover of an empress. And there was also, every time they were together, the illusion that at least the lineaments of Autumn lived again. It was hard to part from her.

"It need not be forever," she said, when he had explained the situation. "Yours is a traveling circus, and I do much traveling myself. This entire continent is but a fraction bigger than your one nation of the United States. So there is every possibility that we will meet again. In Hungary, Austria, Greece, England..."

"I'll devoutly hope so."

"Or you may quickly forget me," she said, with a pretense of cheerful teasing. "There are many beautiful women in Saint Petersburg, among the upper classes, anyway."

"I'm willing to wager my right arm that I'll never forget *you*."

"Nevertheless, I do not wish you to take holy orders and vow celibacy. I shall even help you to meet some of those highborn women. Did you know that the Tsaritsa Maria Alexandrovna is of German birth? Before she wed Tsar Alexander, she was Princess Maximilienne of Hesse. Her family and mine have always been close. I was only an infant when she married and disappeared into darkest Russia. But we have had crown reasons to correspond from time to time. I will write for you a letter of introduction to the tsaritsa, and send it by a ferryman before your circus departs."

"That's kind of you. It will especially please Florian. He is always wanting opportunities to mingle with the élite."

"And you and I will not say good-bye, Zachary, but viszontlátásra, auf Wiedersehen, 'til we meet again. Now—kiss me once more. Then I will go and I will not look back, for I shall have tears in my eyes."

Edge's own eyes were a little blurry when he stood alone in the taproom. He reached for a bottle of brandy, poured and drank a substantial glassful, left a coin on the counter and turned to go. Then he paused, surprised. In the cimbalom in the corner, an apparently overtightened string chose that moment to succumb to its long strain, and broke: *kling-g!* Edge waited until its small, sad, last-ever chime had finished echoing faintly around the big room, and then he left.

7

THE CIRCUS TRAIN, now minus its tail of midway vehicles, made good time going east and a little north across the puszta. The roads were decent, and so was the weather. There was never the slightest hill to climb, and the rivers and creeks were all well bridged or easily fordable. There was only an occasional csárda along the way at which to get a meal of kettle stew, but Magpie Maggie Hag kept her stove continuously banked with coals so it could be fired up in a hurry. She and her women helpers managed competently to keep the whole company fed—if not with sumptuous viands, at least nutritiously—from the supplies stocked in her wagon. She also still slept in there, and everybody suspected that the Hanswurst did, too, since he drove her vehicle and was constantly with her. The old gypsy and the old joey were small people, but they must have been cramped in there, for it had formerly been also the dressing wagon, and still carried, on hangers or neatly folded on shelves, all the costumes of the troupe.

Starting early each morning and not stopping until it was too dark to roll, the circus train made some twenty miles a day, meaning it would take them about twenty days to reach the border at the river Prut. But in less than a week, everybody in the train was thoroughly sick of the puszta—that endless plain of high grass and wild grains, interrupted only at long intervals by minuscule mud villages, where the peasants came out to stare vacant-eyed and slack-jawed at their passing. They also, now and then, passed a farm of domestic grains, where they might see the farmer doing a primitive sort of threshing. A broad circle of mown rye or buckwheat was laid on the ground, and he stood in the center of the circle holding a guide rope while a horse plodded around and around, treading out the grain. There was an infrequent tree or clump of shrub, too, but in this season everything was gloomily colored brown or dun or gray, except for the occasional spangle of bright vermilion wild poppies.

Looking at the flat and uninviting vista ahead, before they took the road one morning, Yount gloomily commented to his Agnete, "Well, this poosta may not be the end of the world, but I do believe I can see it from here."

Standing nearby, Magpie Maggie Hag, who had lately been even gloomier than the others, said, "For some, it *is* end of world."

"Hvad?" said Agnete. "For none of *us*, I hope. We have just lost one companion, not to mention all the midway people."

Abner Mullenax had come to Florian shortly after teardown at Balaton, his one eye bloodshot, and said, "Governor, I ain't no use to you-all no more. I'd like to stay here with the midway folks. One of them shoe-slapper girls is kind of sweet on me, and the whole bunch have offered to pay me a smidgen for doin' odd jobs—carryin' kegs and swampin' out and suchlike—enough to keep me in likker, anyway. Plus peck, if I can live on sausages and pretzels and ices."

"Well, old fellow, you've been with us for a long time, but you've never been indentured. You are free to go or stay wherever you please."

"I like this place, and the locals are friendly. I think it'll be a good spot for Barnacle Bill to drop anchor."

"Won't you be a little hampered by the language problem?"

"Not in bed with my girl. And in a saloon, all you got to do is point at a bottle and crook your elbow."

"True. But Abner, you should have some money put by, in case sometime you do part company with the midway. The *Saratoga* was your contribution to the Florilegium, and we never paid you a cent for it."

"Aw, shucks, forget it. You've kept me on the payroll, when I ain't been nothin' but dead weight for months now."

"No—here—I insist on your taking at least this hundred dollar's worth of forints. Tuck it in a grouch bag."

"Well..." said Mullenax, thirstily licking his lips, and he accepted the wad of money.

"We all wish you happiness here, Abner. Someday surely we will pass this way again, and we'll hope to see you thriving." But Florian sadly doubted that they would ever see Barnacle Bill again, here or anywhere, considering his ever-oftener crooking of the elbow.

Now, far out on the puszta, Florian bawled for the circus train to move out. To Edge's slight surprise, Magpie Maggie Hag climbed up to ride beside him.

"Want tell you something," she said, as they bumped from their camping field up onto the road. "I dukker trouble again with Pavlo Smodlaka. Somewhere. Sometime."

"Oh, hell, what now? Last time, he was convinced that the Démon Débonnaire was a real demon out to get him."

"Now he worried férfifarkas get him."

"Jesus. What is férfifarkas? It doesn't sound any more dangerous than dandruff."

"Don't know word in English. In Spanish maybe hombre-lobo."

"Wolf man? A *werewolf?*"

Magpie Maggie Hag shrugged. "Pavlo speak some Magyar. In last csárda where we stop, he drinking with peasants, tell them he going to Russia. They all look horror. Say he brave man, dare go there, because of férfifarkas. In Russia, they say, some men become férfifarkas. In Russian tongue, oborotyen. Come full moon, such man grows hair all over, four legs, tail, fangs, claws, exact same as wolf, goes hunting other men to eat. Or women, children. Easier to catch."

"Godamighty. And he believed this bunkum?"

"Pavlo believe anything, suspect anything, scared of anything. Even nervous of wife, now. Tells me Gavrila wakes him up in middle of night to criticize his *dreams*. She never do any such thing."

Edge made a noise of amused exasperation. "I'll have a talk with him. Try to persuade him there's no such thing as a werewolf."

"Do that, pralo. I dukker very terrible trouble."

By detouring slightly to the south, the circus could have visited Debrecen, a market town at the crossroads of several trade routes and sizable enough to have provided ample patronage for several days of showing. But Florian said he was damned if he'd unpack and unload the tightly crammed wagons until he had to do it at trainside, and he was anxious to get to that waiting train, for the nights were getting cold and even the daytimes were getting nippy. So the only community in which the Florilegium dallied for a while was a village called Nagykálló, somewhat bigger, cleaner and more attractive than the imbecile-inhabited mud hamlets they had earlier passed through. And they paused in Nagykálló only because it happened to be the home village of the Jászi brothers, and Zoltán, Gusztáv and Árpád together besieged Florian to plead that the company stop and enjoy the hospitality of their relatives and friends.

Florian might have argued, but he was given no chance. The circus train had halted in the middle of the large square around which Nagykálló was built, and a crowd had immediately gathered. All of them recognized the Jászi boys and began an uproar of greetings and welcome-home. Zoltán waved violently to hush them, then belabored the crowd for at least ten minutes with a bellowed, gesticulating recitation of the brothers' adventures since they had left the defunct ranch outside town.

"Now he's telling them," Florian interpreted to the others of the troupe, "how we rescued them from unemployment, disgraceful idleness and possible starvation. We have given them a job they delight in, and have made them stellar artistes, the toast of Lake Balaton, and soon to be *internationally* renowned. He enjoins the villagers to help him and his brothers show their gratitude by wining, dining and putting us up in their houses, and then turning out tomorrow en masse for a festival in our honor."

The crowd roared again, obviously in wholehearted concurrence, and Florian added, with a sigh of resignation, "We can hardly be so boorish as to rebuff such enthusiastic friendliness. They are poor people—homespun smocks, wooden shoes—and yet eager to share with us whatever they have. Stitches, order your Slovaks to find a field in which to stow all our vehicles and tether the walking beasts. Then, except for attending to the animals, the roustabouts might as well relax with the rest of us. No need even to post a watchman."

The villagers pressed in upon the company, plucking at sleeves and crying, "Gyere! Egy vendeget!" So the artistes and crewmen got rather haphazardly apportioned out by ones and twos—the partnered men and women managing to stay together—and were triumphantly borne off to their inviters' houses. The aged mother and father of the Jászi brothers got not only their sons but also Florian and Edge. All of those except Edge spent the remainder of the day in animated conversation. Then, after supping with the family, Florian excused himself and went the circuit of all the other houses entertaining his company, to see if there were questions or problems that he could resolve by speaking Magyar.

Every guest that night got a potluck meal or whatever the host family had been cooking up for itself—in most houses the standard peasant fare of mutton gruel, cabbage, black rye bread and home-brewed beer. But the women of the house clomped about in their wooden shoes on the hard-packed earthen floor, already at work to prepare a grand feast for the next day. They killed and plucked chickens, brought in slabs of beef and lamb from their barns, brought butter and milk and eggs and vegetables from their spring boxes, began peeling and chopping and stirring things. Meanwhile, everybody in every family happily chattered at every circus guest, not a whit discouraged or desisting when the guest could reply only with a wavery smile.

However, when, with the aid of gestures, the hosts made the guests understand that they were to take the family bed or beds, and the family would sleep on the floor, some of the visitors made polite but firm protest. They seized on Florian when he dropped in and made him tell their hosts that they would do no such thing, that they would sleep in their own caravans or wagons. Most of the company, though, were too meek or too overwhelmed by their hosts' pertinacious generosity to refuse the family beds. Long before morning, they wished that they had.

"Bugs!" said Daphne, with disgust and loathing, when the company convened outdoors next morning. "I am covered with welts!"

"Not just bedbugs! Fleas and lice!" said Meli, scratching. "I feel all crawly. I itch all over."

"Now, now," Florian said soothingly, though scratching himself. "It's an old adage; you're not properly circus until you've been properly lousy. Remember where you are, and pity the people, and try not to be too obviously distraught or displeased by the inconveniences. Besides, this short sojourn will make you better appreciate the lodgings I have hitherto arranged for you, and intend to continue providing wherever they are available."

"But we'll be taking these vermin with us when we go!" squealed Clover Lee, scratching. "Into our caravans, onto the train, everywhere!"

"No, we won't," said Edge, scratching. "Just don't go near your vans today. Stay in these same clothes. We'll be sleeping here again tonight and leaving in the morning. Ask your chums who did sleep in their vans last night, and didn't get contaminated, to fetch you fresh clothes to put on tomorrow. But not to fetch them *until* tomorrow. Meanwhile, we'll all do an old army trick. I've already been scouting around, and there's an ant hill down yonder by that linden tree." He pointed.

Daphne said, incredulous, "Bugs, lice, fleas aren't enough?"

Edge ignored her. "At bedtime, strip down to your skin and take your clothes

—never mind if you have to step over the family on the floor. They won't give you a glance. I've noticed that our hosts sleep buck naked and pile their clothes high on a shelf or something. Before you go to bed, take *all* your clothes and go and heap them on top of that ant hill. The ants will have eaten them clean of the vermin by morning. Just make sure you pop anything still crawling on your skin before you put on the fresh clothes your chums bring."

Some of the more modest of the company were scandalized, and bleated. Others thanked Edge. And even the most modest, after spending the whole day scratching, followed his advice that night, and found that it worked as warranted, and was well worth their blushing nighttime run in the nude through a houseful of strangers and through the village lanes to the ant hill by the linden tree.

However, that day's festival was entertaining and absorbing enough that most of the lousy and flea-ridden company scratched only absentmindedly, all their attention on the performances being given in their honor. The first thing they noticed was that overnight a tremendous wooden platform had been erected in the middle of the village square, supported on posts only about a foot high.

"For the dancing," said Florian.

"What do they need that for?" asked Fitzfarris. "The ground here is as flat and hard and smooth as any ballroom floor."

"For resonance. Magyar dancing involves a good deal of stamping and leaping, and on the platform they can thunder more loudly."

The whole village population attended, and so did hordes of country folk, somehow apprised of the occasion during the night and come from miles around. All those who would not be performing, or not yet, sat or squatted on the ground around the platform, giving the Florilegium guests the places where they could see best. Florian sat with Papa and Mama Jászi, so he could ask questions, and he relayed the replies and comments to any interested others of the troupe.

There climbed onto the back of the platform—to face the honored guests—the village musicians, three men in all, wearing their best and best-kept suits of clothes, as was evidenced by the odor of camphor they exuded. The three heaved up an old and scarred cimbalom, at which one seated himself; the two others went away and came back with an accordion and a zither. They warmed up by playing an overture: "There Is But One Girl," already familiar to the circus folk from Beck's rendition. And despite the paucity of instruments, it was well played. Even cimbalist Elemér was seen to nod in approval of the cimbalist onstage.

Then Carl Beck was seen to confer with little Tücsök, and the midget got up and scampered around behind the platform. When the piece was finished, she reached up and tugged at the coattail of one of the men, and spoke to him. The man nodded with enthusiasm, first to her, then out at the circus people. Tücsök scampered back to Boom-Boom. He beckoned to various of his windjammers—the snare and tenor drummers, the tuba and contrabass tuba, the trombone, clarinets, violins, the oboist, and to Hannibal Tyree, the bass drummer, and sent them running to the wagons to get their instruments.

When all those bandsmen returned, they arranged themselves behind the platform, so as not to detract from the village musicians' distinction of being onstage. Then the audience gave a great gasp of awe and rapture. They had never heard anything like it, when "There Is But One Girl" was played again, and thunderously, joyously, with flourishes, by that massed ensemble. Thereafter, when singers took the platform, Beck kept his band silent, not to overwhelm the voices. But when dancers came onstage, if the accompanying music was familiar to Beck and his men, they played in concert from the start. If it was unfamiliar, they let the Nagykálló musicians do the first refrain and chorus, which was enough to enable them to join in, in perfect tune and time, for the next several repetitions.

If only the prettiest Nagykálló females were allowed or cared to perform in public, then there was in this vicinity an extraordinarily high percentage of pretty women and girls, high-breasted and long-legged. One group of them wore short white gowns festooned all over with little silver beads. Another group wore short, brightly colored dresses that were an infinity of tiny pleats. All wore high, soft, white leather boots. The women and girls had arranged their hair in whatever style best suited or pleased them. By contrast, the men had all plastered down their normally curly black hair, uniformly flat and shiny, with fringes of spit curls across their foreheads, and all wore black bandit mustaches like those of the Jászi brothers. Indeed, the Jászi brothers themselves participated in most of the doings on the platform. All the men were shod in high, soft, shiny black leather boots. For the romantic and comic dances, they wore wide, pleated white linen pantaloons and blouses embroidered all over with flowers of red, purple, orange and green. For the more warlike dances, they covered those vivid blouses with bulky, shaggy, colorless sheepskin cloaks.

"You suppose that we are poor people here," Papa Jászi said to Florian. "And we are, we are. These costumes are brought out only—and tenderly, respectfully—on the most special of occasions."

"My company and I are honored," said Florian.

"But poverty has some advantages, however paltry and pathetic," old Jászi went on. "Our people spend most of their lives stumping about in heavy, clumsy wooden shoes. It follows, then, that when they don the soft, light dancing boots, their feet are feather weightless and fleet and nimble."

"Jaj de szép!" exclaimed Florian. "I can see that."

When only the women and girls danced, the group in beaded white did frisky, laughing, coquettish dances. The group in colored frocks did even brisker, louder-laughing and shouting comic dances. At least one of those was danced throughout on the heels of their boots, their toes never touching the platform.

The men's dances were still more energetic. They repeatedly leapt into impossible caprioles, slapping their hands against their boots behind their backs, in front of them or split wide sideways. In one of their comic dances, the men all sat on low milking stools and danced and stamped their feet in rhythm to the music. Then they lifted their feet and held and galloped the *stools* about the platform in intricate patterns, still in perfect time to the music.

For their warlike dances, the men put on—besides the bulky sheepskins— spurs that they jingled and clashed together, to add a whole new instrument section to the band. Then there was a sword dance. The swords were very old, nicked, some slightly bent; but the men must have been up all night polishing them, for they were bright as new. And in that dance, the many ringing, spark-spewing sword fights—each man against another, or one against many, or all against all—added yet another new instrument section to the music.

"Almost all our puszta men's dances," Papa Jászi confided to Florian, "derive from the old verbunkos, the military recruiting dance. The emperor used to send a military band and a troupe of soldier-dancers all about the land. They did such a rousing, exhilarating verbunkos that many of the local young men were stirred to patriotic fervor, and would march off with them to take up military service." He chuckled. "We Magyars are easily moved by emotion."

In between every few dances, the performers stood still to sing—some solo, then all in chorus with the village musicians' accompaniment, then a capella— songs of love, of melancholy, of ancient heroes, anthems from the failed revolution of twenty years ago. They went on like that all day, seemingly tireless, alternating singing and dancing—except for a break at midday, when numerous village housewives went among the crowd, handing out a light repast of little mutton pies and mugs of beer.

The performance concluded at twilight with an explosive climax. A girl singer had just finished a sweet solo about the long-ago lovers King Mátyás and the Fair Ilonka. As her voice and the music trailed off diminuendo, there came a loud rumble of horses' hoofs. Gusztáv, Arpád and Zoltán had gone to get their circus mounts and were galloping headlong around the outskirts of the seated audience, doing their breakneck voltige and shouting war cries as they went. Within minutes, almost every other young man of the village had got a horse from somewhere and joined them, until there was a continuous ring of sheepskin-clad plainsmen doing the voltige—and every one as expert as the Jászi boys—around and around the outside of the square. Beck's band boomed into Liszt's "Battle of the Huns," loud enough to be heard above the tumult.

Then the horsemen, still whooping, thundered in single file out of the square and down a lane. The square was quiet again, except for the people's excited exclamations over this unexpected gala day. The musicians left the platform and the housewives brought from their stoves and hearths and ovens the fare they had been preparing since the night before, setting out trays and platters and bowls and jugs and pitchers, stacks of clean wooden dishes and tin utensils, until the platform was covered all around, to farthest arm's-reach, with food steaming and smoking in the cool twilight air. The Florilegium guests were of course urged to go first to the vast buffet. As he helped himself to liver dumpling soup, beef rolls stuffed with mushrooms, cucumber salad, breaded fried cheese, poppy-seed cake and Debröi wine, Florian remarked to Daphne, just ahead of him in line:

"By God, I'd like to hire and take along every single person who has performed today, if only we had transport for them."

"And if they'd come," said Daphne. "They seem overjoyed that the Jászi brothers are making good in the great outside world, but I rather sense that most are satisfied with their life here. Even sharing it with the bloody vermin."

Next morning, thanks to Edge's prescription, the troupers were able to leave behind their own collection of vermin and boarded their vehicles or mounts in fresh clothes. When the train filed out of Nagykálló, the villagers again gathered to cheer them on their way. But all the brilliant costumes of the festival had been put away for the next such grand occasion, if any should ever again occur. The people were wearing their everyday homespun garb and wooden shoes, the only distinctiveness in their dress being that unmarried girls went bare-headed and the married women wore coifs or kerchiefs.

Two days later, near sundown, the circus train had to ford a creek. The first ten or twelve vehicles did it handily, the water barely reaching their wheel hubs, and climbed easily up the graded bank on the other side. But the Hanswurst was an inexperienced coachman; he had managed to drive Magpie Maggie Hag's kitchen-and-wardrobe-and-sleeping wagon capably enough so far; however, here, he veered just a little to the right as he crossed the ford. When the horses climbed the farther bank, the left-side wheels were on the grade, the right-side wheels humped up onto the higher ground alongside, and the wagon slowly, almost lazily but ineluctably fell over on its left side. The two draft horses braced themselves to keep their feet, so there was a loud, splintering crack as the wagon tongue broke.

Yount, driving the red wagon just behind, halted his Lightning in the middle of the creek and let out a yell to alert the wagons that had already crossed.

"Confound it," he grumbled, hooking his reins onto the dashboard and preparing to get down. "I *told* Maggie she ought to let a Slovak drive her cook wagon. But that old fool Notkin is so set on courting her..."

"Well, it turned over gently enough," said Agnete, beside him. "They couldn't have got worse than shaken up."

But then they saw the smoke spurt from the crevices of the wagon body. Yount leapt into the water and splashed frantically to the farther bank. Other men jumped from their horses or vehicles in the line behind and hastened forward to help. Yount yanked open the cook wagon's back door and smoke billowed out. He had to wait a minute or two for the draft to thin it before he could even see inside, and then he said, "Oh, Jesus," under his breath before shouting to the others, "Get buckets! Anything! Scoop water from the creek in here!"

Yount did not wait for that, though. He crawled inside among the burning costumes and other flammables, lay down on the wagon wall that was now a floor, and, with his feet—feeling the heat even through his stout boot soles—shoved away the wood stove. It had slid across the room, laid itself like a lover on top of Magpie Maggie Hag, embraced her when its iron door swung open, pinned her to the wall and spilled its live coals all over her. Then Yount hastily scrambled out again, his own clothes smoldering here and there, his black beard singed and his face and hands blistered. The bucket brigade took over, and the fire was extinguished and the stove cooled in just a few minutes.

Outside the door, anxiously wringing his hands, Florian asked, "Is she badly hurt?"

"She's not hurting now, Governor, I'm sorry to say," Yount told him. "She'll never hurt again." Rouleau had fetched his rudimentary medical kit and was smearing olive oil on Yount's face and hands.

"Oh, Mag..." said Florian, with a heartfelt groan. "Poor Mag..."

Then, from the front of the wagon, someone gave a shout. Edge and Pemjean sloshed around there and discovered the other casualty. Notkin had not fallen or jumped when the rig turned over, or at least not soon enough. He lay at a slant against the roadbank, on his back, and the edge of the driving-seat board had knifed into and cruelly pinched his belly. Perhaps if not everyone had run directly to the more visible and urgent calamity, someone might have noticed the Hanswurst's predicament and lifted the wagon to drag him loose for some kind of emergency treatment. But, for all his vitality in the pista, he was an old and fragile man. Whatever the cleaver-like board edge had done to his insides, Notkin was as dead as Magpie Maggie Hag.

"Old Mag... old Mag..." Florian kept repeating, wretchedly, as the bucket brigade finished its work and the last smoke cleared.

"Don't go in, Governor," said Yount. "It ain't no pretty sight. Me and Zack will take care of her."

Someone came and told Florian of the Hanswurst's death, as well, and Florian spared some sorrowful words for him—but Florian was clearly more affected by the loss of Magpie Maggie Hag than by any other tragedy that had occurred in the Florilegium since Edge and Yount had been traveling with him.

"She was on the first show I ever joined out with, when I ran away from home," said Florian. "God only knows how old she was *then*. She's looked the same age ever since. Well, she had a long life, a good run. So did Notkin, I guess. But Mag taught me a good deal of everything I ever learned about circus, and she came along with me when I got brash enough to organize my own. She left a fairly decent outfit to join out with mine—and I'd be stretching the truth to brag that mine was even a mud show when it started." He took a handkerchief from his sleeve and dabbed at his eyes. "Been with me... loyal, helpful, hard-working ... all the years since then. Here in Europe, America, here again. I don't know what we'll do without her..."

Then he slogged away from the creek and plodded off into the tall grass to grieve by himself. The other men set the wagon upright and Stitches brought canvases. Edge and Yount tenderly wrapped Magpie Maggie Hag's charred and tiny corpse—tinier even than in life—while Dai shrouded the Hanswurst. The Slovaks dug graves, a toilsome task in the puszta, where the millennia of grass growing, dying, reseeding, growing again, had made the ground an almost impenetrable mesh of roots. But it was done at last, and by then Florian had returned from his solitary mourning.

Edge said, "It's pretty near dark, Governor. Should we put off the ceremonies until morning?"

"No. Maggie always liked the dark. Let's get this ordeal over with. And we'll camp here for the night. Keep them company for at least a little while longer."

At the graveside, some of the people sniffled or wiped at their eyes. Even Nella Cornella, who had long worked with Bernhard Notkin, and the other women, some of whom had known Magpie Maggie Hag for years, only sobbed quietly. But the Jászi brothers, newest additions to the troupe, barely acquainted with either of the deceased, demonstrated their Magyar emotionalism by weeping openly and copiously.

By torchlight, Dai Goesle preached a short and simple service: "Almighty God, with Whom the souls of the worthy, after they are delivered from the burdens of the flesh, do live in joy and felicity, we give Thee hearty thanks for the good examples of these Thy servants, who, having finished their course, now rest from their labors..."

And afterward, as he had had to do all too often, Florian sprinkled a handful of earth into the graves—he also dropped in their conduct books—and spoke the last words, in a choked voice: "Saltaverunt... Placuerunt... Mortui sunt..."

"Zack," Yount said to him, as the Slovaks covered the graves—and doubtless the puszta grass began immediately to overgrow them again—"I don't want to bother Florian with this. He's all broke up. There's several of our women can cook, but it's going to be pretty scant grub from here on. Practically all our groceries was in that wagon. Not too much got burnt, but everything got water-soaked."

"I reckon they can make soup, then, if nothing else."

"Even worse, Zack. Practically all our costumes was in there, too. A lot of them *did* get burnt, or too scorched to be any good any more, or the colors all run or the spangles all ruint by the water. Now, we got cooks to replace old Mag, but I don't think any of our gals can replace her at seamstress work."

"You're right, Obie. Damnation! Well, don't bother Florian with that either, right now. You know what he'd say. We have to work things out as we go along. And it looks like we *will* have to. Maybe we can find a footloose seamstress before we take the railroad train—we're not far from that border town now—and maybe there'll be time before we reach Kiev for her to work up a new wardrobe."

When the other circus women had taken from the wagon some watered comestibles that they could make into soup, and cooking fires had been lit, and Stitches and his assistant carpenters were fitting a new tongue to the wagon by lamplight, Edge climbed inside the wagon by himself, with a lantern, to refold or rehang on the clothes poles what costumes seemed salvageable, and to carry out what other groceries might be dried out and still edible. Then he began to tidy up the personal effects of Magpie Maggie Hag and the Hanswurst, intending to ask Florian—when the Governor was himself again—what disposition to make of them. The two trunks of the old man and woman contained most of their possessions, and they had been scorched and blistered only on the outside; their contents had not suffered from either fire or water. When Edge opened Magpie Maggie Hag's trunk, the first thing he saw—lying on top of everything else, easiest accessible—was a thick, much-thumbed and dog-eared book: *The Ancient Gypsy's Dream Book; or, Every Manner of Omen Mystically Interpreted.*

"Well, I'll be damned," Edge muttered. "Is this what Mag relied on, all this time?"

He tried to recollect some of Magpie Maggie Hag's predictions or onsets of sulking in her bunk. He found himself remembering the very first time he ever heard her "dukker" a dream—that one of Sarah Coverley's, something about falling off her horse and getting enmeshed in a net. And he recalled quite clearly—because it had come so nearly true—that Magpie Maggie Hag had said it foretold Sarah's someday falling into evil doings and being abandoned by her friends.

The *Dream Book* was alphabetically arranged by subject. Edge first looked up Horse. There were a good many dreams that could be dreamt about horses, according to the book, but he found none applicable. He looked under Net; nothing there that fit, either. He thought to try Mesh, and there it was:

"To a young woman, to dream of being entangled in the meshes of a net, foretells that her environments will bring her into wicked ways and consequent abandonment. If she succeeds in disengaging herself from the meshes, she will narrowly escape public disgrace."

"Well, I'll be damned," Edge said again.

Actually, it had been Sarah who had done the abandoning, but still... Had

Magpie Maggie Hag been a fraud all these years? Not if so many of her predictions had come as near true as this one, but that only proved the *book* right. Edge remembered that she'd had one of her spells of seclusion just before they got the news of Lincoln's assassination. Unless that had involved a dream of her own, the book couldn't account for her clairvoyance on that occasion.

"And she never said or did anything," he muttered, "to predict her own dying. Let's see, what else? She dukkered that Pavlo's going to give us trouble over werewolves."

He riffled through the book again. There was no Werewolf listing, and under Wolf only: "To hear the howl of a wolf in a dream discovers to you a sinister alliance"—which either meant nothing at all or could be mystically interpreted in any number of ways.

Edge shrugged, unable to decide if she really had had some gift of soothsaying, or had cribbed all her omen-dukkering from the battered old book, or had in most cases been just a shrewd old woman exercising the wisdom and intuition and experience garnered over a long lifetime. But then, when he sat down with Yount and Agnete to eat the unidentifiable but not-bad soup that the women had contrived to concoct, and the three of them were glooming over this latest disaster to strike the show, Yount chanced to remark:

"And it wasn't two weeks ago that old Mag told me this poosta would be the end of the world for some folks."

Edge twitched, dropped his spoon into his bowl and had to delve to retrieve it. Surely there could be nothing about the *Hungarian puszta* in that old book. He resolved to keep a close eye on Pavlo Smodlaka and an ear cocked for any wolves howling.

Four days later, they arrived at the border town, by which time Florian had pretty well come out of his funk of misery.

"Czernowitz," he announced, when the circus train had drawn up in ranks and files on an empty lot on the outskirts. "Or so it is marked on maps of the Austrian-Hungarian Dual Monarchy. But the inhabitants are mostly Romanian, and call it Cernauti. Now, we've been on short peck for quite a while. First we'll have a bang-up meal at a good inn. Then some of you women go about the markets and mongers and restock our food supply. Others, please go about the drapers' and mercers' shops and buy every kind of fancy fabrics and sequins and other ornamentation you can find. Each of you take along a Slovak or two to carry for you. Meanwhile, I shall look for whatever street passes as Savile Row here, and visit every single tailoring establishment, in hope of discovering a costumier who yearns for far horizons."

He found one, too. In a cramped family shop of father, mother and daughter, he saw at once that the younger woman was deft with the needle at the gown she was working on. Her name was Ioan Petrescu, she was about thirty, but still a spinster, exceedingly plain of face and broad of beam. So much so, she and her parents agreed, that she had little hope of ever snaring a husband here among the "handsome Romanians." Perhaps she would have better luck in Russia, they all said, where *everybody* was even plainer and squatter than Ioan was. She spoke Magyar as well as Romanian and, living this close to the border, a sufficiency of Russian. Also she was a capable cook, but—she said in some surprise, when Florian tentatively raised the question—no, she could claim no powers of divination that would enable her to replace Magpie Maggie Hag in that department.

"Oh, well," sighed Florian, and he went on to settle salary and terms, including a lump-sum payment to the elder Petrescus for the loss of her services. Ioan said it would take her some hours to gather and pack her belongings, to say her farewells to family, other relatives and friends. So Florian arranged to pick her up next morning in his carriage. Then he went to engage comfortable hotel rooms —they would be the last for some time—for the rest of his company.

Shortly before noon on the day after—it had taken that long to load the wagons with all the new supplies the circus women had procured—Florian's Flourishing Florilegium departed from the Kingdom of Hungary. There were no such finicking formalities at their exit as there had been at their entrance into the country. The guards at the sentry boxes on the near end of the bridge merely waved cordially as the procession went past and crossed the river Prut and rolled into Russia.

Россия

I

AT THE FARTHER END of the Prut bridge was a sentry box with a stout barrier pole blocking the road, both box and pole painted in diagonal stripes of white and very dark green with a thin gold line separating the two colors. Beyond was a sprawling guardhouse, flying the Russian flag: a double-headed eagle of dark green and gold on a white ground. Two farm carts heaped with cabbages were ahead of Florian's rockaway, their occupants stolidly waiting for some sentry to take notice of them. So when Florian halted, the circus train stretched behind him all the way across the bridge and some distance back into Czernowitz.

A man ducked under the guard barrier, trotted past the farm carts and came up to Florian, somewhat breathless, agitated and worried-looking. It was Willi Lothar.

"I have been waiting here for the past week," he said.

"We have encountered some delays on the road," said Florian, saving the details for later. "What's the holdup here?"

"The standard discourtesy of every petty administrator in Russia," Willi said sourly. "The soldiers and inspectors are all having their midday meal. Never will they be persuaded to take turns at the table and on duty. I can tell you, Herr Gouverneur, traveling from here to Kiev and back again, I have learned a good deal about Russian incivility and ineptitude. But I must also confess to some oversights and errors of my own. I can only try to excuse them by pleading that this *is* my first visit to Russia."

"Perfectly understandable, Herr Chefpublizist. I have no doubt that we shall all be making faux pas along the way."

"To begin with," Willi said uncomfortably. "I have, at great cost in money and time and interminable red tape and confusion and frustration, procured a special train for us. However, I did not discover until I got here that there is no railway station closer than Khamenets Podolskiy, and that is where it awaits us."

"How far away is that?"

"About sixty versts. Excuse me—I have begun to think in Russian measures. Some forty miles."

"Two days, if we push. That is not intolerable."

"You had better figure on at least four days, Herr Florian. You have not yet seen the condition of the Russian roads."

"Ah, well," Florian said philosophically. "We suffered considerable damage to our wardrobe on the way here. That will give our costumière more time to work on the new costumes."

Willi went on, "During this week that I have been waiting here—and, grâce à Dieu, the commandant and most others of the higher-ranking guards and inspectors speak French—I have been doing my best to... how would you say? ... mit Butter bestreichen all of them."

"To butter them up."

"Ja. I have at least, in this time, got them to unlock their vaults and give me Reisepässe for our whole company, and I have filled in our destinations, purpose of visit—"

"Passports? Russia demands passports? In addition to our conduct books?"

"Ach, ja. And you will need them to get *out* again, plus a certificate from the police that they have no reason to detain you. I obtained a considerable stock of the Reisepässe, not knowing how many you would be on arrival. Each person has only to fill in his personal particulars—as in the conduct books—and then a stamp of visa will be affixed."

"Then your buttering-up has had some good effect."

"But not much," Willi said glumly. "You may yet be stuck here for two or three days, perhaps longer, going through the necessary other formalities. Not to mention the unnecessary ones. I have tried to convince these louts that your tour through Russia will be of great cultural and economic benefit to their country. That you are not the usual gypsylike voyageurs forains. That you have even chartered an entire railroad train. Und so weiter, und so weiter. I have made you sound like the Second Coming. But these people are even more surly, indolent and indifferent than your typical civil servants anywhere else. For one reason, although the nominal commander of this border post is a colonel of the army, the real director and highest authority here is a civilian official of the Third Section. So no other man on the post dares show the least amiability toward a foreigner, let alone accept a bribe or even a cigarette. He would instantly be sent to the salt mines of Siberia."

"What in the world is the Third Section?"

"Tsar Alexander's secret police, accountable only to him personally. You will soon learn, Herr Florian, that there is a bland euphemism for everything grim in Russia. A convict trudging off to lifelong exile in Siberia, for example, is said to be merely 'passing through.' However, the blandly named Third Section keeps watch—and not just at the frontiers; its agents are everywhere—not only for illicit immigrants and undesirable persons and contraband, but also for persons evincing undesirable tendencies, political opinions and even objectionable *thoughts.*"

"Great heavens," muttered Florian. "And we are an aggregation of certifiable eccentrics. Do you think they will let us *in*, Willi?"

"Oh, I think so, but grudgingly. The colonel was clearly impressed when I showed him the receipt for the deposit I paid on the railway charter. We might just pass the word among our company for all to behave discreetly, to do as they are bidden, and not to bridle at any insult. Jules and I, when we meet, must not greet one another too affectionately. The rest of you must be prepared for much interrogation, a search of everything you are carrying, and a generally spiteful dawdling just to cause you delay and distress. Plus a heavy import duty to pay, most likely. I was hoping by flattery and unction to mitigate that, but in vain, I fear."

"Hm. Perhaps the colonel or that éminence grise of the Third Section is a brother in the craft, and I could—"

"Ach, do not, do not, Herr Gouverneur! The brotherhood of Freimaurerei is, as the Russian euphemism puts it, 'disencouraged' here. Every sort of secret society is forbidden. Such societies are rife, of course, but they take care to *stay* secret. Were you to essay any Masonic sign or password, *you* might be on your way to Siberia."

"Hell and damnation. Anything else I should know?"

"Well... everyone might as well throw into the river any books or magazines or newspapers in his possession. It could avert additional delay, for otherwise every page and every sheet of paper must be inspected. All foreign literature, you see, is automatically suspected of being seditious or heretical or at least licentious."

Florian exclaimed, "This is absolutely incred—!" But he was interrupted by a loud whistle blast from a soldier at the barrier pole. The guards had finished their meal, ambled idly out of the guardhouse, picking their teeth, and—after stabbing among the two farm carts' cabbages with their needlelike rifle bayonets—had let those peasants pass. Now the soldiers were beckoning impatiently and imperiously for the circus train to move up.

"I'll go first," said Florian, "and introduce myself and present our conduct books. Meanwhile, Willi, you go down the line and hand out the passports. And all your good advice, as well."

The pole was lifted, briefly, for just the rockaway to pass under and beyond it. Florian got down and started for the guardhouse, but a sentry stopped him with his rifle, barked, "Ostavaitye!" indicated that he was to stay where he was, snatched from Florian the stack of conduct books and himself carried them into the building. There ensued a wait long enough for someone to have read every last word in every last book. Finally the soldier reappeared in the doorway, jerked his rifle in a come-along gesture and barked, "Voiditye!"

There were several officers in the guardhouse office, all still picking their teeth and occasionally belching. Florian addressed the one who sat behind a desk littered with the conduct books. He was also the officer most heavily bedecked with braid, insignia, medals and flowing beard. In his best-remembered Russian, Florian began, "Zdravstvuitye, Gospodín Polkhovnik, it is an honor to meet—"

"Qu'est-ce que ça fout?" growled the colonel, in French rather more fluent than Florian's Russian, and rudely vulgar, and much more to the point. "No need for the social graces, gospodín. Tak, you are the proprietor of that tsirk and the leader of that canaille cluttering my bridge, are you not?"

"Oui, mon colonel. I am proud to be the owner and general manager of Florian's Flourishing Florilegium. We intend to make a grand tour of—"

"S'il vous plaît, c'est peu nécessaire. During this whole past week I have heard little else, from that lèche-cul Lothar of yours, except the greatness of your tsirk and your aspirations to astound all of Russia with it. Right now, simply be so kind as to verify—without rhetoric—these particulars noted in your conduct book." The colonel recited them—name, age, occupation, etc.—and Florian attested that all were truly set forth. The colonel said, "Tak, I do not read well these barbaric foreign languages, but, so far as I can discern, there are no black-mark demerits cited by the authorities of any of the other places you have visited. Very well, Monsieur Florian, *you* are admissible. Give me your passport." The colonel scribbled in it, then stamped it with an inked brass seal. "You may wait outside —and fill in the required blanks in your passport while you do so. Send in the rest of your racaille one at a time."

"Excusez, mon colonel," said Florian, with some ill-concealed indignation. "My rabble, as you keep calling them, are of numerous nationalities. Not many speak French, and none of them, I believe, speaks Russian. I may be useful as an interpreter."

"As you please." The colonel shrugged, then told the sentry at the door, "Odin za drugim."

The guard leaned out the door—all the wagons and cages and vans and animals afoot were being let through the barrier now, and ranked in a field beyond the guardhouse—and curtly beckoned to the nearest trouper, who happened to be Jules Rouleau.

Meanwhile, Florian had leaned his passport against the rough log wall of the room and, with his mason's pencil, was struggling to fill in the blank spaces with Cyrillic script. He again said to the officer, "Excusez-moi, mon colonel. Sostoyániye means 'estate,' I know, but what do I write in that blank?"

"Your *estate*, of course. Your status," the colonel said irritably. "There are only five. Tak, which are you? Noble, merchant, burgher, peasant or cleric?"

"Why, I—I hardly think I fit in any of those categories. I don't suppose any of us do. We are artistes, entertainers..."

"Okh! Put burgher—mestchánye—in all the passports, then. That will suffice." He turned to Rouleau, standing at attention before his desk, and gestured for Jules to point out his conduct book among the heap of them. The colonel picked it up and read, "Yules Rouleau. Français? Nyet. Amyerikanyets." Then he read, with some incredulity, "Aéronaute?"

Florian translated, "Vozdukoplavatol. Monsieur Rouleau is our tsirk's balloonist." Then, yet again, he said, "Je vous fais excuse, mon colonel. But would it perhaps be possible, while you are verifying the conduct books, that your inspectors"—he indicated the numerous other men lounging about, inside and outside the guardhouse, still picking their teeth—"might profitably occupy the same time in the inspection of our train, the calculation of impost and so forth?"

The colonel said negligently, "Skoro budit, gospodín. What is the hurry? There is no point in making out customs declarations and weighing poods and funts until we are assured that all of you are admissible."

Since "skoro budit" meant only "it will happen soon," and was as deliberately imprecise and noncommittal as the Spanish "mañana," Florian could only curb his vexation and seethe silently, and fill out each new candidate's passport after the colonel was done with his routine, and step in to translate when necessary.

"A. Chink?!" exclaimed the colonel, when one of the antipodists stood apprehensively before him. "That is no translation of the name he has signed in his conduct book."

"You can decipher his name, Colonel?" said Florian, in surprise. "We did only the best we could, since none of us speaks or reads Chinese."

"Chinese? You dolt. His name is signed in the Korean alphabet." The colonel looked up at the acrobat, who had begun to tremble slightly, and asked, "Odi so ososse yo?"

The antipodist was visibly startled. He stammered, "H-Hanguk, taeryong. Ch-chip e so Taegu yo. S-sille haessumnida."

"Chossumnida," the colonel said affably, and went into quite a long conversation with him, during which, at the officer's bidding, the Korean separated from the other conduct books those of his two fellows.

"This man's name is Kim Pok-tong," the colonel said to Florian. "Please erase that stupid 'A. Chink' and write it properly in his conduct book and his passport. The other two are his brothers, Kim Tak-sung and Kim Hak-su."

Florian hastily wrote in the names, as well as he could, and said, "You amaze me, Colonel. I could no more tell any Orientals apart..."

"I have served at Vladivostok," the colonel said. "Tak, I took the opportunity to cross the Petra Bay and see something of Korea while I was there. Lovely country, but the people extremely eremitical. Can't understand how these three braved the outside world. Wish I had time to converse with them."

"Bless my soul," murmured Florian.

One by one, the troupers and crewmen survived the interrogation—the colonel noticeably lingered longer in his questioning of the more attractive female artistes—and then, relieved to have that over with, they gathered near their familiar wagons. Only one came out of the guardhouse in high dudgeon, and that was the usually easygoing Hannibal Tyree.

"Cannibal!" he exclaimed, outraged. "Dat ole sojer called me *Cannibal* Tyree!"

"He called me Yules," said Rouleau indifferently. "So he can't read English. So what?"

"Ain't the same thing. Yules don't mean you *eats people!* Jes' 'cause I be's black, dey call me a *cannibal.* Why, even my ole great-gran'pappy back in Afriker wasn't never no—"

"Easy, Herr Tyree, be at ease," said Willi Lothar. "It was an unintentional affront. You see, there is no 'h' sound in the Russian language. They simply cannot aspirate it. So they substitute a velar consonant, usually the 'k' sound. Hence Hannibal—Cannibal."

"Boy, be glad your name isn't Huntley," Fitzfarris said, straight-faced.

But another applicant encountered something more troublesome than mispronunciation. The colonel read from his conduct book, "Nom de théâtre: Maurice LeVie. Nom de naissance: Morris Levy. Okh!" He called to Florian, who was filling out Daphne Wheeler's passport, "Attend us here, please, Monsieur le Propriétaire. This man cannot be admitted. He is an Israelite."

"What of that?" asked Florian. "You have some millions of other Jews in Russia, I understand."

"We got them not because we wanted them," said the colonel. "They simply happened to constitute an offensively high proportion of the population of the Ukraine, and later of Poland, both of which Matushka Rossiya motherly took to her bosom. Tak, our so-called Russian Jews still are restricted to the Pale of Settlement—Poland and the Ukraine. They most certainly are not at liberty to wander about the provinces of Great Russia, as you would have this foreign Jew do."

"Monsieur le Colonel," said Maurice, "I am a *Frenchman*. I have never considered myself to be of any other race or nationality, and I have never observed *any* religion."

The colonel growled, "Tak khram ostavlennyi—vsë khram."

Maurice looked questioningly at Florian, who translated, "An abandoned temple is still a temple."

"Drop your trousers, *Frenchman*," the colonel commanded. "Show us your quéquette." Florian hurried Daphne out of the building. Angry, humiliated, perhaps a little frightened, Maurice let down his breeches and exposed himself. The colonel cried in triumph, "Nu, z gúl'kin húy! Circoncis, évidemment! And you deny that you are a Jew. I daresay you would also deny that you Jews use the blood of abducted Christian infants in the making of your Passover bread."

Maurice said miserably, "Monsieur le Colonel, I have never in my life celebrated the Passover."

The colonel barked orders to his idling subordinates and they snapped from boredom into eager activity, hustling Maurice into a farther room and shutting the door. The colonel's Russian had been rapid-fire, but Florian caught the gist of it. Maurice was to be stripped and examined for any tattoos or other Hebraic cabalistic markings on his body, any insurrectionary Israelite writings or even phials of poison concealed in his body orifices, and then his caravan was to be just as scrupulously stripped and scrutinized. The colonel turned again to Florian and said threateningly:

"Tak, we will suspend further interrogation of your company for now, gospodín. It may well be, if we find anything of seditious or subversive nature among the effects of this Jew of yours, that you *all* can be charged for harboring an enemy of the state."

"I assure you—"

"Do not assure me of anything. That decision will be up to my civilian colleague, Gospodín Trepov, a personal representative of the tsar's chancery. Wait outside."

"Colonel, the Monsieur LeVie is a flying acrobat," Florian said desperately. "I pray that you will not injure him in any way."

"Such things never happen here," the colonel said flatly. "Not even to poseurs like Monsieur *Levy*. Wait outside."

When Florian slouched despondently up to the gathered troupers, Edge asked, "*Now* what's the matter?"

Florian explained, concluding, "If we're not all held culpable, and they let us go on, how can we go without Maurice? We can't abandon him to these brutes. Even if we were that hardhearted, it's one more blow to our already diminished troupe. Goddamn it! I knew that Maurice is a Jew. I simply did not know it would matter here, or I would have falsified his conduct book..." His voice trailed off dispiritedly.

Edge pondered for a moment, then said, "Well, I had intended to save something as a surprise for you, when we got to Saint Petersburg. But I'll get it for you now." He went off to his caravan and returned with a very large ivory envelope. Florian looked with some stupefaction at the two crowns—imperial and royal—emblazoned on it in gold, and at the flowingly handwritten address:

> *Ihre kaiserlich Majestät, die Kaiserin und Zarin Maria Alexandrovna*
> *Reichspalast*
> *Sankt Peterstadt*
> *Russland*

Then, carefully, respectfully, he opened the unsealed flap, unfolded the stiff, handmade paper, and his eyes widened as he murmured aloud, "Gnädige Dame, meine Schwester..." He skipped down to the signature and his eyes really bulged. "Deine Schwester von Gottes Gnaden, Elisabeth Amelie, Kaiserin der Österreich, Königin der Ungarn." In breathless awe, he said to Edge, "And I told you she might be no more than a backwoods Baronin. Jesus!" Then he read the body of the letter and went back to the guardhouse at a trot.

He entered just in time to hear a long groan from the back room, and the colonel snapped, "I told you to stay outside!"

Just as angrily, Florian snapped back at him, "Do you read German?"

"Nyet! Get out!"

Florian laid the letter on the desk in front of the colonel, so the embossed crowns could be seen, but prudently kept his hand on it. "Perhaps the tsar's *representative* reads German."

"Um...ahem...da, I think so," said the colonel. "However, if you hope for conciliation or concession in this matter, I guarantee you that he will refuse. It is what he is for."

Still, the colonel had said that rather uneasily. He got up, went to the door of the other room and cracked it just enough to put his head in. Florian heard him say in Russian, "Desist, men, until further orders. Gospodín Trepov, there is something I think you should see."

He returned with a pudgy man dressed in an ordinary civilian sack suit, with not a single identifying insigne on it. The man's chief distinction was that he was the only Russian that Florian had seen here not wearing a beard. Instead, he had a black mustache like a shoe brush and eyebrows like black caterpillars, seeming pasted there to overhang and hide any expression in his eyes. But when he looked at that deckled sheet of parchment-thick ivory paper— Florian's hand still protectively on it—his caterpillars gave an involuntary leap upward.

Trepov read through the letter, evidently two or three times, then let his caterpillars down again, glowered at Florian and demanded, "How did you come by this?"

"My tsirk's equestrian director—the Sprechstallmeister Edge mentioned therein—happens to be a close personal friend of the Empress-Queen Elisabeth. That should be evident, Gospodín Trepov, from the warmth with which Her Imperial Majesty commends him to your Empress-Tsaritsa Maria Alexandrovna. You will also observe that she requests her sister-in-royalty to extend every courtesy not only to Gospodín Edge, but also to *all his tsirk companions.*"

The man from the Chancery Third Section grunted, then drew the colonel aside for a mumbled conversation. Florian strained hard enough to catch snatches of it.

"Forgery...?"

"Impossible. These oafish durákha? Besides, I have seen the writing in official papers. It is her hand."

"Hungary... no ally..."

"Still... addresses her as 'sister.'"

"Tak, suppose... disappear... them *and* their letter...?"

"Dangerous... duplicate perhaps by post..."

"If they report... complain... the tsaritsa..."

"Tak, we must immediately atone..."

The two of them came back to Florian, each abjectly and oilily rubbing his hands together.

"Had we but known..." said agent Trepov.

"Of course, but *of course* you are all welcome, *most* welcome to Matushka Rossiya," said the colonel.

"Including even the Israelite," said Trepov. "I shall this instant make out the special permit he will require at provincial borders."

"There will be no need for further interrogation," said the colonel. "Simply send in all remaining passports, Monsieur Florian, and I will have my own officers enter the particulars from your people's conduct books, and affix the visas."

"I think also, Zasulich," the agent said to the colonel, "considering that these good folk are, in effect, guests of our tsaritsa they might be exempted from customs inspection and duty. Besides—ha-ha!—do you have any scales that would weigh the poods of two elephants?"

"A good point, Gospodín Trepov. I will make out the customs declaration, Monsieur Florian, and will stamp it 'diplomatic immunity,' to avoid your being held up by any officious petty inspector at any other frontier."

"Perhaps also, since it is getting late," said Trepov, "you and your company would honor us by taking dinner at our officers' mess."

"Your ladies, as well," said Colonel Zasulich. "Females are customarily excluded, but we will, for once, have our own wives attend."

"Then, when you depart in the morning," said Trepov, "we will provide a military convoy. There is a company of Kazháki due to report here tomorrow. They will escort you to Khamenets Podolskiy, so that no ruffians or bandits or wolves will molest your train."

"We accept, gentlemen," Florian said smoothly. "And we are grateful for all these favors. I am happy, too, that I shall be able to give a good report to Her Imperial Majesty regarding the efficiency and hospitality of her subject officials at the Novosielitza border crossing."

The two officials beamed at him, and at each other, and rubbed their hands some more.

All but three of the circus company attended the dinner. Ioan Petrescu declined, because she was working assiduously to restore the salvageable bits of pista costumes, and having to remake many of them entire from the measurements and crude sketches Magpie Maggie Hag had left. Maurice LeVie refused to attend because he was nursing bruises about the kidneys and a twisted wrist —and Nella Cornella stayed with him, to rub arnica on his injuries. Maurice was also, of course, still livid at the treatment he had received and the indignities he had suffered. He swore he would never socialize with any such merdeux savages, *ever!*

"I understand, I sympathize, I agree," said Florian. "However, we now have a special permit that will protect you from any further embarrassments or outrages."

"Je m'en fous et m'en contrefous!" snarled Maurice. "Perhaps, if le roi de cons invites me, the Tsar of Russia himself, *perhaps* I might deign to accept."

Colonel Zasulich had laid on an excellent dinner. Even the zakúska appetizers would amply have fed the entire assemblage: black, red and golden caviar, cold sturgeon in aspic, cheeses, pickles, pâté, paper-thin sliced cold meats— and innumerable bottles of vodka imprisoned in blocks of ice. Many of the circus guests, the females especially, discovered that a single glass of that vodka— drunk the Russian way: tossed down so fast that it flashed past the glottis, directly to the stomach, thence to the brain—was very like hitting oneself on the head with a mallet. So thereafter they drank tea, also in the Russian manner, sipping it from a glass by sucking it through a cube of sugar held in the teeth. Some others, however—Ferdi Spenz, Aleksandr Banat and the three Jászi brothers—were so appreciative of the vodka that they had to be helped or carried back to their vehicle quarters even before the serving of the dinner's next courses—borscht, herring-and-beet salad, elk steaks both grilled and tartare, steamed sausages, morels, a great variety of vegetables and unfamiliar condiments, a strong green Crimean wine, bilberry pie, more tea and vodka and a cranberry liqueur.

Most of the officers and their wives—or their female consorts of unspecified relationship—could speak French. Florian got along well enough in Russian, the Smodlakas could make themselves understood in that language, and Colonel Zasulich even spent some time talking to the brothers Kim in Korean. But those troupers who had to stay mute were not deaf, and they marveled at how abruptly the sound of the native speech had changed, from one side of the river Prut to the other, from the bright and brittle Magyar to the catarrhal Russian, so moist that it seemed sometimes to splutter.

"What is all this 'tak-tak-tak' I keep hearing?" Sunday Simms asked Willi. "Even when these people are speaking French, they seem to throw in 'tak' after every third word. They sound like a roomful of clocks ticking."

"Merely a sort of verbal hiccup, my dear. All it means is 'so,' but it is apparently a national habit to employ it frequently and needlessly. I have heard it everywhere I have been in Russia so far."

The mess waiters did not say 'tak' or anything else. They appeared to be of no Russian nationality at all and evidently did not speak the language. They looked almost as Oriental as the Kims and went about their serving duties without heeding or needing instruction.

"They are Tatars," agent Trepov explained to Edge. "We import them from the Volga provinces, as does every Russian hotel and restaurant, because they are devout Muslims, hence they do not steal nips from the liquor supply. Tak, we of Matushka Rossiya are fortunate in having such a wide variety of nationalities in our vast land, each with its own peculiar virtues or talents. Our Balts, for example, are known for their honesty and punctiliousness, so they constitute most of our estate managers, accountants, clerks. The Letts are especially skilled in building windmills and water mills. And so on."

What conversation there could be between hosts and guests continued to be amiable, mostly trivial, sometimes informative. Jean-François Pemjean commented to the stout but handsome woman who was his vis-à-vis, "Isn't the weather being exceptionally fine for Russia, madame, this late in October? Are you perhaps enjoying a spell of Saint Martin's Summer?"

"We call it Woman's Summer," she replied, with something of a simper. "Báb'ye léto. Because a woman is here considered most attractive in her late maturity. And yes, the weather is being clement. But, for us, tak, it is still only *early* October. Perhaps you are unaware that Russia observes the Julian calendar, which is twelve days earlier than your Gregorian calendar of the West."

At another table, another handsome woman said to Rouleau, "You speak of serfs, Monsieur Yules. That is actually a word from the French. Here they were called krepostnoy. *Were* called, tak, because we have no more such peasants in bondage. Our wise and humane Alexander, who himself owned one million of the krepostnoy, liberated them throughout the land." She added, with frank disparagement of Rouleau's homeland, "That was seven years ago, before your backward and benighted America had to fight a civil war to accomplish the same good for your slaves."

"I don't know that it has accomplished much good for ours," said Rouleau. "When last I saw any freedmen there, they were helplessly adrift, without masters to direct and care for them."

"Tak, I must confess that that is somewhat true even here in enlightened Russia," said the woman. "It will be some time yet before the freed muzhiki rid themselves of their old dependences and their gross unrefinement. Especially their ingrained superstitions." She laughed. "Do you know, if ever a provincial governor or mayor orders a census to count the population that he governs, the muzhiki all flee to the tall timber. Some even commit suicide."

"Par dieu, pourquoi? What superstition can possibly be connected to a census-taking?"

"The muzhiki believe it is done at the instigation of the Antichrist, who wants all their names so they can be damned. At least that one is a religiously inspired delusion, and perhaps excusable on that account. But the peasants also believe in all sorts of heretical and supernatural things, as well, and live in terror of them. The vampír, the oborotyen..."

At another table, Pavlo Smodlaka was anxiously struggling to ask the captain seated next to him for information about one of those very things. "In Magyar, the férfifarkas. You call, I think oborotyen."

"Tak, you have heard of our oborotyen?" said the captain, putting on a somber expression, though his eyes twinkled. "Da, we have that thing. And whatever you have heard probably falls short of the terrible truth. Sometimes, at full moon, there is such a plague of men-turned-wolves that even we, the army, must be called out to hunt them down and destroy them. Tak, for that we must use solid silver bayonets."

The captain went on elaborating, exercising more and more inventive imagination, and Pavlo's jaw gradually gaped until he was spilling chewed morel down his chin.

Colonel Zasulich said to Florian, "I am indeed glad that we resolved the few minor difficulties, and your establishment is now free to entertain our countrymen. I took a stroll among your wagons, and it is obvious that yours is a respectable tsirk, not a ragtag balagan—what I believe you in America call a tína tsirk."

"A mud show, yes," said Florian. "You seem well acquainted with circus terminology, Colonel."

"The tsirk is an honored institution in Russia, Gospodín Florian. We had our first taste of it nearly a hundred years ago, tak, when the Royal Circus of London came to visit Piter—Saint Petersburg. It was warmly received. Partly, no doubt, because Ekaterina the Great immediately took its chief equestrian for the latest in her succession of lovers. Other foreign circuses came after that. Now we have many of our own, from immense spectacles in permanent hippodromes to the shabby balagans that appear at every country fair. But the terminology remains mostly unchanged from that of the West. Tak, our lion tamers give their commands in German. The central ring is the Italian pista. Only a few words are different. What you call a clown or a joey, we call a rizhiy. What you call a midget, like that charming little lady farther down the table, we call a lilliput."

Florian got out his pencil and a piece of paper. "Perhaps, Colonel, you would be good enough to assist me in concocting comprehensible translations of some of our people's noms de théâtre. The Quakemaker, Cinderella..."

"Tak," said the colonel, and they moved their chairs closer together to go through the list.

Later, they two left the others still partying and went to Zasulich's office again, where the colonel generously accommodated Florian by opening his paymaster's safe and exchanging silver Russian rubles and kopeks for Florian's considerable heap of Hungarian koronas and forints, Austrian kronen and gulden. Florian, working the complicated sums in his head, calculated that the ruble was worth about fifty-two cents American and, at one hundred to the ruble, the kopek was worth about half a cent, and he noted that down in his memorandum book.

The next morning, Colonel Zasulich was up and out as early as any of the circus people, and he was a good deal perkier and brighter-eyed than some of them. He arrived at the wagon encampment to announce to Florian and Edge, "Here comes the company of Kazhák infantry. You can hear their marching music down the road. I shall allow them to rest only while you hitch up your teams and form up your train. Then they will be commanded to turn around again and escort you, front and rear of your procession, to the railroad at Khamenets Podolskiy."

Florian and Edge listened for a military band, but that was not what they heard. Half of the approaching company was merely whistling the Russian national hymn and the other half was singing it:

Bozhe tsara krani
Syilni der zharni
Stsar stvouyna
Slavouna slavounam...

"Well, maybe they don't have a band," said Edge, "but that's a pretty rousing anthem. And I've never heard such warbling whistling. What is it they're singing?"

"Um...roughly..." said Florian, "'Our oath to the tsar we pledge with white-hot fervor. Carve it on tree trunks: glory to the Slavic race.'"

As the music got louder, more of the circus folk emerged from their caravans and wagons. When the company marched onto the post parade ground and were halted at attention, still bellowing and whistling, the watchers were able to see how they achieved their peculiarly loud, sweet, harmonic trilling: each of the whistlers had a hole bored between his two front teeth. The company's commander waited for his men to finish a final chorus, then bawled an order that was evidently "Fall out!" The men immediately and efficiently tripod-stacked their long rifles, unslung and let drop their knapsacks, yanked off their tremendous boots, under which they wore no stockings, unbuttoned the flies of their baggy pantaloons and—heedless of the many onlookers, including now all the women of the circus—began pissing on each other's bare feet.

Most of those observing stood stunned for a moment. Then all the women and girls, red-faced, bustled back inside their vehicles.

"The infantrymen always do that after a long march," explained Colonel Zasulich, as unembarrassed as the soldiers. "It rests the feet, toughens them, prevents ringworm and other such foot rots."

Rouleau, restraining a laugh, said to the colonel in French, "I thought the Cossack people were all cavalrymen, real rough riders, like the plainsmen of Hungary and our American plains Indians."

Zasulich said, "You must blame your own Western tsirks and hippodrome shows for fostering that myth about the Cossacks—as you call them. Actually, they are not even one people, or one tribe, or necessarily related in any other way. The word kazhák means only 'brigand,' and in earlier times they roamed and ravaged freely over the steppe. Tak, on the principle that a poacher makes the best gamekeeper, Tsar Pyetr the Great herded them all together and organized them into bodies of soldiers. Very good soldiers they make, indeed. Some, da, are cavalrymen, but not all. Those wild and daredevil riders of whom you speak, da, we have those too, but that sort of horseman is properly called a djigit."

"Another thing," Pemjean said to Edge, "which I just learned last night. If you are keeping a calendar, Monsieur le Directeur, of our appointed arrivals and departures here and there, make sure you adjust it to the Russian calendar. Today is not, as you might believe, the twenty-third of October. It is the *eleventh* of October." He added, in an undertone, "Well, Monsieur Florian *did* say this is a backward country, n'est-ce pas?"

For all that the Kazháks were good soldiers, and readily gave voice to their white-hot devotion to the tsar, they grumbled audibly when the circus was ready to roll and they were commanded to go with it back along the same dreary versts they had just traversed. But they did as bidden, pulling on their great boots again, slinging their knapsacks, shouldering their rifles and forming up, two platoons each fore and aft of the wagon train.

"One last word of advice, Gospodín Florian," said agent Trepov, as they shook hands at parting. "When you get to the railway station, you will be inundated by nosíl'shchiki—volunteer porters. Fend them off. Let only your own men do the work. Those station parasites are not entitled to payment, so if you give them even a small gratuity, it amounts to a gift. By our law, any Russian accepting a gift from a foreigner is committing a punishable crime, and so are you in giving it. However, he *is* entitled to *steal* from a foreigner anything and everything he can get his hands on. I thought you ought to know."

Florian sighed, shook his head in wonderment, thanked the agent, climbed to his rockaway seat and gave the move-out signal. The post officers had all assembled to see the train off, and in unison gave the Russian military salute: the hand snapped to the forehead, then flung high. The Kazháks ahead of the train immediately started marching—now wafting behind them an ammoniac stench strong enough to make Florian's eyes water—while whistling and singing glory to the Slavic race.

2

THE ROAD to Khamenets Podolskiy was made of round slices of log, set close together in the ground like flagstones. Perhaps in mud time when they would be well mired, or in wintertime when they would be gripped solid, the slabs might have made a decent if uneven surface. But now, in late autumn, the dirt road was merely lumpy dirt, and the unsecured log rounds simply lay there at all angles, and teetered and skidded and made a continuous nerve-racking clatter as the circus's animals and wagons went over them. It was a rougher ride than navigating a roiled sea. The Smodlaka children and several of the caged animals were seasick the whole way, and many others suffered bruises and contusions from falling about inside their wagons or caravans. Several times, the whole train had to stop entirely, to repair broken wheel spokes, sprung felloes, torn harness, or to replace thrown horseshoes.

How the new seamstress, Ioan Petrescu, could do her fine stitching in that turmoil was a mystery, but she did, and the journey—it took fully *five* days to go the forty miles—gave her time enough to refurbish all the damaged costumes and make new ones. Those included a set for the Jászi brothers, whom Florian decided to dress in the manner of Edge's former Buckskin Billy, since that would look more "exotic" to Russian audiences than the Magyar csikos dress, which many Russians must already have seen. To give Ioan all the time she required, the other women of the troupe did the cooking at meal stops along the way. The escorting Kazhák troops fed themselves, and spartanly. They lit fires to brew tea, but the only other nutriment anyone saw them take was a fibrous dried meat, like jerky, that they carried in their knapsacks.

Because of the terrible condition of the road, Hannibal and his Slovak assistant put the sheepskin boots on the two elephants, and Stitches made another set for Mustafa the camel. All of those stout boots were shredded and worn through by the end of the journey, so Stitches made new sets, because those walking animals would need them even on paved streets, now that the weather was turning cold. The Woman's Summer ended when the circus was halfway to its destination. No snow fell yet, but the temperature did. The countryside was exactly like the Hungarian puszta—an endless plain of now-brown grass, with only infrequent, bare-limbed shrubs and trees to break the monotony. Every morning the hoarfrosted grass blades looked like standing armies of glittering steel bayonets. Then, when the sun got high enough to evaporate the frost from the grass, it revealed another strange sight: any tree in the landscape naturally cast a shadow, but not a normal dark one; its shadow was silvery-white, because there the frost had not yet melted.

The circus passed through numerous villages, and the resident muzhiks came out to stare in dull-eyed wonder at the unaccustomed apparition. The circus folk did not do much staring in return, as there was little of interest to look at. All the villages were alike: a single row of one-room izba huts lining either side of the road, every izba made of rough-cut, undressed and unpainted logs, their interstices chinked with moss. Only a few had even one window, and only a *very* occasional one—maybe the mayor's—would have glass in it; the other windows consisted merely of oiled paper or even scraped-thin birch bark.

The country peasants were as ugly as their residences. Every man parted his hair in the middle, and the lank, tangled, greasy hanks of it hung down on either side below his shoulders, sometimes as far as the length of his lank, tangled, greasy beard, which might reach his waist. The women were distinguishable only because they had no beards and, whatever their hair was like, they wore babushka kerchiefs over it. Their faces were just as sun- and wind-burned as the men's, and just as coarse of skin, often studded with warts and wens or pitted with old smallpox scars. Both sexes wore thick, gray, graceless belted overcoats of near ground-length and boots of colorless felt, so huge and shapeless that everyone looked clubfooted. The boots and the overcoat hems were clotted with mud and manure. The circus company only rarely caught sight of a young girl or any children—probably the elders herded them indoors, safe from abduction by these unprecedented passersby—and those young ones were sometimes very pretty.

The circus folk did see one thing about those squalid communities that piqued their curiosity. Whenever they chanced to be passing through a hamlet as night was falling, they would see at least one housewife setting on her door-step a crust of bread and a bowl of milk.

"Do the Russians believe in the brownies?" asked Daphne, laughing. "We might almost be in uncouth old Scotland."

"No, not brownies," said Florian. He had lately been spending his evenings with Kapitán Miliukov of the Kazhák company, learning all he could about Russia and Russian ways. "Oh, they believe in enough other kinds of sprites and elves and such. But those food offerings are set out for 'the unfortunates'—men on the run, being hounded by the police or the army or some other authority. Here, as everywhere, the poor and downtrodden are on the side of the underdog. They have a saying: 'He is no thief who is not caught.' Only if a criminal *is* caught and officially convicted do his fellow unfortunates shun and spurn him."

Now and then, the train passed other vehicles on the awful road. Most of them were bulky, solid-wheeled farm carts, but some—perhaps the property of local squires—were more graceful carriages drawn by a troika team. The middle one of that three-horse hitch proceeded at a brisk trot, overarched by the high, wooden dugá yoke, which was always fancily carved and painted, sometimes hung with jingling bells. The two flanking horses ran at an angle, their heads pulled outward by check reins, and they had to run at a canter to match the "root" horse's trotting speed.

"I don't see any purpose in that," horsewoman Clover Lee said critically. "That high yoke must be heavy, and the flank horses must be uncomfortable, having to run at a slant and a different gait."

"I strongly suspect," said Florian, "that the Russian coachmen long ago designed that complicated harness just so they themselves would be respected and irreplaceable—as the only human beings on earth who can hitch and unhitch a troika."

But the travelers saw more novel things than that. Very often there came along the road a man, less frequently a woman, dressed in rags, most of the rags bunched around the feet in lieu of boots, and holding out a pleading palm. "Religious pilgrims," explained Willi Lothar, "going to some shrine somewhere." And he always threw them a few kopeks. But some of the ragged wanderers came along the road frenziedly dancing, whirling, singing and whooping. "Those are also regarded as devout," said Willi, strewing kopeks, "and are called 'the fools of God,' but they are really only pitiful madmen on the loose."

Willi went on, at the campfire that night, "Even many of the truly religious sects here are so fanatical that we would consider them lunatic. There are the monks called skoptsýi, for example, those sworn to total abstinence from sex. It seems they cannot trust themselves to abstain by willpower alone. So they castrate each other. A monk is said to 'take the little seal' if only his testicles are removed—the 'great seal' if he surrenders his penis as well."

Several people around the fire queasily set aside their plates of food.

"Then there is the sect called the Bozhie Lyudi, or People of God," Willi continued. "They also pledge sexual abstinence, but only in regard to their own husbands or wives. It is quite all right to copulate with some *other* church member's mate. And there are the Holy Ghost Worshipers. They must inhale deeply and frequently while they pray, so that they literally *swallow* the Holy Ghost. Many of them faint from that excessive respiration, and they are considered especially touched by the spirit. One of their late members, I was told, is remembered as the most blessed of all. He actually fell down and died from an overdose of the Holy Ghost."

Just once on that road did the circus people stop to purchase a meal, rather than cook their own. That was in a village called Khotin, a community big enough to have two buildings of fair size. They were even painted and sported a couple of glass windows apiece—and each had a sign over its door. The newcomers gazed at those signs, the first display of Cyrillic writing most of them had yet come upon. The writing seemed bewilderingly to comprise familiar letters of the alphabet, but mixed capitals and lower case, plus familiar letters of the alphabet printed backward or upside down, plus a sprinkling among them of totally unfamiliar characters. Florian read the signs to the others: "Pravítyel'stvo Monopóliya Lavka, or State Monopoly Store, meaning it deals in liquor and tobacco. The other sign says Gostínitsa. That is an inn. Let us try it."

The fare they were served—by a buxom, meaty, sweaty and rather smelly woman—was probably no different from what was on the table of every peasant family in Khotin or anywhere else in Russia.

Yount looked suspiciously at his bowl of murky gray-green soup and said, "When she set this down, she called it something like shitsy."

"So would I," said Rouleau, sniffing warily at his.

"The word is 'shchi,'" said Florian, dipping into his without hesitation. "Cabbage soup. Quite good it is, too."

In fact, it was the best part of the meal. The rest consisted of leathery slabs of salt fish, unadorned boiled potatoes, black rye bread like tree bark, raw onions and mugs of what might have been a pale beer, but everyone who tasted it made a sour face and noises of, "Jesus, what is *this?*"

"Kvas," said Florian. "One of the staples of peasant life, I understand. Homemade, and reputedly a most salubrious drink. You merely pour water and a little honey over barley—or even stale rye bread—let it ferment good and rotten, pour off the liquid, and that is kvas."

"By damn," said Yount. "I thought we lived rough during the war back home, when us Cornfeds had to make do with parched-okra coffee and suchlike. But these Russian poor-whites..." He shook his head pityingly.

The wagon train at last arrived at the Khamenets Podolskiy station, to find its railroad train waiting, as promised—and that was an awesomely substantial string of machinery. The Sormovo locomotive was at least four feet higher and two feet wider than any engine the circus people had seen either in the States or elsewhere in Europe. Suspended above its massive black-iron boiler the locomotive had a curious long, thick pipe, almost like a second and thinner boiler, bridging the two bowler-hat-like domes that housed the throttle valve and safety valve. The single driving wheel on either side of the engine was nearly eight feet in diameter, and even the bogie and trailing wheels were nearly the height of a man's chest.

The passenger cars, goods wagons and flatcars were proportionately immense. The coaches did not, like Western European coaches, have a corridor running down one side of the interior, with the passenger compartments opening off it. In this train, the compartments were of a breadth to carry at least ten seated persons in ample comfort on their two facing green-baize seats, for the rooms extended completely from side to side of the coach, with windows and entrance doors on both sides, and narrower doors in the walls beside the seats, opening on the adjacent compartments. For the kondúktor or any other crewman to go any distance along the train without disturbing the passengers, there was a narrow plank catwalk and iron handholds affixed along the *outside* of every car, with gaps between the coupled cars that necessitated the man's making fairly athletic and daring jumps.

The Florilegium arrived at the station about noon. Florian heeded the advice given him by Trepov, shooed away the ragged men and boys vociferously clamoring to be of service and set his own roustabouts to the arduous task of moving the circus from the station platform onto the train.

"If we can do this expeditiously," he said, "we might be loaded by dark. It is only two hundred and twenty miles to Kiev. I should think, since this train will not be stopping at stations along the way, we ought to make that run overnight—and in the dark, so we don't have to look at any more of this dreary prairie."

"Do we sit up all night?" asked Agnete.

"No, Fräulein Eel," said Willi. "I ordered enough coaches that we need put only four persons in each compartment. And, when we are ready to sleep, the back of each seat will be lifted and secured by the train's provodnik, to become an upper bunk. The crewmen, of course, will sleep in the straw with the animals."

So the Slovaks went to work, under the direction of Stitches, Boom-Boom, Hannibal and Banat. It was fortunate that the train's enclosed goods wagons were so big and had broad loading doors, because Hannibal insisted that the circus's horses and the caged and walking animals *not* be ramped onto the flatcars—as were the caravans and supply wagons—but that they ride inside the shelter of the boxcars. It entailed much inching and pinching of wagon wheels and tongues and shafts, and much neighing and roaring and struggling and balking of the animals, and much cursing and frequent cries of pain from the Slovaks, but that was duly accomplished.

Meanwhile, the unoccupied troupers went inside the station and found, to their surprise, that it contained a quite decent gostínitsa—at least far superior to the inn at Khotin—and they had a plain but satisfying meal of sprats, pepper pot soup, pork and dumplings, boiled potatoes and real beer, not kvas. Florian sat Kapitán Miliukov at his table; the rest of the soldiers remained outside, cordoning the train against pilferers or stowaways, and they would eat later, when the Slovaks did. Florian also, after the meal, went into the room adjoining the gostínitsa, another State Monopoly Store, bought twenty bottles of vodka and gave those to the captain. "For your men, by way of thanking them for their services."

"Spasíbo, Gospodín Florian," said Miliukov. "Perhaps, in return, while you wait for your transport to be readied, tak, you and your people will accept my invitation to a fairly uncommon event."

"An event?"

"Da. Come along. It is being held in the square just beyond this station."

The troupe rather puzzledly followed the captain from the station to the square. In its center was an upright stake and stocks, to which a shirtless man was fastened, his arms pinned in the stock openings and tightly roped to stretch all the muscles of his bare back into prominence. He appeared to be a fairly young man, beardless, but his long hair shrouded his face. Several black-robed judges stood about and, at a discreet distance, much of the population of Khamenets Podolskiy. Near the stake stood a giant Kazhák soldier, also shirtless, twisting and limbering a stout whip in his hands. Beside him, some iron tools were stuck in a brazier of glowing coals. At the sight, all the circus women except Monday Simms gave a gasp and hurried back inside the station inn. So did a number of the circus men. Florian asked the captain the reason for this "event."

"The man was convicted as an utterer. The local constabulary requested me, as senior to them in rank, to oversee his punishment and to provide my strongest soldier to do the flogging."

"An *utterer?*"

"Of false coins, tak—a forger, a counterfeiter. He will receive one hundred ninety and nine strokes of the k'nut, then tavró, then shchítsiki. If he lives through all of that, he will be dragged to the city limits and banished."

Before Florian or anyone else could say anything further, or turn and go away, the k'nut-wielding soldier had backed off four or five yards from the stake.

Then he took four or five firm steps forward and sprang high into the air as he brought the whip down with a loud *crack!* That first stroke made only a short cut across the victim's bare skin, from the nape of his neck to his left armpit, but it wrung from him a loud scream. Several more of the troupers and even some of the townsfolk did leave then. Among those who stayed was Monday Simms, and, for the first time in a long while, she was kneading her thighs together.

The knoutmaster backed off again, strode forward, leapt in the air and laid the next stroke exactly half an inch below the first, and parallel to it. He continued like that, each stroke half an inch lower and diagonally longer, until he had striped the shrieking man's back with twenty-five raw red gashes. Then the soldier transferred the whip to his left hand and just as accurately laid on twenty-five more stripes from left to right, crisscrossing the others. When the flogger changed hands again, he laid the slashes perpendicular to the others— changed hands again and whipped horizontally. By this time, the culprit was no longer screaming, and his back was no longer blood red, but a black pulp. During the final ninety-nine strokes, the knoutmaster tried merely to hit any previously unbroken bit of skin remaining among the cross-hatchings, and the victim hung from the stocks, limp and apparently lifeless.

But then Kapitán Miliukov stepped over to him and raised his dangling head, and incredibly the man had life enough to scream again when the Kazhák brought a red-hot branding iron from the brazier and stamped the letter O—for otvyérzheniy, outcast—on each cheek and his forehead. And yet the man lived, while the knoutmaster took a pair of glowing pincers from the brazier, seized and ripped away each of his nostrils, leaving in the middle of his face only a small protrusion of red-gray gristle. When that made the victim scream again, weakly, waveringly, piteously, he was echoed by an almost similar noise from the quivering, starry-eyed Monday Simms.

"Christ!" breathed Yount. "That forger fellow is a stronger man than me and the flogger put together."

"And now he's uglier and more freakish than any Tattooed Man like me," Fitzfarris said thoughtfully.

The outcast was loosed from the stocks and let to thud unconscious onto the cobbles of the square, and Kapitán Miliukov called for volunteers to drag him to the edge of town. Fitz was the only man who stepped forward.

The train was loaded by nightfall, and the circus roustabouts all fed, and the Kazhák company had departed, presumably off again to the border, and the engineer and fireman were getting up steam in the gigantic locomotive, meanwhile ringing its bell and hoo-hooting its whistle, evidently just for the pleasure of hearing them. The Slovaks climbed aboard the straw-strewn goods wagons containing the animals, and the rest of the company got into the compartments. A flagman on the platform swung a green lantern, the engine responded with an uproar of ringing and whooping, and ponderously began to chuff-chuff-chuff up to speed and left Khamenets Podolskiy behind.

The roadbed was not particularly well laid, so there was some heaving, rocking and vibration. Monday Simms might well have been doing her sympathetic vibrations, except that her attendance and excitement at the flogging scene seemed to have drained her of such impulses. For the others, the train ride was like riding a swan boat, after the jolting and careening they had endured on the log-slab road. The only annoyance was the oily smoke and soot that drifted in through every least crevice in the carriages.

At the rear of every passenger car was a cubbyhole in which sat a provodnik, tending and perpetually refilling a big samovar of hot tea, and he periodically came creeping along the car's outside catwalk to inquire if anyone wanted a glass of "chai." At intervals, also, the kondúktor or brakeman or an oiler left the crew car at the tail of the train, to sidle up and down the whole length of it, sometimes apparently doing routine inspection, sometimes perilously carrying a pitcher of tea—and once or twice a bottle of vodka—for the engineer and fire-man. The passenger coaches and even the goods wagons in which the animals and Slovaks rode were at least moderately heated by steam pipes from the loco-motive boiler running under the floors. However, as the night wore on and got colder, the provodnik of each coach came through with lap robes for the passen-gers to wrap themselves in, and later to use as blankets on their bunks. Each was a patchwork of stitched-together scraps of rare and precious furs: mink, sable, ermine. Florian inquired whence came these wonderful coverlets. They were made, said the porter, of bits discarded by the skornyáka workshops that made dress-fur coats, robes and such for Russian rich folks and for export to rich folks abroad.

When the thrill of being again aboard a railroad train had worn off, there being little to look at outside, the passengers began to visit back and forth be-tween compartments. Fitzfarris entered the one in which rode Florian, Edge, Yount and Pfeifer, just as Florian was idly saying, "... wonder what will become of that poor wretch we saw beaten."

Fitz said, "Looks like he'll live, Governor."

"Eh? How would you know that?"

Fitz jerked a thumb over his shoulder. "He's stretched out in the compart-ment that Meli and Jules and I took. Meli and Jules are swabbing his cuts and burns right now, with every medication we're carrying."

"You brought him *with us?!*" Edge exclaimed. "Christamighty, man, what for?"

"What for? Why, to *show*, of course. I'm responsible for recruiting the annex exhibits. I think I'll bill him as the Ugliest Man in the World."

"You'll never get away with it, Sir John," said Florian. "Those O brands are unmistakable. We'll be swooped upon by the first policeman who sees him. We'll be charged with harboring—abetting—God knows what."

Fitzfarris shook his head. "The fellow was as unconscious as a tree stump when we lugged him aboard. He still is. So I took the opportunity to light up a cigar and doctor those brands some, while he couldn't feel it." The other four men regarded Fitz with horrified awe. "I couldn't make them ornamental, but at least they don't look like O's any more. They could be any kind of wicked burn scars. What I figure, when he takes the platform, I'll talk him up as the survivor of a ruckus with Pemjean's bears. Only man ever to escape from *two savage bears,* ladies and gentlemen, with his life—if not much else."

"Hm-m," said Florian. "In Russian folklore, there is an unkillable ogre known as Kostchei the Deathless. You could call him that."

"Perfect," said Fitzfarris. "And it'll make Kewwy-dee and Kewwy-dah look not so tame, besides. The jossers will be more impressed when Pemjean makes those killer brutes skate with Daphne."

Jörg Pfeifer said, "But that man cannot be just a dumb muzhik. He must have some intelligence, to have been a counterfeiter. How do you know he will agree to becoming a sideshow exhibit?"

"Hell, what better alternative has he got?"

"Sir John is right, Fünfünf," said Florian. "Not even a monastery would take in a branded outcast. His only other recourses would be begging or recidivism. The most charitable almsgiver would be loath to give to him. And if he returns to a life of crime, well, he'll certainly be an easy suspect to identify. Caught again, he would surely be condemned to death."

"So we're doing him and us both a favor," said Fitzfarris. "Me, especially. Now I can retire from the limelight. A Tattooed Man damn sure can't compete with *him* in freakishness. I can wear old Mag's makeup and look like a normal human being *all* the time. Meli won't have to wince when people stare at us on the street. I mean, if it's all right with you, Governor."

"Of course, Sir John. Just as soon as Kostchei the Deathless is able to replace you. And I commend your initiative."

"I swear," said Edge, more in wonderment than reproach. "Florian, you and Foursquare Fitz between you must have cornered the market in brass. Whenever I think I know the limits of your outrageousness, one of you comes up with some new and chancy flimflam. Now we're hiring a convict, an Ishmael, shunned in his own land. The man has no conduct book to give him a circus history, no passport to show to border guards—"

"As it happens," Florian said equably, "secret agent Trepov was so eager to ingratiate himself that he slipped me a couple of extra Russian passports, left blank but properly visaed. It also happens that when the Terrible Turk blew our stand, he left in such a hurry and such a fury that he neglected to take along his conduct book. So our new Kostchei the Deathless—whatever his real name— will henceforth be Shadid Sarkioglu in private life." Florian turned again to Fitz- farris. "The man now could pass for any nationality. He certainly no longer has the squat, broad Slavic nose. But take no chances. Cut his hair short, in the Western style. And never let him speak Russian in the presence of strangers. When you introduce him on the platform, you might mention that the shock of his experience rendered the poor man mute for life."

"Right, Governor," Fitz said cheerfully. "We won't know until he wakes up, but just maybe it *did*."

The trip to Kiev lasted rather longer than the "overnight" Florian had hoped for. At every third verst of the way—every two miles—there stood beside the tracks a yellow-painted log cabin in which dwelt a signalman and his family. At the circus train's approaching hoo-hoot, he would pop out, usually accompanied by his whole family—even if they had been in bed, because a passing train was the only event ever to occur in their lives, and the only thing to look at in that desolate landscape—and the man would wave a green lantern to show that, according to his telegraph key, the way ahead was clear. But several times on this trip, the signalman waved a red lantern, the train stopped, its crew got down and swung heavy switch levers, and the train was shunted onto a siding to wait, sometimes for half an hour, to let a regularly scheduled train go by.

There were other stops, some of long duration: to take on water from a tank tower standing stark and lonely on the plain, to take on coal at a division-point railroad town called Vinnitsa. Every time the train stopped, Florian woke up, got out of his fur-blanketed bunk, scattering the soot and smuts that had settled on it and him, and went to inquire, with increasing impatience, what the delay was *now,* and returned to report to his compartment mates, whether or not they were awake or gave a damn.

At the seventh or eighth stop, when Florian got out, the train was in the middle of a featureless immensity of grass extending to the circle of the horizon all around—no water tank, no coal bunker, no signalman's izboushka, nothing. Clearly something had gone wrong with the train itself, for most of the crew were squatting beside one bogie wheel at the end of one of the goods wagons. The moon was rising just then, full and huge and amber, laying a long, golden, shimmering reflection across the prairie, as if the sea of grass really were a sea of water. Simultaneously, there arose from the far distances all around a chorus of mournful baying and howling.

"Volka," one of the trainmen told Florian. "Wolves."

The circus animals seemed to recognize the noise, too, though they probably never had heard it before, for they responded with anxious whinnies and grunts and trumpetings. Then, almost exactly imitating the wolves' baying, there came a howl from one of the passenger coaches. A compartment side door flew open, a naked figure leapt out and began running up the moon's golden pathway, chest-deep in the grass. That figure was followed by a smaller one, shoulder-deep in the grass, and two figures smaller yet, that quite disappeared in the grass. It took a moment for Florian to realize that the first runaway had been Pavlo Smodlaka and his pursuers were Gavrila, Sava and Velja. Pavlo continued to bay, eerily wolflike, as he ran. But the thick grass impeded his progress, while he left a trampled open swath behind him. So Gavrila soon overtook him, halted him, held him, apparently soothed him out of whatever nightmare had impelled him to that flight, and led him back to the train. They and the children climbed again into their compartment and shut the door.

"I wonder what that was all about," Florian said to himself, then in Russian to the train crew, "And what is wrong here, friends?"

When he returned to his own compartment, he reported to the three recumbent, fur-and-soot-covered, deeply sleeping men, "*Now* one of the journal boxes, whatever those are, has developed a hotbox, whatever that is, and must be re-packed, whatever that means. It seems it will take a damnably long time."

And so it was that, though the train very occasionally got up to its top speed of forty miles an hour, over the whole run it averaged a sedate fourteen. But at least the penultimate stop was a welcome one, when in the morning the engineer brought the train to a halt at the station of a village called Fastov, so everyone could debark and have breakfast. Even at that small station, the gostínitsa was a good one and provided a hearty and tasty meal.

From Fastov on, there was more to see through the train windows: rolling farmland, fairly substantial farmhouses, barnyards full of goats and geese, villages of houses that had painted or carved shutters and eaves. The railway frequently ran parallel to a road on which peasants were going to the city, astride mules, asses, horses, in lumbering carts, occasionally in light buckboard-style wagons drawn by a troika hitch. Whether the muzhiks were more prosperous in this area, or because a trip to the city was an occasion for dressing in their best, they were quite gaily attired. The women wore bright bodices and aprons over long print skirts. The men wore their usual baggy sharováry trousers tucked into boots of felt or birch bark, but added vividly colored shirts and high peaked caps. After another few miles, the rolling land began to bulge upward into real hills and, when the train rounded one of those, the passengers could see the series of wooded heights on which stood the city of Kiev. From this distance, it seemed to consist entirely of onion-domed church towers.

"Well, Kiev *is* called 'the Jerusalem of Russia,'" said Willi. "It is where Christianity first took root in this country."

The circus train pulled into the Kiev station about eleven o'clock, and was switched onto a siding where the roustabouts could unload it without disrupting other traffic. That job, like the loading, occupied them until nearly sundown. Meanwhile, Florian settled his charter bill, to date, with the various railroad officials in the stationmaster's office, so the train could go back into regular service, but he made arrangements to have it available again whenever he should decide to make the next run, to Moscow. Now the wagon train and animals afoot had to cross some two and a half miles of the city—the circus did not make parade, but attracted a good deal of attention, nevertheless—to the tober Willi had engaged. It was, as it had been so often in Italy, the infield of a racetrack. This one was called the Esplanáda, and it was finely situated on a height overlooking the broad but sluggish and dirty-yellow river Dnepr.

On arrival there, Banat came to ask, "Pana Governor, do we set up first or go and post paper first?"

"Lord, Lord, neither one," Florian said wearily. "First lay fires, Crew Chief, and heat plenty of water. Let us get the grime off us—and off the animals, as well. And anything else that's filthy, which is probably everything. Tomorrow, we will set up just the chapiteau and its rigging, so the artistes can practice. They haven't worked in weeks; they've got a lot of limbering and unkinking to do. We won't paper until we are ready to give Kiev a good show."

"Speaking of bathing, Herr Gouverneur," said Carl Beck, "the Herr Lothar has told me of a most splendid Bad just down the hill from here, and a miraculous healing hot spring it has. On account of so many miracles, there the Lavra Convent was erected—in all of Russia the convent the most highly revered. It is there to bathe I shall go. Perhaps you and others also would care to come."

"Thank you, Boom-Boom. I am too fatigued even to seek a miracle cure for my fatigue. I'll settle for a tub right here. But take anyone else who wants to go."

So quite a number of the company went with Beck down the hill to the spa near the Baptismal Monument. Not until they had paid their fifty kopeks apiece and got to the disrobing room did they discover that it was communally used by both males and females, and that the men and women all disrobed to the skin, and went together into the hot pool in the grotto. So the circus women—except Clover Lee and the equally unembarrassable Nella Cornella—immediately took their leave, forfeited their fifty kopeks and returned to the tober, preferring a private bath to a sanctified but public one.

A couple of the bath attendants spoke French and managed to make Beck comprehend that, besides the simply miraculous healing bath, the spa offered another, *scientifically* miraculous bath, and other invigorating services, as well.

Beck decided to avail himself of everything offered, but his companions were
satisfied to stay and soak and relax in the communal pool.

One of the extra services was provided by a crone who could easily have
been the Russian fairy-tale witch Baba Yaga. She came to Beck bearing a
hand basket of huge, knobbly, ugly tree mushrooms. With mortar and pestle,
she mashed those into a viscous, pus-like fluid, some of which she spooned
into Beck then and there. It tasted awful enough, he later reported, to be the
good medicine it was warranted to be, for liver and kidney ailments. The
crone poured the remainder of the dreadful substance into a bottle for Beck to
take away with him.

Then she led him to a small, private pool of water, scalding hot, and when
he had gingerly immersed himself, she brought and threw into the water an
entire anthill, complete with its inhabitants. Beck might have bounded right
out again, but the ants perished before they could make the situation even
hotter for him. The pool instantly turned brown-black and unpleasantly pungent, but the French-speaking attendant made Beck understand that the for-
mic acid in the multitude of little ant corpses, plus the turpentine they had
absorbed from living in a pine forest, was far more efficacious than reliance
on mere miracles for easing rheumatism, lumbago, muscle strain and back-
ache. Beck's extended stay in the spa cost him four rubles all together, plus a
scattering of kopeks in gratuities, but he emerged claiming to feel healthier
and livelier than he had in years.

The other circus folk, pleased just to feel clean again and somewhat relieved
of their train-ride cramps, had meanwhile ambled about the neighborhood of the
Lavra Convent—there were quite a few things to see there—before they went
back up the hill.

"Do you know, signori, what they have down there?" Nella Cornella said
excitedly to Florian and Edge. "Many, many caves—le catacombe di Sant'An-
tonio, they are called—and in them are seventy-three saints. All old and dry and
wrinkled like fusilli pasta, but dressed in liturgico finery, as if they might get up
and say mass next Sunday."

"Then Sir John can give his Egyptian Princess a rest while we're here," said
Florian, "if Kiev already has a surfeit of mummies."

"Wait, that is not all!" said Nella. "Right in the middle of one cave, sticking up
from the ground, there is this mummia head of a monk, with one of those tall
hats such as bishops wear."

"A miter."

"Sì, una mitra. And the rest of him is under the ground. He is called John the
Long-Suffering, and he determined to mortify himself to the greater glory of
God, so he had himself buried *alive* that way, just his head sticking up, and the
other monacchi fed him, and he lived like that for *thirty years,* until he died, and
that was seven hundred years ago, signori, and he is still there in the same place!
Maraviglioso!"

"Hell, Governor," Edge said humorously. "We might as well fold up and move
along. How can we possibly rivalize with such splendiferous native attractions?"

"Bah," said Florian. "You heard Nella. The natives have had seven centuries
to get bored with John the Long-Suffering. We will be something new in their
experience."

3

KIEV'S half-million population provided the Florilegium with solidly packed houses for a solid month, even after winter clamped down with voluminous snows, vicious winds and bone-chilling cold. Winter was no novelty to the Kiev citizens, but a "Confederate American" circus was. The people trudged through fresh-fallen snow, or walked gliding and skidding over packed old snow and glare ice, or substituted troika sleighs for their carriages, to get to the Esplanáda, and then sat uncomplainingly in the cold chapiteau until their own combined body heat made it tolerable enough to doff their furs—and for the performers to make their entrance in their skimpy léotards and fleshings.

Florian bought wolf skins—those were the cheapest and most abundant furs—and Stitches Goesle, with his big sailmaking awls and needles, put them together into blankets for the elephants, horses and camel to wear, and immense coverings to go over the other animals' cages, and those were removed only when the animals were performing or on view in the menagerie top. The Slovaks took turns sitting up all night, one man every night, ready to set hay bales smoldering in the chapiteau and annex if snow should fall, which it did about two nights out of five during the remainder of October and into November. Except for that one watchman, everyone else of the company, Slovaks included, slept in the city's Frántziya Hotel.

The Florilegium's only competition in Kiev was the native circus that performed year-round at the Gippodvorets, or Hippo Palace—and that was no competition at all, it being merely an all-horse show, and long familiar to the citizenry. Nevertheless, Florian, Edge, Clover Lee, Monday and the Jászi brothers went to look it over one day, in case it might inspire any innovations in their own acts. It did not. The Russian équestriennes were nowhere near so talented as Monday and Clover Lee, and the djigit or voltige riders were tame compared to the Jászis. The high point of the show was a not very exciting chariot race around and around the arena, run by very Roman-looking charioteers in steel and leather armor and plumed helmets, riding in very Roman-looking open chariots—but, all in all, rather ridiculous-looking, since each of the chariots was drawn by an extremely Russian-looking troika team, with the high dugá bow over the center horse of the three.

Meanwhile, Carl Beck went every day to his anthill bath at the Lavra spa, and even persuaded a few others to try it—Dai Goesle, Jörg Pfeifer, Ferdi Spenz —but once was enough for them. The rest of the troupe took in what sights were worth going to see in Kiev. They stood on the city's one and only bridge for pedestrian and vehicular traffic, to look down at the solidly frozen Dnepr River, and they stood atop the city's highest hill, where the Apostle Andrew allegedly had planted the first Christian cross ever seen in Russia and first preached the Gospel to the pagan Rus tribesmen.

They went to the Ópernyi Teátr to see and hear Glinka's *A Life for the Tsar,* which they found not only incomprehensible but also wearisome, since it lasted for five interminable acts. The scenery and the seventeenth-century costumes were brilliantly done, and the music was stirring, when it was not being overwhelmed by the stentorian singers. But the circus people were more impressed by two phenomena that had nothing to do with the opera itself. At their first entry into the theatre, and at their final exit from it, and at their several exits and reentries during the intermissions—when they went to smoke cigarettes in the ornate lobby—the ushers opened just one of the theatre's many doors, and the entire audience had to crush through it, which made for a good deal of rude shoving and elbowing and grumbling.

"It is the same in every public building here," said Willi. "I do not know if the Russians have a talent and a taste for inconvenience, or if it is deliberately done to toughen the Russian moral fiber, but if a theatre or concert hall or cabaret has *twenty* doors, exactly *one* of them will be unlocked for ingress and egress."

The other noteworthy thing was that the square outside the Opera House—which, on the troupers' arrival, had been quite bare of anything except the gathering operagoers, their private sleighs and carriages and their hired droshkis and karetas—had been transformed by the time the audience emerged at the first interval between acts. The private sleighs and carriages were still there, and so were their half-frozen, red-nosed, patiently waiting coachmen. But the square was now studded with little portable wooden kiosks, set out by the Opera House ushers, and evidently reserved for the coachmen of rich merchants, nobles and other high personages. Inside them, those coachmen had lit the burners under samovars and now, and at every subsequent intermission, served hot tea to their masters and mistresses, when they came out swathed in their minks and sables and martens.

Minks and sables and martens were much on the minds of the women of the circus, particularly after Clover Lee one night returned to the hotel, after having dinner with a Johnny from the seats, *wearing* a superb sable coat. The Johnny, though too old for her consideration as anything more than a one-engagement escort, had turned out to be a wealthy beet-sugar magnate who—Clover Lee gleefully reported—had not pressed upon her any unwelcome advances, but *had* insisted on paying extravagantly for the mere pleasure of her company at dinner.

"He said I needed—I deserved—a better winter wrap than this old loden thing I bought back in Innsbruck or wherever it was," said Clover Lee, tossing the old coat on the back of a chair in the hotel lobby, while the other women goggled incredulously. "So he took me to that street of swanky shops. You know, the Epiphany Boulevard, where we've all yearned in all the shop windows. And he took me to the Frères Couvreux furriers, and Gyorgy—that's his name—Gyorgy never asked the price of anything, and he wouldn't let me ask, either. And the brothers Couvreux, they have all these pretty women of every shape and size, and they picked one my size, and she came out on a little stage, wearing one coat after another, and posing and twirling its skirts about, while one of the Messieurs Couvreux poured champagne for me and Gyorgy—and *oh!* I had such a dilemma, trying to decide between this one and a mink coat just as beautiful. But I think I chose the nicer. Don't you girls think it's nice?"

Through gritted teeth, the other women agreed that it was very nice. From then on, every unattached female among them accepted any invitation she got from any Kiev gentleman who looked reasonably prosperous and not discernibly evil or demented, and who spoke some language comprehensible to her, so she could tell him—over dinner or at the theatre or wherever they went together—about the magnificent gift her sister artiste had received under similar circumstances. But only one of the women succeeded in duplicating Clover Lee's coup d'éclat, and that was the midget Katalin Szábo, possibly because her Johnny, another well-to-do merchant, did not have to lay out a small fortune to buy a mink coat in her size.

As they had in other countries, the handsomer males of the Florilegium also got billets-doux of invitation from ladies in the seats. If the lady was also handsome and the man was unattached, he usually accepted, and afterward expressed no regrets at having done so. None of the men got a fur coat out of those rendezvous, and they were gentlemanly close-mouthed about anything they perhaps did get.

Occasionally, too, a local aristocrat or wealthy pomieshchik would invite the whole company to his city mansion or country seat. Those residences were all sumptuously furnished, in what their owners no doubt believed to be chic and up-to-date Western style. But there was such a clutter of bric-à-brac, and the walls were so chockablock with dismal photographs and mediocre paintings, and the furniture—even when brand-new—was of such a tumid and fustian pomposity that, as Daphne remarked, even Queen Victoria would have felt suffocated in all that dowdiness. Perhaps the best indicator of what the Russian upper classes apparently considered le dernier cri: in the foyer of every great house that the circus people visited stood a stuffed polar bear, erect on its hind legs, holding in its forepaws a silver tray for calling cards.

But the hosts and hostesses, however démodé or dubious their taste in décor, were faultlessly hospitable. The visitors were royally wined and dined and entertained—by folk dancers, or strolling balalaika players, or the lady of the manor herself at a harp or dulcimer or harpsichord—and every guest had at least one servant to wait upon him personally, usually several of them. Since every Russian noble and most of the rich merchants spoke French, a good number of the circus folk could converse with them. For the others, Florian provided translation, commentary or explanation, as required.

During their visit to the estate of a Baron Ignatiev, Yount commented to Florian, "All these serfs working around here may of been freed, but you'd never know it. The baron and baroness, even their snotty little brats, order 'em around sharper than any Dixie massa ever tongue-lashed his darkies. And I just seen the baroness slap a maid in the pantry so hard her whole face is one big bruise."

Agnete added, "Even if I speak kindly to a stable hand, he snatches off his cap as if I were his mistress giving him a scolding. He never lifts his eyes from the ground, and stands there scratching his head like an imbecile."

Florian said, "The head scratching is a mark of respect, as was the tugging of forelocks we've seen elsewhere. But you are right. The muzhiks still act slavish and frightened, even though they are no longer anyone's property. Well, they have reason to be so. I myself just noticed: there is one of them jailed in a privy down at the end of the garden right now, freezing in that stench, for some act of disobedience."

"Don't they realize they're free now?" asked Yount. "Does the zar tolerate his bigwigs still treating the peasants so harsh?"

"He probably would not, if he saw it going on," said Florian. "But the peasants have a fatalistic saying: 'God is a long way up and the tsar is a long way off.' So they put up with the abuses and perpetuate the inequalities."

"The only sign of *equality* that I have seen," said Agnete, "is that both servants and masters are equally humble when they pass that ghastly red-papered corner of the drawing room where all the ferns and the holy pictures are. Everybody, high or low, makes a little genuflection and crosses himself."

"The pictures are called ikons," said Florian. "And that is the krásnyi utol, the beautiful corner. The word krásnyi means both 'red' and 'beautiful.' Every house has a krásnyi corner, every palace, even many shops and offices. You will gratify your hosts if you, too, make at least a respectful nod to the Holy Family when you pass those ikons."

"Undskyld," Agnete said firmly. "I will be damned if I will. These people are hypocrites, pretending piety but behaving most un-Christianly to their inferiors."

Fitzfarris, discovering that the Russians were so devout—or at least pietistic —gave a bread-and-butter gift to every one of the troupe's hosts: one of the Christian-cross-embossed "miraculous eggs of the glukhár," as that bird was here known. The dinner- or party-givers were all ecstatic at receiving such an unusual religious bauble, and most of them immediately set it in an honored place among their multitudinous other gewgaws. One of the troupe's hosts was a Count Bereshkov, a dedicated hunter and outdoorsman, whose mansion's interior decoration included wall-hung trophy heads of every kind of animal from a Siberian tiger to a Pamir mountain goat. He was thrilled to have that unique memento of the glukhár, and was moved to tell the company some enlightening anecdotes about the bird, which Fitz from then on worked into his sideshow presentation of the creature.

"Curious bird, the glukhár," said Bereshkov. "Sometimes, purely out of high spirits, it would seem, the bird slides down a slope of snow with its wings outspread. You can imagine what a strange track that leaves. Any outdoorsman, of course, recognizes it. But the superstitious muzhiks make up all kinds of spooky stories about malevolent fyéyat and kóbol'di to frighten themselves with. Peasants, they will believe in anything."

"Yes," murmured Florian, watching the count fondle the egg.

"The name glukhár means 'the deaf cock,'" Bereshkov went on. "But he is deaf only when he is deafened by his own screaming. And he does that mostly in the springtime, when he is calling for a mate and defying all rivals. So a shooter goes to the woods at dawn, waits until he hears the glukhár's call, then approaches, very cautiously, scuttling from tree to tree each time the cock is bawling and cannot hear. Eventually the shooter gets within view of the glukhár, and the next time it starts bellowing, he cocks and fires his fowling piece, and that call is the glukhár's last."

The one member of the Florilegium company who did not attend any of those invitational dinners or parties—who did not ever leave the tober for any reason —was the newest member, Kostchei the Deathless. After a month of recuperation, he was being exhibited in the sideshow top and, as Fitzfarris had assumed, he was grateful to have even that degrading employment, since it also provided shelter, meals and anonymity. His back had healed, hard and crisscrossed, so it resembled a turtle's carapace, except that it was concave instead of convex. The lacerated skin and muscles had drawn tight as they reknitted themselves, so Kostchei's upper torso, neck and head were arched permanently backward. He looked like a man trying to see to the top of a tall tree. On the annex platform, he was presented completely clothed—Fitzfarris would not show his back, because it had so obviously been flogged.

Instead, Kostchei strode out, the gawkers seeing nothing but the beardless underside of his upraised chin, while Fitz spouted a rodomontade about the man's having entered the cage of the two ferocious Syrian bears, supposing them to be tame, and his being terribly mauled by their teeth and claws, and his miraculous escape with his life but with lifelong disfigurement. Kostchei still stood like that, while Florian translated the story into Russian. Then, as Hannibal thrummed a low and suspenseful mutter on his bass drum, Kostchei very, very slowly bent forward from the waist, to bring his gruesome face into view of the audience—and the audience never failed to gasp in horror and surge back in recoil from that face with no nose and with deeply indented, shiny-gray rosettes of scars covering most of the rest of it.

In truth, it was some while before the rest of the circus company felt at ease around the man. For a criminal, and one who had suffered so, he was good-humored enough, and intelligent and apparently educated; he spoke French in addition to Russian and, over time, learned to speak fair English. Because of his contorted neck, though, his voice was only a strangulated whisper. He never revealed anything of his past history, not even his real name, but seemed content to be known as Kostchei the Deathless in public and Shadid Sarkioglu in private. Most of the time, his fellow artistes saw only the underside of his chin. But he did have to bend forward when he ate with them, and that sight was no inducement to hearty appetite. Eventually, however, the other troupers got as accustomed to him as they were to Tücsök's tininess or Meli's serpents or Fitzfarris's half-blue face. (That last was now to be seen only in the early mornings, before Fitz applied his cosmetic mask of normality.)

One thing that helped Shadid's acceptance into the company—indeed, made him almost a pet of the women members—was his cordial offer of assistance when Sunday confided to him, in French, how the female artistes wished they or their menfolk could afford to buy them furs. Shadid gave what would have been a guffaw, but for his constricted throat; it came out as only thin, piping laughter.

"Mademoiselle Sunday," he said, in his husky whisper, "it is true that the state regulates the price of furs, and sets those prices high. The state regulates many things, but there are always those who circumvent the regulations in one way or another. Besides the state markets, there is what we call the koöperatívnyi market. You ladies want furs? I shall get for you furs, and at poacher's prices. But you must ask permission first of Monsieur le Gouverneur."

"Woe is me," said Florian, when Sunday immediately ran to put the proposition to him. "I might have known. We hire a first-of-May who is an ex-criminal, and soon we are tempted to criminality ourselves. But... well... if Shadid can guarantee that we won't wind up at the stake, as he did..."

So Shadid gave to Fitzfarris an address and a note written in Russian, and Fitz delivered it. The address turned out to be that of a pawnshop conspicuously empty of items for sale. The aged proprietor read the note, nodded, said nothing, but raised three fingers, then ushered Fitz out again. Three days later, after dark, a hooped and canvas-covered wagon lumbered onto the tober and the same old man clambered down from the driver's seat. He dropped the tailgate of the wagon and silently motioned for any who wished to climb aboard and look at the racks down each side of the interior, from which hung perhaps threescore coats of all sizes and every variety of fur.

The pelts were just as fine, and the coats as exquisitely made, as they would have been at a legitimate furrier's establishment, but the prices on their tags were only a quarter to a fifth of what they would have been there. No one could resist such luxuriousness and such bargains. Yount bought for Agnete a mink, and Pemjean for Monday a sable, and LeVie for Nella a stone marten, and Fitz for Meli a mink, and Florian for Daphne a sable. Then, so the unattached women would not be slighted, Florian and Edge chipped in together to buy baum marten coats, almost as elegant, for Sunday and Ioan. And, when Pavlo Smodlaka resolutely refused to "squander money on fripperies" for his women-folk, Dai and Carl sneered at him and paid to buy for Gavrila and little Sava at least a squirrel-skin coat apiece.

Jules and Willi picked out for themselves matching coats of vivid, almost luminescent red fox. When the other men tended to snicker, Willi said haughtily, "There is nothing effeminate about men wearing fur coats. You have seen many in our audiences. And when we get farther north, you will each damn well wish you had one." That made sense, so all the men—all but Pavlo—purchased coats for themselves, but of rather less spectacular gray-and-black badger. Since Kost-chei the Deathless had arranged this windfall, and because he was still on salary holdback, Florian advanced him the money to buy a badger coat for himself, as well.

After that capacity-crowd month in Kiev, the circus's attendance began just perceptibly to fall off. Florian immediately went to the railroad station and made arrangements for his charter train to come and pick up the circus again. Willi Lothar left his calash with the rest of the Florilegium vehicles and he and Rou-leau, wearing their twin red-fox coats, took a regular railroad train to Moscow to engage a tober.

"Aren't you being a trifle impetuous, Governor?" Edge asked. "Kiev isn't ex-actly ostracizing us. We're still turning a more than decent profit. Oughtn't we to milk this stand for all it's worth?"

"If this were summertime, I would," said Florian. "But there are considera-tions that outweigh the red-wagon receipts. We must depend on sfondone at-tendance just to make the temperature bearable in the chapiteau—for our performers no less than the audience."

"And you'll use any excuse, won't you, to hurry on toward Saint Petersburg?"

"Well, I do keep remembering how the tsar blew up that grand old ship in Livorno harbor, just for the benefit of an artist. Who knows what largesse he might bestow on us?"

So, two weeks later, when the Florilegium had been showing in Kiev for eight weeks, the charter train had been made up again and run into Kiev station. The circus once more was laboriously loaded aboard, and the monster Sormovo locomotive hauled it northwestward. Again it was a nighttime departure, and this time there was no breakdown of any part of the train itself on the way. But there were still the intermittent stops for a signalman's red lantern, and for tak-ing on coal, for taking on water, for meal stops at little station gostínitsat, so Florian calculated the average speed on this trip as an only slightly more sprightly sixteen miles per hour. And it was a far longer run—more than five hundred miles—so the circus people were on board the train, except when they got out to eat and avail themselves of the station toilets, that night, the next day and another night. The weather being now so cold that the boiler-steam heating of the compartments was barely perceptible, they rode the whole way, awake or asleep, in their recently bought fur coats, plus gloves, hats, mufflers, and all the patchwork lap robes the provodnik could find for them. The animals in the goods wagons rode in their wolf-skin blankets and cage coverings.

Again there was little to look at in the darkness outside the lamplighted compartments. However, by the next day's dawning, the company had at long last left behind the monotonous grasslands they had been crossing ever since shortly after leaving Lake Balaton, away back in Hungary. The countryside now rose and dipped and had more frequent farms, villages and trees, even forests. The train crossed bridges over many frozen rivers, though none so broad as the Dnepr. The villages, now quilted by snow, looked not so squalid. But the only two cities that the train passed through in daylight—Bryansk and Kaluga—were drab, rusty, smoky aggregations of factories.

It was early morning of the following day when the train approached Moscow, through snow-covered fields that would in summer be the city's market gardens. When the train topped the crest of the Sparrow Hills, the passengers could look across the Moskvá River valley and see the whole panorama of the city—seven-hilled, like Rome and Lynchburg—with the white-walled and many-towered citadel, the Kremlin, its highest eminence. The train rolled through a shantytown that was the suburbs, and into Bryansk Station, and found a siding already reserved for it by the waiting Willi and Jules, who had also taken care of all the paperwork, payment and making of future railroad arrangements with the stationmaster.

"But the best tober I could get," said Willi, "is away up in Petrovskiy Park. From here, we will have to haul a full quarter of the distance around the city and then go northeast on the Tver road."

"Well, since we have arrived so early in the day," Florian said buoyantly, "the roustabouts ought to have us unloaded not long after noon. We shall make parade and go the other way, *three*-quarters of the distance around the city, and entice the Muscovites with a look at the splendor of us."

Lothar and Rouleau looked dubious about the notion, but said nothing, and that is what the Florilegium did—complete with the music of the bandwagon up front and that of the calliope at the rear. Almost all the artistes rode swaddled in their fur coats, but would occasionally flip them open to show their spangled costumes—*very* occasionally, and very briefly, for Moscow was colder than Kiev. The animals in the cages were invisible under their fur coverings, but the horses, the camel and the two elephants, in their wolf-skin blankets, and the elephants and camel in their immense boots, looked even more exotic than if they had marched undressed. Only the Kim brothers, who seemed impervious to *any* inclemency or discomfort, wore nothing but their pista fleshings and did their cartwheels and flips and other acrobatics bare-handed and barefooted along the packed snow of the streets.

The parade proceeded from the railroad station to a wide avenue that looped around most of the central city. It was called Smolensky Boulevard where the circus made a right turn onto it, but, according to the street signs, changed its name every half mile or so. And the paraders soon realized why Willi and Jules had not appeared enthusiastic about their parading. The boulevard, not to mention the intersecting other streets, was excruciatingly ill-paved. Had it not been for the cushioning layer of snow on the cobbles, the riders would have had almost as much of a jolting as they had endured on that log-slab road they had first traveled in Russia. And every street was clogged with a wheel-to-wheel, horse-muzzle-to-tailgate traffic of coaches, wagons, carts, droshkis, troikas and people, people, people, every one of them, riding or afoot, unmannerly shoving and cursing for the right-of-way. Only the fact that many horses shied away from the noise of the parade—and other drivers and pedestrians stopped to gape in amazement—made it possible for the circus to proceed at all. But Florian, in the lead as always, persevered, and the parade succeeded in going counterclockwise the entire seven-mile circuit of the variously named boulevard and then the two miles farther along the Peterburgskoe Chaussée to the Petrovskiy Park.

While they were still on the boulevard, the circus folk could see that Moscow was laid out in concentric circles—or would have been, except that a bend of the Moskvá River intruded, so the main city could be likened to a giant biscuit with a bite taken out of one edge. Occupying all of Moscow's highest hill was the Kremlin—a city-unto-itself of palaces, churches, a monastery, a convent, the Court of Justice, an arsenal and barracks, still other buildings, almost every one topped with domes or turrets or onion-bulbed spires—the whole contained within a triangle of sixty-five-foot-high, crenellated and whitewashed stone walls, one of the walls running close alongside that incurving bend of the river. The Kremlin was the center of the city's concentric part-circles of lesser edifices, and towered over them all.

"As the local proverb has it," Willi later told the others, "there is nothing above Moscow except the Kremlin, and nothing above the Kremlin except Heaven."

The next part-circle outside the Kremlin was called by the natives simply Górod, "the City." That district, also surrounded by a white-washed wall, was the business part of Moscow, all offices, trading concerns, the city's university, banks and the like. Next beyond that was the "White City" of imperial, royal and noble palaces, rich families' mansions, museums, theatres, grand churches and the Imperial Foundlings' Hospital. It was around the dignified White City that the circus folk made their parade. If they looked inward from the boulevard, they could see clear to the Kremlin along the streets that radiated out from it. If they looked the other way, they could see the next outer concentric circle, the "Earth City," so called because of the now crumbling earthworks around it that had once been the outermost ramparts of Moscow. And Earth City consisted of less grand residences, hotels, taverns and market squares. But Moscow had long ago sprawled beyond those ramparts, and the farthest concentric ring, extending all around Earth City and across the river as well, constituting fully three-fourths of the city's area, was the Okréstnosti, the "Suburbs." That name was a typically bland Russian euphemism for what was actually an industrial belt of factories, mills, forges, foundries and the pitiful shacks of their workers, the whole as drab and dirty and mean as the other industrial cities the circus train had passed through—and the Suburbs cast their pall of smoke, soot and noxious smells over the entire inner city, clear to the Kremlin.

"Moscow was once Russia's capital," said Willi, when later he was identifying for the troupers the various things and places they had seen on their one circuit of the city, "and the Kremlin is still the holy place where a tsar must be crowned. But, after Peter the Great built Saint Petersburg and moved his court there, this city stagnated. It now has only about the same population as Kiev. Lately, though, Moscow has aspired to become the industrial and transport center of all the Russias. Hence the unloveliness of it, and the terribly crowded streets, and the noise and dirt and odors."

So the circus people were glad to have their tober well out beyond the Suburb belt, in the trees and clean air of Petrovskiy Park. A short ride by sleigh or wagon from the park was another of Moscow's several railroad stations, the Savelovo, and there was of course a transients' hotel nearby. It had room for all the company, and the hôtelier was more than happy to have guests who would be staying longer than overnight, so he and his kitchen and his maids and porters exerted every effort to make the company's stay pleasant and comfortable.

After the Florilegium's unprecedented Amerikanskiy-parade entrance into the city, the ensuing two weeks brought turnaway crowds. The next week brought straw-house crowds. But then the chapiteau began to show empty seats here and there, then more and more of them. Moscow had two permanent circuses in its Earth City—one pure Russian, the Nikítin; the other run by, and consisting almost entirely of, an émigré Italian family, Truzzi by name—and both of those circuses performed indoors, in commodious and decently heated buildings. Though their seldom-changing programs must have been tiresomely familiar to everybody in Moscow, it was understandable that circusgoers would prefer either of them to a circus that they had to travel at least two miles to see, and then had to provide their own body warmth for heating. Also, to judge from the thick-packed crowds thronging the city streets, the Muscovites had a predilection for clustering close together, as near as possible to the city center, and a corresponding dislike for wide-open spaces.

The artistes all strained mightily to do their turns with every grace and perfection, and to introduce new bits of business into them, in hopes that every other josser would go out praising the show to all of Moscow. Rouleau talked the reluctant Carl Beck into arranging a balloon ascension, and nearly froze to death when the *Saratoga* lofted up to altitudes far colder than ground level. The Emeraldina and the Kesperle, though they no longer had old cuckold Notkin to be the butt of their japes, made their clown routine even bawdier than it had been in Bavaria. Nella memorized and spoke her lines in Russian. Ferdi Spenz, not having the intellect for that, did his part in pantomime. He concealed the inflatable "cactus plant" in his oversized pantaloons and, while lasciviously wooing the Emeraldina, pumped it up to make a prodigious codpiece. At which Nella cried, mock-despairingly, "Bozhe moi! How can a woman keep her most secret closet shut, when every man"—giggle, giggle—"has got such a key to it?" The audiences laughed uproariously, but the audiences continued to dwindle.

So, once more, Florian went to the railroad stationmaster to ask for the making up of his charter train again, and Rouleau and Lothar took an earlier train for St. Petersburg. Meanwhile, the others of the company found time—and courage—to go into the clamorous, bustling, smelly city several times to see its more notable sights.

In the Kremlin compound, they visited the several palace museums, the public rooms of the tsar's own Great Kremlin Palace, the Treasury-and-Armory and the Cathedral of the Assumption, where every tsar had been crowned since the first to assume that title: Ivan IV, called the Terrible. The visitors finished that tour benumbed by the sheer numbers and richness of the buildings' contents—gold and silver and gem-encrusted medallions and diadems and necklaces and tableware, ancient crowns and crown jewels, banners from long-ago battles, antique arms and armor, luxurious old coaches and sleighs, all gold-leaf and fur upholstery. But it was outside the Kremlin that the newcomers found their two favorite things in Moscow. One of them was directly across the river from the Kremlin—the quaintly named Neskuchniy Sad, "the Non-Boring Garden." It was the best-tended and most beautiful park in the city, even in deep winter, with well-sculptured topiary, bosky groves hiding lovers' lanes, a small lake, now frozen over and humming with ice skaters, delicate pavilions on the steps of which old women peddled hot tea and zakuska.

Their other favored place was at the south end of the awesomely vast Krásnyi Square beyond the Kremlin walls. That was St. Basil's Cathedral, another relic of Ivan the Terrible. The interior of it was of no interest, but the exterior was straight out of a fairy tale about gingerbread-and-candy castles. It consisted of a clustered dozen high domes and spires, no two even remotely alike—some onion-shaped, some pineapple-shaped, some saw-toothed, some faceted, some studded all over with pimply knobs, some scaled like fish. All were gilded with gold leaf or painted or tiled in at least two colors each—no two anywhere the same hues—in bands or stripes or spirals. The archway and window shapes were of infinite variety: some round, some square, some rectangular, some oblong, and two, side by side, were framed and painted to represent the eyes of an owl. The onlookers made a number of comments, ranging from admiring to risible to unbelieving, but perhaps Yount's was the most apt:

"Old Ivan couldn't of been so terrible if he built this."

Five weeks after entering Moscow, the Florilegium left it again, from the convenient Savelovo Station, in a chill midmorning. Almost immediately the train was under way, the city dwindled behind and gave place to forests so dense that the train seemed to be tunneling through them. But gradually the forests thinned and there was rolling meadowland, blanketed in snow. Again, the train suffered no breakdowns, but, since there was only the single track between Moscow and St. Petersburg, the two busiest cities of Russia, and many passenger and freight trains had to make use of that track, the circus's train was very often signaled off to a siding to let another pass it in one direction or the other. So again, although the chartered train very occasionally worked up to a decent speed, its effective average was about sixteen miles an hour. And six hours out of Moscow it halted without being flagged down, at the station of a good-sized town, to let everybody disembark for dinner. There, Florian scurried about among his people to tell them at what a significant geographical point they had arrived.

"This town is Tver, a thriving trade center, because it is not only on the Moscow-Saint Petersburg railway, it also straddles that river yonder, likewise a much-traveled trade route. You might want to go and look at it, for that is the river Volga, famed in song and story."

Indeed, the folk song recently published as the "Song of the Volga Boatmen" was already immensely popular throughout Russia. All the troupers had heard it played on balalaikas in restaurants and hotel dining rooms, and Boom-Boom Beck was scoring a version for his windjammers to play. So most of the company did go down to the riverside, and did see the hugely muscled bargemen walking the towpaths along either bank. The river being solidly frozen over, their thick ropes were hauling not barges but sledges heavily laden with grain. Nevertheless, the bargemen did chant that song—though not so musically as a balalaika could play it—with its heavy beat that kept them trudging in step.

The train's crewmen hurried through their meal in Tver, then left the station to do the complicated fastening of a huge horizontal V of a snowplow, point foremost, to the front of their great locomotive. When the circus folk awoke at the next day's dawn, they saw why. The snow on the pasture lands roundabout lay in undulant waves, like desert sand dunes, and this was a region of constant high winds that continuously resculptured the snow dunes and drove them, like real waves, across the railroad tracks. In the infrequent village that the train passed through, where the local church with its onion-domed steeple would ordinarily be the tallest structure in town, the church was no higher than the squat izba huts and shacks of the villagers. Every church in this northland had its onion-domed steeple, all right, but it had been erected on the ground at a distance to the lee side of each church, so as not to endanger the building and its congregation if it should blow over.

The wind also wafted from those farm fields an appalling smell, worse even than Moscow's factory effluxions, the smell of rotten fish. Folding their mufflers around their noses, the circus people expressed the hope that they were not smelling the supposedly immaculate city of St. Petersburg. They were not. But it wasn't until they got to the city that Willi Lothar was there to explain that smell to them.

"The fishermen here in the Gulf of Finland make great catches of herring. Some is sold as food fish, but some of the catch is pressed to make oil, and the useless remains are sold cheap to farmers. In the autumn, after the harvest, the farmers plow those crushed fish into their fields for fertilizer, and the stink is so strong that even the deepest winter snows cannot cover it."

The stench was left behind when the train climbed from the lowlands into the Valdái Hills, covered with birch woods. The woods blunted the ever-blowing winds, and the ground under them was bare of snow and brown of soil, except for the silvery-white "frost shadows" of the trees. Since the birches themselves were silvery white, they seemed not so much to be casting shadows but reflections of themselves, as if the ground had been a calm water.

Then the train was rumbling alongside the broad, frozen river Neva, and through outlying ramshackle residences and immense warehouses—but no factories, no smoke, no soot, no rackety noise or noisome smells. The passengers, now excited enough to be temporarily oblivious to the bitter cold, opened their compartment windows and leaned out, and saw ahead of them the golden spires and domes and broad boulevards and multicolored palaces of the modern "Venice of the North," Great Peter's "Window on the West," the city the travel guidebooks rhapsodized as "Music in Stone," the city called by its inhabitants lovingly, familiarly "Piter"—the capital of all the Russias, St. Petersburg.

4

WILLI AND JULES, in their candescent red-fox coats, were waiting at the Nicholas Station. While the circus train was being shunted onto its assigned siding, Willi said, "Herr Gouverneur, I have got us a fine tober this time." He spread out a plan of the city. "It is in the Tauric Garden, a public park behind the old Potemkin Palace. Only a short way from here."

Florian studied the plan. "Good work, Chefpublizist. But we will not go directly there. It is already past noon, so I shall instruct Stitches and Banat to have their men unload first the animals and cage wagons and the calliope and those other vehicles that can constitute a parade. They will leave the caravans and undecorative wagons until last, and follow us when they are ready. We simply *must* make parade into Saint Petersburg."

"Par Dieu, Florian," said Rouleau. "Stick your nose outside this station. The temperature is fifteen degrees out there."

"Well? Kiev and Moscow couldn't have been much toastier than that."

"But here it feels colder," said Willi, "on account of the pervading dampness. Great Peter built this city on piles in a drained swampland. Even Tsar Alexander's courtiers tolerate it only grudgingly, and only because the tsar himself resides here."

"Ah, but we are not milksop courtiers," said Florian. "We are troupers. If you will ride with me, Herr Lothar, and you with Colonel Ramrod, Monsieur Roulette, you can instruct us, as we go, on whatever you have learned about the city and its ways."

"Very well," said Willi. "The main boulevard of Piter, the Nevskiy Prospekt, is just outside the station here. I suggest we follow it downtown, then turn onto the Morskaya. That is where, every winter afternoon from two until four o'clock, the best people promenade. But the roustabouts and the remaining wagons, when they are ready, can simply go straight north from here to the tober."

"I shall tell Kostchei to ride with them and direct them," said Florian. "We do not want him displayed on parade, anyway."

Even those artistes who rode atop the parade wagons, without the company of Willi or Jules to explain what they were seeing, were able to form some impressions of Piter, most of them favorable, as they waved and smiled to the people who stopped on the sidewalks or halted their vehicles or emerged from buildings to watch them go by. Except for the occasional snow-filled side lane or alley, there was not a street in the city that was less than fifty feet wide, and swept clean of snow, and nicely cobbled, the stones set in swirly patterns. The Nevskiy and other prospekti were fully a hundred feet wide, and were not cobbled but paved with hexagonal blocks of hard wood, also set in patterns. Then and afterward, even with their eyes closed, the troupers could always tell when their vehicle turned from a mere street onto a boulevard by the difference in sound—the metallic rumble of wheel rims on cobblestones; the softer, muted rumble on the wooden paving.

The wonderfully wide Nevskiy Prospekt was lined on both sides with many-storied palaces, mansions, imperial ministries, foreign embassies: buildings of clean white marble or of naturally colored stone or of painted stucco—painted in quite vivid colors—and some were even fronted with a ceramiclike terra-cotta. Many of those grand edifices stood democratically side by side with common public buildings—the City Hall, churches large and small, the Public Library—and even brick-built commercial buildings with shops at their street level: apothecaries, stationers, State Monopoly Stores, restaurants. The more exclusive of those shops bore signs that proclaimed their wares or services in both Russian and French: KONDÍTERSSKAYA/CONFISEUR, TORGÓVETS PLAT'EM/TAILLEUR POUR DAMES. But the façades of all the buildings, even the palaces, were marred by the great pipes, as big around as barrels, that snaked down from the roof gutters, draping over cornices and sills, to ground level. They were a necessary ugliness, to drain the snow that melted from the roofs in winter and the heavy rains that Piter endured in every season.

The paraders now saw, on the left side of the boulevard, a most peculiar building, white-painted, only two stories high but sprawling from one cross street all the way to the next. Its ground level was a row of shops, and so was the upper story, which had an open gallery extending along the row of them. Both the upper and lower levels were enjoying a bustling traffic of people, mostly women, going to and from and into one shop after another.

"The Petersburgers like to believe that they live in the most Western Europe-like and soignée city of Russia," Willi said to Florian. "But right there you can see Russia's Oriental heritage. That building is the Gostíni Dvor. It occupies an entire and immense block. With its extensive frontage and interior courts, it accommodates some two hundred different shops, all selling cheap merchandise for the masses. It is the exact equivalent of an Oriental souk or bazaar." After a moment he added, "As for the upper classes, they not only order their clothes from Worth in Paris, they send them back to Paris to be *laundered*."

Edge remarked to Rouleau, "I notice that almost every cart and coach and carriage has a net slung in front of its dashboard. Is that meant to keep the horses from dirtying these fine streets with their droppings?"

"No. It is to prevent the lumps of snow flung by the horses' hoofs from flying into the lap or face of their drivers." Rouleau went on, "Everyone is very winter-conscious here, even the horses themselves. Observe that one, waiting by the curb there for his driver. All of his own accord, the horse rocks the carriage a little back and forth, to keep the wheels from freezing to the surface of the street."

On its way along the Nevskiy, the parade crossed bridges over three canals, where the waters were unable to freeze because of the constant traffic of goods-laden barges and passenger-laden omnibus boats. The bridges all had decorative wrought-iron railings, and one was especially handsome. Flanking both ends of it were bronze statues of near-naked men leading spirited horses, and so finely detailed was the sculpturing that, as animal-expert Pemjean remarked, the horses' sheepskin saddle blankets really looked like fleece.

Down the center of the boulevard and across those bridges ran two sets of rails, along which, at intervals, going in one direction or the other, there came a horse-drawn double-deck tram that had an outside staircase curving up to the open-air (and, in this January cold, unoccupied) seats on the top deck.

"That is called the Stallion Railway," Willi told Florian. "It carries passengers between the Nicholas Station and the Admiralty yonder on the riverside."

All the troupers could see the soaring, needlelike, gold-leafed spire of the

Admiralty glowing ahead of them, but the parade turned off the boulevard before reaching it—onto the narrower, cobbled Morskaya Ulika, thronged with afternoon promenaders. Those people were well bundled up, but at least one man in ten wore the epauletted, frogged, buckled greatcoat of a uniform. Most of those were military uniforms, the officers wearing also fore-and-aft bicorn hats, or plumed shakos, or a sort of fur turban. Some of them—cavalry officers temporarily afoot—wore sabres in long sharkskin scabbards that clanked and clattered as they dragged along the pavement. Many of the men in less ornamental uniforms, obviously enlisted men, wore bandoliers of cartridges crisscrossing their breasts.

The parade came now to a neighborhood where there were a good many buildings clearly older than those on the Nevskiy Prospekt. These were built only of wood, but had been meticulously painted to simulate brick. However, Willi next directed Florian to take the procession to the right, and again it was among elegant architecture. It came to a vast open square, with a little park in the middle, and in the middle of that was a high-pedestaled statue of the Tsar Nicholas I on a prancing horse. Beyond was the largest and grandest church in all St. Petersburg, the Cathedral of St. Isaac, crowned with a huge, high, gold-leafed dome that shone with almost blinding brightness against the azure sky.

Some ceremony inside it had evidently just been concluded, for a large crowd of well-dressed people was emerging, and all of them stopped on the steps to watch and wave as the parade went by. A number of priests came out onto a gallery above, garbed in black robes and high, cylindrical black hats. As they too watched, but did not wave, one of the priests leaned over the balustrade and, fingering shut one after the other of his nostrils, heedless of his congregation below, twice and copiously blew his nose onto them.

A score or more of shabbily dressed street vendors had been waiting for the church's outpour. They variously carried pails or glass jugs on their heads or, on wooden yokes across their shoulders, metal grills and buckets of coals that they could set down and cook on anywhere. All of them were crying their wares: "Kvas!" "Pirogi!" "Chai!" "Blini!" But even they fell silent and stopped to gawk as the Florilegium went by.

"I assume these folks have seen circuses before," said Edge. "But maybe there's never been an elephant this far north."

"Mais oui, there has," said Rouleau. "More than a hundred years ago, I am told, some Indian potentate presented a whole herd of them to the Tsaritsa Elizabeth. It was necessary to buttress many of the canal bridges to get them into the city. And thereafter that route was reserved for their exercise walks. When the bulls eventually died off, they had so nicely tamped that dirt road that it was paved over and is now the Grecheskiy Prospekt, though many people still call it the Elephant Walk. Our Slovaks are probably driving along it right now; that is the route from the railroad station to our tober park. Also, there is still in business the apothecary's shop on the Grecheskiy that held the imperial warrant to provide the veterinary medicines for those long-ago elephants."

Now the procession passed the Bronze Horseman, the city's most famous and best-loved landmark—a massive, inclined boulder up which rode Peter the Great, about three times lifesize, on a horse that looked even more noble than he did—and just beyond that was the wide promenade running alongside the Great Neva. The river was frozen and black, and such a bitter wind swept up it that the paraders huddled tighter in their furs and other coverings. But there were hundreds of Petersburgers, young and old, out skating and sledding on the river, and they were comparatively lightly clad. Downstream, there was a fancily-wrought iron bridge crossing to the other shore, and that side of the Neva was as crowded as this one with fine buildings and statuary. Below the bridge, various side-wheel and stern-wheel steamers were moored to quays—indeed, were imprisoned there by the ice. As the parade turned upstream on the promenade, the troupers could see in the distance a steam tram puffing black smoke as it went blithely right across the ice toward the farther bank.

"Great heavens," said Florian. "They've actually laid crossties and rails there? And that tram is packed with passengers. How thick must that ice *be?*"

"Well, look yonder, Herr Gouverneur," said Willi. "That artifact still stands where the priests did the Blessing of the Waters a week after Epiphany Day."

It was an elaborately carved altar, topped with a cross, erected beside the river. It was built and sculptured entirely of blocks of ice cut from the Neva, and the blocks of its base were cubes that measured five feet in each dimension.

"That was just a week ago," Willi went on, "so Jules and I were here to watch the ceremony. After the benediction of the river, one of the priests actually *baptized children* in that marrow-freezing water, dipping them down through the hole cut in the ice. One infant he unfortunately let slip, and of course it disappeared at once."

"Great heavens," Florian said again. "I suppose that put a damper on the whole affair."

"Ach, not at all. It was merely a peasant child, and the priest only called 'Drugoi!'—'give me the next.' And the mother and father of the lost infant were not a whit dismayed. They were ecstatic, certain that the child, dying under such auspicious circumstances, had gone straight to the arms of the angels. Then, after the ceremony, all the attending people crowded about the hole to dip up jugs of the now-holy water, to drink or to wash themselves in."

The parade continued northeastward beside the Great Neva, and rather at a trot, both propelled by and fleeing from the cold wind behind. Except for the skaters and sledders on the ice, there were not many people outdoors here to stop and gaze and listen to the band and calliope music. But then the procession passed the two river-facing wings of the huge Admirality building and the spacious courtyard between them, and all the building's windows were filled with uniformed figures watching. Next the parade went by the landing stage of the ice-borne steam tram and was directly under the looming Winter Palace of the tsar. Its three-story and seemingly endless façade was of a brownish red with gold-leafed window cornices, upheld by row upon row of white columns with gold-leafed capitals. Actually, it stood considerably taller than three stories, because its roof bore numerous ornate cupolas and was edged with innumerable giant statues. Its windows, too, were crammed with (presumably) royal and noble onlookers, and their courtiers and servants—so the troupers waved and smiled up at them with special vivacity and warmth.

Then the parade crossed a canal emptying into the Neva, and all the rest of the promenade along here was lined, on the landward side, with palaces. The next was the one called the Hermitage, built by Catherine the Great to house her fabulous collection of foreign paintings, sculptures and antiquities, and to which she could retire—crossing the flying bridge over the canal from her Winter

Palace apartments—to enjoy those treasures in private. Despite the name, the Hermitage was no modest little hideaway; it was two stories high, half the breadth of the Winter Palace's frontage, and just as richly embellished on the outside. Then there was a series of almost-as-sumptuous palaces of this and that Grand Duke and Grand Duchess, separated by courts that obviously would be gardens in the summertime.

From where they now were on the promenade, the circus newcomers could see that the Neva forked on the farther bank. Their parade was proceeding upstream along the uninterrupted south side of the Great Neva but, on the other bank, an arm of it—the Smaller Neva—went off to the northwest and, a little farther upstream, another arm flowed directly northward. So the land they were seeing across the river was actually a number of islands, most of them big ones, set among the many branchings of the Neva delta all the way westward to the Gulf of Finland.

The most prominent structure the paraders could see over there, between the two visible off-branching arms of the river, was the high-granite-walled Fortress of Saints Peter and Paul, the heavy cannons in its embrasures positioned to bombard any enemy coming by water (or ice) up any of those reaches of the Neva. Beyond the wall could be seen only a number of gilded dome tops and one towering gold-leafed spire, needle-thin, like the one on the Admiralty. That, Willi Lothar later informed the others, was the steeple of the Cathedral of Peter and Paul, and that church, he said, was the only even vaguely "saintly" thing inside the fortress, it being the burial place of all the tsars from Peter the Great to Nicholas I, father of the present Tsar Alexander II. Every other edifice within that formidable wall was, said Willi, "secular, to put it mildly"—they being the City Arsenal, the Imperial Mint and the State Prison.

The parade next passed the good-sized park called the Summer Gardens, now all snowbanks and bare trees and a multitude of little wooden houses, one constructed around each of the park's many statues to protect them during the winter. Then the procession left the riverside to take a street that led straight to the Potemkin Palace, uninhabited since the prince's death some eighty years ago, and now used as a stable for a very few—a hundred or so—of the imperial family's horses. Beyond that was the Tauric Garden, named, Rouleau told Edge, after a battle won by Prince Potemkin at a place called Tauris in the Crimea. This park was also snowbound, so all the roustabouts, having already unloaded what wagons they had brought, were shoveling clear what would be the tober area and a broad entrance way to it from the street. They had just about finished that job when the parade brought the rest of the wagons. Before Florian had dismounted from his rockaway, Goesle was there to ask, "Do we set up, now just, before it will be dark?"

"No, Dai, it would be dark long before you could set up. Days are very short here in winter. Besides, everyone is cold and weary. While your lads unload these remaining wagons, I shall go and engage rooms for all of us at a hotel. Post only a watchman, as usual." He turned to Willi. "Have you any recommendation to make, regarding hotels?"

"Well, I was not sure what quality of accommodations you would wish to occupy here. So, for economy's sake, Jules and I put up at the Hotel de France, on Morskaya. We passed it during the parade a while ago."

"Was that the one with the awful sign soliciting patronage?" Florian asked incredulously. "Let us go and get you both out of there immediately."

(The sign had read, in both Russian and French:

> BATH available at any moment!
> Most REASONABLE prices!
> CARRIAGES accessible!)

"I am surprised at you, Baron." Florian almost never used Willi's title. "The Chefpublizist for Florian's Flourishing Florilegium—pinching pennies, inhabiting a sixth-rate hotel. I hope you did not mention that address to any of the officials to whom you applied for our tober and any other necessary permits."

"Nein, nein, Herr Gouverneur," said Willi, chastened. "And believe me, the Hotel de France is far from the worst in Piter. But Jules and I thought... since you have spent so much money on charter trains and the like..."

"I appreciate the thought. And, after our disappointing stand in Moscow, the truth is that I *won't* be able to pay a hefty hotel bill, unless we draw sfondone houses here from opening day onward. But what I have so prodigally spent to get here, I consider an investment well spent. Second only to Paris, Saint Petersburg has been my goal ever since we landed in Europe. Also, I *do* have enough pocket money to be lavish with gratuities to any hotel's staff, and that always impresses the hotel's management. Remember, Willi, a man is oftenest taken by other people at his own estimate of himself and his worth. We must work things out as we go along. And remember another thing. To this place, we come armed with a personal introduction to the tsaritsa. We must have nothing less than the best hotel in town."

Willi shrugged. "That would be the oldest and most venerable, the Evropeiskaya—the Hotel Europe—at the corner of Mikháilovskaya and the Nevskiy Prospekt."

"An excellent address. The Europe it will be, then."

"It is very expensive. The cheapest room with bath is seven and a half rubles a day. Dinner is three rubles per person, table d'hôte."

"Rubbish! We shall dine à la carte. And engage the top-price rooms. Except for the Slovaks, of course. Now, summon Monsieur Roulette to come along with us, to get his luggage, too."

When that had been accomplished, and the three drove on to the Hotel Evropeiskaya, Florian halted Snowball and his rockaway right in the middle of Mikháilovskaya Street, in front of the hotel's stained-glass marquee, blocking and ignoring the numerous other vehicles that had to stop behind him. He flung his reins and an extravagant five-ruble coin to the hotel's dvornik standing at curbside—who would have expected perhaps five kopeks—and said in Russian, "Hold my carriage somewhere in readiness for an imminent departure, there's a good fellow."

The hotel's floridly uniformed privrátnik strode from the doorway, no doubt to protest the blockage of the street traffic, but Florian merely handed him a ten-ruble coin. The man's eyes bugged, and he hastened ahead of Florian to fling wide the double doors and bow him and his companions inside, then personally escorted them to the lobby desk.

Their grand entrance did not go unnoticed by the chief porter at the desk, and he was equally welcoming and obsequious when Florian specified—did not *request*—so and so many suites and rooms with bath facilities, and almost as many without. When Florian spoke in Russian, the chief porter spoke Russian. When Rouleau asked something in French or Lothar in German, or any one of them spoke English, the chief porter obligingly switched to that language, and spoke it fluently. However, his obsequiousness slipped a bit and his eyebrows lifted a little when Florian gave him the heap of passports and he read some of the particulars noted therein.

When Florian departed, went to the Tauric Garden and collected his company and returned with them—a crowd that almost filled the ample lobby—the chief porter seemed disinclined to any more obsequiousness. Most of the company wore fine fur coats, true, but even so they were a motley crew, and other patrons sitting about the lobby stared, even stood up to stare, at the midget Cricket, at the three barefoot Koreans, at the bandit-looking Jászi brothers, at the man inexplicably bent over backward and wearing his hat over his face.

But Florian had returned prepared—and had prepared Edge—for a cool reception. He asked the now stony-faced chief porter for the keys to their several chambers, and in the same breath said, "My company director here possesses a letter written in some language he cannot read, and he will not entrust its translation to any of the rest of us. Perhaps, Gospodín Commissionnaire, you would do him the favor of writing in English what it says?"

Edge already had laid the dual-crown-embossed envelope on the counter, and the chief porter's eyes bugged as the doorman's had earlier done. He read the enclosed message, then—with a quavering hand—wrote on Evropeiskaya stationery an English translation of it. Edge said, "Spasíbo, gospodín," and tucked it away again. From then on, the chief porter was not obsequious, he was servile, and he saw to it that the rest of the staff was, too.

After all the company had refreshed themselves and changed clothes, they reassembled at the hotel's dining room, a vast chamber of pillars, mirrors, murals and potted palms, under a domed ceiling made entirely of stained glass with some kind of illumination above it to make it glow gloriously. Florian slipped a large coin to the maître d'hôtel and requested the best seats for all—rather unnecessarily, as they eventually occupied practically every table in that big room. The maître d'hôtel bowed and went away. He and the captain of waiters were seen to move several parties—they clearly protesting, but ineffectually—with their half-eaten dinners, tableware and all, to a less grand room opening off the main hall. When Florian and company were seated, they ordered à la carte, and unstintingly, and Florian called for the sommelier. He came, with his key on its chain around his neck, and presented his list, and Florian ordered the most expensive wine, without the least notion of what it was or whether it was a suitable accompaniment to everybody's choice of viands.

Over the preliminary zakuska—here, as elsewhere, a meal in itself—Florian said to Edge, seated beside him, "Willi informs me that there is another circus in town, a permanent one, with indoor quarters, like those in Moscow. I think, before anything else, you and I should visit this Tsirk Cinizelli, as it is called, though it is now owned by some Russian named Marchan. I do not expect it to be fearsome competition; Willi says that Marchan is only an upstart who used to be a mere café owner. But then, the first Orfei was only a man of the cloth. And Barnum failed in numerous prosaic businesses before he made his fortune with the great American Museum. Anyway, we ought to see what the Cinizelli is like.

And it will be a professional courtesy to introduce ourselves to Gospodín Marchan."

The next day, when the circus was all set up, and the artistes were again unlimbering on their rigs and in the pista, and the roustabouts had gone out to paper the city, announcing the Florilegium's first performance on the morrow, Florian, Edge—and Fitzfarris, too—went to see the afternoon show of the Tsirk Cinizelli. Its big, solid-looking building was situated alongside the Fontanka Canal, only a four-block walk from the Tauric Garden. The tickets were fairly expensive, but Willi had already apprised Florian of that, and he had priced his own accordingly. At the Cinizelli's ticket window, he bought a four-seat barrière box for ten rubles, forty kopeks. When he handed the tickets to the frumpy old doorwoman who collected them, he gave her also a note he had written and asked her to see that Gospodín Marchan got it before the show was over.

Inside, as Florian could professionally calculate with just a quick look around, the circus had five hundred comfortable chair-seats in its boxes and stalls, and could seat twelve hundred more on the plain plank benches in the circles and galleries. Being a permanent installation, the circus had some features and refinements that no traveling establishment could imitate—a very good lighting system, for one thing, real oxyhydrogen limelights, and overhead as well as pista-level spotlights. The girl ushers who showed the patrons to their seats and gave them the circus's very well printed program folders, were all blonde-haired and quite pretty, and were dressed in provocatively short tulle skirts over spangled léotards. It turned out, when the performance began, that they served—as Fitz's Schuhplattler girls had done—to dance a prologue to the show. Florian remarked that Sir John might recruit another bevy of such girls, perhaps even a matched set of blondes like these.

"To get the girls should be no problem, and to make sure they are blonde shouldn't be difficult, either," said Fitzfarris. He indicated the one who had ushered them to their box. "I think, when you see a fair-haired female with shaggy black fur on her legs, you are justified in the suspicion that she has not always been a blonde."

Edge said, "I had always thought that *all* Russians were tall and fair and blue-eyed. But I've noticed every kind of complexion and coloring, especially here in Saint Petersburg."

"The fact is," said Florian, "that Russia is a congeries of many nationalities, even many races. And of course, this being the capital and biggest city in the country, Piter would tend to attract more of that assortment: Tatars, Mongols, Bashkirs, and so forth. Of the Russians themselves, there are three distinct varieties. It is the Great Russians who are fair of hair and skin, with blue eyes, and they are the most expansive of nature. The so-called Little Russians are slender and dark. The so-called White Russians are rather the Mississippians of this land—poor, ignorant, phlegmatic, slovenly in their habits—probably afflicted with hookworm, as is most of Mississippi. Anyway, they are despised by all those other Russians. They are easily identifiable, because they also suffer from an endemic disease of the scalp, called here the plika polonika."

"Ah, then I *have* seen a lot of those," said Fitz. "Patchy-haired and scrofulous and dirty-looking even when they're washed."

Just then, the gaslights in their box and the others throughout the house—evidently controlled from some central valve—slowly dimmed, while the lights on the pista as slowly brightened, and the usher girls bounded into the pista to dance to the music of a many-piece band in a stand above the entrance door. The Cinizelli was a sufficiently competent and entertaining circus, the three from the Florilegium agreed, while also agreeing that theirs was better.

In this one, animals were in the majority over the human artistes—particularly numerous were trained bears and pigs, which did some amazing tricks. ("Monsieur le Démon Débonnaire must see this," Florian remarked, "and perhaps get some ideas from it.") The human artistes were almost all acrobats or clowns. There was no trapeze act and curiously, for a city so studded with statues of horses, not even a liberty or voltige turn, but only a number of rather mediocre équestriennes doing bareback postures and leaps. The joeys did nothing that Edge or Fitzfarris found funny—certainly nothing as wonderful as the Lupino mirror—but mainly talked and slapped each other for talking back. And that repartee was so very topical that, when Florian translated it to the others, he had to admit that he himself didn't grasp much of the supposed comedy in it.

At intermission, only a small part of the audience adjourned to the cold outdoors for a breath of fresh air. (The interior had got thickly misted and layered with smoke, for everyone, young and old, male and female, smoked cigarette after cigarette during the show.) Those who stayed indoors were regaled by vendors shouting from the arena or prowling among the seats, hawking sheet music of the tunes the band had played, cartes-de-visite of the various performers, jugs of cold lemonade and hot tea, trays of lukewarm pirogiyi and blinis. The Florilegium threesome stayed in their box and shortly were joined by a stoop-shouldered, tangle-bearded, somewhat greasy-looking gentleman—White Russian, thought Edge and Fitzfarris at once—who introduced himself in Russian as Vassily Marchan, and welcomed them to Russia and to St. Petersburg and to his circus.

"Well, having intruded our own into your home territory," said Florian, "we thought it only polite to make ourselves known to you."

"Okh, I do not resent the intrusion," said Marchan. "My establishment has become something of an institution here, tak, like a public toilet, and most of my patronage is repeat patronage. People who enjoy circuses—and, happily, that includes most of Piter—will go to see every circus they can, as often as they can. Tak, neither you nor I should suffer from any divided loyalties among them. After all, this building can hold only seventeen hundred at a time, and the population here is about eight hundred thousand."

"So many? I did not realize," said Florian. "Then Piter is nearly half again as populous as Moscow or Kiev."

"Except perhaps from spring to autumn," said Marchan. "Fully a tenth of Piter's population—and my circus patrons—are peasants, who desert the city to do their spring planting and their summer cultivation and their autumn harvesting. Partly for that reason, tak, I show here only during the winter. Once the weather warms up, I take the circus on the road. To the Crimean resorts, the Ukraine..."

Because Marchan spoke only Russian, Florian occasionally excused himself to turn and translate any parts of the conversation he thought might interest

Edge and Fitzfarris. They did indeed take an interest in one lengthy exchange between the two circus proprietors.

Marchan asked, "Have you seen the Fortress of Peter and Paul?"

"Only from a distance," said Florian.

"Go there. Visitors are allowed, for much of it is a museum of Piter's past. But also in there is the State Prison, and most of the prisoners are not criminals, not murderers or robbers. They are merely unfortunate members of the Land and Liberty and the People's Freedom groups, meaning agitators and advocates of revolution."

Florian, wondering why the man had introduced this topic, said, "There is much dissatisfaction with Tsar Alexander's rule, then?"

"With imperial rule in general," said Marchan. "Alexander is no better or worse, tak, than any tsar before him. But yes, there is much ferment and seething among the masses, and occasionally one of them is brave enough to stand up and shout or even strike a blow. The upper classes scornfully call such revolutionaries Nigilists—believers in nothing—what you in the West, I think, would call anarchists. I recently saw one of them, a woman who was handing out allegedly seditious pamphlets on a street corner, caught by the gorodovói, the uniformed police. They tied the woman's arms behind her back, rubbed pitch in her long hair, set her hair afire, then let her loose to run—and run she did, tak, hoping to make a wind that would blow out the fire—but of course she could not."

"Dear me," murmured Florian. "Barbaric."

"Nyet. She was lucky. She would have fared much worse if she had fallen into the hands of the Third Section."

"No doubt. But why are you telling me these things, Gospodín Marchan?"

"To explain why I became a circus owner. I myself am what the tsar's parasites and bootlickers call a Nigilist, and only in the circus can one express such sentiments without being arrested and imprisoned for it. Let me tell you. Just across the square from this building is the Maryinskiy Ballet Theatre. Most prudently, it always opens its season with the sycophantic Glinka opera *A Life for the Tsar*. Tak, the Maryinskiy and every other theatre, even the cheap cabarets, must have their programs approved by the tsar's censors. Only the circus is exempt. We are considered mere clowns, negligible, inconsequential. We can say what we like, and the audiences may laugh—that is all right with the censors. But perhaps the audiences go away remembering what we say. Listen—" He motioned toward the pista. "Those two rizhiyi are doing a routine I wrote for them myself."

During the conversation, the houselights had gone down, the pista lights had gone up, and the second half of the program was well under way. Two clowns, a white-face and an exceedingly ugly toby, made up to look even uglier, were exchanging ribaldries.

White-face: "How strange. You look extraordinarily like His Imperial Majesty, the Tsar Alexander. *Aha!* Was your mother ever in Saint Petersburg?"

Toby: "No, gospodín. But *my father was!*"

[Uproar of laughter from the seats.]

"Tak, that is merely poking fun at the tsar," Marchan confessed. "But I try to slip into the rizhiy repartee some cogent comments, as well. Listen."

Toby: "Gospodín White-face, would you intercede for me at the tsar's court? Otherwise I have no one to depend on but the Lord God."

White-face: "Okh, you *are* in a bad way. I know of no other personage with *less* influence at the court of Tsar Alexander."

[More laughter from the audience, but some of it sounding a little uneasy.]

"It may seem trifling to you, Gospodín Florian," said Marchan. "But if those few words were spoken in any other public place but a circus, the speakers of them, and all their colleagues, tak, would be to put to interrogation by the Third Section. And interrogation, to the Third Section, means torture. You may ask: why do I indulge in this folly? I will tell you. My father was a muzhik—a White Russian muzhik, the lowest of the low—and a krepostnoy, what you call a serf, a slave. I can remember hearing him and all the other krepostnoyi, when I was a child, repeating the rote lament of every krepostnoy in this land: 'Okh, how sad we are! Okh, how much better it would be, never to have been born!' Lamentation was all they dared do. I at least have attained a position where I can speak just a little bit more loudly, and in public, and in protest. Tak, only a little, but that is something."

He stood up to go. Florian also stood up, and took his hand, and shook it warmly, saying, "I am a foreigner, Gospodín Marchan, not qualified nor entitled to appraise the politics of your land. But I can recognize a brave man, and I salute you. Come to our show and let us entertain you. Under our canvas, there are no upper or lower classes, no oppressors or oppressed. There is only merriment and excitement, to be enjoyed by all. Do come."

Marchan said he certainly would, and shook the hands of Edge and Fitzfarris, and departed. When Florian had translated all that had been said, Edge commented wryly:

"Then, if I present that letter to the tsaritsa, I reckon that will make us all parasites and bootlickers of the tyrannical Tsar Alexander."

"We may be judged, harshly or kindly," said Florian, "but it is not for us to do any judging. We have neither the obligation nor the right to take sides here. We are *circus,* and our only mission is to entertain, whether we show before the blessèd or the damned."

Fitzfarris grinned and said, "Tak."

5

FORTUNATELY for Florian and the rest of the company—and the accounting office of the Hotel Evropeiskaya—the Florilegium *did* show to straw houses right from its first performance in St. Petersburg. In fact, the first two or three shows were merely sfondone, but, from the fourth performance onward, people had to be turned away every afternoon and evening. Gavrila Smodlaka had replaced the late Magpie Maggie Hag at the guichet of the red wagon and, whenever she turned to tell Florian, at his office desk behind her, that she had sold the entire stock of tickets allotted for the performance about to begin, she sounded almost tearful, as if she had committed some fault. But Florian always beamed broadly at the news, and was pleased to go outside and announce in Russian to those still in line that there were no more seats, but that he would be happy to sell them standing room at a cut price, or he would be even happier if they came again another day. Any aristocratic or upper-class ladies and gentlemen would already have bullied their way to the head of the line and procured their tickets and gone into the chapiteau. So the leftovers were all of the proletariat and peasantry, who took their turnaway with a stoical shrug and a whipped-dog grin.

"It seems to be integral to the Russian nature," Florian told Gavrila. "They call it pokórnost—meaning a meek submission to circumstances or higher authority or even a louder voice of command."

Then he was sorry he had told her that, for Gavrila said mournfully, to herself rather than to him, "That word I must remember. Pokórnost. It is how with Pavlo I live."

Despite the ardent reception they were accorded by St. Petersburg's circus fanciers, many of the troupers began to revise the favorable impressions they had first had of the city—and also of their deluxe accommodations. The faucets that fed their hotel-room washstands and plunge baths spewed a water so full of iron that it was rusty brown and almost impossible to make any soap work up a lather in; it left a bather feeling just as rusty, and left a metallic taste in the mouth when the water was drunk. Their pista costumes, which they entrusted to the hotel's laundry facilities, and necessarily often, began to look dingy. That caused them concern, and in their various languages they railed at the maids—and at the old woman privrátnitsa who sat at a table in each corridor, ostensibly to oversee the proper functioning of the domestics on that floor, but seemingly doing nothing but watching with disapproval every guest's comings and goings. The complainants got only amused looks and tolerant shrugs and the words "nizhdý nyet... nitchegó..." meaning roughly "it can't be helped" and "what does it matter?"

But the troupers were much more concerned when they began to feel ill. One after another, they started to suffer recurrent stomach cramps, then bouts of diarrhea alternating with constipation. The sufferers next began to lose vigor, feeling such lassitude that some of their performances became dismally lackluster. A few, those who did the thrill acts—LeVie, Sunday, Clover Lee, Monday, Pemjean—occasionally had to ask Florian or Colonel Ramrod to excuse them from the next show, and often just minutes before they were due to go on, for fear that the cramps or the diarrhea were about to strike when they were variously on the trapeze, on a rosinback horse, on the tightrope or in one of the wild animal cages.

Fortuitously, no two of those artistes ever had to withdraw from the same performance, so the equestrian director was each time able to prolong other acts to make up for the gap. Among the circus folk who worked outside the pista, only Dai Goesle and Carl Beck were similarly afflicted; the Slovaks all seemed impervious to whatever was "going around." Then, when the ailing troupers thought to compare notes on what they had lately been eating and drinking, their consensus was that the blame had to lie with the rusty water they had imbibed in the hotel dining room. Russia was the first country they had yet visited where bottled mineral water was not provided at table, and they had all drunk the Hotel Europe's metallic tap water in preference to the vodka that *was* always and copiously provided. So Florian went storming to the hotel's front desk, demanded his bill and indignantly declared that he was taking his whole company elsewhere.

"Disgraceful!" he fumed. "Supposedly the city's finest hotel! And serving its guests tainted water!"

"Gospodín Florian," said the chief porter, with undeniable sincerity, "all the water in Piter is the same, whether from a pump or a well or a natural spring. It is a burden we have learned to bear. Do not hold it against the Evropeiskaya. Go if you must, but you will find the same water in any other hotel."

Florian had to believe him, but he said with asperity, "You might at least have warned us against *drinking* it, before we all got ill."

At that, the chief porter looked genuinely confounded. He spread his hands and said, "Gospodín Florian, I ask you, man to man. Who would ever have supposed that any reasonable person would drink vodá when there is vódka to be had? Why do you think those two words are so similar? Vodá is only water; vódka is the *good* water. Also there is wine, beer, brandy... even chai has had the impurities boiled out of it." He leaned closer across the counter and said confidentially, because he had to use a street word, "Are you telling me that your people are suffering the dristlíva?"

Since that street word meant literally "the runny shits," Florian replied, "Er ... ah ... the scours ... the flux ... yes."

"Okh, that is easy enough to cure," said the chief porter. "I shall have our house physician prepare a healing potion. Your people will soon be well again. Just tell them, if they must drink water, to boil it first, or to drink only bottled water."

"Well ... thank you, Gospodín Commissionnaire. And forgive my show of temper. We will not be departing. But you might as well give me the bill I requested, and let me settle it to date."

One look at the bill nearly gave Florian an instant attack of the dristlíva right there at the desk. But the Florilegium was, once again, more than solvent; he was able to take his purse from his frock-coat pocket and count out the whole staggering sum in gold imperials, silver rubles and copper kopeks. Thereafter, no longer having to make any false show of affluence, he dispensed only reasonable gratuities to the hotel staff. The maids and waiters and others did not seem dismayed by that; rather, they seemed relieved that this guest had finally come to his senses, and they did not slacken in their good-humored attendance on the company.

The house doctor's potion—or more likely his patients' abstention from drinking tap water—did quickly bring all but one of the troupers back to bonny health. They again performed with verve, and took a renewed interest and delight in their surroundings. Many of them were especially pleased when they discovered that St. Petersburg contained populous communities of other foreigners, with whom they made acquaintance and often visited and could converse in their native tongues.

Each of those nationalities—English, French, German and Dutch—chose to congregate in a separate enclave in the city, apart from each other as well as the native Russians. Only the Germans and Dutchmen had been assimilated to the extent that they were all but Russian in fact, except for retaining their original tongue as a "second language" and their tendency to live clustered together. They spoke Russian everywhere except at home, furnished those homes in the plush-but-dowdy Russian style, observed Russian customs and holidays and in many cases were married to Russians. That was because they were the longest-resident foreigners in the city, being the ninth- or tenth-generation descendants of the shipwrights that Peter the Great had imported from Hamburg and Amsterdam to help him build Russia's first navy and merchant fleet. Those Germans and Dutchmen were the most numerous of the foreign community, totaling some ten thousand all together.

The approximately eighteen hundred resident Frenchmen and fifteen hundred Englishmen were mostly members of their countries' various diplomatic contingents, or were managers, agents, factors of foreign businesses with branch offices in St. Petersburg. The English families all had learned French—it was easier to learn than Russian—to be able to communicate with their local counterparts, and the Frenchmen loftily refused to speak or recognize any language *but* French. So Daphne, Dai, most of the Americans and the other English-speakers of the Florilegium were warmly welcomed into the English homes; and Pemjean, LeVie, Rouleau and Sunday Simms were frequent guests of the French families; and Carl Beck, Jörg Pfeifer, Willi Lothar and—again—Sunday made friends among the Germans. The multilingual Florian, of course, was at home with any and all of those other foreigners.

"A pity that Captain Hotspur is no longer with us," he said. "Ignatz would have enjoyed meeting the local Hollanders. And I understand that there is even a community of gypsies out on one of the farther islands. Old Mag might have liked to meet them."

Clover Lee often enough accompanied the troupers visiting English and French families, but she was, as always, more interested in getting to meet the native aristocrats. As she told Florian:

"Every third residence in this city is the palace of some duke or prince or count. And those men in our audiences who ogle me through those one-eye opera glasses in the handles of their walking sticks, I figure they've got to be toffs. Here, Florian"—she handed him a Piter newspaper—"see if there are any heart-and-hand advertisements that maybe I could answer."

Florian scanned the columns of dense Cyrillic print, and shook his head. "Not unless you want employment as a children's nurse or governess. Odd—they almost all specify English or Scottish governesses. And great heavens, what a long list of quacks offering cures for, er, certain ailments. 'Dóktor Vasiliev, specialist in the scabies grossa...' 'Dóktor Aksakov cures private maladies...' 'Dóktor Chernyshevsky, discreet side entrance in alley alongside office...' 'Dóktor Trediakovsky, for those suffering from the colonel's disease...' Bless my soul, the *colonel's* disease?"

"They all mean the clap, don't they?" Clover Lee said bluntly. "Is that such a scourge here? We never saw such newspaper advertisements anywhere else."

"I doubt that the, um, private maladies are any more prevalent here," said Florian. "Only that the Russians are a little less hypocritical about mentioning them. And evidently a little more prone to confidence in charlatans. Anyway, Clover Lee, I am sorry to disappoint you, but no royals or nobles are advertising for consorts."

"Damn! When are you going to let Zachary present that letter of his, and get us an introduction at court?"

"He and I have discussed that, but we have not decided. If it is likely to eventuate in a command performance, I should prefer to wait until the court moves out of town to one of the tsar's summer palaces. On the other hand, right now is the season for all the court balls and galas and levees."

"Then let Zachary present the letter right now," she urged. "I'd rather mingle with the swells than just frolic on horseback in front of them."

"We'll see, we'll see. We must at least wait until our whole troupe has recovered from our recent indisposition."

The only one who had not yet was Monday Simms. She still had to be excused from an occasional performance, pleading cramps, and, when she did take the tightrope, went only listlessly through her chimney-sweep act. Edge asked her why she did not consult some other physician, instead of relying on the hotel doctor's prescription. At that, Monday looked wary and said she would rather not, that she would be better in time. But, when some more time had passed and she was apparently still ailing, Edge conferred with Florian, and they called Pemjean to the office.

Florian said, "The equestrian director and I are worried about your young lady friend, Monsieur le Démon. She has been urged to see a doctor. Have you any notion why she refuses?"

Pemjean fixed his gaze off in space somewhere, wrung his hands, shuffled his feet like a boy caught in a naughty prank and finally muttered, "Oui, Monsieur le Gouverneur, I know why. A physician would only confirm her condition, and she fears that you would disapprove... perhaps dismiss her from le cirque. Meanwhile, it is I who am seeing a physician."

Edge looked baffled. "What in creation does that mean? Monday has a *condition*, but *you* are seeing a doctor?"

Pemjean muttered, almost inaudibly, "Il y a une polichinelle dans le tiroir."

Edge repeated blankly, "There's a puppet in the drawer?"

But Florian exclaimed, "Mademoiselle Cinderella is *pregnant*? Why, she can't be more than sixteen or seventeen years old."

"Néanmoins..." mumbled Pemjean, looking guilty and ashamed. "Truly, I have tried to convince her that she is too young. That it would be best if she—make no mistake, messieurs, I consider myself a good Catholic—but in this case..."

Florian said, a little coldly, "You recommend what I believe is called a hygienic miscarriage."

"Eh bien, the Dóktor Aksakov is in accord. He speaks French, and I have made him understand the situation. He can administer certain nostrums or, if necessary, use certain implements."

"So that is why you, not she, consulted this doctor—Aksakov? The name is somehow familiar."

Edge said, "Why all the fuss? Young though she is, Monday ought to be able to bear a child without any trouble."

"Mais oui. I have heard that females of her race breed like rabbits from earliest puberté."

"Well, then?" Florian asked. "Are you averse to being a father? Or having such a tie that binds? Or just the bother of it? I must say that I myself am not overjoyed at the prospect of my tightrope artiste being out of action for several months. Still, if Monday *wants* the child..."

"Messieurs, in urging un avortement, I was not thinking of her, or of myself, or of le cirque. I am in fear for the infant." Pemjean ceased his shuffling, squared his shoulders, met Florian's eyes and said, "I was seeing the Dóktor Aksakov—I have been consulting doctors everywhere we have been—before ever I knew that Monday was enceinte. You may remember, when you and I first met, at that hospice d'aliénés in Vienna, I told you I was visiting the clinique there. It is that I suffer from a stubborn affliction of le mal napolitain. La chaude-pisse. La chtouille."

"The clap," Edge said flatly.

Florian said, "Now I remember where I saw the name of your Dr. Aksakov."

Pemjean went on, "I have never confessed to Monday, since a woman can have la gonorrhée and seldom even be aware of it. But I fear, if she bears an infant, it will be born blind or otherwise badly defective. The physician agrees that such is likely, and thinks it best that she—arrange to miscarry."

Florian scratched in his tuft of white beard and meditated for a minute, then said, "So do I, however reluctantly, now that I know all the circumstances. But you must tell the girl the truth regarding the necessity for that drastic action." Pemjean writhed but did not protest. "And, just so that we are all satisfied that she fully comprehends the situation, you will tell her in our presence." Florian summoned Banat and sent him to fetch Monday.

She came, looking a little apprehensive, but not nearly so apprehensive as did Pemjean.

Florian said gently, "There is no need for further pretense of illness, my dear. Monsieur le Démon has confided to us that you are—ahem—in the family way." Monday's fawn-colored cheeks turned rosy with mixed pride, shyness and discomfiture. "However, Monsieur le Démon now has something to confide to *you*."

Fearfully, haltingly, trying to avoid Gallic words and to find the simplest English ones, Pemjean made his abject confession. Monday merely looked confused. Obviously, she had never heard of gonorrhea, or even any of its slang names. Edge said nothing, but he was thinking that the truth about the Terrible Turk's dismissal from the company and Magpie Maggie Hag's subsequent treatment of Meli Vasilakis's ailment must have been kept very quiet indeed, if Monday had heard no female gossip about them. Obviously, too, Monday had never known that there could be any other consequences of sexual congress except plain old pregnancy. So Florian joined in the explanation, using even simpler words. And then, finally understanding—or at least understanding what was now demanded of her—Monday exploded with invective at all three of the men, but aimed her main blast at Pemjean. Weeping and shaking, and talking pure blue-gum, as if she had never had the least bit of education since she'd left Virginia, she shouted at him:

"You *sick,* and you *knowed* you was sick, and you laid with me, and you didn't give a damn if it made *me* sick, and now the *baby* be's sick, too, and gotta be dead! You know what, Frenchman? You a *real* demon, just like that dog-act feller always been sayin'. You know what else? You a real summabitch! I be's damn sorry I ever swapped for you. John Fitz wouldn't never of done such a lowdown thing. I don't *care* if this baby gotta be dead, 'count of I don't *want* none of your get. I tell you what else. That house wagon you been travelin' in, that's still *mine.* I goin' this minute and chunk all your goods out in the snow, and *you* stay out, too, and stay out of *my* hotel room, and stay out of my *sight*, and I hope you stays out in the snow till you freeze your damn sick do-daddy right *off!*"

And she was gone, leaving the red wagon rocking and the men half deafened by the concussion of the door slam. The three sat in silence for a minute. Then Florian cleared his throat and said:

"Three more things, Monsieur le Démon. First and foremost, I will not entrust that girl to any quack who advertises for custom. Forget about taking her to your Dr. Aksakov. I shall have Willi make some discreet enquiries, and I myself will accompany the girl when she goes for the—treatment. Second, whether you make a rapprochement with Mademoiselle Cinderella, or seek a substitute among this company, I *insist*—indeed, I recommend it even if you acquire some Jeannie from the seats—that you take prophylactic precautions when you bed her. Surely you are acquainted with the French use of the baudruche as a sheath."

"Oui," Pemjean said dispiritedly. Then, with wan humor, he added, "I came from a Picard fishing village where all the men swore by the use of eel skins. But our village spawned more bastards than any other village on the coast. Our men were forever forgetting to sew up the eels' eye holes." He forced a laugh, but no one else did. "Excusez, monsieur. You said three things."

"Yes. The third is this. Until and unless you do reconcile with Mademoiselle Cinderella, I advise you never to walk under her tightrope while she is on it. You might also set a Slovak to keep watch over your animals, that she does not slip burrs under their tails to madden them. And when you and they are working in the pista, try to make sure you know where *she* is."

"Ma foi!" Pemjean said dazedly, and dazedly left the wagon.

"I think I'll go for a walk, too," said Edge, shrugging into his big badger coat. "I could use some clean air."

Florian, who had turned to his account books, said offhandedly, "It is snowing. It has been snowing all evening, and the streets won't be swept before morning. Don't flounder into a snowbank and freeze your own do-daddy."

It was after the night show, about midnight, so the pole torches that lined the tober's entranceway had been extinguished. But the foot or so of new snow glowed with its own pale radiance and illuminated the way. Trudging through it, Edge could see, beyond the curtain of big snowflakes falling at a wind-blown slant, another fur-coated figure leaving the tober ahead of him. That person wore a baum marten coat, so it was a female, and was walking more slowly, encumbered by big, floppy, india-rubber galoshes. So Edge soon caught up to her, and found that it was Sunday Simms. When she saw who had fallen into step with her, she smiled welcomingly.

"Are you off to one of your social calls on the foreign community?" he asked.

"No, just out for a stroll," she said. "I do it often, when I want to be by my lonesome. At least when the nights are as warm as this. It can't be much below the freezing mark."

"You don't think it might be dangerous? A pretty girl walking the dark streets by herself?"

"It's never really dark in the city. The Petersburgers keep late hours, so there are plenty of lights. And I don't believe the streets are too full of footpads or assassins. In the daytime I have actually seen the tsar and tsaritsa, on foot, on the Nevskiy Prospekt. They amble along just like the common folk, without any bodyguards or retinue at all. Maybe one or two of their children, and a few servants to carry any purchases they might make on the way."

"You're not quizzing me? What do such exalted beings look like?"

"Well, they're exalted in size, all right. Not fat, but *tall*. I never saw such a colossal family. Every one of them is taller and broader-shouldered even than you are. And the Crown Prince, the young Alexander, must stand six foot five."

"No wonder they don't need bodyguards," said Edge.

"And have you noticed," she asked, "how so many of the common men here wear those shoes with tremendous thick soles and high heels? My guess is that it's because the royal folk are so tall. The short men must consider their short-ness a disgrace."

"Yes," said Edge, amused. "But it doesn't make them look any taller. They just look like small men walking around on brickbats."

He and Sunday had now left the Tauric Garden and come out on Kirochnava Street, which ran east and west. He said, "I'm only out for some late-night sight-seeing myself. If you want to be alone, we'll go separate ways from here."

"No, let's walk together. If you like." She added, with a touch of badinage, "I never feel more by-my-lonesome than when I'm with you."

So they both turned west, toward downtown, but stayed on the inner city streets, not going near the frigid riverside. Even here among the buildings, the ever-blowing southwest winter wind buffeted them and whitened the fronts of their dark coats with blown snow. The wind also prevented the canal waters from freezing, even at this hour when few boats were plying them, dashing the waters up and over their stone brinks, and overlaying the snow on the sidewalks with crusts of ice through which Edge and Sunday crunched, stepping high. The wind also made the streetside lamp standards waver and sway, so the gas lamps swung and squeaked and creaked and jangled. On the otherwise silent streets, they played a not-discordant concert that every visitor to St. Petersburg remem-bered ever afterward as the city's winter-night theme music. While Sunday and Edge only plodded straight ahead through the variously soft and crusted snow, their shadows accompanied them like frisky children. The swinging lamps alter-nately bunched their shadows close about their feet, then elongated them and darted them ahead, behind, sideways, in a continuous and vivacious dance.

The streets and prospekti were empty of people and vehicular traffic, except for the very infrequent lone pedestrian who was not, like Sunday and Edge, out to enjoy the snowy night and its crisp white-wine air, but was hurrying head-down toward shelter somewhere. But indoors, as Sunday had said, the Peters-burgers were not early to bed, so, even where the street lamps were far between, ample light shone from the windows of residences. And there were other lights. The Admiralty's skyscraping steeple was always visible ahead of them, for by night it was illuminated by oxyhydrogen spotlights shining up at it from the building's roof. Its gold coating gleamed brightly, and they could even see the golden crown-and-ship weathervane on its very tip. The steeple's golden light was reflected by the Neva's ice upward to the low-hanging snow clouds, painting them a pale orange, then was reflected downward from them, then upward again by the city's blanket of snow—so that all of central Piter that night was bathed in a peaceful, happy, romantic, almost-magical golden glow.

Edge could not help noticing how that light made even more radiant Sunday's fawn complexion and glinted in the snow crystals caught on her long eyelashes. Then he saw that it also glinted from a pin affixed to her coat lapel, and he said joshingly:

"One of your Johnnies has been giving you jewelry."

She glanced down at it and said, "I bought it myself. These costume pins are all the rage here, among us po' folks who can't afford gold and gems." She unpinned it and handed it to him. It was only steel, but cut in sharp-edged facets and polished to almost sterling-silver brilliance. "They're called Tula diamonds," she said. "The name is half humor, half deprecation. Tula is a steel-mill city down south of Moscow somewhere. The Sheffield of Russia, I guess it is."

Edge looked at her admiringly, as he gave the pin back. "Wherever you find yourself, you seem to get well acquainted with everything about the place. You're a great one for learning things, aren't you?"

"Yes," she said, with no coy show of modesty. "I like especially to learn the *little-known* things about whatever place I'm in. It's been a big help, talking with so many resident foreigners. For instance"—she assumed the bossy voice of a tour guide—"here we are, walking past the School for Court Singers into the big, big and empty Palace Square, a quarter of a mile long and wide."

"Jesus, let's get across it in a hurry," said Edge. "I think *all* the wind has bunched in here. There's hardly a smear of snow on the cobbles."

Sunday ignored him and went on, pedantically, "Now, any guidebook can tell you that that one solitary thing sticking up in the middle of the empty square is the Alexander Column, erected in commemoration of Napoléon's defeat, and that it is made of polished red Finnish granite, and that it is the tallest man-made monolith in the world, and—"

"I believe it, I believe it. Come on, kid, walk faster."

"Don't call me kid." Then she said, not in the tour-guide voice, "Any of that, you can learn from a book, but *I* can tell you a funny thing about the Alexander Column." She laughed. "Timid old ladies won't let their coachmen drive them anywhere near it. They're positive that such a thing, so tall and so exposed to the wind, is bound to topple over one day."

"I believe that, too," gasped Edge, hauling her now at a run across the wind-scoured square, and under one of the soaring arches of the General Staff Building into a sheltered side street. "Whew! I swear, for a child of the tropics, you sure do seem immune to cold weather."

"Tropics? You know as well as I do, Virginia can get just as cold and snowy and blowy in deep winter."

"I meant—" he said, but stopped. He had been about to say something about "Africa," and Sunday knew it, and her eyes flashed as steelily as her Tula diamond.

So they walked on for a time, still side by side but a little apart. Sunday was either angrily or moodily silent, Edge was abashedly and apologetically silent. Meanwhile, he searched his mind for some innocuous subject he could broach, and finally said:

"How is it that you and Monday are so different?"

"We're not," she said morosely. "We are identical—height, weight, breast and waist and hip measurements—right to our identical high-yaller color."

"Oh, confound it, stop that, Sunday! Do you want me to pretend that you're

Anglo-Saxon white as wax? Which of us would be more foolish and preposterous—you for wanting it or me for pretending it? Wouldn't you rather that I
like you just as you are?"

She said meekly, "As long as you—like me, I don't care why."

"Well, when I asked about you and Monday, I was being *admiring* of what
you are, and what you've made of yourself. I mean, you speak English better
than any schoolmarm, and you've worked just as hard on other languages, and
every other kind of self-education. And you're—you're *interested* in things.
Monday is only interested in Monday."

While she thought it over, Sunday moved to walk closer beside him. "I don't
know what accounts for the difference. All three of us were born within an hour
or so, but I came out first. I've sometimes wondered: is there something about
sequence—even in families where the children arrive years apart—the firstborn
getting the most vigor and talent and intellect, and the later ones getting diminishing amounts? It certainly seemed so with us Simmses. Monday came next
after me, and she is content not to strive, just to wait—like that other Cinderella
—for Dame Opportunity to come along and recognize her great worth, and make
her rich or celebrated, or whatever it is she's waiting for. And poor Tuesday, the
last-born—well, you remember. She was totally juiceless, next to invisible."

"Sequence. It's an interesting theory," said Edge. "But then you're making
yourself out to be just a happy accident of nature, not giving yourself much
credit for being what you've become."

Sunday did not comment on that. She had stopped and was looking about,
and now she laughed. "Do you know where we are, Zachary?" It was a neighborhood where all the canals seemed to meet and interconnect, and the islands
among them bore huge, dark warehouses and, between those, rows of very un-
Russian-looking houses with steep, crow-stepped gables. The streets were so
narrow that the wind was only a rushing noise above the rooftops and, down
here, the snow fell softly and straight down. "This is Nóvaya Gollándaya."

"It is, eh? And what is that?"

"New Holland. The Dutch community. We've come way downstream of the
Nicholas Bridge. We'll be walking into the gulf next."

"We'd better turn back east, then," said Edge, and they took a street that
curved in more or less that direction. "Your foreign friends have really taught you
your way around this town."

"Da, sámiy poléznyi," she said merrily. "That means 'yes, most helpful.'
They're teaching me some useful bits of Russian, too. I can even say 'ya lyublyú
tebyá.'" When Edge did not inquire what that meant, she added wistfully, "Except that I don't have anybody to say it to."

Edge said, "Tell me . . ." then hesitated.

"Yes?" Sunday said eagerly.

"Do you and Monday do much sisterly confiding in each other?"

This neighborhood was darker, so far from the Admiralty's golden radiation,
and there were no street lamps. They were walking down the center of the
empty street, keeping their way by just the pale luminescence of the snow itself.
So Edge did not see the exasperated look that Sunday gave him. She sighed and
said:

"We used to, but hardly ever any more. We've sort of grown apart. Why? Is
there something that ought to be confided?"

"No...no...I just wondered." So, thought Edge, with some relief, Monday had not even mentioned her pregnancy. She probably would not, then, spread the word of the troublesome outcome of it.

Sunday went on, "There's a gap that opens and widens between married and single women, even when they're sisters. Of course, Monday is not exactly married, but she's been *practically* married to two different men now. And I'm still a spinster."

"Oh, for God's sake, at your age? A spinster is a dried-up old maid in a mob-cap, sitting in the chimney corner winding flax on a distaff."

"I can hardly wait."

"Maybe here in Piter, where you can socialize with all kinds of people, you'll land yourself a real prize husband. Maybe one of those prosperous English office managers with the furled umbrellas."

This time he did see the look she gave him, for they had stopped atop a short, humped bridge crossing a narrow canal, and on the other shore was a tavern, its brightly lighted windows casting their cheerful beams through the falling snow as far as where Edge and Sunday stood, and they could hear balalaika music and loud masculine singing from over there, too.

"Do you know where we are now?" Sunday asked.

"I haven't the faintest idea."

"Can you make out the signboard over that tavern door?"

Edge peered and said, "There are no words on it. Only what looks like a pair of red lips."

"A rebus, yes. The landlord is named Kissman, and that tavern is much frequented by the young men from the Marine Cadets' School. It's over yonder." She pointed. "Partly because of the tavern man's name and his signboard, and partly because the cadets walk their sweethearts along here, this little bridge is called the Potselúy Móstik, the Bridge of Kisses." There was a long silence. Then she said shyly, "Shouldn't we help the little bridge deserve its name?"

Edge leaned over the railing and looked down at the canal. Its water, unruffled here by any wind, had drawn over itself a thin coating of ice that was no doubt thickening by the minute. Sort of like me, thought Edge. Then, suddenly, there slid from under the Bridge of Kisses a bateau heaped with rutabagas and mangelwurzels, poled along by a solitary muzhik, and the ice crackled and broke as the boat plowed through it.

Edge turned to Sunday, bent and gave her what he intended to be a paternal peck on the lips. But Sunday quickly put her arms around his neck, went up on her tiptoes, hugged him close and kissed him with ardor. Touchingly, she was somewhat inexpert at it, but her lips were tender, the kiss was sweet and lingering and delicious, and Edge wondered why he had resisted for so long. But then he remembered a number of things. He did not fling Sunday away from him, but when she finally stopped kissing and drew a little back so she could say, breathlessly, "Ya lyublyú tebyá," he almost harshly demanded:

"Does that mean what I think it means?"

"It's those famous three little words. They're not so little in Russian, are they? Ya lyublyú tebyá."

"They're not so little in any language, Sunday. One way or another, they can loom pretty big. So don't say them to me. I'm fond of you, yes. You are very dear to me. But I am old enough to be your father. And despite your grown-up ways and talk and appearance, you are still too young to know your own mind."

"Zachary, did I kiss you as if I didn't know what I meant by it?" Her eyes were big and glowing happily in the light from Kissman's tavern. "For a while there, you were kissing back, as if it meant something to you, too."

"Hush. There won't be any more of that. This very night, I've seen how things can go wrong for another girl who was in too much of a hurry to be a woman. You save those words, Sunday, and wait. Sometime you'll find a beau more your own age. More suitable in every way. And when you do, you'll really *know*. You wait and see."

"All right," she said calmly. "I'll do that." She was turned away from the tavern now, so Edge could not see that her brown eyes still glowed warmly, even without the borrowed light. "I'll wait. As long as it takes."

"That's fine. That's showing the good sense I admire in you."

They walked on, and Edge, to atone for his gruffness, companionably took Sunday's hand. It was fur-gloved, so she quickly withdrew it, quickly peeled off the glove, then put her small, bare, warm hand back in his. They continued like that, hand in hand, not talking but sharing a comfortable silence. They crossed another canal and came into another spacious square, and in this one, even at whatever hour this was, there were many people, flaring torches and much activity.

"The Haymarket," said Sunday. The people were almost all peasants, apparently just in from the country, rudely clad in the shapeless long coats and shapeless felt boots. They were putting up stands and stalls and stocking them with bales of hay and hides, baskets of winter vegetables, trays of dried and smoked and salted fish. One of the muzhiks was the rutabaga-and-mangelwurzel man Edge had seen earlier. There were also, moving watchfully among the throng, numerous black-uniformed gorodovóis ostentatiously twirling their truncheons.

Sunday said, "We'd better hurry through here. It's not a nice place to loiter. I'm told it is the haunt of the lowest and criminal classes—ruffians and cutpurses and maybe even cutthroats."

"I've heard of this place, too," said Edge. "In the days before the tsar liberated the serfs, it was just like our Dixie slave marts. A calf might sell here for a couple of rubles, but a sturdy serf sold for as much as a thousand—about the price of a good fieldhand back home."

"What would a young mulatto girl have gone for, I wonder," said Sunday. It was the first time Edge had ever heard her speak of her color *not* in an embittered voice. She quirked her head to smile up at him. "Would you have bid for me, Zachary?"

"I doubt it." Her face fell. "Oh, I didn't mean that the way it sounded. My family, you see, were po' folks, too. We never owned a slave. Not many people in the mountain parts of Virginia ever did. What it amounted to—our Blue Ridge boys fought that damned war, and died doing it, on behalf of the rich, slave-owning plantation families in the flatlands."

"Like the Furfews," murmured Sunday. "You know, it's odd—I can hardly even remember being *owned*. And I'm glad you didn't die, Zachary."

They were past the Haymarket now, and on the broad Sadovaya Street, and they found still more people abroad at this hour. A score or more of women— most of them young and passably handsome, though perhaps too brightly rouged, wearing cheap wolf-skin coats, but with gaudily colored skirts showing below—were wielding twig brooms, sweeping the snow from the cobbles, watched by half a dozen bored gorodovóis.

"My," said Sunday. "I didn't know Saint Petersburg had such a comely crew of street sweepers."

"They're not street sweepers by choice," said Edge. "They save the city the cost of any such crew. I've seen them, or others like them, other times I've gone walking. These are the, uh, ladies of the night, if you know what that means."

"Of course I know. But prostitutes don't usually do *this*."

"Well, they'll have been picked up earlier in the evening by the police for, er, accosting men on the street—or even for walking alone and *looking* like they might solicit. Remember that, Sunday, when you take your own strolls. They've been locked up in the local watchhouse ever since, and they're brought out just before dawn to do this sweeping as their punishment, and then they're let go."

"Poor creatures," said Sunday.

Edge suddenly realized what he had just said. "*Dawn?* If they're out sweeping, it's almost *dawn!*" He also realized that the air was full of the sweet odor that permeated all of St. Petersburg early every morning: the smell of hot, freshly baked bread. "My God, Sunday, we've been walking and talking all night. Where did the time go?"

"The best way time has ever gone for me."

"All night, and we haven't been to bed."

"Well, no," she said, her expression inscrutable. "That would be better yet."

"Soon, soon, little girl. I know you must be damned weary and sleepy. We're not far from the hotel now. If you skip breakfast, you can sleep until time for the noon meal. I do apologize for keeping you up all these hours. I reckon—I reckon I was enjoying the night too much to notice. But I'm sorry."

"Don't be sorry, Zachary. Anything we do, I don't want it ever to make you sorry."

6

"HERR GOUVERNEUR," said Willi. "After diligent but discreet search, I have found a highly respectable physician who is willing to take care of—our medical problem. Not eager, but willing. I presented to him not my Florilegium card but my personal calling card. When I told him that I had inconveniently got a Mulattin with child, and also infected her with der Tripper, he said he was not surprised to hear it from 'one of Bavaria's mad Wittelsbachs.' Here is the address. I told him the girl's father would bring her."

"I thank you for your good offices," said Florian. "Though I don't know if I thank you for putting me in the rôle of father to a Mulattin."

Willi said stiffly, "How do you think *I* felt, in the rôle of her seducer? How many Wittelsbachs do you think must be spinning in their noble crypts at this new blemish I have put on their name?"

"You are right to chide me, Willi. I *am* grateful to you."

So Florian drove Monday to the clinic of the Dóktor Bestuzhev. She was gloomy and nail-bitingly fearful, but apparently resigned. Florian tried to make cheerful conversation with her on the way, but got only grunts in reply. He tried to make cheerful conversation with the physician, too, but got only a disdainful look, and was told to return for his "daughter" on the morrow.

When Florian came back the next day, Monday's usual fawn complexion had paled to beige, and she was weak, but she said the procedure had not been nearly as painful or distressing as she had feared. The doctor this time condescended to speak at least briefly to him, in private:

"I assume you realize, gospodín, that your *miscarried* grandson might have grown up to be another Pushkin. That great poet had some black blood, you know; his great-grandfather was an Abyssinian. Of course, your grandson might as easily have been... Well, no doubt you and his father have done the right thing. In any case, here are the medicaments to rid your daughter of the polkóvnik disease. These calomel pills"—they were a deadly lead color and shaped like little coffins—"she is to take thrice daily. This argyrial solution is for irrigating the interior of her private parts. See that she does it morning and night, without fail."

Driving Monday back to the Tauric Garden, Florian repeated the doctor's instructions and made her promise to abide by them.

"Don't fret," she said. "I'll get myself clean again. I don't want no traces left of that summabitch."

"The others of the company believe that you went to a clinic only to get cured of the intestinal affliction that plagued you longer then the rest of us."

"Awright. I ain't likely to brag on what it was really for. I'm sick of that Mr. Demon and I'm pretty near sick of every man in the world. I been thinkin' of goin' back to bein' a virgin."

"Eh?"

"I even been thinkin' I might join one of them whatchamacallits—places full of nothin' but nuns."

"A convent? I really don't believe they claim to *restore* virginity. Do you feel a sudden religious calling?"

"No. But I can have just as much bed frolic with women as I can with any man, and not worry about havin' sick do-daddies or babies inside of me."

"Well, don't take the veil just yet. We're preparing a couple of surprises to welcome you back to the troupe. One is a new turn for your act. After you've been applauded for the Cinderella routine on the high tightrope, you come down and do an encore. Brutus and Caesar stretch a rope between them with their trunks, and you walk *that*. Dance, somersault, whatever you like."

"Umm... that do sound nice." Then she snapped, "But I do it only if Hannibal be the bull man, you hear? I don't want that Mr. Demon nowhere near me and my act."

It was the contrite Pemjean who had thought up the idea and who was hurrying to train Peggy and Mitzi to do it, but Florian acquiesced: Abdullah would handle the elephants for that one trick.

"You said a couple of surprises."

"What the second will be, I can't say for sure. But today our Chefpublizist—again presenting himself as the Baron Wittelsbach—is visiting the Winter Palace to deliver Colonel Ramrod's letter of introduction to the Tsaritsa Maria Alexandrovna. Or anyway to the highest of her chamberlains or ladies-in-waiting he can gain access to. So we all may be invited to a personal audience, or an intimate tea, a soirée, a full-dress ball, there's no telling. But certainly we *will* soon be mingling with royalty."

"Reckon that do beat minglin' with nuns. Awright, I hurry up and get strong again and get back on that-there rope."

At the tober, Willi had returned from the palace and reported, "I was not, of course, ushered into Her Imperial Majesty's presence, coming uninvited and unannounced as I did. But I put the letter into the hands of a very gracious Countess Varvara Nikolaevich Khvoshchinski, who I am sure can be trusted to deliver it. So now"—he spread his hands—"we can but wait."

Monday was back on the tightrope only two days later, claiming to feel perfectly fit, and appearing to be so, and being introduced to the audience by Florian as Gospozhyá Zolushka, the Russian for "Mademoiselle Cinderella"—in time to be seen and admired by Vassily Marchan of the Tsirk Cinizelli, who that day paid his promised visit to the Florilegium. He, like the rest of the sfondone audience, was more than impressed by her chimney-sweep performance and highly amused by her encore on the elephant-held rope, for the midget Cricket —in Russian she was "Syverchok"—had added a comic fillip to that new turn before it was first presented.

While Gospozhyá Zolushka was taking her bows on the high platform, Abdullah led Brutus and Caesar into the pista, and the midget came with them, struggling to walk with the weight of a coil of thick rope around each shoulder. She was wearing joey makeup and an oversized old coat, a relic of the late Ali Baba. After she gave Brutus an end of rope to hold in her trunk, Syverchok engaged in a tug-of-war with the big bull, doing a parody of the Quakemaker's earlier act. Then the elephant Caesar made a snatch and got an end of the rope on Syverchok's other shoulder. For a brief while, it appeared that the little woman was being dragged asunder—she clutching one end of each rope, the other ends being inexorably pulled by the two elephants backing away from her and each other. The audience, which had been laughing at Syverchok's antics, now gasped at her imminent dismemberment. She was actually lifted into the air as the bulls stretched the two ropes taut between them and she still stubbornly clutched her ends of them. Then the audience laughed again, when the midget slipped out of the coat and dropped lightly on her feet in the sawdust, and it was revealed that the two ropes were really one, threaded through the sleeves of the big coat still hanging there.

By that time, Gospozhyá Zolushka had descended from the platform and mounted to the head of Caesar. Now she danced down the elephant's trunk and onto the stretched rope, did a brisk reprise of her earlier routine and concluded by tripping over the coat strung on the rope, and doing an exaggerated pretense of falling. The audience gasped again, then laughed again, as Monday broke her fall by slipping her own arms into the coat sleeves. Abdullah gave a command, the two elephants slowly moved toward each other and gently lowered Zolushka to the ground—to take another several bows, together with little Syverchok.

Marchan clapped and stamped his feet as enthusiastically as every other spectator, and exclaimed to Florian, "Prevoskhódnyi! I envy you such an array of talent. I have lately added nothing to my tsirk but a dumb strongman. I suppose I could not persuade you to part with some of your performers."

"You suppose rightly, Gospodín Marchan. Indeed, I am ever on the lookout for new artistes, myself. Excuse me, but I must now lead the closing spec."

When that walkaround parade had disbanded, Florian returned to Marchan, who said, "I can well understand that you would not wish to diminish your company, but perhaps you would consent to do so on humanitarian grounds."

"Eh? Do some of them appear to be *mistreated* here?"

"Nyet, nyet, nyet. Of course not. But tell me, how did you acquire those three Korean tumblers?"

"I found them stranded, lost and hungry and bewildered, in Baltimore. That is a port city on the east coast of the Soyedinénnye Shtáti. How did you recognize them as Koreans?"

"I have been some way into Korea, on occasion, when I have taken my tsirk across Siberia. If those men were stranded, and in a seaport, tak, perhaps they were trying to get home again?"

"I have no idea. None of us can speak their language."

"I can, after a fashion. Might I ask them that question?"

"By all means." Florian sent a roustabout to round up and fetch the Kim brothers.

"Meanwhile," said Marchan, "I might mention that we both have new competition. A traveling balagan has set up on the riverside, down by the Bronze Horseman. Nothing to it but a crude, hand-cranked kolesó and an ice-slicked salázki. And of course the usual stalls and tents selling trinkets and sweetmeats and hot tidbits."

"I know what a kolesó is," said Florian. "One of those vertical wheels with the swinging boats. But what is a salázki?"

"Um... some call it the 'English mountain.'" Marchan went on to describe it, and Florian said:

"Ah, yes. What is known in the West as a toboggan slide."

"Anyway, I spoke only in jest about competition. A rubbishy balagan's simple devices attract mostly children."

"I think," said Florian, "I shall go and invite its proprietor to move here to our tober. It might benefit both his establishment and ours. And I *would* like to have a midway out in front of my chapiteau again."

The Kim brothers arrived, looking apprehensive, as they always did at anything unusual. But their faces brightened when Marchan greeted them with "Anyong hasimnika?" and they responded happily, in concert, "Ne, komapsumnida!" Marchan conversed with them for some time, then turned again to Florian. "That was but small talk. I shall now inquire of them if they wish to return to Korea." And he said to the brothers, "Hanguk e tora ka yo. Chip e tora kago sip'o hase yo?"

They looked thunderstruck and cried a babble of "Ne! Ne! Ne!"

"Apparently they do not care to go," said Florian. "They say nay."

"In Korean, ne means yes," said Marchan. "No is ani." Indeed, the Kims were now bounding about, in an evident transport of joy, still crying, "Ne! Ne!" Marchan spoke to them some more, then told Florian, "They do wish to go home, and I have told them that this summer I will be traveling in that direction. I have lately decided to take my tsirk eastward instead of south when we leave Piter. Across Siberia."

"All the way to Korea?" asked Florian, astonished. "Why, that must be three thousand miles from here."

"I shall not get all the way to Korea, nyet. But if I take these men as far as the border of Manchuria, they should have no trouble making the rest of the way."

"Surely there cannot be enough sizable towns between here and Manchuria to make such a tour profitable."

"Truly there are not. But I have traveled there before. You may ask: why do I subject myself and my troupe to such a toilsome journey? Tak, I will tell you. I do it partly from altruism, because the miserable Siberians so seldom get to see any entertainment, or even many outsiders. But partly also—and this I tell you in confidence—because out there are so many Nigilists like myself. Some imprisoned, some in exile, some in hiding. We manage to get together to make plans and plots and schemes."

"Ah."

"Shall I take along your Koreans and help them return home?"

"Well . . ." Florian looked at them, dancing about.

"Ne! Ne! Ne!"

Marchan said, "Since they would be performing for me along the way, it would be only fair if I trade you something for them. Would you care to employ my ten dancing usher girls? They are local wenches, and young, so their parents will not let them travel."

"Well . . . I have *wanted* some dancing girls, but our Sir John has had no success, so far, in finding any for us."

"Done, then. We will exchange, but not immediately. I shall not be leaving until mid-May, tak. The Petersburgers are only now starting to pluck their violets."

"I beg your pardon?"

"Have you not noticed the many farm and household carts carrying the big blue blocks of ice cut from the Neva?"

"Yes. They are blue enough, but hardly violets."

"Nevertheless, that is what they are called: the violets of Saint Petersburg. People cut the blocks to fill their icehouses before the spring thaw makes a jumble of the river ice. So the many carts carrying ice are the harbingers of springtime coming, just as real violets are in warmer climates."

"I see. Well, if you do not depart until May, then the Kim brothers will be with us long enough—" Florian paused. He had been about to say that the Kims would be around to perform before the imperial court, but he decided that that might offend or outrage a dedicated Nigilist, so he lamely repeated, "Long enough."

"You didn't strike your usual hard bargain, Governor," said Edge, when Florian told him about it. "Marchan takes the Kims, and we get the girls he'd have to leave behind anyway."

"I would have agreed, whatever the proposition. Those poor Koreans were so eager to get home again. By the time they do, I suppose they'll have been clear around the world. But let this be an object lesson to you, Colonel Ramrod." Florian put on a look of pious and smug benevolence, but his eyes smilingly belied his solemnity. "When the time comes that *you* are proprietor of this or some other circus, I hope you will remember my small show of compassion today, as vividly as you may remember any of my occasional humbugs and hoaxes, fobberies and fooleries."

Edge snorted. "I'll just hope to hell I never find myself responsible for a whole circus."

"Ah, but you will, you will, lad. After all, I shan't live forever." Florian laughed, as if that remark had been only another bit of humbug. "Well, in the meantime, we can tell Sir John to cancel that advertisement he has been running in the newspapers, and cease his quest for local dancing girls. Where is he?"

"Gone look for girls some more," said Meli, standing nearby. "Him and Maurice." She put on her mink coat over her performing costume, the silver-spangled fleshings like serpent skin. "I go get him. I think now he try that school for noble daughters, and I no trust him"—she smiled to show she did not mean it—"with such a many pretty young Rosithoi."

Although it was not yet six o'clock when Meli left the tober—and although the Petersburgers might be collecting their spring-herald "violets"—it was already nearly dark, and the Slovaks were lighting the entranceway's pole torches. However, Meli did not go along that cleared path. She struck out through the snow that lay north of the tober, to go from the park past the Potemkin Palace onto Shpalernaya Street and follow that to the Smolny Boarding School for Young Ladies of Noble Birth. She was picking her way through a particularly dark arcade along one wall of the palace when, without a sound of warning, two strong hands seized her from behind. Meli let out only a faint "Idoú!" of surprise, assuming that it was Fitzfarris on his way back and playfully ambushing her.

When he turned her around, she saw that it was not Fitz. For a moment, she did not recognize the rough-garbed man. He had shaved off his fierce mustache and grown a heavy beard instead. But she knew his voice, when he said silkily, "Did you think you would never see me again, Hellene woman? Did you think I would just slink meekly away, and leave you free to take another man and forget your dear Shadid?"

"*You!* What you want?"

"What I had. You, whenever I wanted. And I want you now. It was such a pleasant surprise, after all my wanderings, to find my old show here in Saint Petersburg, and to learn that you were still with it."

Meli would not let him see her dread; she said staunchly, "Yes, I have new man now. Him I will tell of you. And he will come and kill you. *He* no Spyros."

"He no Shadid, either," said the Terrible Turk, mimicking her voice. "He is that half-blue Square John, no? You see, I have been watching my old acquaintances for some time. Watching and waiting for this opportunity. You have always preferred half-men, have you not, Hellene? But I am a whole man. Let your half-blue one come for me if he dares."

"You are not man at all. You are okilí."

If the Turk understood the Greek word for dog, he was not insulted by it. "I am glad to see that your new half-man dresses you well. That fine coat will make a comfortable cushion for us on the hard pavement here."

He ripped the coat open down its front, its fur-covered buttons flying everywhere, and threw her flat on her back, and the coat spread on both sides of her like dark wings. Then he stooped, seized the neck of her spangled fleshings, and ripped again, and finally tossed away her last covering, the little cache-sexe pad. Meli whimpered, less from fright than from the impact of the bitter night air on her bare skin.

Shadid did not immediately fall upon her. He took time to look her over, slowly and lasciviously, then said, "You have had so many men now, your göbek must be slack-lipped and loose." He reached up to the roof eave of the arcade—for him it was not much of a stretch—and broke off a long, blunt-pointed icicle. He snapped off that point, so he had a rod of ice as long and as big around as a man's forearm. Meli quailed and flung both her arms protectively across her face, so she was unprepared for what happened next.

Shadid said, in a purring voice, "I am not going to hit you," then rammed the hard, cold thing as far as it would go inside her.

The Slovaks had just finished lighting the pole torches when they heard the scream. They all looked in the direction whence it had come, but could see nothing beyond the glare of the torches. After some mumbling among themselves, they concluded that it must have been one of the horses stabled in the old palace, perhaps frightened by a rat in its stall.

Meli had been able to give just that one scream, then she was paralyzed and benumbed by shock. She could only lie there, on her outspread coat, her eyes bulging, her mouth gaping, unable even to struggle or try to ease herself off the impalement. Shadid held the icicle where it was, and said soothingly, "It will act on you like an alum douche, you will see. When I slip it out, your poor, overused, flaccid göbek will shrink and become sweetly tight for me to enjoy."

The Turk was wrong. When he tried to withdraw the icicle gently, it stayed where it was. It had frozen to Meli's inner membranes, the way a carelessly raised cold tin cup will freeze tight to an unwary lip. Shadid had to yank to get the icicle loose, and it came out with little shreds of pink clinging all around it. The Slovaks on the tober, startled again, and by an even more horrendous scream, told each other that someone must be *branding* the horses over there in the stables.

"You'd have thought we were white slavers," grumbled Fitzfarris, when he and LeVie returned to the Florilegium a while later. "The nuns ran us out of there before Maurice could even find out if any of the schoolgirls spoke French."

"Well, no matter," said Florian. "I've made arrangements to take over the Cinizelli's girls before too long. I'll tell you about that later. Right now, you might want to go after Meli. She went toward that Smolny school to find *you*, some time ago."

"You won't need me for that, ami," said LeVie. "And I've had enough of the cold. I want to thaw out."

So Fitzfarris plodded out again, alone, and a Slovak pointed the way Meli had gone. Fitz followed her track through the snow and nearly fell over her. She was lying halfway between the tober and the palace, at the nearer end of another trail—of red droplets frozen in the snow. With an appalled oath, Fitz bent to her, and she moaned; she was alive, at least. He got an arm under her shoulders and her knees, and lifted her. Meli was almost rigid with cold, and her hands seemed frozen in their clench of the coat about her. But more blood drizzled off the hem of that coat, and congealed almost before it hit the snow. Lurching back toward the tober, Fitz asked, "Meli, can you talk? What the hell happened?"

Her blue eyelids seemed to creak, so much effort she had to make to open them. Panic flared in her eyes, and she tried to convulse her stiff body, nearly making Fitz drop her. But then she saw who it was, and her blue lips murmured his name.

"Yes, I've got you. You're safe now. We'll have you fixed up in no time. But what—who did this to you?"

Meli still had some presence of mind. Her lips trembled and her teeth chattered when she said, "M-m-mu...muzhik..."

"Son of a bitch," growled Fitzfarris.

When he staggered with his burden into the chapiteau, followed by a few goggling roustabouts, he gasped, "It's Meli. She's hurt."

Florian instantly barked at one Slovak, "Quick! Bring any wagon that's got a horse hitched to it!" And at another, "Fetch blankets, furs. The skins off the cages. Anything!" And to Fitz, "Come, Sir John. I know of a doctor not far away."

So, only a quarter of an hour later, Florian was pounding at the door of the Dóktor Bestuzhev's clinic, then wrenching it open and plunging through it without waiting for anyone to admit him. When Bestuzhev appeared, he made no complaint about that unorthodox entrance at such an unusual hour, but only motioned for Fitzfarris to lay the woman down on a couch in the foyer. The doctor flipped open her several coverings, looked at her blue-white, blood-smeared body and remarked caustically to Florian, "Another daughter? You do not take very good care of them, gospodín. You two wait here." He himself scooped up Meli again, and carried her to another room.

Florian asked Fitz, when they both had caught their breath, "Do you have any notion of what happened to her?"

"No. But it had to be rape. All she could say was 'muzhik.' Some bastard peasant waylaid her in the dark. And the damned animals all look alike. We'll never find the culprit."

"I think we will," Florian said slowly. "I think Meli lied."

"*What*? Now look here. You're not going to malign—"

"I'm not maligning, I'm praising her. She lied to protect you. Consider, Sir John. Who was it who raped her before, and raped her repeatedly, and was responsible for the death of her husband? Even in her present wretched condition, Meli was trying to save you from some similar fate."

"The *Turk*?" said Fitz, incredulous. "Christ, we got rid of him way back in Hungary."

"We didn't wipe him off the face of the earth. Now I believe we should have done just that. This very afternoon, Vassily Marchan mentioned that he had recently engaged a strongman for his Tsirk Cinizelli. I paid it no heed at the time, but now..."

"I'll be goddamned," said Fitz. "Well, I'll wait to see what the doctor says. Then I'm going to borrow one of Zack's guns and—"

"Simmer down, Sir John. I am in full accord with your intention. Other considerations aside, we cannot have *two* Shadid Sarkioglus coexistent in Saint Petersburg. But I will not allow you—"

"Damned if I'll wait to be *allowed*."

"Barbaric as this country is," Florian went on, "it does not condone murder. If the Turk doesn't kill you before you can kill him, be assured that the authorities will. And what would your gallantry do for Meli? Only leave her again bereaved."

"Are you advising me to wave the white feather? Go running to the police? Whine for the protection of the law? Accuse the Turk of rape, and maybe see him get off with a few strokes of flogging?"

"No. Only a cowardly mollycoddle would ask the law to do his avenging for him. Besides, that would entail the risk of disclosing that there *are* two Shadids in existence, and might imperil all the rest of us."

"You and your cussed practicality. What *do* you suggest, then?"

"Murder is a capital crime. Dueling is not, if it is done beyond the city limits —south of the Obvodnyi Canal. Dueling is discouraged, yes, but not punished, once it is a fait accompli." Fitz's jaw dropped. "I understand that the Catherine-Court Park is the favored place for pistols at dawn."

Just then the doctor emerged from his inner chamber and said to Florian, "Your daughter will be all right, gospodín." Florian made a noise, but was over-ridden. "She suffers mainly from loss of blood and a shock to her nervous system, but she is a strong woman. There was no frostbite and her internal lacerations will heal. What in God's name happened to her?"

Florian said that, as far as anyone knew, it had been an attack in the dark by an unknown rapist.

"The assailant must have used a broken bottle instead of his own tool," said Bestuzhev. He looked at Fitzfarris. "Is this her man? Tell him that he can take the woman home, but she must rest in bed for a few days. And he is to stay out of her bed. It will be some time before she is again capable of intimate relations. And probably longer before she will want any. I am giving you here some iron pills and fish-liver oil to help restore her blood, and some suppositories that will dull the pain of her insides."

Florian relayed that information to Fitzfarris, then asked the doctor if there was anything else.

"You tell me, gospodín," Bestuzhev said sardonically. "How many more daughters with polovóy problems do you possess?"

So Florian was flushed quite pink when they departed, he and Fitz supporting between them the still quite blue-white but much revived Meli. In the wagon on the way back to the tober, Fitz gently reproached her:

"Why did you try to make me believe it was some lout of a muzhik when it was that same brute Turk again?"

"Ai, Kristos," she said faintly. "Did I speak in delirium?"

"No. But I found out. That's all that matters."

"It is *not* all that matters. Ai, Ziano! Promise me you no get in trouble with this Turk."

"I don't expect any trouble. I'm going to be very gentlemanly and genteel," said Fitzfarris, through his teeth. "The Governor has already convinced me to."

"Then I thank you, Kyvernitis Florian," said Meli, turning to him and laying a pale, cold hand on his arm. "This good man Ziano I no want lose."

The next morning, Fitzfarris came to Florian's office in the red wagon to say, "I'll be going over to the Cinizelli building this afternoon, between shows, to challenge that goddamned Turk."

Florian nodded. "How is Meli?"

"She spent a restless night. Kept waking up with little shrieks. But she's doing all right. Now—as I recollect from what I've read about duels, I'm supposed to slap the bastard with a glove, then dare him to meet me at dawn. Is that the way?"

"That is the melodramatic way. It is sufficient merely to say, in front of some witness, that you challenge him to a duel. But then you must give him time to procure his second or seconds. They and your seconds then consult together to arrange the time and place. *Have* you any seconds?"

"Not yet, but I imagine Zack will agree to come along. He's already cleaning and loading for me two of the revolvers we scavenged from those bummers back in Virginia. Identical Colts, identically loaded, one cartridge apiece. I understand I give the Turk his choice of them."

"Well, actually—" Florian began, but just then the wagon door opened and the Terrible Turk himself strode in, stooping to clear the lintel. Fitz and Florian stared in disbelief. Shadid was followed in by two much smaller men, who, though they wore no makeup, were recognized by Florian and Fitzfarris as the white-face and the toby from the Tsirk Cinizelli.

"Florian Efendi, you still have my conduct book," the Turk said. "I want it back. I have been making do with a temporary—"

Of the two astounded Florilegium men, Florian was the first to find his voice. "I'll say this for you, Sarkioglu. You have more gall than there is in a pista full of tanbark. After what you did last night, do you expect to walk out of here alive?"

"I do," the Turk said confidently. Fitzfarris audibly ground his teeth and made a move forward, but Florian put out an arm to hold him back. Shadid went on, "Would you kill me in front of my clown colleagues? Or kill all three of us? Marchan Efendi might wonder why we do not return, since he knows we were coming here."

"Very well," said Florian, "you will not die *today*." He said to Fitz, "The joeys and I are witnesses. Issue your challenge."

In a tight voice, Fitzfarris said, "Turk, I'm challenging you formally to a duel. Have your seconds meet with mine. He's the Colonel Edge that you already know. I suggest we fight the duel at... where did you say, Governor?"

"The Ekaterin-Dvor," said Florian. "The Catherine-Court Park, south of the Obvodnyi Canal."

"That's the place I suggest," Fitz said, again to Shadid. "And the time I suggest is dawn tomorrow."

"That is satisfactory to me," said the Turk. "And of course I accept the challenge. Perhaps these two clowns will be my seconds. Would you ask them, Florian Efendi? I have little Russian."

Florian did so, explaining the matter at some length. The joeys looked properly awed, but agreed to serve.

"Then it's pistols at dawn at that park," said Fitzfarris. "Colonel Edge will bring the weapons and give you your—"

"A moment, half-blue man. Do you not know the code duello? And, by the way, why are you no longer half-blue?"

"None of your goddamned business. What *about* the code duello?"

"It gives the challenged party the choice of the weapons. And I choose arms."

"All right, damn it!" Fitz snarled. "If you don't want pistols, what *kind* of arms?"

"These," said the Terrible Turk, extending his own upper extremities, and making their muscles ripple and bulge so that they showed even through his coarse, heavy muzhik greatcoat. "Both of us bare to the waist. My arms against your arms."

The natural half of Fitz's face went slightly pale as he looked to Florian, who nodded and said, "I was about to tell you that, when he barged in. He can choose any weapon from howitzers to toothpicks."

The Turk grinned wolfishly. "Half-man, do you wish to withdraw your challenge?"

"Hell, no!" snapped Fitzfarris. "We can go at it right here and now if you want, you son of a bitch."

Shadid gave him a long look and must have decided that Fitz was enraged enough that, this minute, he *might* prove a formidable opponent, at least might wreak *some* damage before he was broken in half. Anyway, the Turk evidently thought it wise to give Fitz time to cool off and repent his rashness and begin to worry. He said, "No, no, not now. We will observe the formalities. Dawn tomorrow, in that park." He turned to Florian. "Now—my conduct book."

"Come for it tomorrow," Florian said coldly. "If you can."

The Turk laughed a booming laugh and was still laughing as he went out, followed by his newly appointed seconds. A long silence ensued in the office. Then Fitzfarris wiped a hand across his suddenly damp forehead and said:

"Jesus. I can shoot a pistol, and sometimes I've hit what I shot it at. But a bare-knuckle brawl against that monster...?"

"Yes," said Florian. "He struck a coup de Jarnac."

"What?"

"A sly blow. It is called that from a long-ago duel in which a certain Monsieur Jarnac—"

"I don't care what it's called. As far as my chances go, *suicide* is as good a word as any. You were right, Governor. All that this will accomplish is to bereave Meli again."

"Now, now, Sir John. If you go into the fray with that despondent attitude, you are as good as dead already. Remember, the institution of the duel originated in what was called the 'wager of battle,' where it was assumed that the gods awarded victory to the opponent who was in the right."

"Come dawn, it'll take the gods to do it, by damn. Well, at least I don't have to go over to the Cinizelli. I can spend all my free time today with Meli. She'll like that, and she won't realize until tomorrow that I've been saying a last long goodbye."

Florian tried hard to think of something else to say that might embolden Sir John for his rendezvous with the Terrible Turk. But only the example of David versus Goliath came to his mind, and that would not serve. David had slung a stone from a distance; he had not had to grapple hand to hand with the Terrible Philistine.

Fitzfarris took out a handkerchief to wipe better at the cold sweat bedewing his forehead. When he did, his hand shook, and he inadvertently rubbed off some of his cosmetic mask. He gazed meditatively at the flesh-colored smear on the handkerchief, then left the office without another word.

At that afternoon's performance of the circus, when Florian marched proudly into the chapiteau at the head of his troupe and animals in the opening Grand Promenade, he glanced idly at the starback section of seats—then stared intently, wondering what the hell the Terrible Turk was doing, sitting *there*. Why had he returned?

Though the man was bundled now in a bulky fur coat, far finer than the muzhik garb he had worn in the morning—and had on his head a fisherman's billed cap, tugged down so far that his features were hidden in shadow—there was no disguising the size of him. Why, Florian wondered, was Shadid not at the Cinizelli, which also showed at this hour? And why was he accompanied now by five or six other people? The Turk leaned here and there among them, speaking to one or several of them, as he pointed to various artistes in the procession. His companions were almost as big as he was—so they did not include his seconds, the two comparatively small clowns—and all were as bundled in furs as Shadid was. Some of them wore hats, also pulled down to shadow their faces, but a couple of them were heavily veiled—indubitably females.

Florian wondered: had Vassily Marchan declared a holiday for several of his troupe, so they could come and gloat with Shadid at the havoc he was going to wreak on Sir John tomorrow? Then why all the pointing and conferring? Were these people perhaps the Terrible Turk's personal henchmen that he had collected during his wanderings from Hungary to here? Was he planning assaults on others of the Florilegium, and identifying them for his henchmen to deal with? But... *female* henchmen?

Florian puzzled and worried and conjectured all during the show. Several times, he managed to sidle over to that starback section to peer more closely at the group. Every time he did, they huddled deeper into their furs and mufflers, and lowered their heads; they definitely did not want to be recognized and did not mind letting him *know* that they did not. Florian said nothing about this to any of his own troupers, but they began to give him queer looks, because—a thing unprecedented—he once or twice bounded into the pista early or late to make his introductions of the acts, and bawled them absentmindedly, haltingly.

At intermission, the mysterious bunch surged out with the rest of the jossers, to the annex tent for the sideshow. While walking with the crowd, then standing in the annex, they contrived still to hunch themselves so they did not too obviously stand taller than everybody else. Florian thought of warning Sir John, but decided that the man already had worries enough. And indeed, Fitzfarris was also distracted and desultory in his presentation of his depleted exhibition, now comprising only the Night Children, the egg-laying glukhár, Kostchei the Deathless, the Egyptian Princess mummy, the midget Syverchok and her little horse, Rumpelstilzchen.

The strange, anonymous group returned to the chapiteau with everyone else, for the second half of the show, and Florian supposed that—if they were going to make any overt move—they would wait for the tober to clear after the performance. He was right. When the show concluded with the final Grand Promenade and the bulk of the audience departed, happily jabbering and laughing, that fur-bundled bunch remained in their seats.

When they were the only jossers left in the pavilion, they stood up and advanced into the pista, apparently with menace. Florian bellowed, "Hey, rube!" and was quickly backed by roustabouts and male troupers carrying tent stakes, whips, sledgehammers, even drumsticks. They and Florian presented a grimly united front as the strange group approached. But the foremost of those persons was veiled—a woman—and she lifted her veil and smiled. She had rather a horselike face, but spoke graciously, trying three different languages:

"Gospodín Florian? Herr Florian? Monsieur Florian?"

Guardedly, he replied in Russian that he was that very Gospodín Florian, so she went on in the same tongue:

"I am the Grafínya Varvara Nikolaevich Khvoshchinski. May I introduce you to Their Imperial Majesties, who are exceedingly eager to meet you?"

Florian stammered, "Why, Countess... Your Grace..." Behind his back, he made urgent shooing gestures with his hands, and his armed men obediently dispersed. "I am honored... you had me mystified... wondering who..."

"Forgive us our secretive behavior," she said. "The tsar and tsaritsa do sometimes prefer to be incognito in crowded public places." She turned to the tallest of the men, and in German said, "Your Majesty, I present to you the proprietor of this establishment: the Herr Gouverneur Florian. Herr Florian: His Imperial Majesty, Emperor, Autocrat and Tsar, Alexander Nikolaevich Romanov, and his consort, the Empress Maria Alexandrovna."

"I am honored," Florian said again, hoarsely, this time in German. He bowed deeply, restraining the impulse to prostrate himself before the tall man and almost as tall woman—not to do that in abject salutation but in sheer relief that there had been no clem.

The tsar said jovially, "Sehr nutzbar macht, das 'Hey, rube!'" and went on to say that he wished he could so snappily muster his own troops when he wanted them. The Countess Varvara introduced the others of the group, one other countess and some counts, ladies- and lords-in-waiting.

The tsaritsa, who was mainly distinctive for her beaky nose, said, "I was delighted to receive that letter from my royal sister Elisabeth. I so much want to meet the Colonel Edge of whom she writes such commendation."

Florian excused himself, turned to hail a roustabout and sent him to bring back Colonel Ramrod, who had departed with the other armed men when no clem occurred.

"We were not exactly spying on you, Herr Florian," said the tsar. "We merely wished to view your regular performance. That is to say, a performance not titivated on our account. But we would wish you to perform for our whole court, when that might be convenient to your troupe."

"Your Majesty's pleasure and command is our convenience," said Florian. He added, "But I assure Your Majesty that we *always* put on the best show of which we are capable, whether it is for royalty or the peasantry. We try never to do less than our best."

Again Alexander humorously remarked that he wished he could command the same from his own underlings.

Edge came and was introduced and also made a sweeping bow. When the tsaritsa had ascertained that he was not fluent in either Russian or German, she said in French:

"My royal sister Elisabeth thinks highly of you." Her eyes twinkled, as if she might have suspected why. "My royal husband has just now invited Monsieur Florian to arrange for us a private court performance of the circus. But may I tender a separate invitation, Colonel Edge, to you and Monsieur Florian and all the rest of the performing troupe, to attend un petit bal bourgeois at the Winter Palace?"

"Avec plaisir, Madame l'Impératrice."

"White tie, at seven of the evening, Sunday, the twentieth of April. You will all be sent billets d'invitation, of course."

"We are honored, Your Majesty. We shall all be there. Everyone who has entertained you today."

Florian wished that Edge had not phrased it quite like that. Unless the gods were awake at dawn tomorrow, and properly attending to their duties, Sir John Fitzfarris would not be attending any palace ball.

7

As everyone on the dueling ground had expected, with dread or with gleeful confidence, the fight was over and done with very quickly.

The Catherine-Court Park was a serene oasis in this industrial suburb of Piter, where all around were tanneries, vodka distilleries, rope and sailcloth manufactories, powered by their waterwheels in the Obvodnyi Canal. The frequent winds off the nearby Gulf of Finland had swept the park almost clean of snow, but now no wind was blowing, and what could be seen in the predawn darkness were well-tended lawns and gravel paths and groves of trees and beds that would be full of flowers in another month or so. However, as the sun rose this morning, it drew from the ground a clammy gray-white mist that swirled thigh high, to make the duelists, the seconds and a couple of spectators seem to be disembodied torsos floating about above the lawn as they prepared for the trial by combat. So the place and the hour provided a properly gloomy and eerie setting for sudden death.

The couple of spectators were Florian and Marchan, who had come because they naturally had an interest in the outcome of the affray, but they took care to stay well out of everyone else's way. While Sarkioglu and Fitzfarris stripped off their overcoats, jackets and shirts, to bare their upper bodies, Edge and the two clowns hovered near to make sure that neither man was concealing a knife or other weapon in his waistband or trouser pocket or boot top. They found nothing. The only thing concealed was the blue half of Fitz's face; even having to rise before dawn today, he had taken the time and trouble to apply his cosmetic mask.

Marchan said, "It is an affair of honor, I understand."

"Not your man's honor, I can tell you," Florian said sourly.

"Then *your* man must hold his honor dearer than life. Regard the two of them. One is slight and lithe—perhaps he would be good at gentlemanly fisticuffs. But the other is as big and heavy and muscled as Hercules. It is a deplorable mismatch. Gospodín, have you prepared a pallet in your carriage, tak, to carry the broken cadaver of your man back to your tsirk?"

Florian ignored Marchan and squinted at the two bare-breasted men, who were about to square off, now that the ground mist was clearing away in wisps and shreds. "Curious," Florian muttered. "The cold has pimpled the invincible Turk with gooseflesh all over. Sir John is shivering, but not otherwise showing the chill. He must be fired with determination."

Then the park's dawn quiet was riven by a roaring war cry from Shadid, and a thunder as he drummed his big fists on his massive chest. Fitzfarris involuntarily took a step back. The Turk lunged forward and Fitz threw his arms high in a protective reflex. That left his own chest vulnerable, and Shadid instantly wrapped his mighty arms around it, either to squeeze Fitzfarris to pulp or to break his back. Apparently flailing in desperation, making the only move he had room and freedom to make, Fitz swiped first one of his forearms, then the other, across the Turk's face. That only made Shadid lower his head and burrow it into the hollow between Fitz's neck and shoulder, where Fitzfarris could not reach to gouge at his eyes, or to do much else besides yank at his back hair. While the Turk had his face protected there, and while he continued to crush Fitz's chest, he also sank his big teeth deep into the flesh at Fitz's collarbone. Fitzfarris was now bent unnaturally backward, very like the deformed Kostchei, and his eyes bulged from the pressure, and his mouth gaped for air that his lungs could no longer pump, and everyone else waited, almost as breathless, to hear his spine snap.

Then, suddenly, the Turk gave another cry—not warlike, but surprised, even distressed. He let go of Fitzfarris and reeled away from him, now using his hands instead to wipe furiously at his face, his eyes, now tight shut, and at his mouth, red with Fitz's blood. He also bore traces of Fitz's makeup. Fitzfarris was free, but for the moment could only crumple to his knees on the grass, gasping for breath and clutching his elbows against his already broken and painful ribs, while blood trickled from his neck.

Shadid was still reeling about, now actually clawing at his eyes and mouth. Then he too went to his knees, and he began grabbing at the grass, scooping from it the mist-deposited moisture to smear frantically on his face. Fitz recovered sufficiently to get shakily to his feet. He stepped over to the Turk and gave him a shove that toppled him over on his back. Shadid seemed uncaring or unaware of his openness to attack; he was still rubbing his wet hands all over his face.

Fitzfarris knelt beside him, drew back his right arm, extended his right hand with fingers straight and tight together, took calculating aim and drove that hand like a spear into the Turk's solar plexus. Shadid gave another cry—of real pain —and now he dropped his hands from his head to clutch at the pit of his stomach. Again Fitz used his rigid hand like a spearhead, and drove it into the Adam's apple of the writhing man. The Turk gave another, weaker, strangled cry, and his whole body convulsed. Fitzfarris used his stiffened hand just once more, this time swinging it sideways, flat, like a blade, with all his strength, at the underside of Shadid's nose. The Turk made no further sound and no more movement except a twitching and quivering from head to foot, and then he lay still. Fitz again got shakily to his feet and, still too breathless to speak, motioned for Edge to fetch his clothes and help him into them.

"Well, I will be damned," breathed Florian.

"Let's gallop back to the tober, Governor," gasped Fitzfarris, when Edge, grinning like a gargoyle, helped him stagger to the rockaway. "So Jules can plug the hole in my neck and strap me back together. I think every last one of my ribs is pulverized."

Edge and Florian helped him up onto the rockaway seat, then sat on either side of him, and they hurried off—leaving the stunned Marchan and his two clowns struggling to lift the limp and heavy corpse of Shadid Sarkioglu.

"All right, tell us how you did it," said Edge.

And Florian said, "I suspected something, Sir John, when I saw that the Turk was covered with goosebumps and you were not."

"Oh, I was. You just couldn't see them." Fitz spoke through teeth clenched against his pain, but he spoke willingly, and with glad pride. "It occurred to me that if I could paint my face with old Mag's makeup, I could paint my upper body and arms, too. So I did, but with more than the cosmetics. Jules gave me carbolic acid from his medicine chest. And Monday offered me some calomel pills she got somewhere. Calomel is only another name for corrosive sublimate, so I powdered the pills and mixed that with the makeup. The carbolic and the calomel just stung my skin a little, but I figured, if I could get some in the Turk's eyes, it would sting a hell of a lot—and evidently it did. But it was his own idea to take a *bite* of that stuff."

"Yes, he deserved what he got," said Florian, and added, not altogether logically, "He chose only arms for weapons, and he broke the code duello when he used his teeth. But that other business, Sir John—killing him by just poking at him...?"

"I had hoped, if I could blind him for a minute, that I might get a headlock on him and break his neck, but Obie said to forget that. He said a strongman's neck is his strongest part. So Obie showed me that trick of using the stiff hand. He said you can kill a man by jamming it up under his breastbone and tearing his guts, or by smashing his Adam's apple so he strangles, or by hitting him hard under the nose. That breaks the bone at the bridge of his nose and drives the splinters up into his brain. But Christ, it took all three to kill *that* big son of a bitch."

"Still, kill him you did," said Florian. "I don't know when I've been more pleased and proud—or more surprised."

"Well," Fitzfarris said modestly, "I had some good advisers to help me do it."

"Hogwash," said Edge, but he was still grinning. "The real truth is that anybody's a damned fool to go into a duel against a cunning and case-hardened old confidence man."

So things settled down to an even tenor again for the circus. Meli was soon well enough to resume her Medusa routine in the sideshow and her struggle with the dragon Fafnir in the blow-off. Monday still lived alone, and seemed to like it. Florian did persuade that balagan to move from the riverside to the Florilegium.

Its proprietor, a Gospodín Tyutchev, ranked his trinket and tidbit and sweetmeat joints along both sides of the entranceway to the chapiteau's front marquee, and put his swinging-boat wheel and toboggan slide on either side at the end nearest the street. He was pleased with the relocation, for it brought him more patronage from the already entertainment-minded jossers than he had enjoyed from strollers on the Neva promenade. Florian was pleased, too, to have a midway again fronting his show, but the stalls and tents were so very shabby and decrepit that he put Dai Goesle and his men to helping the joint keepers patch and paint and furbish them. There was not much anyone could do, though, to improve the aspect of the joint keepers themselves. Men, women and children, they were all ragged, unkempt, bearded where possible and noticeably dirty. They very much resembled the wild "fools of God" who wandered the Russian roads. The circus people, too well remembering their bout with the dristlíva, would never buy anything from those midway joints, but a surprising number of the circusgoers did, even the best-dressed and presumably most finicky of them.

Over most of the next month, the artistes, plus Carl Beck and Dai Goesle, spent much of their free time and a good deal of money in the better shops of the Nevskiy Prospekt and other elegant shopping streets, being fitted for dress suits and ball gowns and buying all the necessary appurtenances. Even Pavlo Smodlaka, for this occasion, "squandered" money on himself, Gavrila and son Velja. (Ioan Petrescu designed and made the gowns for little Sava Smodlaka, for even littler Katalin Szábo and for herself.) All the troupers bought their footwear at Weiss's, the city's best cordonnerie—patent leather, lace-up high shoes for the men, various styles and colors of opera-toed, French-heeled slippers for the women. But there were so many troupers to be dressed that they had to distribute their custom among several different tailleurs and couturiers.

"Even so," said Maurice, "we are probably going to look like pretentious rustics beside the grand uniforms of the gentlemen courtiers and the gowns of those court ladies who order their wardrobes from Warsaw and Paris."

Besides the Slovaks, there were six men of the Florilegium who did not have to scurry about like the others. Edge and Willi Lothar already owned dress wear, but Willi accompanied Jules Rouleau on his shopping expeditions. The Kim brothers, when, with gestures, pantomime and drawings on bits of paper, they were made to understand the nature of a palace ball and the necessity of dressing properly for it, conferred among themselves and then declined. With gestures and pantomime of their own, they conveyed that they would be departing, before too much longer, in the direction of Korea, and in Korea the habiliments of top hat, white tie and tails would be inappropriate, perhaps even derided or vilified, and they would prefer to save their money to take home with them. Kostchei the Deathless also would not attend the ball. Florian did not much want him to, but he felt obliged to point out that the tsaritsa had invited *all* the artistes, and she *had* seen him among them, so she could not have been totally repelled. Kostchei said good-humoredly, "Not only would I be the proverbial skeleton at the feast. Cannot you imagine a tailor going crazy with frustration, trying to fit a tailcoat to my figure?"

Some poor tailor probably *had* gone crazy, several of the troupers decided, by the time he finished making the dress suit specified by Hannibal Tyree. When Hannibal brought it to the tober and proudly displayed it, his colleagues were variously amused and aghast. Though of fine broadcloth, of irreproachable style and cut, the suit was of a color somewhere between pink and pale yellow.

"What y'all gigglin' and gogglin' at?" Hannibal asked. "You folks wears black 'n' white with a pink face up top. I is already black 'n' white—face 'n' teeth—so I wants some *color* in my duds."

"We were overwhelmed, Abdullah, that is all," Agnete said kindly, while the others rearranged their faces and coughed behind their hands. "You paid for your own suit, so you have every right to indulge your personal sense of good taste."

"Yessiree," said Yount, taking his cue from her. "I bet there won't be a uniform in that palace that outglitters you, Hannibal."

While almost everyone else was thus occupied—before, between and after the shows—Edge occupied those times by doing some more solitary roaming about the city. One day he crossed the Neva and visited the Fortress of Saints

Peter and Paul. He viewed with proper reverence the carefully preserved little house of two rooms and spartan furnishings in which Peter the Great had lived while he oversaw the construction of all the other earliest buildings of what would become St. Petersburg. From there, Edge ambled into the fortress's cathedral and inspected the tombs of Peter and the various other tsars and tsaritsas. Then he came across something of rather more immediate interest.

A handsomely dressed young girl was slumped at the foot of a stone cross on which was crucified a stone Jesus. Her head was bowed in her hands, and she was quietly weeping. Edge stood hesitant, wondering whether to approach her and how he might ask what troubled her. But then an old woman did approach, and knelt beside her. The girl raised her tear-streaked face—she was very pretty—and Edge could hear that the two murmured briefly in Russian, then spoke in French. The old woman raised the girl from the floor and led her across the nave. Edge unobtrusively followed and overheard:

"There, my child," the old woman said in French, as she stood the girl before a statue of the Virgin. "If it is that you were betrayed by a man, then pray to Mary, not her son. *Men* only help one another."

Edge was so beguiled by that touching and amusing little occurrence that thereafter, although churches usually bored him, he would at least briefly stop in at any he passed in his wanderings. And so it was that, during Easter week, he stepped into St. Isaac's Cathedral just as the noon mass was commencing, and there saw something marvelous. It made him hurry back toward the tober, but he stopped in a shop along the way to buy a few candles and a spool of black thread. When Carl Beck returned from his latest dress-suit fitting, Edge was waiting to draw him into an earnest consultation—at one point saying, "If we can do it at all, Boom-Boom, we can't do it very often. So we'll save it for the tsar's command performance, whenever that may be. And let's keep it secret from all the others of the company, to surprise them as well."

During the week prior to the ball at the palace, Florian posted notices all about the Tauric Garden to inform the public that there would be no performances on the twentieth of April. As it turned out, that meant no great sacrifice of patronage and receipts. On that day—though it was practically the eve of the short summer of these latitudes, and although the Neva was a river again, with only an occasional ice floe gliding down it—there came an unseasonable and heavy snowfall, so heavy that the streets went unswept, and even the hardy Petersburgers would probably not have braved that weather for the sake of a circus show. The Florilegium troupers were also discomfited by the snowfall. They had intended to ride in droshkis or karétas to the Winter Palace, but now the few vehicles for hire that passed the park—mostly troika sleighs—were all occupied. There was no other way of going there except in the circus's own vehicles, and those, except for Florian's rockaway and Willi's calash, were the vividly painted and garishly lettered wagons—an undignified way, most of them thought, to arrive at the front door of a palace.

However, when they got as far as the Palace Square, it was clear that no one else was likely to notice their mode of transport; there were so many other vehicles—coaches, troika sleighs, berlins, clarences, victorias and every other sort of carriage—converging on the great square from every street and prospekt around it, then jostling and jockeying for precedence at the palace's main entrance.

Also, there was nothing very dignified about the arrival of those other guests. Their drivers bawled at and cursed each other—"Make way, you minétchik, for my lord the Grand Duke!" "To hell with your Grand Duke! Make way for my lady the Princess!"—and the royal or noble or aristocratic occupants of those vehicles leaned from their windows to cry encouragement to their coachmen: "Strike that arrogant ublyúdok with your whip, Vladimir!" Meanwhile, a succession of footmen kept coming out of the palace to assist the fur-swathed guests down from those carriages that did maneuver close to the entrance, and a succession of grooms then led the carriages around to the palace's coach house.

"If this is un petit bal," said Sunday to Meli, "I wonder what un grand bal would be like."

Adding to the throng of vehicles and horses and lookers-on that crowded even this vast square were several troops of mounted soldiers, doing parade-ground drills for the admiration of the arriving guests. Directed by the thunderous commands of their officers, they formed formations and reformed them and column-wheeled-about and oblique-marched, all with admirable precision, making a considerable contrast to the chaotic disorder of the civilians. All the cavalrymen were brilliantly ruddy-cheeked, apparently either from the cold or from enthusiasm to show war-readiness. The horses of each troop were all of the same color, and each troop's color was different from the others'.

"Those on the dapple grays are the Gatchina Guards," Florian told Daphne, who rode beside him on the rockaway. "Those on all-black steeds are the Horse Guards, and those on the chestnuts are the Chevalier Guards."

"You have been doing homework," said Daphne.

"Well, one doesn't want to seem an ignoramus when conversing with the haut monde, as we shortly will be doing."

"I must say, to judge from their behavior here at the front door, one would hardly take them to be the cream of Piter society."

"Ah, well...the Russian temperament. Excitable one moment, melancholic the next."

Anyway, the circus folk all dismounted from their vehicles at a distance from that hubbub, and let the Slovak drivers return them to the tober, with instructions to come back and wait for the partygoers' emergence, at whatever hour that might be. Then they slogged through the churned-up slush of snow to the palace entrance, waited for a break in the procession of aristocrats, and filed in, all in line.

Evidently the doorkeepers and other servants had been told to expect the troupers, and how to recognize them, for the circus people were courteously and hospitably bowed in, and nobody demanded their cards of invitation. That pleased the troupers, for most of them wanted to keep their billets as mementos of the occasion, and some planned to frame and hang them in their caravans. A number of footmen, in white-powdered wigs and a livery of green, red and black, came to relieve the newcomers of their furs and galoshes. Then four hulking *black* footmen appeared, Abyssinian giants, wearing even more exotic costumes of scarlet and gold, with white turbans on their heads. They silently bowed and silently conducted the troupers through several doors and up several massive marble staircases. At either side of every door stood a Chevalier Guard in a uniform of silver, gold and white, unmoving, eyes straight ahead, sabre held rigidly upright at attention. At either side of every sixth tread of every staircase stood a

Kazákh Life Guard, uniformed in red and blue, holding rigidly upright a flaming torch.

Finally the troupe arrived at a grand ballroom and the receiving line where the tsar, the tsaritsa, their two daughters, three of their sons and the wives of the two eldest stood to greet their guests. The Tsar Alexander and his namesake heir-apparent, the Tsesarevich Alexander, wore the sapphire-blue uniform of the Ataman Kazákh Cavalry, with the massive medal of the Cross of St. Andrew—depicting the saint somewhat anomalously crucified on a cross of gold, enamel and diamonds—plus a chestful of other medals and ribbons of decorations presumably awarded by themselves to themselves. The Tsaritsa Maria Alexandrovna wore a dark green taffeta gown, though its fabric was almost indiscernible under its bedizenment of jewels—necklaces, brooches, stomacher—and wore over her shoulder the wide red ribbon of the Order of St. Catherine. The younger tsareviches, their knyagínya wives and the tsarevna daughters were not so splendidly attired, but their garb was by no means tawdry. Except for the two young princess-wives, who were quite petite, the whole family stood so tall that even Obie Yount the Quakemaker felt like a runt when he approached them.

Florian introduced each artiste to the imperial family, all of whom smiled acknowledgment of the troupers' bows and curtsies—their smiles wavering just slightly when they were presented with Abdullah-Hannibal in his pink-yellow dress suit. Only Florian and Ioan could greet their hosts in Russian; several others did so in German or French. When Agnete made her salutation in her native Danish, she was pleasantly startled to have the pretty young wife of the tsesarevich welcome her in the same language. The Knyagínya Maria Feodorovna saw Agnete's surprise, and laughed and said, "I was the Princess Dagmar of Denmark before I married." And when Monday Simms said in English, as precisely as she could, "I am honored, Your Majesties and Highnesses," almost *all* of the troupers were astonished to hear the young Tsarevich Mikhail reply in English, of a sort:

"Och aye, such a verra bonnie lassie is always welcome."

That curious greeting was explained not long afterward. When the last guest had entered the ballroom and the ceremonies of salutation were done, the tsar called for silence and proudly boomed an announcement, which Florian translated for his companions:

"Alexander wishes us all to meet his grandson, who will be brought in by his nurse and displayed for our admiration before he is tucked away for the night."

That was the infant son of the Tsesarevich Alexander and the once-Princess Dagmar: the year-old Nicholas, who would—barring unforeseen circumstances—one day succeed his grandfather and father as emperor, autocrat and tsar. So when the elderly nurse, garbed in a pastel blue uniform, appeared in a doorway with her well-swaddled little burden, the orchestra in an alcove burst loudly into the "Bozhe Tsara Krani" anthem. The male Russian guests cheered "urá!" and all the females ooh-ed and aah-ed. Several of the ladies crowded about the nurse to coo over the baby and tickle his nose and chuck him under the chin and ask motherly questions. The princeling goo-gooed amiably at his admirers, but the old nurse could only say to those querying her in Russian and German and French:

"Ye'll forgi' me, Your Graces, but I canna speak aught but English."

Florian chuckled. "And now we know where the Tsarevich Mikhail learned *his* English. You remember, Clover Lee, how those advertisements for nannies specified English or Scottish. They must be quite the vogue here."

Daphne said, "And apparently the Russians can't tell the difference between them."

When the little prince had been borne away again, the orchestra played softer music, and footmen circulated through the crowd, bearing trays of crystal flutes of champagne. The adults of the imperial family also circulated, each of them trying to converse at least briefly with every guest. The Florilegium folk mingled, too—Florian and Willi as casually as if they were very much at home in such surroundings, the other troupers more shyly, until they discovered that they were rather in demand. It transpired that not only the tsar and tsaritsa had seen the circus perform; so had almost everyone else present, and each of those was eager to talk to any artiste with whom conversation in some common language was possible.

"Tiens!" said the Tsarevna Alexandra. "Do you mean to tell me, Monsieur Pemjean, that you and all your colleagues and animals and—and everything— travel in just twenty-some vehicles?"

"Oui, altesse. As I recall, twenty-six at last count."

"Drôle de chose! Why, when our family goes traveling—no more than six or eight of us—we require four *hundred* carriages."

"Incroyable! Whatever do you carry in them?"

"Well . . . simply so that we may dine properly, we must have our forty cooks and all their kitchen equipment, must we not?"

"Gospodín Tyree, that is a very striking suit of formal clothes," said a dowager who was almost as gaudily dressed as he, but in gems from the vaults of the jewelers Sazikov. "Tell me, is that color a new American fashion?"

Hannibal preened and said grandly, "We's a *Confed'rate* Amer'can circus, ma'am. Dis here's a *Confed'rate* Amer'can fashion."

"Do tell," she said, impressed. "I must make a note." Dangling on a golden chain from one of the lady's plump wrists was what Hannibal had taken to be an ordinary fan. But she now opened it, and it was a sheaf of very thin ivory leaves, pivoting fanwise. With an attached tiny pencil, she scribbled on one of the ivory pages. "I *must* remember to tell my husband, the duke. He does *so* like to be the first in Piter to introduce any new and exotic style of dress."

The orchestra was now playing a Strauss waltz, and most of the elderly or infirm guests moved toward the walls of the ballroom so the younger and spryer ones had room to dance. The middle of the great chamber became a gentle maelstrom of swirling skirts and coat tails, the many-colored gowns and uni- forms contrasting with the starkly elegant black and white of dress suits. The couples moved in their graceful swoops and checks and figures as rhythmically as if they all had rehearsed together in advance to make the lilting music *visible*.

Clover Lee was waltzing with a handsome young captain of the Chevalier Guards, one of the officers who had been directing the cavalry dressage exhibi- tion in the Palace Square earlier. She might not have accepted a mere captain's invitation to dance, except that he had introduced himself as "Kapitán the Graf Evgeniy Suvorov." And now Clover Lee was wondering if she might not be wast- ing her time with this captain-count. Seeing him close, in the radiance of the crystal-cascade chandeliers above, she realized that the ruddiness of his cheeks

—what had appeared, outdoors, to be a manly high coloring—had really been achieved by a liberal application of rouge. Somewhat scathingly, she remarked on that fact.

"Da," said Suvorov, managing a small shrug while he danced. "All of us officers must do it so. The emperor likes his troopers to look warlike, burned by sun and wind and cold."

Clover Lee looked about. There were many other officers waltzing, some of them with her sister artistes; and, sure enough, they were all rouged. So maybe, she thought, she was *not* wasting her time. Knowing that she had sounded critical of the rouge, Clover Lee now hastened to praise Evgeniy's resplendent uniform, and added, "I wish I could get my circus tights to fit so snugly."

"Ah, you refer to the breeches? Actually, they are a torment, Mademoiselle Coverley. Elk skin, they are, and we should be disgraced if they showed a singe wrinkle or crease. So, before they are put on, they are well wetted and smeared inside with soap. Then it requires at least one other fellow officer to help haul them onto—er—onto the bare extremities, where they dry excruciatingly tight."

"Captain Suvorov! You are *naked* underneath them?" Clover Lee tried to sound scandalized, and demurely lowered her eyes—though only to keep the count from seeing the mischievous merriment in them. "Should you be telling a modest maiden stranger such naughty things?"

The waltz ended and the dancers thanked the musicians with a polite patter of applause. Clover Lee waited to be either escorted off the floor or asked to dance again. Instead, the young Captain Suvorov stammered, "It—it seems a little warm in here." That was true. Because of the unseasonable weather, the servants working inside the palace walls had stoked and fired up the big tile stoves in the corners of the ballroom. They were burning an aromatic wood that nicely perfumed the whole ballroom, but the heat had become a trifle oppressive. Suvorov, however, looked warmer than the heat would have accounted for. "Perhaps—perhaps you would care for a refreshing stroll, mademoiselle. I could—I could walk you to the coach house and show you a most remarkable sleigh..."

He swallowed nervously and seemed unable to believe his good fortune when Clover Lee smiled, took his arm and said, "Let us do that, Evgeniy. I've never been shown a remarkable sleigh before."

When the next waltz commenced, almost all of the other troupers had got over their shyness and were taking the floor—Pemjean with the Tsarevna Alexandra, Hannibal with the dowager duchess, Pfeifer and Goesle and Beck with other ladies of the court, Fitzfarris and Yount and LeVie with their own women. Little Katalin danced with Velja Smodlaka, but even that child was rather too tall for her.

Numbers of the guests not dancing left the ballroom for another across the hall. That one was equally vast, and in its middle was a table the size of the Florilegium's pista—a ring of tables, actually, linen-clothed and crowded with sterling silver samovars, crystal decanters, stacks of gold-inlaid porcelain tableware, snowy serviettes, silver flatware, and salvers and tureens and bowls displaying what appeared to be every finest sort of viand that ever came from a kitchen. There was one gap in the ring, at its far side, and a constant procession of scullions trotted in and out through it, to the kitchens and back. Whenever a hot dish among the buffet array threatened to cool, or a cold dish to get tepid, it was instantly whisked away and a replacement brought.

Inside the ring of tables was a tremendous round table piled with extra supplies to replenish those on the outer ring. It was decorated, besides—heaped with hothouse flowers, from the center of which heap towered a massive, rough-hewn block of plain ice. Between the inner and outer tables waited a score or so of white-uniformed servers, ready to ladle into dishes the helpings of any delicacy a guest pointed at, and to fill glasses with tea or goblets with wine or flutes with champagne.

Florian approached the buffet with the Tsaritsa Maria Alexandrovna on one arm and Daphne on the other. His rapt gaze took in the flamboyant spread of food and drink, then moved upward past the bank of flowers to the centerpiece, and he wondered what significance there might be in an unsculptured square pillar of ice. But then Daphne gasped, and at the same moment Florian descried the figure frozen inside that block. Seen through the rough-cut ice, it was wavery, but discernible as the figure of a young girl wearing a peasant costume—the bright and ornate costume she would have worn to a country festival. And that had been artfully disarranged: the skirt rucked up on one side to show a bare and shapely leg, the blouse pulled down from a shoulder to expose nearly all of one breast.

"Do you like the centerpiece, Monsieur Florian, Madame Wheeler?" asked the tsaritsa. "Our chef d'embellissement sometimes confects a cake in the semblance of Saint Isaac's Cathedral, or does the Admiralty in spun sugar. This morning he was inspired by the unseasonable snow to take for the motif of tonight's ball an old Russian folktale. It tells of a poor krepostnoy girl—a serf—who was gathering firewood on a mountain when she fell through the snow into a crevasse. She emerged a hundred years later and a hundred versts away, frozen in the wall of a glacier, still as young and beautiful as the day she perished."

"A poignant tale, Your Majesty, and the chef has illustrated it most magically. He has achieved a really lifelike model of the girl within."

"A model?" said the tsaritsa. "Why, I suppose...really, I never thought to ask..." Florian felt Daphne's hand tremble on his arm, and the tsaritsa disengaged hers, saying briskly, "Now, do enjoy yourselves. I must excuse myself to have a word with old Admiral Count Gordeyev yonder."

"I think I have lost my appetite," Daphne said in horror, when the tsaritsa was out of hearing. "Florian, that is a...real...live...girl frozen in there. Anyway, she was alive this morning. Frozen, just to amuse—"

"Hush, my dear. Perhaps she is artificial. Let us assume she is. At least take some food, not to be conspicuous. You need not eat it if you cannot."

They selected a modest repast—caviar, cheek of herring soup, broiled livers of peacock, flake pastry and a Crimean wine. When the server had prepared their plates, he did not hand them to Florian and Daphne, but to a footman who was suddenly at their side. That servant bowed them to an unoccupied one of the many small tables that filled the rest of the big room. He set down their plates, held their chairs for them and bowed himself away. Daphne had only just taken a large, restorative draft of her wine when the footman was back again, bringing a third plate bearing the identical viands they had selected; then he bowed himself away again without explanation.

"What is the extra plate for?" asked Daphne.

"I don't know," said Florian. "Perhaps it is the custom. To anticipate our wanting second helpings."

"I don't even want firsts," said Daphne, shuddering again and averting her eyes from the ice block. But she did begin to nibble at a cracker heaped with caviar.

The coach house next door to the palace was almost as stately and well appointed as the palace itself, but chill and dark inside. Captain Count Suvorov lit a lantern to guide Clover Lee to the "remarkable sleigh." That description, she decided, was a considerable understatement. The vehicle was on runners and its front end had all the attachments necessary for hitching horses to it, but there its resemblance to a sleigh ended. It was, in fact, the biggest and most luxurious caravan Clover Lee had ever seen.

"It was built to the order of Ekaterina the Great," said Suvorov. "It required four spans of four horses apiece to draw it."

"And I bet even sixteen horses couldn't go faster than a walking pace with that load," said Clover Lee, in awe. They climbed inside and went through the sleigh's interior, which was lined with porcelain, fine woods and decorative tiles.

Suvorov identified the various features. "This is Ekaterina's sitting room, where she rested on this chaise longue while the sleigh was in motion. This is the dining room. This is the bedroom and, off it, the lavatory..."

"Ah, truly a voluptuous-looking bed," said Clover Lee. "I wonder, is it comfortable?"

Captain Suvorov looked *not* quite comfortable, and babbled on, "No one uses the sleigh nowadays. The muzhiks would think the imperial family overweeningly pretentious if—"

"It *is* a fine, big bed," said Clover Lee, reclining on it, languorously, invitingly. "Catherine must have had good times here."

"Ahem. Mademoiselle, it is cold in this place. Perhaps we should return to the ball."

Clover Lee sat up and said indignantly, "Do you mean you actually did invite me out here only to show me Great Catherine's sleigh? You had no other diversion in mind?"

"In mind, yes, mademoiselle," Suvorov said wretchedly. "But also in constricting elk-skin breeches. I should have to summon the stable boys just to—"

"Oh, never mind!" snapped Clover Lee, flouncing angrily off the bed. "I wouldn't want your bare shanks to get cold. By all means, let us return to the ball."

Florian and Daphne discovered the reason for the additional plate that had been set beside theirs. Tsar Alexander had entered the dining hall and was drifting from table to table, pausing to sit for a brief while at each. Every table had an extra plate, so he could take just a bite, and the table's other occupants could afterward claim truthfully that they had dined with the emperor. When Alexander came to sit with Florian and Daphne, he glanced at what they were eating—Daphne still nibbling at a caviar cracker, Florian spooning up soup— and himself took a dab of caviar and a sip of soup, while expressing in not very fluent French the hope that they were enjoying themselves.

Florian assured him that they were, and Daphne refrained from any comment on the presence of a dead serf girl at the feast. Then Alexander said in German, "Herr Florian, would you accompany me to my chambers for a private conversation? Perhaps the Frau Wheeler would excuse our impoliteness and accept Marshal Krylov's invitation to dance?" Apparently in response to some invisible signal, a middle-aged Horse Guards officer, stout and wearing Dundreary whiskers, was there and bowing to Daphne. Florian explained to her in English, and she made a moue of mystification, but obediently went with Krylov to the other ballroom.

The tsar, waving away the various guards and servants who started to join him, led Florian up another marble staircase and through various magnificent rooms and halls to his own suite, where the door was flanked by two catatonically rigid sentries of the Golden Company of Imperial Grenadiers. The tsar's rooms were scant on furniture, but every piece was exquisite. Alexander went first to his Karelian birchwood sideboard, on which stood a ewer and basin, each cut from a single solid amethyst. He poured water and washed his hands, explaining, "I had to shake hands just now with the Emir of Bokhara. I always wash after being touched by someone of another religion."

Then he waved Florian to an armchair, took the one opposite, leaned forward and said, "You are from Alsace, a land long ambiguous of national identity. Your circus's second in command, Colonel Edge, is a Virginian. In effect, now a man without a country. The others of your troupe comprise an assortment of nationalities."

"Your Majesty is well informed."

Alexander made a dismissive gesture. "The Third Section of my chancery keeps a detailed dossier on all foreigners, resident or transient. For example, I know that you brought your circus through what is now being called the Seven Weeks' War—adroitly dodging between the opposing armies. I gather that you personally favored neither Austria nor the Prussian-Italian alliance in that war. However, I daresay you know why it was fought."

"Circus people are apolitical, Your Majesty, but not ignorant. Everyone in Europe is aware of Chancellor Bismarck's ambition to weld together a Reich of all the German-speaking peoples."

"Of which people I happen to be one, Herr Florian. You will have noticed that German is the everyday language of this court. My mother was a Prussian, my grandmother a Württemberger, my great-grandmother an Anhalter. My own empress wife is a Hessian, so my sons have even less Russian blood than I do. When I address King Wilhelm of Prussia as 'cousin,' it is no idle court formality."

"I am sure, Your Majesty, that the world understands why you supported Prussia in that Seven Weeks' War."

"Which is more than Wilhelm did. He is an old man, and all he wants is a peaceful old age. So he has handed the reins to his scheming chancellor. Now Bismarck has humbled Austria and established Prussia as preeminent among the Germanic lands. He has already absorbed Schleswig-Holstein and Hanover. And he can count on adding to his confederation those other states—Hesse, Baden, Saxony—which previously disdained his idea of an empire. Next, of course, Bismarck will want to seize Alsace and, by doing so, flaunt the German people's superiority over the French. He will find or contrive some pretext for a war with France. In a year or thereabouts, I should estimate. And, if he wins that war, I shall be expected to rejoice on behalf of my cousin Wilhelm, and call him no longer king but Kaiser. However"—Alexander held up a hand as if Florian had untimely applauded—"I cannot ignore the fact that Prussia lies just the other side of Russia's Polish and Lithuanian borders. If or when my cousin is emperor of a united and powerful German Reich, I should find him a most uncomfortable next-door neighbor."

"Are you saying, Your Majesty, that you would support France in a contest against Prussia?"

"Surely you do not expect me to answer that directly." Alexander leaned back in his chair, steepled his fingers and said, "France is a mob. It has always been a mob. Frenchmen are at their most French when they are in a mob. Their royal courts and their councils and their clergy have been only better-washed mobs. Louis Napoléon is nothing but an opportunistic arriviste. Nevertheless, he did retrieve the imperial crown from the quagmire of republicanism."

"So you feel an imperial kinship."

"To preserve the Russian empire, I must be concerned with the fate of other empires. When Bismarck pushes the European states about like chess pieces, he endangers the very concept of monarchy. France teems with Communards who await only an excuse to topple the throne there once again. My own Russia has its lurking Nigilists and People's Freedom cults, agitating for the same kind of overthrow. My emancipation of the krepostnoyi did not curb their desire to shed imperial blood. Meanwhile, Russian emigrants living in western Europe have formed what they call a Populist party, also preaching revolution, and at a safe distance from my reach. Our young people who go to study abroad get infected with those radical notions, and come home carrying the fomites of that disease. If Prussia defeats France in a war, the French Communards will have their excuse for rising against Louis Napoléon, calling him inept and impotent. It could mean revolutions again, like those of 1848, in almost every kingdom and empire. Including mine."

"If I read your intentions rightly, sir, you would stay aloof from a war between Prussia and France—but meanwhile try to maintain a balance between those two powers, so that neither is preeminent in Europe."

"Exactly. It is fortunate, for my purpose, that the French are very fond of eating snow partridge."

Florian blinked. "I beg your pardon?"

"The biggest and tastiest birds of the partridge family. We have an abundance of them in our mountains, and we regularly export them to the Paris markets. They are plucked and cleaned, then shipped in wicker baskets packed with oats, to prevent the birds' getting bruised."

"I am sorry, Your Majesty, but I do not quite—"

"Every customs office at every border from here to France is eternally vigilant against contraband. They scrupulously search and inspect most goods going through. But those officers have got so accustomed to our baskets of birds in oats that they routinely let them pass. And among those oats can be concealed communications in cipher, to be sifted out by my Third Section agents in Paris. I have succeeded in getting many messages to Louis Napoléon by that means, unknown to my cousin Wilhelm and the ever-watchful Chancellor Bismarck, unknown to Napoléon's own ministers and advisers, unknown even to my own diplomatic officers in Paris and elsewhere."

"Ingenious, Your Majesty," said Florian, wondering why he was being told these things.

"Unfortunately, Louis Napoléon does not always appreciate my good advice, or take the measures I recommend. I suppose I cannot blame him. I might be equally suspicious if foreign secret agents were to bring me similar advices. However, if the messages came by way of a third and demonstrably disinterested party... and I can think of none more politically innocuous than your circus, Herr Florian. You have been overheard to say that your next destination will be Paris. When do you plan to be there?"

Florian was taken aback. He had made that remark more than once, but he could not remember any strangers being within eavesdropping distance at any of those times. He collected himself and said, "I have made no firm plans, Your Majesty. We will not leave Saint Petersburg until after we have enjoyed the White Nights of midsummer here. Probably we will depart when the winter again approaches. But I have not yet given thought to our route."

"To go overland from here to Paris would be an arduous journey and take a hellishly long time. Suppose you went by ship, direct to some western Baltic port."

"Well, we have traveled by merchant vessel before. But now we have become such a large and cumbersome aggregation—"

"A line-of-battle ship would accommodate you easily."

Florian blinked again. The tsar explained, "All of the world's heads of government have been invited to attend or send emissaries to the grand opening of the Suez Canal in November. My ambassador will depart from here in September, and of course I am sending him in fitting style, aboard my newest steam battle cruiser, the *Pyëtr-Velík*. Your circus could accompany him as far as, say, Kiel in Schleswig-Holstein."

"Your Majesty makes a very generous and inviting offer. But if your warship is steaming all the way around Europe to Egypt, why should we not stay aboard until—oh, perhaps Le Havre, whence it is a much shorter run to Paris?"

"Because—to be blunt, Herr Florian—I shall ask you to pay for your passage, in a manner of speaking. It requires your crossing the German lands to enter France."

"I had assumed, sir, that you intended for us to carry some message. But are you wishing us to *spy* along the way? I fear we are all inexperienced at such—"

"I shall ask only that you keep your eyes open. If no one else is capable of that, your ex-cavalry colonel Edge certainly should be. I would tell you and him beforehand what to look for."

"Well..."

"Naturally, you will wish to think it over and talk it over with Colonel Edge. I should prefer, though, that not too many of your people know all the details of this proposal."

"I promise to be most discreet, Your Majesty."

"I shall give you plenty of time to consider, before we meet again—and we had best meet under social circumstances, as we did tonight. Suppose we set a date for your circus to perform for my court, when we have removed to one of our summer palaces. You mentioned the White Nights. So let us fix the engagement for one of those longest days of all the year." Alexander leaned to a table on which sat a desk calendar. "The ninth of June? The court will be then at Peterhof. Would that be satisfactory?"

"Eminently so, Your Majesty."

"You can give me your decision then, as to whether you wish to avail yourself of my offer of sea transport. If you do so desire, I will give you and Colonel Edge some messages and a few instructions. I will give you also a persuasive letter of introduction to His Imperial Majesty Louis Napoléon. That should help advance the fortunes of your own enterprise, Herr Florian, but bear in mind that you might, at the same time, be influencing the course of history. For the better, I believe." The tsar stood up; so did Florian. "You leave first, mein Herr. I think you can find your way again to the ballroom. From now on, we should be seen seldom together."

Florian bowed himself out, between the two still-rigid Grenadier sentries. He went back the way he had been brought, until he came to a corridor in which there were no guards or servants or anybody else to see him. There, very sprightly for a man of his age and build, he leapt into the air and clicked his heels together.

8

ONE DAY in the middle of May, Vassily Marchan drove onto the tober with a wagonful of fresh-faced, wide-eyed girls, his dancing ushers. Each of the girls had her performing costume wrapped in a knotted big kerchief. They got down from the wagon and looked about with apparent pleasure at being there.

"I brought them to get acquainted with your establishment, Gospodín Florian," said Marchan. "And perhaps your dirizhér will wish to rehearse their music with them. Other than that, tak, you need have no concern about them—not even feeding or quartering them. They go to their homes for meals and sleep."

"Excellent. But before we conclude this exchange, Gospodín Marchan, tell me one thing. Will their parents allow them to travel as far abroad as Peterhof?"

"Agá! You have been accorded an imperial command performance! Da, the girls can go that far. It is only some thirty versts from here. You can all go there and back by railroad train in a day. That railway was the first ever built in Russia—naturally—it being for the tsar's convenience."

"We shall go by road. Make parade into Peterhof. And go a few days early, to show in any village or villages along the road."

"There is only Prival between here and Peterhof. You would not wish to set up there. The perpetual wind off the Gulf of Finland would carry away your chapiteau."

"Oh, I intend to leave all our tops in position here, for we shall be returning to finish out the summer season. At Peterhof—and at Prival—we will show in the open air. My canvasmaster and engineer are already making extra poles and gumshoes and guys to support the aerial rigging."

"I shall explain to the girls, then, that they will be away from Piter for some days. They will surely get their parents' permission, when they know it is at the tsar's behest."

"Thank you, gospodín. And here come your Kim brothers. Be good to them; they are fine fellows."

The Koreans, frisking and beaming, piled their few belongings in Marchan's wagon, then went about vigorously shaking hands and bowing to everybody of the Florilegium, even the Slovaks, and saying over and over, "Anyong-hi kesip-sio." All the female artistes also kissed the Kims on the cheek as they shook hands, and said, "Good-bye. Good luck. Travel safely. Happy homecoming."

As the wagon rattled off, with the brothers still waving back at the tober, Ioan Petrescu took charge of the new girls. She shepherded them away from the appreciative ogling and murmured commentary of the male troupers, to the dressing wagon, to see if their costumes needed any refitting or furbishing.

It was not until the next day that Hannibal, who now had the formerly shared caravan all to himself, came to Florian carrying a half-full sack. "Sahib, dem Chinks left somep'n. A bag o' that macaroni they was always fryin'."

"Good Lord. If they've had that ever since Italy, it must be full of weevils and mold by now. But thank you, Abdullah. I'll be going downtown later. I'll drop it off at the Cinizelli, if it has not yet departed."

It had. There was only an aged dvornik left as custodian, and he was a Kalmuk who barely spoke Russian. He waved his hands at the emptiness of the building's interior and said, "Podí k' Krimu."

"Podí, eh?" said Florian. "Gospodín Marchan wastes no time. Wait—what was that? Gone to the Crimea? You mean Korea, old man."

"Koréya? You crazy, gospodín? Nobody goes Koréya. Marchan *always* go Krimu in summer."

"I would like to think it was only tit for tat," Florian grumbled afterward to Edge. "We did cost Marchan his strongman. But clearly he was lying from the moment he suggested the exchange."

"Well, you said those Kim boys were going around the world. They're just going the long way around. At least they won't be backtracking westward... with us spies."

With some exasperation, Florian said, "Call it scouting, not spying. I truly do not understand your objection to my accepting the tsar's proposal. Good heavens, man, you've done ranging duty in two wars already."

"You don't reckon two wars are enough in any man's lifetime?"

"Confound it! We may be helping to *prevent* one."

"And we may be risking our necks. But look, Governor, it's your decision to make, and I'll abide by it. I just want to go on record as the loyal opposition."

The days got longer and longer—*unnaturally* longer, it seemed to most of the circus company. By the first of June (as reckoned by the Russian calendar) the sun was not dipping below the horizon until nearly midnight—what the dancing girls told Florian was called at this season "the noon of night"—and then dipped only long enough to let the city rest in a long twilight and a very brief night. The night did not get fully dark until about half past midnight, and stayed that way for only about three hours before it began to lighten again. Early or late in the twenty-one-hour day, people walked about trailing unbelievably long, thin, black shadows, as if they were dragging fallen steeples around with them. When the moon rose, it was always gilded by the nearby sun, sometimes flushed to vermilion or scarlet or crimson.

The Petersburgers took every advantage of the warm long days and the balmy White Nights. At almost any hour, the streets and prospekti were thronged with strollers. The upper-class folk, who had paraded on the sheltered Morskaya in the wintertime, now arrogated to themselves the broad and airy

Nevskiy Prospekt, and there displayed a no longer fur-muffled variety of ladies' fine gowns, jewels and hair styles, gentlemen's side-whiskers, chin whiskers, eccentric whiskers and some beards so long that they were worn tied under the cravat.

At almost any hour, too, the riverside promenade was lined with fishermen leaning over the balustrade with extremely long poles, and they usually were standing deep in "summer snow," the drifts of white fluff dropped by the poplar trees that also lined the promenade. Younger Petersburgers swam in the Neva, but not venturing too far from the bank into that turbulent current. On several nights in succession, when the circus performers emerged from the chapiteau after the night show—which now was actually a twilight show—they saw bonfires burning at intervals along the riverbank. Numbers of young men and women, wearing old clothes but with wreaths of flowers on their heads, were jumping over those fires and into the Neva. Florian inquired of the usher girls about that, and translated to the rest of the company:

"An old custom, they say. Those are all young bachelors and spinsters, and every one's wreath is distinctive enough to be recognizable. When the jumpers hit the water, they let the wreaths float loose. Then, at dawn, in a couple or three hours, they'll go downstream to search for them. Each can tell—or so say these girls—from the position and condition of his or her wreath whether he or she will be married before this time next year."

"Maybe some of *us* ought to try that," Clover Lee muttered to Sunday. But if they did, they did not report the outcome of it.

The warm weather brought to the swamp-encircled and often rain-drenched city one almost intolerable bane: a superabundance of mosquitoes. Sometimes the circus's audiences seemed to be continuously applauding, they were so frenziedly slapping at mosquitoes. The aerial artistes, and those ground performers who also had to maintain an undistracted concentration and balance, could work only after they had slathered themselves with an insect-repellent mixture that Ioan compounded for them, of oil of cedar and spirits of camphor—and then they reeked so that they quite repelled even each other.

"No wonder the zar has summer palaces everywhere except here," growled Yount, after he had whacked his shaven head so often and so angrily that he was groggy.

"Yes," said Katalin. "I imagine, out there beside the gulf, the sea wind sweeps away the vermin. Well, we will soon know, Obie. We start for Peterhof tomorrow."

The roustabouts worked through most of that night, having to use lanterns only during the darkest two hours or so, to take down the chapiteau's aerial rigs and take up its pista curbing, and pack into wagons everything that the circus was taking to Peterhof. They left standing the chapiteau and its tiers of seats, the menagerie and sideshow and dressing tops. Three Slovaks were delegated to stay and take eight-hour shifts as watchmen around the clock. Florian also was leaving behind every wagon that was not needed for transport or quarters, including the red wagon.

"But how I sell tickets at Prival?" Gavrila asked anxiously.

"It would be futile to try," said Florian. "We shall be performing in the open, freely visible to all who want to watch. I do not mind giving that show gratis. It will be the first time that most of our people have worked under no pavilion but the sky. That rehearsal should preclude any misadventures when we similarly perform on the palace grounds. I just hope it doesn't rain during either show."

The rains held off, but there had been so many previous deluges that the road from Piter to Prival was fifteen versts of mud. The circus did not make parade; it had to struggle just to make progress. Sometimes the mud was ooze, into which the wagons sank nearly to their wheel hubs, and Peggy and Mitzi had often to nudge them free. Sometimes the mud was sticky, and on those stretches the wagon wheels accumulated it and got begummed to such thickness and heaviness that they had to be stopped and scraped clean. Jörg Pfeifer, pressed into that job with every other ablebodied man of the train, said peevishly, "The tsar has a railroad to ride on, so he doesn't give a Furz for the scheissegal roads his people have to use."

When they were again rolling, Edge remarked to Sunday, riding beside him, "Now that we can see this north country not covered with snow, it's really an earth-colored land, isn't it? Where the mud is not brown, it's black or it's ocher. And where the ground isn't mud, it's grit. Even the people's clothes are earth-colored. You can't tell the peasants from the scarecrows, unless they're walking."

"Notice something else, Zachary?" said Sunday. "No farmhouse has a garden or a window box of flowers. Even the wild flowers are few and puny and pale. You're right. It's a gritty country."

By the clock, it should have been nighttime when the train got to Prival, but of course the sun was still well up. The name Prival meant merely "stopping place," for that was where troops marching between St. Petersburg and Peterhof customarily paused for refreshment, an overnight rest and perhaps a roll in the hay, if they were desperate enough to utilize the scrawny or obese peasant women with the vapid faces of cows, muddy complexions and real mud all over the rest of them. Fortunately for the circus, the frequent troop movements had trodden and compacted a firm drill ground amid the surrounding sea of mud. So Florian stood up on his rockaway and announced to the collected and vacuously gaping villagers that his circus would set up and show on that ground after dark, if any of them wanted to stay awake late enough to see it. In the meantime, he said, his troupe would be pleased to pay for a meal.

There was a mess hall for the transient soldiers, so the company dined there —the artistes first, while Goesle, Beck and Banat supervised the roustabouts in their first setup of center poles that did not have to support canvas. They also fitted together the curb sections to make the pista, and spread straw inside it, and outside it ranged the carbide-fired footlights and spotlights.

Gusztáv Jászi scowled at the food set before him and said in Magyar, "Almost I would rather be out there laboring than eating this ürülek." The troupe had been served the same meal the villagers were accustomed to give the passing soldiers, and what they themselves ate day after day—in short, the only meal they could provide. It consisted only of buckwheat porridge, boiled cabbage, black rye bread, salted cucumbers, tea and kvas.

"Consider it *not* shit, and certainly not food, but merely sustenance," said Ioan in the same language. "To sustain you as far as Peterhof, where again we shall be feasting."

The entire population of Prival did stay up to squat in a circle beyond the pista and watch the show, though they watched it with the same torpor that a troop drill would have inspired in them, and never applauded or laughed once.

The artistes didn't much mind that; in fact, they rather wished they could achieve the impassivity of the audience. They waited nervously while the ex-Cinizelli usher girls danced their overture. Then, from their first march out of the darkness into the lighted pista, doing the opening Grand Promenade, the artistes felt almost naked in the breeze blowing constantly from the north and with nothing but black emptiness and some twinkling stars above them. Even the marching elephants, camel, horses and terriers rolled their eyes uneasily upward. As Boom-Boom conducted his bandsmen, he had to make repeated lifting gestures of his hands, bidding them play ever more forte, so the music would not sound thin in all that space. Only the calliope of the Slovak "professor" did not have to exert itself; that instrument was designed for the wide-open outdoors.

However, once the artistes were performing, the familiar surrounding glow of limelight and their concentration on their work enabled most of them to forget the absence of a roof, and almost all of them easily adjusted to the novel ambience. Colonel Ramrod, for the first time in his shootist exhibition, had to allow for windage—and he supposed that so did Maurice and Sunday on the traps, Monday on the rope, Daphne and Yount on their high velocipede, even little Cricket inside her rolling globe. Only Pavlo Smodlaka seemed still agitated, unable to accept the new circumstances. The night was not warm, with the breeze coming off the gulf, but Pavlo sweated oilily in the limelight, and fumbled his commands to the dogs and the albino children and his wife, and kept glancing up at the sky, which had begun ruddily to lighten in the east. But Terry, Terrier and Terriest went unperturbed and efficiently through their brisk routine, as they probably could have done without any commands at all.

Because the audience was so apathetic, and because the sideshow people had often before exhibited outdoors, Florian did not interrupt the program for an intermission. The pista performers worked straight on through all their acts to the closing spec. That was marched to the "Bozhe Tsara Krani" anthem, and Rouleau had memorized the Russian words to sing, but not one of the villagers stood in salute. So Florian himself pranced around the perimeter in front of the squatting spectators, pounding his own hands together. Thus prodded, the villagers came half-alive and clapped halfheartedly. As Goesle slowly dimmed his lights and the troupers disbanded, the muzhiks also got up and drifted toward their izba huts, with something of the air of having been finally excused from an ordeal.

"Merde alors," muttered Rouleau. "I hope the open air does not similarly stupefy our audience at the palace."

"No fear," said Willi. "Peasants are un merdier, indeed. We will not be performing to peasants at Peterhof. Ah, regardez—the moon rises. A full moon tonight, red as blood."

"And listen," said Rouleau. "A wolf is baying in the far distance." That mournful, long-drawn ululation had barely died away when it was echoed, and loudly, and close by. Immediately the elephants began trumpeting, the cats roaring, the hyenas barking, the horses whinnying. Rouleau exclaimed, "Putain! That one must be right here near the tober—after the animals, perhaps!"

He and Willi went running from the drill ground to where the wagons, caravans and cages had been ranked. Other people were running, too, and still others were leaning from their van doors or windows. At one of the caravans, the lamplight spilling from its open door showed two figures struggling together. Edge was the first to get there and was momentarily relieved to see that it was only Gavrila trying to restrain her daughter, who appeared to be trying to bolt into the darkness.

"Where are you off to, kid?" Edge demanded. "What's going on, Gavrila?"

The woman's face was contorted and tear-stained. "Sava wishes to run and find her father."

"Jules, hold the girl here. All right, Gavrila, where has her *father* gone off to?"

"The moon—" she sobbed.

"What? Oh, come *on*, Gavrila."

"The moon rises full. Pavlo makes wolf noise. He runs into night. Velja I could not stop, he runs after to catch. Is terrible, Zachary! Every time moon comes full, even in city, Pavlo get neudoban—strange."

"She's right," said Florian. "I saw him run away like this once before."

"By damn," said Edge. "I remember now—old Mag telling me to watch out for something he might do. The crazy bastard thinks he's a werewolf. What do we do, Governor?"

"Everybody fan out," Florian said to the now considerable gathering of circus men. "Head for the moonrise yonder. Try not to fall in any swamp. Let Pavlo run if he wants to, but find the boy and bring him back. There *are* wolves out there."

The men dispersed into the night, all except Edge, who went to arm himself first. The villagers had also been aroused by the commotion, and a crowd of half-dressed peasant men stood dumbly looking on. Florian told them about the demented man and asked if they would help search for him. They only continued to stand and stare bovinely, so he added, "On sam voöbrayet sobóy oborotyen."

"Oborotyen!" the muzhiks repeated, in a gasp, and showed the first emotion they had shown yet—a mixture of awe, horror and, curiously, almost gleeful eagerness. They did not, however, run impetuously toward the moonrise. They went to their huts, got fully dressed and, when they returned to Florian, were carrying staves, scythes, wooden pitchforks and, sensibly, lighted candle lanterns. The headman of the village also carried a small dagger, which he showed to Florian, saying reassuringly, "Syeryebró."

"Silver? My God, don't kill the man! He only imagines he is a werewolf. Only *imagines* it. Voöbrayet—*voöbrayet!*"

The peasants merely gave him a leave-it-to-us wave and went off with their lanterns and weapons. Florian stayed, trying to comfort and calm Gavrila and Sava, and shooed the rest of the company back to their own quarters. The genuine wolf, still off in the far distance, howled at the crimson moon from time to time, but now there was no echo to its baying. Florian wished Pavlo *would* give voice again. It might distress his womenfolk to hear it, but it would help the searchers locate him.

Perhaps an hour passed, and the sun was also about to rise, the day already lightening, when one of the villagers returned from the manhunt, came up to Florian and said guardedly, "Est' sumashédshiy."

Gavrila asked urgently, "Florian, does that mean they found Pavlo? Velja?"

"Probably Pavlo. This one said 'crazy man.' You two get inside your caravan and lock the door. Don't open it to anyone but me."

Florian waited to make sure they obeyed, then followed the muzhik. They went some distance from Prival, and the day got light enough that the guide blew out his lantern. They came to the other villagers, gathered in a huddle, and they parted to let Florian see Pavlo. He lay on the swampy ground on his back, the silver dagger hilt-deep in his chest. Pavlo's mad eyes were still open and glaring, and his lips were curled in a lupine snarl that bared his teeth. There was very little blood about the neat dagger puncture in his breast, but his teeth, lips and beard were shiny and clotted with red smears and gobbets, as if in his dying he had vomited up blood and bits of his insides.

The village headman was explaining to Florian what had happened when there was a rustling in the brush nearby, and Edge emerged from there, a revolver at the ready in each hand. When he had taken in the situation, he uncocked the pistols, let them hang at his sides, and walked over to look stonily down at the dead Pavlo.

"I told them not to kill him," said Florian. "But they claim he rushed upon them—out of that thicket you just came from—gnashing his teeth and flexing his fingers like a wolf's claws. They *had* to kill him, they say. One stunned him with a club and the headman expertly dispatched him with the dagger in his heart. They are all thanking God that it was a silver dagger. I don't know whether to berate them or—"

"Hell, you ought to give every man of them a gold medal," said Edge. He raised one of his pistols and fired three times in the air. "That should fetch the other fellows."

"Why call them in? The boy is still out there somewhere."

"No, he's not. He's in that thicket." Florian made a move, but Edge stopped him. "Don't go and look, Governor. I wish I hadn't. Christ, I thought a *real* wolf had got him."

Florian stared at Edge, swallowed several times, finally sighed and managed to say, "Well, before the others get here, let us make it look as if that *is* what happened."

So the late Pavlo was made tidy of face and messy of body. They closed his lunatic eyes and snarling mouth and scrubbed the blood and other substances from his lips and beard with a handful of leaves. Then Edge plucked loose the dagger from his chest, took a deep breath and—to the mystification of the watching peasants—used the dagger to do some additional, deliberately inexpert hacking at Pavlo's torso, so that his clothes got drenched with blood and the nature of his wounds was not easily discernible. The muzhiks may by now have thought *all* these foreigners insane, but one of them readily parted with his shabby felt cloak when Florian offered him a gold imperial for it. Edge took the cloak into the clump of bushes and, after a minute, returned with it enfolding a limp small burden that he did not then or afterward unwrap. When the other circus men, by ones and twos, found Florian and Edge, they were shown only Pavlo's body and were informed that the wolf they all had heard howling had killed both father and son. The men somberly shook their heads, Yount and one of the Jászis picked up Pavlo between them, Edge still carried Velja and the whole crowd returned to Prival.

When Florian announced himself at the Smodlaka caravan and was admitted, he asked Sava to wait outside for a little while, then broke the news to Gavrila as gently as he could, and with the same merciful lie. She turned pale, abruptly sat down on a bunk and groped for a vial of smelling salts which she had apparently already been resorting to. Florian took from a pocket a flask of vodka he had thought to bring along. While Gavrila alternately sniffed at the salts and choked down the liquor, Florian went on:

"It was impossible to tell, my dear, which of your unfortunate menfolk the wolf attacked first. But I would guess it seized the smaller, the pursuing Velja. When Pavlo heard the cries, that must have cleared his addled mind, and he turned back, attempted to wrest the boy from the beast, and in so doing got mortally injured himself."

With an effort, Gavrila said, "So—at last of his life—he was not madman, he was hero."

"That seems to be the fact, dear lady. Exactly so."

She gave him a long and expressionless look, and Florian tried not to squirm or avoid her gaze. At last she said, "The wolf, then. Where is it?"

"Er, the wolf? Why, the wolf ran away. It fled from the muzhik who found the bodies. He said he did not give chase because he feared the brute must be rabid. To have attacked a child and then a grown man."

"Yet it runs from next grown man," Gavrila said dully. Florian tried to add some other touch of verisimilitude, but she only shook her head. "No matter. You go now, please. Send in Sava and I try tell her."

Florian did so, and, after a respectful interval, also sent Agnete and Meli to keep the grieving Smodlaka women company. The Florilegium stayed at Prival long enough for all those who had been involved in the commotion to get a few hours of sleep. Then the Slovaks resumed their interrupted teardown of the poles, rigging, lights and pista, and repacked the wagons. Agnete came to Florian to say:

"Gavrila mourns her son, of course, and deeply, but—perhaps this I should not say—I think she feels that the wolf paid her some recompense in ridding her and Sava of that awful Pavlo."

"No need to be bashful about saying it, Miss Eel. I rather imagine that many of this company would concur in that opinion. Is there anything we can do for the poor woman?"

"She did ask that Velja not be buried in this dreadful place. She said nothing about the disposition of Pavlo's remains. And she hopes that the tragedy will not make you decide against the gala parade as we approach Peterhof."

"Gallant Gavrila. A real circus lady. Go tell her, please, that we *will* make parade, since she allows it. I have already ridden to the other outskirts of this village, and the road beyond is a well-kept corduroy. Tell Gavrila also that, when we get to Peterhof, I shall ask Alexander's permission to bury Velja in some beautiful place on the palace's own grounds. Just one other thing, Miss Eel. Dissuade her—*restrain* her, if necessary—from any attempt to take one last look at her son. Persuade her to remember him as she knew him."

In the late afternoon of the eighth of June, the Florilegium parade reached the entrance of Peterhof, with its calliope whooping and band blaring, the horses prancing, terriers cartwheeling, clowns frisking and all the artistes—except Gavrila and Sava—atop the wagons, garbed in their gayest pista costumes, Clover Lee even wearing her fluttery mantle of white doves. Peterhof was not ringed about by any walls or gates. The only way Florian knew that they had arrived was that the corduroy road here became a broad, well-cobbled avenue through a village some ten times the size of Prival and composed of buildings much grander than Prival's izbas. At the far side of that village was a handsome gatekeeper's lodge—albeit sans gate—and beyond that the avenue could be seen to branch into several other paved roads and graveled drives. Florian drew his rockaway to a halt at the lodge, and the gatekeeper emerged to salute and shout in Russian, over the music, "Welcome, Gospodín Florian and your entire Tsvetúshchiy-Bukyét. You are expected."

"Thank you, my good man," Florian shouted back. "Which road to the palace?"

"*The* palace, gospodín? There are *forty-two* of them hereabout."

"Oh? Including these, I suppose." Florian indicated the buildings of the village.

"Pólno! These are but the houses and schools and conveniences for the thousand servants of the various palaces."

"Well, I do not know exactly at which one we are expected."

The gatekeeper began to tick off on his fingers: "Nu, there is the Great Palace, the Monplaisir, the Farm, the Cottage, the Hermitage, the Château de Marly..."

"I venture to guess that the tsar awaits us at the Great Palace."

"If you like, I will ride with you to guide you."

Florian beckoned him up to sit on the other side of Daphne, and the parade went on, still whooping and blaring and cavorting, though the avenue now was empty of people. It ran through a great park, in which the gatekeeper-guide pointed out and named the groves of maples, limes, chestnuts, fruiting trees and flowering shrubs. Among them, on greenswards or beside reflecting ponds, were set magnificent edifices, some of which were modestly named but nowise modest in execution. The Cottage was a palace of vaulted lattice arches, stained-glass windows, white marble terraces, balconies and staircases. The Hermitage merited its retiring name only because it was surrounded by a moat and guarded by a drawbridge. Monplaisir was a tremendous but exquisitely delicate structure, comprising mainly great expanses of window, in which the multitude of panes were of "moon glass" that reflected rainbows in all the pastel colors of mother-of-pearl. Almost every building was topped with a wrought-iron representation of the spread-winged, double-headed eagle symbol of the Russian Empire.

"But if you walk all the way around one of those roof images, gospodín," said the guide, "you will count *three* heads. That was done so that, from whatever angle it is viewed, the eagle displays the proper and proud double head."

And every palace had at least one fountain in front of it. The rotating Sun Fountain sprayed from a golden disk a flashing, spiral sun-wheel of water; the Wheat Sheaf Fountain sprayed columns that rose, then diverged in the semblance of a shock of grain; the Bells Fountain somehow cascaded sheets of water downward to limn the curves of four huge and transparent bells.

"The main palaces," said the guide, "are occupied, in season, by the imperial family and their nearer relations. The outlying and lesser palaces are for more remote ducal uncles, aunts, cousins. Whenever the tsaritsa announces 'Tomorrow we will all breakfast at the Chinese Pagoda—or the Ukrainian Dacha, or whichever other pavilion—no one dares decline. So those minor royals must come galloping many versts, early in the morning, from their palaces in all corners of these seven thousand acres."

The parading troupers were already agog. But then the guide directed the train around to the north façade of the Great Palace, where it came to a halt, and all the musicians stopped playing, as if awestricken, and there Florian exclaimed—expressing the sentiment of every one of his company—"My God! And we thought we had seen palaces before!"

The actual Great Palace building was imposing enough: more than a fifth of a mile from end to end, of rose-red stone interspersed with white pilasters, rising through three tall stories of windows and arches and pediments to a rust-red iron mansard roof. The palace fronted on a glossy white marble terrace of equal length and commodious breadth. But even more spectacular was the view the palace looked out upon.

From the plateau of the terrace, the ground fell away to the north, and from below the balustrade descended two staircases that might have been built for Titans, except that they were not for walking on. Each was forty feet from top to bottom and forty feet wide, but consisted of only six broad, steep steps, down which flowed gleaming sheets of water—to which more water was added on the way by jets spouting from gilt-bronze statues and bas-reliefs of nymphs and naiads lining both sides of both staircases. Those waters eventually fell into a series of granite-bowled basins, each the size of a goodly pond, around which stood more gilded statues—dolphins, Tritons, lions, Perseus, gladiators, a bare-buttocked Venus Callipyge—most of those also spewing aloft fountains of water. In the farthest and biggest basin, the centerpiece was a gilded, twice man-sized Samson wrenching open with his hands the jaws of a proportionately tremendous gilded lion, and from the lion's upward-gaping jaws towered the grandest fountain jet of all, a plume sixty feet high.

"A symphony in water!" Florian marveled. "But what kind of hydraulic machinery does all this require?"

"None whatever," said the guide. "It was cleverly designed so that gravity does it all: the waterfalls, the fountains, the jets and sprinklers."

Beyond Samson's pond, the collected water flowed more tranquilly into a wide, granite-banked canal that ran between lawns and groves, straight as an arrow, for half a mile—spanned by several high-arched footbridges—to where it debouched into the silver gulf, on the far horizon of which could be seen a dim blue line that was the coast of Finland. Where the canal joined the gulf, there lay at anchor a steam cutter flying the blue-cross-barred white ensign of the Imperial Navy.

"Whenever the tsar is in residence here," said the guide, "he keeps always a ship ready there, to hasten him to Saint Petersburg if an emergency should require his presence. And—ahem—speaking of His Imperial Majesty, gospodín, he is standing patiently waiting for your attention."

"Oh, dear me!" said Florian, swiveling his gaze from the vista below to look toward the palace.

Alexander, his empress and a numerous host of other men and women stood on the steps of the Great Palace's central entrance, smiling at the train of vehicles, evidently admiring it and commenting on it to each other. Florian leapt down from his rockaway seat, hurried over to doff his top hat in a sweeping bow to the tsar and tsaritsa, and to make salutation on behalf of the whole Florilegium.

While he was attending to the formalities, the other troupers lined up beside the wagons and, from there, bowed to the august company on the palace steps. They were loath to approach too close to those finely dressed ladies and gentlemen, clad as they were in their gaudy or frivolous or too-revealing pista costumes.

When, after a rather lengthy conversation with the tsar and tsaritsa, Florian returned to the train, he was accompanied by two palace grooms, and he spoke first to Dai Goesle:

"Canvasmaster, we will be showing tomorrow in the Upper Park, which is around on the other side of the palace. But not until late in the night, when it is dark, so there will be no hurry about setting up tomorrow. These servant lads will show the drivers to the coach houses, and help them feed and water the animals, then will take all your roustabouts and Carl's windjammers to the kitchens for their own feeding." As he spoke, Florian was drawing Goesle away from the other troupers. "Leave all that to the underlings, Stitches, and you get dressed to dine with us in imperial style." And now Florian dropped his voice to a confidential murmur. "However, after dinner, can you procure enough decent wood to knock together a small coffin for Velja before morning?"

"I daresay. But . . . for the child, just? What about his da?"

"Hush. I'll see to him myself." Then Florian returned to the others and told them, "There is no need for you to unpack everything immediately, but do get out your dinner garb before the wagons are stowed. Their Majesties have assigned to each of you a maid or valet to show you to your rooms in the palace and help you change for dinner."

Finally Florian went to the Smodlaka caravan, where Gavrila and Sava had ridden in seclusion all the way from Prival, and told them the same.

"Thank you, but I think we not hungry for dinner," said Gavrila. "Or for happy company. We stay here tonight, if you please."

"As you like, my dears. However, I will have one of the maids bring you some zakúska snacks, in case you do begin to feel the need of nourishment. And I hope you both will be in better fettle by morning. I have already asked the tsar about a burying place for little Velja, and Alexander is being more than generous. He is not only allotting us a site, but also lending us his court chaplain and chapel for the funeral services."

"Yes, we be there," said Gavrila, touching a handkerchief to her eyes, which were almost as pink as those of her albino daughter. But she asked nothing about the arrangements for her late husband, and Florian likewise said nothing.

9

THE TROUPERS were as dazzled, when they entered the dining hall, as if they had walked suddenly into a blaze of limelight. Everything in the great room was white or nearly transparent, and made even brighter by the still-high summer sun shining in through the translucent white draperies at the floor-to-ceiling windows. The walls were covered with white satin, the parquet floor was of basswood pickled to make it even whiter, the wall and ceiling moldings of animals, cupids, flowers and fruit were of white gesso. The room's many chandeliers and sconces were of crystal pendants tinged with just a touch of lavender to make them visible. The linen on the three long tables and the porcelain of each table's thirty place settings and the tables' carnation centerpieces all were white. A string orchestra of musicians in white—wigs, frock coats, knee breeches and stockings—played softly in one corner.

"And thank goodness," murmured Daphne, as the troupe, their hosts and the other guests sat down to dine. "No block of ice this time."

The room had a characteristic that the newcomers had already noticed in the other chambers and halls they had passed through on their way to this one. Every room of this Great Palace was so very high that it made echoes, not from wall to wall but from floor to ceiling and back. The curious effect was that anyone's footsteps or the scrape of a chair leg on the parquetry resounded hollowly and at length, while every sound made at an intermediate level—the string music, the table conversation—was muted and had to be carefully listened for.

Although the Florilegium's newest troupers were able to speak in Russian to their table partners, those native dancing girls conversed in an even more muted tone than that of the foreigners. Possibly it was because they were ordinary Russian girls in the presence of their next-to-Almighty, or possibly it was because they were embarrassed that their dinner dresses were not luxuriant gowns but common holiday-wear sarafán frocks. The Tsaritsa Maria Alexandrovna, after trying in vain to elicit more than shy mumbles and gulps from one of those girls, turned to Florian on her other side and inquired where *he* had learned to speak Russian.

"I was once married to a Russian woman, Your Majesty. Or, rather, she was charitably called my wife. I should frankly confess—like my other marriages, that one was not formalized by ceremony or certificate."

"Okh, you amoral artistes!" the tsaritsa scolded, then asked, "Would she be again in Russia, do you suppose? Would you like to see her again? Surely the tsar's agents could quickly find her for you."

"Perish the thought, madame! I had as lief join the cult of the great-seal skoptsyí. For that matter, crossing Hungary, too, I almost tiptoed for fear I might arouse another onetime wife who might be lurking there. And I shall tiptoe across Schleswig-Holstein to avoid a certain Dane."

Tsar Alexander was passing the table just then—he was again circulating to visit and eat something at each of the separate tables—and, when he heard Florian mention Schleswig-Holstein, he paused to clap a conspiratorial hand on Florian's shoulder, but made no remark. Nor did he refer at all that evening to the proposal he had made during their April tête-à-tête.

The imperial family and the other guests seemed disposed to sit on, after dinner, and make small talk. But many of the circus folk had had little sleep the night before, and all had had a road journey this day, so Florian asked and got the hosts' permission for his company to retire from theirs. Most of the troupers went to bed in their palace rooms, but Florian and Edge sat up late, until the night was full dark but the moon had not yet risen.

Then they went together to the coach house and the baggage wagon where Pavlo Smodlaka's body lay wrapped in a tarpaulin. They carried it between them, around the wing of the palace and down from the north terrace past the cascading waters. They several times had to put down their burden to rest and catch their breath, and they several times encountered patrolling sentries. Those guards were apparently too surprised to bark a challenge, seeing two men in formal dress lugging a rolled tarpaulin at this hour of morning. But each time, Florian said in Russian, hoarsely and breathlessly, "Preparing for tomorrow's circus, chasovóy," and each sentry shrugged and let them pass.

"I feel a little silly, doing this in full fig," panted Edge, at one rest stop.

"Well, it makes us less conspicuous," panted Florian, "in case any insomniac is watching from the palace windows. And I'll wager we're a damned sight more stylish pallbearers than any other werewolf ever had."

Finally, and unceremoniously, they slid their burden into the water where the Samson basin spilled into the canal, and watched it drift gulfward.

"Well, that's that, and good riddance," said Edge. "You don't think there's a chance some watch officer on that cutter out there might see him go past?"

"I doubt it. I doubt that he'd raise an alarm if he did. He couldn't tell whether Pavlo came from here or from the Neva delta. And as many dead bodies float down the Neva as down any other river of Europe. Come on, we've earned some sleep."

Next morning, the artistes dressed in their best street clothes and, after breakfasting in their rooms, were led by their servants to the palace's church wing. Gavrila and Sava joined them and, though Gavrila had no widow's black to wear, the two had somewhere procured black veils. The service was held not in the capacious church nave but in a small chapel to one side. The tsar, his elder son and even some of the guests from outside the family also attended. The palace's resident priest and his acolytes conducted the funeral mass, and an organ droned suitable soft music at the proper intervals. Goesle had built a good coffin and Edge personally, in private, had laid Velja in it and nailed down the lid. There had been no time to stain or paint the raw wood, so the palace servants had heaped flowers completely over it.

There were some looks exchanged among the circus folk when they saw only the one coffin before the altar, and some curious glances were cast at Florian. But he appeared to be as satisfied as if Pavlo had conveniently evaporated, so no one made any remark, and no one cared enough about Pavlo to inquire what *had* happened to him. The chaplain considerately made his service short, since so few of those attending could follow the formulary of a Russian Orthodox mass. Then the tsar gave his arm to Gavrila, the tsesarevich to Sava, and escorted them out a side door of the chapel.

There was waiting a platoon of the Golden Company, and the musicians from the night before, now in somber black. With the black-robed and black-hatted priest and his censer-swinging acolytes going in front, Velja's coffin was borne by Yount and the Jászis, two men to a side. Behind came a considerable cortège: Velja's mother and sister accompanied by an emperor and a crown prince, the circus company and the splendidly caparisoned honor guard, all walking in solemn cadence to a string rendition of Chopin's funeral music.

The grave had already been dug, near the Adam Fountain, "where the boy can look down the avenue," said Tsar Alexander, "to the view of the Gulf of Finland." Since the priest spoke at the graveside, and made repeated signs of the cross over it, and did the first sprinkling of earth into it, Florian on this occasion only murmured the Latin epitaph to himself and those close enough to overhear.

Afterward, the mourners dispersed in various directions, the guardsmen and musicians marching briskly off, most of the troupers heading for the tober. But

Florian and a few others strolled with the Alexanders, père et fils, while they pointed out notable features of this Lower Park. When the group of walkers came to a grove of young oak trees, in which one tree was ringed by tulips in brilliant bloom, Jörg Pfeifer asked, "Is that not an oddity, Your Majesty? Tulips flowering still in June?"

"Go and look closely at them," said the tsar, and he and his son covered their mouths to hide smiles. But then they laughed uproariously. As Pfeifer bent over the tulips, they spouted water up at him and the oak branches overhead spewed jets that showered down on him. Jörg spluttered, cursed and staggered away from the artificial tree and flowers, to slump onto a park bench nearby. The tsar and tsesarevich roared even more loudly, for the bench immediately spouted water from its back and seat, thoroughly drenching Pfeifer before he could leap off it. When he returned to the group, wringing out what bits he could reach of his suit, Jörg said through his teeth, but as graciously as he could:

"When the good Lord made Your Majesty an emperor, He deprived the world of a promising clown."

"Ach, do not praise me, Herr Pfeifer. Those trick automata, actuated by your weight—they were built at the order of Peter the Great."

Meanwhile, Edge was at the tober in the Upper Park, the vast courtyard of lawns and ponds sheltered from the gulf wind by the bulk of the palace and its southward-extending wings at either end. He was again consulting with Carl Beck, and now also with Dai Goesle, who of course had had to be let in on the surprise being prepared.

"I've soaked and dried the thread," said Edge, "and I brought along plenty of candles. We just have to place them. Now... do we set off this spectacle right at the start of the show?"

"Nein," said Beck. "First are the dancing girls. Tonight to the 'Volga Boatmen's Song' they will dance. For that the footlights they will require."

"Suppose we do it like this, just," said Goesle. "As soon as they've done dancing, I will quench the footlights, so the pista will be dark when Boom-Boom swings into the anthem for the come-in."

"Fine," said Edge. "Then, at that same instant, Carl, you strike the match. If everything goes as intended, we'll be doing our most spectacular spec ever."

"Ja, ja," said Beck. "Now, excuse me, please. The Gasentwickler I must go and charge."

"You're going to send up the balloon?" Edge asked. "Hell, the minute Jules rises above the palace roofline, that north wind will take him. And he won't find any contrary winds at any altitude to fetch him back again. We'll have to chase him clear to Kiev."

"Nein, nein. Only on a tether am I letting him go. Up and down many times, a royal passenger taking each time." And Beck trotted off.

"Thrill rides for the jossers," murmured Edge. "Good idea." Then he looked critically at his equipment for the surprise, and said to Goesle, "We're out of the wind here, but there are still gusty drafts. How about protective reflectors on the candles?"

Goesle cried, "Dammo, Zack man, there's a thousand of them! To cut that many pieces of tin—"

"No need, Stitches. When your crew have got everything set up, send them down to the gulf shore. There should be shells there—clam shells, mussel shells, any kind will do."

"It's deuced glad I am we're not doing this every night," grumbled Goesle. "But do it we will."

At that moment, Florian emerged from a back door of the main palace building and called Edge over to tell him, "The tsar would like to discuss again the proposal he made, and I must make my decision. Since you constitute the loyal opposition, I think you ought to be present."

So they went together up the marble stairs and across the Portrait Gallery to the Eastern Study, where Imperial Guards flanked the doorway but Alexander waited alone within.

Florian said, "I brought my second in command, Your Majesty, because I cannot, in conscience, commit my company to this undertaking without his concurrence in it. And Colonel Edge says frankly that he is opposed to enlistment as a spy."

"Okh! *Shpión?*" said Alexander, with a laugh. "Nyet, nyet!" He continued in German, "Tell the colonel that I am not asking any of you to *spy*. For one thing, you will not be acting on my behalf. For another, if I *did* wish to acquire information from abroad, I could get it without spying."

When Florian had translated that to Edge, the tsar went on:

"Only here in my own Russia do I find spying necessary, and it is right here that my Third Section has to do most of its work. Naturally, they keep close watch on my government ministers, high military officers and all my relatives. Palace coups have been known to occur in the past. And those agents also keep close watch among the masses, because the lower classes of Russians are the most secretive, suspicious, mistrustful and untrustworthy of human beings. But *foreigners?* Pah! They are so foolishly careless of their secrets and their schemes that it takes no professional spy, only a clear-eyed observer, to recognize all their designs, read the intentions of their councils, unravel their chinoiseries. Since the time of Peter the Great, we rulers of Russia have known all foreigners to be so, and we have taken advantage of that fact. For example, speaking of chinoiserie..."

Alexander stood up, motioning for the others to remain seated, and walked to one of the walls of the study. They were covered with embroidered silk, clearly Oriental and showing scenes of what appeared to be everyday Oriental folk going about their everyday labors. The tsar drummed his fingers on one of the panels and said:

"In Peter's time, the art of making porcelain was known only to the Chinese. In all of Europe, porcelain was so rare that it was treasured as diamonds or emeralds are today. Bits of it were set in goldwork and worn as jewelry. The Chinese adamantly refused to divulge to any Occidental the method of making porcelain. However, one intelligent Russian, traveling in China, quite fortuitously found out the whole process. In a draper's shop there, he saw for sale some bolts of silk tapestry depicting *every step* of porcelain making. A child could have read them like an ázbuka. That sharp-eyed tourist purchased the fabrics, sent them to Great Peter, and they became the textbook of instruction for Russia's ceramicists. Then they were hung on these walls. You see them around you this minute. And you dine here on Russian-made porcelain."

"I take your point, Your Majesty," said Florian. "But what sort of fortuitous discoveries would you hope we might make in the German lands?"

"If Bismarck is setting his aim next on Alsace, he must already be making preparations on his side of that border. His General von Moltke will soon be moving troops and armaments there. Count them. Or they may travel by night, not to be noticed. But your circus company often camps by the roadside for the night, nicht wahr? A battalion or a regiment marching past you would pay no more heed to you than they would—excuse me for saying so—to an encampment of gypsies."

"Doubtless true, Your Majesty."

"Now, even a professional spy wanting to know the strength of such a troop on the move might have to count heads. The artillery and other weapons he would certainly have to scrutinize carefully in order to describe them. But I am quite sure that Colonel Edge could ascertain those things at a glance."

"It's likely," said Edge. "And if we should get any such information, what are we supposed to do with it?"

"Memorize it," said the tsar. "Write nothing down. If the information is only inside your head, it cannot be discovered during any searches of your train by sentries, border guards, anyone else."

"And then?"

"When you get to Paris, communicate it to no one but the Emperor Louis Napoléon and to him alone, in absolute privacy. Not even his henpecking harridan Eugénie is to know."

Edge said skeptically, "Your Majesty, we just stroll into his throne room and request a private audience? We gypsies?"

"Warum nicht? He will be eager to hear your report, after he reads this letter of introduction I have written for you." Alexander picked a large sheet of parchment off a table and handed it to Florian. "That will not be untimely discovered by any officials, because you will *flaunt* it at them. It may even make your every border crossing easier, as the Empress Elisabeth's letter eased your way into my domains."

"It is most flattering of us, Your Majesty," said Florian, with delight. "Louis Napoléon should receive us with open arms—as a circus—even if we did not bring privy information."

"And there is more to that letter than you or any border guard can perceive. It was written at my dictation by my French scribe. Even he does not know what I later inserted between the lines."

"A secret message, Your Majesty?" said Florian, peering at the document from various angles. "Invisible ink?"

"The very best," the tsar said, with some pride. "My own urine. It dries invisible on the parchment, but Louis Napoléon knows that heating will turn it brown. Please, when you present it at border crossings, do not lay it near a stove or lamp."

"We will take the utmost care of it."

The tsar said pointedly, "The letter still lacks my signature and seal. I have yet to hear your decision."

Florian looked at Edge, who said, "If it's what you told me, Governor—the possible avoidance of a war—then I withdraw my opposition."

Florian bowed deeply to Alexander and said, "We will be, as Your Majesty phrased it, Your Majesty's clear-eyed observers."

The tsar nodded, took back the parchment and sat down to the table, on which were writing implements. He chose a pen, inked it, wrote his name with a flourish at the bottom of the letter, sprinkled sand on that and blew it off. He lit a stick of red wax, let it dribble onto the parchment, took up a chunky piece of dark-blue lapis lazuli, gold-speckled with pyrites, and pressed its intaglio end into the hot wax. He surveyed the resulting seal, handed the letter again to Florian, then yanked the lapis lazuli open to reveal that it was also a container of personal-hygiene instruments. He took out an earspoon, leaned back in his chair and began lazily delving inside one hairy ear.

"Just one thing, Your Majesty," said Florian, carefully rolling the parchment. "Colonel Edge and I know that we will keep our word, but how do you? We could use this letter as entrée to the French court, and tell the emperor nothing at all, or invent a Mischmasch of lies. Are you always so trusting of your deputed agents?"

"Nyet," the tsar said negligently. "Of course I trust *you* two gentlemen. Just the same, I hope you will allow me one precautionary measure. A new artiste will be joining your troupe at Kiel."

"*Eh?*"

"Oh, a very pleasant young lady, of good family. For personal reasons, she wishes to emigrate from Russia. So, from Kiel to Paris, you will have her services, with no salary to pay; she enjoys an independent income."

"But—but what does she do? What is her Spezialität?"

"I think you will find that evident when you first set eyes on her. And she will accept any rôle you wish to assign her."

"Well... well, why does she not join us sooner? In Piter, so we can work her into our program."

"She has reasons for not caring to appear in public in her home country. She will join you at Kiel. Now, gentlemen, I believe it is getting on toward the hour we ought to start dressing for dinner."

"Damnation," muttered Florian, as he and Edge left the palace. "I do not like having a supernumerary artiste thrust upon me."

"Hell, you practically begged for it, suggesting that we couldn't be trusted. I'm just glad he didn't demand that we leave hostages for a guarantee."

Florian sighed. "Well, we will make the best of it. Work things out as we go along."

The circus entertainment commenced that evening even before dinner was over. The polite and quiet table talk was abruptly interrupted by a loud, false-feminine voice raised in complaint and, not at all muted by the room's vastness, its petulant squeal brought a general silence and craning of necks. Fitzfarris had taken from his pocket Little Miss Mitten and, his head thrown back to get the up-and-down echo effect, was conducting a comic quarrel with her in a mélange of memorized French and German, with a sprinkling of Russian. Probably few in the dining hall could understand the whole routine, but it put them all in a jolly humor. And after dinner, the crowd of royals and nobles poured out onto the tober in the Upper Park, to exclaim over the beauty of the now inflated balloon.

Rouleau went up first with Clover Lee as a passenger, to demonstrate the safety of the *Saratoga,* and Carl Beck had his Slovak crewmen anchor the rope when the balloon had cleared the palace roof and the wind made it strain to go southward. The Tsesarevich Alexander insisted, over his mother's expressed anxiety, on being the first of the family to "fly." When he came down again, effervescing with enthusiasm over the experience and the view from up there, everybody else—even his mother—took a turn. By the time they had all done so, the twilight was deepening to dark, the Slovak anchormen were nearly exhausted from the repeated hauldowns, and the gas in the bag had cooled so that the balloon was logy in its ascents. Beck politely vetoed any second rides, and Rouleau pulled the ripcord to collapse the balloon for repacking in its wagon. Meanwhile, the palace servants brought out chairs—every kind from thronelike seats for the imperial family to Chippendale chairs for the guests—and set them on the grass at a comfortable distance around the pista and the grouped bandsmen.

The show was spectacular, right from its overture, the energetic dance of the usher girls. In unison, they repeatedly bounded into the air and there touched fingers to toes while their legs were extended together before them or spread wide apart at their sides. When the girls were not in midair but on the ground, they squatted low, swung their knees together from side to side, or, with amazing rapidity, did the v'prisyádku, kicking out and drawing back one leg after the other. When they stamped in rhythm, they were stamping only on pista straw, but Abdullah's bass drum provided the stamping noise for them.

In conclusion, the girls, shiny with sweat and tremulously smiling, made low curtsies in the direction of the tsar and tsaritsa. Goesle closed his gas valve to dim and kill the footlights, and the tober went totally dark. A moment passed, and Beck struck a match. By its light, he gave his band the downbeat to crash into the "Bozhe Tsara Krani." Simultaneously, from that one small flare of light, a streak of fire flashed around and around the pista and up one of the high poles and across the tightrope and down the other pole. The flame had no sooner whizzed about than it went out, but left behind it a countless multitude of candles burning and making glow the translucent shells stuck onto them. The curbing of the pista and the perimeter of the promenade space outside it, the two center poles and the tightrope all were outlined with those points and nimbuses of light. The audience burst into applause, pounding their hands to the beat of the Russian anthem, while Florian strutted out of the darkness, leading the whole Florilegium in its Grand Promenade between the two circles of candles on the ground.

When the spec was making its final circuit around the outside of the pista, some of the Slovaks scurried about to relight Goesle's footlights and spotlights. Others, as unobtrusively as possible, snuffed the candles on the ground and climbed the center poles to remove the candles stuck upon them, and shook the tightrope to dislodge all the candles stuck along its length. Then Colonel Ramrod returned with his horses to the limelight to do his liberty act. That was followed by Florian, Fünfünf, the Kesperle and the Emeraldina, doing their repartee comedy routine in German. Then, while the Quakemaker was being trampled over by Brutus, Florian had his first chance to say:

"Colonel Ramrod, I am told that that marvelous opening illumination was your doing. How did you come to invent that?"

"I didn't. I saw it done in a church in the city, and I just copied it. Boom-

Boom helped me figure out how. All it took was cotton thread soaked in vitriol and aqua fortis—making the thread into guncotton is what it amounted to. The thread was looped around the wick of each candle, and every wick was touched with coal oil so it would catch fire in a flash. But please, Governor, don't say let's do it regularly from now on. Stitches and his Slovaks would all blow the stand."

The show's every act was received with loud acclaim, and the artistes put into every act every bit of business they had ever conceived, plus a few new ones. The Jászi brothers for the first time rode a galloping "Saint Petersburg Courier" in a three-man pyramid, one standing on the shoulders of the other two, and they standing on separate steeds while all the other horses of the show thundered between them. Little Syverchok made her Enchanted Globe do more mysterious gyrations and bounces than ever before. Terry, Terrier and Terriest now entered the pista adorned as a troika team—the middle dog wearing a high-bowed dugá yoke—drawing Sava in the little chariot. And Gavrila, though her smile must have been forced, gamely put the dogs through their whole succeeding repertoire of tricks.

When Florian declared intermission, it meant only time enough for the spectators to light fresh cigarettes, while the Slovaks set up Sir John's platform inside the pista, and then he presented his sideshow there. He had already done his ventriloquy act, and he had only one Night Child to exhibit, but the audience seemed sufficiently entertained by Meli's doing her Medusa routine, Syverchok's mock-liberty act with Rumpelstilzchen, and Meli's returning to wrestle erotically with her Fafnir python. Then Sir John quite stunned the spectators by summoning the one trouper they had not already met socially—"Kostchei Byesmyértni!" —who came lumbering from the darkness behind the band, and, in the glare of the spotlight, slowly bent forward to display his frightful face. It was even more frightful than usual. Kostchei's dark eyes burned like coals when he glowered out at the tsar who had dictated Russia's laws and punishments and, however unknowingly, had made Kostchei look as he did.

The pista program resumed with Mademoiselle Butterfly's trapeze act, and she added only a small touch to that, but an affecting one. When Sunday climbed the rope ladder to her platform, she wore a yellow rose in her hair. She stood up there, gracefully posed, one hand lightly holding her bar, and Beck waved his band to silence, as she had asked him to do. Silhouetted by Goesle's spotlight against the night sky, in that total silence, Sunday surreptitiously detached one petal of her yellow rose. It fell slowly, drifting back and forth, twirling and dipping out of the spotlight into dimness, then brightening again when the footlights caught it, and finally settling gently onto the pista. No amount of Florian's bombast could so effectively have made the audience realize the distance between the girl and the ground. The moment the petal touched the straw, the band lilted into "There Is But One Girl," and Sunday swung out into space, and the audience gasped at her daring.

When the show at last concluded with the come-out spec, marched to the band's reprise of "Bozhe Tsara Krani," with Monsieur Roulette singing the words, the whole audience—except, of course, the tsar being sung to—stood up respectfully and reverently. Then the spectators broke ranks to mingle excitedly with the sweaty and tired but triumphant artistes, and to shake their hands and lavish them with compliments.

"You were right, Herr Florian," said Alexander. "All other considerations aside, Louis Napoléon certainly should welcome your circus *as* a circus. I congratulate you on its dazzling competence. Before you leave tomorrow, I wish to distribute some few small tokens of our appreciation."

So, after breakfast next morning, when the train was made up and waiting on the great marble terrace, the whole company lined up there at attention. The tsar and tsaritsa went along the line of them, handing out gifts from trays and baskets borne by their servants. The gifts were considerably more extravagant than any other monarch had dispensed to them. Each of the circus women received a gold and enamel Easter egg, faithful copies of those made a century before by Great Catherine's legendary goldsmith Posier. The eggs could be opened for access to their contents: a phial of perfume, rouge, some heart-shaped beauty spots, powder and a tiny puff. Each male trouper was given a chunk of moss agate, the stone sheared flat on one side to display an uncannily lifelike "landscape" scene drawn by the stone's own grain. Those were also open-able to disclose toothpick, earspoon and tweezers, all of gold. Banat and the other Slovaks were flabbergasted when even they received gifts: a fine astrakhan fur hat apiece.

"September eleventh," said the tsar, taking Florian aside for one last conference, "is the festival of Saint Alexander Nevsky, therefore my own name day and a public holiday. It will also be the day you leave Saint Petersburg. Most of the population will be congregated in the Palace Square to watch the ceremonies and participate in the festivities there, so not many people will be on the streets to see when and how you depart. One of my aides will come to lead your circus train down the riverside to a harbor where you will board the fleet cruiser *Pyëtr-Velík*. Good-bye, then, Herr Florian, and good luck. Do-svidánya."

Not making parade now, but making its best speed, the circus train was again at Prival by midday, and no one was inclined to tarry in that ill-omened place, so the train went right on through. The rain having held off for some days, the dirt road beyond Prival was no longer mud, except in a few and easily nego-tiable places, so the circus was back on its tober in St. Petersburg by nightfall. The three watchmen who had stayed behind, having already had some dinner, pitched in to start unloading the wagons. So Florian hailed droshkis and karétas to take all the hungry others of the company to the Hotel Europe. There he treated them to a minor feast to celebrate their having captivated the court of the tsar. When they were all replete and relaxing over tea or brandy, Florian made his announcement of their date and means of departure from Russia. That evoked a concert of cheers, for everyone apparently had been dreading a long haul overland. Then, before the company returned to the tober, Florian sent Banat to find a shop in which to buy three more astrakhan hats for those three Slovaks who had missed out on the gift giving.

The next three months passed uneventfully and almost monotonously. The performers did their two shows a day and spent much of their free time, as always, in practice and improvements. The clowns worked on new knockabout routines. Gavrila taught her dogs new tricks, and so did Pemjean teach his cats and bears. Monday practiced new comic capers on the tightrope. Ioan continued to augment every artiste's wardrobe with new costumes, and to embellish the older ones. Goesle and his carpenters fret-sawed and painted fancy filigree roof crests that could be attached to the tops of wagons and cages for parades and the pista promenades, or removed for ordinary road travel. The usher girls, disinclined to work when they didn't have to, occupied their free time in entertaining, in unoccupied wagons or unfrequented corners of the park, the circus's numerous bachelors, from the Jászis to the Slovaks. Anyway, no one was idle.

The days shortened and the nights lengthened. By late August, the sun seemed grudgingly to bestir itself in the morning, and rose only halfway to the zenith before sinking again. On the last day of August, Florian sent the roustabouts to paper the city with posters announcing that the Florilegium's final performance would take place on the ninth of September.

"Well, well!" said Florian, going over the books in his office and rubbing his hands together. "Even after the expense of those rail charters and the luxury hotel, we are leaving Russia much wealthier than we were when we entered it." So when, after the last show on the ninth, he paid off the usher girls, he generously gave each of them a bonus, because they would be unemployed until the knavish Marchan returned from the Crimea.

Everyone and everything of the Florilegium was ready to go by dawn of the eleventh, and that was well, for the tsar's emissary arrived not very long after dawn, in a carriage emblazoned with the imperial arms. He was a grizzled navy komandór, wearing a bicorn hat of the Admiral Nelson persuasion, and the petty officer who drove the carriage wore a tarred pigtail of Nelson vintage. When Florian greeted the komandór and said simply, "Lead on, sir," the officer said, "I have something to deliver first, gospodín. In private."

Florian took him to the office, and the petty officer followed, carrying a satchel that was apparently very heavy, for he dropped it with a thud on the wagon floor. The komandór waved him out again and said to Florian, "With His Imperial Majesty's compliments. The tsar thought you might have incidental expenses while traveling at his behest, and wishes to defray them in advance."

"Bless my soul," muttered Florian. He stooped, unlatched the bag and was so overcome that he nearly pitched headfirst into it. "Gold imperials! Why, there must be ten thousand rubles' worth here!" But then he recovered his composure and said only, "His Majesty is widely known for his generosity to the arts. Please convey to him our thanks, Komandór."

"If you will stow them somewhere safe," said the officer, "we can be on our way."

"The satchel will be safe here until we are on board. Let us go."

The carriage led the circus train through the nearly empty streets and skirted the main city, following the Obvodniy Canal, crossing a short bridge onto Ryezvi Island and proceeding to the far side of it, to the Gutuyevskaya Docks, the closest a deep-draft vessel could approach to the city. The *Pyëtr-Velík* was moored there, steam already up in preparation for working its hoisting machinery. The cruiser was screw-propelled like the collier *Pflichttreu*, but it was twice as big and it was immaculately clean. There were monstrous turret guns fore and aft, but those were capped at their muzzles, since the ship was off on a peaceable mission. Also the cruiser's ammunition magazines were empty, so all of the Florilegium's caged and walking animals could be quartered and sheltered belowdecks—and most of the wagons and caravans as well; only a few had to be tied down on the open deck. The ship's steam-driven winches and windlasses made the loading fairly easy and quick of accomplishment.

The appointments of the warship were of course spartan, but on this voyage it was leaving ashore most of its combat seamen, so there were enough empty officers' deck quarters to accommodate the circus women, four to a cabin. The circus men had to make do with bunks crowded and stacked close together belowdecks in the ratings' compartments, but at least there were separate compartments for the troupers and the Slovaks. Except for the deck cabins occupied by the ship's captain and chief officers, there was only one cabin allotted to male passengers, those being the tsar's ambassador to the Suez Canal dedication ceremonies—a Count Gendrikov—and his three accompanying aides.

The boarding and stowing went so efficiently that the *Pyëtr-Velík* cast off from the dock in early afternoon, and about four hours later was steaming past Peterhof on the port side, the Great Palace easily visible to the passengers. By the next morning, the land on that side of the ship was Russia's province of Estonia and, two days later, the cruiser steamed from the Gulf of Finland into the open, gray, bleak Baltic Sea.

The weather discouraged the circus people from disporting themselves on deck. They emerged from their quarters only to take an occasional walk for exercise and fresh air—Florian frequently strolling with the Count Gendrikov, asking him questions about Egypt, which the count knew well, in case the Florilegium might someday go there. The Slovaks came on deck only to heave overboard the collected animal droppings, and otherwise stayed below, playing cards. The Russian Navy's food was dreary, too, tending mostly to salt fish, fried cheese and boiled cabbage. But all tolerated the inconveniences, because Florian assured them that this voyage would last little more than a week.

Florian asked of his company just one chore out of the ordinary while they were at sea. As soon as he had the opportunity, he told Edge of the unexpected bounty bestowed by the tsar, and said, "I wish to put that away to be our communal grouch bag, for emergency use only. But it must be put *well* away. Whenever we have to pass through the customs barrier of some kingdom or duchy, I can account for our other money, if necessary, by producing my receipt books. But a satchelful of gold Russian imperials would be difficult to explain and would be a mighty temptation to confiscation. How do you suggest it best be hidden?"

"That's easy, Governor. Tuck it under the straw of old Maximus's cage wagon. I'd like to see any customs officer go rummaging in there."

"Excellent idea. Let us confer with the canvasmaster and le Démon Débonnaire."

So, after Goesle had done some measuring from outside the cage, he and Pemjean climbed into it together, and Pemjean kept Maximus distracted while Goesle cut out a section of the flooring. Two days later, the two climbed into the cage again, Goesle fitted a box into that hole, deposited the satchel in it, replaced the flooring as a lid and scattered the lion's straw bedding over it again.

A few nights after that, Florian passed the word that all the troupers and roustabouts were to assemble on deck after they had eaten dinner. When they were convened, he told them, "Any of you who have been keeping calendars, take note. Today is no longer the Russian September eighteenth, but the West-

ern September thirtieth. And the captain informs me that tomorrow, the first of
October, we shall make landfall at Kiel."

10

AS THE *Pyëtr-Velík*'s derricks deposited one after another of the Florilegium's
vehicles on the wharf, Florian said, "Where is that so-called artiste the tsar is
saddling us with?"

"I doubt she'd be hanging around the docks," said Edge. "This is no place for
a lady."

Kiel harbor was all smoke, steam, bustle and noise. There were ships arriving, ships departing, ships taking on or discharging cargo, with sirens hooting,
anchor chains rattling, windlasses ratcheting. Steam cranes worked with frantic
clangor, steam pile-drivers jarred the wharfside area with their massive thumps.
The iron-shod horses and iron-rimmed wheels of heavy drays rang and rumbled
on the cobbles. Gang bosses shrieked whistle blasts and invective at stevedores
who cursed back just as vehemently. It may have been no place for a lady, but
the lady arrived nonetheless.

"I'll be damned," said Edge, as that most extraordinary lady came down the
gangplank from the *Pyëtr-Velík,* walking with the aid of a cane. She had waited
until every circus person and animal and bit of gear was on the dock, to be the
last to come ashore.

"She must have stayed inside her cabin all the way from Piter," said Florian.
"God knows she'd have been hard to hide anywhere else."

The young woman came up to them and introduced herself in English. "I am
Olga Somova. I am here to join your circus."

"And we welcome you, Gospozhýa Somova," said Florian, with unfeigned
sincerity. "Why did you not make known your presence aboard the ship, so we
could earlier have got acquainted?"

"I did not want the mariners gaping at me all the way. The steward who
brought my trays snickered often enough. And I did not want the Count Gendrikov to know that I was—well—finally acknowledging myself to be a freak. He
would laugh at the idea of my joining a circus. And he would spread malicious
gossip."

"May I inquire, gospozhýa, exactly how tall *are* you?"

"Three arshín and a vershók," she said, not as if she were proud of it.

Florian quickly calculated and said admiringly, "Seven feet and almost two
inches. My, my! Not quite as gigantic as the famous Anna Swan, but a more
than adequate giantess."

Olga Somova flinched slightly at the word. She was an exceedingly pretty
young woman, with wide, clear blue eyes, high cheekbones and a satin complexion. Her black hair was worn in prim coils on either side of her head. She
was not fat or musclebound or massively boned, but a nicely proportioned
woman on a fantastically large scale, just as Katalin Szábo was in miniature.

"It is why I must use a cane." she explained, and blushed as she did so.
"My—my lower extremities are of normal size and shape. They would have to be

hideously huge to support my great height and weight unaided. I weigh nearly seven poods, you see."

"Close to two hundred and fifty pounds," said Florian. "About ideal for your height, I should say. But we will make sure, gospozhýa, that you have to stand or walk no more than necessary."

"I thought spies were supposed to be invisible," said Edge, to let her know that they were aware of her real reason for joining them. "Aren't you in the wrong line of work, Miss Somova?"

"I am not really a spy. I am only to telegraph to the tsar from each stopping place between here and Paris, so he will know your itinerary. And in Paris, when you report to the French emperor, I am to telegraph the tsar that you did so. That is all. And, since I tell you frankly what I am to do, *am* I really a spy? Those things I had to agree to do, in order to procure the visa to leave Russia. Such a visa is not easily come by. Except for Jews, which the tsar is happy to get rid of, he does not let his subjects emigrate whenever they please." She glanced anxiously back at the cruiser, as if fearful that the ship's captain or the count might still order her to return.

Florian said, "If you are only unwillingly an agent for the tsar, and if you are only unwillingly acknowledging your, um, individuality, and if you are doing both only in order to emigrate, then you must have some very compelling motive for emigrating."

"For a woman, Gospodín Florian, the most compelling. I seek a husband. Perhaps in lands where I am not already known as a figure of fun, an anchoress forever in hiding..." She shrugged her broad but shapely shoulders.

"I see. And how is it that you speak English?"

"I speak also French and German. When one has no social life—and from childhood I have not—one has ample time for studying."

"I daresay. Well, Gospozhýa Somova, may I have your passport? I must go and wave the tsar's letter at the officials of the office of Einwanderung yonder, and get all our other papers properly endorsed. Then we are repairing to a hotel —the Adler has been recommended—and there I shall introduce you to your new colleagues."

The Kiel immigration officers were of Prussian efficiency but also of Prussian thoroughness, so it was quite some time before Florian emerged from that office. He came out muttering, and with his arms full.

"Just *look* at all these papers and these signatures and stamps and seals. And they entitle us only to travel within this Prussian province of Schleswig-Holstein. No doubt we will have to go through the same damned rigmarole at the border of every damned province. Such officious formalities are something new, since I was last in these parts."

Right now they still had to run the gantlet of the customs officers, but that ordeal was made easier by having each trouper present for inspection only the personal luggage he or she was taking to the hotel, while Banat and the other Slovaks remained with the wagons and caravans and animals and equipment, stored in a dockside warehouse, until the Florilegium should be ready to roll. Willi Lothar was let to go first through customs so that he could depart straightaway in his calash to investigate the possibility of the circus's showing here in Kiel.

Finally all the artistes had cleared customs and had collected many more documents full of stamps and signatures. Then the rockaway, with Florian and Daphne on the seat and the giantess inside, led the rest of the troupe in a train of hired Droschken to the Hotel Adler. And there, after going to their rooms to bathe and refresh themselves, the company gathered in the dining room to be presented to Olga Somova—"a first-of-May gift from Tsar Alexander," as Florian introduced her.

Fitzfarris was overjoyed to have such a splendid new exhibit for his sideshow. After greeting her, he took Florian aside and said, "What'll we call her, Governor? How about 'Olga the Volga Ogress'?"

"Please, Sir John," said Florian, looking pained. "Have some regard for her dignity. I suggest, at least while we are in these Teutonic regions, calling her Brunhilde, after that superhuman princess of the legend."

"Fine, fine!" said Fitz. "Now where's Ioan? I want to tell her an idea I've got for Brunhilde's platform costume."

As he hurried off, Kostchei the Deathless sidled up to Florian and said confidentially in Russian, "Call the giantess what you like, gospodín, for Olga Somova is not her name either. She is the Princess Raisa Yusupova."

"Good heavens! Really? How do you happen to know that?"

"The Yusupov family is among the most prominent in Russia. And you must admit, Raisa is a prominent member of it. Forgive the feeble pun."

"The tsar did say that she came of good family."

"A richer family even than his own Romanov line. The Yusupovs are wealthy beyond measure."

"If that is so, why has she come abroad to seek a husband? Surely her money and lineage would have made any Russian aristocrat ignore her—ahem—overwhelming stature."

"No doubt," Kostchei said drily. "But perhaps the Princess Yusupova wishes to be courted by some man who is unaware of her wealth and distinction. Even a commoner, if he wanted her for herself alone."

"You are right. I was being crass. It is likely that a big woman would have a big heart."

Willi Lothar returned while they were all at dinner, and came straight to the table shared by Florian, Edge, Daphne and Olga. He was formally introduced to the giantess, but only absentmindedly kissed her hand before reporting with some urgency, "Herr Gouverneur, I have disappointing news. There is already a circus showing here in Kiel. The Zirkus Renz of Berlin."

"Ah, well. We can't have everything our own way. And Kiel is not a particularly enchanting city. I shan't be sorry to move on."

"We will lose more stands than this one. I have ascertained that this whole north country is rife with circuses, playing their last autumn dates before moving south for the winter. Besides the Renz, there is the Zirkus Strassburger, the Krone, the Carmo, the Sarrasani. I have not been able to find out their exact stands and dates, but we are surrounded by competition."

"Hm," said Florian. "I certainly do not want to go up against any of them day-and-date. But neither do I want to dash ahead of them and unfairly skim the cream from the cities already on their planned routes. Let me think. If the Renz is now showing here, then its logical next stop southward would be Hamburg. So perhaps Bremen, over to the west, is not on its schedule. Tomorrow, Willi, ride for Bremen and find out. We will meet you there. If Bremen is circus-fresh and not already committed, we will stop and show. Otherwise, we shall simply go elsewhere."

"Bremen is about a five-day drive from here," said Willi. "Will you be close behind me?"

"Not right on your heels. I imagine I will waste most of tomorrow just getting our train through customs inspection and off the dock. Now go find yourself a table, Willi, and have some decent food. Kill the aftertaste of all the salt fish we have consumed."

When Willi went away, Edge said to Florian, "I'll come with you tomorrow, Governor. While you're busy with the customs people, I'll mosey around the harbor. If I'm supposed to be on the lookout for suspicious matériel, it might be interesting to see what kind of goods are being landed here." Then he turned to Olga and said, with a touch of taunting, "You can telegraph to your puppetmaster from the hotel desk, Miss Somova. And you can assure him that we're keeping our end of the bargain."

The giantess blushed, but said nothing. Daphne looked puzzled by those cryptic remarks, and glanced questioningly at Florian. But he offered no elucidation, so she likewise said nothing.

At every overnight stop during the circus train's journey to Bremen, whether at an inn or merely by the roadside, Ioan worked on the costume for Brunhilde. Its most striking feature was its helmet. Ioan procured from one of the inns a tin pot that would fit comfortably upside-down on Olga's head when she let her long hair down, and Goesle removed the pot's handle and polished it to a fine gleam. A night or two later, when the train was camped near a dairy farm, Fitzfarris borrowed from engineer Beck a stout hacksaw, and disappeared into the darkness. When he came back he seemed uncharacteristically fidgety, until the train took the road next morning and got a good many miles down it. And that night he cemented a nicely curved and pointy black horn onto either side of the pot-helmet.

To go with that, Ioan made a dress of heavy silver bouclé resembling chain mail, and at its front were two padded, stiff, silver-spangled, assertively Valkyrean breast cups that exaggerated Olga's already impressive bosom. Meli Vasilakis contributed her late husband's longest sword for Olga to carry, and Goesle made for her a silver-painted wooden shield with a sharp boss in its center. Olga's only reservation about her costume was that the dress's skirt was overlong, but Fitzfarris assured her there was a reason for that.

Meanwhile, Stitches produced a new banner for the sideshow, representing Brunhilde the Giantess and Cricket the Midget standing side by side, with Olga depicted more immense and Katalin more puny than they were in actuality. The two women complained, not about that, but about their being so *badly* painted; the pictures bore no least likeness to them. Goesle could only apologize; the fairly expert Korean painter was gone, and the only other portraitist available—admittedly, not much of one—was an aspirant Slovak.

"Never mind the banner, ladies," Fitzfarris said cheerfully. "The jossers will be that much more stunned and pleased when they see you in person, and see that you're both beautiful. And Olga, try not to give me any funny looks when I introduce you, because I'm going to talk you up as being over *eight* feet tall."

"But I am not. Anyone with eyes can measure."

"Not when you're standing above everybody on a platform. And I'll make sure you look that tall. I'll have our biggest trouper, the Quakemaker here, walk under your arm."

"Now, hey," said Yount. "*That* tall she ain't. I'd have to stoop some."

"Wait and see, Obie, wait and see."

The city of Bremen was in the Grand Duchy of Oldenburg, so, to everybody's vexation, there was another lengthy procedure to go through at that border. The officials inspected all their papers and goods and vehicles—though none probed the straw where old Maximus paced grumbling back and forth—and there was another copious issuance of documents, and an interminable stamping and signing of them. Fortunately, all that bother was not for nothing. When they reached Bremen and met Willi, he was pleased to inform Florian that no other circus was in the city, or due to be, and he had secured a tober for the Florilegium in the beautiful Bürgerweide park.

So it was there that Brunhilde made her début, with some evident stage fright, but competently enough, after all the rehearsals Fitzfarris had put her through. Immediately before her appearance, little Cricket did her turn with Rumpelstilzchen. While the midget took her bows, Sir John lifted the dwarf horse off the platform and, unnoticed by the applauding crowd, set a sturdy wooden box up there behind Cricket and sprinkled on it some of his lycopodium. When the clapping subsided, Cricket remained there, as Sir John bawled in German, "Now, ladies and gentlemen, from her legendary flame-encircled castle, the mighty *Princess Brun*-HILDE!" and touched a lighted cigarette to the flash powder. Using her sword as a cane, Olga hastily mounted the stair that had been added for her behind the platform. When the lycopodium smoke cleared, she was standing beside the midget. Cricket remained only long enough for the audience to marvel audibly at the disparity in their size. Then she retired, and Fitz, below the platform, went on with his memorized patter:

"...So admirably feminine are the curves and proportions of the Princess Brunhilde, ladies and gentlemen, that an observer may not immediately appreciate that she stands eight feet and eight inches tall! However, to demonstrate it unmistakably, I shall ask the tallest man among you to ascend the dais. Sir, you there!" And he pointed to Yount, planted among the crowd. "It will be seen that you have no slightest difficulty in walking fully erect under the giantess's extended arm."

When Yount heaved his bulk onto the front of the platform, Brunhilde smilingly stepped back as if to make room for him. In so doing, she stepped up onto the box behind her, and her overlong skirt made her increase in stature imperceptible, but the grinning Yount *was* able to stroll about under her outstretched sword arm.

"Why, it was not fearsome or embarrassing, after all," Olga said delightedly to Fitzfarris, when she had been roundly applauded and the sideshow was over and the jossers had returned to the chapiteau. "It was almost a pleasure, pretending for the first time in my life not to be smaller but to be bigger even than I am." She was bubbling so, with relief or whatever emotion, that she turned and smiled at Kostchei the Deathless and said, "Do you, sir, also find it easier to bear your—your difference—when you are here among others who are just as different from those normal folk?"

Kostchei started, rolled his eyes, gesticulated in dumb show, then fled precipitately.

"Er... Princess Brunhilde," said Fitz. He remembered Florian's injunction that the mutilated ex-criminal not speak to strangers—and Kostchei evidently regarded Olga as a stranger. "You're forgetting, that poor fellow is mute. Struck dumb, as I said just now, by the shock of his battle with the bears."

"Oh," said Olga, looking bemused. "I thought that was only a story for the spectators, like my being a princess. True, I have never heard that man speak. But I did think I had seen him in conversation with others."

"Pantomiming, no doubt," said Fitz, and went to caution the Deathless to be on his guard when the giantess was about.

After only a week in Bremen, Florian ordered the circus torn down and moved along. Inasmuch as it was drawing straw houses at every performance, and because all the troupers liked the old city of Bremen, several of them insubordinately demanded to know if Florian had any good reason for the hurry.

"Two," he said. "I want to get as far south as possible before winter comes. More important, Paris is our ultimate destination, and I want us well settled there before winter really clamps down. What I emphatically do *not* want is to hear any more quibbling with my decisions."

So the train continued along a rather zigzag southerly route, making only brief stands and long runs between them. On those moves, Edge was keeping his eyes open, as bidden. There were indeed occasional bodies of troops to be seen on the road, marching or in military wagons. Edge kept count of their numbers and memorized their various insignia in expectation that some of Louis Napoléon's officers would be able to identify the armies, corps, brigades, regiments to which they belonged. Quite often, the circus's road paralleled a railroad, and now and then a goods train would rumble past, laden with tarpaulin-covered but recognizably military equipment, and Edge could discern the nature of some of that. Several times, whether he was sleeping at an inn or in his own caravan by the roadside, Edge's eyes would even come open in the middle of the night, when he heard many hoofs or exceptionally heavy wheels going by, and he would get up and creep as close as he could get unseen, to determine what that traffic consisted of.

Every time the Florilegium prepared to leave a town where it was showing, Willi Lothar went first, to make sure it would not trespass on some other circus's scheduled stand. So Florian frequently bypassed a big city to show in a smaller one nearby—Hildesheim instead of Hannover, where the Zirkus Krone had already reserved a tober; Darmstadt instead of Frankfurt, where the Carmo would soon be setting up. The short stands and long runs that the journey entailed were not so irksome to the travelers as were the frequent and tedious interruptions of it, which occurred wherever the train had to cross a border, and there were many of those.

To go from Bremen to Hildesheim meant crossing from the Grand Duchy of Oldenburg into what only recently had been the Kingdom of Hannover, but was now just one more of Prussia's provinces—and again the circus company and its every accoutrement had to be subjected to Prussian-scrupulous inspection and

Prussian-detailed documentation and Prussian-grudging consent to pass. To go from Hildesheim to Kassel meant entering only another Prussian province, Kur-hesse, but the company might as well have been refugees from an enemy land, for they had to undergo the identical Prussian ritual there, too. Then, when they journeyed from Kassel to Darmstadt in the independent Grand Duchy of Hesse, they *were* coming from a country that the Hessians had reason to detest—the Prussia that was hungering to swallow Hesse—so at this border the circus troupe had to endure an even more searching, suspicious interrogation and scrutiny. The next run was to Karlsrühe in Baden, another independent Grand Duchy, and at this border again...

"Good *Jesus!*" Clover Lee exploded. "Every single one of us is already carry-ing enough documents that Saint Peter would wave us straight in through the Pearly Gates without asking a question!"

"Easy, my girl," Florian said with equanimity. "This is our very last border crossing in the German lands. Besides, think of the trouble and delay we *might* have suffered, if we didn't have the tsar's impressive letter to show as our chief credential." And, with the flourish of a fencing master, he presented it to the Badener guard blocking the road.

Karlsrühe, too, got only a week's enjoyment of the Florilegium before Florian told Goesle and Banat, "Bust the lacings, my lads, we're moving on."

This time Willi was not sent on ahead. The train went south through the Schwarzwald, *truly* a Black Forest at this time of year, its firs, pines, cedars and junipers hardly describable as evergreens, they were so dark under the gloomy and lowering gray sky. At Freiburg, the winter's first snow was falling. The troupe spent a night in a comfortable inn there, and next day they no longer went southward; Florian turned west through the still falling snow. At midday the train came to a broad river and a bridge, with a Badener sentry post at its nearer end, from which no official emerged to bar their way across. The far end of the bridge was invisible in the haze of snowflakes, but Florian stood up on his rockaway seat to point, and to call to all the travelers behind:

"This, my hearties, is the river Rhine. When you can see the flag flying yonder it will be the tricolor. I, an Alsatian, welcome all of you to Alsace. To France!"

FRANCE

I

As the troupe neared the Alsatian end of the bridge, a stockaded group of buildings appeared through the snow—almost a minor fortress, bristling with weapons pointed across the Rhine and swarming with armed soldiers. When the train was halted inside the garrison compound, Florian gathered up his armload of credentials: the company's conduct books, the letter from Tsar Alexander, the Russian passports everyone now owned, and all the other possibly pertinent documents—Prussian visas, Hessian visas and so on—to lay them all before the officials of the Bureau d'Immigration. But, before he could do so, Pemjean and LeVie came and handed him two more booklets, Pemjean saying, "Here, Monsieur le Gouverneur, you will have to show our internal passports, as well."

"Internal passports? What the devil are these?"

"They permit us to travel within France," said LeVie.

"What? A Frenchman needs permission to travel about his own country? I never heard of such a thing."

"An innovation since you left here, I suppose," said Pemjean.

"It is unbelievable!"

"It is a fact of life. A foreigner, once admitted into France, has rather more liberty of movement than we Frenchmen do."

Florian shook his head as he went to the office, bearing his sheaves of paper. But there he brisked up and said with warm good cheer, to the official to whom he presented the documents, "Bonjour, Monsieur le Fonctionnaire! But how good it is to be home again! To stand on French soil and speak French to a fellow

696

Frenchman. To see the beloved tricolor rippling overhead. To breathe the sweet air of Alsace. To hear—"

"Assez!" interrupted that functionary. "None of these foreign passports bears an entry visa for France. Why did none of you procure them from some French consulate on your way here?"

"It was through my own fault, as leader of the company, monsieur. I was unaware of the apparently many new restrictions imposed since I—"

"Ignorance of the law is no excuse."

"Je suis désolé. But this is the Bureau d'Immigration. Surely you yourself, monsieur, can provide the visas." Florian looked about the office, where the four or five other civil servants were idly lounging about, and said, "Or perhaps I am interfering with more urgent activities?"

"Of a certainty," snapped the official. "We are commanded to be constantly alert against any hostile moves from those boches across the river. How can I be alert if I am inundated in paperwork? C'est insupportable."

Nevertheless, albeit indolently, he went at the chore. With lackluster deliberation, he examined each trouper's conduct book, and only when he was unable to discern anything derogatory among the numerous and multilingual comments entered therein would he affix a visa stamp to that trouper's Russian passport. Florian, though not invited to sit, did so, and settled down for a weary wait. Then the man came to Florian's own conduct book and said, with malicious pleasure:

"As you have remarked, monsieur, you are Alsatian-born. Why do you not possess an internal French passport? If I cared to do so, I could charge you with infracting the law just for traveling from the middle of the bridge to this office."

"I have been abroad for many years, and was unaware until just—"

"Ignorance of the law is no excuse."

"However, I trust you can provide me with such a passport, Monsieur le Fonctionnaire?"

"Oui, oui," said the man, with exasperation. "Yet *more* work heaped upon me, when my attention and faculties are supposed to be undistracted from the boche menace. Very well, monsieur, kindly produce two witnesses who will vouch for your respectability, solvency and moral rectitude." He glanced contemptuously out the window at the circus company. "None of your foreign canaille will serve for that purpose."

"Among that canaille," growled Florian, "are two French citizens—"

"Subjects."

"Two French subjects of good repute and standing. You have their internal passports there before you."

The official sniffed and said, "I suppose they will have to do."

So Pemjean and LeVie came in and swore, with upraised right hands, that Florian was not likely to attempt to unseat Napoléon III, or to commit gross indecencies, or to become a charge upon the public charity. They also signed papers to that effect, and were dismissed, and the official, with many a sigh of being sorely put upon, laboriously began to fill out Florian's internal passport.

When, at long last, he finished his languid writing, signing, stamping and collating of papers, and shoved the heap across his desk, Florian gathered them up and said sweetly:

"Allow me to commend you, monsieur, on your strict punctiliousness and efficiency." The man looked surprised, but pleased. "You are proof of a long-standing theory of mine—that officiousness is always in inverse ratio to the importance of the office."

"Ah, merci, monsieur! Importance of the office, yes, indeed. Merci beaucoup. No hard feelings, eh? Bon voyage, monsieur, et bonne chance."

Not until Florian could show the douaniers of the next-door customs office that the company's immigration papers were all in order would they bestir themselves to begin inspecting the train for items they could tax or refuse entry. Since they gave evidence of being as refractory as the immigration official, Florian again had Willi and his luggage cleared before everyone else, and sent him on along the road, with instructions:

"In this snow and with this accursed delay, the rest of us will never reach Colmar tonight, but you can. Try to engage for our tober the big, open Champ de Mars right in the center of the town."

Then Florian turned to where Edge was arguing with the customs men, and not very successfully.

"Here, Governor, you take over. My French professor never taught me the cuss words I need here. These bullyboys want to bar everything from Fitz's fool bird to my own firearms. They say there are already enough coqs de bruyère in this country, and they won't allow any weapons to civilians. Damn it, I thought the Russian and Prussian border keepers were obnoxious, but..."

"Allow me, my boy." And to the inspectors he said briskly, "Allons donc, Messieurs les Douaniers, c'est assez cet enculage de mouches!" They bridled at being so indelicately told to cease their finicking objections. But then Florian was holding before them the letter from Tsar Alexander, and they were more awed by it than the immigration official had been. "You will take note, messieurs, that we are on our way to an audience with the emperor. He will doubtless be interested to hear whether we were cordially received into his realm." Florian went on at length in that vein, and perhaps some money changed hands, and eventually the whole circus train and company were let to pass with all their goods intact and untaxed.

The troupers' initially sour opinion of France was considerably ameliorated when the next day dawned sunny and bright. Before they left their roadside camp, the artistes dressed in their finest pista costumes, then bundled themselves in furs or cloaks. The calliope's professor stoked its firebox, Goesle fixed the new filigree crests on all the wagons, Beck's windjammers got out their instruments and Hannibal put the sheepskin boots on the camel and elephants. Then the train proceeded, with an azure sky overhead and the white-blanketed fields on either side glittering as prismatically as a fairy landscape. As the procession neared Colmar, the road was lined on either side with purple-barked weeping beeches, their drooping fronds hung with snow so that they looked like sculptures of marble and amethyst. The town itself, when it appeared in the distance, was an inviting sight—sharply vertical church spires and steeples and towers rising above tile or thatch roofs that were wavy and swaybacked with age.

The train paused while the artistes doffed their wrappings—the sun was now warm enough for that—and the bandsmen got settled upon their wagon, and the professor opened the calliope's boiler valves. Then the Florilegium made loud, cheerful, colorful parade into its first French town. As it racketed between the outlying houses—from which spilled wide-eyed housewives hastily wiping their hands on their aprons, and a multitude of wide-eyed children in smocks and wooden shoes—Willi was waiting there, and swung himself up beside Florian on the rockaway.

"I could not get the Champ de Mars, Herr Gouverneur. Perhaps it was a wide open space when you were last here, but now it is a park full of close-set trees and some ghastly statuary."

"I suppose I shouldn't be surprised," said Florian, a little sorrowfully. "I see much here that is new to me."

"However, I did obtain the smaller Jardin Mequillet, if you know where that is."

"Of course I know. And that will do very well. Thank you, Willi."

Florian did know his way about, and he led the parade up and down all the streets that were not too narrow for passage, collecting a tail of excited followers, mostly children but quite a few adults among them. The troupers noticed that the streets, where they had markers, were sometimes named in French, sometimes in German—the rue des Clefs, for example, leading into the Place des Unterlinden. Colmar was a quaintly cozy city. Except for the rectilinear public edifices and churches, the buildings seemed seldom to have a straight line or a right angle to them. Not only did their roofs sag, their walls bulged or dimpled here and there, so the houses resembled loaves of bread dough in various stages of leavening. Their windows were small, and many were round, with half-moon shutters. Several of the buildings had dates chiseled above their low doorways; one inn-and-stable was dated 1529. Narrow canals twisted through the city, with swans floating serenely on them, as white as the snow on the canal banks.

At last the parade halted at the little park Willi had engaged, and the Slovaks immediately started the unloading and setup, and the collected townsfolk stayed to watch. Florian asked Edge and LeVie if they would join him in a stroll when they had got into street clothes—"I have a reason for asking, gentlemen"—and, as they went off to change, he said to Beck:

"Chief Engineer, it looks as if this fine weather will hold at least through tomorrow. Can you and Monsieur Roulette arrange a balloon ascension to celebrate our arrival in France?"

"Ja, not too cold it is. But acid I have none. Where, in a small city like this—?"

"The Université de Technologie is up that way," Florian said, pointing. "I'm sure its Ecole de Chimie will oblige you."

"As soon as rigging is done, with wagon I shall go there."

When Florian and his invited companions left the park, they were five, for Daphne had come along with him and Nella with LeVie.

"I never imagined," said Florian, "that I should ever have to ask for tutelage regarding my own native country. But that is what I would like to ask of you, Maurice. Having been taken unawares by that business of the internal passports, I realize that I am rather out of touch with modern France. Now, Louis Napoléon and I are about the same age, and in my youth, when he was only the pretender to the diadem of his famous uncle, I followed his varying fortunes—his intermittent exiles and imprisonments and restorations to favor—and his ascent to the figurehead presidency. I have not been in France since he contrived to become emperor by public acclamation. Therefore, tell me, Maurice, anything you know about the man inside the imperial ermine."

"And," Edge said, "I'd like to ask something. Everybody knows about the great Napoléon the First. But this one is Napoléon the Third. I never heard of any Napoléon the Second."

Florian said, "That was Bonaparte's son, cousin to the current emperor. He was only a child when his father was overthrown, and he died young, so he never got to rule anything. Louis could legitimately call himself the second, but there is a popular joke as to why he is Napoléon the Third. People say that when he was campaigning to be acclaimed emperor, he ordered every town to hang out banners ... like this..." Florian knelt and with a finger wrote in the snow: VIVE NAPOLÉON!!! "So the exclamation points, they say, were mistaken for a Roman numeral."

"Alors," said LeVie, while the others chuckled. "As soon as Louis became emperor, he cast about for a suitable empress. He hoped for someone like a Hohenzollern, but of course all the ancient families spurned him as a parvenu. So he settled for the Countess Eugénie of Spain, about half his age, as beautiful as a porcelain doll, and just as empty in the head. Granted, brainlessness is often a virtue in a woman—eh, Nella?" She giggled, pouted and pinched his arm. "But *not* in an empress who wields much influence over an emperor. For many years now, Louis has suffered from the bladder stone. He is prematurely old, doddering, dull, a layabout—not even any longer the lecher he was in his first years as emperor— while Eugénie is still giddy and flighty. And meddlesome in state affairs."

"Brain maybe I do not have much," muttered Nella. "But meddle I do not never."

"Eugénie is vain and imperious. Louis is as monotonous as a metronome," LeVie continued. "I illustrate. Eugénie will not let her hairdresser attend her, which he must do several times a day, unless he arrives wearing knee breeches and a sword at his belt. And Louis? He insists that, on every one of his castles, the ivy on the walls be trained to grow in even undulations."

"Yes," said Florian. "You have illustrated them for me."

"Some people refer to Eugénie and Louis as 'Loquèle et Lourdeur.'"

Florian laughed, but Daphne looked blank and said, "If that is a mot, my French is not up to it."

"Well," said Florian, "a free but apt English translation would call them 'Twitter and Thud.'"

The group had come now to the Champ de Mars and Florian said, "Willi was right. This is a full-grown park—fountains, statues—and it used to be an empty drill ground. I see there's a monument to old General Rapp... and one to Admiral Bruat. Rapp was an aide-de-camp to that first Napoléon, if any of you care, and Bruat was a hero in the Crimean War. Two Colmar boys who made good."

As the group followed Florian through streets that got ever narrower, his tour-guide oration got more grandiloquent—accompanied by sweeping flourishes of his top hat—in a deliberate parody of his own pista bombast:

"*Friends!* Messieurs et mesdames! Together we have visited the courts of emperors and kings. We have walked in the Forum where once the mighty Caesars trod. But *now,* ladies and gentlemen, I take the greatest pleasure and gratification in introducing to you the one site in all of Europe most deserving of your admiration and veneration. *Here,* mein Herren und Damen..." They were in a street that was little wider than an alley. Florian brandished his hat at an old stucco house of two stories and a low dormer attic under the eaves. "Here—rue du Lycée, number eight—*here* is the humble birthplace and boyhood home of the world-famous showman and entrepreneur..." His voice caught, and he concluded almost shyly, "... yours truly."

His companions made various exclamations—of surprise, delight, even awe.

"Yes, indeed," Florian said softly. "It appears to be all residential flats now. When I lived here as a boy, the street floor was a cobbler's shop. The cobbler and his family lived on the upper floor and rented the attic. That is where we resided; we could afford no better habitation. But my father did not, like most fathers, drag me off to drudge beside him in the Jacquard mill at the age of eight or nine. Somehow he scraped up francs enough to send me to the Lycée des Jésuites— yonder, at the end of the street—where I acquired what little formal education I ever had."

"If a general and admiral can merit statues," said Daphne, "your house should have a bronze plaque, at the very least."

"Ah, well, my dear, this neighborhood is famous for other things besides me. Colmar is a fair-sized city now, but you are standing on the spot where *it* was born—as a mere Roman outpost called Columbarium." Florian paused. "We would have had a straighter run to Paris if I had brought us across the Rhine at Strasbourg. But I couldn't resist coming on south to here, to see the old place again." He sniffled slightly. "I had even hoped I might encounter some of the playmates of my youth and... by God, can that be *Kestenbaum?*"

They had come out of the alley into the small square fronting the lycée. On a bench there, warming himself in the afternoon sun, his papery eyelids closed, his veined and ropy hands clasped over the crook of a cane, sat a withered and white-bearded old man.

"Heavens," Daphne said faintly. "If he was a playmate, Florian, you are far, far older than you look."

"No, no, of course he wasn't. Grown man, a currier, lived next door. Kestenbaum! Lucien Kestenbaum, is that you?"

The old man's eyes opened, rheumy and dim. His toothless mouth opened and creaked, "Eh?"

"M'sieu Kestenbaum, je m'appelle Florian. Vous rappelez-vous du temps passé? Florian! Me remettez-vous?"

"Ah... ah, oui. Herrchen Florian." He gave some gasps that might have been laughter. "Le petit *Balg* Florian du numéro huit. Je me rappelle parfaitement les alten Zeiten."

Kestenbaum's speech was such a mixture of French and German words, and of French words with German accent or vice versa, that neither Edge nor Daphne could follow it. Somehow LeVie could, and he translated:

"The old man says yes, he remembers the Florian *brat* from the house number eight, long ago. Now he is asking, 'Do you see him ever, monsieur? How does he fare? Has he done well? Ma foi, we had always such high hopes for him.'"

Florian unabashedly dabbed at his eyes, then leaned close to the old man's face and said loudly, "C'est moi, m'sieu. C'est Florian. *Je suis* cet Florian-là. Moi. Ici."

"Horreur! Mais non!" exclaimed the old man. He recoiled and his eyes opened wide and red-rimmed. "Chose fausse! Florian, il est ein Jüngling, fort et réjoui."

"He refuses to believe," said LeVie. "Florian, he says, is a youngster, chipper and spry."

"Vous êtes ein garstig alte Kauz aux cheveux gris!" railed Kestenbaum, spraying spittle. "Menteur! Schwindler!"

LeVie went on, "He says this stranger accosting him is an impostor, an ugly old codger with gray—"

"No more," Nella whispered in compassion, laying a hand on LeVie's arm. "Tell no more. The Signor Florian this minute *looks* old."

Kestenbaum angrily waved his cane about as he continued to expostulate. Florian murmured some few more words to him, tucked a circus ticket into a pocket of his shabby coat, and came away. He and the others walked a distance in silence, then he sighed and said:

"That young Florian, *did* he do well? Did he vindicate the high hopes? Or did he just get old? There are no monuments or plaques for mere circus men, that is certain."

Daphne, walking at his side, leaned over and kissed his cheek. Edge said, "Remember what Cato replied, Governor, when somebody asked him why Rome had put up no statue to *him*."

On their way back to the Jardin Mequillet, they encountered various of their Slovaks, tacking or pasting up Florilegium posters—these worded in German, leftovers from the circus's tour through Austria and Bavaria—while Colmar townsfolk clustered about, to read and discuss them.

"That reminds me," said Florian. "The rest of you go on, while I seek out a printing establishment. Those German posters and our German program books will serve here in Alsace, but we shall need new ones as we proceed into France proper. Oh, and when you get to the tober, tell Boom-Boom to rehearse the band in 'Partant pour la Syrie.' That will be our promenade anthem from now on."

Though none of those five troupers spotted old man Kestenbaum at the next afternoon's performance, he could have been there unnoticed, for that show drew a turnaway crowd. And—as Daphne pointed out to Florian—the audience cheered and applauded as it surely never would have done at any reappearance of those *other* hometown heroes, General Rapp and Admiral Bruat.

As prelude to the evening show, Monsieur Roulette took the *Saratoga* aloft— with Monday concealed in the gondola so Sir John and Sunday could do the "disappearing girl"—and floated over a good deal of Alsace before bringing it down again. When he did, he missed the tober—deliberately, because the Mequillet park was so small and so packed with gawking spectators—landing instead on the paved court of the Ecole Normale just across the street, so the "reappearing girl" was visible to the marveling crowd. Also, he managed that landing without having to yank the ripcord and collapse the balloon. So the roustabouts simply towed the *Saratoga*, its basket bouncing lightly along the ground, back to where it belonged. The next day's weather being just as fine, and Beck having an ample supply of acid and shavings for the Gasentwickler— and, as he said, "the Herr Gouverneur's natal city a second salute deserving"— he topped up the balloon's gas content and Monsieur Roulette, with Sunday aboard this time, made another ascension that evening.

The Florilegium's subsequent shows were just as crowded, the Colmar folk now joined by country families attracted by the sight of the *Saratoga*—and were just as enthusiastically applauded, for the troupers were determined to show everybody in Florian's hometown a performance no less perfect than they had shown to Alexander II or would show to Napoléon III. At her every appearance, Mademoiselle Butterfly—now Mademoiselle Papillon—did that suspense-building trick of letting a flower petal silently drop the long, long way to the pista floor before the music thundered and she launched into her trapeze act. In the sideshow,

Sir John gave Princess Brunhilde more to do than just stand tall and be admired. Now she fought a mock duel with Cricket—here called Grillon—the giantess flailing her long sword, the midget wielding a dagger not much bigger than a hat pin.

Only one act was not being elaborated, but gradually shortened: the klischnigg contorting of Miss Eel, now dubbed Mademoiselle Anguille. She still performed with incredible elasticity and sinuous grace, but lately she could work for only a short while before her laboring lungs had to rest. And she could no longer hide the coughing spells that racked her afterward, during which Yount could only embrace her and clumsily pat her back and look concerned.

Florian claimed that he never again in Colmar espied anyone whom he recognized from his boyhood. Edge thought he might be lying about that, just to avoid approaching any such person and perhaps again being accused of imposture. However, it was undeniably a fact that, at the nearby Park-Hôtel, where Willi had engaged rooms for the company, Florian's various identity documents were received by the desk porter as casually as were those of all the other troupers, and Florian was no more or less assiduously served by the hotel's maids and dining-room waiters. At the circus, none of the jossers ever erupted from the seats to hail him with glad cries, and none was ever heard to remark that the name so flamboyantly painted on the chapiteau marquee evoked any recollection of a onetime local lad also named Florian. Nevertheless, it was not melancholy or bruised self-esteem, said Florian—only his eagerness to move on toward Paris— that made him order teardown after a single week's stand in Colmar.

So the circus train went on westward across the Haut-Rhin, then traversed the départements of the Vosges, the Haute-Marne and the Côte-d'Or, on the way crossing rivers whose names were familiar to at least the better-educated members of the company—the Moselle, the Saône, the Marne, the narrow upper waters of the Seine—besides a number of less famous streams. The circus made only short stands: four days in the substantial city of Epinal, two days at the little spa of Bourbonnes-les-Bains—and there mainly to please Carl Beck, so he could spend his every free hour pickling himself in the saline hot baths—then a couple of days apiece at Langres and Châtillon.

From one to the next of those communities was a three- or four-day run, but the traveling was easy. There were few troublesome highlands to toil over; most of the way the train was crossing a plateau of rolling meadows and farmlands. Where that land was not covered with snow, it was all brown and tan, and everything that its human inhabitants had put onto the land seemed deliberately selected to harmonize with its colors. The small horses grazing in the meadows were dark brown of coat with pale yellow manes and tails. The cattle and sheep of that region were inexplicably but identically cream colored. The farmhouses, stables and byres were all of warm tan stone, and roofed with dun-colored thatch. The villages, a dozen or so houses huddled close about a single church spire, were predominantly brown and tan. The larger towns in which the circus stopped, either to spend a night or to set up for performing, were likewise mostly of tan stone, but the buildings were roofed with reddish-brown tiles shaped like tongues and laid overlapping, so every roof looked fish-scaled.

Since those towns seldom had such a horde of travelers descend upon them at one time, hence possessed no grand hotels, the company apportioned itself out among several inns. Those were always remarkably alike, every one seeming to be owned by a widow lady of formidable dimensions and creaking corsets, commanding a staff that consisted of her numerous beefy daughters. There was never an identifiable husband or any sons to be seen, or any other male domestic except perhaps an ancient who tended the stables and yard. The accommodations in those inns were usually modest, frequently rustic or worse, but Madame l'Aubergiste never apologized for any shortcomings. Every proprietress received the guests as if they were supplicants and she were the Empress Eugénie—though not so regally that she ever failed to request that "le quibus" be handed over in advance. Then she would lead the guests to their rooms, which, through some constructional quirk common to every inn, were always at the end of a long, dark corridor. On the way, Madame would light the wicks of the hallway's sconce lamps, and then would snuff them all as she departed, sternly instructing the guests to use their bedside candle stumps to light their way when they came downstairs to dinner or whenever they had to go out to the "hangar d'aisance."

"Governor, I dislike to say this about your countrymen," grumbled Fitzfarris, after he had been fiercely scolded by one landlady for some trivial misfeasance of his, "but they're as humorless as Bibles and as unlovable as lawyers."

"Come, come, Sir John," Florian said pleasantly. "The common folk of France are kindly, charming and warmhearted people, *except* when they are disgruntled about something—the state of the nation, say, or the ineptitude of the government. Or the rankling condescension of their social superiors, or the impudence of their social inferiors. Or the presence in their midst of foreigners of any breed. Or the speaking of bad French—which is to say the speech of anyone born more than ten miles north, east, west or south of their own birthplace. Or they may get unhappy about the paltriness of their income, or furious at not having grasped some opportunity to screw an extra sou out of some commercial transaction. Or a Frenchman may be out of sorts for any number of other reasons. And it goes without saying that he *is* eternally disgruntled for one or several or all of those reasons. In brief, the common Frenchman is much like the common man or woman anywhere in the world."

Florian could be jovial, for he had just finished dining and was leisurely smoking a good cigar. All the company had to agree that just to enter a country inn's dining room was enough to overcome any deficiencies of their accommodations. One breathed the commingled aromas of wine, garlic, melting butter, wood smoke, sliced onions, furniture wax, cigar smoke, robust coffee, even the smell of fresh printer's ink on the newspapers being perused by other diners—perhaps the town's Monsieur le Maire or Monsieur le Notaire, in long black frock coat and yellow shoes fashionably curled up at the toes—stout men whose presence guaranteed that this was a damned good place to dine.

The beefy, red-faced waiter-daughters might waddle gracelessly with their trays from kitchen to tables, but nymphs on tiptoe bearing cornucopias could not have brought more ambrosial fare. The wine might arrive in a wooden pitcher, but it would be a genuine crisp Moselle or Rhine. The first course might come in wooden bowls, but it would be a clear-topaz bouillon or a bronze-brown onion soup. The main dish might be only a pot-au-feu, to be eaten with a dull pewter spoon out of a rough earthenware porringer, but *what* a pot-au-feu it would be. And then there was the incomparable, crusty French bread, and rich golden butter that had the slightest taste of hazelnut to it. And afterward would come a creamy Coulommier cheese, some green almonds, a mug of eyeball-extruding black coffee and perhaps a prunelle liqueur.

The town of Auxerre in the département of Yonne was the end of the Florilegium's directly westward traveling—from here it would turn northwest. Florian, who had been getting increasingly excited and fidgety with every step nearer Paris—more euphoric than his colleagues had ever seen him—declared this turning-place to be a major milestone of the journey, and Auxerre deserving of a parade entry. Outside the town, the air was bitterly cold, so the artistes had to hide their pista costumes under heavy wraps. But, once the procession had passed through the beautifully clock-towered archway that was Auxerre's entrance, the air almost magically became warm enough that they could shed their outerwear and show all their spangled grace and glory. The change of temperature, they soon realized, was an effect of architecture, not magic. Auxerre's streets were narrow enough at street level; they got progressively narrower overhead, because the old building fronts were like upside-down staircases, each upper story projecting beyond the one below until, at their tops, the houses on opposite sides of the street all but leaned eave-to-eave. That made the streets almost into tunnels, holding out the winter cold and holding in the warmth emanating from all the houses' hearths and stoves.

Willi had arrived in advance and, after the parade had been admired and hurrahed by the people on every negotiable street, he led it to the tober he had engaged near the riverside. The circus was set up, the town was plastered with posters and, next day, the citizens of Auxerre gave the Florilegium an even warmer welcome than their streets had done. So Florian was pleased to accord the town three days of performances and—since Beck was able to procure here his gas generator's necessities—as a bonus, an ascension of the *Saratoga*.

After the three days, when Florian announced that they would tear down and move on, nobody groaned at the prospect of taking the road again, for he also said, "From here we follow the river Yonne downstream. Three days' journey will bring us to Montereau, and we will show there—for the last time in the provinces, because at Montereau the Yonne flows into the Seine. And three days more of following the Seine will bring us to the bourn dreamed of by every circus artiste on earth. Paris, my friends, Paris at last."

2

T H E Y met their first Parisian before they got to Paris. On the tober at Montereau, where the Florilegium showed for three days, Rouleau was approached and addressed in French by a small, slight, very well-dressed gentleman with a waxed and pointed black goatee and mustache, and eyes almost equally black, bright and sharp, with a square monocle in one of them.

"Monsieur Roulette? I heard of your balloon ascensions out here in the provinces, so I have come from Paris just to meet and greet a fellow French aéronaute. I am Nadar."

"Bon jour, Monsieur Nadar. Actually, I am not a Frenchman but a créole américain, and my real name is Jules Rouleau."

"Eh bien, Nadar is only *my* nom-du-métier. I am by birth Félix Tournachon."

"And your métier is ballooning?"

"Oh, I do many things. I earn my living as a photographer, but ballooning I *prefer* to do. I have sometimes combined the two occupations. I believe I am the first ever to take a photograph from the air. Of the Arc de Triomphe, that was. No easy endeavor, you will appreciate, a long exposure from such an unsteady platform. I must have used two dozen plates before I succeeded."

If Monsieur Nadar was a typical Parisian, Rouleau soon decided, then a Parisian was incapable of giving a simple answer to a simple question, but elaborated every statement with far more information than had been asked for. However, Nadar's loquacity contained much of interest, at least to a fellow balloonist, for he went on:

"Some years ago, I built the biggest gas-inflated aérostat ever made—I called it *Le Géant*. It carried not a gondola basket, but a veritable two-story cottage made of wicker. On its first ascent, I took up in it a dozen persons besides myself, including the Princesse de la Tour d'Auvergne."

"Mon Dieu, monsieur! Compared to you, I am a rank dilettante."

"Ah, well. The second time I made an ascension in *Le Géant,* I made two mistakes. I took up also my wife. And I made a very rough landing. Hélas, Madame Nadar made me abandon the balloon, and I have not been aloft since. An embarrassing admission for the founder of the Société d'encouragement de la locomotion aérienne. We sociétaires are few—myself, Flammarion, the brothers Godard—and I believe there is not nowadays a gas aérostat being flown anywhere in France. So you and yours will be a most welcome sight in our skies."

"I regret that you will not witness an ascension here, Monsieur Nadar. We could not procure the chemicals for our generator. But I will, of course, be going aloft in Paris, and I gladly invite you to accompany me whenever you wish."

"And I gladly accept." Nadar added, a trifle petulantly, "Then I need not have left Paris at all, eh? I try to do so as seldom as possible. I detest equally the countryside, the riding of railroad trains and the cold of wintertime. Just to go from my residence to the Gare de Lyon today, I had to send my valet first to find a voiture, then to find two or three fat porters to ride around in it and get it well warmed before I got into it."

Keeping a straight face, Rouleau said, "You need not endure such nuisances to return there, monsieur. You can ride with me and our advance man, the Baron von Wittelsbach, in his own carriage. We are departing this very afternoon, and the baron is plump enough to warm the carriage to your requirements, I think. Come and meet him."

Willi was in conversation with Edge and Florian. When Rouleau introduced Nadar, there was no need to explain to Florian who he was.

"Of course! The famous photographer of the famous! I have seen and admired much of your work, Maître Nadar. But what brings you out here? Are you quitting salon portraiture to do bucolic scenes? Genre studies of peasants?"

"Heaven forfend!" cried Nadar, so horrified that his monocle fell to the end of its ribbon. "Once, just once, I espied in the markets of les Halles a handsome country woman. I asked her to sit to me. She refused. And do you know why? She was of the firm conviction that the camera could see through her clothes! Non, non, messieurs. Give me the most decadent duchess or the most shameless courtisane, any time, rather than the pure and puritan peasant—of any country—who believes beauty is obscene. La plus belle, to the country mind, is la poubelle."

Edge idly commented, "I haven't seen many young ladies anywhere in these provinces that I would consider plus belle, so how can the peasants consider them garbage?"

"Ah, mon colonel, these days any country girl who has any beauty at all runs off to the city. You see, most of the great Parisian courtisanes rose from obscure origins, ascending by way of various bedroom stairs. La Jeanne aux Violettes was a bottle washer in a winery; today she is famous for having inspired Flaubert's *Salammbô*, and is currently the mistress of the wealthy Monsieur Barouche. And Blanche d'Antigny was the daughter of a common laborer; now she takes daily baths in champagne. Juliette la Marseillaise, who frequently entertains while clothed in nothing but her long blonde tresses, started life as a wool picker. Perhaps, Colonel, you would be professionally interested to know that the renowned Marguerite Bellanger was originally a circus bareback rider. Later, she was famous in several army barracks as Margot the Frolicsome. Later still, the remark was widely quoted that 'she holds an extremely important position under the emperor.' Voilà, now she has a mansion in the rue des Vignes."

"Well. . ." said Edge, somewhat dazed by such an unsolicited wealth of information.

"Donc, every other female nonentity aspires to do the same, and so the country coquettes flock to Paris. They dress in what they think is fashionable—Sébastopol blue or Magenta fuchsine—and they wear their hair in the tire-bouchon made popular by Eugénie, and they walk with 'the Alexandra limp,' imitating the Princess of Wales. But *all* those fashions are ludicrously out of date in Paris now. Eugénie wears her hair these days in a chignon dusted with gold, and of course country girls cannot afford gold dust. They cannot afford more than a single drink of cassis or absinthe, over which they sit for hours in the public houses of the boulevard des Italiens, hoping to be discovered by some prince or pasha or social lion. The bistros call them contemptuously les grog-chasseuses, the cheap-drink huntresses. And it is well said that, if the palace is the brain of Paris, and Notre-Dame is the heart, and les Halles the stomach, then surely the boulevard des Italiens is le clitoris de Paris. Simply visit the zincs along that boulevard, Colonel Edge, if you seek easy conquests."

"I don't, really. And anyway I'm a nonentity myself."

"No matter. The country gonzesses are so pathetically eager to acquire the social graces and urban polish that they will fall down horizontal for any man who is passably well-spoken. Someone has described a day in the life of such a girl—s'habiller, babiller, se déshabiller."

Florian interrupted Nadar's own babillage to say, "Just now the colonel, the baron and I were discussing where to set up our circus in Paris. It might be that the emperor would care to have some say in that, since we are bearing to him a letter of introduction from his imperial counterpart, Alexander of Russia. I think, monsieur, you are well acquainted with Louis Napoléon?"

"Exceedingly so," said Nadar, with an exaggerated air of ennui. "I suppose you wish to know if he is as degenerate as is commonly reported. Oui, Louis is a whore." Nadar yawned languidly behind a glove. "Not, however, one of the *great* whores."

"What I meant, monsieur," Florian persisted, "is that I believe you have easy access to His Imperial Majesty. And perhaps—"

"But of course I do. I am the court portraitist, after all. I have photographed every member of the imperial family, not to mention every one of His Majesty's amantes. Some of them, to paraphrase the venerable Hugo, visage masqué, con à nu—and some not masqué at all. In one study I did of the Comtesse de Castiglione, she is reclining on her black satin sheets, wearing a pensive look, nothing else. His Majesty was pleased to autograph for her a print of that picture with the message, 'I send you a kiss on all four of your cheeks.'"

Willi Lothar and Jules Rouleau were regarding Nadar with awe and admiration, as he continued his virtuoso display of insouciance. But Florian, with a touch of desperation, interrupted again:

"I thought, monsieur, that you might graciously consent to introduce the baron to Louis Napoléon—under your auspices, so to speak. Willi can present our billet d'introduction and thereby perhaps inspire His Majesty to allot our circus a better location than we could otherwise procure."

"By all means. I shall be happy to do so, in gratitude for the comfortable transport and congenial companions taking me back to the city."

So Florian hurried off to get the tsar's letter and Edge sent a Slovak to hitch up the calash, while Nadar went on prattling to the fascinated Willi and Jules.

"His Majesty may even maliciously allow you to set your circus on the estate of a certain lady with whom he is lately disenchanted. She was once so refined that she would not be laid on any but a bed of rose petals and hundred-franc notes. She claimed to be so sensitive that she could not masturbate with anything harsher than the tip of an artist's fine sable brush. Also, she enjoyed the reputation of being a fastidious and high-principled lady, because she never had two lovers at the same time. Of late, however, she has required ever more and coarser stimulation, until now—it is said—she has had her physician permanently clamp golden rings onto her labia and each of her nipples, for her lovers to manipulate and yank and twist..."

Florian returned with the parchment rolled for Willi to carry, and the driver came with the calash. Nadar was still unquenchably gossiping, now about someone else, as he climbed in with the other two men:

"...His lifetime of buggery has left the poor marquis's posterior muscles so slack that he is these days fecally incontinent. He dares not leave his chambers for even so much as a stroll about his own grounds. Meanwhile, his poor marquise, who once enjoyed the distinction of having been the first love of several generations of schoolboys, now has only one consoling companion..."

"My God," Edge muttered to Florian. "Is he the world's most outrageously inventive storyteller? Or is Paris really what he makes it sound like: Sodom and Gomorrah rolled into one?"

Nadar's voice trailed off as the calash rolled away. "...Eau de Cologne she calls it, but everybody knows it is Holland gin..."

Florian shrugged. "It is more than twenty years since I was last in Paris." He tugged his little beard meditatively. "You know, the Book of Genesis is quite explicit about the sin of Sodom. But I have always wondered *what* went on in Gomorrah. I suppose we shall soon find out."

Four days later, he led the Florilegium along the Quai de Bercy on the east bank of the Seine. But, even after he had passed the word down the train of wagons— "We have just crossed the city line, from Charenton into Paris"—none of the troupers could see anything like the splendid metropolis they all were anticipating. There was no snow on the ground that day, and none falling, but a leaden sky hung low and gloomy overhead. The river was also dull gray, and there was only grayness on both sides of it: a pall of gray smoke and, shrouded in it, slab-sided factories with high chimneys, ramshackle boat-building yards, grimy brickworks, smelly stock-yards, stinking garbage dumps, reeking abattoirs and gray, bleak, squalid warrens of huts and shanties. The people who slunk out, to stare in silence at the passing train, were gray people—gray from hair to complexion to homespun clothes and wooden shoes. Even the children, with pinched faces and hollow eyes but protruding little paunches, were so encrusted with coal smoke, industrial dust and miscellaneous other filth that they were as gray as their elders.

Florian said to Daphne, who sat beside him, wearing her sable coat over her pista costume, "We shall wait to make parade until we are out of les bas quartiers."

"In England we call them slums," she said, looking pityingly at the children.

"Is that so? Perhaps the term somehow derives from the cheap slum goods peddled on circus midways... Hello, this bridge wasn't here in my day."

Florian had to halt Snowball abruptly where the Pont National met the quai, so the toylike Petite Ceinture railroad train could chug and clatter past on its interminable stop-and-start circuit of Paris, around what had once been the city's line of outer walls.

"You will see a lot of new things in Paris," said Daphne. "And a lot of old ones gone. The Baron Haussmann has been drastic in his renovation of the city, and parts of it are still as torn up as Vienna was. At least he has razed all the slums in the middle of Paris, even if that meant leveling many landmarks. There are new boulevards, new squares, new parks, new bridges." She laughed. "Nevertheless, the oldest bridge in Paris is still known as the Pont Neuf."

The Florilegium's wagons, caravans and animals were now on the Quai de la Rapée, and the urban scenery began to improve slightly. On the other side of the river was the immense Gare d'Orléans, plumed with the steams and smokes of the many trains arriving, departing, waiting, being shunted about the yards. On the landward right side of the quai stood multistoried brick or stone residential buildings, and their inhabitants came outside or threw open their windows, even on this chill gray day, to get a better look at the circus procession. The occupants of the lower floors appeared healthy and were decently dressed; those leaning from upper windows looked less so. LeVie told Nella that everywhere in Paris, even in the most stylish quarters, the lower-floor residences were the most expensive, hence housed the more prosperous and better-class families. The upper floors, which required climbing stairs, cost decreasingly less in rent according to their altitude, so the very poorest and socially insignificant tenants lived always on the topmost floor—thus, though they might not appreciate the fact, enjoying the best view and the freshest atmosphere.

The riverside quais and the streets leading down to them were crowded along here, mainly with people on foot, and not many of them looked as "typically Parisian" as had Monsieur Nadar. There were gypsies in layers of gaudy fabrics, Algerian Arabs and Moroccan Berbers in sweeping robes, beady-eyed and beak-nosed Armenians, bearded and ringleted Polish and Russian Jews, little yellow Cochin-Chinese. Peddlers maneuvered pushcarts through the crowd and bellowed their wares: oysters "à la barque!" eggs "à la coque!" chestnuts "tout bouillant!" Flower girls shrilled, "Fleurissez vos amours!" Frowsy old ladies pushed smoking little stoves on wheels, on which simmered hot sausages or apple fritters or fried potatoes.

Where the quai crossed the waters of the Port de Plaisance that extended all the way from the Seine to the Place de la Bastille far distant on the right, Florian halted the train and called down the line, "From here we make parade!" The bandsmen got out their instruments from where they had been carefully keeping them warm—especially the ones with metal mouthpieces—and the professor opened the valves of his calliope boiler. The artistes took up their positions and graceful poses on the various wagons, but here, as they had done on other wintry occasions, they only intermittently opened their cloaks or furs to give the street crowds glimpses of their skimpy costumes and bare flesh. Now the circus stepped out more briskly, to its clamor of music, along the Quai Henri IV, which jinked farther to the right where the Seine parted around its two great midstream islands.

"The Ile Saint-Louis and the Ile de la Cité," said Sunday. "Once upon a time, those were *all* of Paris."

"You sound like you had been here before," said Edge, beside her.

"Thanks to Jules's tutoring," she said modestly. "Of all Europe, he has always laid most emphasis on France and Paris. So I'm glad to be here at last. I can hardly believe I really am."

The central city was as overhung and veiled with smoke as its outskirts had been, but the newcomers now could see it at least in planes of silhouette ahead of them. Sunday continued to point out to Edge the various sights and landmarks she recognized from her geography and history books or from Rouleau's descriptions—the high spire and towers of Notre-Dame in mid-river, on the Left Bank the even higher steeple-topped dome of the Panthéon and, beyond that, highest of all the edifices in Paris, the cupolaed dome of the Invalides. Away off on the Right Bank, overtopping the whole city, and visible even from this distance upriver, was the conical hill of Montmartre, but it was otherwise undistinguished, bearing only a scattering of small buildings and rustic windmills.

The farther the parade went along the quai of continuously changing names —it was now the Quai de l'Hôtel de Ville—the thicker and more tumultuous became the street traffic, and the parade's involvement made it ever more tumultuous. The street policemen at every crossing had to do frenzied whistle blowing and arm waving to hold up other carriages and carts as it came by, and many of the civilian horses shied or reared in their traces at sight of the elephants or scent of the cats. Some of the policemen shook their fists at Florian and shouted profanely—"Démerde-toi!" "Foutez le camp!"—but others goodnaturedly waved the parade on past. The pedestrian passersby, when they were not dodging kicks from panicked horses, likewise goodnaturedly waved and cheered.

The drivers of the circus wagons let Florian worry about making a way through the throngs, and simply stopped or moved on when his rockaway did. The troupers on the wagon seats or beds or tops kept their graceful poses, and mechanically waved and smiled and blew kisses, and absentmindedly flicked open their coats or cloaks to flash their spangles and skin, for they were meanwhile ogling Paris as raptly as the Parisians were ogling them. Right now, they were on the Quai de la Mégisserie, and staring at the shops that lined its right side, for every one of those was a pet shop. The sidewalks outside them were piled with stacked glass bowls and tanks glinting with goldfish, or wire cages full of canaries and parrots, or stouter cages containing kittens and puppies, those having lively hysterics at the sight, smell and commotion of the circus's passing.

Everywhere there were flags flying. The several bridges across the Seine were lined with flag-bearing standards; flags flapped from the window staffs of apparently patriotic shopkeepers and householders; gonfalons hung lengthwise down the streets' lampposts. Most were the familiar red, white and blue, but some of the flags were dark green, patterned with golden figures too small to make out from a distance. Edge asked Sunday if she knew what they were, and she did.

"Golden bees. The Napoleonic symbol. When Maître Jules told me that, I asked him if it meant B for Bonaparte, and he nearly caned me for my ignorance. I was forgetting that a bee in French is une abeille."

As the street traffic got thicker and thicker, especially where streams of vehicles and people poured from the bridges onto the quais, the circus more frequently had to stop and wait for a break in the torrent. But it always got one. No traffic-directing policeman could long endure the booming of the band or the caterwauling of the calliope, stalled at his street crossing, without doing everything in his power to clear a way for the parade to go on. When the train was held up in a jam of vehicles on the Quai du Louvre, one of those vehicles deftly extricated itself from the pack and deftly inserted itself right into the circus train, behind Florian's rockaway. It was Willi's calash, and Rouleau got hastily out of it, before the parade could move on again, to climb up beside Florian and Daphne.

"Willi is getting very expert at intercepting us," Florian said admiringly. "Where do I go from here, Monsieur Roulette?"

"Turn off the quai at the Place Concorde, circle around that and then go up the Champs-Elysées."

"Come, come. I would have done that without being told. Where else should a parade make parade in Paris? But where are we going ultimately?"

"The emperor has most generously given us a splendid tober in the Bois de Boulogne, at—"

"What? Out in the *forest?*"

"Perhaps it was a forest, mon vieux, in your prehistoric youth. But now, after what the locals call the 'haussmannisation' of Paris, the Bois is all lush parklands and lakes and ponds and carriage drives and pavilions and monuments. As lovely as the Prater."

"Ah. Of course. I should have assumed something of the sort."

"We are to pitch—most fittingly, I think—right at the monument marking the historic place whence the first untethered balloon carried men into the sky, nearly two centuries ago. Very near the drive that all the fashionable folk take to the racecourses at Auteuil or Longchamps. Also very near a lake suitable for watering the stock."

"Well done," said Florian. "And have you and Willi engaged hotel rooms for us all?"

"Er, yes..." said Rouleau, a little warily. "The last time we arrived in an imperial capital, it was *you* who insisted that Willi engage only the best, and so he has done that here, as well. This hotel, Florian, you must see to believe. But, heh heh, wait until you see the prices. The new Grand Hôtel du Louvre on the boulevard des Capucines."

"Ooh!" Daphne cried ecstatically. "That was just a-building when I was last here. Is it as swanky as it promised to be?"

"Swanky. The very word. All plush and mahogany and shining brass. The servants wear cork-soled shoes so they'll walk silently. They are not summoned by bell pulls, but by push buttons that communicate by some kind of electrical apparatus. However, the objet de luxe is the ascenseur. Only guests are allowed to use it, but people come from all corners of the earth just to marvel at it."

"Ascenseur?" said Florian. "A mere hoist? You make it sound more like an indoor balloon."

"Almost the equivalent. No guest of the Grand Hôtel need ever climb any stairs unless he simply wants the exercise. The ascenseur is a small room suspended on cables from machinery powered by steam. Step into it on the ground floor and you are gently lofted to any upper floor you choose. Or lowered from upper to ground. Fantastic."

"It sounds as if Willi has chosen well," said Florian. "We *should* have the most modern and best accommodations—being, as it were, guests of the emperor."

"That reminds me," said Rouleau, gesturing toward the Tuileries Palace that they were then passing. "His Majesty wishes to see you and Zachary as soon as you can leave the setting-up to the underlings."

"Oh? And did he receive you graciously?"

"Mais oui. Nadar most expeditiously arranged our audience the very day we got here, and Louis Napoléon greeted us with every courtesy. But then—curious thing—after he read that letter from Alexander, he took it to the fireplace and appeared about to *burn* it. Willi and I wondered if something in it had angered him. But evidently not. He merely read it through again, and granted us the tober in the Bois, and directed his chamberlains to see to anything else we might require. Then he told us to have Monsieur le Propriétaire Florian and Monsieur le Directeur Edge attend upon him—these are his words—as soon as you possibly can." Then Rouleau made Daphne jump, by loudly and joyfully breaking into song to the Offenbach tune the band had just begun playing:

> Nous allons envahir
> La cité souveraine,
> Le séjour de plaisir...

It was the longest parade the Florilegium had ever made, both in mileage covered and time expended, partly because Paris was so big in area, partly because the parade took the most populous thoroughfares. For all the vastness of the Place de la Concorde, and although vehicular traffic there was allowed only one-way movement, counterclockwise, and despite every exertion the harried policemen could make on the circus's behalf, the progress there was glacial. The circus train had to go three-quarters of the way around the Place to turn off into the Avenue des Champs-Elysées, and, since three-quarters of the Parisians' vehicles turned there, too, the subsequent pace was not much more rapid.

The bandsmen had taken a much needed breather during the slow circuit of the square, but resumed making music with admirable vigor as they went along the broad avenue between the ranks of bare-branched chestnut trees. Behind the trees, sometimes behind intricately wrought iron fences, sometimes behind small lawns or gardens as well, stood almost side by side the massive but architecturally artful mansions of royals and nobles, and the smaller but just as handsome residences of lesser aristocrats and mere plutocrats.

The day's chill could not deter the fashionable folk of Paris from making their afternoon promenade on the Champs-Elysées—some afoot on the wide sidewalks under the chestnuts, others riding in the most elegant equipages the circus people had ever seen on one stretch of pavement. There were stately barouches and broughams and victorias, racy phaetons and daumonts and coupés, old-fashioned shandrydaus and the new, low-slung C-spring landaus. One small carriage, a high-wheeled stanhope, was *not* very elegant; it flaunted advertising placards on both sides and the back—"*La Capote CONVERTIBLE de M. L'Inventeur Dauzat!*"—and the driver, presumably M. Dauzat, every few minutes worked a cumbersome crank to raise up or fold down his stanhope's hood and demonstrate its ease of convertibility on the hoof, as it were.

The promenaders, walking or riding, were superbly dressed. The men wore curly-brimmed top hats, fur-collared overcoats and glossy patent-leather shoes, with spatterdashes over them to preserve their gloss. The women mostly wore their hair in Empress Eugénie chignons—either a small chignon under a capacious hat or a large chignon with only a little pancake of a hat perched on top. If the women were not totally enveloped in sable, mink or other fine fur, their coats and what could be seen of their gowns were of the textiles and colors stylishly named for French expeditions, battles and even foes: Shang-haï and Pékin and Canton fabrics, Solferino red, Crimée aqua, Bismarck brown, Prussian blue. But the most remarkably dressed were the children, some of whom rode miniature goat-drawn carts beside their parents or governesses. Little boys and girls wore glengarry caps and Scottish tartans, plaids over their shoulders and kilts below —or trews on some of the boys—and a few even had hairy sporrans hanging from their belts and toy dirks in their stocking tops.

"Oh, yes," said Rouleau, when Daphne remarked that she had not noticed that fashion when she was earlier in Paris. "Doubtless those nannies with the tykes are Scots. Anything Scottish is currently as popular here as it was in Saint Petersburg."

"I am astonished," said Florian, "that the French would take up any fad shared by any other nationality. They are usually most idiosyncratic—I might say eccentric—in the things on which they choose to fasten their regard. For example, there was the great French poet Lamartine. Not only a poet, but a polymath: man of letters, diplomat, legislator, very nearly President of France. And what did his countrymen choose to admire most about him? The shapeliness of his hands and feet." Florian amusedly shook his head. "I shall not find it at all curious if the French audiences attending our circus should give their wildest applause to, say, one of the hyenas, or the Devil's Fiddle in the band, or even a particular tent pole."

The parade continued on, up the avenue's Chaillot Hill incline to its top, the Place de l'Etoile, the great open "star" of which the points were the twelve avenues radiating downhill from it, and in the center of which stood the Arc de Triomphe. The circus train left the Champs-Elysées and turned right to merge with the slow counterclockwise whirlpool of vehicles circling the arch, and all the troupers gaped up at that bulky, soaring edifice. Even those who had not been in Paris before had probably seen pictures of the monument, and perhaps were aware that it was the biggest victory arch in the world, but—since most published pictures showed its central barrel vault straight on—they were surprised to see how *thick* the arch was, about a third as deep as it was wide, and with barrel-vaulted arches going sidewise through it, as well.

Florian led his procession around two-thirds of the perimeter of the Place, then turned right again, into the eighth starpoint avenue he came to, the avenue du Bois de Boulogne. It was not crowded and creeping with traffic, so the train proceeded along it more rapidly—though still with music, waves and smiles for everybody on the sidewalks—and came eventually to the Porte de la Muette, what had once been a gateway in the old city walls and was now an entrance to the Bois. Rouleau showed Florian the historic balloon-ascension marker, because it was modestly small and easy to overlook. The circus drew up on that expanse of lawn, the band ceased playing, the calliope wheezed down to silence and the drivers began to maneuver their wagons and caravans into their accustomed backyard ranks.

"Don't even think of setting-up this evening, men," said Florian. "Just unload a couple of wagons in which the company can ride to the hotel. Willi, will you lead them there, when they have all changed into street clothes? And then, once everyone is settled at the hotel, Monsieur le Démon Débonnaire, will you take Abdullah and his assistant handlers on to les Halles? Show them where they can purchase feed and grain—and you yourself purchase any cat's meat or other provisions your own animals may require. Colonel Ramrod, while all that is being attended to, will you also change clothes and join me right now in paying a call requested by His Majesty Louis Napoléon? If Paris hasn't been too greatly altered, I know a shorter route back to the Tuileries. The sooner we get this over with, the sooner we two will be able to relax with the others."

3

THE ROCKAWAY went at a trot through the drives, past the statues and fountains and the few evening strollers in the Tuileries' public gardens, then was halted by a sentry at the entrance to the palace gardens. When Florian gave his name, the sentry disappeared into his box, where apparently he had a telegraph apparatus, for he popped out again almost immediately to give a formal salute with his musket and let the rockaway go on. There were guards also flanking the palace entrance, but they too merely presented arms, while a flunky hastened down the steps to take Snowball's reins. By the time Florian and Edge had mounted the broad stairs, the palace's grand chamberlain was there to meet them, wearing a richly embroidered scarlet livery and his huge key of office on a chain of gold and green acorns around his neck—the Duc de Bassano himself, who usually left to the under-chamberlains every duty except the direction of great court balls and receptions. Gushing politenesses all the way, the duke led them up various stairs and along various corridors to Louis Napoléon's study, and the emperor actually stood to greet them when they entered.

He could have been a stouter elder brother of Monsieur Nadar. He wore the same sharply waxed and pointed mustache and beard, his graying hair similarly tufted out into little eaves above his ears. But his skin was an unhealthy color, the whites of his eyes were tinged with yellow and he stood in a stooping posture. His clothes, like Nadar's, were very well cut and of the best black broadcloth and white linen, but they were hardly imperial; he could have been a bourgeois dressed for church.

"M'sieu Florian, Colonel Edge, I am delighted to meet you." He waved them to boulle chairs and quickly sat down again himself. His chair was one of the new, bulbously padded leather "confortables," and he stiffly raised his legs to rest his feet on a matching leather pouf. "I hope you will forgive the urgency of my summons, but I did want at least one interview with you in private." Edge would have supposed that an emperor could demand privacy whenever he wanted it, but Louis added significantly, "My empress-wife will return any day now, from the festivities at the Suez Canal."

His study was a masculinely homely room, but old-womanishly overheated. The walls were all bookshelves, interrupted only where there stood a huge desk for the emperor and a smaller one for his secretary. In the center of the room was a divan-jardinière, a circular sofa built around a towering plant stand, and the plants on it were white roses and white lilacs in full bloom. But if those had any perfume, it was smothered by another and sickly odor that permeated the room. And that was explained when Louis fitted a cigarette into a gold holder and lighted it—and continued to smoke one after another while they conversed—for the cigarettes had been steeped in some kind of asthma reliever, and smelled awful.

Urgency notwithstanding, the interview commenced with small talk, the emperor saying, "I heard your circus parade go by, messieurs, earlier this afternoon, playing 'Partant pour la Syrie.'"

"What else *would* we play, under the windows of the palace?" said Florian, with a smile. "What else but the country's most popular anthem?"

"The country's, not mine. I loathe the damned song."

"Oh?" said Florian, caught off guard. "Well . . ."

"Perhaps you are unaware that it was my mother who composed it," Louis went on. "It may be a good piece of music; I would not know; I have no ear. But I loathed my queen-mother Hortense, and the song perpetually reminds me of her. It is impossible to have fond memories of a mother who presented you with a bastard half-brother, and presented her husband, your father, with another man's get. Happily, both she and the bastard are dead now. He was, by a polite fiction, called the Duc de Morny, and he once collaborated with that Jew Offenbach in composing an operetta for a court ball, and making it very offensive. Ever since, I have detested Offenbach's music, as well."

"In which case, Your Majesty, we shall certainly strike from our repertoire—"

"Oh, no. You cannot stop every other band and orchestra in France from playing those tunes—or the people from singing them. You might as well play them, too."

To turn the talk to a more lightsome topic, Edge ventured the comment, with a gesture at the jardinière, that he had never before seen roses and lilacs in bloom in midwinter.

"Hothouse-forced," said the emperor. "In artificial heat and total darkness to bleach them white. Unfortunately, if one plants them outdoors, they revert to their ordinary and coarse colors."

Since that subject seemed also depressive to His Majesty, Florian broached the reason for their summons to attend upon him. "You have read the Tsar Alexander's letter, sire . . ."

"Oui." He reached to a table to pick it up, which requred the scattering of some playing cards laid out in a complicated game of patience. Louis scanned the parchment, tweaked the points of his mustache and said, with a wry smile, "Every other monarch in Europe addresses me in the traditional style, as 'Monsieur mon frère.' Alexander alone still refuses to recognize my legitimacy; his letters always begin 'Mon cher ami.' I am not offended. I rather prefer it. A man *chooses* his friends, but, as I know too well, he cannot choose who is to be his brother." Louis leaned back almost supine in his easy chair. "Well, now. The covering letter of course lavishly commends your circus, as you are aware. I do hope you are pleased with the site I allotted to your emissaries."

Florian assured him of that. Louis went on to proffer his chamberlains' assistance in providing any other conveniences the circus might require, and then extended an invitation to the whole troupe to attend the next palace ball, which would be planned when Her Majesty Eugénie had returned from abroad. Florian accepted, with gratitude, on behalf of his company.

"Now," said the emperor, back to business. "You are also aware that the letter contained interlineations in invisible ink." He paused, frowned and said, rather peevishly, "Alexander is forever giving me advice, but he refuses to give me the formula for that very useful secret ink."

Florian and Edge also refrained from divulging it.

"His concealed message this time consists only of a caution. In effect, that I *must not* go to war with Prussia, whatever provocations those boches may goad me with. Really, messieurs, that is very like being told that I should not leap out that window yonder, three stories above the courtyard bricks. I have no intention of doing so; I need not be warned against such a rash act. Nevertheless, I *can* imagine a situation—say a fierce, consuming fire on this floor of the palace— that would *force* me to jump from a window, bon gré, mal gré, and to hell with good sense and good advice."

Florian murmured that yes, any exigency was conceivable.

"However, the tsar adds that you, Colonel Edge, may be able to give me additional reasons for not going to war. Please do."

"Your Majesty will wish to take notes," said Edge. "Would you care to summon a—?"

"I shall take them down myself." The emperor reached to the table for pencil and paper, discarding a top sheet on which apparently he had been keeping score of how many games of patience he had won and lost. "For the time being, messieurs, this conversation is strictly entre nous."

So Edge recited from memory: what forces he had seen grouping or traveling east of the Rhine, identifying each unit in the only way he could, according to its composition—infantry, cavalry, artillery, supply—and the insigne each displayed on flags or wagons or uniforms. He gave his best estimate of the number of men and officers in each of those units, and told where it was emplaced or where it appeared to be headed, and what supplies it carried, as an indication of how long it expected to be in the field. He told what small arms the infantry and cavalry outfits carried, and what pieces the artillery units had at trail, and, judging from the wagons and caissons, how much ammunition was available for those arms. He described two obvious supply depots he had glimpsed, and extrapolated from them the Prussians' probable logistical preparations for maintaining their troops at a considerable distance from any homeland base. Louis Napoléon took notes of everything, not interrupting, nodding approvingly at intervals, and Florian regarded Edge with open admiration.

"Most immediately significant, I think," said Edge, "is the matter of ordnance. The infantry and cavalry of the Prussians, and evidently all their allies, carry the breech-loading Dreyse rifles and carbines. Every artillery piece I saw was also a breech-loader, and made of stout Krupp steel. But here in France—for example, at the frontier post where we crossed the Rhine, and where the Prussians might, too—I have seen only muzzle-loading rifles and cannons. Worse yet, Your Majesty, your army's cannons are all of *bronze*. They must date from the Crimean War."

"N'importe pas," the emperor said airily. "We are gradually equipping our troops with Chassepôt's breech-loading rifles. But there is no hurry about that, because we fear no duels between individual soldiers carrying individual rifles. We fear not even the steel artillery. We have the new Montigny mitrailleuses. You will not have seen any of those guns, Colonel, because they are being kept most secret until they are needed."

"Mitrailleuses?" said Edge. "Pardon, Majesté." He turned and said to Florian in English, "To the best of my recollection, mitraille means grapeshot. Yes, it's almost the same in Spanish: metralla." Florian could only shrug, so Edge turned again to Louis and said, "With all respect, Your Majesty, there is nothing new about la mitraille. But it is effective only at close range, when discharged into a close-packed body of troops, and—"

"The name is misleading, Colonel. Deliberately so, to delude the enemy, if he should hear of it. Monsieur Montigny's new gun is a rapid-firing *long*-range weapon. It employs ball-cartridge ammunition, fed by previously loaded disks into *thirty-seven* clustered barrels, the cluster rotated by a hand crank. The barrels fire in swift sequence and spew a lethal storm of lead. No troops can stand against that, no matter the quality of their individual weapons."

"I cannot doubt Your Majesty," Edge said diplomatically, "since I have not seen Monsieur Montigny's invention in action. However, I have encountered the similar machine invented by Gatling. He was a Carolina man, but we Confederates were glad he offered his gun to the Yankees, and didn't burden us with it. The Gatling had only ten barrels, but they were forever jamming. I hate to think what thirty-seven—"

"I have seen the Montigny gun work," Louis said stiffly. "It does work."

"Even so, I must tell Your Majesty one thing," Edge persisted. "Any weapon cranked by hand is absolutely incapable of holding an accurate aim. And the longer its range, the more widely and randomly that lead will be scattered. Not a storm, but a sprinkle."

"Your criticisms have been noted," said the emperor, now quite frigidly. "I will have my ordnance officers make an expertise upon them. Is there anything else you wish to tell me?"

"Yes, sir. The Prussians also have a secret weapon. At least, I doubt that you know about it. I just happened to get a glimpse."

"Qu'est-ce que c'est?"

"Not a what, Your Majesty, a who. The Prussians seem to have the American General Philip Sheridan on their side."

Louis Napoléon no longer regarded Edge frigidly, but with blank bewilderment. So did Florian.

"I spotted him at one of those supply depots I told you about. He wasn't in uniform, but I couldn't possibly mistake that squat little bastard. He was being shown around by three or four Prussian generals, and none of them paid any attention to an innocuous train of circus performers plodding past at the time. I was flabbergasted to see Little Phil there, but he would have been a damned sight more so, if he had looked up just then, to see me driving a circus wagon through Kurhesse—a Confederate he'd fought against in the Shenandoah Valley, and stood next to during the stacking of arms at Appomattox."

The emperor breathed, "C'est incroyable."

"Now, the last I heard of Sheridan, he was military governor of Missouri, and making life hellish for the Indians there. Before that, he was military governor of poor, defeated, whimpering Louisiana, and he made life so hellish in those parts that even President Johnson was appalled, and yanked the son of a bitch out of there. Maybe Little Phil is on leave, and he's just enjoyably lending the Prussians an unofficial helping hand. Or maybe his old commander and new president, Ulysses Grant, has sent him over here for some shifty reason of his own. But I will say this. If Phil Sheridan is acting as adviser to the Prussians, I hope to hell that France doesn't have to go to war with them. If it does, I hope to hell France doesn't lose, because Sheridan likes nothing better than to trample on anybody that's down—and that is the advice he will give the Prussians."

There was a long minute of silence in the room. Then Louis Napoléon said, with malevolence:

"This Sheridan cochon has once before beset me and hindered me and given me ample cause to abhor him. Barely a month after that Appomattox of which you speak, Colonel Edge, this Sheridan had a division of American troops on the Mexican border, making feints and noises of menace at the monarchy I was trying to establish there. Meanwhile, Washington was sending me fierce threats and ultimatums. Well, Maximilian was far too inept to defend Mexico against an American invasion, and I could hardly direct such a war myself, from across an entire ocean. Besides, I must say frankly that—after the Confederacy fell—I considered the Mexican venture no longer worth my while. I had undertaken it, really, as a gambling proposition, and at least partly to please my empress-wife. Eugénie is of Spanish blood, you know; she still dreams Spanish dreams of a Mexican conquest."

He sighed and was silent again, ruminating. Then he resumed:

"The venture could have succeeded. It should have done. If only your Confederacy had won the war, Colonel, the venture *would* have succeeded. The Confederate States of America would then have had, at their back door, a nation as firm and friendly as France herself, an ally that soon would have helped the Confederacy subsume the Northern states and eventually Canada as well. But now, what kind of a Mexican neighbor has the United States got for its busybody officiousness? As a result of Washington's threats and Sheridan's threatening presence on the border, I withdrew my French troops and my support of the infant monarchy. Maximilian was overthrown and executed, *his* empress-wife is now a raving lunatic, and Mexico is back in the chaos of republicanism and revolutions, ravages from which it may never recover. So, you see, I already owe General Sheridan retaliation for his part in that débâcle." Louis Napoléon pounded a fist on his chair arm. "And *now*—is the fils de putain again conniving against me? Just beyond my own Alsatian border? C'est intolérable!"

But suddenly his livid face cleared, then actually brightened. He leaned abruptly forward and grinned bloodthirstily at Edge. "Sheridan is a cavalryman. So were you, and you have fought him before. How would you like to fight Sheridan again, Colonel? And best him this time!"

"I would not, Your Majesty, thank you all the same."

Louis Napoléon's grin became a scowl and his voice got tight. "It is not generally considered polite—or wise—to say a flat and unequivocal no to an emperor, Colonel Edge."

"Forgive my manners, Your Majesty. But I am not one of Your Majesty's subjects, and I have probably already violated some international rule of war, by bringing you the information I just—"

"And Sheridan? What is *he* doing? Foutre! If Bismarck and his General von Moltke can enlist a foreigner's aid, surely I can do the same. I will consult with the Maréchal MacMahon as to what brevet commission can be accorded you. Something higher than a lieutenant colonelcy, I daresay."

This time rudely, without asking the emperor's pardon, Edge turned from him to Florian and said in English, "I told you that somebody's neck would be at risk, goddamn it." Florian was expressively rolling his eyes, but Edge paid no heed. "I'll be goddamned if I'll be dragged into another goddamned war, and especially one that's—"

"Allow me to interrupt, Colonel," said Louis, also speaking English, "before you make some lamentable lapse into imprudence. During my various exiles, I lived for some years in London and briefly in New York. I can probably even swear in English as fluently as you."

"In any language, Your Majesty, I still must decline any further involvement. I have done all that I will do."

"Hold a moment. You spoke just now of goddamned war. But there *is* no goddamned war. With you as our countermeasure to the bellicose Sheridan—to help us anticipate his thinking, the advice he would give the Prussians—perhaps that would *avert* any goddamned war."

"Your Majesty," Edge said wearily, "I heard that exact same argument from the Tsar Alexander, which is the only reason I have meddled as much as I already have. I beg to be excused. I am done with war and rumors of war."

"Ah, well," said the emperor, spreading his hands. "I shall not importune. God grant there will *be* no war, in which case this discussion has been only academic. However, if war does come, I trust that all my subjects will rally to the tricolor." He rose to shake hands, and added, "Also all good men enjoying the hospitality and benefactions of the tricolor."

"That was not said idly," Florian remarked, when he and Edge were again on the rockaway and leaving the palace gardens, now lamplit in the night. "I imagine he *could* command conscription in a national emergency. You could be vulnerable, Zachary, since you are, after all, something of a stateless person. I doubt that the local American consul would intervene on behalf of an ex-Confederate. I have seldom observed American consulates doing anything for staunch *Americans* in difficulties abroad."

Edge only grunted.

"Now, understand, Zachary," Florian continued, as he turned up the rue des Pyramides, "I am not recommending any course of action for you. I only point out what you must already know: that volunteers fare immeasurably better than conscripts. The emperor all but offered you a marshal's baton. Are you familiar with the history of Count Rumford?"

"No."

"He was a Massachusetts boy by the name of Benjamin Thompson, a royalist during the American Revolution, who became a British cavalry colonel, and got himself knighted Sir Benjamin for it. Then he served the Prince of Bavaria as an army officer, eventually minister of this and that—and got made a count. He took the un-Bavarian name from his wife's hometown in New Hampshire. So, you see, it *is* possible to go far and rise high in the service of a foreign prince. In the meantime, Count Rumford continued with his chief interests, scientific experiments, just as you could keep on as a circus—"

"That's all I care to be. I want nothing to do with other people's wars."

"Well, you have had your share of them, true. But I should think that would make you rather casual about war. Even eager, like a fire horse hearing the bell and hastening to be harnessed."

"Confound it, Florian!" Edge turned on the rockaway seat to face him squarely. "A long time ago, I told you how the Comanche cavalry broke and ran at Tom's Brook. Well, I didn't just watch that rout. I was part of it. I was one of them, one who broke and ran. I still do it sometimes, in my dreams. I'll never put myself in another situation where I might actually do that again."

Florian drove on, to the broad avenue de l'Opéra, lined with glowing lamp globes. Not until after he had turned into that avenue did he speak again:

"Sergeant Yount, too?"

"You'll have to ask him. I was too busy to notice, right then, and I've never inquired in all the years since. Maybe Obie would accept that marshal's baton from the emperor, if you're keen on somebody getting it. He could probably do better in the job than I could."

"Zachary, there is no earthly way you can persuade me that you are a coward. I have seen you face armed men... cope with tragedy... heartbreak... And besides, as I recall, you were a captain at the time of that fiasco. You finished the war as a lieutenant colonel, so you hardly spent the rest of it in hiding."

"I never had to make another cavalry charge, either, so I don't know whether I'd have turned tail again. After the Thirty-fifth was disbanded in disgrace, Obie and I spent the final six months of the war doing routine patrol duty around the ditchworks at Petersburg. And trying, like every other man there, not to get hit by an artillery kettle or a sniper's ball. Lots of them did get hit, and that's how I got my promotions. By way of attrition, not from doing any heroics."

"Still, there *were* heroics before the—before the disbandment. You've never bragged, but, by your own account, the Comanche cavalry was—"

"Sans peur et sans reproche. Yes. Every man of us had reason to hold his head high. Before. So now, whenever I dream about that shameful rout, I wake up and I fetch out all those other memories, and I polish them on my sleeve, and I try to shine them up so they'll put that other memory in the shade. Maybe they do. Maybe, on balance, I *wasn't* a coward. If that's so, I don't have to do any more heroics to prove it, and I sure as hell won't risk any more Tom's Brooks."

They neither of them said anything more, and the rockaway finally pulled up in front of the Grand Hôtel du Louvre, at the corner of the boulevard des Capucines and the rue Scribe. There was a considerable throng of carriages and voitures milling about there. The hotel, like the palace, had flunkies to dash forward and take charge of the guests' private vehicles, and lead them off to some coach house somewhere. Florian and Edge entered the immense, high, richly gleaming lobby and looked around with pleasure at the potted palms and plush lounge seats and impeccably dressed other guests. It was a striking contrast to the provincial inns they had been lately inhabiting; indeed, the Grand

Hôtel was the grandest hotel they had seen anywhere. Willi was waiting in the lobby and, when he approached, Florian asked:

"Is everyone accommodated, Herr Chefpublizist?"

"All but Kostchei the Deathless and the Princess Brunhilde. I could not persuade them to accept the rooms I had reserved here for them. They both insist that they prefer to bide at the tober, with the Slovaks. I suppose they are timid of being conspicuous among these elegant people and surroundings. Kostchei stayed at the Bois, but the giantess is yonder, behind those palms. She wishes to have a word with both of you before she goes back out there."

"Damn. Those two should have got accustomed to their freakdom by now, and inured to embarrassment. Well, come, Zachary." They left Willi and threaded their way through the chatting and smoking and laughing groups of people. "Olga doubtless wishes to make her final telegraph report to the tsar."

On the way across the spacious lobby, Edge sauntered slowly enough to overhear snatches of the chatter going on, and he decided that Monsieur Nadar's bright, brittle and wicked gossip had truly been but a foretaste of the conversational standards of Paris.

"... Complained of his wife to his friends at his club. He said she was witless, a spendthrift, a scold, et ainsi de suite. Then one of his friends stood up and declared, 'I cannot allow you, mon ami, to criticize my mistress in this fashion!'..."

A willowy young man with curling-iron-crimped yellow hair was saying, with lissome gestures, to another willowy young man:

"... Too decrepit to be any longer attractive to lovers, so he stays now secluded in his mansion, and nobly calls himself 'le reclus de Passy.' But, my dear, the *rest* of us titter and call him 'le reclus de Passé.'..."

A woman of late middle age, but well caulked and enameled against erosion, was saying to an attentive trio of gentlemen:

"... Rather a checkered past, to put it charitably. But she swears to me that, before the wedding, she will *tell all* to her husband-to-be."

"Quelle candeur," said one of the men.

"Quelle folie!" exlaimed another.

"Quelle mémoire," murmured the third.

Olga was seated on a corner divan, deep within a minor forest of palms, but, even in concealment, she was hunched to make herself look smaller.

"Gospozhýa Somova," Edge said to her, "I have delivered my collected intelligences to Louis Napoléon, and he seems disposed to follow Alexander's good advice. Is that all you will need to report, or shall I give you the gist of our conversation?"

"Nyet, Gospodín Edge. The tsar should be satisfied to know that you completed your errand, and to good effect. I shall have the desk porter telegraph the message."

Florian said, "I believe, gospozhýa, this terminates your obligation to the tsar, also. Does that mean you will be leaving our company?"

"Well..." she said uncertainly. "Sir John has begged me to stay on in his annex show until he can find another monst—until he can find a replacement exhibit. I shall be glad to do so." Her smile was slightly tremulous. "I had planned no further ahead than getting out of Russia. Where I will go now, and what I will do, I have not yet decided."

"We will be grieved when you do leave us, Olga," Florian said kindly. "But when you depart, I hope you will step out proudly, not sidling into corners like this and being ashamed of your regal stature."

She managed to laugh a little. "It is that all the French are so *small*. In Russia there were at least a few *men* not too much shorter than I. Here, I feel like a lighthouse towering over a fishing village."

"Very likely the original Brunhilde felt the same. So *think* of yourself as a Princess Brunhilde among the runts, and look haughtily down at them. That will make them look up to you, and with reverent admiration, not ridicule."

"You can be sometimes a very wise man. Gospodín Florian," she said gratefully. "I shall try. But, for a few nights at least, while I work up my courage, let me remain at the tober."

"As you wish, my dear." Florian snapped his fingers at a hotel page boy and sent him to have a voiture ready at the door when Olga had got her message off to St. Petersburg.

Then Florian and Edge obtained their room keys from Willi, and rode the Grand Hôtel's unique and famous ascenseur up to their floor. At this, as at all hours, the lift was crowded with guests—and guests of guests—who had found some excuse to ride in that little room of leather-quilted walls and gilded lamp sconces. The men in the ascenseur with Edge and Florian were trying to look nonchalant and blasé, but one woman clutched at her companion and girlishly squealed "Not so *fast!*" at the machine's professionally imperturbable operator.

In their rooms, where their luggage had already been deposited, Florian and Edge had a quick washup, then took the lift down again to the mezzanine dining room. Almost all of the troupe had already dined that night, but the several chiefs had waited for their Governor. So Florian, Edge, Fitzfarris, Beck, Goesle and Lothar took a large table—and a meal both epicurean and gargantuan— while they planned for the Florilegium's stand here in Paris.

Over the apéritifs, Florian said, "Canvasmaster Goesle, have your roustabouts start draping the whole city with posters, as soon as they've finished setting up tomorrow. That will probably take them three or four days to do, so mark the posters to announce that our show will open five days from tomorrow."

"Aye. We can make good use of that time. Get some of our more travel-worn gear in tiptop shape and shininess."

"Very good," said Florian. "Chief Engineer, you lay in the necessaries for the *Saratoga,* a good supply of them. And, in your capacity of Kapellmeister, another charge upon you. I just this evening learned that the emperor is not enamored of that 'Syrée' anthem we have been using for opening and closing. So think about a substitution, and rehearse your windjammers in it."

Beck considered and, by the time the escargots were served, he suggested, "For the opening walkaround, perhaps some of Auber's overture to *Fra Diavolo* we can play. And the more bouncy bits of his 'Grand Pas Classique' for the closing spec. Jolly music and very French, those pieces are. Surely by now old Maître Auber is dead and cannot object. The rehearsals as public concerts in the park I will do. More advertising of the circus that will make."

Over the vichyssoise, Willi said, "Whether the composer Auber is dead, I do not know. But we should be seeing on our tober a number of other composers, also artists and poets, who frequently take the circus for their theme. Monsieur

Nadar seems to know them all, and he promises to bring them to attend our performances. He says they are all weary of the other circuses that have been showing in Paris for so long."

Over his roast duck, asparagus and pâtés cuites, Fitzfarris said, "I'd like to know more about those other circuses. On almost every street corner here, there's a sort of large round pillar, evidently put up just to be plastered with posters, because every one of them is. One poster that I saw was advertising a Cirque d'Hiver. As well as I could decipher it, that circus is doing some kind of spectacle about 'Robin des Bois,' which I take to mean Robin of the Woods."

"Actually French for 'Robin Hood,'" said Florian, over his endive salad. "And those large round things, Sir John, are public pissoirs. Yes, the Cirque d'Hiver performs every winter—and in summer becomes the Cirque d'Eté—and has been a Paris institution for as long as I can remember. It has its own permanent building, like the Cinizelli in Saint Petersburg. I don't know how many other permanent circuses may exist here now."

"I have investigated," said Willi. "Not counting such things as the little Temple of Magic, where old Robert-Houdin performs conjuring tricks, and the one-man clown show of Deburau at the Fantaisies Parisiennes, there are three others in competition with us. All three are owned by a Monsieur Degeau, and all are sycophantically named to flatter the royal family: the Cirque de l'Empereur, the Cirque de l'Impératrice and the Cirque du Prince Impérial. They also are indoors, and Monsieur Nadar says they are all mediocre. They vary their programs mainly by trading an occasional act between one and another."

"We ought to reconnoiter, though," said Edge, as an apricot mousse was set before him. "Just to see how they compare with us. They'll be sending scouts to our tober, surely."

"Yes," said Florian. "And let us do that before our own opening day, for we will be too busy thereafter. However, no point in any one of us having to sit through all of them. Sir John, you take the Cirque d'Hiver. Colonel Ramrod, you visit the Cirque de l'Empereur. I will canvass the other two, and then we will all compare notes. Now, gentlemen, here is our coffee. I suggest that we indulge also in some fine Trichinopoly cigars, and the most venerable cognac the sommelier can find among his cellar's cobwebs, and all together raise a rousing 'santé' to our success here at the pinnacle of the world."

4

THE FIRST TIME Florian encountered Kostchei on the tober next day, he upbraided him as he had done Brunhilde, for declining to join the other troupers at the Grand Hôtel.

"Damn it, Kostchei—or Shadid—you have the same rights as every other artiste. And if the hotel should in any way make you feel unwelcome there, I shall simply threaten to withdraw all—"

"Ni mudí, gospodín," Kostchei interrupted, as offhandedly as his strangled voice could manage. "It is not my own tender feelings I protect. I merely do not wish to turn the stomachs of all the fine folk at the—"

He was in turn interrupted. He and Florian had been speaking in Russian and had not noticed another presence nearby. But suddenly Olga was looming over them, staring intently at Kostchei and not roughly but firmly backhanding Florian out of the way.

"Timoféi?" she asked, breathless, hopeful, unbelieving.

"Okh, t'fu própast..." the man growled, turning his terrible face away.

"It *is* your voice, even changed. You *are* Timoféi!" gasped the giantess, still staring down at him. The mutilated man said nothing, but looked beseechingly at Florian. He got no help there, for Florian was also goggling, transfixed. "You do not deny it," the woman said, and tears started down her face. "You are Timoféi Somov."

"Nyet," he said finally, his voice more choked than ever. "I *was* Timoféi Somov. I am now Kostchei Byesmyértni, who was many times killed but never died."

"Timoféi... Timoféi..." she sobbed. "How did you...? This is why you never spoke in my hearing. It was *not* an accident with the bears, was it? *What did this to you?*"

"I did."

"What? But how? What happened?" She brushed the tears from her cheeks, but fresh ones came. "All I knew was that you went away... I waited..."

"I went away to become rich," he said, with abject despair. "I became this instead."

She blinked. "To become rich?"

"To be worthy of you. Because you were the Princess Raisa Vasiliyevich Yusupova, and I was only Timoféi Somov."

"Oh, my dear," she said softly, and enfolded his contorted body in her arms. "Did you *never* know? Do you not know *now*? Why do you suppose I chose the name Somova?"

Florian quietly tiptoed away.

The other artistes, though they practiced and rehearsed assiduously every day, as long as the daylight lasted, took advantage of their free nighttimes to sample some of the enjoyments available in Paris. They postponed the mere ogling of landmarks and monuments, and instead went to theatres and ballets and cabarets, where the show times would conflict with those of the Florilegium when its performances began. Because they had not much time before opening day, they crowded in two or three entertainments each night.

A number of the male troupers—and some Slovak crewmen, as well—went out together a couple of times, in what Fitzfarris called a "stag rut." Their first foray was to a back-street café called the Alcazar, to see "les déshabillées"— doing acts with titles like "Mimi's Bath" and "Fifi at Her Toilette." If the men had hoped to see beautiful naked women, they were disappointed. The performing soubrettes were pretty enough, but the "undress"—for example, in the turn called "Lulu's Bedtime"—consisted of Lulu's appearing on stage fully clothed, then slipping into a nightdress of tent dimensions and opacity, and, accompanied by suggestive music, merely peeling teasingly out of her other clothes underneath it, and never showing more flesh than her face and hands.

So the stags next visited the café chantant Eldorado, across the river in St-Germain, where the woman known only as Theresa sang songs that Fitzfarris had been told "make even the sterner sex blush to listen to." She did sing them, too. She sang "Batifolez, mesdemoiselles!" and she sang all thirty-six bawdy verses of "De la gargouille," and she sang a song that had long been popular and once had been innocent, "C'est dans le nez que ça me chatouille," but Theresa put some new interpretations into those lyrics. None of the circus men in attendance commanded enough French to appreciate all the ways in which Theresa claimed she could be tickled "dans le nez," so they were less scandalized by the performance than by its audience. Except for some waiters and barmen and a burly chucker-out stationed at the door, the circus men were the *only* men in the café Eldorado. All the other patrons were women, and rather severely dressed women, but not old-maidish women, for almost all of them were smoking, and some were smoking cigars.

Fitzfarris and company next visited the Bal Mabille, which advertised performances of the indecent chahut dance imported from Algeria, better known now by the Parisian slang word for rumpus, "cancan." The music was rowdy enough, and the dancers, both male and female, flung themselves about with mad abandon and apparent bonelessness, and the girls did kick their skirts and their legs incredibly high—but, contrary to rumor, they wore ruffled pantalettes under the skirts.

When the stag herd left the Mabille, even the Jászi brothers and the Slovaks were agreeing with Fitzfarris: that every tableau vivant he had ever devised for his annex was much more provocative than anything they had yet seen in Paris. To assuage their disillusionment, the men stopped at a drinking place cheerfully designated on its signboard AU RENDEZ-VOUS DES SPORTIFS. It turned out to be the lowest sort of den, with only tin cups to drink from, and those chained to the zinc counter to prevent their being stolen. There the men sampled that other fiendish bequest from Algeria, absinthe. They again agreed: it was like drinking licorice cough medicine—but several of them had to be helped to walk the rest of the way to the tober.

The women of the troupe went to more refined entertainments: to hear the two greatest divas of the time—Adelina Patti as *La Traviata,* Christine Nilsson in *Mefistofele*—and to see the new but highly acclaimed young actress Sarah Bernhardt portraying a minstrel boy in the most successful play of that season, *Le Passant.*

The women also, early on, found the many-storied Magasins du Printemps, which clearly had been the model for the Nagyáruhaz Párizsi shopping place that had had them agog in Pest, for the Printemps was an even vaster aggregation of all manner of shops as "departments" under one roof. It was the most gorgeous commercial building in all of Paris; even its exterior was a fantasy of domes, statuary, enameled tiles and gilding. It was Clover Lee who discovered, not far from the Printemps, the city's several "passages." Before Haussmann, those had been merely narrow alleys, and served as little more than depositories for ash bins, jumbled trash and sleeping drunks. Nowadays they were elegantly paved, roofed over with arching glass, lighted with gas sconce lamps, and were lined from end to end with fashionable jewelry shops, rare book dealers, art galleries, glovemakers, couturiers and the like.

Meanwhile, Florian, Edge and Fitzfarris managed to take time off from their tober duties to visit the other circuses showing in Paris—and to ascertain that they offered not much competition to worry about, their current programs consisting mostly of trick horseback riding and rather tame animal acts. The Cirque

d'Hiver's "Robin Hood" spectacle, Fitz reported, was only a sort of half-baked
Wild West show, only with the riders green-costumed as Merrie Men and waving
longbows while they rode.

"Fairly sparse audience, too," he added. "And all of them riffraff, in the very
cheapest seats. Which, by the way, were only little stools, and I'm happy we don't
have any such things. When an audience dislikes an act, they tend to fling the
stools at it."

Things were no better elsewhere. At the Cirque de l'Impératrice, Florian
reported, the chief attraction was some apes in ladies' riding habits doing a horseback quadrille, and, at the Cirque du Prince Impérial, eight horses ridden by
monkeys dressed as jockeys. Edge returned from the Cirque de l'Empereur to
report that its stellar and closing act consisted of a plain old barnyard goat doing
acrobatics.

"Pretty *good* acrobatics," he admitted. "But if the emperor ever sees that, the
manager had better change the name of his establishment."

"Well," said Florian, "we seem to be the only *real* circus in town right now. At
least unless and until the great ropewalker Blondin or the even greater trapezist
Léotard should finish their foreign tours and come home to Paris. If they do, I'll
outbid every other circus owner for their services. In the meantime, gentlemen,
we ought to do a booming trade. Gavrila has been selling tickets from the red
wagon ever since we arrived, and our first *four* shows are already sold out."

Now and then, a member of the company, out sightseeing, would have a
small adventure. The band's cimbalist, Gombocz Elemér, after a hard day's practice, was one night strolling in the precincts of Notre-Dame, where there were
always wandering street singers, barrel-organ grinders, stilt walkers, bawling
peddlers of food, drink, plaster madonnas, glass-bead rosaries and chromos of
the Last Supper. A blind man was playing a xylophone, and playing it so badly
that his upturned cap on the pavement contained only the decoy few sous he
had put into it himself. Elemér considered for a moment, then stepped behind
the xylophone, plucked the little mallets from the man's hands—making him
bleat a helpless protest—and began to play, as frenetically and loudly and melo-
diously as he ever had on his cimbalom.

One after another passerby stopped and curiously looked, then smiled at the
happily flailing Elemér and the blankly bewildered man with the AVEUGLE placard on his chest. As Elemér jingled and jangled a very merry rendition of "Ave
Maria," coins began to clink into the cup almost as rapidly as the arpeggios he
was playing. A considerable crowd collected as he continued with some bits of
Bach and Liszt masses, played at a pace more exuberant than reverent. When
the shabby old cap was overflowing with coins, he stopped—the crowd applauding and cheering—and handed the cap and the sticks to the blind man. The
beggar's face went blissful when he felt the weight of his takings. Then he
reached out to stop his benefactor's walking away, and Elemér paused to acknowledge his thanks, but what the blind man whined was:

"M'sieu, are you not going to give me something for the loan of my xylophone?"

That same night, Florian escorted Daphne and Clover Lee to the opening of a new ballet. They dressed in their best evening clothes and took a fiacre to the Opéra in the rue le Peletier, where the posters all over the façade proclaimed "Première! COPPÉLIA; ou, *La fille des yeux en émail!*" Very shortly after the curtain rose, on the scene of a quaint town square, the lovely young heroine Swanilda danced out from the door of one of the stage houses. As she swooped into a graceful valse lente, Florian and Clover Lee leaned forward and peered, then whispered:

"Isn't that—? That is someone we have seen before!"

"It is. We have. But where?"

Daphne looked from them to the ballerina, in puzzlement.

"Rome!" said Clover Lee.

"Yes!" said Florian. "She was the pretty little protégée of that balletmaster from whom you took lessons."

"Maestro Ricci. But the girl had a name as long as my arm."

"Giuseppina Bozzacchi," said Daphne, consulting her playbill.

"That's it," said Clover Lee. She added, with some envy, "And now look at her. Making her début as prima ballerina on the first night of a brand-new ballet. In *Paris.*"

"Pity we didn't recognize the name on the posters," said Florian. "We should have brought flowers. Well, we can be her claque—although, if I'm not mistaken, from what I've seen of her dancing so far, she won't need any prompted applause. And we can go backstage afterward to congratulate her. If she remembers us."

"But of course I remember you," the glowing Giuseppina said in French, when they had finally made their way through the crush of well-wishers. "You two are probably the only people in Paris who ever saw me dance a Summer Blossom."

"You were but one of many, then," said Florian, kissing her hand. "Now you are what the Signor Ricci predicted you would be, la prima di tutto, with a star on your dressing-room door. And with all Paris at your feet, to judge from the audience response. Heavens, those dozens of curtain calls and those tons of flowers thrown! And all this at—what tender age?"

"Oh là, monsieur! I will be seventeen on my next birthday."

"Hélas, une ancienne!" Florian said in mock dismay. "Nevertheless, I hope and I fully expect that, like la Taglioni, you will still be première danseuse in your forties."

For such a child, Guiseppina was womanly perceptive. Clover Lee, her elder by at least a couple of years, was regarding the banks and heaps of flower baskets and bouquets filling the dressing room, and looking at them wistfully, as if at a fame that had already passed her by.

"I stole from you, mademoiselle," the girl said brightly, to Clover Lee's bewilderment. "Do you remember how Maestro Ricci had me attend those circus performances? Well, I took particular notice of a fouetté you did while standing on your horse. You had to do it with *utmost* care, so as to be always kicking in the direction the horse was cantering."

"Er... oui..."

"And tonight, did you not see me do the very same move? When Swanilda pretends to be the mechanical doll coming to life? As the toymaker vitalizes

Coppélia into dancing, I imitate that concentrated movement of yours, to convey her clockwork preciseness."

"Well..." said Clover Lee, again cheerful. "You're welcome to it. And I have added to my own act some folk dances on horseback. So may I steal a few of those comic steps you do in Coppélia's Spanish bolero and Scottish fling?"

"Mais certainement," said the girl, smiling. "Pour *vos* beaux yeux en émail de saphir."

Nevertheless, next day, Clover Lee again found reason to feel twinges of envy. It was the day before the Florilegium's opening, and Edge let her have only a short practice session, so that Bubbles and herself might have plenty of resting time. So Clover Lee bathed, changed clothes and went out walking. And, as she idled through the departments of the Printemps and through the arcades of the Passage des Princes, she frequently heard people talking praisefully of "l'étonnante petite Giuseppina." Perhaps that contributed to Clover Lee's flare-up later that afternoon, when the usually unfaultable facilities of the Grand Hôtel for once went amiss.

"Just *look* at this!" she wailed to wardrobe mistress Ioan. "My very best and newest léotard and frill skirt. They were ruby red when the maid took them to launder. And *now* look—pale petal pink!"

"Pierde. Ruined," Ioan agreed, shaking her head. "No time make new costume before show tomorrow."

"And I wanted to catch every eye." Clover Lee sniffled, then snarled. "Pink! About as vivid as a baby girl's bonnet."

"Bad mistake. Wash woman maybe used eau de javelle."

"Hell, she must have used *lye!* They haven't only faded, they've shrunk and gone nearly transparent. In my fleshings, I can barely get *me* into the léotard now. There's no room for even a breast bandeau or a cache-sexe. I'll be showing every curve and nub and crack I've got. Even in that candy pink, I sure won't look like any *baby* girl."

"In pink, be glad you got pink nipples and pale bush, too," Ioan said pragmatically. "But maybe better you wear other costume."

"Damned if I will. I'd planned to wear this for the opening show, and I'm going to. If I get arrested for indecency tomorrow, the damned hotel can pay my fine."

But Clover Lee recovered her usual good humor that night, when, escorted by Fitzfarris, she and other Americans of the troupe—Edge escorting Sunday, Rouleau with Monday—went out on the town for one last and special pre-opening treat: to see the drama that had been playing to packed houses for some two and a half years, *La Vie et la Mort d'Abraham Lincoln*. For all their effort to be on their best behavior, the Americans could not help grinning and chuckling and sometimes guffawing at so many scenes that the other playgoers in the house frequently leaned to glare at them or to hiss shushing noises. What occasioned the most hilarity—among the Americans, not the enraptured rest of the audience—was the third act, in which Honnête Abe sternly rebuffed a young man who asked his niece's hand in marriage, that young man being Jean Wilkes Booth. It took four more acts for the rejected Booth's indignation to reach the boiling point, at which time—in Act VII—he crept into the theatre box of Monsieur le Président and Madame Lincoln (while they were watching *King Lear*), shot the obdurate uncle-president and leapt from the box crying, "Sic semper tyrannis!"

"Mon dieu, that was the only factual bit in the whole damned farce," said

Rouleau as they left the theater, still laughing and still being glared at by others of the audience.

"But hell, that spoiled the whole play for me," said Edge. "He could at least have yelled 'Sic semper avunculis.'"

"By damn," Yount said to Florian next day, when the first patrons began arriving on the tober. "Miz Smodlaka must of sold out all them tickets to nobody but the nobs and swells." The people were indeed as dandily dressed as if they were attending the Prix Lutèce race at Longchamps, and many came in splendid private carriages. Yount went on, "Governor, I think you'd better send a couple of the Slovaks running to play flunky, toot dee soot."

"To play flunky *what?*"

Yount looked proud. "Never thought I'd speak any piece of lingo you wouldn't know, Governor. Been doing some study on my own. Seen it in Sunday Simms's French book. Toot dee soot. Means real quick. Right away."

"Ah, yes, of course. My mind was elsewhere. And thank you, Monsieur le Tremblement-de-terre, but Crew Chief Banat already has instructions to deal with the jossers' horses and carriages. Meanwhile, I applaud your ambitions toward self-improvement. And speaking of improvement, how fares Mademoiselle Anguille?"

"I think the resting time here has done her good. She's fixing to work her full tour of duty at every show again. Says she's done enough malingering."

"Well, good. But you keep an eye on her. Make sure she does not overtax herself."

The Florilegium had, as yet, no sanctioned midway of slum joints on this tober. But opening day had attracted every sort of street peddler and entertainer —pushcarts and push stoves selling things to eat and drink, quick-sketch and silhouette-cutter artists, organ-grinders, fire-eaters, guttersnipe children dancing while one of them played a jew's-harp, and other musicians of every kind of instrument and degree of talent, including Elemér's blind xylophonist. The musicians soon gave up and departed, unable to compete with the stentorian calliope. Goesle and Rouleau circulated among the others, selecting those they would allow to stay. They directed one of the more spectacular fire spouters to perform by the front-door marquee, where the Gluttonous Greek had once served as a beacon. The vendors of the less noxious-looking cookery and beverages and less trashy gimcracks they let line the entranceway. But they shooed off every parasite whose presence lowered the tone of the establishment, and all the mere mendicants who had nothing to contribute but their sores and mutilations.

Edge circulated, too, wearing his Colonel Ramrod uniform, but he wandered among the paying patrons. Most of them were occupying their wait until show time by inspecting—many through monocles or lorgnons—the animals in the menagerie tent. As he watched, Edge reflected on the variety of audiences the Florilegium had shown to: people of so many different racial or national characteristics, and modes of dress, and customs, and languages, and temperaments. And all the time, barring some losses and additions to its company and equipment, the Florilegium had stayed the same. Everywhere it went, it took with it the familiar sounds of canvas flapping, of ropes and poles creaking, rigs and harnesses jingling, heavy wheels rolling, animals whuffling or snorting or rumbling; the familiar odors of those animals and their feed bins and their droppings, aromas of hay and tanbark, of greasepaint and the sweat of hard work, the sharp smells of burned gunpowder, hot lamps and the balloon generator's chemicals; the familiar sights of garish banners billowing, and the tents brilliant in daylight or glowing after dark, and the pista full of action and color or, afterward, empty and asleep in dreams and memories. And always, everywhere, those least and tiniest things in the circus, but the things that said unmistakably "circus"—flashing their bright glints to pick out this or that face in the crowd, and dappling with their reflections the faces of their own wearers—the spangles, the spangles...

We are a floating island, thought Edge. It moors for a time on any and every kind of coast, and briefly brightens it with spangled light. Then it floats away from the landbound and commonplace, itself remaining always uncommon, undimmed and unchanged by any encounter. Edge started suddenly, his reverie broken when the calliope went silent and Beck's band rollicked into "Fra Diavolo." And Colonel Ramrod went to the chapiteau's back door, to line up the opening Grand Promenade.

It was only two o'clock in the afternoon, and the interior of the big tent was only shaded, not at all dark, but Florian had decreed that the pista curbing, the center poles, the lungia boom and the tightrope again be spangled with instantly-lighting candles, as had been done at Peterhof. "This is *opening day in Paris,* my lads! No less deserving of spectacle than a tsar's command performance!" So, when Boom-Boom gave the downbeat, Thunder charged in at the gallop, Colonel Ramrod brandishing his cavalry sabre, and Boom-Boom touched a match to the improvised fuse. With a sort of rippling effect, the candles became lines and circles and swoops of diamond points of light, as the rest of the troupe paraded in. Even without full darkness, it was spectacular enough that the band's triumphal music was hardly louder than the audience's exclamations and gasps of delight.

The Grand Promenade, to grand applause, eventually exited through the back door, and some of the more scantily clad artistes ran to the dressing tops to put on robes, but all immediately returned to the backyard. Even those who would not perform until the second half of the program did not, as usual, wander off to nap or otherwise pass the time. All the troupers clustered close to the back-door marquee, listening eagerly for the audience's response to the early acts. So did even the black-overalled roustabouts, who customarily waited only stolidly for their cues to move props or cages or rigging. And all those people loitering in the backyard were gratified to see the chapiteau's canvas quiver—almost billow—to the crowd's repeated, prolonged explosions of clapping and cries of "bis! bis!" for encores.

When the liberty horses of "Colonel Retouloir" came cantering from the tent in blanket-number sequence at the finish of their act—with a roar of noise following them—Florian also popped out right behind them, ordering the Sovaks to mix them up and herd them in again. And the backyard listeners could hear the horses get even more applause when they repeated their milling and wheeling and curvetting to sort out their numbers. When they again emerged in sequence, Colonel Retouloir bowed himself out with them, and barely had breath enough to blow the whistle for the next performer.

"That's me," said Fünfünf, and someone shouted, "Crack their ribs, white-face!" as he went cartwheeling inside to do his comic repartee with Florian and was received with a crash of clapping.

"I think," the Emeraldina said cautiously, "it is a hit we are making."

"Yes, *ma'am!*" said Abdullah, one big ebony-and-ivory grin. "Give a listen. Joey's got dem rubes cacklin' awready. Dis show go' run overtime, sho'!"

When Terry, Terrier and Terriest came flip-flopping out the back door after their act, Gavrila and Sava had them merely circle and go flip-flopping in again for a repeat of their performance. Next was the combined strongman-and-klischnigg act and, to judge from the reception, it could have gone on indefinitely, but the equestrian director—out of concern for Mademoiselle Anguille's frailness—finally whistled it off. She showed no sign of debility, though, when she lissomely bowed herself out of the tent. She was followed by the elephant Brutus, led by Monsieur Trembling-of-the-Earth, and *he* was so nearly staggering that someone in the backyard raucously hailed him, "Hey there, Monsieur Trembling-of-the-Knees!"

"You said it!" he panted, joyously. "Old Peg here . . . she was beginnin' to look worried . . . jossers made me have her tromp across me . . . so many times. Whoo-ee! And listen yonder, Agnete . . . they *still* want us back again!"

"Ikke lunkent," said the shining-eyed, rosy-cheeked Mademoiselle Anguille, with something like awe. "Better than any audience yet, these Parisians like our show."

"Mais pourquoi pas?" said Monsieur Roulette, with rather too elaborate a pretense of yawning.

But Sir John Fitzfarris unabashedly exulted, "Hot damn! We're a success in *Paris!* Nobody can call us a high-grass or a mud show, not ever again!"

During the trapeze act, the backyard listeners heard, besides applause and cheers, what sounded like angry shouts and protests, and they wondered if something had gone wrong. However, when Maurice LeVie and Mademoiselle Papillon at last danced out the back door, he was laughing and she was bubbling with excitement:

"You should have seen it! The jossers kept me up there on the trap for so long that Maurice feared I'd faint. So he came lurching out as the Pete Jenkins, and the whole audience jumped up and started cursing him. When Zachary and the crewmen chased him and grabbed him, a mob of big men came running from the seats to help. Maurice had to scramble up the lungia rope in a hurry, or he'd *really* have been manhandled and thrown out."

"But then," said LeVie, "when I stripped off my tramp rags, the audience so laughed at themselves that they would have demanded an encore . . . if a second surprise had been possible."

"I could have encored, too," said little Grillon, somewhat wistfully, after her performance in the Globe Enchanté. "But once I stand up to take my bows, I cannot mystify the crowd again."

Meanwhile, every act that *was* capable of elaboration or reprise was encouraged and almost commanded by the audience to do so, as Abdullah le Hindou confirmed when he emerged from the chapiteau, streaming sweat. "Dey had me jugglin' till I juggled most ever'thing in reach 'cept our two bulls. And dem Jazzy brothers, dey just done rode voltige till de *hosses* about give out. Dem Jazzies *never* gits tired."

"I was worried that the Parisians would find my act boring," said Daphne,

now known as Madame Patineuse. "After all, Plimpton skates and penny-far-
things are no novelty here. But they *adored* the skate-dancing, especially when
the bear joined in. *And* my careening about on the velocipede with Obie. I believe they'd have made him repeat his dive into the fiery vat, if the Slovaks hadn't
already quenched the flames."

Even during the mid-program intermission, the crowd seemed insatiable.
They first flocked to the side of the chapiteau where a few crewmen were commencing the inflation of the *Saratoga,* and the people stood about making admiring comments, although the balloon was as yet no more than a barely puffed-up
pile of fabric. Then they went to gather about the annex top, where Sir John had
set his platform outside because the tent could not contain the whole audience
and the hour was now so late that the sideshow could not be done in shifts.
Every exhibit, monster and phenomenon was vigorously applauded as Sir John,
with a patter of memorized French superlatives, introduced the coq de bruyère
and its miracle eggs (now embossed with the cross of Lorraine), the albino Enfant des Ombres, the mummified Princesse Egyptienne. Then Florian had to
step in to translate, when Sir John himself and the ventriloquized Mignonne
Mademoiselle Mitaine went well beyond their rehearsed French squabble into
English insults and ripostes.

Every other sideshow performer also had to stay overlong on the boards. La
Méduse worked her snakes until they were as limp as strings. Grillon and Rumpelstilzchen were kept even longer at their liberty act. Brunhilde strode through her
smoke cloud with a genuine smile, seeming to have lost every remaining trace of
self-consciousness, and unhesitatingly made herself look ungainly and ludicrous
in the sword fight with Grillon. Then, when she descended from the platform, she
had to whisper to Timoféi, about to mount it, "Wipe that smile off *your* face, my
dear, or you will not look properly the horrible Kostchei l'Impérissable."

Le Démon Débonnaire opened the second half of the chapiteau program by
putting Maximus, Raja, Rani, Siva, Kewwy-dee, Kewwy-dah, Brutus and Caesar
through every trick they had ever learned—and then, by popular demand, had
to put them through their repertoire again. When he finally tottered out into the
backyard, the Slovaks following with the caged and haltered animals, he told the
troupers in the backyard, "Tiens, I twice even relit the cats' fire hoops. Now, par
Dieu, we are all—the animals and myself—more débiffé than débonnaire."

Mademoiselle Cendrillon was, by audience acclaim, kept so long on the
tightrope that the perky chimney sweep had to invent, on the spot, several new
comic prances and larks and postures. When, during the Lupino mirror closing
act, the jossers all but toppled out of their seats, convulsed by the antics of
Fünfünf and the Kesperle, the two clowns surpassed themselves in doing mirror
images of each other's antics, far beyond any they had ever done before or could
ever have rehearsed. Even the equestrian director, watching incredulously, had
to conclude that the joeys must somehow be reading each other's mind.

The audience's response to every single performance, both inside and outside
the chapiteau, had been galvanizing and inspiriting to the performers involved,
and might have made every single one of them feel like the topmost star of the
circus. However, all those uproars had been halfhearted compared to the concus-

sive cheers and clapping evoked by Clover Lee's équestrienne act, which occupied no star spot on the program, but came midway through the second part.

When, at that point, Florian bawled through his megaphone, "Et maintenant... *la Procession des Nations!*" Clover Lee rode in on the cantering Bubbles, this time appearing first in a costume of red, white and blue, with the Phrygian cap of Liberté on her head—"*la belle France!*" The applause had begun then, and at such an initial volume that, when it increased for each of her transformations, Florian's bellowing was almost inaudible—"*Liesse de l'Ecosse!*"... "*Luxe de l'Espagne!*"—during which Clover Lee, in glengarry, plaid and kilt, then in toreador costume, imitated Coppélia's dances as well as could be done on tiptoe atop a cantering horse.

The crowd's exhilaration came close to mass paroxysm when—at "*l'Equestrienne américaine, Mademoiselle Clover Lee!*"—she flung off the last disguise and rode revealed in her exceedingly revealing pink léotard and gossamer frill. But it was not her near nudity that so excited the audience, for she gave the people little chance to gape. The roustabouts were ready with her garlands and garters, and she became just a pink blur as she leapt and dived and somersaulted. When the act concluded, with her riding at a stand around the pista, the flock of doves following and fluttering and hovering about her, Clover Lee for once did not take her acclaim with her arms raised in the V. Instead, she let a couple of doves settle on her hands, and used their fluttering wings to cover her more conspicuous and indecorous exposed places.

It was at that point, the only time during the show, that the spectators brought out the flowers they carried—expensive hothouse blossoms, at this time of year—and flung them in such profusion that they quite carpeted the riding area outside the pista curbing. As Clover Lee continued to circle the tent, with doves alighting on her shoulders and bright hair and a mantle of them trailing behind, her horse's hoofs trod and mashed the flowers to attar, and added—to the circus odors Edge had earlier been cataloguing in his mind—a new, pervasive, fragrant perfume. Clover Lee's face was now as radiant as Guiseppina's had been at her curtain calls, and she threw away all attempts at modesty when she let go of her concealing doves to blow kisses to the audience with both hands.

"By damn, Governor," said Fitzfarris, and he had to say it very loudly to be heard over the ambient tumult, "I was thinking of recruiting some cancan girls to be our overture dancers. But they would look like nuns alongside Clover Lee."

Florian shook his head and shouted back, "Ioan Petrescu told me Clover Lee did not deliberately choose to display her charms so flagrantly. And anyway—you saw—she was doing her best *not* to exploit them. No, it wasn't any wantonness that set this audience on a roar. They simply *like* Clover Lee and her act. Better than any other, it seems. I have said before, there is no telling what the French public will choose to fasten its fancy upon."

When the closing Grand Promenade was over, most of the men in the audience, and not a few women, hastened again to Sir John's annex, everybody trying to be among the first to see the Amazone Pucelle in the toils of the Dragon Fafnir. The first several score of jossers to crowd inside the tent kept the maiden and the python dragging out her ravishment to an almost opera-seduction length, until the people waiting in line set up a clamor of impatience, and the maiden had to succumb to Fafnir with rather unmaidenly abruptness. Meanwhile, in the chapiteau, the

roustabouts were hurrying to place new candles and connecting fuse for a repeat of
the instant-lighting spectacle at the night show. And outside, the coaches and
carriages of patrons with tickets to that show were beginning to arrive.

Some of those newcomers, along with jossers from the afternoon audience,
were loudly admiring the *Saratoga*. It was not yet fully inflated, more carrot-
shaped than pear-shaped, but it now stood erect, the vermilion-striped bag and
its gondola looking very like an exclamation point beside the horizontal spread of
the green-striped chapiteau. Florian was going about the tober yelling through
his megaphone that Monsieur Roulette's balloon ascension would shortly take
place, and that all those patrons who had already seen the show but wished to
stay and witness that event were welcome to do so.

"I, for one, most certainly shall," said Nadar, materializing from the crowd
and taking Florian by the arm. "I trust Jules has not forgotten his inviting me to
come along."

"I am sure he has not, monsieur. It will add great prestige to this ascension if
you will allow me to announce that Paris's own world-famous aéronaute is aboard."

"By all means. And while we wait, Monsieur Florian, would you gather your
sous-chefs and principal artistes? Some of my friends attended your opening with
me, and now would wish to meet all of you."

Florian went off and brought back Edge, Beck and Fitzfarris. He told Nadar
that the artistes would join them as soon as they had changed into fresh clothes.

"Mais non, monsieur!" exclaimed a small old man who was now standing
with Nadar. "The others, bien, but *not* the aphrodisiaque Mademoiselle Clover
Lee! That one must never wear any different garb. Always she must wear pink,
and of that generous transparency."

Nadar laughed and said, "The Maître Auber has still an eye for beauty and an
appreciation of the aphro—"

Carl Beck blurted tactlessly, "Auber? Mein Gott! Dead you are supposed to be!"

"I regret to disappoint the supposers, monsieur."

"Das ist... I mean..." said Beck, trying to cover the gaffe. "We would not
your music have played without your permission asking. If alive you were."

"We should all be so alive at his age," said Nadar. "Do you know, messieurs, I
was recently present in the maître's studio when he was at the piano rehearsing
the beautiful soprano Bernardine Hamaker in the music of his *Le Philtre*. He
told her, 'Didine, you carry the melody, while I play only the left-hand part.' And
she stood singing while le vieux put his right hand under her skirts. He absolutely brought her to climax, there and then."

"Amazing concentration, that woman," said the old man. "Never missed a
note the whole time."

"Neither did you," said Nadar. "I ask you, messieurs, what do you think of
this man? Still lubrique at the age of eighty-eight."

"I am not eighty-eight," Auber said firmly. "I am four times twenty-two."

"But... the music?" Beck persisted. "You have no objection to our playing it,
Komponistmeister?"

"None whatever. I thought your renditions very... spirited. I am not jealous
of my brainchildren, no. Some composers are, of course, and here is one of them.
A good thing you did not play *his* music. May I present my confrère, le Maître
Jacques Offenbach?"

The master looked not at all as merry as his music, but was quite wooden-faced. He nodded only minimally, as if being careful not to dislodge his pince-nez, when each of the circus men was presented by name. After they all had expressed their pleasure at meeting him, he replied not very cordially:

"I must tell you frankly, messieurs, I am here only because Félix *would* not cease importuning. Really... an American circus..." Words failed him; he made a gesture of weary distaste.

Edge asked, "Which is it you dislike, Monsieur Offenbach? Americans or circuses?"

"Both. Since you ask, Colonel Edge, I tell you. And before you ask why, I shall tell you that, also. Two Americans have stolen a piece of my music, put abominable English words to it, and made it into a vulgar circus song. It *was* the chef-motif of my *Papillon*. Now it is 'The Daring Young Man on the Flying Trapeze.' I sincerely hope that I—and my solicitors—will not hear you people playing the damned thing."

"You will not, monsieur," Edge assured him. Then he added a prick of the poniard. "His Imperial Majesty has intimated that he would be best pleased if we play nothing whatever of yours."

Offenbach's pince-nez fell off.

"Ah, Maître Auber!" called another man, approaching the group. He was distinguished-looking, wore a diamond stickpin in his cravat and carried a platinum-headed cane. "When I heard that you were indisposed last week, I sent some of my hothouse grapes. I thought they would be easy nourishment for a toothless old gourmand. But I never received any thanks. Did you not enjoy them?"

"I did not, James," Auber said grumpily. "I do not like my wine in pills."

"Ingrate!" the newcomer said fondly. "Very well, I shall send a case of my best in bottles." The man turned to Florian and said, "I so much enjoyed the exercices du cirque, Monsieur le Propriétaire, perhaps you also would accept some of the liquid produce of my vineyard."

"Of course, monsieur," said Florian. "I am always pleased to make the acquaintance of a good wine."

"Only good ones, eh? Well, the general opinion is that my Château Lafite yields not a bad Médoc."

"Good heavens—!" said Florian.

"Allow me to present," said Nadar, "the Baron James Rothschild."

"I am honored," said Florian. "We all are. Your calling your Lafite-Rothschild not a bad Médoc is like calling the Arc de l'Etoile not a bad traffic stanchion."

The other troupers began to arrive, by ones and twos, dressed to meet the visitors in their best street clothes, if only briefly, before they had to change into costume again. They were all so vibrant and effervescent after the show's tremendous success that even the wooden Offenbach began to unbend. Auber immediately seized upon Clover Lee, took her apart from the group and talked to her with much animation and many gesticulations, probably on the subject of her pista attire. Others of Nadar's acquaintances also arrived, including one fairly young man who carried a sketch he had made during the show. It was a charcoal drawing of Mademoiselle Cendrillon on the tightrope, and now its creator looked uncertainly from Sunday to Monday Simms, who were standing side by side. Finally he shrugged, laughed and turned the picture so they could see it.

"That's me!" squealed Monday.

Her sister hissed in her ear, "C'est moi."

"Then it is yours, mademoiselle, with my profound compliments," said the artist, handing it to Monday with a deep bow.

"Gol-lee!" she breathed, overwhelmed. "I never had no kind of picture of *me* before." She squinted at the signature. "I surely do thank you, M'sieu Door."

"Doré. And take care, mademoiselle, the charcoal will smear as easily as your chimney-soot makeup. If sometime you are free to visit my atelier"—he handed her his card—"I shall be happy to blow upon the picture some fixatif, to preserve it."

Nadar was regaling the group, regardless of its now mixed nature, with some more of his esoteric gossip, in language most forthright: "Did you see the Comtesse Walewska in the seats? I wonder if *she* saw anything at all. Of the performance, I mean. When she gets that preoccupied look on her face and sits up very straight with one hand behind her and hidden by her wrap or muff, you always know she is putting her syringe up her backside. The dear lady started by drinking paregoric, to relieve her female problems. But then she required laudanum, and eventually graduated to pure opium and God knows what else. She remains fastidious, however, about having needle punctures disfigure her arms, so she takes her doses intra rectum, and *I* think she manages it very discreetly in public."

Fitzfarris was in conversation with a young man who had been introduced by Nadar, rather archly, as "Monsieur Renoir, who used to paint fans and window blinds, and now paints nude women." So Fitz had evidently decided he was the man to query as to where he might engage some cancan girls for the circus, girls who would be a trifle less prudish than the ones he had so far seen.

"Try the Folies Bergère, monsieur," said Renoir. "It is a new café revue, and therefore struggling for custom and notoriety. So it requires its soubrettes to show, ahem, rather more of themselves than can be seen elsewhere. Naturally, the girls it hires must be—how shall I put it?—quite devoid of prejudices. And they are so pitifully paid that you could doubtless hire them away at no considerable cost."

"Look out," said someone in the group, warningly. "Here comes Verlaine."

"Ah, the Poet Nauseate," said Nadar.

"Dear God," muttered Rothschild. "Drunk and disheveled, as usual. Please permit me, mesdames et messieurs, to take my leave. Paul will only want to borrow money, and he holds the Chinese belief that anyone who ever saves another's life is thereafter obliged to sustain him forever. Here, Félix"—the baron shoved a roll of notes at Nadar—"*you* rescue him this time." And he was gone.

When the very young man shambled up to the group, he *was* a bit drunk; he was also the most casually dressed person on the tober that afternoon, to the point of being very nearly shabby. Nadar introduced him merely by pronouncing his name again, and then began a capsule description of him:

"This poet's work being unpublishable in any civilized country—"

"Ne faites pas attention," said Verlaine, slurring his words and addressing nobody in particular. "My publisher is in Belgium."

"Just as I said. For that reason, young Paul has an alternate profession. His reputation is already so vile that it can no longer be sullied, and anything, however nasty, will be believed of him. So now, if a scandal threatens, and some gentleman's good name is at risk, that gentleman has only to pay Paul a pittance to take the blame and the opprobrium for him."

"I have composed a new poem," said Verlaine, with a hiccup. "Any generous gentleman here who will part with a small donation, his name I will *not* put in it." He struck an attitude and began reciting in a monotone:

Je suis foutu. Tu m'as vaincu.
Je n'aime plus que ton gros cu
Tant baisé, léché—

"Jésus," said Nadar. "Here." He thrust Rothschild's money at Verlaine. "Don't put *anybody's* name in it."

"Ah-h..." said the poet, rapturously smacking his lips as he began to count the bills.

Rouleau was suddenly among the group, wearing his green and yellow acrobat's fleshings. He cheerfully announced, "The *Saratoga* is ready to go! Monsieur Nadar, are you?"

"I am, indeed. Take me away from these sordid environs."

So all of them, laughing, went to the launching place, and the crowd on the tober clustered as close as was prudent. Florian gave a florid speech, with many praiseful references to France's own Montgolfier inventors of the aérostat, and many compliments to the daring of the Montgolfiers' successors, Messieurs Roulette and Nadar. Those two gentlemen bowed and were heartily hurrahed, and then they climbed into the basket. For this ascension, Boom-Boom had not convened his band, but had himself taken the place of the professor at the calliope. He roared into "Le Phénix" so abruptly and loudly that the entire crowd jumped, and so did the *Saratoga,* as the roustabouts cast off its anchor ropes. The *Saratoga* kept on going up, though. As it rose from the late afternoon shadows of the Bois into the last level rays of the setting sun, it seemed to burst into an even brighter blaze of vermilion and white against the purpling sky, and the spectators gave another grand hurrah.

"A smooth launching, Governor," Goesle observed.

"We are *all* well and truly launched this day, Stitches," said Florian, sounding as happy as a man could be.

5

AT THE NIGHT SHOW, Clover Lee's act again sent the crowd into rampant delirium. There could not have been many repeat patrons left from the afternoon attendance to communicate to the new audience their enthusiasm for the girl. Nevertheless, she was once more the artiste most frenziedly applauded, called back for encores, and the only one deluged with flowers. Clover Lee had been unsure whether it was her scandalous costume that had made her so popular in the afternoon, but there was a show-business maxim: never to change "anything that once brought you good luck." So she had hastily rinsed and wrung out the pink léotard and skirt and worn them again for the night show. And this time, too, she did her best—staying in constant motion, using her doves for concealment—to minify the effect of her inadvertent immodesty. Even so, this time, too, that did not at all lessen the audience's uproarious acclaim.

"It is as I said," Florian told her, when she had finally been allowed to leave the pista that night. "There is no accounting for French enthusiasms. They quite simply adore you, my dear. I *would* suggest that you have Ioan immediately make you some less skintight léotards, but have her make sure they are all that exact same shade of pink."

Ioan did. So, at succeeding shows, Clover Lee was able to add the underwear
of bandeau and cache-sexe that properly obscured what she had called her
"every curve and nub and crack." And still, at every show, the crowd's passion
remained undiminished. Within a few days, Clover Lee found that her popularity
extended beyond the circus tober. Whenever she spent a free morning browsing
among the Paris shops and passages, anonymous in street dress, she still overheard murmured mentions of "l'étonnante Giuseppina," but now she heard as
often admiring comments about "la fantasque Clover Lee." That was celebrity
enough to make her rejoice, but one morning, a week or so later, when she was
strolling the aisles of the Magasins du Printemps, she discovered that she had
attained something like apotheosis. She almost ran back to the Grand Hôtel.
Florian and Rouleau were sitting in the lobby, smoking cigars and chatting.

"So Offenbach offers a rapprochement?"

"Yes. He came to say he would allow us to play his music, and before he left
he was almost begging us to. Anything, he said, except that 'Daring Young Man'
travesty of—"

"Florian!...Jules!" Clover Lee panted, quite out of breath. "Guess what! In
the Printemps...in a showcase...there's a fine evening gown...in *my* pink
color..."

"Well, well," Florian said indulgently. "If you want it, my dear, surely you can
afford it. You don't need my permi—"

"No, no, no!" She was gasping and laughing at the same time. "Remember,
Jules? A long time ago...way back in Virginia...you told how the trap artiste
...Léotard...had so many things...named in his honor...?"

"Why, yes," said Rouleau. "Just recently, I saw a pâté Léotard on a restaurant
carte."

"And I said...if I ever got famous in France...maybe they'd name something after *me*? Remember?"

Florian and Rouleau regarded her quizzically. Clover Lee left them in suspense for a minute, while she got her breath back, so that she could say with
proper dignity and pride and impressiveness:

"That gown in the Printemps showcase. It's got a placard on it: 'robe de soir,
brocart de couleur à la mode, *Clover Pink!*'"

"No!" both the men said together.

"Just like that. In English. Clover Pink. And underneath, in smaller letters, I
guess for anybody who doesn't know what it means: 'couleur de rose de trèfle.'
The pink color of clover."

"Bless my soul!" said Florian. "Why, if this is true, my girl, you have earned
us a recognition more to be treasured than any command performance." She
laughed joyously and ran off to the ascenseur, hurrying to spread the news
upstairs. Florian said to Rouleau, "I only hope the child is not deluding herself
on the basis of mere coincidence. After all, a clover blossom *is* pink."

But it proved to be no delusion. The Printemps, second only to the custom
couturiers, was the harbinger and promoter and often the instigator of popular
fashions. Within another week, boutiques in all the better districts of Paris were
displaying gowns or peignoirs or scarves or gloves done in that pastel color and
duly labeled CLOVER PINK or even CLOVER LEE PINK, and the ubiquity of it soon
made unnecessary any translations of the label into French. In the following
weeks, the color suffused other things besides wearing apparel. The city's pre-

mier saddlery and tack shop, Hermès et Fils, set in its show window a handmade sidesaddle, and that was in the distinctive Hermès caramel color, but it was perched upon a saddle blanket of Clover Pink. Susse's art gallery put in its windows a group of watercolors by Constantine Guys, all on circus subjects, and behind and about the ornate frames Clover Pink satin was draped and swagged. The custom perruquier Raymond Pontet put in his window a fanciful costume-ball wig of Clover Pink. The épicerie Fauchon, the Printemps of food stores, offered—among its ortolans from Italy, truffles from Périgord, pâté de foie gras from Strasbourg and other such delicacies—a Clover Pink saumon fumé, Clover Pink bonbons and Clover Pink petit fours biscuits. In the dining hall of the Hôtel Grand one night, everyone of the Florilegium was grandly served a new sweet concocted by the kitchen's chef de sucrerie, a Clover Pink strawberry mousse. The crowd in the stands at every show of the circus was liberally dotted with Clover Pink—hats, coats, blouses, scarves—and on the Paris streets Clover Lee was among the few females to be seen not wearing *something* pink. She resolutely refused to wear her hallmark color anywhere except in the pista.

From her first performance in Paris, Clover Lee had been receiving communications from the Johnnies in the seats, as she had in other places. After every show, Banat or one of the other Slovaks would bring her bouquets or boxes of candy and accompanying notes. She had accepted two or three of the earlier invitations to dinner or the theatre, but had found the Johnnies unworthy of a return engagement. However, when her Clover Pink became the rage of all Paris, Clover Lee began to receive more precious gifts—bits of good jewelry, bottles of expensive perfume, cases of rare wines—and the accompanying envelopes often bore embossed crowns, coronets or heraldic designs. In times past, Clover Lee would have leapt to accept the invitations enclosed in such envelopes, but now she returned only polite thanks and regrets, while she pondered: how to turn her dizzying popularity to best account?

She went one morning to the Hôtel Crillon, where Giuseppina Bozzacchi was residing. The two girls sat long in earnest converse, for Giuseppina was also being besieged by invitations signed with notable names, and was equally uncertain which to accept, if any. Next, Clover Lee accosted Monsieur Nadar, who was an almost daily visitor to the Florilegium tober, and asked his advice. Nadar looked through her collection of billets received so far and made some comment on each one, if only a scornful sniff, and began separating them into two piles.

"An unbridled libertine, this Comte Zichy." Tossed aside. "This one would merely want a pretty young woman as a disguise, so to speak, while he prowls after pretty young men." Tossed aside. "A confirmed debauché, this Chabrillan." Tossed aside. "This Persigny, he is already married—he for her money, she for his title. So, should he ever wish to bestow the title on you, chérie, you would both be penniless." Tossed aside. "And this one, who signs the billet as the Marquis de Persan, is really the *Marquise* de Persan. A member of that circle called 'the little Eldorado of Saint-Germain.' Quite a distinguished circle in some respects—it includes the Princesse Troubetskoi, the Comtesse d'Adda—but I do not think you would wish to join it." Tossed aside.

When Nadar was done, Clover Lee was left with a thin sheaf of envelopes, but was assured that their senders were at least all males, heterosexual, unmarried, possessed of unsmirched credentials and at least a modicum of unattached wealth. So thereafter, when any of those sent another gift and another invitation,

Clover Lee would not immediately decline it. She maintained contact with Giuseppina, and for some months the two girls kept messengers rather frequently trotting between the Bois and the Opéra or between their separate hotels, bearing notes on the order of "I have two eligibles for midnight supper, a minor prince and a count. Would you care for one of them?" And generally, when the girls did accept invitations, even from certifiably acceptable Johnnies, they arranged to go out in a foursome. That was not so much for the sake of safety or even propriety; Clover Lee and Giuseppina had together decided that it added to their aspect of inaccessibility and uninterest, and therefore would make them more sought after by the *most* eligible and wealthy and titled suitors.

During that winter, many others of the circus company also received gifts and notes from the seats—and not only the women troupers, but the men, too, including some who had *never* attracted such notice before. Of course, such polished and jaunty performers as Jean-François Pemjean, Árpád, Gusztáv and Zoltán Jászi could almost take their pick of smitten Parisiennes after almost every show. But the older and less dashing types—Jörg Pfeifer, Carl Beck and Dai Goesle—also had a sufficiency of admiring females to keep them entertained in their off hours. The decidedly unbeautiful Gombocz Elemér was often to be seen on the boulevards, driving the fancy phaeton of a decidedly handsome matron who sat affectionately close beside him. The lowly Slovak "professor" of the calliope was frequently invited by fluttery spinsters to attend their "musical soirées."

But Clover Lee continued to be the cynosure of all eyes, of male and female Parisians alike. And, when the chimney-smoke gray pall of winter lifted off the city, the fad of wearing Clover Pink was more than ever in evidence, because that color went so well with the Paris spring's pale pink misty mornings, and the pale blue mists that wafted along the Seine as the waters warmed, and the pale green mists that were the sprouting of grass in the Bois and leaf buds on the chestnut trees along the Champs-Elysées.

The people of the Florilegium had seen spring arrive in many different places on the planet, but not many of them had experienced it here, and so were unprepared for the beauties and delights of an April in Paris. After the pink mornings, the sky became a clear, windswept aqua color, and at night it went not to black, but to a deep, rich violet. The Champs-Elysées, even before its trees had fully greened out, was an avenue all of color and of all colors: crocuses, daffodils and tulips banked on both sides, along its central dividing strip, in the circles at street crossings. To walk past the flower stalls on the quais around La Cité was to risk giddiness from the commingled perfumes; to stand in the fruit market near Ste-Chapelle was to court intoxication from the aroma of wild strawberries; to walk along the Quai St-Bernard was to chance *real* drunkenness from the fumes of the brandy barrels being unloaded from the river barges.

Springtime in Paris was no novelty to Florian, but something had been added since last he had seen April burgeon here. The cafés, estaminets, brasseries and restaurants not only flung wide their street doors, they erupted *out* of them, setting tables and chairs on the very sidewalks, as many as they could squeeze along their frontage without blocking pedestrian traffic entirely. Florian expressed surprise, and Nadar, who was walking with him, explained:

"It started with the Great Exposition of 'sixty-seven, when so many foreigners and country folk crowded into the city. And you know, ami, how very greedy is every innkeeper. They simply acquired extra tables and chairs and appropriated the sidewalks outside their doors. They were roundly damned at first, by every poor soul who was forced to walk in the slops of the gutters and maybe have a hoof or a wheel crushing his foot. But now these have become an accepted thing. And even I must agree, a sidewalk table in fine weather is a pleasant place to sit long over a coffee or a liqueur, a smoke and a newspaper, to chat with friends or merely to cultivate the languid arts of the flâneur and observateur."

Gavrila Smodlaka and Katalin Szábo had, for different reasons, not previously shown the least inclination to make new men friends, but now, possibly inspired by the hedonistic gaiety of their fellow troupers—or of springtime Paris itself— they ventured out of their self-imposed solitariness. At any rate, when Gavrila was approached by a middle-aged, pleasant-faced expatriate Yugoslav gentleman who addressed her not just in Serbo-Croat but in her own native "kaj" dialect of Serbo-Croat—"Mogu li da se predstavim, gospodja? Moje ime Jovan Maretić"— she accepted his invitation to dinner. She did express some misgivings about leaving Sava unattended, but the girl rather petulantly said that she was certainly now old enough to be left on her own, even perhaps to make some friends of her own. And it was, in fact, at Sava's insistence that Gavrila continued thereafter to go out with the Gospodín Maretić once or twice a week.

Little Katalin-Cricket-Grillon was the recipient of almost as many bouquets and candy boxes and messages as was the star artiste, Clover Lee. Katalin kept all the gifts and opened all the accompanying envelopes. But some of the notes she immediately tore up, telling her curious sister troupers only that they were "disgusting." Others she laughed at and showed around; they were impassioned scrawls obviously written by moon-calf boys who must have thought that she was only a precociously developed girl of their own age. A few notes Katalin kept at least briefly, while she went to peek in the chapiteau's back door and have the Slovak who had brought the notes point out the senders of them. None was a midget like herself, but an occasional one of the men apparently looked tolerable enough; anyway, Katalin would have the Slovak bring him around to the backyard. There, well away from any possible eavesdroppers, she would briefly converse with him. When she did, one man after another looked incredulous and shocked, and hurried away. Only one of them, at last, did not flee, and from him she accepted an invitation to dine. She continued to accept other invitations from him: to the Opéra, to cafés-concerts, to the Théâtre Lyrique. Florian, as curious as anyone else, finally asked Katalin why this particular gentleman, of all those she had interviewed, seemed satisfactory to her. The little woman hesitated to reply, until Florian swore he would tell no one else.

Then she said simply, "He is impotent."

Even the dumpy and plain and always behind-the-scenes Ioan Petrescu made a romantic attachment. Dai Goesle somewhere found and brought to the tober a master of plumbery, who had invented a privy closet that did not depend solely on a pit dug underneath it, but employed a zinc tank containing solvent chemicals. Such a donnicker, Goesle told Florian, would not have to be so frequently moved, its old pit filled and a new one dug; the chemical tank would dissolve much of the deposited waste and to some degree deodorize it, as well. So Florian enthusiastically commissioned the Maître Delattre to provide fully six of the contrivances for the use of the circus patrons and company, and assigned a number of Slovaks to help him. It was while the master plumber was supervising that job of construction that he met Ioan and, despite the considerable language barrier, by the time the donnickers were finished he and she were regularly going out on the town together.

Fitzfarris, following the painter Renoir's advice, eventually visited the Folies Bergère, taking along Maurice LeVie to act as interpreter. At that café, by judiciously dispensing some of the nowadays much-in-demand circus tickets, they managed to insinuate themselves backstage. And there it required no great deal of persuasion and salary dickering to hire away the three prettiest girls in the Folies troupe. Those three promised also to round up some of their girl friends who were presently unemployed or engaged elsewhere. ("On the streets, no doubt," LeVie said in English to Fitzfarris, who replied, "Hell, I don't care where we get them.") So, after some more culling and selection among those convened girl friends, Fitz proudly presented to Florian a bevy of ten handsome, shapely and willing cancan dancers.

When Florian asked the girls if they possessed conduct books, he was slightly nonplussed when they handed him, instead, what they called their brèmes—or "flatfish"—the white cards issued by the police department, in which were listed the dates of their periodic medical examinations.

"Well," said Florian, after he had sent the girls on to Ioan to be fitted for costumes, "they may be putains, but at least they are not poivrières."

"Eh?" said Fitzfarris.

"They are prostitutes, but they are not pepperpots. They will not pepper our company with, ahem, embarrassing infections."

"And they're damned good-looking, besides." Fitz added gleefully, "What's more, they *will* dance the cancan with absolutely nothing under their skirts."

"Now, now, Sir John. If you wish to add them to your blow-off show, you may have them dressed as you like—or undressed. But when they dance in the pista they must be decently covered underneath. I shall instruct the wardrobe mistress to see that they are."

It took Ioan a week to do the girls' gowns. Those were all identical in style— tight and cut daringly low on top, with knee-length, billowy, flouncy skirts and many underskirts—but each dress was of two colors, and there were no two colors alike among the ten dresses. So when the girls danced the prelude to every show, they made a dazzling kaleidoscopic mêlée in the pista. Their frenzied, shouting, screeching fling-about of high kicks, backbends, struttings, sudden splits— danced to Maître Offenbach's rowdy cancan from *Orphée aux Enfers*—could hardly have been more rousingly erotic if they had danced stark naked. Later, after every show's come-out, the girls repaired to Sir John's annex for a "men only" postlude to the Maiden-and-Fafnir tableau. Between times, the girls proved Renoir's assertion that they were "quite devoid of prejudices" by making themselves available, at colleague-bargain prices, to all the males of the company—Hannibal, Banat, other Slovaks—who had not secured female consorts from the seats. Then they changed into their own clothes and disappeared from the tober, either to their own living quarters in the city or to work the late-night streets.

Some of the flirting and importuning Johnnies from the seats would hardly have been approved by Monsieur Nadar, if his counsel had been sought by those female troupers who succumbed to their blandishments. One night, when Jovan

Maretić brought Gavrila back to the hotel after a midnight supper at Fouquet's, she said good night to him and rode the ascenseur upstairs—then almost immediately rode it down again, returning to the lobby in time to find Maretić still there, buying a cigar at the bureau de tabac. She ran to him, clutched his sleeve and said in panic:

"Sava! Moj kći! Ona ne ovo u mojoj!"

"Not in your room? Perhaps she is merely wandering about the hotel."

"Ne, Jovan! Her street coat and muff and all are gone!"

"Then perhaps she went for a stroll. You must not—"

"It is after midnight! She is only eleven years old!"

"Still ... let us not take alarm, Gavrila. Let me think what is the best thing to—"

Just then, Sava came through the street doors into the nearly empty lobby. She wore a beatific smile, but it was directed at nobody and nothing in particular. She walked somewhat unsteadily, and her clothes appeared to have been hastily and untidily put on. She did not notice Gavrila and Jovan until her mother exclaimed:

"Sava! Where have you been?"

"Ah there, mati!" the little girl greeted her, with woozy cordiality, clearly having difficulty in focusing her pink gaze. "And Gospodín Maretić, hello." She looked more than ever waxily transparent, and her breath smelled of anise. "I was out."

"So we can see. *Where?*"

"With my friend Paul. Never told you about Paul? We've been out lots of times. This time he gave me a nice syrup drink. Four or three of them."

"Is Paul some little boy?"

"Not likely," grunted Maretić. "She reeks of absinthe."

"And this time he wrote me a poem. Just for me." Sava produced a wrinkled and stained piece of paper. "See, mati?"

Gavrila glared at it. "Jovan, can you read this?"

He had some trouble making out the drunken scribble, where many words had been crossed out and others interpolated. But he managed to read aloud a couple of the lines—"Mignons, pâles, doux tétins d'enfant ... d'elle pas encore en puberté"—then he swallowed and read the rest to himself.

"Well?" demanded Gavrila.

"Well ..." Maretić coughed. "Whoever he is, he seems to have a rather, um, intimate knowledge ... of the child's, er, body."

"Sava!" Gavrila said hoarsely. "What—what did you and this man *do?*"

"Went to his rooms. Not very nice rooms. Drank syrup drinks." She put a hand to her lips to cover a delicate burp, then grinned happily and fluttered her white eyelashes. "Next we went to bed and did what you and Papa used to do at night."

Gavrila flicked an embarrassed glance at Maretić, who fixed his own eyes on a distant upper corner of the lobby ceiling. Then she said to Sava, with wan hopefulness, "You cannot mean that. I am a grown woman, your father was a grown man."

"Paul is a grown man. But grown women are bulgy and hairy, Paul said. Paul said he would not wish me any more grown. And Paul said I did every woman thing that a grown woman could." Sava assumed a quite grown-up womanly look of sly and smug self-satisfaction. "Be-*cause* I was ver-ry, ver-ry careful to do the way you used to do with Papa." Gavrila did not again glance apologetically at Maretić; she only sagged and looked old. Sava went on, now mumbling blurrily, "Paul said his name is the same as Papa's. French for Pavlo. D'you know that?"

Her mother said wretchedly, "You must be making stories, child. You are *only* a child. It is impossible...unthinkable..."

Maretić coughed again and said, "Unthinkable, perhaps, but I regret to tell you, not impossible. To judge from what the man wrote so explicitly in this—"

Gavrila snatched the paper from him, snatched Sava protectively close to her and almost snarled, "Jovan, please go away now! I will show this paper to Gospodín Florian. He will know what to do. But you go away. I thought I was through with men forever. I *should* have been. Now I *am*. Zbogom, Jovan."

Sava echoed sleepily, "Zbo'm, Jovan."

"I go away," said Maretić, bowing. "But I will not stay away. I say dovidenja, not zbogom. Forgive me for telling you this at such an inopportune moment, Gavrila, but I believe your little family needs a man."

The next morning, Monsieur Nadar was again on the tober, and Florian produced the grubby piece of paper Gavrila had earlier given him. Nadar propped his square monocle in his eye, read the poem and said, "The abominable Verlaine, no doubt about it. Why do you show me this?"

"The abominable Verlaine, if it was he who wrote that, last night raped an eleven-year-old."

"Indeed? An eleven-year-old what?"

"Our enfante des ombres. The little albino girl."

"A female human being? Paul must have been dead drunk and desperate. Would you wish the police informed, then? I know a high-ranking inspecteur."

"No, no. I wished only to be certain of the fiend's identity. And please, monsieur, *try* not to talk of this sad incident. If any other man on this tober were to know of it, Verlaine would be hunted down and butchered. As it is, I shall myself merely horsewhip him to tatters the next time I encounter him."

"Tarare, ami! Do not spoil a good whip and do not risk an attaque d'apoplexie for yourself. Paul Verlaine might bed anything that is warm and cannot get away, but he much prefers les éphèbes. You have read the poem. Clearly he uses the girl only because her body is as featureless as a boy's. But now, zut alors, he has made a woman of her. She would be repugnant to him from now on. He will stay well away from her vicinity. The child need never fear him again, and the rest of you will probably never see him again."

Nadar was right. Verlaine was not again glimpsed, on the tober or anywhere else in Paris, by anyone of the troupe. And that same day, Florian had only just left Nadar when Gavrila came to him again to say:

"I am sorry, gospodín, I make so much shout at you this morning. That was before Sava waked. When she awake, she have terrible headache, sick stomach, but she no remembers why. Even she asked me why she little bit sore—down there—and got little bit blood. I quick tell lie. Tell her she yesterday try do split like cancan girl. First lie I ever tell Sava in her life."

"Entirely justified, Gavrila, and quick thinking. How fortunate, the child has had a loss of immediate memory. Not unusual after heavy intoxication. To what point of yesterday *does* she remember?"

"She visits rooms of man named Paul. No more. She wakes in own hotel room."

"Be glad, then, that the bastard got her drunk. And do not so much as hint at what did occur. Perhaps in time she will even forget the man and his name. Let us hope so. Meanwhile, make her stay in bed until she feels better, and you go back there and stay with her. We will work around your slanging-buffers act until—"

"No, gospodín, I work." Gavrila blushed slightly. "Not all men bad men. Very good man is watching over Sava right now. Better father even than her father."

In the ladies' dressing tent, where the two Simms girls were laying out their costumes for the day's first show, Sunday idly asked her sister, "Where are you spending your free time these days? You don't browse among the shops with any of the other women, and I never see you being squired anywhere by any Johnnies."

Monday laughed and said, "Lookit here." She reached for her street coat, took from it a chamois grouch bag that clinked richly, and upended it on the dressing table, pouring out a heap of gold coins. "I makin' more money now outside the show than I am in it."

"Gracious," said Sunday, staring. "How?"

"You 'member that man what drawed my picture?"

"Monsieur Doré, yes."

"I call him Gus, now. I went to his place like he told me, so he could put somethin' on that picture to stop it smudgin'. Seen a lot of him since then, and a lot of his picture-drawin' chums." She giggled. "They done seen a lot of me, too."

"Monday!"

"Gus is makin' pictures for a book he says is about the idles of a king. So I done posed to be all the fine ladies in them pictures, and them I done with fancy costumes on. But Gus's chums—Edgar and Edward and August and John-Baptist —they likes to draw me without no costumes, and they pays better for that."

"Monday! You actually undress for strange men?"

"Uh huh. They say they purely adores my skin color. They say there ain't many French women my color."

"How would you know what they're saying? You don't have more than half a dozen words of French."

"Oui, oui," Monday said sarcastically. "I don't never need much more than that. Oui, oui. But most of them talks some American. And lemme tell you, sis, they don't make fun of *mine*, neither, like you always doin'. Them gentlemens think a Southern accent is ladylike and *cute*."

"Then they ought to find Hannibal Tyree absolutely darling. But never mind that. Is posing in the nude *all* you've done? All they've paid you for?"

Monday snorted. "Hell, no. You reckon they'd pay gold just for lookin' at brown meat? They likes to sample it."

"And you let them? All those men you mentioned?"

"Well, not all at once. And sometimes there's other women posin', and they joins in." She added vaguely, "One way or another."

"Monday, that's..." Sunday waved her hands helplessly. "Doing it promiscuously, and for money, why, that's just plain—"

"You hush up! I swear, I'm go' stop callin' you sis and start callin' you auntie. You ain't got no man what cares a damn to get *you* undressed, so you want *me* to not have no good times neither."

Sunday sighed. "Maybe you're right. Maybe that is so."

"Keepin' yourself pure and innocent for that Zachary Edge, what's too old for you, anyhow. Maybe he's too old for anybody. I don't see him squirin' no Janes from the seats, even."

"He took me to dinner chez Vefours the other night."

"Along with Mr. Florian and Daphne Wheeler. Now *ain't* that romantic!" Monday looked at her sister with narrowed eyes. "I'm go' show you somethin' I been savin'. It's in the caravan. Stay here."

Monday was gone only a few minutes. She returned with a yellowing, folded piece of paper.

"You 'member after Miss Auburn died, old Zack parceled out her belongin's?"

"Of course. I still have her music box."

"He guv me a picture she'd had. It was a long time before I noticed this-here tucked in the back of the frame. I reckon old Zack was confused in them days, and forgot he'd stuck it there. Anyway, I judge Miss Auburn must of wrote this back when she thought she'd die natural, a good while before she decided to kill herself."

Monday handed the paper to Sunday, who said uncertainly, "It probably wasn't meant for anybody but Zachary to see."

"Well, it's got your name in it. So who got a better right to read it?"

Sunday opened it, her hands trembling a little, and slowly read aloud a part of it. "'...Zachary, I could have written this same sentiment, but another woman did it so much better. When I am dead, my dearest...sing no sad songs for me...'" Sunday sniffled, then read on in silence until she was halfway down the page. "'Of course, you may meet someone outside the circus, some truly fine and great lady, perhaps...'"

Monday said unfeelingly, "Like that fine, great countess he got so stuck on."

Sunday looked up and said loyally, "That was only because she reminded him so much of Autumn." She went back to the note. "'But, Zachary, among our own company—'" and stopped with a gasp.

"I told you," said Monday. "That Miss Auburn really must of liked you. I never in my life heard of no white woman sayin' so many nice things about no high-yaller wench. *And* throwin' her at her own white man."

In a shaky voice, Sunday said, "I wonder if Zachary ever read this."

"I wouldn't reckon *she'd* left it where I found it. You mean he ain't never said nothin' about it?"

"No. And don't you, either, Monday. But I guess this is still your property." She held out the note.

"Hell, it ain't no use to me. I'll tell the truth, sis. I only been keepin' it hid from you for spite, 'cause nobody never said *I* was brilliant and goodhearted and all them other things. It's yours, now. It ought to make a pretty powerful argument if you really want to bag the—*why you tearin' it up?*"

6

MAISON
DE L'EMPEREUR   *Palais des Tuileries, le 3 mai 1870*
Premier Chambellan

Monsieur Florian,

Par ordre de l'Empereur, j'ai l'honneur de vous prévenir que vous êtes invité, ainsi que...

"Well," said Florian, with hearty satisfaction, as he showed to his chief subordinates the exquisitely engrossed invitation just presented to him by a liveried messenger. "I had been wondering if the emperor had forgotten us. But we are all invited—except the Slovak crew, of course—together with any civilian consorts or other guests we may wish to bring, first to dinner at the palace of Saint-Cloud and then to a costume ball in the Grand Trianon at Versailles. On the first of June. According to the chamberlain's note, many other leading lights of the performing arts will also be at the dinner. And I should guess that a thousand or so of the aristocracy will be at the ball. Would you gentlemen spread the word around the tober? Ascertain exactly how many will be attending—including outside guests—so that I may inform the chamberlain."

"A costume ball," said Edge. "Does that mean pista costume?"

"For any who wish to wear it," said Florian. "But I imagine that most of us will wish to assume a different persona for a change, with the excuse of such a grand event."

"I think," said Willi, "some one of us should invite also the Monsieur Nadar. He will be useful in identifying for us the other guests."

"You mean giving us the latest and nastiest gossip about them," said Florian, with a smile. "Yes, definitely he must come along. Very well, go and tell the troupers. The big night is more than three weeks off, but that may be short notice for the females who wish to acquire ornate outfits for the occasion. And Stitches, will you prepare posters announcing that the Florilegium will not be performing that day? Also the day preceding, for our preparation, and the day after, for our recuperation."

When the others left the office, Fitzfarris lagged behind. "I'd like a private word, Governor, about the cancan girls."

"Dear me. I am afraid, Sir John, that they would be as out of place at a formal dinner as the Slovaks would be."

"Oh, I agree. It isn't that. I wanted to tell you that the girls came to me in a group to demand an increase in salary."

"What? We're paying them half again what you said they were earning at that squalid café revue. And they must be making even more than that from their, um, extracurricular activities."

Fitzfarris said uncomfortably, "Well, yes, they were for a while, but now they're not. I don't know exactly how to broach this, Governor. The girls' spokesman—no, that's not right—I guess you'd call her the spokesputain—anyhow, she said they've lost all their backyard trade. They claim that an amateur putain is, er, giving herself free to all comers."

"Heavens! One amateur is doing the work of ten professionals? But I have seen no sidewalling stranger anywhere in the backyard."

Fitzfarris took a deep breath and said, "The competitor is described as 'ce petit blanc ver.' If I comprehend correctly..."

"'That little white maggot?' Good God, that could only be—"

"Yes. I find it incredible, too, but the girls insist it is so. I haven't called Sava to account yet, or her mother. I wouldn't know how. That's why I'm dumping the problem in your lap. I'm sorry."

"Don't be," said Florian, looking troubled. "The rôle of this company's paterfamilias is mine, after all. But go quickly and send Gavrila to see me."

Edge was also being privately consulted, by Clover Lee, to whom he had just imparted the news of the forthcoming gala evening.

"I already knew it was being planned," she said. "I heard from a—from a friend at court. He'll be at the ball, too. But I'd like to ask a favor of you, Colonel Zack. Would you meet him, somewhere off the tober, before I introduce him to Florian at the ball? I've got a reason for asking."

"All right. When and where?"

"Sunday tells me you've got a favorite café, where you sometimes take your noon meal."

"Yes, but it's no place for entertaining company. Le Commerce, down by the fish markets of les Halles. If your friend is some duke or count, that's hardly—"

"That will do fine. Nobody there would be likely to recognize him. Tomorrow at noon?"

Fitzfarris had no sooner asked Gavrila to report to Florian—reason unspecified—than he was confronted with another situation that was, at least briefly, disquieting. When he told Brunhilde and Kostchei of the imperial invitation, they both begged to be excused—he on the usual grounds, that he refused to spoil everybody else's appetite, she because her family was too well-known by too many people in imperial court circles, and her presence in the guise of a circus exhibit might cause embarrassment all around. Fitz was not surprised at their declining, but he was fairly staggered when the giantess went on:

"Timoféi and I do not mind occasional retiracy, since we have each other for companionship. And we have decided to make permanent the having of each other. Sir John, we are planning to be married."

Fitzfarris's calculation took only a moment: there went twenty-five percent of his sideshow.

"Well," he said unhappily, "ever since you've been with us, we have all gone along with calling you Olga. But of course we all know who you are, Your Highness, and that you're a wealthy woman. I suppose we can't complain, now that you've found a husband to your liking, if you choose to enjoy your fortune—and good fortune—in permanent retiracy. But this show will certainly be the poorer for your leaving."

"Okh, nyet, nyet!" Kostchei exclaimed, in some alarm. "You would not *dismiss* us because we marry?"

"Why, no. Hell, no. But I assumed you two would go off and buy a palace somewhere. Live happily ever after, that sort of thing."

Brunhilde laughed with relief, and said lightly, "The ogre and the ogress, haunting a gloomy castle, deep in a dark forest? That would be *too* much privacy and solitude. Nyet. Here we have made friends, Sir John, who do not regard us as monsters. And here we can *see* other people, and give them enjoyment or a brief frisson, yet we do not have to mingle with them and pretend to be like them. This is the life we wish to continue living, if you will keep us on."

"Damned right we will!" said Fitzfarris, now exhilarated. "And *won't* we get newspapered when you two get married! I can guarantee, Florian will arrange the most bang-up wedding you could ever—"

"Okh, please, no!" begged the giantess. "That would make a travesty of it. Also, my family in Russia would certainly die of mortification at such notoriety."

"Oh. Well. I guess you're right," said Fitz, though dashed. "What a waste. It would have beat Tom Thumb's wedding by a country mile."

"We wish no panoply at all, no public notice. Just a civil ceremony in some municipal office. If you can find out the proper procedure, Sir John, we would be grateful."

"Yes. All right. I'll inquire around."

Gavrila danced into the red wagon, saying ebulliently, "John Fitz tells me the so grand news. Please, it will be allowed if I invite Gospodín Maretić?"

"Of course it will. It is partly of your friend Maretić that I wished to speak to you. Sit down, my dear." Florian fidgeted with some things on his desk for a minute, then said cautiously, "It appears that little Sava did not entirely forget *everything* that occurred on the night she was, er, abducted. Indeed, it seems she has developed a taste for repeating some of those things." He tugged at his tuft of beard. "I suppose a mother would be the last to know."

Gavrila put up a tremulous hand to hide her trembling lips. Florian had to go on and tell her of Sava's reported activities, but he refrained from mentioning her reportedly limitless voracity, and its effect on the earnings of fully ten professional whores.

"With a *Slovak* she does it?" Gavrila said, almost retching. "Svetog Vlaha! But... but... perhaps, gospodín... you would consider to expel him? Such a man like that?"

Florian did not explain that he would have to discharge his entire work crew and his band and his bull men and only God knew who else. Instead he said, "I think, this time, it is not any one man's fault. Now it is Sava's. Or, more accurately, it is her problem, her affliction. What the medical profession calls cytheromania. The girl needs supervision. If she invites intimacies—considering her tender age and beguiling dewiness and her undeniable uniqueness—it would be a strong man who could refuse her."

Gavrila said miserably, "I cannot watch every minute."

"I am aware of that. Which brings me to Gospodín Maretić. You called him a good man and, from what I have seen and heard of him, I fully agree. Has he perchance asked you to marry him?"

"Very almost," she mumbled. "If I would give him to suppose I might say yes, he would ask."

"Then why don't you? And say yes when he does."

She looked almost as shocked by that as by the revelation of Sava's indiscretions. "Because he is not *circus!* He is blagajnik, caissier, clerk in bank. He never can join out with circus."

"Then I fear you must consider the advantages of leaving it."

"After all my *life?*" she wailed.

"A terrible decision to face, I know. And a wrenching move, if you make it. I myself should not ever wish to contemplate it. But Maretić evidently earns a good living at bank clerking. You need not work at all. And a safe and settled existence should soon make up for the loss of spangles and excitement and applause."

"But... but... the pasovi?"

"The terriers? Does Maretić dislike dogs?"

"No, no. He likes."

"Well, then. Other families have household pets. Yours would simply have extraordinarily *talented* pets."

"With audience of one man."

"Confound it, woman, look here! We are not talking about you or the dogs or the jossers or the circus, or the deprivation of any of those. We are talking of what is best for Sava."

"Is so. I being selfish. Silly."

"The child was born different from other people, at least in appearance. She had an unloving father, who came to a deservedly terrible end. At the same time, Sava lost her brother, who was the only other person quite like her, in her immediate world. Then the first friend she ever made outside the tober took brutal advantage of her. Small wonder the girl has turned—well, unruly. But she could be redeemed. With a home, family, school, security. Understand, I am not commanding you to marry. And I sympathize with your reluctance to give up the only kind of life you have known. I sympathize also with Gospodín Maretić. He may be taking on more responsibilities than the typical bank clerk would expect to meet in a marriage. Thank God, he is a good, sturdy Yugoslav, not a vaporing Frenchman prone to pitapatation. I only urge you, Gavrila, to consider what is best for you to do. If it *is* marriage, then do not dally too long. Meanwhile, I am issuing strict hands-off orders, as regards Sava, to every man in this tober. But Sava herself I cannot command or control. You must do that, and *it must be done.*"

Clover Lee and her friend were late in arriving at the café le Commerce the next day, so Edge already had a platter and carafe in front of him on his sidewalk table and, while he ate, was reading Paris's only English-language newspaper, *Galignani's Messenger*. The Commerce's outdoor tables were set close together, and not one of them was unoccupied, and those patrons who were not noisily talking or laughing or bellowing for a "garçon!" were almost as noisily eating—slurping bisques and soups, cracking the shells of crabs and lobsters and langoustes and écrevisses, clashing cutlery and crockery and glassware. Waiters with trays held high scuttled sideways amongst the tables, crying loudly, "Par'n, 'sieurs, 'dames!" but jostling the diners' elbows and knocking hats askew, regardless.

The noise and commotion did not end at the café's curbside, for there was the rue Coquillière. On it, great grays drawn by great horses and oxen rumbled by, laden with barrels packed in salt and ice. The porters afoot made nearly as much noise, for they wore wooden sabots, and they clumped along under the weight of everything from baskets overflowing with sprats to entire sturgeons as big as themselves. They also shouted jolly insults at each other, frequently collided and then exchanged very unjolly invective. In the street's overall miasma of raw fish, slopped guts and scales and slime, seaweed and salt water, le Commerce was rather an olfactory oasis, smelling much more sweetly of *cooked* fish, wine, coffee, frying butter, onions, capers, shallots and garlic, garlic, garlic.

Edge hurriedly got to his feet, fumbling with and dropping his newspaper and serviette, when Clover Lee and a handsome gentleman of about thirty—both of them dressed as for a palace presentation—appeared beside his table.

"Zachary, may I present my good friend Gaspard, Comte de Lareinty? Gaspard, the Colonel Zachary Edge."

Edge swallowed his mouthful, murmured, "Your Grace," and shook the man's hand.

"Zut, Zachary, call me Gaspard. Or Jasper, if you prefer the English version. After all, I am very nearly already a proxy member of your circus family. Sit down, sit down. Finish your déjeuner."

Edge waved a hand rather apologetically at the hectic and inelegant surroundings, and said, "All my life, I never could get enough oysters. So here in Paris I just gorge on them, and this place serves the best." He indicated his platter, pyramided with oysters on the half shell: the bright green Fines de Claire, the dull green Portugaises, the silvery Belons and, added by the chef for their colorful contrast, some vividly orange mussels.

The count screwed a monocle into one eye, gazed about at the rough-hewn and rudely dressed other diners and said patronizingly, "Un estaminet des pieds-humides. Singulier, oui."

"The oysters do look good," said Clover Lee, as the count held a chair for her. "But I never eat before a performance. Perhaps, Gaspard, an apéritif?"

The count raised a hand and snapped his fingers without even looking up. He may have been unrecognized in this milieu, but, while all about were futilely bawling, "Garçon!" he had a waiter instantly at his side. He ordered an absinthe for himself and a nonintoxicating cassis for Clover Lee.

Edge quickly finished off his shellfish, so the waiter could clear away the platter when he brought the drinks. The count made a small ceremony of tilting the pony glass of clear absinthe into the goblet of clear water and watching the combination turn to an iridescent white-opal color. Edge took a draft of his wine and looked encouragingly at Clover Lee.

"Well, you must have guessed, Zack," she said, a little nervously. She peeled the glove off her left hand to display the ring set with a diamond the size of that finger's nail. "Gaspard and I are affianced."

The count sipped at his drink and, as if he were not at all the subject of discussion and appraisal, said feelingly, "Ah! When we get to paradise, amis, we shall find it to be only the hour of apéritif, infinitely prolonged."

"I'm happy for you, Clover Lee," said Edge. "I wish you good luck and every joy. And you I congratulate, Gaspard. And surely neither of you requires my consent."

"What we'd like to ask of you," said Clover Lee, "is that you be our go-between, so to speak. You see, Zack, as the Comtesse de Lareinty, I would be—well, leaving the circus, making my home in Paris."

The count commented airily, "It is better to die at thirty in Paris than to live to be a hundred anywhere else."

"So you want me to break the news to Florian," said Edge.

Clover Lee said, "Of all the artistes on the show, I've been with it longer than anybody except Jules and Hannibal. I'm afraid the dear old Governor may take it badly."

"Hélas," said the count, "but every man must sometime endure his mauvais quart d'heure."

"Yes," said Edge. "It may give Florian a bad quarter of an hour. But you know, Clover Lee, he's never wanted anything but the best for all his company. And he knows how eager you've been to—"

"Oh là!" Clover Lee said merrily, but hastily, to forestall anything Edge might have added. "I was overwhelmed to be proposed to by a man not only fine and good and handsome, but also of noble lineage. I would never have expected such an honor." As she said that, she fixed Edge with a significant cobalt gaze. "I have tried and tried to impress upon Gaspard the fact that I am unworthy, that I am only—"

"Most frank and honest she has been, Zachary," said the count, and Edge's eyebrows involuntarily went up a little bit. "I have cited to her previous examples. The Comtesse de Chabrillan was once, like Clover Lee, an équestrienne of a circus, le Cirque Franconi. And the Marquise de Caux was and still is a singer, la Diva Patti. Now, those women were wealthy in their own right and they purchased those husbands with titles. But this one"—he laid a hand affectionately on hers—"I quote to you, Zachary, her exact words. She said, 'I am but a poor maiden, Your Grace. The innocence you admire is all I have of dowry to bring to a marriage.'"

"Ah," said Edge, unable to think of any other comment, and Clover Lee now was not meeting his eyes.

"However," the count went on, "much as I appreciate Clover Lee's skill and grace in the circus—and her rightfully earned celebrity—she need not and cannot continue to be in the public eye. La Patti must, in order to support her Marquis de Caux. To the contrary, I am financially well fixed. More important, my family is of a certain distinction, and I myself hold rather a prominent position in His Majesty's retinue..." He shrugged expressively.

"Gaspard is the emperor's military aide-de-camp," Clover Lee explained.

"I understand the situation," said Edge. "Caesar's wife, and all that. But Gaspard, if you hold such a high military appointment—with all the rumors of impending war—is this quite the time to be thinking of taking a wife? A hostage to fortune?"

Gaspard said suavely, "I am a Frenchman, mon colonel. Death? Capture? A Frenchman surrender? *Never!* I shall run away."

The count's previous and sententious pronouncements had not much endeared him to Edge, but that remark made Edge smile. Unfortunately, that, as usual, made Edge look as grim as if he had taken the frivolity seriously. The count in turn looked somewhat affronted, and said stiffly:

"I was but jesting, of course."

"Oh, he knows it, Gaspard," said Clover Lee, laughing. "The colonel always looks ugliest when he is best pleased. Then we have your blessing, Zachary?"

"Unreservedly. Now you and I had better be heading for the tober to dress. I'll beard the Governor at the first opportunity."

He waited until Florian was relaxing alone in his caravan, after the show's come-out, and broke the news.

"I don't know how happy Clover Lee is likely to be," Edge added, "married to a jasper named Jasper, whose conversation consists mainly of café banter and banalities. But she has always yearned for a wealthy man with a title, and she's sure got the genuine article in this one."

"Far be it from me to stand in the way of true love," Florian said, a little wryly. "But I do begin to have the feeling that the whole Florilegium is about to fall apart into domesticity. I think you have not yet been apprised of a couple of other instances." He told Edge about the plans of Kostchei and Brunhilde, and about the problem with Sava, and the possibility of its being solved by Gavrila's getting married. "I next expect our wardrobe mistress to come and tell me she is retiring to become Madame Plumber Delattre. Or for Monsieur Roulette and the Baron Wittelsbach to announce that they are setting up housekeeping together."

"Well, don't make it all sound like the end of the world, Governor. I imagine we can do some more recruiting of new talent, when and if we have to."

"I suppose so," Florian said fatalistically. "Anyway, no one will be deserting before the emperor's dinner and ball. After that, we shall see."

Once again, as had happened in St. Petersburg, the troupers wanting dinner dress and ball costumes had to scatter their custom among a variety of clothing establishments, because every one of those in Paris, from Worth and Dobergh to the least back-street seamstress, was inundated with orders. The ladies' couture shops were especially crowded, and, as often as not, the crowds included burly and watchful men. They were the flunkies who had brought their mistresses' diamonds, emeralds and rubies to be sewn onto bodices or headdresses or whatever, and would not depart until they took the gem-finished goods with them. But with the participation of Ioan Petrescu, who worked all day, every day, and by lamplight into the wee hours of the morning, all the artistes were properly outfitted by the eve of the great day. Some of the women said, "Dear Ioan, you have labored so hard for the rest of us. But what of your own ball costume?"

"Ah," she said, rubbing her red eyes. "That, my Pierre is making for me."

"A *plumber* is making your costume? What in the world are you going as?"

"You will see," said Ioan, with a weary but happy smile, and would give no further hint.

The palace of St-Cloud was only a couple of miles beyond the farther edge of the Bois de Boulogne. The circus folk went there in hired fiacres, wearing their dinner dress, and a single Slovak driver trailed along with one of the baggage wagons carrying their costumes for the ball afterward. The so-called palace was nothing like the majestic pile in the Tuileries Gardens, but was merely an immense, homey, comfortable country house set on a hill in a park, and from that height overlooking all of Paris. As the troupers descended from their voitures in the twilight, they pointed out to one another the edifices they could recognize from this distance: Notre-Dame, the Panthéon, the Invalides, their own chapiteau in the Bois.

"You must forgive me, my dear Florian," said the emperor, as he greeted the party, "for neglecting you all this time. I was forced to spend my entire winter and spring dealing with the most depressing state business."

"Not depressing, *distressing,*" his empress sharply corrected him. Eugénie was almost twenty years younger than Louis Napoléon, barely on the shady side of forty, and still a handsome woman, though in a hard, brittle sort of way, as if she had been recently varnished. Standing a few steps behind her, as he would be throughout the whole night's festivities, was a massive Nubian manservant in gold-embroidered robes.

Louis and Eugénie introduced the circus people to the only other royals present: their son, the Prince Imperial, Eugène Louis, only fourteen years old, but manly and mannerly; and the emperor's stout, bald, jowly cousin Jérôme, Prince Napoléon. The newcomers saluted those personages with bows and curtsies, and properly addressed the princes respectively as "Your Imperial Highness" and "Your Highness." But Monsieur Nadar was such a familiar figure in these precincts that he addressed only the emperor and empress formally; he called the young prince "Lou-Lou" and the elderly one "Plon-Plon."

Plon-Plon only cursorily acknowledged the introductions of everyone else, he was so eager to fasten upon Clover Lee. She had, for this one night, decided to wear her distinctive color outside the tober, and was radiantly garbed in that very same Clover Pink brocade gown she had first seen in the Printemps. "Mademoiselle," said the prince, bowing so that he nearly plunged his fleshy nose into the cleft of her décolletage, "I have attended three of your performances, and been enchanted, enraptured, enslaved. I insisted that my cousine seat us side by side at table this evening."

"But I wish now to make one change in the seating at the premier table," said

Engénie, to whom Edge had considerately spoken in Spanish when he was presented. She beckoned to the big black servant and said, "Scander, the colonel was to sit with Mademoiselle Leblanc. Please put his place card at *my* right hand." To Edge she said coquettishly, "I hope you will not mind, Monsieur le Colonel, conversing with a dull Spanish matron, instead of a beauteous young actress. Anyway, your charm would have been wasted on Léonide. She is even duller than I, and inaccessible if you *had* charmed her, for she is already the mistress of the Duc d'Aumale. Now come, all of you, and meet the other guests."

Most of those were milling about and sipping apéritifs in a great drawing room with vast windows that gave a panoramic view of Paris dimming and disappearing in the dark, being replaced by a galaxy of innumerable points of light sparkling against the night's purple velvet. The guests included a goodly number of dukes, counts, marquises, some accompanied by wives—"not necessarily their own," Nadar remarked, sotto voce—and the other invited performing artistes. There was the actress Léonide Leblanc, famed more for her sensuous beauty than for any talent at acting. There was the boyish and frizzly-haired Sarah Bernhardt, who consumed liqueurs and cigarettes one after another. There was the exceedingly pneumatic Adelina Patti, her bosom constantly threatening to levitate out of her décolletage à la baignoire. There was Hortense Schneider, the star comédienne of almost all of Offenbach's operettas, now some years past her full bloom. And there was the very young, very pretty Giuseppina Bozzacchi, who immediately ran to embrace Clover Lee.

As the emperor and empress genially and informally managed the complex criss-cross of introductions, the roomful of guests bobbed and surged in bows and curtsies so that the gathering resembled a fairly turbulent sea. In the meantime, as expected, Nadar gave to any of the troupers who were nearby and cared to hear a pithy précis on this guest and that.

"There is an amusing anecdote involving Hortense Schneider. In her prime, she was nicknamed for that arcade of shops downtown, 'le Passage des Princes,' because she had horizontally entertained not only Louis Napoléon, but also the Khedive of Egypt, Tsar Alexander of Russia, heaven knows how many other crowned phalluses. Well, one time, the Khedive Ismail was taking the waters at Vichy, and got very bored, so he told his secretary, 'Send for Schneider.' The secretary, being new at the job, summoned *Adolphe* Schneider, the munitions maker who supplies most of Egypt's armaments. Adolphe came by the first train, was met by the khedive's entourage, hastened to an apartment brimming with flowers, conducted to a perfumed bath. After an interval, Ismail entered, himself all perfumed and powdered and ready for a frolic. And there, wallowing in bubbles, was this naked, fat, bald, walrus-mustached old Adolphe. I would have given anything to have been a fly on the wall."

Fitzfarris, laughing, asked, "Well, what happened?"

Nadar shrugged. "For an Egyptian, Ismail was of almost French sang-froid. He gave Schneider, then and there, a large order for a shipment of new weapons to his army. What else would *you* have done?"

Nadar was by no means the only person present who was prattling waggishly or waspishly. Gossip was clearly the common coin of conversation at court get-togethers.

"... Everyone, but everyone, is still tittering about the way she earned the Grand-Croix de la Légion d'Honneur. She slipped from the ballroom with the

Duc de Loury and returned, an hour or so later, with his medal unknowingly caught in the ribbons of her bodice. La Légionnaise de Déshonneur, they call her now. Even her husband."

"... Has a lover for every separate day of the week, and each must pay part of her upkeep. The duke who has Wednesdays pays her rent, Count Thursday pays her milliner, Marquis Friday stocks her wine cellar, and so on. Monsieur Saturday is not a man of means—only a third-rate opera tenor—but he also must pay his way. So he personally pedicures her corns and bunions."

"... Started her career in the lowest harborside bordel. Today she spends five thousand francs a month just on the cleaning of her Chantilly laces."

"... When Carpeaux asked her to sit to him for a sculpture, she consented only if she could pose standing erect. Carpeaux told her that would be a tiring position, and asked why she insisted on standing for so many sessions upright. She said, 'It rests me.'"

"Messieurs, would you come with me?" Louis Napoléon asked Florian and Edge. "I wish to show you a thing of great curiosity before we are called to dinner."

As the two followed him up a flight of stairs, the emperor asked, as if by the way, "Colonel Edge, will you still refuse even to consider resuming your old profession of warfare?"

"Still, Your Majesty."

Louis Napoléon led them along a corridor and opened a door into a lamplit room that smelled of acrid chemicals and looked rather like a combined studio, workshop and laboratory. Its furniture consisted mostly of easels and tripods and worktables, the latter cluttered with various kinds of apparatus and littered with bits of unidentifiable machinery.

"We call this the grown men's playroom," said the emperor, with a smile. "That box yonder, for example, is Plon-Plon's latest toy, the appareil Dubroni. My cousin believes it will make him a greater photographer than Nadar, but do not ask me how. All I know is that he is forever pouring smelly liquids into its orifices. That other and complicated object was Plon-Plon's previous hobby. He bought it of a fairground charlatan who called it a Hydro-Oxygen Gas Microscope. For some while, Plon-Plon made an atrocious nuisance of himself, going about with a pin and pricking people's fingers. He would examine and compare under the microscope the blood droplets from, say, an unmarried girl and a married woman, an ascetic friar and a confirmed drunkard..."

"Very interesting, Your Majesty," said Florian, trying to sound very interested.

"And *this,* the appareil Casilli, is *my* current plaything. No toy, this, but a most ingenious and useful invention. Maître Casilli calls it the Pantelegraph. Would you believe it, messieurs? By means of this contrivance, a préfet de police can send a drawing of a criminal's face, or a facsimile of his handwriting, to the préfecture of any other arrondissement in Paris, in all of France, and even— thanks to the transatlantic cables—to the police agencies in all the Western hemisphere. Imagine that! A sketch, a scribble, can be translated into the dots and dashes of the code Morse, transmitted and reassembled into the identical likeness again. No criminal will evermore be able to elude justice simply by fleeing beyond a city's limits or a nation's boundaries. He can be recognized and apprehended by any policeman anywhere."

"*Very* interesting, Your Majesty," said Florian.

However, His Majesty himself seemed suddenly to lose interest in that electrical marvel. He went over to an ordinary easel, pulled a string, and a cloth chart unrolled and flopped down to hang the length of the easel. It was a large-scale map of eastern France and the abutting Germanic states.

"Another hobby of mine, messieurs." He lighted one of his noxious asthma cigarettes and with it pointed at the map. "I study the terrain of my empire, I estimate the risks to it, I assess its vulnerabilities. Perhaps, Colonel Edge, you would be so kind as to comment on one recent cause for concern. My military attaché in Berlin sent me an enciphered message. His spies have concluded that Prussia's General von Moltke now has four armies of one hundred thousand men apiece. It is the attaché's opinion that, in case of war, von Moltke would invade simultaneously westward across the Rhine into Alsace and southward across the frontier of Lorraine." The emperor's gestures describing those anticipated thrusts left trails of cigarette smoke, like battle smoke, to mark them. "A pincers, so to speak, closing upon the city of Nancy. It would effectually bite off that entire northeast corner of France. What think you, Colonel?"

Edge looked long at the map, and rubbed his chin thoughtfully. Finally he nodded. "It would seem to fit, Your Majesty, with what observations I was able to make."

"And would you know how best to counter such a plan of attack?"

"In my time, Your Majesty, I was only a tactical commander, not a strategist. But I reckon I could, in the event, tell you how Jubal Early would have done it. Or Phil Sheridan, for that matter."

"And by unhappy coincidence, von Moltke *has* General Sheridan to advise him. Hélas, I do *not* have General Early. And, hélas de beaucoup, *you* have retired from any and all military involvements."

"I have, Your Majesty."

"But ah, I was forgetting something!" exclaimed the emperor, seeming abruptly to lose interest now in the map. "I did not prove to you, messieurs, how efficiently the Casilli Pantelegraph operates." He took their arms and hustled them again to the table where that apparatus reposed. "For absolute proof that it worked, I wished to experiment, using absolute strangers. So I hope you will forgive me, Monsieur Florian, that for practice I used the persons of your circus company. It was only because, you see, I did know that they were strangers to Paris—and to the Paris police."

Florian and Edge regarded him in silent stupefaction as he began to shuffle among a pile of papers on the table.

"So the office of the Procureur Général detailed a detective agent, who has considerable skill with the pencil, to attend your circus and there to make surreptitious sketches of various men of your troupe, men he selected purely at random. Only the men, messieurs; chivalry prohibits intrusion on the privacy of ladies, even ladies of public pursuits. After the performance, that agent professed himself to be an admirer of those male performers, and requested autographed mementos. Later, I was present in person at the Préfecture de Paris when those several pictures and signatures were put through the wonderful appareil Casilli, and thereby telegraphed to all the countries your circus has toured. Lo and behold... ah, yes, here they are."

He abstracted two papers from the pile he had been rummaging in and laid them on the table before the stunned Florian and Edge. One picture, sketchy though it was, was unmistakably the scarred and noseless face of Kostchei the Deathless; the scrawl of Cyrillic script below it was presumably his signature. The other picture was not so readily recognizable until one read the autograph —John Fitzfarris—and then it obviously *was* he, wearing his cosmetic mask to conceal his own disfigurement.

The emperor went on, quite casually, "By almost immediate return of telegraph, the excellent Third Section of the chancery of my friend Alexander of Russia identified the man Timoféi Somov as a convicted utterer of false coinage, who was flogged, mutilated and ordered into exile. Unfortunately, the American states have no agency nearly so efficient as the Third Section. Response from Washington was a long time in coming. However, the authorities there seem to think that the other man, Fitzfarris, is of some interest to various jurisdictions—civil governments in the North, military in the South—as a suspect in several instances of swindling, employing the postal system to defraud, I forget what else."

Florian cleared his throat, but his voice was still husky when he said, "Somov has expiated his crime, Your Majesty, and Fitzfarris is a thoroughly reformed character."

Louis Napoléon looked unutterably wounded. "Mon cher ami, I have not the least doubt of it! You would not have such men traveling with you, otherwise. Surely you do not think I had any base motive in making this trivial experiment! I grant you, I was somewhat surprised at the outcome of it. Nevertheless, I assure you, Monsieur Florian, that I have commanded the préfet to seal all the records pertaining to it."

"But not to destroy them," Edge said in a tight voice.

"And do you, too, suspect me of ulterior motives, Colonel? You must understand that even I cannot interfere in the official duties of the police. One of their duties is to keep apprised of any persons resident in Paris who might, however remote the possibility, constitute a risk to public peace or state security at some future date. If a war should eventuate, for example."

"At which time, such persons could be at hazard," said Edge, "unless perhaps some other person went ransom for them. Say, by agreeing to help in the prosecution of the war. If a war should eventuate."

"There you are!" the emperor said jovially. "If. You and I both said *if.* Now come, messieurs, let us go down to dinner."

7

THERE WAS still a clamor of chatter, gossip and laughter downstairs, but a couple of noises of complaint were audible over all.

The Empress Eugénie was complaining, in an imperially loud voice, "His Majesty and I nowadays have to avoid strolling about the Orangerie outside *our own gardens.* The Tuileries terrace there has lately become a trysting place for those awful tapettes—you must excuse the word—prowling after other men. I should not find them so distasteful if they were gay and decorative, like the grog-chasseuses prowling the boulevards for *real* men. But the tapettes all look so drearily and uniformly *melancholy.*"

Sarah Bernhardt was complaining, in a voice trained to reach the galleries, "I wish to prove myself as a tragédienne, but the managers insist on frothy and simpleminded plays to appeal to the common man. I tell them: *the common man*? Merde alors, so many things are brought down to his level that the wretched pignouf will remain *forever* common!"

When the servants saw the emperor coming downstairs, a steward rang a gong, and the clamor diminished as the crowd filed two by two into the dining hall. Eugénie was on Edge's arm, Hortense Schneider on Louis Napoléon's, Clover Lee on Prince Jérôme's, and tiny Katalin went with her hand held high to lay at least her fingers on the arm of the young Crown Prince Eugène.

At the table where the emperor and empress sat at the head and foot, Louis Napoléon immediately and pridefully commanded all the other diners to examine their place settings before any food was put upon their dishes. The plates, saucers, cups, utensils and even the wine and water goblets were all made of a metal that shone like well-polished pewter.

"But so amazingly light of weight," the elderly Marquis de Gallifet said wonderingly, lifting a plate. "What is it, Your Majesty?"

"A metal only recently refined. Rarer still than gold, and I am the only person yet to possess a complete dinner service of it. It is called alumine."

"Laissez donc," murmured the very young Marquise de Gallifet. She giggled and essayed a naughty pun. "I thought alumine was an astringent used by lâches women to tighten their lâches parts and pretend maidenhood."

Louis Napoléon gave her an exasperated look. "The salts of alumine are medicinal, yes, but the metal itself has until now been only a laboratory curiosity. This imperial dinner service is the very first practical use ever made of it." How practical it was the others later disputed, most thinking it looked tawdry and agreeing that it tainted every food and drink with a metallic taste.

All those at the premier table would also have enjoyed their meal much more if Adelina Patti had not been among them. She and her husband, Henri, had not been separated, as had other couples, to provide each with a stranger for a conversational partner. It might have been supposed that la Diva Patti would have preferred that, since her husband was twice her age, only half her size and distinctive merely in having no discernible distinction. But the empress was obviously familiar with the peculiar crotchets of this couple, and, as hostess, had had the Marquis and Marquise de Caux seated side by side.

La Diva was no invalid, and was plainly capable of feeding herself; indeed, her considerable poitrine suggested that she was *very* capable of it. But out in company, as the company observed, her husband did the care and feeding of her. The other diners partook of numerous different wines during the meal, all of them excellent—or they would have been, if they had not had to be drunk from the metal goblets. But Henri waved away every waiter who proffered a decanter, and himself poured for Adelina only champagne, and only brut champagne, and only the Dom Pérignon brand of champagne. Every dish that was brought by the table flunkies, the marquis first sampled, then, if he approved, said, "Here, ma chère Adi, you may have some of this," and himself put the helping onto her plate. None of the watching circus folk could guess—and never did find out— whether Henri so sedulously attended upon Adelina because she was his sole means of support, or whether she required that service of him, like his title, as a contract condition of the marriage.

Meanwhile, Eugénie and Edge conversed quietly in Spanish, and the empress was perhaps less discreet in her native tongue than she would otherwise have been. She first confided that the "depressing state business" that had occupied His Majesty for so many months had in fact consisted of his feebly ceding much of his own power to "those damned Third Party leftists" in the Corps Législatif.

"We are rapidly becoming nothing but a parliamentary empire," she said bitterly. "I refuse to be deposed, as was my cousin Isabella in Spain. And I would far rather be a rue de Rivoli shopgirl than to be a mere figurehead empress like Victoria. Ever since Louis was first afflicted with the bladder stone, he has been getting more lax and dull and timid and unenterprising."

Edge said placatively, "Seguro, no totalmente, Vuestra Majestad." He was only partly being diplomatic; he was also thinking of the not at all timid threat the emperor had made upstairs.

"¡Sí, totalmente!" Eugénie insisted. "He no longer even ruts among his mistresses. As for the despicable Third Partyists—Ollivier, Gramont, Gambetta—and the uncouth street mobs agitating for republicanism, and the coarse caricatures of His Majesty—*and of me*—that constantly appear in comic papers like *La Vie Parisienne,* why, any other monarch would by now be greasing the guillotine. For such contemptible subversives, show them the world upside-down, I say! But not he!" She broke off to exclaim in puzzlement, "¿Qué pútrida purgación es este?"

The table flunkies had served to everyone else—and the empress's ever-present black Scander had served to her—the dinner's fish course, turbot in some kind of creamy sauce, and she had just tasted hers and made a face at it. Edge took a bite of his own; it was curiously almost candy-sweet. Most of the others at the table were also looking askance at their turbot and at each other. Henri de Caux had already waved the dish away; for once, the others envied Adelina his attentions. Only the emperor appeared to have noticed nothing amiss and was heartily eating his.

The dining hall's chief steward came running to the table in a panic, his face pale, sweat beading his forehead. "Oh, Your Majesties!" he wailed, wringing his hands, almost weeping. "An apprentice sous-chef made a ghastly mistake. Instead of the sauce hollandaise for the turbot, he poured the egg custard intended for the sherry trifle. Inexcusable, inexcusable! Le chef-saucier is about to take a cleaver to his own head. Forgive the mistake, Your Majesties, Your Graces." He was frantically snapping his fingers. "Garçons! Remove these vile dishes!"

"Nonsense," the emperor said placidly. "I find it quite good." He went on imperturbably eating, and waved dismissively at the steward. "Simply serve up the hollandaise with the trifle."

The steward reeled away in horror, the other guests rolled their eyes and resumed eating the fish, and Eugénie, under her breath, swore a terrible obscenity in Spanish.

"There, you see?" she said to Edge. "The old clod puts up with anything. It is I who will have to make sure that that bungling apprentice is boiled with his own next custard. And I will be cursed and called 'l'inquisiteur espagnol.' Oh, I hear it often enough, behind my back. I tell you, Señor Coronel, there is only one way for Louis to regain his imperial rights and powers, to deserve again the admiration and affection of his subjects. That way is to wage a war, and win it. Fortuitamente, we have at hand the perfect excuse for a declaration of war against Prussia."

Edge mildly suggested that there never could be any *perfect* excuse for a war.

"There is! Ever since Queen Isabella fled from Spain, the Spanish people have been consulting and arguing and holding plebiscites to determine what kind of government they should have. Now, very wisely, they have decided on the resumption of a monarchy. They are casting about to find an acceptable new occupant for the throne. There are several possible candidates. But the Prussians—can you conceive of such barefaced audacity?—are offering to Spain one of their hateful Hohenzollerns!"

"I was reading about that in a newspaper, just the other day. A Prince Leopold, it said."

"A blood cousin of King Wilhelm! You see what the Prussians hope to do? Surround us! Put a knife to our back! But they shall not. If my imperial husband, if the Corps Législatif, if no *other* Frenchman has what the French call le cran, their 'horseradish'—es decir, los cojones, excuse the expression—then *I* shall see to it that no Hohenzollern ever plumps his fat Teutonic culazo on the throne of my native Spain."

"You would deliberately provoke a war on that account, Your Majesty?"

"I would! Remember, I am not only an empress, Señor Coronel, I am a *mother*. I must think not just of France or of Spain or of Louis Napoléon or even of myself. I must think of *dynasty*." She lowered her voice but, even so, spoke with the maternal ferocity of a she-bear. "Unless there is a war, my son will never be emperor."

When the sweet was served, the trifle in hollandaise sauce, not even the emperor could eat it. So everyone made do with hothouse-forced Montreuil peaches, Fontainebleau grapes and Montmorency cherries, with which they drank—all but La Patti—the delicate, sweet, white Vouvray wine that could be enjoyed nowhere outside France, because it was too fragile to travel. The dinner concluded with coffee and liqueurs, and then there was no separation of the sexes—the women to a withdrawing room, the men to cigars and port—because it was almost midnight. They all resumed their wraps and their carriages, to proceed to Versailles.

Even in the dark, the long line of private and hired vehicles, with the circus wagon at the tail, cantered the five miles in only half an hour, and went directly through the park—not by way of the château—to the terrace of the Trianons. There, the night was not dark, for all the great trees had among their branches little lanterns of many colors, turning their leaves to millions of shimmering spangles of different hues against the deep purple sky, and making even the bats that fluttered about look like huge, iridescent butterflies. Beyond the trees, the tall, many-paned windows of the Grand Trianon shone golden with the light of the innumerable chandeliers within, and from those windows poured a flood of music, because most of the ball guests had arrived earlier and been dancing for some hours.

The carriages deposited their occupants at the terrace, where servants waited to carry their baggage of costumes, then the vehicles went on to wait among the thousand or so others already ranked along the marble promenades of the Grand Canal. The arrivals were met by the titled chief flunky of the evening, Comte Walsh, who informed them that changing-rooms, valets and maidservants awaited them in the Petit Trianon. They all went there and, of course, it was the men who dressed and emerged first, and crossed the terraces to the columned and arched arcade of the Grand Trianon, where liveried pages escorted them to the grand entrée. That door, like the doorway to every separate chamber within, was flanked by sentries of l'Escadron des Cent-Gardes à Cheval, every man of them at least six feet tall, uniformed in sky-blue tunic, white breeches and black topboots. Their plumed helmets and their breastplates were of steel, burnished so bright that many ladies loitered to lean close and use them as mirrors in which to touch up their rouge or a straying lock of hair.

At the grand entrée, everyone spoke his or her name to an enormous liveried butler, who bawled it over the music to the assemblage inside. Evidently the guests, though in bal travesti disguise, were not expected to be anonymous and unrecognized. Some of their costumes, though, required some guessing or explaining.

"I know who I'm supposed to be," Edge said to Florian, "but who the dickens are you?"

"Certainly not Dickens," said Florian, who wore a sort of motley, carrying under one arm a small brandy keg and in the other hand a gigantic bone he had begged from the St-Cloud kitchen. At intervals, he tore from it with his teeth a shred of meat, so that his mouth and little beard were shiny with grease. "From your robes and shepherd's crook and those fearsome whiskers, I take you to be your biblical namesake. The prophet Zechariah? Yes. And am I not equally obvious? I am Rabelais's Gargantua, the giant of the unappeasable appetite."

"Hell, instead of the bone, you should have brought along the turbot and the trifle."

"And Goesle yonder, with the harp, is a Welsh bard," Florian went on. "And Abdullah, in all that war paint, is somebody he never even heard of, Chaka of the Zulus. It was Monsieur Roulette who gave him the idea. Jules and Willi, incidentally, are inside that single and singular costume just arriving on four legs. They are supposed to be the Siamese Twins."

Almost every other man at the ball was also a comic or grotesque figure. Prince Plon-Plon wore a clerical white collar, with little gray windows painted around it, and, depending from it, a neck-to-floor gray smock vertically striped with painted white columns, and he had pasted a carved little steeple to the top of his bald head; he was portraying the domed Panthéon. The old Marquis de Gallifet was got up as a medieval apothecary, and the chief feature of his costume was that he carried an enema syringe big enough to have purged the real Gargantua. But the women were mostly dressed as either mythical or historical females, and mostly those famed for their beauty. The Duchesse d'Estrées was Helen of Troy, the Princesse Rimsky-Korsakov was Amphitrite. The Empress Eugénie, when she finally made her entrance, was immediately recognizable as the Lebrun portrait of Marie Antoinette, wearing crimson velvet edged with sable and a towering silver-white headdress, in the heights of which were perched wee golden birds. Prince Lou-Lou was dressed as her page, in tight hose of white silk, with a short crimson velvet cloak thrown over one shoulder. The emperor disdained any disguise; he merely wore one of his dress uniforms and a domino mask.

When the circus women appeared in their costumes, they overshadowed most of the aristocratic ladies, in beauty or originality or both. Clover Lee was again a vision in Clover Pink, but that was now augmented by clover green. She had a pink band holding back her cascade of corn-silk hair, and a scandalously tight, low-cut pink bodice, but her full skirt was all of clover leaves—four-leaf clovers individually scissored from green baize, bunched and stitched so close together that the girl looked like a woods nymph emerging from a bank of real clover. Prince Jérôme, eyes gleaming, mouth watering, came lumbering eagerly up to her, but only to find himself being introduced to "le Comte de Lareinty, my fiancé," at which the steeple on the prince's dome seemed to wilt and droop.

Agnete Knudsdatter came as Andersen's mermaid, in skintight fleshings that made her look naked from the waist up and, from the waist down, blended into a wondrous tail of silver spangles and gauzy fins. She had to be carried from place to place by Yount—garbed as her prince and wearing a gilt crown to hide his unprincely shaven head—but wherever he set her down, Agnete astounded the onlookers by moving as sinuously as any mermaid afloat in her proper element. Sunday and Monday Simms came as the Gemini and, though they in no way resembled twin *boys,* they were classically dressed for those rôles, in diaphanous short tunics that bared their long legs and, for that matter, did not much hide the rest of them. They had silver-sequin stars all through their black curls, and each carried a tin-tipped spear. They were so twin-identical that even Edge did not know which was which until one said:

"Good heavens, is that *you,* Zachary?"

And the other said, "Hell, sis, I *told* you he was gettin' old."

"Who are you supposed to be? Moses? Father Time? Why in the world would a good-looking man want to hide in a long gray beard and a nightgown?"

Edge said defensively, "It saves me having to ask anybody to dance, and making even more of a fool of myself."

"Won't dance, even," said Monday. "I *told* you he gettin' old."

Gavrila Smodlaka and her escort, Jovan Maretić, and daughter Sava had come as a family of angels, and a handsome trio they made: each in a fine white gown, each with a gilt-circlet halo held overhead by an *almost* invisible wire, each with immense folded pinions painstakingly made by Gavrila herself of real feathers. Gavrila was, of course, the angel Gabriel, and so carried a horn—the battered cornet that had once been the Florilegium's only band instrument. Jovan was Michael, and so carried a great sword, courtesy of the absent Brunhilde.

However, it was plain and dumpy Ioan Petrescu whose arrival was the most noticeable. She had not brought her plumber Delattre, but wore his handiwork, a suit of armor hammered out of tin, complete from helm to sollerets. She clanked and jingled and clattered as she walked, and did not much improve the Trianon's parquet floors, but even the quadrille just then being danced was interrupted while everybody applauded her.

"Well, my name is Ioan," she said shyly to Florian, her voice muffled behind the visor. "So Pierre say I be Ioan of Arc."

"A felicitous conceit," Florian said, raising his glass of champagne. "I toast your maître de plomberie."

"Except I no can dance," she said. "Also no can drink, because I no can pee."

Monsieur Nadar, who was only a head, hands and feet protruding from a sphere of vermilion-and-white striped silk held globular by bent bamboo ribs inside, was asked by several people what kind of egg he represented, and peevishly had to explain that he was the balloon *Saratoga.* Whenever he was not thus occupied, he was identifying other personages for the circus troupers, or merely making wicked commentary on them.

When two late arrivals, the eminent Anglo-French diplomat Waddington and his very large and very dowdy American wife, were boomingly announced by the butler—"Monsieur et Madame Waddington!"—Nadar looked at them, or, specifically, at her, and murmured, "Beaucoup de wadding, mais peu de ton."

At another time, he remarked, "The oak-bound gentleman dancing with Giuseppina is the much-honored Chimiste Pasteur." The man was wearing a beer barrel; Giuseppina was ethereal in the gossamers of Aurora. "He has already made the French silk industry independent of the Orient. Now he is working to make French-brewed beer good enough to put the Bavarians out of business. But I am surprised that he got invited here. The last time Pasteur was a guest at the Tuileries, he brought along a tank full of frogs, to demonstrate some experiment on which he was then engaged. The frogs escaped among the company—men cursing, women swooning—it was like that plague of Egypt. I'll wager some of the creatures are still hopping about the palace."

The other conversations to be overheard roundabout were, in the main, remarks on how deliciously perfect the late spring and early summer weather had been this year in all of France, and what abundant and splendid wine vintages it ought to bring forth in the autumn. But there was also much gossip, just as candid and bitchy as Nadar's.

"... Such a charmingly naïve little ninny. I said to her, 'But my dear, you have just announced your betrothal. Why are you wearing mourning?' Do you know what she replied? 'Eh bien, madame, my mother always told me that marriage meant a maiden's losing something. So I have done the best I could. I have lost a distant cousin.'"

"... No, indeed, Eugénie does not hesitate to meddle in state matters. When King Christian appointed the Baron Bronck ambassador to France, the king made him swear never to reveal here his, ahem, sexual proclivities. So, immediately on arrival, the baron acquired a courtisane who, for a price, accompanied him everywhere in public, and privately let him use her chambers for his liaisons with tapette lovers. Then, one day, driving with the woman in the Bois, he politely doffed his hat to the empress in her carriage. She later remarked, 'How odd that the Baron Bronck has never formally presented his wife at court.' Someone told her that the woman was not his wife, but his mistress, and Eugénie flew into one of her twittery rages. 'He dares to salute me in her presence? And forces me to return the bow?' She fired off a venomous note to King Christian, the poor baron was withdrawn, and now he languishes in obscurity, for having done no more than obey the orders he was given."

The dawn was dimming the lantern lights in the trees outside the windows, but the dancers and drinkers and gossipmongers were still making merry, when Florian came to draw Edge aside and say confidentially, "I think, Colonel Ramrod, you had better round up our people in preparation for departure. I shall make our excuses to the emperor and empress, on the ground that we must rest for tomorrow's performances."

"Well, yes, we ought to. But what are you mumbling for? Is there some other reason for us to leave now?"

"You might as well know. Little Sava went missing while her mother and Jovan were engaged in a minuet. She has only just been discovered. In the shrubbery outside, with her angelic gown up around her waist for the accommodation of the Marquis de Gallifet. The old lecher wasn't even employing *himself*, but that immense clyster syringe, to—"

"Hell, *you* round up the people, Governor, while I go and wring his scrawny neck."

"No need. When last seen, the marquis was being pursued across the lawns by an avenging angel wielding a mighty sword. If Jovan catches him—the wings do somewhat impede his speed—I'd like to be well away from here, just so we won't be connected with any attendant bloodshed. Get the others, and let us depart as unobtrusively as possible."

As the cavalcade of voitures and single circus wagon went back through the park of Versailles, where the fields were dotted with grazing sheep and cattle, cozy little cottages and byres—the restored and preserved relics of Marie Antoinette's "milkmaid" period—Yount yawned prodigiously and remarked to Agnete curled up half asleep at his side:

"I didn't notice, coming this way in the dark. But now, in the daylight, I feel like I've been here before. It's almost spooky. The trees are some different, and it's summer, not spring, and there's no smell of old gunsmoke. But this could be the countryside around Appomattox."

8

FROM VERSAILLES, only Florian went directly to the tober, to instruct the crewmen on the resumption of performances on the morrow. He had been there just a little while when a voiture came at top speed through the Bois and, before it even halted, Jovan Maretić leapt out to accost him. Maretić was in street dress, now carrying his costume, which looked rather the worse for wear, the wings especially, but Maretić still had the avenging look in his eye.

He did not say whether he had ever caught the miscreant marquis or what, if anything, he had done to the man. Instead, he said brusquely, "I come to return this damned zbrka to Gavrila. I am done with playing angel."

"She is at the hotel, gospodín. Almost everybody went straight there to sleep or rest."

"Then to you I tell what I will tell to her." Maretić spoke in an uncertain amalgam of French, English and Serbo-Croat, but there was nothing uncertain in his tone. "I will have no more zakasnjenje—no more barguignage—no more shally-shilly. Gavrila must marry me, odmah—immediately, tout de suite. That divjli child of hers must be soumise—chastised, made tame."

"Well, yes, I have recommended to Gavrila that a firm hand—"

"Even if it spoils some of the child's porcelain complexion sans couleur, her bottom must be *tanned*."

"Quite so, quite so. Best thing for her."

"However, that I cannot do until I am legally her otac, her père. So Gavrila and I marry. D'accord?"

"D'accord, franchement."

"When we marry, you lose them from your predstava, your cirque. You do not object?"

"Point du tout. We shall all regret the loss, of course, but Gavrila and Sava both deserve the better life you could give them. If I may make a suggestion—there are others of our company preparing to marry. Perhaps I can contrive to have all the épousailles done at one time, and thereby save everybody a good deal of fil rouge et routine."

"I do not care if it is done by papal decree or the lowliest clerk, so it is done."

"It will be arranged, I promise, as soon as everyone concerned is awake again. Join us at the hotel tonight, gospodín."

During that afternoon, as the troupers emerged by ones and twos from their rooms, Florian held private converse with several of them. Then he convened his chiefs in the Grand Hôtel's men-only smoking chamber off the lobby, to tell them:

"Gavrila Smodlaka and her friend Maretić will be getting married. Meaning that we lose her, the Night Child and the slanging buffers from our program. We will also lose our star équestrienne to the Comte de Lareinty, whom I believe all of you met last night. The Princess Brunhilde and Kostchei the Deathless will likewise be marrying, but they will stay on the show. Also, I have just been informed by Ioan Petrescu that her Monsieur Delattre has proposed marriage to her."

"Ach y fi," muttered Goesle. "There must be something in the air of Paris, to be sure."

"Nobody to *me* has proposed," grumbled Beck.

"Well," said Florian, "you too can have Monsieur Delattre, in a manner of speaking. He has offered to abandon his plumbery business, to join out with us, if we will have him. I wished to ask you, Chief Engineer, before I accepted him."

Beck exclaimed, "He would become Zirkus, im Ernst? Then I say ja! Ja, gewiss! He can of the Gasentwickler take charge, now that Jules is twice a week up in the *Saratoga* going. Also, always there is tinkering of the Dampforgel pipes to be done. Not to mention the donnicker Klosetts in good repair he can keep. Ja, him we can use."

"I was hoping you would say so. Otherwise, we should lose our invaluable wardrobe mistress."

Fitzfarris said, "Governor, I've already been looking into marriage arrangements on behalf of the Deathless and the giantess. Since you told me about Kostchei being of interest to the police, I figured it might be best if this got done someplace where it wouldn't attract too much official notice. So Zack and I went out to the city fringes, to Montmartre."

"No problem at all," said Edge. "The mayor there will do the hitching of them himself. Quick and quiet. And I gather that none of the rest of Paris pays much attention to anything that happens out in that eighteenth arrondissement."

"Very good," said Florian. "Then would you two please approach Monsieur le Maire again? Ask if he'll do four couples all at once."

"Four couples?" Edge and Fitz looked puzzled.

"Why not? Would you dock a dog's tail a little bit at a time, on the theory that it hurts him less?"

"But who are the four?" Fitzfarris counted on his fingers. "There's Brunhilde and Kostchei, Ioan and Pierre, Gavrila and Jovan..."

"And Clover Lee and Gaspard."

"What? In that shabby little office?" said Edge. "Surely *they'll* want pomp and revelry, fuss and feathers."

Florian shook his head. "The count confided to me last night—and evidently Clover Lee doesn't mind—that he wishes his family to remain unaware of his marriage until it is a fait accompli. He says that *then* there will be a panoplied church ceremony and a grand fête at the family palace." Florian sighed. "I only hope this is not an inauspicious start to the new Comtesse de Lareinty's wedded life."

"Well...if that's what they want..." said Edge. "Fitz, we'll ride out there first thing in the morning. If the mayor is agreeable, Governor, we can herd all the lambs to the slaughter before show time tomorrow."

The next day, everyone of the company except the crewmen left the tober, and Aleksandr Banat took over the wicket of the red wagon, in case any early-arriving jossers wanted tickets. Naturally, every trouper was going to attend the mass wedding, so it was necessary to avoid the appearance of making parade and thereby attracting notice on the streets. Florian sent the several principal couples in separate fiacres, and groups of their colleagues and well-wishers in others, plus his own rockaway, the vehicles leaving the tober at intervals and taking different routes from the Bois to the Butte Montmartre. They all met again at the base of that hill, at the Place Blanche, where the pavements ended, and in train climbed a dirt road that wound among the scattered habitations—a few modestly pinkwashed cottages, but mostly dilapidated shacks and huts—past the ramshackle towers of mills with immense sailcloth-and-lattice sweeps creakily turning in the breeze of the heights, and among the goats and cows supported by the few patches of grass that grew between the limestone outcrops and stunted trees. Halfway up the hill, the carriages stopped at the mairie of Montmartre, a town hall not much more impressive than any other building thereabout.

The four happy couples did not, of course, get wed in a bunch; for one reason, there would not have been room for all of them in the mayor's office. There certainly was not room for the accompanying celebrants, who had to be satisfied with crowding into the hallway outside his office, lining the rickety stairs to the upper story or leaning in the open ground-floor windows from outside. And they had to share even those vantage places with clerks and greffeurs and such from the other civic bureaus, all wearing paper cuff-protectors and inky pens tucked behind their ears, who also crowded about and made appreciative noises throughout the several ceremonies, mainly by sucking their teeth.

The troupers had come dressed in their best street clothes, and even that made them a spectacle in this mean quarter of the city, but some of them would have created a sensation anywhere. Edge and Fitzfarris had evidently forewarned Monsieur le Maire of the peculiar nature of some of the applicants, because he managed to evince no surprise, awe or nervousness when he recognized before him the famous "Clover Pink" girl and the first noble of the empire ever to set foot in this mairie—or when he was confronted by a beautiful bride who towered over a contorted and noseless bridegroom, or when he discovered that that bride was of even bluer blood than the French count, or when that bride's maid of honor proved to be a pretty midget who came barely to her knee. As if these were everyday occurrences, the mayor employed only routine dramatics and gesticulations as he read to each couple the dispense de bans and the pacte de mariage—involving automatic naturalization as Frenchwomen of those brides marrying French subjects, absolute prohibition of divorce and so on—and each couple in turn mumbled their I-comprehend's and I-do's and I-will's. In every ritual Florian stood as symbolic father to the bride, and Sava as flower girl, strewing fresh petals about for each couple, while Nella served as Ioan's maid of honor, Daphne as Gavrila's, and Sunday as Clover Lee's. The mayor's madame did her routine duties—providing motherly sniffles and eye dabbings during each ceremony, then witnessing the marriage certificate signatures afterward—

as stolidly as if all the principals were only local goatherd bumpkins or the even lowlier resident artists and poets.

When everything was concluded—the signing and stamp affixing and wax sealing of papers—and Monsieur le Maire had kissed the brides and Madame le Maire all the bridegrooms except Kostchei, who ducked outside, the troupers within the building threw confetti and rice, and even the municipal office workers threw bits of torn-up blotting paper. When the couples emerged from the mairie, they had to be confettied and kissed some more by their fellow artistes. Then the eight newlyweds, even irreligious Clover Lee, went on uphill to the humble little Church of St-Pierre standing alone and lonely on the very brow of the butte, to light a candle and say a prayer for their future. That climb was too steep for the voiture horses, so the brides and bridegrooms had to go afoot, and the Princess Yusupova-Somova had to support her new consort all the way, because his backbent posture made him liable to topple over backward. While the other troupers waited at the mairie, chatting with the civil servants, Carl Beck ambled on around the hillside to the rather ill-kept and unkempt Cemeterie du Nord, to pay his respects at two graves there—that of his countryman poet Heine and the still freshly sodded one of his colleague musician Berlioz.

When the company had convened again, the train of carriages took them only a short way back down the hill, to stop at the Moulin de la Galette, the one mill on which the sweeps were not revolving, their lattices' sails entirely furled. According to the notices newly painted on the wooden gate and wattle-and-daub wall around the mill, the Galette's proprietor, "M. Debray," had converted the establishment to a "salon-cabinet-café" offering everything from "Bière" to "Siam."

"Siam?" someone said wonderingly.

"A bowling game," said Florian. "But we are not here to play. I reserved the place for the wedding déjeuner."

So they all sat at the tables outdoors in the walled yard, and Madame Debray cooked in the kitchen that had formerly been the grinding room at the base of the mill tower, while Monsieur Debray and a number of little Debrays trotted back and —delivering omelettes and terrines and crépinettes and coffee and hot chocolate and green-gold Muscadet wine and, of course, the house specialty, galettes. ("Well, I'll be dogged!" Yount said happily. "Good old home-style hoecakes!") The ancient clapboard mill tower and its idle great sweeps rocked and creaked as if unhappy in retirement, but those noises could not dampen the merry chatter and laughter of the celebrants. At any rate, *most* of their chatter was merry. Fitzfarris was still lamenting the forgone opportunities of having "newspapered" this unique quadruple event, and Florian was saying to Clover Lee, rather ruefully:

"I expect, Comtesse, that our shows today will be pelted with vegetables instead of flowers, when the jossers fail to see the pink-clad équestrienne who has for so many months been our star attraction and the toast of all Paris."

"It's nice to be called countess, but not by my foster father," she said affectionately. "And stop your bellyaching. You've still got the best circus in Paris. Anyway, you said yourself that fads come and go here. For all you know, Clover Pink may have gone right out of fashion during the three-day layoff."

The meal over, the carriages took the whole company to the bottom of the hill, and there in the Place Blanche stopped again while good-byes and kisses and handshakes and embraces were exchanged among those staying with the Florilegium and those departing. The belongings of the new Comtesse de Lareinty had already been collected by the count's manservant from her hotel room and her tober caravan, and taken to the Gare St-Lazare, whence those two new-lyweds would entrain this very day for their lune de miel at Deauville by the sea. Gospodín Maretić was taking the new Gospodja and Gospodjica Maretić to his apartment, in some dull bankerish neighborhood over on the Left Bank, to get them accustomed to it before they moved their possessions and their dogs from their caravan. Brunhilde and Kostchei were returning to the tober to work as on any ordinary day, but the new Madame Delattre was taking an extra day off to help Pierre pack everything he would be removing from his plumbery workshop and his chambers above it, out in the quartier Marais.

So, after the vehicles of the departing parties had rolled away, Florian again instructed the others to take diverse routes back to the Bois. He and Edge were atop his rockaway, Daphne and Sunday riding inside, and, when they got as far as the boulevard de Courcelles, they found ragamuffin newsboys running about in unusual excitement, waving their newspapers and shouting, "Querelle à Prusse!" Florian halted Snowball long enough to reach down and buy a paper. He quickly scanned the front page, grimaced, handed the paper to Edge and said, "Well, the empress was not just twittering to you. Prussia *has* proposed its Prince Leopold as the new king of Spain, and France *is* making truculent de-mands that his nomination be withdrawn. A tense situation." He clucked the horse onward again. "Nous verrons."

At that day's two shows, the equestrian director had le Démon Débonnaire draw out his various animal acts to extra length, to make up for the loss of the terrier turn, and Monday elaborated her haute école riding on Thunder, to make up for the loss of the bareback performance. No one in the audience threw any vegetables; they *had* as usual brought flowers to throw, so they threw them in appreciation of the work of Mademoiselle Papillon and Maurice LeVie on the trapeze. However, a few jossers, on their way out after the show, did inquire of doorkeeper Banat what had become of "la fille de rose-de-trèfle." He told them the truth, that she had gone off to become a countess, and all exclaimed some-thing like, "Ah! She deserved such reward. A happy ending to her career!"—and made no complaint at having been deprived of her performance. Within a few days, affirming Florian's opinion of Parisian fads, the Clover Pink items began to disappear from store windows and the dress of women on the streets.

That rage was immediately succeeded by another, called by the upper classes "l'arte pugilistique" and by the lower "la boxe." Prizefighting, formerly sneered at as just one of the national aberrations of la perfide Albion, was now the chief topic of conversation at every zinc and every café table. Almost every theatre short of the august Opéra erected onstage a roped and padded square, engaged professional pugilists and referees and conducted their contests by the English Queensberry rules—including timed rounds, gloves for the fists and no use of the feet. The lowest cabarets squeezed their tables closer together, made room to rope off a space in the middle of them and called that "un ring de boxe." They commandeered from the streets every "fort" market-porter and any other brawny ruffian who was willing to strip to the waist and do a combination of la boxe and la savate—fighting with bare knuckles and brass-toed work boots or wooden sabots, in savage "rounds" that terminated only when a man was knocked down—each fighting for nothing but the prospect of a few francs' prize if he beat an opponent unconscious.

Acknowledging the fad, equestrian director Colonel Ramrod resurrected the parody prizefight once done by the long-dead joeys Ali Baba and Zanni. He allotted the turn to Ferdi Spenz and Nella Cornella, and the audiences received that act with even more hilarity, now that it involved a well-built, pretty female pummeling a runty and ill-favored male, with the white-face Fünfünf again cholerically but ineffectually playing referee:

"No, no, Mam'selle Emeraldina! You never hit a man when he is down!"

At which she would knock the Kesperle clear across the pista, then, grinning, lie down herself before he could stagger back again and try to retaliate—and the jossers would rock in their seats.

Meanwhile, on the streets, the crieurs des journaux continued to bellow about a somewhat comparable brawl in the international political arena. "Retraite de Prusse!" was the latest shout, a glad one, for Bismarck had bowed to French pressure and withdrawn the Hohenzollern prince as a contender for the Spanish crown.

But France in general, the cities especially, and the Florilegium in particular soon had another contingency to deal with. The summer weather had earlier excited much comment on its clement warmth and clear skies. But now that warmth intensified, day by day, until it became a hot and airless drought. The long garden that was the avenue of the Champs-Elysées—roses and geraniums of every hue, begonias and peonies and fuchsias of prodigious proportions—began to droop and shrivel and lose its bright colors. The chestnut trees lining the sidewalks let their leaves hang limp and dispiritedly shed their blossoms like a continuous dry pink rain beneath their arching boughs. Edge now made a practice, before every afternoon show, of climbing the rung-and-rope ladder to the trapeze platform—he had got adept at this since the long-ago time when Autumn had shown him how—and one day he descended from there to tell Florian that he was canceling both the trap act of Maurice and Sunday and the tightrope performance by Monday.

"They'll be risking a dead faint," he said. "Until this ungodly heat subsides, Governor, I won't let anybody work up there near the peak except during the night shows."

"I will not gainsay the equestrian director," said Florian, but he looked concerned. "We're going to be stretching the rest of the acts almighty thin to fill. And not all of them *can* stretch. This damnable weather is taking its toll of poor Miss Eel. Her klischnigg turn gets more and more painful for her. I am seriously thinking of sending her on furlough to the mountains. But in that case, the Quakemaker would certainly want to go with her." He blew a long breath of resignation. "Still, there are worse things to worry about."

He unfolded from under his arm the day's Le Monde to display its headline: NOUVELLE DEMANDE PAR FRANCE.

"Now what?" asked Edge.

"France's new demand is that Prussia *guarantee* that it will not ever again propose Prince Leopold for the throne of Spain. Damn it all. That's asking Prussia to abase itself, and to no good purpose. I wonder if it's the hot weather that is making tempers so irascible. Or is the weather merely reflecting the heating up of this squabble among monarchs?"

"Hell, I can tell you what it is," said Edge. "It's the Empress Eugénie's doing. That woman just won't let well enough alone."

A day or so later, two throngs of Parisian men and women—lower-class peo-ple, to judge from their dress—went trooping up and down the streets of the central city, the six or eight stronger men in each group carrying a platform on which stood a gaudily gilded and painted wooden statue, one male, one female. Whenever the effigies chanced to meet in their peregrinations, the carriers tilted them so they bowed politely to one another.

"What in the nation is going on?" asked Yount.

"Those are the images of Saint Marcellin and Sainte Geneviève," Pemjean told him. "The people haul them out of their shrines and parade them around to petition for a change in the weather. They seem to think that if the saints *feel* how hot it is outside their churches—or cold, or wet, or whatever—then Gene-viève or Marcellin or both will exert their influence on the elements."

But the saints did not oblige. The summer heat only got worse, and Edge eventually had to order the roustabouts to furl up the sidewalls of the chapiteau during the afternoon performances, lest the audience faint. Another day or so later, Florian returned from a trip downtown to report:

"The Carnavalet Museum has hung a giant thermometer outside, and it shows thirty-eight degrees. Centigrade, that is. On the American scale, that would be exactly one hundred. Intolerable!"

"Well," said Edge, "Maurice and Sunday and Monday are likely to kill me, but I'm going to keep them off during the night shows, too, from now on."

"It is also intolerable that we have such a scanty program to show," said Florian. "We *must* have more acts. You and Sir John and I will again take turns canvassing the other circuses in town, reassessing their talent to see if any is worth abducting. Equestrian acts, animal acts—give your serious consideration to everything except apes. I still refuse to have jockos in my show."

So, the next afternoon, Edge went out into the sweltering heat, bound again for the Cirque de l'Empereur. On the way, he encountered another news crier shouting with vigor, and this time just one word: "Insulte!" So he bought a *Quotidien de Paris* and read as he walked. He did not have to worry much about colliding with other pedestrians, for there were few people out afoot in these scorching days. The biggest word on the front page was the same that the boy had been bellowing: INSULTE! The news was that the Chancellor Bismarck had replied to the latest French demand with a flat "Nein!"—he would not promise that Prussia's Prince Leopold would never again be a candidate for the Spanish crown. And this blunt boche refusal, said the *Quotidien,* was an affront to France's good intentions, to France's altruistic desire to keep the peace, to France's pride, to France's commercial interests, to France's national honor, to France's standing among the powers of Europe, to the cran of France's men and the gentle nature of France's women...

Evidently to everything but France's noble sauces, thought Edge, as he tossed the paper into a trash bin outside a greengrocery.

When he bought his ticket at the circus building, Edge saw there a poster boasting of a new artiste on the program, a "Mademoiselle Mystère!... Merveille des âges!... Vainqueur du continent!" and other such pufferies, but the poster was equally a mystery in giving no clue as to what she did in the way of an act.

Edge sat through the same series of turns he had seen months before—over-talky and not wildly funny patter clowns, dull animal acts—and he took note that the acrobatic barnyard goat had been demoted. It now closed the program's first half, before the intermission, indicating that the new Mademoiselle Mystère must have the stellar close of the whole show, so Edge sat on through the second half, hoping she would make his stay worthwhile.

The equestrian director introduced her with almost Florian-florid superlatives—the wonder of her time, the astonisher of even the most jaded connaisseurs du cirque, and so on and so on—but still keeping a mystery Mademoiselle Mystère's specialty. Then the circus band, sizable but mediocre compared to Beck's, blared a fanfare. From the arena's back door entered just another équestrienne, a rather brassily blonde woman balanced on one foot on a cantering horse. The band swung into a galop as she commenced her postures and cavortings. The only thing novel about her was that she wore—besides a spangled léotard, flesh-colored tights and a tulle skirt—a papier-mâché mask covering her whole face. It was the mask of a Columbine, with bright red, round rouge spots on the cheeks, spike-lashed eyes and cupid's-bow mouth.

Edge had a starback in the front row of seats, so he was close enough to the pista to realize that, if the woman was a mademoiselle, she was no young one. She was competent and graceful enough on the rosinback, but workmanlike, not sprightly and vivacious. Neither was her costume or her horse very young. Her léotard was missing sequins here and there, and her fleshings were a trifle baggy at knees and elbows—or maybe her knees and elbows were. The horse was not so ancient that it stumbled, but it was slow and slightly erratic of gait. Edge sighed and stood up to leave. He had his back to the pista when the music changed, from the opening galop to a more lilting tune. No one was singing the words to it, but it was the music to which, a very long time ago, Monsieur Roulette had warbled, "As I sat in the circus and watched her go round . . ."

Edge returned and resumed his seat, and watched closely. After the closing promenade, he made his way unchallenged through the arena's back door and prowled until he found her dressing room. Sarah had on a somewhat threadbare wrapper over her costume, but she still wore the paper mask. Its expression was perkier than her voice when she said:

"I saw you right away, at ringside, but it was too late to signal the windjammers to change my music."

"Why do that? You would almost certainly have met some one of us, if not me. Somewhere in town, if not here. You must have known we've been in Paris for months."

"Yes. But I had hoped that I could come and go again undetected. Monsieur Degeau here engaged me for only three weeks. My services are not exactly in clamorous demand." She reached out to shake his hand. "Hello, Zachary. It's good to see you again."

"An old friend doesn't get a kiss?"

"No. Gerald wouldn't like it, if he should walk in."

"Gerald?"

"You saw him perform, with the moth-eaten dancing bear. Orphée et l'Ours. In England they were Bruno and Bruin. That's where we last got work. I was Miss Masked Mystery there."

"You can drop the mystery with me. The mask, too."

"No. I never take it off—not until I'm in our room at the pension. Even the Governor Degeau has never seen me without it. That's probably the only reason he hired me. When you don't have much left of beauty or talent or youth, you have to dream up some device. Surely you noticed that I've slowed considerably, that I have to dye the gray in my hair now. So my only sellable device is my mysteriousness. That—and the bear—at least get me and Gerald the occasional short engagement, like this one, at mud-show salary. But bugger all that." She made a grandly dismissive gesture and assumed an air of gaiety. "I can rejoice in the tremendous success my little girl Edith has made of herself. Imagine! Her name is a byword. Clover Lee Coverley—Paris's all-time best-loved équestrienne!"

"Have you been to the show to see her work?"

"No. I told you. I'm avoiding detection." She turned away, to fidget distractedly with something on her dressing table. "I haven't seen her. No."

"Just as well you didn't come. She's blown the stand."

"What?" The mask jerked back toward Edge, and Sarah's blue eyes blinked behind its eyeholes.

"Also, she's not a little girl any more," Edge said, with a broad grin. "She's even dropped her baby-talk name. She is now Edith, Countess of Lareinty. And she's on her honeymoon at Deauville."

"Well, I'll be damned," said Sarah, with a laugh of relief and delight. "And wipe off your grin, Zachary; *that* hasn't improved over the years. So Clover Lee really did it, did she? I'm glad one of us did. And I *predicted* it, remember? Ever so long ago."

"I remember. You said to hell with morals, you'd teach her manners fit for a state ball. Well, she'll be enjoying plenty of those."

"And you, Zachary? Have you yet married your lovely Autumn?"

"Not yet." He went quickly on, "You'll be happy to know that Clover Lee didn't get just a tinsel title. Her Gaspard de Lareinty is a wealthy man, so she's well fixed for life. Why, if ever *you* felt like retiring and settling down, Clover Lee could—"

"No."

Edge looked exasperated. "No, no and no. That's all you've said to me. If I invite you to rejoin the Florilegium—and bring along Gerald if you like—would you say no to that, too?"

"Yes."

"Damnation. Clover Lee's departure is the reason I'm here today. I'm hunting for replacement acts. And look here, Sarah. There's nobody left on the show that you might not want to meet again. Pepper and Paprika are both dead. Others are, too, or gone elsewhere. But lots of your old friends are still with us—Jules and Fitz and Hannibal and the Simms girls. And you know Florian would welcome you with open arms. We've still got your Snowball, a damn sight better mount than that nag you're riding here. We're a first-rate show now. We can afford the finest costumes and props and trappings." Having told her nothing but the truth, so far, Edge now tried to slip in one small untruth. "You're as good an équestrienne as you ever were. You'd be Madame Solitaire again and—"

"Don't talk balls to me, Zachary. You used to know better. Thank you for the offer, but no, thanks. I'll stick to the gypsy life with my third-rate Gerald among the third-rate shows. He and they are not much, but neither am I. Now please go, old friend, and *please* don't mention to anyone—not even Autumn—that I still exist."

"But *why*, Sarah?"

She sighed. "You always did require convincing, damn you." She began to undo the tapes that held her mask on. "I used to complain about horses forever flinging their dumb heads back and bashing me in the nose. Well, one of them did it once too often." She took the mask off, and Edge wished he had a mask to put on, to hide the expression that must have come over his own face. Sarah would still have been a beautiful woman, except that she now had a monstrously oversized nose the texture of cauliflower and mottled red and purple. "All those breaks and bruises caused a condition the doctors call bacchia," she said, quite levelly and coolly. "And it gets worse all the time. *Now* will you believe that I do not want to be found or rescued or even remembered?"

Edge nodded, silently shook her hand again and went to the door. She was putting the mask on again when he turned to say, "Good-bye, then, Sarah. Good luck. If there's ever anything I can—"

"One thing. You can tell me this. Does Clover Lee speak of me? Often? Ever?"

Edge briefly considered trying another lie, then rejected it. "No. Not ever."

"Good," said the Columbine mask. "Don't you, either. Good-bye, Zachary."

On his way out, crossing the pista, Edge paused for a moment. The arena was as empty as the Florilegium chapiteau had been the very first time he saw the Big Top set up. There was here no canvas overhead or roundabout, but there was sawdust underfoot and the smells were much the same. He could close his eyes and, in the hollow silence of the place, almost hear a faint echo of that once brave and winsome music:

Solitaire is the Queen of all riders, I ween,
But alas, she is far, far away...

When he got back to the tober, Sunday was reading aloud from a newspaper to some other troupers grouped about her, translating an editorial in the day's *Le Gaulois*: "...If France does not force Prussia to yield to her demands, there is not a woman in Europe who would ever again consent to take a Frenchman's arm..." Florian was one of the group, and he looked up expectantly at Edge's approach.

"No luck, Governor," Edge said. "Nothing at the Cirque de l'Empereur we can use."

"Perhaps this is not your day for luck," said Florian, with a long face. "I'm sorry to tell you, but a flunky from the Tuileries has been here. You are commanded to present yourself before His Majesty Louis Napoléon."

"Oh, Christ. Well, I can't say I haven't been expecting it. But I've already missed one show today. He can wait until—"

"No, no, my boy. If you keep him waiting overnight, he will know that you deliberately delayed obeying. Whatever his present mood may be, that would not improve it. I will again take over your directorial duties at tonight's show, and somehow we will again contrive to fill in for your shootist turn, if you are not back by then. You go and see what the emperor wants."

"I know what he wants," Edge growled. "But I'm damned sure not going off to his war, and I don't care how many women refuse my arm on account of it."

9

"AH, our reluctant cavalier," said Louis Napoléon, when the chamberlain ushered Edge into the study. There were two more persons present, one of them the Empress Eugénie. Edge was at first surprised to see that the other was Gaspard de Lareinty, in military uniform, but then he remembered that the count was the emperor's aide-de-camp.

"Your Majesties, Your Grace," he said, bowing to them.

The emperor said, without preamble, "Would you have any conscientious objections, mon colonel, to merely *discussing* war?"

"No, Your Majesty."

"Capital," Louis said drily. "Gaspard, the maps, please."

As de Lareinty began unrolling the charts on various easels about the room, Edge asked, "Is there definitely to be a war, then?"

Before her imperial husband could reply, Eugénie snapped, "Judge for yourself. Our operative across the border informs us that telegraphs are flying in all directions, putting the civilians of Prussia and its allies on a wartime alert, mobilizing their Home Guards, rationing civilian supplies, and so forth. Also we have a copy of a comment made by that vile Bismarck to his sycophantic parliament. Listen." She produced a paper and read, "'We Prussians are not so confident in our prowess that we rely on it utterly. We also take into account the fact that we can depend on the French to behave stupidly and cowardly.' ¿Eh, Señor Coronel? ¿Le gusta esta mierda?"

"Come, come, my dear," said Louis. "No vulgarity. Let us not lower ourselves to the level of the barbarians. Yes, Colonel Edge, in view of all the relevant circumstances, I have today telegraphed to King Wilhelm my formal declaration of war." He sighed. "Now...if you will regard the maps. I already showed you how the boches have disposed themselves at our frontiers. Gaspard, will you describe the present array of our own forces?"

The count, using his swagger stick for a pointer, explained, "We have five corps, under the Maréchal Bazaine, between Metz and the border, and two corps near Strasbourg under the Maréchal MacMahon. You can see by the standard symbols, Colonel, the forward disposition of our artillery batteries, our horse and foot, vis-à-vis those of the enemy. Here, here and here are our battalions held in reserve. Every one of our infantry companies, incidentally, contains a heavy-weapons platoon, and each squad in that platoon is armed with the Montigny mitrailleuse, to give long-range rapid-fire cover for each advance of the riflemen."

"Any comments, Colonel?" asked the emperor.

Edge went close to the charts and moved from one to another, studying them intently, while the empress impatiently tapped her foot, and Louis and de Lareinty waited impassively. Finally Edge said, "I repeat, Your Majesty, I am no strategist, and far be it from a retired colonel to anticipate the plans of your field marshals. However, if you are asking for only tactical advice..."

"Please give it," said the emperor.

"Well, I should guess that the Prussians will hope to use their formidable modern artillery to decimate and demoralize your forces with intensive barrages from great range, long before your men ever see the spikes on their soldiers' helmets. So—"

"Frenchmen are not so easily demoralized," Eugénie interrupted acidly. "And we have cannons, too."

All three men gave her an annoyed look, and Edge said, with what patience he could, "An artillery duel between bronze muzzle-loaders and steel breech-loaders would be disastrous for the French. Even if your guns had the same range and accuracy—which they do not—and even if they could be as quickly reloaded and rapidly fired—which they cannot—they would very soon overheat to uselessness. Meanwhile, your foot and horse would be immobilized, unable to move forward through that rain of high-explosive shells thrown by both sides. They would be standing targets, or more likely would be breaking ranks and scattering for safety."

"But artillery alone never won a battle," said de Lareinty. "The boches *must* let up the bombardment eventually, to make their own advance."

"Yes, when your own foot soldiers are dispersed or hugging the ground, when your cavalry horses are panicked, when all your forces are disorganized," said Edge. "Yes, then the Prussians would advance."

"Ah, but we have the mitrailleuses!" crowed the emperor. "They would hold the enemy at bay for as long a time as we should require to regroup."

"No doubt those would have an initially terrifying effect on the enemy infantry," Edge said diplomatically. "But a tactical effect, I think not. Very quickly the Prussian soldiers will realize that those machines can only spray, not be aimed—that a man risks being hit only by a random ball. Then they will again advance, far more confidently than they would against even antiquated single-shot muskets... with marksmen behind them."

Eugénie blazed at him, "You are talking sheer defeatism! Denigrating our brave men and our most modern weaponry. That is seditious and subversive and—"

"Chut, madame!" Louis said sharply. "He may only be talking sense. Kindly let him continue. Colonel Edge, you have been unequivocal in telling us what things we cannot do. Have you any suggestions as to what we *can?*"

Edge looked again at the maps. "As regards Strasbourg, frankly, I do not. The situation there will depend on whether your Marshal MacMahon intends to forge across the Rhine or to prevent the Prussians from doing so. But up here in the northeast"—he tapped the map of the Lorraine area—"you and the Prussians are facing each other across a fairly level terrain where there is no impediment to a sudden charge. I would assume that the lethal Krupp cannon there are already targeted on your forward positions..." He looked at de Lareinty, who nodded and said:

"We also assume so. And ours are targeted on all their positions, of course."

"Then I suggest reaiming yours, specifically at the Prussians' cannon batteries. And I would *make* a sudden charge. Close immediately with the enemy, and you will nullify their artillery advantage. A sudden lunge forward—your infantry charging directly for the enemy lines ahead, your cavalry on either flank—and the Prussian cannons cannot quickly reaim at that moving tide of men, but your own artillery can be lobbing shells at *them*. Meanwhile, I would expect the enemy to send out their cavalry to blunt your infantry's spearhead assault. So have your mitrailleuses ready to concentrate on that counterattack; their spray of lead *can* be effective against large targets like horses. And if that rapid fire mows down or repulses the Prussian troopers, your own cavalry and your infantry will have an unobstructed field to the enemy lines." He paused and gave a slightly deprecating shrug. "Of course, from then on, it would not be a battle between modern machines. It would be a very old-fashioned kind of combat. Men and horses, rifles and sabres and bayonets, a man-to-man contest of the individual soldiers' strength and courage and—well, cran, as you call it."

Eugénie gave a sniff that was more than slightly deprecating. "And what *would* the world think of us?" she demanded. "Discarding all the technologie de plus modernes, to fight like—like the Franks of the Dark Ages! We should be laughed at by every up-to-date nation."

Edge dared to say, "No one laughed, madame, at the Frank called Charlemagne." Then he said to the emperor, "I hardly need point out, to a commander of Your Majesty's experience, that things can look easy on a map and quite otherwise on the actual ground. The enemy may do something totally unforeseeable, the weather may turn bad . . . those much-praised mitrailleuses may misfire."

The emperor muttered, "You *will* still harp on that string."

"However," Edge went on, "if the tactics I have suggested should prevail, I think I would go right on through and beyond the Prussian positions—with no delay for mopping up or herding prisoners to the rear or pillaging or celebration —and strike hard for their city of Saarbrücken." He pointed to the map. "Leave only your artillerymen on the battlefield. Let them abandon their old cannon and turn the captured Krupp pieces around, to bombard that city's defenses ahead of your attacking colums." Edge stopped there and spread his hands. "But such larger designs are matters for your strategists."

There was a while of silence in the room, the emperor and the count looking pensive, the empress looking rather sulky. Then Louis Napoléon said to de Lareinty, "Qu'en pensez-vous, Gaspard?"

"Ce me semble pratique, Majesté."

"Aussi à moi. Go yourself to tell Bazaine. I should not wish to entrust the message to cipher or to a courier. Repeat the colonel's suggestions to the maréchal in every particular—but only as suggestions, mind you, and no need to cite their source. Let Achille think, if he likes, that they are a consensus of the General Staff. And make it plain that he is free to act on them or not, as he chooses. But go at once."

"I am there, sire!" the count said crisply. He bowed to the emperor, to the empress, even to Edge, then whisked from the room.

"Well, damn," muttered Edge. "I wanted to ask him how he is enjoying married life."

"The marital life must take second place to the martial life," said the emperor in English, as smugly as if he had uttered a ringing epigram. "Now, Colonel, I wanted to ask *you*—again—will you still not consider a commission? Perhaps to command that fine cavalry as it sweeps the field from Metz to Saarbrücken . . . as you claim it can."

"It can do it, Your Majesty, and without me. I thank you again for the inestimable honor of the offer, but I still must decline. I am rather over-age and under-ardent to take the field again."

"How now?" said Louis Napoléon. "*I* shall be going to the front, and I must be twenty years older than you. My son will be going with me, and he is nearly thirty years *younger* than—"

"Lou-Lou?" cried Eugénie, aghast. "Surely you would not risk—"

"Madame!" He coldly cut her off. "While this may be very much your war, the conduct of it shall be mine. And the Prince Imperial will have his baptême de feu."

"But he is only fourteen! He is our only child!"

"And this may be the only war in his lifetime. Every man should have his steel tempered and honed by at least one war. Eugène Louis shall not be deprived of taking part in this one."

"It is insane that *you* should think of going. An old man, ailing, in pain, shuffling about like a pantomime pantoufle. What use can you possibly—?"

"I do thank you, my dear, for your wifely solicitude."

"But to take the boy! Have a thought for the succession, Louis. If something should happen to him . . ."

"It will not, without happening also to me. In which case, I daresay, Prince Plon-Plon would be crowned by acclamation."

"Dear God!"

"And in which case also, madame, you would live out your days as the Dowager Empress, admired and revered by all, for having inspired such devotion in both of your menfolk that they went willingly to fall in a war that you insisted must be waged. Now let us say no more of it. We are embarrassing an inadvertent witness to this airing of shabby family linen."

The admonition was unnecessary; Eugénie had gone livid and speechless with fury. Louis Napoléon turned again to Edge.

"When I summoned you today, mon colonel, I was prepared to exert duress. I could have offered you your choice: accept a commission or endure internment for the duration of the war. Or I could have used chantage, threatening action against those questionable colleagues of yours. Or, as a resident foreigner in wartime, you could have been conscripted as a mere ranker, or worse, into a labor battalion. But I will do none of those things."

"I am grateful, Your Majesty, but I am also curious. Why will you not?"

"Partly because you have imparted constructive criticism and possibly valuable advice. When we win the war, s'il plâit à Dieu, you will have fought for us as well as if you had done so in person. If we should lose the war, à Dieu ne plaise, I shall be in no position to blame or punish you for it. But also—as my wife's termagant concern for the dynasty repeatedly reminds me—this *is* in large part a family affair. I have no right to involve a stranger against his will. So go in peace, mon colonel, and may you enjoy more peace than I have known."

On his way back to the Bois, though the night had brought not much alleviation of the day's enervating heat, Edge found the streets thronged with people. They were jabbering excitedly, as the newsboys ran among them, wildly waving their newspapers and barking more loudly than ever: "Guerre!" "La Guerre Déclarée!" Edge did not trouble to buy a paper, but everybody at the tober seemed to be reading one—troupers and jossers alike—for he arrived there during the intermission of the show.

Florian naturally expressed glad relief on hearing that his equestrian director had been exempted from military service. And he chuckled, though a little wryly, when he pointed to his newspaper's headline and remarked, "I have always wondered why, in almost every European language, the word 'war' is female in gender."

Edge said, "I think it's apt enough in this case."

"Perhaps tragically so. Not only has Louis Napoléon been goaded and prodded into going to war, against the good advice of everybody from the Russian tsar on down, it is he—not King Wilhelm—who has *declared* war. So, as Tsar Alexander feared, if France should be defeated, the onus will be on Louis alone."

"Well, at least it won't be on me. During this one, for a happy change, I'll only be shooting at gourds and saucers and such. I'll go and get into costume to do it this very night."

Ten days after the declaration of war, His Imperial Majesty Louis Napoléon donned his best uniform—and His Imperial Highness Eugène Louis a uniform tailored to his boy size—and they entrained for Metz, where the emperor would personally take command at the still quiescent northeastern front. To make their departure without fanfare or public fuss, Louis Napoéon had his private train call for them at the St-Cloud station. So most Parisians did not know they had gone until that evening's newspapers announced that the Empress Eugénie would be Regent of France during the emperor's absence, and that the Deputy Emile Ollivier would serve meanwhile as Premier of France. A good many Frenchmen openly grumbled at that—a female given nominal rule over them, and the real reins of government in the hands of the not-at-all-beloved Ollivier—but most Frenchwomen were more sentimentally affected by the reported farewell words of Eugénie to her son: "Lou-Lou, do your duty."

That same day, a mahogany clarence drawn by four matched bays drove onto the Florilegium tober. Its doors were emblazoned with the de Lareinty arms, and its footman handed down from it a blonde young woman gorgeously caparisoned in Worth silks and laces.

"Clover Lee!" several nearby troupers cried in gladsome greeting. Some others had the presence of mind to bow or curtsy—though with broad smiles on their faces—and say, "Your Grace!"

Then the young woman astonished those troupers, not to mention her own coachman and footman. As if she had been deranged by the long spell of hot weather, Clover Lee began to undress on the spot, tossing back into the carriage each garment she took off. But, when she had doffed the last outer covering, she stood revealed in a gold-spangled and flesh-colored costume—one of her old, pre-Clover Pink léotards and tights. Finally, she kicked off her needle-toed dongola slippers, spoke a word to the footman and, as the clarence rolled away with her discarded garb, she danced barefoot up to Florian.

He said admiringly, "Madame la Comtesse, you have not forgotten how to make a stunning entrance."

She said, "Hell, yonder goes the countess," gesturing at the departing carriage. "For the time being, I'm plain Clover Lee again. I'd like to come back to work—for a while, at least. As long as Gaspard is away."

"You are most certainly welcome, and more than welcome, you know that. However, are you sure that is what you want? I am aware that the count is off on military duty, but what of his family? Are they not likely to be...er...?"

"Horrified?" Clover Lee said blithely. "That Edith de Lareinty is displaying her charms in public? Well, they probably would be, except that they don't even know about Edith *or* Clover Lee yet. Gaspard and I were still at Deauville when the emperor yanked him back here to help run the war. So I haven't met any of the noble clan, not even my mother-in-law. I can't very well go around to them all and introduce myself, and I'm bored with twiddling my thumbs in solitude. Until they do know who I am, and expect me to behave like a proper countess, well... what the hell? I might as well do as I please, and enjoy myself."

"I would be the last to dissuade you. Our company is much depleted, and I imagine that even the hungriest out-of-work artistes are staying well away from western Europe until this war is over. You are back on the show as of tonight's performance, my dear. Ask Colonel Ramrod where he wants to respot your act, and see Madame Delattre for any costumery you may require. Meanwhile, I shall inform the hotel to have a room for you, and tonight we will all celebrate your return with a veritable banquet there."

Clover Lee was boisterously welcomed back by all the other troupers and crewmen and bandsmen who had not seen her arrive, and her horse Bubbles whickered with delight. Then she was hustled off by her sister artistes—away from the men—so they could gigglingly inquire of her what it was like to be married to a count, what the resort of Deauville was like, what it was like to be gowned by Worth, etc., etc. After a while, Monday Simms even got Clover Lee farther aside, away from the other women, to ask a question so intimate that she couldn't quite ask it:

"Did your husband...? You know, when you and him...? I mean, was he mad on account of...?"

"Because I wasn't a virgin?" Clover Lee said, with a laugh. "Why, girl, I made sure beforehand that he wouldn't even know."

"You did? *How*? You ain't quizzin' me?"

"Not a bit. A long time ago, after my very first man—'way back in Italy—old Maggie Hag told me how to fix myself for my wedding night."

"No, is that so? I wish you'd tell *me*. I ain't got no husband in sight, but just in case I ever does. Me, I'm spraddled wide open down there, like Mammy must of been, after she squirted out us three pickaninnies all at once."

"All right." Clover Lee glanced conspiratorially about. "Well, the first thing, you go to an apothecary shop and buy a man's shaving kit. Like you're buying it to give to some man, but that's only so the clerk won't know what you're buying it for. Then you throw away everything in it—brush, razor, soap—everything except the shaving stick. Or the styptic pencil, sometimes it's called. Then, when the time comes..." As Clover Lee's voice lowered, Monday's eyebrows raised.

"Our emperor takes command at Metz," Sunday translated from *Le Siècle*, a few days later, to a group of listening troupers. "He orders immediate drive into... Terre-Sarre? What is that?"

"Called in German the Saarland," said Jörg Pfeifer. "Across the border from Lorraine."

"Well, those are the headlines," said Sunday, and went on into the body of the news story. "Two August. By instantaneous telegraph report from our intrepid correspondent at the front. On the brilliantly decisive order of His Imperial Majesty Louis Napoléon, the formidable Second Corps of the French Army this day, under command of the always courageous General Frossard, supported on its flanks by elements of the gallant Third and Fifth Corps, began an inexorable advance from the department of the Moselle into the enemy's territory of the Terre-Sarre, where the defending Prussian Second Army's artillery batteries are being overrun, their horse squadrons and foot battalions falling back in disorder... Whew! That's all one sentence."

"I'll be damned," muttered Edge. "They're doing it." Everyone turned to look at him, and he hastily added, "If any newspaper reporter can be believed."

Evidently this one could. The next morning, though it was only a Wednesday, all of Paris was awakened by the triumphant clangor of every church bell in the city. Crowds poured into the streets, to seize the still-wet newspapers flung by the newsboys bawling "Grande victoire!" and "Prussienne défaite!" The headlines read variously: CAPITALE DE TERRE-SARRE SAISIE! and C'EST À NOUS, LA CITÉ SAAR-BRÜCKEN! and the appended news stories gave the details. The Prussians' retreat had been so precipitate and disorganized that their sappers had had no chance to blow up or block the bridges over the Saar River. The gallant French had stormed straight into the city of Saarbrücken, and were now in firm occupation both of it and its chief suburb of St. Johann. Furthermore—so judged the several newspapers' several intrepid correspondents; they all used the word "inexorable"—the juggernaut French advance should continue onward from there to the Saarland's second city of Kaiserslauten "dans le coeur du pays des boches."

As if the tumult of bell ringing had roused some long-sleeping weather god, the remorseless heat that had gripped the city for more than a month was broken at last. A suddenly rising east wind sent trash and newspapers and hats and loose roof shingles scuttering about the city, and sent the Florilegium's roustabouts running to guy the five tents with extra ropes. The wind piled clouds up from the eastern horizon into the bleached-out sky, and as soon as those clouds had covered the city, the bottom fell out of them in a drenching deluge. The circus's Slovaks went running again, this time to tighten all the tent guys as the parched canvas soaked up the water and began to sag.

But the cloudburst, far from dampening the ardor of the Parisians, only gave them an additional reason to rejoice. They continued to crowd the avenues and boulevards, slapping each other on the back, standing each other drinks, parading in groups that roared the "Partant pour la Syrie" anthem and carried tricolored flags, and strove to wave them, but managed only to flap them soggily. And, well before show time, the Florilegium's chapiteau was full, while multitudes were being apologetically turned away from the tober. Those people rebuffed only shrugged cheerfully and slogged off through the downpour to other circuses or theatres or cafés, or just to buvette grogshops to get drunk, for all of Paris was celebrating this day.

"Well, I reckon they've got something *to* celebrate," said Edge. "Old Louis Napoléon seems to have the war well in hand."

"And as long as he does well at that, all France will shout his praises," said Florian. "*Exactly* as long as he does well. The French are notoriously fickle, mercurial and short on loyalty. The moment the armies suffer a setback or the emperor makes one misjudgment, his people will shout just as loudly for his hide—or his head. Ah, well. I shall not play the pessimist. Sufficient unto this day are the revels thereof."

But the following day was as dolefully sobering as any revel's morning-after. The newspapers that, on Wednesday, had described the French invasion of the Saarland with words like "formidable" and "inexorable" were, in Thursday's early editions, more cautiously referring to "difficulties" and "impêchements." The rain that had so blessedly come to Paris, and was still falling, was still, not so blessedly, falling in the locale of battle as well. So the roads over which the French had made their advance to Saarbrücken, and the roads leading in every direction out of it, were now all quagmires, and the French were not so much occupying the city as marooned in it.

By the Thursday afternoon editions, the newspapers were no longer praising the French army and its officers and its emperor-commander, but were freely using terms like "inefficacité" and "défaut de prévoyance." It was now apparent that the French invasion had been done rather *too* well, but with dismally inadequate planning to support it, once done. The fighting forces had far outdistanced their commissary and quartermaster and ordnance trains, and those trains, miles behind, were now bogged down to their horses' bellies and wagons' axles in the roads churned to mud. The victorious soldiers in Saarbrücken could feed themselves and their mounts by confiscation from the civilian population, but they could not similarly feed their weapons. And it now transpired that the French had been prodigally wasteful of lead and powder during their advance. The much-vaunted Montigny mitrailleuses in particular, reported the correspondents, had proven extravagantly spendthrift of cartridges. So the occupying forces were not only marooned in Saarbrücken, they also lacked the ammunition to defend their position there.

The Parisians still crowded the streets, to snatch up every new edition of the papers as they came out, but the people's faces were as gray as the rain, and there was no more singing or cheering or flag waving. There were, instead, many mutterings about the emperor's presumption in having taken command from the generals who *might* have known how to conduct a war, which Louis Napoléon demonstrably did not.

"What did I tell you?" Florian said to Edge.

"And what should I have told *him*?" Edge said, though only to himself. "Don't ever outrun your supply lines, Your Majesty? Hell, any new-harnessed shavetail ought to know that."

By Friday morning, the rain had stopped, and the day dawned sunny but refreshingly cool, the city washed sparkling clean, and all the Champs-Elysées flowers newly bright and beautiful. But the people's faces still were glum, for so was the morning's news. The papers reported that the rain had also stopped in the east, and the roads over there had dried sufficiently to support troop travel. Unfortunately, a fresh Prussian army, the First, was hurrying southward from a place called Merzig, and would reach Saarbrücken before any French reinforcements or supply trains could. So the occupiers of the city were making an abrupt departure to avoid being trapped there—coming back over the border the way they had gone, toward their earlier positions outside Metz. That news was bad enough, but the afternoon papers disclosed—with frank contempt, derision and thickets of exclamation marks—that the French had left Saarbrücken in such unseemly haste that *their* sappers, too, had criminally neglected to blow the Saar bridges behind them.

"Jesus Christ," growled Edge. "So the Prussians can march right back in, without even getting their jackboots wet. And you can bet they won't let that city be taken again by any surprise maneuver. All the French accomplished was to put the enemy on sharper alert. The emperor would have done better to keep his men in garrison, practicing close-order drill. Or cutting up those damned mitrailleuses for bayonets."

However, the afternoon newspapers of Saturday, the sixth of August, brought better tidings from another part of France, to exhilarate the Parisians again and make them forget, for a little while, the bungled opportunities in the Saarland. "Autre bataille, autre victoire!" bellowed the crieurs, and the people grabbed for the papers. The new battle had been instigated by two of the Prussians' allied forces, the Bavarian Fifth and Eleventh Corps, which had surged across the northern border of Alsace on the day before, but by this morning the Maréchal MacMahon already had his French First Corps in position to oppose them, and his Seventh Corps was rushing to the battlefield from Colmar. At noontime, according to the latest telegraphed communiqués from the newspapers' intrepid correspondents, the French were annihilating the Bavarian boches by the thousands.

Again the people of Paris paraded and sang and danced in the streets, and hundreds of them continued to make merry all night. By that time, the French government ministries and the newspaper offices, as well, knew that those first reports from Alsace had somehow been garbled and misread, and that the celebrators in the streets were actually doing a danse macabre. The Premier Ollivier and the numerous newspaper publishers had received later telegrams correcting and totally contradicting the earlier ones—but such august personages were not at all eager to confess the dreadful mistake of their impetuous announcements of a great victory.

It was not until the newspapers put out their routine Sunday morning editions that Paris learned the truth: it was the Bavarians who were annihilating the French. Of the thirty-seven thousand men the Maréchal MacMahon had thrown into that battle in Alsace, more than twenty thousand had died in a day. Worse, when MacMahon, in desperation, had summoned General de Failly's Fifth Corps for reinforcement, it had arrived on the scene only to decide that the situation was already beyond retrieval, and had retired without engaging at all. That entire Fifth Corps, together with what débris remained of the First and Seventh, was now in pell-mell retreat westward, with the whole Third Army of the boches in hot pursuit, and nothing to stop their advancing clear to the Moselle River.

The Parisians might have responded to that news in any number of ways— with pride and sadness for those who had fought bravely and died, with scorn and shame for those who had run, with apprehension for the fate of the other French armies around Metz, which were now about to be flanked by the enemy racing for the Moselle south of them. The Parisians chose instead to respond with wrath at the government's deceit in keeping the catastrophe a secret for as long as it could.

A great mob gathered and raged outside the Hôtel de Ville, and did not depart after venting its feelings, but grew in size and clamor and ugliness as more and more people joined it. Before that Sunday was out, announcements were printed and posted in every public place, and the newspapers rushed special editions to the streets. Emile Ollivier had resigned as Premier and War Minister, and Her Majesty the Regent had proclaimed as his successor the Comte de Palikao. Ollivier had been nothing but a lawyer and a politician. The old count was a much-decorated and widely respected former cavalry general. The mob in the Place de l'Hôtel de Ville consulted among themselves, and agreed that the government was in strong and honest hands again, and quietly dispersed and went home.

I O

FOR THE NEXT WEEK OR SO, neither the Paris newspapers nor the government ministries could publish more than sketchy bulletins on the progress of the war. That was not because of any official timidity or duplicity, but because the front-line battles, advances, retreats, marches and countermarches were so frequent, so fast-moving, fast-changing and often so confused that the correspondents and even the French armies' own liaison officers could not always keep track of them.

The Maréchal MacMahon continued to retreat from the east, along the way gathering up his battered and scattered three corps, and every so often fighting rear-guard actions against the boche Third Army in pursuit. But that Third Army seemed to be chasing him only leisurely, even detaching a sizable piece of itself to surround and lay siege to the Alsatian capital of Strasbourg. So Louis Napoléon sent word to MacMahon to withdraw fully a hundred miles west, to Châlons on the river Marne, and the emperor, the prince imperial and their immediate entourage took train from Metz to make rendezvous with him there. The official explanation was that Louis Napoléon and MacMahon together would reorganize, reinforce and revitalize that army unstrung by defeat and retreat. But a different story bandied in high places was soon rife among all the Parisians: that the emperor really had wanted to bring that army *and himself* safely all the way home to Paris; that he had been prevented only by the Empress Eugénie's telegraphing a stern command to him, to be a man and stand firm *somewhere* between his capital city and the oncoming boches.

Meanwhile, in the northeast, the Maréchal Bazaine, after having almost taken Saarbrücken, appeared not to know what to do next with his five corps, but only loitered about in the neighborhood of Metz, while King Wilhelm and General von Moltke menacingly built up their forces on the farther side of the Saar River.

The fifteenth of August, a Monday, should have been France's most festive summer holiday, the annual commemoration of the birth of Napoléon the Great. This year, as usual, everything was in readiness to make la Ville Lumière even more of a City of Lights than ordinary, with a full million extra globe gas lamps affixed to building façades, statues and monuments—twelve thousand lights to outline the Arc de Triomphe alone—and immense dark-green banners were stretched on lines high across every avenue, bearing the fancily worked letter *N* and spread-winged eagles and golden bees. Bands and orchestras and choirs were all tuned and rehearsed, street vendors were well stocked with everything from flowers and sweets to cheap felt bicorn hats à la Napoléon, and the cafés had crowded even more tables onto the sidewalks outside their doors.

"During the Fête Nationale," Florian had told his company—including the first-of-May Delattre, who, when he was not exercising his plumbery skills about the tober, now occupied the ticket window of the red wagon—"it is traditional for all theatres and cafés and other such establishments to offer their entertainment free of charge. We will abide by that custom at both of the day's shows."

Unfortunately, on this fifteenth of August, the morning newspapers again announced bad news. For once, the correspondents at the northeastern front had sent a full report of the latest battle—and France's latest humiliation. The Maréchal Bazaine had yesterday been (again) in the process of repositioning his five corps around Metz when suddenly, from over a hilltop, had surged a part of the Prussians' Second Army. The fighting had been fierce, and the French had "given a good account of themselves," so that the opponents' casualties had been about equal, some four thousand men dead or wounded on each side. Nevertheless, when nightfall gave them the opportunity, the French had slipped away from the engagement to flee to shelter under the heavy guns of the Metz fortifications.

Premier de Palikao quite rightly decided that it would be inappropriate for Paris to celebrate simultaneously the anniversary of the great Napoléon's birth and the news of another French retreat, so he decreed that the city's festive lamps not be lighted, and requested his fellow citizens to refrain from revelry on this equivocal occasion. The people did not promenade in jubilation, but they did not all stay at home, either. Some thousands of Parisians took to the avenues and boulevards in what looked suspiciously like not a spontaneous but a previously arranged demonstration—waving the red flag of revolution instead of the tricolor, singing "La Marseillaise" and shouting anti-imperial slogans.

"What goes on?" asked Yount, watching.

"Those would be the local Communards," said Florian.

"What the hell is a Communard?"

Daphne laughed and quoted, " 'What is a Communard? One that has yearnings.' " Yount looked baffled, so she explained, "An Englishman described them in doggerel a long time ago. I still remember the old verse:

> What is a Communard? One that has yearnings
> For equal division of unequal earnings.
> Idler, or bungler, or both, he is willing
> To fork out his penny and pocket your shilling."

Florian also laughed and, since Yount still looked baffled, he explained further, "The Communards are the extremists among the many who want France to be a republic again. The republicans in general wish to abolish all the titles and privileges of royalty and nobility and other aristocracy. The Communards insist on abolishing not only the classes, but also all other distinctions—wealth, social status and so on. No man would be richer than any other, and a fish peddler at les Halles would be as respected as a professor at the Sorbonne."

"Would that be bad?" Yount asked.

"Oh, it might not be so regrettable, if that were what *everyone* wanted. But the Communards, like any religious sect, are so cocksure of the rightness of their own beliefs that they brook no disbelievers. Given any opportunity, the Communards would impose on everybody their own brand of the Promised Land, and they would do it not by persuasion or by vote, but by *force*. Myself, I should much prefer an optional Hell to an obligatory Heaven."

On that day, though, the marching throngs made no show of force. After they finally got tired of tramping about, waving their red flags and yelling their insulting opinions of the emperor, the empress and all of the imperial establishment, they—along with practically everybody else in Paris—decamped to the free entertainments of the cafés and the theatres and the circuses.

Still, the Premier de Palikao seemed to have taken a serious view of that blatant Communard demonstration. The next day, posters appeared to announce that the Premier of France, having consulted with His Majesty by telegraph, was appointing for the city of Paris a military governor, to be in charge of public law and order, safety and welfare, for the duration of the wartime emergency. The Parisians grumbled, as they always did, but not even the Communards could complain too much, for the governor was to be General Louis Trochu, widely known as a liberal. There was no reason to suppose that his appointment was anything more than a gesture of admonishment for all to be good and do right.

Then there came more disheartening news from the northeastern front. The Maréchal Bazaine, after having spent so much time indecisively shuffling his troops around and about Metz, had finally come to a decision. Because the entire Prussian Second Army was now in that vicinity, he would *depart* from Metz, leaving only a sufficient garrison for the city forts, moving the bulk of his five corps to join forces with those of the emperor and the Maréchal MacMahon at Châlons, whence the combined armies would spread out north and south to present an impregnable front against further Prussian incursion.

However, the Prussians had anticipated the withdrawal from Metz. When, on August 16, the French troops took the road to the westward, two of their cavalry divisions in the lead, they had gone only ten miles—as far as the village of Vionville—when they met the patrolling enemy cavalry, two divisions of *them*. Cavalry charged against cavalry, more than two thousand horsemen to a side, and the battle raised such a great cloud of dust that it became a confused mêlée —here and there, two opponents sabre-dueling to the death, while about them herds of other riders milled hither and yon, looking for an enemy group to fight, and several times almost engaging other groups from their own side.

Meanwhile, the French and Prussian commanders hastened to throw into the fray every other soldier of infantry and artillery that they could rush to the scene. Between nine o'clock that morning and seven o'clock that evening was fought the fiercest battle of the whole war—the Prussians' eventual deployment of forty-seven thousand riflemen, eight thousand cavalrymen and more than two hundred artillery pieces versus the French deployment of eighty-three thousand rifles, eight thousand sabres, four hundred cannon and twenty-four mitrailleuses. Both in riflemen and in heavy guns, the Prussians were outnumbered two to one, but that deficiency was offset by the more rapid and accurate fire of their breech-loading weapons.

When the battle ended in the dust and smoke and darkness of nightfall, it *might* have been called a French victory, because the outnumbered Prussians quit fighting from sheer exhaustion, while the French did still have enough energy to move. However the only moving they did was to *retreat again,* seven miles back the way they had come. They breasted a long ridge of ground and, once that was between them and the enemy, they settled to rest for the night in the little valley beyond. But they had fallen back in such helter-skelter fashion that all their units were intermingled and confused and, in the dark, unregroupable. Even when their officers placed pickets on lookout for any reappearance of the boches, those officers themselves were so disoriented that many of them put their guards out to the north and east, although they had left the entire enemy army behind them to the west and south.

The woeful news brought the Communards to the streets again, this time joined by soberer citizens. The hordes of men and women marched throughout the city and milled about the Hôtel de Ville, ranting against the emperor, his marshals and other officers—and the shamefully wretched performance in the field of their own sons and husbands, whom they had sung and cheered off to war less than a month before. To that roar of criticism and vilification, the Premier de Palikao and Governor Trochu publicly replied only by posting notices of feeble reassurance and pleas for patience. But privately they were engaged in other measures, and the Florilegium's Dai Goesle was one of the first to realize that. He had gone for a stroll through the Bois de Boulogne, but came hurrying back to the tober to tell Florian:

"I was thinking for a minute, just, that we were about to have competition, Governor. A Wild West show, by Saint Dafydd! Come and give a look."

Several other troupers followed them, and, on the farther side of the lake, sure enough, rough-clad men on horseback were herding cattle onto the lawns of the Bois. But the animals were far too numerous to be for show and, behind the cattle, came also droves of sheep, driven by horsemen and dogs. They were all coming down the northern paths of the park, and evidently had been brought in from the countryside by way of the sparsely populated Puteaux district of the city, to attract as little public notice as possible. Florian contemplated the extraordinary scene and said:

"It appears that General Trochu is prudently stocking the city to make it self-supporting, in case the Prussians should get this far. Perhaps he has good reason to fear that they *will* get this far." He turned quickly to Hannibal Tyree and said, "Abdullah, take this money. Take Slovaks and wagons. Go to les Halles and buy from your usual suppliers as much as possible of oats and hay and cat's meat, both fresh meat and dried or smoked. There is sure to be a run on such fodder. Go immediately."

Hannibal took plenty of francs with him, and returned with plenty of supplies, but reported that they had cost him *all* of that plentiful money. "Dem feed merchants done already hiked up de prices, Sahib."

"It was only to be expected," said Monsieur Nadar, who was visiting Florian in the office wagon. "The prices will go far higher yet. Any plausible excuse will serve for a Frenchman to gouge his customers, preferably foreigners, but his fellow Frenchmen will do." He added languidly, "You may depend on it: if the boches do not lay waste to France, the French will."

Within hours, the unobtrusive importation of livestock into the Bois was known all over the city, so Trochu abandoned any pretense of secrecy, and the herdsmen drove their animals right through the boulevards of Paris and across the Seine bridges to stock also the Luxembourg Gardens on the Left Bank. Meanwhile, housewives, and husbands who could be badgered into it, and servants of every aristocratic household were hurrying to market with baskets, handcarts and all available children to help carry things. They frantically bought every kind of comestible, clothing, wine, lamp oil and, though this was mid-August, even winter-weight blankets and buckets of coal.

Of course, for all their swift action, the buyers had not got to the shops and stalls before the vendors had taken down their customary price cards and put up new ones scrawled with cutthroat prices, and had hidden away all their best and scarcest merchandise to save for themselves and their favored customers. The besieging buyers cried outrage and cursed the sellers, but took what they could get—often coming to blows among themselves over any coveted or last-in-stock item—and they paid the prices demanded. So, by the next day, every sort of vendor, from those of the dignified Printemps and the exclusive passage boutiques to the least pushcart peddler, had raised all prices again, beyond mere avarice to outright rapacity.

That gave the Communards another war cry. Now, as they surged about the city, they alternated their fulminations against the emperor and his minions with execrations of "the callous capitalist bourgeoisie!" and, before long, had amended that, howling instead that the money-grubbing gougers must all be "the filthy youpins!"—a cry that was enthusiastically taken up even by the execrated bourgeoisie. It was bellowed in the streets and could be heard spoken even in more civil tones at café tables, by presumably level-headed moderates, diehard imperialists and the most fervently anti-Communard conservatives: "à bas les youpins."

"That's right, blame the yids, the Abies, the sheenies," said Nadar with disgust. "No matter if the barbarians are at the gates, the French can ignore that— no matter how indecently the French are behaving toward each other, they can excuse themselves—simply by making scapegoats of the youpins."

"It has been ever thus, monsieur," Maurice LeVie said wearily. "And not only in France, hélas."

From then on, there was seldom an identifiable Jew to be seen in public. The cafés of the rue Cadet, which formerly had been both the social-gathering and business-dealing places of Paris's diamond merchants, now stood empty of patrons. Jacques Offenbach hastily left Paris for Italy, and thus earned himself a double damnation, for having cravenly deserted the city in these dire days, and for having been such a prominent fixture of it until now. The Parisians who had for so long acclaimed the man and his music now contemptuously referred to him by the name he had been born with, Jacob Eberst, and reminded each other that his father had been not just a Jew, but a synagogue cantor, and of Cologne, of *Prussia*. Military Governor Trochu finally had to take cognizance of the furor over that one Jew, and did so by banning performance of any of his works, on the ground that Offenbach's lighthearted operettas "had diverted the French public's attention from reality."

Attending to reality was unpleasant. Another great battle had been fought outside Metz, and this one had ended with the most catastrophic defeat yet for the French. With his entire army—except for the multitudes of dead, wounded and captured—Maréchal Bazaine had retreated *inside* the city of Metz. The victorious Prussians had gleefully surrounded the city, not attempting to overwhelm it, but only to keep the French bottled up in there. For King Wilhelm and General von Moltke to lay siege to the city did not require a great many of their men, and the remainder of their army was now free to advance unimpeded through the heartland of France, which they immediately set about doing.

That news set off the worst-ever panic and hubbub and anger in Paris. The mobs rampaging through the streets naturally included Communards, but also disillusioned citizens, frightened citizens, irate citizens of every class and age and sex and occupation and political inclination. They tore down all the golden-bee banners, hacked away the fancy stone N's that decorated public edifices and monuments, threw stones at the windows of the Hôtel de Ville and of the buildings housing minor ministries. The newspapers echoed the public's latest and most sardonic condemnation of Louis Napoléon: "First the emperor left the government at Paris, then he left the army at Metz! Now the one is enfeebled and the other lost!"

The poorer folk among the stampeding mobs yelled another complaint: the price of every commodity for sale in Paris was now so astronomically high that only the wealthy could afford to feed and clothe themselves. Governor Trochu had stocked the city with forty thousand beeves and two hundred thousand sheep in the Bois and the Luxembourg Gardens, plus warehouses full of flour and coal and ammunition. Why, demanded the people, did not the governor now arrange for distribution of some of the staples among the families who could not afford to buy?

Trochu's response was not meant to be broadcast, but it was overheard and immediately repeated all over Paris: "Damn the ungovernable city people! Oh, for some good, illiterate, biddable peasants!" And the only action he took was to safeguard those emergency supplies by setting a chain of armed sentries around every herd and warehouse, around the clock. To do that, he had to summon to active duty the Home Guard—or what was mockingly called la Garde Sédentaire—men aged thirty-one to sixty, too old for army service but conscriptable into the Home Guard under wartime regulations. Most of the men available were nearer sixty than thirty-one, and they came but grudgingly to duty—their pay for it being only a bottle of wine and thirty sous per day—but, once they were given the authority of uniforms, they diligently stood guard and they did carry weapons, so the rabble made no attempt at rustling cattle or sheep.

While the masses clamored and marched and painted ribald, wrathful, revolutionary slogans in blood-red on building façades, there was another, very quiet and less noticeable traffic in the streets. It consisted of the nobles, aristocrats and rich bourgeois making their own preparations against any calamity. The rich men took their fortunes of French francs to the Jewish diamond dealers and money changers—who had gone to ground but could be located without much trouble—and exchanged the francs either for easily concealable and portable diamonds or for foreign currencies (including Prussian marks) that would not be liable to distressing fluctuations. The rich women took their jewels and furs and objets d'art to the city's monts-de-piété. Those pawnshops, which heretofore had made loans of a few francs or even a pitiful few sous on the pledged goods of the poor—from cheap, thin wedding rings to mattresses—now found themselves presented with real valuables, and having to take them in pawn for necessarily sizable sums. The women's theory was that not only did they receive cash in hand; their treasures were being stored under government protection until such time as danger was past and they could be redeemed. So many had recourse to the monts-de-piété that the government funds—originally meant for the succoring of the poor—were rapidly depleted. Governor Trochu had to order that henceforth the pawnshops would accept no article valued in excess of fifty francs. So the upper classes joined the lower in grumbling about Trochu's martial-law strictures. The lower classes cursed him with expletives; the upper more genteelly took to calling him "Governor Trop Chu."

Sunday Simms had rather prided herself on having acquired considerable fluency in French, but she confessed to her former tutor Jules Rouleau that the epithet Trop Chu escaped her comprehension.

"Aha!" said Rouleau. "I was always telling you to give special practice to the irregular verbs. 'Chu' is the past participle of the verb 'choir,' meaning to fall, to succumb."

"Oh? Then Trop Chu would mean Governor Much-Fallen?"

"Well, more slangily, Governor Irresolute—Governor He-Who-Yields—he who backs down under pressure."

While they were talking, there came across the tober a young man in captain's uniform, painfully limping with the aid of a cane, and carrying one arm in a sling. He looked around in some bewilderment, then inquired of Sunday and Rouleau if there might be such a person as a Comtesse de Lareinty hereabouts.

"Wait where you are, Captain," said Sunday, so he would not have to limp to the backyard. "I'll bring her to you."

When the two girls came, Rouleau, who had been conversing with the visitor, gave a slight twitch of his head to draw Sunday aside and leave Clover Lee alone with him.

"Madame... Your Grace..." said the young officer, with understandable hesitancy, since he was addressing a presumed countess in an extremely abbreviated garb, mostly of spangles. "You—you are Edith de Lareinty? Gaspard often boasted to us that he had wed a beautiful circus artiste, but we never quite believed him."

"You should have," Clover Lee said brightly. "He did. And I am the Edith he married."

"Yes. Well. I was invalided home, you see," said the captain, still hesitantly. "So I was enjoined to bring you word of him."

"Oh, good! I mean... I'm sorry *you* got wounded. But how is Gaspard? Is *he* safe from harm?"

The captain swallowed and said, "Never will he be more safe from harm than he is now, Your Grace."

Clover Lee started to smile, then blinked, then moved her lips several times before she could say, "He is...? You mean...?"

"He rests now in the deserving soldier's last long bivouac. He is buried at Châlons-sur-Marne."

Clover Lee's eyes brimmed. "How—how could it have happened? I thought an aide-de-camp was a headquarters officer. Always safe behind the lines, like the generals and the emperor."

"You must understand, Your Grace, that Gaspard lately had to be His Majesty's eyes and arms and legs. The emperor is so afflicted with his internal ailment that he is now unable to sit a horse. He no longer leads an army, but must be carried in its baggage train. So Gaspard had to perform all liaison functions for him, meaning he *was* often at the very forefront, and at hazard. It was a sniper's bullet that felled him. I am sorry to be the one to bring such—"

"No. No, it was g-good of you to come," said Clover Lee, as her eyes brimmed over. She swiped at her face with the back of her hand. "I th-thank you, Captain."

The young officer threw a glance of appeal to where Rouleau and Sunday stood at a distance, and they came quickly. As Sunday put an arm around her, to lead her off to grieve in private, Clover Lee was trying to laugh through her tears, saying brokenly, "I remember—Gaspard once—he joked, he said—*I get killed? Wounded, captured? Never! I am a Frenchman. I shall run away...*"

"Please, monsieur," said the captain, when he and Rouleau were alone. "The count lived long enough to dictate and sign this." He fumbled awkwardly inside his tunic with the hand that held his cane, and produced a sealed envelope. "Would you give it to Madame la Veuve de Lareinty when she is more composed?"

"Why not stay, mon capitaine, and see the show as our guest? You can watch the countess herself perform, and afterward give her the letter yourself."

"Surely, monsieur, she would not be capable..."

"Stay and see. The count did not shirk. Neither will she."

And of course she did not, but performed flawlessly, her smile and vivacity undimmed, her horse Bubbles and her canopy of doves always under her control. She could even smile bravely at the captain, after she had taken her bows and Rouleau brought him to the backyard. The young officer handed over the last message from her late husband, and said:

"Your artistry was most marvelous to see, chère madame. Small wonder the count was bewitched by you. A performance delightful, a thing of which to tell our comrades—Gaspard's and mine—when I return to serve with them. If I do. If they are still alive."

Clover Lee opened the letter in private, and frowned over it for a while, then waited until the show was over and took it to Florian in the red wagon.

"I can read poor Gaspard's signature, shaky though it is. But my French is nothing to brag about, and neither is the handwriting of whoever wrote this for him. I didn't want to show it to Sunday or Jules, in case it's *real* private and sentimental. If it is, Sunday or Jules would get to crying. Would you read it to me?"

Florian scanned the two pages and said, "Feminine hand. Evidently he dictated it to a nurse, and I imagine she was also under strain, writing in haste, hence the scrawl. There's nothing sentimental in it, my dear, all very business-like." Clover Lee looked a little cast down to hear that. "Remember, the man was...he did not have much time. So he confined himself to the necessary, and even that must have cost a heroic effort. Surely he would have added some tender last words, if he could have done."

"Oh, that's all right," Clover Lee said huskily. "After all, we weren't together long enough to...I mean to say, it wasn't any grand passion. I'm sorry he got killed, but I can't really feel bereaved."

"Well, now that he is gone, you will *have* to introduce yourself, on your own, to the rest of his family, and—"

"And show my marriage certificate as my credentials? What's the point? I'd still be a stranger to them, an interloper. Besides, they'll be hurt enough by Gaspard's death. I wouldn't want to add the shock of telling them that he left a circus bareback rider as his widow."

"Your attitude does you credit. But you haven't even asked what *is* in this letter. Nothing sentimental, granted, but a good deal of generosity. It is an admirably concise disposition of his holdings and possessions and entitlements."

"Oh, God, I sure don't want to get into any squabble over his share of the family estate. No, I had the fun and glory and vanity of being a countess for a little while. I can truthfully say that I got what I long ago set out to get. Now I'll just go on being who I really am. Doing the work I do best and enjoy most."

"You *remain* the Comtesse de Lareinty, and fully entitled to everything that goes with that rank. You can easily forgo Gaspard's share of any family inheritance, and still never have to work another day in your life. He already had his own estimable fortune—bequeathed, it says here, directly from his grandparents on his mother's side. And this letter leaves it all to you. It is, in effect, a holograph will and testament, quite incontestable by any of his blood relations."

"Oh."

"You don't care? It lists bank accounts, investments, income from various estate tenants, a château in Puy-de-Dome..."

"And if word of that got out, I'd have every titled pauper in France congregating to comfort the widow, like so many leeches. Anyhow, the way this war is going, it's likely to wipe out everything Gaspard owned. Please, Florian, let's just keep that letter a secret, until and unless I have reason to make use of it. In the meantime, I'll be Clover Lee, équestrienne."

Florian looked at her, long and fondly and admiringly. "I remember when you were as puny and gawky as a new-foaled filly, and just as giddy and frisky. You have matured into quite a commonsensical young lady. More deserving of a noble title than most nobles I have known. I should feel unreservedly proud and glad of that, except..."

"Except what? Would you want me giddy and foolish again?"

"Oh, no, no." He sighed. "It is only that your growing up reminds me that I am growing old."

Again the war news published in Paris got sketchy, as the emperor and the Maréchal MacMahon led their army out of Châlons to relieve the beleaguered Bazaine at Metz, and moved so rapidly that the correspondents were hard put to keep up and, along the way, find opportunity to telegraph their reports. But the brief bulletins that did get through were enough to be discouraging. The French army traveled only two-thirds of the way east from Châlons to Metz before it was blocked. The one major town en route was Verdun, which the army had expected to use for its staging place on the Meuse River. But the advance cavalry scouts had to report that Verdun had already been ringed by the enemy and laid under siege; that the rest of the Prussian forces had bypassed it and were still advancing, now well west of Verdun. So MacMahon had no hope of helping Bazaine or of getting any help from him. There was nothing that could be done but to attempt a diversionary action: the French turning north along the Meuse, deliberately provoking skirmishes with the Prussians to make them also turn and follow northward—which at least detoured them from forging straight westward to Paris.

In such reports as reached the Paris papers, the correspondents were uncharacteristically respectful in their comments on the leaders of this one and only French army still in the field. What little could be done, said the reporters, MacMahon was gallantly doing. And the emperor, they said, was obviously suffering terrible internal pain from being forever on the move, but he stayed staunchly with his troops and was never heard to make complaint.

Louis Napoléon was not being accorded even that faint praise in his capital city. The Paris protests and demonstrations went on unabated. Vicious caricatures of the emperor were drawn on walls, and caricatures of the Napoleonic eagle, clutching a bloody soldier in its talons, captioned "le dernier vol de l'aigle." That was rather a clever play on words, Pemjean explained, when he and some other troupers came upon one of those eagle pictures, since dernier could mean either "last" or "vilest," and vol was properly "flight," but in street slang meant "theft." While the angry crowds still harassed and pelted with stones and gutter dung the government offices at the Hôtel de Ville and the Palais-Bourbon, they now also, for the first time, mobbed the Tuileries, pressing as close to the palace as the cordon of guards would let them, to shout invective at "the Spanish Inquisitor!"—the woman whom all France, and not entirely unreasonably, held responsible for this war.

Even Florian's Flourishing Florilegium now, for the first time, was affected by the city's turmoil. It quit giving afternoon performances, because its potential audience was out raising hell in the streets all day. The circus showed only at night, when those people, weary of demonstrating but flushed with pride at their public-spirited exertions, were ready for some relaxing entertainment—and were grateful that the Florilegium was almost the only establishment in Paris that had not raised its prices.

Premier de Palikao and Military Governor Trochu did their best to calm the people and allay their fears and resentments, but that best was very little and accomplished very little. The authorities could only post announcements that the boches *were* still being held at bay, and that Paris herself was well prepared for any onslaught. There was enough food, supplies and ammunition stored, they insisted, to maintain the city for a whole month. According to the government posters, the city's Home Guard now numbered two hundred thousand, and all the Gardes Mobiles—the trained militia—had been summoned from every suburb, town and village for miles around, to concentrate in Paris, to the number of another hundred thousand. Also, volunteer outfits had bravely sprung into existence from some unlikely sources, and were intensively training and drilling to become fighters. There was the Légion des Volontaires, consisting of all the city's Polish émigrés, and les Amis de France, consisting of all the Belgians, Englishmen and Italians resident in the city—and even les Francs-tireurs de la Presse, comprising journalists, poets, novelists and feuilletonistes who, apparently unsatisfied with merely writing about war, now wished to experience one.

Such announcements were received by the masses with vulgar raillery and scoffing. *Everybody* knew how pompously and struttingly useless were reservists and militiamen and resurrected old veterans and half-baked volunteers. For the Garde Mobile, the people coined the derisive term "les moblots." As for foreigners—and writers, merde alors!—who in his senses would trust them to put up any kind of fight for Paris? Even among the officials publicly lauding those impromptu defense forces, there seemed to be some barely suppressed risibility. When Governor Trochu ordered a mass review of all those irregulars, in a grand march along the Champs-Elysées, the sidewalk watchers could scarcely contain their mirth at the motley and slovenly parade. And Trochu's wonderfully ambiguous commendation of the troops, after it was over, was greeted and repeated with glee by everybody else in the city: "Mes soldats, never has any general had before his eyes such a spectacle as you have just given me."

A few days afterward, though, even the derisory laughter was silenced. The mobs were still in the streets, but they were glum and somber now, no longer taking joy in their riotousness. MacMahon's army, the newspapers reported, had gone north along the Meuse as far as it *could* go without having to retreat from France altogether and fall across the border into Belgium. By the thirty-first of

August, it had rallied about the town of Sedan, to make a stand there—and the emperor had been carried into the town itself, for the attention of the surgeons. Arrayed against the French were awesomely overwhelming forces led by King Wilhelm, Prince Friedrich Karl, General von Moltke and other generals: Bose, Manteuffel, Zastrow, Goeben. Indeed, every highest-ranking enemy except the Chancellor Bismarck was there in person, to be in at the kill, and they had even brought along with the lions a scavenger jackal in the person of the American "observer," General Philip Sheridan.

One of the first Prussian shells fired at the French lines, early in the morning of the first of September, wounded the Maréchal MacMahon, and command passed to General Auguste Ducrot. That general's expressed opinion of the situation, despite the soldierly earthiness of its language, was duly reported by telegraph to Paris: "Nous sommes dans un pot de chambre, et nous y serons emmerdés." The good citizens of Paris immediately began daubing walls with caricatures of Louis Napoléon seated trouserless on a chamber pot. Along the city's boulevards and in the passages were certain elegant boutiques that had earned a particular distinction, and for years had proudly displayed it on their signboards and show windows. Now their proprietors were scraping away or defacing the gold-leafed legend: "Purveyors to His Majesty the Emperor."

It would be a suspenseful two days before Paris heard what happened next at Sedan. But, by the afternoon of that same first of September, seventeen thousand French soldiers and nine thousand Prussians lay dead, dying or severely wounded around the outskirts of the town. Frenzied and confused fighting was still going on when, at about four o'clock, the French General Wimpffen happened to glance behind him at the town he was defending, and was appalled to see a white flag flying from its highest church steeple. Thinking it the doing of some panicky civilian townsman, he sent his aide running to tear down the shameful rag. Wimpffen himself also hurried into the town, to the sickbed where Louis Napoléon lay in agony, to plead that His Majesty show himself on the ramparts to inspire his desperately battling soldiers. The emperor weakly and sadly demurred; the battle was over, he said. He had already telegraphed to the Regent and the Premier of France that he was surrendering his army and himself. It was by his own order that the white flag flew from the church steeple; let it stay; let the killing and the dying cease.

However, all the telegraph lines out of Sedan had been cut, either deliberately by the besiegers or by random shellfire. So Louis Napoléon, Prince Lou-Lou and their retainers were under house arrest under Prussian guard, the French army had been unconditionally surrendered and had been disarmed— the victors magnanimously allowing all officers to retain their swords—before the Prussian engineers repaired the telegraph lines and, on September 3, let the emperor's final message go through to Paris.

Well before the newspapers could learn and publish the terrible news, that message had somehow been disclosed by someone in the premier's office, and had flashed about the city far faster than telegraph keys could have repeated it. Thus there now collected in the Tuileries gardens the vastest and most turbulent mob yet, surrounding the palace, pressing threateningly close upon the cordon of guards, thunderously stamping their boots in unison and chanting in a cadenced roar, "Déchéance! Déchéance!" before a messenger from the Hôtel de

Ville could slip unobserved, by way of the Louvre museum, through a private passage into the palace, to give the Empress Eugénie her own first look at her husband's telegram:

"The army is defeated. Having been unable to be killed among my soldiers, I have had to constitute myself prisoner to save the army. Napoléon."

The roar outside the palace—"Dethronement! Overthrow! Abdication!"— went on all night. If any of the crowd went home to sleep, it was unnoticeable, because there were ample replacements. And by the next day, September 4, there could hardly have been any person indoors anywhere in Paris or in the most remote suburbs, for even country people poured into the city. From the Florilegium tober, the circus company watched in wonder as accordion-necked old farmers and muscular young farm laborers and meat-faced farm women, dressed in coarse homespun and wooden sabots, some carrying wicked-looking scythes and sickles, came afoot or in farm carts drawn by mules or oxen, across the Bois de Boulogne from the western countryside and, sparing not even a curious sidelong look at the circus spread, moved implacably toward the center of Paris. By midmorning, the combined city and country folk thronged the streets and made almost a solid mass in the Tuileries gardens, in the Place de la Concorde, about the Palais-Bourbon and the Hôtel de Ville.

At the latter place, the Premier of France and the Military Governor of Paris gloomily contemplated the situation. The Empire of France had fielded two great armies; one was now uselessly barricaded inside Metz and the other, including the emperor himself, had surrendered at Sedan. There was no organized force to stop the boches between the river Meuse and this very building, outside which the crowd yelled over and over, "République! République!" Finally, fatalistically, at midday, General Trochu, Governor He-Who-Yields, admitted into the Hôtel de Ville the leaders of the various republican factions, from moderate Third Partyists to the Communard extremists, and all those men began wrangling as to how a new government could quickest be instituted and which among them would constitute it. Meanwhile, overhead, a young Communard had scaled the building's façade to haul down the tricolor from the flagstaff there. He had not thought to carry up with him a red flag, so he simply ripped from the tricolor its white and blue panels, and ran the remaining ragged red strip back up the halyard.

Three other things were happening at the same time.

At the Tuileries, the Empress Eugénie, lately Regent of France, dressed in modest black and heavily veiled, went with her maid along the private passage from the palace to the Louvre, went down the museum stairs and out a side door into the Place St-Germain-l'Auxerrois. The two women slipped unrecognized through the milling crowds and hailed a common voiture. The maid was carrying five hundred francs, the empress's luggage consisted only of two handkerchiefs, as they rode away from the palace.

A hundred and thirty-five miles to the northeast, at Sedan, the Prince Imperial Eugène Louis, lately heir apparent to the throne of France, helped his father climb, gasping and groaning, into a Prussian army carriage, then said farewell to him. Two Prussian guards took the inside seat facing Louis Napoléon, a Prussian coachman whipped up the horses, and the emperor began the long, long ride out of France—toward Kurhesse and imprisonment.

Also at Sedan, King Wilhelm was drafting for the Herrenhaus at Berlin his recommendation that General von Moltke be created and styled the Graf von

Moltke, while the general himself was issuing the orders that would send all his armies westward, destination Paris. The "observing" General Philip Sheridan tendered some advice in that regard, and other officers then present later repeated it to still others, until it eventually reached the ears of a correspondent of the newspaper *Le Gaulois*. He, as a noncombatant, was not interned or guarded or even restrained from exercising his trade, and no Prussian officer tried to prevent or censor him when he telegraphed to Paris what Sheridan had suggested to von Moltke:

"Inflict on the enemy's army as telling blows as possible, then cause the civilian population such suffering that they must force their government to sue for peace. The people must be left nothing—nothing but their eyes with which to weep."

I I

" 'REPUBLIC PROCLAIMED!' That's the headline," said Sunday, translating the news for a group of troupers in costume. She skimmed through the story, summarizing as best she could. "First, the Premier de Palikao was offered the dictatorship of France for the duration of the war. But he declined and suggested instead the formation of a Council of National Defense. So that's what the government will be called. Until the wartime emergency is past, and elections can be held throughout the country and the French people's will can be known."

"Hell, the people's will is already pretty clear," said Fitzfarris. "I gather they want anything but an emperor. I was downtown a while ago, and went by the Tuileries palace. It's chalked all over with sarcastic notices like 'National Property' and 'Free Admission' and 'Rooms to Let.' "

"For the duration of the emergency," Sunday went on, "General Louis Trochu will be acting President, Monsieur Jules Favre will be acting Foreign Minister, Monsieur Léon Gambetta acting Minister of the Interior and Monsieur Adolphe Thiers acting Chief of Deputies." She laughed. "I know who the president is— old He-Who-Yields—but I never heard of any of those others."

"Mostly former deputies and Third Partyists," said Pemjean. "At least, thank God, none of them is a rabid Communard. I would guess that the President, Trochu, will continue to be pliable, merely a figurehead. The Foreign Minister will be the government's mouthpiece to the people, and the real rule will be in the hands of Minister Gambetta."

"You must be guessing right," said Sunday, still scanning the newspaper. "Here's an account of a long speech by Monsieur Favre, addressing the public." She grinned and raised her fist in a mock-heroic gesture as she read, " 'We shall not cede an inch of our territory or a stone of our fortresses...' He seems to go on saying that same thing over and over in different words."

"Then either Favre is crazy," said Jörg Pfeifer, "or he thinks his people are. Everybody knows the Prussians are already halfway across France. And French fortresses are falling everywhere."

A sudden loud whistle blast made the whole group start. "Whoops!" said Clover Lee. "Let's get lined up for the come-in, or Zachary'll be laying siege to all of *us*."

After the show was over that night, while the rest of the troupe made off for the hotel and a late supper, Florian and Edge tarried in the office wagon, sipping wine and smoking, and Edge commented:

"It's a good thing we've still got 'Confederate American' painted on our wagons and the marquee and all. I hear the street mobs were furious when they found out that it was a Yankee who spirited the empress out of the country."

Florian chuckled. "Her American dentist, of all unlikely people." Then he said soberly, "Yes, the mobs would dearly have loved to give Eugénie the Marie Antoinette treatment. But now she is safe in England, and the headhunters are frustrated, so no doubt there'll be anti-American sentiment for quite a while."

"Do you think we ought to get out of here while we can? After all, Governor, we've done what we came to do. Paris was the pinnacle we aimed at—the Mecca of all the circuses in the world—and we got here and we've had our triumph. Hell, we even put a new phrase in the French vocabulary: Clover Pink. And we've made a lot of money. So, now, do we stay or clear out before the Prussians invade?"

"I believe the Prussians will come only to goose-step up and down the boulevards for a while. To be able to say, as you just did, that they accomplished what they set out to do. King Wilhelm has no quarrel with the French people themselves. His objective was to curb the power of the French emperor, and he has absolutely annihilated it. Now, between Britain in the west and Russia in the east, there is no great power except Prussia and its allies. Wilhelm—or, more precisely, his Chancellor Bismarck—has everything he wanted: a federation of Germanic peoples, and no other European nation able to contest that federation's preeminence. So this new government of France must sue for peace. Its Chief Deputy Thiers is already off to visit Vienna, Florence, maybe Saint Petersburg, asking that the other heads of state help to arbitrate satisfactory peace terms."

"Well," said Edge, "not everybody in Paris is so sanguine about any early truce. Do you know what they're doing now? Their army is shot to hell, but the French Navy hasn't been bruised by this war at all. So they're bringing ships' cannoneers from Dieppe and Calais to man the guns of the forts around Paris."

"No harm in being prepared against an attack on the city, even if it never occurs. A good bristling defense of the capital should help France's bargaining position in the peace negotiations. But, unless Thiers fails utterly in his emissary mission, Wilhelm and his armies will be coming here only to do a sort of victory dance while the treaties are being signed."

"Then the Florilegium will stay?"

"I think it best, Zachary. Even if I am being overly optimistic—even if this government proves inept in its dealing with the enemy, if it fails to secure a peace, if it recklessly goes on prosecuting the war—our staying here would be less chancy than taking to the road. Which way would we go? There would be troops of both armies marching and skirmishing God-knows-where, not to mention the usual hordes of freebooters and looters, no respecters of friend or foe. I think our circus train would be much more liable to mishap on the open road than it is right here in the Bois."

"Probably so."

"And there are other considerations. These are dark days for the Parisians, and they have been most generous in their patronage of our circus. I think we owe them the favor of our continued presence. Ever since Offenbach's entertainments were banned, every other theatre from the Opéra to the Odéon has not dared to stage any lighthearted plays or operettas. Even the Comédie-Française is presenting only lugubrious heroic dramas and dolorous tragedies. We are offering almost the only fun and frivolity to be found in the entire city. And, not incidentally, that means prosperous sfondone houses for us. If, when the victors do march in, every Parisian circusgoer retires to crepe-hung gloom and isolation, well... we can doubtless expect replacement audiences of Prussians. They liked us well enough when we showed in their own lands."

To acknowledge that there was still a war in progress and no longer a French Empire in existence, Florian did order a few topical changes in the circus's ambience and program. He had Stitches Goesle put pennants fluttering from the tops of the tents' sidepoles—alternately tricolor and red pennants—and had Boom-Boom Beck play for the opening and closing specs neither the imperial "Partant pour la Syrie" nor the revolutionary "Marseillaise" but the noncontroversial "Champs de la Patrie." However, he defiantly kept Offenbach's *Orfée* music for the dancing of the cancan girls before every performance.

Midget Grillon's dwarf horse was no longer introduced as Rumpelstilzchen, but as "Petit Poucet." On the other hand, the two hyenas were given even more recognizable German names than Anwalt-lawyer and Berater-lawyer; their cage in the menagerie tent now bore a large sign identifying them as "Hyène Wilhelm" and "Boueur Bismarck." The joeys contrived a routine in which Fünfünf was King "Vilain," Ferdi Spenz was Emperor "Lourdeur" and Nella Cornella was "La Belle France." The two mock monarchs abused, manhandled and all but raped poor France, until she flirtatiously inflamed their jealousies and provoked them into a duel with pistols borrowed from Colonel Ramrod. The act was more vulgar than funny, but the audiences invariably roared with laughter, especially when the two rogues shot each other "dead." The jossers also—even though there must have been many petty gougers in their ranks—thought it hilarious when, in the sideshow, Sir John played a poor peasant, with his Miss-Mittened hand as a snappishly greedy greengroceress:

"Mon Dieu, madame! You ask *four francs* for a cabbage? Why, the fruitier across the street sells them for a franc apiece."

"Then buy across the street, pignouf!"

"Hélas, he is all sold out."

"Tiens! When *I* am sold out of cabbages, I also ask only a franc apiece."

Those topical routines were hardly masterpieces of satire, but they were at least more mirthful to contemplate than what was happening outside the chapiteau. Every day's newspapers brought more despondent bulletins. The Prussian armies were continuing their approach to Paris, but with grim deliberation rather than impetuosity. After subduing the three largest cities to the east of Paris—Châlons, Reims and Troyes—the enemy armies split to encircle the capital at a distance. On the way, they easily took smaller communities—Sens in the south, Compiègne in the north—and detached sufficient forces to besiege and isolate any cities that put up any resistance—Chartres in the south, Amiens in the north—while their main forces simply went on by, to loop an iron noose around Paris, then gradually to tighten it, moving closer to the city on all sides. Meanwhile, the traveling emissary, Thiers, was having no success in pleading for diplomatic intervention from foreign powers. All were unanimous in declining to arbitrate on behalf of a dubiously self-appointed "government" of France.

The only lightsome items appearing in the Paris newspapers in those September days were the letters from readers—including some respected scientific men—putting forth ingeniously bizarre methods and "inventions" with which to best the Prussians, when and if they arrived. One writer suggested that, since there were not enough firearms or even swords to supply every ablebodied man in the city, a factory should immediately be set to manufacturing wooden lances of the jousting sort. Another writer proposed that every woman in Paris be issued a thimble tipped with a poison needle, which, by slaying any boche who assaulted her, would simultaneously defend her honor and the city as well. Any kind of poison would serve for that, said the writer, but he recommended as most suitable—what else?—prussic acid. Several patriots suggested floating blazing waves of "Greek fire" down the surface of the river Seine, and others suggested using the river itself as a weapon, by pumping poison into the water where the Seine debouched from the city, thereby to kill all the boches and their horses that drank from it downstream. Others thought it would be a good idea, if worse came to worst, to let loose the lions, tigers and other ferocious animals from the menagerie in the Jardin d'Acclimatation.

By September 16, the city was ringed on three sides, from Taverny in the northwest around to Lagny in the east and to Villeneuve in the south. A good number of people were leaving Paris, by cart and carriage and charabanc, along the westerly roads still open; one of the last persons to slip *into* the city was Deputy Louis Thiers, returning from his ineffectual peace mission. Two days later, the Prussians were in the Argenteuil suburb north of Paris proper, and at Le Bourget, and along the S-bend of the Marne River east of the Charenton district—and had not only taken Versailles, southwest of the city, but also were arrogantly setting up their main headquarters in the great château there. On September 20, the two encircling arms of their armies met at St-Germain-en-Laye, west of Paris, and the city was entirely surrounded, none of the enemy's siege lines farther than nine miles from Notre-Dame.

There then ensued a suspenseful wait for the attack that almost everyone was sure would come. For several days, Paris seemed a deserted city, with practically its entire population staying indoors. On the streets were only patrols of soldiers, sédentaires and moblots, to discourage burglars, looters, secret agents planting bombs, spies gathering information for the enemy, or any other such miscreants.

Florian was one of the few who still maintained that the Prussians would not lay waste the city, but simply wait for it to surrender. However, since every other public gathering place in Paris had battened down for the expected blow, and since the public itself was secluded in private, the Florilegium also suspended operations. And, in case Florian was wrong, Edge ordered precautionary measures. After all, he pointed out, the circus was situated in one of the more exposed positions on the fringe of the city—for the enemy had by now occupied the hill and palace of St-Cloud, whence they could look across the intervening three miles of suburbs, Seine and Bois, and actually *see* the tober.

So Edge loaded with real ammunition all his weapons, and even Florian's antique underhammer buggy rifle, and allotted the various firearms to the men who could best use them—himself, Yount, Fitzfarris and the three Jászi brothers. Those six men, plus all the Slovaks—armed with sledgehammers, axes, tent stakes—camped at the tober, while everyone else of the company stayed more safely and comfortably at their hotel in the very middle of the city.

Now and again a cannon boomed, from one direction or another, and made every citizen jump nervously. But those shots were from Paris's own ring of forts, and were fired only to let the enemy know that the city was prepared to defend itself. The Prussians had established their lines well beyond the range of those old bronze muzzle-loaders, so the fort commanders fired only occasionally, conserving their ammunition for a time when it might have some effect. Scouts sent out from the forts returned to report that the boches were bringing their own artillery from the east, and setting the guns in position—mostly south and east of the city—and those heavy steel, breech-loading cannon did have the range to belabor the forts that could not reach them. But, for the present at least, and almost contemptuously, the boche gunners did not deign to answer the biteless barks of the French cannons.

From the Hôtel de Ville issued a constant stream of newspaper notices and wall posters, adjuring the Parisians to keep calm and be brave, and not to listen to rumors but only to official pronouncements, and to await with stout hearts the deliverance that must surely, eventually come from French armies being levied in the provinces. For a short while, the Paris public *did* get some official bulletins of events taking place elsewhere in the country, because it was now made known that the government's engineers—before the Prussians had encircled the city and cut all other lines of communication with the outside world—had secretly laid a telegraph cable along the bed of the Seine. It extended underwater beyond what were now the siege lines in the south, so there continued to be communication—in cipher—between the Hôtel de Ville and secret agents out there. However, the government naturally passed on to its citizens only the more inspiriting bits of news, such as they were: the reassurance that many French cities—Chartres, Tours, Amiens, Le Mans, Strasbourg and others—were still holding firm against the enemy assaults on them. And a great deal of newspaper space and wall space was given to cheer the Parisians with the ringing war cry of General Antoine Chanzy, who was feverishly organizing a new Army of the Loire at Orléans: "The boches have only Paris; we still have France!"

The underwater telegraph line was in operation for only a few days before the Prussian sappers discovered its existence, dredged up a length of it and tapped their own keys into it. Either because they could not decipher the transmissions or, more likely, because they could and found that the information going in and out of the city was useless to them, they cut the cable. Thereafter, deprived of even the news their government thought fit for them to hear, the Parisians had to depend on rumors, which were plentiful. The government hurriedly and authoritatively squelched some of them, but let others proliferate without comment, and doubtless itself fostered some of them "for the good of public morale."

One of the first rumors to go about—when the city had been surrounded for more than a week but no enemy assault had yet been made—was that the boches were purposely, maliciously, cunningly prolonging the suspense, in expectation that the city folks' nerves would snap and they would be reduced to hysteria and helplessness by the time the attack *was* made. The government did nothing to kill that rumor, since it very well could be true, and instead encour-

aged the citizenry to show that they were *not* demoralized, and could not be. So
the people again ventured out of their residences into the streets. A few cafés,
then several, then many of them set out their streetside tables; some places of
entertainment unboarded their doors; a number of people even visited the Florilegium's tober to inquire when its ticket window would reopen.

There was no delusion that Parisian life would resume and go on as before;
the general feeling was only that life might as well go on as long as it could,
before the inevitable onslaught of the boches. So the merchants also opened
their shops and stalls, and the pushcart vendors again appeared on the streets,
but now they were not demanding outrageous prices for their wares. Quite the
contrary, their prices were lower than they ever had been, and those prices were
cut and cut again as the days went on and the suspense continued to mount.
The shopkeepers told their customers, with an air of great patriotism and self-
sacrifice, that they much preferred to empty their shelves in supplying their
beloved fellow Parisians, even at crippling personal loss, than to have any dealing
with any Prussian customers, should the city be occupied. The merchants did
not mention that they expected any occupying Prussians to be not customers but
confiscators, plundering and paying nothing at all.

The shopkeepers' avidity to make what money they could, while they could,
might also have been owing to another rumor. Since the government had managed secretly to lay a telegraph cable, people asked each other, might it not also
have managed to dig a tunnel from the city underneath the enemy lines and out
to the countryside? The query soon became a statement: that there *was* such a
tunnel, and through it flocks and herds and vegetable carts would be driven,
when necessary, to keep the city provisioned. The newspapers ridiculed that
notion, since it would have meant a project of about the magnitude of the oft-
discussed Channel tunnel, and would have taken years, and could hardly have
been done on the sly. But plenty of Frenchmen stubbornly went on believing in
it, and many even searched for the tunnel's entryway.

The government and the press let two other rumors go unchallenged. One
was that the boches occupying Versailles were looting the community, enslaving
all the males and raping all the females—including the nuns of the parishes of
Notre-Dame and St-Louis—and were carrying off to Berlin all the art treasures
of the château and the Trianons. The other rumor involved the gunboat *Farcy,*
which the French Navy had brought upriver just before the city was blockaded.
Paris need not fear the boches at all, went that story, because the gunboat could
freely cruise the sinuosities of the Seine throughout the city, the Ourcq Canal
and the Marne through Charenton. It would, almost unaided by the forts' cannons, bombard to rubble every Prussian artillery battery from Argenteuil to St-
Cloud to Meudon, etc., etc. That belief was no doubt comforting to the citizens,
except to any who strolled to the quai where the *Farcy* was moored, and took a
look at the stumpy howitzer that was its one and only gun.

Monsieur Roulette had not taken the Florilegium's *Saratoga* aloft since the
sixth of August, when Florian had ordered an ascension to help the city celebrate that day's news—false, as it had turned out—of the Maréchal MacMahon's "victory" in Alsace. For the subsequent month and a half, the *Saratoga* had
been folded away under its tarpaulin in the balloon wagon, hidden in the hope

that Paris would forget its existence, lest it be requisitioned for some kind of war use, or just as a source of prime silk.

So a group of the artistes, emerging from their hotel on a golden morning in late September, were rather pleasantly surprised to see another balloon in the sky. It was far to the southeast of the city, and not wafting about in free flight, but apparently anchored and being used for observation. As best they could make out from that distance, it was about the same size as the *Saratoga*, but was a faded yellow in color. What they could not make out was whether it was on the French or the Prussian side of the siege line, so Florian and Rouleau went off to Monsieur Nadar's photographic atelier to ask if he knew anything about it.

"Mais oui. It is my *Céleste*," Nadar said proudly. Then he went on, with his customary loquacity, "You need not have feared for your *Saratoga*, mes amis. Whenever the authorities—whenever *any* Frenchmen—think 'balloon,' they naturally and immediately think also 'Nadar!' I donated to the Gardes Mobiles three old ones I have long had stored in a warehouse. They were all in sad disrepair, and the *Céleste* is the only one that the quartermasters have yet been able to restitch and revarnish for service. The work was of course done under my supervision, but it was done hurriedly—haphazardly, I fear—and she was inflated with coal gas at the Gare de Lyon, then run up on a tether from the Quai de Bercy, to see if the observer she carries can make out what the boches are doing south of Charenton, in the way of preparation for an assault. Eh bien, with all the hurry, the *Céleste* is still extremely épuisée, and I frankly confess that I rejoice that *I* am not aloft in her. The observer, I gather, wishes that *he* were not. The only notes he has dropped from the gondola, since he has been up there today, say that the boches are doing absolutely nothing down below, except pointing and taking rifle shots at him. He is too high for the bullets to reach him, but he dreads the onset of a crise de nerfs. Pah! Were I he, I should be much more afraid that the suspension hoop's old linen ropes might fray and part and drop the gondola out of the sky."

"But the boches are doing absolutely nothing, eh?" murmured Florian. "It is as I anticipated. They do not plan to attack the city, simply to squat around it until Paris runs out of provisions and patience, and surrenders from pure ennui. Very well. To do our small part in relieving the ennui, our circus will resume its performances."

"And I," said Nadar, "am working on an invention of wartime utility, in collaboration with a colleague, Monsieur Dagron. *Our* contribution to relieving the ennui."

"Nom de Dieu," groaned Rouleau. "Not, I hope, one of those timbré notions like Greek fire or prussic acid."

"No, no," said Nadar, laughing. "An eminently practical photographic invention. But we shall not boast of it until we have perfected it."

"I look forward to hearing of it," said Florian. "And, monsieur, since you are so familiarly connected with the military, you are probably the most trustworthy source of information in Paris. I should be grateful if you would keep us apprised of any new circumstances that might affect our own situation."

"Most assuredly I will," said Nadar.

However, the troupers could see for themselves the next and portentous circumstances, a few days later. Across the lake from their tober, where the cattle and sheep were pastured and guarded, the herdsmen rode about, separated out some two score of the fattest beeves, then drove them past the circus lot, out of the Bois and through the Place de la Muette, clearly heading for the markets at les Halles.

"The city's food stock must be getting low already," Edge commented, "if they're starting to carve up their reserves."

"And those reserves won't last long in a city this size," said Florian. "When they're gone, surely the city will capitulate and this war will end."

"The food may last longer than you think, Governor," said Sunday. "Haven't you seen this afternoon's papers?" She handed him her copy of *Le Moniteur.* "The government is starting what it calls rationnement of the available meat. So it will stretch, but everybody will get a fair share of what there is. Each person will have a card, with tickets to be torn off for each week's allotment."

"It sounds like a decent system," said Edge.

"No, it doesn't, damn it," said Florian. "It sounds as if the government intends to hold out against surrendering, as long as possible."

"If that's what the people want," said Sunday, "and if they're willing to tighten their belts, what's wrong with that?"

"The longer the Prussians have to wait, my dear, the stiffer will be their terms for peace. Or they may get weary of waiting—it was France who declared this war, remember—and choose to wreak vengeance."

Sunday turned to Edge. "You've had experience of cities under siege, Zachary. Richmond, Petersburg. What do you think of Paris's chances?"

"Well, if the French are anything like the Confederates, it won't be lack of food that makes the people give in. They'll tighten their belts until the buckles scrape their backbones. But winter is coming soon, and winter brings sickness. Any kind of food, people can find substitutes for. Medicines, they can't."

"It says here," Florian read from the newspaper, "that heads of households are to apply to their local préfectures for the ration cards for all family members. I suppose I qualify here as head of household, so I shall go there with everybody's documents. Inasmuch as we are still being well fed at the hotel, we'll not be using the meat ration, so we will save that for the cats and bears and zekes. But other things than meat will soon be in short supply, so let us conserve our other fodder. I would not ordinarily desecrate a handsome park, but if government cattle can pasture in the Bois de Boulogne, so can ours. After dark, anyway. Colonel Ramrod, please instruct Abdullah to have his boys sneak out our road and ring horses, the bulls, the hump and the convicts—on halters, where necessary—after every night show, to graze and browse their fill of grass and shrubbery."

"Right, Governor," said Edge. When Florian had gone bustling off, Edge gazed appraisingly at Sunday and said, "Miss Butterfly, you continually surprise me. When you left Virginia, you couldn't have *spelled* Richmond and Petersburg, and you'd probably never even heard of them, let alone the Yankee siege of them."

"I do a lot of history reading, you know that. And not just about Europe. I want to learn about the country I came from, as much as the ones I find myself in."

"No book told you *I* was at those places."

"No. Well..." She looked away from him, and said in some slight embarrassment, "You know how gossip gets about. Everybody heard how you turned down a commission in the emperor's army, and refused ever to fight any more. And some wondered if..." She looked him in the face again. "I was sure you were no coward. Lord, the very first day I ever laid eyes on you, I watched you outshoot three other armed men, just to protect the rest of us. But... well... I shouldn't confess this, but I asked Obie. About what you did in your soldier days. That's how I knew you'd been under siege before. Obie told me everything—even what you did down in Mexico. How you found two troopers unhorsed and wounded by an ambush, and you gave them your own horse, and you stayed, all by yourself, holding off the Mexicans while they got safe away, and then you kept shooting even after you got wounded yourself, until a relief troop came. And how that earned you the Certificate of Merit and your colonel's commendation to officers' school and—"

"Whoa, whoa. History's one thing, but all that stuff is *ancient* history. Why should it make any difference to you, if I've ever been a coward or if I haven't?"

"It doesn't, really. I'd be in love with you anyway. I only want to know all I can about the man I—"

"Sunday... Sunday..." he sighed, shaking his head. "Not only am I old enough to be your father. Now you've just been reminding me that I was *killing men* before you were born."

"If I hadn't been born when I was, I would never have met you. And ever since I've known you, I've grown up as fast as I could. Maybe—Zachary, maybe we'll keep pace from now on."

Edge said, almost to himself, "There are other things." He turned and looked off across the city to the heights of Montmartre. "Just last night, I dreamed... we were standing up yonder, and she was pointing out things to me. The way she used to do in other high places... the tower in Pisa, the cathedral in Vienna. It was a pure pink spring day, and she was wearing that yellow dress of hers. I told her, look, we're finally here, Paris at last, and we can start all over. But she said no. She said it sadly—she didn't want to say it—but no was what she said, and I couldn't understand why. In the dream, you see, I didn't remember, but she did. She knew she was dead."

Sunday blinked her eyes very rapidly several times, to clear them, though Edge was not looking at her, and she swallowed several times before she could say, and softly, "I wouldn't ever intrude on your memories. Or your dreams. Or your privacy. I would only be there when you wanted me." And when Edge finally turned, she had gone away.

While Florian and most of the ordinary householders of Paris were hastening to apply for their ration cards, the merchants of Paris were just as hastily doing another volte-face. Given the evidence that the city was going to try to endure the siege, and that what supplies were already in the city were all there *would* be, the vendors—not only meat sellers, but also vendors of every kind of food, clothing, fuel and other commodity—again changed their prices, from yesterday's unprecedented lows to unprecedented new heights.

Since the government was also financially hard-pressed, it did not simply distribute its hoarded stocks to the public at large, but sold them to the retailers for whatever prices *it* could get, hence was in an ethically weak position to enforce any bans on civilian gouging. The result was that, from then on, the poorer people got less and less of worse and worse goods, while those who could and would pay the prices demanded found that the siege caused them extravagant expense but not much deprivation. The cafés and restaurants served what meals their patrons could afford—from absolute swill in the cheapest estaminets to filet mignon, perhaps just a *trifle* tough, in places like Vefour's, the Jockey Club and the Grand Hôtel du Louvre.

At the circus, during one afternoon show, Florian was standing near the back door of the chapiteau, watching le Démon Débonnaire put Brutus and Caesar through their "bridge" routine, when Nadar appeared beside him and asked:

"Have you, Monsieur Florian, any loved ones abroad who might be worried about your safety here in Paris?"

"Eh? No, not I. Not a soul in the world. What kind of question is that?"

"I thought you might wish to communicate with them. Via the world's first airborne mail."

"Eh?"

"There is no longer any postal service by road or rail. The boches have cut Paris's only telegraph line to the outside world. The government fears that our being isolated will be worse for the public morale than anything else we might lack in the way of sustenance or creature comforts. You know how we Frenchmen *must* converse."

His own conversing was just then drowned out by the audience's applause for Pemjean, Peggy and Mitzi. Florian drew Nadar out the door to the quieter backyard. Rouleau was out there and, when he saw the visitor, ambled over. Nadar went on, addressing both men:

"Since the boche troops are doing nothing worth the balloon observer's observing, our Minister of Posts, Monsieur Duroux, is appropriating the *Céleste*. He will send it, loaded with mail, over the enemy lines to somewhere in the unoccupied provinces. It will of course carry mostly official messages, but any citizens prepared to pay a high tariff may also send personal letters."

"To *where* in the unoccupied provinces?" Rouleau asked.

"Alors, that is hard to say. As you are aware, the prevailing winds here are westerly, and would carry an aérostat toward the Prussian-held areas. The Balloon Post, which is what Monsieur Duroux has named it, must await an easterly wind. And I, the expert adviser on this project, will ascertain the proper day and hour by sending up expendable miniature balloons made of oiled paper. Then, of course, if the aéronaute does succeed in flying westward over the enemy lines and landing in some safe place far beyond, he will not be returning. He cannot reasonably expect to land near any source of gas to reinflate his aérostat."

"Well, the idea is ingenious and daring," said Florian, "but it strikes me as slightly slapdash. You have one balloon, which can make only a one-way flight, delivering the post perhaps to some peasant village where no one can read—"

"However, once he is safely beyond the Prussians, the aéronaute can proceed overland, with his precious burden, to—say, to General Chanzy at Orléans—or to any city that does have communication with the rest of France and the world."

"And then what?" asked Rouleau. "They have no way of communicating here. You will not even know whether your one-time, one-way Balloon Post landed safely *anywhere*."

"Aha! That, yes," said Nadar, holding up a finger. "The aéronaute of the *Céleste* will carry with him also a number of carrier pigeons. One or more of them should get back with the good word. Meanwhile, a second of my balloons is being refurbished and prepared for service. If the first flight is successful, there will be another, and then many more. My *third* balloon is being carefully taken to pieces, so that its gores will serve as patterns. A whole corps of seamstresses is being assembled, and we shall turn the Gare d'Orléans from a railway station to a balloon-making factory. It might as well be; no trains are going in or out of it; but coal gas it *can* provide. Those balloons produced in quantity will be done cheaply—using only calico for the bags and hemp for the nets and ropes; there is not enough silk and linen to be had—and God knows what their clack valves and other fittings will be like, manufactured by conscripted and thick-fingered mechanists. But the mass aérostats are not intended for repeated use or ex-tended service, only to make a single flight apiece."

"Again I say ingenious," said Florian. "But I still fail to see the merit in sending letters and official messages *out,* if none can come back *in.* A homing pigeon can carry only—what?—surely not the weight of a single letter."

"Fifty grams. Not quite two of your American ounces. Hence the invention, of which I earlier spoke, contrived by Monsieur Dagron and myself. We photo-graph a page of writing. Then we take the negative plate and, by means of a diminishing lens, focus it down almost to a pinpoint and onto one minuscule portion of a sheet of sensitized rice paper. On a single, sheer, nearly weightless piece of rice paper only so big"—he framed a small rectangle with his fingers—"we can reduce to print an entire Paris newspaper, or the equivalent in personal letters, enciphered government documents, whatever."

"But who can read them?"

"Anyone—with a limelight lanterne magique and a compensating magnifier lens. If the first Balloon Post is successful, then the second flight will carry Dagron along. He will establish himself at the government délégation at Tours, as my outside communicant, but he will also teach the process to any other photographer in France who wishes to imitate it. Thus our outgoing aérostats can carry, in miniature, all the mail and news of Paris, and the homing pigeons can each bring back here a substantial quantity. No doubt two or more birds would carry duplicate packets, to allow for loss to hawks, hunters, accidents..."

"Fantastic," murmured Rouleau.

"The new slang word is éléfantasque," said Nadar, with a smile, gesturing back to where he had just seen Brutus and Caesar. "Possibly inspired by the people's elephantine hunger. Another new and popular slang word is queue."

"Queue?"

"Queue. From the tail on that letter of the alphabet. Does it not perfectly describe the line one has to stand in at every shop and stall, sometimes for hours, waiting to buy anything at all? And by the way, I must remark that neither your elephants nor yourselves seem yet to be suffering from any scantiness of proven-der."

"We make do," said Florian. "It is horrendously costly, living at the Grand Hôtel and diverting our market rations to our animals—and without ever raising our admission prices—but we do it. I only hope that our living well is requited to those who cannot, by the thrills and mirth we provide them so cheaply. And thank you, monsieur, for telling me about the queue. I must work that new popularity of the word into one of our comic turns. We do try to keep up with the times. Listen."

He led Nadar back inside the door flap to hear Fünfünf and the Kesperle engaged in one of their patter routines.

"You were doing *what*, pignouf?" demanded the white-face.

The toby meekly shrugged and said, "I was teaching my horse Mouflard to live without food in these hard days."

"What? How?"

"Eh bien, I merely fed him less and less. And finally nothing."

The audience tittered and Fünfünf barked, "Well?"

"Such a great loss," whimpered the Kesperle. "Just as Mouflard learned to live without eating"—sob—"he died."

The audience roared with laughter.

I 2

THOSE who saw the *Céleste* take the first slow steps of its epochal voyage were the night people of Paris—market porters, whores, garbage pickers. The balloon had been inflated by night and then, its gondola weighted with many extra sandbags, it was anchored atop a heavy brewery wagon. Before dawn, four dray horses began the long haul across the whole northern extent of the city toward the Butte Montmartre. Since that took some three hours, by full daylight people crowded every curbside to watch and marvel and cheer. With the immense, pale-yellow bag bobbing above the roofs of most of the buildings on its route, it must have excited similar wonderment in any Prussians watching through glasses from St-Cloud.

The balloon's wagon was followed by a carriage in which rode the Minister of Posts and his chief adviser to the Balloon Post, Monsieur Nadar, and the experienced aéronaute who had volunteered for this mission, a Monsieur Mangin, and, as an interested observer, the Florilegium's Monsieur Rouleau. In the carriage was also a small crate of six homing pigeons, cooing and fluttering sleepily, and a canvas bag carrying a hundred and twenty-five kilograms of dispatches from the Hôtel de Ville, hopefully addressed to the government offices in Tours. Monsieur Mangin held on his lap his few special provisions for the journey: a hamper of sandwiches and wine, a pocket compass and a small aneroid barometer.

Behind the carriage came another wagon, bearing a dozen or more of the biggest and burliest porters recruitable from les Halles, because the horses could get the *Céleste*'s carrier only halfway up the steep Montmartre. From there, the porters lent their weight and muscle to the sandbagged basket and manhandled it—the bag above bouncing and heaving—the rest of the way to the bare earthen square before the Church of St-Pierre. Mangin accompanied the handlers, concerned that they not scrape the gondola against a rock outcrop or get the suspension ropes tangled with any tree or windmill. But Nadar hurried on ahead, Rouleau with him, to where his assistants had been sending up the trial paper balloons since dawn, some of them let to float free, others on strings. So Nadar was pleased to be able to report to Mangin, when he and the aérostat and its bearers got to the top of the hill:

"Conditions are favorable, mon confrère. There is an east wind between one thousand and fifteen hundred meters. You must, in any case, achieve an altitude of a thousand meters before you are over the enemy lines, to go beyond their range of rifle shot. Since the merdeux coal gas is so logy of lift, we do not want you drifting before you get up there, so we will pay you out on the tether. Here on the hilltop, we are at about one hundred meters. Therefore, when you feel the rope stop your ascent, you will know that we have counted off nine hundred, and your aneroid should indicate approximately one thousand. At that point, you cast off the tether, and get higher if you can. After that, ami, you and the *Céleste* are on your own. God go with you."

The launching was done with little ceremony, except for the Minister of Posts standing at a respectfully stiff salute, hand to forehead, the whole time. The gondola was attached to the end of the rope wound in a bulky coil on an iron windlass securely spiked to the hard ground, the extra sandbags were detached and then the rope let unwind. The balloon rose at only a slight angle from the vertical, while Nadar counted the turns of the big windlass crank in the hands of his assistants, making allowance for the *Céleste*'s slight sidewise drift and the bellying slack of the rope, and at last called, "Halte!" In just a moment, the balloon high overhead gave an exultant leap higher yet and nicely to the west-ward. And a moment after that, the loosed rope came tumbling down, and the Minister Duroux had to drop his salute and make an undignified jump to avoid being hit by it.

As the balloon dwindled westward, Nadar watched it through a pair of field glasses. The others on the hilltop could hear a far-off crackle of rifle fire, and then the cannons of Fort Valérien out there squandered a fair number of boom-ing shots at the enemy, intended only to disturb the riflemen's aim. Nadar said, "Mangin is dropping sand to gain more altitude." Then he chuckled, said, "He is dropping something else, too," and handed the glasses to Rouleau. Jules focused on the now distant yellow bag and said in puzzlement, "What is it? Is he sprin-kling *confetti* on the boches?"

"Four thousand of my calling cards," Nadar said proudly. "I thought the sa-lauds ought to know who is at least partly to be credited for this grand coup d'éclat."

Then Nadar, Duroux and Rouleau all hurried back down the hill to their carriage and, in it, to the rue de Berne house of the elderly pigeon fancier who had lent his birds to the enterprise. They would have gone right on up to his roof, but the old man said, "Patience, messieurs, your messenger cannot even have landed anywhere yet. Stop and let my old woman make breakfast for you."

So they did, though it wasn't much of a meal. By now all the market staples were being adulterated by government edict—the coffee eked out with ground acorns, the petit pains baked of a flour that was "officially" a mixture of wheat, oats and rice, but tasted and chewed more like hay. Then they and the old man climbed up to sit impatiently among the dovecotes and chimney pots and wash lines. They waited until after midday, came downstairs again for a meal of sawdust-tasting sausage, more of the straw bread and some very acid wine, re-turned to the roof and waited—rather anxiously now—until finally, near sunset, the first pigeon came flapping home.

The old man reached into the roost where it had settled, gently brought it out, gently detached the little tin tube from its leg and, with a bow, handed that to the Minister of Posts. Duroux opened it with slightly tremulous fingers, unrolled the wee ribbon of paper and read, with a smile of triumph:

" 'Landed safely eleven o'clock Craconville near River Eure.' Mon Dieu, it took him only three hours to traverse more than eighty kilometers! 'Proceeding muleback Rouen, thence railway Tours. Vive la République!' Messieurs, mes amis, the Balloon Post is a success!"

"Truly a success," said Rouleau, when he got to the tober and recounted the day's events to the troupers who came crowding about him. "A second pigeon arrived shortly afterward, bearing a duplicate of the message. Mangin was to release three on landing, and save three to send from Tours."

"We all watched the *Céleste* go over," said Agnete. "Det var vaeldig, Jules, but not nearly so fine as your *Saratoga*."

"However, the *Saratoga* has never made such a long flight," Rouleau said, a little wistfully. "Something like fifty miles. And on an errand of genuine importance."

"Quatsch! Be not envious," said Willi. "It and you have never been shot at, either."

"No," Rouleau conceded. "There is that to be grateful for."

Two days later, the troupe watched another balloon go westward high above the Bois. Nadar had not even waited to make sure that any of Mangin's other pigeons returned from Tours before launching this second of his restored old balloons, the *Neptune*. He was eager to get this one off, for it carried, besides the volunteer aéronaute, Nadar's photographer-colleague Dagron, with his reducing-camera apparatus. The first homing pigeon brought the good news that the *Neptune* had landed safely at Mantes, also on the river Eure and well beyond the Prussian lines.

When, eventually, the various other pigeons brought word from Tours that both aéronautes, Dagron and all the Paris-sent mail had arrived there—and that Dagron was hurrying to set up his equipment to miniaturize newspapers and letters for transmittal *to* the city—Nadar launched yet another balloon. He had no more of his old and proven ones to send. This grandly named *Les États-Unis* was the first of the hastily mass-manufactured calico products from the new "balloon factory" in the Gare d'Orléans. At least its volunteer pilot was an expert, Louis Godard, as famous for his aerial exploits as was Nadar himself. So he made the *États-Unis* perform its mission efficiently also, landing safely, like the others, near the Eure, and Godard proceeding overland to Tours.

But this left in Paris no other experienced aéronautes, so the next of the calico balloons to go westward, the *Ville-de-Florence*, had for its pilot a certain Gaston Tissandier, who was an estimable chemist but only a novice balloonist. It was afterward unclear whether Tissandier made some mistake in his valve-working aloft or whether the *Florence* burst a seam in midair, because the pilot's report of the accident was written hastily, briefly and almost illegibly, with his left hand. What was certain was that the *Florence* had plummeted untimely to the ground, and very near an encampment of Hessian soldiers. Tissandier had suffered only a broken right arm in the crash, and had had time to scrawl the left-handed message and get a pigeon away with it, before the Hessians came to capture him and the eighty kilograms of Balloon Post in his charge.

The Paris newspapers, which had published praiseful and euphoric accounts of the successful balloon flights, suppressed the news of this failure. But Nadar came to the Florilegium tober in person, to tell Rouleau and Florian of what had happened to the *Ville-de-Florence*.

"I feel it only fair to be frank," he said, "because I have come also to ask you,

Monsieur Rouleau, to volunteer yourself, and you, Monsieur Florian, to volunteer your *Saratoga*." Rouleau looked interested, but Florian frowned, so Nadar quickly went on, "Not for the Balloon Post, messieurs. For that, we can continue to take our chances with unsound craft and inept aéronautes. No, I ask you to lend your aérostat and your habilité for a much more vital mission. One in which we cannot risk calamity."

"If you could be more specific...?" said Florian.

"Today's pigeons from Tours brought the first of what Dagron and I have dubbed the 'micromessages.' Tomorrow's newspapers will publish the first news from the outside world that we have had in all these weeks of siege. For proof, I tell you in advance these few news. The Italian Army has taken Rome from Pope Pius, and King Victor Emmanuel has proclaimed it the new capital city of a *totally* unified Italy. Prosper Mérimée has just died at Cannes and, in Bavaria, Richard Wagner has just married the daughter of the Abbé Franz Liszt."

Florian noted with amusement that Nadar, like all Frenchmen, pronounced Liszt "Lits," but he remarked only, "We thank you for the news, though I fail to see what it has to do with our—"

"The micromessages also bring distressing news of the war's progress and the general political climate in the provinces. I am not at liberty to divulge state secrets, but I can tell you this. The government's feeble délégation at Tours is incapable of rallying the unoccupied parts of France to the support of our new republic. Someone from Paris, from the Hôtel de Ville, someone of high rank in the Council of National Defense, must get *out* of Paris, so that he is visible to the whole of France and can take control of it."

"Literally *fly* out of here?" exclaimed Rouleau. "Old President Trochu?"

"No, the president deems his presence here necessary to the city's survival of the siege. Just as well, ami." Nadar laughed and stressed the pun: "Surely you would not want your fine balloon *trop chu* from out of the sky!" Rouleau and Florian dutifully laughed, too. "And Foreign Minister Favre refuses to go, unashamedly confessing that he is terrified at the thought of ascending from the ground. So it will be Minister of the Interior Gambetta."

"From what I hear on the streets," said Florian, "no one would care if *he* fell out of the sky."

"He is not a popular man, true, and not likable, but if anyone can integrate the factions of the government it is Léon Gambetta. Now, I grant, friend Jules, that in just a few hours' flight with him, you will doubtless come to loathe him. Nevertheless, I ask you—the Republic implores you—to make that flight. Yours is a stalwart silk balloon, much more trustworthy than our patchwork factory products. Also you have the hydrogen generator, so the *Saratoga* will be much more nimble and maneuverable than ours full of sluggish coal gas."

Rouleau looked at Florian and raised his eyebrows inquiringly.

"Well..." said Florian. "We are not making use of the thing, and are not likely to, until France gets back to normal. Very well, I will lend the *Saratoga*. However, any volunteering of your services, Monsieur Roulette, must be done by yourself."

"Oh, I am willing enough," said Rouleau, trying hard to dissemble what was really eagerness. He even said modestly, "But, if so much depends on the pilot of this flight, Monsieur Nadar, I should defer to you, as being by far my superior in matters aérostatique."

Nadar looked offended. "What do you take me for, monsieur? I should be happy to defy Madame Nadar's meddlesome command that I refrain from flying ever more. But I would never be so presumptuous as to purloin a colleague's conveyance—and cheat him of the glory of putting it to such splendidly patriotic derring-do!"

"Well," said Florian, "since this may be the *Saratoga*'s last ascension from Paris for some time, we ought to make one hell of a spectacle of it. I shall go and have a word with my chiefs."

Thus it was that, on a bright blue morning in October, while an inflated Balloon Post calico balloon was slowly towed by the brewery horses northwestward from the Gare d'Orléans toward the Butte Montmartre, a flamboyant circus parade went noisily northeastward from the Bois de Boulogne toward the same destination. Florian left behind on the tober only the caged animals and most of the crewmen. As always, he led the parade in his rockaway, with Boom-Boom and the windjammers roaring martial music in the band wagon right behind. On the wagons following, the artistes were all in costume, waving and smiling. In the middle of the procession strode the two elephants, Brutus hauling the wagon in which the *Saratoga* lay folded, Caesar drawing the two generator machines in tandem. All of the circus's riders—Colonel Ramrod, Clover Lee, Monday and the Jászi brothers—were mounted. The colonel and Monday put their horses to fancy steps, and Clover Lee, Árpád, Gusztáv and Zoltán did stands and poses as they rode. Abdullah, Fünfünf, the Emeraldina and the Kesperle were afoot, capering and doing acrobatics. Daphne was on her Plimpton skates and the Quakemaker on the velocipede, both of them wheeling in and out of the line of march, among the watchers who crowded the sidewalks, in and out of shop doors. The calliope brought up the rear, bellowing so loudly that it had to be audible out at St-Cloud, and the Prussians there must have marveled more than ever at the antics of their besieged but irrepressible foe—seeing the calico balloon bobbing its way along behind the rooftops, apparently to the accompaniment of all that uproarious music.

The parade pulled up at the base of Montmartre and remained there in the Place Blanche, the band and the calliope taking turns playing for the entertainment of the great crowd that had followed, while only the elephants drew their wagon and tanks on uphill to the halfway point. There, Rouleau and Beck and the *Saratoga*'s Slovak tenders began its laying out and the charging of its generators. In the meantime, Nadar's porters muscled the Balloon Post's aérostat past them and on to the top of the hill. This one was an unadorned white bag, except for its crudely painted-on name, *George Sand*. It could have gone off straightaway, for Nadar's assistants had already determined that the wind aloft was in the right quarter. But Nadar had decreed that both balloons should depart together, and had installed an extra windlass of rope for that purpose, reasoning that a dual launch would confuse and make even more ineffectual the rifle fire from the enemy lines.

So, while the *Saratoga* slowly filled, Rouleau stood and smoked cigarettes—which he would not be able to do once he was near either balloon—and chatted with the *George Sand*'s aéronaute, a Monsieur Revilliod, and with his own two passengers-to-be, the Minister Gambetta and his secretary, Monsieur Spuller.

Those two men wore heavy fur coats and an air of ill-concealed apprehension, and they nervously eyed the two aircraft and anxiously inspected and reinspected the cargo they were taking along: satchels of clothing and personal belongings, satchels of official papers, a bale of political tracts, baskets of sandwiches and wine, a crate of six pigeons. Léon Gambetta was as unprepossessing in person as he was in reputation—short, fat, bearded, of swarthy and oily complexion, looking very much what he was, the son of an immigrant Genoese grocer—and, for a time, Rouleau wondered how the man could nervously eye both of the far-apart balloons at once, until he realized that Gambetta's left eye was of glass, and disconcertingly independent of his good one.

By the time the *Saratoga* was fully inflated and lugged up to stand alongside the *George Sand,* almost all the circus troupers had also climbed the hill to say their farewells to Rouleau. Only Kostchei the Deathless stayed below, because hill climbing was such a chore for him. Most of the male artistes gave Rouleau a hearty handshake and encouraging slaps on the back. The females—and Willi —each gave him a warm embrace and a kiss on the cheek. Florian said mocksternly, "You keep the old *Saratoga* safe now, my lad, until you can bring it back to us or we can come to you." Rouleau said he would and promised to correspond by way of the micromessage pigeons, then climbed into his gondola.

So did Gambetta and Spuller, nervous or not, and their luggage was handed in by the Slovaks, and Rouleau disposed it for best balance. Then Rouleau and Revilliod exchanged "ready" nods, then nodded also to Nadar, who cried, "Allez houp!" and his men pulled the windlasses' crank pins. As the two ropes unspooled and the balloons rose side by side, Gambetta—though crouching protectively low in the basket and clutching tight to its rim—summoned up courage enough to shout to the people rapidly dwindling below him, "Vive la France! Vive la République!"

Down in the Place Blanche, the collected crowd raised a mighty huzzah and the band and calliope together thundered into what must have been history's loudest-ever rendition of "Champs de la Patrie." When Nadar gestured to stop the windlasses, everyone was bent backward almost like Kostchei, keeping watch of the double ascension. Then the two ropes came tumbling down, and the balloons leapt up and away—the more buoyant *Saratoga* immediately going both higher in the sky and faster to the westward than the *George Sand.* A minute or two later, the tumult of band-calliope-and-crowd noise was outshouted by the dramatic booming of cannons at Fort Valérien, and, if the Prussians were frustratedly sniping with their rifles out yonder, that noise was not at all to be heard.

The circus troupers were accustomed to the sporadic cannon shots from the various Paris forts, but here on the heights of Montmartre the concussion of those shots was unexpectedly jolting. Both the clay hill underfoot and the crisp air roundabout seemed to rock at each explosion and to quiver for a good while afterward. Since everyone else was still straining to look upward, no one noticed that Monday Simms was not. She had a beatific smile on her face, her eyes were glazed and unfocused and she was blissfully rub-rubbing her thighs together.

It had been nearly noon when the balloons got off, so it was not until that night, during the circus's late performance, that Nadar arrived in the chapiteau to report to Florian. The first pigeons, he said, had come from both the *Saratoga*

and the *George Sand,* announcing that both had landed intact and well beyond
the reach of the boches. When Florian pressed for details, Nadar shrugged and
said:

"Eh bien, Monsieur Rouleau *did,* unfortunately, set his gondola down in the
top branches of a tree. He and Gambetta and Spuller had to clamber down, in
full view of a crowd of amazed, admiring and amused peasants. It was hardly the
way the French government's minister-at-large would have wished to make his
first appearance among the countrymen he hopes to lead."

"Oh, drat," muttered Florian. "Monsieur Roulette must be mortified."

"I wager he is not," Nadar said blithely. "I told both of you that, even on short
acquaintance, he would probably come to detest Léon Gambetta. I would lay
money that Rouleau put him atop that tree deliberately. Anyway, they all got
down unscathed, if undignified. Then they got the balloon down unharmed, as
well, and they and it are now en route to Tours. So is the other aéronaute,
Revilliod, with his Balloon Post cargo."

Florian waited until the act in progress was finished—Mademoiselle Papillon
and Maurice LeVie on the trapeze—and the performers had taken their bows,
then stepped into the pista with his megaphone to trumpet the good news. The
audience applauded, cheered and stamped as if they had just witnessed another
tremendous circus feat—and so did all the circus company.

So the city was no longer deaf and mute to the rest of the world. The
Balloon Post worked better than even the Minister Duroux might have hoped
—balloons continuing to be sent off every three or four days, and the carrier
pigeons returning with Dagron micromessages. There was a return to almost
normal interchange of personal letters between the Parisians and their relatives and friends elsewhere, and the Paris newspapers were able to publish,
not too tardily, news of what battles against the Prussians were still going on
in various parts of France, plus non-war news from provincial French papers
and even from foreign ones. Much of the news that came in was bad—for
example, that the city of Toul had fallen to the enemy as long ago as the
eighteenth of September, and Strasbourg on the twenty-eighth. And some of
the good news was almost as depressing—for example, the revelation that the
boches occupying Versailles were *not* looting the château and the Trianons,
and *not* raping nuns or anybody else. They were being very well behaved,
indeed, and the Versailles shopkeepers were so prosperously thriving on Prussian custom that they were freely expressing disdain of Paris's "stupide, ob-
stiné" resistance to a similar occupation.

Some of the news from overseas was merely interesting news—that the Arc-
tic explorer Nordenskiöld had penetrated into the icy interior of Greenland, that
a certain Schliemann claimed to be excavating in Turkey the true site of the
ancient city of Troy. But other items might have been variously received by various readers—for example, the news that in an election in the Utah Territory
women had voted, and that in Lexington, Virginia, the great General Robert E.
Lee had died. The latter item touched a chord of sympathy in every circus
trouper who had been with the Florilegium when it visited that obscure little
town, and the news genuinely saddened some of them, most notably Edge and
Yount. It also grieved most Parisians, since practically all of them had been

pro-Confederate during that American war, but it doubtless caused no mourning at Versailles, where General Philip Sheridan was still keeping company with the Prussian high command.

Winter came early and bitter to Paris. After the crisply invigorating first weeks of October, it turned so cold that, on the night of the twenty-fourth, the icy blue and green draperies of the aurora borealis undulated eerily in the Paris sky, a sight never seen in the lifetime of the oldest citizens. People thronged the streets that night, pointing and making hushed exclamations of awe. But the next night no one was out looking at the heavens, for any northern lights would have been invisible above the clouds pouring rain. The rest of October and the rest of the winter continued like that, days of steely cold alternating with slightly milder ones that merely dumped or drizzled a chill rain. So, except for the occasional morning hoarfrost, there was never any snow or ice, only coldness, then wetness, then coldness again. At the Florilegium's tober, the ground underfoot would one day ring like slag and the next day be unpleasantly mushy to walk on, like decayed flesh, and the roustabouts were forever having to tighten or slacken the tent guys. Also, the Bois de Boulogne, like every other park space in Paris, now continuously exuded a clammy gray mist that smelled like fungus. But that was perfume compared to the miasmas and frequent overflows that oozed up from the overworked sewers under the city streets.

The householders who had hoarded fuel soon ran out of it, and the government could not peddle its stocks of coal, even at the prospects of profiting from it, because the coal was needed for, among other things, the generation of gas for the Balloon Post. Many of the poorer dwellings had no heat whatever, and all commercial buildings were prohibited from having any, and the few rich families that had not fled the city before the siege were not saying what provision they might have made for heating their mansions. But even such a palatial establishment as the Grand Hôtel du Louvre now provided a modicum of heat and hot water only for the four hours before midnight, to give its guests a fairly comfortable time in which to undress, bathe and get into bed. It also suspended indefinitely the operation of its proudest amenity, the steam-powered ascenseur.

Eventually the Ministry of Resources gave the Parisians permission to cut firewood anywhere they could find it. The people immediately seized on the handiest, which meant the trees growing on the city streets. While men took saws and axes to the trunks, children clambered about overhead, breaking off and taking home what branches they could. When a tree was felled and cut up and carted away, the women came to gather every dropped twig and scrap of bark. Even the venerable chestnuts lining the Champs-Elysées, the lindens of the Luxembourg and Tuileries gardens disappeared. Only then did the wood scavengers hie themselves as far afield as the parks of Vincennes, Montsouris, the Butte Chaumont and the Bois de Boulogne. The Florilegium's troupers, fond of "their" Bois, were glad that it, though as large as all the other parks together, actually suffered least. True, all of its old and big trees were taken, but so much of that onetime forest now consisted of new plantings that the saplings and shrubs were not worth the scavengers' trouble of cutting.

Even in these drear days, the mass of Parisians still frequently left their own chill quarters, braving the even colder and danker outdoors, to flock to the theatres and indoor circuses. That might have seemed inconsistent with the prevailing misery, but actually the people did it as much for the warmth of crowding together in one chamber as for the entertainment. The theatres were still showing only "significant" plays and operas like *Hernani* and *Le Prophète*, and even the circuses leaned to "inspirational" horseback pageants like "Le Cid Defeats the Moors" and "Charge of the Light Brigade." The Florilegium's canvas chapiteau *had* to be full to be warm—but full it was, at every show, with people who were weary of heavy-handed propagandisme and came for sheer fun and diversion.

Florian's refusal to conform to the killjoy climate of the time brought not only sfondone houses, but also a new performer. Clover Lee's longtime best friend outside the company, young Giuseppina Bozzacchi, came to tell Florian that she was unemployed and bored—and half frozen, sitting most of every day in her Hôtel Crillon, which was also skimping on heat. *Coppélia* had closed, at the first official frown on frivolity, and no other ballets were being mounted, ballet being notoriously incapable of conveying "significance." Giuseppina said she would be happy to do any sort of dancing for the circus, even join the cancan girls, and demand no pay, just to keep limber, and to be warm for a few hours each afternoon and evening, and to feel herself still an artiste.

Florian was delighted to welcome her, and insisted on her taking a salary, and of course would not waste her talent on the cancan. But she could hardly do ballet in the sawdust, so Florian and Kapellmeister Beck devised a routine in which Giuseppina again impersonated a mechanical toy. She was billed and announced as "The Music-Box Dancer" and performed atop the pista's padded curbing, doing several circuits of the ring, almost entirely en pointe, the way music-box dolls did, while cimbalist Elemér played, solo, a very creditable imitation of a music box tinkling one of Offenbach's barcarolles. For all the depression of wartime, the Parisians had not forgotten the pretty and gifted Giuseppina, or lost an iota of their adoration of her, so her little divertissement was far more pleasurably received than any of the "meaningful" epics being staged downtown.

Giuseppina continued to reside at the Crillon, as the other troupers did at the Grand Hôtel du Louvre, and none of them complained of the austerities imposed at either place. Not even the oldest and ricketiest guests of the Grand complained of having to climb the stairs instead of riding up and down, because all the premier hotels were now charging so much for meals that their luxurious accommodations came cheap by comparison. And the patrons of their expensive dining halls *were* still eating, which was more than many Parisians could boast nowadays. If the "cotelettes de veau" advertised on the dinner carte were frequently recognizable as filets of filly, they were at least meat.

For those who had to buy their meat in the markets, the allowable ration had now shrunk to fifty grams per person per day, and by now horsemeat was no longer the pitiful resource of the very poor; it was practically the only meat to be found. The government helped out here, by selling to the knackers all its horses not absolutely necessary to the defense forces, and those horses requisitioned as "voluptuary surplus" from the stables of rich families who had left town and could not protest, and all the horses that had once constituted the imperial stables—including the famous pair of trotters that had been a gift from Tsar Alexander to Louis Napoléon.

"Those two horses," said Florian, "Louis told me were valued at fifty-six thousand francs, nearly twelve thousand dollars American, enough to purchase a fine house and grounds. Now they wind up on the butchers' scales at the same government-mandated price as the meat of a worn-out cab horse, fifty centimes the kilogram."

But even at that official price—and the butchers invariably demanded at least four times as much—horsemeat was beyond the reach of the poor families who had used to depend on it. So stray dogs and cats began to vanish from the streets, and so did unguarded pets. The city's pigeons and starlings, having now so few trees to perch in, became the prey of birdlime traps and wire snares laid on park lawns and windowsills. About this time, two more linguistic terms came, like "queue," into everyday usage: "osséine" and "seine de la Seine," but only the latter had anything to do with the river. Osséine was a market product promoted by the Bureau of Public Health as a meat substitute for the poor, and affordable by them. Affordability was its only attraction; osséine was a repellent gelatin of boiled-down horse hoofs and bones, which could either serve as a nauseous replacement for olive oil or be dissolved in hot water to make a disgusting sort of bouillon.

"Seine de la Seine" meant what it sounded like: netting for fish in the river. As in happier days, old men and other idlers still dangled fishing poles off the quais and bridges, but, as always, their catches were infrequent, undependable and, at best, only one fish at a time. So more people more determinedly descended on the river with home-woven nets, to seine for more copious hauls. They caught them, too—for a while at least, until the Seine got full of drift ice that tore up their nets—but their catches were mostly of dace. Dace were hardly epicurean fare and, besides, were on average so small that, subtracting scales, fins, guts and bones, even a copious haul might make only one meal for one family.

The nouveaux fishermen soon found it easier and more productive to bait hooks or traps with tallow or osséine and to fish in the sewers or in the garbage-strewn alleys—for rats. They did, and they caught them, and some of the more fastidious set up as vendors to sell the catches, earning enough to afford for themselves other provender. But many who caught the rats and all who bought them did so to cook and eat them, and they declared rat to be rather more palatable than dace, much more palatable than osséine, and a hell of a lot more palatable than nothing at all.

The curators of the Jardin d'Acclimatation had always before fed their zoo cats and other carnivores on horsemeat. Then, when that meat began to appear on tables even at the luxury clubs and restaurants, they bought dogs and cats to feed the menagerie. But, when butchers of dog and cat flesh also became fixtures in the Paris markets, the government finally decided that it could not, in fairness to the hungry lower classes, go on maintaining those merely decorative dependents. An official order came down for the slaughter and sale of the zoo animals themselves, even unto the two elephants, Castor and Pollux, that had been the pets of a generation of Paris children. In so acting, the government turned a handsome profit for its defense treasury, because, when those exotics were auctioned, the butchers bid them up to prices far in excess of what the Jardin had paid for them. Then the meats were sold at retail at prices that only the very rich households and the most expensive dining establishments could pay. It became, among the upper classes, très distingué to be able to say casually, "We dined on a salmis of camel hump at Voisin last night," or "The count and countess served us an émincé of elephant trunk"—or haunch of zebu, yak tongue, galantine of cassowary, civet of tiger, whatever, as long as the zoo delicacies lasted.

Some others of the haut monde thought it more chic and clever to make demonstration, however transparently opportunistic, that their hearts were with The People. They had their clubs or favored restaurants lay on at least one meal of what the poor folk were eating—horse, dog, cat, even rat—and resolutely sat down to eat those things, and made sure that the newspapers carried full and glowing reports of their having done so, with an appended list of the ghastly carte de diner: "Consommé de la moelle de cheval, rable de chien Alsatien au jus, saucisse des ratons aux fines herbes..." Then *they* went about complacently remarking that a saddle of dog was quite as good as mutton, that jugged cat was indistinguishable from jugged hare, that rat made as good a ragoût as squirrel, or facetiously arguing the comparative tenderness of horse and mule steaks.

If such well-publicized condescension was intended to persuade The People to be content with their miserable lot, it did not, for the Communards were much more effectively agitating in the low quarters in the city. Whenever they could whip a crowd to enough of a frenzy that it had the strength to march in protest, march they did. And the Communards made sure always to march the mob, bearing the ominous red flags of revolution, through the upper-class and bourgeois neighborhoods, before converging on the Hôtel de Ville to shout vituperation at President "Trop Chu" and the "imitation-imperialist" government in general. Some of those marchers, never yet disabused of belief in the "secret tunnel," loudly demanded that it be utilized, that relief provisions be brought in from outside and freely distributed. Others, usually the Communard agitators themselves, just as loudly yelled that the tunnel *was* being employed, but only to supply oysters and champagne and other dainties to the decadent favored few. That shout always made the whole crowd even more furious and started them throwing rocks.

"Totally irrational, totally French," Florian said drily, to his chiefs convened in conference. "However, these two latest deliriums sweeping the city—the plutocrats' caprice for eating jungle meats, and the proletariat's more understandable demand for *anything* to eat—could mean problems for us. I hear that the other circuses, like the public menagerie, are selling off many of their animals—exotics, curiosities and even trained ring stock. I do not know whether they are doing it to snatch a quick profit from the rich who desire those peculiar meats, or to show a pretended sympathy for the unfed unfortunates, or simply and honestly because they can no longer afford to feed their beasts."

"Gott behüte!" growled Beck. "On the hotel bill of fare next, baboon Braten will be."

Everybody grimaced, and Florian went on, "So far, Abdullah and le Démon Débonnaire and their assistant handlers have managed very well in sustaining our own menagerie, not luxuriantly but sufficiently, on the feed we earlier stocked and the pasturage here in the Bois and our pooled civilian meat rations. But, with both the government and the other circuses turning their food-consuming animals into consumable food for human beings, some zealous do-gooders are likely to look on us as harboring, almost literally, dogs in the manger."

"Come on, Governor," said Fitzfarris. "I know—from away back in Baltimore —that you don't give a damn for the opinion of do-gooders."

"True enough, I don't. I would much rather butcher a zealot than a horse, or even one of your mouse-game mice. And I will no more sacrifice our loyal and longtime animal companions than I will any of our human artistes. Oh, if times got bad enough, Sir John, I might consider feeding to the carnivores your de-crepit old Auerhahn—or the ostriches or the hyenas—except that it would be an exercise in futility. Such stringy creatures are all but inedible even by other creatures. No, we will keep our animals as long as we can keep ourselves."

"Mind you, Governor, that might not be too long," said Goesle. "I was about to tell you, now just, that when Hannibal came back from his buying trip today to les Halles, he brought word from his regular cat's-meat man. That butcher, and all the other shops, I take it, will soon be not accepting coin and paper of the realm."

"What? Confound it, why not?"

"They are all coming fidgety over the current situation. They say, if the peo-ple's unrest causes *this* government to fall, the French franc will be worthless. And if the boches occupy the city, they say, the Prussian mark will be the only good money. So they are now distrustful of *any* coin or paper, until things settle down."

"More goddamned rumors."

"Aye, and ill news has healthy legs."

"What do they want, then? Marks? We have still a goodly quantity of them, not yet exchanged for francs. Even a fair amount of rubles and koronas and kronen."

"They want gold, Governor. The one currency that endures through any war or revolution."

"Then, damn it, we'll pay them in gold. Unplug that hidden cache under Maximus's cage floor, Dai, and take out a handful of those Russian imperials the tsar donated. Each of those little coins is worth about forty francs, so a mere handful should sustain us for some time."

"Aye, aye, Governor."

Florian pondered and frowned for a moment, then said, "I fear it will make us look even more callous to the misery of the common folk, spending *gold* to keep animals alive. Nevertheless, I will not unbend. Most of the Paris citizenry, I rejoice to say, are dedicated circus-fanciers, or at least people of reason, who would support my position. However, at the top and at the bottom of that citi-zenry are those with their own positions to defend or aggrandize. At the top is the government, anxious to maintain its appearance of solicitude for all and sundry..."

"Not *quite* all," said Willi. "Only those who can vote, whenever elections are finally held. That does not include our animals, or even most of *us*."

"Correct," said Florian. "Meanwhile, at the bottom are the Communards. They would happily contrive to discover 'bourgeois betrayal of the masses' in a

Kindergarten, if that would stir up trouble to their advantage. Either of those extremes, top or bottom, might put pressure on us to dispose of our stock and menagerie to the meat markets. And either the government or the Communards could claim it was 'for the good of all,' and take credit for it."

"We don't have to give a damn about pressure, either," said Fitzfarris, "if we have the bulk of the public on our side."

"Perhaps not. However, when pressure fails, any group of fanatics might decide to take upon themselves the disposal of our animals—especially if they are famished fanatics. I think it would behoove us to be on the qui vive for any such developments. Colonel Ramrod, I suggest that you again issue loaded fire-arms to the responsible members of our crew, and schedule guard watches here at the tober around the clock."

"Consider it done," said Edge. "Anything else on your mind, Governor?"

"Not right now. I think... before very long... we shall have to ask the Balloon Post to repay the favor we did it. But I'll take that up with Monsieur Nadar, next time he drops around."

The Balloon Post was one of the few things in Paris still functioning without serious breakdowns, or not too many of them, at any rate. When the surrounding Prussians learned that one of the aérostats had carried Minister Gambetta safely out to the unoccupied provinces, they sent a hurried message to the gunworks at Essen in the Rhineland. Very soon thereafter, they were provided with a new and specially Krupp-designed cannon, the first ever capable of being cranked almost to the vertical, and firing a Shrapnel shell that could be time-fused, in theory anyway, to explode at a predetermined altitude. The sixteenth balloon sent off from Paris had to waft its way across the siege lines through suddenly appearing little black clouds, and those proved to be composed of gunsmoke and flying metal shards. That aérostat made it without mishap, but the aéronaute later reported, by homing pigeon, serious wear and tear on his nervous system.

"I'm sure glad I ain't the cannoneer on that gun," said Yount, when he heard of it. "Time fuse is a tricksome thing. That gunner has got to cut the length of it before the shell is rammed in the breech, and he's got to *hope* that firing the gun will light the fuse, and *hope* he didn't cut the fuse so short that the shell goes off right over his own head, and *hope* he didn't cut it so long that the shell falls *back* on his own head before it goes off. All in all, I druther be out ahead of that gun than behind it."

The Minister of Posts, though, was more respectful of the new contre-aérostat cannon, and ordered all balloon flights from then on to be launched only after dark. That turned out to be no great help to the aéronautes. For one thing, the little paper test balloons had to go up in daylight to be visible, and whatever winds they indicated up there might change after dark. Then, when the big balloon was launched, it was never *entirely* invisible to a ground observer. To the aéronaute, however—and nowadays he was always a novice—the ground *was* so hard to see that he could never be sure of how high he was or even, some-times, which way he was drifting. Meanwhile, the new Krupp gun would be lobbing up shells to explode in his general vicinity, and the Fort Valérien guns would be making their uproar to distract the Prussian gunners, and the com-bined commotion was enough to make any Balloon Post volunteer regret that he had ever volunteered.

"Nevertheless, ami," Nadar said proudly, as he and Florian stood watching a night performance of the circus, "considering the almost impromptu commencement of the Balloon Post, and all the handicaps it must labor under"—he ticked them off on his fingers—"shoddily made aérostats, totally untested until they have gone beyond recall; their having to rely on slow-lifting coal gas; their limited maneuverability under the best of conditions; the inexperienced pilots flying them through hostile fire—zut alors, the Balloon Post has tallied a remarkable record of successes against its few failures."

"I have been meaning to ask you—" Florian started to say.

"No need to ask, mon vieux, I will tell you. So far, we have lost only four. One balloon floated out over the Atlantic and has not been heard of since. Three have fallen into enemy hands. But"—he raised a finger—"owing to a mistake of the aéronaute or a structural fault, not shot down by enemy fire. The others have all landed safely and in friendly territory. One of them, indeed, in a quite distant friendly country. To tell the truth, it inadvertently set a new record for balloon flight—some twenty-four hundred kilometers, clear across the North Sea, landing in Norway. I daresay that young aéronaute is still thawing out, but I also daresay he is elated by his achievement. It will be a very long time before that record is surpassed."

"Well, what I wanted to ask—" Florian began again, but stopped to say, "Hark! One of your balloons must be leaving right now." Over the band music and crowd noise, they could hear the heavy rumble of the Fort Valérien guns and the harsher bark of the Prussians' contre-aérostat cannon.

"Oui," said Nadar, "et regardez-là." He discreetly jerked his head to direct Florian's attention to Monday Simms, standing nearby. She was waiting to go on next, as Mademoiselle Cendrillon, and meantime was smiling to herself, eyes closed and thighs chafing together. "I have a physician friend," Nadar said confidentially, "who tells me that many of his female patients behave thus when the cannons boom. The concussion or the vibration causes a sympathetic frisson in their delicate petites choses. Some women, he says, respond only to the firing of a particular one of the cannons, so they have given pet names to the various guns—Big Joséphine, Big Camille and the like. Do you suppose, ami, that is why we men wage war? At the instigation of women who want the thrill of it?"

"I should not be in the least surprised. Except that we were waging war long before it made any such noises."

"C'est vrai. But we were speaking of the Balloon Post's successes. So far, it has carried various other important passengers besides the Minister Gambetta, and perhaps a million letters, newspapers, dispatches—and hundreds of pigeons, most of which have dutifully flown back bearing their cargoes of micromessages. Incidentally, what think you of the news of Gambetta? Did I not say that the man, for all his deplorable lack of the social graces, has a driving energy and a talent for organization? Twelve new army corps he has mustered and equipped and armed! A whole new Army of the Loire!"

"Admirable, yes," said Florian. "But I don't know what good it can do. One of your pigeons also brought the distressing news that General Bazaine has surrendered Metz and his whole army that had been bottled up there. The new Army of the Loire may hold what ground it has, but with Bazaine's army gone, it cannot possibly recover what ground the boches have taken."

"Still, the longer France can stand against Prussia, the better terms we might negotiate for peace."

"Let us hope so," said Florian, not very hopefully. "This stolid holding out is costing Paris dearly. The cold and the damp and the ever-worsening malnourishment are now, I hear, causing widespread illness."

Nadar shrugged. "Among the better classes, only maladies de poitrine—la bronchite, la grippe—no worse than in any other winter. They do say there may be épidémies among the lower classes. One hears rumors even of la peste—worse, even la vérole. But what can one expect of types who eat rats?"

"If the plague and the smallpox *are* breaking out," said Florian, "they may start in the low quarters, but they may very well not stop there."

"Best raise your circus admission prices, then," Nadar said offhandedly. "Keep out the canaille, so they do not exhale their foul fomites upon your better patrons and your own artistes. I do hope"—and he moved a step away from Florian—"you have not already noticed any symptômes épidémique among your troupe."

"No. But, in one case, une maladie de poitrine, yes. I wanted to ask you about those passengers the Balloon Post sometimes carries. One of our young ladies, the Mademoiselle Knudsdatter—you know her—Miss Eel, our contortionist..."

"Ah, oui, and I am aware that she is constitutionally frail of the lungs."

"Well, this wretched weather will kill her if it continues, and if she continues to perform, as she has insisted on doing. However, I have—after considerable intense persuasion—procured her man's permission to send her abroad, and her own acquiescence in leaving Paris, if that is possible. I should like to get her away to a sanatorium, or at least to some clear, dry mountain heights."

"Mais certainement," said Nadar. "The Balloon Post is heavily indebted to you and your establishment. I can easily arrange her passage... if she is willing to take the risks involved."

"I think she would prefer to fall or be shot down from the sky than to die of slow strangulation. And if by chance she got wafted all the way to Scandinavia, there could be no more salubrious place for her."

"C'est déjà fait accompli. Simply have her pack the smallest possible bag of the fewest possible essentials, and I shall have her aboard the next departing aérostat. I shall also immediately inform you when a pigeon brings word of her safe landing and whereabouts. She and her man—that is the Monsieur Earthquake, no?—can thereafter exchange billets-doux by the Balloon Post. Ah, how fortunate for us all that it exists!"

13

MISS EEL gave one last performance, at an afternoon show, and outdid herself to make it a sensationally sinuous, boneless, nearly unbelievable demonstration of contortion—though it left her so weak and gasping for breath that she could barely take her bows to the applause—and then said her good-byes to the company. Yount drove her in the rockaway to Montmartre, and helped her make the arduous climb to the top of the hill. Then they exchanged hugs and kisses and mutual adjurations to "take care of yourself," until Monsieur Nadar declared that the wind was right and the evening now dark enough for launching. Yount lifted

Agnete into the basket beneath the brown bag—all the balloons were now being made of dark-colored calico—and the tether rope was uncranked to the thousand-meter altitude. Then Yount stood, head back, hands prayerfully clasped, watching the diminishing dark blob as long as he could see it, and not even noticing when the cast-off rope tumbled down around him.

When he could no longer see the balloon, he began to see little explosive flashes in the sky, each followed after a moment by the harsh cough of that one Prussian cannon out there—at which Yount unclasped his hands and wrung them instead—and, in a minute, the fort's guns started their rumbling. Yount and Nadar waited with the other Balloon Post crewmen until all that noise ceased, indicating that the aérostat was either downed or was safely beyond the enemy's reach. Then the two men walked together downhill, the Frenchman making cheerfully reassuring noises, and Yount drove back to the Bois, while Nadar went off to await the arrival of the first pigeon. Yount got to the tober in plenty of time to don his leopard skin for the night show, but he looked so bereft that his fellow troupers rallied to cheer him up.

"She'll be all right, Obie," said Sunday. "A lot better off than if she'd stayed here."

"I just wish I could of gone with her."

Fitzfarris said, "Well, you couldn't, big fellow, even if that balloonist had dumped *all* his official freight. Hell, they'd probably have to build an oversized craft to lift you alone."

"And if she and you went off separately, Obie," said Edge, "you'd land separately, neither of you knowing where the other was. You might both have to wander all over France, and still not get together. This way, at least, you can write to one another, by way of the post and the pigeons, and stay in touch."

"I reckon," mumbled Yount. Then he emerged from his despondency to remark on something he had noticed. "You know what, Zack? That whole hill up yonder now is a hive of artillery pieces. Them sedentaries and mob-lots ain't been as layabout as we all thought. They've set up factories—like the balloon one—in the train stations, and they've been forging railroad iron and brass into cannons and mortars and shot. Nadar and me talked to some of the fellows. They say, if it comes to it, that hill's going to be the last-ditch defense of Paris." He added, as an afterthought, "They was all wearing red shirts or neckerchiefs along with their uniforms."

"Damnation," said Florian. "I don't like the sound of that. The Communards might consider those guns their private armory, and Montmartre their private fortress."

Edge asked, "Do you mean they'd be crazy enough to destroy their own city, just to deny the Prussians the fun of doing it? Or they'd refuse to honor any truce the government makes with the enemy? They'd go on fighting? Or what?"

"Who knows? But I do know that one of the reasons for rearranging Paris was to eliminate the narrow and crooked streets, because earlier revolutionaries erected barricades in them. Haussmann laid out all the long, straight avenues so the government troops would have a clear field of fire, to rout any such insurrectionists. However, if the insurgents were to hold the one height overlooking the whole city..." Florian made a face and briskly dusted his hands. "Well, no sense in borrowing worries from the morrow. We have a show to do tonight. Let us get on with it."

Whatever appprehension Yount was feeling about Agnete, he did not let it interfere with his work, but performed with his usual competence and bravura. When the show was just over—the chapiteau emptying out and most of the troupers getting ready to hurry to the hotel to partake of its last room heat and hot bath water—a fiacre came clattering onto the tober. Nadar bounded from it, shouting, "Monsieur Earthquake, be at ease! The first pigeon made a quick trip this time." He waved a flimsy little strip of paper. "Voilà, your lady landed safely near Mézières. From there she can take train for anywhere she pleases."

Yount sighed out a couple of bushels of air and said, "Well, that takes a bigger load off me than I've ever had piled on. Makes me feel good." He turned and said expansively, "Hey, Fitz, tell you what. I know it's your night to play corporal of the guard, but let me take it for you, and you go on with Meli to the hotel. I ain't got nobody to go home to."

So Yount stayed on the tober with the armed Jászis and Slovaks that night. Next noontime, when the first of the troupers began to gather again at the Bois, Yount hurried to meet Florian and report "all secure," but added, in an undertone, "I want to show you something, Governor, before any of the females hear about it. Come to the menagerie top."

Florian had arrived in company with Jean-François Pemjean, so they both followed Yount into the animals' tent. He kicked aside some straw and said, "You ever see a man lay as flat as that?"

"Bon Dieu de merde!" exclaimed Pemjean, regarding the corpse stretched prone there, a large knife clutched in one of its hands.

"Yes, as a matter of fact, I have," Florian said soberly. "So I can guess what happened. But tell me, anyway."

"Well, we've always supposed we was to be on guard against a mob raiding us. So the boys was posted around the perimeter, as usual. We didn't figure on a single sneak, and he got past us somehow. Poor bastard probably thought he'd just carve himself a haunch off a horse or something. But we heard a hullabaloo from here. Horses neighing, cats roaring, elephants trumpeting. We all come running, just in time to see Mitzi make a snatch with her trunk at this fellow. Never poked her tusks at him."

"Bulls seldom do, except when they fight each other."

"She plucked him off his feet and laid him real neat on the ground in front of old Peggy, damned near like they'd rehearsed it. And then, before we could do anything, Peggy just kneeled down, put her forehead on the man's body and— by God—did a *headstand* on him. You never heard such a sound. Like stepping on a quail nest with chicks in it, only the biggest nest and chicks in all creation. Crackle and squoosh."

"I've heard it. I've known this to happen on other shows."

"Well, then old Peggy stood up again, and her and Mitzi shook hands with their trunks, and all the other beasts quieted down nice and peaceful. Couple of the Slovaks puked, and they're all still right shaky. But me and Zoltán hauled the body over here to the side, and left the knife in his paw, in case you want to show the police."

"No, I don't think we'll trouble the police with this," said Florian. "What we probably ought to do is hang him up on the marquee, as a caution to others."

"We could feed him to my cats," Pemjean suggested. "It would be only poetic justice."

"Jesus, Demon," said Yount. "You'll make *me* puke."

Pemjean shrugged and pointed to the dead man. "Like him, one swallows one's scruples when there is nothing else to swallow."

Florian said thoughtfully, "This one we can't bury under the pista, or the bulls would never step into it again. For now, Quakemaker, you and the boys roll him in a tarpaulin and hide him somewhere. After dark, we'll drop him in one of the holes where a park tree was uprooted, and tamp him out of sight. Tell the guard detail to be alert from now on for lone poachers like this one, but not to rule out mobs of them, either."

Pemjean said, as they left the tent, "Mobs of poachers may soon be the only mobs we will be seeing here, Monsieur Florian, unless this damned siege ends, one way or another. People used to come to see us because we offered the only diversion to be found. But I think now the only reason they still come is that ours is the only establishment in Paris still willingly accepting francs and sous and centimes. And those who come are the people not yet too weak from hunger or sickness to make their way out here."

That may have been true, for the Florilegium's attendance began to dwindle, gradually but steadily, as the wicked winter wore on. Despite ever more severe edicts issued by the government, the markets and shops continued to sell their wares first to those who could pay in gold or foreign currency. The poor, with only their life savings of commonplace francs to spend, had to settle for the dregs, the crumbs and the leftovers—when there were any. Most of the city's physicians and apothecaries were just as venal, treating first their well-paying patients and selling first to them the diminishing stocks of medicines. Whether or not it was true that the rich never suffered from anything worse than hypochondria, their appropriation of the available medicaments turned out, in time, to be hardly in their own best interests. Real and fearsome diseases—diphtheria, typhoid and smallpox—afflicted the unattended and undernourished poor, and, unchecked in those neighborhoods, inevitably spread into the more genteel districts.

When the government could no longer ignore the several contagions that were threatening to become plagues, the Bureau of Health tried an expedient that was at least more ingenious than issuing futile demands and prohibitions. While it was patently impossible to import food into the city, it *might* be possible to import medical supplies—so the Balloon Post carried to the provinces a plea for those necessities, and suggested a method by which they could be sent. They were, too—considerable quantities of medicines, packed into hollow zinc globes and floated from towns upstream on the Seine and its tributaries. The Prussians even compassionately refrained from shooting the metal spheres out of the water when the things floated through their lines. So some of the medical supplies did get through, but only a meager fraction. Too many of the globes were crushed or punctured and sunk by the drift ice in the river. Others kept going, right through Paris and on seaward, because the ice tore away the nets rigged in the city to catch them.

One afternoon, young Giuseppina failed to appear for the afternoon show, so afterward her good friend Clover Lee hurried to the Hôtel Crillon to see if she was ailing. When Clover Lee returned to the tober and Florian's office, she was without Giuseppina, and looking baffled and worried.

"She's gone. Just plain gone. And not only won't the hotel manager tell me where she went, he claims *she was never staying there.* It's a damned lie, and I told him so, to his face. Hell, I've visited her rooms many a time. What can be going on?"

"Hm," said Florian. "Is it possible that the girl finally settled on one of those wealthy noblemen who have been courting her for so long? Could she simply have eloped and, for reasons of her own, decided to cover her tracks?"

"You know better, Florian. Pina's a trouper. She'd never do such a thing without giving notice. She'd certainly have told *me.*"

"True. It does seem odd. Hold on." Florian rummaged through his files and came up with an old copy of the *Era,* then riffled through its pages and said, "Ha, I thought I remembered seeing it here. Yes, her engagements-agents are the Messieurs Paravicini and Warner, of London, and they have a branch office here, in the rue de la Paix. No number given, but that street is only two blocks long; you should have no trouble finding it."

Giuseppina was absent also from the night performance, so the next morning Clover Lee went straight from her hotel in search of the agency. Again she returned very shortly, almost in tears, but seething with anger, too.

"Where is Zachary?" she demanded of Florian. "I want him to strap on a pistol and go back there with me. Can you imagine? The son of a bitch at that office said oh, yes, he knows of the lovely signorina, and has long admired her, but his company *have never been her managers,* and they know nothing of her whereabouts! Another goddamned liar! Where is Zachary?"

"Easy, my dear, easy. I agree that this is all becoming most mysterious, but I think crafty investigation might serve better than brute force to get to the bottom of it. And for craftiness, let us call in Monsieur Nadar. He knows everyone and everything in this city."

"Well, let's hurry. Pina has a birthday coming up." She showed him a gaily wrapped package. "I bought her this present, and I've been carrying it all over town for these two days."

Even for Nadar, it took nearly a week to uncover the truth, and he looked both sad and uneasy when he came to report to Florian and Clover. Almost with trepidation, he addressed her by her title:

"Madame la Comtesse, I must apologize for my compatriots. It was cruel of the hotelkeepers to do it as they did. But you must understand... a premier hotel... the establishment had its reputation and its other guests to protect. Therefore, when the Mademoiselle Bozzacchi fell suddenly ill, and required the attention of the resident physician, and he made an examination diagnostic, and recognized that the child was suffering from la petite vérole—"

"Smallpox!" exclaimed Florian, and Clover Lee gasped.

"Oui. So, quite naturally, the hotel management whisked her out of there, and secretly, not to alarm the other guests, and have since done everything possible to keep quiet the circumstances."

"Oh, *quite* naturally," Clover Lee repeated, through gritted teeth. "They might have lost business... even money. How very French. And she was the dancer who was acclaimed and fêted by all Paris, not a year ago. Well, damn it, where did they whisk her *to?*"

"To the women's hospice, La Salpêtrière."

"Hospice? Is that a hospital?"

"Not exactly, Your Grace," Nadar said miserably. "A hospital is for treatment and cure. A hospice is for the comfortable last confinement of the incurable."

"This is monstrous!" snarled Clover Lee. "You take me there, monsieur. Take me immediately."

"It is a long way from here, Your Grace. It is, after all, a place of isolation of contagion. I will take you, of course, if you insist. But do you think it wise? To expose yourself to—?"

"Take me there! You can wait outside. And, Florian, while I'm gone, find that document of mine. You know the one I mean." She snatched up the now slightly wilting birthday package, then all but snatched Monsieur Nadar off the tober and into a voiture, and they were gone.

Florian had the Comte de Lareinty's testament-letter waiting when Clover Lee returned to the red wagon, some hours later. But she returned without either Nadar or Giuseppina, and still carrying her gift package, and with tear-stains on her face. So Florian said nothing; he merely held out the paper to her. She shook her head and waved it away.

"I don't need it. Pina died just before I got there. Today. Her seventeenth birthday."

"I can't possibly tell you how sorry I am, my dear."

"And she died in a *pesthouse*. In a lazaretto, as if she'd been a beggar and a leper. Just because she was too sick to realize, and protest, and insist on private treatment. Do you want to know what that place is like? One of the nursing sisters told me they have to mix carbolic acid into the rubbing alcohol, or the attendants will *guzzle* it all."

"I truly am sorry, and so will be everyone else of the company. If only it hadn't happened so suddenly. If she could have got word to us..."

"Well, at least I was able to claim the remains, so she won't be *whisked off* again—and maybe to some potters' field. I've already made the arrangements for a proper interment."

"And all of us will attend, of course, just as if she had been with us always. Meanwhile, it might make you feel a trifle better, Clover Lee, if you consider this. Giuseppina may have preferred *not* to survive the smallpox. It is very possible that she would not have been...beautiful afterward. But tell me. Why did you want me to get this document from my files?"

Clover Lee gave a bitter laugh. "I was going to make use of it, but it's too late now. I was going to get hold of some of the money Gaspard left, and go and *buy* that double-damned hotel, and throw everybody there out of his job, from the manager down to the bootblacks, and give the place to Giuseppina, to burn it down if she wanted to. But now...what the hell..."

Florian gazed at her with admiration. "I think you *ought* to make use of the paper. Not such a Draconian use, perhaps, but to affirm your title, anyway. I've said before and I'll say again: nobility becomes you, my dear. You have not only a noble heart, you have nobly imperious instincts."

"To hell with that, too," she said dully. "If the upper classes could forget and abandon Pina so easily, and the business classes worry that a dying girl is an impediment to their business, I don't want anything more to do with any of them. If I had the spunk, I'd help the Communards overthrow them."

"Please don't say that. If you think the nobility and the bourgeoisie are bad, I hope you never have much experience of the French lower classes. But right now, my dear, why don't you go back to the Grand and rest? We'll gladly excuse you from tonight's performance."

"Damned if you will. I've already missed one today. Pina never would have, if she could have helped it. The least I can do is go on with the show and...and ...celebrate her birthday."

With that, she burst into weeping and hurried from the wagon, so blinded by tears that she did not see or greet Edge, just about to enter. He stood for a moment in the door, looking after her, then turned inquiringly to Florian, who said:

"Our little music-box dancer is dead. Clover Lee is quite broken up about it."

"I heard where she had gone to. I'm sure sorry. I liked that Giuseppina, ever since we first met her back in Rome. And maybe I ought not to intrude practicality at a time like this. But Clover Lee has just come from visiting a smallpox ward. I had a mild dose of it once, so I'm immune to it, but not everybody here is. And God only knows what variety of other infections the jossers are bringing in here twice a day. Do you think, Governor, it might be prudent for us just to close up shop until the world gets back to normal? I'm not suggesting, only asking."

"My answer is no—unless you and the others choose to overrule me, in which case I would bow to the majority decision. We may be eternal birds of passage, with no home habitat, but—if you'll allow me the avian metaphor— wherever we light we cast our lot with the local birds, however briefly, for good or ill. Most of the illnesses going about, Zachary, are afflicting the famished and the feeble. All of us are still being adequately nourished, and all of us still with the show are physically stronger than even normal healthy people. I think we are not in much danger of falling prey to the prevalent infections. Remember, we constitute almost the only bright aspect of this desolate city. Also one of the few warm places in it. Unless I am overruled, I say we continue to show as long as we have a single artiste capable of performing, and a single josser paying admission to see that performance."

"Nobody would dream of arguing with you, Governor. You're the strongest of us all. We'll carry on, and we'll just hope that things do get better."

But things did not; they got worse.

Ever since the Prussians had first drawn shut their encircling siege lines, the commanders of the city's defense troops had intermittently tested the strength of those lines. They sent small forces—of army regulars, not the conscripts and reservists—to make probes and patrols in various directions. Those forays frequently resulted in fierce and bloody skirmishes with the enemy, but only short ones, the French always quickly retreating inside the city again. To date, they had only proved that, though the Prussians and their allies clearly had had to spread themselves thin to form that encirclement of fully fifty-eight miles, their thin line was no weak one.

But now came a pigeon from Tours, bearing the heartening news that the Gambetta-organized Army of the Loire, under the generals Chanzy and Bourbaki, was pushing north from Orléans toward Fontainebleau. President-and-General Trochu decided that, if his Paris troops could just force a breach in the enemy lines, make the thirty miles to Fontainebleau and join that approaching army, those combined forces *might* be able to peel away the blockade entirely. So he mustered every available (and dependable) man in the Bois de Vincennes on the southeastern edge of the city, and, on the twenty-eighth of November, sent them charging across the Marne River bridges toward the enemy-held suburb of Champigny.

It was Paris's one shining moment in that dark winter, but too brief a moment. Its soldiers fought with such valor and desperation that, on the last day of November, they *took* Champigny. Then the evicted boches paid their gallant foes the compliment of asking that December first be a day of truce, for both sides to bury their dead and succor their wounded—the combined casualties amounting to thousands. That was mutually agreed upon, and the Prussians brought their ambulance wagons and field-hospital teams for their fallen comrades. But the French had gone into that battle with so little preparation that the Paris Compagnie de Transport Public had to send out its street omnibuses and charabancs for that purpose.

The next day, the furious fighting resumed, and, on the day after, the French were beaten. What was left of them went reeling back across the Marne and into the city, and the only briefly broken siege line was closed again. Anyway, the reports brought from Tours by later pigeons made it evident that the attempted emergence of the Paris troops would have come to nothing even if it had succeeded. The French Army of the Loire, on its way north, had run into the boche Army of the Meuse, had been severely mauled and even cut in half, into two disorganized forces that fled separately—under General Chanzy to the northwest and under General Bourbaki to the southeast—neither of them even trying to get anywhere near Fontainebleau.

But the beleaguered city's one show of temerity and defiance seemed finally to have exhausted the Prussians' patience. Now they opened up their long-range Krupp guns, first pounding to rubble the fort on Mont Avrons, then beginning to bombard the other forts east and south of Paris, and, as each fort was evacuated by its outgunned defenders, the siege lines moved closer and closer to the city's boundaries.

"Damn," said Florian. "I knew, if Paris kept on stubbornly holding out, von Moltke would come in and take it."

"Well, they won't be shelling the city itself for a while," said Edge. "Just the outer ring of forts."

"What? Shell the city?" said Florian, looking surprised. "I meant there would probably be hand-to-hand fighting in the streets. Surely the boches would not be so barbaric as to bombard *the city!* Drop explosives on unarmed civilians? Why, that would be unprecedented. A violation of every humane rule of war. An atrocity unheard of ."

"The hell you say," grunted Yount. "Maybe you never heard how Sherman shelled Charleston, or how Meade did it to Petersburg, but you *saw* what was left of civilian property in the Shenandoah after Little Phil done his Burning. Well, them Prussians have got Sheridan out there with 'em, and he don't respect *no* rules of war—not in *anybody's* war, I'd judge."

"Christ," muttered Florian.

"But they won't start slinging their pumpkins into the city just yet," Edge said again. "There are too many open squares and parks, and they're all soggy from this winter's rains. The shells would just bury themselves and not do much damage when they exploded. Those cannoneers will wait and hope for a cold spell, to freeze all the open ground, so the shells will go off on impact, or skitter around before they explode, and inflict the most havoc possible."

"Christ," Florian muttered again.

Edge was right. The cannonade continued, but concentrated on the forts. The only effect in the city was to give pleasurably thrilling sensations to Monday Simms and to other women likewise susceptible to vibration and concussion. However, the first week of January brought a change in the weather. The monotonous alternation of cold and rainy days ceased; the sky cleared to ice-blue and the air stayed colder-than-ice cold. The parks and lawns and unpaved market squares of Paris no longer got mushy underfoot; they froze to iron solidity.

Not until then did the Prussians elevate their guns for maximum range— about four and a half miles for those firing the big fifty-six-pound shells—and started lobbing the missiles at random. One of the first to hit Paris exploded near a parochial school in the Vaugirard district and sheared a young girl student neatly in half at the waist, not otherwise disarranging her school uniform. Another fell in the Montparnasse cemetery, shattering and scattering tombstones, but not disturbing its occupants. Another took the head off an old woman chestnut vendor, and another killed fully six people waiting in a queue for their ration of straw bread and horse-hoof osséine.

But that first bombardment by daylight seemed intended only to show what the Prussians *could* do, if they chose. Thereafter, they did not commence their barrages until about ten o'clock each night and, though they sent a missile every four or five minutes, kept it up for only about four hours. During those hours, most Parisians were indoors, safe from having a shell land directly on them or near enough to cause injury. And, when one did hit a building, it could blow a sizable hole in the roof or outside wall, but the explosive power of black powder was not strong enough to do much damage to the inside—or to any occupants of the building, once they learned to stay away from the upper floors, windows and exterior walls. Because the Prussians still had their heavy guns positioned south and east of the city, most of their shells fell in the residential areas on the Left Bank. One that exploded in the Places des Invalides was the only missile that came anywhere close to the city's center, and only a few flew across the river to fall around Auteuil, a mile or so south of the Florilegium's tober.

So, after the initial shock and alarm—and outrage, that the City of Light could be thus insulted and mistreated—most of the citizens came to regard the cannonade with a stoic fatalism. After all, it was causing far fewer casualties each day than were the various diseases and sheer starvation. Street urchins scurried to the scene of every new explosion and gathered up the shell fragments to peddle as souvenirs. In better-class families, the parents would allow their children, as a special treat for being good, to "stay up late and watch the bombardment."

Only the Communards refused to regard this new molestation calmly. It gave them another excuse to be troublesome, and they again whipped up mobs of the lower-class folk to march along the avenues, to mill about in the Place de la Concorde and eventually to surround the Hôtel de Ville. They pelted that building with rocks and excrement, shouted vilification of President Trochu, his "neo-imperialist" government and its inability either to fight for Paris or to defend it adequately. Several times, those crowds included armed sédentaires and mob-lots, in guard uniforms but with the addition of red kerchiefs, and on one occasion those men got so carried away by the mob leaders' rhetoric that they fired at the building's windows. The bedeviled government officials had to call out their own troops—loyal regulars—to disperse those rioters, and that was done by firing at *them*. A number of Communards and their followers were killed or wounded, which gave the remainder of them another cause for outrage. So the marches and demonstrations went on, making more disturbance of the city's peace than the enemy's cannons could do.

President Trochu did make one overt protestation of his own against the bombardment, after a shell fell on the Hôpital de Ste-Anne one night. He sent a messenger the next morning, under a white flag of safe conduct, to the Prussian headquarters at Versailles, deploring and condemning such a heinous atrocity. General von Moltke sent the messenger back with a note of cool reply: that he hoped soon to be close enough to Paris that his bombardiers could more easily see and therefore respect the red crosses.

"I bet you anything," growled Yount, when Sunday read that from the news-paper, "it was that damned skunk Sheridan told him to say such a hateful thing."

The Florilegium's troupers had got used to doing the second half of every nighttime show to the every-few-minutes *boom!* and *boom!* of von Moltke's guns, then the ghostly, eardrum-fluttering *whoofle-whoofle-whoofle* of each flying shell, and then the thunder of its explosion, frequently loud enough to drown out Beck's windjammers and sometimes even the noise of the calliope, if it was playing. But only once did the bombardment interfere with the show.

It was a night during the second week of January and the performance was nearly over, Mademoiselle Cendrillon doing her next-to-close act on the tight-rope, when a number of the Prussian cannons, instead of spacing out their shots with their usual clockwork regularity, for some reason fired in quick sequence. Though distant, that drumroll of noise overwhelmed the band's Strauss accompaniment of Monday's chimney-sweep personation. The unusually loud, long burst of gunfire made the whole audience—which tonight filled about half the house—glance off to the southward, and made Monday pause in her cavorting. Perhaps none of the jossers noticed, but the equestrian director and the other troupers loitering about the pista saw how Monday shut her eyes and stopped in the middle of the rope, her legs trembling under her.

It was clear to those watchers that Monday *tried* to control herself, biting down on her lower lip and clutching hard to her vibrating balance-pole chimney brush. When the echoes of the gunfire died and the "Cinderella" music could be heard again, Monday shook her head to clear it, and began hastily but unsteadily to move along the rope toward the security of the guidon platform ahead of her. But she paused once more, when there came that eerie whoofling noise of the several shells on their way—and the heads of all the audience turned in unison to follow that sound, as if they could actually see the missiles boring through the night sky—and then there was the sustained, appalling roar and concussion of their explosion, in what seemed a minutes-long sequence. That was too much for Monday; her face went as blank as if she had suddenly gone to sleep; her whole body convulsed and she toppled from the rope.

Two men were already lunging into the pista. The devil-costumed Démon

Débonnaire was a step closer than the equestrian director, so it was he who flung his arms under the girl, enough to break her fall just slightly, and they hit the ground simultaneously, Pemjean in a sprawling dive, Monday landing flat on her back with a deadweight *thud!* In the echoes of the explosions, that sound, like the band's music, was inaudible to the crowd, and probably few of them had even seen the fall. As Monday's battered stovepipe hat came gaily swooping and sideslipping down after her, Edge made the crossed-arms X signal to Boom-Boom, then bent to the prostrate girl. By the time the audience gave its attention to the pista again, the band was blaring away in the "Wedding March," and Fünfünf, the Kesperle and the Emeraldina were already doing their knockabout routine in preparation for the show-closing Lupino mirror act.

Pemjean got up unassisted and, with Edge, knelt beside Monday. She had been knocked breathless, but she was conscious. Her eyes were open and there was a smile on her chimney-soot-smudged face, and she reached up both her hands to give a reassuring touch to both men. They slid their arms under her from either side and locked hands to make a chair lift. While Florian was apologizing to the crowd, through his megaphone, for "the boches' rude interruption of the mademoiselle's performance," Edge and Pemjean—with Sunday anxiously following—carried Monday to the backyard and to the ladies' dressing tent. When they gently laid her on the cot in there, she had got her breath back and said, almost dreamily, "It was... the best one ever..." Then she blushed and said, almost angrily, "But I ain't gonna do *that* no more."

"She sure as hell won't," Edge reported to Florian, back in the chapiteau. "Not ropewalk *nor* do that thigh-rubbing business, it looks to me. I don't think she realizes it yet, but she's as limp as a corpse from the hips down. You'd better inquire if there's a doctor in the house."

Florian gestured for the band and the clowns to halt—which required Fünfünf and the Kesperle to freeze in their comic postures on either side of the mirror frame. Then Florian announced to the crowd that, although the Mademoiselle Cendrillon had been no worse than shaken by her boche-caused mishap, he personally would feel better if a physician would confirm that fact—if there happened to be a physician present—and if he would oblige. A man got up from the starback seats, carrying a small black satchel, and the audience applauded *him* as he went to meet Florian at the pista curb. He introduced himself, loudly enough to be heard by everyone in the chapiteau, as le Docteur-Médecin Étienne Landgarten, then added in a low voice for Florian only, that he required his fee paid in gold, and paid in advance. Not very well concealing his disgust, Florian gave him two Russian imperials and waved for Edge to lead him to the dressing top.

There, the doctor did not bother to clear the tent of the several other troupers worriedly gathered, and did not ask that his patient be undressed at all, but did only some perfunctory poking about her torso. The he stood up and said, in English, to no one in particular:

"Keep her supine on the cot, strapped to it, and keep her well warmed, but get her to hospital. The hospitals at least still have plenty of muscular attendants, if nothing else, and this patient will require forcible correction of her spine, then protracted immobilization. That is all that can be done for her. Adieu et bonne chance."

He turned to go, but Sunday asked, "Doctor, can you tell us what is—what is hurt?"

"A country midwife could tell you that," he said superciliously. "Comminution of the ninth and tenth thoracic vertebrae. Total and irreversible paraplectic anesthekinesia, with eventual atrophy of the pelvic extremities. Likely repeated episodes of dyspnea, with hazard of asphyxia. Also every likelihood of decubitus ulcers, lifelong fecal impaction and incomplete micturition. With such extensive somesthetic deprivation, she will risk many inadvertent and self-inflicted traumata. Does that suffice to dispel your ignorance, mademoiselle?"

Sunday could only blink, but Monday widened her eyes in alarm, and perhaps in wonderment that she could so suddenly have been afflicted ▼ith so much. Pemjean growled and uncoiled his red-clad length from where he had been kneeling beside the cot. He took hold of the doctor's cravat with both hands, knotted it tight in his fists and lifted the man so his toes were almost off the ground. Glaring like a genuine demon, Pemjean said, in a low voice but one that would have cowed a fractious tiger:

"Un poème épique, Monsieur le Docteur. But now, you pète-sec, you tell us in plain language. How is the girl hurt? What can we do about it? What will be the outcome?"

The doctor could only make strangled noises until Pemjean set him down again, still holding firm to his cravat.

"Alors..." the man rasped, and with difficulty but with frightened alacrity went on, "The...subject female...has crushed two bones of her spine. They contain vital nerves, which have been damaged beyond repair. She must be stretched, by main strength, to realign those bones, then kept stretched while they heal. The bones will, that is to say, but not the nerves. She will eventually be able to get about in a wheelchair, but she will never again have any sensation or capability of movement below the waist. Her unused legs will gradually shrivel. Because some of the damaged nerves are those of her diaphragm, she will sometimes have trouble drawing breath, and must be constantly tended, to shift her position in bed or chair so that she does not suffocate—also to prevent the ulcerations called bedsores. Also, since she will have no feeling in those lower parts of her body, she must be guarded against burns or cuts or, ahem, female infections that may occur without her awareness. Further, since her bowels now have no control either to contain or extrude, she will—she will leak those substances, but never sufficiently to empty them all out, hence she would be liable to systemic poisoning by her own bodily wastes. So a nurse must give her regular enemas to empty the intestines, and must press upon her abdomen to empty the bladder..."

"I druther be dead!" Monday wailed.

"No, you would not," Pemjean said to her, then gave the doctor a brisk shake. "Anything else? Speak!"

"Nothing else, nothing else, monsieur. With those attentions, she should live long. Not ambulant, but not invalid and not—at least, after the forcible correction—not in any extraordinary pain. Please, may I go now, monsieur?"

Pemjean paused, as if considering. "My cats have not had a decent meal in weeks. But I think they would reject such swill as you. Oui—démerde-toi!" And he flung the man out of the tent.

"Well done, Jean-François," Edge said to him. "Sunday, you stay here with your sister. Keep her bundled up warm, and don't let her move so much as a finger. I'll have Banat ready a wagon to take her to the hospital, and Florian will send somebody ahead to engage the best one in the city. Now, everybody else, get back to the chapiteau for the closing walkaround. And Monday, you stop your crying. You ought to know better than to believe a quack sawbones like that one, whatever he says about *anything.*"

"Yessuh, Mr. Zack," she said, sniffling. Sunday bent and whispered something to her, so Monday added, "Oh, and before you go... Mr. Demon... I ain't said thank-you yet." It was, in fact, the very first time she had spoken to him since St. Petersburg. "Wasn't for you, Mr. Demon, I *would* be dead, most likely. You done a good deed."

"I owed you a good deed, chérie," he said softly, and went away.

A little while later, it was he, Florian and Edge who drove the wagon—and Monday on her cot in back, Sunday beside her—to a small, private and expensive clinic, the Centre Médical Marmottan, not very far from the Bois. They all hovered while the attendants carefully carried Monday inside, and while a sympathetic physician—quite unlike the other one—tenderly probed her all over. When Dr. Tonnelier stepped away from her cot, pensively stroking his beard, Florian murmured, not to be overheard by the others:

"Monsieur le Docteur, something called 'forcible correction' was recommended. Will that be extremely painful for the girl?"

"It would be, yes. Excruciating. It always has been. Painful enough to make the strongest of male patients scream like the damned in the inferno. Are you, monsieur, a dedicated French patriot?"

"Eh? What has that to do with this?"

"Forcible correction, which is not very different from the medieval torture rack, is the French method. Hence most French surgeons swear by it, and will consider no alternative method. However, here at the Marmottan—if I do not offend your French sensibilities by telling you this—we prefer the more humane method introduced by the, ahem, detestable boches. The German name for it is Modellierverbessung, if I am pronouncing that correctly."

"Ja. Er, oui. Modeling correction."

"Just so. Unlike the French method, quite painless for the patient. Tedious, I grant, but no more so than the French method's aftermath. Rather a gentle invention, n'est-ce pas?—to come from such a vicious people as the boches?"

"If it serves, and does not hurt, I wouldn't care if it was invented by the Hun Attila."

"Nor would I. You and the mademoiselle's other friends may even watch the procedure initiated, as soon as the nurses have her disrobed and prepared."

So they saw Monday put to bed inside an overhead device of guys, weights and pulleys that rather resembled the circus's lungia, her body stretched in an easy but insistent traction between her pillowy neck brace and padded ankle yokes. The doctor and his assistants did a great deal of finicky adjusting of the various wires and of numerous bolsters wedged under and about her body. But never once did Monday cry out, groan or even complain. She actually smiled a time or two, and once mumbled, "Ain't never had so much nice attention paid to me before."

When he was satisfied with the traction arrangement, Dr. Tonnelier told Florian and the others, "Adjustments will continually be made, both to expedite the healing process and to give the girl the comfort of frequent small changes of position. The modeling correction usually takes from four to six weeks. The Mademoiselle Simms is young and pliant and healthy; I should say she will be out of that bed in four. But not—you already know this—not back on her feet, not ever again. Once she graduates to a wheelchair, well, from then on, she must adjust and adapt to that life. That is not in my métier as a surgeon. It will be only her near and dear who can help her with that."

"We understand," said Sunday.

"We shall see to it," said Pemjean.

Sunday stayed on, to keep her sister company during her first night in hospital. The others said "au revoir" to Monday and the kindly physician, and departed, to return the horses and wagon to the tober. On the way back there, Pemjean said again:

"I owed Monday a good deed. And I have long prayed for a rapprochement. I only wish it had not had to happen so."

"Don't feel too bad, Jean-François," said Edge. "A long time ago, *I* loved a woman who walked the tightrope. Before you joined out with us; you never knew her. I was always terrified that she would fall, the way Monday did tonight. Now, by God, I wish she *had*—instead of what did happen. I would rather have had the care and keeping of just the half of her, than to have lost her altogether."

"Aussi moi-même," said Pemjean, and he turned to Florian. "Please, Monsieur le Gouverneur, you will not discharge the girl? Now that she is—?"

Florian snapped, "What an obscene question! Certainly not!"

"Then I should like to be entrusted with the attending of her. Perhaps she has now forgiven the wrong I did her, but still I owe amends. If she will let me, I will care for her, all her life long."

"Well..." said Florian, with a sidelong look at him. "If you and she are going to resume where you left off, there is one thing I should wish to know..."

"Am I cured of my unspeakable disease?" said Pemjean, with a wry smile. "I cannot be certain, monsieur. But that first doctor tonight, for all his stupid emmerdement, did speak the truth in one respect. Monday has no longer sensation in those parts. She is, in effect, châtrée—and therefore, so will I be. She may sadly miss that delicious aspect of life, and I confess that so will I. But it does assure that never again will I make her suffer any torments such as I once inflicted. Even if I should wish to be so cruel, and I do not."

"In that case, she is yours," said Florian. "And both of you have my sincerest blessing."

They rode for a while in silence through the empty, dark streets where, at this hour, not even the grunting of distant guns was to be heard. Then Florian spoke again, and in tones of woe:

"I swore that our Florilegium would go on showing here as long as we had a single artiste capable of performing. I begin to wonder if the Fates are maliciously determined to hold me to that brash oath, and dwindle our company down to *just* one. We have so recently lost Miss Eel... Signorina Giuseppina... Monsieur Roulette and the *Saratoga*. Now Mademoiselle Cendrillon. And just this morning, Madame Alp confided to me that she is pregnant."

"Qui?" said Pemjean, and Edge said, "Madame Alp?"

"Yes. Of course, that will only briefly discommode us, at the time the child is actually born. In the meanwhile, it should make Madame Alp look even more sensationally gigantic in exhibition."

"Governor," said Edge, "we left Madame Alp back in Baltimore, some six years ago."

"Eh?" Florian seemed momentarily disoriented. "Did I say Madame Alp?" He scratched in his little beard and looked embarrassed. "Dear me. Maybe the Fates are suggesting that *I* retire, by crippling me with senility. I meant, of course, the Princess Brunhilde."

"Ah," said Pemjean. "And she is with child? Quelles bonnes nouvelles!"

"Yes. She and the Deathless are ecstatic, and so should all of us be, on their behalf. Anyway, as I say, her delicate condition will not for some while be taking her out of our sideshow. But she will require medical attention when that time comes, and medical consultation even before. That means more expense, because I most certainly would pay any amount to keep her from having to rely on some charlatan like Dr. Lustgolden, or whatever the oaf's name was. But I tell you frankly, gentlemen, I begin to worry about expenses. That box of Tsar Alexander's imperials is getting low. True, we have in our red-wagon treasury a wealth of French francs. But they are practically unspendable at present, and who knows whether they will ever be of value again. If they remain worthless..." He shook his head and sighed. "Then, considering our diminished company and that imminent impoverishment, the Florilegium has very nearly come full circle. Back to the mud show it was, Colonel Ramrod, when you first met it on that Virginia creek bank. Yes? Well... say something."

"Damned if I will. I'm not paying the least attention to your jeremiad, Governor. As long as you're still addressing me by my circus name, I know damned well you haven't lost your perennial optimism. Or your ability to ride a cataract like a cork. And as long as you've got that, the rest of us are all right."

"Ah, well, I thank you for your confidence, and I hope it proves justified. Yes, yes... we must simply work things out as we go along. If only this miserable war would end!"

14

THE WAR ENDED, not abruptly and decisively, but with a fitful sputtering, like the last few sporadic bangs of a string of firecrackers.

Battles were still going on all over France—at St-Quentin in Picardie, at Le Mans in Maine, at Belfort in Alsace—when, on the eighteenth day of January, Wilhelm gave notice to the world that he considered France effectually conquered, his armies victorious and his people preeminent in Europe. On that day, at an age when most monarchs might have been thinking of handing over their rule to a successor and retiring from the cares of state, the seventy-three-year-old Wilhelm proclaimed himself no longer merely King of Prussia but Emperor of the new German Empire. He did so in the presence of his son, Crown Prince Friedrich, his Chancellor Bismarck, General the Graf von Moltke and numerous other dignitaries, including the admiring General Philip Sheridan. When the news reached Paris the next day, by a Balloon Post pigeon, Florian remarked with resignation:

"Well, we shall no longer be speaking of Prussians, Hessians, Bavarians and such distinctions. From now on, they are all Germans. And here goes my poor shuttlecock Alsace again, back across that border. Wait and see."

The rest of Paris took the news not so resignedly. It was bad enough that Wilhelm had announced his accession to Kaisertum on the sacred soil of France. What was even more shocking, demeaning and galling to every Frenchman was the fact that he had held that ceremony in their historic landmark, the proud château of Versailles, and even—quelle horreur!—in its venerated Hall of Mirrors.

Now it was not only the forever disgruntled Communards, but all the citizens of Paris, who demanded of their government *some* action, *any* action. So, that same day, the remnants of the city's regulars, under General Bergeret, made one more spasm of desperation and tried again to break through the German siege lines. This time they struck westward, trooping through the Bois de Boulogne— and past the solemnly watching company of the Florilegium—to cross the Seine toward the suburb of Buzenval, as if they intended to press on to Versailles itself and confront the detestable Wilhelm in person.

But the roads on the other side of the Seine, untraveled these many months, were frozen and glazed. They also led uphill, and had to be climbed. Even the cavalry horses were hardly able to keep their footing, and the cannons and their caissons could not move at all. Practically the only soldiers advancing were the wretched infantrymen, without either artillery or effective cavalry support. In a frantic effort to provide them with something *like* artillery, the army engineers also hastened to the fore, to throw—by hand—fused and capped sticks of the new demolition explosive called dynamite. But the dynamite was as frozen as the contested ground, and failed to explode. The battle became a shambles. Perhaps seven hundred of the Germans holding the siege line were killed or wounded, but four *thousand* of the Frenchmen were. The survivors trudged back across the Seine bridges, through the Bois, past the circus tober and into the city again, to try no more.

That one last abortive effort gave the Communards yet another excuse to denounce the government as incompetent, and to lead their mobs again upon the Hôtel de Ville. There, another shooting affray with the guards left a few of the protesters lying on the ground when the rest dispersed, shaking their fists, their rifles and their red flags. The government, beset by siege without and riot within, finally confessed itself incapable of holding or being upheld by the capital of the Republic of France. On the twenty-third of January, Foreign Minister Jules Favre and his chief aides, with a military escort bearing the white flag, rode from Paris to Versailles, to ask the High Command of the combined armies of the German Reich for the granting of an armistice, during which the terms of the city's surrender might be discussed.

The sad news of that imminent capitulation went by balloon to the government's delegation at Tours, and thence to the rest of France. However, the rest of France had never even been invited to recognize the authority of that self-appointed government. Also, it was no secret that most Frenchmen of the provinces were indifferent—if not spitefully pleased—whenever they heard of *any* catastrophe afflicting the high and mighty Parisians. So the news from Paris did not make any of the French soldiers still battling the Germans in the provinces throw down their weapons in either despair or sympathy. Meanwhile, the news had to go all the way to Switzerland to reach General Charles Bourbaki and his sizable piece of the whilom Army of the Loire. He had done nothing with that army except to get chased by the Germans all over southeastern France, until now he had led it into safe hiding. Rather than suffer the further humiliation of surrendering—there being no enemy in Switzerland to whom to surrender, in any case—he chose a more honorable end for a French officer-and-gentleman.

"'... And did it as ineptly as he has done everything else during this war,'" Sunday read from *Le Moniteur,* then glanced up to tell the listening troupers, "Those are the newspaper's words, not mine. It goes on, 'According to the pigeon-borne dispatch, the general shot himself in the head. Those of us who have long suspected that Bourbaki's head is his least vital organ are not surprised to learn that the general managed thereby to wound himself only slightly, and is already on the mend.'" Sunday looked up again, to remark to Florian, "You've always said, Governor, that the French respect their leaders and warriors only as long as they're winning."

"Alas, I fear that they have had few leaders to respect at all, even for a little while, during this war. And of the warriors, those deserving respect are mostly dead, poor fellows."

On the twenty-eighth of January, the armistice was declared, but with no indication of how brief or lengthy it might be. So practically every man, woman and child in Paris who could move—by carriage, voiture, wagon, horseback or afoot—streamed out of the city toward the countryside, barely glancing at the German guard posts on the now unblocked roads.

"The people are not making a mass escape," said Florian, watching the hordes pouring westward through the Bois. "They are carrying no belongings."

"Whatever they're doing," said Edge, "what do you think we ought to do? Tear down and get out while we've got the chance?"

"I think not. For one thing, we still have no idea where best to go. The nearest unwarring places are the Low Countries, but there is still fighting going on between here and there. For another thing, we cannot just leave Mademoiselle Cendrillon in the hospital here. Also, at last report by the pigeon post, Miss Eel was in a Montreux sanatorium and Monsieur Roulette with the *Saratoga* in Tours. If we take to the road, we cannot communicate to them our whereabouts, for our eventual reunion. No, we had best stay right here until the war is entirely over."

Clearly the Parisians had decided to do the same, for all those who had left the city came straggling back before nightfall, laden with country hams, milk, butter, long loaves of real bread, sheaves of firewood and buckets of coal, every other kind of provision they had lacked for so long. The people made the same foraging trip on subsequent days, and so did Hannibal Tyree, Jean-François Pemjean and their menagerie Slovaks, taking out every empty circus wagon, and coming back with meat for the cats and snakes, fish and honey for the bears, grain and hay for the other animals, plus all manner of fresh foods and delicacies for the humans of the company. Hannibal and Pemjean did complain that the country folk had become just as avaricious and sharp-trading as any Parisian vendor—but at least they accepted francs in payment of the astronomical prices they demanded. So, while the armistice lasted, everyone in Paris was again well fed, clothed and warmed—or everyone who could afford to be. And that dropped the price of horseflesh, dog, dace and other such iron rations, so that the poorer people of Paris could at least again afford to stave off starvation.

During that time, too, many restaurants and cafés-concerts reopened their doors, while the Florilegium continued to show as before, but now to increasing audiences again. Several of the artistes were "doubling" or even "tripling" to make up for those absent. Clover Lee now wore Monday's Spanish costume and did the haute école riding in addition to her rosinback turn. Sunday resumed doing the slant climb, with old Jörg Pfeifer as her cross-over partner, to replace her sister's tightrope act. In the sideshow, Fitzfarris delightedly expatiated at length to the jossers on the fact of Princess Brunhilde's pregnancy, and—in a hushed and awful voice—invited them to speculate on what the offspring of a giantess and the horrible Kostchei might look like when it arrived. Olga and Timoféi endured that embarrassment with circus stoicism, but then Fitz proposed a further audacity:

"Hey, Princess, Deathless, how about this? We'll have your kid earning its keep before it's even here. We'll sell tickets to the jossers, chances on a raffle game. Have them guess the day it'll come—or better yet, the *weight*—the winner to get a big prize out of the takings. Hell, maybe we can even figure some way for them to guess what the kid will look—"

"Sir John," said Kostchei, in a hushed and awful voice. "You utter one more word and guess what I will make *you* look like."

So Fitz went away, crestfallen, and, while he made up some cross of Lorraine eggs for the coq de bruyère to have laid, moped in self-pity at people's unappreciation of his efforts to do his best for them.

Probably Foreign Minister Favre was feeling just as Fitzfarris did. The armistice went on for nearly a month, during which Jules Favre must have decided that he was the most universally despised of men. Whenever he went to Versailles, his attempts to negotiate lenient terms were received by the Germans with open contempt, because both Kaiser Wilhelm and Chancellor Bismarck were well aware of his government's unpopularity, the seething unrest in Paris and the perpetual dissension among the numerous Republican factions. To every one of his proposals they replied stiffly, "Yours is a government by back-alley brawl. How can we expect it to respect any agreement?" And, whenever Favre returned to Paris, he passed on almost every street corner a Communard, atop a market box or a statue pedestal, haranguing an attentive crowd:

"*You*, comrade citizens, overthrew the vile emperor! But *you* have been betrayed by the even viler Republic..."

"*You*, comrade citizens, are now being surrendered by Favre to the clutches of our longtime enemies, the vile boches..."

"*You*, comrade citizens, are being abased in the eyes of our even older enemies, the even viler *English!*"

That last was guaranteed to provoke a comradely angry response from all listeners. True, the English had ostensibly sided with France in this war, and true, the English had even sent relief when and whither it was possible. But it was also true that an English shipment of winter boots for the French soldiers had turned out to have paper soles. And was it not also true that Queen Victoria was a blood cousin of Kaiser Wilhelm? So the crowds roared cries of outrage and ire and mutiny: "A bas la République!" and even—ominously—more and more often, "Vive la Commune!"

By the middle of February, Monday Simms was out of her traction bed, transferred to a wheelchair and being taught by the hospital attendants how to maneuver it. She told her visiting colleagues, "Y'all don't know how good it feels not to be looking at a ceiling all day long. I bet I done counted every crack in that plaster. But it ain't no fun and games trying to roll this-here chair neither. All my stren'th used to be in my legs—ropewalking, horse riding. Now I gonna get arms like Obie Quakemaker's."

But she found that that was not necessarily so; Pemjean was willing and eager to roll her anywhere she wanted to go about the hospital. When she was released from there, Pemjean, Florian and Edge came for her with a newly purchased wicker wheelchair to be her very own. (Wheelchairs being one commodity that had not exorbitantly increased in price, Florian had been able to buy the best one in the shop.) Thereafter, at the hotel, on the street—and, eventually, when she was hale enough, on the tober—Pemjean was Monday's constant attendant and chair pusher, until one day Clover Lee took him aside and said sternly:

"Look here, Monsieur Démon, you're going to turn that girl into a professional invalid. Lazy and petulant and demanding."

"Madame la Comtesse," said Pemjean, with hauteur, "you speak of the woman I love."

"Well, you love your old Maximus, too, I think. He's damn near rigid with rheumatism now, but if you refused to let him do his jumps—sad though it is to watch him—you know he'd just pine away and die. Jules Rouleau was once stuck in a wheelchair, but nobody would have dared to treat *him* like a baby in a perambulator. Pretty soon, he was as fleet on wheels as he'd been on his feet. You do take good care of Monday's other needs. But one thing she needs, you're not letting her have, and that's self-reliance."

Although with some misgiving, Pemjean took Clover Lee's advice, and increasingly absented himself from Monday's side. For some while, she was inclined to sit wherever her chair had been put, so she could whine and grouse about being neglected, but everyone else deliberately ignored her. Before long, necessity and boredom impelled her to propel herself about. And, before much longer, she was doing it with agility, rapidity and apparent enjoyment. Only Pemjean knew how often she wept at night, and lamented, "What I am is me at one end and a log at the other."

During this time, Foreign Minister Favre had doggedly gone on trying to negotiate with the Germans, but finally had to accede to their terms. On the twenty-sixth of February, he and Premier Adolphe Thiers rode together to Versailles to sign with Chancellor Bismarck the "preliminaries of a peace." Trochu remained behind in Paris, to send what remained of his loyal regular troops about the city to disarm all the units of the Home Guard. He deemed it highly advisable to get that done before the citizenry learned the distressing terms of the agreement being signed.

The majority of the moblots and sédentaires happily handed over their rifles and their artillery pieces, only too pleased to be relieved of militia duty. But an alarmingly numerous minority of them flatly refused to relinquish their arms. They were the men who had worked to forge the weapons in the improvised railroad-station factories, and now claimed them as personal property. Most of the men were the guards of Montmartre, Belleville and other working-class districts, and wore with their uniforms a red shirt, sash or kerchief. Trochu's regulars were both outnumbered by "the Reds" and outfaced by their stony solidarity, so the arms-collecting troops could only return to the Hôtel de Ville to report that they had pulled the teeth of all the militiamen except the most volatile and dangerous, the Communards.

Trochu made no further attempt at that, because by now the terms of the peace preliminaries were known all over the city, and the city was again on the boil. What Favre and Thiers had agreed to was nothing less than the abject surrender of Paris, with only the one mitigating condition that the Germans would not occupy it in perpetuity. Thirty thousand of the enemy troops would march into the city on the first of March, and would camp here until the surrender was formally ratified by the whole National Assembly, then they would depart. No doubt some Parisians were glad for the small mercy of having their city spared the indignity of long occupation, but most of them—naturally including the ever obstreperous Communards—were furious at this newest "betrayal" by the Republican leaders. For one thing, they told each other heatedly, this agreement was tantamount to a confession that all of France was now defeated. But there were still French armies in the field, some still fighting, and there were some cities still bravely holding firm against German siege, and for those armies and those cities this unelected government had no right to speak.

"Well, it is as I said," Florian told his chiefs. "The Germans will make only a token march of triumph, in and out again. Unless, God forbid, the diehard Communards should take a notion to fire on them. What mainly worries me is the possibility of there being a *civil* war here, as soon as there is no longer any German presence to damp the revolutionary ardors. Nevertheless, let us show our respect for poor defeated Paris. We will give no more performances after the last day of February, the eve of the victors' marching in. Then we shall stay shut down, lying low, until we see what turn events take thereafter."

By rights, the first day of March should have been as dark a day in fact as it was in most Parisian hearts. But when the Germans came strutting in, they brought with them a seemingly traitorous springtime, the bitter winter having disappeared all at once, the day unseasonably balmy and bright. So the sun made the Krupp-steel cannon barrels gleam, and made the bayonet points and helmet spikes flash spanglelike sparkles, while the warm breeze made the immense banners and standards undulate voluptuously. Von Moltke led the troops of cavalry, the companies of infantry, the batteries of artillery, and each separate unit had its own brass band, alternately playing Schubert's "Military March" and—so the goose-stepping troops could bellow their *halli-hallo!* singing to it—"Die Wacht am Rhein." The officers wore gaily plumed hats and chests full of medals, every last man's uniform was crisp and pipe-clayed, every horse was impeccably groomed and its flanks checkerboard-brushed. With all their swagger and swank, the conquerors had at least had the good grace not to bring General Sheridan with them.

Though the procession entered Paris by way of the Bois, just north of the

Florilegium's tober, none of the troupers went to watch. And when it proceeded on along the avenue de l'Impératrice, that boulevard was also almost empty of oglers. When the parade reached the Place de l'Etoile, von Moltke gave only four Prussian regiments the honor of marching through the Arc de Triomphe; all the rest—Bavarians, Saxons, Hessians and other allies—had to be content with merely circling that monument. Then the procession went on along the avenue des Champs-Elysées, likewise almost empty of Parisians, until it halted in the Place de la Concorde, and there disbanded. Most of the German units stayed there to pitch their shelter-half tents, and some of those soldiers when, dismissed from ranks, did a victory dance around the Strasbourg statue. Other units were marched off to camp in the gardens of the Tuileries, the Carrousel and the Palais Royal, but all stayed on the Right Bank, and all punctiliously set up rope barriers to divide their "occupied Paris" from "free Paris."

The reason that the city streets were only *almost* empty of spectators was that every Parisian had stayed patriotically aloof and indoors—except those Parisians who had something to sell, and they were numerous. As soon as the German soldiers were off parade and free to trade, every café owner in the occupied areas threw open his doors to them, every pimp and prostitute from all the twenty arrondissements and eighty quarters descended upon them, and they were assailed by vendors peddling everything from pretzels to plaster replicas of the Arc de Triomphe—and clocks. Somehow the word had gone about the city: "No German can resist a clock," so there came clockmakers, pawnbrokers, burglars and penurious householders, offering bracket clocks, case clocks, porcelain clocks, enameled clocks, even Black Forest cuckoo clocks. And whoever had started the rumor had been right; the Germans bought them, and paid handsomely for them, even the cuckoo clocks.

Whether the Republic's Assembly was more anxious to get rid of the Germans or to end that shameless display of Parisians pandering to them, the legislators ratified the preliminary peace agreement in record time, by the very next day. And on the day after that, the Germans packed up their belongings, their clocks and other acquisitions, shouldered arms, formed up in parade and marched out again. It may have been unfortunate for the French Republic that the unusually fine weather did not depart with them. If the month of March had turned to its usual blustery chill, the ensuing events might not have occurred. But no sooner had the Germans cleared the city limits than the red-sashed militiamen flocked from their outlying districts into the city's center to punish those citizens who had consorted with the enemy. Encountering no resistance or interference from either police or soldiery, the Communards used their rifle butts to smash the furniture, bottles and glassware in a few of the German-serving cafés and estaminets, then beat a number of prostitutes nearly to death, but refrained even from scolding any of the women's pimps, the pimps being known to carry knives or razors.

With their blood up now, with the weather continuing wonderfully mild, with—oddly or not—still no official restraint in the form of police action, the Communards widened the scope of their punitive campaign. From the consorters-with-the-Germans, they went on to every other enemy and political opponent they had ever had or imagined, and every person or institution that they had collectively or individually yearned to get even with. While the more recent enemies, the Germans, were efficiently leaving Versailles and rolling up their siege lines—to move en masse to a position east of the city—Paris was enjoying far less peace and tranquillity than it had known in the worst days of the cannon bombardment. Over the next two weeks, mobs of the Communards surrounded the Hôtel de Ville, the Ministry of Foreign Affairs and other government buildings, pelting them and their cowering guards with every kind of missile, from cobblestones to horse turds, that would not draw return fire. Other mobs roamed the streets, breaking into and looting any mansions the owners had vacated and left insufficiently guarded, ransacking the boutiques that had catered to those élite folk—and even poor père-et-mère shops, if the proprietors were Jews, or foreigners, or Frenchmen known to be unsympathetic to the Communard cause, or if they were owed money by anyone in the mob.

For all the inviting beauty of the early-budding springtime, almost everyone except the rampaging rabble stayed huddled indoors. The Florilegium, like almost every other gathering place, remained closed to the public, and all the company kept close to their hotel, except for the tober-patrolling Slovaks and Jászi brothers, plus Edge, Yount or Fitzfarris, who again took turns as "corporal of the guard." Since no mobs had yet attacked there, Edge found that job as boring as any army garrison duty, so he began to enliven it by teaching every man who could sit a horse to do some simple cavalry arms drills, and even taught the band's trumpet windjammer some of the American cavalry bugle calls.

One night Monsieur Nadar appeared at the Grand Hôtel du Louvre, for once not in sartorial splendor, not even sporting his square monocle, and told Florian, with rather less than his customary casualness, "I waited until after dark to come, because the streets are not quite so perilous at night. And, even at hazard to my own well-being, I decided I ought to come and recommend that you move your company out of this establishment."

"Why? Is it on the looting list?"

"I do not know. But your residence here marks you as persons of affluence, a dangerous thing to be nowadays. Look at *me*, ami, wearing clothes of peasant tiretaine for disguise. I strongly urge that you remove your people to the safety of your circus ground. And even there, be not conspicuous in dress or display or consumption. Once more the cry is for Liberté, Egalité, Fraternité. So anyone evidencing wealth or luxury or authority or prestige or privilege—even of intelligence above the average jackass—is liable to be, let us say, cut down to égalité with the masses. Also be careful of your women. The common louts, convinced of their equality with even the highest-born lady, will rudely fraternize and take every sort of liberty with her."

"Come, come, monsieur. We have entertained those people. They surely cannot bear us any ill will."

"Can they not? Precisely *because* you have entertained them, you have shown yourselves not to have a sour and solemn outlook on life."

"I should hope we don't. What of that?"

"The most rabid revolutionaries, mon vieux, are always the most hidebound reactionaries. I am not making an epigram. It is the lower class that revolts, and I ask you—what, besides ignorance and the belief that ignorance is a virtue, are the distinctive traits of the lower class? Intolerant prudery, bigoted piety and the certainty that its constipated morality should be everybody's."

"Well, that is one way to achieve equality for all, by damn. The denying of liberty to all."

"Just so. Your troupers are not of acceptable joylessness, therefore they are in danger. Get them out of it and away to safe seclusion."

No one of the company minded at all the move to the tober, and their living again in caravans, in such a benevolent springtime, when the Bois was bright with greenery and flowers. Florian minded least of all, because the cost of accommodations at the hotel had been the greatest drain on the Florilegium's treasury. The troupe took with them plenty of provisions, so they should not even have to venture into the city to dine. The permanent inhabitants of the tober, the roustabouts, who had for so long been making their own meals, were glad to have the rest of the company present, for Ioan Delattre, Meli Vasilakis and Daphne Wheeler cheerfully pitched in to make one of the now seldom used dressing tents into a cookhouse wherein to feed everybody. Goesle even made for it a flagpole with a halyarded pennant, so the cooks could hoist that at mealtimes and draw the time-honored shout from all over the grounds, "Flag's up!"

"Just like the old, old times," Florian remarked to several people, but not entirely happily. "Come the full circle, we have."

Once on the tober, the artistes were constitutionally unable simply to laze about. Every one of them began practicing, to work out the kinks incurred during this latest layoff, and to experiment with new tricks and turns. Le Démon Débonnaire tried an act combining mixed breeds of cats—having old Maximus stalk from his own cage into that of Raja, Rani and Siva, where he was to stand still while the three tigers vaulted back and forth over him. And it worked without contrariness from either the lion or the tigers. True, the venerable Maximus seemed a little downcast at having been demoted from performer to prop, but he seemed almost grateful for his work having been eased without removing him from the pista, where he could still enjoy attention and applause, so he took his semiretirement graciously enough.

The Jászi brothers somewhere procured a quantity of old sabres, and blunted their points and edges, then conscripted half a dozen of the roustabouts that Colonel Ramrod had already taught to stay in a saddle, and worked them into a horseback sabre duel in which—once the Slovaks had got over being terrified by the wild Hungarian recklessness of the mêlée—Arpád, Gusztáv and Zoltán convincingly "dueled to the death" with twice their number of opponents. They then applied to Florian for permission to bill that act as "The Gallant French Spahis Challenge the Vicious German Uhlans" and, having got his permission, next applied to wardrobe mistress Ioan for the making of proper uniforms for all participants. When Ioan set herself to that job, her plumber husband, Pierre, who had just finished putting all the tober's donnickers in prime condition, obligingly took her place in the cookhouse—but not until after Florian had made him give his hands and clothes a good scrubbing.

The bustling busyness of everyone else on the tober infected even Monday Simms. She surprised the equestrian director by rolling her wicker chair up to him and saying:

"Colonel Zack, that Thunder horse of yours, when I rode him, he done most of his fancy stepping to touches of the quirt. Not too many of 'em to knee squeezes or heel kicks. And I bet I could learn him to do *all* of 'em to a touch or maybe a word. If I was to be strapped in the saddle..." And she looked up at him imploringly.

Edge thought about it. "Well, I don't know what the good doctor would say to such daredevilry. But I sure admire you for proposing it, and I'm damned if I can see how it could hurt you. Hell, yes, let's go ask Stitches if he can work up some kind of harness for you."

While various of the circus's crewmen left the Bois at intervals, taking wagons to fetch fresh supplies of this and that, the only trouper who went beyond the park every day was Sunday Simms. Each morning she would stroll as far as the nearest street kiosque or crieur, to buy a newspaper and to hear what she could of the latest gossip and rumors, in order to keep the company informed of events in the city and the rest of France.

Her reports and her readings-aloud from the papers indicated that the government leaders, for some while yet, tried to ignore the still-rampaging Communards and their followers, evidently hoping that those were only ragtag mobs venting their spleen in random vandalism, and that they would eventually weary of the sport. But then, to its alarm and chagrin, the government learned that the depredations were being directed and coordinated by a Communard "Comité Central" and that the mutinous militia was now dignifying itself as a "Garde Nationale." Belatedly recognizing that the unabating turbulence was not inchoate rioting but organized revolution, the Hôtel de Ville made one last attempt to quell it.

On the seventeenth of March, the government's regulars, commanded by no fewer than four army generals, marched to the main stronghold of the Garde Nationale, the Butte Montmartre, to demand the surrender of the artillery pieces that now studded it from top to bottom. And again the red-sashed men refused —laughed, said some observers—at which the generals drew up their troops, had them level their rifles and ordered them to fire on "the damned rebel Reds." The troops did not exactly decline to shoot at fellow Frenchmen; about half of them simply did an about-face, with the leveled rifles now aimed at their officers. They calmly declared themselves defectors to "the people's cause" and actually arrested—"by authority of the Commune"—two of the generals and numerous other soldiers of lesser rank who were too slow in fleeing the scene.

The next day, a Communard stump court gleefully put on trial the hapless generals Lecomte and Clément-Thomas for "crimes against the people," summarily found them guilty and sentenced them to be stood against a wall and shot. The execution was attended by most of the inhabitants of Montmartre and the surrounding working-class districts, all cheering lustily. While that was going on, the leaders of the government—demoralized by finding that they no longer had enough loyal soldiers even to protect themselves, let alone to maintain the tottering Republic—decided abruptly not to be government leaders any more, at least not in Paris, and were hastily decamping from every government office. Adolphe Thiers was the first out of town, at a gallop, in a carriage escorted by a troop of cuirassiers, and he did not stop until he was safe inside the château of Versailles, itself only recently evacuated by the German High Command.

There ensued ten days of anarchy, probably a confusing time even for residents of the central city, and more so to the circus company out in the Bois, because the newspapers began to be only infrequently distributed, and some of them not at all, and any of their accounts of events were fragmented and incoherent. So were the rumors and gossip that Sunday managed to glean. But the general import was that the Communards were taking over the city and, while doing so, were either shooting on sight or taking prisoner every noble and political and military and bourgeois personage they considered inimical to them. The reason for the newspapers' increasingly undependable publication was that most of them were shutting up shop, either voluntarily or by mob demand, because they had not supported the Communard cause. Soon the only papers Sunday could find on the kiosques had names like *Le Journal de la Commune* and *Le Cri du Peuple,* and contained more "Hourra pour nous!" than news.

The Florilegium's most trustworthy source of information was Monsieur Nadar, who came out to the tober from time to time. But his communiqués were sometimes of such a nature that he imparted them only to Florian and Edge.

"It is as I said, mes amis. The rabble are equating nobility with immorality, and vice versa, and not entirely mistakenly. But they are employing bestial measures to stamp out both. Have you heard what they did to the Marquise de Persan?"

"No."

"She was one of the ladies of 'the little Eldorado of Saint-Germain.' Those females, although most are married, have always preferred the company of their own sex. Alors, the mob caught the marquise imprudently out for a stroll. Before imprisoning her with their other high-ranking hostages, they paraded her through the streets stark naked and grotesquely mutilated. They did to her what their grandfathers did to a Princesse Something-or-other, eighty years ago, during the Terror. In the manner of Red Indians taking scalps, they cut out and peeled off the marquise's, ahem, chevelure pubienne, and stuck it on her face for a goatee."

Florian said, "Dear God, don't tell us any more."

"Eh bien, what is even more disgusting is that the canaille have *their own* perverts, and not only leave them unmolested, but elevate them to positions of responsibility. You have noticed the rapid extinguishment of newspapers? That is the doing of the Commune's recently appointed Censeur de la Presse—and guess who that is. A onetime acquaintance of one of your troupe. The Poet Nauseate. Paul Verlaine."

Edge also said, and even more feelingly, "Dear God, don't tell us any more."

Meanwhile, the other troupers enjoyed their remoteness from the storm, and delighted in the lovely springtime, and carried on with their occupations. Dai Goesle and Ioan Delattre made the supportive harness Monday had requested, and made it so cunningly that, although it comprised quite a number of straps to hold her on the saddle, plus a stiff back brace to hold her erect, it would be unnoticeable to any jossers who weren't professional riders themselves. The back brace, for instance, was hidden by a short cape that Ioan added to Monday's Cordobesa costume.

Jean-François Pemjean anxiously gnawed his knuckles, the first time Edge lifted Monday onto Thunder, but not for long, for she quickly had the horse in hand. She admitted afterward that she had felt vertigo for a moment, but then "it was like I never been off of him." Edge thought it probable that Thunder also had to adjust to the feeling of having a half-lifeless burden on his back. But Monday and the horse had to rehearse for only a matter of days before Thunder had learned to help keep her balanced in the saddle, and had learned also to do all his sedate or prancing steps of haute école to merely manual and vocal commands.

"I'd say you two are ready to show, whenever we do show again," said Edge, one bright morning, lifting her down from Thunder and settling her in her wheelchair. "But you go yourself and ask the Governor if he agrees."

Edge politely remained at a distance while they held a rather long colloquy. When Monday at last rolled herself away, smiling, Edge went over to Florian, and saw that he was frowning uncertainly.

"I hope you told her yes," said Edge. "The kid may never be any tower of intellect, but she sure shows more get-up-and-go nowadays than she used to. It almost seems that her accident made a new person of her."

"New person. Yes," Florian said distractedly. "But I worry. Maggie claims she is perfectly capable of returning to work, but she is also dukkering something bad about to happen."

"Well, if she—what? *Maggie*? Maggie Hag?"

"She says she doesn't know how she knows. And it is certain that she has not the least grasp of local politics, so I fear that she may foresee some calamity of a circus sort. She says she just *feels* that something dire is in prospect."

"I reckon I'd take her word for it, Governor," Edge said drily, "if she's taken all the trouble to come back from the hereafter to warn you."

"Eh?" said Florian, looking confused.

"Governor," said Edge, regarding him with some concern. "Magpie Maggie Hag has been dead and buried for two and a half years."

"Maggie? Did I say Maggie Hag? Well, well. Heh heh heh . . ." Florian paused to collect himself. "I meant to say *Monday*. Monday Simms. I meant to say that Monday has begun to *behave* like old Mag. The way Maggie used to, that is. Dukkering, I mean."

"Oh?"

"Yes. Of course, as you say, she seems physically almost improved by her accident, and naturally I gave my permission for her to perform again. But then she cautioned me to watch out for something bad in the offing. It makes me wonder if the accident addled her mind. Or if perhaps it endowed her with some gift—some extra sensitivity—as compensation for her infirmity. I suppose we'll simply have to wait and see."

"Yes," said Edge, still looking searchingly at him.

"It's just one more thing," said Florian, with a long sigh, "to make me feel that we have come full circle. Back to the bygone days of yore. Lord help us, next I'll be hearing someone doing old Maximus's roaring for him again . . ." And Florian wandered off, despondently shaking his silver-gray head.

15

THE CITY'S DISORDER at last began to subside, until, on the twenty-eighth of March, the Garde Nationale and other Communards actually stood orderly and quiet. In fact, that day they stood at attention, in disciplined ranks—from the Place du Châtelet to the Place de l'Hôtel de Ville, and along all the streets, quais and avenues between—while brass bands played and red flags flapped everywhere. The ordinary folk of Paris also joined the throng, many of them emerging into the open for the first time in ten days or so. The focus of all that attention was a platform that had been erected to extend the porch of the Hôtel de Ville. Up there, looking as solemn as their black serge suits, stood the mayors of all the arrondissements of Paris, who had until now been the only legal authorities left in the city. In front of them stood another row of men, also in sober dress except for the diagonal red sashes across their shirt fronts, the Communard eminences whom the convened mayors had helped select to constitute the city's new government.

One of them, Henri d'Assy, stepped forward to announce to the crowd packed in the Place, "Camarades! Citoyens! The Comité Central has now been dissolved and—let us rejoice—the Commune is proclaimed!"

The camarades and citoyens, most of whom had lately been living in hiding from the savage minions of these very men, boisterously applauded and cheered: "Vive la Commune!" They continued to roar approval as one speaker after another stepped forward to posture and pontificate.

"Today, citoyens—seventh day of the month Germinal of the year seventy-nine since the proclamation of the First Republic—today Paris opens the book of history to a blank page, and thereon inscribes her radiant name!"

"Vive la Commune!"

"Too long we have suffered, citoyens, under the archaic laws of the rest of France! From this day forward, Paris will be a city apart—liberated from the petty meddling of rustic provincial legislators!"

"Vive la Commune!"

"Incroyable," muttered Florian, one of a few troupers who had come to look on. "The Germans out at Chelles must be astounded and convulsed with hilarity by such a spectacle. The Parisians are hailing the third government they have had in less than eight months."

"I think," said LeVie, "the Parisians would hail any régime that is not already being subverted by some number of themselves. As soon as any faction starts to denounce and undermine this one, the cheering will stop and the citywide booing will commence."

"This one may not let any booing commence," said Pemjean. "The press is stifled, the religious and military schools are closed, there have been hundreds of dissenters put under political arrest. Nobles, magistrates, generals, clerics—even the Archbishop of Paris. And Mazas Prison is well called the antechamber of the scaffold."

"Also," said Florian, eyeing a notice posted on the wall behind them, "I see that all internal passports are being called in, for verification of their authenticity. Damn! The new bureaucrats are sure to do their best to find fault with every paper issued by the old."

As the troupers made their way through the street crowds back toward the Bois de Boulogne, they saw café waiters setting tables out on the sidewalks, and even saw men pasting up theatre posters announcing forthcoming programs.

"You see?" said LeVie. "As long as the Parisian masses are unhindered in their making of money from each other—or from anybody, even their enemies—they do not greatly care who occupies the throne or the Hôtel de Ville."

Florian said, "Then I suppose we might as well take the same attitude, and open our own front door again. But first, I shall see what this business of the internal passports might portend."

He waited a few days, until the mingled commotion, celebration and uncertainty in the city had died down. Then, leaving all the artistes at practice and rehearsal, all eager to get back to work, Florian drove off in his rockaway to the central préfecture, carrying the company's sheaf of passports. But he was back very soon, looking exasperated. Edge was in the red wagon, reloading his revolver after having done some target practice, when Florian came in to rummage in his office trunk, grumbling meanwhile:

"Just as I feared, confound it. Heretofore, we have had to deal only with red tape. Now it is Red red tape."

"They found some fault with our documents?"

"Zachary, you *know* that finding fault is the first duty of any civil servant, *and* his chief delight in life. Add to that the Frenchman's dislike of strangers and the Communard's distrust of everybody, and you have bureaucracy thrice compounded. When I handed in our passports, Rigault scratched out the printed word 'Empire' on all of them, and scribbled in 'République' instead—and added an 'e' to the 'Français.' The typical picayune paltering of a desk clerk, and I thought that would be an end to it. But then Rigault held onto the passports and demanded that I fetch our conduct books, as well."

"Rigault?"

"You remember, when the mobs were first pillaging private property, we wondered why the police never intervened. Well, now I know why. This Raoul Rigault was installed by the Trochu government as its Préfet de Police, but he was a Communard all the time. Now he styles himself the Procureur de la Commune, and seems determined to be the most obnoxious of the bunch. It is he who has ordered all those political arrests, so we had best be wary of him. Most of us are foreigners—one of us is a Russian princess, another a Bavarian baron—and, of our few genuine Frenchmen, one is a Jew." Florian finally came up with the conduct books. "I shall take these to Rigault. Let the artistes go on with their rehearsal, Colonel Ramrod, and please oversee it for me. But we dare not announce our reopening or do any other damned thing without the procureur's approval."

Edge put his pistol in his belt holster, followed Florian from the wagon and ambled into the chapiteau, whence came a loud boom-and-oompah of music. Beck was rehearsing his band in the "Radetzky March," which he had chosen to accompany the sabre duel of the Jászis and their Slovak opponents. All nine of those men were also in the tent, on horseback in the pista, flailing away at each other, because this was their first practice in the new uniforms Ioan had made for them. When that rehearsal came to an end and Beck dismissed his band, Edge ambled out of the tent again, into the backyard, where Monday had been putting Thunder through his paces. She signaled to Edge that she too was ready to dismount, so he went to unstrap her and her back brace from the saddle and settle her in the wheelchair. As Monday, carrying her harness in her lap, trundled herself away to the dressing top, Edge led Thunder to hand him over to one of the Slovak bandsmen who were just then emerging from the chapiteau. But he halted when he was hailed in French—"Holà! Garçon!"—by one of a body of strangers who had trooped onto the tober.

Edge politely waited as they approached, though they had obviously mistaken him for a stable groom. The dozen men were all carrying holstered pistols or slung rifles of various sorts and various degrees of antiquity, but the men wore no uniforms. The one who had shouted spoke again, inquiring where he might find this establishment's proprietor. Edge replied, in French, that Monsieur Florian was in the city on business, and asked if he, the establishment's director, could do something for the messieurs.

"If you would, citoyen," said the spokesman. "We are of the Committee of Public Safety. We are informed that you have among your company a certain noblewoman, the Comtesse de Lareinty." He added, with a man-to-man leer, "We are also informed that she is a female of great beauty. Une blonde dorée." Then he quit leering to say, very businesslike, "She is required to accompany us."

"Required, monsieur?"

"For interrogation, citoyen."

"Regarding what, monsieur?"

"You will address me correctly, as citoyen. And you will not question the actions or motives of the Commune's Committee of Public Safety. Produce the countess, and do it this instant."

The circus band's trumpeter had come across the yard, goggling at the armed intruders, to take Thunder's reins. But Edge held onto them, as he said coldly to the Frenchman, "I do not believe there is any countess here. What is more, I do not much believe that there is any Committee of Public Safety here, either. Show me some kind of warrant or identification."

"Pignouf! We need show you nothing. You need but to obey! Bring us the countess!"

Edge did not really care whether or not this was an authentic committee, for he was remembering what Nadar had related about the Communards' horrific treatment of another noblewoman, and *those* had been authentic Communards. So he was merely parrying for time while he uneasily considered the odds: twelve well-armed men against him, his one revolver and the Slovak, armed with nothing but a trumpet. Everyone else of the company seemed to have chosen this time to be absent or invisibly occupied elsewhere, or had given only a glance at what looked like a peaceable colloquy, and had gone on about his business.

"Bring the countess!" the man commanded again. "Or be arrested yourself."

Edge said, "I'll be damned if I will," and, without taking his eyes off the group, said to the Slovak in English, "Sound 'to horse.'"

The trumpeter obediently did so, and the newcomers all started and goggled at *him*. But the flourish of noise was brief and produced no discernible effect except to bring a few of the circus company peering from the doors of caravans or wagons, then disappearing again. Edge hoped mightily that Clover Lee de Lareinty—and every other "female of great beauty"—would remain in safe concealment.

The committee's spokesman jerked his head at the trumpeter and said menacingly to Edge, "Tu fais péterade, citoyen? You try to ridicule us by blowing farts? And you dare to impede an officer of the Commune in the performance of his duty? Very well, you also will come with us. But first, go and get the countess."

"I don't go and I don't come until you show me something to prove who the hell you are."

"Then you are under arrest. I shall find her myself."

The man gestured, and all his followers drew their pistols or unslung their rifles to point them, and the Slovak sidled around behind Edge. But then the spokesman hesitated, and glared about the yard uncertainly. He had seen some of the circus company, but he could not know how many there were all together, or if they were armed and prepared to repel intruders. However, he stood unde-cided for not long, because now there came around a corner of the chapiteau one of the circus's females of great beauty. It was Sunday, returning to the tober after purchasing the afternoon newspapers, and looking quite the lady herself in a handsome street gown and hat. Before Edge could call a warning, the committee leader gave a shout, and four or five of his men darted over there to seize the girl.

The leader, now holding a pistol aimed at Edge, backed a little away from him, grinning wolfishly. "We came for a noblewoman. Voilà, we have one. Any-thing that happens to her now, whoever she is, will be your own fault—and that of the real Comtesse de Lareinty, so cowardly hiding. This one will serve in her stead, so we need not arrest you, citoyen. Simply stay where you are and stay quiet until we are well away."

Sunday had dropped her newspapers when she was seized, and those were merrily scattering and wafting about the backyard. But she had not cried out and she was not struggling against her captors; she merely looked over to Edge as if for instructions. All the rest of the committee—except the leader, still grinning and holding Edge at bay—cautiously backed over there to bunch about the girl, forming a cordon with weapons bristling outward. Edge stood unmoving for a moment, weighing alternatives. Then he shrugged and said to the Slovak, "Sound the 'charge.'"

The committee had evidently decided that the Slovak was only a harmless prankster, so none of them shot him when he blared the bugle call. And he had not even finished it when there came an even louder noise—men shouting and hoofs pounding—and nine horses and riders erupted from the back door of the chapiteau. They were so compactly grouped that they brought part of the canvas sidewalls flapping loose on both sides of the door, poles and ropes and stakes flying. In the same instant, Edge vaulted to Thunder's saddle, his revolver in his hand.

The committee men all spun to face the chapiteau, and briefly froze where they stood—perhaps not so much stupefied by the sudden charge as by its ap-pearing to consist of mingled French and German cavalrymen. Then the men sprang apart, and Sunday flung herself prone on the ground, for she knew what her captors did not: that a running horse, even a stampeding horse, will take care not to tread on a prostrate and apparently helpless human being in its path. The moving men, however, were fair game, and the Jászis might have done no more than ride them down, chasing and trampling them. But the men's leader whirled again on Edge and, before he could reaim his pistol, Edge shot him in the chest. Seeing that, the Jászi brothers did not restrain themselves, and their companion Slovaks followed their lead, leveling their sabres as they charged after the men. The sabre points were blunted, but the impetus of the charge drove even those dull tips clear through the bodies of five or six of the men, spattering blood and gobbets of gore.

There was a great deal of noise: the Jászis shouting wild Hungarian war cries; the Frenchmen who had been wounded, but not mortally, shrieking or groaning in pain; the yet uninjured Frenchmen, in a panic and forgetting that they still held weapons, wailing as they tried to flee. And, running to the fray, came other circus men, shouting "Hey, rube!" Over all of that, Edge managed to bellow, *"Don't let any get away!"* So the mounted circus men who still had sabres used them, and those afoot used tent stakes as clubs. Meanwhile, Edge rode Thunder to where Sunday still lay prone inside the churning crowd. He leaned from his saddle, she reached for his hand and he swung her up behind him. By the time he had carried her the short distance to the chapiteau, the battle was over, and the dozen intruders were either lying limp or writhing in agony on the ground.

As Sunday slid down from the horse, Edge said, "Get inside and don't look out." Without waiting to see if she obeyed, he whirled Thunder back to the scene of combat. Obie Yount, tent stake in hand, was standing over one fallen man. Edge said, "Sergeant, you and I will finish this job. The rest of you men—*scatter*. You haven't fought anybody. You haven't seen anything. You know nothing of what has happened here. Make sure all the women are indoors and that they stay there until further notice."

The Slovak trumpeter, still on the field, conscientiously finished *his* job by blowing "Retreat," then vanished with the rest. Yount, the only circus man remaining, ignored the various piteous utterances of the Frenchmen still conscious, brought his tent stake smartly up in the rifle salute and said, "Orders, sir?"

Edge dismounted with a heavy sigh and said, "The coup de grâce, Sergeant. I hate to do it, but we can't leave any of these to tell the tale. If you want to be excused, just say so."

"Oh, hell, Zack," said Yount, "think of 'em as Injuns," and with his stake neatly broke the neck of the man at his feet.

When they both were done with that grisly business, Yount volunteered to collect some of the company's most trustworthy old-timers, to bury the bodies undiscoverably far in the brush of the Bois. So Edge went to his caravan to wash the blood and powder stains off his hands and shirt. While he was at that, there came a knock at his door. He opened it and Sunday entered; her dress also had blood on it, and mud and grass stains as well.

"I came to say thank you. I still don't know what that was all about, but I know you saved my life. Or saved me from what the novels call a fate worse than death."

"No, from being mistaken for a noblewoman by the Communards."

She considered that, then shuddered slightly. "It probably *would* have been worse than just death, wouldn't it? Well... I'm sure you'd have saved anybody, in that case. But thank you."

"I only wish I hadn't had to do it at all. Those men may have deserved and needed killing, but it wasn't any pleasure for me. And God knows what the repercussions are likely to be."

"It was my fault, for walking straight into their hands the way I did. If I hadn't come back from—"

"No, no. They were out for trouble, and they'd have got it, one way or another. You weren't to blame, Sunday. Don't you feel bad about it."

"I wasn't, really. I was thinking how bad you must feel. You wanted not ever to risk leading another cavalry charge, because you thought you might—because you thought it might turn out wrong. And commanding a cavalry charge is what you've just now done."

"I... why, yes, I reckon it was, pretty near..." Edge looked a little surprised and dazzled by the realization. "I didn't even hesitate. I wonder why." He looked long and thoughtfully at Sunday. "Maybe... maybe because it was you that stood in danger." And his face creased in the smile that made everybody flinch or quail—everybody except Sunday, who now smiled shyly back at him. He went on, "You wouldn't know, but a long time ago Autumn left me a letter. She said that if I ever took up with anybody else of this troupe—"

"I do know. My sister showed me the letter."

"You've read it? And you've never said a word?"

"Come, Zachary. What in the world could I have said? What could I have said that I didn't say on the Kissing Bridge in Saint Petersburg?"

There was a long silence. It was Edge who broke it:

"I wish there were a bridge like that here."

Sunday said softly, "There always has been. Everywhere. You don't have to see it. Just cross it."

Edge pondered, and finally said, "Yes. It's about time. If I've crossed Tom's Brook at last, I can surely do that. Could you, Sunday? I mean—not now, when we're both smeared with blood—but sometime, could we cross that bridge together?"

She smiled again, radiantly now, and stood on tiptoe to kiss him. "As you said, you dear old slowpoke, it's about time."

They were interrupted by another knock at the caravan door. It was Gusztáv, reporting in his rudimentary English, "Edge úr, is come Florian úr. Ask where is everybody goddammit hell. We no say. Better you tell."

"Yes," said Edge, uncomfortably. "Thanks for not breaking the bad news to him yet." He said to Sunday, "While I'm doing that, you go and get rid of that dress. Burn it. I'll buy you a new one." He gave her a quick hug and left with Gusztáv.

But he could think of no better way to broach the news to Florian than to suggest, "Maybe now it *is* time for us to skedaddle out of Paris, Governor. I'm afraid I've just worn out our welcome." And he recounted the afternoon's events, concluding, "If Monday Simms really is becoming a Maggie Hag gypsy, maybe this was the something bad that she dukkered."

"Oh, Lord," said Florian.

"I still don't know whether they were really some kind of Communard highups or just a bunch of bummers. There were no insignia, no official-looking papers on any of the bodies. I incline to the bummer theory. If they were out to capture or kill or mutilate somebody of nobility, they could have demanded Princess Olga or Willi von Wittelsbach. But they didn't want a mountain-sized woman or an effeminate fat man, they wanted a pretty girl to play with. That doesn't strike me as genuine government business."

"Genuine or spurious, no matter," said Florian. "When the whole government is nothing but the dregs of society risen to the top, there's not much to prefer between the lawmen and the outlaws."

"What puzzles me is how they knew about Clover Lee being the Comtesse de Lareinty. She's never flaunted the fact."

"Oh, it is not impossible that Nadar perhaps gossiped in the wrong circles. Or any of our own people could have bragged of it in some low grogshop. Or that loathsome Verlaine might have got wind of it while he was lurking around young Sava. He is now high in the councils of the Communards. And of course Gaspard de Lareinty was high in the councils of the emperor, so any of his family might be marked for Communard vindictiveness. *If* those men were acting officially. If they were not, well, as you have surmised, it made a plausible excuse to abduct a beautiful girl for even more nefarious reasons."

"Whoever they were, there were twelve of them, and they're all being put under the sod right this minute. I'm sorry, Governor. Maybe, if you had been here, you could have buffaloed them with your Masonic jargon or something. But I had to decide for myself, and in a hurry."

"You did quite right, my boy. Quite right. As I trust you always will do... when I am no longer here at all."

"Don't talk like that. I've already got enough worries, thank you."

"Come, come, Zachary. Have you no respect for circus lore and tradition?"

"Well... sure. But what's that got to do with—?"

"Then do you not remember the very first time we met? In that Virginia creek bottom? It seems a long time ago, now, but surely you remember." Florian smiled reminiscently and a little sadly. "It was also the first time you met the bull Brutus. She saluted you with her upcurved trunk, and I told you then what that portended."

Edge thought back and finally said, "Yes, I remember. It does seem a long time ago, doesn't it? You said it meant that someday—" He broke off, shook himself and said almost angrily, "Confound it, Governor, if you want to talk morbidity, how's this for morbid? Those dozen dead intruders—*somebody's* bound to miss them. Their bummer chums, if not the Committee of Public Safety. And that somebody is probably going to know where they went last, because they didn't come here on the spur of the moment. And that somebody is probably going to be asking us what became of them."

"Perhaps not immediately." Florian heaved a deep sigh. "Let us devoutly hope not, for we cannot pull up stakes and leave, as you recommend. The Procureur Rigault is now holding our passports *and* our conduct books. No one is being allowed to leave Paris. It seems Paris is at war again."

"Again? You mean still. Are the Germans resuming the siege?"

"No, no. The war with the Germans is over. Have you not seen the afternoon newspapers?"

"They sort of got lost in the shuffle."

"The news is just in. Or Verlaine is just now letting it be printed. The very last little hold-out French fortress fell, two or three weeks ago—Bitche, in Lorraine—and France is irrefutably defeated. The details of the final and formal surrender are now being thrashed out."

Edge said incredulously, "The mighty German Reich is dealing with this puny up-jumped Commune?"

"Of course not. Still with the Republican government, of which Adolphe Thiers is now President."

"*What* Republican government? It got run out of here."

"But not entirely out of France. It has relocated in Bordeaux. Thiers is communicating with the Germans by messenger and telegraph."

Very gently, as if speaking to a child, Edge said, "And meanwhile, Paris is at war again? With whom, Governor?"

"With France, damn it all." Florian added, with some testiness, "And don't look at me like that. It is true. Before the French forces in the field could disband, Thiers ordered a good many of them to Versailles, to prepare to retake Paris for him. They ought to be in position by now, and about ready to storm the city."

"Jesus Christ Almighty. France against herself."

"So far, Verlaine has kept that news out of his tame press. But I had it from Rigault just now, because that is the reason for the ban on travel. And anyway it will be public knowledge as soon as the shooting commences, meaning any minute. The Commune is frantically slamming every Paris gate while it frantically tries to organize a resistance. Hence our being bottled-up here, along with all the other unhappy citoyens."

"I don't think I want to hear the word citoyen any more."

"Well, persons, then. And we can hope that all those persons will be sufficiently preoccupied by this newest turn of affairs that they won't notice that twelve persons have mysteriously gone missing. Ah!—the flag is up. The ladies have dinner ready. Come, Colonel Ramrod, let us carry on as though nothing untoward had happened."

While the company dined in the cookhouse that evening—the second of April, a mere five days since the Commune had been proclaimed —they heard the boom of cannon again, and not so very far away. The forts of Vanves, Mont Valérien and Issy, west and southwest of the city, were being bombarded, and this time by French artillery. The Germans, still settled on the other side of Paris, may have been bemused to see their own siege replaced by one apparently of brother besieging brother, but the Parisians themselves were soon aware that there was no brotherliness involved. Adolphe Thiers, infuriated at having been made to flee, was burning for revenge, and not only on the Communards who had supplanted him, but on the entire ingrate city. So his "Versaillais" forces were all composed of country Frenchmen from the provinces, who never had borne any love for Paris and could be counted on to show no hesitancy in the taking of it.

They did not simply blockade the city and wait for it to yield, as the Germans had done, nor did they mannerly confine their bombardments to the nighttime hours. Day and night, while their heavy artillery kept the forts harassed and busy, the Republican forces ran repeated attacks of cavalry, infantry and lighter artillery right up to the city limits, from Gentilly to St-Cloud. Almost every day, a number of shells fell in the Bois de Boulogne, blowing shrubs and saplings to splinters, or throwing waterspouts up from the ponds, or exploding in a pretty burst of flower petals. None of the shells ever flew as far east across the Bois as the Florilegium's tober, and none of the troupe ever complained that the cannonade was preventing their reopening the show—because it was also keeping the Bois cleared of other people, including anybody who might have been curious about the whereabouts of that lost "committee."

But other committees went on with their work, war or no war. Some simply resumed the pillaging of houses formerly occupied by the nobility, the rich and the "oppressors of the people"—and began with the rue St-George ex-residence of Adolphe Thiers. Others rounded up more people for "interrogation," meaning imprisonment or worse. Some were arrested for what was called treason, as in the case of General Bergeret, because he had failed in making Paris's last desperate try to break the German siege at Buzenval—regardless of the fact that that had happened in a war already concluded. Others, such as the Magistrate Bonjean, were hauled in simply because they had held office under the imperial or the Republican régime, or both. And still others—almost all the clerics in the city—were arrested because the Church was an abomination to the Commune. The aged curé of the Madeleine was thrown into Mazas Prison, where Archbishop Darboy already languished; lesser priests were only put under house arrest. The city's nursing nuns were allowed to go on working—the hospitals could not have functioned without them—but they had to wear red sashes over their habits. One Commune committee began the job of demolishing what it regarded as the city's most egregious symbol of tyrannical rule: the towering column in the Place Vendôme, on which were depicted the exploits of Napoléon the Great, and which was topped by a statue of him. Those particular Communards may have been the most dedicated of all, for they had undertaken a laborious piece of work, sawing through a thirteen-foot-thick column of granite plated with bronze.

Most of Paris's shops, merchants and vendors had had opportunity to lay in ample stocks of goods, between the enemy Germans' unblocking of the roads and their fellow Frenchmen's blocking of them again. So there was no immediate want among the people—except, as usual, among the poorest of them—and the weather continued wonderfully clement. Some of the city's bourgeois institutions tried a pretending of normality and even the traditional gaîté parisienne; indeed, the Gaîté Théâtre opened with a vaudeville, but it soon closed its doors again when its patrons turned out to be all Communards insisting that égalité and fraternité accorded them the liberté of not paying for tickets. Others of the bourgeoisie simply gave up and left town, going north through St-Denis, where there were no Versaillais troops attacking and no German troops encamped. Despite the ban on travel, that could be accomplished by slipping five francs to any sentry of the Garde Nationale who might bar the way—so long as the escaper went afoot, with no horse, carriage, luggage or anything else the guards could confiscate.

Whatever low opinion Florian, Edge and others might have held of the Communards, no one could fault the fervor with which they fought for their cause. Not only their Garde Nationale and their recruits from the regular army ranks, but also civilians of every age rallied to the defense of Paris. Some of their tactics may have seemed unnecessary, such as the building of barricades in almost every street, just because their revolutionary forefathers had done that—and some were patently foolish, such as the digging of ditches at intervals across the avenue de l'Impératrice, in the hope that any invading enemy cavalry would fall into them—but there was no doubt of the defenders' sincere resolve. The inner barricades were mostly guarded by old men, young boys and women, and many of the women, emulating Mademoiselle Liberté in Delacroix's revered painting, chose to wear Phrygian caps and to tear their bodices so that one breast hung exposed. Since almost all the women were big and brawny brutes, their leathery dangling dugs were obviously meant to be inspiring, not titillating, to their male companions-in-arms.

The uniformed troops of Paris's outer bastions managed to repel all the early sorties of Thiers's Versaillais and, whenever those fell back, even pursued them well beyond the city limits. That was brave, but foolhardy, because on each of those occasions some of the Communards would venture too far, and get flanked and captured. And their captors, instead of interning them at Versailles as prisoners of war, would often carelessly "lose" them to the Versailles citizens. Since those people had been reviling the Parisians as "stupides" and "obstinés" ever since the time of the German siege, they now enthusiastically mauled any of the prisoners they could get their hands on—cracking their skulls, tearing off their ears, kicking them to pulp and otherwise demonstrating their contempt. When those atrocities became known in Paris, Procureur Rigault gave notice that, for every Communard who died at Versailles, he would execute three of the hostages he held in Mazas Prison.

"I swear," said Yount, when Sunday read that news from *Le Cri du Peuple,* "I ain't never seen *any* ruckus before—not in Mexico or Yankee land or even in the Injun territories—where *everybody* involved was so pure-damned dastardly villainous."

"Oh, they're not all villains, Obie," she said mischievously. "Here's a report that a certain Mademoiselle Papevoine has been declared a Heroine of the Commune because, right out on the barricade where she is assigned to serve, she has succored the intrepid defenders of Paris by sexually satisfying as many as eighteen of them in one spell of guard duty."

"Miss Sunday!" exclaimed Yount, scandalized. "You oughtn't to be reading such trashy newspapers!"

However, there was at least one authentic hero in the upper echelons of the Commune, according to Monsieur Nadar, the only city dweller who came out to the Bois nowadays. On a night in May, he, Florian, Edge and Fitzfarris were playing a game of piquet by lamplight in the cookhouse, and listening to the ever-nearer rumble of cannon in the west, when Nadar said:

"It is expectable that the governing Communards should take advantage of their parvenu status to settle old scores, or to slake their bloodthirstiness, or to line their pockets. But the one man who could be plundering every bank and cashbox in Paris—the Finance Minister Tourde—is remaining faithful to the precepts of an ideal communisme. He continues to reside in his lowly back-street tenement flat, and his wife still pursues her lifelong career of taking in washing."

"More fool he," said Fitzfarris, who was dealing the cards, and flagrantly cheating. "When there are plums to be picked, I say pick plums. Me, I'm going stale for lack of opportunity, goddammit."

"Yes, carpe diem and caveat emptor," said Florian, with a laugh. "Remember, Sir John? That time you and I posed as doctors seeking study specimens, and got us that freak from that asylum?"

"No," said Fitz.

"No? You don't remember?"

"No, we didn't do it. I remember you once talking about something of the sort."

"Indeed? I could have sworn..." Florian fumbled distractedly with his hand of cards. "Ah, well. Some earlier time, I suppose, some other confidence man..."

"Eh bien," said Nadar. "If the Minister Tourde is going to dip into the till, he had better make haste. Carpe diem, as you say, mon vieux. There won't be many more days. The Communards are showing fanatical courage and determination, but the one commodity that the city did not stock during the interregnum was ammunition. It is fast running out. The Commune must fall before much longer."

"It can't fall too soon for me," muttered Edge, but he did not elaborate on the remark, for Nadar had never been told of the fracas with the alleged Committee of Public Safety.

The next day, when Sunday brought the newspapers to the tober, before she read them to any other interested parties, she came to Florian to say solemnly:

"I wanted to give you my condolences, Mr. Florian. The big news today is about the surrender of France to the Germans. It's all settled, and Jules Favre has gone to Frankfurt to sign the treaty with Chancellor Bismarck."

"And why, Miss Butterfly, am I especially to be condoled?"

"France will pay Germany some incredible amount of indemnity. But worse, it's giving Germany *your Alsace*. And a piece of Lorraine besides. I'm truly sorry, sir."

"Well... thank you for saying so, my dear. But perhaps Alsace will not mind too much. There is little honor in claiming French nationality these days. No doubt the Communard press is making great ado about that concession, to whip up public sentiment once more against the Republican government. Nevertheless, it comes as no surprise to me." He scratched morosely in his little beard and said, more to himself than to her, "What does begin to surprise me is my having reached an age when so few things *can* surprise."

And in truth, when Sunday left him, Florian was looking quite old and bowed. For the first time she could remember, he was showing every one of his years.

16

WHEN the out-gunned Garde Nationale began to pull back from its forts and outer lines, and the Versaillais pressed ever closer, the Commune leaders seemed to have decided not to *let* the city fall, but spitefully to pull it down around them. A great crowd assembled in the Place Vendôme on the sixteenth of May, to jeer and cheer as the finally sawed-through column was toppled and shattered, Napoléon's laurel-crowned head breaking off and rolling into the gutter. Two days later, the Communards squandered some of their dwindling gunpowder and dynamite to blow up the once-imperial École Militaire on the Champ de Mars. But they had sufficient explosives only to make a mess of the interior; the classic old façade and walls stayed standing. So thereafter the Communards resorted to simple incendiarism; civilians were recruited to be pétroleurs and pétroleuses, for two francs apiece per day, going about to douse coal oil throughout the lesser public buildings and to set match to them.

On the twenty-first of May, the advance units of the Versaillais pushed their way into Paris from the west, entering through the Point du Jour, to the south of the Bois de Boulogne. The Florilegium company watched from their tober as a throng of Communard defenders rushed to that front—a mixed gang of Garde Nationale, regular soldiers and civilians, bearing every kind of weapon from modern rifles and ancient muskets to scythes and clubs—running along the boulevard Suchet, down the eastern side of the park. What was most conspicuous about that hurrying procession was that it was led by several dozen feeble and ragged crones. Those women were not going voluntarily to combat; they were beggars and derelicts who had been snatched up from their alley abodes. The old wretches were being shoved along as a shield for the armed Communards, on the assumption that the Versaillais would be more gallant than *they* were, and would not fire on aged women. That assumption proved to be erroneous, as was evident to the circus folk when they heard the shooting begin at the southern end of the Bois.

"Jesus," growled Yount. "Like I said, in this war there ain't nothing *but* villains."

By nightfall, the Versaillais had fought their way through the fashionable residential districts of Auteuil and Passy as far as the Iéna bridge, one mile directly east of the Florilegium tober. But night could not really be said to have fallen. On the orders of Procureur Rigault, the pétroleurs had torched the two great palaces, the Tuileries and the Palais Royal, and all of Paris was bathed in the lurid light of their burning.

That unnaturally bright night gave way at dawn to an ominously dark day, the sun and sky hidden by a pall of smoke. The day got even darker when Rigault ordered the burning of other landmark buildings—the Hôtel de Ville, the Quai d'Orsay, the Palais de Justice, the Louvre library. What had been the city's heart was one vast pyre, and the pillars of smoke made a beacon for the Versaillais troops to aim at, as they advanced now on both sides of the Seine, that day pushing as far as the Arc de Triomphe on the Right Bank, the Invalides on the Left.

The fighting having so quickly gone right past and beyond the Bois, the Florilegium was safely behind the lines, and the troupers were content to stay there on the tober, uninvolved and unendangered, while they waited for whatever the outcome might be. For several more days, they could hear the sounds of battle gradually moving farther off toward the middle of the city, and from over there rose ever more columns of smoke and flame from the ever more edifices torched by their "defenders." As the Communard forces were inexorably pushed backward and backward—along the stylish Faubourg St-Honoré on one side of the river, through the warrens of Montparnasse on the other—they were at last making use of their plethora of barricades. They fought from behind one until they were overwhelmed, then fell back to another, and their womenfolk behind them pried up the streets' paving blocks and flung furniture out of buildings to erect yet more barricades.

President Thiers himself approached as close as the captured fort of Mont Valérien, west of the Bois. When he looked out toward the center of Paris—being destroyed to keep him from taking it—he passed the word to his generals: "Je serai sans pitié," and pitiless were his Versaillais in consequence. As they had not hesitated to shoot down the old street women fronting the mob at the Point du Jour, they now did not hesitate to kill wounded and helpless opponents, opponents trying to surrender, bare-breasted Mesdemoiselles Liberté, and anyone else they encountered who even looked capable of being an opponent. And in consequence of that, an irate Procureur Rigault ordered the execution of all of his more illustrious hostages: Archbishop Darboy, Curé Duguerry, Magistrate Bonjean, General Bergeret and forty-three others. Then, wearing the uniform of a major of the Garde Nationale, Rigault left the Préfecture Centrale, ordered it and its next-door Arsenal burned, and went off to direct the defense of his own home district.

Whatever brief defense he may have arranged was among the last waged by the Commune, for all the Left Bank was in the hands of the Versaillais by the next morning. The only fighting still going on was in the farthest eastern working-class district of Belleville. Whenever there was a lull in the shooting there, the combatants could hear a Bavarian regiment, encamped just beyond the city limits, passing the time by playing a band concert. That same day, the Florilegium troupers watched the main body of the Republican forces march past the Bois to occupy Paris. They were led by a stern-faced, ramrod-erect mounted officer who, said Yount, "looked as soldierly as General Lee," and who was identified for him by LeVie as the Maréchal MacMahon.

On Saturday, the twenty-seventh of May, the Versaillais overran the very last Communard barricade in Paris—in the rue Ramponeau, between the height of Chaumont and the Père Lachaise cemetery—and found that it was being defended by one lone man. But the Florilegium company could still hear small-arms fire, sporadic bursts and single shots, from every part of the city—and, distantly from the eastern part, regular volleys of massed rifle fire at deliberate intervals, about five minutes apart.

"What can that be?" someone asked.

"Firing squads, I'd reckon," said Edge. "The other shooting must be ferret parties, cleaning out the last diehards. But I can't believe that so many Communards could be holed up and holding out."

That was explained by Monsieur Nadar, four days later, when he made his first trip out to the tober since the invasion had begun. He was once more nattily dressed, from silk hat to suede spats, again wearing his monocle and jauntily twirling a walking stick. And, as usual, he was able to give a wry and gossipy account of much that had been happening beyond the Bois.

"Those were firing squads, oui, as you surmised, Colonel Edge. In the Père Lachaise there is a wall admirably suited to the purpose. And the other frequent shots you still hear are, as you surmised, those of the vengeful provincial soldiers snuffing every last spark of the Commune—and, hélas, many other sparks as well. They ordered out practically every inhabitant of the city for questioning and inspection—including even my august self and the formidable Madame Nadar, can you conceive of it?—and then shot every man wearing any fragment of a Garde Nationale uniform, even military boots that he might innocently have scavenged, and every woman found to be carrying a taper or a box of allumettes, because she *might* have been a pétroleuse. Now the Versaillais are going through the military hospitals, starting at one end of each ward, marching down it and giving the coup de grâce to all the bedridden—the Communard and the German wounded alike. Zut alors, but the rustics are enjoying their visit to the metropolis."

Yount growled yet again, "Like I said, nothing *but* villains."

"Ah, well, the fortunes of war," sighed Florian.

"Mais non, ami," said Nadar. "I agree with the Monsieur Earthquake. I myself am ashamed of my compatriotes. I illustrate. When the Procureur Rigault went to the barricades, he was captured by a Versaillais patrol. As an officer, and an anonymous one, he might only have been taken as a prisoner of war. But he defiantly announced his identity and was instantly shot through the head, his body left lying in the street. The monster deserved it, God knows, but he at least showed courage and conviction. When the patrol moved on, the district residents crept from their hiding places to kick and spit on his body. And *those* were Rigault's own working-class neighbors, who had formerly been boastful of their local-boy-made-good, and had sycophantically cheered his many vile malfeasances while he was in office. Merde et plus de merde!"

"But the Commune *is* finished, surely," said Florian. "That blot on the escutcheon of France is erased."

"The Commune is finished, oui, but the blot may be a long time fading," said Nadar. "The Commune endured for seventy-two days and, by my best estimate, it took the lives of perhaps five hundred Parisians in that time. Now the Versaillais have rounded up some fifty thousand prisoners. The good and decent Maréchal MacMahon would transport them all to Nouvelle Calédonie, to spend the rest of their lives boiling down coconuts into copra. But MacMahon is unable to control his soldiers' indiscriminate killing, because it is encouraged by the wrathful Thiers. *That* toll may amount to twenty thousand. Four times the amount of blood shed in Paris's previous most shameful episode, the Terror of eighty years ago."

Edge made a face of disgust, but said, "Well, if you feel secure enough to go strolling about like a boulevardier, Monsieur Nadar, I think I might go downtown and take a look around, too."

"Ah, in truth there is much to see. Even the new ruins are pittoresque. The rubble of the Tuileries, the Hôtel de Ville—the stones are no longer merely stone-colored stones. The oil that burned them has beautifully glazed them. Red, green, blue. However, Colonel Edge, I would advise you not to venture out just yet. No one should be abroad who does not speak impeccable French, who cannot prove himself incontrovertibly a Frenchman *and* a staunch supporter of President Thiers."

"Yes, you stay here, Zachary," said Florian. "I can more plausibly portray a Frenchman and a hypocrite. I shall go out and gauge the mood of the populace." He paused and looked around at his gathered chiefs. "But, in the meantime, there is nothing to impede our resuming rehearsals and preparations for commencing to perform again. Paris will want—nay, she will *need* some recourse to recreation when this long nightmare is finally over. To celebrate the deliverance of the city, to salve the wounds of fratricidal strife, to ease the people back to normality. Yes! We shall reopen on the very first day that is feasible."

He beckoned to Stitches Goesle, took out a piece of paper and his old stump of mason's pencil and began sketching.

"Canvasmaster, have your crewmen start painting posters. Like this, to announce a grand *victory parade* of Florian's Flourishing Florilegium. As many as your Slovaks can turn out. We will start the men papering the city at the earliest possible moment."

"Aye aye, Governor," said Goesle, watching him scribble.

"Ah, l'optimiste," murmured Nadar, with a smile. "Eternellement l'optimiste."

But Fitzfarris said, "Governor, mightn't you be a little premature? How do we know this nightmare *is* about to end? For Christ's sake, this is the fourth government we've lived under since we got here. What makes you think it'll be the last? Or that Paris will *ever* be normal?"

"Call it an old circus man's intuition, Sir John," said Florian. "I just *know* the city will soon be circus ripe. I just *feel good* about it. Now, you go and see that all your phenomena and monstrosities are fit to make parade. The Princess Brunhilde has been having spells of morning sickness, but she ought to be getting past that stage of her pregnancy by now. Go and find out. But please, inquire with delicacy."

Fitz said haughtily, "When have I ever been anything but considerate to anybody?" and stumped off toward the annex tent.

Florian went on, turning to Beck, "Kapellmeister, go and muster your windjammers. Teach them some politically neutral victory marches. Perhaps the 'Garry Owen'... 'Marching Through Georgia'..."

"Ja wohl, Herr Gouverneur."

"And will you, Colonel Ramrod, in my absence, see to the others? Get Abdullah and his assistants to currying and polishing the animals for parade. Get your artistes into costume and make sure their dress doesn't need any attention from the wardrobe mistress."

"Right, Governor."

"Eh bien," said Nadar, "I can see that everything is back to normal *here*. And I look forward, messieurs, to seeing all of you en grande tenue, when that great parade day comes."

He continued to chatter to Florian as they went off together: "I must tell you, mon vieux, that even Frenchness has been no certain guarantee of safety in these recent times. One of the last men to die on the barricades, I regret to report, was dear old Maître Auber. Poor Daniel, his mind was severely disturbed by the long privations. It finally snapped, and in his derangement he ran out among the fighting in the rue Saint-Georges. Can you imagine some Frenchman taking aim with a rifle at that frail and white-haired old gentleman? Yet that is what occurred. On the other hand, some genuine French traitors have eluded the avengers. The Communard painter Courbet, the abominable Paul Verlaine, they somehow slipped out of the city into safe hiding. Hélas, it is always the wrong people who die..."

In the tober's backyard, when Pemjean emerged from his and Monday's caravan, garbed in his red Démon Débonnaire costume, he said to Edge:

"Monsieur le Directeur, could the Mademoiselle Cendrillon be excused from this review of the company? She is slightly indisposée."

"I hope it's nothing serious. Nothing to do with her back or—"

"No specific complaint, I think. In her words, she merely feels bad *about* something, and wishes to be left alone."

Edge muttered, "Oh, Lord. Maggie Hagging again."

"Comment?"

"Nothing, nothing. Let's go and see how your animals are."

At the menagerie top, Hannibal was looking uneasy.

"Mas' Zack, Mr. Demon, I think somep'n done spook our critters. Cats all pacin' de cages, even rickety old Maximus. Hosses whickerin' and actin' contrary, even dem zebra hosses. And jist look at dem bulls."

The two elephants had their eyes closed and were both making a noise like a low, meditative hum, while they rocked in unison from left legs to right, their trunks swinging loosely from side to side. Edge could not be sure whether he felt an emanation of the animals' agitation or a Maggie-type premonition, but his back hair prickled. Still, not to alarm Hannibal, he asked only:

"Are you sure nobody has been slipping loco weed—larkspur, or something like that—into their feed?"

"Nawsuh, Mas' Zack. Dese animals ain't sick or pizened, dey *spooked*. I ain't never seen 'em act like dis. I be feared to lay brush on any of 'em."

"All right, Abdullah, leave them be. I'll ask the Governor to take a look at them, when he gets back. Meantime, you and your boys keep watch. All night, if necessary, in shifts. And let me know immediately if they get any more restless."

The company occupied the rest of the day at practice and rehearsal, and in going over their costumes and gear and rigging and props, and handing a few articles to Ioan or Stitches for repair or improvement. At evening, when the flag went up, all repaired to the cookhouse for dinner and, afterward, scattered to their caravans, wagons or tent pallets. It was well after dark when Florian finally returned. Finding the tober quiet, dark and almost deserted, he apparently decided not to make his usual round of inspection, but went straight to his own caravan. Edge had looked in on the menagerie from time to time and—finding the animals still wakeful and unsettled, but no more—he saw no need to bother Florian about them. He left a Slovak staying on watch there, and went to bed himself.

But he and the others of the company were wakened next morning—or yanked forcibly from sleep—by a noise as horrendous as the calliope had ever made. It was compounded of elephants trumpeting, cats roaring, hyenas yapping, horses whinnying, bears bawling and even the ostriches hissing what noise they could. It brought the men pelting toward the menagerie, most of them clad only in their underwear, while nearly every woman of the troupe leaned to peer wonderingly from her van's door or window. At the menagerie, the Slovak watchman had fled to the outdoors, and he stood there, eyes bulging, pointing into the tent and gibbering incoherently. But when the men crowded inside, the animals had all gone as suddenly silent again. Some were munching on wisps of hay or leftover scraps of other food; the rest were settling down to sleep at last. While the men stood about, regarding the animals with bewilderment and mumbling curses, they were galvanized anew by the sound of a woman screaming—"*Florian! Oh, God! Florian!*"—and they all rushed out again into the backyard.

"He came in late," Daphne told the collected company, after the other women had soothed and calmed her somewhat. "He had dined with Nadar in the city. He was weary, so we... we went to bed. But then he slept badly." Daphne sniffled, and dabbed a handkerchief at her nose. "I supposed that he was talking in his sleep—until I sat up and looked, and his eyes were open. He spoke... quite clearly, not in a sleepy way." She paused for a moment, to remember. "He was talking about people... no, not about them... he was talking *to* them. People from before my time on the show. Solitaire and Pepper and Hotspur. And some

I'd never heard of before. Names like Zip Coon and Billy the Kink... if I heard
him right..."

She said those names half questioningly, and looked around at the others.
Clover Lee and Hannibal Tyree nodded, unable to speak.

"I finally fell asleep, so I don't know whether he ever did. But when I woke,
this morning, he was already up and getting dressed. Putting on his most spiffy
pista clothes. He... he bent down to give me a kiss, then he clapped on his good
gray topper, and gave it a brisk tap. He threw open the door... and I could see
that it was a beautiful day..."

She paused again, mopped at her eyes with the handkerchief and swallowed
several times before she could continue:

"Well... some of you must have seen him standing there. And he spread his
arms. As if he were grabbing... hugging the day. Then he disappeared... and
that frightful animal noise came blaring in. I leapt to the door... and he was
lying at the foot of the steps." She wadded the handkerchief against her lips to
stop their trembling. "Then... some of you came... and brought him back inside..."

"Obie," said Edge. "Take the rockaway and go fetch a doctor."

Yount said gently, "Zack, Mr. Florian is dead. Can't no doctor—"

"I know he's dead, goddammit. I want to know what he died of. Go get that
Dr. Tonnelier who treated Monday Simms. At the Marmottan hospital. It's not
far."

"Zachary," said Pemjean, also gently. "That was a bone doctor. He would
hardly—"

"He was a good doctor. He'll do. You go with Obie and show him the way."

"It was what you call in English a stroke, Monsieur Edge," said Tonnelier.
"Which, in English, is short for 'a stroke of God's hand.' Or, to employ the medical jargon, it was an intracranial hemorrhage, the bursting of a blood vessel in
the brain. The—the engorgement and empurpling of his head are sufficient
signs diagnostic, and I need not do autoptic surgery to confirm that. It accords
also with what you told me of his recently wandering memory and occasional
confusions. And it *can* be aptly called a stroke of God's hand, for it took him
instantaneously."

"Painlessly?"

"That, I cannot say. The wisest physician in the world will never know that
until he has such a seizure himself. But quickly and mercifully, yes. Monsieur
Florian was spared any gradual enfeeblement of his mind or crippling of his
body, such as could have occurred if the hemorrhaging had continued to be only
a slow leakage. So be glad for your friend. Just give him the privacy and decency
of a closed coffin at the funeral. That way, no mourner will remember him looking otherwise than he did in life. Quite a handsome old gentleman, I recall. Will
you wish me to make out the certificate of death? You will require that, and
many other particulars, for the formalities of burial arrangements."

"Don't bother, Doctor. We'll see to the arrangements without involving the
authorities."

"Monsieur Edge, in accordance with my license to practice, I must protest
and deplore any irregular or extraordinary procedures. But what the hell, as you

say in English. We live—and die—in extraordinary times, n'est-ce pas?"

"And the deceased was an extraordinary man. Thank you, Doctor."

"Is there anything else I can do? I have already looked in on the young lady who was, er, in his company at the time. She will survive the experience; she is English. Beaucoup de sang-froid."

"Well . . . I'd like your professional opinion on something. Florian seemed not to suspect that he was about to die. At least, he didn't go around declaiming any memorable last words."

"Invent some, then. He was an entertainer, and every entertainer ought to have his curtain line."

"I daresay circus legend will provide plenty of those for him. What I want to ask you—the *animals* seemed to be expecting his death. Also one of our younger female troupers. Is that possible?"

"There are more things in heaven and earth, Horatio, than the wisest physician will ever apprehend. But the lower animals, and of course that includes the females of our own species, are closer to nature than are you and I, monsieur. I should see nothing impossible in their instincts' giving warning of the imminent loss of one near and dear. However, I am French. You must puzzle out the prodigy according to your own lights."

"*Not* in a proper cemetery we will bury the Herr Gouverneur?" exclaimed Beck, in horror. "But, Herr Direktor, no mere trouper he was! Consider. In the Montmartre cemetery lies Heine, in the Père Lachaise lie Abélard and Héloïse. Distinguished company he would have!"

"Come on, Boom-Boom," said Edge. "You know verdammt well that if Florian was buried anywhere but under his own pista, his ghost would haunt every circus on earth, from now until Kingdom Come. Just go and tell Elemér to pick some nice, gentle cimbalom pieces to play at the service. And Stitches, would you do up a canvas shroud? Use a piece of our striped sidewall; he'd like that. And then prepare your preachments, while I do the laying out of him."

"To be sure. Of what denomination was the Governor?"

"Your guess is as good as mine. He either recognized none of them or he recognized all of them—and I don't mean just the Christian ones. The only thing I'm sure he was, was a Freemason. Is there such a thing as a Masonic funeral ceremony?"

"If there is, lad, I fear I don't know it."

"Well, preach something nondenominational. You've done it often enough before."

"Aye. And will I be carving a headboard for the Governor?"

"That might be fitting, yes."

"Do you know his dates, then?"

"Only the last one. He never said when he was born. I reckon just his name and R.I.P. will do."

"And what was his name, then? The all of it."

Edge looked blank. "Well, I'll be damned." After a moment, he laughed. "More than six years, and I never even wondered: was Florian his first or his last name? Let's ask Clover Lee and Hannibal. They were with him longer than anybody except maybe Jules Rouleau."

But Clover Lee was equally baffled. She could only blink her reddened eyes and say, between sniffles, "Isn't that a hell of a thing to realize? We never called him anything but Mr. Florian."

Hannibal, whose eyes were all but bleeding, helpfully suggested, "Maybe Mister *be's* his fust name?"

"Wait," said Clover Lee. "His conduct book is bound to have it, or his passport."

"Except God only knows where they are," said Edge. "Probably all our papers burned up when the Central Préfecture did. I've already searched the red wagon. There's no other information there. You know, this is really wondrous, when you think about it. Trust Florian to be unique. Every other trouper on this show has two or three different pista names, besides their real ones, and he never even had a *whole* name."

Goesle asked, "Then I carve on the headboard 'Florian,' just?"

"Never mind the board, Stitches. It wouldn't last long, anyway, after we've gone. And right outside the tober there's that little stone marker where the first balloonist went up. If any of us ever come back here and want to pay our respects to Florian, we won't have any trouble finding the place where he rests."

The members of the company were all in pista dress when they stood about the hole in the pista ground and the piled earth and sawdust on opposite sides of it. The troupers wore their full—or skimpy—spangled costumes, the bandsmen were in uniform, the roustabouts in their best black overalls. Abdullah and Le Démon Débonnaire had brought inside the chapiteau all the menagerie, both the walking animals and the caged ones, even the coq de bruyère. The ring horses and Brutus and Caesar wore their performing tack and adornments, and all the animals were being as quiet and well mannered as if they recognized the solemnity of the occasion. Although it was midafternoon, Stitches and his men had lighted every one of the carbide lamps, and now one of the Slovaks shone the spotlight on the tent's back door, as Colonel Ramrod led in two of the road horses, drawing one of Beck's wheeled generator tanks for a catafalque, the jauntily green-and-white shrouded body lying on a pallet on its flat top. The spotlight followed its slow progress into the pista, while Elemér Gombocz, off to one side, quietly trilled "Träumerei" on his cimbalom.

When the catafalque was halted beside the waiting grave, the troupers and crewmen went up, one after another, to bid Florian farewell. Some murmured quietly, some found it hard to say anything at all, some spoke loudly enough to be heard.

"Governor," said Sir John, "I kind of envy you the celestial wonders and marvels you've got *now* . . . to talk-up to the celestial rubes. Good-bye, old friend."

"Dear Florian," said the Princess Brunhilde, "you were the first person ever to make me feel really like a princess. Do-svidánya, mílyi drot." And Kostchei the Deathless echoed that.

"Istenhozzád, barát Florian," said the midget Tücsök, and Elemér and the Jászi brothers echoed that.

"Sbohem, Nadrzízený," said Banat, and the other Slovaks and the Kesperle echoed that.

"Khairete, Kyvernitis Florian," said Meli the Medusa.

"Addio . . . ed arrivederci, caro Florian," said the Emeraldina.

"Voi ruga, Florian mosneag," said wardrobe mistress Ioan.

"Glückliche Reise, Freund Florian..."

"Adieu, ami, et bon voyage..."

"Taraf, Mas' Sahib, taraf," said Abdullah. Then he turned, weeping, to explain to any who did not know, "Taraf be's elephant talk. Means... come back."

Clover Lee said no audible farewell to Florian. Instead, she plucked a couple of the sequins off her léotard and laid them on the shroud at his head, where they glittered gaily in the spotlight beam.

When all had done, Canvasmaster Goesle stepped up beside the pallet, bowed his head, folded his hands, closed his eyes, waited for the others to do the same and said:

"Here we are again, Lord. This time, we're here to tell You that our friend and fellow trouper Florian has made his teardown, now just. He has hit the road for the long run to the final tober on his route sheet. Now, Lord, You already know that the very last thing Florian ever did on this earth was to fling wide his arms to embrace the last day You blessed him with. Such a man, Lord, does not need our commending, even to the All Highest. But when he gets there, Lord, do sit down from time to time and have a jar and a jaw with Florian. Of course we are mindful that You are Governor of the grandest circus of them all—Yours being this world here, full of artistes and players and jugglers and acrobats and rope-dancers and risk-chancers and mountebanks and musicmakers and freaks and roustabouts and slum-joint keepers and clem brawlers and confidence men and every kind of menagerie animal there is—all of them prancing about Your great round pista or lining Your capacious midway or gathered in Your multitudinous pavilions. Maybe, Lord, alongside the immensity of that circus, this one of Florian's seems no more than a mud show. Nevertheless, Florian can tell You a thing or two, Lord, and not just tober gossip and outrageous yarns and bawdy jokes—though You'll enjoy the hearing of those, to be sure. He can also slip You a handy word of advice, now and again, that will help You keep Your troupers and crewmen working their best... and being happy at their working... and all the while loving the Governor of them... Amen."

Goesle started to raise his head, then lowered it again and added, "Dammo, Lord, I nearly forgot. Let us ask of You one small favor for our friend. When he approaches the Pearly Gates, please have Saint Peter open them all the way, so Florian can enter in style. Let him make parade, Lord."

While Stitches had been speaking, a couple of the Slovaks had been unobtrusively fixing rope tackle to Florian's pallet. Now they pulled on another line, and the pallet was lifted by the lungia boom, was gently swung over the open grave and gently lowered into it. For the first time during the ceremony, Colonel Ramrod stepped forward, took a handful of sawdust—not earth—sprinkled it down onto the green-and-white shroud and haltingly, huskily said the last words:

"Saltavit... Placuit... Mortuus est..."

And some of the troupers whispered a translation for some others:

"He danced about. He gave pleasure. He is dead."

"If I could have everybody's attention," said Edge, as the Slovaks quietly went to work to fill the grave and smooth the sawdust over it, "while we're all here together... or most of us are. Herr Lothar, I reckon you can vote on behalf of Monsieur Roulette, and Quakemaker, you can vote for Miss Eel. Anyway, let's all decide what's to happen next. I've got some ideas I'd like to expound, but I can be outvoted. So... those of you who can understand my English, please translate to those who can't."

He waited until they were all properly attentive.

"Now, I've gone through the office cashbox and all of Florian's papers and ledgers and files. I haven't had a chance yet to look into the box underneath Maximus's cage yonder, but, as soon as I do, I'll be able to report, to the penny, how our finances stand. One thing I *can* tell you right now is that Florian didn't leave any kind of will or testament or the least scrawl to indicate his wishes for the Florilegium. So I figure the only fair thing is for everybody—including the roustabouts—to get an equal share of everything. If any of you feel that the shares ought to be apportioned according to star standing or length of hitch on the show, you can say so and we'll put it to a vote, but please save the objections until I've said my piece."

No one spoke, but everybody was gazing at him intently—and oddly, it seemed to him.

"If you all agree, each of us would keep everything we each own or that has been part of our act—caravans and draft horses, props, rigs, costumes, performing animals. Everything else we would divide. The cash on hand, plus whatever cash the other properties might fetch on the market—the stock and menagerie animals, the canvas and poles, seats and lights, wagons and so on. I think it's likely that the other circuses here in Paris will want to rebuild and restock in a hurry now, so they might buy us out at a good price. And that brings me to another point. Some of you may already have circuses in mind, elsewhere in Europe, that you'll want to apply to. But these Paris circuses will be also wanting new acts and artistes, so they'll probably jump at the opportunity to sign up any... what's the matter?"

He had become aware of the rising mutter and growl among his audience.

"What's the *matter!?*" cried Clover Lee. "You're talking about dismantling and selling Florian's *Florilegium!*"

There were other, similar cries, in several languages and varying degrees of disapprobation.

"Well, hell," said Edge, "we can't just walk off and leave it."

More cries: various renditions of "Who is walking off?"

"Then what—?" Edge tried to say, but Fitz overrode him.

"Zack, it sounds to me like nobody intends to blow the stand, and nobody's going to blow them *off* it. I bet, if you asked for a show of hands, you'd raise every one, including hoofs and paws."

"Sir John, this is all very fine and loyal. But who is going to pay the salaries into those hands? And put the feed into those—?"

"Same that has paid always," said Nella. "Il Florilegio."

"If it is a question of money, Gospodín Zachary," said the giantess, "I would be happy..."

"I could help, too," said Clover Lee de Lareinty.

"Look here, everybody," Edge said patiently. "I've told you. Florian made no provision for the disposition of the Florilegium. He didn't even have any family that we can find and saddle with it. Nobody *owns* this estab—"

He was shouted down: "We are the family!" "We own it!"

"Our own little Commune, eh?" said Edge. "You saw what a mess the other one made of things."

More shouts: "No Commune!" "Zum Teufel mit jedem Kommune!" "Elect a government!" "Oui, plébiscite!"

"Oh, hell, Colonel Zack," Yount boomed over all. "It's as clear as can be. When a troop's CO falls in the field, the next senior rank takes over. And you've been Florian's second in command for ever so long."

"Except this isn't the military, sergeant. This is a—a floating island. Populated by civilians. And civilians don't take kindly to having martial law imposed on them."

"It need not be martial and it need not be imposed," said Jörg Pfeifer. "You mentioned voting, Herr Direktor. Sehr wohl, if we vote that you assume Florian's place, will you do it?"

Edge looked uncertain.

Daphne spoke up. "I don't pretend to be Florian's widow, but his confidante, yes, I was. I know he would have wanted you to carry on, Zachary. And so do you."

"I just don't know if I could, Daphne. Who the hell could aspire to fill Florian's shoes?"

"You *gotta,* Mr. Zack!" urged Monday. "Else I can't never do no horseback act again."

Hannibal also chimed in. "You *gotta,* Mas' Zack! You wouldn't chuck us Amer'cans out in dis furrin land."

"Well..." said Edge.

"And what of all the posters my lads have painted?" Goesle demanded. "For the big parade. Do we tear them up, then?"

"Well..." Edge said again.

"A brave man," said little Katalin, "should not be afraid of appearing immodest or forward. It merely makes you look coy, Colonel Zachary, and wanting to be courted and wooed. Leave that to us women."

Several people laughed; so did Edge, but uncomfortably.

"Allow me," said Willi Lothar, striding to the front of the assemblage. "Let us spare the colonel's blushes. Zachary, why do you not step outside? While all this is explained to the non-speakers of English, and while we argue any pros and contras, and while we put the matter to a secret ballot. Alles in Ordnung."

Edge shrugged in resigned acceptance, and left the chapiteau by the front door. He went well beyond the marquee, out of earshot of any discussion inside, and strolled about, as the beautiful day drew toward its close. He lit a cigarette, and had not even finished it before Yount emerged as the tidings bearer.

"Well, Obie?"

"Why ask? I don't have to tell you it was unanimous." Yount was carrying Florian's parade-dress gray top hat, and now handed it to Edge. "Everybody wants you to run the show. Like Foursquare said, even Meli's snakes would of raised a hand, if they had any."

Respectfully turning the hat in his hands, not putting it on his head, Edge said, "I just don't know if I can do it, Obie."

"The hell you say. Why, I've knowed you to take on tougher—Jesus Christ! *Look a-yonder!* Now, ain't that-there a *sign,* Zack? You can't tell me that ain't a *sign!* The good times are a-coming!" He ran back into the chapiteau, yelling, "Hey, everybody! Get out here and look! Come quick!"

They poured out onto the midway, looked where Yount was pointing and, all together, heaved a great sigh of wonder and welcome. High up over the park's greenery, brilliant against the blue sky, hung the vermilion-and-white striped globe of the *Saratoga.*

"Lieber Himmel!" breathed Beck. "Ein Gaswerk somewhere he found..."

"Good old Jules," breathed Clover Lee. "He came back just as soon as it was safe."

"By damn," breathed Yount. "I wonder if maybe he's picked up Agnete and brought her..."

"Just in time for the parade," breathed Sunday.

"The parade, yes..." said Edge, thoughtfully. Then, briskly, "All right, people. As long as you've voted us back in business, let's get to business. Banat, run some of your men out there to catch Monsieur Roulette's anchor rope. He's coming down, and he's probably out of practice."

"Da, Pana Nadrzízený."

"Meli, would you and Ioan get the cookhouse stove fired up? Monsieur Roulette may be hungry for some good circus grub. I know I am."

"Amésos, Kyvernitis."

"Stitches, what do those posters of yours say, exactly? About the parade."

"Right here I have one," said Goesle, taking it from a Slovak and unrolling it.

"Hm. 'Watch for the grand victory parade, coming soon,' Well, hell, let's not leave it uncertain. What is today's date—the first of June? Let's make it definite, for the day after tomorrow." He scribbled on the bottom of the poster, "SAMEDI 3 JUIN," and realized that he was writing with the old stub of mason's pencil he had found in the late Florian's vest pocket. "Have the boys put that on all the posters, big and bold and visible."

"Aye aye, Governor."

Somehow Sunday managed to say all in one breath, "Don't you think the proprietor of Florian's Flourishing Florilegium, Combined Confederate American Circus, Menagerie and Educational Exhibition ought to have a wife?" And then she laughed, breathlessly.

"Florian didn't."

"Florian had *three* wives that he admitted to. Four, if you count Daphne. More than that, I'd bet. He just never married any of them. And I didn't say anything about our getting married. No applying to Monsieur le Maire for certificates and witnesses and everything. Only being husband and wife."

After a pensive silence, Edge said, "You realize...we could never go back home again."

"Virginia is only where I came from. For one third of my life, Zachary, my home has been where you are. That's the only home I'll ever want. And there's all the rest of the world to go to. Places that don't care..."

He nodded. "I remember Florian talking about maybe touring the Low Countries. And Egypt. And there's Meli's Greece that we haven't been to. And old Maggie Hag's Spain and Agnete's Denmark."

"And Daphne's England," said Sunday, and instantly thought, *Autumn's England,* and wished she had not reminded him. So she made haste to say brightly, "Well, it's time to get into costume for the parade. The show comes first. As for anything else . . . we've got the rest of our lives to decide."

"Yes. We'll just—just work things out as we go along. Today you'll ride with me on the rockaway. Come on, let's make parade."

S A L T A V E R U N T

P L A C U E R U N T

M O R T U I S U N T O M N E S

Acknowledgments

For basic research, technical advice and other sorts of assistance, this book and I are indebted to numerous individuals and institutions:

Dr. Györgyi Berenyi, IBUSZ, Budapest
Jim Bonde, Marine World/Africa USA, Redwood City, California
The Clown and Circus Museum, Vienna
Wylma Davis, Librarian, Virginia Military Institute
Gloria Doyle, Baton Rouge, Louisiana
Donald Dryfoos, Donan Books, New York, New York
Peggy Hays, Librarian, Washington and Lee University
Hester Holland, Linda Krantz and Grace McCrowell, Rockbridge (Va.)
    Regional Library
Albert F. House, Circus Fans Association of America
Natalia Kousnetzova, Curator, Leningrad State Circus Museum
Don Marcks and his *Circus Report* magazine
Jack Niblett, Oldbury, Warley, West Midlands, England
Robert L. Parkinson, Director, Circus World Museum and Library,
    Baraboo, Wisconsin
Robert M. Pickral, M.D., Lexington, Virginia
Emanuela Radice, Rome
Charles Sens, Library of Congress
Alexey Sonin, Artistic Director, Leningrad State Circus
Dr. Mihály Szegedy-Maszák, Institute of Literary Studies,
    Hungarian Academy of Sciences
Gordon Van Ness III, University of South Carolina

...and especially to my intrepid interpreter in the USSR, Zoia Belyakova, who had to cope
    with the rigors of my being in Russia during an uncommonly frigid season in Soviet-
    US relations.

For actual under-the-Big-Top, in-the-ring, on-the-road and behind-the-scenes experience, lore, instruction, action and adventure, I owe thanks and more than thanks to:

Jim Roller, Elaine Roller, the performers and crewmen of the
    Roller Brothers Circus of Arkansas
John Pugh, Renée Storey, the performers and crewmen of the
    Clyde Beatty-Cole Brothers Circus of Florida
Hellmuth Schramek, the performers (especially Banda Vidane) and crewmen
    of the Circus Krone of Munich
Louis Knie of the Circus Knie of Switzerland
The performers and crewmen of Elfi Althoff-Jacobi's Österreichischer
    National-Circus
The quaint little traveling remnant of the once-mighty Circus Renz of Berlin
The performers and crewmen of the traveling Cirque Dumas of France
The Spanish Riding School, Vienna
The performers and crewmen of the Fővárosi Nagycirkusz of Budapest
The performers and crewmen of the Leningrad State Circus
The curators and docents who allowed me access to the understandably
    restricted Treasure Rooms of the Hermitage, Leningrad
The performers and crewmen of the Mayak Traveling Circus of the USSR
Rinaldo Orfei, Cristina Orfei, Freddy and Jackie Bovill, Peter and Sue Motley,
    Rae Dawn Stevens, Adriano, all the other performers and the crewmen
    of the Circo Orfei of Italy...

... with a special, deep, adoring bow to that golden lady, the beautiful, talented and gracious Liana Orfei

                                                                        G.J.